Wolf Among Wolves

Wolf Among Wolves

Hans Fallada

Translated by Phillip Owens

Restored, and with additional translations
by Thorsten Carstensen and Nicholas Jacobs

MELVILLEHOUSE
BROOKLYN, NEW YORK

Wolf Among Wolves
First published as *Wolf Unter Wölfen* by Rowohlt, Berlin, 1937
© Aufbau-Verlagsgruppe GmbH, Berlin 1994 (Published with Aufbau;
"Aufbau" is a trademark of Aufbau Verlagsgruppe GmbH)
First translated into English by Phillip Owens and published by
G. P. Putnam's Sons, New York, 1938

This restored, unabridged edition © 2010 Melville House Publishing
Additional translations by Thorsten Carstensen and Nicholas Jacobs.
Afterword © Thorsten Carstensen

Melville House Publishing
145 Plymouth Street
Brooklyn, NY 11201
www.mhpbooks.com

ISBN: 978-1-933633-92-3

First Melville House Printing: April 2010

Library of Congress Cataloging-in-Publication Data

Fallada, Hans, 1893-1947.
  [Wolf unter Wölfen. English]
  Wolf among wolves / Hans Fallada ; translated by Philip Owens ; this
unabridged edition restored with additional translations by Thorsten
Carstensen and Nicholas Jacobs ; afterword by Thorsten Carstensen.
     p. cm.
  ISBN 978-1-933633-92-3
  1. Germany—History—1918-1933—Fiction. 2. World War, 1914-1918—Social
aspects—Germany—Fiction. 3. Germany—Social conditions—1918-1933—
Fiction. 4. Germany—Economic conditions—1918-1945—Fiction. I. Owens,
Philip. II. Title.

PT2607.I6W613 2010
833'.912—dc22

                                                      2010001949

A Word to the Reader

The author has been reproached by some readers of his novel *Once We Had a Child* for making his hero, Johannes Gäntschow, such a brute. He has read this complaint with some astonishment, for as he wanted to portray a brutal man he could not depict a kind one. To avoid similar complaints the author warns in this preface (which can be glanced through in a moment at any bookstore) that *Wolf Among Wolves* deals with sinful, weak, sensual, erring, unstable men, the children of an age disjointed, mad and sick. All in all, it is a book for those who are, in every sense, adult.

Another not superfluous observation is that this is a novel, and therefore a product of the imagination. Everything in it—characters, events, places, names—is invented, and even if time or place should seem to point to a definite person, the novel is nevertheless only invention, fancy, fiction, story.

While not aiming at a photographic likeness, the author wished to picture a time that is both recent and yet entirely eclipsed. It behooves the rescued not altogether to forget past danger, but, remembering it, to appreciate doubly the happy issue.

H. F.

A Note on the Text

Philip Owens' translation of *Wolf Among Wolves* was published by Putnam's in New York and London in 1938. For reasons that are not entirely clear, the book was heavily edited in translation: hundreds of passages, including entire paragraphs, were edited out the first English edition. This new edition restores the novel by comparing the abbreviated English edition with the original German text published by Rowohlt Verlag in September 1937. New passages have been translated by Nicholas Jacobs and myself and added to Owens' impressive original.

THORSTEN CARSTENSEN,
New York University

CONTENTS

Part One—The Unquiet City

Part Two—The Land Afire

Part One

The Unquiet City

Chapter One

Awake in Berlin—and Elsewhere

I

A girl and a man were sleeping on a narrow iron bed. The girl's head rested in the crook of her right arm; her mouth, softly breathing, was half open; her face bore a pouting and anxious expression—that of a child who cannot understand why it is sad.

She lay turned away from the man, who slept on his back in a state of utter exhaustion, his arms loose. Tiny beads of sweat stood out on his forehead and in the roots of his curly fair hair; the handsome defiant face looked somewhat vacant. In spite of the open window the room was very hot, and the pair slept without blanket or covering. This is Berlin, Georgenkirchstrasse, third court-yard, fourth floor, July 1923, at six o'clock in the morning. The dollar stands for the moment at 414,000 marks.

II

Out of the dark well of the courtyard the smells from a hundred lodgings drifted into their sleep. A hundred noises, faint as yet, entered the open window where a dingy curtain hung motionless. On the other side of the courtyard barely twenty-five feet away, a refugee child from the Ruhr suddenly screamed.

The girl's eyelids quivered. She raised her head; her body grew rigid. The child wept quietly, a woman's voice scolded, a man grumbled—and the girl's head sank back, her limbs relaxed, and she slept.

In the house there was movement. Doors banged, feet shuffled across the court. There was noise on the stairs; enamel pails knocked against iron banis-ters; in the kitchen next door the tap was running. On the ground floor a bell rang out in the tin-stamping shed; wheels hummed, machine belts slithered.

The pair slept on . . .

III

In spite of the early hour and the clear sky, a dull vapor hung over the city. The stench of an impoverished people did not so much rise to the skies, as cling sluggishly to the houses, creep through every street, and seep through windows into every mouth that breathed.

In the neglected parks the trees let fall faded leaves.

An early main-line train from the east approached Schlesische Bahnhof—the wreck of a train, with rattling windows, broken panes and torn cushions. Its carriages clanked over the points and crossings of Stralau-Rummelsburg.

Rittmeister Joachim von Prackwitz-Neulohe—white-haired and slim, with bright dark eyes, retired cavalry captain and tenant of a manor—leaned out of the window to see where they had come to, and started back: a spark had flown into his eyes. "Miserable dust heap!" he muttered angrily, dabbing with his handkerchief.

IV

Fires had been kindled with limp yellow paper and matches whose heads jumped off or which stank. Bad coal or damp rotten wood smoldered; adulterated gas spluttered, burning without heat; blue watery milk warmed slowly; bread was doughy or too dry; margarine, softened by the heat of the flats, smelled rancid.

The people ate their carelessly cooked food as hastily as they slipped into garments cleaned, shaken and brushed too often. Hastily they skimmed the newspapers; because of the rise in prices there had been riots, disturbances and looting in Gleiwitz and Breslau, in Frankfurt-on-the-Main and Neuruppin, in Eisleben and Dramburg, six killed and a thousand arrested and therefore public meetings had been prohibited by the government. The State Tribunal had sentenced a princess to six months' imprisonment on the charge of being accessory to high treason and perjury—but the dollar stood at 414,000 as against 350,000 marks on the twenty-third. Salaries would be paid at the end of the month, in a week's time. What would the dollar be then? Would there be enough to buy food for a fortnight? For ten days? Three days? Would one be able to pay for shoe leather, gas, fares? Quick, wife, here's another 10,000 marks. Buy something with it—a pound of carrots, some cufflinks, the phonograph record "Yes, we have no bananas," or a rope to hang ourselves with—it doesn't matter what. Only be quick, run, don't lose a second.

V

The early sun was also shining upon the manor of Neulohe. The rye stood in the fields, the wheat was ripe, oats were ready, too. Across the fields a few tractors rattled, lost in the expanse of country. Larks were warbling and trilling overhead.

Forester Kniebusch, bald but with his wrinkled brown face thickly bearded, left the heat of the open field for the wood. Walking slowly, he adjusted the rifle sling on his shoulder with one hand and with the other wiped the sweat from his brow. He walked neither happily, hurriedly, nor powerfully. He walked in his own way, the way he walked in his own forest—light-footed, soft-kneed, cautious, noticing every twig on the path, to avoid stepping on it; he wished to walk quietly.

In spite of all his caution, however, at a turn in the path he met a procession of handbarrows emerging from behind a thicket. Men and women. Their barrows were loaded with freshly cut wood; not branches, only solid trunks were good enough for them. The forester's cheeks flushed angrily, his lips trembled, and his faded eyes lit up with a gleam of their bygone youth.

The man with the leading barrow—Bäumer, of course—gave a start. Then he went on. The barrows of stolen wood clattered past with hardly a yard to spare, the people looking straight in front or aside as if the forester were not there, motionless, breathing heavily. . . . Then they disappeared behind the thicket.

"You are getting old, Kniebusch." The forester could hear the voice of Rittmeister von Prackwitz.

Yes, he thought gloomily, I am so old that I would gladly take to my bed and die. He thought it and walked on.

He was not to die in his bed, however.

VI

Alarm bells were shrilling in Meienburg Penitentiary, the warders ran from cell to cell, the governor was telephoning the Reichswehr for reinforcements, the staff were buckling on their pistol belts and seizing rubber truncheons. Ten minutes ago No. 367 had thrown his bread ration at the warder's feet, screaming: "I insist on having bread, regulation weight, and not this damned plaster pulp!"

And this had precipitated the uproar, the riot. Yells, shouts, wails, singing and howling came from twelve hundred cells. "Grub! Grub! We're starving!" The little town of Meienburg crouched beneath the shining white walls of the penitentiary. That uproar penetrated into every house, through every window. And there came a frightful crash. A thousand prisoners had beaten their stools against the iron doors.

Warders and orderlies ran through the corridors, trying to calm the rebels, unlocking the cells of the well-behaved prisoners. "Be reasonable . . . nobody in Germany gets better food . . . the dollar . . . the Ruhr . . . harvest crew will be organized at once and sent to the big estates. A packet of tobacco every week, meat every day . . . for the well-behaved."

Slowly the noise died down. "Harvest crews . . . meat . . . tobacco . . . good conduct." The news trickled into every cell and calmed the rumbling stomachs with hopes of repletion. And there was the prospect of the open sky, perhaps of escape. The last of the rioters, those who were still goading themselves into fury, were dragged by warders to the solitary confinement cells. "Well, then, see if you can live without the plaster pulp."

The iron doors crashed to.

VII

In Countess Mutzbauer's apartments in the Bayerischen district of Berlin, the lady's maid Sophie was already awake in spite of the early hour. The room which she shared with the still-sleeping cook was so narrow that, in addition to the two iron beds, there was space only for two chairs, and she had to write her letter on the window sill.

Sophie Kowalewski had beautifully manicured hands, but they guided their pencil awkwardly. Downstroke, upstroke, pothook, comma, upstroke, downstroke . . . Ah, she would like to say so much! How she missed him, how slowly time went, still three years to wait and hardly six months gone! But Sophie, daughter of the overseer at Neulohe, had not learned to express her feelings in writing. If Hans had been with her, if it had been a question of talking or touching, she could have expressed anything, have made him mad with a kiss, happy with an embrace. But as things were . . .

She looked into the distance. How she would like to convey her feelings to him through this letter! Out of the windowpane a reflected Sophie stared at her, and involuntarily she smiled. A dark curl or two fell loosely over her forehead. Under her eyes, also, the shadows were dark. She ought to be using these hours to sleep thoroughly—but was there time for this when everything faded away, everything decayed before it was completely clear? Live for the moment, then. Today you were still alive.

However tired she might be in the mornings, her feet painful, her mouth stale from the liquors, the wine, the kisses of the night before, by evening she was again attracted to the bars. Dance, drink, and riot! There were plenty of gentlemen, flabby as the 100,000-mark notes, each fifty times a maid's wages, stuffed in their pockets. Last night, too, she had been with one of these gentlemen—but what did it matter? Time ran, flew, galloped. Perhaps in the repeated embraces, in the features which bent over her, greedy and restless as her own, she was looking for Hans (now in prison). . . . But he, shining, swift, superior to them all, had no counterpart.

Sophie Kowalewski, who had escaped to the city from the hard work on the farm, was looking for—she didn't exactly know what—something that would grip her even more. Life is unique, transient, she thought, when we die we are dead for a very long time, and when we get old—even over twenty-five—men will no longer look at us. Hans, oh Hans. . . . Sophie was wearing madam's evening dress and didn't care whether the cook saw it or not. Just as cook had her pickings from the tradespeople, so she, Sophie, lifted silk stockings and underwear from her mistress; neither could throw stones at the other.

It was nearly seven o'clock—so a quick finish. "And I remain, with passionate kisses, your ever-loving future wife, Sophie." She did not attach any value to the word wife. She did not even know if she wanted to marry him, but she must use the word so that he would be given her letter in the penitentiary.

And the convict, Hans Liebschner, would get the letter, for he was not one of those who had been put into solitary confinement for roaring too madly. No, in spite of being scarcely half a year in prison, he had been promoted to orderly against all rules and regulations. And now he talked with particular conviction about harvest crews. He could do so. Neulohe, he knew, was not far from Meienburg, and Neulohe was the home of a nice girl called Sophie.

I'll wangle it all right, he thought.

VIII

The girl had awakened.

She lay, her head propped on her hand, looking at the window; the dingy curtain did not move. She believed she could smell the reeking heat from the courtyard. She shuddered a little—not from the cold, but because of the horrible heat and the foul stench. She looked at her body. It was white and faultless; wonderful that anything could remain so white in such a corrupt atmosphere.

She had no idea what the time was; from the sounds it might be nine or ten, or even eleven o'clock—after eight the noises were very much alike. It was possible that the landlady, Frau Thumann, would come in soon with the morning coffee, and she sought, in accordance with Wolfgang's wishes, to get up and dress decently and cover him up also. Very well, she would do it at once. Wolfgang had surprising fits of propriety.

"It doesn't matter," she had said. "The Thumann woman is used to such things—and worse. As long as she gets her money nothing worries her."

Wolfgang had laughed affectionately. "Worry, when she sees you like that!" He looked at her. Such glances always made her tender—she would have liked to draw him toward her, but he continued, more seriously: "It's for our sakes, Peter, for our sakes. Even if we're in the mud now, we would really be stuck in it if we let everything slide."

"But clothes don't make one either respectable or not respectable."

"It isn't a question of clothes," he had replied, almost heatedly. "It's something to remind us that we're neither of us dirt. And when I've struck it lucky, it'll be easier for us if we've refused to accept things here. We mustn't come down to their level." He was muttering by this time. Again he was thinking how he would "pull it off"; lost in his thoughts, as so often before. He was often miles away from her, his Peter.

"By the time you've brought it off I shan't be with you," she had once said, and there had been silence for a little while, till the meaning of her words penetrated his brooding.

"You'll always be with me, Peter," he had replied, "Always and always. Do you think I'll forget how, night after night, you wait up for me? That I'll forget how you sit here—in this hole—with nothing? Or forget that you never ask questions, and never nag me, however I come home? Peter"—and his eyes shone with a brightness which she did not like, for it was not kindled by her— "last night I almost brought it off. For one second a mountain of money lay before me. . . . I felt it was almost in my grasp. Only once or twice more. . . . No, I'll not pretend to you. I wasn't thinking of anything definite—not of a house or a garden or a car, not even of you. . . . It was like a sudden light in front of me. No—more like a beam of light in me. Life was as wide and clear as the sky at sunrise. Everything was pure . . . Then," he hung his head, "a tart spoke to me, and from that moment everything went wrong."

He had stood with bent head at the window. Taking his trembling hand between hers, she felt how young he was, how young in enthusiasm and despair, young and without any sense of responsibility.

"You'll bring it off," she said softly. "But when you do, I shan't be with you."

He pulled away his hand. "You'll stay with me," he said coldly. "I forget nothing." And she knew then that he was thinking of his mother, who had once slapped her face; she hadn't wanted to stay with him because of that. But now she would be staying with him forever. He hadn't yet succeeded indeed, and she had known for a long time that he was not going the right way about it. But what did it matter? Though there could still be this dirty room and she couldn't know from one day to another what they were going to live on, or whether they could have any clothes or furniture—from one o'clock this morning she would be tied to him.

She reached out for her stockings and began to slip them on.

Suddenly she was seized by a terrible anxiety. Everything might have gone wrong yesterday, utterly wrong; the last 1,000-mark note lost. But she dared not to get up to make sure. With burning eyes she looked at Wolfgang's clothes hanging over the chair near the door, trying to guess the amount of money in them by the bulge in his right-hand coat pocket.

The fees have to be paid, she thought anxiously. If the fees aren't paid it can't happen.

It was fruitless, this study. Sometimes he kept his handkerchief in that pocket. Perhaps new notes had been issued—500,000-mark notes, 1,000,000-mark notes. And what would a civil marriage cost? One million? Two million? Five million? How could she know? Even if she had been brave enough to reach into the pocket and count, she would still know nothing! She never knew anything.

The pocket was not bulging enough.

Slowly, so that the bed springs did not creak, cautiously, anxiously, she turned to him.

"Good morning, Peter," he said in a cheerful voice. His arm pulled her to his breast, and she put her mouth against his mouth. She did not want to hear what he said.

"I'm entirely broke, Peter. We haven't a single mark left."

In the silence that followed the fires of love grew brighter. The stale air of the room was purified by a white-hot flame. In spite of everything, merciful arms raise lovers from the struggle, the hunger and despair, the sin and wickedness, into the clean cool heaven of consummation.

Chapter Two

Berlin Slumps

I

Many streets round Schlesische Bahnhof are sinister. In 1923, to the dreariness of the facades, the evil smells, the misery of that barren stone desert, there was added a widespread shamelessness, the child of despair or indifference, lechery born of the itch to heighten a sense of living in a world which, in a mad rush, was carrying everyone toward an obscure fate.

Rittmeister von Prackwitz, in an over-elegant light-gray suit made to measure by a London tailor, looked almost too conspicuous with his lean figure, snow-white hair above a deeply tanned face, dark bushy eyebrows and bright eyes. He walked with fastidiously upright carriage, careful not to come into contact with others, his gaze directed to an imaginary point far down the street, so that he need not see anything or anybody. He would have liked to transport his hearing also, to, say, the rustling harvest-ripe cornfields in Neulohe, where reaping had scarcely started; he had tried not to listen to scorn and envy and greed calling after him.

It was as if he were back in the unhappy days of November 1918, when he and twenty comrades—the remainder of his squadron—went marching down a Berlin street in the neighborhood of the Reichstag and suddenly, from window, roof and dark entry, bullets had pelted down on the small party; an irregular, wild, cowardly sniping. They had marched on then as he now did, chin pushed out, lips compressed, staring at an imaginary point at the end of the street, a point they would possibly never reach.

The Rittmeister had the feeling that, in the five years of lunacy which followed, he had in reality always been marching on like this, eyes fixed on an imaginary point, waking as well as sleeping—because there was no sleeping without dreams during those years. Always a desolate street full of enmity, hatred, baseness, vulgarity; and if against all expectation one came to a turning, there opened up only another similar street, with the same hate and the same vulgarity. But there again was that point which had no real existence and was a mere figment of the imagination. Or was that point something which did not exist outside, but within himself, in his very own chest—let him be frank:

in his heart? And perhaps he marched on because a man must, without listening to hate and vulgarity, even though from a thousand windows ten thousand evil eyes are watching him, even though he is quite alone—for where were his comrades? Perhaps he marched on because only thus could a man fulfill himself and become what he had to be in this world—himself.

Here in Langestrasse near Schlesische Bahnhof in Berlin, accursed city, Rittmeister von Prackwitz was haunted by the sensation that, although confronted by ten blatant coffee-house signs advertising nothing but brothels, the goal of his march was at hand. He, who much against his will had come here to hunt up at least sixty laborers for the harvest, could soon lower his eyes, stand at ease and feel with the Lord God: "Behold, it was very good."

Aye, a good, almost a bumper harvest stood in the fields, a harvest which those famished townspeople could very well do with, and he had had to leave it all in the charge of his bailiff, a somewhat dissipated young fellow, and go up to town to bed laborers. It was strange and utterly incomprehensible that the greater the misery in the city, the scarcer the food, and the more the country offered at least a sufficiency, the more people made for the city like moths attracted by a deadly flame.

The Rittmeister burst into a laugh. Yes, indeed, it really looked as if the heavenly rest after the sixth day of creation was near at hand. Or was it a *fata Morgana*, a mirage of an oasis, seen when thirst became unbearable?

The female in whose face he had unthinkingly laughed emptied behind him a pailful, a barrelful, nay, a whole vatful of filthy abuse. The Rittmeister, however, turned into a shop over which hung a dilapidated signboard with the words: "Berlin Harvesters' Agency."

II

The flame rises up and sinks; it is extinguished; happy the hearth that retains the glow. The glow dies down, but there is still warmth.

Wolfgang Pagel sat at the table in his field-gray tunic, now extremely worn and old. His hands rested on the bare oilcloth covering. "Madam Po has scented it," he whispered, winking and nodding at the door.

"What?" asked Petra. "You're not going to call Frau Thumann Madam Po, or she will throw us out," she added.

"That's certain," he said. "There won't be any breakfast today. She's scented it."

"Shall I ask her, Wolf?"

"Don't bother. He who asks won't get. Let's wait."

Wolgang tilted the chair, rocked back and started to whistle: *Arise, ye prisoners of starvation. . . .* He was quite unconcerned, unworried. Through the window—the curtain was now drawn—a gleam of sun entered the dreary gray room, or what is called sun in Berlin; all the light which the smoke-blanket lets through. As he rocked to and fro the sun lit up sometimes his wavy hair, sometimes his face with its sparkling gray-green eyes.

Petra, who had on only his shabby summer overcoat dating from pre-war times, looked at him. She was never tired of looking; she admired him. It was a wonder how he managed to wash in a little hand-basin with less than a pint of water and still look as if he scrubbed himself for an hour in a bath. She felt old and used up compared with him, although she was actually a year younger.

Abruptly he stopped whistling and listened to the door. "The enemy approaches. Will there be any coffee? I'm frightfully hungry."

Petra would have liked to tell him that she, too, had been hungry a long time, for the scanty breakfast with its two rolls had been her only food for days—but no, she didn't want to tell him that.

The shuffling footsteps in the corridor died away, the outer door slammed. "You see, Peter, Madam Po has merely taken herself to the toilet again. That's also a sign of the time; all business is transacting in a circuitous manner. Madam Po runs around with her pot."

He again tilted back the chair, starting to whistle unconcernedly, gaily.

He did not deceive her. She could not understand by a long way all he said, nor did she listen very attentively, even. She was alive to the sound of his voice, its softest vibration, of which he himself was hardly aware; and she could tell that he was not feeling so gay as he would like to appear, nor so unconcerned. If only he would unburden himself; in whom should he confide if not in her? There was no need to feel embarrassed, he did not need to tell her lies, she understood him—well, perhaps not altogether. But she approved of everything in advance and blindly. Forgave everything. Everything? Nonsense, there was nothing to forgive, and even should he start to race at her or to strike her, well, it would have its reason.

Petra Ledig was an illegitimate child, without a father; a little salesgirl later, just tolerated by her now-married mother as long as she handed over her salary to the last halfpenny. But there came a day when her mother said: "With this rubbish you can buy your own food," and shouted after her: "And where you sleep, that's your own affair also."

Petra Ledig (it may be assumed that the pretentious name of Petra was her unknown father's sole contribution to her equipment for life) was, at twenty-two, no longer a blank page. She had ripened, not in a peaceful atmosphere, but during the war, postwar and inflation. Only too soon she knew what it meant when a gentleman customer in her boot shop touched her lap significantly with his toe. Sometimes she nodded, met this one or that of an evening, after shop hours, and courageously steered her little ship a whole year without floundering. She even managed to pick and choose to a certain extent, her choice being decided not so much by her taste as by her fear of disease. But when the dollar rose too cruelly and all that she had put by for the rent was devalued to almost nothing, then she would parade the streets, in deadly fear of the vice squad. She had made the acquaintance of Wolfgang Pagel during such a stroll.

Wolfgang had had a good evening. He had a little money, he had been drinking a little. At such times he was always cheerful and ready for anything. "Come along, little dark thing, come along!" he had shouted across the street, and something like a race took place between Petra and a mustachioed policeman. But a taxi, a frightful contraption, had carried her off to an evening quite pleasant but really not very different from any other evening.

The morning had come, the gray, desolate morning in the room of an accommodation hotel, which always had such a depressing effect. The sort of occasion when you ask yourself: "What's the use of it all? Why do I go on living?" As was proper, she had feigned sleep while the gentleman hurriedly dressed, quietly, so as not to wake her. For conversations on the morning after were unpopular and distressing, because you discovered that you had nothing to say to the other person and, more often than not, loathed him. All she had to do was to look through her eyelashes to see whether he put the money for her on the bedside table. Well, he had put the money down. Everything was going as usual, not a word of another meeting, and he was already at the door.

She did not know how it happened or what had come over her, but she sat up in bed and asked in a low and faltering voice: "Would you—would you, sir—oh, may I come with you?"

At first he had not understood and had turned round quite startled. "Excuse me?"

Then he had thought that she, perhaps new to such a situation, was ashamed to pass the proprietress and the porter. He had declared that he was willing to wait for her if she made haste. But while she hurriedly dressed, it appeared that it was not a question so simple as that of leaving, unmolested, the house for the street. She was used to that. (She had made no pretenses from the first moment.) No, she wanted to stay with him altogether. Wouldn't it be possible? "Oh, please, please!"

Who knows what he was thinking? He was no longer in a hurry, though. He stood there in the gloomy room—it was just that horrible hour, shortly before five in the morning, which gentlemen always choose for leaving, for then they can catch the first streetcar to their lodgings and freshen themselves up before their work; and many pretend to, or actually do, have a nap, so as to leave the bed disturbed.

He drummed with his fingers thoughtfully on the table. With greenish eyes shining out from beneath his lowered brow, he looked contemplatively at her. Did she think he had any money?

No. She hadn't thought of that. It would be all the same to her.

He was a second lieutenant in the war, and without a pension. Without a job. Without a fixed income. In fact, without any income.

It was all right. That wasn't her reason for asking.

He did not inquire why she had asked. Indeed, he did not ask any more questions, anything at all. Only later did it strike her that he might have asked a lot of questions, very disagreeable questions. For instance, whether she made a habit of begging men to let her go with them; whether she was expecting a baby; thousands of disgusting things. But he stood there and looked at her. Already she was convinced that he would say "yes." Ought to. Something very mysterious had urged her to ask him. She had never thought of such a thing before, nor was she at that time the least in love with him. It had been quite an ordinary night.

"'Oh, Constance, is it done?'" said he, quoting the title of a popular comedy hit. For the first time she noticed the humorous wrinkles round his eyes, and that he winked when he joked.

"Oh, certainly," she rejoined.

"All right," he said, drawling the words. "What is hardly enough for one is barely sufficient for two. Come along. Are you ready?"

It was a strange sensation, descending the stairs of a repulsive bed-and-breakfast house by the side of a man to whom one now belonged. When she stumbled over a badly laid stair carpet, he had said "Upsey" quite absent-mindedly. Probably he did not realize she was with him.

Suddenly he had stopped. She remembered it vividly. They were downstairs in the false marble splendor and stucco of the entrance. "By the way, my name is Wolfgang Pagel," he said with a slight bow.

"Pleased to meet you," she replied in the correct manner. "Mine is Petra Ledig."

"Whether you'll be pleased I don't know," he had laughed. "Come on, little one. I shall call you Peter. Petra is too Biblical and too stony. But your surname's good enough for me and can stay as it is."

III

Petra was still too much taken up with what was happening to pay much attention to the sense of Wolfgang's words. Later she learned from him that Petra meant "rock," and that it had first been borne by the disciple Peter, on whom Christ had founded his church.

Altogether she learned a good deal during the year she lived with him. Not that he behaved like a teacher. But it was inevitable that, during the long hours of their being together—for he was without a genuine occupation—he should talk a good deal with her, if only because they could not always sit in silence side by side in their dreary room. And when Petra gained confidence, she often asked a question, either to stop him brooding or because it gave her pleasure to hear him talk. For instance: "Wolf, how do they make cheese?" or: "Wolf, is it true that there is a man in the moon?"

He never laughed at her, nor did he ever refuse to answer her questions. He replied slowly and carefully, for the knowledge he had gained at the military college was of no great consequence. And where he was not informed, he took her with him and they went into one of the big libraries and he consulted their volumes. She would sit quietly, some little book in front of her, which, however, she did not read, and look about her awestruck at the big room in which people were sitting so still, so gently turning the pages, as quietly as if they were moving in their sleep. It always seemed like a fairy tale that she, a little shopgirl, an illegitimate child, who had just been on the point of going under, was now able to enter buildings where educated people, who had surely never heard of the rottenness with which she had been forced to make such an intimate acquaintance, were sitting. By herself she would never have dared to come, although certain poor creatures allowed to sit along the walls showed that not only wisdom was being sought here, but also warmth, light, and just that which she, too, sensed in these books—a profound peace.

When Wolfgang had learned enough, they went out and he told her what he had gleaned. She listened and forgot it, or remembered it but not accurately—that, however, was of no importance. What mattered was that he took her seriously, that she was something other than a creature whom he liked and who was good for him.

Sometimes, when she had spoken without thinking, she would exclaim, overwhelmed by her ignorance: "Oh, Wolf, I'm so terribly stupid. I'll never learn anything. I shall remain stupid forever."

Even then he did not laugh at the outburst, but entered into her feelings in a friendly and serious spirit, declaring that fundamentally it was unimportant whether one knew how cheese was made or not. For one would never know how to make it as well as the cheesemaker did. Stupidity, he believed, was something quite different. If one didn't know how to arrange one's life, how to learn from one's mistakes, but got annoyed, repeatedly and unnecessarily, about little things, knowing that they would be forgotten in a fortnight; if one could not get on with one's fellowmen—that was stupidity, real stupidity. His mother was a striking example. In spite of all her reading and her experience and intelligence, she had succeeded, out of sheer love, through knowing what was best for him and tying him to her apron string, in driving her son out of the house, he who was really patient and easy to get on with. (So he said.) She, Petra, stupid? Well, *they* hadn't quarreled yet, and even if they had no money, they hadn't spoiled their lives on that account, nor sulked. Stupid? What did she mean?

What Wolf meant, of course. Spoiled their lives? Sulked? They had had the most glorious time, the most beautiful time of her whole life. Nothing could be more beautiful. As a matter of fact, she did not mind whether she was stupid or not—despite what he said, clever was out of the question—as long as he liked her and took her seriously.

A rough passage? Nonsense! She had learned often enough in her life, and especially during the last year, that to be without money need not spoil one's existence. At this very time when everybody's thoughts turned on money, money, money, figures stamped on paper, paper with more and more noughts printed on it—at this very time the little foolish girl had made the discovery that money was of no value. That it was absurd to bother one's head about it for a moment; that is, about the money which one hadn't got.

(Perhaps she was not quite so indifferent this morning, for she was hungry enough to be nearly sick, and at half-past one the rent had to be paid.)

If she had taken thought for the morrow, she could never have had a peaceful moment by the side of Wolfgang Pagel, former second lieutenant, who had managed for more than a year to provide a livelihood for both, with practically no working capital, from the gaming tables. Every evening at about eleven o'clock he gave her a kiss and said: "So long, little girl," and went, she only smiling at him. For she mustn't say a word, in case it brought him bad luck. At first, when she realized that this eternal nightly absence did not mean "going out on the loose," but was "work" for both their livelihoods, she had sat up till three or four . . . to wait for him; and he would return pale, with nervous movements and hollow temples, his glance unsteady, his hair wet with perspiration. She had listened to his feverish descriptions, his triumphs when he won, his despair when he lost. Silently she had listened to his complaints about this or that woman who had purloined his stake money, or his brooding astonishment as to why, on that particular evening, black should have turned up seventeen times in succession, and have hurled him and Petra, almost on the threshold of wealth, back into poverty.

She did not understand anything of the game, his game of roulette, however much he told her about it (he had refused point-blank to take her with him). But she understood quite well that it was a kind of tax which he paid to life for having her, that he was so kind, so imperturbable, because in the hours at the gaming table he could spend his energy, all his despair over his spoiled and aimless life, the only life he knew.

Oh, she understood far more; she understood that he deceived himself, at least when he assured her passionately again and again that he was not a gambler. . . .

"Tell me, what could I do instead? If I were an accountant scribbling figures into a book I'd only get a salary on which we should starve. Shall I sell boots, write articles, become a chauffeur? Peter, the secret is to have but few needs and thus time to live your own life. Three or four hours, often only half an hour at the roulette table, and we can live for a week, a month. I a gambler? It's a dog's life! I would rather carry bricks, instead of standing there, holding myself from being swept off my feet by a run of luck. I am as cool as a cucumber and calculating; you know they call me the Pari Panther. They hate me, they scowl when they see me because there's no change to be got out of me, because I take away my small gains every day, and once I have them, finish! No more play!"

And, with a marvelous inconsequence, having quite forgotten what he had just said: "Only wait! Let me pull off something really big! An amount which is worthwhile! Then you'll see what we'll do. Then you'll see I'm no gambler. I shall never be caught that way again. Why should I? It's the lowest kind of drudgery; no one would voluntarily take it on—if he's not a gambler."

Meanwhile she saw him coming home, night in, night out, with hollow temples, damp hair, gleaming eyes.

"I nearly brought it off, Peter," he cried.

But his pockets were empty. Then he would pawn everything they had, keeping only what he stood up in (during such times she had to stay in bed), and go off with just enough money in his pocket to buy the minimum of counters—to return with some small winnings, or occasionally, very rarely, with his pockets stuffed with money. When it looked like the end of everything, he always brought in some money, she had to admit; much or little, he brought some.

He had some "system" or other connected with the rolling of the roulette ball, a system of chance, a system which was based on the fact that the ball often did not do what, according to the probabilities, it ought to do. This system he had explained to her a hundred times, but as she had never seen a roulette table she could not properly understand what he told her. She also doubted whether he always kept to his own system.

But however that might be, till now he had always scraped through. Relying on this, she had for a very long time managed to lie down and go quietly to sleep, without waiting up for him. Yes, it was better to feign sleep if by any chance she were still awake when he returned. There was no sleep that night if, straight from the game, he started to talk.

"How can you stand it, my girl?" Frau Thumann would say, shaking her head. "Out every night and with all your dough in his pocket. And they say the place is alive with classy tarts. I wouldn't let my man go."

"But you let your husband go up a building, Frau Thumann. A ladder may slip or a plank give way. And tarts are everywhere."

"Lord, don't suggest such things with my Willem working on the fifth floor, and me being already so nervous. But there's a difference, lass. Building's necessary, but gambling's not."

"But suppose he needs it, Frau Thumann."

"Needs it! Needs it! I'm always having my old man telling me what a lot he needs. Cards and tobacco and floods of beer, and, I dare say, little bits of fluff as well, but he don't tell me that. I tell him: 'What you *do* need is me to take you in hand and the pay envelope from the contractor's office on Friday nights. That's what you need!' You're too good to him, my girl, you're too soft. When I look at you of a morning when I bring in the coffee, and see you making eyes at him and he don't notice you at all, then I know how it'll end. Gambling as work—I like that! Gambling's not working and working's not gambling. If you really mean him well, my girl, you take his money away and let him go building with Willem. He can carry bricks, can't he?"

"Good God, Frau Thumann, you talk exactly like his mother. She also thought I was too kind to him and encouraging him in his vice, and she even slapped my face once for that very reason."

"Slapping ain't the right thing either! Aren't you her daughter-in-law? No, you do it, see what I mean, for your own pleasure, and if it gets too much for you, then you hop it. No, slapping's not nice, either; you c'n even go to the law about it."

"But it didn't hurt at all. His mother's got such tiny hands. My mother was quite different. And anyway . . ."

IV

A wooden barrier divided the room of the Berlin Harvesters' Agency into two very unequal parts. The front part, in which Rittmeister von Prackwitz stood, was quite small and the entrance door opened into it. Prackwitz had hardly room to move.

The other and larger part was occupied by a small, fat, darkish man. The Rittmeister was not sure whether he looked so dark because of his hair or because he had not washed. Gesticulating, the dark fat man in dark clothes was speaking vehemently with three men in corduroy suits, gray hats, and cigars in the corner of their mouths. The men replied just as vehemently, and although they were not shouting it seemed as if they were.

The Rittmeister did not understand a word; they were speaking Polish, of course. Though the tenant of Neulohe employed every year half a hundred Poles, he had not learned Polish, apart from a few words of command.

"I admit," he would say to Eva, his wife, who spoke broken Polish, "I admit that I ought really to learn it for practical reasons. Nevertheless I refuse, now and forever, to learn this language. I absolutely refuse. We live too near the borders. Learn Polish—never!"

"But the people make the most insolent remarks to your very face, Achim."

"Well? Am I to learn Polish so that I can understand their insolence? I haven't the slightest intention of doing so."

And thus the Rittmeister did not understand what these four men were negotiating so vehemently in the corner, nor did he care. But he was not a very patient man: what had to be done had to be done quickly—he wanted to go back to Neulohe at noon with fifty or sixty laborers. A bumper harvest stood in the fields, and the sun shone so that he thought he could hear the crackling of the wheat. "Shop! Shop!" he called out.

They talked on. It looked exactly as if they were quarreling for dear life; the next moment they would be flying at each other's throats.

"Hey, you there!" called the Rittmeister sharply. "I said 'Good morning.'" (He had not said good morning.) What a crowd! Eight years ago, even five, they were whining before him and slavishly trying to kiss his hand. A damnable age, an accursed city! Wait till he got them in the country.

"Listen, you there," he rapped out in his curtest military voice, banging the counter with his fist.

Yes—and how they listened! They knew that sort of voice. For this generation such a voice still had significance, its sound awakened memories. They stopped talking at once. Inwardly the Rittmeister smiled. Yes, the good old sergeant major's bark still had its effect—and most of all with such scum. Presumably it penetrated to their miserable bones as if it were the first blast of the last trumpet. Well, they always had a bad conscience.

"I need harvesters," he said to the fat, swarthy man. "Fifty to sixty. Twenty men, twenty women, the remainder boys and girls."

"Yes, sir." The fat man bowed, politely smiling.

"An efficient foreman reaper, must be able to deposit as security the value of twenty hundredweights of rye. His wife, for a women's wage, to cook for them."

"Yes, sir."

"I pay single fare and your commission; if the people stay till after the beet harvest their fares won't be deducted. Otherwise . . ."

"Yes, sir. Oh, yes, sir."

"And now get a move on. The train goes at twelve-thirty. Be quick. Pronto. Understand?" And the Rittmeister, a weight having been taken from his mind, nodded even toward the three figures in the background. "Get the contracts ready. I'll be back in half an hour. I only want some luncheon."

"Yes, sir."

"Then everything's settled, isn't it?" he concluded. Something in the attitude of the other puzzled him; the submissive grin did not appear so much submissive as deceitful. "Everything's in order?"

"Everything's in order," agreed the fat man, with a gleam in his eyes. "Everything will be done in accordance with the gentleman's instructions. Fifty people—good, they're here. Railway station, twelve-thirty—good, the train leaves. Punctually to your orders—but without the laborers." He grinned.

"What?" the Rittmeister almost shouted, screwing up his face. "What are you saying? Speak German, man! Why without laborers?"

"Perhaps the gentleman who can give orders so perfectly will also order me where to get the people. Fifty people? Well, find them, make them, quick, pronto, presto, what?"

The Rittmeister looked more closely at his man. His first bewilderment was over, as was also his anger, now that he sensed the other was out to annoy him. He knows German well enough, he thought, as the fat man gabbled on grotesquely, but he doesn't want to.

"And those in the background?" he asked and pointed at the three men in corduroy from whose lips the cigars were still hanging. "You are surely foremen? You come with me. New quarters, decent beds, no bugs."

For a moment it seemed to him deplorable that he should have to advertise himself in this manner. But the harvest was at stake, and it might rain any day. Yes, today even, for here in Berlin there was something like thunder in the air. He could no longer rely on the fat, swarthy man; he had alienated him, probably by his commandeering voice. "Well, what about it?" he asked encouragingly.

The three stood there motionless as if they had not heard a word. They were foreman reapers, the Rittmeister was sure of it. He was familiar with these struck-out jaws, the fierce but rather gloomy look of the professional nigger-driver.

The swarthy man was grinning; he did not look at his men, he was so sure of them. (Here is the street, the Rittmeister thought, and the point at which to look. I must march along.) Loudly: "Good work, good pay, piecework, good allowances. What do you say to that?" They were not listening. "And for the foreman thirty, I say thirty, good genuine paper dollars down."

"I'll arrange for the men," cried the dark man.

But he was too late. The foreman reapers had moved over to the barrier.

"Take mine, sir. Men like bulls, strong, pious . . ."

"No, don't take Josef 's. They're all lazy scoundrels, won't get up in the morning; strong with girls but slackers with work . . ."

"Sir, why waste time with Jablonski? He's just out of jail for knifing a steward."

"You dirty dog!"

A cataract of Polish words fell between them. Were they going to pull out their knives? The fat man was among them, talking, gesticulating, shouting, pushing, glaring at the Rittmeister, toward whom the third man was stealing, unnoticed.

"Good paper dollars, eh? Thirty of them? Handed over on departure? If the gentleman will be at Schlesische Bahnhof at twelve o'clock I'll be there, too, with the people. Don't say anything. Get away quickly. Bad people here!"

And he mingled with the others. Voices screamed. Four figures swayed to and fro, tugging at each other.

The Rittmeister was glad to find the door so near and unobstructed. Relieved, he stepped into the street.

V

Wolfgang Pagel was still sitting at the oilcloth table rocking the chair, whistling absent-mindedly his whole repertoire of soldier songs, and waiting for Frau Thumann's enamel coffeepot.

In the meantime his mother sat at a handsome Renaissance table in a well-furnished flat in Tannenstrasse. On a yellow pillow-lace tablecloth stood a silver coffee service, fresh butter, honey, genuine English jam—everything was there. Only, no one was sitting in front of the second cover. Frau Pagel looked at the empty place, then at the clock. Reaching for her napkin, she drew it out of the silver ring and said: "I will begin, Minna."

Minna, the yellowish, faded creature at the door, who had been over twenty years with Frau Pagel, nodded, looked at the clock and said: "Certainly. Those who come late . . ."

"He knows our breakfast time."

"The young master couldn't forget it."

The old lady with the energetic face and clear blue eye, from whom age had not stolen her upright bearing nor her firm principles, added after a pause: "I really thought I should see him for breakfast this morning."

Since that quarrel at the end of which Petra, least concerned of any, had had her face slapped, Minna had daily set a place for the only son. Day after day she had had to clear away an untouched plate, and day after day her mistress had voiced the selfsame expectation. But Minna had also noticed that the repeated disappointment had not in the least diminished the old lady's certainty that her son would appear (without herself making any advances). Minna knew that talking did not help, and so she kept silent.

Frau Pagel tapped her egg. "Well, he may come during the course of the day, Minna. What are we having for lunch?"

Minna informed her and madam approved. They were having the things he liked.

"In any case he must come soon. One day he's sure to come to grief with that damnable gambling. A complete shipwreck! Well, he shan't hear a word of reproach from me."

Minna knew better, but it was no use saying so. Frau Pagel, however, was also not without intelligence nor without intuition. She turned her head sharply toward her faithful old servant and demanded: "You had your afternoon off yesterday. You went—there—again?"

"Where's an old woman to go?" Minna grumbled. "He is my boy, too."

Frau Pagel angrily tapped her teacup with her spoon. "He's a very silly boy, Minna," she said harshly.

"You can't put old heads on young shoulders," answered Minna, quite unmoved. "When I look back, Madam, at the silly things I did in my youth . . ."

"What silly things?" her mistress called out indignantly. "You didn't do anything of the kind. No, when you talk like that you mean me, of course—and I won't stand it, Minna."

Minna thereupon kept silent. But when one person is dissatisfied with herself, then another person's silence is like fuel to a fire—silence more than anything.

"Of course, I oughtn't to have slapped her," Frau Pagel continued warmly. "She's only a silly little chit and she loves him—I don't want to say like a dog its master, although that expresses it exactly. Minna, don't shake your head. That's it exactly . . . (Frau Pagel had not turned round to look, but Minna had really shaken her head.) She loves him as a woman oughtn't to love a man."

Frau Pagel stared furiously at her bread, put the spoon in the jam and spread it finger-thick. "To sacrifice oneself!" she said indignantly. "Yes, of course! They all like to do that. Because it's easy, because there's no trouble then! But to tell the painful truth, to say: 'Wolfgang, my son, there must be an end to this gambling or you'll never get another penny from me'—that would be true love."

"But, madam," said Minna with deliberation, "the child has no money she could give him, and he's not her son, either. . . ."

"There!" Frau Pagel called out furiously. "There! Get out of the room, you ungrateful creature! You've spoiled my breakfast with your everlasting back talk and contradiction. Minna! Where are you going to? Clear away at once. Do you think I can go on eating when you annoy me like that? You know quite well how easily upset I am with my liver. Yes, take away the coffee, too. The idea of coffee! I'm upset enough as it is. The girl can be a daughter to you for all I care, but I'm old-fashioned, I don't believe that one can be spiritually pure if before marriage . . ."

"You just said," replied Minna, quite unmoved by this outburst, for such outbursts were part of the routine and her mistress calmed down as quickly as she flared up, "you just said that if you love someone you sometimes have to tell them disagreeable truths. Then I have to reply that Wolf isn't Petra's son."

Whereupon Minna stalked off, the tray rattling in her hand, while as a sign that she expected to have peace and quietness in "her" kitchen, she slammed the door.

Frau Pagel understood quite well and respected her old servant's familiar hint. She only shouted after her: "You old donkey. Always feeling insulted. Always losing your temper about nothing at all." She laughed; her anger had evaporated. "Such an old donkey, imagining that love consists of saying disagreeable things to the other person." She crossed the room. Her outburst had taken place only after she had finished her breakfast, and she was therefore in the best of spirits. The little quarrel had refreshed her. Stopping before a small cabinet, she selected a long black Brazil cigar, lit it carefully, and went across to her husband's room.

VI

On the door of the flat, over the brass bell-pull (a lion's mouth) was a porcelain name plate: "Edmund Pagel—Attaché." Frau Pagel was getting on for seventy, and it therefore didn't look as if her husband had made much progress in his career. Attachés advanced in years are unusual.

Edmund Pagel, however, had gone as far as the most efficient councillor or ambassador—that is, as far as the cemetery. When Frau Pagel went into her husband's room, it was not to visit him but only those reminders of him which were renowned far beyond the walls of the little home.

She flung the windows wide open; light and air flowed in from the gardens. In this small street, so close to the traffic that of an evening one could hear the elevated railway enter Nollendorfplatz station and the buses rumbling day and night, there was a straggle of old gardens with tall trees—long-forgotten gardens which had scarcely changed since the 'eighties. Here it was good to live—for aging people. The elevated might thunder and the dollar climb—but the widowed Frau Pagel looked tranquilly into the gardens. Creeping vine had ascended to her windows; down below, everything grew, flowered, seeded—but the frenzied, restless people yonder with their turmoil and commerce did not know it. She could look and remember, she need not hurry, the garden would remind her. That she could live on here, that she did not need to hurry, was the doing of the man whose work was in this room.

Five-and-forty years ago they had seen each other for the first time, loved and married. Nothing was as radiant, as happy, as swift as Edmund, when she looked back. It always seemed as if she were running with him in a beautiful breeze down streets full of blossoms. Branches seemed to reach down to them over walls. They ran faster. The sky soared over them from the top of a hill full of houses. . . .

As long as they kept running, the blue silk curtain in front of them would continue to open.

Yes, what characterized Edmund was his speed, which had nothing hasty about it, but it came from his strength, his sense of perfect well-being. They reached a meadow with crocuses. For a moment they remained motionless on the festive green and purple carpet, and then bent to pick the flowers. But hardly had she had twenty in her hand then he came to her, swiftly, with no rush, light of step, with a whole big bouquet.

"How did you do that?" she asked breathlessly.

"I don't know," he said, " I feel so light, like I'm blowing in the wind."

They had been married for quite a while when in her sleep the young wife heard a cry. She awoke. Her husband was sitting up in bed, looking altogether changed. She hardly recognized him.

"Is that you?" she asked, very softly lest her words turn the dream into reality.

The strange yet familiar man tried to smile, an embarrassed, apologetic smile. "Forgive me if I have disturbed you. I feel so strange. I can't understand it. I'm really worried." And after a long pause, while he looked doubtfully at her: "I can't get up."

"You can't get up?" she asked skeptically. It was a joke, some nonsense of his, of course, a poor joke. "It's impossible that all of a sudden you can't get up."

"Yes," he said slowly and seemed not to believe it himself. "But I feel as if I had no legs. Anyhow, they are numb."

"Nonsense," she cried and jumped up. "You have caught a chill, or they've gone to sleep. Wait. I'll help you."

But even as she spoke, even as she walked round the bed to him, terror pierced her. . . . It's true, it's true, she realized.

Did she realize it? The old woman at the window shrugged her shoulders. How could she realize the impossible? The fleetest, the happiest, the most vivid creature in the world, not to be able to walk, not even to stand. Impossible to realize that!

But the icy sensation had remained; it was as if she were inhaling more and more of coldness with every breath. Her heart tried to resist, but it, too, was getting cold. Round it an armor of ice closed tightly.

"Edmund!" she called imploringly. "Wake up, get up!"

"I can't," he murmured.

He really could not. Just as he sat that morning in bed, so he had sat, day in and day out, year after year, in bed, in a wheeled chair, in a deck chair . . . sat, entirely healthy, without pain—but could not walk. Life which had started so flamboyantly, swift shining life, the smile of good luck, the blue sky and flowers—all was all gone and done with. Why could it not return? No answer. Oh, God, why not? And, if it had to be, why, then, so suddenly? Why without any warning? He had passed happily into sleep and had miserably awakened, to incredible wretchedness.

Oh, she had not lain down under it; no, she hadn't given in for a moment. All the twenty years this had lasted she hadn't given in once. When he had long abandoned every hope, she still dragged him from physician to physician. Reports of a miraculous cure or a newspaper notice were enough to rekindle her optimism. In succession she believed in baths, electrical treatment, mud packs, massage, medicine, miracle-working saints. She wanted to believe in them, and she did believe.

"Don't bother," he smiled. "Perhaps it's just as well as it is."

"That's what you'd like," she cried angrily. "To give in, to bear it patiently. That's too easy. Humility may be all right for the proud and fortunate who need checking. I hold with the ancients who fought the gods for their happiness."

"But I am happy," he said good-humoredly.

She didn't want that kind of happiness, however. She despised it, it filled her with anger. She had married an attaché, an active man on good terms with his fellow men, a future ambassador. On the door she had fixed a plate: "Edmund Pagel, Attaché," and it would stay. She would not have a new one made: "Pagel—Artist." No, she had not married a color-grinder and a paint-dauber.

He sat and painted. He sat in his wheeled chair and smiled and whistled and painted. Angry impatience filled her. Did he not understand that he was wasting his life on these stupid paintings at which people only smiled?

"Let him alone, Mathilde," said the relatives. "It's very good for an invalid. He has occupation and amusement."

No, she would not let him alone. When she married him there had been no talk of painting; she didn't know that he had ever held a paintbrush in his hand, even. She hated it all, down to the smell of the oil paints. She was always knocking against the frames, the easel was always in her way; she never resigned herself to it. His pictures she left in boarding houses, at watering-places, in the attics of their flats; his charcoal sketches lay around and were lost.

Occasionally, in the midst of some work or worry, she would glance from the narrow prison of herself at one such picture on the wall as if seeing it for the first time. Then something seemed to want to lightly touch her, as if something asleep were waking. . . . Stop! Oh please stop! Everything was very bright. A tree, for instance, in the sun, in the air, against a clear summer sky. But the tree seemed to rise up, the wind to blow gently. The tree moved. Was it flying? Yes, the whole earth was flying, the sun, the play of light and air—everything was light, swift, soft. Oh, stop, you relentless, bright world! She came closer to the picture, and the curtain in front of the mysterious stirred. It was linen, smelling of oil paint, earth, firm earth. But the wind was blowing, the tree waved its branches, life was in movement.

Painted by a cripple, created out of nothing by a man who knew and loved movement, it is true, but who was now no more than a cumbersome body that had to be rolled out of bed into a chair. No, do not stop, we're fleeing, we're flying.

Yes, something stirred in the dreaming woman about to be illuminated by an intuition that in this picture her husband was living, immortal, brilliant, swifter than ever; but she turned from it. There was nothing left now but canvas and paint, a flat surface colored in accordance with certain rules; nothing of movement, nothing of the man.

More watering-places! Still more physicians! What did the world say? Two or three exhibitions—no one heard anything about them, saw anything of them; and no pictures were ever sold—thank God, there was no need of that. Now and then, on one of their restless journeys through the health resorts of the world, someone would seek them out; some young man, taciturn, awkward, gloomy, or another breaking out into a flood of words, with nervous movements, to announce a new era; such people did not encourage her to regard her husband's pictures seriously.

"The day is so beautiful; let us go for a drive."

"The light is good. I should like to paint another hour."

"I almost forget what it's like outside. I shall die for lack of air."

"All right, sit by the window, open it—I've been wanting to paint you for a long time."

That was his way—friendly, serene, never angry, but not to be moved either. She talked, implored, got furious, made it up again, used wiles, asked for forgiveness. He was as a field over which pass wind, storm, sunshine, night frost and rain, accepting everything without seeming to change, yet in the end producing a harvest.

Yes, the harvest came. But before it ripened something else happened, something for which she had fought, scolded, struggled, begged, for twenty years: one day he stood up, made a few steps, faltering at first, and then, with the same somewhat embarrassed, apologetic face of twenty years before, said: "I really think I can."

The affliction vanished as it had come, just as incomprehensibly. All her eagerness, her zeal, had not been able to effect its departure; it had been beyond human influence—it was enough to make one despair.

Meanwhile half a life—the better half—had passed. She was in her early forties, a forty-five-year-old husband at her side. An active life, an eager life without rest, full of plans, full of hopes, had slipped away. Now the hopes were fulfilled and there was nothing more to desire. All her plans, all her cares, had lost their meaning. A whole life had crumbled to dust in the moment Edmund got up and walked.

Incomprehensible heart of woman! "Here is your painting, Edmund. It only wants a few more touches. Won't you?"

"Painting, yes, painting," he said absent-mindedly, glanced at it, and went out, where his thoughts had already gone.

No, there was no time now to paint for even half an hour. He had had time, twenty years, to be ill, patiently, without complaint; now he had not a minute to spare. Outside, the whole of life was waiting for him in a whirl of festivities each more splendid than the other, hundreds of people with whom it was glorious to talk, beautiful women, girls who were so bewitchingly young that a thrill went down one's spine just to look at them . . .

And wasn't he himself young, really? He was five-and-twenty; what had happened didn't count, a mere waiting around. He was young, life was young; pick and taste the fruit. Stop, please stop! Go on. . . .

Painting? True, it had helped him, it had been an excellent pastime. Now nothing more was needed to pass away the heavy burden of time. Down its torrent raced, sparkling, shining from a thousand eyes, thrilling to a million songs—with him, still with him, forever with him. Sometimes he started up at night, supporting his burning temples in hot hands. He thought he could hear Time rustling by. He ought not to sleep; who dared sleep when Time glides away so quickly? To sleep was time lost. And softly, so as not to wake his wife, he got up, went into the town, went once more into the town where the lights shone. He sat at a table, looked frantically at the faces. That one? Or you—? Oh, don't rush away—stay for a while!

She let him go. She heard him, but she let him go, in the day as well as the night. At first she had gone with him; she, whose hope was now fulfilled. She saw him at the garden party of a family with whom they were on friendly terms; at a dinner, immaculately dressed, slim, quick, laughing, with gray hair. He danced faultlessly, with assurance. "Forty-five," something said within her. He chatted and joked always with the youngest, she observed. It was horrifying. Just as if a dead man had come to life, as if a corpse with its mouth full of dust were reaching out for the bread of the living. Stay for a while! That memory which her jealous heart had clung to for twenty years and which had been her happiness and life, that memory of early, splendid days faded now, and she could not recall them.

The night surrounded her like a prison wall without a gate. On the bedside table the clock ticked away a useless time which had to be endured. A trembling hand switched on the light, and his bright sketches greeted her from the walls.

She looked at them as if for the first time. In this she was like the world, which at that time had also begun to look at his pictures. Their day had suddenly come, but for their creator it was already over. Paradox indeed that, when he was creating for twenty long years, he was the only one who saw his work. Now came the world, with letters and reproductions, with art dealers and exhibitions, with money and golden laurels—but the once-flowing spring of his interest was dry.

"Yes, paintings," he said, and went.

The woman who was expecting his child lay in bed, and now it was she who gazed at the paintings. It was she who now saw his true image in them. His fleetness, his cheerfulness, his interest—all had gone. Gone? No, they were here, enhanced by the glory that eternity gives to life.

There was one painted shortly before his "recovery," the last to be finished before he put away his brush. He had made her sit at an open window; she sat motionless, as hardly ever in her active life. It was her picture, it was she when she was still with him, painted by him when she still had significance for him. Nothing but a young woman at a window, waiting, while the world rushed by outside. A young woman at a window—his most beautiful picture.

Painted by him when he was still with her. Where was he now? One morning in a vibrant world full of the sun's splendor (but the sun paled for her), he was carried home, disheveled, dirty, the clever hands contorted, the jaw fallen, dry blood on his temple. Policemen and detectives were very tactful. It had happened in a street, the name of which of course conveyed nothing. A fatal accident—yes, an accident. Say no more.

Time, you must fly. Hurry, hurry. And now the son. The father was a radiant star which shone benignly for a long time and was extinguished suddenly. He was extinguished. Let us await the son. A spark of hope, the promise of a fire. Alone no longer.

The woman at the window, an old woman now, turned around. Certainly there was the picture. Young Woman at a Window, Waiting.

The old woman put the stub of her cigar in the ash tray.

"I have the feeling that the silly boy will really come today. It is time he came."

VII

Frau Thumann, spouse of the bricklayer, Wilhelm Thumann, bloated and flabby, in loose garments, with a bloated, flabby face which nevertheless wore a soured expression—the Thumann woman shuffled with the inevitable chamber pot across the corridor to the toilet on the half-flight of stairs below; a toilet serving three families. She was entirely without scruples concerning the harboring of girls of the worst reputation and their hangers-on (at present, temperamental Ida from Alexanderplatz was living in the room opposite the Pagels), but she was full of sanitary niceties about the toilet.

"And now they've discovered them bacticilli, dearie. They could have let 'em alone, but as they've gone and done it, and we ain't got the most wonderful people here either, and sometimes when I go to the toilet I c'n hardly fetch my breath, and who knows what's flying about! An' once there was a blackbeetle there which looked at me in such a nasty way. . . . No, trust me, dearie, I know bugs when I see 'em. You can't tell me anything about them, dearie—I was born and brought up among bugs. Since they *have* been discovered, though, I says to my Willem: 'Pot or no pot, health's the most important thing in life.' I says to him: 'Be careful! The beasts jump at you like tigers and 'fore you know where you are, you bring in a whole microcosmetic of 'em.' But I tell you, dearie, we're made in the rummiest way. Since I've kept to the pot I'm running about with it all day. Not that I'm complaining, but it is a bit funny. Our young gentleman who's got the little pale dark girl—she isn't his wife, but she imagines she will be one day, and some of them relish their imagination like a cake from Hilbrich's—he always calls me Madam Po. Only she tells him not to, which I find decent of her. But he can call me what he likes, for all I care. What does he say it for? 'Cause he likes his little joke. And why does he like his little joke? 'Cause he's young. When you're young you don't believe in nothing, neither in parsons, which I don't either, nor in these bacticilli. And what happens? Just as I rush about with the pot, so they hurry to the Health Committee, but what with, I don't care to say. We all know what it is, though some of 'em call it only a catarrh. And now, silly as they are, they suddenly become wise to it. And as regards the catarrh, don't they wish they could sneeze and someone would say to them, 'God bless you'! But it's too late then, and that's why I'd rather trot about with my pot."

So the Thumann woman, frowsy and voluble, with an acid complexion, was shuffling with her pot along the corridor.

The door of the Pagels' room opened and revealed young Wolfgang Pagel, tall, with broad shoulders and slim hips, fair and cheerful, in a field-gray tunic with narrow red stripes. It was a material which, even after five years' wear, still looked good, with a silver gleam like the leaves of the lime tree.

"Good morning, Frau Thumann," he said quite pleasantly. "How about a little chat about coffee?"

"You! You!" said the Thumann woman indignantly, pushing past with half-averted face. "Don't you see I'm busy?"

"I beg your pardon. It was an urgent inquiry as the result of hunger. We'll gladly wait. It's only about eleven o'clock."

"Don't bother to wait till twelve, then," she replied, and stood in the doorway, waving her pot in a portentous manner. "The new dollar comes out at twelve and, as the man in the greengrocer's cellar said, it'll come out strong and Berlin'll slump again. Then, without batting an eyelid, you can put down another million marks on the table. Coffee without cash—nothing doing!"

Thereupon the door closed; sentence had been pronounced. Wolfgang turned back. "She may be right, Peter!" he said reflectively. "By the time I'd persuaded her about the coffee it would have been twelve o'clock, and if the dollar is really going up—what do you think?"

He did not, however, wait for a reply, but continued, somewhat embarrassed: "Make yourself comfortable in bed, and I'll carry the things straight to Uncle's. In twenty minutes—at most half an hour—I'll be back again and we'll breakfast comfortably on rolls and liver sausage—you in bed and I on the edge. What do you think, Peter?"

"Oh, Wolf," she said weakly, and her eyes became very big. "Today!"

Although they had not said a word about it this morning, he did not pretend to misunderstand her. Rather conscience-stricken, he replied: "Yes, I know it's silly. But it's really not my fault. Or almost not. Everything went wrong last night. I already had pretty fair winnings when I had the mad idea that zero must win. I don't understand myself at all. . . ."

He stopped. He saw the gaming table before him, nothing more than a worn green cloth on the dining table of a good middle-class room; in one corner stood a great hulking buffet with carved pinnacles and knobs, knights and ladies and lions' mouths. For the gambling hells of those days led a nomadic existence, always in flight from the department of the police which dealt with them. If they thought the police had smelled out the old meeting place, then the very next day they would rent a dining or drawing room from some impoverished clerk. "Only for a few hours tonight when you're not using the room. And you can lie in bed and sleep; what we are doing is no business of yours."

So it happened that the prewar room which a head accountant or departmental chief's mother-in-law had furnished became, after eleven o'clock at night, the meeting place of evening dresses and dinner jackets. In the quiet, decent streets, touts and drummers collected their clientele—provincial uncles, sizzled gentlemen undecided where to go next, stock-exchange jobbers who had not had enough of the daily exchange swindle. The house porter had his palm oiled and slept soundly; the outer door could be opened as often as they liked. In the sober passage with the tarnished brass clothes-hooks, a little table stood with the big box of chips, guarded by a bearded, melancholy giant, looking like a sergeant major. A cardboard notice "HERE" on a door indicated the toilet. They spoke in whispers, everybody realizing that the people in the rest of the house must not notice anything amiss. There were no drinks. They had no use for "drunks" because of the noise they might make. There was only gambling—sufficient intoxication in itself.

It was so quiet that even behind the entrance hall one could hear the humming of the ball. Behind the croupier stood two men in dinner jackets, ready at any moment to step in and settle an argument by the dreaded expulsion into the street, by exclusion from the game. The croupier wore a tail coat. But all three resembled each other, he and the two birds-of-a-feather standing behind, whether lean or fat, dark or fair. All had cold, alert eyes, crooked, beaky noses, and thin lips. They rarely talked with each other; they communicated by glances, at most by a nudge of the shoulder. They were evil, greedy, insensible—adventurers, cut-purses, convicts—God alone knew. It was impossible to visualize them leading a private life with wife and children. One could not imagine how they behaved when alone, getting out of bed, looking at themselves in the mirror while shaving. They seemed born to stand behind gaming tables—evil, greedy, insensible. Three years ago such people had not existed, and in a year's time none of them would be left. Life had washed them up when they were needed. Life would carry them away, whither no one knew, when the time came. Life contains them, as it contains everything else necessary to it.

Round the table sat a row of gamblers: the rich people with fat pocketbooks which were to be gutted, the beginners, the greenhorns. They always found a seat—the three silent, alert birds of prey saw to that. Behind stood the other gamblers in a crowd two or three deep. To place their stakes on the little peep of table which they could command, they reached over the shoulders of those in front, or under their arms. Or, above the heads of the others, they handed their chips to one of the three men, with a whispered instruction.

But, in spite of the poor view and the crowding, there was hardly ever a dispute, for the gamblers were much too immersed in their own game, in the spinning of the ball, to pay much attention to others. And besides, there was such a diversity in the counters with which they played, that even when there was a huge throng only two or three at the most played with the same color. They stood close together, beautiful women and good-looking men among them. They leaned against one another; hand touched bosom, hand brushed silky hips—they felt nothing. Just as a great light kills a lesser, so the crowd heard only the whirring of the ball, the click of the bone chips. The world stood still, lungs could not breathe, time stopped while the ball spun, clattered, ran, turned toward a hole, changed its mind, jumped on, rattled . . .

There! Red! Odd—twenty-one! And suddenly the breast heaved again, the face softened; yes, she was the beautiful girl. "Your stakes, ladies and gentlemen, your stakes. That is all." And the ball rolled, clattered . . . the world stood still.

Wolfgang Pagel had elbowed himself into the second row. He never got any farther forward; the three birds of prey saw to that, exchanging glances of annoyance as soon as he entered. He was the most undesirable type of gambler—playing carefully, never letting himself be carried away, the man with so small a working capital in his pocket that it was hardly worth looking at, far less winning. The man who came evening after evening with the firm determination to take enough from the bank to live on the following day— and who mostly succeeded.

It was useless for Pagel to change his club, although at that time the number of gambling hells was as the sands of the sea, just as everywhere there were heroin and cocaine, "snow," nude dances, Franch champagne and American cigarettes, influenza, hunger, despair, fornication and crime. No, the vultures at the top of the table recognized him at once. They recognized him by the way he came in, the detached scrutiny which, passing from face to face, rested at last on the table. They recognized him by his exaggerated, his feigned indiffer- ence, by the way he played his stakes, by the intervals between them intended to even out the chances and take advantage of a run; they recognized a like bird to themselves, in different plumage.

This evening Wolfgang was nervous. Twice, till he succeeded in squeezing in with a party, the touts had closed the door in his face in the hope of driving away an undesirable gambler. The man with the sad sergeant major's face pre- tended not to hear his request for chips, and Wolfgang had to control himself so as not to make a scene. In the end he got the chips.

He saw at once that a certain lady of the demimonde, called by habitués the Valuta Vamp, was present in the gaming room. There had been encounters in other places with this pushing and impudent girl, because, when she had a run of bad luck and was near the end of her resources, she did not hesitate to use the stakes of her fellow gamblers. He would have liked to go away—he had let a chip fall to the floor, a bad omen, because it meant that the room wanted to keep his money. (There were many omens of this sort—mostly unlucky.)

Nevertheless, since he was already there, he went to the table to play within the limits he had imposed on himself. As with all gamblers, Wolfgang Pagel was firmly convinced that what he was doing was not real gambling and "did not count." He firmly believed that one day, in a flash, the feeling would possess him: your hour has come. In that moment he would be a real gambler, the pet of Fortune. Whatever he staked, the ball would hum, the money flow to him. He would win everything, everything! Sometimes he thought of this hour, but not very often, just as one doesn't want to lessen the enjoyment of a big piece of luck by savoring it too often in advance. And when he did think of it, he felt his mouth go dry and the skin over his temples tighten.

He thought he could see himself, leaning forward with shining eyes, the notes collecting between his open palms as if blown there by the wind; all this paper representing huge amounts, noughts upon noughts, an astronomical number of noughts, wealth beyond realization.

Till that hour came he was only an unpaying guest of Fortune, a starveling who had to be content with the lean chances of even odds. This he was more than content to put up with, for the prospect of something big allured him.

On this evening he was, for him, not badly off. If he played cautiously he ought to be able to take home quite a good profit. Wolfgang Pagel had based his system on careful observation. Of the thirty-six numbers of the roulette, eighteen were red, eighteen black. If one didn't take into consideration the thirty-seventh chance, zero (in which case all the stakes went to the bank), the chances for red and black were equal. According to the theory of probabilities, if roulette were played throughout eternity red must turn up as often as black. It probably would. But the manner in which red and black alternated during the course of one game seemed to be governed by a much more mysterious rule, which might be guessed at partly by observation, partly by intuition.

Wolfgang stood watching the table, as he always did before he staked for the first time. He would see, for instance, that red turned up, then red again, and so on for the fourth, fifth and sixth times; it might continue to turn up ten times running, in very rare instances even longer. Red, always red. It was against all sense and reason, it contradicted every theory of probabilities, it was the despair of all gamblers with a "system."

Then all at once black turned up; after six or eight turns of red came black. Came twice, thrice, then red again, and next occurred a tiresome, everlasting alternation between red and black, black and red.

But Wolfgang still waited. No stake could be risked until he felt sure there was a chance of success.

Suddenly he felt something within him tighten; he looked at the little space of table within his view. He felt as if he had been so carried away by his thoughts that he had not been following the game. Nevertheless he knew that black would turn up thrice in succession; he knew that he must stake his money now, that a run of black had started. He staked.

He staked three, four times. Further he did not dare go. Red turning up twelve or fifteen times was an exception, but it was that which meant the big winning chances: allowing the stake to stand and so double the winnings. Letting it stand again and double itself . . . again and again until it had reached a fabulous figure. But his capital was too small, he couldn't risk a failure, he had to be content with dull safety. The night would certainly come, however, when he would stake on and on and on and on. He would *know* that red would turn up seventeen times; he would stake seventeen times and no more.

And then never gamble again. With the money they would start something quiet, an antique shop, for instance. He had a flair for such things; he liked to handle them. Life then would flow gently and quietly. There would be no more of this horrible tension, none of this dark despair, no more vulture-like faces scrutinizing him angrily, no more doubtful ladies stealing his stake money . . .

He had found at the other end of the table a place away from the Valuta Vamp, but it did not help him. Just as he was staking he heard her voice. "Make room. Don't spread yourself all over the place. Others also want to play!"

Without looking at her he bowed and quit the field, found another place and started again. He was thinking that tonight he must be particularly cautious—he must take home more than usual; tomorrow at half-past twelve they intended to marry.

All right. She was an excellent girl; no one would ever love him so unselfishly, just as he was, and without comparing him with some tiresome ideal. So they would marry tomorrow; though why, he didn't really know at the moment. It didn't matter, it would turn out all right. But he wished he could pay more attention to the game. Just now he shouldn't have staked on black at all. Lost! Lost! Well . . .

Suddenly he heard the malignant voice again. She was quarreling now with another man, speaking in high-pitched and indignant tones. Yes, of course, her nose was quite white, she sniffed snow, the bitch. No use starting a row with her; even when she was sober she didn't know what she wanted or was doing. And now she knew less than ever.

He looked for another place.

This time everything went well. Staking cautiously, he made up what he had lost. Indeed, he could now pocket his original capital and operate with the winnings. Beside him stood a young fellow with unsteady eyes and fidgety movements, unmistakably playing his maiden game. Such people brought luck, and he succeeded in passing a hand, his left hand, across the young fellow's shoulder without his noticing—which increased the chances of winning. In consequence he let the stake stay on one game longer than he would otherwise have dared. Again he won and the vultures cast evil glances on him. Good.

He now had enough for tomorrow, even for a couple of days longer, if the dollar didn't mount too high—he could go home. But it was still very early. He would only lie awake for hours, analyzing the game, and be filled with remorse at not having exploited this chain of good luck.

He stood quietly there, holding the counters he had won, listening to the ball, the voice of the croupier, the gentle scratching and scraping of the rakes on the green table. He felt as if he were in a dream. The clacking of the ball reminded him of a water wheel. Yes, it made him drowsy. Life, when one felt it, reminded one of water, of flowing water; πάντα q∑ῖ, everything flows, as he had learned at grammar school before he went to the military college. Flows past, too.

He felt very tired. Besides, his mouth was as dry as leather. Damned nonsense that there was nothing to drink here; he'd have to go to the water tap in the lavatory. But then he wouldn't know how the game went. Red—black—black—red—red—red—black . . . Of course, there was nothing but Red Life and Black Death. Nothing else was being handed out or invented. They might invent as much as they liked—beyond Life and Death there was nought. . . .

Nought.

Of course! he had forgotten zero; that existed, too. The even-odd gamblers always forgot zero, and their money vanished. But if zero existed, then it was Death—a reasonable assumption. Red then was Love, a somewhat exaggerated emotion. Certainly Petra was a good girl. I'm feverish, he thought. But I suppose I'm feverish every evening. I really ought to drink some water. I'll go at once.

Instead of that he shook the counters in his hand, hastily added those from his pocket and, just as the croupier called: "That's all," put everything on zero. On Nought.

His heart stopped. What am I doing? he asked himself. In his mouth the sensation of dryness increased unbearably. His eyes burned, the skin tightened like parchment over his temples. For an inconceivable time the ball hummed around; he felt as if everybody were looking at him.

They all look at me. I have staked on zero. Everything we possess I have staked on zero—and that means Death. And tomorrow is the marriage.

The ball went on spinning; he could not hold his breath any longer. He breathed deeply—the tension relaxed.

"Twenty-six!" called the croupier. "Black, odd, passe." Pagel ejected the air through his nose, almost relieved. He had been right—the gaming room had kept his money. The Valuta Vamp had not disturbed him for nothing. She was saying in a loud whisper: "Those poor fish, they want to play but they ought to play with marbles." The vulture-like croupier shot him a sharp, triumphant glance.

For a moment, Wolfgang stood still, waiting. The feeling of relief from agonizing tension passed. If I had just one more chip, he thought. Well, it's all the same. The day will come.

The ball whirled round once more. Slowly he went out, past the mournful sergeant major, down the dark stairs. He stood for a long time in the entrance hall until a tout opened the door.

VIII

What could he tell his good little Peter? Almost nothing. It could be compressed into one sentence. At first I won, then I had bad luck. So there was nothing special to report; of late it had been like that frequently. Of course, she could hardly gather anything from that. She thought, perhaps, it was somewhat similar to losing at cards or drawing a blank in a lottery. Nothing of the ups and downs, good fortune and despair, could be made comprehensible to her; she could be informed of the result only—an empty pocket. And that was all. But she understood much more than he thought. Too often she had seen his face when he came home of a night, still heated with excitement. And his exhausted face while he slept. And the evil changes in it when he was dreaming of gambling. (Didn't he really know that most nights he dreamed of it, he who wanted to persuade both her and himself that he was not a gambler?) And his thin, remote face when he had not listened to her, absent-mindedly asking: "What did you say?" and still not hearing—that face which expressed so clearly what he was thinking that it seemed one could touch it, as if it had become something tangible. And his face when he combed his hair in the mirror and suddenly saw what sort of a face he had.

No, she knew enough. He did not need to say anything, nor to torment himself with explanations and apologies.

"It doesn't matter, Wolf," she said quickly. "Money never meant anything to us."

He looked at her, grateful that she could have spared him this explanation. "Of course," he said, "I shall make up for it. Perhaps this evening."

"But," she replied, for the first time insistent, "we have to go at half-past twelve to the Registry Office."

"And I," he said quickly, "have to take your clothes to Uncle. Can't the registrar marry you as someone seriously ill in bed?"

"You may have to pay for invalids as well," she laughed. "Surely you know that not even death is free."

"But perhaps invalids can pay afterward," he said, half smiling, half reflectively. "And then if he doesn't get his money, well, a marriage is a marriage."

For a while both remained silent. The vitiated air in the room, ever hotter with the climbing of the sun, felt unpleasantly dry to the skin. The noise of the tin-stamper seemed louder. They heard the tearful voice of Frau Thumann gossiping with a neighbor in front of their door. The over-crowded human hive of the house buzzed, shouted, sang, chattered, screamed and sobbed with multifarious voices.

"You know, you needn't marry me," said the girl with sudden resolution. And after a pause: "No human being has done so much for me as you."

He looked away, a little embarrassed. The window glistened in the sun. What have I really done for her? he thought, bewildered. Taught her how to handle a knife and fork—and speak correct German.

He looked at her again. She wanted to say something more, but her lips trembled as if she were struggling with tears. Her dark glance was so intense that he would have preferred to look away.

But she had already spoken. "If I thought that you only felt you ought to marry me, I wouldn't wish it."

He shook his head slowly.

"Or to spite your mother," she continued. "Or because you think it would please me."

He shook his head again. (Does *she* know, then, why we are marrying? he wondered, amazed and lost.)

"But I always feel that you would like it, too, because you feel we belong to each other," she said suddenly, forcing the words out with tears in her eyes. Now she spoke more freely, as if the most difficult part had been said. "Oh, Wolf, my dear, if it isn't so, if you marry me for some other reason, don't do it—please don't do it. You won't hurt me. Not so much," she corrected hurriedly, "as if you married me and we didn't belong to each other after all."

"Oh, Petra, Peter, Peter Ledig!" he cried in his den of selfish solitude, overwhelmed by her humility and her loveliness. "What are you talking about?" He took her, embracing and rocking her like a child, and said laughingly: "We haven't got the money for registrar's fees, and you talk about one's deepest feelings."

"And am I not to talk about them?" she murmured, lowering her voice, nestling her head on his breast. "Am I not to talk about such things because you don't talk about them? Always, every moment, every day, I think, even when you hold me in your arms and kiss me, as you are doing now, that you're very far away from me—from everything."

"Now you're talking about gambling," he said, and his embrace relaxed.

"No, I'm not talking about gambling," she denied hurriedly, and leaned closer to him. "Or perhaps I am. You must know that I don't know where you are or what you are thinking about. Gamble as much as you like—but when you don't, couldn't you be with me a little? Oh, Wolf," she cried, and now she had moved away, holding him above the elbows and looking firmly at him, "you always think you ought to apologize about the money or explain something. There's nothing to explain and there's nothing to be sorry for. If we belong to each other, everything's all right; and if we don't, then everything is wrong—with or without money, marriage or no marriage."

She looked hopefully toward him, she yearned for a word; if only he had held her in his arms in the right way, she would have understood him.

What does she really want of me? he had been thinking. But he knew. She had given herself to him entirely, right from the start, from that first morning when she had asked whether she could come with him. Now she begged him to open for once his dark, remote heart. But how can I do that? he asked himself. How am I to do it? He felt a sudden relief. That I don't know how shows she is right: I don't love her, he thought. I merely want to marry her. If I hadn't staked on zero there would have been money for the registry office; there wouldn't have been this discussion. Of course, now I know it, it would be better if we didn't marry. But how am I to tell her? I can't retreat. She's still looking at me. What am I to tell her?

The silence had become heavy and oppressive. She still held his arms, but loosely, as if she had forgotten she was holding them. "Peter!" He cleared his throat.

The outer door creaked, and the shuffling of Frau Thumann was heard.

"Quick, Wolf, shut the door," said Peter hurriedly. "Frau Thumann's coming and we don't want her now."

She had let go of him. But before he could reach the door of their room the landlady came in sight.

"Are you still waiting?" she asked. "I've told you: no money, no coffee."

"Listen, Frau Thumann," said Wolfgang hurriedly. "I don't want any coffee. I'm going immediately with our things to Uncle's. In the meantime give Petra rolls and coffee. She's half dead with hunger." Not a sound from Petra. "And with the money I'll come at once and pay you everything, keeping only what I need for my fare to Grunewald. I've an old army friend there, Zecke is his name, von Zecke, who'll certainly lend me some money."

He risked a glance into the room. Petra had sat down quietly on the bed, sat there with bent head; he couldn't see her face.

"Is that so?" the Thumann woman replied, half a question, half a threat. "The girl shan't lack for breakfast, not today nor tomorrow—what about the wedding, though?" She stood, an overflowing form in shapeless garments, the chamber pot in her hand—the sight of her was enough to destroy anybody's desire for weddings and respectability forever.

"Oh," said Wolfgang lightly, and recovered himself. "If Petra's breakfast comes along, the wedding will come along as well." He glanced at the girl, who did not move.

"You'll have to stand in line at the pawnshop and Grunewald's a long way," said the Thumann woman. "I'm always hearing about the wedding, but I'd prefer to see it."

"It's all right," cried Petra and got up. "You can be sure about the money and about the wedding, too. Come, Wolf, I'll help you pack the things. We'll take the small suitcase; then the man will only have to glance at it to see everything is there as usual. He ought to know it well by now." And she smiled at him.

Frau Thumann looked keenly from the one to the other, like a wise old bird. Immensely relieved, Wolfgang cried: "Peter, you're splendid. Perhaps I can really get it through by half-past twelve. If I find Zecke at home, he'll certainly lend me enough to take a taxi. . . ."

"Certainly," replied the Thumann woman for Petra. "An' then she gets out of bed and into the registry office with a man's overcoat on and nothing beneath. We're very clever, aren't we?" she flashed out. "I'm tired of hearing about it, and what's worse, there's no end to the silly little geese who believe you fellers when you tell such yarns. And I know the girl. She'll sit about the kitchen pretending to help me, but she won't want to help me, not a scrap; only wants to keep an eye on the kitchen clock, and when half-past twelve comes she'll say: 'I feel he's coming, Frau Thumann.' But he won't turn up; he'll probably be with his high-born pal, and they'll be having a quiet drink an' smoke. If he's got it in his head at all, it'll be: 'They marry people every day, anyhow.' And what don't happen today needn't happen tomorrow by a long chalk!"

And thereupon the Thumann woman shot a devastating look at Wolfgang and a contemptuous, pitying one at Petra, made a flourish with the chamber pot which was period, exclamation and question mark combined, and closed the door. The two stood there, hardly daring to look at each other, for, however one might regard the landlady's outburst, it was not pleasant.

Finally Petra said: "Never mind, Wolfgang. She and all the others can say what they like; it doesn't affect the issue. And if I was in a tearful mood a moment ago, forget it. Sometimes one feels quite alone, and then one is afraid and would like to be reassured."

"And now you don't feel alone, Peter?" asked Wolfgang, oddly moved. "Now you don't need reassurance?"

She looked at him, forlorn and confused. "Oh, you are with me. . . ."

"But," he urged, "perhaps Madam Po is right. At half-past twelve I'll be sitting and thinking: 'One can be married any day.' What do you think?"

"That I trust you," she cried and lifted her head and looked at him confidently. "And even if I didn't, what difference would that make? I can't tie you down. Marriage or no marriage—if you want me everything is all right, and if you don't . . ." She broke off, smiled at him. "Now you've got to hurry, Wolf. Uncle closes at twelve for lunch, and perhaps there's really a line." She handed him the suitcase, she gave him a kiss. "Good luck, Wolf."

He would have liked to say something, but could not think what.

So he took the case and went.

Chapter Three

Hunters and Hunted

I

At Neulohe Manor the little bailiff Meier, nicknamed Black Meier, was so tired out by eleven or twelve in the morning that he could have fallen into bed as he was, in coat and leggings, and have slept till next day. He sat, however, and nodded drowsily in the long dry grass at the edge of a rye field, well hidden from view by a group of pine trees.

He had been up since three o'clock that morning, handing out the fodder in the steaming stables, supervising the feeding, watching the milking, looking to the cleaning of the cattle. At four o'clock he had got in the rapeseed, which must be carted in the morning dew, so that it does not droop. At a quarter to seven, standing, he had swallowed a cup of coffee and some food. And from seven onward the usual routine. Then a message had come from the rye field that both reaping and binding machines had broken down. He had hurried thither with the smith, had tinkered with the machines; now they were rattling again; still rattling—how tired he was! He was tired not only because of yesterday: now he was also tired from today. How he would like to drop asleep, bask in the sun! But before twelve he had to be in the sugar-beet field to see whether the overseer, Kowalewski, and his gang were doing the hoeing properly and not scamping the work.

Meier's bicycle lay in the ditch a few yards away. But he was too lazy to get on it; he simply couldn't. His limbs and especially his throat felt as if they were smothered by a thick layer of fatigue. When he lay quite still this fatigue rested more lightly on him, so to speak, but if he moved only a leg, it irked as if made of bristles.

He lit a cigarette, puffed at it contentedly and gazed at his dirty and worn-out shoes. He needed new ones, but the Rittmeister was an unapproachable man, and 500,000 marks was an unheard-of salary for a bailiff. If he waited for the dollar rate on the first of the month, perhaps he would not even be able to have the shoes soled. There were many things needed on Neulohe Estate—two more on the staff, for instance—but the Rittmeister was a great man and had discovered that he could do everything himself. The hell he could! Today he had gone to Berlin to fetch harvesters; in any case he couldn't rout a poor bailiff out of his morning nap. One was curious what sort of people he'd bring back with him. That is, if he brought any at all! Oh, damn—!

Meier lay back, his cigarette slipped into the corner of his mouth, and he pushed his trilby hat over his eyes as protection against the burning sun. . . . The women in the beet field could pickle themselves with their Kowalewski, for all he cared; they were a cheeky lot. Kowalewski, though, had a smart daughter; one would not have thought it of him. She ought to come from Berlin here for a holiday again; he could manage her all right. How warm it was! As hot as an oven. If only there was no storm! Otherwise all the crops, would get soaked, and he would have to clear up the mess. They ought to have got them in before, of course, but the Rittmeister was a great man and a weather prophet besides. "It won't rain, don't bring in the crops, selah!"

Thank God, the reaping and binding machines were still clattering, and he could go on lying here. But he mustn't fall asleep or he wouldn't wake up before evening, and the Rittmeister would hear about it at once and tomorrow he'd be thrown out. That wouldn't be too dreadful; at least one could sleep one's fill for once.

Yes, indeed, that Kowalewski girl wasn't bad; she was sure to be up to her tricks in Berlin. But Amanda, Amanda Backs was by no means a back number either. Little Meier turned on his side, at last having repressed the uncomfortable thought that the Rittmeister had not actually said that the crops should not be brought in, but rather that one should be guided by the weather.

No, Meier did not want to think of that now; he preferred to think of Amanda. He felt more alive, drew his knees up and grunted with pleasure. This caused the cigarette to drop out of his mouth but it didn't matter; he didn't need a cigarette, he had Amanda. Yes, they called him Little Meier, Black Meier—and when he looked at himself in the mirror he had to admit they were right. Big, round, yellowish owl's eyes looked from behind thick lenses; he had a flat nose, blubber lips, ears that stuck out and a forehead hardly two inches high—as far as that goes, the man himself was hardly five feet.

But that was just it: he looked so odd, so grotesque, had such a comically ugly mug, that the girls were all keen on him. When he had been still quite new at Neulohe and Amanda and her girl-friend had passed him, the friend said: "Amanda, you'll need a step to reach up to him." But Amanda had replied: "That doesn't matter, he has such a sweet kisser." That had been her way of declaring love; the girls here were like that, impudent and of a divine casualness. Either they were keen on you or they weren't, but in any case they didn't make a fuss about it. They were grand.

Look at yesterday evening when Amanda had climbed through his window—as a matter of fact he wasn't keen himself, he was too tired and the mistress had rushed out of the bushes! Not the Rittmeister's lady—she would only have laughed, being herself not a bad sport—but the old lady, the mother-in-law, from the manor house. Any other girl would have shrieked or hidden herself or called on him for help; not so Amanda. He could remain out of it and be amused. "Yes, madam," Amanda had said quite innocently. "I only want to check up the poultry accounts with the bailiff; he never has any time during the day."

"And you climb through his window for that!" the old lady, who was very pious, had shrieked. "You shameless creature."

"But the house is already locked up," Amanda had replied.

And as the old lady still hadn't got her bellyful and couldn't see that she was no match for the young of today, even with the help of religion and morals, Amanda had simply added: "This is my free time, madam. And what I do in my free time is my own business. And if you can find a better poultry maid for such low wages—but you won't find one—then I can leave, of course; but not till tomorrow."

And she had insisted that he shouldn't shut the window. "If she wants to stand there and listen, let her stand there, Hans dear. It's all one to us, and perhaps she gets some pleasure out of it. After all, she didn't get her daughter in solitary prayer."

Little Meier sniggered and pressed his cheek against his arm as if he were feeling the soft but firm body of his Amanda. Such a sport! She was just the right sort for a poor devil and bachelor. No soft stuff about love, faithfulness and marriage, but good at her work and ready with her tongue; so downright and free-spoken that sometimes she made you wince. But this was not surprising when you came to consider that she had grown up in the four years of war and the five years afterward.

"If I don't snatch my food myself I don't get any. And if I don't smack you, you'll smack me. Always stand up for yourself, young man, even against that old woman. She's had her good times—why shouldn't I have mine, just because they started a potty war and an inflation? It's enough to make a cat laugh. After all, if I die, then as far as I'm concerned the world's at an end. And she'll have to squeeze out the tears which she'll shed over my grave as a good girl; and as for the tin wreath which she'll slap on my worm-chest, I shan't be able to buy myself anything with it, and therefore we'd better be happy while we can. What do you say, Hans dear? Be sorry for the old woman and gentler with her? Well, who's been kind to me? They were always boxing my ears, and if my nose bled, so much the better. And when I cried a bit I was told: 'Shut up or you'll get a few more where that came from.' No, Hans, I wouldn't say anything if there was any sense in it, but it's just as silly and idiotic as my hens who lay eggs for our pleasure and then in the end are thrown into the stewpan. Not me, thank you! If you like it, do; but don't ask me."

The girl was right. Little Meier laughed once more and fell into a deep sleep and would have slept on till the evening dew—blow the work, blow the Rittmeister—if it hadn't suddenly become extremely hot and even suffocating.

Starting up—no longer with a weary movement but leaping onto both feet—he saw that he had been lying in the midst of the excellent beginnings of a forest fire. Through the voluminous stinging smoke he saw a figure jumping about and stamping and beating out the flames; and he himself was jumping now, and stamping and beating them down with a fir branch, shouting: "It's burning nicely."

"Cigarette!" said the other man, and went on extinguishing the fire.

"I might have been burned to death," laughed Meier.

"And no loss either."

"Sez you," cried Meier, coughing with the smoke.

"Shut up, man," ordered the other. "To be suffocated isn't fun, either." And the two with all their might continued to put out the fire, the bailiff straining his ears in the direction of his two reaping and binding machines, to hear if they were still rattling. For it would not have been pleasant for him if people had noticed anything and told the Rittmeister.

Contrary to all expectations, however, they were carrying on their work, which in other circumstances would have annoyed the bailiff, for it showed that the fellows were drowsing in their seats and leaving not only the work but also the thinking to the horses, and, that, as far as they were concerned, the whole manor of Neulohe, with all its buildings and eight thousand acres of forest, might have burned down. On returning, they would have gazed at the ashes of the stables as if witchcraft had been responsible. But this time Meier did not get annoyed; he was happy about the ongoing clatter and about the subsiding smoke.

At last Meier and his rescuer faced each other, rather out of breath, across a blackened patch as big as a room. The rescuer looked a little neglected, with a flutter of reddish whisker round nose and chin; he had keen blue eyes, was still young, and dressed in an old gray tunic and trousers, although with a handsome yellow leather belt and an equally handsome holster. And there must be something—not merely lollipops—in it, that is, in the holster, for it swung so heavily.

"A cigarette?" asked the incorrigible Meier and held out his case, for he felt that he, too, should do something for his rescuer.

"Hand us one, comrade," said the other. "My paws are black." "Mine, too," laughed Meier, and he fished out a couple between the tips of his fingers. Smoking, the two sat down comfortably in the grass under the scanty shade of fir trees a little way from the charred spot. They had learned enough from their recent experience for one to use an old stump as an ash tray, and the other a flat stone.

The man in field gray inhaled a few times, stretched his limbs, yawned unceremoniously and said, profoundly: "Yes . . . Yes . . ."

"Things are not too good," agreed Meier.

"Not too good? Lousy," exclaimed the other, screwing up his eyes to look at the country quivering in the heat. Seeming utterly bored, he flung himself on his back in the grass.

Actually Meier had neither time nor inclination to share in another morning nap, but he felt nevertheless obliged to stay with the man a little longer. So as not to let the conversation fade away entirely, he remarked:

"Hot, isn't it?"

The other merely grunted.

Meier looked at him sideways and hazarded: "From the Baltic Army Corps?"

But this time he did not get even a grunt for reply. Instead, something rustled in the fir trees and Meier's bicycle appeared, pushed by Forester Kniebusch, who threw down the cycle at Meier's feet. Wiping away the sweat, he spoke. "Meier, again you've left your bicycle in the road. It isn't even yours, but belongs to the estate, and if it runs away, the Rittmeister'll storm at you. . . ."

And then he saw the blackened patch and flew into a temper (for with a colleague he could indulge in what he dared not risk where wood thieves were concerned), and started to blackguard Meier. "You damned lousy dolt, you've been smoking your cursed stinking cigarettes again and setting fire to my trees. You wait, my little friend, that's the end of friendship and cards of an evening— duty is duty, and the Rittmeister's going to hear all about it tonight. . . .

But it was fated that Forester Kniebusch should not end all his sentences, for in the grass he now discovered the highly suspicious fellow in shabby field gray, apparently sleeping. "Have you caught a tramp and incendiary, Meier? Splendid, that'll mean praise from the Rittmeister, and he'll keep his mouth shut for a while about slackness and inefficiency and being afraid of the laborers. Wake up, you swine," he shouted, and kicked the man heavily in the ribs. "Get up and to jail with you."

But the other only pushed his field cap off his face, shot a keen glance at the angry forester, and exclaimed, even more sharply: "Forester Kniebusch!"

It was surprising for Black Meier, and even more amusing, to see the effect of this simple form of address on his brother-at-cards, that sneaking rabbit, Kniebusch. He jumped as if struck by lightning, the angry words sticking in his throat, stood instantly to attention and said humbly: "Herr Lieutenant!"

The man slowly and deliberately rose, brushed the dry grass and twigs from his tunic and trousers and spoke. "A meeting this evening at ten at the village magistrate's. Inform our people. You can bring the little chap along, too." He straightened his belt and added: "You're to report what serviceable arms and ammunition are available in Neulohe. Understand?"

"Certainly, sir," stammered the old graybeard, but Meier noticed that he had received a shock.

The mysterious individual, however, nodded briefly at Meier, saying: "All in order, comrade," and was lost to sight among the bushes and young firs in the wood. He had disappeared like a dream.

"Confound it," exclaimed Meier, his breath taken away, staring into the green depths. But everything was still again, shining in the noonday glare.

"Yes, confound it; that's what you say, Meier," the forester exploded. "But I'm to do the running round the village this afternoon, and I've no idea whether they're agreeable or not. Some pull long faces and say it's all nonsense and they had quite enough with Kapp. But," he continued, even more depressed if possible, "you've seen what he's like. Nobody dares to say it to his face, and when he whistles they all come. I alone hear their objections."

"Who is he?" Meier was curious. "He doesn't look so marvelous to me."
"I don't know," the forester rejoined angrily. "It doesn't matter what he calls himself. He won't tell us his right name, you bet. He's just the Lieutenant."

"Well, lieutenant doesn't mean such a lot nowadays," reflected Meier, who, however, had been impressed by the way in which the other had dealt with the forester.

"I don't know whether a lieutenant is a lot or a little. Anyhow, people obey him," grumbled the forester. "And they're surely planning something big, and if it succeeds then it's all over with Ebert and the whole Red gang," he added mysteriously.

"Now, now!" said Meier. "Many have tried to bring that about. But red seems to be a fast color. You won't scrape it off so easily."

"This time it will be," whispered the forester. "It's said they have the Reichswehr behind them and they called themselves the Black Reichswehr. The whole district is swarming with them, from the Baltic Corps and Upper Silesia, and from the Ruhr, too. They're called fatigue parties and they're supposed to have no arms. But you yourself have seen and heard. . . ."

"A *Putsch!*" said Meier. "And I'm to join? I would have to think it over a good deal first. I'm not doing anything just because somebody says to me 'All in order, comrade,' you can bet your life."

The forester paid no attention to him. "The old governor has four sporting guns and two three-barreled ones. And a rifle. The Rittmeister . . ." he said uneasily.

"Exactly," cried Meier, relieved. "What's the Rittmeister's attitude? Or doesn't he know anything about it?"

"If only I knew," was the doleful reply. "But I don't. I've asked all over the place. Sometimes the Rittmeister travels to Ostade and drinks with the Reichswehr officers. Perhaps we'll come a terrible cropper, and if things go wrong I'll lose my job and end my days in jail . . ."

"Now don't start weeping, old walrus," laughed Meier. "It's quite simple. Why shouldn't we ask the Rittmeister whether he wishes us to join or not?"

"My God," ejaculated the forester, and threw up his arms in despair. "You're really the biggest idiot in the world, Meier. The Rittmeister doesn't know anything about it, and we'll then have given it away to him. You've read in the newspapers: 'Traitors punished by the secret tribunal, the *Vehmgericht*,' and you know how I . . ." He suddenly realized what he was saying, the sky turned black, and he went cold with fright. "And I, the chump, have betrayed everything to you. Oh, Meier, do me a favor, give me your word of honor here and now that you won't tell anybody. I shan't tell the Rittmeister you set fire to the forest. . . ."

"First of all," said Meier, "I didn't set fire to the forest—your Lieutenant did. If you betray him you know what'll happen. And, secondly, suppose I had set fire to it; well, I'm going this evening at ten o'clock to the village magistrate's to belong to the Black Reichswehr. And if you betray me then, Kniebusch, you know how traitors are dealt with by the *Vehine*."

Meier stood there, grinning in the middle of the path and looking impudently and defiantly at Kniebusch, the old coward. If the *Putsch* story does no other good, he thought, it puts paid to this miserable sneak—he'd better not risk saying another word about me to the old gentleman or to the Rittmeister.

The forester, however, stood facing him, alternately paling and flushing. He may have been thinking: I've managed in forty years of service to get along; with many scares and having much to put up with, but always hoping that life would become simpler. But, instead, it gets more and more complicated, and now even in my sleep I wake up with a start, fearing that something terrible has happened. I've never felt like that before. Before, it was only the timber accounts and wondering whether I'd added up correctly; or when the old gentleman wanted to shoot a buck and was waiting for it in ambush, whether it would come along that day as it usually did. But now I lie awake in the darkness with my heart beating quicker and quicker. Timber thieves and lieutenants about the place and this rotter getting cheeky, and a *Putsch* coming off. . . . It will end by my being in the soup, although I have nothing against the President of the Reich. . . .

But aloud: "We're comrades, Meier, and have played many a game of cards together. I've never yet said a word about you to the Rittmeister, and what I said about the forest fire only escaped me in anger. I'd never have given you away, of course not."

"Of course not," and Meier grinned insolently. "Now it's nearly twelve and I won't have time for the beet field. But I must be present for the fodder, and so I have to cycle. You can run behind me, Kniebusch, you won't mind that, will you?" And Meier got on his bicycle and pushed off, calling out: "All in order, comrade," and was gone.

The forester stared after him, shaking his head gloomily and wondering whether to take the private path instead of the road to his house. On the road he might come across timber thieves, and that would be embarrassing.

II

The pawnbroker sat on a high stool writing in his account books, while an assistant negotiated in an undertone with two women, one of whom grasped a bundle of feather beds wrapped in a sheet, the other holding a black dummy figure like those used by dressmakers. Both had sharp faces and the elaborately unconcerned look of those who only rarely visit a pawnshop.

The shop itself, situated on the mezzanine floor of a busy building, looked, as always, dirty, dusty and disorderly, although it was scrupulously tidied. The light filtering through the frosted windows was gray and dead. As usual, a huge safe stood wide open, revealing a heap of small packets wrapped in white paper, suggesting costly jewels. As usual, the keys were in the lock of the little wall-safe which held the pawnshop's cash. From dozens of errands it was so familiar that Wolf took it in without looking. It was quite usual, too, for Uncle to glance at him over his gold-rimmed eyeglasses and then continue writing.

Wolfgang Pagel turned toward the assistant, who apparently could not come to terms with the woman wishing to pawn her tailor's dummy. Lifting his suitcase onto the table he said in a low voice, but lightly: "I'm bringing the usual. Just have a look." And he unlocked the case.

Everything was really there as usual, everything they possessed—a second pair of trousers very worn in the seat, two white shirts, three dresses of Petra's, her underclothing (scanty enough), and the gem of the collection, a small real-silver handbag of hers, probably the gift of an admirer—he had never asked.

"Three dollars as usual, isn't it?" he added, just to say something, for he thought the assistant was looking rather hesitatingly at the things. The man, however, replied: "Yes, Herr Lieutenant."

And then when everything seemed settled, a high-pitched voice from the office stool exclaimed, quite unexpectedly: "No."

Both Wolfgang, who was known there only as the Lieutenant, and the assistant, looked up surprised.

"No," said Uncle once more, and shook his head firmly. "I'm sorry, Herr Lieutenant, but this time we can't oblige you. It doesn't pay us. You always come and fetch the goods the next day, and we have all that bother—and, besides, these dresses are going out of fashion. Perhaps another time, when you have got something . . . more up to date."

He glanced once more at Pagel, pointed his pen at him—at least it seemed so—and went on writing. Without looking up, the assistant slowly closed the suitcase, snapping the catches. The two women looked at Wolfgang, embarrassed and yet somewhat malicious, like schoolboys with a fellow pupil who has been reprimanded by the master.

"Listen, Herr Feld," said Pagel briskly and crossed the pawnshop toward the man, who calmly went on writing. "I've a rich friend in the West End who's sure to help me out. I only want the fare. I'll leave the things here and on my way back this evening, before you close, I'll drop in and pay back the money. Fivefold if you like. Or tenfold."

Uncle looked reflectively at Wolfgang through his glasses, frowned and said: "I'm sorry, Herr Lieutenant. We don't lend money here, we only advance money on pledge."

"But it's only the miserable few thousands for my fare," insisted Wolf. "And I leave you the things."

"I am not allowed to retain the articles without a pawn ticket. And I don't want to take them in pawn. I'm sorry, Herr Lieutenant." And the pawnbroker looked at Wolfgang with a puzzled frown as if he wanted to judge from his face the effect of his words; then he nodded slightly and returned to his books. Wolfgang, too, had frowned and nodded slightly as if indicating that he didn't take the refusal too badly. But, turning toward the door, he was struck by an idea, and once more went up to Herr Feld. "Look here, Herr Feld," he said. "Buy the things from me. For three dollars. Then the poor mind will be at rest." It had occurred to him that the rich Zecke was sure to help him out with a largish sum, and it would be a huge joke to surprise Peter with an entirely new outfit. What would be the use to her then of the old rubbish? No, away with the lot.

Herr Feld went on writing for a while. Then he stuck the pen in the inkpot, leaned back a little and said: "One dollar—with the case, Herr Lieutenant. As I said, the things are not up to date." He looked at the clock on the wall. Ten minutes to twelve. "And at yesterday's dollar rate."

For a moment Wolfgang felt like flaring up. It was the most impudent swindle in the world; and he ought to consider Peter, too, her only possessions at that moment being some toilet articles and his very ancient summer overcoat. But just as quickly came the thought that Zecke would give him money. And if he didn't, he had always managed to get some, somehow. With a quick gesture which was to show how little it mattered, he said: "All right, then. Hand out the dough. Four hundred and fourteen thousand." It was really nothing when he considered that yesterday evening he had gambled away almost thirty millions on zero. And one had to laugh at such a microbe as this Feld, who toiled for such muck, for such ridiculous amounts.

Uncle, wicked tough Uncle, the microbe, slowly climbed down from his office stool, went to the safe, rummaged in it for a while, and then paid out Wolfgang four hundred thousand marks.

"But where are the fourteen?"

"It's usual to deduct four per cent for cash payment," said Herr Feld. "Really, only three hundred and ninety-eight thousand are due to you, but I make a present of the two thousand because you're an old customer."

Wolfgang laughed. "You're smart, Uncle. You'll get on, you see if you don't. Then I'll be your chauffeur. Yes?"

Herr Feld took it seriously. "Me be driven by you, Herr Lieutenant?" he protested. "No, not even free, since nothing matters to you, not even your things. Oh, no." And once again the pawnbroker: "At your service when you have something else, Herr Lieutenant. Till then!"

Pagel rustled the notes and said laughingly: "Perhaps this will help me to get a car of my own."

The pawnbroker still looked uneasy, and returned to his writing. Smiling, Wolfgang stepped into the street.

III

After the loathsome negotiations at the Harvesters' Agency the Rittmeister felt that he deserved a little repose. But where could he go so early in the morning? This was an hour at which he had not hitherto been about in Berlin. Finally he thought of a hotel café in the Friedrichstadt where one could sit comfortably and perhaps see a few well dressed women.

And the first person whom he met in the hall of the hotel was, of course, an acquaintance. (Prackwitz always met acquaintances in the parts of the town he frequented—of course not at Schlesische Bahnhof. Or acquaintances of acquaintances. Or relatives. Or acquaintances of relatives. Or comrades from his regiment. Or comrades from the war. Or mere privates. He knew all the world.)

This time it was actually someone from his own regiment—Oberleutnant von Studmann.

Herr von Studmann stood in the hall, irreproachably dressed in a frock coat and brilliantly polished shoes (at such an early hour). He might have seemed momentarily embarrassed at the meeting; but the Rittmeister, in his pleasure at having found a companion for the two hours he had to wait, noticed nothing.

"Studmann, old chap—splendid to see you again. I've got two hours to spare. Have you had your coffee? I'm just going to—for the second time, that is; the first at Schlesische Bahnhof didn't count—it was ghastly. When did we meet last? In Frankfurt, at the officers' reunion? Well, never mind; in any case, I'm glad to see you again. But do come along; it's quite comfortable here, if I remember rightly."

Oberleutnant von Studmann replied in a low voice, distinct yet somewhat troubled: "With pleasure, Prackwitz—as soon as I'm free. I'm—er—reception manager in this joint. I must first attend to the guests coming by the nine-forty train."

"Damn!" exclaimed the Rittmeister, just as softly, but quite downcast. "The inflation, I suppose? These swindlers! Well, I know all about it myself."

Von Studmann nodded gloomily, as if he were past words. At the sight of that long, smooth, energetic face, Prackwitz was reminded of a certain evening when they had celebrated Studmann's Iron Cross, First Class, at the beginning of 1915; actually the first I.C. First Class which had been allotted their regiment. . . . He would have liked to recall the face, laughing, cheerful, gay, and eight years younger, of this same Studmann, but the latter was already saying: "Certainly, porter, at once." With a regretful gesture he turned from von Prackwitz and advanced on a rather bulky lady in a dust-colored silk coat. "Please, madam?"

For a moment the Rittmeister watched his friend standing there, leaning toward the lady and listening with a serious but friendly expression to her vigorous wishes or complaints. A deep sadness welled up within him, a formless, all-pervading sadness. Not good enough for anything better? Shame came over him, as if he had seen his friend doing something degrading. Quickly he turned away and entered the cafe.

Here prevailed the early forenoon silence, when only residents were there and the general public had not yet entered. In ones or twos the guests were dotted about at the tables. A newspaper rustled, a couple spoke in subdued voices, the little silver-metal coffeepots gleamed, a spoon clattered against a cup. The waiters, not yet busy, stood at their stations; one of them was carefully counting the silver, avoiding every unnecessary sound.

The Rittmeister soon found a seat to his liking. So good was the coffee, which arrived shortly after it had been ordered, that he resolved to give Studmann a few words of appreciation. But he rejected the idea. It might embarrass him. Oberleutnant von Studmann and a really fresh-made pot of hotel coffee!

He tried to make out why this feeling of embarrassment should overcome him again, as if Studmann were doing something illegal, even indecent. It was a job like any other. We're no longer so narrow-minded that we consider one kind of work inferior to another, he thought. If it comes to that, I live at Neulohe only by the grace of my father-in-law, and I've the deuce of a job to scrape the rent together. So what's the reason for it?

Suddenly it occurred to him that it might be because Studmann did this work only from sheer necessity. A man must work, certainly, if he wanted to justify his existence; but there ought to be freedom in the choice. Hated work, done only for the sake of the money, soiled. Studmann would never have chosen this job himself, he thought. He had no choice.

A feeling of impotent hatred overcame Rittmeister Joachim von Prackwitz. Somewhere in this town there was a machine—naturally a machine, for men would never submit to be prostituted for such a purpose—which vomited paper day and night over the city and the people. "Money" they called it; they printed figures on it, beautiful neat figures with many noughts, which became increasingly rounder. And when you had worked and sweated to put by a little for your old age, it all became worthless paper, paper muck. And for the sake of this muck his old friend Studmann had to stand in the hotel hall bowing and scraping. Good, let him stand there, let him bow and scrape—but not because of this muck. With painful clearness the Rittmeister recalled the kindly, serious face of his friend, as he had just seen it.

It suddenly grew dark, and then there was light once again. A small rapeseed oil-lamp dangled from the rough beams. It cast its warm reddish glow directly upon Studmann's face—and this face laughed, laughed. The eyes sparkled with joy; a hundred little wrinkles twitched in their corners.

The joy of restored life is in that laugh, said a voice within the Rittmeister.

It was nothing, only the memory of a night spent in a dugout—where had it been? Somewhere in the Ukraine. It was a rich land; pumpkins and melons grew in the fields in hundreds, and of this royal abundance they had fetched some into the dugout, laying them on the shelves. They slept. A rat (there were thousands of rats) pushed a pumpkin down, and it fell on the head of a sleeper, on his face. He had yelled in fright, the pumpkin bouncing onward. There they lay, wide-awake, breathless, cowering in their blankets in the expectation of shell splinters from a direct hit. Moments of mortal fright—life rustles by and I am still alive. I want to think of something worthwhile, my wife, child, my daughter Vi. I have still got a hundred and fifty marks in my pocket; it would have been better if I had paid my wine bill; the money is now lost—and then von Studmann's laugh: "Pumpkin, a pumpkin!"

They had laughed, laughed. Life restored was in that laughter. Little Geyer had wiped his bleeding nose and laughed too. Geyer was his name. He fell a little later; pumpkins were exceptions in the war.

But at the time it had been genuine fear and genuine danger and genuine courage. To tremble—but then to leap up, to discover that it was only a pumpkin and to laugh again! At oneself, at the fright, at this absurd life—to march on, down the street toward the non-existent point. To be threatened, however, by something which vomited paper, to be enslaved by something which made the world richer in noughts—that was shameful. It was painful for the man who did it; and it was painful for the man who watched the other do it.

Prackwitz scrutinized his friend. Von Studmann had entered the café and was listening to the waiter who a moment ago had counted the silver so carefully and now was holding forth excitedly. Probably a complaint about some colleague. From his own experience Prackwitz knew this kind of bickering. It happened with his staff at Neulohe. Quarrels forever; eternal tale-bearing. He would much have preferred to manage with only one employee and at least be spared that annoyance. He must really get an additional man, however. The thefts were increasing, and Meier could not cope with them, while Kniebusch was old and worn-out. Later, though. There was not enough time now; at twelve he had to be at Schlesische Bahnhof.

The waiter was still talking, talking himself into fire and fury. Kindly, attentively, von Studmann listened. Now and then he said a word, nodded at other times, shook his head. There was no more life in him, concluded the Rittmeister. Burnt out. Exhausted. But, he thought with sudden fright, perhaps I, too, am burnt out and exhausted—only I don't know it.

Quite surprisingly, Studmann said a single sentence and the waiter, entirely put out of countenance, stopped. Studmann nodded once more at him and then came to his friend's table.

"So," said he and sat down, his face immediately becoming more animated. "I think I've half an hour. If nothing happens." He smiled at Prackwitz. "But actually something always does."

"You have a great deal to do?" Prackwitz asked, a little confused.

"Good heavens," Studmann laughed abruptly. "If you ask the others, the elevator boys or the waiters or the porters, they'll tell you that I've nothing to do, that I only stand about. And yet in the evening I'm as dog-tired as when we had squadron drill or the Old Man put us through our paces."

"I suppose there's an Old Man here, too?"

"One? Ten, twelve. Managing director, three directors, four assistant directors, three head clerks, two confidential clerks . . ."

"Stop, please."

"But on the whole it isn't so bad. It has much in common with the army. Orders. Obedience. A perfect organization. . . ."

"But civilians only," murmured Prackwitz disparagingly, and thought of Neulohe, where obedience did not always follow upon orders by a long way.

"Naturally," acknowledged Studmann. "It's somewhat freer than at that time, easier. Therefore, more difficult for the individual, I would add. Someone gives an order, and you don't know exactly whether he has a right to give it. No clearly defined authority, you know."

"But it was sometimes like that with us," argued Prackwitz. "An officer with special instructions, you know."

"Certainly. But on the whole you can say it's an amazing organization, a model large-scale undertaking. You should see our linen presses. Or the kitchen. Or the checking-in department. Amazing, I can tell you."

"So you get some fun out of it?" the Rittmeister asked cautiously.

Studmann's animation died away. "Dear, dear, fun? Well, perhaps. But that doesn't matter. We have to live somehow, go on living after all that's happened. We must go on living. In spite of the fact that at one time one had other ideas."

Prackwitz cast a searching look at the clouded face of his friend. Why "must," he thought, a little annoyed. Then he found the only possible explanation. "You're married? Got children?" he asked.

"I?" Studmann was surprised. "No, no. What an idea!"

"No, no, of course not," said the Rittmeister rather guiltily.

"After all, why not? But it didn't turn out like that," said von Studmann, pondering. "And nowadays? No, when the mark becomes worthless daily, when one has one's work cut out to scrape together a little money for oneself—"

"Money? Muck!" said the Rittmeister sharply.

"Yes, of course," replied Studmann in a low voice. "Muck—I quite understand. I also understood your question of a moment ago—or rather your thoughts. Why I'm doing this against my will, as you think, for such muck." Prackwitz wanted to protest, in some confusion. "Oh, don't talk, Prackwitz," said von Studmann, for the first time with feeling. "I know you. Money—muck! That's no mere inflation wisdom of yours; you used to think like that before. You? We all did. Money was something that went without saying. We had our allowances from home and a few pence from the regiment. One didn't talk about it. And if now and then one couldn't pay immediately for some article, the man just had to wait. Wasn't it like that? Money wasn't worth thinking about." Prackwitz shook his head and wanted to make an objection, but Studmann went on hurriedly. "Please, Prackwitz, roughly speaking, it was like that. But nowadays I'm quite sure we took up a wrong attitude, not having the faintest idea of the world. Money, I've discovered meanwhile, is something very important, something which is worth thinking about."

"Money!" exclaimed von Prackwitz indignantly. "If it were real money. But this paper stuff . . ."

"Prackwitz," said Studmann reproachfully, "what do you mean by real money? Such a thing doesn't exist at all, just as there exists no unreal money. Money is simply the basis of existence, the bread we must eat every day for the sake of living, the clothes we must wear so as not to freeze to death . . ."

"But that's mysticism," cried Prackwitz angrily. "Money's quite a simple matter. Money is only—used to be, I mean—if you had a sovereign, but notes were all right, too. They were different then because you could exchange them for gold. . . . Well then, money, I mean any kind of money, you know . . ." He became furious with himself, stammering and stuttering; one ought to be able to say clearly and distinctly what one so clearly and distinctly felt. "Well," he finished, "if I have money I want to know what I can buy with it."

"Naturally," said Studmann, who had noticed nothing of his friend's confusion, busy with his own thoughts. "Of course we took up the wrong attitude. I've discovered that ninety-nine per cent of mankind have to torment themselves about money; they think of it day and night, speak of it, spend it, save it, start anew—in short, money is the thing round which the world revolves. It is only inexperience which makes us indifferent to money, not willing to speak about the most important thing which exists."

"But is this right?" cried Prackwitz, in despair at his friend's present frame of mind. "Is this noble? Merely to live in order to satisfy one's private hunger?"

"Of course it isn't right, of course it isn't noble," Studmann agreed. "But we're not consulted; that's how it is now. And if it's like that, then we oughtn't to close our eyes but should devote our attention to it. If we don't find it noble, then we must ask ourselves how to alter it."

"Studmann," asked von Prackwitz, bewildered and despairing, "Studmann, you haven't become a Socialist, by any chance?"

The former first lieutenant looked for a moment as perplexed and as startled as if he had been suspected of a murder. "Prackwitz," he said, "old comrade, the Socialists think about money just as you do. Only they want to take it away from you, so that they can have it. No, Prackwitz, I'm certainly not a Socialist. And won't become one either."

"But what are you?" asked von Prackwitz. "You must eventually belong to some group or party."

"Why?" asked von Studmann. "Why must I?"

"Well, I don't know," said von Prackwitz, a little perplexed. "We all eventually belong to something, for the elections if for no other reason. Somehow one has to subordinate oneself, to toe the line. It's, so to speak, orderly."

"But if no order exists for me?" asked von Studmann.

"Yes," said Prackwitz. "I remember that I had a chap once in my squadron, a crank we always said—what was his name? Grigoleit, yes, Grigoleit. A proper orderly kind of man. But he refused to touch a carbine or a side-arm. Imploring him didn't help, reprimands didn't help, punishments didn't help. 'Yes, Herr Lieutenant,' he'd say—I was a lieutenant, it was before the war. 'But I'm not allowed to. You've your code and I've mine. And because I've my code I'm not permitted to disobey it. One day my code will be yours.' And such cranky pacifist stuff. But he was a decent sort, not one of those shirkers who shout, 'No More War' because they're cowards. . . . Well, we could have made his life a perfect hell for him, of course. But the Old Man was reasonable and said: 'He's only a poor idiot,' and so he was reported as unfit for service, sub-section fifteen you know, because of insanity."

The Rittmeister paused, meditating, perhaps recalling the fat, round-headed Grigoleit, with his platinum-blond hair, who did not at all look like a martyr.

Studmann, however, burst out laughing. "Oh, Prackwitz," he cried, "you haven't changed a bit. And now in all innocence you've certified me as suffering from imbecility and insanity! Without even noticing. That reminds me vividly how you tried to console our Old Man, when he cut a very poor figure in the maneuvers, with the story of a major who even fell off his horse in front of the assembled general staff and still wasn't kicked out of the service. And do you remember . . ."

With that the two friends lost themselves in mutual reminiscences, and their voices became more animated. But that didn't matter. The café had begun to fill, and the waiters were busy running about with beer glasses amid a hum of voices. The two men's conversation was just one of many.

After a while, when they had remembered enough and laughed enough, the Rittmeister said: "I would like to ask you something, Studmann. I live so much alone on my bit of land and meet only the same people. But you are here in the capital and in such a swell place at that you must surely hear and know more than any of us."

"Ah, but who knows anything nowadays?" asked Studmann, and smiled. "Believe me, even Prime Minister Cuno hasn't the slightest idea what will happen tomorrow."

But Prackwitz followed up his idea. He sat there, leaning back a little, his long legs crossed, smoking in ease and comfort. "You think, perhaps, I'm free from your worries—Prackwitz has an estate and is a great man. But I'm not very secure. I have to be very cautious. Neulohe doesn't belong to me; it belongs to my father-in-law, old Herr von Teschow—I married little Eva Teschow long before the war—I beg your pardon, you know my wife, of course. Well, I've rented Neulohe from my father-in-law—and the old boy didn't let me have it for nothing, I can tell you. Sometimes I've frightful worries. In any case, I must be very prudent. Neulohe is our only means of existence, and if things went wrong, the old man doesn't love me and he'd take away my bit of land on the least provocation."

"And what would happen to you?"

"Well, you know, I'm no hermit, and Eva still less, so we've our scrap of social life in the district and, of course, also with the comrades of the Reichswehr. And one hears all sorts of things and all sorts of rumors."

"And what do you see and hear yourself?"

"That something's on the boil again, Studmann. I'm not blind. The countryside is full to the brim with people—fatigue parties they call themselves, but you've only to look at them. 'Black Reichswehr' goes the whisper."

"That may be because of the Allied Powers and the Control Commission, commission for snoopers."

"They may be burying arms, of course, digging them up again and fetching them away; that might account for it. But it's not only that, Studmann; there's a good deal more than rumor, and there's more going on than before. No doubt they are enlisting supporters among the civilian population, maybe in my own village—the proprietor is usually the last person to hear that his house is burning. Neulohe borders on Altlohe, where there are many industrial workers; that means, of course, war to the knife between them and us of the manor and the farmers at Neulohe. For one side has the food and the others the appetite, and it's like a powder barrel. If it goes up in the air, I shall go with it."

"I can't see quite how you can prevent it," said von Studmann.

"Prevent it? . . . But perhaps I'll have to decide whether to join with them or not. One doesn't want to stand out against one's friends. They're the old comrades in the Reichswehr, Studmann, and if they're taking a risk in order to get us out of the mire and I haven't gone in with them, I should die of shame. Yes, but perhaps it's only talk, worked up by a few adventurers, a hopeless *Putsch*—and to risk for that one's estate, living and family . . ." The Rittmeister looked questioningly at Studmann.

"Haven't you got anybody in the Reichswehr whom you could ask in confidence?"

"Good heavens, Studmann. Naturally I could ask, but who knows? In this sort of thing only three or four people are ever really in the know, and they won't give a definite reply. Did you ever hear of a Major Rückert?"

"No. In the Reichswehr?"

"You see, Studmann, that's just it. This Rückert is said to be the man who . . . But I can't even find out whether he belongs to the Reichswehr or not. Some say yes, others no, and the very cute just shrug their shoulders and say: 'Perhaps.' he doesn't know himself!' And this sounds as if others were backing him. It's enough to drive me crazy."

"Yes," said Studmann, "I understand. If it's necessary you'd join in at once; but if they're crazy adventurers—no, thank you."

"Quite."

Both were silent. But Prackwitz still looked expectantly at Studmann, the former first lieutenant and present reception manager (nicknamed "Nursie" by the regiment). He had turned out to be a man with very curious, even suspicious, views about money and God-ordained poverty. . . . Looked at him as if expecting from his reply liberation from all doubts.

And finally Studmann said slowly: "I think you oughtn't to worry, Prackwitz. You must simply wait. We learned that from the war. You worried and were afraid only when you were in reserve or lying quietly in the trenches; but once you got the order to advance, then you were all right and went ahead and everything was forgotten. You won't miss the signal, Prackwitz. We learned in the trenches to wait quietly without brooding over it—why shouldn't you do the same now?"

"You're right," said the Rittmeister gratefully, "and I'll remember it. It's funny that we seem to have lost the art of waiting. I think it's this idiotic dollar. Rush, hurry, quick, go and buy something, make haste, run."

"Yes," said Studmann, "to chase and be chased, hunters and hunted at the same time—that makes people so bad-tempered and impatient. But there's no need to be either." He smiled. "But now I must be off; I'm not quite free from it myself. I see the porter beckoning me; perhaps a director is already chasing after me to inquire why I'm nowhere to be seen. And I shall chase after the chambermaids, so that the rooms of the departures will be free at twelve. So, good hunting, Prackwitz. And should you be in town tonight at seven and have no engagement—"

"By then I'll be back in Neulohe some time," said von Prackwitz. "But I've been tremendously pleased, absolutely tremendously pleased, to have met you again, Studmann, and if I come to town again . . ."

IV

The girl was still sitting on the bed, alone, motionless, idle. Her head drooped; the line of the shoulder, nape and head was feminine and soft. In the small bright face the lips were parted, and the eyes gazing at the worn floorboards saw nothing. Under the overcoat, which had fallen open, the skin glimmered light brown, firm.

The room was stuffy, full of smells. The house was wide awake now and carried on its routine; shouting, calling, weeping, banging doors, clattering up and down the stairs. In this house Life manifested itself mostly in noise and decay. In the copper workshop on the ground floor could be heard the screech of sawing copper, sounding like cats, or children being tortured. Then it was almost quiet again, with only the whirring and humming sound of the leather transmission belts.

The girl heard a clock strike twelve. Instinctively she raised her head toward the door. If he was going to look in after the pawnbroker's, bringing her something to eat, he ought to come now—he had mentioned something of having breakfast together. But he did not come, and she had a conviction that he would not. He was certain to go straight to his friend's. If he got money he would come later; but he might also go straight on to the gambling club, and she wouldn't see him until the early hours of the morning, either penniless or with money in his pockets. Anyway, she would see him again.

And then it hit her: Was it so certain she would see him again? He'd always gone away and he'd always come back. Whatever he'd done, or wherever he'd been, he always ended up with her in Georgenstrasse. He would cross the court-yard, go up the steps—and reach her, either excitedly happy or utterly exhausted. I've never made any demands on him, she thought. Why shouldn't he come back? I was never a burden to him. But was this true? Had she not, in fact, made a demand, unspoken but insistent, that he should always return to her?

Even my love can become a burden to him, she reflected, filled with unut-terable sadness, and then he won't come back.

It grew hotter and hotter. She jumped up from the bed and went to the mirror. Yes, there she was—Petra Ledig. Hair and flesh, a sudden attraction, desire, consummation—the world was full of it. She thought of the thou-sand rooms in which at this hour the morning desire awakened. Kisses were exchanged, women were slowly undressed, bedsteads creaked, the transient sigh of lust escaped. And people separated at all hours in a thousand rooms, parted from one another every minute.

Had she believed she was secure? That it could continue? In her heart she knew, had always known, that it wouldn't. In the streets people were all in a hurry, rushing to catch their trains, to meet their girls, to spend their money before it became valueless. What endured, then? How could love endure?

All was futile on which she had set her heart. That they should be married this morning had seemed important enough for her to make a scene about it. Could it change anything? And if she sat there hungry and in debt, was that any reason why he should return? Did it matter in what condition she was deserted—whether, for example, she had a car and a villa in Grunewald, or not? The significant fact was that he did not come back. Whether she jumped out of the window or sold shoes again or walked the streets was all the same in that case.

She remained standing in front of the mirror and looked at herself as if looking at a dangerous stranger she had to be careful of. The figure in the mir-ror looks very pale, a brownish pale, and as if consumed from the inside. Its dark eyes shone, its hair hanging, with some loose locks, over its brow. She looked at herself breathlessly. It was as if everything was holding its breath. The house seemed to heave another sleepy sigh and then go silent. She herself still breathed. She shut her eyes and an almost painful shudder of happiness ran through her. She felt how warm her cheeks grew; they became hot. A good warmth, a lovely heat! Oh life, oh, love of life! It's led me from here via there, to here. Houses, faces, beatings, rows, dirt, money, fear. Hear I am, oh, sweet, sweet life! He can never leave me again. I have him inside me.

Life whirred, life bussed tirelessly up and down, stirring in every stone. It overflowed from the windows. It looked askance and it railed. It laughed—yes, it laughed as well. Life—wonderful, sweet, everlasting life! He can never leave me again. I have him inside me. Never thought of it, never hoped for it, never wanted it. I have him inside me. Life was racing, and we were just racing along with it. We never arrived anywhere. Everything slid away from us. Everything was lost. But something remained. Grass doesn't grow over all footprints, not every sigh is in vain. I remain. And he remains. We!

She had opened here eyes and now looked at herself. This is me, she thought for the first time in her life: she pointed her finger at herself. She was now without fear. He would return. He, too, one day would understand that she was "I" as she understood it. Now that she was no longer "I" but "We," she understood it too.

V

When the Rittmeister visited Berlin one of his chief amusements was to stroll along Friedrichstrasse and a stretch of the Leipziger, and look at the shops. Not that he made large purchases, or intended to—no, the show windows amused him. To the eye of a provincial they were so wonderfully arranged. In some windows there were delightful trifles which simply dragged you into the shop for the pleasure of pointing at them and saying: "That one." And in others were to be seen such frightful atrocities that you were moved again and again to laughter. Often he was tempted to carry such an article home, to see how Eva and Vi would be amused at, say, a man's head made of glass, the mouth serving as an ash tray. (One could also connect the head with the electric light and it would glow horribly red and green.)

But the experience that, after a few days, these curios stood about the house unnoticed, had made the Rittmeister cautious; he was now content to laugh by himself. If he wanted to take a present back—one may be ever so retired and white-haired a cavalry officer and yet like to stop before a lingerie shop to choose something silky or of lace. It was delightful to buy some trifle of that kind. Every time he entered such a shop the trifles had become lighter and more fragrant, ever more delicate in tint. You could squeeze in one hand a pair of knickers into a tiny ball, and it would spread out again, softly rustling. Life might have become gray and dismal, but female beauty seemed increasingly fragile and delicate. That brassiere made entirely of lace! The Rittmeister could well remember the gray drill corsets of prewar days, into which a husband had to lace his wife as if he were reining in a restive horse.

Or he entered a delicatessen shop. However worthless money might have become, here all the showcases were bursting: green asparagus from Italy, artichokes from France, fattened geese from Poland, Heligoland lobster, corn cobs from Hungary, English jams—the entire world had rendezvous here. Even caviar from Russia was back again; and foreign money, procurable only out of "friendship" and at exorbitant rates even so—here one could eat it up by the hundredweight. It was very puzzling.

After his talk with Studmann, the Rittmeister had plenty of time, so he strolled once again into his old haunts. But this time his joy was damped. Life went on in Friedrichstrasse rather as one imagined it must in an Oriental bazaar. Dealers, beggars, strumpets: almost shoulder to shoulder they stood on both sides of the pavement. Young men displayed suitcases filled with shining cut-glass bottles of perfume. One, yelling and shouting, flourished braces. A woman, disheveled and dirty, handled long, shimmering silk stockings which she offered, with an impudent smile, to the gentlemen. "Something for the little lady, Count. Put them on her yourself, and see what fun you'll have for that miserable bit of paper, Count."

A policeman came in sight, looking peevish beneath his lacquered military shako, and to keep up appearances the cases were shut and opened again as soon as his back was turned. Under the house walls, beggars squatted or reclined, all war-wounded, to judge from the placards they carried. But the very young ones could only have been in school during the war, and the old men must have been invalided out long before. Blind men whined monotonously; the palsied shook their heads and arms; wounds were exhibited, terrible scars gleamed fierily on scaly gray flesh.

But the girls were the worst. They strolled about calling, whispering, taking people's arms, running alongside men, laughing. Some girls exposed their bodies in a way that was revolting. A market of flesh—white flesh bloated with drink, and lean dark flesh which seemed to have been burned up by spirits. But worst of all were the entirely shameless, the almost sexless: the morphine addicts with their contracted pupils, the cocaine sniffers with their white noses, and the cocaine addicts with high-pitched voices and irrepressibly twitching faces. They wriggled, they jigged their flesh in low-cut or cunningly-slashed blouses, and when they made room for you or went round a corner they picked up their skirts (which, even so, didn't reach their knees), exhibiting between stockings and drawers a strip of pale flesh and a green or pink garter. They exchanged remarks about passing men, bawled obscenities to each other across the street, and their greedy eyes searched

among the slowly drifting crowd for foreigners who might be expected to
have foreign currency in their pockets.

Amid vice, misery and beggary, amid hunger, fraud and dope, young girls
who had hardly left school flitted from the shops, carrying cardboard boxes
and bundles of letters. They missed nothing, and it was their ambition to be as
insolent as those others, to be got down by nothing, to be scared at nothing, to
wear skirts just as short, to snatch as much foreign currency

"You can't get us down," said their glances. "You old people can't take us
in," they said and flourished their boxes. "At present we're only shopgirls,
sales-girls, office-girls. But it only needs a man to cast an eye on us, the little
chap here or the fat man there with the mutton-chop whiskers, flaunting his
paunch in a pair of checked flannel trousers—and we drop our boxes in the
street, and sit this evening in a bar and have a car tomorrow."

The Rittmeister felt as if he heard them all running and shouting: "Nothing
has any value but money. Money. But in point of fact money has no value; the
greatest possible enjoyment has to be squeezed out of it moment by moment.
Why save oneself up for tomorrow? Who knows where the dollar will stand, who
knows whether we shall be still alive tomorrow? By tomorrow younger, fresher
girls will be in the running. Do come, old man, you've got white hair certainly—
but it's all the more important not to waste any time. Come, dearie."

The Rittmeister caught sight of the entrance to the Arcade from Unter den
Linden to Friedrichstrasse. He always liked to look at the waxworks—so he fled
into the Arcade. But he might have come from purgatory into hell. A closely
packed crowd surged through the radiantly lit tunnel. The shops paraded huge
pot-boiler pictures of naked women, repulsively naked, with revoltingly sweet
pink breasts. Chains of indecent picture-postcards hung everywhere. There
were trick novelties which would have made a hardened roué blush and the
lewdness of the photographs that furtive men stickily pressed into one's hand
could not be rivaled.

But the young boys were by far the worst of all. In their sailor suits, with
smooth bare chests, cigarettes impudently sticking in their lips, they glided
about everywhere; they did not speak, but they looked at you and touched you.

A tall fair woman in a low-cut dress, very elegant, pushed through
the crowd, accompanied by a train of such lads. She laughed loudly, spoke
emphatically. The Rittmeister saw her quite close too, his eyes falling on the
shamelessly uncovered and thickly powdered breast. Laughingly she looked
at him. The pupils of her eyes were unnaturally enlarged, her lower eyelids
painted blue-black. Shuddering nausea overcame him at the realization that

this rigged-up woman was a man; she was the female for this repulsive crowd of loungers, and yet she was a man.

Regardless of others, the Rittmeister forced his way through the crowd. A whore shouted, "The old man's got a screw loose. Emil, sock him one. He biffed into me." But the Rittmeister was already outside and had caught a taxi. "Schlesische Bahnhof," he directed and leaned back into the cushions exhausted. Then he pulled out of his coat pocket a white, freshly laundered handkerchief and slowly wiped his face and hands.

He forced himself to concentrate on something entirely different—and what was of more interest than his worries? Indeed, it wasn't easy to manage Neulohe these days. Quite apart from his father-in-law being a rat (and on top of that his mother-in-law with her religiosity), the rent was really too high. Either nothing grew, as last year, or, if anything did grow, one had no laborers, as this year.

But after the conversation with poor Studmann, who had also been tainted by wrong views and was by way of imbibing cranky ideas, and after his little walk through Friedrichstrasse and the Arcade, the Rittmeister thought of Neulohe as an untouched island of purity. To be sure, there were eternal worries, trouble with the farm hands, trouble with the taxes, money troubles, trouble with workmen (and the worst of all was the "in-law" trouble). But at least there was Eva, and Violet, known from her babyhood as Vi.

Certainly Eva was a bit too vivacious: the way in which she danced and flirted with the officers in Ostade would once have been regarded as improper and Vi also had picked up a rude manner (it was often enough to make her grandmother swoon)—but what was this compared with the misery, the indecency, the demoralization which manifested itself in Berlin in broad daylight? Rittmeister Joachim von Prackwitz was made otherwise and had no intention of changing: in his view a woman was of finer stuff than man, she was a delicate creature, one to be protected. Those girls in Friedrichstrasse, they were no longer women. A real man could think of them only with horror.

In Neulohe they had a garden where they sat in the evening. The manservant Hubert brought shaded candles and a bottle of Moselle; at the worst the phonograph with its "Yes, we have no bananas" gave a townish flavor to the foliage and the blossoms. But the women were protected. Pure, clean.

One could no longer go with a lady to Friedrichstrasse, in particular when that lady was one's daughter. And to think that a splendid fellow like Studmann wanted somehow to make this street scum happy, to place himself in some respects on the same footing, merely for the reason that he had to earn money as they did! No, thank you. At home in Neulohe one might think that the *Deutsche Tageszeitung* exaggerated when it called Berlin a morass of infamy, a Babel of sin, a Sodom and Gomorrah. But when you'd had a sniff of it you realized that those remarks were an understatement. No, thank you!

And the Rittmeister calmed down so far that he lit a cigarette and, contented with the business he had concluded and the prospect of an early return home, approached the station.

His first action was to go to the refreshment room and have a couple of strong cognacs, for he had a presentiment that the sight of his newly engaged harvesters would not be an unmitigated joy. But it wasn't so bad after all: as a matter of fact only what he expected. The faces were perhaps rougher, more impudent and shameless than before—but what did that matter, as long as they worked and got in the harvest? They oughtn't to have too thin a time—decent allowances, every week a sheep slaughtered and once a month a fat pig.

Only, the foreman was just the kind of man utterly obnoxious to him, treading on those below, bending the knee to those above. He cringed before the Rittmeister, spewed out a flood of half-German, half-Polish words praising the strength and efficiency of his men, and then kicked a girl's behind unexpectedly when she didn't get through the door ` quickly enough with her bundle.

Incidentally, when the Rittmeister wanted to get a party ticket, it turned out that the foreman had brought with him not fifty but only thirty-seven hands; and in reply to the Rittmeister's questions he again poured out a welter of confused phrases which became more and more Polish and less and less intelligible. (Eva was quite right, of course. He should have learned Polish, but he hadn't the slightest intention of doing so.) The foreman seemed to be affirming something; he tensed his upper-arm muscle and looked laughingly, coaxingly, with his small, mouse-quick eyes at the Rittmeister. In the end Prackwitz shrugged his shoulders and bought the ticket. Thirty-seven were better than none, and in any case they were trained agricultural workers.

Then came the noisy departure to the platform; the boarding of the waiting train; the abusive guard who wanted to push into the carriage a bundle which was blocking the door, although it was being pushed out again, together with the girl who carried it; the quarrel between two lads; the wild gesticulations and cries of the foreman who meanwhile was incessantly addressing the Rittmeister, asking, demanding, begging his thirty dollars.

At first the Rittmeister was of the opinion that twenty were sufficient, since a quarter of the people had not turned up. Hotly they bargained and finally, when the last man had found a place in the train, the Rittmeister, tired of the argument, counted out three ten-dollar notes into the foreman's fist;

who now brimmed over with gratitude, bowed, hopped from one foot to the other, and finally contrived to snatch the Rittmeister's hand and kiss it fervently. "O Lord, holy benefactor."

Somewhat disgusted, the Rittmeister looked for a place in a second-class smoking compartment right in front. Sitting down comfortably in the corner he lit a cigarette. All in all, he had done a good day's work. Tomorrow the harvest could begin in real earnest.

Rumbling and puffing, the train got under way, steamed out of the sooty, neglected hall with its broken windows. The Rittmeister was waiting for the guard to pass, as he then intended to have a nap.

At last the man came, punched the ticket and gave it back. He did not go, however, but stood as if expecting something.

"Well?" asked the Rittmeister sleepily. "Rather hot outside, what?"

"Aren't you the gentleman with the Polish reapers?" asked the guard.

"Certainly." The Rittmeister sat up.

"I only wanted to report," said the guard with a trace of malicious joy, "that they all alighted at Schlesische Bahnhof. Made themselves scarce."

"What?" shouted the Rittmeister and leaped toward the compartment door.

VI

The train gathered more speed. It dipped into the tunnel; the lighted platform was left behind.

Pagel sat on the fire extinguisher box in the overcrowded smoking carriage and lit a Lucky Strike from the packet he had just bought with the proceeds of their goods and chattels. Splendid! He had last smoked on his way home from gambling the night before; therefore this cigarette tasted all the better. "Lucky Strike," it was called. If his school English had not quite forsaken him it meant that this fortunate cigarette ought to be an omen for the rest of the day.

The fat man over there snorted angrily, rustled his newspaper, looked around restlessly—all that won't help, Pagel thought; we know it already: the dollar is valued at 760,000 marks, an advance of over fifty per cent. The cigarette merchant, thank God, didn't know it or else he couldn't have afforded this cigarette. You too have backed the wrong horse, fatty; your snorting gives you away, you're furious. But it won't help you. This is an ingenious, entirely modern postwar invention; they rob you of one-half of the money in your pocket without touching the pocket or the money. Yes, brilliant brains, brilliant brains. The question now is whether my friend Zecke has backed the right or the wrong horse. If he's backed the wrong one he may be rather hard of hearing, though this isn't certain; but if devaluation has suited his purpose he won't mind parting with a handful of 1,000,000-mark notes. Even 2,000,000-mark notes had been current for a day or two; Pagel had seen them in the gambling club. For a change they were printed on both sides and looked like genuine money, not like those scraps of white paper printed on one side only. People were already saying that these 2,000,000-mark notes would forever remain the highest denomination; and because of such a fairy tale the fat man snorted, having perhaps believed in fairy tales.

It was unlikely that Zecke had backed the wrong horse. As long as Pagel could remember Zecke had always backed the right one. He had never made a mistake in summing up a teacher; he had had a hunch as to what questions would be asked, what themes would be set, in the examination papers. In the war he had been the first to organize a magnificent system of leave in order to distribute Salvarsan in the Balkans and in Turkey. And when this business became precarious he was again the first who, before he gave it up entirely, filled the Salvarsan packages with rubbish. Then he had exported sixth-rate singing and dancing girls to the Bosphorus. A choice fellow, all in all; a fool in some respects, in others as sharp as a needle. After the war he had gone in for yarn—what he now dealt in, Heaven alone knew. It didn't matter to him—he would have made a corner in bull elephants had there been any money in them.

Really, when one came to think of it, there was no reason why this so-called friend should give away his money—Pagel admitted it. He had never hitherto attempted to touch him. But another feeling dwelt also in Wolfgang Pagel's breast—the feeling that Zecke was now "ripe," that he would undoubtedly do what was expected of him. A gambler's instinct, so to speak: a hunch, the devil knew why. He would certainly give the money. There were such moments. Suddenly you did something which you would not have done yesterday at any price. And out of that automatically followed something else—for instance, this evening you would win a tremendous sum—and again everything was suddenly changed. Life would run at right angles to its hitherto straight course. One could buy twenty tenement houses in the city (the hovels were to be had for next to nothing) or open a giant super bar (eighty girls behind the counter)—not a bad idea, indeed; or for a change you need do nothing at all, sit and twiddle your thumbs, take a real rest, eat and drink well and enjoy Peter. Or still better, buy a car and travel with Peter all over the world. Show her everything—churches, paintings, everything; the girl had potentialities— of course. Did anybody deny it? He didn't, in any case; a splendid girl, never awkward! (Or hardly ever.)

Retired Second Lieutenant Wolfgang Pagel alighted at Podbielskiallee and sauntered down a street or two to the Zecke villa. In the heat. Lazily and leisurely. Now he stood in front of the house; that is to say, in front of the front garden, the laid-out grounds, the park. And not directly in front of it; there was, of course, a wrought-iron railing and some hewn stone (let us say limestone) in the form of pillars. And a very small brass plate was also there, inscribed with nothing else but "von Zecke," with a brass bell-push. Well polished. One couldn't see much of the house—it was hidden behind bushes and trees; one only got an impression of big shining windows and of a gracefully designed housefront, not too tall.

Pagel took a look at the whole bundle of tricks; there was plenty of time. Then he turned round and had a look at the villas on the other side. Pompous. So here dwelt the grand folks who could not under any circumstances live in a backyard off Alexanderplatz. Himself Wolfgang Pagel considered capable of both; at one time Dahlem, at another Alexanderplatz; he didn't mind which. But perhaps he was living not in Dahlem but in Georgenkirchstrasse just because he didn't mind.

He turned round again and eyed the name plate, bell-push, flowerbeds, lawn, house-front. It remained a puzzle why Zecke should burden himself with such stuff, for after all it was a burden, owning a house, a huge villa, almost a palace, which eternally demanded something of you: either to pay the taxes or have it done up or see about electric current failing or the coke that had to be bought. Zecke, in any case, must have changed a good deal. Formerly he, too, would have thought it a burden. The last time he saw him Zecke had had two very elegant bachelor rooms in Kurfürstendamm (with girl-friend, telephone and bath)—and that was more in keeping with him. Not this.

Possibly he was married. Any incredible change in a friend was explained by the fact of his having married, of a woman being there. Well, one would probably see her, and she would guess immediately that this old friend of her husband's wanted to touch them for some money. Whereupon she would treat him with a mixture of annoyance and contempt. But for all he cared she could do as she pleased; the man who in the evening prowled about as the unwanted gambler was proof against female moods.

He was just about to ring the bell—one had to do it sooner or later, however pleasant it might be to stand lazily in the sun and think of the nice sum of money which he was going to lift from Zecke presently—when he remembered in time that he still carried nearly a hundred thousand marks in his pocket. To be sure, there was the saying that money is attracted by money, but this proverb was not properly worded. It ought to run—a lot of money attracts a lot of money.

And that hardly applied to the sum Pagel was carrying. In the circumstances it would be better if he stood before Zecke utterly penniless. One pleaded for a loan much more convincingly when one hadn't even got the fare home. For his hundred thousand he could get, say, two small cognacs, and these would add weight to his application for a loan.

He sauntered down the street, went to the right, then the left, again right, and to and fro; but it proved difficult to convert his money into alcohol. In this very smart residential district there seemed to be neither shops nor taverns. Everything, of course, was brought to the door; such people' kept wine and schnapps by the cellarful.

Pagel came across a newspaper seller, but he didn't want to invest his money in newspapers. No, thanks, he didn't want to have anything to do with them. When he read the headline: "Trade Barriers Lifted in the Occupied Territory," it didn't matter to him. Do what you liked about it, it was bosh anyway.

Next he came across a flower girl selling roses at a bus stop. The idea of appearing with a miserable bunch of roses before Herr von Zecke, who had a whole garden full of them, was so attractive that Pagel almost bought some. But he shrugged his shoulders and walked on. He was not quite sure whether Zecke would see the funny side of it.

The money must be got rid of, however. So much was certain. He would most have preferred to give it to a beggar—that always brought luck. But here in Dahlem there were no beggars; they found it better to sit in Alexanderplatz among the poor, who always managed to spare something.

For a time Wolfgang followed an elderly skinny lady whose worn short jacket, with its faded lilac facings and black bugles, gave him the impression of a poor woman ashamed to beg. Then he gave up the idea of pressing the money into her hand. It would be the worst possible omen if he did not rid himself of it at the first try, but had it thrust back on him.

Finally the dog turned up. Pagel was sitting, enjoying himself in a quiet way, on a bench, and he whistled to a stray brown-and-white fox terrier. The dog was brimming over with whimsical energies; he barked at the cajoler defiantly; challengingly; then, suddenly becoming amiable, he put his head scrutinizingly on one side and wagged his stump of tail. Wolf had almost got him when, in a flash, he was yelping joyfully on the other side of the ornamental gardens, while a maidservant swinging a leash hurried after him, calling in a despairing voice: "Schnapps, Schnapps."

Confronted by the choice between the peacefully smoking man and the excited girl, the terrier decided in favor of the man. Beseechingly he pressed his nose against Pagel's leg, and in his eyes could be read an invitation to a new game. Wolf shoved the notes under his collar just as the girl approached, hot and indignant. "Let our dog go," she gasped.

"Ah, Fräulein," said Wolfgang, "we men are all for Schnapps. And," he added, for in the fresh summer dress there was a pleasing girl, "and for love."

"Oh, you!" said the girl, and her annoyed face changed so suddenly that Wolfgang had to smile. "You've no idea," she went on, trying to put the dancing, barking terrier on the lead, "what a lot of trouble I have with the dog. And gentlemen are always speaking to me—but what's this?" she asked, surprised, for she had felt the paper under the collar.

"A letter," said Pagel, departing. "A letter for you. You must have noticed that I've been following you every morning for a week. But read it later, when you're alone. It explains everything. So long."

And he went hastily round the corner, for her face was shining too brightly for him to wish to see her discover the truth. And round another corner. Now he could probably slow down, safe. He was sweating again; as a matter of fact, however slowly he walked, he had been sweating ever since alighting at Podbielskiallee. And suddenly it struck him that it was not the warmth of the sun which made him so hot; at any rate, not the sun only. No, it was something different, something quite different. He was agitated, he was afraid.

With a start he stopped and looked round. Silently in the midday light the villas stood within the shelter of the pines. Somewhere a vacuum cleaner was humming. Everything he had done up to now to delay pressing the bell had been inspired by fear. And the fear had started much earlier than that; otherwise he would not have bought his Lucky Strike cigarettes instead of breakfast for both. Had it not been for fear he would not let the pawnbroker have their things. "Yes," said he, and went slowly on, "the end is at hand." He saw their situation as it really was—in debt, with nothing for the following day, Petra almost naked in a stinking den, he himself in the wealthy quarter in his shabby field-gray tunic, and not even the fare home in his pocket.

I must persuade him to give us money, he thought. Even if it's only a very little.

But it was lunacy, utter madness, to expect a loan from Zecke. Nothing that he knew of Zecke entitled him to expect him to lend money—with very little prospect of getting it back. Suppose he said no? (And he would, of course, say no, Wolfgang needn't worry himself about that.)

The long, rather wide avenue, at the end of which Zecke's villa was situated, opened before him. He went along slowly at first, then quicker and quicker, as if he were running down a steep hill toward his fate.

He must say yes, Pagel thought. Even if he gives ever so little. Then I'll finish with gambling. I can still become a taxi driver—Gottschalk has definitely promised me his second car. Then Petra will have an easier time, too.

Now he was quite close to the villa; he saw again the limestone and railings, brass plate and bell-push. Hesitatingly he crossed the street. But he would say no, of course . . . Oh, damn, damn!—for at the end of the street he saw a girl approaching; the fox terrier straining and yelping at the leash revealed who she was. And between the argument there and the request here, hunter and hunted, he pushed the button and sighed with relief when the electric door-catch softly burred. Without a glance at the approaching girl he carefully pulled the door to behind him and breathed again as a turn of the path brought him under the cover of bushes.

After all, Zecke could only say no, but this wench could make an infernal row—Wolfgang hated scenes with women. You never knew where they would end.

VII

"So here you are, Pagel," said Herr von Zecke. "I've rather been expecting you." And as Wolfgang made a gesture, he added: "Not exactly today—but you were due, weren't you?"

And Zecke gave a superior smile, to Pagel's annoyance. Zecke, it occurred to him, had always loved an affectation of mystery; he had always had this supercilious smile, so irritating to Wolfgang. Zecke smiled in that way whenever he considered himself particularly smart.

"Well, I only mention it," grinned Zecke. "After all, you're sitting here—you won't deny that. Well, never mind. I know what I know. Shall we have a schnapps and a cigarette and a look at my pictures?" Pagel had glimpsed the pictures on entering.

They were sitting in a big, very well-furnished sun-porch. A couple of doors opened on to the terrace, steeped in the glowing sun. Through them could be seen a lawn bright with summer; but it was, nevertheless, pleasantly cool inside. Light, radiant and dark at the same time, and, above everything else, cool, filtered through green venetian blinds.

They sat in pleasant chairs, not in those smooth, cold leather things which one now saw everywhere, but in deep, roomy easy-chairs upholstered in some flowery English material—most likely chintz. Books a third of the wall high, and above them pictures, good modern paintings, as Pagel had seen at once. But he did not react to Zecke's question. He realized that the atmosphere was not unfavorable, that his visit somehow suited Herr von Zecke. Zecke, of course, wanted something, and so he could quietly wait and be a little difficult. (He would get his money!) He pointed at the books. "Nice collection. Do you read much?"

But von Zecke was not so silly as all that. He laughed heartily. "I read? You're still the same old joker, aren't you? Wouldn't you like me to say yes, so that you could bore me stiff with what's written in Nietzsche, there!" His face changed, became pensive. "I believe they're quite a good investment. Full-leather binding. You have to see how to invest your money in stable values. I understand nothing of books—Salvarsan's simpler—but I've got a little student who advises me . . ." He deliberated a moment, probably considering whether the little student was worth the money he paid him. Then he asked: "Well, and the paintings?" But Pagel was not biting. He indicated some carvings, figures of apostles, a Virgin and Child, a crucifix, two Pietàs. "You're collecting medieval wood-carvings also?"

Zecke pulled a doleful face. "Not collect, no. Invest money in. But I don't know what's happened, it's beginning to amuse me. Have a look at this one, the fellow with the key, Peter, of course. I got him from Würzburg. I don't understand anything about it, it doesn't look much, not at all impressive and so on—but I like it. And this Angel light-bearer—the arm's probably restored. Do you think I've been done?"

Wolfgang Pagel cast a searching glance at von Zecke. He was a little man; in spite of his twenty-four or twenty-five years he was already rotund and, his hair having retreated at the temples, his forehead was high. In addition he was dark—and all this annoyed Wolfgang, together with the fact that von Zecke liked carvings and that his pictures seemed to cause him real concern. Zecke was a profiteer, nothing more, and he had to stay one. For a man like that to take an interest in art was ridiculous and disgusting. Wolf was most indignant, however, at having to ask this transformed Zecke for money—Zecke was capable of giving it out of sheer decency. No, the man was a profiteer and must remain so, and if he lent money he ought to take exorbitant interest; otherwise Wolfgang wanted to have nothing to do with him. He didn't want to receive money as a gift from a man like Zecke. Looking disapprovingly at the torch-bearing angel, he said: "So now it's the turn of angels—you no longer deal in variety tarts?"

At once he saw from Zecke's reaction that he had gone too far, that he had made a fatal mistake: They were no longer at school, where one had to put up with such familiarities, where they were considered to be a form of sport. Zecke's nose turned pale, while his face remained extremely red, a sign known to Pagel from those earlier days.

But if von Zecke had not yet learned to read books he had learned to control himself (and in this respect he was far ahead of Pagel). He behaved as if he had heard nothing, put the angel slowly down, gently stroked the probably restored arm, and said: "Yes, yes, the pictures. You must still have some very fine ones at home, of your father's."

Aha, so that's what you're after, thought Pagel, completely satisfied. "Yes, some very fine specimens are still there," he replied.

"I know," said Zecke, pouring out another schnapps, first in Pagel's glass, then in his own, and seating himself comfortably. "So, if you're in need of money—I buy paintings as you can see . . ."

That was a facer, a belated reply to his impertinence, but Pagel did not show it. "I don't think we're selling any."

"You're not quite informed there." Zecke smiled charmingly. "Only last month your mother sold 'Autumn Trees' to the art gallery in Glasgow. Well, your health!" He drank, leaned back satisfied and said innocently: "Well, what's the old woman to live on nowadays? What she had in stocks and shares is worth less than nothing today."

Zecke didn't grin, but Pagel felt very strongly that the designation of "good friend" which only that morning he had applied to him was an overstatement. He had already been stung by two darts, and he wouldn't have long to wait for the third. True, von Zecke had always been a snake, a bad enemy, so it would be better to advance to the attack himself—then the matter would be settled and finished with. Trying to speak as easily as possible, he said: "I'm a bit hard up, Zecke. Could you help me out with a little money?"

"What do you call a little money?" asked Zecke.

"Well, not much, a trifle to you. What do you say to a hundred millions?"

"A hundred millions," murmured Zecke dreamily. "I didn't make as much as that on all the variety tarts."

The third blow, and this time it really seemed a knockout. But Wolfgang Pagel did not so easily take the count. He started to laugh, heartily and unconcerned. "You're right, Zecke. Splendid! I talk big and then it turns out I only want to touch you for money. But, you know, something put my back up immediately I came in. I don't know whether you understand what I mean . . . I live in a kind of hole in Alexanderplatz, you know!" Zecke nodded as if he knew. "With nothing at all . . . and then to come here amidst all this splendor! Not at all like the parvenus and profiteers, but really well done, and I don't believe the arm's restored either."

He stopped to look scrutinizingly at Zecke. He couldn't say more, he simply couldn't bring himself to say another word. But when Zecke didn't make a move, he added: "All right, don't give me any money, Zecke. I don't deserve any; I've behaved like an idiot."

"I don't necessarily say no," explained Zecke. "I only just want to hear what you have in mind. Money is money, and you don't want it as a present, do you?"

"No, as soon as I can you'll get it back."

"And when will that be?"

"Under favorable circumstances, if all goes well, tomorrow."

"Really," said Zecke, not particularly enthusiastic. "Really. Well, let's have another schnapps. And what do you need the money for?"

"Oh," said Pagel, getting confused and annoyed, "I've got a few debts with my landlady, trifles really—you know, a hundred millions sounds a tremendous lot, but one way and another it's not much more than a hundred dollars, not so alarming."

"So, debts with the landlady," said Zecke quite unmoved, his dark eyes looking attentively at his friend. "Anything else?"

"Yes," replied Pagel vexed. "I've also got a few things in pawn." In the same moment it occurred to him that this was really not quite true, but in speaking he hadn't considered the distinction between what's sold and what's pawned, and so he left it at that. It really didn't matter one way or the other . . .

"So, a few things in pawn," said von Zecke, still scrutinizing him. "You know, Pagel, I must ask you something else—you must excuse me. Money's money after all, and even a very little, a hundred dollars, for instance, is to some people quite a lot—for instance, to you."

Pagel had made up his mind to take no notice of these pin-pricks, for, after all, the main thing was to get the money. "On with your questions!" he said peevishly.

"What are you doing? I mean, what are you living on? Have you got a job which earns you something? Are you a traveler on a commission basis? Employee with a salary?"

"At the moment I've got nothing," said Pagel. "But at any moment I can get a job as a taxi driver."

"Indeed." Zecke seemed quite satisfied. "If you want another drink please take one. I've had enough for one morning. A taxi driver, then . . ." And this shady profiteer, this vampire, this criminal (sand instead of Salvarsan!) started to prod him again. "Taxi driver—a good job and handsome earnings, no doubt." (How the venomous monkey sneered!) "But surely not so much that you can return my money tomorrow? You said, tomorrow if all goes well, you remember? But taxi driving doesn't pay so well, does it?"

"My dear Zecke," said Wolfgang getting up, "you want to torment me, isn't that it? But the money's not so important as all that." He was almost shaking with fury.

"But, Pagel!" cried Zecke, startled. "I torment you? Why should I? Look here, you purposely haven't asked me for a gift—otherwise you would have got a couple of notes long ago. You want a loan and you made statements about repayment—so I ask you how you figure it out, and you start a row. I don't understand."

"I spoke without thinking," said Pagel. "In reality I could only pay the money back in weekly installments, perhaps about two millions a week. . . ."

"That's of no consequence, old boy," cried von Zecke cheerfully. "That's of no consequence with old friends like ourselves. The chief thing is that you don't lose the money gambling. That's the position, isn't it?"

The two looked at each other.

"It isn't the slightest use shouting," said Zecke, at once hurriedly and softly. "I'm so often shouted at that it has no effect. If you want to assault me you'd better do it very quickly—you see, I've already rung the bell. Yes, Reimers, the gentleman would like to go. Show him out, will you? So long, Pagel, old friend, and if you want to sell a painting of your father's I'm always at home to you, always. . . . What's the matter, have you gone crazy?" For Pagel had started to laugh with unrestrained amusement.

"Good God, what a swine you are, Zecke," he said laughing. "It must have hurt you damned hard about the tarts if you have to discharge your venom in this way. Your chief used to trade in music-hall tarts," he told the man behind him, a cross between master and servant. "He doesn't wish to acknowledge it anymore, but it still hurts if it's mentioned. But, Zecke," went on Pagel, with the dead earnestness of the expert, "I'm inclined to the view that this torch-angel's arm is stuck on, and badly, too. I should like to do—this . . ."

And before Zecke or his man could prevent him, the figure had lost its arm. Von Zecke screamed as if he himself felt the pain of amputation, and the servant made to attack Pagel, who, despite inadequate nourishment, was still a powerful young man. With one hand he warded off the manservant, in the other he held the angel's amputated arm with its lamp socket. "This gross forgery I would like to keep in remembrance of you, my old friend Zecke," said Wolfgang pleasantly. "You know—The Light That Failed—and so on. So long, and do enjoy your lunch, both of you."

Pleased and satisfied, Pagel made his exit. If von Zecke really wished to enjoy the the thought that he had not given him any money, he would also have to remember the angel's arm now in Pagel's pocket. And the pain would outweigh the pleasure.

VIII

Unmolested he arrived at the gate of Zecke's villa, and as he pulled it open, saw a girl standing outside, a girl with a terrier straining at its leash, a girl with a very red face.

"Good heavens, Fräulein, you're not still standing here!" he cried in dismay. "I had completely forgotten all about you."

"Listen," said she, and her anger had lost none of its heat through her long wait in the sun. "Listen," and she held out the notes, "if you think I'm that sort of a girl, then you're wrong. Take your money."

"And so little!" said Pagel quite unconcerned. "It wouldn't buy even a pair of silk stockings. . . . No," he added quickly, "I don't want to pull your leg any longer. In fact, I want your advice."

She stood there gaping at him, the notes in one hand, the leash with the fox terrier in the other—utterly confounded by the change in his manner. "Listen," she said once more, but the threat in her voice had lost its vigor.

"Let's go," suggested Pagel. "Come along. Don't be silly, come a part of the way with me, Lina, Trina, Stina. I can't do anything to you in the street and I'm not crazy either."

"I've no time. I ought to have been home by now. My mistress . . ."

"Tell your mistress Schnapps ran away, and listen. I've just been with that fine fellow in the villa there, a school friend of mine, trying to borrow some money. . . ."

"And then you put your money in my dog's . . ."

"Don't be a goose, Mitzi."

"Liesbeth."

"Listen, Liesbeth. Naturally, I didn't get anything with you standing outside with my money. A fellow can't get any money as long as he has any left, and that's the reason I stuck what I had in the dog's collar. Do you get me?"

It took her quite a while, however. "So you haven't been running after me for a week, then, and you haven't put in a letter either. I thought the dog had lost it. . . ."

"No, no, Liesbeth." Pagel grinned impudently, but was nevertheless feeling abject. "No letter—and I didn't want to buy your chastity with the money, either. But the question I want you to answer is this: what am I to do now? I haven't got a penny. I have a dirty hole in Alexanderplatz for which the rent isn't paid, and my girl's sitting there as a kind of pledge, dressed in nothing but my summer overcoat. And I sold all our things to get here."

"Serious?" asked the girl. "No more kidding?"

"No more kidding. Dead serious."

She looked at him. She gave the impression of being unbelievably fresh and clean, in spite of the heat—she smelled, so as to speak, of Sunlight Soap. Perhaps she wasn't as young as he had at first thought, and in addition she had a rather determined chin.

She realized now that it was indeed serious, looked at him, then at the money in her hand.

Will she give it back to me? he wondered. Then I'll have to go to Peter and do something. But what I'd better do I really don't know. I'm not keen on anything. She shall tell me.

The girl had smoothed out the money and put it in her pocket.

"There," she said, "you must come with me first. I'm going home now—and you look quite done—in to me and as if you could do with a bit of lunch in our kitchen. The cook won't mind, nor the mistress. But to think that your friend's sitting in your room in your summer overcoat and perhaps nothing in her stomach, either, with a rude landlady into the bargain! And a chap like you puts money in dog collars and wants to pick up another girl right away—you men are rotters, upon my word you are."

She was talking faster and faster, dragging at the dog, walking more and more hurriedly, not doubting for a moment that the young man was coming with her.

And follow her he did, he, Wolfgang Pagel, son of a not-unknown painter, former second lieutenant, and gambler at the end of his tether.

IX

The letter had come by the second post at eleven o'clock, but Frau Pagel was still out attending to various details, so Minna had put the letter on the console table under the mirror in the hall. There it lay, a gray envelope of embossed, rather imposing handmade paper; the address written in a bold, stiff handwriting, and every free space on the front and back covered with 1,000-mark postage stamps of various denominations, although it was merely a local letter.

When Frau Pagel returned from town, somewhat late and hot, she cast only a fleeting glance at the letter. Ah, from cousin Betty, she thought. But I must first see about the lunch. I'll know soon enough what the old gossip wants.

Not till she was sitting at table did the letter come to her mind and she sent Minna for it—Minna who, as always, was standing behind her in the doorway, while as usual the cover was laid for Wolfgang at the other end of the table. "From Frau von Anklam," she said to Minna over her shoulder and tore open the envelope.

"Goodness, it can't be so urgent, madam, that you should let your food get cold."

But from the silence, the rigid attitude, the flabbergasted way in which Frau Pagel stared at the letter, she guessed that it was important after all. Silently, without moving, Minna waited quite a long time; then she coughed, and at last said meaningly: "The food is getting cold, madam."

"What?" Frau Pagel almost shouted, turning round and staring at Minna as if she were a total stranger. "Oh, yes." She recovered herself. "It's only . . . Minna, Frau von Anklam writes me. . . . It's only—our young master is getting married today." And then it was all up. The head with its white hair lay on the table; that back which will power had kept erect was now bent—and the old woman wept.

"Good God!" said Minna. "Good God!

She came nearer. Certainly she did not consider this marriage to be so very bad, but she understood the pain, grief and desolation of her mistress. Cautiously she put her work-worn hand on Frau Pagel's shoulder and said: "It needn't be true, madam. Not everything that Frau von Anklam says is true by a long way."

"This time it is," whispered Frau Pagel. "Somebody read the banns after they had been put up and told her about it. Today at half-past twelve."

She raised her head and looked as if for help at the walls, recollected herself, and glanced at the watch on her wrist. "It's half-past one," she cried. "And the letter has been waiting a long while. I could have known of it in time!"

True suffering finds food in everything, even in the unreasonable. That she had not known in time, that at half-past twelve she had not been thinking, Now they are being married . . . this increased Frau Pagel's grief. With streaming eyes and quivering lips she sat there, looked at her Minna and said: "Now we needn't lay a place anymore; Wolf is gone forever, Minna. Oh, that terrible woman. And now she is Frau Pagel, just as I am."

She recalled the path she had traveled under this name, a stormy, hurried, flowery path at first. Then the endlessly long years at the side of her paralyzed husband who, growing more and more of a stranger, had painted contentedly while she pursued the health which he no longer seemed to crave. Finally she remembered the awakening, the resurrection of the man with the graying temples, who had entangled himself in the most absurd coxcombry and had been carried home shamefully killed. . . .

Every step on this long road had been painful; no year had passed without trouble; sorrow had been her bedfellow and grief her shadow. But out of that she had become a Pagel; out of the sweet illusions of youth there had arisen the determined woman who now and forever was Frau Pagel. In heaven she would still be a Pagel; it was impossible that God would ever make her anyone else. But all for which she had fought so hard, this metamorphosis, this agonizing fulfillment of her destiny, had fallen into the lap of that young thing as though it were nothing. As casually as they had met, so were they united. "Whither thou goest, I will go; and where thou lodgest, I will lodge. My people shall be thy people, and thy God my God: where thou diest, will I die, and there will I be buried; the Lord do so to me, and more also, if aught but death part thee and me." Yes, so it was written; but they knew nothing of that. To be Frau Pagel was not merely a name, it was a destiny. They, however, had stuck up a notice, had the words "half-past twelve" inserted, and that was all there was to it.

Minna said, to console her (but she was right all the same) : "It will only be at a registry office, madam, not a church."

Frau Pagel sat up. "Isn't that so, Minna; you think so too? Wolfgang hasn't properly considered the matter, he does it only because the girl's forced him. He too doesn't consider a registry office sufficient; he wouldn't cause me that pain."

"It's no doubt," explained the inflexibly honest Minna, "because the registry office is compulsory, while church is not. He'll be short of money, the young master.

"Yes," said Frau Pagel and heard only what pleased her. "And those who have come together so hurriedly will just as lightly part."

"The young master," ventured Minna, "has always had too easy a time. He's no idea of how a poor man earns money. First you made it easy for him, madam—and now the girl does. Some men are like that—all their life they need a nursemaid—and what's so extraordinary, they always find one."

"Money," repeated the old woman. "They will have hardly any money. A young thing is vain, likes to dress nicely. If we were to give her money, Minna?"

"She would only give it to him, madam. And he would gamble it away."

"Minna!" Frau Pagel was shocked. "What are you thinking of? He'll not gamble any more now, when he's married. There may be children."

"There could have been children before, madam. That has nothing to do with gambling."

Frau Pagel did not want to understand; she was staring across the table at the empty seat.

"Do clear away, Minna," she cried. "I can't look at food any longer. Here I'm eating a little pigeon—and he has married." She wept again. "Oh, Minna, what are we to do? I can't go on sitting here in my flat as if nothing had happened. We must do something."

"Suppose we went there?" suggested Minna cautiously.

"Go there? Us? And he doesn't come here! And he hasn't even written to tell me he's going to get married! No, that's quite impossible."

"There's no need to behave as if we knew anything."

"I deceive Wolf? No, Minna, I won't start that now. It's bad enough to realize that he doesn't mind deceiving me."

"And suppose I went there alone?" Minna again asked warily. "They're used to me, and I'm not so particular about a bit of deceiving."

"That's bad enough, Minna," said Frau Pagel sharply. "Very disgusting of you. Well, I'll lie down now for a short time. I've a terrible headache. Bring me a glass of water for my tablets."

And she went into her husband's room. For a while she stood before the picture of a young woman, thinking perhaps: She can never love him as much as I did Edmund. They may separate very, very soon.

She heard Minna go to and from the other room, clearing away. She's an old donkey, she reflected angrily. She was to bring me a glass of water; but no, first she must clear away. Well, I won't do what she wants. She has her afternoon off the day after tomorrow; she can do what she likes then. If she goes today the girl will know at once why. One knows how mercenary these young girls are. Wolf is a fool. I'll tell him so, too. He thinks she's taking him for his own sake, but she has seen the flat and the paintings; she's known for a long time what prices they fetch. And that this picture really belongs to him. Funny, he's never asked me for it. But that's just like Wolf. He isn't calculating.

She heard the water tap flowing in the kitchen. Minna probably wanted to bring some ice-cold water. Quickly she went to the sofa and lay down, covering herself with a blanket.

"You could have brought me the water five minutes ago, Minna. You know that I'm lying here with a frightful headache."

She looked angrily at the old servant. But Minna wore her most wooden expression; you couldn't read her thoughts if she didn't want you to.

"All right then, Minna. And be very quiet in the kitchen—I want to sleep a little. You can have your afternoon off today. You may leave once you've finished the dishes. Leave the window cleaning till tomorrow; you're bound to make a noise. You'll make such a clatter with the pails that I shan't be able to sleep."

"Good-by, madam," said Minna and went, closing the door very softly, avoiding any clatter. Silly woman, thought Frau Pagel. How she stared at me—just like an old owl! I'll wait till she goes, then I'll hurry along to Betty's. Perhaps she was at the registry office or sent somebody there—no one's so inquisitive as Betty. And I'll be back before Minna-no need for her to know everything.

Frau Pagel glanced once again at the painting on the wall. The Woman in the Window was looking away from her. Seen thus, the dark shadows behind her head made it seem as if a man's lips were approaching the nape. Frau Pagel had seen it often like that; today it annoyed her.

This damned sensuality, she thought. It spoils everything for the young people. They are always taken in by it.

It occurred to her that, since the couple were married, half of the picture belonged to the young wife. Was it not so?

But only let her come! I wish she would. I slapped her once and there is more waiting for her. . . .

Almost smiling she turned over, to fall asleep the next minute.

Chapter Four

An Oppressive Afternoon in Town and Country

I

"Listen," said the Governor, Dr. Klotzsche, to the journalist Kastner, who had chosen that day of all days to visit Meienburg Penitentiary during his tour through Prussia's strongholds. "Listen. You need attach no importance to the gossip you hear from the townsfolk. If ten prisoners make a noise, in this reinforced concrete building it sounds as if it were a thousand."

"But you telephoned for the Reichswehr," the journalist pointed out. "It's unbelievable!" Governor Klotzsche was about to fly into a rage over Press spying, which went as far as listening-in to trunk calls, when he remembered that this Herr Kastner carried a letter of introduction from the Minister of Justice. Besides, although Cuno was Reich Chancellor, his position according to rumor was shaky, and it was therefore wiser not to be on bad terms with the Social Democratic Party whose Press Herr Kastner represented. "It is unbelievable," he continued, but in noticeably more moderate tones, "how gossip in this town exaggerates the putting into force of a regulation. If there is unrest in the penitentiary, I have as a precautionary measure to inform the police and Reichswehr. Within a very short time I was able to cancel the warning. You see, Herr Doctor—"

But even that title did not soften this man. "Still, in your opinion there was a possibility of serious unrest. Why?"

The Governor was extremely annoyed, but it didn't help. "It was on account of the bread," he said slowly. "It wasn't good enough for one of the convicts, and he shouted. And when they heard him, twenty others joined in."

"Twenty, not ten then," corrected the journalist.

"A hundred for all I care," cried the Governor, whose gall was overflowing. "For all I care, sir, a thousand, all of them! I can't alter it; the bread's not good, but what am I to do? Our food appropriations are four weeks behind the mark devaluation. I can't buy the best flour—what am I to do?"

"Deliver decent bread. Make a row with the Ministry. Incur debts on behalf of the administration and don't worry. The men are to be fed according to the regulations."

"Certainly," said the Governor. "I'm to risk my neck so that my gentlemen get the best of food. And the unpunished population starves outside, what?"

But Herr Kastner was not accessible to irony and bitterness. Seeing a man in convict garb polishing the corridor floor, he called to him, suddenly very amiable. "You there. Your name, please?"

"Liebschner."

"Herr Liebschner, tell me quite honestly—how do you find the food, in particular the bread?"

The prisoner glanced swiftly from the Governor to the gentleman in mufti, uncertain of what they wanted to hear. You couldn't tell; the stranger might be from the Public Prosecutor, and if you opened your mouth too wide you fell in the soup. He plumped for caution. "The food? I like it."

"Ah, Herr Liebschner," said the journalist, who was not speaking with a prisoner for the first time, "I'm from the Press. You needn't be afraid of me. You will come to no harm if you speak frankly. We shall keep an eye on you. What was wrong with the bread early this morning?"

"I beg your pardon," cried the Governor, pale with fury. "This borders on instigation . . ."

"Don't be ridiculous," Herr Kastner barked. "If I'm asking this man to speak the truth, is that instigation? Speak freely—I am Kastner from the Social Democratic Press Combine. You can always write to me."

But the prisoner had made his decision. "Some will always grumble," said he and looked frankly at the journalist. "The bread is the same as it ever was and I like it. Those here who complain the loudest go shortest when they're outside and haven't a whole pair of trousers to their behinds."

"So," frowned the journalist, visibly dissatisfied, while the Governor breathed more easily. "So! What have you been sentenced for?"

"Fraud," replied Herr Liebschner. "And then they say harvest crews are to go out; tobacco and meat as much as you like."

"Thanks," said the journalist curtly, and turned to the Governor. "Shall we continue? I should like to see a cell. Besides, I don't set much store by an orderly's gossip; they're all afraid of losing their jobs. And fraud! Frauds and bullies are the most untrustworthy people in the world."

"But at first you seemed to attach importance to this swindler's evidence." Behind his fair beard the Governor smiled.

The journalist paid no attention. "And then harvest crews. To do work for the big agrarians which even the Poles consider themselves a cut above. And for wretched wages. Is that an arrangement of your own?"

"No, not at all," said the Governor pleasantly. "It's a decree of your Party comrade in the Prussian Ministry of Justice, Herr Kastner."

II

"Frau Thumann," said Petra, firmly buttoned up from top to toe in the shabby summer overcoat, and without taking any notice of the lodger from the room opposite, the jaunty but debauched Ida of Alexanderplatz, who sat at the land-lady's kitchen table soaking delicious glazed brioche in her milky coffee, "Frau Thumann, haven't you anything for me to do?"

"Lor', girl," groaned Madam Po at the sink. "What do you mean by some-thing to do? D'you want to watch the clock to see if he's coming, or do you want some grub?"

"Both," said Ida in a voice hoarse with drink, and sucked her coffee audi-bly through a lump of sugar in her mouth.

"I've already cleaned the fresh 'errings and you don't do the potato salad as Willem likes it—and what's left?"

Madam Po glanced round, but nothing occurred to her.

"I've been working my guts out so I'd be at the church door in time for the grand wedding, and now it's twenty to two and the bride's still hopping round in a man's overcoat and bare legs. I'm always being cheated of something."

Petra sat down. She felt queer in the stomach, a tugging sensation with a hint of pain to come, a weakness in the knees and now and again a flush of per-spiration which couldn't be altogether caused by the sultry air. Nevertheless she felt quite contented. An enormous and happy certainty was within her. She could let them talk as they liked; her previous pride and shame were gone, she knew whither she was going. What mattered was not that the path was difficult, but that it led to a goal.

"Sit down gently on the chair, my lady," jeered the dashing Ida. "Or else it won't bear you till the bridegroom comes to take you to the wedding."

"Don't be too hard on her in my kitchen, Ida," cautioned Madam Po at the sink. "Up till now he's always paid his way, and you have to be kind to paying guests."

"But there's an end to everything, Thumann," said Ida sagely. "I under-stand men. I know when the dough gets short and he wants to hop it—hers has hopped it today."

"Don't say that, Ida, for God's sake," wailed Frau Thumann. "What am I going to do with a girl with bare legs, with nothing on but an overcoat? Oh, God," she screamed, and flung a pan down with a clatter. "I've no bloody luck. P'raps I'll have to buy her a dress to get rid of her."

"Buy a dress?" said Ida contemptuously. "Don't be a mug, Thumann. You only need tell a policeman certain things—by the way, there's one living in the front part of the house—tell him, for instance, she's swindling—and off she goes to the police station and Alexanderplatz. They'll give you a dress there, Fräulein—you know, a dark blue uniform and cap."

"Why try to worry me?" said Petra peaceably. "No doubt you've been thrown over once too." She had not intended to say it, but out of the fullness of the heart the mouth speaketh—and she had spoken.

Ida gasped as if someone had struck her in the breast.

"She got you there!" giggled the Thumann woman.

"Once, Fräulein?" said Ida loudly. "You say once? You mean a hundred times. No, a hundred's not enough. The times I've stood with icy feet while the hand of the big clock moves on and on until it dawns on me, silly fool, that someone has done the dirty on me once more. But," and she changed over to truculence, "for all that, a girl who even on her wedding day hasn't a rag to put on needn't rub it into me. A girl who can't keep her greedy eyes off the brioche in my mouth and counts every gulp of coffee I take! A girl like that . . ."

"Go on, go on!" rejoiced the Thumann woman.

"And besides, is it right that a girl like that should come in such a miserable state, into a strange kitchen and ask, as if she were Lady Mud herself, 'Can I help?' Those with nothing must beg. My father used a stick to impress that on my back; and if you'd said: 'Ida, I'm starving, give me a roll,' you'd have had one. And another thing, Frau Thumann. I pay you a dollar daily for your bug walk, and there's not even a night light on the stairs, and what with the gentlemen always complaining about it—it isn't for you to laugh and shout: 'She's got you there, my girl.' You ought to protect me, and when someone like that gets fresh, a woman who sleeps with her bully buckshee, just for fun, and you, Thumann, have to see where you can get the dough—she's too good to work, she won't walk the streets and get cash, she's too good for that—no, Thumann, I'm surprised at you; and if you don't chuck out that impertinent hussy on the spot, laughing at me for not always having been lucky with the gentlemen, then I'll clear out."

The dashing Ida stood there flushed with anger, a brioche in her hand, getting redder and redder the more it dawned on her how greatly insulted she was. Frau Thumann and Petra looked quite disconcerted at this storm, arisen none knew why or how. (And the dashing Ida, if only she had thought it over, would have been just as surprised at the way her speech had ended.)

Petra would have preferred to get up and go back to her room, lock the door, and throw herself on the bed. But she felt fainter and fainter, there was a ringing in her ears and everything swam before her eyes. The angry voice was speaking from a distance, but then again it came close, shouting into her very ears. Everything swam again. Then fire ran down her nape and back; the sweat of weakness broke out. Now she reckoned it up, she had for some days eaten practically nothing, except when Wolf had had some money; a sausage with salad, or rolls and liver sausage, on the edge of the bed. And, since yesterday morning, nothing at all, though it was important now that she should have plenty to eat. She must try to get to her room as quickly as possible, lock the door, lock it firmly, not open it even if the police knocked; open it only when Wolfgang returned. . . .

In the distance she heard Frau Thumann wailing: "See what you've done, my girl. People like you who've nothing mustn't talk away other people's livings, and Ida's a first-class lady who brings me her dollar every day—you mustn't throw mud at a girl like that, understand? And now get out of my kitchen quickly, or you'll get more than you bargained for."

"No," shrieked Ida. "That's no good, Thumann. Either she goes or I go. I won't be insulted by the likes of that—out of the flat with her, or I move this minute."

"But, Ida, my child," wailed Frau Thumann. "You see what she's like; so much spit on whitewash, not a stitch on and nothing in her belly—I can't turn her out like that."

"Can't you, Thumann? Can't you? All right, we'll see about that—you can watch me go out of your front door, Frau Thumann."

"Ida," begged Madam Po, "do me a favor. Just wait till her chap comes back. Then I'll get rid of them both. Get out of her sight, you fool, you," she whispered agitatedly to Petra. "If she don't see you, she'll cool down."

"I'm going," whispered Petra. All of a sudden she could stand and could see the open kitchen door as a black oblong against the passage. But she could not distinguish the faces of the women. She went 'slowly. They were saying something, ever quicker and louder, but she didn't hear it clearly, did not grasp it. . . .

But she could walk, however—from the bright stuffy heat slowly toward the blackness which led to the gloomy corridor with "her" door; she only needed to enter, lock it, and then to bed. . . .

She passed it as if in a dream, however, her feet disobeying her. I ought to have made the bed, she thought, casting a glance at the room, and passed. Close by was the front door. She opened it, stepped over the threshold, and closed the door behind her.

The blurs right and left were the faces of women neighbors. "What's the row at your place?" asked one.

"Have they chucked you out, Fräulein?"

"Lord, she looks like a warmed-up corpse."

But Petra only shook her head—if she spoke she would wake up and find herself again in the quarrelsome kitchen. . . . Softly and gently, or the dream would vanish! . . . She held the railing cautiously, and descended a step. It was a real dream stair; one went down and down.

She had to hurry. Upstairs a door opened; they were calling to her. "Wench, don't be so silly. Where are you going with nothing on? Come upstairs. Ida forgives you, too."

Petra made a gesture of dissent and went still lower, lower—to the bottom of a well. But down below was a shining gate—as in a fairy tale Wolfgang had told her. And now she passed through the bright gate, out into the sun, across sunny courtyards . . . and now she was in the street, an almost empty sunny street.

Petra looked up and down it. Where was Wolf?

III

At one o'clock, immediately on starting work, the bailiff Meier went to the sugar-beet field. It was as he had feared. Kowalewski, the overseer, had been slack and let the women merely scratch the soil, leaving half the weeds behind.

At once little Meier went crimson and started to curse him. "You damned swine, standing about flirting with the women instead of keeping your eyes open, you miserable old fool," and so on, the well-known and frequently repeated formula upon every irregularity.

Without a word of excuse Kowalewski let the torrent pass over his almost white head, and had meanwhile pulled up one or two of the weeds with his own hands.

"You're not here to cuddle the girls, but to watch them," Meier shouted. "But naturally you prefer a cuddle."

An utterly unfounded accusation. But Meier, having scored off the old man amid the laughter of his men, vanished among the firs, where his crimson complexion returned to its usual color—a healthy tan—and he laughed till his belly shook. He had given it hot and strong to the old fool: the telling-off would have its effect for at least three days. You had to learn the trick of shouting furiously without feeling angry, or else the laborers would be the death of you.

The Rittmeister, although an old officer and used to drilling recruits, had not this knack. When angry he turned as white as snow and as red as a lobster, and after every such explosion he was played out for twenty-four hours. Queer old bird—great man, indeed!

It would be interesting to see the workers he turned up with, supposing he brought any at all. If he did, they were bound to be excellent, because the Rittmeister had engaged them—and he, Meier, would have to cope with them. Complaints would be useless.

Well, it would pan out all right. He, little Meier, had always got on with great men. The most important thing was that he should bring a few nice girls along, too. In her way Amanda was quite all right, but Polish girls were still more impulsive and passionate, and, above all, they had no grand ideas. Black Meier sang absent-mindedly: "Both the rose and the girl want to be plucked."

"Young man, you're not alone!" At the deep voice of his employer's father-in-law, Bailiff Meier started with fright. Geheime Ökonomierat von Teschow was standing on the path beneath a fir tree.

Below the waist the old gentleman was sufficiently clad, particularly for such oppressively hot weather; that is to say, in top boots and coarse green trousers. But from the middle upward he wore over his enormous corporation only a Jager shirt with a colored piqué front, which showed his gray, shaggy, sweating chest. Higher up again there was a grizzled reddish beard, a red bulbous nose, two cunning cheerful eyes, and on top a green hat decorated with a goat's beard. The whole was Geheime Ökonomierat Horst-Heinz von Teschow, owner of two estates and eight thousand acres of forest.

And, of course, the old gent was carrying a couple of sturdy branches—his hunting carriage was probably somewhere round the corner. The bailiff knew that he hated all fawning and false refinement, and was no enemy of his. Therefore he could speak undaunted. "Been looking for a bit of firewood, Herr Geheimrat?"

In his old age Herr von Teschow had leased both his estates, Neulohe to his son-in-law and Birnbaum to his son, keeping for himself only "a few fir trees"—that is how he described his eight thousand acres of woodland. And just as he insisted on the highest possible rent ("donkeys if they let themselves be fleeced"), so he kept his eyes as sharply on his wood as the devil does on a lost soul. Nothing was to be wasted; on every expedition he would, with his own hands, load his hunting carriage full of firewood. "I'm not such a nob as my fine son-in-law. I don't buy firewood, not even from my own firs—I look for it. A perquisite of the poor, haw, haw, haw!"

This time, however, he was not inclined to air his views on the gathering of firewood. Branches in hand, he contemplated the young man who barely reached his armpits. Almost anxiously he inquired: "Up to your tricks again, eh, my boy? My wife's on about you. Is the plucked rose the Backs wench?"

As well-behaved and polite as a good son, little Meier replied: "Herr Geheimrat, we've only been checking the poultry accounts."

At once the old gentleman flushed purple. "What have my poultry accounts to do with you, sir? What has my poultry girl to do with you? You're employed by my son-in-law, not by my maid, understand? Nor employed by me."

"Certainly, Herr Geheimrat," said little Meier obediently.

"Why must it be my wife's maid, Meier, my boy, you Apollo, you?" the old gentleman lamented again. "There are so many girls about. Consider the feelings of an old man. And if it must be, why must you do it so that *she* sees it? I understand everything; I've been young myself once. I, too, didn't sweat it out; but why must I have all this trouble because you're such a Casanova? I'm to fire you. It's impossible, I told her; he's not my employee. I can't sack him. Sack your maid. No, it's impossible, she's only been seduced, says she; and besides, she's so efficient. Good poultry maids are hard to find, but bailiffs are as numerous as the sands of the sea. So now she's sulking, and as soon as my son-in-law comes back she'll be at him—so there you are."

"We only went through the poultry accounts," maintained little Meier, for "Never admit anything" is the slogan of all petty criminals. "Fräulein Backs is no good at adding up—so I helped her."

"All right," laughed the old man. "She'll learn it all right. Totting up, my lad, what?" And he laughed uproariously. "By the way, my son-in-law has phoned to say that he's got the laborers."

"Thank God!" said Meier hopefully.

"Only the trouble is, they gave him the slip; probably he's been ordering them about too much. I neither know nor understand anything about it. My granddaughter, Violet, spoke to him on the phone. He's held up at Fürstenwalde—does that make sense? Since when was Fürstenwalde part of Berlin?"

"May I ask a question, Herr Geheimrat?" said little Meier with all the politeness he kept in reserve for his superiors. "Am I to send conveyances to the station this evening or not?"

"I've no idea," said the old man. "I'd better not interfere with your affairs, my son; if you make a mistake you'd like to say it was under my orders. No—ask Violet. She knows. Or doesn't know. One can never tell the way things are run with you."

"Certainly, Herr Geheimrat," said the well-behaved Meier. One had to be on good terms with the old man. Who knew how long the Rittmeister would last with the rent he had to pay? And then perhaps the old man would engage him, Meier.

The Geheimrat whistled shrilly on two fingers for his carriage. "You can put the branches on my cart," he said graciously. "And what about the sugar beet? You're only hoeing now, aren't you? Won't grow, eh? You heroes have probably quite forgotten the sulphate of ammonia, eh, what? I wait and wait, nobody spreads manure. I think—leave them alone; a clever child knows without being told. And have a good laugh at you all. Good morning, sir."

IV

The atmosphere of Police Headquarters at Alexanderplatz was stifling. The corridors stank of fermented urine, rotten fruit, unaired clothes; people stood about everywhere, dull figures with wrinkled gray faces, hopeless or madly excited eyes; the tired policemen were apathetic or irritable. Rittmeister von Prackwitz, blazing with fury, had had to approach a score of people, rush, through dozens of corridors, go up and down numberless stairs till he was sitting, half an hour later, in a big untidy, smelly office. Hardly a couple of yards away the metropolitan railway rattled outside the window; one heard it more clearly than one saw it through the grimy panes.

Von Prackwitz was not alone with the official. At a neighboring desk a pale-faced, big-nosed ruffian was being examined by a plain-clothes officer concerning some pocket picking. In the background, at another desk, four men whispered together; one could not tell whether any of them were criminals, for all were in shirt sleeves.

Controlling his fury, the Rittmeister made his report as brief and as exact as possible, very vigorous and almost loud when his fury at having been taken in got the better of him. The official, a pale, worn-out civilian, listened with lowered eyes without interrupting. Or else did not listen. In either case he was very busy all the time trying to stand three matches against each other so that they would not fall down.

When the Rittmeister had finished, the man looked up. Colorless eyes, colorless face, short mustache, everything rather sad and dusty, but not unsympathetic. "And what are we to do about it?" he asked.

The Rittmeister was greatly shocked. "Catch the fellow," he shouted.

"But why?"

"Because he hasn't kept his contract."

"But you didn't make a contract with him, did you?"

"Yes, I did. By word of mouth."

"He'll deny it. Have you got witnesses? The man from the Agency will hardly confirm your statements, will he?"

"No. But the fellow, the foreman, has cheated me out of thirty dollars."

"I would prefer not to hear that," said the official in a low voice.

"What?"

"Have you got a bank certificate entitling you to possess foreign currency? Were you allowed to buy it? Are you permitted to dispose of it?"

The Rittmeister sat there rather pale, biting his lips. So this was the assistance the State gave you! He had been cheated—and all he got was threats. Everybody possessed foreign currency instead of rubbishy marks—he would like to bet that the gray man before him had some in his pocket, too.

"Don't bother about the man anymore, Herr von Prackwitz," advised the official. "Suppose we did catch and jail him? The money would be gone, and you wouldn't get the laborers anyway. Day after day, hour after hour, these cases are reported. There's a daily list of persons wanted—as long as this. It's useless, believe me." Suddenly he became quite official. "Of course, if you wish, there's the matter of the fare money. . . . You can prosecute for that. I'll file it."

Von Prackwitz shrugged his shoulders. "And I've got my harvest waiting out there," he said finally. "You understand, no end of food, sufficient for hundreds of people. I didn't give him the foreign currency just for fun, but simply because one can't get workers."

"Yes, of course," said the other man. "I understand. So let's drop the matter. There are plenty of agencies around Schlesische Bahnhof—you're sure to get laborers, but don't pay anything in advance, or to the agent either."

"All right," said the Rittmeister. "I'll try again."

The big-nosed thief at the next desk was weeping. He looked repulsive. Undoubtedly he wept because he could think of no more lies.

"All right and many thanks," said von Prackwitz, almost against his will. And in a subdued voice, almost sympathetically, as if to a fellow sufferer: "How do you get on with all that?" and he made a vague gesture with his hand.

The other raised his shoulders and then dropped them hopelessly. He made to speak, hesitated, and finally said: "Since midday the dollar's stood at seven hundred and sixty thousand. What are people to do? Hunger's painful."

The Rittmeister likewise shrugged hopelessly, and without another word went to the door.

V

Weaponless, without even thinking of defense, he let himself be pushed and shoved—not even protecting his neck from the blow that threatened. Carry on, man, you leaf on life's stream. Its swift currents bear him to calmer waters; but a new eddy engulfs him, and nothing remains but to let himself be whirled to destruction or to another respite—who knows?

Petra Ledig, half-naked and cast out, could with a few words have calmed the storm raised by the two women in the back kitchen. The matter was not really so serious. Life could have returned to its past, had it not been for a stubborn silence which hid pride as well as despair, hunger as well as contempt.

Nothing compelled Petra Ledig to pass by the open door of her room. She could have entered and turned the key had she wanted to. But the eddy wafted the leaf onward. For too long it had been lying in a quiet corner by the water's edge, at the most sometimes agitated by a ripple. Now the wave lifted the acquiescent leaf into the utterly unknown, onto the street itself.

It was the afternoon, perhaps three o'clock, perhaps half-past three; the workers had not yet left their factories, women were not yet shopping. Behind their windows, or in dark, musty back parlors, the—shopkeepers dozed. No customer was in sight. Too hot!

A cat lay blinking on a stone step. Across the street a dog looked at her, but decided that she was not worth troubling about, and yawned, displaying his rose-pink tongue.

The still blinding sun looked, through the haze, like a red-hot sphere boiling over. Whether it was the walls of a house or the bark of a tree, a shop-window or a pavement, clothes drying on a balcony rail, or a horse's urine in the roadway—everything seemed to groan, sweat and smell. It was hot. Red-hot. The girl, quietly standing there, thought she heard a soft monotonous sound, as if the whole town were simmering.

With her tired eyes blinking in the light, Petra Ledig waited for an impetus which would carry the leaf onward, no matter whither—anywhere. The town hummed in the heat. For a while she stared across at the dog, as if he could supply this; and the dog stared back, then flopped down, extending all four legs, to sigh with the heat and fall. asleep. Petra Ledig stood and waited, making no effort one way or another. Even a blow would have been relief. The town hummed with the heat.

And while she was standing in the unbearable heat of Georgenkirchstrasse waiting for something or other to happen, her lover, Wolfgang Pagel, sat waiting in a strange house, in a strange kitchen—waiting for what? His guide, the spotless Liesbeth, had disappeared somewhere in the interior of the house; and another young girl, to whom she had whispered a sentence or two, stood at the electric cooker with its chromium-plated fittings. A pot was boiling diligently on the hot plate. Wolfgang sat waiting, hardly waiting indeed, his elbow supported on one knee, his chin in his hand.

He had never seen such a kitchen. It was as large as a dance hall, white, silver, copper-red, its saucepans a dull black; and the working part was divided from the sitting-room part by a waist-high railing of white wood along a kind of platform. Two steps down, and you had cooker, kitchen table, pots, cupboards.

In the raised part where Pagel sat stood a long snow-white dining table and comfortable white chairs. Yes, there was even a fireplace of beautiful red bricks with fine white joints.

Wolfgang sat above; below, the strange girl was busy with the stove.

Indifferently he looked through the high bright windows, framed by vine leaves, into a sunny garden—to be sure, there were bars to the windows. And, he thought absently, just as crime is shut up behind bars, so wealth also shelters behind them, feels secure only behind the railings of banks, the steel walls of safes, the wrought ironwork -also in its way a barrier—and steel grills and burglar alarms of its villas. Odd resemblance—not so strange actually. But I'm so tired. . . .

He yawned. The girl at the stove was looking at him. She nodded, smiling but serious. Another girl, also not unsympathetic—plenty of girls about and nods and sympathy: But what on earth was he to do? He couldn't sit here forever. . . . What am I really waiting for? he thought. Not for Liesbeth. What can she say to me? Work and pray; the early bird catches the worm; we rise high on work and industry; work is the citizen's ornament; no sweets without sweat. Or the dignity of labor, and the laborer is worthy of his hire; therefore he ought to be a laborer in the vineyard; work and don't despair is the best medicine . . .

Ah, thought Wolfgang, and smiled weakly as if he were nauseated, what a lot of proverbs man has prepared to persuade himself that he must work and that work is good for him, though he would much prefer to sit here with me, doing nothing, waiting for something, I don't know what. Only in the evening at the gaming table when the ball buzzes and clatters and is about to fall into the hole—only then do I know what I'm waiting for. But when it's fallen, whether into the hole I want or another, then I no longer know.

He stared into vacancy. He hadn't a bad brain; he had ideas, but he had gone to seed and was lazy, he didn't want to pursue a thought to its logical conclusion. Why should he? I'm like that and I'll stay like it. Wolfgang Pagel forever! Stupidly he had sold their last possessions merely to visit Zecke, to borrow money. But, arrived at Zecke's, he had just as stupidly, for the sake of a malicious word, destroyed his chances of getting that money. And, again stupidly, he had gone with the first person he happened to run into, and that was why he was now sitting here—in stagnant water, a leaf without a purpose, the image of all leaves without a purpose. He was not without talents, not without good feelings, not unkind, but he was indolent—just as old Minna had expressed it, he wanted a nursemaid to come and take him by the hand and tell him what to do. For the last five years he had been nothing more than an ex-second lieutenant.

His presence had probably been made known by Liesbeth. A stout woman came in—a woman, not a lady—She cast a swift, almost embarrassed glance at Wolf, and announced from the cook stove that the master had just telephoned. They would eat at three-thirty sharp.

"Good," said the girl at the stove and the woman left, not without casting another glance at Wolfgang. A stupid inspection. He would clear out at once!

The door opened once more and a liveried manservant came in, an important fellow. Unlike the fat woman, he did not need any excuse; but, crossing the kitchen, ascended the two steps and went up to Wolfgang at the table. He was an elderly man with a fresh-complexioned kindly, face.

Without any embarrassment he held out his hand and said: "My name is Hoffmann."

"Mine is Pagel," said Wolfgang after a momentary hesitation.

"It's very close today," said the servant in a friendly, low, but very clear and trained voice. "May I bring you something to drink—a bottle of beer?"

Wolfgang pondered a moment. "May I have a glass of water?"

"Beer makes one sleepy," agreed the -other and fetched the water. The tumbler was on a plate and a piece of ice swam in the water; everything was done in style here.

"Yes, that's good," said Wolfgang, drinking greedily.

"Take your time," advised the other, always with the same kind seriousness. "You can't drink up all our water—nor the ice," he added after a pause, and the corners of his eyes wrinkled. However, he fetched a second glass.

"Many thanks," said Wolfgang.

"FräuleinLiesbeth is engaged for the moment. But she will come soon."

"Yes," said Wolfgang slowly. And pulling himself together—"I'd rather go now, I'm quite refreshed."

"Fräulein Liesbeth is a very good girl, very good and very efficient."

"Yes," agreed Wolfgang politely. Only the thought of his money in this Fräulein's pocket still held him there; those few notes so recently despised would take him back to Alexanderplatz. "There are many good girls," he acquiesced.

"No," declared the other. "Forgive me for contradicting you: the sort of good girl I mean is rare."

"Yes?" inquired Wolfgang.

"Yes. For one ought not to do good just for the fun of it but because one loves what is good." He looked at Wolfgang again, but not quite so kindly. (Queer fish! thought the visitor.)

"Well, it won't be long now," the servant concluded, and he left the kitchen just as gently, as deliberately, as he had entered. Wolfgang felt that although he had hardly said anything he had not given the man a good impression.

Now he must move a little; the girl from the stove came with a tablecloth, then a tray, and started to lay the table. "Stay where you are," she said. "You're not in my way."

She too had a pleasant voice. It struck Wolfgang that the people in this house spoke well. They spoke very good German, clearly and distinctly.

"There's your place," said the girl as Wolfgang gazed absent-mindedly at the paper napkin in front of him. "You'll have your lunch here."

He made a vague but defensive gesture. Something was beginning to disturb him. The house was not far from Zecke's mansion, yet far removed in other ways. But they ought not to talk to him as if he were a patient, or rather as if he were somebody who had committed a crime in a fit of madness, and must be spoken with cautiously so as not to provoke him again.

"You won't disappoint Liesbeth, will you?" the girl said. And after a pause: "The mistress is agreeable."

She laid the table, the silver clinking—not much, though, as she was very neat-handed. Wolfgang did not stir; a kind of paralysis caused by the heat, no doubt. So he was being treated as some sort of beggar from the street, a hungry man who was given a meal with the consent of the lady of the house. In his mother's case, the beggar was not allowed into the kitchen; Minna would make some sandwiches and at best a plate of soup was handed out through the door, to be eaten on the landing.

Well, here at Dahlem they were more generous, but it didn't matter much to the beggar. Whether he was outside the door or in the kitchen, a beggar was a beggar, now and forever after. Amen.

He hated himself for not going. He didn't want food. What did he care about food? He could eat at his mother's; Minna had told him that a place was always laid for him. It wasn't that he was ashamed, but they ought not to talk to him as if he were a patient who had to be considerately treated. He wasn't ill. It was only that damned money. Why hadn't he taken those miserable scraps of paper out of her hand? He would be sitting in the subway by now . . .

In his nervousness he had taken out a cigarette and was just about to light it when the girl said: "Please not now, if you can possibly do without it. After I have sent the lunch up to the dining room it will be all right. The master has such a delicate sense of smell."

The door opened and in came a little girl, the daughter of the house, ten or twelve years old, bright and cheerful. She certainly knew nothing of the evil gray town side. Probably wanted to have a look at the beggar. Beggars seemed to be a rarity in Dahlem.

"Papa is already on the way," said the child to the girl at the cooker. "In a quarter of an hour we can eat. What have you got, Trudchen?" "Inquisitive!" laughed the girl and raised a lid. The child sniffed eagerly at the steam. "Oh, merely those old green peas again," she said. "No, tell me honestly, Trudchen."

"Soup, meat and green peas," said Trudchen tantalizingly.

"And?" urged the child.

"Curiosity killed the cat," laughed the girl.

Such a world still exists, thought Wolfgang, half smiling, half desperate. And I had only forgotten it because in Georgenkirchstrasse I lost sight of it. But children innocent and unspoiled, and real innocence, still exist. What the pudding's going to be is important, even though hundreds of thousands of people have given up asking about their daily bread. Looting at Gleiwitz and Breslau, food riots in Frankfurt-on-the-Main and Neuruppin, Eisleben and Dramburg . . .

He eyed the child with suspicion. It's a swindle, he thought, an artificial innocence, a carefully protected innocence—just as they have bars in front of their windows. Life will reach her in spite of all this. What will remain of her innocence in two or three years' time?

"Good day," said the child. She had only just noticed him, perhaps because he moved his chair in order to get up and go. He took the hand which she extended. Beneath a frank handsome forehead she had dark eyes. "You're the gentleman who came in with our Liesbeth?" she asked, looking at him seriously.

"Yes," said he and tried to smile at so much earnestness. "How old are you?"

"Eleven," she answered politely. "And your wife has nothing on but your overcoat?"

"That's so." He still tried to smile and appear at ease. But it was damnable to hear one's shortcomings from the mouths of others, especially from a child's. "And she has nothing to eat—and won't be able to get anything, not even a pudding with macaroons."

She remained unaware that he had intended to hurt her. "Mamma has so many clothes," she said meditatively. "Most of them she doesn't wear at all."

"Quite right," he said, feeling rather shabby with his cheap talk. "Such is life. You haven't learned that in school yet, eh?"

He felt lower and more miserable than ever before those serious eyes.

"I don't go to school," said the child, assuming an air of importance. "I'm blind." Again that look. "Papa is also blind. But Papa used to be able to see. I have never been able to, at all."

She stood before him—and he, so quickly punished for his cheap sneering, felt still more strongly that she was looking at him. No, not with her eyes, but perhaps with her candid brow, her pale curved lips; as if this blind child could penetrate further than did Petra with her eyes.

"Mamma can see. But she says she would prefer not to, as she never knows what Papa and I feel like. We wouldn't let her though."

"No," agreed Wolfgang. "You don't want that."

"Fräulein and Liesbeth and Trudchen and Herr Hoffmann can tell us what they see. But when Mamma tells us, then it's quite different."

"Because it's your Mamma, isn't it?" said Wolfgang cautiously.

"Yes. Papa and I are both Mamma's children. Papa, too."

He kept silent, but the child expected no reply. The subjects she was speaking about were so self-explanatory that there was nothing for him to say about them.

"Has your wife a Mamma—or has she nobody?"

Wolfgang stood there, a very thin smile round his lips. "Nobody," he said decidedly. If only he could get away. Knocked out by a child exposing his unkindness, his want of character.

"Papa will certainly give you some money. And this afternoon Mamma will go and see your wife. Where is she?"

"Seventeen Georgenkirchstrasse," said he. "Fourth floor," said he. "At Frau Thumann's," said he. Something welled up within him. If only she could get some help! She ought to be helped. She was worthy of all help. Evanescent world in which you have your being, poor thing, both entangled and entangling. Just as you suddenly feel she is freeing herself from you, you notice how useful she was to you. Expelled into the dark, with clear light still existing far away. But now it goes out. You're on your own, and don't know whether you can and will return or not. Poor Petra . . . He was indeed a beggar; and now that the chance of help had arrived he felt that it would be of no use to him, because he was hollow, burnt out, empty.

"I must go now," he said to the kitchen. He shook hands with the child, nodded, said: "You know the address?" and went. Went into the sultry, the confined, tumultuous town, once more to try and hold his own in the struggle for money and bread. For what? For whom? He did not know and was not to know for a long while.

VI

The Manor, as it was called in Neulohe, was the old gentleman's house. Rittmeister von Prackwitz lived about half a mile farther on near the farmyard
and among the fields, in a small villa of six rooms, speculative-builder style; a
jerry-built erection of the early inflation period, the plaster already in flakes.
The Manor—which the old gentleman wouldn't leave, if only because he wanted
to stay near his beloved firs and incidentally keep an eye on his son-in-law was
a ramshackle yellow building also, but with three times as many rooms as the
younger people had and at any rate a real terrace and steps, a sun porch with
French windows, and a park.

Black Meier passed the Manor. He had no business there and was not
looking for any, wishing to avoid the angry old lady. He was bound for the staff-
house (situated uncomfortably close to the Manor) where he had an office and a
bedroom—the other rooms stood empty because of the Rittmeister's economy
campaign. (Yet the Rittmeister was a great man!) Since he wanted to question
the young Fräulein about her telephone conversation with her father, he went
first to his room to wash his hands and face, and sprinkled his chest profusely
with a scent called Russian Leather, which was obviously the right thing for the
country, since it was advertised as "Pungent, Manly, Dashing."

He looked at himself in the mirror. That time was, of course, long past
when he had felt ashamed of his small stature, blubber lips, flat nose and bulging eyes. Successes with women had taught him that to be handsome was not
essential; on the contrary a somewhat odd appearance attracted the girls as
surely as a salt-lick attracted the deer.

Naturally Violet would not be so easy to deal with as, for example,
Amanda Backs or Sophie Kowalewski. But little Meier believed—again not
in agreement with his employer's view—that little Vi, although only fifteen years old, was a bitch. Certain glances, a young bosom consciously
displayed, certain expressions—sometimes bold, sometimes of the deepest innocence—these could not be misunderstood by such an experienced
wencher. It was natural, when you came to think of it. Old Herr von Teschow was said to have thrashed a lover out of the bedroom of her mother,
then unmarried, a discipline which the mother subsequently tasted herself. So people said. Well, the world was large and everything possible. Like
mother, like daughter. To call the little bailiff, because of his thoughts in
front of the mirror, an intriguer and a rascally seducer would be an exag-
geration. His thoughts were not plans; only day-dreams full of youthful
vanity. He had a young puppy's ravenous appetite; he would have liked to
bite at everything—and Violet was very handsome indeed.

But, as with a puppy, his fears were as big as his appetite, and he was afraid of a thrashing. He was bold enough with Amanda Backs, who had no relatives; but he would never be able to behave like that with Vi, who had the support of a quick-tempered father. Although in his dreams he had arranged everything, including an elopement and a secret marriage, he still funked the return to his father-in-law's, for he could conceive of no homecoming which would be at all satisfactory; the young wife would best manage that interview. He need have no fear of Vi, nor respect for her; once she had slept with him she would be no better than he was. Aristocratic origin peeled off as varnish did from mass-production furniture, revealing the common pine beneath.

Black Meier grinned at himself in the mirror. "You're a gay dog" may have been the meaning of it, and, as confirming his valuation of himself, he remembered that the Lieutenant had spoken to him this morning in a more comradely tone than to the sneaking Kniebusch.

Meier greeted himself in the mirror, waved a friendly hand at his reflection—"Good luck go with you, child of Fortune"—and marched off to Violet von Prackwitz.

Frau Hartig was tidying up in the office. The coachman's wife, still comely, would probably also like to have her fling; but women over twenty-five were as old as the hills, and Hartig was about twenty-seven, the mother of no less than eight children. Today her lips were compressed, her eyes sparkled, and she frowned. That didn't bother Meier; but, just as he was about to pass by, the iron reading lamp fell from the desk with a thundering crash and the green shade broke into a thousand fragments.

So Meier had to stop and say his piece.

"Well," he grinned, "broken glass brings us good luck-does this apply to you or to me?" She gave him an angry glance. "What's the matter with you? Is it the weather? It's close enough for a storm." And he looked mechanically at the barometer, which had been dropping slowly but steadily since midday.

"I don't want any of your dirtiness," cried the woman shrilly. "Do you think I'm going to tidy up any longer after you two?" And she slipped her hand into the pocket of her apron and showed him three hairpins. (In 1923 bobbed hair had not yet conquered the great plains.) In your bed they were," she almost shrieked. "You filthy beast! But I won't tidy up that, I'll show it to the mistress."

"Which one, Frau Hartig?" laughed Meier. "The old one knows about it already—and she's praying for me at this moment; the young one has guessed and'll laugh all the more." He looked at her with a superior and mocking air.

"Such a common bitch, too," shrieked Frau Hartig. "Can't she have a look in the bed before she clears out? But no, I'm to tidy up after a poultry maid! Creatures like that have no shame."

"Oh, yes, they have, Frau Hartig," said Black Meier seriously. Then he grinned again. "What handsome red hair your youngest son has, exactly like the head stableman's. Is he to become a coachman like his father, or stableman like his stepfather?" And with that Meier marched off, giggling to himself, pleased as Punch, while Frau Hartig, still angry but already partly mollified, stared at the three hairpins in her hand. He was a rotter, but he knew his way about, small as he was.

She looked at the hairpins once more, then stuck them resolutely in her own hair. I'll get hold of you yet, she thought. Amanda won't rule forever.

Cheerfully she cleared away the fragments of the lamp shade, of a sudden firmly convinced that they would bring her the good luck.

Meier, too, was thinking of the broken glass and the good luck it would almost immediately bring him. In the best of moods he arrived at the Rittmeister's villa. First he peeped into the garden, for he would much prefer to meet Vi out of earshot of her mother; she was not there, however. This was not difficult to establish since, although the garden was not small, one could see all over it at a glance. Already partly dried up, it had been recently created by Frau von Prackwitz and conjured up at a moment's notice from a bare field.

Nothing, by the way, could better symbolize the position in Neulohe or the gulf between owner and tenant than a comparison of Teschow's park with Prackwitz's garden: in the former were sumptuous trees a hundred years old, abounding with foliage and sap; in the latter a few bare sticks with scanty and fading leaves. In the one were wide green lawns; in the other a thin dry grass struggling hopelessly against advancing mare's-tail, couch-grass, and meadow heartsease. There a fair-sized lake with rowboat and swan; here an artificial stone basin filled with green ditchwater. In one place a growth inherited and full of promise for the future; in the other, growth hardly born, yet already withering. (Still, the Rittmeister's a great man!)

Bailiff Meier was just about to ring the bell when he heard a call from the side. A ladder led up to the flat roof of the kitchen annex where stood a deck chair and a big garden sunshade. It was from there that the voice had called, "Herr Meier!"

Meier stood to attention. "At your service."

An ungracious voice from above: "What's the matter? Mamma is quite done up by the heat and wants to sleep. Don't you dare disturb her."

"I only wanted to ask, Fräulein . . . Herr von Teschow told me that the Rittmeister had telephoned." Rather angrily: "It is about the conveyances . . . Am I to send them to the station or not?"

"Don't shout like that," shouted the voice from above. "I'm not one of your farm girls. Mamma wants to rest, I tell you."

Meier looked despairingly at the flat roof. But it was too high to see anything of the girl he had eloped with in his dreams and married; only a corner of the deck chair and part of the sunshade. He decided to whisper as loudly as he could. "Am I to send conveyances—this evening—to the railway?"

Silence. Meier waited.

Then from above: "Did you say anything? I could only hear "Run away."

"Haw-haw-haw." Meier guffawed dutifully before repeating his inquiry somewhat louder.

"You're not to shout," came her command.

He knew quite well that she only wanted to torment him. He was merely Papa's bailiff. Had to do what he was told. Had to stand and wait till it graciously pleased Fräulein. You wait, my dear, one day you'll have to stand and wait—for me.

However, he now seemed to have been kept waiting long enough, for she called to him (surprisingly loud, too, for such a considerate daughter): "Herr Meier, aren't you going to speak? Are you still there?"

"Certainly, Fräulein."

"I thought you'd melted in the sun. You're hot enough for that."

There, she knew all about it, of course. But no harm done, it only whetted the appetite.

"Herr Meier!"

"Yes, Fräulein?"

"If you've stood there long enough perhaps you will notice a stepladder, and come up here and tell me what you really want."

"Yes, Fräulein." And up the ladder. "Yes, Fräulein" was always good, flattered her and cost nothing, stressed the social gulf between them and permitted everything. One could peep into her low-necked dress while saying, very humbly: "Yes, Fräulein." One could even say it and kiss her. "Yes, Fräulein" was smart and gallant, like the officers at Ostade.

He was now standing at the foot of her deck chair, blinking obediently, yet with insolence, at the young mistress who reclined before him clad in nothing but a very short bathing suit. At fifteen, Violet von Prackwitz was already fully developed—over-developed if one considered her age, her heavy bosom, fleshy hips and vigorous bottom. She had the soft flesh, the too-white skin of the lymphatic, and, in addition, somewhat protruding eyes like her mother's, of a pale blue, a sleepy blue. The dear innocent child had raised her naked arms, stretched herself; it didn't look at all bad, the bitch was handsome and, hang it all, what a body to cuddle.

Sleepily, sensually, through half-closed eyes, she searched the bailiff's face. "Well, why are you looking like that?" she demanded. "At mixed bathing I wear nothing else. Don't be stupid." She studied his face.

"Mamma ought to see us both here. . . ."

He struggled with himself. The sun burned madly, vibrated, dazzled. Now she stretched herself again and he made a step toward her. "Vi, oh, Vi."

"Why, oh why?" she laughed. "No, no, Herr Meier, you'd better stand nearer the ladder." And now she was the daughter of the house again. "You're funny. You seem to imagine things. I have only to call out and Mamma's at her window." Then, when she saw that he obeyed her: "You needn't send carriages to the station today. Probably tomorrow morning to meet the first train. But Papa will telephone again."

A moment ago she had understood quite well, the cheeky bitch. Had only wanted to exhibit herself and torment him. But wait, I'll get you yet.

"Why don't you gather in the harvest?" asked the young girl who was to be eloped with and secretly married.

"Because the laborers have to sheave it first." Rather surly.

"And if there's a storm and it all gets wet, Papa will be in a terrible temper."

"And if I bring in the crop and there's no storm, he'll also be in a temper."

"But there will be a storm."

"One can't be certain."

"But I know."

"So Fräulein wishes me to get the crop in?"

"Not at all." She laughed boisterously, her full bosom positively jumping in her bathing dress. "So that you could blame me afterward if it doesn't suit Papa! No, blunder as much as you like, but don't put the blame on others."

She looked at him with an air of benevolent superiority. This flapper of fifteen years was amazingly impudent. Why? Because she happened to be born a von Prackwitz, heiress of Neulohe—for no other reason.

"Then I can go, Fräulein?" asked Black Meier.

"Yes, be sure and don't neglect your work." She had rolled on one side and looked at him mockingly.

He moved off.

"Hi, Herr Meier," she called.

"Yes, Fräulein?" There was nothing he could do about it.

"Are you carting manure?"

"No, Fräulein."

"Then why do you smell so queer?"

It took him quite a while to grasp that she meant his perfume. Then, without a word, but red with fury, he turned round and descended the ladder as quickly as he could.

What a bitch! One oughtn't to have anything to do with such a bitch. The Reds were quite right—against the wall with the whole insolent rag, tag, and bobtail! Aristocracy be damned! Insolence, impudence, nothing but arrogance. . . .

He was down the ladder, walking away with short, furious legs. Then a voice sounded again, a voice from heaven, the voice of the young lady: "Herr Meier!"

He started, full of fury—and again he couldn't do anything about it. "Yes, Fräulein?"

Her voice was very ungracious. "I've told you three times you're not to shout like that. You'll wake Mamma." Then, impatient: "Come up again."

Meier climbed the ladder once more, full of bile. Yes, hopping up and down like a tree frog, with you calling the weather. But wait till I get you. I'll jilt you and leave you with a baby, without a penny. Nevertheless he stood smartly upright. "Please, Fräulein?"

She was no longer thinking of showing her body off, but was reflecting, although she had practically decided. Only she was uncertain how to tell him. In the end she said as innocently as possible, "You're to deliver a letter for me, Herr Meier."

"Yes, Fräulein."

Suddenly it was in her hand. Whence she had taken this longish envelope of blue paper was a mystery; as far as one could judge at Meier's distance it was unaddressed.

"You're going this evening to the village?"

He was utterly taken by surprise and quite uncertain of himself. Was this merely conversational, or did she know something? That, however, was impossible.

"I don't know. Perhaps I will. If you wish it, Fräulein, certainly."

"A gentleman will ask you for a letter. Hand it over."

"What gentleman? I don't understand."

Suddenly she became exasperated. "You needn't understand anything. You're simply to do as I tell you. A gentleman will ask you for the letter and you'll give it to him. That's quite simple, isn't it?"

"Yes, Fräulein," he said. But it sounded rather feeble—he was so much wrapped up in his own thoughts.

"Then that's everything, Herr Meier." And she handed him the letter. He could hardly believe it, but he held the letter in his hand, a weapon against her. You wait, my little lamb. Any more of your sauce. He pulled himself together. "It shall be done, Fräulein."

And again he descended the ladder.

"I should say so," her voice challenged him from above. "Or else I shall tell Grandpa and Papa who it was started to burn down the wood."

The voice stopped. Meier paused midway, so as not to miss a word. There! And that was that! "Burn down." A shot in the heart. Bravo! Splendid for fifteen years old. She had a future before her.

"And the Herr Lieutenant doesn't like jokes, either," added the voice—and now he heard her fat, lazy flesh rolling over on the other side, the deck chair groaning. Fräulein Violet von Prackwitz yawned comfortably up there while Herr Bailiff Meier got on with his work.

Right you are, he told himself, that's O.K. by me.

But he did not get on with his work immediately. Deep in thought he trotted along to his room, the letter in the outside pocket of his linen jacket and his hand on its smooth surface all the time. He must feel that he had really got the letter, that it was there, this letter which he would straightway read. She had said little enough, the artful bitch, but she had said enough for him. Quite enough. So she knew the Lieutenant, that mysterious, somewhat raged but overbearing gentleman who convened nocturnal meetings at the village magistrate's, and before whom Forester Kniebusch stood to attention. And she had met this Lieutenant between twelve and three today, or else she could not have known about the fire.

If, therefore, this Lieutenant nodded in such a friendly way to Herr Bailiff Meier, it was not because he thought Black Meier so much more efficient than that old slacker Kniebusch, but because he knew that Meier had already been chosen for go-between. The Lieutenant, it seemed, knew his way about in Neulohe. A secret agreement of long standing.

You have gone far, you two, thought Meier. I can picture it all. And when I've read the letter—you're a fool, nevertheless, you proud silly goose. Do you think I shall hand it over without having a look at what you've written? I want to know, and then I'll consider what to do. Perhaps I'll tell the Rittmeister—what's a bit of a forest fire against that? You won't have me by the short hairs on that matter. But I don't think I'll say anything to the Rittmeister after all. You're so silly that it never occurs to you that a fellow like the Lieutenant will jilt you. You need only look at him, of course, to see that. Then I'll be there—no, my child, I don't mind. I don't take offense. It's not much fun and a lot of trouble to break in young horses—it's better they should know their paces first. You shall pay me then for every impertinent, arrogant word, for every "Yes, Fräulein"—and for this letter above all. How does one open letters? With steam, I've heard, but how can I quickly manage that in my room? Well, I'll try to open the flap with a knife, and if the envelope gets spoiled I'll take one of my own. Yellow or blue— he'll hardly notice which. . . .

He reached the office. Without even taking off his cap he sank into the chair at the desk. Putting the letter on the worn ink-stained baize, he stared at it. He was damp with sweat, his body was limp, his mouth parched. He was utterly exhausted. He could hear the hens clucking in the farmyard, the dairy-men clattering with pails and milk cans in the cow barn. He should think so—high time for milking!

The letter lay before him, the flies buzzed monotonously; it was unbear-ably close. He wanted to look at the barometer on the wall (perhaps a storm would come after all) but he didn't look up. It was all the same to him!

The letter, the clean blue rectangle on the stained baize. Her letter.

Lazily, carelessly, he seized the paper knife, drew the letter nearer, and put both down. He wiped his sweating hands on his jacket.

Then he took the paper knife and slowly, one might say luxuriously, inserted the blunt point into the small gap under the flap. His gaze was intent; a light, satisfied smile hovered about his thick lips. Yes, he could open the letter. By careful pushing, lifting, pressing, he loosened the carelessly stuck flap and saw a corner of the writing. There were tiny fibers which did not want to yield—but at the same time he saw Vi as he had just seen her on the deck chair . . . She stretched her body, her plump white flesh quivered . . . she threw up her arms and tiny curls glistened in the armpits. . . .

Black Meier groaned.

He was staring at the letter which he had opened meantime—but he was absent, half a mile away on a flat sun-baked roof—flesh to flesh, skin to skin, hair to hair. "Dearest!"

A wave subsided, shining with the colors of beautiful, living human flesh lit up by the evening sun. . . . Black Meier groaned again. "Well, I never," he wondered. "That bitch must have made me quite crazy. But it's the heat as well."

The envelope had opened without tearing. It would not be necessary to gum the flap—Fräulein Violet had fastened it so carelessly. Well, let us read it. . . . But first he wiped his hands on his jacket—they were wet with perspiration again.

He drew the paper out of the envelope and unfolded it. The letter was not very long but, for all that, it was full of meat.

Dearest! My dearest darling! My only one! You have only just gone and again I am quite crazy about you. I tremble all over and vibrate, so that I have to shut my eyes over and over again. Then I see you. I love you *sooo* much. Papa definitely does not come home today, so I will wait for you between eleven and twelve at the pond by the swan-house. See to it that the silly meeting is finished by then. I am longing so terribly for you.

100,000,000 kisses and even more. I press you to my heart which beats quite madly.

Yours, VIOLET.

"God," said little Meier and stared at the sheet. "She really loves him. Loves him so with three o's and yours underlined. A kid still wearing her nappies! He'll play her up. Well, all the better."

He copied the letter on the typewriter, meticulously counting the noughts in the sum of kisses. ("Sheer inflation—she's up to date") and refastened the envelope.

The copy he put into Volume 1900 of the *District Gazette*, the letter itself in his coat pocket. And now he was completely satisfied. And quite ready to carry on with the farming. He looked at the barometer. It had again dropped a little.

Would there be a storm? Should he get in the crop? Nonsense, she was talking rubbish.

He went out to his mowing machine.

VII

"I thought you would look me up today, my poor Mathilde."

Frau von Anklam, over seventy, the white-haired and shapeless widow of a major general, had emerged with difficulty from the easy-chair in which she was passing her afternoon nap. She held her visitor's hand in hers and looked compassionately and anxiously out of her large brown eyes, still beautiful. At the moment she spoke in a dramatic manner, as if at a death; but she could also speak in another key—that of the regimental commander's wife who keeps the ladies of the regiment in order and propriety.

"We're getting old, but our burdens don't lighten. Our children tread on our laps when they are young. Later, on our hearts."

(Frau von Anklam had never had children. Nor could she bear with them.)

"Come, sit on the sofa, Mathilde. I'll ring—Fräulein will bring us coffee and cake. Today I sent out for a Hilbrich cake; he still has the best. Only it isn't worthwhile for myself alone—forty thousand marks in fares, you understand, forty thousand! Robbers, that's what they are. Yes, Fräulein, pastry and coffee, very strong—my cousin has had bad news. Yes, dear Mathilde, I've been sitting in my chair and thinking about things. Fräulein thinks I've been sleeping, but of course I haven't. I hear every sound in the kitchen, and when a plate's broken in the washing-up I'm there at once. Does your Minna break much, too? It's still the old Nymphenburg china which Grandfather Kuno received on his diamond wedding from the dear late Emperor—there's enough left for an old woman, but one has to think of one's heirs. I really promised it to Irene, but lately I've not been sure. Irene has such strange views about the bringing-up of children. Perfectly—how shall I describe it?—revolutionary."

"And the news is absolutely true, Betty?" asked Frau Pagel, erect and slender. However sympathetic a close relative might be, it could not be told from her face and behavior that she had wept.

"The news? What news? Oh, *the* news. But dear Mathilde, when *I* especially wrote to you about it." This rather as commander's wife, but yet sympathetic. "Certainly it's true. Eitel-Fritz happened to be there and read it with his own eyes. The banns, they call it, don't they? Not that I know what business he had there, of course. I was so excited that I didn't ask him. But you know Eitel-Fritz, he's so original, he goes to the oddest places. *Attention! La Servante!*"

Fräulein appeared with the tray and the coffee set of Nymphenburg china from grandfather's diamond wedding. The ladies became silent. Without a sound, Fräulein, elderly and mouse-gray, laid the table.

She was always "Fräulein"—all these changing faces were nameless at Frau Major General von Anklam's. Fräulein set the table, and Fräulein darned. Fräulein read aloud and Fräulein described something; above all, Fräulein listened. Fräulein listened from morn till even. Stories of regimental ladies long dead and forgotten ("I told her: 'Dear child, I decide what tact is'"); stories of children long ago in possession of their own children ("And then the sweet little angel said to me"); stories of relatives long alienated; tales of promotion and dismissals; of orders and decorations; of wounds; of marriage tangles and divorces—the rag, tag, and bobtail of a life spent entirely in gossip and tittle-tattle about intimate, the most intimate, things.

Fräulein, colorless and mouse-gray, listened, said: "Yes," "Oh, no," "Really," "Charming"; but when Her Excellency had visitors she heard nothing. Frau Major General whispered with the last remnants of her Lausanne finishing-school French: "Attention! La Servante!" and the ladies fell silent. When there were visitors Fräulein had no existence, as was fitting. (When the visitors were gone everything was recounted to her.)

But after the first silence Frau von Anklam did not remain silent by any means—that was not done either. She talked of the weather. ("It is close today, perhaps we shall have a storm; perhaps yes, perhaps no.") She'd once had a Fräulein with rheumatic twinges in her big toe before a storm—very strange, was it not?

"It always came true, and once when Fräulein was on her holiday (you know we had our estate at that time) we had a tremendous hailstorm which smashed down the whole crop. Well, if Fräulein hadn't been on holiday we should have known about it in advance-and that would have been so good, wouldn't it, dear Mathilde? But, of course, Fräulein was on her holiday."

"Yes, everything is all right, Fräulein, thanks. You may now press the lace frill on my black taffeta dress. It's already pressed I know, Fräulein. It's not necessary to tell me that. But it's not done as I like it. I like it to be as light as a breath of air. Fräulein, as light as air! So please do that, Fräulein."

And the door had hardly closed behind Fräulein before Frau von Anklam turned sympathetically to Frau Pagel. "I've considered and reconsidered the matter, dear Mathilde, and I stick to my opinion. She is simply a low, vulgar creature."

Frau Pagel started and looked anxiously toward the door. "Fräulein?"

"Mathilde,, do concentrate a little. What are we talking about? Your son's marriage! If I were to be so absent-minded . . . I always told the ladies of my regiment. . . ." Frau Pagel still hoped to learn something definite, but what she hardly knew. She succeeded in putting in a word. "The girl is perhaps not entirely bad. . . ."

"Mathilde! A creature! Only a creature!"

"She loves Wolfgang—in her way."

"I don't wish to hear anything about it. No indelicacy in my house!"

"But Wolfgang gambles, Betty, gambles everything away."

Frau von Anklam laughed. "To see your face, dearest Mathilde! Boys always play a little—you mustn't say 'gamble,' it sounds so vulgar. All young men play a little. I remember that time we had the regiment at Stolp—there was a lot of playing among the young fellows. Excellency von Bardenwiek said to me: 'What are we to do, Frau von Anklam? We must do something about it.'

I said: 'Excellency,' I said, 'we'll do nothing of the kind. As long as the young people play they're not making fools of themselves in another way.' And he agreed with me at once. . . . Come in."

There had been a gentle knocking at the door. Fräulein put her head in: "Ernst is back, Excellency."

"Ernst? What does he want? These are peculiar manners, Fräulein! You know I have a visitor, don't you? Ernst—the idea of it!"

In spite of this outburst Fräulein still dared to say something. Like a mouse in the trap she squeaked. "He has been to the registry office, Excellency."

Frau von Anklam brightened up. "Oh, of course. He shall come in as soon as he has washed his hands. What a long story you make of everything, Fräulein. Fräulein, one moment, don't always run away at once, so heedlessly. Please wait for my instructions. First give him a spray or two of eau-de-Cologne; yes, the toilet eau-de-Cologne. One never knows whom he has met there."

Alone with her cousin again, she said: "I wanted to find out how the wedding went. I considered for a long time whom I could send to such an affair, and I sent our Ernst. Well, now we shall hear." And her eyes shone. She moved her heavy body to and fro in anticipation. She was to hear something new, something more for her lumber-room of memories. O Lord, how splendid!

Ernst, the servant, entered: an elderly man, diminutive, close on sixty, who had been in Frau von Anklam's service for a lifetime.

"Wait at the door," she called. "Stay at the door, Ernst."

"I know that, Excellency."

"Immediately afterward have a bath and change every stitch. Heaven knows what bacteria you have picked up, Ernst. Come on, do tell us about the wedding."

"There was none, Excellency."

"You see, Mathilde—what did I tell you? You get excited about nothing. What did I tell you only three minutes ago? She's quite a common person. She has thrown him over."

"Might I ask Ernst a few questions, dear Betty?" said Frau Pagel faintly.

"Certainly, dear Mathilde. Ernst, I don't understand you. You stand there like a stick. Don't you hear that Frau Pagel wants to know everything? Speak. She has of course thrown him over. Go on, what did he say to that?"

"Pardon me, Excellency. I believe the young gentleman didn't turn up either."

"You see, Mathilde, what did I tell you? The boy is all right, the bit of playing does him no harm; on the contrary, he is absolutely sensible. One doesn't marry such a person."

At last Frau Pagel got in a word. "Ernst, is it certain? Was there definitely no wedding? Perhaps you arrived a little too late."

"No, madam, certainly not. I was there in time and waited till the end, and also asked the clerk. Neither of them turned up."

"You see, Mathilde."

"But why should you think, Ernst, that it was my son?"

"I wanted to be sure, madam. Something might have happened. I ascertained their address from the registry office. So I went there, madam. . . ."

"Ernst, be sure to have a bath immediately and put on fresh linen."

"Yes, Excellency. The young gentleman has not been seen since this morning. And the girl has been turned out of doors because the rent hadn't been paid. She was still standing in the doorway."

Frau Pagel stood up suddenly. Once more she was full of decision, energetic and unyielding.

"Thank you, Ernst. You have reassured me. Excuse me, dear Betty, for leaving without ceremony, but I must go home at once. I have the feeling that Wolfgang is sitting there waiting for me, full of despair. Something must have happened. O God, and Minna is also out! Well, he still has the key of the flat. Excuse me, I'm quite confused, dear Betty."

"Manners and deportment, dear Mathilde! Deportment in every situation of life! Naturally you should have stayed at home on such an afternoon; of course he's waiting for you. I, myself, wouldn't have gone out on such a day. And above all—please, Mathilde, one moment, you simply can't run off like that—be firm. No false kindness. Above all give him no money, not a penny. Board and lodging and clothes—that's all right. But no money; he'll only lose it at play. Mathilde—Mathilde! Go. Don't stand on ceremony. Listen, Ernst. . . ."

The Thumann woman of the upper classes talks on and on. . . .

VIII

The dog slept, the cat slept, Georgenkirchstrasse slept.

Petra Ledig stood in the shadow of the doorway leading to the courtyard. The street vibrated in the merciless white heat; the hard light hurt her eyes; what she looked at seemed to lose its outlines and dissolve. She shut her eyes, and her head was filled with darkness shot through with aching flashes. She heard clocks strike the hour—it was good that the time passed. At first she had thought she must go somewhere or do something, but as she felt the moments slip away in a daze, she knew that she need only stand and wait. He must come, he might come any moment, he was bringing money. Then they would set out. Round the corner was a baker's, next to a butcher's. She imagined she was biting into a roll; it crackled, its crisp amber shell breaking, splinters of crust round the edge, and the inside white and spongy.

Now intruded red objects; she tried to recognize them, which she could do with shut eyes, for they were within her brain, not without: small round circles with reddish spots. What could they be? And suddenly she knew—they were strawberries. Of course, they had moved on; she was at a greengrocer's. The strawberries lay in a basket. They smelled fresh—oh, how fresh they smelled. The strawberries lay on green leaves which were cool, too. . . . Everything was very cool and very fresh, with the sound of water also clear and cool. . . .

She tore herself away from her fantasy with an effort, but the water ran so insistently, and splashed down in such a way that it seemed to have something to say to her. Slowly she opened her eyes, slowly she recognized the doorway in which she was still standing, the vibrating street—and at last saw the bowler-hatted man who was saying something to her, an elderly man with sallow face and yellow-gray mutton-chop whiskers.

"What do you say?" she asked with a great effort, which she had to repeat because at first only a tiny unintelligible sound came from her parched mouth.

Many had passed her while she stood there. If they did notice the figure in the shadow of the open door they only hurried on all the quicker. It was a poor district in a starving age, and everywhere, at any hour of the day, stood women, girls, widows, miserable bodies rigged up in the most ridiculous rags, hunger and misery in their faces. To find a buyer for that miserable body was the last hope of the war widows done out of their pensions; working-class women whose husbands, even the soberest and most industrious, were tricked out of their wages by every devaluation of the mark; girls, some almost children, who could no longer witness the misery of their younger brothers and sisters. Every day, every hour, every minute, they slammed the doors of wretched hovels in which hunger was their mate and worry their bedfellow; they slammed doors behind them in finality and said: "Now I will do it. Why preserve myself for a greater misery, the next influenza epidemic, the medical officer and the bone house? Everything flows, hurries on, makes haste, changes—and am I supposed to keep myself?"

There they stood, in every corner, at all hours, insolent or cowed, talkative or silent, begging: "Only a cup of coffee and a roll."

Georgenkirchstrasse was in a poor district. Gas company collector, middleman tailor, postman—they hurried all the quicker when they saw the girl. They didn't pull a face or make an insolent remark or joke: they had no thought of scoffing. But they hurried past lest a word of supplication should reach their hearts and move them to make a gift which should not be given. For the same trouble awaited all of them at home: black care rode on everybody's shoulder. Who knows when my wife, my daughter, my girl will be standing there, at first in the shadow of the door and next time in broad daylight? If you hurry by and see nothing, no whisper reaches your ears. You are alone, I am alone, we die alone—so each for himself.

But now somebody had stopped before Petra, an elderly man in a bowler hat, a yellow owl's face and yellow owl's eyes.

"What?" she asked, this time quite distinctly.

"Well, Fräulein!" He shook his head somewhat disapprovingly. "Do the Pagels live here?"

"Pagels?" So he didn't want anything of that sort, he was inquiring after the Pagels. The Pagels, several Pagels, at least two of them. She would have liked to know who he was, what he wanted; perhaps something important for Wolfgang. . . . And she tried to pull herself together. This gentleman wanted something. He mustn't discover that she belonged to Pagel, she who stood in the doorway thus. "The Pagels?" She sought to gain time.

"Yes, the Pagels. Well, you don't seem to know. Been having a drop or two, what?" He winked. He seemed to be a good-hearted man. "You oughtn't, Fräulein, not during the daytime. It's all right in the evening. But it's bad for you during the day."

"Yes, the Pagels live here," she said. "But they're not at home. They're both out." (For he mustn't go up to the Thumann woman; what he would hear there might be detrimental to Wolfgang.)

"So? Both out? Probably to the wedding, eh? But then they must have arrived late. The registry office is closed now."

So he knew that, too. Who could he be? Wolfgang had always said he had no acquaintances.

"When did they go?" the gentleman continued.

"About half an hour ago, no, an hour ago," she said hastily. "And they told me they weren't coming back today." (He mustn't go up to the Thumann woman. No!)

"So they told you that, Fräulein?" the gentleman asked, suddenly suspicious. "You're probably on friendly terms with the Pagels?"

"No, no," she protested hastily. "They only know me by sight. They only told me because I'm always standing here."

"So . . ." said the gentleman thoughtfully. "Well, thank you very much." And he went slowly through the doorway toward the first courtyard.

"Oh, please," she called in a weak voice and even took a few steps after him.

"Anything else?" he asked, turning round; but he didn't come back. (He intended to go up in any case.)

"Please," she implored. "The people up there are bad. Don't believe what they tell you of Herr Pagel. Herr Pagel is an excellent and very respectable man I've never had anything to do with him, I only know him by sight."

The visitor stood in the sunlit courtyard. He looked at Petra keenly, but he did not recognize her in the shadowy doorway; a slight, weak figure, the head bent forward, the lips half open, hands laid imploringly on her breast, anxiously awaiting the effect of her words.

He fingered his yellow-gray beard thoughtfully. After a long silence' he said: "Don't worry, Fräulein. I don't believe everything I'm told."

It did not sound ironical, perhaps it was not intended for her at all. It sounded almost friendly.

"I know the young gentleman quite well. I knew him when he was so high." And he indicated an impossibly short distance from the ground. Then, without another word, he nodded at her and vanished in the passage to the second courtyard.

Petra, however, slipped back to her sheltered corner behind the open door. She knew now that she had made a mistake; she should not have given any information at all to this old gentleman who had known Wolfgang as a child. No, she ought to have said: "I don't know whether the Pagels live here."

But she was too tired, too shattered, too ill to think about it any more. She only wanted to stand there and wait till he came back; then she would read in his face the information he had gleaned. She would tell him what a wonderful man Wolfgang was, that he had never done anything wicked, never done anybody any harm. . . . She rested her head on the cool wall, shutting her eyes, and this time almost unwillingly felt descend upon her the darkness which meant relief from her ego, her troubles, while in her mind she endeavored to accompany the old gentleman across the courtyard. And then upstairs to Frau Thumann's door. She thought she could hear him ring, and now she wanted to concentrate on his conversation with the landlady. . . . She would talk, that woman! Oh, she would talk, reveal everything, fling mud at them both, lament over the lost money. . . .

And suddenly she could see their room, the ugly den gilded by the rays of love. . . . There they had laughed, slept, talked, read. . . . Wolf stood brushing his teeth at the wash stand. She said something. . . .

"I can't hear," he shouted. "Talk louder."

She did.

"Louder." He went on brushing his teeth. "I can't hear a word. Louder still."
She obeyed, he brushed, the soap foamed.

"I said much louder."

She obeyed and they laughed.

Here they had been together; she had waited for him, never in vain. . . .

And she saw the street in one quick stab and knew that she was walking along . . . fairy fountain . . . Hermannspark . . . on, still farther on . . . And now she was in the country, with fields and forests, bridges and bushes . . . And again towns full of houses with doorways, and again land and water, vast oceans . . . and distant lands and country and town; unimaginable. . . . The myriad potentialities of life at every corner in every village . . . "To thee will I give all the glory of them." Her brain grew confused. "And I will worship before you if you will give me back our room and the vigil for him within it."

Slowly the world went dark. Everything was extinguished. The world was obscured. Dark shreds floated away, hiding her. . . . At one moment she thought she could still see the curtains in the room, yellow-gray, and hanging limp and motionless in the immense sultry heat. Then they too were swallowed up in the night.

The servant Ernst laid his hand on her shoulder and said admonishingly: "Fräulein, please, Fräulein."

Petra saw him from a long way off and, as if she had been urgently waiting to put the question ever since he had gone, asked at once: "What did they say?"

The man shrugged his shoulders. "Where has the young master, gone to?" She hesitated and he said soothingly: "You needn't feel embarrassed with me. I'm only his aunt's servant. I needn't tell her everything."

"He has gone to get some money." He couldn't learn anything worse from her than he had heard upstairs.

"And hasn't come back?"

"No. Not yet. I'm waiting."

They were both silent for a while, she waiting for what fate and perhaps this man had in store for her, he undecided whether to go away and report to his mistress. He could guess without difficulty what Frau Major General von Anklam thought of this girl, and what she would say to active help. All the same. . . .

Ernst stepped slowly through the doorway on to the street to look irresolutely right and left, but the man they expected was nowhere to be seen. For a moment he entertained the thought of simply going away. The girl would not hinder him at all, he believed; it was an easy solution; any other might bring him into difficulties with Her Excellency. Or cost him money—and the less the value of the small capital which Ernst had for a lifetime saved up, the more firmly he held on to it. In his small room at home he would fill one tea canister after another with notes and their incredible figures.

Nevertheless. . . .

He looked up and down the street once more, but there was no one.

Hesitatingly, almost a little indignant with himself, he went back to the doorway and asked with reluctance: "And suppose the young master doesn't bring any money?"

She looked at him with a slight movement of the head—revived by the vague prospect, suggested in the servant's words, that Wolfgang would still return, even if penniless.

"And suppose he doesn't come back at all, what will you do then?"

Her head fell forward, her eyelids closed—without uttering a word it was clear enough that she would then be indifferent to everything. "Fräulein,"he, said uncertainly, "a manservant doesn't earn much. And I've lost all my savings, but if you would like to take this . . ."

He tried to push a note for 50,000 marks into her hand; he had taken it out of his worn, thin pocketbook. And as she withdrew her hand, he went on more insistently: "No, no, you must take it. It's only for the fare, so that you can go home." He stopped short and pondered. "You can't go on standing here like this. Surely you've got some relative to go to?"

He broke off again. It struck him that she could not possibly get on a streetcar in such a get-up, legs bare to above the knee, slippers down-at-heel, a man's miserable overcoat displaying too much of her breast.

He stood there embarrassed, almost angry. He would like to help her but—how could one help her? He couldn't exactly take her with him, dress her, and then what? "O God, Fräulein," he said, suddenly downcast. "How could the young master have let things get to this?"

But Petra had understood only one thing. "So you also think that he won't come back?"

He shrugged his shoulders. "How can I tell? Have you quarreled? Weren't you going to get married today?"

Marry! Yes. She's heard the word but hadn't given it any further thought. "We're getting married today," she said, and laughed vaguely. She remembered that today was the day she would be getting rid of the name Ledig, which had always been something like a stain. She remembered it when she woke up, didn't dare look for his wallet, and was sure of it all the same. It would happen today! Then the first doubts came—his indecisive attitude when she first urged him, then demanded, then begged. . . . And how she already felt when the door slammed—Well, it won't be today after all.

Suddenly (and incomprehensibly, because hunger had caused her burning head even to forget that, though it had happened)—suddenly, in front of the mirror, she realized, she knew that he might well have gone, but that he would still remain with her, in her forever. What had happened next—the humiliating begging in Frau Thumann's kitchen, the squinting at Ida's brioche, the expulsion, the endless passive waiting in the corridor—that was all caused by hunger, that crafty enemy of body and brain that had made her forget what she never should have forgotten, that he was in her.

What was the matter? Was she bewitched? So far she had always managed to get along. Her mother may have been as brutal as she could be—a few tears and Petra went on. The fascinating gentlemen with knife-sharp creases to their trousers may have proved vulgar and stingy she had set her teeth and gone on. Wolfgang might return or might not return—that was dreadful, yes. But for twenty-two years she had eaten humble pie for her own sake, and now she was standing there doing nothing, bespoken and not called for, when, for the first time in her life, another being was dependent on her, on her alone—no other woman in the world could replace her. It was absurd.

A stream of thoughts entered her mind, so that she was almost overwhelmed. After hunger had immersed her poor head for a time in dark, vague dreams, it now made it over-active, wide awake and clear—everything seemed simple. She had somebody to look after, and because this somebody was within herself she must first of all look after herself—this was obvious. Everything would then come right again.

And while she was thinking this, she was already thinking about other things. She was already making her plans—the things to be done immediately and the things later. And therefore she said suddenly, clear and decided: "Yes, it's nice of you to give me the money. I can make good use of it. Many thanks."

The manservant looked at her dumbfounded. Only the fraction of a minute had passed since he reminded her that today she had intended to marry. Ernst could not guess the train of thought this one remark had evoked, or what she had experienced and planned in these few seconds. He saw only the change in her face, which was no longer vacant but full of life and had even regained some of its color. Instead of a hesitating mutter he heard energetic tones, almost a command. Without any hesitation he put the money in her hand.

"Well, Fräulein," he said, a little angry, "so you're alert again. Why? The registry office is closed by now. I really believe you've had a drop too much."

"No," she replied. "An idea has occurred to me, that's all—I haven't been drinking. I appear strange to you because I've eaten nothing for a long time and that makes one queer in the head."

"Eaten nothing!" Ernest now waxed really indignant. All his life he had had his meals regularly at the appointed times. "Nothing to eat! The young master oughtn't to do such things."

She looked at him with a half-smile. She knew what was passing through his mind, what he was indignantly thinking and feeling, and she had to smile. When the well-trained servant, grown gray in dealings with the upper circles, actually took up her side against the young master, she perceived how widely separated men were. The young master could have ill-treated her, deceived her as much as he liked, jilted her—all this would not have made the servant so angry (nor most of his fellow-beings). But that he should have starved her—no, that was not done.

Ernst was eyeing her attentively. She could guess the big step which he was about to take, and therefore she made it easy for him. "If you would bring me a few rolls," she said. "Just round the corner is a baker's shop. And then you needn't bother about me anymore. As soon as I've eaten something I'll manage all right. I've an idea."

"Of course I'll fetch you some rolls," he said eagerly. "And perhaps something to drink. Milk, eh?"

He hurried off, went into three, four shops—butter, bread, rolls, sausages, a few tomatoes. . . . He no longer thought of his savings. . . . The fact that a human being was hungry and with nothing to eat had quite confused him. The young master oughtn't to have done it, he thought again and again. She may be no better than she should be, but to let her go hungry—no!

He hurried, harassing himself and the sleepy shopkeepers; everything had to be done urgently. He would have liked to say: "Please, it's for somebody who is starving." But when he returned he was still more perplexed, for she was no longer there. Neither in the doorway, nor in the street, nor in the courtyard. She had gone.

He decided to go up to Frau Thumann once more, certainly not with much pleasure, for she, in her unrestrained scandal-mongering had only too dismal a likeness to Her Excellency Frau Major General Bettina von Anklam. But he encountered no one but Ida, by now dressed half professionally, half in deshabille—who rather frightened him. For the young lady inquired very ungraciously whether he hadn't a screw loose, because: "That bitch doesn't come here again, I'll see to that. If she rings here, I'll give it to her. I don't know what such people imagine!"

Ernst descended again, went through the courtyard, came again to the doorway.

No one stood in the shade there. Shaking his head he went into the street: no one. He couldn't take these bags of food, this bottle of milk, back to his mistress. Fräulein would be sure to see them, and was certain to tell Her Excellency.

He returned, piled up his purchases in the darkest corner behind the door, and then walked away, not without looking round several times. Only when he was sitting in the subway did he cease to think back and, instead, thought of the future. What should he tell Her Excellency?

After careful consideration he decided to say as little as possible.

Chapter Five

The Storm Breaks

I

About three o'clock the police sergeant, Leo Gubalke, returned from his allotment near the rolling-stock depot of Rummelsburg to his flat in Georgen-kirchstrasse. He had ample time to change for duty and for a thorough wash, but not enough for the nap he had hoped to have. His very strenuous spell of duty lasted from four o'clock in the afternoon till two o'clock in the morning, and it was always better if he had a little sleep beforehand; it was good for his work and, above all, for his nerves.

Oberwachtmeister Gubalke was alone in his two-roomed flat. Since morning his wife had been at the allotment (North Pole estate); his two girls had gone there direct from school. Into the kitchen he brought the big tub which his wife used for the washing, and scrubbed himself slowly and carefully from top to toe.

It was an old controversy between them as to how best to wash all over. He himself started at the top and proceeded downwards: head, neck, shoulders, chest and so on, till he arrived at the feet. This was truly methodical and clean, for nothing which had already been cleansed was affected by the washing of the next part. Besides, it was economical, since the soapy water, as it flowed downwards, soaked those parts of the body to be dealt with later.

Frau Gubalke did not wish to grasp this method or, if she did, avoided it. She washed herself unsystematically: now the back, then the feet, now the chest, next the thighs. Oberwachtmeister Gubalke had to deal with hysterical women nearly every day, yet he was firmly convinced that women could be sensible if they wanted to. But, in any case, their sense was quite different from men's, and to try to convince them of something about which they didn't want to be convinced was absolutely useless.

She was a marvelously tidy woman, Frau Gubalke. The kitchen was spick and span, and Gubalke knew that in every carefully closed drawer, behind every reliably shut cupboard, each article lay in absolute order. But she would not get any system into the care of her body. Women were like that. Well, then, if that be so, it was no use attempting to alter them, otherwise they easily got irritated. The father, however, had scored a victory in that both the children washed according to his method.

The Oberwachtmeister was a man in the early forties, ruddy, on the plump side, very orderly, not without benevolence, if it could be afforded. He no longer felt any particular enthusiasm for his calling, although it satisfied his sense of order. Whether he cautioned chauffeurs for driving contrary to the law, or took a drunk and disorderly to the police station, or warned a prostitute off the prohibited Königstrasse, he was keeping Berlin in order and seeing to it that everything was ship-shape in the streets. But public order, naturally, could never rise to the heights of private order as exemplified in his flat, and perhaps it was this which damped his pleasure in his work. He would have preferred to sit among the records and be responsible for registers and card indexes. There, with the aid of pen and paper, and possibly a typewriter, he could almost have attained his ideal of the world. But his superiors had no wish to take him off the streets. This man, cool and collected, perhaps a trifle slow, could hardly, in these difficult and chaotic times, be replaced.

While Leo Gubalke scrubbed his pinkish fat till it was crimson, he reflected once again how he could so wangle it as to fulfill his frequently expressed desire for a transfer to indoor duties. There were various ways and means of achieving this, even when opposed by superiors; for instance, cowardice—but, of course, cowardice could not be entertained for a moment. Or excitability, to get rattled—but Oberwachtmeister Gubalke would never, of course, lose his self-control in front of people in the street. One could also become too particular, report every trifle, drag everybody to the police station—but that would not be fair to his colleagues. Or one might commit a serious error, some colossal blunder which would compromise the police and delight some of the newspapers—this would certainly disqualify him for outdoor work. But he was too proud of his uniform and the force to which he had belonged for so long.

He sighed. If one considered the matter closely, the world was surprisingly full of obstacles for a man who believed in order. Hundreds of things which the less scrupulous did every day were out of the question for him. On the other hand, he had the pleasurable feeling, without which a man could not live, that he was not only keeping the world in order, but was in harmony with it himself.

Gubalke carefully wiped the tin tub till the last drop of water was soaked up, and then hung it on its hook in the lavatory. He also wiped the kitchen floor, although the few splashes would dry all the same in the disquietingly close atmosphere. Then he buckled on his belt and, last of all, donned the shako. As always, Leo Gubalke examined himself in a kitchen mirror about the size of the palm of your hand; and, as always, he confirmed that he couldn't see clearly in this whether the shako was being worn in the way prescribed by the regulations, or not. And thus to the dark corridor in front of the big mirror. It was annoying to switch on the electric light for such a short period (the consumption of current was said to be highest at the moment of switching on), but what could one do?

At twenty minutes to four he was ready—at one minute to four Oberwachtmeister Leo Gubalke would report for duty. He went downstairs. He had on one white glove, the other was held loosely in his hand. And now he approached the doorway and Petra Ledig.

The girl was leaning against the wall, her eyes closed. When she had asked Ernst to bring some rolls and he had gone to fetch them, she was possessed by an overwhelming vision of their proximity. She thought she could smell their freshness; something of their wholesome taste entered her stale and weary mouth. She had to swallow, and choked.

Again it grew black inside her head, her limbs yielded as if they had no firmness, her knees gave way; there was a continual trembling in arms and shoulders. Oh, please do come! Please do come! But, imprisoned in her torment of hunger, she did not know whom she was longing for—servant or lover.

Oberwachtmeister Gubalke had naturally to stop and have a look. He knew the girl by sight, for she lived in the same house as he did, although in the back part, and officially he knew nothing to her detriment. Still, she was lodging with a woman who occasionally harbored prostitutes, and she lived, unmarried, with a young man who apparently had no occupation but gambling—a professional gambler, if one could go by women's gossip. All in all there was no reason to be either severe or lenient, and the officer watched her impartially.

She had had too much to drink, of course; but she was near her room and she would, somehow, get upstairs. Moreover, his spell of duty did not start till four; he need not have seen anything, which was all the easier as this was not his beat; neither had she noticed him. And Gubalke was about to go away when a violent fit of retching threw her body forward. He saw straight into the opening of the overcoat—and looked away.

This wouldn't do. He couldn't overlook this; all his clean and orderly life rose in revolt. Tapping the sick girl's shoulder with his gloved finger, the Oberwachtmeister said: "Well, Fräulein?"

His calling, which had made the policeman skeptical of his fellow-beings, had also undermined confidence in the validity of his own observations. Till now the Oberwachtmeister had believed the girl to be dead drunk, and her dress, or rather state of undress, confirmed this belief. No girl who attached the slightest value to what was seemly about or around herself could go like this into the street.

But the look she gave him when he tapped her shoulder, that burning yet sane glance as of a creature in torment who spurns her torment—that glance dispelled any idea of drunkenness. In quite a different tone he asked: "Are you ill?"

She leaned against the wall, seeing but dimly the uniform, shako, and his ruddy full face and reddish stubby beard. She was not sure who was speaking to her, what she was to answer, to whom she should answer. But perhaps an orderly man, who has to struggle all day and every day with a disorderly world, understands better than anyone what proportions disorder can attain. From a few answers uttered with difficulty the Oberwachtmeister had quickly built up a picture of the state of affairs; he understood that she was only waiting for a couple of rolls, that the girl then intended to go to Uncle's round the corner, who would certainly help her out with a dress, and that she would then look up some of her chap's friends or relatives (she had the fare in her hand)—in short, that the scandal would in all probability be removed in a few moments.

The Oberwachtmeister gathered all this, found it reasonable, and was just about to say, "All right, Fräulein, I will let it pass for once," and report for duty, when he was painfully struck by the thought: When would he actually arrive at the station? A glance at his wrist-watch showed that it was three minutes to four. Under no circumstances could he be at the station before a quarter past four, and he would thus be a quarter of an hour late for duty, and with what excuse? That he had, without taking any official action, gossiped for a quarter of an hour with an improperly dressed female? Impossible; everybody would think that he had overslept.

"I'm sorry, Fräulein," said he officially. "I can't let you go about like this. You must come along with me first."

Gently but firmly he placed his gloved hand on her upper arm and gently but firmly led her into the street where it had been impossible for him to let her go unofficially. (Order often brings the paradoxical in its wake.)

"Nothing will happen to you, Fräulein," he said soothingly. "You haven't done anything wrong. But if I let you go alone in the street like this it might become a public nuisance or worse, and then you will have committed an offense."

The girl went with him willingly. Nothing about the man who was leading her in a not unkind manner made her uneasy, although he wore a uniform. The Petra Ledig who had been, not so very long ago when she was walking the streets without a permit, unreasonably afraid of every policeman, now observed that, at close range, policemen were not alarming, but even fatherly. "They haven't provided for such a contingency in the police station," he was saying, "but

I will see that you get something to eat at once. The men in the registration department are usually not very hungry, and I shall get hold of a piece of bread and butter there." He laughed. "Someone else's piece of stale bread and butter in a crumpled sandwich paper isn't too bad. When I bring my girls something of that kind they get quite excited about it."

"Yes," said Petra. "I was always pleased when Herr Pagel used to bring me some."

At the mention of Herr Pagel the Oberwachtmeister put on his official face. Though men had to stand together, particularly against women, he did not approve of this young gentleman, who among other things was said to be a gambler. He intended—but he would not tell the girl—to investigate the conduct of this young swell. Herr Pagel seemed not to be behaving very correctly, and it would do such a ne'er-do-well good if he realized that someone had an eye on him.

The Oberwachtmeister had fallen silent and stepped out smartly. Willingly enough the girl followed him, glad to get away from being stared at. And the two vanished toward the police station. In vain the manservant, Ernst, comes with his rolls; in vain Frau Pagel's maid, Minna, makes her inquiries; in vain there sets out from Dahlem a luxurious Maybach with a lady and a blind child. In vain, too, is Wolfgang Pagel in a final quarrel with his mother.

For the present Petra Ledig has been removed from all civilian influence.

II

Without any particular haste Wolfgang Pagel had walked from the villas of the rich at Dahlem through the crowded streets of Schöneberg to the old West End—quite a walk. In many of the streets there was hardly a pedestrian; they were abandoned and as if dried up by the sun. At other times he passed along roads full of traffic, swarming with people, and he, the aimless, was carried along by those with a purpose.

Above hung a blanket of vapor made of the heat and exhalations of the city. Walking along Dahlem's avenues of trees he had cast a clearly-defined shadow, but the more he mingled with the crowd the more his shadow paled, until it was gray and indistinguishable from the granite setts. His shadow was extinguished not only by the seething crowd surrounding him and by the ever higher and narrower housewalls, but by the blanket of vapor growing thicker and the sun, paler. The heat continuously poured into the overheated town, completely obliterating his shadow.

No clouds could yet be seen. Perhaps they lurked behind the rows of houses, crouched under the hidden horizon, ready to ascend and pour forth fire, thunder and flood, Nature's unavailing incursion into an artificial world.

But Wolfgang Pagel walked no faster, for all that. At first he had set forth without a definite goal, merely because he felt he could no longer sit in that lordly kitchen. But when at last the object of his pilgrimage became clear, he went no quicker. He had always been easy-going, slow by nature and by habit; before he replied to a question he liked to make a gesture with his hand, since that postponed the answer a little.

And he was walking slowly now—it postponed the decision a little. In the kitchen, during the conversation with the blind child, he had still been of the opinion that he must leave the responsibility for Petra to others, because he himself could not help her. To help a girl without clothes or food, and in debt, could only mean one thing—money—and he had none. But then it had struck him that he did have money, if not in coin then in what was equally valuable. To put it concisely, von Zecke had presented him with an idea: he owned a painting. This painting, Young Woman at a Window, indisputably belonged to him. He remembered his mother telling him before he went to the Front: "This painting now belongs to you, Wolf. At the Front you must always remember that Father's finest picture is waiting here for you."

Wolfgang did not like this picture, but it had a market value. He would not oblige Zecke; there were art dealers in plenty who would gladly take a Pagel, and he decided to approach a big dealer in Bellevuestrasse. There they would certainly not lower themselves to cheat him, since a Pagel was a good proposition without that.

He would receive for the picture numerically an unheard-of sum, hundreds of millions, probably (perhaps even a milliard), but he wouldn't touch a penny of it; not one note was to be changed. He would go on foot to Georgenkirchstrasse—that little bit extra wouldn't mean much to one who had walked from Dahlem into town. No, not one note should be changed. He would overwhelm his waiting Petra with the whole enormous sum.

Pagel walked through the scorching town of Berlin without haste, without stopping, running over his plans time after time, for there were various aspects to be considered. Most of all he thought about the moment when he would count out on the table an immense sum in notes; or, better still, he would let them rain down on the girl in bed so that she would be entirely covered by the money, covered with money in that filthy den. Often he had day-dreamed of this moment, imagining that it would be his winnings. Well, it would be instead money from the sale of his father's painting. Money gained by gambling—snatched so to speak from the three birds of prey—that would have been better still. However, *that* idea was now definitely finished with; he would think of it no more.

So he marched on, Wolfgang Pagel, ex-second lieutenant, ex-gambler, ex-lover. Again, he had done nothing, only gone, gone from here to there, and back again. In the morning he did go, and made plans, but only these last ones were the right ones. His were the most excellent of intentions, and therefore he could walk without hurrying. He was completely satisfied with himself. He would sell a picture, turn it into money, and give the money to Peter—magnificent! Not for one moment did it occur to him that money might perhaps mean nothing to his Peter. He was bringing money, a lot of money, more money than she had ever had in her life—could a man do more for his girl? The world rushed on, the dollar rose, the girl starved—but he walked at his ease, for what he proposed to do was as good as done. He wasn't in any hurry, there was time for everything: we have always muddled through somehow.

He turned into Tannenstrasse, a blind alley. A few steps more and he unlocked the front door and ascended the familiar stairs to his mother's flat. There was no change: the porcelain name plate on the door, older than himself, with the missing corner which he himself had knocked off with a skate very long ago; the habitual odor in the corridor, its dark chests, oak cupboards, temperamental grandfather clock, and high up on the walls his father's sketches seeming to float above the dark world as bright as clouds. But the splendid asters in the two china-blue vases on the old-fashioned mirror-table were an innovation, and when Wolfgang looked more closely he found a note from his mother. "Good day, Wolfgang," he read. "There is coffee in your room. Make yourself comfortable. I had to go out urgently."

For a moment he was taken aback by this greeting. From Minna's reports he knew that his mother expected him every day, every hour almost—but this was too much—he had pictured her as hopeful rather than assured. It entered his mind not to touch the coffee but to take the painting and go; yet he did not fancy that either— it was too much like a thief in the night. He shrugged his shoulders and the pale man in the greenish mirror opposite did likewise; a trifle embarrassed, Wolfgang smiled at himself, screwed up the note and dropped it into his pocket. His mother, missing it, would guess that he was here—and look for him. The sooner the better.

He went to his room.

Here were flowers, too, this time gladioli. Dimly he remembered having once told his mother that he admired them. And of course she would remember that and put some there for him; he was still expected to like them. And he was also intended to feel how much his mother loved him, since she could think of all this.

Yes, she was great at such things; she weighed and measured love. If I do this, then he has to feel that. Yet nothing was further from his mind than to respond. Gladioli were not really beautiful, but stiff and artificial in their pale colors—mere painted wax. Peter would never love by double entry.

Why is Mamma so exasperating? he reflected, pouring out a cup of the hot coffee. (She must have just placed it there. It was a marvel they had not met on the stairs or in the street.) I'm absolutely furious with her. Is it the house, the old familiar smell, the memories? I've only realized, since I lived with Peter, how she has always tied me to her apron strings and lectured me. . . . Everything she wanted was good; every friend I chose was unsuitable. And now this dramatic reception . . . Yes, I've already noticed there's another note on the desk. And over the chair hangs a newly pressed suit and underwear. A silk shirt with the studs put in. . . .

He prepared his third roll, which tasted excellent. The coffee was strong and mild at the same time; its rich flavor gently took possession of the whole palate, quite unlike Madam Po's insipid yet harsh decoction. (Was Peter having her coffee too? Of course, she must have had it long ago. Perhaps she was now having her afternoon coffee.)

Stretching himself comfortably on the settee, Wolfgang Pagel tried to guess what was written on the slip of paper. Something like this of course: "You must choose your tie for yourself; they are hanging inside the wardrobe door." Or "The bath water is hot." Yes, something like that would be written there.

And when he did look he read that the bath-stove was alight. Angrily he thrust this crumpled note with its fellow. That he had summed up his mother so well didn't please him but only made him angrier still.

Naturally, he thought, I can sum her up so well because I know her so well. Possessiveness. Bossiness. When I came home from school I always had to wash my hands and put on a clean collar, because I'd mixed with the "others"—and we were different, better. This note of hers is an insult to me, but above all to Peter, a calculated insult. It's not enough to change my clothes, I must also have a bath. Because I've been with a creature whose face Mamma slapped outright. Insolence! I won't stand it.

He stared furiously round his old room with the yellow birch desk, the birch bookshelves and the half-length green silk curtains hanging before them. The birch bedstead glittered like silver and gold. Everything was light and joyful—and outside the window there were trees, too, old trees. Everything was so tidy, clean and fresh; when one thought of the Thumann hovel one realized why this room was kept so neat and ready. The son was to compare the one with the other: that is how you live with the girl, but this is the care that your loving mother has for you. Sheer insolence and provocation!

Stop! He tried to control his anger. Stop. You're running away with yourself, the horses are bolting. Part of it's true; her flowers and notes are distasteful, but the room itself never looked different. Why am I so furious then? Because I can't help remembering that Mamma slapped Peter? Nothing of the sort. With Mamma one couldn't take such a thing seriously, and Peter didn't take it seriously either. It must be something else. . . .

He went to the window. The nearest houses stood a good way off and one could see the sky. Dark sinister clouds were piling up, high on the horizon. The light was dismal, there was no breeze, not a leaf stirred. On the mansard roof opposite he saw a couple of sparrows squatting, puffed up and motionless; those quarrelsome chaps, too, were cowed by the impending threat in the sky. He must get away quickly. It wouldn't be pleasant running in a storm with the picture under his arm.

And suddenly he understood. He visualized himself with the painting, wrapped in some used brown paper, walking to the art dealer's. He couldn't even afford a taxi. He was carrying an object worth millions, perhaps even milliards, huddled under his arm—as if he were a thief. On the sly, like a drunkard secretly taking the bedding from his wife and home to the pawnbroker.

But it is my property, he argued. I needn't be ashamed.

But I am ashamed, though. Somehow it isn't right.

Why isn't it right? She has given it to me.

You know very well how attached she is to it. That's why she gave it to you. She wanted to tie you all the closer to her. You will hurt her terribly if you take it away.

Then she oughtn't to have given it to me. Now I can do what I like with it.

You've been in a bad way often enough before. You've often thought of selling it and you never did.

Because things were never so bad as they are now. They've come to a head.

Oh! have they? How do others manage who haven't got a picture to fall back on?

Others would never have got to these straits. Others would not have let their affairs drift until they became desperate. Others would not in the last resort hurt their mother to give bread to their mistress. Others would not have gambled without any misgivings—without any misgivings because they had a picture in reserve. Others would have looked for work in time and would have *earned* money; would not have gone so casually to the pawnshop or asked for a loan or begged; would not have gone on taking and taking from a girl without ever thinking of what they could give her in return.

The sky was growing darker and perhaps sheet lightning was already play-ing, only one could not see it through the haze. Perhaps thunder was already muttering in the distance, but it could not be heard. The town thundered and roared even louder.

"You are a coward," a voice whispered. "You are a poor devil, who has wasted his twenty-three years. You had everything here, love and gentle care, but you fled. Youth is afraid of happiness. It doesn't want it. Because happiness means peace, and youth is restless. But where did you run to? Did you run to Youth? No, you went to the place where the old foregather, those who no lon-ger feel the prick of the flesh, who have no passion left. . . . You went into the desert of artificial passions and yourself became arid, unnatural, prematurely old. You are a coward. And for once you have to make a decision, yet there you stand and hesitate. You don't want to hurt your mother and yet you want to help Peter. You would prefer your mother to ask you, implore you with desperate gestures of entreaty, to sell the painting. But she won't do that, she won't spare you the decision; you will have to act like a man. There is no middle course, no shift, no compromise, no shirking. You have let things drift too long—now you have to decide—the one or the other."

The clouds rose higher and higher. Wolfgang Pagel still stood irreso-lutely at the window. He was good to look at, with his slim hips and broad shoulders, the image of a warrior. But he was not a warrior. He had an open face, with a good forehead, a straight nose—but he was not frank, not straight. Many thoughts struggled within him; all were disagreeable and tormenting. All demanded something of him, and he was angry at having to deal with them.

Others have better luck, he thought. They do what they like and don't bother. With me everything is difficult. I shall have to think it all out again. Is there no way—must I choose between Mother and Peter?

For a while he stood his ground; this time he did not wish to evade his responsibilities. But gradually, as he found no solution although everything clamored for a decision, he grew tired, lit a cigarette, and took another mouth-ful of coffee. Softly he opened the door of his room and listened. The flat was silent; Mamma was not back yet.

His hair was fair and curly, his chin was not a very strong one—he was soft, he was indolent. And now he smiled. He had made up his mind. Once again he had avoided a decision. He would take advantage of his mother's absence to remove the painting without a scene. He smiled, suddenly very satisfied with himself. The thoughts that had tormented him were gone.

He went straight across the corridor toward his father's room. There was no time to be lost, the storm was about to break, and Mamma might come back at any moment.

He opened the door and there, in the big armchair, sat Mamma, black, stiff and upright.

"Good afternoon, Wolfgang," she said. "I'm so pleased to see you."

III

He was not at all pleased. On the contrary, he felt like a thievish servant caught red-handed.

"I thought you were out shopping, Mamma," said he lamely and gave her a limp hand which she pressed energetically and meaningfully. She smiled. "I wanted to give you time to feel at home again; I didn't wish to overwhelm you at once. Well, sit down, Wolfgang, don't stand about so irresolutely. . . . You've no engagements at present; you aren't here on a visit, you're at home."

He sat down obediently, the son once again under maternal command and care. "Only on a visit. Just for a few minutes," he muttered, but she did not hear him, whether intentionally or not he was to learn later.

"The coffee was still hot, was it? Good. I had only just made it when you came. You haven't bathed and changed yet? Well, there's plenty of time. I can quite understand that you wanted to have a look at your home first. It's your world after all. Our world," she modified, watching his face.

"Mamma," he began, for this emphasis on the world that he belonged to, the insinuation that the Thumann flat was Petra's world, annoyed him—"Mamma, you're very much mistaken . . ."

She interrupted him. "Wolfgang," she said in a changed, a much warmer voice, "Wolfgang, you needn't tell me anything or explain anything. I know a good deal, I don't need to know more. To clear the situation up once and for all, however, I'd like to admit here and now that I didn't behave well to your girl-friend. I regret some of the things I said and even more what I did. You understand me! Is this enough, Wolfgang? Come, give me your hand, my boy."

He scrutinized his mother's face. He could not believe it at first; he knew his mother, knew her face and there was no doubt she meant it sincerely. She had repented. She had made her peace with him and with Peter—she was therefore reconciled, and Heaven alone knew how it had come about. Perhaps the suspense of waiting for him had softened her.

It was incredible. He held her hand. "Mamma," he said, "that's very nice of you. But perhaps you don't know yet that we intended to marry today. It's only . . ."

She interrupted him again—what readiness, what eagerness to meet him halfway! She was making everything easy for him. "It's all right, Wolfgang. Now everything is settled. I'm so glad to see you sitting here again."

An immense relief overwhelmed him. A moment ago he had stood at the window of his room tormented by doubts as to which of them he should hurt—his mother or Petra. Except these alternatives there seemed to be no escape. And now everything had altered; his mother had seen her mistake, and the way into this orderly home stood open to both of them.

He got up, he looked down on the white parting in his mother's hair. Suddenly he was seized by something akin to emotion. He swallowed and wanted to say something, and cried out that he wished life were different, no, that he wished he were different, then he would have behaved differently.

The old woman sat at the table with an immobile wooden face. She didn't look at her son, but she rapped her knuckles smartly on the table. It sounded wooden. "Ah, Wolfgang," she said, "don't be childish, please. In the Easter term when you hadn't moved up to a higher form you always cried out 'I wish . . .' And when your engine was broken you were sorry afterwards about the way you had treated it. But that's futile, and you're no longer a child. Retrospective repentance is useless, my boy; you must learn in the end that life goes on, ever on and on. One can't change the past, but one can change oneself—for the future."

"Certainly, Mamma," he said like a good boy. "I only wanted to . . ."

But he did not finish. The outer door opened and shut hurriedly, more than hurriedly. Steps hastened along the corridor . . .

"It's only Minna," explained his mother.

Their door opened without a preliminary knock; it was flung open, and Minna stood in the doorway, elderly, gray and shriveled.

"Many thanks, Minna," said Frau Pagel quickly, for at the moment she did not wish to have any news from Georgenkirchstrasse; she had got here all that had interested her there. "Many thanks, Minna," she therefore said, as severely as possible. "Please prepare the supper immediately."

Minna, however, for this once was not the obedient servant; her eyes were angry and suspicious, her yellowish cheeks flushed. She didn't look at her mistress, her hostile stare was directed at the hitherto beloved young master.

"Shame on you," said she breathlessly. "Shame, Wolfgang. So you are sitting here?"

"Are you mad?" Frau Pagel cried indignantly, for she had never experienced such behavior from her Minna in all the twenty years of their life together. "You're disturbing us."

But no notice was taken and Wolfgang at once comprehended that something had happened "there." A misgiving overcame him. He saw Peter, and Peter saying to him "Good luck, Wolf" as he went with the suitcase to the pawnbroker's. She had given him a kiss . . .

He took Minna by the shoulders. "You've been there? What's the matter? Tell me quickly!"

"If you say another word," cried Frau Pagel, "you're dismissed on the spot."

"You needn't dismiss me, madam!" said Minna, outwardly calm. "I'm going anyhow. Do you think I'd stay in a place where the mother encourages the son to do wrong and the son obeys her? Oh, Wolf, how could you have done it? How could you have been so wicked?"

"Minna, what's come over you? How dare you! You old . . ."

"You can call me what you like, I'm used to it, madam. Only I always thought that you called me names only in fun. But now I know you mean it; you think that we're different, that I'm just out of the kitchen and you're a fine lady."

"Minna," shouted Wolfgang, and shook the old servant vigorously. She was quite beside herself. "Tell me what has happened to Peter. Is she . . . ?"

"Oh? Do you really care, Wolf, even though you've run away from her on her wedding day and sold all the clothes off her body and left her with nothing but a shabby overcoat? The one from your husband, madam—and nothing underneath, no stockings, nothing . . . And so the police have arrested her. And what's the worst of all, I'll never forgive you for it, Wolf, she was starving. She was retching again and again and almost fell down the stairs."

"But where do the police come in?" Wolfgang shouted despairingly, shaking Minna as hard as he could. "What have the police to do with it?"

"How should I know?" Minna shouted back, and tried to free herself from the young master who was unconsciously holding her still tighter. "How do I know what mess you've got her into? Of her own accord Petra's done nothing wrong; I know her too well for that. And the vulgar person who lives on the same floor is going about saying that it serves Peter right because she considered herself too good to walk the streets. But I gave her something!" For a moment Minna stood there triumphantly. Then she said sullenly: "God bless her for not doing it, though you and all you menfolk don't deserve anything better."

Wolfgang let go of Minna so suddenly that she almost fell. She became silent at once.

"Mamma," he said agitatedly. "Mamma, I haven't the least idea what's happened. I can't make it out at all. I left about midday and tried to borrow some money. It's true that I sold Petra's clothes and that we owed the landlady money, and it's possible that she hasn't had much to eat lately. I admit I didn't notice. I was very often away from there. But what the police have to do with all this!" He was speaking in lower and lower tones. It would have been much easier to tell all this to Minna than to his mother sitting there so wooden, so hard, and, incidentally, just under that particular painting. Well, that was done with, that was all over.

"Anyway, whatever may be the matter with the police, I'll settle it at once. I'm quite certain, Mamma, that there's no real trouble—we've done nothing, nothing. I'll go there at once. It must be a mistake. Only, Mamma . . ." It grew increasingly difficult to speak to the dark woman who sat there quite unmoved, distant, hostile. . . . "Only, Mamma, unfortunately I'm at the moment without any money whatsoever. I need some for the fare, perhaps to settle with the landlady on the spot, for bail, I can't tell; things for Petra, too, food." He stared intently at his mother. There was need for haste. Peter must be freed, he must leave at once. Why didn't she go to her desk and fetch the money?

"You're worked up, Wolfgang," said Frau Pagel, "but, in spite of that, we mustn't act rashly. I fully agree with you—something must be done for the girl at once. But I don't think you in your present condition are the right person to do it. Perhaps there will be lengthy explanations with the police—and you are somewhat lacking in self-control, Wolfgang. I think we should call up my solicitor, Justizrat Thomas. He knows all about such matters; he'll settle it quicker and more smoothly than you."

Wolfgang looked at his mother's mouth as if he must not only hear the words she uttered but also read them from her lips. He passed his hand over his face; it felt so dry, the skin really ought to rustle. The hand, however, came away damp.

"Mamma," he pleaded, "I can't let this matter be settled by your lawyer and meanwhile sit here calmly, have a bath and eat my supper. I ask you to help me this once in *my* way. I must settle the matter myself, help Peter myself, fetch her out myself, speak with her myself."

"That's just like you," said Frau Pagel, again rapping her knuckles on the table. "I have to remind you, Wolfgang, unfortunately, that if you have asked me once to do what you want in your own way, you have asked me a hundred times. And whenever I did so, it was always a mistake."

"Mamma, you can't compare this case with some childish trifle."

"Dear boy, whenever you wanted anything all the rest was only a trifle. But this time I won't yield, it doesn't matter what you say, if only because these negotiations would bring you into contact with the girl. Be glad you got rid of her; don't start all over again because of some mistake on the part of the police, or because of some foolish backstairs gossip." She glanced sourly at Minna, who was standing in the doorway—her accustomed place. "Today you have finally separated from her. You've given up this ridiculous wedding, you've returned to me, and I've received you without any question or reproach. Am I now to witness you and the girl come together again, in fact help you to do this? No, Wolfgang, on no account!"

She sat erect and gaunt, looking at him with flaming eyes. She had not the slightest doubt in her mind, and her will was adamant. Had she ever been gay and free? Had she ever laughed, ever loved a man? All was past and gone. Gone! His father had scorned her advice, but she was not disconcerted; she had persevered. And should she now give way to the son? Do what she did not approve of? Never!

Wolfgang looked at her. He was rather like his mother. With his lower jaw pushed forward, his eyes glistening, he said very gently: "I didn't quite catch that, Mamma. Today I've finally separated from Peter?"

She made a hasty movement. "Don't let's talk about it. I require no explanations. You're here, that's enough for me."

And he, more gently if possible: "So I've given up this ridiculous wedding?"

She scented danger, but it did not make her cautious, only aggressive. "When the bridegroom doesn't turn up at the registry office," she said, "then one can draw a certain conclusion."

"Mamma," retorted Wolfgang, sitting down on the other side of the table and leaning across it, "you seem to be very well informed about my comings and goings. You ought to know then that the bride didn't turn up either."

Outside it had grown quite dark. A first gust of wind swayed the treetops, a few yellow leaves whirled through the window. In the doorway stood Minna, forgotten by mother as by son. And now there was a flash of lightning and the tense faces gleamed and were blotted out in a deeper gloom. There was a rumble of distant thunder.

The elements wanted to break out, but Frau Pagel tried to control herself. "Wolfgang," she pleaded, "we don't want to argue about the extent you've separated from Petra. I'm convinced that if this incident with the police hadn't occurred you would have almost forgotten about her. Leave this matter to a lawyer, I beg you, Wolfgang, and I've never asked you so earnestly before. Do what I want for once."

The son heard the mother pleading as he had pleaded with her a few minutes ago, but he paid no attention. In the gloom her face was dim. Behind her head the sky lighted up in sulphur-yellow, fell back into darkness and flashed anew.

"Mamma," said Wolfgang, and his will was strengthened more and more by her resistance, "you're very much mistaken. I didn't come here because I had separated, partly or entirely, from Petra. I came because I wanted money for this ridiculous wedding."

For a moment his mother sat motionless. But, however hard the blow was, she did not show it. "Well, my son, then I can tell you that you come in vain," she replied bitterly. "You shan't get a penny for that purpose here." Her voice was very quiet but unfaltering. Still more quietly and without a trace of excitement, he replied: "I know you, and I never expected a different answer. You love only those people who want to be saved in your way, though one cannot congratulate you on the salvation you yourself have achieved."

"Oh," groaned the woman. This was a mortal blow—to her whole life, her whole being, her marriage and motherhood—struck by her own son.

But this cry of pain excited him all the more. Just as, in the world outside, oppressive heat and stench had simmered together since the early hours of the morning and were now at boiling point, so had possessiveness, an old woman's assurance, the arbitrary exploitation of her position as mother and as guardian of the money, long been simmering together in him. But what made his anger dangerous was not these things, nor his mother's contempt for Petra (who, without this, would not have had such significance). From his own weakness, from his own cowardice, came the hottest glow. And he had to revenge himself for having given way to her a hundred times. He was terrible now because he had been so afraid of this scene. His anger was shameless because it had been his intention to smuggle the painting away.

"Oh!" His mother's groan had released in him a deep joy. It was a hungry age, a wolf age. Sons turned against parents, one hungry pack bared its teeth against another—who is strong shall live! But the weak must die. And let me do the killing!

"And I've also to tell you, Mother, that when I came into the room so quietly a moment ago, I was under the impression that you were out. I wanted to take away the painting secretly, *the* painting; you know which one I mean—the painting you gave me."

"I've never given you a painting!" she said very quickly, but with an unmistakable tremor in her voice.

Wolfgang heard it clearly. But he talked on. He was drunk with revenge, shameless.

"I wanted to sell it secretly. Get a lot of money for it, nice money, a heap of money, foreign money, dollars, pounds, Danish kronen—and give it all to my dear good Petra." He was sneering at her, but also at himself. He was a fool. Ah! this was even better than gambling; it excited him, inflamed him— to talk into the darkness against the lightning and the almost incessant threat and rumble of thunder far away. Out of the primeval origins of all human existence, liberated by this evil age, rose the earliest hatred of children for their parents. Youth against Age, recklessness against slow deliberation, blood against cold flesh. . . .

"I wanted to take it away without your knowing, but that, of course, was nonsense. It's just as well to tell you everything once and for all—everything. . . . And after I've spoken I'll take away the picture."

"I won't give it up," she cried, jumping to her feet and standing in front of it. "No!"

"I'll take it," he said undaunted, and remained seated. "I'll carry it off before your eyes and sell it, and Petra shall get the money, all of it."

"You won't take it by force!" There was fear in her voice.

"I shall take it by force," he cried, "since I intend to have it. And you'll be sensible. You know I want it, and that I'll get it, too."

"I'll call the police," she threatened, wavering between telephone and picture.

"You won't call the police," he laughed, "because you know quite well you gave me the picture."

"Look at him, Minna," cried Frau Pagel, and now she had forgotten that it was her son standing there. She saw in him the male, the male who always acted contrary to common sense, woman's enemy from the beginning of time.

"Look at him! He can't wait to get back to his girl! To deliver her from the police! It's all lies and acting. She interests him as little as anything else. He only cares about money." She mocked him. "Nice money, much money, dollars, pounds—but not for the dear, beautiful, good Petra in jail, for Fräulein Ledig; no, for the gaming table."

She stepped aside, surrendering the picture, stood at the table, rapped it hollowly. "There, take it. That's the worst I can do for you, to let you have it. Sell it, get money, a heap of money. And that will show your silly, obstinate, cantankerous mother to be in the right again—you won't make the girl happy with it. You'll lose the money gambling, just as you've gambled away everything else—love, decency, feeling, ambition, the power to work." She stood there breathless, with flaming eyes.

"Anyhow, I thank you, Mamma," said Wolfgang, suddenly dead tired of quarreling and talking. "And that's the end of that, eh? And of everything else, too. I'll send for my things this evening; I don't want to burden you with them any longer. With regard to your prophecies, though—"

"Take everything," she shouted, trembling in every limb as she watched him remove the picture from the wall. "Don't you want some of the silver for the bride's dowry? Take it. Oh, I know you Pagels," she cried, and was once more the young girl she had been long, long before her betrothal and marriage. "Outwardly kind and gentle, but inwardly greedy and barren. Go! Go quickly! I don't want to see you any more. I've sacrificed my life to you and in the end you've thrown mud at me, father as well as son, one the image of the other. . . . Yes, go, without a word, without a look. Your father was like that, too; he was too grand for arguments, and when he wanted to do anything at night which would give him a bad conscience, he used to creep out of the room in his stocking feet."

Wolfgang was already going, the picture under his arm. He had looked round, intending to ask Minna for brown paper and string, but she stood stiffly in the doorway. And he was, above all, conscious of his mother's voice, that shrill, merciless voice, like a cracked bell, eternally clanging since his childhood.

He would carry the picture as it was. He must get away before it rained.

But as he crossed the threshold of the room to the accompaniment of that wild raving voice, the old servant, that silly goose whom one could never please, burst forth in his very face: "Shame on you! Shame on you!"

He shrugged his shoulders. He had done it for Petra; it was Minna's opinion also that he ought to have done something for the girl. But never mind, let them talk.

He was out of the flat, the door was closed. Once he had chipped a corner off its porcelain name plate. He went downstairs.

How much would he get for the picture?

IV

On this twenty-sixth day of July, 1923, the divorced Countess Mutzbauer (*née* Fräulein Fischmann) wished to go into the country to have a look at some farms with her present friend, a Berlin cattle dealer by the name of Quarkus.

Quarkus was a man in his late forties, stocky, with dark curly thinning hair, fleshy forehead, and a roll of fat at the back of the neck; a married man for almost a quarter of a century, and the father of five children. At first he had regarded the inflation favorably, since it had made him richer and richer, a few months changing a man with a weekly turnover of a wagon-load of pigs and two dozen cattle into a wholesale dealer whose buyers traveled into South Germany and even into Holland. Before the cattle, paid for in advance, arrived in Berlin, indeed even before they were dispatched, their value had risen twofold, threefold, and even fivefold, and Quarkus had always proved to be right when he had told his buyers: "Pay what the people ask you—it's little enough."

At first, raking in the money had given Herr Quarkus undiluted pleasure, creating in him a distaste for the Schultheiss pothouses, the Bötzow taverns and the Aschinger saloons; and he had become a generous, even popular, client of all the bars in the old Friedrichstadt and the new West End, asserting with conviction that one could eat really decently in only three of all Berlin's restaurants. Thus, when it came about that a genuine countess embraced him, he felt that no earthly desire of his remained unfulfilled.

But the richer he grew and the less importance money held for him, the more thoughtful became cattle dealer Quarkus. His unscrupulous optimism which hitherto had relied, without worrying about the future, on the continued fall of the mark, became dashed at the sight of this currency leaping round the dollar in bounds which would have carried a flea over Ulm Cathedral.

"There's a limit to everything," he muttered when he learned that his pigs had brought him in twentyfold the purchase price. At a time when hundreds of thousands did not know where to find the money for a piece of bread, he became sleepless with the worry of how to invest his.

An expression whispered on many sides—real values—reached his ear. Nobody can free himself from his early training. The lad Emil (the name Quarkus had attained significance for the surrounding world only from his twenty-fifth year onwards) had had to drive one cow along many German highroads, and look after three pigs; he had been a cattle drover before he became a cattle dealer. Longingly the thin hungry youth had looked at the farmhouses beside the highroad, where the doors emitted such an alluring smell of fried potatoes and bacon. Whether it hailed, rained, snowed, or was cold enough to freeze your very eyelashes, the farms always sprawled comfortably along the roadside, their broad thatched or tiled roofs promising protection, warmth and comfort. Even the ox which Emil Quarkus drove could notice this; when it rained it lifted its head, stretched out its tail and lowed yearningly for the farmyards.

What for the boy had been the epitome of all security and comfort, now became a refuge for the man. At a time when the mark was bounding, leaping, crashing, nothing could be more secure than a farm—excepting five or ten farms. And Quarkus was resolved to buy them.

Countess Mutzbauer, *née* Fräulein Fischmann (which she did not naturally divulge to her friend Quarkus) was, of course, more in favor of an estate with a castle, terrace and racing stable. But about this Quarkus was adamant. "I have bought enough cattle from manors," he said. "I don't want to buy their worries, too."

He was sure that if he went to a farm with a bag full of notes—better still with a trunk—asked to buy a cow, bought ten, threw his money around and bragged about it and used it as a bait, then no owner would be able to resist him. And after buying ten cows he would buy the cowhouse, the straw, the land on which the straw grew, and ultimately the whole farm. And when he told the owner that he could remain and carry on with the farming, doing what he liked with the produce, that farmer would think him cracked and would find other sellers for him, more than he wanted. Till the day dawned when the mark—well, nobody could conceive what the mark would be like on *that* day—it baffled imagination. Whatever happened, however, the farm would be there. The farms, rather.

Such were, roughly, Quarkus's reflections as frequently outlined to the Countess. Actually, since the manor had been turned down, she took very little interest in the matter, but she was too wise to be disinterested enough to let her friend travel by himself. It was always better to be on the spot, for vulgar women, to whom money was as necessary as dung to the dung-beetle, were to be found everywhere. Moreover, if he bought ten farms, an eleventh might perhaps be thrown in as her pickings; and though the idea of her owning a farm was about as reasonable as her possessing a locomotive, yet it could always be sold—in fact, one could sell anything. (Countess Mutzbauer had already sold, in turn, three cars which she had been given by her friend, and had treated him to the magnificent explanation: "You're too much of a gentleman, Quarkus, to expect me to put up with such an old-fashioned car." And he was really too much of a gentleman—besides being uninterested in such points.)

The notion of the eleventh farm, however, had reminded the Countess that her chambermaid, Sophie, came from the country and toward midday, having slept thoroughly, she rang for her and conducted the following conversation:

"Sophie, you come from the country, don't you?"

"Yes, Frau Countess, but I don't like it."

"Do you come from a farm?"

"No, Frau Countess, from a manor."

"You see, Sophie, I told Herr Quarkus that he should buy a manor. But he says he only wants a farm."

"Yes, Frau Countess, my Hans was just like that, too. When he had enough money for Habel and partridges, then he only wanted Aschinger with pea soup and bacon; men are like that."

"So you, too, Sophie, think that a manor is much better?"

"Of course, Frau Countess. A manor is much bigger, and when it belongs to you, you don't need to work yourself but employ people."

"On a farm one has to work?"

"Terribly hard, Frau Countess; and work which ruins the appearance."

Hastily the Countess decided to forgo the eleventh farm and accept instead the gift of a diamond ring. And with that decision she lost all personal interest in the trip or the purchase, and thus any reason for taking Sophie with her as adviser.

"Listen, Sophie, in case Herr Quarkus should ask you, don't tell him that. That's no need to dissuade him; it only spoils his pleasure and won't stop him buying."

"Just like my Hans," said Sophie with a sigh, reflecting sadly that the police would never have nabbed Hans Liebschner if he had followed her advice.

"All right, Sophie. Then everything is settled. I knew you understood all about the country. Herr Quarkus and I are going to buy a farm, and I thought of buying one for myself. Then I would have taken you with me. But if a farm is no use . . ."

Too late Sophie realized that she had spoken too soon. A trip by car into the country with the rich Quarkus would have been very agreeable. She changed her tune. "Of course, Frau Countess, there are all sorts of farms—"

"No, no," said the former Fräulein Fischmann. "You've explained everything splendidly. I'm not buying."

Since there was nothing more to be gained here, Sophie looked for an advantage on the other side. "So Frau Countess will probably be away for some time?"

Yes, Countess Mutzbauer would hardly be back before tomorrow evening.

"Oh, if the Frau Countess would then be so kind . . . My aunt at Neukölln has been seriously ill and I ought to have gone to see her before. . . . Could I have this afternoon off? And perhaps till tomorrow midday?"

"Well, Sophie," said her mistress graciously, although she took the sick aunt in Neukölln about as seriously as Sophie did the acquisition of a farm by the Countess, "it's really Mathilde's turn for a day off, but as you've given me such good advice . . . Don't upset Mathilde, though."

"Not at all, Frau Countess; if I give her a cinema ticket she'll be quite happy. She's so mean. Only recently the cobbler said to her: 'Fräulein, don't you ever go out? The soles of your shoes are still good the second year of wear-ing!' But she's like that."

Perhaps the cook Mathilde was really like that with regard to stinginess, days off and the cinema; Sophie Kowalewski may have reported correctly, but she was mistaken in her forecast of the way in which Mathilde would receive the news about that particular afternoon off. Sophie had spoken quite casu-ally about the paltry cinema ticket with which Mathilde would let herself be appeased; but nothing of the kind, nothing of the kind at all! Mathilde stormed. She wouldn't have it. What? She, the economical and steady one, was to sac-rifice herself for a whore who went with any lounge-lizard for three drinks! Oh, no! Unless Sophie immediately gave up this outing obtained in such an underhand manner, she, Mathilde, would go at once to the Countess, and what the Countess would then hear, Sophie might only too well imagine. Such filth wouldn't pass without reason over her lips. At which point Sophie began to defend her client in front of her friend.

Oh, stout, easy-going Mathilde! Sophie could not understand why she was furious. Previously she had allowed her free days to be passed over a dozen times, had forgone them voluntarily or involuntarily, and when she sulked for once, a box of sweets or a cinema ticket had always appeased her. Had the oppressive heat driven the old woman mad? For a moment Sophie wondered whether she ought not to give in. If Mathilde opened her mouth to the Count-ess there might be a pretty stink. Not that Sophie was afraid of that. She could make short work of a drunken man who kicked up a row, and such could be almost as bad as a quarrelsome woman.

So she considered for a moment. . . . Then she spoke coldly and mali-ciously: "I don't know what's biting you, Mathilde. Why do you want to go out? You haven't anything fit to wear."

Oh, how sweetly this oil sizzles, how the flame rises higher and higher. "Nothing to wear! Of course, if I could use my mistress's wardrobe, as some of us do . . ."

"You'd do it, Mathilde. Only nothing fits you. You're so terribly fat."

Even in 1923 it was a serious insult to call a woman plump—not to men-tion fat. Promptly Mathilde burst into tears. "Whore, strumpet, bitch!" she screamed, and rushed off to her mistress. Herr Quarkus had just come in, and they were about to set out for the country.

Sophie, shrugging her shoulders, stayed behind. It was all one to her, whatever happened. All of a sudden she had had quite enough of the life here, although a minute ago she would not have wished to leave. But it was like that nowadays, there was no stability; what was valid one moment was not so the next. (Never was the fatal gas tap turned on so often and so impulsively as in those days.)

Suddenly she felt how dog-tired and worn-out she was, and how attractive the thought of a couple of weeks' holiday with her parents in Neulohe. That would be really fine: to sleep as long as you liked, do nothing, drink nothing and, above all—for a change—no gentlemen. Besides, you could show yourself off to envious school friends of bygone days as a finished woman-about-town—especially just now when they were working themselves to death over the harvest. Finally, and most important, quite close to Neulohe was Meienburg, where stood an establishment which little Sophie had formerly looked at with horror but which now sheltered her Hans. Suddenly she was seized by a mad longing for him; her whole body was a-tremble. She must go to him, she must live near him, she must sense him once again—at the very least she must see him. It ought to be easy to get into touch with him. Warders were only men after all. . . .

Sophie had stopped cleaning the silver—why do anything now? She'd leave today anyway; finish with the joint! With satisfaction she heard Mathilde's guttural whine interspersed with the sharp, irritated voice of the Countess, and occasionally Herr Quarkus's hoarse tones. If they came and made the slightest criticism there would be a showdown. What a showdown! They would have no option but to get rid of her on the spot—not without her month's wages, though. And that great gawk Mathilde could whistle for her free day—she would have to do all the work herself.

With reluctance Countess Mutzbauer sent her friend Quarkus to fetch Sophie from the kitchen. Certainly she wanted no quarrel with her chambermaid, least of all in front of her friend. There had been, some time ago, rather an odd burglary in the flat, and though Herr Quarkus had generously replaced the lost jewelry, he had wanted then and there to get in touch with the police. It would not be pleasant if Sophie explained the ramifications of that theft. Even more painful, of course, would be an account of certain bedroom visits. Countess Mutzbauer was convinced that her gentleman friend would not be broad-minded in the latter respect; and even though one should never shed tears over a lost lover, there being as many good fish in the sea as ever came out of it, she was terrified of a good thrashing.

But what was to be done? Mathilde, in front of Herr Quarkus, had given an exact account not only of the freedom with which Sophie used her mistress's wardrobe as well as underwear (the Countess had known this all along) but also of an orgy which had taken place in the Mutzbauer apartments during a two-day absence of the mistress, an orgy, besides, in which strange bullies and tarts had taken part, also her own liqueurs, cigarettes, champagne, and—here Herr Quarkus leaped up with a "Damn"—unfortunately the Mutzbauer bed, too.

Against all sense and reason the Countess hoped that Sophie would be reticent. On her side, at least, nothing would be done to make matters worse.

Whereupon in the first three minutes the very worst happened. There was a frightful row, an infernal stench. Emil Quarkus, the cattle dealer, was certainly not squeamish and during his life had had to put up with a lot of unpleasant things; moreover the times were not propitious for cultivating a thin skin. . . . But what these three women said to each other stank more than all the dunghills of his future farms rolled into one.

And Quarkus, too, shouted and stormed. With his own hands he threw them out of the room in turn and, howling with fury, fetched them in again for cross-examination, exculpation. He bashed their heads together, separated the clawing women, telephoned for the police and immediately canceled the call, inspected Sophie's trunks, and had almost at once to rush to her ladyship's bedroom where murder seemed to be in progress. Then, picking up his hat, he marched off with the contemptuous exclamation: "You damned women, you can kiss my arse," left the flat, got into his car, and made the chauffeur stop at once, it having occurred to him that under no circumstances could he leave his jewelry with that vulgar woman. . . .

The upshot was that he sat on a couch utterly exhausted, incapable of anything more. Her cheeks still red and her eyes flashing, Countess Mutzbauer paced up and down and mixed a pick-me-up for her Emil.

"Such vulgar women! All abominable lies, of course. It's good that you dismissed them on the spot, Quarkus." (He had done nothing of the sort.) "You're quite right not to call in the police." (He would dearly have loved to do so.) "In the end your wife would have learned of it, and you know what she is!"

Mathilde was sitting on her hamper in the kitchen, sniveling quietly as she waited for the carrier to fetch it. Then she would go by subway to her brother-in-law who lived off the Warschauer Brücke. Her sister wouldn't be very joyful over this surprise because, as things were, the wage of a streetcar conductor was already insufficient. But, in possession of a fair pile of foreign currency which Quarkus, softened by her good cooking, had obtained for her bit by bit, she felt secure against any sisterly displeasure. As a matter of fact, dismissal at this moment suited Mathilde; she would now have time to do something for her illegitimate offspring, the fifteen-year-old Hans Günther; that morning she had read in the newspapers of his arrest as ringleader of a mutiny in a Berlin institution for young delinquents, which was the reason for her anger when Sophie had annexed her day off. Now she had her free day after all. She was content.

Even more content, however, was Sophie Kowalewski. Through the gathering storm a taxi took her toward the Christian Hostel in Krausenstrasse. Accompanied by gentlemen, Sophie did not object to the most filthy accommodation hotel; but as a young lady traveling alone she was cognizant only of the Christian Hostel. She was going for her summer holiday, her trunks were packed with her ladyship's nicest possessions, she had her wages; also she had sufficient money saved up and she would get in touch with her Hans, perhaps even see him. Yes, she too was content.

Only Herr Quarkus was not quite as happy as the three women. But he was not properly aware of it, and in any case he had to go and buy farms immediately. The mark pursued him faster than any female.

V

Forester Kniebusch walked slowly through the village of Neulohe, his pointer on a lead. One never knew what might happen; most people, anyhow, were incredibly more afraid of a dog than of a man. Old Kniebusch had always disliked going into the village—his house lay a little back from the road on the edge of the forest—and today he was particularly peevish. He had put off as long as practicable the rounding-up of the villagers for the ten o'clock meeting at the village magistrate's, but now that the entire western sky was black with storm (from Berlin, of course; what else ever came from there?) he had to set about it. Needs must; he had to be careful not to offend anybody.

Thank heaven the village of Altlohe didn't come into the picture so far as this secret military business was concerned. Only miners and industrial workers (therefore Spartacists and Communists) lived in Altlohe; that is, thieves who robbed the fields, wood stealers and poachers, in Herr Kniebusch's opinion.

He was quite well aware why he had refused to notice the wood stealers that morning. They were Altlohers who became aggressive on the slightest provocation and openly proclaimed a doctrine akin to the right to steal. Forester Kniebusch was also quite well aware why he had left his rifle at home but taken his dog with him—a weapon only infuriated the people and made them even more dangerous. Still, a dog might mean a torn trouser leg, and trousers were expensive!

Depressed, the forester slunk through the village threatened by the coming storm. "I would like to die peacefully in my bed," he had again said to a wife almost paralyzed by rheumatism. She had nodded. "We are all in God's hands," she had said.

"Oh, you!" he would have liked to reply, for he had been certain a long time that God had nothing to do with all this ghastly confusion. But, after a glance at the colored Lord's Supper on the wall, he had preferred to keep silent. In these days one could not say even to one's own wife what one really thought.

He had pictured his old age differently. If the war and this damnable inflation had not come, he would long ago have been living in his own little house in Meienburg, letting duty and the wood thieves look after themselves, occupied only with his bees. But anyone could easily figure out how simple it was to starve to death on an old-age pension in these days. And as for the savings-bank book (hidden from thieves between the sheets in his wife's linen cupboard), showing a total savings of over 7,000 marks scraped together coin by coin during forty long years of service, that did not bear looking at or thinking of, if tears were not to come at once into the eyes. Had there been no war that sum would have meant a little house in Meienburg, neat as a doll. And then there had been the first mortgage on the magistrate Haase's farm here in Neulohe, a sound investment, for the interest of 4 per cent on the 10,000 marks Kniebusch had advanced was paid promptly. Some of this advance had been inherited, most of it saved; and it yielded 400 marks yearly, which would have been a welcome addition to Kniebusch's old-age pension.

But that was past and done with. Incomprehensibly past and done with. The old man had had to continue running about, working, watching, trying to worm his way between the encroachments of the people and the reprimands of his employer. And this wearied man, so much in need of peace and retirement, was now terribly afraid of having to retire—for what could save the old couple from starving to death? Their two sons had fallen in the war, and their daughter, married to a railway clerk at Landsberg, did not know how to get food enough for herself and her children. Only when a pig was to be killed did she write to her parents, to remind them of the promised share of fat.

And so the old man had to carry on, fawn, flatter and humble himself to avoid dismissal at all costs. And when that fool of a Lieutenant beckoned, he could do nothing but click his heels and reply submissively: "Very good, Herr Lieutenant." How was he to know whether his employer approved or not?

It was dreary walking round the village. The men whom the forester had to see were still in the fields, though it was time for feeding the cattle, nearly six o'clock. Or, sweating, they hurried past him with hardly an acknowledgment. There was not a moment to spare; they must get in all the crops they could before the storm broke.

Thus the forester had to leave his message with their womenfolk, and they, of course, said exactly what they thought. He was undoubtedly crazy, trying to call a meeting at the height of the harvest! He didn't, of course, have such a bad time; he wasn't aching in every limb; he could go for a walk while others worked themselves to death. He got up at six in the morning, their men at half-past two. They had no intention of delivering such a stupid message; he must go and look for bigger fools. They stood with their arms akimbo and the forester got it hot and strong. He had to persuade and beg them to give the message about the meeting at ten o'clock, and when he finally left he was not at all sure whether it would be delivered.

Some women, however, pursed their lips and listened in silence, though with angry, narrowed eyes. Then they turned away, but he heard them mutter that an old man like that should be ashamed to take part in such plottings. Hadn't enough people been killed already in the World War? An old crock like him ought rather to be preparing for a peaceful death.

The forester's face grew ever more troubled, almost bitter, the farther he went, muttering also. He had to give expression to his wrath somehow, and he was accustomed to talking to himself. Otherwise he had nobody in whom he could confide; his wife quoted texts at him on every occasion. He ground his almost toothless jaws in impotent anger. He suffered all the more because he was so helpless.

He arrived at the village square, round which Haase's farm, the grocer's shop, the inn, school and the clergyman's dwelling were grouped. His business was not really with these people. Grocer and innkeeper were much too cautious to associate themselves with a venture which might offend their customers; the organist Friedmann was much too old; and Pastor Lehnich always behaved as if he were not of this world, although he was very good at adding up what was due him. The village magistrate must be in the secret, however, otherwise the meeting would not have been convened at his house.

Nevertheless Forester Kniebusch stood irresolutely in the square, looking across at Haase's farm; it might be a good idea to face up to the magistrate for once and discuss the mortgage and its interest. But before he could decide on this a window in the inn flew open and the ugly head of little Black Meier popped out, spectacles glittering and face flushed. "Well, Kniebusch, old hen, come along and drink to my departure from Neulohe," he shouted.

The forester was really not in a mood for drinking, and knew, too, that Black Meier, when drunk, was as vicious as an old bull; but the greeting sounded very much like news, and he could never resist that. He had to know everything, so that he could trim his course accordingly. Therefore he entered the inn, where his dog crawled under the table, prepared to wait silently with canine submissiveness for one hour or four, whichever it might be. The forester knocked on the table warningly. "I've no money on me!" he said.

"Neither have I," grinned Black Meier, who had been drinking hard. "In spite of that I'm going to treat you, Kniebusch. And willingly. They're all out in the fields and so I've taken a bottle of cognac from the buffet, but I can get you some beer if you prefer it."

The forester shuddered at the possible consequences of such arbitrary behavior. "No, thanks, Meier. I'll have nothing."

Immediately Meier flushed a deeper crimson. "Oh, you think I pinched it? You think I won't pay for what I drink? I'll have none of that, Kniebusch. Just tell me of one occasion when I've pinched anything, or . . ."

The alternative was never divulged, for the forester immediately assured him that everything was in order, and that he would like a cognac.

"A cognac's nothing at all," shouted little Meier, and in spite of mild opposition, he poured out with professional skill a glass of beer and fetched a box of cigars. For himself he brought a packet of cigarettes.

"Your health, Kniebusch. May our children get long necks!"

The forester knitted his bushy brows at this toast, which reminded him of his two fallen sons. But it was futile to protest to such a man as Black Meier. "What has happened since midday to make us celebrate your departure?" he asked instead.

Meier turned glum. "The storm," he growled. "A miserable filthy Berlin storm. We never get a storm with a west wind. But we do today."

"Yes, there'll be a heavy downpour in about ten minutes," said Kniebusch and looked toward the dark window. "Didn't you bring in the crops? The whole village is working at it."

"I can see that, too, you great ass!" Meier shouted angrily. And it would really have been difficult not to notice it—another heavily loaded wagon had just raced across the village square and disappeared into Haase's farm.

"But it is not certain that the Rittmeister will sack you," Kniebusch remarked consolingly. "Of course, in your place I'd have got the crops in."

"If you were me you'd be so clever that you'd have been in two places at the same time," Black Meier screamed furiously. He drank hastily, then spoke more calmly. "Any fool can be wise after the event. Why didn't you tell me at midday that you'd have got the crops in, eh?" He smiled with a superior air, yawned, and drank again. Then he looked at the forester with screwed-up eyes, winking mysteriously, and said with meaning: "Besides, the Rittmeister won't chuck me out only on *that* account."

"No?" replied the forester. "By the way, did you notice whether Haase is in his farmyard?"

"Yes," said Black Meier. "He went in a moment ago with the Lieutenant."

This did not suit Kniebusch at all. If the Lieutenant was there, then it would be no use speaking with Haase about the mortgage. And yet it was absolutely necessary. In five days' time the half-yearly interest was due again, and he could not be put off with a two-hundred-mark note slipped into his hand.

"Are you deaf in both ears, forester?" shouted Meier. "I've been asking you how old Vi is."

"The young Fräulein? She was fifteen last May."

"Oh, Lord! Oh, Lord!" Meier pretended to lament. "Then the Rittmeister is sure to chuck me out."

"Why?" The ever-wakeful curiosity of the tale-bearer and spy stung Kniebusch. "What do you mean?"

"Oh, don't bother!" Meier made a magnificently disdainful gesture. "You'll learn everything soon enough." He had another drink and looked at the forester through his narrowed eyes, grinning impudently. "But the girl has a magnificent bosom, I can tell you that, Kniebusch, old rake."

"What girl?" asked the forester, dumbfounded. He could hardly believe his ears.

"Well, that young thing Vi," said Black Meier negligently. "A sweet little bit, I can tell you. What a welcome she gave me a short time ago in her deck chair. On the roof of the kitchen annex, mind you, with only a bathing costume on. And then she undid her shoulder-straps—like this—and then—well, don't let us talk about it. Once a gentleman always a gentleman."

"You're mad, Meier," remonstrated Kniebusch. "You're boasting. You're drunk."

"Oh, yes, I'm boasting!" said Black Meier, with a show of indifference. "Oh, yes, I'm drunk! But if anybody asks you, Kniebusch, then you can tell him from me that here"—he pointed to his breast well beneath the armpit—"Vi has a tiny brown mole, and it's a sweet cuddlesome spot, Kniebusch, I tell you that in confidence."

Meier looked expectantly at the forester. "That you've seen her in her bathing dress, Meier, I can well believe," said Kniebusch. "Several times lately she has been lying about like that on the kitchen roof and Madam won't have it; I know that from Armgard the cook. But that she should have behaved as you suggest . . . no, Meier, I can't swallow that. You must tell that to a bigger fool than Kniebusch." The forester grinned conceitedly, pushed away his tumbler and rose. "Come along, Cæsar!"

"You don't believe me?" Black Meier shouted, leaping up. "You've no idea, Kniebusch, how crazy women are about me. I can have them all, all of them. And little Vi . . ."

"No, no, Meier," said Kniebusch smiling contemptuously and making a deadly enemy of little Meier for life. "You're all right for a dairy maid or poultry maid, perhaps. But for the young Fräulein! No, Meier, you're just drunk."

"Shall I prove it to you?" Meier almost screamed, beside himself with alcohol, wrath and humiliation. "Shall I show it to you in black and white? There, can you read, you silly idiot? There! Your young Fräulein wrote that to me." He had pulled the letter out of his pocket and opened it. "Can you read? There. 'Your Violet.' 'Your' underlined, you gaping owl. There, read: 'Dearest! Most dearest!! My one and only!!!' See the exclamation marks? There! No, there's no need for you to read it all—only this. 'I love you sooo much!'" He repeated it: "'Sooo.' Well, is that love? What do you say now?" He stood there triumphant. His thick lips trembled, his eyes were aflame, his face was flushed.

But the effect of his words was not at all what he had expected. Forester Kniebusch stepped from him toward the door. "No, Meier," he said. "You oughtn't to have shown me that letter and told me all that. What a swine you are, Meier! No, I wish I hadn't seen it; I don't want to know anything about it. It's as much as my life's worth. No, Meier," and Kniebusch looked with open hostility in his faded eyes, "if I were you I'd pack my trunk and clear out without waiting for notice, and get away as far as possible. If the Rittmeister learns . . ."

"Don't talk so big, you old rabbit," said Meier peevishly, but put the letter back into his pocket. "The Rittmeister won't hear about it. If you keep your trap shut . . ."

"I'll keep my mouth shut," said the forester and really meant it. "I'm having nothing to do with it, believe me. But you won't keep *your* mouth shut. . . . No, Meier, be sensible for once and clear out. And quickly at that—Ah, it's really starting now."

The two had been paying no attention to the weather and the increasing darkness of the sky. But now a flash of lightning made the inn parlor as bright as midday, a crash of thunder deafened them, and the rain came pelting down as from a thousand sluice gates.

"You aren't rushing out into the storm?"

"I am," replied the forester hurriedly. "I'm running across to Haase's. I wouldn't like to stay here." And was already gone.

Meier saw him disappear into the rain. About the parlor hung the smell of spirits, sour beer and dirt. Slowly Meier opened one window after another. When he passed the table where they had been sitting he involuntarily took hold of the bottle and raised it to his lips, shuddered at its smell, and let the spirit gurgle out on to the village square. Returning to the table, he lit a cigarette and withdrew the letter from his pocket. The envelope was now damaged beyond use. With the cautious movements of the half-drunk he laid the letter on the table. It was crumpled and he tried to smooth it out. What on earth am I to do? What on earth am I to do? he thought wearily.

The letter was growing wet beneath his smoothing hand. He looked. It had been placed in a pool of cognac and the writing was quite smudged.

What on earth am I to do? he thought again.

He stuffed the messy scrawl into his pocket. Then he took his stick and went into the pouring rain. He must go to bed, sleep himself sober.

VI

Kniebusch hurried as quickly as he could through the heavy rain to Haase's farmstead. However unpleasant it was for an old man to get wet to his skin, it was ten times better than sitting with that fellow, Black Meier, and listening to smut.

He stopped on the sheltered side of Haase's barn. In his present state he could not appear before the magistrate. Panting, he wiped his face meticulously and tried to comb out his wet beard. But while he did all this mechanically he was thinking, just as Black Meier yonder: What on earth am I to do? What on earth am I to do?

Once again he felt aggrieved that there was not a soul to whom he could pour out his heart. If he could have told only one person about this crazy business he would have felt easier. But as it was, what he had heard rankled till it was hardly bearable. It was like a sore place on a finger against which one kept on knocking; it was like an eczema which one had to scratch, whether it drew blood or not.

Forester Kniebusch knew from many a bitter experience how dangerous was his growing propensity to gossip; it had often caused great mischief and involved him in the most unpleasant scenes. In this case, however, there was really nothing much to tell—only the drunken talk of a fellow who was mad after women, little Meier.

Having dried himself in the shelter of Haase's barn he was about to enter the house when the whole thing was revealed to him: he saw Meier in the inn pulling the letter out of his pocket, tearing it open, reading it . . .

Kniebusch gave a long and high whistle, although it actually took his breath away. His dog by his side, shivering with the damp cold, started and pointed, forepaw raised as if he smelt game. But Forester Kniebusch went on further than his dog; he'd spied the black-coated hog, the wretched boar, in its damp hide and put a bullet through its head. Black Meier had told a lie. "It isn't possible otherwise," he muttered to himself. "This chap with his blubber lips and our young Fräulein—no, I couldn't swallow that. And it wasn't necessary to swallow it, either. The foolish braggart and liar thinks I don't see through him. Tears the letter open before my eyes, yet already knows what is written in it. Tells me he has just been with Fräulein Violet and has got a letter from her in his pocket. Of course she's given him a letter, but to deliver to someone else, and the fellow's read it on the quiet. Yes, I must think this matter over quietly and thoroughly. I shall be surprised if I don't get to the bottom of it all, and most surprised if I don't use it as a rope to hang you with, little Meier. You won't be able to call me a rabbit and gaping owl much longer. We'll see then who'll be in a funk and gape!" Kniebusch turned round and faced the inn. But the inn was not to be seen, because the rain was so heavy.

It's better not to do anything rash, he reflected. The matter had to be considered carefully, for obviously he must so manage things as to get into Fräulein Violet's good books. She might be very useful to him one of these days.

Thereupon Kniebusch whistled shrilly the call, "Quick march, advance" and marched off, straight into the magistrate's living room. He didn't even leave the dog on the brick floor of the kitchen as usual, but let it make muddy circles with its wet paws on the waxed and polished floor. So sure of victory was he.

But in the living room he got a shock, for not only was the tall Haase sitting there, but in the hollow in the middle of the old sofa lounged the Herr Lieutenant as large as life, his old field cap on the crocheted elbow rest, and he himself shabby and unkempt. He was doing himself well, though, with a large cup of coffee and fried eggs and bacon, and soaking pieces of bread in the fat, like a plain honest countryman. But six o'clock in the evening was really not quite the right time to eat fried eggs.

"Order executed," reported the forester standing to attention, as he did to anybody he believed invested with authority.

"Stand at ease," ordered the Lieutenant. And then, quite friendly, a big piece of egg on his tin fork; "Well, forester, still running about on your old legs? The orders passed on and carried out? Everybody at home?"

"That's just it," said the forester dolefully, and told of his experiences in the village, and what Frau Pieplow and Frau Paplow had said.

"Old fool!" The Lieutenant calmly went on with his meal. "Then you'll have to leg it through the village again, when the men are at home, understand? To tell the women such things! I always said there's no fool like an old one." And he went on eating.

"Yes, Herr Lieutenant," said the forester obediently, concealing his fury. He might very well ask this young chap what right he had to snap at him, and why he was entitled to give him orders—but it wasn't worth while, he'd leave it. Instead, he turned to the tall and wrinkled Haase who had been sitting in his big chair as silent as usual, listening without turning a hair. Kniebusch spoke to him not at all kindly. "Ah, Haase, since I'm here I'd like to ask you about my interest. It's due in five days' time and I must know what you intend to do."

"Don't you know?" asked Haase and looked nervously at the Lieutenant, who, however, seemed to be interested in nothing but his fried eggs and the bits of bread which he was chasing across the plate. "All that's set down in the mortgage."

"But, Haase," entreated the forester, "we don't want to quarrel, old people like us."

"Why should we quarrel, Kniebusch?" asked Haase surprised. "You receive what is due to you and, besides, I'm not as old as you are by a long way."

"My ten thousand marks," said the forester in a trembling voice, "which I lent you on your farm was good prewar money—it took me twenty years to scrape it together. And on the last rent day you gave me a bit of paper—I still have it at home in a drawer. Not a stamp or a nail have I been able to buy with it."

Kniebusch could not help himself; this time it was not the infirmity of age but an honest grief which brought the tears to his eyes. He was looking at Haase, who slowly rubbed his hands together between his knees and was just about to answer when a curt voice from the sofa called "Forester!"

The forester wheeled round, torn from his grief and entreaty. "Yes, Herr Lieutenant?"

"Matches, forester."

The Lieutenant had finished eating. He had soaked up the last smear of fat from his plate, swallowed the last dregs of coffee. And now he lay stretched out on Haase's sofa in his muddy boots, his eyes shut. A cigarette in his mouth, he demanded a light.

The forester gave it him. With the first puff of smoke the Lieutenant looked straight into the tearful eyes of the old man. "Well, what's the matter?" he asked. "I almost believe you're crying, Kniebusch?"

"It's only the smoke, Herr Lieutenant," replied the embarrassed forester.

"Well, that's all right, then," said the Lieutenant, shutting his eyes and turning over.

"I really don't know why I listen to your eternal bleating, Kniebusch," declared Haase. "According to the mortgage deed you're to get two hundred marks. Last time I gave you a thousand-mark note, and because you had no change I let you keep the lot."

"I couldn't buy a nail with it," repeated the forester doggedly.

"And this time I won't be hard on you, either. I've already got a ten-thousand-mark note ready for you, and you needn't give me any change. I'm like that, although ten thousand marks are as much as the entire mortgage."

"But, Haase!" cried the forester. "That's simply adding insult to injury. You know quite well that this ten-thousand-mark note is worth much less than a thousand marks six months ago. And I gave you my good money!" Grief almost broke his heart.

"What has that to do with me?" cried Haase angrily. "Did I turn your good money into bad? You must apply to the authorities in Berlin—it isn't my fault. What's written is written."

"I only ask for justice," begged the forester. "I've saved for twenty years, denying myself everything, and now you offer me a bum-wiper in exchange."

"So?" said Haase venomously. "You say that, Kniebusch? What about the year of the drought when I couldn't scrape the money together? Who said: 'What's written is written'? And what about the time when fat pigs cost eighteen marks per hundredweight and I said: 'The interest is too high, you must reduce it'? Who answered: 'Money is money, and if you don't pay, then I'll distrain on you'? Who said that? Was it you or somebody else?"

"But that was quite different, Haase," said the forester dejectedly. "There was very little in it, really, but today you don't want to give me anything at all. I don't ask you to give me the full value, but if you gave me twenty hundredweights of rye instead of the two hundred marks—"

"Twenty hundredweights of rye!" Haase laughed loudly. "I believe you've gone mad. Twenty hundredweights of rye! That's more than twenty million marks."

"And yet not nearly as much as you ought to pay me," insisted the forester. "In peace time it would be nearer thirty hundredweights."

"Yes, in peace time," said the magistrate, quite ruffled, for he realized that he could not easily rid himself of the forester, who now seriously threatened his purse. "But we haven't got peace now, but In-fla-tion—and everyone must look after himself. Anyway, Kniebusch, I've had quite enough of your eternal bleating. You're also for ever gossiping about us in the village, and not long ago you said at the baker's that the magistrate didn't pay his interest, but could afford to eat roast goose. Don't argue, Kniebusch—you did say it; I hear everything. But tomorrow I'll cycle to Meienburg and I'll send you your interest, through my solicitor, two hundred marks exactly, and in addition you'll get notice of repayment of the mortgage, and on New Year's Eve you shall get your money, ten thousand marks exactly—and I don't care how little you can buy with it. Yes, I'll do that, Kniebusch, for I've had enough of your eternal moan about your savings. I'll do it, you see. . . ."

"You'll do nothing of the kind, Haase," came a sharp voice from the sofa, "and it will have to do." The Lieutenant was sitting upright, wide awake, the cigarette still alight between his lips. "On the last day of the month you'll give the forester his twenty hundredweights of rye, and we'll draw up a contract in writing in which you bind yourself to make the same payment as long as this muck called money is current."

"No, Herr Lieutenant, I won't do it," said the magistrate resolutely. "You can't order me to. Anything else, but not that. If I tell this to the Major—"

"He'll give you a kick in the behind and throw you out. Or put you up against a wall as a traitor—everything is possible, Haase. Look here, my man," cried the Lieutenant briskly, jumping up and buttonholing the magistrate. "You know our aims and objects, yet you, a veteran soldier, want to take advantage up to the last moment of the swinish actions of the scum in Berlin. You ought to be ashamed of yourself, Haase." He went back to the table, took another cigarette and bawled: "A light, forester!"

Kniebusch, a thousandfold relieved and cringingly grateful, rushed up to him. Giving the Lieutenant a light he whispered: "It ought to be written down also that the mortgage can't be terminated. Otherwise he'll pay me off with the rotten money—and it's all my savings." Self-pity overwhelmed him, gratitude at this unexpected rescuer made him abject. Kniebusch wept again.

The Lieutenant observed this with distaste. "Kniebusch, old water-tap," he said, "clear out—or else I won't say another word. Do you think I care about you? You and your miserable cash mean nothing to me. It's the Cause; the Cause must be kept clean."

The bewildered forester went over to the window. Wasn't his case as clear as daylight? Why must he be snapped at?

The Lieutenant turned to the magistrate. "Well, what do you say about it, Haase?" he asked, puffing at his cigarette.

"Herr Lieutenant, why should I be placed in a worse position than the others? In this district they are all clearing off their mortgages. And Kniebusch is not a person who deserves special consideration."

This time the lieutenant replied, "It isn't a question of Kniebusch: it's you, Haase. You can't fill your pockets through the swindling of the Berliners and overthrow them because of those same swindles. That's as clear as daylight; every child understands that; you understand it, too. And in there," he tapped Haase lightly on his waistcoat and the magistrate draw away uneasily, "in there you know quite well that you're in the wrong."

A terrible struggle was taking place in the other's heart. In the course of a long, strenuous life he had learned to hold on to what he had got, but he had not learned how to be generous. At last he said slowly: "I'll write that I won't repay the mortgage and that I'll pay him the value of ten hundredweights of rye every six months. . . . The farm doesn't yield more, Herr Lieutenant, times are bad."

"Shame!" said the Lieutenant in a low voice and looking very gravely at the old man. "You don't want to burden your conscience with the entire guilt, but you'll profit by the smaller guilt all right, eh? Look at me, man! I'm not much to write home about, but there is one thing . . . I possess nothing at all, Haase; for five years I've possessed nothing except what I stand up in. Sometimes I get my pay, sometimes I don't. It's all one to me. If you believe in a cause, then you give up everything for it—or you don't believe in it. If that's the case, we've no more to say to one another."

Haase was silent for a long time. At last he said peevishly: "You're a young man, and I'm an old one. I've a farm, Herr Lieutenant, and I must look after it. We Haases have been living here since time immemorial, and I wouldn't like to meet my father and grandfather in the hereafter if I'd played fast and loose with the farm."

"And if you retain it by fraud, that wouldn't matter at all?"

"It isn't fraud," cried the magistrate heatedly. "Everybody does it. Besides, Herr Lieutenant," and his face wrinkled in a grin, "we're human beings, after all, and not angels; my father now and again sold a horse as a good draught animal when it wasn't. We are cheated and we cheat for once—I think that God does forgive, too; it isn't just a bit of writing in the Bible."

The Lieutenant had already started another cigarette. What the magistrate thought about God didn't interest him. He was more concerned that things should first improve in this world. "A match, forester!" he ordered, and the forester, who had been playing with the tassels of the curtains, sprang forward.

"Take cover," ordered the Lieutenant, and Kniebusch jumped back into the curtains.

"If you don't do what I tell you," declared the Lieutenant stubbornly—for he could be just as obstinate as an old farmer—"if you don't do what is the simple duty of every decent fellow, I've no use for you in our Cause."

"I always thought *you* needed us," rejoined the magistrate, unmoved.

"And if you aren't with us, Haase," the Lieutenant continued, undaunted, "and we take command in a month or two, do you think that matters will turn out so very much in your favor?"

"Lord!" said Haase, unperturbed. "If you're going to punish everybody who hasn't been with you, Herr Lieutenant, there will be a deal of weeping and wailing in all the villages. And you won't be appointed Minister of Agriculture, either, Herr Lieutenant," he mocked.

"All right," said the Lieutenant curtly, and picked up his cap from the sofa. "So you don't want to, Haase?"

"I have said what I'll do," repeated the other stubbornly. "I won't give notice and I'll give the equivalent of ten hundredweights of rye."

"We've finished with each other, Haase," said the Lieutenant. "Come along, forester; I'll tell you where the meeting's taking place this evening. Not here, anyhow."

Haase would have liked to say something more, but he pressed his thin lips together. The Lieutenant was no bargainer; you could not beat him down; he demanded everything or nothing. But since the magistrate did not wish to grant him everything, he remained silent.

The Lieutenant stood in the doorway of the house and looked across at the farm. Behind him, silent, stood Forester Kniebusch and his dog. The Lieutenant might have been reluctant to step out into the lessening, but still sufficiently heavy, rain. But he wasn't thinking of the rain at all; he was looking absent-mindedly at the open barn floor, where, before knocking off for the day, they were hurriedly unloading the last cartful of rye saved from the storm.

"Herr Lieutenant," said Kniebusch cautiously, "you could, perhaps, hold the meeting at Farmer Bentzien's."

"Bentzien, yes, Bentzien," said the Lieutenant thoughtfully, and watched the unloading. He could hear the rustle of the dry straw. He had not been in the Great War—too young for that—but he had served in the Baltic Provinces and Upper Silesia and had learned the lesson that tenacity of purpose decides the issue. He had told the magistrate that they had finished with each other; Haase might think so, but the Lieutenant hadn't yet finished with him. "Benzine," he muttered. "Wait for me here, forester," he said hastily.

And with that he went into the house again.

Less than five minutes afterwards the forester was called inside. Haase sat at the table and wrote a confirmation that he forewent his right of extinguishing the mortgage and that he pledged himself to pay an interest of forty hundred-weights of rye in two half-yearly installments. The magistrate was inscrutable, and the Lieutenant was inscrutable, too. The forester could have sobbed with joy, but was afraid to, lest the agreement be rescinded. So he hid his feelings, with the result that he made a face like red lacquer nutcrackers.

"So that's that," said the Lieutenant and scrawled his name as witness. "And now go and call the people together, Kniebusch. Here, of course! Farmer Bentzien? Benzine doesn't come into consideration now!"

And he laughed maliciously. The magistrate, however, remained silent.

The conversation between Lieutenant and magistrate had been very brief.

"Tell me, Haase," the Lieutenant had said on re-entering, "it has just occurred to me—what about the fire insurance?"

"The fire insurance?" asked Haase dumbfounded.

"Yes, of course." The Lieutenant spoke impatiently, as if a child ought to understand the reason for his question. "How much are you insured for?"

"Forty thousand."

"Paper marks, what?"

"Ye-e-e-es." Very long drawn-out.

"I think that's about forty pounds of rye?"

"Ye-e-e-es."

"Isn't that damnably careless? With a barn full of dry hay and straw?"

"But there isn't any other insurance," the magistrate had cried despairingly.

"Oh, yes there is, Haase," the Lieutenant had said. "That is, when you've called in Kniebusch and written down what I tell you."

Whereupon the forester was called in.

VII

Retired Oberleutnant von Studmann, reception manager, had a very unpleasant experience that afternoon in the hotel. About three o'clock, at a time when travelers do not arrive by train, there appeared in the entrance hall a rather tall, powerfully built gentleman, faultlessly dressed in English cloth, a pigskin case in his hand. "A single room on the first floor, with bath but no telephone," he demanded.

He was told that all the rooms in the hotel had telephones. The gentleman, who seemed to be a little over thirty, could contort his pale, clean-cut face into most horrifying grimaces. This he did now to such effect that the porter started back.

Studmann came closer. "If you wish it, the telephone could of course be removed from the room. At any rate . . ."

"I do wish it!" the stranger barked. Then, without any perceptible change of mood, he asked gently that the electric bell in his room should also be disconnected. "I dislike modern technical apparatus," he added frowningly.

Von Studmann bowed without speaking. He was expecting a demand that the electric light be cut off, but the gentleman either did not regard electric light as belonging to modern technical apparatus, or he had overlooked the point. Preceded by the bedroom waiter with the registration form, he went upstairs muttering, followed by a page with the pigskin case.

Von Studmann had been in a metropolitan caravanserai long enough not to be surprised at any request from a visitor. His composure was not easily ruffled; there had been the South American lady, traveling alone, who had screamed for a commode for her little monkey; there had been the distinguished elderly gentleman who, emerging from his room in pajamas at two o'clock in the morning, had requested in a whisper that he be furnished with a lady, at once, please. ("Don't pretend; we're all men.") Nevertheless something about this new visitor warned Studmann to be careful. Ordinarily the hotel was patronized by ordinary people, and ordinary people prefer rather to read of scandals in the newspapers than to experience them. The reception manager's instinct warned him. He was not affected so much by the silly requests as by the grimacing and shouting, and the man's restless glances, now arrogant, now furtive.

However, the reports which von Studmann received a little later were satisfactory. The page had been given in tip an entire American dollar; the visitor's pocketbook had been extremely well lined. The bedroom waiter brought the registration form. The gentleman had inscribed himself as "Reichsfreiherr Baron von Bergen." Süskind, the waiter, had also taken the precaution of asking to see the stranger's passport, which he was entitled to do in accordance with a regulation issued by the police. The passport—an internal one, issued by the district authority at Wurzen—seemed to be in order. The Gotha Almanac, which was then consulted, confirmed at once that there were really Reichsfreiherren von Bergen; they were domiciled in Saxony.

"So everything is all right, Süskind," said von Studmann and shut the Gotha.

Süskind shook his head doubtfully. "I'm not sure," he hazarded. "The gentleman is queer."

"What do you mean by queer? An impostor? If he pays it doesn't matter to *us*, Süskind."

"An impostor? Certainly not. But I think he's cracked."

"Cracked?" repeated von Studmann. Süskind had had the same impression as he himself. "Nonsense, Süskind. Perhaps a bit nervous. Or drunk?"

"Nervous? Drunk? Certainly not. He's cracked."

"But why? Has he behaved in an extraordinary way?"

"Not at all," admitted Süskind readily. "That grimacing and tomfoolery mean nothing. Some people think they can impress us that way."

"Well, then?"

"One has a hunch, Herr Director. When the woven-fabric merchant hanged himself in Room 43 I had a feeling . . ."

"For God's sake, Süskind, don't talk of the devil or you'll see his imps. Well, I must get on. Keep me informed, and be sure to keep an eye on the gentleman."

Von Studmann had a very strenuous afternoon. The new dollar rate had not only necessitated refixing all the prices, but the entire budget had to be calculated anew. Studmann sat on pins in the directors' boardroom. Vogel, the managing director, debated laboriously and at length, whether they should not, as a precaution against further dollar increases, add a certain amount to the present charges so as not to become "impoverished."

"We must maintain our stores and establishment, gentlemen. Maintain them." And he set forth that the stock of alabaster soft soap, for instance, had fallen in the past year from seventeen hundredweights to half a hundredweight.

In spite of his superior's disapproving glances, Studmann kept on dashing out into the hall. From four o'clock onwards the whole staff had to deal with the reception of a rush of incoming guests, and this stream met and blocked another stream of people who had suddenly made up their minds to depart.

Studmann gave only a brief nod when Süskind whispered that the gentleman in No. 37 had taken a bath, gone to bed, and had then ordered a bottle of cognac and one of champagne to be taken to his room.

So he's a drinker, he thought. If he starts a row I'll send the hotel doctor up to give him a sleeping draught.

And he hurried away.

When he next left the boardroom again, the managing director was holding forth on the ruinous effect preserved eggs were having on the hotel trade. Nevertheless, under present conditions, it should be considered whether or not a certain stock . . . since the supply of new-laid eggs . . . and unfortunately also of chilled eggs . . .

Idiot, thought von Studmann, rushing away, and was surprised to find himself so irritable. He ought to be used to all this dawdling by now. It must be the storm.

Süskind stopped him. "It's starting, Herr Director," he said, his face lugubrious above his black tie.

"What's starting? Be quick about it, Süskind. I've no time to waste."

"The gentleman in No. 37, Herr Director," said Süskind reproachfully. "He says there's a slug in the champagne."

"A slug?" Von Studmann could not help laughing. "Nonsense, Süskind, he's pulling your leg. How could there be a slug in the champagne? I've never heard of such a thing."

"But there *is* a slug in it," Süskind continued, worried. "I saw it with my own eyes. A great big black slug."

"You saw it?" Studmann suddenly became serious. He began to think. That there should be slugs in the champagne in this establishment was quite impossible. "We don't sell adulterated champagne here. He must have put it in himself by a trick. Take him another bottle and don't charge him. Here—for the butler." And he scribbled a wine slip.

"Watch him, Süskind, see that he doesn't play us a trick again."

Süskind bowed his utterly perplexed head. "Wouldn't you like to go yourself? I'm afraid. . . ."

"Nonsense, Süskind. I've no time for such rubbish. If you can't settle it yourself, take the butler with you as a witness, or anyone else you like."

Studmann was already gone. In the hall the famous iron magnate, Brachwede, was shouting that he had rented an apartment for ten millions daily, and on the bill he had been charged fifteen. The magnate had to be informed of what he already knew, that is, the rise in the dollar. Here Studmann had to persuade, there to smile, elsewhere to give a stern hint to a page to be more careful; he had to superintend the transportation of a crippled lady in the lift; to refuse three telephone calls. . . .

The mournful Süskind stood behind him again.

"Herr Director. Please, Herr Director," he begged in a truly old-fashioned nerve-racking stage whisper.

"What's the matter now, Süskind?"

"The gentleman in 37, Herr Director. . . ."

"What is it this time? What is it? Another slug in the champagne?"

"Herr Tuchmann (this was the butler) is just opening the eleventh bottle—there were slugs in all of them."

"In all of them?" von Studmann almost shouted. Feeling that the hotel guests had their eyes on him he lowered his voice. "Have you gone mad too, Süskind?"

Süskind nodded gloomily. "The gentleman is screaming that he won't stand black slugs, he's screaming. . . ."

"Come along," Studmann cried and rushed up to the first floor, heedless of the dignified demeanor which the assistant director of so distinguished an establishment ought to maintain in every situation. Süskind, the woe-begone, followed him. Together they sprinted through the puzzled guests—and at once the rumor circulated, whence nobody knew, that the coloratura soprano, Contessa Vagenza, who was to have appeared that evening in the big concert hall, had just given birth to a child.

They arrived simultaneously at No. 37. In view of the information he had received, Studmann was of the opinion that he need not concern himself with time-wasting formalities—he knocked and entered without waiting for an invitation, closely followed by Süskind, who was careful to shut the baize inner door so as to deaden the noise of a possible dispute.

The room was a large one, the electric light full on. The curtains of the two windows were closely drawn. The door leading to the bathroom was shut—also locked, as was to be discovered later. The key had been removed.

The guest was lying in the wide modern bed of chromium steel. The sickly yellow of his skin, which had so struck Studmann in the hall, looked more ghastly still against the white of the pillows. He wore crimson pajamas made of what looked like a costly brocade, its thick yellow embroidery seeming pale against the bilious face. One powerful hand, displaying a strikingly handsome signet ring, lay on the blue silk counterpane. The other was hidden beneath the cover. Von Studmann saw, too, on the table which had been pushed up to the bed, a display of cognac and champagne bottles which astounded him. A much larger number must have been brought up than the eleven mentioned by Süskind. At the same time he realized that the over-anxious waiter had not been content with the butler as a witness; near the table stood a small but embarrassed group of people consisting of a page, the chambermaid, an elevator boy and a gray female who was probably in temporary employment as a charwoman.

For a moment Studmann wondered whether he should, as a preliminary, turn out these witnesses to a possible scandal, but a glance at the guest's face, which was twitching uncontrollably, showed him that speed was called for. So he went up to the bed, introduced himself with a bow, and waited for results.

At once the twitching stopped. "Very unpleasant." The guest spoke through his nose in that arrogant military manner which von Studmann thought had become extinct long ago. "Extremely unpleasant for—you. Slugs in the champagne—filthy."

"I see no slugs," said von Studmann after a glance at the champagne glasses and bottles. What perturbed him was not this silly complaint, but the look of unbridled hatred in the guest's dark eyes, eyes which were impudent and cowardly at the same time, an expression Studmann had never seen before.

"They *are* there!" screamed the guest so suddenly that everybody started. He was sitting up in bed, one hand clawing at the quilt, the other still covered.

On your guard, said von Studmann to himself. He's up to something!

"They've all seen the slugs. Take this bottle; no, that one."

With an appearance of unconcern Studmann held the bottle up to the light. He was convinced that the champagne was quite in order, and that the guest knew it as well as he did. For some reason which Studmann did not know yet, but would probably soon learn, he must have bamboozled the waiter and the butler.

"Look out, Herr Director," Süskind shouted. Studmann wheeled round. But it was too late. Absorbed in looking at the bottle, Studmann had lost sight of the guest who, with incredible deftness, had slipped out of bed and locked the door. He stood now with the key in one hand, a revolver in the other.

Von Studmann had been some years at the Front—a weapon aimed at him was not unduly disturbing. What did frighten him was the expression of hatred and despair on the mysterious stranger's face. At the same time this face was without a grimace, but it smiled, and a very sneering smile it was, too.

"What's the meaning of this?" Studmann asked curtly.

"It means," said the guest in low but distinct tones, "that the room is now under my control. Who disobeys will be shot."

"Are you after our money? The result would be hardly worth your while. Are you not the Baron von Bergen?"

"Waiter," said the stranger. He stood there, magnificent in the pajamas of crimson and yellow. "Waiter, pour cognac into seven champagne glasses. I shall count up to three and anyone who has not emptied his glass by then will stop a bullet. Now, hurry!"

With a look of entreaty toward von Studmann, Süskind obeyed.

"Why this unseemly jest?" von Studmann asked indignantly.

"You're to drink," said the hospitable one. "One—two—three—drink, will you. Drink up!"

He was shouting again.

The others looked at Studmann. Studmann hesitated. . . .

The stranger shouted again. "Empty your glasses!" He shot, and it was not only the women who screamed. Alone, von Studmann would have risked a struggle with the man, but he checked himself in consideration for the distracted people present and the hotel's reputation.

He turned round and remarked calmly: "Drink, then," smiling encouragement at the anxious faces; and himself drank.

There were several gulps of cognac in each glass. Studmann got rid of his quickly, but he heard the others behind him choking and panting.

"You must drink it all up," said the stranger aggressively. "Who doesn't is to be shot."

Von Studmann couldn't turn round, he had to keep an eye on the guest. He was still hoping that the man would look away for a moment and thus make it possible for him to snatch the weapon.

"You sent your bullet into the ceiling," he said politely. "I must thank you for your consideration. May I ask why we're to get drunk here?"

"I don't want to shoot, though I don't mind either way. What I do want is that you should get drunk. Nobody will leave this room alive until every drop of alcohol has been swallowed. Waiter, pour out the champagne."

"That's it," said von Studmann, who was determined to keep the conversation going. "That's what I understood. But I am interested to know why you want us to get drunk."

"Because I like my little joke. Now drink."

Someone from behind pushed a champagne glass into Studmann's hand. He drank. "Oh," he said, "because it amuses you? All right." And then as nonchalantly as possible: "I presume you know that you're insane?"

And the other just as imperturbably: "For six years I've been declared incapable of managing my own affairs and have been put into a loony house. Waiter, now let's have say half a glass of cognac. I don't want to hurry you. I want the pleasure to last longer," he explained. And again imperturbably: "I couldn't stand the shooting at the Front. They were shooting only at me. Since then I shoot alone. Drink!"

Von Studmann drank, and felt the alcohol rising like a fine mist into his brain. Without turning his head, he saw, out of the corner of his eye, Süskind at the other end of the room stealing toward the bathroom door. But the Baron had also seen him. "Unfortunately locked," he said, smiling, and Süskind, with a regretful movement of his shoulders, vanished out of the assistant director's range of vision.

Von Studmann heard a woman behind him gasp and the men whispering. "Look out, look out!" something was saying within him. Then his head was quite clear again.

"I see," he said. "But how do we come to have the honor of drinking with you in this hotel if you are put away in an institution?"

"Cleared out," the Baron laughed. "They're such fools. Won't the old chap curse when he fetches me back! I made a fine job of it, apart from the attendant whose nut I cracked. It's going too slowly," he muttered peevishly. "Much too slowly. Another cognac, waiter. A full glass."

"I'd prefer champagne," Studmann hazarded.

It was a mistake.

"Cognac," the visitor screamed. "Cognac! Who doesn't drink cognac will be shot. It's all the same to me!" he shouted significantly to Studmann. "Under paragraph fifty-one I can't be punished. I'm the Reichsfreiherr Baron von Bergen. No policeman can touch me. I'm insane. Drink!"

This is going badly, thought von Studmann desperately as the oily stuff trickled down his throat. The women are already laughing and giggling—in five minutes the lunatic will have got me, too, where he wants to have us, the sane groveling like crazy animals before the insane. I must see if . . .

But there was nothing to see. With undivided attention the fool stood by the door, the pistol in his hand, his finger on the trigger, very much on guard.

"Pour out," he ordered again. "A full glass of champagne to refresh the palate."

"Right-o, mister, right-o," someone called, probably a page, and the others laughed their assent.

"You're a gentleman." Studmann made another attempt. "I suggest we let the two ladies go. None of the others will try to get out. I give you my word of honor."

"Ladies out—nothing doing!" someone bawled from behind. "Isn't that so, kitten? We don't get a treat like this every day."

"You hear?" the Baron answered. "Another drink—cognac this time. And sit down. That's right—on the sofa. Come, on the bed, too. You will also sit down, Herr Director. Come on! Do you think I'm joking? I'll shoot! There!" The revolver spoke again. There were screams. "So—another drink. And now make yourselves comfortable. Coats and collars off—you over there, take off your apron, girl. Yes, you can take off your blouses if you like."

"Herr Baron," remonstrated von Studmann, "we're not in a brothel. I refuse to . . ." But he realized that, under the influence of alcohol, will and deed were no longer running parallel; his frock coat now hung over the back of a chair, and he was fumbling with his tie. "I refuse," he objected once more, feebly.

"Drink," shouted the visitor. With a sneer: "In five minutes you won't refuse any longer. Champagne this time."

There was a crash and clatter of breaking glass. Süskind had fallen across the table, then dropped to the floor. Now he lay there, gasping, obviously unconscious.

The giggling butler, his fat paw clasping the girl's breast, sat on the bed. The elderly charwoman held a boy in each arm; she was as red as a turkey-cock and no longer aware of the world around her.

"You're to drink," screamed the madman. "You, mister, it's your turn to pour out. Champagne!"

In three minutes I'm lost, thought Studmann, reaching for the champagne bottle. In three minutes he would be as far gone as the others.

In his hand the bottle felt cool and firm, and suddenly his head cleared. It's quite simple, he thought.

The bottle changed into a bomb. He pulled out the pin and threw it at the other's head. He leaped after it.

The Baron dropped key and pistol, and flopped to the floor. "You mustn't touch me," he shouted. "I'm insane. I'm protected by paragraph fifty-one. Don't hit me, please don't, or you'll make yourself criminally liable. I'm immune." And while, in a drunken fury, von Studmann thrashed the miserable creature, he thought angrily: I've been taken in by him, after all. He's only a coward, like those who messed their trousers at every barrage. I should have punched his mug the first minute.

Then his stomach turned against beating the soft cowardly whimpering thing on the floor. Catching sight of the key, he picked it up, staggered to his feet, opened the door and stepped outside.

The large gathering of people who had sought shelter from the storm in the big hall of the hotel were startled at the appearance on the first-floor landing of a man with bleeding face and torn shirt sleeves, reeling along the gorgeous red stair carpet. At first only a few saw him, but soon an expectant silence caused others to turn round, too, and they in their turn stared as if they could not believe their eyes.

The gentleman stood swaying on the top of the stairs, glaring down into the crowded hall. He seemed not to know where he was. He mumbled something which no one could understand, but the silence spread until the music from the adjoining café could be clearly heard.

Rittmeister von Prackwitz got up from his chair and gazed at the apparition with amazement.

The hotel employees looked up, stared, wanted to do something about it, but were at a loss.

"Fools!" shouted the drunkard. "Mad! They think they're immune. But I thrash them."

He called down again to those staring up at him. "I'll thrash you, you fools."

He lost his balance. "Upsey," he chirped and managed the next six steps. Then he tumbled forward, rolled down the staircase and came to rest at the feet of the visitors, who fell back. He lay motionless and unconscious.

"Where shall we take him?" Rittmeister von Prackwitz muttered, gripping him under the armpits.

Suddenly the staff surrounded the casualty. The guests were edged away, and Studmann—Prackwitz with him—was taken down the stairs to the corridor leading to the storerooms and kitchen quarters. Preliminary rumors circulated. "A young German-American. Not used to alcohol; prohibition, you know. Dollar-millionaire, dead drunk."

Three minutes afterwards everything was normal again; people gossiped, were bored, asked for their letters, telephoned, had a look at the storm.

VIII

Between six and seven o'clock in the evening, when Wolfgang Pagel stepped out of the art dealer's in Bellevuestrasse, it was still raining, though not so heavily. He looked up and down the street, uncertain. Taxis were available at the Esplanade Hotel as well as by the Rolandsbrunnen; they would have taken him quickly enough to Petra, but an obstinate caprice forbade him to touch money which was dedicated to her.

He pulled the old army cap firmly on and set out. He could easily be with Petra in half an hour. A little while ago, although penniless, he had had a free ride by tram to Potsdamerplatz. Although the picture he carried made him conspicuous to any conductor, the evening rush heightened by the weather had enabled him to travel without paying his fare. Now, with an incredible sum in his pockets, he dared not risk such a free trip; if he were caught he would be forced to take a ticket and thus break in upon his millions.

Pagel whistled contentedly as he walked along the endless garden wall by the Reich Chancellor's palace. He knew quite well that this deliberation about fares or no fares was ridiculous and that it was more important (and also more decent) to bring Petra speedy help—but he shrugged his shoulders. He was once more the gambler. He had made up his mind, come what might, to stake only on red; and he would stake only on red. The devil might come for him, the chances might be against him as much as they liked. But red would win through. Petra's case would come to a satisfactory end only if he carried out his intention to place the 760,000,000 marks intact in her hands. But if 10,000 marks or only 1,000 were missing, then the black consequences could not be foreseen.

Perhaps silly, certainly superstitious—but how could you be sure? This life was so complicated, turned up so unexpectedly, contradicted every rule of logic, every careful calculation—was there not a chance of catching it out by means of superstitions, wild ideas, absurdities and follies? Very well then, Wolfgang, it was all right; and if it wasn't, it would work out just the same. Whether one made a mistake according to logic or folly was the private amusement of each individual. He, Wolfgang Pagel, plumped for folly.

As I am, so I remain, forever and ever. Amen.

Seven hundred and sixty million marks. A good round thousand dollars. Four thousand two hundred prewar marks. A nice little sum in the evening for one who at midday had had to beg Uncle for a single dollar. For whom two rolls and a very battered enamel can of adulterated coffee were beyond hope in the morning.

Pagel arrived at the Brandenburger Tor. He would have liked to pause for a moment to get out of the everlasting rain and dry his face, but it was not possible—the arches were thronged with beggars, hawkers and war-wounded. The rain had driven them from the entrances of the Tiergarten and the Pariserplatz into this shelter, and if Pagel were to place himself among them his inability to say no would endanger the inviolable treasure. He therefore fled from himself and the entreaties of the beggars into the rain again—hard-hearted out of weakness not hardness, like many another.

He carried himself rather stiffly, his hands guarding the pockets of his tunic. The money was in danger of getting wet. He did not forget for a moment that he was carrying a sum of 760 millions on him. A quarter of this sum, that is 250 dollars, was in good American notes, magnificent paper dollars, the most coveted currency in the Berlin of the day. . . .

I could afford to let the whole town dance tonight, he thought, and whistled contentedly. The remainder—570 millions—was in German notes, some of it in incredibly small denominations.

But the way it had been got together! It had been difficult enough to drag this sum out of the art chap that evening. No such amount of money was available in the place, nor could they send to the banks—they were closed by then. An advance certainly, and the balance tomorrow morning, nine-thirty, by messenger to any place in Berlin which Herr Pagel might designate. Herr Pagel would trust them for this sum, would he not? And at that the dealer, a massive man with rather a red face and a black Assyrian beard, had looked along his walls in affectionate pride.

Wolfgang followed this glance. He was sufficiently the son of his father to be able to understand the man's pride in, and affection for, his pictures—this man who looked as if he had no concern with art.

Across the road, two blocks farther along by Potsdamerstrasse, the "Sturm" gallery also sold pictures. He had stood there now and then with Peter for quite a time and looked at these Marcs, Kampendocks, Klees and Noldes.

Sometimes he had had to laugh or to shake his head or to complain, for many of the works were merely a colossal impudence—those were the times of Cubism, Futurism, and Expressionism. Scraps of newspaper were stuck together and made into pictures, and the world was carved up into triangles which one itched to put together again like a jigsaw puzzle. But sometimes, standing there, one had been thrilled. A feeling was stirred, you were affected, a chord had been touched. Would these rotten times give birth to something living?

But here at this rich man's, who bought pictures only if he liked them, and who was not greatly interested in their sale, here one saw no such experiments or gropings. Even in the reception room there was a Corot, some pond bathed in reddish light; and redder still the cap of the solitary ferryman who was poling his boat off an embankment. There was a magnificent van Gogh, an immense expanse of green and yellow field and an even wider expanse of blue sky already darkened by the threat of an oncoming storm; a Gauguin of mild brown girls with beautiful bosoms; yes, and a Pointillist like Signac, a Rousseau, childlike and awkward, a peaceful animal scene by Zügel, Leistikow's red sunny pine trees. These, however, were far removed from the experimental stage—they had been tested by the understanding, judged worthy of love, and were now loved. You could trust this man.

But Wolfgang Pagel equally realized that here he could demand whatever he wanted. He could be so unreasonable as to require them, after six o'clock in the evening, where there was no money left in the establishment, to scrape together a sum of 760 millions. He was as wet as a drowned cat when he first entered and produced the picture from under his tunic, where he had endeavored to shelter it from the storm. The gentleman, soft as an over-ripe plum, who had been shown it, said in matter-of-fact tones, but with a suspicious glance: "Certainly, a Pagel of the best period. You are selling on account of whom?" And Pagel felt that they would buy the picture on any condition and that he could dictate his own terms.

On his reply that he was selling on his own account, the over-ripe plum had called in the proprietor who, without making the slightest ado about the man in the tunic (in these times the most unlikely and shabby creatures sold most unlikely and precious possessions), had briefly remarked: "Set it down over there. Of course I know it, Dr. Mainz. Family property. An uncommonly good Pagel—sometimes he transcended himself. Not often—three or four times. . . . Mostly he's too pretty for me. Too slick and smooth, eh?"

He had turned to Wolfgang. "But you don't understand anything of that sort, do you? You only want money? As much as possible?"

Under the sudden attack Pagel started. He felt himself blushing crimson.

"I am the son," he said as calmly as possible.

It was sufficient.

"I'm tremendously sorry," the dealer said. "I admit I'm an ass. I ought to have seen the likeness, especially about the eyes—about the eyes if nowhere else. Your father has often been here. Yes, in his wheel-chair, to see some pictures. He liked pictures. Do you also like pictures?"

Again this abrupt, sudden—well, it was really an attack. At least Wolfgang felt it so. He had never considered whether the picture he had taken away from his mother was a good one or not. Fundamentally, the dealer had guessed correctly; even if he were the son, the transaction was only a question of money—although the money was for Peter.

With vexation mingled with sadness he realized that he really was the man he was estimated to be.

"Yes, I like them quite well," he replied, sullen.

"It's a very fine work," said the dealer pensively. "I've already seen it twice; no, three times. Your mother didn't want me to look at it. Does she agree to a sale?"

Again an attack. Pagel became annoyed. God, what a fuss about a picture, barely half a yard of painted canvas. A picture was something to look at if one wanted to; one wasn't compelled, it wasn't necessary. One could live without pictures; but not without money.

"No," he said crossly. "My mother doesn't agree to a sale."

The dealer looked at him politely and waited in silence.

"She made me a gift of this"—with feigned indifference—"thing here; one makes presents to members of one's family, you know. As I needed money, I remembered it. I'm selling it," he added emphatically, "against my mother's wishes."

The dealer listened quietly; then he announced casually, but in a noticeably colder voice, "Yes, yes, I understand, of course."

The over-ripe Dr. Mainz, who had vanished unnoticed, now re-entered. The dealer looked at his assistant (fine arts degree), and the assistant nodded briefly. "In any case," said the dealer, "your mother raises no objection to its sale. I have just had her rung up," he added, in answer to Pagel's inquiring glance. "Now please don't think I'm suspicious. I am a man of business, a prudent man of business. I don't want any trouble."

"And what will you pay?" Pagel asked abruptly. His mother could have prevented the sale with a word. She had not done so, and Wolfgang felt that the break was final. He could go his own way; from now onwards and forever his way was alone. She had no further interest in him.

"I'll pay," said the dealer, "a thousand dollars; that is, seven hundred and sixty millions of marks. If you would let me have the picture on commission I would exhibit it here and sell it on your account, and you might get a very much higher figure. But if I have understood you correctly, you need the money at once."

"At once, within an hour."

"Now, let's say tomorrow morning," smiled the dealer. "That's pretty prompt. I'll send my messenger with the money to whatever place you like."

"Now!" said Pagel. "This very hour. I must . . ."

The dealer looked at him attentively. "We've sent our cash in hand to the bank," he said kindly, as if he were explaining to a child. "I don't keep money here overnight. But tomorrow morning . . ."

"*Now*," said Pagel and laid his hand on the frame of the picture, "or the sale will not come off."

He had correctly summed up the situation. True, the dealer disapproved of a rebellious son who took away from his mother and sold a cherished picture; true, since he had learned that fact the temperature of the conversation had fallen; but in spite of his disapproval he would not for one moment hesitate to make use of that combination of circumstances to buy. This man with the black Assyrian beard, tall, assured and rich, had his weak spot—we all have. There was not the slightest reason for Pagel to feel ashamed; on the contrary. He (Pagel) was forced to sell; the big man was not obliged to buy.

Pagel spoke quietly. "I must have the whole amount in half an hour. I need the money this evening, not tomorrow morning. There are other buyers . . ."

The art dealer made a gesture which signified that this picture at any rate was no longer the concern of any other dealer. "The money shall be found somehow. At the moment I don't exactly know how. But it will be found."

He whispered to his assistant, Mainz, who nodded and went out.

"Please come with me, Herr Pagel. Yes, you can leave the picture here—I have bought it."

Pagel was shown into the dealer's office, a large gloomy room. Here the only pictures on the walls were some bold and dashing charcoal drawings by an unknown artist.

"Please sit down. Over there. Here are cigarettes. Whisky and soda I'll put within your reach. It may take"—slightly sarcastic—"even thirty-five minutes. So make yourself comfortable—come in!"

One after another the employees of the establishment entered, beginning with the historians of art with their degrees and ending with the totally unlettered charwomen who had by now started their evening work. Dr. Mainz had instructed them, and they went without a word to their employer's desk, pulled their fortunes out of pockets, waistcoat pockets, purses or wallets, and laid it down while their chief counted. "Dr. Mainz, one million four hundred and thirty-five thousand. Fräulein Siebert, two hundred and sixty thousand. Fräulein Plosch, seven hundred and thirty-three thousand. I thank you, Fräulein Plosch."

There must have existed in this firm a good relationship between employer and employee, for everyone gave as a matter of course. These shorthand-typists, accountants, gallery attendants, forwent what they had intended to do that evening. Sometimes they cast a look at the gentleman in the chair who was drinking whisky and soda, and smoking; it was not a look of hostility, but of detachment. Immaterial to them why this man in the shabby tunic needed money so urgently that they had to forgo their evening pleasures; but it did concern them if a picture which their chief wanted to buy was taken away from the firm. The giving up, counting, noting down of the money, was taken by both sides quite naturally; without exaggerated thanks or facetiousness and without embarrassed explanations on the side of the employer—a naturalness which almost induced Pagel to explain and excuse himself, to say that he really needed the money that evening, that his girl was in prison and he ought . . .

Yes, what ought he to do? Have money at once, at any rate, plenty of money! Wolfgang Pagel said nothing.

"Stop, Fräulein Bierla," said the dealer. "I see you have still fifty thousand in your purse. Excuse me, but this evening we have to scrape together every mark."

Embarrassed, the beautiful brunette muttered something about fares.

"You don't need any money for fares. Dr. Mainz has ordered taxis for closing time. The drivers will take you wherever you want to go."

The paper money piled up. The dealer, rummaging in his own pocket-book and emptying it, said disparagingly to Dr. Mainz: "If you read the newspapers and listen to what people say, you hear that everyone is swimming in money. It's in every pocket, it crackles in every hand. But here is what twenty-seven people, you and me included, carry on them. Not even seven hundred marks in peace time. A ridiculously exaggerated affair, this era of ours. If the people saw clearly, for once, how few figures stand in front of so many noughts they wouldn't allow themselves to be so bemused."

Dr. Mainz whispered something hurried and urgent.

"Yes, of course, telephone immediately. Meanwhile I'll go to my wife. I'm sure to get money there."

While Dr. Mainz telephoned some Herr Director Nolte, who ought to be receiving 250 paper dollars that evening, but was now asked to wait till tomorrow morning, Pagel reflected what an unaccustomed disorder had been brought into this place by his demand. But he realized with surprise in what an orderly fashion the disorder was being cleared up, without noise or bustle—taxis waiting at the door, every employee being driven where he wanted, the individual amounts neatly noted on a piece of paper. . . . In the moment disorder arose everything was being done to remove it in the shortest possible time.

I've also let disorder arise, he thought gloomily, but it never occurred to me to remove it. It has increased, has invaded spheres of which I never dreamed. Now all my life is in disorder.

He remembered how often he had asked Petra to dress before Frau Thumann brought in the morning coffee. I've always played a part to myself and, above all, to her, he thought. Disorder is not turned into order by putting a blanket over it. On the contrary—it is turned into something which no one dares to defend. Into a lying, cowardly disorder. Did Peter understand that? What did she really think? Was that the reason why she put so much value on our marrying? For the sake of order? She always did what I suggested, without protest. Fundamentally I know nothing about what she really thought.

The dealer returned, laughing and flourishing a fat wad of notes.

"At my house everyone's staying at home tonight. My wife's delighted; she was going to some ghastly first night, followed by a celebration of the dramatist already bursting with his own importance. She's glad that we can't go now, and is telephoning all the world enthusiastically, declaring that we're without a penny—tomorrow I shall read about my insolvency in the newspapers. And you, Dr. Mainz?"

It appeared that Dr. Mainz, too, had been successful. Herr Director Nolte would wait for his 250 dollars till tomorrow morning.

"A thousand dollars—seven hundred and sixty millions," said the dealer. "It took," he pulled out his watch, "thirty-eight minutes to collect, however. I must apologize for the eight minutes."

Why does he scoff at me? thought Pagel, exasperated. He should rather ask me why I need the money. People often do find themselves in situations where they need cash immediately. People very easily find themselves in such situations, but the question of responsibility also arises. Am I to blame for the blunders of the police? He became annoyed.

"It's rather a lot of paper, but such is the spirit of our age," the art dealer smiled. "Shall I have it tied up for you? You would rather put it in your pockets? It's raining hard. Well, you'll probably take a taxi. . . . Immediately to the right, as you go out of the door, in front of the Hotel Esplanade. . . . Or shall I call one?"

"No, thank you," Pagel had replied grumpily, stuffing the notes into his pockets. "I'll walk."

And now he was passing through Königstrasse, wet through, his hands protectingly over his two outer pockets. People might get angry with him as his mother did, or mock him as this picture chap did; they might get into difficulties as Peter did; but he was going to do exactly what he wanted, and full steam ahead. He wouldn't break into the money; he had no intention of taking a taxi even though his pockets were bursting with money. If he didn't want to, then neither rain nor necessity could force him.

Nor did he go straight to the police station where Petra was confined; he went first to Frau Thumann, to look round. Now as ever he was convinced that there was plenty of time for everything. He was like a mule: the more he was thrashed the more obstinate he became.

Or was he, perhaps, afraid of what he would learn at the police station? Was he afraid of the shame he would feel when he saw Petra in such a deplorable situation?

Whistling, he crossed Alexanderplatz and turned into Landsbergerstrasse. What would give Petra greater pleasure—a tobacco shop or a flower shop? Or perhaps an ice-cream bar?

IX

Oberwachtmeister Leo Gubalke was not the sort of man who, on duty or off, was inclined to interference, spite, or bickering. That terrible temptation was not his which besets a man into whose mouth the words of power are placed: "Obey or die!" Although now and then he was subject to those petty meannesses from which no self-esteem is immune, it was always his exaggerated sense of order and punctuality which led him astray.

It was this which had made him remove Petra Ledig from the doorway in Georgenkirchstrasse. It was this which, in reply to his superintendent's reproachful "What's the matter with you, Gubalke? You—of all people—twenty minutes late," made him report: "An arrest. This girl is connected with gamblers."

These last words, which he would never have uttered had he not been delayed—nothing being further from his thoughts than to do harm—were for some hours all that the police station knew about the arrest. Oberwachtmeister Gubalke had only wished to remove a half-naked girl from the streets, intending to give her a seat in the police station, and then get her something to eat. During the course of the evening he would have found out what sort of girl she was, would have begged some garments for her from a relief committee and, after a lecture on order and unseemly conduct, discharged her into the world again.

And instead of carrying out these good intentions, Herr Gubalke had reported that she was connected with gamblers. An unpunctuality which can only be excused by a kind heart and compassion remains an unpunctuality; this remark about gamblers turned the unpunctuality into a necessary official action. Until the moment when that remark, never to be recalled, escaped his lips, Gubalke had not even dreamed of ascribing to the girl any complicity in the vice of gambling, which he knew about only through women's gossip. But man is a weak creature and with most of us—men and women alike—the tongue is weakness's weakest point. Under the necessity of justifying himself, Gubalke entangled Petra's fate with that of a gambler; and, as a finishing touch, turned a single gambler into gamblers.

It is certain that the Oberwachtmeister did not realize the far-reaching consequences to Petra Ledig of these few words. Hastily he buckled on his pistol, hooked on his rubber truncheon and thought only of going as quickly as possible to the assistance of his comrades in Kleine Frankfurterstrasse, in trouble with some street gangs. He was in such a hurry that he did not even look at the girl on his way out. If he thought of her again, it was certainly not with a bad conscience. At any rate she had been removed from the street into the safety of the police station, and at the latest he would be back in a couple of hours to deal with the matter.

Unfortunately, two hours later the Oberwachtmeister was lying in hospital at the Friedrichshain, mortally wounded, his bowels lacerated by a murderer's bullet. He died the most disorderly, filthy and lingering death which could finish off such a clean and orderly man. The case of Petra Ledig was forever beyond his influence.

Nevertheless he did influence it. By the time the news of Gubalke's murder reached the agitated police station, Petra Ledig had spent two hours there, unmolested and almost unperturbed. Except for a trifling incident, nothing worth mentioning had happened to her. An indifferent man or other in uniform, neither kind nor unkind, had pushed her into a small cell rather like a cage in the Zoo, with three solid walls, and a fourth of bars facing the charge-room. To her request that they should bring her something to eat, no matter what, as the Herr Wachtmeister had promised, the indifferent man at first mumbled that they had no facilities there, and that she must wait until she arrived at Alexanderplatz. After a while, however, he appeared with a thick crust of dry bread and a cup of coffee. He handed them to her between the bars.

Nothing better could have been given the half-starved Petra as her first nourishment. The stale and very hard crust compelled her to nibble away at extremely small fragments, which had to be chewed for a long time. In the beginning she was assailed again and again by waves of nausea. The stomach refused to keep down the food, to restart its activity. Huddled on the bench, her eyes closed, her head pressed against the corner of the cell, Petra heroically attacked her nausea, one sweat of weakness following another. Again and again she forced the food back into her stomach. I must eat, she thought dully, exhausted but unyielding. She was not eating for herself alone.

The crust of bread, which a three-year-old child would have managed in five minutes, lasted almost half an hour. But when she had finished it a physical warmth filled her, a feeling akin to spiritual bliss.

All this time she had not been conscious of the world around her, but now that she felt restored she began to take an interest in the life of the chargeroom. That world held no shocks for her. Anyone who came from the place she had come from could not be afraid of greed or vulgarity, vice or drunkenness. All was part and parcel of human life, an expression of it, as was indeed Wolfgang's smile and embrace, pleasure at a new dress, or the display in the window of a flower shop.

Nor did anything happen in the next half-hour to frighten her. They brought in a starved-looking youth who, as the half-audible examination showed, had tried to steal a pair of shoes from a department store; a drunken bilker; an unhappy woman in a shawl who, it seemed, took furnished rooms only with the intention of stealing something from them; and a man who sold gold-plated watches as solid gold, and found buyers by pretending that this unique opportunity was the result of picking a pocket.

All this wreckage washed into the charge-room underwent examination with composure; the prisoners wandered resignedly into cages which were locked behind them by the uninterested man in uniform.

Then the noise started. Two policemen brought in a woman, dead drunk and raving. They almost had to carry her. With benevolence—or what looked like it—they listened to the most filthy abuse; the girl, they said, had filched the pocketbook of her equally drunk gentleman escort, whom a third policeman now brought in. Rather pale and stupid-looking, he evidently grasped very little of what was going on outside him, because he was too preoccupied with what was going on within him. He was very sick.

The girl's drunken screaming prevented any of the evidence being recorded; the yellow, half-audible secretary could not prevail on her to keep quiet. Again and again she flew, with her long, red-lacquered, dirty nails, at the faces of the policemen, the secretary and her gentleman friend.

This girl Petra recognized with genuine fear, reminded of a time in her life which she had believed forgotten, and was ashamed of. She knew her, not by name, it is true, but from her activities in the better part of the West End, Tauentzienstrasse, Kurfürstendamm and, after the restaurants had closed, also in Augsburgerstrasse. On her beat she was called "The Hawk," probably because of her thin curved nose and her unreasoning hostility to any rival.

In those bad days before Petra had asked Wolfgang to take her along with him she had encountered the Hawk on several of those rare occasions when, the lack of money having become too frightening, she had herself gone on the hunt for a paying gentleman. Probably about that time the Hawk had been placed under police supervision and from then on had, with a noisy hatred which stuck at nothing, persecuted any girl who did not belong to the "profession." When she discovered someone poaching on her beat, accosting a gentleman or even only glancing at him, she would try first to bring in the police. If that did not succeed or no policeman was near, she would seek to lower the intruder in the eyes of her gentleman, starting from a bad accusation and going on to a worse; at first accusing her of being a thief, next of having a venereal disease, and so on and so on. Her ultimate weapon had been a howling screech, an hysterical yell of rage stimulated by cocaine and alcohol to an inconceivable pitch, whereupon the other's gentleman took to his heels.

Petra had had always the feeling that the Hawk disliked her particularly, and persecuted her with an especial hatred. Once she had escaped assault only by headlong flight through the dark streets to Victoria-Luise Platz where she found a hiding place behind the half-circle of pillars. Another time, however, she had not been so lucky. The Hawk had dragged her out of the taxi into which she and a gentleman were stepping, and there had been a free fight (the gentleman escaping in the taxi). Petra's dress had been torn to shreds and her umbrella broken.

All this was very long ago, almost a year—or was it more than a year? Petra had experienced so much since then; the gates of another world had opened to her, and yet she looked at her enemy with the same old fear. That enemy had changed, too, but for the worse. Drugs—cocaine and alcohol—had done their work on her; and the removal of her beat from the rich West End to the East End spoke eloquently of her fading charms. The smooth round cheeks had become haggard and wrinkled, the soft red mouth cracked and dry; every movement as jerky as a mad woman's.

She screamed, spilling her venom, an incessant abuse. Whenever the yellow secretary asked a question she started again, as if the filth within her were continually and mysteriously renewed. At last he made a gesture to the two policemen, and they removed her from the charge-room to the cells, one of them saying quietly: "Come along, little girl, and sleep it off."

She was just about to start her screaming again when she caught a glimpse of Petra through the bars. She stood still. "Have you got that bitch at last?" she shouted triumphantly. "Thank God! The damned whore! Is she already under supervision? What a sow! Takes all the gentlemen away from a decent girl and infects them, that tart, that dirty tart! She walks the streets, Herr Wachtmeister, day and night, and the filthy bitch is a mass of disease."

"Come along, girl," said the policeman quietly and, finger by finger, disengaged the clinging hand from the bars of Petra's cell. "Have a proper sleep."

The secretary had risen from his desk to approach them. "Take her away," he said. "One can hardly hear oneself speak. It's snow—when it's worn off she'll collapse like a wet rag."

The policemen nodded; between them they supported the girl and took her away. Except for this assistance she was upheld only by a senseless fury which fed on anything. Even when she could no longer see Petra she still shouted abuse over her shoulder.

The secretary cast his sick tired glance (the whites of his eyes were yellow, too) on Petra, and asked in low tones: "Is it a fact? Have you walked the streets?"

Petra nodded. "Yes, a year ago. But not now."

The secretary also nodded, wearily. He went back to his desk. But he stopped again, turned round. "Have you got a disease?" he asked.

Petra shook her head energetically. "No, never have had."

The secretary nodded again, sat down at his desk and continued his interrupted writing. Life in the charge-room went on. Some of the arrested might have been afraid, fidgety and worried; perhaps the drunkards were tormented by visions; but outwardly everything went smoothly and well.

Until shortly after six o'clock, when the telephone announced that Oberwachtmeister Leo Gubalke was mortally injured in the stomach and would probably die before midnight. From that moment the aspect of the police station completely changed. Doors were continually banging; officers, in plain clothes or uniform, came and went. One whispered to another, a third joined in, a fourth cursed. And at half-past six Gubalke's comrades returned, those he had wanted to help in their fight with the two gangs, the fight in which he was wounded by the only shot fired. The whispering continued. The desk was banged; a policeman stood grimly in a corner, swinging his rubber truncheon; the looks cast at the prisoners were no longer indifferent but stern.

Those, however, which were cast at Petra Ledig were of particular intensity. Everybody had been told by the secretary that she was "Leo's last official act." Gubalke, because he had arrested this girl, had been twenty minutes late.

Had he been punctual and turned out with the others, in closed formation, he might not have been hit by the murderer's bullet. In fact it was certain.

The man who was in this moment suffering a painful and slow death was thinking, perhaps, of his wife and children. Possibly, in his extreme pain, he was pleased to remember that his girls at least washed themselves as he did, and that he had left behind him a part of his being, a tiny symbol of what he regarded as order. Or he may have thought, in the valley of the shadow of death, that now he would never sit in a tidy office and keep orderly records, or he remembered his allotment garden, or he wondered whether the burial club, at the present rate of devaluation, would pay out enough money for a decent funeral. The dying man might be thinking of a variety of subjects, but the chances that he was thinking of Petra Ledig, his "last official act," were very scanty.

And yet he, dying, took possession of this case, singled it out from all the others. His colleagues saw in Petra not an ordinary girl but the reason for the dying man's having been twenty minutes late. Gubalke's last official act must have been important.

The tall, heavy, melancholy-looking superintendent with the sergeant major's mustache came into the room, stood beside the secretary's desk and asked significantly: "Is that the girl?"

"That's the girl," confirmed the secretary in a low voice.

"He told me that she had dealings with gamblers. Nothing else."

"I've not yet examined her," whispered the secretary. "I wanted to wait till—he came back."

"Examine her," said the superintendent.

"The drunken woman who made such a row recognized her. She's walked the streets. She admitted it, but maintained that it was some time ago."

"Yes, he was very observant. He saw everything which was not in order. I shall miss him very much."

"We shall all miss him. He was an excellent worker and a good comrade, and not at all pushing."

"Yes, we shall all miss him. Examine her. Remember that the only reference he made was to gamblers."

"I'll remember. How could I forget it? I'll put her through it."

Petra was led to his desk. If she had not already noticed the significant glances or realized by the way they stood round her cell that something was amiss, the manner in which the yellow secretary now spoke to her must have revealed that the atmosphere had changed and to her disadvantage. Something must have happened to make them think badly of her—could it have something to do with Wolf? This uncertainty made her timid and embarrassed. Once or twice she referred to the kind Wachtmeister "who lives in our house," but the blank silence with which this appeal was met by the superintendent and the secretary frightened her the more.

As long as the examination concerned herself alone, and she could stick to the truth, everything went fairly well. But when the question cropped up as to her friend's means of subsistence, when the word "gambler" fell on her ears, then she felt cornered and confused.

Without hesitation she admitted that she had accosted men several times ("Perhaps eight or ten times, I can't remember exactly"), had slept with them and received money for it. But she did not want to admit that Wolfgang was a gambler for money, and that this had been their main resource for some time. Since he had never made any secret of it she was not even sure whether gambling was illegal, but she preferred to be on the safe side and prevaricated. Even on this point the dying man had done her a disservice. The word "gambler" had a meaning here in the East End of Berlin quite different from what it had in the West End. A girl of doubtful character who walked the streets and had a permanent friend and also "had dealings with gamblers" could mean only one thing in the East End: she was the companion of a cardsharp, that is to say, a three-card trickster. In the eyes of the two police officers she was a girl who acted as a decoy for her friend and brought in victims to be fleeced.

In a police station in the other part of Berlin this reference to gamblers would have had a more obvious significance. The West End—everybody knew it—swarmed with gambling clubs frequented by half the Smart Set and certainly the whole of the demimonde. The police section which dealt with this evil hunted down these clubs night after night, but it was a Sisyphean labor— for every ten closed there sprang up twenty new ones. The gambling public was not prosecuted, otherwise half the population of the West End would have been imprisoned; the promoters and the croupiers only were arrested, and all money confiscated.

If Petra had explained that her friend frequented a West End gambling club, the police in the East End would have had no further interest in the matter. But she evaded their questions, affected ignorance, lied, was caught out once or twice and thereafter kept silent out of sheer bewilderment.

If the dying man had not held the threads of the case in his hands it would probably have petered out. There could not have been much in it; a girl who lied so clumsily and blushed at every lie, contradicting herself, could hardly be the decoy of an artful confidence man, or the accomplice of a dangerous criminal. But there was always the possibility that some grave but unknown matter might lie behind it all. Petra was shouted at, admonished in a fatherly manner, warned of consequences and, when all this did not make her speak frankly, led back to her cell.

"Send her to Alexanderplatz with the seven-o'clock van," decided the superintendent. "Draw their attention in the minutes to the importance of the case."

The secretary whispered.

"Certainly, we can try and get hold of the fellow. But he's sure to have bolted by this time. Anyhow, I'll send a man to Georgenkirchstrasse at once."

Thus, when at seven o'clock the green police van stopped outside the police station, Petra, too, was put in. It was raining. She found herself sitting next to her enemy, the Hawk, but the secretary was quite right—the cocaine had worn off and the girl was in a state of collapse. Petra had to support her during the ride or she would have fallen off her seat.

X

He turned out of Landsbergerstrasse into Gollnowstrasse. He left behind Weinstrasse on the right, Landwehrstrasse on the left. To the right again he came to Fliederstrasse, a small street with but few houses. Here on the corner stood a low schnapps bar which Pagel had never before entered.

He ordered a glass of vermouth at the counter. It cost seventy thousand marks and tasted of fusel oil. He paid and went as far as the door before remembering that he had no more cigarettes. Lucky Strikes? They had none, but they had Camels. Not bad either, thought Pagel. He lit one and ordered another vermouth.

For a while he stood at the counter shivering in his wet clothes. The fuseloil vermouth didn't help much, so he took a double cognac, which tasted horribly of raw spirit. But a slight warmth was kindled in his stomach and slowly spread; an artificial warmth, not bringing that quiet happiness which Petra had felt after eating the crust of bread.

Pagel stood there indolently, looking with indifference at the smelly barroom with its noisy crowd. Apathy had seized him. He was convinced that already, before he had lifted a finger to help Petra, everything had miscarried. It didn't matter in the least that the carefully guarded money had now been broken into. Indeed, he would have preferred it to flow from him, if possible, without his having to make any effort—for what could money do? But if money couldn't help, what did? Must there be any help? Did anything matter?

As he stood there, so he would have preferred to stand forever; each step he took brought him nearer to a decision which he did not wish to make, which he wanted to delay as long as possible. It occurred to him that he had really done nothing else the whole day long but put off that decision. First of all he must have money, then he would go forth in grand style. Now he had the money—and he stood calmly waiting at the counter.

A young lad wearing a peaked cap down over his ear came up to him, sniffed the smoke from his cigarette and begged for one. "I'm mad on English cigarettes. Don't be so stingy, you; at least give me your fag end." Smiling, Wolfgang shook his head, and the face darkened. The lad turned away. Wolfgang put his hand into his pocket, extricated a cigarette, shouted "Catch" and threw it. The other caught it and nodded curtly. At once there were three or four lads round Pagel, also begging for cigarettes. Hastily he paid at the counter, noticing their eyes fixed on his thick wad of money, and as he went out he pushed aside with his shoulder a lad who tried to jostle him.

Pagel was now only three minutes' walk from his room and this time he did not dawdle. But as he rang Madam Po's bell he felt the stimulus which the encounter in the dram-shop had supplied dying away; boundless sadness fell on him again. It seemed to weigh him down as the dark storm clouds had done that afternoon.

In the corridor he heard Madam Po's repulsive shuffle and her phlegmy cough, noises which somewhat dispersed the cloud of sadness, and he felt that he would punish this woman for what had happened—no matter what it was.

Cautiously the door was put on the jar, but he kicked it wide open and towered over the startled woman. "Oh, Lor', Herr Pagel, what a fright you gave me!" she complained.

He stood silent, perhaps waiting for her to speak, for her to start to tell him what had happened. But he had obviously filled her with fear, for she didn't utter a sound, only smoothed her apron with her hands.

Suddenly—a second ago Pagel himself hadn't known that he would do it—his shoulder pushed aside the woman as it had done the lad in the schnapps bar, and without hesitating he went along the dark corridor toward his room.

Frau Thumann rushed up behind him. "Herr Pagel! Herr Pagel! Listen to me a second," she whispered.

"Well?" He turned so suddenly that she was again scared.

"Lor', what's the matter with you, Herr Pagel? I don't understan' it." She was very flustered. "It's only that I've let your room. To a girlfriend of Ida's. She's in it now—not by 'erself. You understand? Why are you looking at me like that? You want to frighten me. You needn't, I'm frightened enough already. If only Willem'd come! You ain't left anything there, and your girl having been fetched away by the coppers . . ."

She was under way again, was Madam Po. But Pagel listened no longer. He pushed open the door of his room—had it been locked he would have broken it open—and went in.

On the bed sat a half-naked female, prostitute, of course—on the same narrow iron bed in which he had slept that morning with Petra. A young man of no better appearance than substance was just unbuttoning his braces.

"Get out!" said Pagel to the startled pair.

Frau Thumann was lamenting in the doorway. "Herr Pagel, this is the last straw. I'll call the police. This is my room and you not having paid I need money too. No, Lotte, don't talk, the man's cracked. They took his girl to the police station, and so he's gone off his rocker."

"Shut up!" said Pagel sharply and punched the youth in the back. "Hurry. Get out of my room! Look sharp!"

"I must really ask—" The youth made a timid show of resistance.

"I'm just in the mood," said Pagel softly but very distinctly, "to give you a good hiding. If you and that whore are not out of my room in one minute . . ."

His voice failed. He was shaking from head to foot with fury. He had never for one moment intended to claim this damned filthy hole, but it would suit him admirably if this bloody counterjumper said one single word of opposition.

He did not, however. Silent and flurried, he buttoned up his braces, fumbled with his waistcoat and jacket . . .

At the door Madam Po was wailing. "Herr Pagel! Herr Pagel! I don't understand you! You're an educated man an' we always got on so well, an' me wanting to give a roll and a pot of coffee to your girl, only Ida wouldn't stand for it. . . . Besides, everything was Ida's fault, I'd got nothing against you. Lor', now he sets my place on fire!"

Pagel, paying no attention to her, had been standing by the window, absent-mindedly watching the girl putting on her blouse in a great hurry. Then it occurred to him that he was no longer smoking. Lighting a cigarette, he eyed the burning match in his fingers. Beside him was the curtain, the repulsive, dingy curtain which he had always hated. He touched it with the match. The hem scorched and writhed, then burst into flame.

The girl and the Thumann woman screamed, the man made a step toward him, then hesitated.

"So!" said Pagel and crumpled the curtain up, thereby extinguishing the flame. "This is my room. What do I owe you, Frau Thumann? I'll pay to the end of the month. Here!"

He gave her some money, any odd amount, a couple of notes, it didn't matter. He was putting the wad back into his pocket when he noticed the girl looking at it with a pathetically covetous look. Supposing she knew, he thought with satisfaction, that this was only one of six such packets—and the least valuable at that.

"There!" he said to the girl and held it out.

She looked at the money, then at him, and he realized that she did not believe him. "All right, then," he said indifferently and put the money away. "You're a fool. If you'd taken it you could have kept it. Now you won't get anything."

He went to the door. "I'm going to the police, Frau Thumann. In an hour I'll be back with my wife. See that there's something for supper."

"Certainly, Herr Pagel. But you haven't paid for the curtain yet. A quarter of an hour ago a copper was looking for you. I told him you had 'opped it."

"Good. I'll go there now."

She hurried after him. "And, Herr Pagel, please don't take it amiss. You'll hear about it any'ow at the station. I only said you were a bit behind with the rent, and straightaway they made me sign something about fraud. But I'll take it back, Herr Pagel, I didn't mean it. I'll go at once to the police and take it back. I didn't want to do it, but he made me. I'll be there right away. I must first get rid of the girl. A fool like her wouldn't never have earned the rent, and you've seen what sort of a gent that was, Herr Pagel, with a dickey on . . ."

Pagel was already descending the stairs; the devil takes the hindmost, and so it was quite in keeping that Frau Thumann had laid a charge on account of fraud. It didn't matter to him, but as regards Petra . . .

He returned. Madam Po had started to report the events to a neighbor on the landing. "If you're not at the police station in twenty minutes, Frau Thumann," he said, "there'll be the devil of a row."

The yellow secretary at the police station had had a bad day. It was a severe bilious attack, as he had feared in getting up that morning. Dull pressure in the region of his gall-bladder and a feeling of nausea had warned him. He knew quite well, and the surgeon had told him often enough, that he ought to report sick and undergo a course of treatment. But what married man nowadays could afford to let his family depend on sick benefits which lagged so far behind the devaluation?

The excitement of the Gubalke case had brought on a real bilious colic. He had hardly been able to finish the records for the transfer of the prisoners to Alexanderplatz at seven o'clock, and now he was huddled in the lavatory while they were calling for him outside. He could have screamed with pain. Of course he could go home if he was ill; no superintendent, and his least of all, would have any objection; but one couldn't leave one's duty so suddenly, especially at this hour when the heaviest tasks of the police started. The shops had closed, throwing thousands of businessmen and employees on the streets; hundreds of restaurants displayed their illuminated signs, and the lust for amusement swept people off their feet. He would stick it till he was relieved at ten o'clock.

He was sitting at his desk again. With some anxiety he noticed that, although the bilious attack and the pain had stopped, their place was taken by a state of utter irritation. Everything annoyed him, and he looked almost with hate at the pale spongy face of a street-vendor who, without having a license, had sold some toilet soap of dubious origin out of a suitcase and, when reprimanded by a policeman, had started a row. I must pull myself together, thought the secretary. I mustn't let myself go. I'm not to look at him like that.

"It is forbidden to offer goods for sale in the street without a hawker's license," he said for the tenth time, as gently as possible.

"Everything is forbidden," the hawker shouted. "You ruin a chap. Here you're only allowed to starve to death."

"I don't make the laws," said the secretary.

"But you're paid to carry out the lousy laws, you and your fat job," the man shouted. Just behind him stood a good-looking lad in a field-gray uniform, with an open, intelligent face. He gave the secretary strength to endure such abuse without exploding. "Where did you get the soap?" he asked.

"Find out!" the vendor bawled. "Why must you interfere with everything? You only want to ruin the likes of us, you corpse-maggot. When we're dead you'll have a good feed." And his abuse did not cease even while a policeman was pushing him toward the cells.

The secretary shut the lid of the soap case sadly and put it on his desk. "Yes?" he said to the young man in the field-gray uniform, who, frowning and with his chin thrust out, had watched the hawker being taken away. His face, the secretary now noticed, was not so frank as he had first thought it; there was defiance in it and foolish obstinacy. The official was familiar with the expression which some men assume whenever a policeman uses force against a civilian. Such men, the born kickers against the pricks, see red, particularly when they have been drinking a little.

This young man had himself under control, however. With a sigh of relief he looked away as soon as the iron door closed on the corridor. He jerked one shoulder in the tightly fitting tunic, went up to the desk and said in a challenging but otherwise reasonable voice: "My name is Pagel. Wolfgang Pagel."

The secretary waited, but nothing further was forthcoming. "Yes?" he said. "What do you want?"

"You are expecting me," replied the young man angrily. "Pagel. Pagel from Georgenkirchstrasse."

"Why, yes," said the secretary. "Yes, of course. We sent a man along. We should like to have a talk with you, Herr Pagel."

"And your man has compelled my landlady to make a charge against me."

"Not compelled. Hardly compelled," the secretary corrected. "We have no special interest in accepting charges. We're stuffed up with them." He was determined to keep on good terms with this young man.

"Nevertheless you've arrested my wife for no reason," said the young man vehemently.

"Not your wife," the secretary corrected again. "An unmarried girl, Petra Ledig, isn't that so?"

"We wanted to marry at lunch time," said Pagel flushing. "Our banns were put up at the registrar's."

"But the arrest didn't take place till this evening. So you weren't married at midday?"

"No. But we can soon change that. I had no money this morning."

"I understand," said the secretary slowly. "But an unmarried girl for all that!" his gall trouble made him add.

He looked at the green ink-stained baize before him, then selected a sheet from the pile of papers on his left. He avoided glancing at the young man, but again he could not resist adding: "And not arrested without a reason. No."

"If you mean the charge of fraud, I've just paid the bill. In ten minutes the landlady will be here to withdraw her statement."

"So this evening you have money," was the secretary's astonishing reply.

Pagel felt like asking the sallow man what business that was of his, but he refrained. "If the statement is withdrawn," he said, "there will be nothing to prevent Fräulein Ledig from being discharged, then."

"I believe there is something," said the secretary. He was tired out, sick of all these things, and terribly afraid of a quarrel. He would have preferred to be in bed, a hot-water bottle on his belly, and his wife reading him the serial in today's newspaper. Indeed, there would inevitably be a scene with this agitated young man whose voice was becoming more and more strained. Stronger, however, than his need for rest was the irritability which was oozing out of his gall-bladder and poisoning his blood. But he held himself in. Of all his points he chose the weakest, so as not to enrage this Herr Pagel any further. "When she was arrested she had no home and was dressed only in a man's overcoat." He watched Pagel's face to see the effect of his words. "It was causing a public nuisance," he explained.

The young man had become very red. "The room has been re-engaged and paid for," he said hurriedly. "So she will have a roof. And with regard to her clothes, I can buy the necessary dresses and underclothes in a few minutes."

"So you have enough money for that? Quite a lot of money?" The secretary was sufficiently a detective to pin a man down to anything he casually admitted under examination.

"Enough for that, anyhow," said Wolfgang vehemently. "So she will be discharged?"

"The shops are now closed," replied the secretary.

"Never mind. I'll get her some clothes somehow." And almost beseechingly: "You'll discharge Fräulein Ledig?"

"As I said, Herr Pagel, we should like to have to talk with you, quite apart from this matter. That's why we sent an officer along."

The secretary whispered for a moment with a man in uniform, who nodded and vanished.

"But you're still standing. Please take a chair."

"I don't want a chair. I want my friend to be discharged at once," Pagel screamed. But he pulled himself together immediately. "Forgive me," he said in lower tones. "This won't happen again. But I'm very worried. Fräulein Ledig is a good girl. Anything you may have against her is my fault. I didn't pay the rent, I sold her dresses. Do please set her free."

"Sit down," said the secretary.

Pagel wanted to flare up, but thought better of it. He sat down.

There is a method of examination by which criminologists can crush most men and certainly the inexperienced. This method is far removed from gentleness or humanity. It cannot be otherwise. The examiner has in most cases to discover a fact which the examined person does not want to admit, has to browbeat the questioned man till he admits the fact against his will.

The secretary had before him a man who was the subject of a vague accusation that he lived by card-sharping. This man would never confess to the truth of this accusation if he were in a calm and collected frame of mind; in order to make him lose his head he had to be provoked. Often it is difficult to find something which enrages the accused to the extent of making him lose his powers of reasoning. In this case the secretary had found the something which he needed: the man seemed to be genuinely concerned about his girl. That must be the lever to open the door to a confession. But such a lever could not be used gently; kindly consideration would not liberate the farmers of East Prussia from a three-card trickster. One had to attack him vigorously: the young man had self-control, he hadn't flown into a rage, he had sat down. "I have a few matters to inquire about," said the secretary.

"Certainly," replied Pagel. "Ask what you like, as long as you promise me that Fräulein Ledig will be discharged this evening."

"We can talk about that later."

"Please promise me right away," begged Pagel. "I'm worried. Don't be cruel. Don't torture me. Say yes."

"I'm not cruel," replied the secretary. "I'm an official."

Pagel leaned back, discouraged and irritated.

Through the door came a tall, sad-looking man in uniform. He had heavy pouches under his eyes and an iron-gray sergeant major's mustache. This man stepped behind the secretary's chair, took a cigar out of his mouth and asked: "Is that the man?"

The secretary leaned back, looked up at his superior and said in an audible whisper: "That's the man."

The superintendent nodded slowly, subjected Pagel to a detailed scrutiny and said: "Carry on." He continued to smoke.

"Now to our questions," the secretary began.

But Pagel interrupted him. "May I smoke?" He was holding the packet of cigarettes in his hand.

The secretary rapped on the table. "The public are forbidden to smoke in this office."

The superintendent puffed vigorously at his cigar. Angrily, but without losing his temper, Pagel put away his cigarettes.

"Now to our questions," said the secretary again.

"One moment," interrupted the superintendent, putting his big hand on the other's shoulder. "Are you examining the man about his own case or the girl's?"

"So I also am concerned?" Pagel asked with surprise.

"We shall see later," said the secretary. And to his superior, again in that ridiculously audible whisper: "About his own case."

They treat you like dirt, do what they like with you, thought Pagel bitterly. But I won't be upset. The main thing is to get Petra out this evening. Perhaps Mamma was right, after all. I ought to have employed a lawyer. Then these fellows would be more careful.

He sat there outwardly calm, but inwardly uneasy. The feeling of despair, as if everything was in vain, had not left him since he had been in the schnapps bar.

"Now to our questions," he heard the persevering secretary repeat. It had really begun.

"Your name?"

Pagel gave it.

"Born when?"

Pagel told them.

"Where?"

Pagel said where.

"Occupation?"

He was without an occupation.

"Address?"

Pagel gave them the address.

"Have you your identity papers?"

Pagel had.

"Show them."

Pagel showed them.

The secretary looked at them, the superintendent looked at them. He indicated something to the secretary and the secretary nodded. He did not hand the papers back, but put them down in front of him. "So," he said, leaning back and looking at Pagel.

"Now for the questions," said Pagel.

"What?" demanded the secretary.

"I said 'Now for the questions,'" Pagel replied politely.

"Right," the secretary said, "Now for the questions. . . ."

It was not clear whether his irony had made any impression on the two officials.

"Your mother lives in Berlin?"

"As can be seen from the papers." They want to confuse me, he thought, or they're stupid. Yes, they're definitely stupid.

"You don't live with your mother?"

"No, in Georgenkirchstrasse."

"Wouldn't it be pleasanter to live in Tannenstrasse?"

"That's a matter of taste."

"Have you perhaps fallen out with your mother?"

"Not quite." A complete lie was difficult for Pagel, and this case was not sufficiently important for one, anyhow. But to tell the truth was impossible; it would have resulted in an unending chain of questions.

"Possibly your mother doesn't want you to live with her?"

"I live with my friend."

"And your mother doesn't want that?"

"She is *my* friend."

"And so not your mother's? Your mother disapproves of the intended marriage?"

The secretary looked at the superintendent, the superintendent looked at the secretary.

How clever they must feel to have found this out, Pagel was thinking. But they're not stupid. No, not at all. I'd like to know how they do it. They find out all there is to know. I must be more careful.

"Your mother has private means?" the secretary began again.

"Who has private means in the inflation?" countered Pagel.

"Then you support your mother?"

"No," said Pagel angrily.

"So she has enough to live on?"

"Certainly."

"And possibly supports you?"

"No."

"You earn your own living?"

"Yes."

"And that of your friend?"

"Yes."

"How?"

Stop, stop! Pagel thought. They want to catch me. They've heard something. But nothing can happen to me; gambling's not punishable. It's better not to mention it at all, though. Peter, I'm sure, has given nothing away.

"I sell things."

"What do you sell?"

"For instance, my friend's possessions."

"Whom do you sell them to?"

"For instance, the pawnbroker Feld in Gollnowstrasse."

"And if there's nothing left to be sold?"

"There's always something to be sold."

The official pondered a moment, looking up at his superior, who nodded slightly.

The secretary took a pencil, stood it on its point, eyed it reflectively and let it fall. "Your friend doesn't sell anything?" he asked casually.

"Nothing!"

"She sells absolutely nothing at all?"

"Nothing at all."

"You know that one can sell things which are not necessarily goods?"

What on earth, thought Pagel, dumbfounded, could Peter have sold for them to ask such foolish questions?

"I, too, didn't mean only such things as clothes," he said.

"What, for instance?"

"Pictures."

"Pictures?"

"Yes, pictures."

"What do you mean by pictures?"

"Oil paintings."

"Oil paintings. . . . Are you an artist, by any chance?"

"No—but I'm the son of an artist."

"Oh," said the secretary dissatisfied. "You sell your father's paintings. Well, we'll talk about that later. I only want you now to confirm that Fräulein Ledig sells nothing."

"Nothing. What there is to sell, I sell."

"It's possible," said the secretary, and his bilious pains tormented him acutely—this young fool put on too many airs for his liking—"it's possible that Fräulein Ledig sells something behind your back—without your knowledge?"

Pagel repressed the inquietude and misgivings which arose in him. "Theoretically it would be possible," he admitted.

"But in practice?"

"In practice impossible." He smiled. "For we don't possess very much and I should at once notice if the smallest trifle were missing."

"Oh?" said the secretary. He looked round at the superintendent, who returned the glance—it seemed to Pagel as if the shadow of a smile showed in their eyes. His uneasiness, his apprehensions increased. "We agreed, did we not"—the secretary half closed his eyes—"that one can sell not only tangible things, such as goods and paintings but—other things?"

Again this menace, now hardly veiled. What could Petra have sold?

"For example?" said Wolfgang crossly. "I can't conceive of any intangible things which my friend could have sold."

"For example . . ." the secretary began and looked up again at the superintendent.

The superintendent shut his eyes, at the same time moving his melancholy face from right to left, as if to say "No." Pagel saw it clearly. The secretary smiled—the moment had not yet come to tell the young man, but it was close at hand. "For example—we'll come to that presently," he said. "First let's get back to our questions. So you admit you get your livelihood by the sale of paintings?"

"Gentlemen!"—and Pagel got up and stood behind his chair, gripping it with both hands. Looking down at them he saw the knuckles show white against the reddened skin. "Gentlemen!" he said resolutely. "For some reason unknown you're playing cat-and-mouse with me. I won't stand it any longer. If Fräulein Ledig has done anything foolish I alone am responsible. I haven't looked after her sufficiently, I've never given her any money, probably not even enough to eat; I'm responsible for everything. And if any damage has been done I can make that good. Here is money." He tore at his pockets, he threw wads of notes on the table. "I'll pay for whatever damage has been done, but tell me at least what has happened."

"Money, a lot of money," said the secretary, and looked with anger at the preposterously mounting pile of notes. The superintendent had shut his eyes, as if he wanted to avoid seeing the money, as if he could not bear the sight.

"And here are two hundred and fifty dollars," Pagel cried, himself overwhelmed by the heap of money. It was the last wad to be thrown on the table. "I can't think of any damage which nowadays couldn't be repaired with that. I'll give you the lot," he said obstinately, "if you'll let Fräulein Ledig go this evening." He, too, was staring at the money, the monotonous white or brown of the German notes, the bright colors of the American.

The man in uniform let in Frau Thumann, Madam Po, her slatternly fat quivering in her loose garments. At a time when women's skirts barely reached the knee, a draggle-tail skirt reached to her heels. Her flabby gray face trembled, her underlip hung down, revealing the inner side.

"Thank heavens I'm still in time, Herr Pagel. How I did run. I was in such a to-do lest you should set my place on fire again as you threatened you would. I'd have been in good time but just as I was in Gollnowstrasse and thinking of nothing else but you and getting here in time, a car ran into a horse. Then I 'ad to stop, of course. All its guts outside and I says to myself—Auguste, take a look at that. They always say not to compare man and beast, but they must be pretty like inside, and then I thought to myself, you've always something wrong with your bladder and that oats-engine's got a bladder too. . . ."

"So Herr Pagel threatened to set your flat on fire if you didn't come here at once and withdraw your charge?"

But Frau Thumann wasn't born yesterday; she talked a lot but she couldn't be pinned down to anything. She had seen the money on the table, had acquainted herself with the situation, and was already gabbling on. "Who said that? He threatened me? I never said so, I demand that be showed on record, Herr Lieutenant. You put that in your own pipe and smoke it. Threaten me! And Herr Pagel such a pleasant, kind gentleman! I wouldn't have signed that statement against 'im and 'is girl if that man of yours hadn't talked me out of my senses. It's the law, he says. 'Ow can it be the law when I get my money? There can't be any talk of fraud then. No, I want my statement back, I make you responsible for that. . . ."

"Silence!" thundered the superintendent, for the secretary's halfhearted attempts at interruption were of no avail against this flood of talk. "Please go out of the room, Herr Pagel. We'll talk this matter over with your landlady herself."

Pagel looked at them for a moment, then at the money and papers on the table. He bowed and stepped out into the corridor. Opposite him was the door of the registration office; toward the street, just inside the exit, was the charge-room. He could see people in the street, where it seemed to have stopped raining. A cool breeze entered and strove with the stale air in the corridor.

Pagel leaned against the wall and lit the long-desired cigarette. They haven't arrested me yet, he thought, or else they wouldn't have let me go out by myself.

Inside, Frau Thumann's voice was rambling on, but tearfully. From time to time the bark of the superintendent could be heard—how well the melancholy man growled! But he had to; in his job one had to. And their letting him out proved nothing. All his money was lying there on the table; they knew quite well that nobody would run away from so much money. But why should they arrest him at all? And what was the trouble about Petra? What could Petra have sold?

He racked his brains. He wondered whether she might have sold some of Frau Thumann's belongings, bed linen or the like, to buy herself food. But that was all nonsense. Madam Po would have blurted it out long ago. Except for that, Petra had had no chance of taking anything.

Absent-mindedly he went to the exit; the air in the corridor had given him a headache, and the voices in the secretary's room disturbed him.

He stood in the street. The asphalt was shining like a mirror. Difficult day for taxi drivers, he thought as the cars passed him cautiously, feeling their way. No, I shouldn't like to be a taxi driver. But what on earth would I like to be? I'm no use for anything. I've wasted the whole day and now I shan't get Petra out, after all—I feel it. What can she have done?

He remained on the curb. Lights were reflected on the wet asphalt, but there was no light to guide him. Then somebody knocked into him, and it was Madam Po, of course.

"Lor', Herr Pagel, it's a good thing I saw you standing 'ere. I thought you'd hopped it. Don't do that, whatever you do. Fetch your good money. Why should you leave it to those fellows? I don't know, and never will, why they call themselves policemen, with a copper's sharp eye and a good wage and all that, and then somebody pulls their legs, telling 'em that you're a sharper with the three-card trick. You know, they squeeze the card like this and chuck it on the table and the other's got to guess what it is. . . . The blinking fools! A gent like you. But I've given them an earful. All above-board gambling, I told 'em, good class with the bank and gents, men in tail coats, only those who rake in the money, not you, of course. Ain't I heard about it often enough through the door when you were telling Peter? . . ."

"What's the trouble about Peter?"

"Well, you know, Herr Pagel, the trouble about her—well, I don't know either. They won't say a word, but there's something queer. The fraud charge and so on, that's finished with, they had to give it back to me, and I've torn it to pieces in front of Mister Yellow Eye—Mister Yellow Mug. An' about the curtain, I told them that was only a tipsy joke of yours, and if you'd like to give me something toward a new one . . ."

"I must get my money first," said Pagel and went back.

The secretary was now alone. Yes, interest in his case had slackened. It seemed that the dying man had made a mistake, after all; it wasn't an important matter, only a trifle. And this was no time for trifles. The secretary was no longer in a mood to employ his detective technique. Leo Gubalke's last official act had been wiped out before the dying man had drawn his last breath.

With indifference the secretary examined the copy of the art dealer's purchase note. It would be in order. He did not even ring up. It was too improbable that a man could win a thousand dollars in a couple of hours by the three-card trick. "But you're not to gamble," he said wearily and gave Pagel back the purchase note. "Games of chance are prohibited by law."

"Certainly," said Pagel politely. "I shan't gamble any more. May I stand bail for Fräulein Ledig?"

"She's no longer here," said the secretary, and for him she no longer existed, indeed. "She's already at Alexanderplatz."

"But why?" shouted Pagel. "Tell me why?"

"Because she indulges in lewd practices without being under police supervision," said the secretary, tired out. "Moreover, she is said to have a venereal disease."

It was just as well that there was a chair near—Pagel gripped it so hard, he thought it would break. "That's impossible," he managed to say at last.

"She's been recognized," explained the secretary and made to get on with his work. "By another girl of the same profession. Besides, she admitted it."

"She admitted it?"

"She admitted it."

"Thanks," said Pagel. He let go the chair and went toward the door.

"Your money, your papers," called the secretary impatiently.

Pagel made a renunciatory gesture, then thought better of it and pushed the lot back into his pockets.

"You'll lose your money," said the secretary indifferently.

Pagel repeated his gesture and marched out.

Only five minutes later, in the midst of his scribbling, did it occur to the secretary that he had given Herr Pagel false, or at least misleading, information. Petra had admitted to having practiced lewdness a few times about a year ago. She had not admitted to having a venereal disease.

The secretary deliberated a moment. Perhaps it wasn't so bad after all. Perhaps he wouldn't marry her now. One shouldn't marry such girls. Never!

And he returned to his writing. The case Ledig, the last official act of Oberwachtmeister Leo Gubalke, was wiped out as far as he was concerned.

Chapter Six

It Is Still Sultry after the Storm

I

After the first assault of junior and senior hotel staff, peace reigned round the friends von Prackwitz and Studmann. The reception manager lay sleeping on a rather dilapidated sofa in a basement room of the hotel. His was the leaden and ugly sleep of the drunken, with dropped jaw and wet mouth, a puffy face and a skin which looked suddenly stubby, as if he had not shaved for some time. Across his forehead was a red scratch received while falling down the stairs.

Von Prackwitz looked at his friend, then at the room into which he had been carried. It was not an inviting place. A big electric mangle took up most of the room, empty laundry baskets were piled up in one corner, against the wall leaned two ironing boards.

A waiter peered in—everybody seemed to think that he was entitled to do so without a word of apology, to make frivolous remarks, even to laugh. "Surely Herr von Studmann has a room of his own in the hotel?" Rittmeister von Prackwitz inquired angrily. "Why hasn't he been taken to it?"

The waiter shrugged his shoulders. "How should I know? I didn't bring him here," he said with an inquisitive glance at the sleeper.

Von Prackwitz restrained himself. "Please send me someone from the management."

The waiter vanished. Prackwitz waited.

And nobody came. The Rittmeister waited a long time. He leaned back in the kitchen chair, crossed his legs and yawned. He was tired out. He felt that he had gone through a good deal since his train, coming from Ostade, had entered Schlesische Bahnhof that morning; too much, in fact, for a simple countryman unfamiliar with cosmopolitan excitements.

In the hope that it would cheer him up he lit a cigarette. No one came. Surely the management must have learned that the reception manager and assistant director, after some incoherent remarks, had fallen downstairs in full view of the crowded entrance hall. Nevertheless none of the gentlemen of the management troubled himself about it. The Rittmeister frowned, wondering what lay behind this matter. Von Studmann had not fallen downstairs through an accident which might happen, by some cruel trick of fate, to the most noble. The intrusion of the junior staff, the absence of the senior, the breath of the sleeper, all gave the game away—Oberleutnant von Studmann was drunk, dead drunk. Was still drunk. Von Prackwitz wondered if Studmann had become a drunkard.

Had Studmann become a drunkard? It was possible. Everything was possible in these accursed times. But the Rittmeister immediately rejected this idea. Firstly, no confirmed drunkard ever fell downstairs—that happened only to the amateur; secondly, no big hotel would employ a drinker.

No—and Rittmeister von Prackwitz paced up and down the ironing room—there was more to it than that. Something unexpected must have happened, which he would hear about in time, and it was quite useless to rack his brains at present. The important question was, how would it affect Studmann? From the behavior of the staff Prackwitz concluded that the results would be unpleasant. Well, he would defend his friend with tooth and nail as long as Studmann was in no fit state to defend himself.

With tooth and nail! The Rittmeister was pleased with this warlike phrase. But should this turn out to be useless (and one knew these unfeeling money-makers), perhaps it was as well. He might be able to persuade him . . .

He thought of his lonely walk through Langestrasse to the Harvesters' Agency. He thought of the many solitary walks he had taken since he had left the army, always toward that imaginary point in his mind's eye. He remembered how often he had felt the need of a comrade. At the military college, in the army, during the war, there had always been friends with whom he could chat, fellows with similar sentiments, similar interests, the same sense of honor. Since the war all this had vanished, however—everyone was for himself alone; there was no concord, no community of feeling any longer.

He won't like to come as my guest, reflected the Rittmeister, going on to think of other things. Why should he fool himself. He had made a blunder that morning at the Harvesters' Agency; and he had made another blunder in giving the dollars to the foreman at Schlesische Bahnhof. And his behavior at police headquarters was possibly not altogether wise; moreover, after endless chasing about and talking, he had allowed an agent, an hour ago, to palm off on him sixty people whom he would not have a chance of inspecting before the following morning—all because he had wanted to bring this nauseating business to a conclusion. That, too, was perhaps not very wise.

Well, he was hot-headed and impulsive, rushing at things tooth and nail, although afterwards he always became bored with them. Besides, some matters he did not entirely grasp; perhaps his father-in-law, old Geheimrat von Teschow, was right—he would never become a real businessman.

The Rittmeister threw the stub of his cigarette into a corner and lit another. Yes, he mortified himself, he smoked this rubbish instead of his favorite brand. If his wife bought herself a couple of pairs of silk stockings he quarreled with her. But when the cattle dealer came and haggled with him over fat oxen, talked for one hour and bargained the next, allowed himself to be sent away and then came back again, wouldn't go and was humble when he was barked at—yes, then Herr von Prackwitz gave way. He became bored, and sold the fine oxen at a price which made the old Geheimrat, when he heard about it, exult. Who thereupon said, of course: "Excuse me, Joachim, I mustn't interfere with your business. Only I've never had money enough to be able to chuck it out of the window."

No, he could easily convince Studmann that at Neulohe he would be a very necessary and very useful assistant, who could not be too highly paid, friendship apart. Meier wouldn't be there much longer. What Violet had said on the telephone a little while ago (when he rang up about the carriages for the following morning) was beyond a joke. Meier, it seemed, hadn't brought in the crops, but had drunk himself silly during working hours. The Rittmeister's blood boiled at the thought. He was too easygoing with such fellows. Meier would go out on his ear.

His glance fell on his sleeping friend, and the Rittmeister's sense of justice forced him to admit that the friend too had got drunk during working hours. But with Studmann it was, of course, quite different. There must be special circumstances, surely.

But in the end nothing stood in the way of assuming that special circumstances obtained in the case of the Bailiff Meier as well—he also was not accustomed to being drunk while on duty.

"Of course, just while I'm away!" said the Rittmeister to himself. But that didn't sound right either, because he was often away without this kind of thing happening. And so he lost himself again in speculation about Studmann, on the one hand, and Meier on the other.

Thank heavens, there was a knock, and an elderly gentleman in dark clothes entered, who with a bow introduced himself as Dr. Zetsche, hotel physician.

Von Prackwitz in turn introduced himself and explained that he was an old army friend of Herr Studmann. "I happened to be in the hall when the accident occurred."

"Accident, yes," said the doctor, rubbing his nose thoughtfully and look-ing at the Rittmeister. "So you call it an accident?"

"If somebody falls downstairs, isn't that an accident?"

"Intoxication!" stated the doctor. "Complete inebriation, alcoholism. The scratch on his forehead is not serious."

"Do you know . . ." the Rittmeister began.

"Give him some Eumed or Aspirin or Pyramidon—anything which is handy when he wakes up."

"But there's nothing handy," said the Rittmeister, glancing round the ironing room. "Couldn't you arrange for my friend to be taken to his own room? It was a bad fall."

"It is a bad case. There are six people upstairs just as drunk, all of them employees of the hotel. An orgy under your friend's leadership. And the only participant who wasn't drunk—Herr Reichsfreiherr Baron von Bergen, one of the guests—was knocked down by your friend."

"I don't understand it," said the Rittmeister, dumbfounded by these revelations.

"I don't understand it either," said the doctor firmly. "And I don't wish to understand it."

"But do explain to me . . ."

"There's no explanation," said the doctor imperturbably. "A guest, a Reichsfreiherr, knocked down by a drunken reception manager!"

"There must have been special circumstances," insisted the Rittmeister. "I've known Herr von Studmann for a long time and he's always done his duty, even in the most difficult situations."

"Doubtless," replied the doctor politely, retreating before the other's agi-tation. With his hand on the doorknob he also became agitated. "One of the females was half naked—in the presence of the Reichfreiherr!" he shouted.

"I insist," cried the Rittmeister in a loud voice, "on Herr von Studmann being taken to a room fit for a human being."

He hurried after the retreating physician.

"I hold you responsible, doctor!"

"I refuse to take any responsibility," shouted the doctor over his shoulder, "for this orgy and its participants." And he dashed down a side corridor, fol-lowed by the Rittmeister.

"He's ill, doctor."

But the doctor had reached his goal. In a most sprightly manner the old gentleman leaped into an ascending lift. "He's drunk," he shouted, his feet already level with the stomach of his pursuer, who would have liked to lead him back by force to his duties. But in vain; the defaulting physician had escaped.

Von Prackwitz, who despite all his energy had been unable to do anything for his friend except the insignificant task of ordering some Pyramidon, uttered a curse and made his way back to the ironing room. However, the confusion of white corridors, all with the same doors, rendered him helpless. Searching for the doctor, he hadn't noticed into which particular hole he'd bolted. He looked hesitantly here and there, up and down all the corridors at least once. If he persisted he would find the right door. He remembered quite clearly having left it open.

Up and down he went—white doors, white corridors. His sense of direction led him to believe that he was farther and farther from his goal, but in the end even the number of cellars in a grand hotel must be finite. But there were the stairs. Had he passed them before? Should he go up or down? He went up, sure that it was wrong, and met an elderly female, with a rather severe look behind a pince-nez, who was putting clothes in a cupboard in total solitude.

The woman turned round at the sound of his footsteps and inspected the stranger.

Counscious that he was there quite illegitimately, von Prackwitz addressed her very politely. The laundry woman nodded her head gravely without saying a word. Von Prackwitz was decisive: "If you please, how do I get to the ironing room from here?"

His polite smile didn't in the least soften the woman's severe look. She seemed to reflect, then made a large gesture with her hands: "There are many ironing rooms here. . . ."

Von Prackwitz tried to describe this one to her, without having to mention Studmann. "There are wash baskets in the corner," he said. "Oh, yes, and a chaise-lounge with blue flowers on the covering." And he added, not without a little bitterness, "It was pretty threadbare."

She reflected again. Eventually she said coldly, "I don't think we have a chaise-lounge in disrepair. Everything is immediately repaired here."

This was not exactly the information von Prackwitz wished to hear upon his inquiry. However, in his present and in his former jobs he'd always had to do with people, and the type who is never able to answer a question precisely was well known to him.

Despite this, he tried again. "So where is the hotel lobby?" he asked.

The answer was prompt: "Hotel guests are completely forbidden to enter the service rooms."

"Totally," said the Rittmeister seriously.

"What—?" she almost shouted, and quite lost her control and bearing, becoming a bit flustered, like a chicken.

"Totally or, better still, strictly forbidden," corrected the Rittmeister. "Not completely. So, good evening and many thanks!"

He addressed her with dignity, as if she was the commander of a regiment and he a young lieutenant. He left. Completely or totally confused, she stayed.

The Rittmeister was now more comfortable being lost. He'd been enlivened by the little incident. It was true that he'd once again not been able to do anything for his friend. This he regretfully admitted. Nevertheless things like that do one good. Besides, he was now walking on carpets, and if he was perhaps farther and farther from Studmann, he seemed to be approaching inhabited regions of the hotel.

The Rittmeister stood before a row of doors in dull polished oak: massive doors, doors inspiring confidence.

"Cashier I," he read. "Cashier II." And went on. There came the Service Cashier, Buying Departments A and B, Staff Inquiries, Registrar, Physician. He looked disapprovingly at the physician's plate, shrugged his shoulders and went on.

"Secretariat." Still farther, he decided.

"Director Haase."

The Rittmeister hesitated. No, not there. Farther along.

"Director Kainz." "Director Lange."

"Managing Director Vogel."

The Rittmeister knocked perfunctorily and entered.

Behind the desk sat a large man dictating to a very good-looking young secretary at the typewriter. He hardly looked up when the Rittmeister introduced himself.

"Pleased-to-meet-you-please-take-a-seat," he said with the absent-minded unreal politeness of a man whose profession it is to make the acquaintance of a stream of new people. "One moment, please. Where did we get to, Fräulein? Do you smoke? Then please help yourself."

The telephone rang.

"Vogel speaking—Yes, his doctor? What's his name? What? Please spell it. What's his name? Schröck? Medical Superintendent Schröck? When will he be coming? In five minutes? All right, bring him to me at once. Yes, that will be all right, I'll have time. I've only to dictate something and a short interview." He looked vaguely at the Rittmeister across the telephone. "Say in three minutes. All right. Under no circumstances is he to be taken to No. 37, but brought straight to me. Thanks." The receiver was replaced. "Where did we get to, Fräulein?"

The young secretary muttered something and the managing director went on with his dictating.

You can only spare me three minutes, thought the Rittmeister angrily. You wait, you'll be mistaken. I'll show you. . . . But he heard a name, started and listened intently.

The director was dictating quickly and mechanically. "We very much regret that Herr von Studmann, whose personal and professional qualities we have learned to appreciate during his eighteen months' service in our Berlin organization . . ."

He paused for breath.

"One moment," cried the Rittmeister and rose.

"One moment," murmured the director. "I'll be finished immediately. Where did we get to, Fräulein?"

"No, Fräulein," protested the Rittmeister. "Excuse me. If I understand you rightly you are dictating a testimonial for Herr von Studmann. Herr von Studmann is a friend of mine."

"Splendid," said the director calmly. "Then you'll take care of him. We were in a fix."

"Herr von Studmann is lying on a worn-out sofa in an ironing room," complained the Rittmeister. "There's not a soul to look after him."

"Very regrettable," admitted the director. "A mistake which I must ask you to excuse owing to the momentary confusion created by the occurrence. Fräulein, telephone that Herr von Studmann is to be taken to his room without attracting any attention. Without attracting any attention, Fräulein, please. Without attracting any attention!"

"You want to sack Herr von Studmann," cried the Rittmeister indignantly, pointing to the notebook. "You can't condemn a man without hearing his defense."

The managing director spoke without any show of feeling. "Herr von Studmann will be taken at once to his room."

"You can't dismiss him straight away," cried von Prackwitz.

"We're not dismissing him," contradicted the other. Von Prackwitz had the impression that this gray giant could not be touched by any emotion, any entreaty, any human feeling. "We're granting Herr von Studmann an extended holiday."

"Herr von Studmann doesn't need a holiday," the Rittmeister assured him, intimidated by this unassailable man.

"Herr von Studmann does need a holiday. His nervous system has gone to pieces."

"You judge without hearing him," the Rittmeister declared with less conviction.

"In the room occupied by Reichsfreiherr Baron von Bergen," said the managing director as monotonously as if he were reading from a statement, "we found nineteen champagne bottles, of which fifteen were empty. Four cognac bottles—empty. Two hotel pages—completely intoxicated. Two adult male employees—also completely intoxicated. An insufficiently clad chambermaid—dead drunk. A charwoman in our temporary employ—dead drunk. The guest, Herr Baron von Bergen, quite sober but with a black eye and almost unconscious as the result of several brutal blows on the head. Doubtless you know how we discovered your friend Herr von Studmann."

Abashed, Rittmeister von Prackwitz bowed his head.

"On the one hand," said the managing director a little more cordially, "your loyalty to your friend does you honor. On the other hand, I would ask—does a cultured man with a sound nervous system share in such a bacchanalia?"

"But there must have been some reason for it," von Prackwitz cried despairingly. "Otherwise Herr von Studmann would never . . ."

"Can you think of any reason which would have made you take part in such an orgy, Herr von . . . ?"

"Prackwitz," prompted the Rittmeister.

"Herr von Prackwitz. You will understand that we cannot any longer employ in our organization a man so compromised, if for no other reason than the bad example to our staff."

There was a curt, important knock. The door flew open and in stormed a little bowlegged old man with a tall forehead, shining blue eyes and a faded beard, which no doubt had once been fiery. He was followed slowly by a thick-set man whose jacket fitted so tightly across his shoulders that he looked like a prize-fighter.

"Have you still got him?" croaked the fiery old man. "Where is he? For God's sake don't let him get away. Türke, see about it! Make haste! Don't let him escape. Run! I've been chasing this boy all over Berlin for the last twenty-four hours. I don't believe there's a haunt in this wretched town into which I haven't stuck my nose, damn it!"

He took hold of the above-mentioned nose and looked breathlessly at the dumbfounded people round him. The thick-set man in the tight jacket, presumably Herr Türke, stood behind.

Probably because his profession had accustomed him to the most extraordinary examples of the human species, the managing director was the first to emerge from stupefaction.

"Vogel," he introduced himself. "I presume I'm speaking with Dr. Schröck?"

"No, I'm speaking with you," shouted the old man, letting go his nose. The transition from calmness to rage was so sudden that all—except the imperturbable Herr Türke—were startled. In that bowlegged body a fiery temperament must be concealed. "I've been asking you for the last three minutes whether that fellow's still here."

"If you mean Reichsfreiherr Baron von Bergen," began the managing director, "I know he's in Room 37."

"Türke," screamed Dr. Schröck, "did you hear that? Room 37! Go and fetch the young rotter, alive or dead! Look out—you know how tricky he is. Don't forget he locked your colleague in his room!"

The thick-set one nodded. "He won't get away with it this time. He couldn't have done such a thing to me, sir." Leisurely he departed.

"An excellent male nurse," muttered Dr. Schröck. "A man without a trace of sentimentality." Suddenly his anxiety returned. "He can't have got away by any chance?"

"No, no," the managing director reassured him. "He can't get away. Things have happened, unfortunately." He gave a glance at the Rittmeister. "I'll report to you as soon as I've dealt with this gentleman."

With a sigh of relief Dr. Schröck sank into a chair, and mopped his forehead. "He can't get away then, thank God. Something's happened. Wherever that fellow goes something happens." He gave a sigh of resignation. "Police? Public prosecutor?"

"No, no," the managing director assured him. "The gentleman is sure to apologize." He glanced with annoyance at the Rittmeister. "We'll make good any damage. One of our employees unfortunately so far forgot himself as to strike the Baron."

The old man leaped out of his chair. "Where is he? Who is it?" He pointed to the Rittmeister. "Did you?"

"He apparently threw a champagne bottle at his head," wailed the managing director.

"Splendid," cried the old man. "A champagne bottle! Magnificent! Not you? Your friend? Let me meet him. I must thank him. It isn't possible? Why isn't it possible?"

"Your charge seems to have made my friend—and half a dozen other people—mysteriously drunk."

"There you are," said Dr. Schröck. "The usual dirty business." He sat down resigned. "I'll arrange everything, nobody shall suffer. You, my dear managing director, seem to have been dazzled by the title of Reichsfreiherr and so on. Let me tell you this Reichsfreiherr is the most irresponsible, pampered, vulgar, sadistic little beast in the world. And a coward at that."

"Dr. Schröck!" implored the managing director.

"That's the truth! He imagines that because he's been put under restraint as a result of his extravagance, and was acquitted in some scandal because of paragraph fifty-one, he can do what he likes. He's lazy and without respect, without a trace of human feeling." Dr. Schröck flared up. "The fellow ought to be whipped morning and evening; he ought to be put in prison or at least in a State asylum. There they'd cure him of his nasty tricks!"

"But he's in your sanatorium—this poor fellow."

"Unfortunately," grumbled Dr. Schröck. "Unfortunately. I offer him to my colleagues as if he were sour beer, but they won't take him, although he pays more than any other patient. Patient! My goodness, he's just a vicious monkey. When I take him back to my institution, behind bars and locked doors in the ward for troublesome cases, of course, he'll be tolerable for a month or two— especially if your friend has given him a good hiding."

"A quarter of an hour ago he was nearly unconscious," interposed the managing director.

"Excellent! But he'll soon be overbearing again. He teases harmless patients into a frenzy, annoys the attendants, steals cigarettes, drives me and my assistants mad. . . . And he's by no means stupid, he's devilishly cunning. He's always escaping. Watch him as much as we like, he always finds some fool. Borrows money or steals it. . . . And I can do nothing," said the old man gnashing his teeth. "I can't get rid of him. As he's not in full possession of his mental faculties, the law's on his side." He sat there, grown suddenly older and exhausted. "For twenty-four hours I've been chasing him in my car." He looked round. "If only I could get rid of him," he groaned despairingly. "But then, as likely as not, he'd regain his freedom—no, I couldn't take the responsibility. However, let's at least try the ultimate remedy—expense. Perhaps his mother—he has only one mother, unfortunately—will get tired of paying for him. Herr Director, may I ask you for a bill, a detailed account?"

"Yes," said the managing director, hesitating. "There's been a lot of alcohol consumed, champagne, cognac . . ."

"Nonsense." Dr. Schröck grew angry. "Those are trifles. Champagne, cognac! No, every person the fellow's harmed is entitled to damages. I hear of half a dozen persons whom he's made drunk. . . . Your friend, for instance, I think?"

"I don't know whether my friend . . ." began von Prackwitz awkwardly.

"For Heaven's sake," cried the incensed Schröck, "don't be a fool! Excuse me, I shouldn't say that, of course, but really don't be a fool! The greater the expense the sooner there's a chance of his mother locking him up one of these fine days in a well-guarded lunatic asylum. You're doing a service to mankind."

The Rittmeister looked at the managing director, then at the typewriter in which the testimonial was still inserted. "My friend, who is assistant director and chief receptionist here, is to be discharged by the hotel management because he was intoxicated while on duty," he said.

"Excellent," cried Dr. Schröck, but this time the managing director interrupted him.

"I must contradict Herr von Prackwitz," he said hastily. "We're granting Herr von Studmann a long holiday, say three months, even six months. During that time Herr von Studmann, in view of his efficiency, will easily find another position. We do not dismiss him for drunkenness on duty," he explained firmly, but without emotion. "We simply ask him to look round for another field of activity because in no circumstances must a hotel employee make himself conspicuous. Unfortunately, Herr von Studmann, when he fell down the hall stairs insufficiently clad and completely intoxicated, made himself very conspicuous in front of many employees and still more guests."

Dr. Schröck was satisfied. "Together with an indemnity for a lost position we must consider the question of damages. That pleases me immensely; I see light. I shouldn't be surprised if that didn't put paid to young Bergen. How do I find your friend? At your place? Many thanks. I'll make a note of your address. You'll be hearing from me in two or three days' time. Splendid. By the way, we pay, of course, in stable currency. I assure you that you can't put in for too much in the way of expenses. Oh, don't worry. Do you think I mind? Not a bit. It hurts nobody, I only wish it did."

The Rittmeister rose. Life was a strange thing. Somebody had actually fallen downstairs for once and got rid of his troubles. Herr von Studmann could come to Neulohe as a man free from worry, as a paying guest if he liked. He, Prackwitz, would be no longer alone.

He took his leave, Dr. Schröck once again regretting that he was not allowed to shake Studmann's hand for knocking the Baron down.

As von Prackwitz approached the door it opened and there stumbled in, guided and supported by the attendant Türke, a creature bedizened in red and yellow, exceedingly wretched to look at, with his black eye and swollen face, contemptible with his hang-dog glance.

"Bergen!" said Dr. Schröck in a voice like a crow's. "Bergen, come here!"

The coward broke down, fell on his knees. His gorgeous pajamas were in strange contrast with his miserable appearance. "Dr. Schröck," he begged, "don't punish me, don't send me to a lunatic asylum. I've done nothing. They drank the champagne quite willingly."

"Bergen, to begin with, you are deprived of your cigarettes."

"Please don't do that, Dr. Schröck! You know I can't bear it. I can't live without smoking. And I only shot into the ceiling when the gentleman didn't want to drink."

Von Prackwitz closed the door softly, and the miserable creature's wails, a child without a child's purity and innocence, died away. If only I were back in Neulohe, he thought. Berlin makes me vomit. No, it's not only the printing of money which has gone mad. He looked down the clean corridor with its dark polished oak doors. It all had the appearance of soundness, but inside it was rotten. Was the war still in everybody's bones? I don't know, and anyway don't understand.

Walking slowly along the corridor he came into the hall and inquired for his friend's room. A lift took him up to just beneath the roof. There von Studmann sat on the edge of his bed, his head in his hands.

"I've a rotten hangover, Prackwitz," he said, looking up. "Have you time to come with me into the open air for half an hour?"

"I've all the time in the world," said the Rittmeister, suddenly cheerful. "Both for you and the open air. But first let me put on your collar. . . ."

II

The little bailiff, his head thick and muddled with drink, had thrown himself on his bed just as he was, with mud-stained boots and clothes soaking wet with the rain. Through the open window he could see that it was still pouring down, and he could hear someone scolding from the direction of the cowhouse and the pigsty. What are they doing? he thought. What's the matter with them? My God, I want to sleep. I must sleep and forget; when I wake up I shall find out it's not true!

He put his hand over his eyes and it was dark. Ah, this darkness was good! Darkness was the void; where the void is, nothing is; nothing has happened, nothing has been messed up.

But the darkness lightened into gray and the gray became brighter. Out of the brightness appeared the table, the bottle, the glasses . . . the letter!

Oh, God, what was he to do? Little Meier pressed his hand more firmly against his eyes. It grew dark again. But flaming wheels of many colors were circling in that darkness, faster and faster, till he felt giddy and sick.

He sat up and stared about the room, which was still light. He loathed it. How familiar it all was! The stinking slop-pail beside the washstand! The photos of nude girls around the mirror! He had cut them out of magazines and pinned them on the wallpaper, and he was sick of the sight of them. How he loathed his present life and what had happened! He would like to get out of this situation; to be something quite different. But what could he do? He sat there with protruding eyes and a swollen face. There was nothing that he could do. Everything was going to collapse about him. He must just stay still and wait— and he hadn't wanted to do anything bad! If only he could sleep . . .

Thank God, there was a knock at the door of the adjoining office, to break the monotony. "Come in," he growled, and when the person outside hesitated, he growled still louder: "Come in, you fool!" And was immediately frightened. Suppose it was somebody he oughtn't to call a fool—the Geheimrat, or Frau von Prackwitz—then he'd be in the soup again. What a life!

But it was only old Kowalewski, the overseer.

"What's the matter?" Meier shouted, delighted to have someone on whom he could vent his fury.

"I just wanted to ask a question, bailiff," said the old man humbly, cap in hand. "We had a telegram from our daughter in Berlin; she's coming tomorrow morning by the ten-o'clock train—"

"So that's what you wanted to ask, Kowalewski?" sneered Meier. "Well, now you've asked it, you can go."

"It's only about her luggage," said the overseer. "Is a carriage going tomorrow to the station?"

"Of course," said Meier. "Tomorrow quite a lot of carriages are going to the station. To Ostade and Meienburg and Frankfurt, too."

"I just thought whether one of our carriages could also fetch her luggage," explained Kowalewski.

"Ah, that's what you thought! You're a mighty fine cock, overseer, talking about 'our' carriages."

The overseer was not discouraged. He had experienced generations of bailiffs, and this one was perhaps the worst of the lot. But a poor man had to beg a hundred times before one of the powerful said "Yes" for a change; and sometimes little Meier was quite different. He was like that; he liked to have his little joke; one ought not to blame him for it.

"It's only because of her box, bailiff," he begged. "Sophie doesn't mind walking at all; she likes walking."

"But she likes to lie down on her back still better, eh, Kowalewski?" grinned Meier.

Not a muscle of the old man's face twitched. "Perhaps a farmer will be going to the station," he meditated, half-aloud.

Meier, however, was satisfied. He had vented a bit of his rage, he had felt not altogether without power. "Well, clear out, Kowalewski," he said graciously. "The harvesters and the Rittmeister are arriving by the ten-o'clock train. There'll be room for your little Sophie. Hop it, you stinking old crow," he shouted, and with a muttered "Very many thanks" and "Good evening," the overseer retreated.

Black Meier was alone again with his thoughts. "If only I could at least sleep..." he growled to himself, his ill-temper returning. "Any damned fool can sleep when he's drunk as much as I have, but not me; I never have any luck, of course."

But perhaps he had not drunk enough. In the inn he had been quite tight; the trouble was, it had blown off by now. He could go back again, but he was too lazy for that. Besides, he would have to pay for all he had had there, and he shuddered at the thought of the reckoning. Well, Amanda was sure to put in an appearance this evening, and she could go and fetch him a bottle of schnapps. It would give her something to do; he couldn't bear the thought of women today. If Vi hadn't made such an exhibition of herself, he wouldn't have behaved so stupidly. But that sort of thing was enough to drive a man mad.

Meier lurched from his soiled, damp bed and stumbled round the room. He had remembered that the forester had told him to pack and get away as soon as possible.

His boxes lay on top of the wardrobe. He had two small suitcases, a cheap dilapidated one of fabric-covered cardboard and a smart leather case which he had taken away with him on leaving his last job—it had only been standing about doing nothing in a loft. Meier squinted up at this suitcase; the cheapness of its acquisition always pleased him.

When you look at a suitcase you think of traveling. And when you think of traveling the money for the fare occurs to you. Thus it was that, without having looked through the half-open office door, Meier had a vision of the safe, bulky and painted green, the gilded decorations of which had become a dirty yellow with the years.

Usually the Rittmeister kept the key and only on pay days or for some special expenditure would fetch from it the necessary money. Meier was, of course, utterly reliable in money matters, but the Rittmeister was a great man and mistrustful! It would serve him right if he came a real cropper through his suspicions.

The bailiff pushed the office door open with his shoulder and planted himself thoughtfully in front of the safe. Yesterday evening the Rittmeister had checked the amount in hand twice over—the safe held quite a handsome packet of money, more than Bailiff Meier could earn in three years. Lost in thought, he fingered the key in his pocket. But he didn't take it out. He didn't unlock the safe. No, I'm not such a fool as all that, he thought.

Whatever he did was always on the safe side; he might possibly be sacked, but he couldn't be jailed for it. To get the sack didn't matter. One always got a new job after a while; an employer never stated in his testimonial the real reason for dismissal. But Meier had a lively aversion to jail.

I'd only squander the money in a week or two, he told himself. Then I'd be broke and couldn't get another job, because they were looking for me. No, certainly not.

Nevertheless he stayed before the safe for a long time; it fascinated him. A way out of the dirt, he thought. They don't catch everybody, by a long way. They say you can get false papers quite cheaply in Berlin. I would only like to know where. How long will it take before the Lieutenant learns that I haven't delivered the letter? Well, tonight those two are going to miss each other. You'll have to go to bed hungry, dear Vi. Meier grinned with malice.

There was another knock, and he jumped away from the safe and leaned negligently against the wall before calling out: "Come in," this time politely. But all his trouble was unnecessary; once again it was no one of any consequence— only the charwoman, the coachman's wife with the seven urchins, Frau Hartig.

"Your supper, Herr Meier."

Meier did not want her to see the soiled bed in the next room (Amanda could tidy it up a bit later); he was in no mood for a dust-up now. "Put it on the desk," he said. "What is it?"

"I don't know why the women think so much of you," said Frau Hartig, taking the lid off the dish. "Now Armgard is starting, too. . . . A roast and red cabbage in the evening for a bailiff. . . ."

"Rot," said Meier. "I'd have preferred a herring. Whoa! Look at the fat! To tell the truth, I've had a drop too much."

"I can see that," confirmed Frau Hartig. "Why can't you men lay off the booze? Supposing women did the same! Was Amanda with you?"

"What next! I don't need her for boozing." He laughed, suddenly quite lively and in high spirits. "What about it, Hartig? Would you like the grub? I can't eat tonight."

Frau Hartig beamed. "My old man'll be pleased. If I quickly cook a few potatoes to go with it, it'll be sufficient for us both."

"No," drawled Meier by the wall. "That's for you, Hartig, not for your old man. Do you think I want him to get strong on it? You're crazy. No, if you want the food you must eat it here. On the spot!" He looked hard at her.

"Here?" she asked, returning his stare.

Their voices had changed, become almost soft.

"Here!" answered Black Meier.

"Then," said Frau Hartig in even lower tones, "I'll close the windows and draw the curtains. If somebody saw me eating here . . ."

Meier didn't answer, but he followed her with his eyes as she closed the two windows and carefully drew the curtains. "Lock the door as well," he added softly.

She looked at him, then she did so. She sat down in front of the tray on the desk. "Well, it'll taste good to me," she said with simulated vivacity.

Again he did not reply. He watched her as she put the meat on the plate, then the potatoes, then the red cabbage. Now she ladled gravy over it all. . . .

"Hartig, listen," he said quietly.

"What is it?" she asked without looking up, apparently only concerned with her food.

"Yes, what was I going to say?" he drawled. "Yes, where do you button up your blouse—in front or at the back?"

"In front," she whispered, starting to cut the meat. "Do you want to have a look?"

"Yes," said he, adding impatiently, "well, get on."

"You must do it yourself," she replied. "Or else my food will get cold. Ah you . . . ah. . . . Yes, darling . . . such good food . . . yes . . . yes. . . ."

III

Violet von Prackwitz was having supper with her mother. The manservant stood stiffly by the sideboard. Räder, although not much over twenty, was of the "serious servant" type. He was obsessed by the notion that his employers would one day move out of their jerry-built place into the old people's mansion, where he would no longer be the manservant but the butler. Therefore, in spite of his faultless demeanor, he regarded the old Geheimrat and his wife as people who withheld from his master and mistress something which by right belonged to them. Most of all, however, he hated old Elias, who lorded it over the silver at the Manor. How could anyone bear to have a name like Elias, anyway! His own Christian name was Hubert, and his employers called him by it.

Hubert had one eye on the table, in case they needed anything, and both ears on the conversation. Although he did not move one muscle of his somewhat lined face he was filled with glee at the way in which the young Fräulein was duping her mother. For, as Hubert had little to do, what with Armgard the cook and Lotte the servant, he made it his business to be acquainted with all that went on, to see everything, to know everything. Hubert knew a great deal—he knew, for instance, exactly how the young Fräulein had spent her afternoon. Which madam didn't know.

"Have you seen to Grandpapa's geese this afternoon?" Hubert heard Frau von Prackwitz ask.

Frau Eva von Prackwitz was a very good-looking woman, perhaps a trifle plump, though one noticed it only when she stood beside the tall, lean Rittmeister. She had all the sensual charm of a woman who was glad to be a woman and who, in addition, loved country life, and whom the country seemed to reward for this with an inexhaustible freshness and cheerfulness.

Vi pulled a reproachful face. "But, Mamma, there was a storm this afternoon."

Hubert understood. This evening Fräulein Violet was playing the role of a small girl, which she particularly liked to do whenever she had been up to some very grown-up mischief. This would stop her parents from thinking any wrong of her—that is, from thinking of her aright.

"You would really do me a favor, Violet, if you kept an eye on Grandpapa's geese. You know Papa gets so annoyed when the geese get into his vetch. And the storm only started at six o'clock."

"If I were a goose I wouldn't like to be in Grandpapa's old damp park with its sour grass," declared Vi with a childish pout. "I believe the park stinks."

Hubert, who well knew how often and how gladly the young Fräulein stayed secretly in the Geheimrat's park, was enchanted by the naïveté of this precautionary reply.

"But, Vi, the word 'stink'—and at table!" Frau Eva's calm and smiling glance passed over Räder's wooden yet far from youthful face.

"All right, Mamma. I won't go there, I think it st—smells of corpses."

"Stop it, Vi!" Frau Eva knocked on the table very energetically with the handle of her fork. "That's enough. Sometimes I think you might be a little more grown-up."

"Yes, Mamma? Were you more grown-up when you were my age?" The girl's expression was completely innocent—nevertheless the servant wondered if the artless young person had possibly heard a rumor of her mother's youthful pranks. There was a story about the old Geheimrat thrashing a farmer's boy out of his daughter's bedroom window; and perhaps it was true. At all events, Hubert found that Frau Eva's next question fitted in very well with the rumor. "What had you to say to Meier that took such a long time this afternoon?" she asked.

"Pooh!" said Vi disparagingly and pouted again. "Old Black Meier." She laughed. "Imagine, Mamma, all the girls and women in the village are said to run after him, and yet he's as ugly as—I don't know, as old Abraham." (Abraham was the he-goat they kept in the stable, in accordance with the old cavalry idea that he banished disease.)

"The dessert, Hubert!" admonished madam still calmly, but with rather dangerously flashing eyes.

Räder marched out of the room, not without regret. Fräulein Vi had made a slip. And now she would certainly get a good talking-to. She had been piling it on a little too much in her exuberance; madam was not a fool by any means. Hubert would have liked to hear what the mother said, and above all what the daughter answered. But Hubert was not one to eavesdrop; he marched straight away to the kitchen. Granted common sense, there were many ways of learning what one wanted to know. One needn't shake, by eavesdropping, an employer's confidence in an exemplary servant.

Old Forester Kniebusch sat at the kitchen table, waiting.

"Good evening, Herr Räder," he said very politely, for the detached and taciturn manservant was regarded as a power in the land. "Is supper finished yet?"

"The dessert, Armgard," said Räder, and started to arrange the plates on the tray. "Good evening, Herr Kniebusch. Whom do you want to speak to? The Rittmeister doesn't come back till tomorrow."

"I only wanted to see madam," said Kniebusch cautiously. After long deliberation he had come to the conclusion that he had better lay his knowledge before the older generation. Fräulein was too young to be of any real use to an old man.

"I'll announce you, Herr Kniebusch," said Räder.

"Herr Räder," asked Kniebusch, "could it be arranged that Fräulein Vi is not present?"

Räder's face showed even more furrows. To gain time he snapped at the cook: "Get on, Armgard. I've told you a hundred times that you're to arrange the cheese dish before I come."

"In this heat!" sneered the cook, who hated him. "The butter balls would stick to each other."

"You need not take the butter out of the refrigerator until the last moment. But if you're still only cutting up the cheese!" And in low tones to the forester: "Why shouldn't the young Fräulein be present?"

Kniebusch became visibly embarrassed. "Well, you know . . . I only thought . . . not everything is fit for a young girl's ears."

Räder regarded the embarrassed man with the inscrutability of an idol. "What's not for young girls, Herr Kniebusch?" he asked, but without any noticeable inquisitiveness.

Kniebusch turned red with the sheer labor of inventing a lie. "Well, Herr Räder, you understand, when one is so young and the rutting season on . . ."

Räder gloated over his confusion. "There's no rutting now," he said contemptuously. "All the same, I understand. Thanks. Uniform—u-ni-form is the password."

With expressionless fishy eyes he looked at the intimidated, confused forester. Then he turned to the cook. "Well, ready at last, Armgard! But if madam scolds, then I shall tell her whose fault it is. Don't speak to me, I've nothing to say to you." And he went away with the tray in his hand, grave, far from youthful, rather mysterious. "We'll have a word later, Herr Kniebusch," he said and vanished, leaving the forester in the dark as to whether he was to be announced or not.

"What a swelled head that donkey has!" grumbled the cook. "Don't have anything to do with him, Herr Kniebusch. He pumps you—and afterwards tells everything to the Rittmeister."

"Does he always behave to you like that?" inquired the forester.

"Always," she exclaimed. "Never a good word to Lotte or me. The Rittmeister's not nearly so grand as that ass. He won't even eat at the same table with us." She stared at the forester, who muttered something unintelligible. "No, he carries his plate to his room. I believe, Herr Kniebusch," she whispered mysteriously, "he's peculiar. He has no interest in women. He's . . ."

"Yes?" The forester was curious.

"I don't want anything to do with such a creature," asserted Armgard. "Do you think he would as much as touch the Rittmeister's cigarettes!"

"Yes, doesn't he?" asked the forester hopefully. "All servants do. Elias always smokes the old gentleman's cigars. I know the smell because the Geheimrat sometimes gives me one."

"What? Is that true about Elias? I'll rub it in to the old rascal. Fancy pinching cigars from the master and then storming at me because I haven't wiped my boots properly at the Manor entrance!"

"For God's sake, Armgard, please don't say a word to him. I might have made a mistake." The old man fell over himself with anxiety. "It's probably quite a different cigar, and you've just said that Hubert smokes the Rittmeister's cigarettes. . . ."

"I haven't said anything of the kind. I said quite the opposite. He doesn't smoke, he doesn't drink, and he doesn't listen at doors; he thinks himself much too grand for all that, the silly fool."

"I'm much obliged to you," a voice rasped, and the two looked intensely startled at Räder's face. (Old Frog Face, thought Armgard furiously.) "So I'm a silly fool! It's good to know what people think of you. Go to madam, Armgard;

she wants to talk to you. Not that I should have told tales about the cheese, anyway; you're too stupid for me to bother about. You can tell her, however, that in your eyes I'm a silly fool. . . . Come, Herr Kniebusch."

And, obedient but very depressed by all the complications of domestic life, the forester followed with an embarrassed squint at the cook, who, crimson with rage, fought back her tears.

Räder's room was only a narrow strip of floor in the basement, between the coal cellar and washhouse. It was another reason for his grudge against Elias, who had a proper large two-windowed room in the upper story of the Manor, very cozily furnished with antique furniture. Räder's room contained only an iron camp bed, an iron washstand, an old iron folding chair from the garden and an old wobbly deal wardrobe. One couldn't tell that a human being lived in the room. No article of dress was visible, nor the smallest utensil of the occupant's, not even soap or towel in the washstand, for Hubert Räder washed himself in the bathroom.

"There," he said. "There, you can sit down on the chair till she comes. Then you can get up and give her your seat."

"Who's coming?" asked Kniebusch, confused.

"You're not to be such a chatterer, Herr Kniebusch," declared the servant with serious disapproval. "A man doesn't chatter—above all, with women."

"I haven't said anything at all," the forester maintained.

"Naturally she has to wash her face first, because she's been crying, but when she's finished with madam she'll come."

"Who's coming, who's with madam?" asked the forester, completely confused.

"A uniform is a uniform," the servant informed him. "My livery, of course, doesn't count, nor your green one, because you're only in private service. If you were a Government forester, that would be different."

Kniebusch, completely lost, agreed. "Yes, yes." He was still hoping, of course, that he would in the end understand something of Räder's enigmatic remarks.

"A civilian shouldn't get mixed up with uniforms," announced the servant earnestly. After pondering a long time, his brow puckered, he opened the door a little and listened. Then he nodded, went across the room to the forester and said in a low voice reproachfully: "You're a civilian, Herr Kniebusch, and you want to get mixed up with uniforms."

"Certainly not," cried the forester, aghast.

"Have you ever considered, Herr Kniebusch, what the Geheimrat loves most?" went on the servant, returning to his post by the door.

"No. . . . Why? I don't understand what you're getting at, Herr Räder."

"Don't you really?"

"No. But I believe he loves his forest most."

The servant nodded. "Yes, he won't want to give it away before he dies. And to whom will he leave it?" He looked expectantly at the forester.

"There's the old lady," pondered the forester, "and there's his son at Birnbaum. And here is the Rittmeister." He considered the case.

"Well, whom will he give the forest to?" questioned the servant condescendingly, as one who puts a very easy question to a backward schoolchild. "Or will he split it up in two or three portions?"

"Split up—his forest?" Kniebusch was full of contempt. "No, don't imagine such a thing, Herr Räder. If they split the forest after his death I believe he'd come out of his grave and pull up the boundary stones. But he'll have written down somewhere what he wants done with it."

"And who will he have set down, Herr Kniebusch?" the servant persisted. "Perhaps the old lady?"

"Certainly not. She's always saying that she won't go into the wood because of the snakes. No, Herr Räder, she won't come into it at all."

"Or the son in Birnbaum?"

"I don't think so, either," said the forester. "He hasn't a good word for him, because he's much too grand for his liking and is always asking for money. And now he's gone and bought a racing car . . . so that he can run away from his debts, as the old man grumbled."

"So the old man knows about the racing car," meditated the servant. "You told him that for certain, Herr Kniebusch."

Red in the face, the old man wanted to protest, but Hubert paid no attention. "Then madam upstairs will inherit the forest," he said conclusively, pointing with his thumb to the ceiling.

"Even when he can't stand the Rittmeister?" queried the forester anxiously. "And this business with the geese will also turn out badly."

"Who, then, will inherit the forest?" persisted the servant.

"I don't know," said the forester, perplexed. "There are his sister's children in Pomerania, but—"

"What about his grandchild?"

"Who?" The forester's jaw dropped. "What do you mean? Fräulein Violet is only fifteen." But Räder continued to stare at him. "Of course," went on Kniebusch thoughtfully, "she's the only one whom he takes with him when he goes shooting, that's true. . . . And when he measures the timber, she's got to go with him with the yardstick and tape-measure. Oh, God, Herr Räder, nobody knows yet, and the young Fräulein herself may not know either."

"And you've wanted to get mixed up with uniforms," said Räder contemptuously.

Before the forester was able to protest, however, there were hasty steps in the corridor and Vi walked in. "Thank God I managed it, after all. I couldn't get away before. Armgard has been sobbing out to Mamma that you're always so unkind to her, Hubert. Are you really so unkind?"

"No," replied Hubert seriously. "I'm only strict with her and I don't lower myself with females at all."

"Good God, Hubert, how serious you're looking, like a carp in the pond. I'm sure you live on vinegar. I'm merely a female myself."

"No," declared Hubert. "First of all, you're a lady and then you're my superior, so I can't lower myself with you, Fräulein."

"Thank you very much, Hubert. You're really magnificent. I believe you'll burst with vanity and pride one of these days."

She looked at him, very pleased, with her slightly protruding bright eyes. Suddenly she became graver and whispered mysteriously: "Is it true, Hubert, what Armgard told Mamma—that you're a fiend?"

Unmoved, Räder's fishy eyes looked at the inquisitive girl. Not a trace of color rose in his wrinkled gray cheeks. "But Armgard didn't say that in front of you, Fräulein," he maintained. "You've been listening at the door again."

Violet also was not in the least embarrassed. With surprise the forester saw how familiar this odd pair were. Räder was much cleverer than he had thought. He must be on his guard with him.

Vi laughed. "Don't be silly, Hubert. If I didn't do a bit of listening I wouldn't hear anything. Mamma tells me nothing, and recently when we saw the stork in the meadow and I asked Papa if it were really true, he went quite red. Lord, poor Papa, how embarrassed he was! And so you're a demon?"

"Here is Forester Kniebusch," interposed Räder, unshaken.

"Yes, of course. Good evening, Kniebusch. What's the matter? Hubert behaves mysteriously, but, as a matter of fact, he always behaves like that. What's the matter with you?"

"Lord, Fräulein," said the forester miserably, for he saw to his horror the moment coming when he had to tell his tale. Already everything was confused and he no longer knew what he had really seen and what he had only surmised. And neither had he the courage to tell everything to her face; maybe Black Meier had not been bragging and she really loved him. Then he would be nicely in the soup.

"I really don't know. . . . I only wanted to ask . . . I've caught a glimpse of the stag which the Rittmeister wants to get so much, and if the Rittmeister is coming home this evening . . . He was standing in the clover, but now he has gone into Haase's field . . ."

Vi looked at him attentively. Räder, however, eyed him coldly and contemptuously, waiting quietly till the forester had got himself completely bogged. Then he was unmerciful. "It's about the un-i-form, Fräulein. If I hadn't been here he would have told madam and not you."

"Kniebusch," said Violet, "you ought to be ashamed of yourself. Always sneaking and telling tales behind one's back. . . ."

And now the forester had to reveal everything, if for no other reason than to exonerate himself; starting with the errand round the village, down to the summons into the inn. His account of Meier's drunken twaddle was faltering and exceedingly embarrassed. He would have liked to beat about the bush, but could not succeed. Vi and Räder were unrelenting investigators.

"No, you're leaving something out, Kniebusch. Tell me everything. I promise you I won't blush."

Nevertheless she did blush. She leaned against the wall, she half closed her eyes, her lips trembled, and she breathed quickly. But she did not falter. "Go on, Kniebusch—what did he say next?"

And now came the affair of the letter.

"Did he read it all out? What did he read to you? Tell me every word he did read. . . . Oh, and you were idiot enough to believe that I'd written that to him? Him!—That cad!"

Now came the part about the encounter at Haase's.

"What? You saw the—gentleman and you told him nothing? Didn't even give him a hint? Of all the fools, Kniebusch, you're the biggest!"

The forester stood confounded and guilty. He, too, realized that he had done everything wrong.

"Haase was present," Räder interposed.

"True, but he could have passed him the letter."

"The forester didn't have the letter." (Räder again.)

"Oh, yes, I'm quite muddled. But Meier still has it—is still sitting in the inn, perhaps, and showing it to others. . . . You must set off at once, Hubert."

"Meier has been back in his room for a long time," said Hubert imperturbably. "I myself told you that he came back quite drunk from the inn some time after six o'clock. But I suggest the un-i-form. . . ."

"True. Go off, Hubert, and tell him. You're bound to find him; he's sure to be still at Haase's. No, tell him nothing at all; merely tell him that I must speak to him at once. But where? Tell him at the old place. . . . How can I get away, though? Mamma won't let me go out so late."

"Hush! Madam is coming," the imperturbable Hubert warned her.

"Well, what kind of a plot is going on here?" asked Frau von Prackwitz, standing very surprised on the threshold. "I've been looking for you everywhere, Violet, and I find you here!" She glanced from one face to the other. "Why do you all look so embarrassed? I want to know what's going on. Will you tell me, Vi?" she added in a sharper tone.

"Excuse me, madam, if I speak." It was Räder. "There's no longer any purpose in not telling madam."

Breathless silence. Despairing hearts.

"To tell the truth, madam, it's about the buck."

"About what buck? What's this nonsense? Vi, I ask you—"

"Yes, the buck in the clover, which the Rittmeister was talking about," said Räder. "Forgive me, madam, for having heard about it. It was the day before yesterday, at supper, when I was serving the tench." His persuasive, slightly pedantic voice shrouded everything in a mist. "And the buck suddenly disappeared just when the Rittmeister was stalking it; and you've heard about it yourself, madam, the Rittmeister set great store on it."

"I still haven't heard what this assembly is about."

"Well, today the forester's seen the buck, madam, in Haase's field, and it will have to be shot this evening, because it never stays anywhere. And so we thought, as the Rittmeister is away, that Fräulein should surprise him. It was not right of us, madam, to want to do it secretly . . . but it was my suggestion that we should wait till madam had gone to sleep, because there's the full moon, which would be sufficient light for a rifle, Herr Kniebusch says. . . ."

"Stop that droning of yours, Hubert!" said Frau Eva, visibly relieved. "You're a terrible man. For days on end one wishes that you would open your mouth, but when you do, one only wishes that you'd close it again as quickly as possible. And you might be a little nicer to the maids, Hubert; no gem would fall from your crown if you were."

"Certainly," said Räder calmly.

"And you, Vi," she continued severely, "you're a proper goose. Had you told me, the surprise for Papa wouldn't have been any the less. Really, as a punishment I ought not to let you go; but if the buck is in Haase's field only for this evening . . . You're not to leave her for a moment, Kniebusch. . . . God, what's the matter with you, Kniebusch—why are you weeping?"

"Ah, it's really only the shock, madam, the shock of seeing you in the doorway," wailed the old man. "And then I've no self-control. But it was a joyful shock, they're tears of joy. . . ."

"I think, Hubert," said madam dryly, "you'd better get ready to go with them, or else, if they meet a wood thief in the forest, our good Kniebusch will burst into tears of joy again and Vi will have to look after herself."

"Oh, Mamma. I'm not afraid of wood thieves and poachers."

"You'd better be more afraid of some other things, my dear Violet," said Frau von Prackwitz energetically. "Above all, you ought to be afraid of secrecy. Then it's arranged that Hubert's to go with you."

"Certainly, Mamma," said Vi obediently. "Just a second. I'll change my dress."

With that she ran upstairs, leaving her mother with the two men, giving them a good talking-to for having "secrets with a mere child." Frau Eva did this very thoroughly, but she was not quite satisfied with the result, having a womanly intuition that there was something wrong. However, since Vi was still only a child, it couldn't be really bad, and she made herself easy with the thought that Vi's misdeeds had so far turned out to be all rather harmless. Her worst wickedness to date had been cutting her beautiful long hair into an Eton crop. But such a crime, thank God, could be committed only once.

IV

The women's section in Alexanderplatz prison was shamelessly overcrowded. When the prison had been built they had painted the air capacity of each cell on its green iron-plated door: so-and-so many cubic meters inscribed there as adequate for one occupant. Then they had put in a second bed; but that had happened so very long ago that two beds in the one cell were regarded as normal by even the oldest officials. Then came the inflation, and more and more women prisoners. Two further beds were placed in the cell, so that with one stroke the capacity of the prison was doubled. But now, for a long time, that, too, had been insufficient. As the endless procession of women came day after day in the green police van, they were pushed higgledy-piggledy into the cells. In the evening a couple of mattresses and a couple of woolen blankets were thrown after them—let them manage with that.

Seldom had Petra Ledig felt lonelier and more abandoned than in that overcrowded prison. It seemed as if it would never get dark.

True, she did not belong to the class of girl for whom prison means shame and the end of all things. She lived a commonplace existence; she knew that life was a difficult matter for those who were poor and friendless, who never knew what was coming to them, or from which point of the compass the winds of misfortune would blow.

She knew quite well, after the second very superficial examination at headquarters, what she was accused of, and she knew that these accusations were partly out of date, partly untrue. But she did not know what the consequences might be. It might mean the workhouse, or the surveillance card, or weeks or months in prison. Her future lay in the hands of men who were as strange to her as if they had been beings from another world.

She was led at once to the medical officer. The women stood in an endless line outside his door, and in the end it was announced: "No more examinations. The medical officer has gone home."

So Petra was led back to her cell and she discovered that, meanwhile, supper had been issued and her share eaten up by the others. It didn't matter very much; she had eaten enough for the time being at the police station. She listened with only half an ear to her fellow prisoners accusing one another—it might well be that the Hawk had stolen her portion, as the fat woman in the lower bed said (already the senior inmate, of two days' standing).

But never mind. It would be better if they didn't talk about it, for the Hawk became wild again and attacked Petra with noisy abuse. To have been put in the same cell with her was unpleasant, but that, too, must be endured. The girl couldn't go on forever with her shouting and raving. When she had first come in she had still been as limp as a wet rag, but now she was restless once more. Again and again she attacked Petra and wanted to beat her. But she no longer had as much strength as formerly; alcohol and cocaine having done their work, Petra could ward her off with one hand. Although she made no reply, nevertheless the Hawk stormed more and more furiously.

That was tiresome. Under these continual attacks and this shouting Petra could not think as she would have liked to. There was the matter of Wolfgang—would he return that night? Would he ever return? She knew what the authorities thought of her and what they would tell him at the police station. What would he then think of her? In his place she would have come all the quicker, but with him you never could tell.

She looked around the cell. She would have liked to ask the gray-haired woman on the bed about the visiting hours, but the Hawk was shouting louder than ever. It seemed, as a matter of fact, not to disturb the others at all, not even to interest them. Two nut-brown gypsies with impudent, restless, bird-like eyes were squatting side by side on one corner of a mattress, whispering loudly, with many gesticulations; they looked at nobody else in the cell. The tall pale girl in the other lower bed had already crept under her blanket: one saw only her shoulders convulsively shaking. No doubt she was weeping. On the stool perched a little fat woman who, scowling, picked her nose.

The gray-haired woman sitting on the edge of her bed looked up and said angrily: "Shut up, you silly bitch. Sock her a couple, jail-birdie, so that she spits teeth."

The title "jail-birdie" was meant for Petra, probably because she was the only person there who wore the blue prison dress. She had been given it immediately on her arrival.

But Petra didn't want to hit the Hawk. It was useless; the girl was beside herself with the craving for cocaine or alcohol. Already the warders had knocked on the cell door twice and demanded silence, and each time the Hawk had leaped forward and begged: "Oh, please, do give me a drink. Only one, just a very small one. You can do it, boys. You yourselves like a drink now and then. Oh, please do give me one, boys."

But their footsteps had died away; she got no response—at most, one of the warders laughed. Then the Hawk was seized with a fit of rage, battering the iron door with her fists and shouting abuse after the men.

Slowly, however, she changed. Gradually the sky outside the cell window grew dark and the electric light over the door brighter; it became increasingly apparent that the girl no longer knew where she was. Probably she believed herself in hell. Like a caged animal she rushed from wall to wall, blind to her companions. Incessantly she muttered to herself. Suddenly she stopped and shrieked in a high-pitched tone, as if in terrible pain.

Again the warders knocked; again their reprimand gave new impetus to the tormented creature's heart-breaking appeals and furious abuse. This time she collapsed before the door; her head resting against its iron panels, the miserably ruffled Hawk crouched there as if she were intently listening. She started to mutter to herself: "Something's running, something's scuttering in my belly. Oh, so many legs! They want to get out—my whole body is full of them, and now they want to get out."

With trembling fingers she tore her clothes, trying to free her body. "Ants," she moaned, "transparent red ants. They're running about inside me. Oh, leave me in peace. I haven't got anything. I can't give you any snow."

She leaped up. "Give me snow," she shouted. "You're to give me snow, do you hear? You've got snow."

With a faint cry the gray-haired woman fell down backwards; without any attempt at resistance she lay whimpering beneath the raving girl.

The gypsies interrupted their unintelligible whispering and looked on with a grin. The tall girl's shoulders stopped shaking. Slowly she turned her head and looked with frightened eyes at the other bed, prepared at any moment to crawl completely beneath her blanket. The fat, gloomy woman on the stool grumbled. "Do stop that row! How can one think when you make such a noise?"

Petra jumped up. It was easy to pull the emaciated creature off the woman lying beneath; it was impossible, however, to disengage the clinging hands from the victim's hair.

"Will you be quiet, you women!" yelled the warders outside. "Now they've got each other by the hair, the miserable creatures. You wait, you'll get such a thrashing."

Petra turned and called angrily: "Come in. The girl is in a fit. Do help us!"

For a moment there was silence. Then a polite voice spoke up. "We're not allowed to, Fräulein. After locking up we're not allowed to enter the women's cell. Otherwise it would be said at once that we were carrying on with you." And another voice added: "It might be a trick on your part. We're not taken in by that."

"But this can't go on," protested Petra. "She's half mad. There must be a wardress in the place. Or a doctor. Do send for a doctor, please."

"They've gone by now," said the polite voice. "She ought to have complained when she was admitted, then she would have been taken to the sick ward. You five will be able to manage her."

It did not look so. The gypsies sat mute, the fat woman squatted sulkily on her stool, the tall girl had crawled beneath her blanket, and the old woman was groaning beneath the Hawk's claws.

For a short time the assailant had been lying, quietly sobbing, beside the old woman; now she started to scream again, tugging mechanically but fiercely at the other's wisps of hair. The old woman also screamed.

"You must help!" cried Petra indignantly, kicking the iron door till it clanged. "Or I'll make such a noise that the whole prison will start shouting."

It had almost come to that already. Many cells were resounding with angry cries for silence. A woman started to sing the Internationale in a high-pitched voice.

The door flew open; two armed warders wearing felt shoes so as not to disturb sleeping prisoners stood in the doorway.

"We won't come in," said one, a tall, blue-eyed man with a ginger mustache. "We'll tell you what to do. You look quite sensible, Fräulein. Quick, take a pinch of salt out of the cupboard."

Petra hurried. "You old scarecrow on the mattress," ordered the warder, "take the woolen blanket and help a bit. You, too!"

The gypsies jumped up, grinning, and did what they were told.

"You there, the little beauty on the bed," called the warder in the doorway, "up with you now. You'll get some snow."

With a shout of joy the Hawk leaped up and staggered toward the warders. "You're splendid fellows!"

The old woman sat up groaning, feeling her scalp cautiously.

"Keep off," cried the ginger mustache to the Hawk. "Keep your distance!" He gave her a scrutiny. "Yes, she's not acting. She's a dope-fiend right enough."

Scared by his command, encouraged and made obedient by his promise, the Hawk waited. Her arms hanging limply, she looked at the men with a cringing hopeful expression. Petra and the gypsies also waited. But the tall pale girl crawled beneath her blanket to get away from the warders' glances, and the fat woman grumbled. "Oh, hop it with your rubbish. Let me think in peace."

"Lie down flat on the floor, you!" ordered the ginger warder. "Yes, go on. Or else you won't get any snow."

The girl hesitated; then with a moan she lay down.

"Keep your arms close to your body," ordered the warder. "Do as you're told. Now roll her in a blanket. Tighter! Tighter! Very tight, as tight as you can. Rubbish, it won't hurt her. Show her the snow, so that she doesn't resist! The salt, I mean, you fool. Show it to her, she believes it all right. Yes, my lamb. You'll get it presently, only be good for a moment."

The girl moaned. "Oh, please, please! Don't torture me so. Give me the snow," she implored.

"Just a moment. Now the other blanket—no, roll it round her the other way. Turn her over like a parcel. It won't kill her by any means. You there, the fat one on the stool, take your finger out of your nose and help. Fetch two sheets from the upper beds—yes, my dear; in a moment. Don't you see what a lot of snow there is? You'll get your shot presently."

In accordance with the warder's instructions, they knotted the sheets like ropes around the parcel. The girl submitted willingly. She didn't lose sight of the hand which held her salvation, the cocaine, the salt. "Please give it to me," she murmured. "How can you be so cruel? It's so beautiful. . . . I can't stand it anymore."

"There," said the warder after a moment's scrutiny. "That'll do. Well, it's really unnecessary because she'll find out at once, but never mind, give her the salt."

"Yes, the snow. Please, please, the snow!"

Hesitatingly, reluctantly, Petra held her palm with the salt on it under the Hawk's nose. And witnessed, oddly moved, the change in that tormented face.

"Nearer," the girl whispered with a compelling glance. "Hold it right under my nose." She sniffed it in. "Oh, how good it is." Her sharp contorted features smoothed themselves out, her eyelids sank. Where there had been dark hollows, soft flesh filled out the cheekbones. The deep furrows round her mouth vanished; the cracked lips became fuller; she breathed rhythmically. What bliss!

But it's only salt, Petra thought, disturbed. Common cooking salt. But she believes in it and so it makes her young again. And a sudden thought-association made her think of Wolfgang, of Wolfgang Pagel, whom, as she now realized quite well, she had been expecting, minute by minute, the whole evening, in spite of everything. How did others see him?

"There, she's starting again!" said the warder in an undertone.

The girl's face, close to that of the kneeling Petra, changed frightfully. The mouth was a dark deep cavern; the eyes stared with rage and anger.

"You beasts, you swine!" she shrieked. "That's not snow. You've cheated me. Oh—oh—oh!"

Her whole body struggled, her head reared up. The face became crimson, then blue, with her efforts to get free. "Let me go!" she screamed. "I'll show you!"

Petra had recoiled—such hatred, such despair showed on the face which had been so contented only a moment ago.

"No fear, my girl," said the warder. "That'll hold you. Take care, you in blue, you're the most sensible of the lot. Let her lie on the ground; don't set her free whatever she says. And see that she doesn't bash her head in on the stone floor, she's quite capable of it. If she screams too loudly put a wet towel over her mouth, but don't let her choke."

"Take her out of this," said Petra angrily. "I don't want to do that. I'm no wardress. I don't want to torture people."

"Don't be silly, you in blue," said the warder imperturbably. "Are we torturing her? It's the snow which does that. Did we make her an addict?"

"She ought to be in hospital," said Petra indignantly.

"Do you think they'd give her snow there?" rejoined the warder. "She's got to get rid of the craving in here or somewhere else. Is she still a human being? Have a look at her."

And indeed the Hawk hardly looked human, a trembling, raging thing, sometimes full of fury and hate, sometimes weeping and despairing; at other moments beseeching as a child beseeches who believes that the person pleaded with can do everything.

"I'll see if I can get her a sleeping draught from the sick ward," said the ginger one reflectively. "But I don't know whether there's anybody there who has the key to the medicine chest. These are times, I can tell you. . . . So don't depend on it!"

"You can always give her salt occasionally," interposed the other. "She'll be taken in by it at least a dozen times. People are like that. Well, good night."

The door was pushed to, the lock groaned under the keys, the bolt grated. Petra sat down beside the patient, who with shut eyes was flinging her head from side to side, ceaselessly, quicker and quicker. . . . "Snow," she whispered. "Snow, snow, good snow. . . ."

Again and again she'll be taken in by salt, thought Petra gloomily. "People are like that!" He's right, people *are* like that. But I don't want to be like that anymore. No!

She looked at the door. The peep-hole blinked like an evil eye. Wolf won't come, she thought resolutely. He has believed what they told him. I'll not expect him any longer.

V

At the Manor in Neulohe the old people, the von Teschows, had supper every day punctually at seven o'clock. At half-past seven they finished, and the maids had only to wash up and tidy the kitchen, which, at the latest, would be finished by eight. As the old lady would remark: "Even a servant must have her free time in the evening."

True, at eight-fifteen came evening prayers, which everybody in the Manor had to attend after a wash—except old Herr von Teschow who, of course, to his wife's perpetual annoyance, had always, just at this very hour, an urgent, absolutely essential letter to write.

"No, this evening it's really impossible, Belinde! And besides—for your sake I listen every blessed Sunday to what old Lehnich tells us from the pulpit. I must say it sounds quite nice, but it doesn't give me any clear ideas, Belinde. And I don't believe you get any, either. The only notion I get is that we shall one day be angels flying about in heaven, you and I, Belinde, in white shirts like the pictures in the big illustrated Bible . . ."

"You're mocking again, Horst-Heinz."

"God forgive me, not in the least. And I'll meet my old Elias there, and he too will be flapping around and singing eternally, and then he'll whisper to me: 'Well, Geheimrat, you're lucky. Had I told the Lord about your red wine and the wicked language you've used at times . . .'"

"True, Horst-Heinz, very true!"

"And all without any class distinction and on the most familiar footing, in a kind of nightshirt and with goose wings. Excuse me, Belinde, they really are goose wings. It ought to be swan's wings, but swans and geese are very much the same."

"Yes, go upstairs by all means, Horst-Heinz, and write your important business letters. I know you'll only sneer—not at religion, but at me. Well,

I don't mind that; I can stand it. Perhaps it's better so. Because if you really mocked at religion you would be an outcast forever and ever—but if you sneer at me you're only being discourteous. And you can do that, for we've been married forty-two years and I'm thus quite used to a discourteous husband!"

With that the old lady bustled off to the chapel, leaving the old gentleman laughing on the landing. The deuce, I've got it again hot and strong, he thought. But she's right—and I'll go to one of her meetings tomorrow or the day after. It livens her up a bit, and once in a while one ought to do something for a wife, even though one's been married for forty-two years. If only she wouldn't get the hiccups as soon as she's upset. It's exactly like somebody getting a cannon at billiards—I can't stand that clicking sound, and I can't bear her hiccups—I keep on waiting for them. Well, I'll do some of my accounts. I fancy my son-in-law pays much too little for the electric current . . .

With that the Geheimrat went upstairs to his study and three minutes later was wrapped in the smoke of a Brazilian cigar, immersed in his belligerent accounts, an old but incurable fighter. The accounts, however, were belligerent because he wanted them to assault his son-in-law with. Who, according to his father-in-law, paid much too little for everything; and according to himself, much too much. Electricity included.

Neulohe was not connected up with any area system, but generated its own current. The generating machine, an up-to-date crude-oil Diesel motor, with its batteries, stood in the Manor cellar, and because of this was not leased to the son-in-law, who was the chief user, but retained by the old gentleman for himself, although he burned only "three miserable lamps in his old hut." The arrangement about the price of the current was also quite simple: each party had to pay his share of the cost according to the amount consumed.

But even the simplest, clearest arrangement fails when two parties cannot stand one another. Old Herr von Teschow considered that his son-in-law was no farmer, but a grand Herr von Have-Not, who wanted to live comfortably on his father-in-law's pocketbook. Rittmeister von Prackwitz regarded his father-in-law as a grasping skinflint, and a good deal more "plebeian" than he could bear, at that. The old gentleman saw his ready money dwindle in the inflation and, as the savings of years became worthless, all the more desperately did he chase after fresh sources of revenue. The Rittmeister noticed how, month by month, it became more difficult to carry on, saw the money which came from the harvest vanishing in his hand, was worried, and found the old gentleman miserly in that he was forever coming along with new claims, objections and reproaches.

On the whole, Geheimrat von Teschow found that his son-in-law lived much too well. "Why doesn't he smoke, as I do, cigars which one can draw at for an hour? No, he must have cigarettes, those coffin-nails which stain your fingers and are puffed away in three minutes. After the war he came here with only an officer's trunk, and no more in it than his soiled linen. No, Belinde, if anyone pays for his cigarettes it's us—but of course, he doesn't pay for them at all, he buys them on credit."

"All young people smoke cigarettes nowadays," Belinde remarked, thereby rousing her husband properly. Wives—in fact married people generally—have a special knack of making irritating remarks.

"I'll teach him! He's not as young as all that any longer," cried the Geheimrat finally, nearly blue in the face. "My dear son-in-law shall learn how difficult it is to earn money."

And so the old gentleman was sitting at his desk and calculating with the idea of earning more money himself. He reckoned what his electric-light plant would cost if he purchased it today at a dollar rate of 414,000 marks, and this purchase price he distributed over ten years. For the plant would certainly not last any longer, and even if it should, he wanted to write it off within that period.

Quite a pretty little sum stood on paper; even charged at the rate of only a twelfth part every month, it still showed a huge figure with very many noughts.

My son-in-law will stare tomorrow morning, said the Geheimrat to himself, on reading these glad tidings. He won't have any money, of course; the little he still had will have been left behind in Berlin. But I'll press him so that he starts threshing soon; then I'll get the threshing money out of him, and he can wait and see how he'll get through the winter.

The hatred the old man felt toward his son-in-law was incomprehensible. Formerly the two had got on quite well, when the Rittmeister was still an officer living in some remote garrison, or later, during the war, when they had met once in a while. Hatred had only arisen since the son-in-law had lived in Neulohe as its tenant. Since the Prackwitz's family life had played itself out under the eyes of the old gentleman.

The old gentleman was not entirely foolish and obstinate, for he realized how much the Rittmeister toiled and worried. But his son-in-law was a retired cavalry officer and not a farmer, for which reason he often got hold of the wrong end of the stick, and clumsily at that. Moreover, he was often too easy-going and sometimes impulsive. Besides which, he wore suits made to his measurements by a very expensive London tailor, and shirts which were buttoned from top to bottom ("Revoltingly effeminate"—although no woman ever had such a garment), while the old Geheimrat wore only coarse homespuns and Jaeger shirts. Yes, there were ten or twenty objections to the Rittmeister. But each by itself, or the sum of them, was insufficient reason for such a hatred.

Geheimrat von Teschow had finished his calculations; he would write the letter to his son-in-law after having a look at the *Oder-Zeitung*. But he did not get as far as reading, for the first glance showed that the dollar no longer stood at 414,000, but at 760,000 marks. That really ought to have annoyed him—he should have looked at the newspaper before starting his calculations—because now he would have to do them all over again. Yet he was not annoyed. With a sense of enjoyment he set about the new reckoning—it meant that his son-in-law would only have to pay more.

I'll finish him off yet, he thought for a fleeting moment, and the hand which held the pen stopped short, as if it had been frightened. Then it went on with its writing, and the Geheimrat shrugged his shoulders. What a foolish idea! Of course he was not out to ruin Herr von Prackwitz. Prackwitz had only to pay what was right; more was not demanded. For all the Geheimrat cared he could live in the place as he liked, in his silk shirts and breeches!

Through the old Manor sounded the melancholy, yet sometimes almost frivolous, tones of the organ. Geheimrat von Teschow nodded, keeping time with his feet, hurrying up the music. Faster, Belinde, faster! People would fall asleep if she didn't go faster.

"For he's not only the Rittmeister von Prackwitz—he's also our only daughter's husband," Belinde had said recently. That was just it! That was the very reason! How like a woman to speak about it as if it were the most natural thing in the world! Our only daughter's husband!

Now when the old Geheimrat goes through the village and sees a girl, he crows aloud the length of the village street: "Oh, what a charming child! Come over here, my little sweet. Let's have a look at you. You really are a charmer, my little one. Goodness me, what eyes you've got!"

And he strokes her cheeks and chucks her under the chin, all in front of the whole village. And in front of the whole village he goes with her to the shop and buys her a bar of chocolate, or he takes her to the Inn and treats her to a sweet drink. Then he puts his arm around her waist, right in front of everybody. Then he lets her go and goes into the forest smiling with satisfaction.

But he wasn't smiling because of the girl who, embarrassed yet flattered, had really been delightful. No girl exists anymore on earth who could warm up his old blood. He was smiling because he had once again thrown dust in people's eyes. Pastor Lehnich will hear about it, and he'll whisper it to Belinde—and Belinde, poor old hen, will run around as if she's swallowed a ruler. And no one, but no one, will have any idea.

Except one—the old man himself knows very well. She also feels it; even more, she knows it. He hardly ever sees her anymore, and never by herself. And after the beginning of the bad times, as this problem quite unexpectantly began, he naturally didn't bother to meet her anymore. No, the Geheimrat knew alright: Hot fires don't burn in old men anymore. He was nothing but a spark time smothered by ashes.

When a Rittmeister von Have-Not and Cannot but Wants-a-Lot comes along, it must be made clear to him—we haven't brought up our daughter for your benefit. That's amazing conceit, thinking we have brought up a daughter, a girl second to none, just for your pleasure. And not only that—one hardly passes the Villa without hearing you shout at Eva. No, my dear son-in-law, we'll show you; and it doesn't matter to us that the price of our current is exactly eleven times as high as that of Frankfurt power station; you'll have to pay up, although—no, *because*—you are our daughter's husband.

With angry determination the old man set down his figures. What did he care whether there would be a quarrel? The more quarreling the better. And he would also make another hole in the park fence, so that Belinde's geese could get into his son-in-law's vetch. Belinde, up till now, had poured oil on the troubled waters, but if her son-in-law harmed her geese, as he had threatened to do, then she would no longer act as peacemaker.

Yes, Herr Geheimrat Horst-Heinz von Teschow was just in the right mood to write this letter to his son-in-law. It must, of course, be restrained, concise and businesslike, as suited the matter, for one ought not to mix family feeling with financial arrangements.

"Extremely sorry, but the increasingly more difficult conditions on the money market force me, etc. etc. Enclosed statement. With best regards, Yours, H. H. von Teschow." There! That would do it! Finished! Elias could take the letter across first thing tomorrow morning. Then the gentleman would find it on his return from Berlin. The hangover which he was sure to have brought with him from that place would help in rubbing him up the wrong way.

Herr von Teschow was about to ring for Elias when the organ pealing from below reminded him that devotions were still under way; Belinde was going it tonight very thoroughly. Undoubtedly she had a black sheep in her flock, one who must be guided to penitence before bedtime. He could not call Elias, then. And yet he would very much have liked to see the letter on its way.

As a matter of fact, he knew, of course, who the black sheep was—the little poultry witch, Amanda, with the shining red cheeks. She and Meier with the blubber lips. Recommended as an engaged couple. Well, they're long past the engagement stage, and well into the marriage bargain. Well, what did it matter?

The Geheimrat grinned a little, and it occured to him that it would be much better to hand the letter to Meier for delivery. That would annoy his son-in-law acutely, for he knew quite well that the old gentleman was fond of an occasional chat with the bailiff. And when he got such a letter through such a go-between he would think, of course, that his father-in-law had already discussed its contents with him. But he would be much too grand to ask his employee right out, naturally, and that again would add to his annoyance.

The old gentleman put the letter in his shooting jacket, took his stick and shaggy hat and went slowly downstairs. The evening devotions seemed to be over; two of the maids passed him on their way upstairs, looking very amused—not at all in a pious mood—rather as if some comic incident had occurred. Von Teschow was about to inquire but changed his mind. If Belinde heard him talking on the stairs she would possibly come out and ask him where he was going, and offer to accompany him. No, better not.

He stepped out into the park, now fairly dark, just made for his purpose. He knew, of course, exactly where his wife's geese always discovered a hole in the fence, since only the day before yesterday he had stopped it up at her request. But what is shut can be opened, he told himself, and cautiously rattled at the fence. He must find a loose stake which could be broken away.

Suddenly, while he was so employed, he had the feeling that somebody was watching him. Quickly he turned round, and something like a human form did indeed stand near the shrubs. The old gentlemen's big bulging eyes still saw quite well, even in the dusk. "Amanda!" he called.

But nobody answered, and when he looked more closely there was no human form at all, only the rhododendron and jasmine in the background. Well, never mind. If she had been there it need not and it must not matter to her; he had only been looking to see whether the stakes were firm. But for that evening he refrained from loosening them, and went instead to the staff-house and Meier.

But he preferred not to enter the place; unlike his wife, the old Geheimrat had not the slightest inclination to see things which violated a sense of decorum. With his stick he knocked at the open window. "Hi, Herr Meier! Kindly stick your esteemed nut out of the curtains," he shouted.

VI

Amanda Backs, the poultry maid, would have preferred to cut evening prayers as she had often enough done before, usually for the more general reason of boredom and of previous engagements, but this time because she could guess at whom madam would be praying and preaching. The fat cook and Black Minna, however, did not allow her out of their sight.

"Come, Amanda, we'll help you count the hens, and then you can help us with the washing up."

"I seem to hear the word scram," said Amanda, meaning by that just what her mother had meant with her "Make yourself scarce."

But the pair never left her a minute—it was obvious that they were dancing to madam's tune.

"Always the same," said Amanda Backs, scolding the few belated hens who, with agitated cacklings, hurried from the meadow to the coop. "You wait, I'll close the shutter before your very beaks and then you'll find out how the fox says 'Good Night.' You oughtn't to behave so foolishly, Minna. The cook weighs at least two hundredweights, and so it's difficult enough for her to get a man—you can't blame her for standing about like an angel made of soft soap. But you with your six ragamuffins with at least ten different fathers!"

"Indeed, Amanda! Don't be so low," protested Black Minna. "Madam means well."

"I seem to hear the word scram," said Amanda Backs again, breaking off the discussion. That the old lady should have appointed Black Minna as spy was really too ridiculous. But everyone knew how childishly she fussed over that aged slatternly female. Whenever Minna got into trouble again—and the old lady noticed it only when the midwife arrived, although with such a scraggy, bony woman it had long been apparent to everyone else—then the mistress flew into a passion, abused the woman and once again cast her off forever and ever, telling her to remove from the almshouse where she lived, as utterly incorrigible.

Then Minna would shriek and carry on terribly. Sobbing, she would load her possessions on a little handcart—not everything, however, only enough to impress madam, but not forgetting a single one of her many children—and march through the village howling, and singing hymns. For the last time she would call at the Manor, push the brass bell-knob and ask Elias with many tears to give the dear good lady her blessings and gratitude. And could she be allowed to kiss her hands in farewell?

Thereupon Elias, who knew this play by heart, would say "No." Whereupon Black Minna wept even more bitterly and departed with her fatherless children into the cold wide world, as far away as the curbstone at the Manor gateway. There she sat and wept and waited and, according to the extent of her mistress's anger, had to sit one, two, or even five hours, and sometimes as long as half a day.

But she knew she would not wait forever, and if she had not known by experience, she could always tell by the curtains in the house. For the old lady opened and closed them with her trembling hands and could not refrain from gazing on her erring sheep.

But if the scandal happened to be a bad one, and Frau von Teschow had learned from the village magistrate via her husband that this time three men were definitely involved and perhaps even five—not to mention those who were shielded out of "sympathy," for in her relationships Minna distinguished between "sympathetic" men and casuals—then madam hardened her soft, worldly-unwise heart, thought over all this Sodom and Gomorrah business and remembered how often Black Minna had promised to mend her ways.

Then she would let fall the curtain and say to her friend, old Fräulein von Kuckhoff, who lived with her: "No, Jutta, this time I won't relent. And I won't look at her out of the window." And old Fräulein von Kuckhoff, with the black velvet ribbon round her neck, would energetically nod her little vulture-like head and remark in her flowery but precise manner: "Certainly, Belinde—constant dropping wears away even a stone."

Yes, and half an hour had barely elapsed when there would be a gentle knock at the door. "Pardon me, madam, but I have to report that she's exposing herself," old Elias announced.

And indeed, when the two ladies rushed each to her window, there sat the poor homeless creature on the curbstone, her blouse unbuttoned, feeding the youngest fruit of her sins.

"Jutta, we cannot take the responsibility of this new scandal," her mistress would sigh. And Jutta would remark obscurely: "Wasps do not attack bad fruit," which Frau von Teschow then regarded as approval of her intentions.

"No, Elias, I'll go myself," she would say hurriedly, for although Elias was now well in his sixties it was uncertain whether he was a match for such a temptation. So old Frau von Teschow personally went down to the sinner who, when she saw madam step out, quickly did up her blouse. For her mistress might perhaps notice that it was only stageplay; Black Minna couldn't feed any of her children, and had brought them all up on the bottle. That, however, was something madam did not need to know.

Then Minna and her mistress would go to the almshouse, the old woman walking beside the ridiculous barrow-load of furniture, the idea never entering her head that people would sneer or laugh. She had softened and humbled her heart, reminding herself how even she had almost yielded to temptation forty years ago when smart Lieutenant von Pritzwitz had wanted to kiss her behind the door—at a time when she was as good as engaged to Horst-Heinz.

And when she had accompanied Black Minna across the threshold of the almshouse, she was at the stage of understanding and forgiving all. Even if she were not quite so silly as to take the sinner's tears at their face value, she nevertheless thought in her heart: She does mean it a little, after all, and she's a tiny bit sorry—how do I know how much repentance God demands of us?

That, then, was how old Frau von Teschow thought and acted—and even Amanda Backs would have regarded it as nice and kind, if only madam's good heart had been inclined as lovingly and forgivingly to all sinners. But man's heart is strange—and why should an old woman's heart be any different? What she forgave an artful female like Minna ten times, she would not once overlook in a young girl.

And in Amanda Backs least of all. For Amanda was brazen and shameless in her speech; she smiled joyously at all men; wore skirts so short that they were hardly skirts at all; never wept over a mistake; never repented, and never sang a hymn, only popular songs such as "What are you doing with your knee, dear Hans?" and "What a woman dreams in spring" . . .

No, Amanda knew quite well what was in store for her at the prayer meeting. But that Black Minna should have been assigned as her supervisor roused her to especial anger, and for a moment she seriously considered whether she should lock the two women up in the coop and slip off to her little Hans—it would be a glorious joke.

But however forward and impudent Amanda was with her tongue, she was prudent and circumspect in deed—which a poultry maid, of course, has to be above all things. For poultry are the most difficult creatures in the world, ten times more temperamental than a circus full of wild beasts, and obey only level-headed persons. Yes, out of Meier's window yesterday evening Amanda in her rage had talked big and threatened to leave madam—but all the same (the human heart is indeed strange) she was fond of her little blubber-lipped Hans Meier, and even the Garden of Eden itself would have appeared desolate without him.

So she didn't slam the door of the hen house but contented herself with chasing out the two wingless hens, and brought her subjects to roost with a click and a cluck, counted their heads and found that none was missing. "There, you old hens," she said emphatically, "since you have helped me so wonderfully I'll scrub your pots for you in return."

"Lor', Amanda," groaned the fat cook, her whalebone corset creaking, "if one didn't know you were only joking . . ."

"And how do you know that?" asked Amanda Backs very aggressively. Aggressively she walked between the two women, who had now fallen silent, aggressively she bounced along in her short skirt. For she was very young, and the bitter experiences of her childhood had not been able to rob her of an appetite for life or of the freshness of youth; to be young was good fun and rows were fun and love amused her—if her mistress imagined she could rob her of this fun by hymns and prayers, then she was very much mistaken.

Such thoughts as Amanda's might well carry one over the scrubbing of the sootiest pot, but they were not quite suitable for evening prayers in the Manor. By this time people had been sitting there quite a while—the usual crowd, a rather imposing assembly. For madam saw to it that not only those who were in her service came to these meetings, complete with chick and child, but that any villager who wanted a little firewood from the forest in the winter, or to gather berries and mushrooms there in summer, obtained permission for this only by sitting through many a service. Pastor Lehnich often did not have so many parishioners in the church of a Sunday as the old lady did evening after evening in her chapel.

"And you, Amanda?" she had asked. Amanda, starting out of her sinful thoughts, had stared around, and knew nothing of what was happening. The little geese on the back benches, the ones in their early 'teens who laughed at everything, had of course begun to snigger. Madam, however, spoke quite mildly. "And your verse, Amanda?"

Oh, yes, they were having "singing in turns." That meant that everybody had to name from the hymn book a verse which was then sung by all; which often led to a medley of vesper songs, dirges, hymns, penitential chants, hymns of the Passion, hymns of Jesus, and christening hymns. But it entertained them and livened up the wearisome evening. Even the old lady at her organ got red in the face, so quickly did she have to turn over the pages of her music book and leap from one melody to another.

"'Commit thy ways unto the Lord,'" Amanda called out hurriedly before the sniggering could turn into laughter.

Madam nodded. "Yes, you should do that, Amanda."

Amanda bit her lips for mentioning a first line that had given her mistress such an opening. She was rather flushed as she sat down.

But at least there was no pause, for Frau von Teschow knew this hymn by heart. The organ struck up at once and all joined in immediately. And then it was the turn of Black Minna, who was sitting next to Amanda—that hypocrite chose, of course, "Out of my deep anguish I cry to Thee."

And they were singing again.

Amanda Backs, however, allowed herself no more day-dreams, but sat there erect and watchful; she did not want to be laughed at again. For quite a while nothing happened. All went on with their singing—in the end without any enthusiasm, because they grew bored and the old lady had become tired and more and more frequently struck a wrong note or didn't keep time. Then the organ started to whistle strangely and groan; the little geese on the back benches sniggered again, and Frau von Teschow turned crimson.

She's getting tired, thought Amanda. There's not much left of her, actually. Perhaps she doesn't feel disposed to make a long story about me, and I can quickly get to my Hans!

Amanda Backs had no idea how the sins of others can warm up an old woman, how the errors of her sisters can revive her. For one moment it looked as if the mistress wanted to make an end of the meeting. But she changed her mind. Stepping before her little flock, she cleared her throat and said, rather hurriedly and somewhat embarrassed: "Yes, dear children, now we can say the Benediction and go quietly home, every one of us, and sleep with a good conscience in that we have ended our day well. But is that true of us all?"

The old woman, no longer embarrassed, looked from one face to the other. She had stilled the motions of that conscience which warned her that she was about to do something strictly prohibited.

"Yes, is this true of all of us? Looking at Neulohe and even more at Alt-lohe, where they are most likely still sitting in the pothouse, then we can well be satisfied with ourselves. But, if we look more closely within, what do we see? We are weak human beings, and every one of us errs every day. It is a good thing then if we confess our sins in public and tell our assembled fellow Christians in what way we have transgressed. Only our sins for one day! I myself will make the start."

With that old Frau von Teschow quickly knelt down and at once prepared herself in silent prayer for an open confession. Through her flock there rippled a barely concealed agitation, however, for not one among them was ignorant that Pastor Lehnich, and even the superintendent at Frankfurt, had strictly forbidden madam to confess her sins in public. It was quite against the spirit of Christ and Luther, and smelled of the Salvation Army, the Baptists, and above all, of the objectionable auricular confession of the Roman Catholic Church!

But if none of those present got up and marched out as a protest—and old Fräulein von Kuckhoff or Elias were the ones to do it boldly—it was because they were all of them on tenterhooks to hear the old woman. Hardly one of us can listen to the sins of others without a thrill. Each person there hoped that it would not fall to his lot to have to confess after madam, and everyone quickly rehearsed his recent sins, both secret and revealed, and thought that he would not come off too badly.

The one person, however, who knew definitely that she would be among the two or three whom Frau von Teschow would subsequently call upon, and who knew that the pastor's and superintendent's prohibitions had been disregarded on her account only—that particular individual sat very tensely, though without showing it. In a bad temper she listened to the old woman stammering; she must be very agitated, she was mixing her words up and constantly hiccuping. People would have laughed had it not been for the excitement. Frau von Teschow counted it as sinful that she had read another installment of the wicked serial in the newspaper—hiccup—that she had been impatient with her dear husband—hiccup—and that she had again kneaded margarine into the butter intended for the servants—hiccup!

Amanda Backs listened to all this with an impatient, scornful face. People listened to this silly stuttering, ten times more thrilled than if they were hearing God's word, and yet the whole confession was only a sham. In spite of her show of piety, madam didn't mention the things that really mattered. As for the margarine, they had all tasted it for themselves—there was no need to tell them about that. The bit about the serial was rubbish, and everybody in the house knew how often she quarreled with her "dear husband." It was all eyewash. Madam ought rather to confess that she had staged this performance solely for the purpose of dealing a blow at her, Amanda Backs. That would, indeed, have been a confession! But madam didn't see it like that at all.

In her excitement the cook was panting like a boiler; her cheeks were flushed crimson, and her whalebone casing creaked. Minna looked stupid and dull, her mouth gaping as if she expected it to be filled with roast chicken.

Amanda Backs's cheeks also reddened, not with excitement and shame, but with defiance and anger. Madam was now brazenly talking about yesterday evening, when she had surprised a girl (alas, a girl of her own household) as she was climbing into a man's room in the darkness (hiccup).

A downright start went through the whole assembly, and Amanda saw the faces rigid with sheer astonishment and anticipation. Now it was coming!

But no, not yet. Madam, interrupted by many hiccups, accused herself of letting anger get the better of her, so that she had warmly rebuked the girl and threatened her with dismissal, instead of considering that we were all sinners, and that this erring lamb should be guided patiently to the fold. Ruefully she confessed that she had neglected her duty, since this young girl had been

entrusted to her care, and she begged that He might strengthen her with for-
bearance and long-suffering in her struggle against evil. . . .

Amanda, utterly contemptuous and very angry, listened to this twaddle.
Hardly had Frau von Teschow said the last "Amen" and risen from her knees
(certainly she had not had time to indicate by word of mouth or movement of
finger the next who was to kneel down on the little stool of repentance and
prayer), when Amanda rose with bright red cheeks and eyes dark with anger,
and said that madam need not trouble herself, she (Amanda) knew very well
who was referred to in all this talk, and there she stood, and perhaps madam
was satisfied.

On top of these words, however, Amanda Backs, in a perfect fury, turned
on Black Minna, who was pushing her forward so that she should be clearly
seen by the whole assembly. "Will you take your muddy paws off my clean
dress? I won't be pushed forward—and least of all by you! The confession and
penitence in this show have nothing at all to do with God!"

Having, with this angry hiss, crushed Minna, her enemy, Amanda turned
again to the assembly and said (for she was now well wound up) that she had
climbed through a window last night and, so that they should know everything down to the smallest detail, it had been the staff-house window, Bailiff
Meier's window. And she was not ashamed of it, and she could point to at least
ten women present at the meeting who had climbed through other windows to
other fellows! And with that she lifted her finger and pointed at Black Minna,
who thereupon cowered down with a screech on her bench. And Amanda lifted
her finger again, but before she could point it the bench where the younger
girls sat in the dark corner at the back fell over with a crash, so exceedingly
occupied had they all been in making themselves inconspicuous.

Then Amanda Backs laughed (and, alas and alack, a good many people
joined in), but unexpectedly her laughing turned to weeping. Furiously she
cried out: "It would be better if you paid us a decent wage." And, sobbing unrestrainedly, she rushed out of the chapel into the dark park.

In the meeting place many other things besides the bench had crashed
down, the old lady's views and beliefs among them. Trembling she sat in her
chair, gulping wretchedly; and this time even her old friend Jutta von Kuckhoff
stood before her and said mercilessly: "You see, Belinde, you can't touch pitch
and remain undefiled."

People, however, were making their way as fast as possible out of the
chapel. They were looking very quiet and almost dumbfounded, but, alas,
there was no doubt that before they reached home they would have recovered
their powers of speech. And there could be no doubt about who was destined

to be the subject of their gossip—it would not be Amanda Backs, the victress in the combat.

She, tear-stained and still very agitated, was running about the park, not feeling at all victorious, but calling herself donkey and goose for having mismanaged her own and Hans's case. Once she stopped, because she saw someone who turned out to be the old Geheimrat fumbling with the fence. She had wanted to take her courage in both hands and ask him for mercy, but her experience—young though she was—warned her not to ask anybody for anything.

However, roaming in the park, she became calmer, washed her face in the cool pond water and went to her Hans; and arrived just as the Geheimrat was knocking at the window and calling for Bailiff Meier. And heard, in Hans's room, a frightened woman scream out.

VII

The dusk was thickening into darkness. It was after nine o'clock and the street lamps were already lit. From the window of Wolfgang's room Frau Pagel looked out into the gardens now almost shrouded by night. In the background, however, there were twinkling lights and a reddish glow over the town—perhaps the mother was reflecting under which of the distant lights her son now sat squandering the filched money.

Impatiently she turned round to Minna, who was packing a trunk. "Hurry up, Minna," she said. "He may come any moment for his things."

But Minna did not look up from the shoes with their carefully inserted trees. "He won't come, madam," said she, placing the shoes in their small linen bags.

Frau Pagel grew angry. Minna's answer sounded almost as if she were being talked out of expecting her longed-for visitor. "You know quite well what I mean," she replied curtly. "Then he'll send somebody for his things."

Minna, unruffled, unflurried, went on with her packing. "There was no need to give him your best cabin trunk, madam. You won't have a decent one to go away with next spring to Ems."

"Silly creature!" said Frau Pagel, looking out of the window. She couldn't see the street for the treetops, but in the deep silence she heard every footstep, every approaching car.

"Shall I put the bathing wrap in, too, madam?" asked Minna.

"What? Oh, the bathing wrap! Of course. Everything which belongs to him is to be packed."

Minna made a sour face. "Then I must go up into the loft and fetch his books. I don't know whether the porter is still up. I couldn't manage the heavy cases by myself."

"There's time for the books," said the old woman, annoyed by these continual difficulties. "You can ask him whether he wants them, when he comes."

"He won't come, madam," said the old servant, monotonously dogmatic.

This time Frau Pagel had not been listening; this time she had no need to get angry at her maid's obstinacy. Leaning out of the window, she strained her ears, listening for one footstep. . . .

The maid, although she had her back to her mistress, felt that something was happening. She stopped her packing, turned round, a bathing suit in her hand, and saw the listening figure. "Madam!" she said pleadingly.

"Wolfgang!" Frau Pagel called out of the window, doubtingly at first, then with certainty. "Wolfgang! Yes, wait, my boy, I'm coming. I'll let you in immediately, I'll open the front door for you at once."

She wheeled round, her face flushed, the eyes under the white hair shining as of old.

"Hurry, Minna, the key! The young master's waiting. Run!" And without heeding Minna's imploring words, she ran into the dark corridor, switched on the light, seized some keys at random from the shelf beside the console table and, followed by Minna, ran downstairs.

She tried the house door, but the keys did not fit. "Quick, Minna, quick!" she called feverishly. "In case he changes his mind—he was always changeable."

Minna, who had fallen silent, pressed the handle, and the house door, which had not been locked, opened. Frau Pagel ran through the small front garden and pushed open the little iron gate which led to the street. "Wolfgang, my boy! Where are you?"

A solitary wanderer, some crank who longed for fresh air and the smell of growing things rather than for bars and noise, started with surprise. In the glow of the solitary gas lamp he saw before him a white-haired, very agitated old lady; behind her an elderly maid with a bathing suit in her hand. "Yes?" he inquired stupidly.

The old lady stopped short and turned away so suddenly that she almost fell. Throwing him an angry glance, the elderly maid with the bathing suit followed her, took the old lady by the arm, and the two vanished into the house.

They don't lock up, observed the wanderer to himself. Queer old hens, to scare a chap so! And he went his way, looking for an even quieter street.

The two old women went slowly upstairs without exchanging a word. Minna felt madam's hand on her arm tremble violently, and she noticed how difficult her mistress found the stairs. The flat door stood open, the landing was brightly lit. Minna closed the door. She was not sure whether her mistress preferred to go into the young master's room or to her own; it would certainly be better if she had a rest after all this excitement. But Minna, stubborn, obstinate Minna, had learned in her life one lesson which most women never learn—the lesson that there is a time for speaking and a time for silence. This was a time for silence.

Gently she led her mistress across the corridor until a gentle pull at her arm revealed that she wanted to go into the young master's room again. The trunk stood open before them. A drawer had been pulled out; on top was the young master's blue-and-white striped bathing wrap.

Frau Pagel stopped on seeing this. She cleared her throat. "Take out the bathing wrap, Minna!" she said coldly.

Minna did so and put the garment on the sofa.

"Take out everything," said Frau Pagel more angrily. "You must start packing all over again, Minna. I find I can't spare my trunk."

Without a word Minna began the unpacking, her mistress, with a severe, hard face, watching her. Perhaps she hoped for some slackening, some slightest indication of the servant's taking up an attitude about the matter; but Minna's face remained expressionless, her movements were neither particularly quick nor particularly slow.

Suddenly Frau Pagel turned away. She wanted to escape to her own dark room. But she could not get as far as that. The tears burst forth, blinding her, and she leaned against the lintel weeping unrestrainedly.

"Ah, Minna, Minna," she whispered. "Am I to lose him, too, the one person I love?"

But the old servant who during a lifetime had thought and worked only for her mistress's benefit, who had fetched and carried according to her mistress's whims, and who was at the moment again forgotten—the old servant seized her mistress's hand almost imploringly: "He'll come again, madam," she whispered consolingly. "Our Wolf will certainly return."

VIII

Sophie Kowalewski, Countess Mutzbauer's former chambermaid, had spent a very pleasant evening at the Christian Hostel. Up to supper time she had rummaged among her things, triumphantly examining as final proprietor all that she had carried off from her former mistress, by no means a little. Sophie could feel that she was expensively turned out. Neulohe, when it saw all this finery, would burst with envy.

Having examined her possessions, she now dressed up in them, for she had to wear something suitable for the evening meal in a hostel. With the instinctive adaptation to environment which was Sophie's strong point, she chose a blue dress and a shantung silk blouse. For truly religious people the skirt was possibly a little too short, but nothing could be done about that now. She possessed no skirt which was longer; however, she made up her mind not to cross her legs. The low front of the blouse she corrected with a light-colored silk modesty vest.

Only a very little lipstick, only a hint of red on her cheeks, and Sophie was ready. She went downstairs to the dining hall. The texts on the wall, some in poker-work, some in colored cardboard, delighted her. The tables had ugly but elaborately carved legs, and the tablecloths were of gray crêpe paper. Where the crêpe had been stained it was covered by a paper serviette. This was economical, practical, and exceedingly ugly—in Sophie's opinion.

The soup was thin and originated from a soup cube, and to make up for this the green peas were thickened with too much flour; the pork chop was far from large and the fat had a smell. This execrable food Sophie, the spoiled Sophie, ate with the greatest pleasure. It was fun for her to be living with the pious. So this was how they lived, inflicting privations on one another solely for the purpose of mortifying the flesh and standing well with the Lord, Who, after all, did not exist.

With particular interest Sophie looked at the waitresses, trying to make out whether they were fallen women who had been rescued or whether they really liked their present occupation. If they had ever fallen, she decided, it must have been very long ago—they were all so elderly. And they all looked discontented. This place couldn't be—as advertised in the text above the side-board—a fat green pasture.

When the meal was over, it was half-past eight—one couldn't go to bed so early. For a while Sophie stood irresolutely at the dining-hall window, looking at the rain-soaked Wilhelmstrasse. She had been out only in the West End; perhaps for a change she might have a look at the places of amusement in the Center. But no—she decided to go to bed early that night and generally to be perfectly steady throughout her entire holiday. Going out that evening was out of the question. Thank heavens, she had discovered a door marked "Writing Room," and thus knew how to pass her evening. She would inform her friend Hans that his sister would soon be visiting him.

In the very bare, poorly-lit writing room only one person was sitting—a white-haired gentleman in a long black frock coat—a pastor, surely. As she entered he started up in confusion from his newspaper, or from his nap over the newspaper, and stammered something. Decidedly he was embarrassed; possibly he was in doubt as to whether he should stay in the room alone with such a nicely dressed girl.

Gliding past him with a daughterly smile—at least Sophie considered it as such—she lifted herself into the revolving chair at the desk, thinking that this old sermon-spouter looked one of the soft sort. Pastor Lehnich in Neulohe was of a different breed. She had a distinct remembrance of his heavy hand when she had not learned the hymn verse or, worse still, when she had been caught with the boys.

But neither softness nor age nor religion seemed to prevent the white-haired gentleman from looking up from his paper every so often and peering at her legs. Angrily she pulled down her skirt as far as it would go—that is, as far as the knee. She considered that, for a pastor, his behavior was incorrect. Otherwise it amused her to watch men stealing glances at her legs, but it was not fitting for a pastor; he had something else to do than to find her legs attractive—he didn't draw his salary for that.

Catching the old gentleman out for the third time, she looked at him severely. At once he turned red, muttered something, and rushed headlong from the room.

Sophie sighed. She hadn't quite meant that. Occupying the writing room in solitary state was rather dismal.

However, the writing paper bore the heading "Christian Hostel," which was pleasing. She supposed that such a letter would be handled at the penitentiary with respect, that it would, without fail, get her the longed-for visitor's permit. As a precaution she slipped at least a dozen of the sheets and envelopes into her handbag; they would certainly come in useful one of these days.

However, not even the most pious superscription could free her from the labor of writing; as in the morning, so in the evening—it was a hard task and a long one.

But at last she finished. She hadn't written much, only four or five sentences, but they were sufficient to prepare Hans Liebschner (and the penitentiary officials) for his "sister's" visit. How Hans would grin over this letter! How amusing the visit would be if—and he could do it marvelously—he treated her as a sister. She already felt his mocking brotherly kiss, under the policeman's very eyes, or whoever looked after a penitentiary.

It was half-past nine and there was nothing more to be done but go to bed. Slowly she undressed. Although she had been tired all day long, she was now wide awake. Not a trace of the desire to sleep was left. Outside, cars glided beneath her window. She could almost see, while she peevishly undressed, men entering bars, pompously or with an affectation of nonchalance, nodding to the girls and climbing on to their high stools, ordering their first cocktail or whisky.

But under no circumstances would she go out tonight. She was resolved on that. And was therefore glad to find a little black book with red ends on the bedside table. It bore in gold letters the title *The Holy Scriptures*.

Since her confirmation Sophie had never had a Bible in her hand, and then her preoccupation with this book had been limited to learning verses and—more often—to looking for seductive passages. But this evening she had leisure for once; so she took up the Bible and, in order to deal with it properly, started to read from the beginning. (If it turned out to her liking, she would pack this excellent free holiday reading in her trunk.) It would be interesting to find out what there really was to this famous book. The narrative of the Creation awoke only a moderate interest—for aught she cared it might have happened like that or it mightn't—it was unimportant, anyhow. The important thing was to be here oneself—thanks to the creation of Adam and Eve in the second chapter, and the fall from grace in the third.

So this was the famous Fall of Man with which a girl was so often bored in bars by educated men (as long as they were on their best behavior). Sophie rediscovered everything—the Tree of Knowledge, the apple and the snake. But she didn't at all agree with the Bible version of what had taken place. If you carefully read what was written you would realize at once that God had never forbidden woman to eat of the Tree of Knowledge. Certainly, He had forbidden man to eat of it, but that was before woman had been created. To punish woman for something which had not been forbidden to her at all was a fine thing! That was exactly what men would do!

If it starts like that, she thought, what can you expect? It's a put-up job—only a fool would be taken in by such rubbish. And those chaps still go on preaching to you nowadays. Well, let them come to me about it! . . . She shut the book angrily. . . . What! Take it with me on my holidays? I shouldn't think of it for a moment. I should only get annoyed. That's why they leave the book about so freely—there's no demand for it!

She switched off the light.

It was very warm; the air in the room was oppressive. She rose and opened the windows. She could hear the streetcar bells clanging; when the streetcars turned into Krausenstrasse they always rang the bell. She heard footsteps, sometimes those of a solitary pedestrian, very distinct; at other times a noisy confusion. Cars came with a roar and a hoot, to scurry on . . .

Her body started to itch; she scratched herself here, she scratched herself there; she turned over on this side, turned over on that. Then she forced herself to lie still. She assumed a sleeping position—on her right side, both hands under her right cheek. She closed her eyes. Sleep was nearly there. But she was thirsty, and had to rise and drink a glass of water which tasted stale. Again she lay down and waited for sleep, in vain recalling how tired she had been that morning, her mouth foul with liquors, her feet aching. Then she had had to struggle against sleep as she forced herself to write a few lines to Hans, while behind her the cook, that clumsy creature, snored loudly. She began to count up to a hundred.

Similarly thousands of others lay in their beds, harassed and restless. Those who had spent their last penny. Those who had sworn by their morning hangover that they would never again go out at night, but would sleep soundly instead. They were those who'd grown tired of eternal youth and had given up looking for something night after night whose name they didn't even know. Like Sophie, they tossed restlessly from side to side. It was not the craving for alcohol nor the longing for embraces which kept them awake and finally urged them to get up; no, they could not remain alone and find peace. The darkness of their rooms reminded them of Death. They had heard and seen enough of Death; for four years, at home and abroad, people had been dying. And they themselves would die soon enough—would die much too soon. At present they were alive and wanted to feel so.

As did the others, Sophie Kowalewski got up, dressed hastily as if she had to keep a most urgent appointment—some important matter which she must not miss at any price—went quickly downstairs and out into the street.

Where should she go? She looked up and down the street. It doesn't actually matter where she goes. She knows inside her: It's always the same. But she remembered that she once wanted to see the drinking places in the town center. So she goes slowly (as she is among people, she suddenly feels she's got plenty of time) towards the center of town.

IX

A long quiet stroll through the Tiergarten had cleared the head of von Studmann, the former reception manager. It had also given Rittmeister von Prackwitz the opportunity of painting to his friend a picture of Neulohe, surrounded by woods and remote, almost on the Polish frontier in fact. He had not intended to paint the place rosier than it was or to deceive his friend. But somehow, compared with this riotous and perverse city of Berlin, the Manor of Neulohe now appeared quieter and purer than in reality—every face there

known to him, every character in the last resort clear-cut, and in nothing contaminated by the madness of the times.

In the midst of the ostentatious shops with their marble fronts, illuminated signboards and advertisements, although the façades above were
crumbling and decaying, Prackwitz found it easy to say: "My buildings, thank
heavens, look quite different. Not handsome, but solid honest-to-God red
brick." And looking at the scorched lawns, the weed-ridden flower beds of the
Tiergarten, for which no money was available in spite of the flood of money
everywhere, he was able to say: "We, too, have had a drought. But we're having
quite a good harvest in spite of it."

The rose gardens in the Tiergarten were stripped of their roses and badly
damaged. There seemed to be florists who supplied themselves, not from the
markets, but from the parks. "There's a bit of pilfering at our place, but, thank
heavens, not this devastation!"

They sat on a bench. The dry air had already sucked out the moisture from
the soil. Before them stretched the New Lake, dotted with bush-clad islets, and
above them the treetops were motionless. From the Zoological Gardens they
heard the roar of wild beasts.

"My father-in-law," said Herr von Prackwitz dreamily, "still retains eight
thousand acres of woodland. Although the old man is so stingy in many ways,
he's generous over the shooting—you could kill many a handsome buck."

Yes, in the increasing dusk Neulohe changed to a quite very remote island,
and Herr von Studmann was not unreceptive to such a delineation. That morning he had rejected the idea of a flight into the country. But the afternoon, with
its varied experiences, had proved that life today could break the nerve of a
soldier who had been four years at the Front. It was not so much the grotesque
painful incident with Reichsfreiherr Baron von Bergen—thank God, utter
madmen were not as yet so common in contemporary life that one was forced
to reckon with them daily—but the incident had laid bare in a frightful manner
the inhuman nature of that hotel industry to which von Studmann had devoted
his energies and zeal. It had been his belief that, in carrying out his duties
conscientiously, he had earned, if not affection, at least respect. He had, however, seen himself the object of shameless, insolent curiosity, from the most
recently engaged elevator boy to the managing director. If the temperamental
Dr. Schröck had not intervened with his somewhat unusual views on lunatics,
he (von Studmann) would have been discharged without any consideration
whatever and at a moment's notice, as if he were some sort of criminal.

As it was, he had, on his way out, been intercepted by the managing director who, in spite of his monumental appearance, had taken a very serpentine

course between on-the-one-hand and on-the-other; a gratuity—in good foreign currency, of course—was now pressed on him, and the warmest recommendations assured him later. "Yes, my dear colleague, I believe this rather trifling though exceedingly disagreeable incident will turn out to your advantage. If I have understood Dr. Schröck rightly, he expects you to put in a very heavy claim for damages—a very heavy claim."

"No," said Herr von Studmann, emerging from a reverie on his bench in the Tiergarten, "I shouldn't like to take advantage of that young scamp's moral weakness."

"What?" asked von Prackwitz, starting. He had just been talking of wild-boar hunting in Neulohe. "No, of course not. I understand that quite well. It's not necessary either."

"Forgive me," said von Studmann, "I was still here in my thoughts. In Berlin. I've been doing very stupid work. Rather like charring—one gets tired out and next morning everything is dirty again."

"Of course. Female work. At my place . . ."

"Excuse me, I couldn't live with you either and do nothing. A real job of work . . ."

"You'd be a great help," said von Prackwitz pensively. "I told you this morning about the various political and military complications. At times I'm rather isolated—rather perplexed."

"So many people are running away from their jobs," went on Studmann. "To work, to do anything at all, has suddenly become idiotic. As long as people received a fixed tangible value at the end of the week or the month, even the most boring office job had some reason. But the fall of the mark has opened their eyes. Why do we live? they suddenly ask. Why are we doing anything? Anything at all? They don't see why they should work merely to be paid in a few worthless scraps of paper."

"This devaluation is the most infamous cheating of the nation ever known," said von Prackwitz.

"This afternoon opened my eyes. If I really came to live with you, Prackwitz, I'd have to have a real job. Hard work, you understand!"

Von Prackwitz racked his brain. Horse-breaking, he thought. But my nags already have more exercise than is good for them. Scribbling in the office? But I can't ask Studmann to make out the pay sheets. In his mind's eye he saw the Manor office with its old-fashioned green safe and ugly deal shelves full of out-of-date law books. A hideously dusty and neglected hole!

Von Studmann was more practical than his friend. "To my knowledge," he prompted, "they have agricultural students on many estates."

"They do exist," confirmed Prackwitz. "A terrible crowd. They pay a premium—otherwise nobody would take them on—keep their own horse, stick their nose into everything, understand nothing, don't lend a hand anywhere, but hold forth very grandly about agriculture."

"Well, then, not that," decided von Studmann. "What other openings are there?"

"All sorts of things. For instance, bailiffs who hand out the fodder, supervise the feeding, milking and grooming of the animals, keep stock books, work with the threshing machine. Then there are outdoor bailiffs who arrange about the plowing, manuring and harvesting, all the fieldwork, and have to be present . . ."

"On a horse?"

"Bicycle," replied von Prackwitz. "At least at my place."

"So you have a bailiff?"

"I'll sack him tomorrow, he's a lazy drunken fellow."

"But not because of me, Prackwitz. I couldn't become your bailiff straight away. You'd say, 'Studmann, manure that rye,' and upon my soul it'd be a difficult job for me. I haven't the slightest idea about it—except for natural manuring, which would be insufficient, I fear."

The two men laughed heartily, and stood up. Von Studmann's brainstorm was over. Prackwitz was sure his friend would join him. Walking along, it was agreed that von Studmann should come to Neulohe as something in between a student, a confidential clerk and a supervisor.

"You'll travel with me tomorrow morning, Studmann. You'll have your things packed in half an hour, if I know anything of you. If only I could get hold of another sensible fellow now, to take charge of the people I've engaged today, the harvest would do very well. Oh, God, Studmann, I'm so glad! My first happy hour for I don't know how long. Listen, let's go to some decent place and have something to eat; it'll do you good after the wretched drink. What do you say to Lutter and Wegner's? Fine! Now, if I could get another man, also from the army if possible, an ex-sergeant major or someone like that, who knows how to handle people . . ."

At Lutter and Wegner's they went into the cellar restaurant. The army man whom the Rittmeister needed was sitting at a small corner table. He had not been a sergeant major but a second lieutenant and at present was rather drunk.

X

"There's Second Lieutenant Pagel!" said von Studmann.

"There's Bombshell Pagel!" said Prackwitz.

And both saw vividly again that scene which had made this same Pagel unforgettable among their many comrades of the World War, or rather, for that war was over, of the last desperate attempt by German troops to hold the Baltic Provinces against the Red onslaught. It had been in the spring of 1919, during that wild attack of the Germans and Letts which finally liberated Riga.

Young Pagel, looking hardly older than a schoolboy, had been one of Rittmeister von Prackwitz's motley detachment. He may have been seventeen, but more probably was only sixteen. Intended for an officer's career, he had been thrust from the military college at Gross-Lichterfelde into a delirious world exhausted with fighting and no longer wishing to have anything to do with officers. Uprooted and not knowing what to do, the boy had wandered farther and farther into East Prussia until he fell in with men whom he might call comrades but was not forced to address as "Comrade."

This beardless youth who had never before smelled gunpowder was both moving and ridiculous in his delight at being among veterans who spoke his language, wore uniforms, gave and accepted orders, and really carried them out, too. Nothing could damp his ardor or his desire to get acquainted with all there was to know in the shortest possible time—machine guns, mine mortars, and the one and only armored train.

Until it came to an attack; until hostile machine guns as well as friendly ones started to rattle and the frist shells whined overhead to burst in the rear; until the enthusiastic schoolboy play turned into reality. Then Prackwitz and Studmann had seen young Pagel turn pale and silent, flinching at every scream of a shell and ducking his head.

With a glance the two officers had understood each other. To the boy they said nothing. Green with terror, with sweating brow and wet hands, he was fighting against his fear; to them he was a bridge between the present and those inconceivably remote days in August 1914, when they themselves had heard this screaming for the first time, and had flinched. All had to go through that experience; everybody, once and for all, had to fight down the terrified cur within. Many lost this secret battle, but the majority were victorious and from that time were masters of themselves.

With young Pagel the result was at first in doubt. One could have spoken to him, shouted at him, and he would have heard nothing. His ears perceived only the wailing overhead; he looked hither, thither, like someone in a nightmare; in the midst of the advance he hesitated. Now he looked back.

"Yes, Pagel, that's right, the damned Reds are getting the range. They're landing them nearer. Yes, we're in for it now, Second Lieutenant!"

And then the first shell was already in their lines—automatically Studmann and Prackwitz flung themselves down. But what was the matter with Pagel? Young Pagel stood looking at the shell hole, his lips moving as if he were mumbling some incantation.

"Lie down, get down, Pagel!" screamed von Prackwitz.

Up went the earth in a welter of dust, fire and smoke—the explosion rent the air.

Fool! thought von Prackwitz.

A pity! thought von Studmann.

But—and one could hardly believe one's eyes—a shadow, a motionless figure was standing in the fog and smoke. It became clearer, leaped forward, picked something off the ground, shouted furiously "Blast it," let it drop, took his cap to hold it by, rushed up to Prackwitz, clicked his heels and said: "Beg to report, Herr Rittmeister, a shell splinter!" And in very unmilitary language: "Damned hot!"

He had—forever—vanquished the cur in himself.

Forever?

This scene, this rather ridiculous yet heroic deed of a very young man, was clearly recollected by the two as they saw Pagel sitting, apparently rather the worse for drink, at a corner table in Lutter and Wegner's. "There's Bombshell Pagel!" they called out.

Bombshell Pagel looked up. With the hesitating movements of the drunken, he pushed back his glass and bottle before rising to his feet and said without surprise: "The officers!"

"Stand at ease, Pagel," said the Rittmeister smiling. "We're no longer officers. And you're the only one of us who still wears his uniform."

"Certainly, Herr Rittmeister," said Pagel stubbornly. "But I'm no longer on duty."

The two friends exchanged an understanding glance.

"May we sit at your table, Pagel?" asked von Studmann. "It's rather crowded down here, and we want something to eat."

"Please do," said Pagel and sat down quickly as if standing had become very difficult for him. The other two, sitting down, spent some time choosing their food and wine.

Then the Rittmeister raised his glass. "Your health, Pagel! To old times!"

"My respectful thanks, Herr Rittmeister, Herr Oberleutnant. Yes, to old times!"

"And what are you doing now?"

"Now?" Pagel looked slowly from one to the other as if he had to think very carefully about his answer. "I'm not sure. . . . Something or other." He made a vague gesture.

"But you must have been doing something during these four years," said von Studmann. "Perhaps you've started something, been employed, achieved something, eh?"

"Certainly, certainly," assented Pagel politely. And with the malicious insight of drunkenness, he added: "May I be permitted to ask, Herr Oberleutnant, what you have achieved during these four years?"

Von Studmann started, was about to be angry, then laughed. "You're right, Pagel. I haven't achieved anything. As you see me here, I have only six hours ago suffered complete shipwreck again. I really shouldn't know what to do if the Rittmeister wasn't taking me back to his manor—as a kind of apprentice. Prackwitz has a big estate in Neumark, you know."

"Shipwrecked six hours ago," repeated Pagel, not noticing what was said about the estate. "That's strange."

"What's strange, Pagel?"

"I don't know. . . . Perhaps because you're eating duck and barberries, therefore it seems strange."

"With regard to that," said von Studmann, in his turn malicious, "you're sitting here and drinking Steinwein which, by the way, taken in such quantities is far too heavy. Duck would be much better for you."

"Of course," Pagel readily agreed. "I did think about it. But eating's so terribly boring, drinking's much easier. Besides, I've something on hand."

"Whatever you may have on hand, Pagel," remarked Studmann casually, "food will serve your purpose better than drink."

"Hardly, hardly," replied Pagel. And, as if to prove his point, he emptied his glass. But since this demonstration made no impression on the others, their faces being still skeptical, he added by way of explanation: "I have to spend a lot of money."

"By drinking you'll certainly not be able to spend much more, Pagel," interposed von Prackwitz, more and more annoyed by the casual attitude of Studmann, who was rather encouraging this young puppy. "Don't you see, man, that you're full to the brim already?"

Von Studmann winked at his friend as a hint to desist, but Pagel remained surprisingly calm. "Possibly," he said. "But that doesn't matter. I'll get through my money all the easier."

"So it's something to do with women," von Prackwitz cried angrily. "I'm no moralist, Pagel, but to be in such a drunken condition—that's not good."

Pagel made no reply except to fill his glass again, empty it and refill it deliberately. Prackwitz made a furious gesture, but von Studmann was not in agreement. His friend was an excellent fellow, but certainly no psychologist; he was not observant, and he always thought that everybody must feel as he did. And when things were not just as he wished them he would flare up at once.

Seeing Pagel refill his glass, Studmann was very painfully, and therefore very vividly, reminded of a certain room—No. 37. There, too, glasses had been filled and emptied in a similar manner, and he also clearly remembered a look of fear and insolence which he had observed then. He was not at all sure that Pagel, in spite of his heavy drinking, was actually drunk. Certainly, however, he didn't like being questioned and would probably much prefer to be alone. But Studmann had no intention of allowing himself to be influenced by Pagel's indifferent or even hostile mood. He sensed they had met the former second lieutenant in a critical situation; now, as before, they had to keep an eye on him. And von Studmann, who that afternoon had suffered a defeat, swore to himself not to fall for any tricks that night, but to throw the champagne bottle hand grenade in good time—there were many kinds of precedents for such actions.

Pagel was smoking, apparently lost in thought and not altogether conscious of the others' presence. In an undertone Studmann informed Prackwitz of his scheme and was answered by an impatient gesture of refusal, but in the end Prackwitz agreed.

Pagel tilted the bottle over his glass, but no wine flowed forth. Avoiding their eyes, he attracted the waiter's attention and ordered another bottle of Steinwein and a double cherry brandy.

The impatient Prackwitz started to speak, but Studmann placed an imploring hand on his knee, and the other maintained an unwilling silence.

When the waiter brought the wine Pagel asked for the bill. The charge, either because of the guest's condition or because he had been drinking there for some hours, was heavy, indeed extortionate. Pagel pulled a wad of bank notes out, selected a few, gave them to the waiter and refused the change. The man's unusually servile thanks gave a hint as to the size of the tip.

Again the two gentlemen exchanged glances, the one angry and the other pleading for patience. They still said nothing, however, but continued to observe Pagel, who now drew from every pocket large and small bundles of notes, piling them on top of each other. Then he took his paper serviette, wrapped it round them, searched his pockets again for a length of string, and tied the parcel up. Pushing it aside, he leaned back as after a task finished, lit a cigarette, swallowed the cherry brandy and poured out a glass of wine.

Then he looked up. His expression was remarkably gloomy and uncompromising, and his glance rested mockingly on the two friends. At once Studmann was aware that Pagel was only showing off. His drinking, his apparent indifference to them, the provocative display and wrapping up of his money—all was histrionics, performed for their benefit.

The lad is utterly wretched, though Studmann, strangely moved. Perhaps he would like to tell us about his trouble or ask our help, but he can't get himself to do so. If only Prackwitz wouldn't . . .

But the white-haired choleric Prackwitz could no longer restrain himself. "It's rotten, Pagel," he shouted, "the way you're behaving with that money. You mustn't treat money like that."

Studmann got the impression that Pagel was pleased with this outburst, although he did not show it.

"If I may be permitted to ask a question, Herr Rittmeister," said the young man, mouthing the words with exaggerated politeness, "how *does* one treat money?"

"How?" screamed the Rittmeister, the veins in his forehead swelling and his face almost purple with fury. "How does one treat money? In a proper manner, Second Lieutenant Pagel! Properly, conscientiously—as one ought to, you understand? You don't carry it about loose in your pocket, you put it in a wallet . . ."

"There's too much of it, Herr Rittmeister," said Pagel apologetically. "No wallet would be large enough."

"One doesn't carry so much money about with one," shouted the Rittmeister at white heat. Already people were looking at them from the adjoining table. "It isn't right. It isn't done."

"Why not?" asked Pagel like an obedient inquiring pupil.

Studmann bit his lips so as not to burst out laughing. Von Prackwitz, however, had too little humor to understand that his leg was being pulled.

"As soon as I've drunk my wine I'll try and get rid of the stuff as quickly as possible," said Pagel apologetically. He drank, an amused boyish smile spreading over his face. He looked very much as he did on his first day in Courland, so Studmann thought—no trace of a resemblance to Reichsfreiherr Baron von Bergen. Taking hold of the packet of money, Pagel hesitated and then impulsively held it out to the Rittmeister. "Or would you like it, sir?"

Rittmeister Joachim von Prackwitz started out of his chair, his face flushing crimson. It was an insult, a deliberate insult, all the more heinous in that it came from a former second lieutenant. An officer, and particularly a Rittmeister von Prackwitz, may leave the Service, but he still retains his old conceptions and views. Studmann and Prackwitz were good friends, but the friendship originated at a time when one was a captain and the other a lieutenant; and it continued on that basis. If the first lieutenant wished to criticize the captain he had to do so while carefully observing the formalities proper between a superior officer and his subordinate. Pagel, however, was not even a friend of von Prackwitz; he had said something very unpleasant, even insulting, to his face, without preparation and without observance of the proper forms. Rittmeister von Prackwitz therefore exploded. Something dreadful might have resulted had not von Studmann laid a firm hand on the Rittmeister's shoulder and forced him back into his chair. "He's stupidly drunk," he said in low tones. And sharply, to Pagel, "Apologize at once!"

The boyish smile faded slowly. Pagel looked thoughtfully at the angry Rittmeister, as if he were not quite clear as to what had happened, then at the parcel of money in his hand. His face darkened. Putting the money back again on the table near him, he reached for his glass and drank hastily.

"Apologize?" he said sullenly. "Who attaches any importance nowadays to such tomfoolery?"

"I do, Herr Pagel," cried the Rittmeister, still very angry. "*I* have retained my manners, whether others consider them antiquated and foolish or not. *I* attach importance to this tomfoolery!"

"Let him alone, Prackwitz," suggested von Studmann. "He's overwrought, he's drunk, and perhaps he intends to do something vicious."

"I'm not interested," cried the Rittmeister furiously. "I'll let him alone with the greatest pleasure."

Pagel glanced quickly at Studmann but made no reply.

Studmann bent across the table and said in a friendly way: "If you were to offer me the money, Pagel, I'd accept it."

The Rittmeister made a gesture of extreme astonishment. Pagel, however, hastily reached for the packet of money and drew it nearer.

"I'm not going to take it away from you," said Studmann, rather mockingly.

Pagel turned red, ashamed of himself. "What would you do with it?" he asked sullenly.

"Keep it for you—till you felt better."

"That's not necessary. I don't need money anymore."

"Exactly what I supposed," agreed the Oberleutnant calmly. "How was it that you, too, suffered shipwreck six hours ago, Pagel?" he inquired with an exaggerated indifference.

This time the young man went completely crimson. With an almost painful slowness the flush, starting from his cheeks, spread over his whole face. It crept under the high and creased collar of his tunic, and went up into the roots of his hair. Suddenly one could see how very young he was, how terribly he suffered under his embarrassment. Even the angry Rittmeister looked at him with new eyes. Pagel, however, annoyed at his very obvious confusion, asked defiantly: "Who told you that I had suffered shipwreck, Herr von Studmann?"

"I understood you so, Pagel."

"Then you've misunderstood me. I—" But Pagel broke off, dissatisfied with himself, his blush having betrayed him completely.

"Of course you're not doing well, Pagel," said von Studmann mildly. "We can see that, the Rittmeister as well as myself. You're not an habitual drunkard. You're drinking for a definite reason, because something's gone wrong, because—oh, you understand me quite well, Pagel."

Pagel tilted his wineglass. His bearing was less tense, but he made no reply.

"Why don't you want us to help you?" Studmann asked. "I let the Rittmeister help me this afternoon without any hesitation. I, too, had a very unpleasant upset. . . ." He smiled at the remembrance of his fall. He had no actual recollection of it, but Prackwitz had described, very caustically, how he had rolled downstairs in the hotel. Studmann was clear that his case was different from Pagel's—albeit only physically.

"Perhaps we could advise you," he continued persuasively. "It would be better still if we could help you in a practical way. When we were advancing on Tetelmünde you fell down with the machine gun and you didn't hesitate for a moment to accept my help. Why can't what held good in Courland hold good also in Berlin?"

"Because," said Pagel morosely, "we were fighting for a cause. Today everybody fights for himself—and against everybody else."

"Once a comrade always a comrade," said von Studmann. "You remember, Pagel, don't you?"

"Yes, of course." Pagel bent his head as if he were deliberating, watched expectantly by the other two. Then he lifted his head. "I could say a good deal against it," he said with his clumsy yet distinct articulation. "But I don't want to. I'm terribly tired. Could I meet you somewhere tomorrow morning?"

In a few words the two friends reached an understanding. "We are leaving Schlesische Bahnhof for Ostade shortly after eight tomorrow morning," said von Studmann.

"Good," said Pagel. "I'll also be at the station, perhaps."

He stared into space as if everything had been settled. He put no questions: it did not seem to interest him why they were leaving, where they were going, or what was to happen.

The Rittmeister shrugged his shoulders, dissatisfied with this half-promise. But Studmann persisted. "That's something, Pagel. But not entirely what we would like. You've something on your mind; you spoke just now about getting rid of your money."

"Affairs with women," muttered the Rittmeister.

"It'll soon be midnight. Between now and tomorrow morning at eight o'clock you've got something on hand, Pagel, the result of which appears so uncertain that you can't give us a firm promise and also don't want us with you."

"Wretched women," muttered the Rittmeister.

"I differ from Prackwitz," said Studmann, noticing that Pagel was about to reply. "I don't believe that some dubious affair with a woman is behind it. You're not the kind of man for that." Pagel lowered his head, but the Rittmeister snorted. "I should be grateful, we should be grateful, if you would allow us to spend the next few hours with you."

"It's nothing special," said Pagel, now won over by the other's tactful insistence. "I only want to make a test."

The former lieutenant smiled. "A challenge to Fate, Pagel?" he said. "The former Second Lieutenant Pagel submits to God's judgment! Oh, how enviably young you still are!"

"I don't consider myself so enviable," growled Pagel.

"Of course not, and you're quite right," agreed Studmann hastily. "So long as one is young one regards Youth as a misfortune. Only later does one discover that Youth is happiness. Well, how about it? Are we coming with you?"

"You won't prevent me from doing what I want to do?"

"No, of course not. You must behave as if we aren't present."

"And the Rittmeister agrees?"

Rittmeister von Prackwitz muttered something, but it was enough for Pagel.

"All right, come with me if you like." He cheered up a little. "It might perhaps interest you. It's—well, you'll see. Let's go by taxi."

They set off.

Chapter Seven

Full Moon on an Oppressive Night

I

Amanda Backs stood panting among the bushes.

"Well, Herr Meier, what a strange voice you've got. You're bleating like a woman," squeaked the Geheimrat in his thin old voice.

Black Meier's head popped out of the window. "Herr Geheimrat," he explained, "that's only because I was awakened suddenly. When I'm asleep I've always got a high-pitched voice."

"It's all the same to me," said the old man. "I only hope, when you get married, your wife believes in this high-pitched voice! I've got a letter here, Herr Meier."

"Very good, Herr Geheimrat, I'll deliver it."

"Now don't be in such a hurry, young man. You shall get back to your bed in a minute. This letter is for my son-in-law."

"Certainly, Herr Geheimrat. I'll give it to him tomorrow morning as soon as he arrives from the station."

"No, that won't do. His wife will be present. This is a business matter, you understand?"

"Yes, Herr Geheimrat. So I'll give it to him . . ."

"Wait a moment, young man. Never mind about the bed creaking. I expect it's getting bored, eh?"

"Yes, Herr Geheimrat."

"Well now! And you won't catch a cold at the open window; you're used to draughts. By the way, do you always sleep without a nightshirt?"

"Herr Geheimrat, I . . ."

"Better stick to 'Yes, Herr Geheimrat'—that's safer, isn't it? You think I can't see in the dark. I can see as well as an old tom-cat."

"It was so hot, Herr Geheimrat—you'll excuse me."

"Of course I'll excuse you, my son. I quite understand that you're feeling hot, not having brought in the crops and having a drop too much afterwards— yes, you'd certainly feel hot."

"Herr Geheimrat!"

"Well, what can I do for you? Do you know, my son, I've changed my mind. I'll get Elias to take the letter. I'm inclined to think you'll have too much on your mind tomorrow."

"Herr Geheimrat!" (Pleadingly.)

"Well, good night, Herr Meier, and do put on a nightshirt. I believe I saw Amanda in the park."

The old man shuffled off. In the bushes, her heart thudding, stood Amanda. She had always known that her Hans was not worth much and was always running after every skirt; but she had thought that she could keep him straight if she was always there when he needed her. . . . But, nothing doing, no such luck!

Little Meier still leaned out of the window. Once more he had pleaded "Herr Geheimrat!" as if the old man could be of any help, and as if having the letter entrusted to him would have altered anything. . . . From where she stood Amanda could plainly see him hanging out of the window. He was so stupid. Why did she always take up with such silly, spineless fellows who were no good at all? She didn't understand it. It made her miserable.

And now the female in his room started to whisper.

Hans turned his head round and said roughly: "Shut up!" That rather pleased Amanda; his insolence to the other woman showed that he could not care very much for her. He would not have dared to talk to herself like that; she would have boxed his ears. She would very much like to know who the other woman was, however. It was no one from the Manor; they had all been at the prayer meeting.

"For Heaven's sake dress quickly," she heard Hans say. "If Amanda comes there'll be the hell of a row. That would just about finish it."

Amanda almost burst out laughing. He was as silly as ever. The row was waiting outside his very window, but he'd noticed nothing. Hans was always wise after the event. But she would like to have had a few words with the female—everyone in the village, not to mention the people on the estate, knew by now that she went herself with Meier.

The woman inside did seem to be in a hurry—Amanda heard her moving about. Now her head was beside his.

"Shut the window and switch the light on. I can't find my things," she grumbled.

Who could it be? One couldn't recognize a whisper like that.

"Hush!" said Meier, so loudly and roughly that even Amanda started. "Can't you keep your trap shut? If I turn on the light they'll think I'm awake."

"Who'll think that? Your Amanda?"

Was it the Hartig woman? That would be the limit. The coachman's wife with her eight children stealing a girl's young man! If so, she'd be in for it.

"That's none of your business. You've got to hurry up!"

"But my things . . ."

"I'm not turning on the light. You must manage the best way you can."

Complaining, the second head vanished from the window. Amanda was now almost certain that it was Frau Hartig. But almost certain is not quite sure. Amanda was in no hurry; she could catch Hans at any time. Now she had to intercept the woman first. Even if she stood there all night, she must get her. She would have to come out through the door or the window—one must be patient!

It was strange that, although Amanda had grown so angry in the prayer meeting, now when there was much more cause for it she couldn't feel really angry. Least of all with Hans. He was a fool and remained a fool, and if she didn't look after him he would do stupid things. Neither was she furious with the woman. Indeed, she was surprised at herself. But perhaps she would be furious when she knew who it was and had had a talk with her. Amanda hoped to be in good form. The woman was not to imagine that she could annex someone who by rights belonged to another.

So she waited patiently or impatiently, according to her thoughts from one moment to another, until—and not without relief—she at last saw the visitor climbing out of the window. The relief was derived from the fact that this proved that Hans could not care much about the woman; she had no power over him if he was too lazy to unlock the front door for her. The woman, too, did not waste much time on an affectionate farewell or look round, but steered straight for the corner of the house in the farmyard.

That's that, thought Amanda Backs, and followed. The bailiff's windows were thereupon shut rather noisily, which annoyed her, for a shut window on such a warm night could only signify that Herr Meier didn't want any more visitors—which Amanda took personally.

"Wait for me, you Hartig woman!" she called.

"You, Mandy?" asked the coachman's wife, peering at her. "How you frightened me! Well, good night! I must go. I'm in a hurry."

"Let me come with you," said Amanda, and hurried with her across the farmyard toward the coachman's dwelling. "I'm going the same way as you."

"Are you?" asked Frau Hartig and walked more slowly. "Yes, a girl like you on her legs from morn till night—madam won't get another like you so easily."

"I don't put my legs up as easily as some people," said Amanda, with meaning. "Well, get along; your husband will be waiting for you."

But Frau Hartig stopped. They were in the middle of the farmyard. To the right were the pigsties in which there was still an occasional rustling (the sty doors stood open because of the heat); on the left was the midden. The two women, however, stood so that Amanda was facing the coachman's dwelling at one end of the farmyard, while Frau Hartig looked toward the other end, where she could see a light burning in the bailiff's window—and, of course, it annoyed her that he should have turned on the light after all.

"Besides, Mandy isn't the right way to address me," said Amanda Backs after a longish pause.

"I can call you Fräulein Backs, if you prefer it," said Frau Hartig submissively.

"Yes, *Fräulein*," was the retort. "I'm not yet a Frau—I can go with whom I like."

"So you can," acknowledged the coachman's wife. "Any master or mistress would be glad to have a poultry maid like you."

"Shall we have it out now or shan't we?" cried Amanda and stamped.

The coachman's wife remained silent.

"I can talk to your husband if you like," said Amanda threateningly. "I've heard that he's already wondering how you get such varied children."

"Varied children," echoed Frau Hartig with a forced laugh. "How strange you are, Mandy."

"You're not to say Mandy. I don't want to hear it from you."

"I can say Fräulein Backs if you like."

"Then say it—and besides, it's a shame for a married woman to take away a girl's young man."

"I haven't taken him away from you, Amanda," pleaded Frau Hartig.

"Yes, you have. And one would think that a woman with eight children has got her share."

"Lord, Amanda," said the coachman's wife, conciliatory, "you don't know anything about what it's like to be married. You imagine it quite different from what it is."

"Don't talk rubbish, Hartig," cried Amanda threateningly. "You can't fool me that way."

"When one's got a steady man," explained Frau Hartig, "one thinks all that's over. But you get that queer feeling again . . ."

"What queer feeling? Don't talk nonsense."

"God, Amanda, I'm not talking nonsense. You must know what it's like when you feel as if you had a prickling all over your body, and no peace whatever you do, and everything's got to be done in a blazing hurry, as if you hadn't a moment to spare—and then you find that you've been standing about with a swill pail in your hand for a quarter of an hour without knowing where you are!"

"I've nothing to do with swill," said Amanda Backs cuttingly. But actually she was no longer feeling so hostile; she was giving due attention to what she was hearing.

"No, of course not," assented Frau Hartig.

"And you've got your husband whenever you feel like that. So you oughtn't to put a spoke in my wheel."

"But, Amanda, that's just what you can't foretell," exclaimed Frau Hartig eagerly.

"What can't you foretell?"

"That your husband can't help you in that at all. If I'd known as a young girl what I know today, I'd never have married, you can believe me."

"Is that really so?" meditated Amanda Backs. "Don't you like your husband at all?"

"Lord, yes, of course—he's quite nice in his way. And quite steady, too. But I don't like him that way anymore. That queer feeling stopped as far as he was concerned a long time ago."

"So you like—Hans—Bailiff Meier—much more?"

"God, Amanda, what are you thinking about? I've told you already that I'm not taking him away from you."

Amanda's voice was thick with rage. "So he was the first to start—I mean, Meier?"

Frau Hartig remained silent for a while, thinking it over. In the end, however, she decided in favor of the truth. "No, Amanda, I won't tell you a story. I wanted him first—and a man feels it. And then he was a bit drunk . . ."

"So he was drunk, too! But I don't quite understand—if you don't like him at all?"

"Well, you know, Amanda, I don't understand it either, but when one has that queer feeling, and at the same time can't help being inquisitive . . ."

"But you mustn't!" Amanda prepared to end the scene with a tremendously severe lecture which, to tell the truth, would have turned out milder than at first intended. When all was said and done, she understood Frau Hartig quite well. . . . But she broke off.

Three persons were walking across the farmyard in Indian file—a man, a woman, then another man. . . .

They walked through the farmyard in the darkness without a word or a sound—and Amanda Backs and Frau Hartig gaped.

When the first man had approached the two women, he stopped and said in a peremptory voice: "Who's standing there?" At the same time there shone on them the light of a flashlight held by the woman in the middle. (The moon had not risen very high yet and the stable buildings were still intercepting her light.)

"Amanda," said Amanda Backs calmly, while the coachman's wife automatically shielded her face with her hands as if she had been caught in some criminal offense.

"Hurry up and get to bed," said the man in front, and noiselessly and stealthily the three figures passed by the women, crossed the farmyard and disappeared round the corner of the bailiff's house where, as Frau Hartig saw, the light had gone out during her dispute with Amanda.

"Who was that?" she asked, dumbfounded.

"I think it was the young Fräulein," replied Amanda thoughtfully.

"The young Fräulein in the dead of night with two men!" cried Hartig. "I'll never believe it."

"The man behind might have been the servant. The one in front I don't know. He isn't from here—I never heard that voice before."

"Extraordinary!" said Hartig.

"Extraordinary!" said Backs.

"What business is it of his if we stand here?" asked Amanda loudly. "He's nothing to do with the place and yet he orders us to bed."

"That's it," echoed Frau Hartig. "And the young Fräulein allows him to order us about."

"Where did they go to?" Amanda stared across the farmyard.

"To the Manor?" suggested Hartig.

"No. Why should they go to the back door? The young Fräulein needn't enter the Manor by the back way," snapped Amanda.

"Then there's only the bailiff's . . ." suggested Frau Hartig.

"That's what I'm thinking," Amanda frankly admitted. "But what are they after, behaving so strangely, one behind the other, and so quietly—as if they wanted nobody to see them?"

"Yes, it was strange," agreed Frau Hartig. And added: "Shall we go and have a look?"

"You'd better get back to your husband," said Amanda Backs severely. "If anyone is having a look in the staff-house, it's me."

"But I should like to know so much, Mandy. . . ."

"You're to call me Fräulein Backs. Besides, what will your husband say to your being away so long? And your children."

"Pooh!" said Frau Hartig indifferently.

"And what's more, you're to leave my Hans alone. Another time I shan't be so easy-going. If I catch you again . . ."

"You can be sure you won't, Amanda. I swear it! But you'll tell me tomorrow, won't you?"

"Good night," said Amanda Backs curtly and went toward the dark staff-house.

The coachman's wife stood for a moment there, looking enviously after her. She was thinking how lucky such young unmarried girls were and how little they knew it. Then she sighed and went toward her home, to her scuffling children and nagging husband.

II

Frau von Teschow, after the shock of that evening's devotions, felt a craving for peace and quietness. She wished to see and hear nothing more, only to go to bed as quickly as possible.

Supported on one side by Fräulein Jutta von Kuckhoff, on the other by Elias, she staggered upstairs into the big mahogany bedroom with its three windows. Fräulein von Kuckhoff undressed her trembling, tearful friend, and at last Frau von Teschow lay in her wide mahogany bed, looking no bigger than a child, with her little wizened bird's head, a white nightcap over her thin hair and a loosely knitted bed-jacket round her shoulders.

"Oh, my Lord and my God, Jutta," she wailed, "what a world! God forgive me for passing judgment—but how shameless the young people are! What will Lehnich say? And Superintendent Kolterjan?"

"Everything is good for something, Belinde," said Jutta sagely. "Don't agitate yourself any more. Are you still feeling cold?"

Yes, Frau von Teschow was still cold. Fräulein von Kuckhoff rang for Elias, who received an order to get two hot-water bottles from the kitchen.

"Oh, Elias!" The servant was just about to leave.

"Yes, madam?"

"Tell the cook to make me a cup of peppermint tea. Yes—and very strong. And with plenty of sugar. Yes. Oh, God!"

"Very good, madam."

"Oh, Elias!"

"Yes, madam?"

"Perhaps she'd better make me some mulled wine, not peppermint tea. Peppermint tea makes one belch so. But no water, only red wine. Red wine already contains water. Oh, God! And a little nutmeg. And *one* clove. And plenty of sugar. Elias, you'll see to it for me, won't you?"

"Certainly, madam."

"And, Elias, one moment! She's to put a dash of rum in it—I feel so ill. Not much, but naturally one must be able to taste it. Not too little, Elias, you understand?"

Elias, bald and getting on for seventy, understood quite well. He was going away when a faint call from the invalid reached him in the doorway. "Oh, Elias!"

"Yes, madam?"

"Please come nearer. . . . You can inquire in the kitchen—but not as if it came from me, quite casually . . ."

Elias waited. Madam must be feeling very ill; she could hardly talk. It would be better if she had her mulled wine quickly, but he couldn't give the order yet. Frau von Teschow still had something on her mind.

"Elias—do ask—but without attracting attention—whether she—you know whom I mean—has gone to bed. Yes, do ask, but without attracting attention."

For a while the invalid still felt very poorly, and Fräulein von Kuckhoff had plenty to do, what with proverbs and advice, or warming the cold hands between hers, or stroking the aching forehead. Then the hot-water bottles arrived and the mulled wine smelling strongly of rum—its fragrance alone revived Frau von Teschow. Sitting up in bed, she received, with compressed lips, the message that "she" had gone out.

"Thank you, Elias. I'm very sad. Good night. I don't suppose I shall sleep."

The old servant assumed a suitably troubled expression on hearing this farewell, wished madam good night, and sat down in the anteroom. He must wait for the Geheimrat, to take off his boots. Then his duty would be ended.

But the waiting was not too tiresome for him; he had his own interests. He pulled out a thick pocketbook, formerly brown, now almost black, and a long list with many numbers, names and words. A packet of brown bank notes came out of the pocketbook, the list was unfolded, and he started comparing, marking and writing.

That evening was a bad one for his old mistress, but a good one for him. He had that day succeeded in buying up five prewar brown red-stamped 1,000-mark notes.

Like many Germans, particularly elderly people, faced by the monstrous fantasy of inflation, Elias, too, refused to believe in a general devaluation. A man who had been saving assiduously for more than fifty years had to retain something; it was impossible that the whirlpool should swallow up everything. And it did not require much thought to convince him that "real money" from prewar times would remain "real." This was already borne out by the statement on the notes themselves that they were redeemable at the Reichsbank for gold.

And gold was "real." Money which had been issued during or after the war was not, of course, "real." It was the war which had started the fraud of "linen" shirts made of paper and "leather" shoes of cardboard!

When old Elias first noticed the signs of inflation, he began to buy 1,000-mark notes. There were always people who could not think so deeply as he did. Certainly he had heard that the Reichsbank in Berlin no longer redeemed these notes for gold; but that, of course, was only bluff, intended for fools. The Reichsbank wanted to call in its own notes cheaply—to save its scanty gold. Elias, however, being no fool, did not hand over his notes cheaply to the Reichsbank. He waited; he could afford to wait; one day he would receive gold, as was plainly stated on the notes.

Thus it started—in the beginning as a capital investment. Then Elias found that this investment had its own science; in his old age, without knowing it, he discovered the delights of collecting.

There were so many kinds of brown 1,000-mark notes! Of course, one learned at the very outset that only notes with the red stamp were valid. Those with the green stamp originated during the war or postwar times and should not be collected. But there were notes with one red stamp and some which bore two red stamps; bank-notes with no fiber strips and notes with a blue fiber strip on the left side and others with the strip on the right side. There were notes bearing eight signatures, some with nine, and some even with ten. There were notes with the series letters A, B, C, D, followed by seven and eight figures. Yet it was the same brown 1,000-mark note, pictures and text never changing—but with what a multitude of variations!

Old Elias jotted down and compared; he was now no longer collecting brown 1,000-mark notes, he was collecting variations, differences, distinctions. His big, round, smooth head grew crimson over his task. He beamed when he found a specimen which he had not seen before. He was firmly convinced that its distinctive features were secret signs made by connoisseurs for connoisseurs. They possessed a significance. He who knew how to interpret them would be rewarded with much gold thereby.

Let the old Geheimrat laugh at him! With all his cunning the old gentleman understood nothing of these secret matters. He believed what the people in the banks told him; he believed what was printed in the newspapers. Old Elias was not so credulous, and for that reason he was richer than his master; he possessed more than a hundred thousand marks in gold currency—or in currency as good as gold.

Tonight he was very happy; he had three perfectly new specimens among his recent purchases, among them a note from the year 1876. He had not known of any 1,000-mark notes of such an early date—his earliest hitherto was of 1884. He would think twice before going so far as to change these notes for gold. They were so beautiful with their engravings of human forms which, as he had heard, represented Industry, Trade and Transport.

"Industry, Trade and Transport," he murmured and stared at the notes awe-struck. The labor of a whole people! Except that Agriculture was not included, which seemed a pity.

What would he do with gold? He could not carry about with him over a hundred thousand marks in gold. With gold he would be in a state of perpetual anxiety—whereas this paper money was so beautiful.

The old servant was happy. Each note was carefully folded before it found its way back into his pocketbook. The bank-note presses in Berlin harassed the people in an ever-increasing delirium—but they had presented Elias with happiness, great happiness. With beautiful notes.

The mulled wine had had its effect. From her pillows Frau von Teschow, feeling more lively, spoke to her friend: "Would you read to me, Jutta?"

"From the Bible?" asked Fräulein von Kuckhoff, quite agreeable.

But this suggestion did not find favor tonight. The evening devotions directed to the conversion of an erring girl had miscarried; the Bible and its God were rather in disgrace.

"No, no, Jutta—we must continue with Goethe."

"Gladly, Belinde. The keys, please."

Fräulein von Kuckhoff received them. On the top shelf of the wardrobe, with the hats, was hidden a thirty-volume edition of Goethe in half-calf—Frau von Teschow's confirmation present to her granddaughter, Violet von Prackwitz. Violet's confirmation already belonged to the distant past, but it was impossible to predict when the Goethe would be handed over to her.

Fräulein von Kuckhoff took down the seventh volume: *Poems. Lyrical. I.* It looked oddly swollen. Nearby, Fräulein von Kuckhoff placed scissors and paper.

"Paste, Jutta!" Frau von Teschow reminded her.

The friend added the little pot of paste, opened the book and at the marked place started to read the poem of the goldsmith's journeyman.

After the first verse Frau von Teschow nodded approvingly. "This time we're lucky, Jutta."

"Wait and see, Belinde," said Fräulein von Kuckhoff. "Never count your chickens before they are hatched."

And she read the second verse.

"Good, good!" nodded Frau von Teschow and found the subsequent verses praiseworthy.

Till they came to the lines:

> Her little foot peeps in and out,
> And calls to mind what is above;
> I recollect the garter, too,
> I'm giving to my love. . . .

"Stop, Jutta," cried Frau von Teschow. "Again!" she lamented. "What do you think, Jutta?"

"I told you so," declared Fräulein von Kuckhoff. "What's bred in the bone will come out in the flesh."

Frau von Teschow waxed indignant. "Even present-day writers aren't worse. What do you say, Jutta?" But she did not wait for a reply. Sentence was passed. "Paste it up, Jutta, paste it up well—suppose the child should read it!" Fräulein von Kuckhoff was already pasting up the lewdness. "Not much left, Belinde," she said and held up the volume for scrutiny.

"It's scandalous." Frau von Teschow was very indignant. "And such a man regards himself as a classic! Oh, Jutta, why didn't I buy a Schiller for the child? Schiller is much nobler, far less carnal."

"Don't forget the old proverb, Belinde—'No rose without its thorn.' Schiller, too, is not good for young people. Think of 'Intrigue and Love,' Belinde. And then that female, that Eboli woman. . . ."

"True, Jutta. Men are all like that. You've no idea the trouble I've had with Horst-Heinz."

"Yes," said the Kuckhoff. "Every pig to its sty. Well, I'll read on."

Thank God, next followed the poem about Johanna Sebus, the rescuer. That was really noble; but why the poet referred to *Johanna* Sebus as "Sweet Susan" was not clear.

"He ought to have written 'Sweet Hannah,' oughn't he, Horst-Heinz?" For the Geheimrat had just come in. Smirking, he watched the two little women. "He may have considered Hannah as too common," he suggested after a close examination of the point. In socks and shirt sleeves he paced up and down the room, the book in his hand.

"But why 'Suschen'?"

"I think, Belinde, Suschen is an abbreviation of Sebuschen. And Sebuschen, you know, Belinde—well, what do you think, Jutta?" The Geheimrat was serious, but the corners of his eyes were twitching. "Sebuschen, Buschen, Busen, Bosom; that, too, sounds indecent, don't you think?"

"Paste it up, Jutta, paste it up. Suppose such thoughts occurred to the child!" cried Frau von Teschow excitedly. "Oh, there's simply nothing left. . . . Horst-Heinz, you must get rid of the Backs woman on the spot."

"On the spot I'm only going to bed. Besides . . ."

"I'm going at once," grumbled the Kuckhoff. "Let me just lock up the Goethe."

"The Backs woman is already out of the house. I saw her a moment ago in the park."

"You know quite well what I mean, Horst-Heinz."

"If I know, then there's no need to tell me, Belinde." And with a warning clearing of the throat: "Fräulein von Kuckhoff, may I point out that I'm just about to take off my trousers?"

"Horst-Heinz! Give her time; she must first say good night."

"I'm going. Good night, Belinde, and don't worry any more about the meeting. Sleep well. Are the pillows comfortable? The hot-water bottles? . . ."

"Fräulein von Kuckhoff! I'm taking off my pants, and then I shall be in my shirt. A Prussian Geheimrat in his shirt! You don't want to—"

"Horst-Heinz!"

"I'm going at once. Sleep well, Belinde. Good night. The Seidlitz powder . . ."

"Sebuschen—Sweet Bosom!" cried the Geheimrat, now only wearing his shirt. He shrank, however, from shedding this last veil. . . . Every evening the same comedy with the two old hens! "Oh, these women!" he shouted.

"I wish you good night, Herr Geheimrat," said Fräulein von Kuckhoff with dignity. "And He created man in His image—that is, a long time ago."

"Jutta," weakly protested Frau von Teschow against this disparagement of her Horst-Heinz; but the door had closed behind her friend and not a moment too soon.

"What was the matter with the evening prayers?" inquired the Geheimrat, diving into his nightshirt.

"Do not evade the issue, Horst-Heinz. Tomorrow you must dismiss the Backs."

The bed groaned under the old gentleman. "It's your poultry maid and not mine," he said. "Do you want to burn the light much longer? I want to sleep."

"You know I cannot bear agitation, and when such a person becomes insolent . . . You ought to do me a favor for once, Horst-Heinz."

"Was she insolent during prayers?"

"She's immoral," said Frau von Teschow furiously. "She's always climbing through the window to the bailiff."

"I believe she's doing it tonight as well," said the Geheimrat. "Your prayers seem to have had no effect, Belinde."

"She must go. She's incorrigible."

"And then the to-do with your poultry starts again. You know the position, Belinde. No one else has lost so few chicks or had so many eggs either. And she uses less feed than anyone."

"Because she's hand-in-glove with the bailiff."

"True, very true, Belinde!"

"So she gets much more feed than she notes down."

"We can't grumble about that; it's our son-in-law's corn. No, no, Belinde, she's efficient and has a lucky hand. I wouldn't give her notice if I were you. What business is it of ours what she does of a night?"

"Our home must remain pure, Horst-Heinz!"

"But she goes to him at the staff-house; he doesn't come here."

"Horst-Heinz!"

"Well, it's true, anyhow."

"You know quite well what I mean. She's so brazen!"

"She is," admitted the Geheimrat, yawning. "However, that's always the same. The efficient people put up with the least nonsense. That little fellow Meier, her friend—you can kick him in the behind for hours on end and he only grows more polite."

Since Frau von Teschow refused to hear any coarse expressions from her husband, she missed the word "behind." "Then tell Joachim to send the fellow away. Then I can keep the Backs."

"If I tell my grand son-in-law to fire his employee," said the old gentleman pensively, "he'll keep him till his dying day. But cheer up, Belinde, I believe Amanda's friend will be fired tomorrow. . . . And if he isn't, then I'll praise him up, and he'll have to pack his trunks at once."

"Do so, then, Horst-Heinz!"

III

Man is not free from the prejudice of investing other creatures with his own failings; for instance, there is said to be no truth in the story that the ostrich when frightened hides its head in the sand. Yet some people certainly shut their eyes to an approaching danger and then maintain it does not exist.

After the departure of Frau Hartig, Bailiff Meier had turned on the light to look for something to drink. His fuddled brain, the rebuff by the old Geheimrat on whose favor he had been relying, the approaching quarrel with Amanda—all these awakened in him the desire to drink. He wanted to think no more of the whole filthy business, as he put it.

Having secured the windows against a surprise attack by Amanda, he stood for a moment looking at his untidy room, with its disheveled bed and scattered garments. He felt his brain to be just as ravaged and, what was more, a sharp pain stabbed his forehead. He knew there was nothing to drink in his room, no cognac, no schnapps, no beer—but when someone felt as he did, then there was always something to drink, if only he could remember where it was.

But the only idea which came to him was that of returning to the inn and fetching a bottle of schnapps. He shook his head peevishly. He had long ago concluded that he didn't want to be seen there again because of the bill. Besides, he had nothing on—that sly old dog the Geheimrat had noticed that. The others would also notice if he went to the inn like that. He looked down at himself and began to chuckle gloomily. A fine sight! What rubbish! Wouldn't touch it with a barge pole. "Shame doesn't lie in the shirt," he said aloud. He had heard this saying once and remembered it because it seemed to justify any shamelessness. But now he had to look for his shirt, and he started to kick the clothes about on the floor in the hope that it would emerge. But not so. Instead he ran a splinter into his foot.

"A swinish mess," he cursed, and that reminded him of the pigs, and the pigs reminded him of the veterinary medicine-chest in the office, and the medicine-chest suggested Hoffmann's ether drops. But there wouldn't be enough to drink with any effect, anyway, and there might be none left in the chest at all.

Hoffmann's drops! Since when had Hoffmann's drops been given to pigs? On a lump of sugar, perhaps? He had to laugh at this idiotic idea; it was too silly.

He wheeled round, suspicion and fear in his face. Was somebody in the room laughing at him? It had sounded exactly like it. Was he alone? Had the coachman's wife gone? Had Amanda arrived or would she be coming? He looked round the room with his bulging eyes—the gap between seeing and perceiving was so vast that he had to look at an object for a long time before his brain registered it as wardrobe or curtain—bed—nobody in it! Nor under it, either!

Laboriously he arrived at the conclusion that no one was in the room. But how about the office? Was somebody watching him there? The door stood open; the darkness beyond gave him the impression that someone might be lying in ambush.

Was the other door to the office locked? The curtains drawn? Oh, God! Oh, God! Such a lot to be done, and he hadn't found his shirt yet. Would he never get to bed?

With hasty uneven strides, naked Black Meier went to the office and shook the outer door. It was locked, as he had thought; the curtains were drawn, too. Switching on the light, he looked with hostility at them. Of course they were drawn—it was utter rubbish—they were trying to rattle him. The curtains were drawn and would remain so. Let anyone dare to touch his curtains! They were his curtains—*his!* He could do what he liked with them—if he tore them down it concerned him alone.

In the deepest agitation he made for the unfortunate curtains—and the medicine-chest of deal, painted brown, entered his field of vision.

"Hallo! There you are at last." Black Meier grinned contentedly. The key was in the lock, the little door had learned to obey and opened at the first attempt, and there in two crowded compartments were the whole doings. In front stood a big brownish bottle, with something written on the label. But who could read a chemist's scrawl? No, it was printed—it amounted to the same thing.

Meier took the bottle, withdrew the stopper and smelled the contents.

He took another sniff. He stood there inhaling the ether vapor, while his body started to tremble. Supernatural clarity spread over his brain, he was conscious of an understanding and insight such as he had never known before. He sniffed and sniffed—it was bliss.

His face became haggard, his nose pointed, wrinkles appeared in his skin. His body shuddered. Yet he whispered: "I understand everything—everything! The world . . . bliss . . . clarity . . . blue."

The ether bottle dropped out of his trembling hand, fell to the floor and broke. Still intoxicated, he stared at it. Then he went quickly to the switch, turned off the light, entered his room again, switched off the light there, groped his way to the bed and threw himself down.

He lay without stirring, with closed eyes, surrendering completely to the bright visions within his brain. The shapes became dimmer, gray mist drifted over them. Darkness approached from the boundaries of consciousness, grew blacker and blacker. Black Meier slept.

IV

"You ought to know who's got the key," the Lieutenant stormed.

Three persons stood before the dark staff-house. Räder had tried the handle, but the door was locked.

"Herr Meier has the key, of course," he said.

"There must be another," insisted the Lieutenant. "Fräulein, don't you, by any chance, know who has the second key?" Although the situation between them left no room for doubt, he continued to address Violet as Fräulein.

"The second key will be with father," said Vi.

"And where does he keep it?"

"In Berlin." In reply to an angry gesture, she added: "Papa is in Berlin, Fritz!"

"He won't have dragged the key of this hovel all the way to Berlin! I *must* go to the meeting."

"If we go afterwards . . ."

"And let him run off with the letter in the meantime? Is he in there?"

"I don't know," said the offended Hubert. "I've nothing to do with the bailiff, Herr Lieutenant."

The Lieutenant felt he could die of impatience and fury. These damned love affairs were always hampering men. He had absolutely no use for women at this juncture. And how helpless Vi stood there; not a scrap different from the hopelessly stupid servant! He had to do everything himself. What was she going to suggest now?

"There's a window open upstairs, Fritz," she said.

He looked up. Yes, a window was open in the gable.

"Splendid, Fräulein. Now we shall pay the young man a visit. Here, you, I'll lift you up on the chestnut tree. From that branch you can easily climb into the room."

But Räder stepped back. "If Fräulein will excuse me, I'd rather go home."

The Lieutenant cursed. "Don't be so silly, man. Fräulein is present."

"I've given you my willing assistance, Fräulein," said the servant with invincible determination and taking no notice of the Lieutenant, "and I hope you won't forget it. But I must really go home to bed."

"Oh, Hubert," begged Vi, "do me a favor. When you've opened the front door you can go home at once. It'll only take a moment."

"It is, so to speak, a punishable offense, Fräulein," the servant protested respectfully. "And just now two women were standing by the dungheap. I would much rather go to bed."

"Oh, let the fool go, Violet!" cried the Lieutenant furiously. "He's messing his trousers like a whole company down with dysentery. Clear off, my lad, and don't spy about in the bushes."

"Thank you very much, Fräulein," said Räder, imperturbably polite. "I wish you good night." And with a steady stride (without acknowledging the Lieutenant) he vanished round the corner.

"What a boor," the Lieutenant grumbled. "Really, Violet, I'd like to be for a Sunday what he fancies himself to be the whole week long. Now help me on to the tree. If the trunk weren't so beastly slippery with the damp I could manage it alone. But what that idiot can do you can do also."

While Vi was helping her Lieutenant on to the tree, Räder, softly whistling to himself, his hands in his jacket pockets, went across the farmyard. He had eyes in the back of his head and thus saw in the shadow of the stable the person who wanted to pass him.

"Good evening, Fräulein Backs," he saluted very politely. "Still about so late?"

"You, too, are still about, Herr Räder!" the girl retorted, but stopped.

"Yes. But I'm going home to bed. When do you get up in the morning?"

Amanda Backs paid no attention to this question. "Where did Fräulein go to with the gentleman, Herr Räder?" she asked inquisitively.

"Everything in its turn," said the unyouthful Räder, pedantically. "I asked you, Fräulein Backs, when you get up in the morning."

If Amanda had not been a true woman she would have replied, "At five," and could then have required the answer to her own question. However, she said: "It can't interest you, Herr Räder, when I get up," and thereby prolonged the argument.

But in the end, after considerable dispute, Herr Räder learned that Amanda's time for getting up was governed by the sun, because chickens wake at sunrise, and he heard that in July the sun rose about four o'clock and that Amanda had to be outside by five at the latest.

This he thought was rather early; he himself got up at six and sometimes later.

"Yes, you," said Amanda rather contemptuously, for after all, a man who tidied rooms was, for that very reason, contemptible. And now he was expressing the opinion that she ought to be in bed. "Where was Fräulein going so late with the gentleman?" she asked sharply. "She's only fifteen and she ought to have been in bed long ago."

"I don't know when Fräulein goes to bed," said Räder. "There's probably no time fixed."

Amanda did not despair. "And, anyway, who was the gentleman, Herr Räder? I don't know him at all."

Räder, however, was of the opinion that he had done his duty. Fräulein must be, by now, inside the house with her Lieutenant. He couldn't do any more to protect them from spies.

"No, you probably don't know the gentleman," he confirmed. "We have so many gentlemen visitors. Good night!" Before Amanda could put a fresh question he had gone on.

Angrily she stared after him, trying to make up her mind to go home. In spite of young Räder's being so clever, she was beginning to feel that he had been pulling the wool over her eyes, and as Herr Räder had a good opinion of himself and rarely talked with her, he wouldn't have fooled her without some end in view. There must be something behind it.

Thoughtfully Amanda walked on. She left the farmyard, turned the corner of the dark staff-house and stopped before her young man's windows.

A short time ago those windows were open and had then been closed. A short time ago, when she looked for a moment across the farmyard, a light was burning in his room. Now there was no light. Amanda told herself that it was quite in order; her Hans was sleeping. It was better to let a drunken man sleep; and sleep, in view of her argument with Frau Hartig, would be better for herself, too. There was really no sense in stirring up any more strife—she was not like that. Frau Hartig wouldn't take up again with her Hans—of that Amanda was convinced.

So she could let him sleep, and herself, too—she needed rest, a good rest. But she was itching with curiosity; she felt so worked up that bed didn't attract her, although she was longing for it. At other times she knew what she wanted, but now, even though she wished to let him sleep, she nevertheless felt like tapping at the window, just to hear his furious sleepy voice, and know that all was well. . . . She wanted to and yet she didn't. . . .

"Oh, well, I'll tap," she decided. And in that moment saw in Hans's room a little beam of light, as if from a flashlight. Involuntarily she stepped aside, although she had seen by the light that the curtains were drawn. A similar beam had been directed at her a little time ago, when she was standing with Frau Hartig at the dungheap. Precisely similar!

She stood racking her brains, trying to puzzle out the connection between the torch, Fräulein and the unknown gentleman, and what they could be doing so late and so secretly in Hans's room. She saw the beam of light move, go out, light up again, dart about. . . .

But she was not the kind of person to stand for long inactive and wondering. She went to the front door and cautiously pressed the handle. When she leaned against the door, it yielded.

Amanda tiptoed into the dark corridor and closed the door behind her.

V

The Lieutenant, through the gable room and down the loft stairs, reached the hall of the staff-house, where the beam of his flashlight showed him that the key, luckily, was in the door—he turned it, and Violet slipped in after him.

The office, it is true, was locked, but here Violet knew her way about: the double key lay in the little tin letterbox on the office door, and that was easily opened—a convenient solution for Meier. Like that, he didn't have to get up in the mornings, if the foreman fetched the key from the office. The two entered. There was an overpowering stench in the office. Shining his lamp on the broken bottle, the Lieutenant said: "Chloroform or alcohol. I hope the fellow hasn't done himself in. Don't tread on the broken glass, Violet!"

No, he had not done himself in. Their ears told them that. Black Meier was snoring and wheezing terribly.

Violet laid her hand on her friend's arm and felt safe in the disgustingly close room. More than that—she found this whole nocturnal excursion, this commotion over a letter of hers, "ever so interesting," and thought Fritz "terribly dashing"! She was fifteen; her appetite for life was great, and Neulohe very boring. The Lieutenant, of whose existence her parents were unaware (she herself knew him only by his Christian name), had been met on her walks in the forest. She had liked him at first sight. This hasty, often completely absent-minded, yet generally cool and insolent man, from whose reserve broke now and again an ever surprising and consuming fire—this Lieutenant seemed to her the epitome of all manliness and silent heroism. . . .

He was quite different from all the men she had yet known. Even if he were an officer, he in no way resembled the officers of the Reichswehr who had asked her to dance at the balls in Ostade and Frankfurt. The latter had always treated her with extreme courtesy; she was always the "young lady" with whom they chatted airily and politely of hunting, horses, and perhaps of the harvest.

In Lieutenant Fritz she had as yet discovered no politeness. He had dawdled through the woods with her, chatting away as if she were some ordinary girl; he had taken her arm and held it, and had let it go again, as if this had been no favor. He had offered her his dented cigarette case with an indifferent "Like one?" as if the strictly forbidden smoking was a matter of course, and then, when lighting her cigarette, he had taken her head in his hands and kissed her—just as if it were all part of it. "Don't make a fuss," he had said, laughing. "I find girls who make a fuss simply detestable!"

She did not want him to think her "simply detestable."

One can warn a young person of dangers and perhaps even protect her from them—but how about the dangers which, like everyday things, do not look at all like dangers? Violet never really had the feeling with Lieutenant Fritz that she was doing anything forbidden, that she was ever really in danger. And when *it* had happened, and something like an instinctive resistance, a panic fear, did indeed threaten to seize her, he had said with such genuine indignation: "Look here, Violet, don't kick up a fuss! I can't for the life of me stand this silly gooselike pretense! Do you think it is different with any other girl? That's what you're in the world for! So come on!"

"Is *that* what I'm here for?" she had wanted to ask. But then she realized she was being merely stupid. She would have been ashamed not to do what he wanted. Just because he thought so little of her, because his visits were so short and irregular, just because all his promises were so unreliable ("I was going to be here Friday? Don't be silly, Violet; I've really got other things to think about besides you!"), just because he was never polite to her, just because of all that, she had succumbed to him almost without resistance.

He was so different. Mystery and adventure hovered around him. All his faults became merits to her because others did not have them. His coldness, his sudden desire which disappeared just as rapidly, his off-hand manner that was only skin-deep, his complete lack of respect for anything in the world—all this was reality, frantic love, manliness!

What he did was right. This casual fellow who traveled about with a vague commission to mobilize the country-folk for all emergencies; this cold adventurer who was not concerned with the object of the struggle, but only with the struggle itself; this mercenary who would have fought for any party so long as there was unrest—for he loved unrest and hated quiet, which immediately left him unoccupied, out of his element, not knowing what to do with himself—this dashing jack-of-all-trades was the *hero!* And he might have set a world alight— he would nonetheless remain the hero to her!

The way he now, with the flashlight in his hand and her lightly trembling fingers on his arm, directed the beam on to the disarranged bed with the naked man on it, the indifferent way he said to her: "Better look away, Violet!" and covered up the fellow; the way he growled: "Swine!" and then told her to sit by the bed, adding: "See whether he wakes up! I'll take a quick look through his things!"—this camaraderie which was a shabby thing, hardly concealing ruth- lessness, lack of respect, and roughness—all this she found marvelous.

She sat on her chair. It was almost completely dark, the moon scarcely penetrating through the grayish-yellow curtains. The man in bed wheezed, snored and groaned, invisible to her, and then began tossing about, as if in his sleep he sensed his enemies. Behind her the Lieutenant was going through the things, cursing loudly; it is difficult to find anything in an unfamiliar room with a flashlight in one's hand. He rustled about, stumbled over chairs; his torch danced suddenly across the window and went out. Then the rustling started again. . . .

Yes, she had to be early in bed of an evening. Now and again she was allowed to go to a dance till eleven o'clock, till twelve at the latest, or to go shooting, with 'special permission and accompanied by the forester and the servants. In the afternoons, on alternate days, her mother spoke French and English with her. "So that you shall keep up with things, Violet. Later on you will have to go into Society—not like your Mamma, who is only a farmer's wife." Oh, how thin, how false, how dull the world at home seemed! Here she sat in the bailiff's malodorous room, and life smelled of blood and bread and dirt. It was by no means, as parents, governesses and vicars pretended, a gentle, friendly, polite business; it was dark . . . a wonderful darkness. And out of the darkness came a mouth with glistening white teeth. The eye-teeth were pointed, the lips were thin, dry, saucy. O mouth, man's mouth for kissing, ravenous teeth for biting!

Parents, grandparents, Altlohe and Neulohe, Ostade with its garrison, the autumn fair in Frankfurt-on-the-Oder, the Café Kranzler in Berlin—narrow world, servile world, world forever standing still. One sits at a little marble table, the waiter bows, Papa and Mamma argue whether their dear daughter can stand another cream puff, the impudent fellow at the next table stares, and the dear daughter looks away—of that ordered world only the ruins are left.

For another life has broken into it, and the past no longer counts. This life is swift and brilliant. Infinite fire, mysterious adventure, a wonderful darkness, in which one may be naked without shame! Poor Mamma who has never known this! Poor Papa—so old with your white temples! For me ever new paths, ever different adventures! Stupid ugly Black Meier, good for nothing but to get himself a little quarter of an hour's thrill and then be severely punished for it.

"Is that the scrawl?" asked the Lieutenant, shining his torch on a damp smeared sheet of paper. "The fellow has drowned it in spirits!"

"Oh, please give it to me!" she cried, suddenly ashamed of her emotional scribblings.

"By no means, my child!" he replied. "You won't send it traveling again and get me to run after it!" He had already put the letter in his pocket. "And I tell you this, Violet, you are not to write to me again. Never. Not a word!"

"But I wanted you so much!" she cried and threw her arms round his neck.

"Yes, of course, I understand—understand everything. Tell me, you don't keep a diary, do you?"

"I? What do you mean? A diary? No, of course not."

"Well, I think you're lying. I shall have to inspect your room sometime."

"Oh, do! Fritz, do come to my room sometime; it would be wonderful of you if you had been in my room!"

"Good! Good! We can arrange it. But now I must hurry off to the meeting. They'll be cursing."

"Today—will you come today? After the meeting? Oh, please, Fritz, do come."

"Today? Absolutely impossible. I've got to come back here again after the meeting—chat with the fellow, hear whether he has told any others about the letter." He became thoughtful.

"Yes, Fritz, go for him properly. You must make him afraid; otherwise he will tell everything. He's too disgusting and mean."

"And you yourself recommended him to me as a messenger—" began the Lieutenant, but controlled himself and stopped. There was no use in reminding women of an error they had committed, in starting a quarrel with them. It always immediately passed beyond all bounds. A different, a much more frightening, thought had occurred to him: the man there might not merely be able to babble about the letter—he knew other things. Perhaps Kniebusch had not kept things to himself. . . .

"No, I have got to talk to him later," he said once again.

She seemed to have guessed his thoughts. "And what will you do with him then, Fritz? If he has betrayed you?"

The Lieutenant stood quite still. Even this silly little goose had thought of it, had sensed the danger which was always threatening the Cause, which everyone feared: betrayal. As yet hardly anything had been said; outside a very small circle hardly anyone knew exactly what it was all about, what was intended. Hints were thrown out, loose phrases. Dissatisfaction, hatred, despair, sufficiently abounded in the country. The printing presses in Berlin hurled a new wave of bitterness abroad with every new spate of paper money. Thus a few words were enough, the muffled clank of arms . . . almost nothing. But the traitor did not need to be well informed, he did not need to know much; if he told the *Landrat* that someone was running around inciting people, that he had even heard today that the weapons were to be counted in the village . . .

The Lieutenant let the ray of his torch fall on to the sleeper's face. It was not a good face, not one that could be trusted. He had had the right instinct when he didn't want to have this fellow in it. . . . But that was Violet. She had suggested that he would be such a convenient, unnoticeable go-between, always with access to the Rittmeister's house and always to be found in the fields, in the woods. . . . And on the very first occasion the affair went wrong! Always these women had to put their oars in. They had nothing on their minds but their so-called love.

The Lieutenant turned round abruptly. "You are going to bed at once, Violet," he said angrily.

She was quite frightened by his tone. "But Fritz, I wanted to wait for you here. And then I've also got to speak with the forester about the buck."

"Here? Don't be ridiculous. How can you think of it? Supposing the fellow wakes up, or someone comes in?"

"But, Fritz, what do you want to do then? If he wakes up now and notices his letter is gone, my letter, I mean, and he gets angry with us, he'll run off and tell everything to Grandpa or Mamma."

"Now please stop it, Violet! Please! I'll see to all that. I shall deal with him after the meeting—and properly, I can tell you!"

"But supposing he runs away before?"

"He won't run away. He's drunk."

"But supposing he does run away before?"

"For God's sake, shut up now, Violet!" The Lieutenant almost shouted. Then, since he himself had had a fright, he added in a whisper: "Come along now, be sensible. You can't possibly wait here. Keep watch for me outside the house—I shall be back here in an hour."

They went out together, felt their way through the dark room and along the dark passage. Now they were in the open again. It was night, full moon and peaceful; the air was very warm.

"Blast the moon! Everyone can see us! Go into the bushes there. In an hour, then."

"Fritz!" she called after him. "Fritz!"

"What's the matter? Can't you be quiet?"

"Fritz! Aren't you going to give me a kiss? Not even one?"

"Damn and curse!" he muttered. Aloud: "Afterwards, my child, afterwards we'll make up for everything."

The gravel crunched and he was gone. Violet von Prackwitz stood in the bushes where Amanda Backs had been standing. Like the latter she kept her eyes on the window of the staff-house. She was a little disappointed but at the same time very proud of standing guard like this.

VI

Forester Kniebusch wandered along slowly, gun on back, through the dark forest. The full moon was already fairly high, but here below, among the tree trunks, its rays made visibility only more uncertain. The forester knew the forest just as a townsman knows his house; he had walked here at all hours of the day and night. He knew every bend of the path, every juniper bush which—eerily like a ghost—appeared amidst the trunks of lofty pine trees. He knew that the rustling he had heard came from a hedgehog hunting for mice, but even though everything was familiar, he did not like going through the wood *now*.

The forest had remained unchanged for ages, but the times had changed and the men with them. To be sure, there had also been timber thieves in the past. Yet they had always been the same questionable characters whose business was shady and whose reputation was even shadier. One had caught them, they were what they were, and because they were like that, they landed in jail. It hadn't been necessary to get worried about them; in the end it was they who always did the worrying and paid the penalty of their misdeeds.

But had there been such a thing in the past as a whole village, man by man and house by house, going off to steal wood? You ran about and watched and worried yourself to death, and if you eventually caught one of them, then you were either seized with fear of revenge or with a feeling of shame that such a man should have joined thieves.

In the days of Forester Kniebusch's youth, during his first years in Neulohe forest, there had been a notorious poacher in the district: Müller-Thomas, who afterwards hanged himself in his cell in Meienburg prison. With this fellow there had been a long life-and-death struggle. Cunning had fought against cunning and strength against strength, but it had been a struggle with more or less the same weapons. . . . Today, however, they went "hunting" in swarms, with army pistols and rifles! They started the game wherever they found it; they spared no pregnant female animal or one suckling its young—they shot at pheasants, even at partridges, with bullets! If they had poached for poaching's sake like Müller-Thomas, or for a joint to still their hunger, that wouldn't have been so bad. But, murderers that they were, they killed simply from the desire to kill. Murderers and destroyers!

The old man had now left the dense part of the forest and was walking along a small glade between plantations of pine trees. The little trees were fifteen years old; they should have been thinned out two or three years ago, but one could not get the men. So the plantations had become impenetrable thickets, a mass of thorny branches, uprooted trees fallen in all directions. Even in the daytime one could scarcely see three yards into them. Now in the moonlight they stood there like a black wall. . . . Whoever had an enemy coming along this path need only conceal himself in the thicket and he could not possibly miss his man. In vain the forester told himself that no one could be expecting to see him coming along this glade now; this was a quite unforeseen errand he was on, and had he kept his mouth shut it would never have come about. So no one could possibly be lying in wait for him in the thicket.

And yet he walked stealthily. He knew where the mossy patches ran, on which one could walk softly, and whenever a twig cracked under his foot he stood still and peered around with beating heart. He had long since put his pipe in his pocket, for one can smell tobacco a long way off in the forest; and he held his three-barreled gun ready to shoot, for even an uncertain shot was better than none at all. He was a very old man. He would much rather have gone into retirement long ago, but that had not been possible. And now he had to walk among the plantations at night because a silly girl couldn't take care of her heart and her letters. It was a thoroughly foolish business. He wouldn't be able to spot the buck, and if he did he would miss it. And should he be able to bring it down that wouldn't be anything—neither the Rittmeister nor his wife would have been surprised if Fräulein Violet said that her stalking expedition had been in vain. "You see, you would have done much better to stay in bed, Vi," was the most the Rittmeister would have said, and teased her a little.

But no, they didn't think of that. They actually sent him off after the buck; he had to chase around while the three of them settled their business with that cursed Meier. Whom did they have to thank for their information? Why, himself! Who had got this conceited, thoughtless Lieutenant away from Haase? Why, he himself! And then this young prig could say uppishly: "We don't need you here, Kniebusch. You go off and shoot the buck. But don't go playing the fool here among the bushes; otherwise I'll have something to say to you!"

Fräulein Violet had stood there, she had heard every word of this arrogant speech. She might have been a little grateful to an old man, but no, she merely said: "Yes, do that, Kniebusch, and try and see that I have something to show Papa tomorrow."

So there was nothing to say except: "Certainly, Fräulein," and about face into the woods. Therefore he would never learn what did actually happen to Bailiff Meier tonight. Meier would certainly not open his mouth, Räder the manservant would also keep mum, tomorrow the Lieutenant would have disappeared as if blown away, and Fräulein Violet wasn't one for telling things, however much she liked having things told to her.

Then what had resulted from that calculated tale-bearing which was to have benefited him so much? A nocturnal stalk through the forest and the undying hatred of little Meier! And he could be a really poisonous toad when he was angry.

Forester Kniebusch stood still, sighing. He mopped his brow—it was hot, very hot. But it was not the sultry damp heat in the forest which made him so warm, it was annoyance with himself. For the thousandth, for the ten-thousandth time in his life, he swore firmly to see and hear nothing of whatever might happen to come to his knowledge. He would just go his own way in the few years that he had still to live; he would never again be wise and clever and cunning and calculating. Never again!

As if putting a period after this immovable resolution a shot resounded through the forest, like an "Amen" in church.

The forester started, listening without moving a foot. It was a rifle shot: the crack was sharp like the crack of a whip. And it was the rifle shot of a poacher. For who else could be abroad in the forest at this time?

These two things were certain; but the forester could not decide quite so certainly the direction from which the shot came. The lofty forest wall round the glade re-echoed the sound hither and thither, playing ball with it. Yet the forester could almost have sworn that the report came from the direction in which he was going, from Haase's field where Fräulein Violet's buck was browsing. Someone else had fired at it.

The forester had not moved from the spot where he had stopped to mop his brow and heard the shot. He was in no hurry. He was filled with an iron determination. He was a man, he did just what he wanted and nothing else. Slowly he hung his gun over his shoulder, slowly he drew his short pipe from his pocket, filled it and, after a little hesitation, struck a match. Puffing strongly, he carefully pressed the tobacco down once again, snapping-to the nickel lid of his pipe and set off. Purposefully and steeled with determination, he walked steadily away from the place where the shot had rung out. Don't scald your lips in another man's pottage. Amen.

Yet the fact is that some people, whether they like it or not, are forever pursued by new events, while others wander through life and hear nothing, getting their bread only when it is stale. The forester, after all, had made not the slightest effort in the afternoon to find out about Fräulein Violet's letter. On the contrary, he had turned from Meier's babbling with abhorrence, not wanting to listen to his loathsome bragging—and yet he had learned everything about it.

The forester who smoked so contentedly as he put distance between himself and the poacher, with a grin at his own cunning, was very calmly resolved to traverse slowly the least dangerous parts of the forest until he could quite credibly affirm that every effort and every patient endeavor had been in vain— there was no buck to shoot. This old coward of a Kniebusch, however, was condemned to shoot his buck, and without a rifle!

For the new event from which he so zealously fled came rapidly cycling between the lofty pines down a defile which no moonlight could brighten. Up this defile walked the forester, smoking.

The impact was violent. But while for Kniebusch there was enough soft sand to spare for his old bones, a large rock lay waiting for the cyclist, who struck it first with his shoulder, at which he let loose a powerful oath, although he didn't know then that his collarbone was fractured. Next his cheek passed over the rough stone so that the skin was scraped off and the raw flesh burned like fire. But this he hardly noticed, for his temple had made the acquaintance of a sharp-edged projection, and a temple is just as sensitive as sleep—both are easily wounded by disturbance. The cyclist, already lapsing into unconsciousness, groaned and was heard no more.

Worthy Forester Kniebusch sat in the sand rubbing the thigh which had borne the brunt of the collision. He would very much have liked to see the other man get on his bicycle and set off again. He, Kniebusch, would have raised no objection and asked no questions, so steely was his resolve not to poke his nose into things anymore.

In the darkness he peered at the other man. Since, however, it was too dark to see anything at all (only someone who knew the forest inside out would dare to cycle down this pitch-black defile) he gradually began to imagine that he saw something, a dark figure which, like himself, was sitting in the sand and rubbing its body.

Forester Kniebusch therefore sat still and peered, now quite certain that the other was also sitting still and peering, that the other was waiting only for him to go away. At first he was undecided, but, on considering the matter, he admitted that the stranger was right. The forester, being to some extent in an official position, ought to go first and thereby signify that he had no wish to pursue the case.

Slowly, quietly and cautiously he stood up, keeping his eye all the time on the black patch. He took a short step, and another, but at the third he fell over for the second time, and naturally right on top of the man from whom he was backing away. The black patch had been deceptive; the forester sat directly beside, even partially on top of, his latest discovery.

His greatest desire now was to jump up immediately and run away, but he had fallen on the bicycle, and this gave rise to some confusion of clothes, pedals, chain, gun strap and saddlebag, quite apart from the pain which his sudden collapse onto thin steel bars and jagged pedals had caused.

Completely shaken in body and spirit, the forester sat there, and if at first he still thought of getting away he yet could not help gradually noticing that the body on which his arm rested was somewhat more motionless than it would have been in the case of a conscious man.

Quite a little time passed, however, before Kniebusch could bring himself to switch on his electric torch. Once this had happened, though, and the beam discovered a pale unconscious face, skinned on one side, things moved more quickly. From the realization that this was the notorious rogue, Bäumer of Altlohe, delivered into his hand as helpless as a lamb, to the resolve to take the wretched poacher and rowdy to the lock-up, was only a step.

With rope and straps the forester made Bäumer into a parcel such as no girl in a store could have tied better or more securely, and all the while he reflected that by this "arrest" he would gain much credit with the old Geheimrat and the young Rittmeister, seeing that Bäumer was an arch rogue, a ring leader, a master thief, a poacher, an absolute thorn in the flesh of every landowner—all of which was proved by the staggard in his rucksack and the gun on his bicycle. Much more important than this credit, however, was the fact that in this risk-less manner he was disposing for a long time of his most dangerous enemy, one who had often threatened to give him a beating should the forester ever dare to search his little wood cart. It must truly have been an act of divine providence, that rightly upsets and softens every steely resolve, which had given, helpless into his hands, an enemy who was a match for three men. And thus the forester tied the knots with a feeling of satisfaction such as if he had just experienced the greatest stroke of luck in his life.

Fräulein Jutta, of course, could have told him that one should not praise the bacon until the pig has been slaughtered.

VII

Wolfgang Pagel looked up and down the dark street near Wittenbergplatz, deserted except for a few hurrying pedestrians. It was shortly after midnight. There, where the square broadened out, a man was leaning against the wall of a house; he wore a cap, smoked a cigarette and, despite the summer heat, had his hands in his pockets—everything as it should be.

"That's him," said Wolfgang nodding. He felt suddenly cold—he was so near to his goal. Excitement and expectation gripped him.

"Who's that?" asked von Studmann without much interest. It was a boring business to be dragged through half Berlin at night, dog-tired, just to be able to look at a fellow in a cap.

"The spotter!" said Wolfgang, ignoring the weariness of his two companions.

"I admire your knowledge of Berlin," grumbled Rittmeister von Prack-witz. "It's undoubtedly most interesting that that fellow is called a spotter. Do you mind at last telling us what you really have on?"

"Soon," said Wolfgang, continuing to peer ahead.

The spotter whistled and disappeared into the brightness of Wittenberg-platz. A key rattled in a street door very close to the three men, but no one appeared.

"They have locked the street door; it's still the old house, No. 17," explained Pagel. "Now the police are coming. Let's take a stroll round the square in the meantime."

But the Rittmeister turned rebellious. Stamping his foot he exclaimed heatedly: "I refuse to be a party to this nonsense any longer, Pagel, if you don't explain to us at once what you are planning to do. If it's anything shady, then no thanks! I openly confess that I'm longing for my bed, and Studmann probably feels the same."

"What's a spotter, Pagel?" Studmann asked quietly.

"A spotter is someone who keeps a look-out to see whether the police are coming and whether the air is clear in general. And the man who locked the door quickly just now was the tout, who persuades people to come up."

"So it's something illegal!" cried the Rittmeister still more heatedly. "Thanks very much, my dear Herr Pagel. Count me out! I don't like having anything to do with the police, another point in which I'm old-fashioned."

He broke off, for the two policemen had come up. They were strolling along side by side, one sturdy and big, one little and fat, the storm straps of their shakos under their chins. The chains on which their rubber truncheons hung clinked softly. The noise of their hobnailed boots was re-echoed by the walls of the houses.

"Good evening," murmured Pagel politely.

Only the tall one who passed nearest to the three turned his head a little, but he did not answer. Slowly the two pillars of order passed down the street. Only the sound of their hobnail boots disturbed the silence of the three. Then they turned into Augsburgerstrasse, and Pagel made a gesture of relief.

"Yes," he said and felt his heart beat more calmly again, since he had feared that there might be some hindrance at the last moment. "Now they are gone we can soon go up."

"Let's go home, Studmann!" said the Rittmeister irritably.

"What's up there?" asked Studmann, nodding his head in the direction of the dark house.

"Night club," said Pagel. He looked toward Wittenbergplatz. From its brightness reappeared the spotter, coming slowly down the street, hands in pockets, cigarette in mouth.

"Disgusting!" exclaimed the Rittmeister. "Undressed women, watery champagne, nude dancers! I said it the moment I saw you! Come along, Studmann!"

"Well, Pagel?" asked Studmann, paying no attention to the Rittmeister. "Is that so?"

"Not at all! Roulette. Just a little roulette."

The spotter had stopped some five paces away from them under a lamp-post. He was looking thoughtfully at the light, whistling "Mucki, call me Schnucki!" Pagel knew that the fellow was listening, knew that he, the worst patron of all gambling clubs, had been recognized, and trembled lest he should be refused admittance. Annoyed at the others' hesitation he shook the packet of money in his hand.

"Roulette!" cried the Rittmeister in astonishment. He came a step closer. "But is that allowed?"

"Roulette!" Von Studmann, too, was surprised. "And with that sort of swindle you put questions to Fate, Pagel?"

"The game's played fair," murmured Pagel in protest, his eye on the spotter.

"There has never yet been anyone who admitted that he lets himself be cheated," Studmann objected.

"I once used to play roulette, as a very young lieutenant," the Rittmeister said dreamily. "Perhaps we can just have a look at it, Studmann. Of course, I won't risk a penny."

"I don't know," said Studmann hesitantly. "It must be crooked. The whole sinister atmosphere. You see, Prackwitz," he explained with some embarrassment, "I've naturally also gambled from time to time. And I don't like . . . Hang it, once you've tasted blood and are in the mood I'm in today . . ."

"Yes, of course," said the Rittmeister, making no move to go, however.

"Well, are we going up?" Pagel asked the two undecided men, who both looked at each other inquiringly, eager and yet not eager, afraid of the swindle, but more afraid of themselves.

"You can take a look at it, gentlemen," said the spotter, pushing his cap carelessly higher and strolling nearer. "Excuse me for butting in." He stood there, his pale face lifted to them, his little dark mousy eyes darting critically from one to another. "Won't cost you anything to look. No charge for playing, gentlemen, no cloak-room fee, no alcohol, no women. . . . Just pure gambling."

"Well, I'm going up now," said Pagel firmly. "I've got to play today."

Unable to wait any longer, he went hastily to the street door, knocked, was let in.

"Wait a minute, Pagel!" the Rittmeister called after him. "We're also coming."

"You ought to go with your friend, really," the spotter said persuasively. "He's got his head screwed on all right; he knows how to play. Hardly an evening goes by without him clearing off with his winnings. We all know him."

"Who? Pagel?" cried the Rittmeister, astonished.

"We don't know what his real name is, of course. With us the gentlemen don't introduce themselves. We just call him the Pari Panther, because he always gambles only on pari. . . . And you should see how! He's a real gambler, he is! All of us knows him. Let him go on ahead; he won't lose himself in the dark. I'll show you the way up."

"So he plays a lot, does he?" von Studmann cautiously inquired, for Pagel's case was beginning to interest him more and more.

"A lot?" said the spotter with unmistakable respect. "The bloke never misses an evening. And he always skims off the cream! We get infuriated with him sometimes. But he's cool, I tell you; I could never be as cool as that bloke. It's a miracle the way he can stop when he's got enough in his pocket. I really oughtn't to let him go up at all, they dislike him so much. Still, it doesn't matter today, since you gents are with him."

Von Studmann began to laugh heartily. "What are you laughing like that for?" the Rittmeister asked, at a loss.

"Oh, sorry, Prackwitz," Studmann said, still laughing. "I always like hearing pretty compliments of that sort. Don't you understand? They let the cool cunning Pagel go up because he is bringing us two idiots with him. Come along. I feel like having a fling now. Let's see whether we two can't also be cool and cunning." And still laughing, he took the Rittmeister by the arm.

The spotter also laughed. "I seem to have put my foot into it proper. Still, you gents ain't offended. And seeing as you're not, you might perhaps give us a tip now. I don't know, but from the looks of both of you, you won't be coming down them stairs again with a fortune in your pockets." On the landing he adroitly shone a light on the wallet which Prackwitz was searching for a tip.

"He really believes we won't have a penny when we come out, Studmann," the Rittmeister said irritably. "What a bird of ill-omen!"

"Wishing people a bit of bad luck has always helped in gambling," said the spotter. And in a soft, persuasive tone: "I say, Baron, just another little note. I see you don't know our rates yet, and me always standing with one leg, so to speak, in Alexanderplatz police station."

"And me?" The Rittmeister, very angry at being reminded once more of the unlawfulness of this enterprise, was on the verge of exploding.

"You?" said the spotter sympathetically. "Nothing will happen to you. The most that happens to players is to lose their cash. Those who entice them into gambling have to go to jail. You see, I'm enticing you, Baron."

A dark figure came down the stairs.

"Psst, Emil! These are the two gents with the Pari Panther. Take them upstairs; I'm going to keep a look-out. I've got a queer feeling in my stomach as if something might happen!"

The three men ascended. In a hollow whisper the spotter called after them: "Hi, Emil! Listen!"

"What do you want? You know you're not to make a row!"

"I've already touched 'em for a tip! Don't milk 'em a second time!"

"Oh, get off with you—better keep your eyes skinned!"

"Trust me, Emil. I'll keep a good look-out, even if the ship sinks!"

He disappeared into the dark regions.

VIII

Wolfgang Pagel was already sitting in the gaming room. In some mysterious way the news of the large sum of money which the Pari Panther had exchanged for counters had made its way from the vestibule to the vulture-like croupier and his two assistants, and had obtained for him a place near the head of the table. Yet Pagel had changed only a quarter of his money with the gloomy sergeant major. Carelessly and hastily he had stuffed away the rest of the notes and had entered with his hand burrowing about in the cool bone counters in his tunic pocket. They rattled softly, with a pleasant dry sound. And this sound at once called up the image of the gaming table: the somewhat indifferently spread green cloth with the embroidered yellow numbers, under electric light that always seemed very peaceful despite all the noise going on around; and the spinning and rattling of the ball, the soft hum of the wheel. Wolfgang sucked in the air with a deep, almost relieved, breath.

The gaming room was already full. Behind those sitting on chairs there stood two crowded rows of players, although it was still early. Wolfgang had only a vague impression of all those tense white faces as he was conducted by one of the croupier's assistants—a favor never before enjoyed—to the chair which had been vacated for him. Passing a woman, he suddenly became aware of the almost overpowering strength of her perfume, which seemed to him strangely familiar, and to his irritation discovered that, although he would now have liked to concentrate on the game, he was completely distracted, his brain entirely bent on finding out the name of the perfume. Through his head darted a host of words like Houbigant, Mille Fleurs, Patchouli, Ambra, Mysticum. Not till he sat down did it occur to him that he probably didn't know the name of the perfume at all; that it only seemed familiar to him because it was the perfume of his enemy, the Valuta Vamp. He thought he now remembered this woman smiling at him.

Although he had a seat, Pagel refused to let himself glance at his surroundings or the gaming board. Slowly and deliberately he laid down a packet of Lucky Strikes bought at Lutter and Wegner's, a box of matches, and a silver cigarette holder—a kind of miniature fork on a ring which slipped over the little finger and was supposed to prevent the fingers from getting yellow. Then he counted out thirty chips and placed them in front of him in piles of five—he still had a whole heap more of them in his pocket. Not looking up yet, he played with them, enjoying their dry rattle as if it were a beautiful music. Then—the resolve had arisen in him just as abruptly as the first flash of lightning darts out of a stormy sky—he suddenly placed a whole handful of counters, as many as he could grasp, on number twenty-two.

The croupier gave him a quick, dark glance, the ball rattled, rattled endlessly—and the sharp voice rang out: "Twenty-one—odd—red."

Perhaps I'm making a mistake, he thought, strangely relieved. Perhaps Petra is only twenty-one. Suddenly he was in a good mood and no longer distracted. Without regret he saw the croupier drag away his stake. Vaguely he felt as if he had, with these counters, sacrificed in accordance with Petra's age, bought himself free from her and could now, without taking her into account, play as he liked. He gave a faint smile at the croupier, who was attentively regarding him. The man returned his smile almost imperceptibly, his lips hardly moving beneath his bristly beard.

Pagel looked around him. Directly opposite, on the other side of the table, sat an old gentleman with a face so sharply featured that, in profile, his nose looked like the blade of a knife, its end a threatening point. This stagnant face was terrifyingly pale; in one eye perched a monocle, over the other the paralyzed lid drooped. The man had whole heaps of counters lying in front of him, and little packets of bank notes as well. When the croupier called, his slender well-kept hands hastily seized counters and money and with bent fingertips distributed the stakes over a large variety of numbers. Pagel's glance followed. Then he looked away quickly and contemptuously; the pallid gentleman with the restrained face had completely lost his head. He was playing against himself, staking on zero and on numbers, on odd and even, simultaneously.

"Eleven—odd—red. First dozen," called the croupier.

Red again! Pagel was convinced that black would now turn up. With rapid decision he placed all his thirty counters on black and waited.

It seemed an eternity. Someone withdrew his stake at the last moment and then put it back again. A profound, deathly aversion seized Wolf. Everything was going so slowly; this game which had filled his life for the past year suddenly seemed idiotic. There they sat around like children and waited breathlessly for a ball to fall into a hole. Of course it fell into a hole! Into one or into another, it made no difference. There it ran and clattered—oh, if only it would stop rolling, if only it would fall in! The monocle opposite glittered maliciously, the green cloth had something magnetic about it. If only he were rid of his money! What stupidity to have hungered for this game!

Pagel was rid of his money. The thirty counters disappeared under the croupier's rake. "Seventeen" had been called out. Seventeen—also a very nice number. "Seventeen and Four" was far better than this silly game. For "Seventeen and Four" one needed a little common sense. Here one only had to sit and await sentence. The silliest thing in the world—something for slaves.

With a jerk Pagel stood up, pushed his way out through those standing behind him and lit a cigarette. First Lieutenant von Studmann, who was leaning against a wall, asked with a glance at his face: "Well? Finished?"

"Yes," said Pagel sullenly.

"How did it go?"

"Moderately." He puffed his cigarette greedily, then asked: "Shall we go?"

"Certainly! I don't want to see or hear anything of this business. I'll go and get von Prackwitz away at once. He wanted to watch for a little, just for amusement."

"Just for amusement! All right, I'll wait here."

Studmann pushed through the players while Pagel took his place against the wall. He felt limp and tired. So this was what the evening, long hoped for, was really like; the evening when, with a great gambling capital, he would be able to stake as he liked! Things never came together. Today, when he could have played as long as he liked, he had no desire to. First there's no beaker, and then there's no wine, he thought. He was finished at last with gambling; he felt he would never again have any desire for it. Now he could peaceably travel into the country early tomorrow morning with the Rittmeister, presumably as a kind of slave driver. He would miss nothing here in Berlin. No risk of that! One did this, one could do that: everything was equally meaningless. Interesting to observe how one's life melted away, rendering itself meaningless, just as the money that was always pouring forth from the presses also became meaningless. In one short day both mother and Petra were lost, and now even gambling, too. It had become completely meaningless. . . . Really, one might just as well jump from a bridge under the next train—it was just as sensible or senseless as anything else.

Yawning, he lit himself another cigarette. The Valuta Vamp stepped up to him. She seemed to have been waiting for that. "Will you give me one?"

Without a word Pagel offered her the packet.

"English? No, I can't smoke those; they're too strong for me. Haven't you any others?"

Pagel shook his head with a faint smile.

"I can't understand how you like smoking those! They've got opium in them!"

"Opium is no worse than cocaine," said Pagel provokingly, looking at her nose. She couldn't have sniffed much today, her nose wasn't white. Of course, he had to remember the powder; naturally she had powdered herself. . . . With calm, objective curiosity he looked at her.

"Cocaine! You don't think I take that, do you?"

Something of the old hostility made her voice shrill, although she was now doing her utmost to please him. And she really looked pleasant. She was tall and slim; her breasts in the low-cut dress seemed small and firm. Only, the woman was wicked; one shouldn't forget that. Wicked. Greedy, avaricious, quarrelsome, rotten with cocaine, cold. Wicked beyond measure. Peter hadn't been wicked, or perhaps she had been—yes, Petra had been wicked. But one hadn't noticed it much; she had been able to hide it for a long time, until he had found her out. No, she too was finished.

"So you don't take snow? I thought you did!" he said off-handedly to the Valuta Vamp and looked around for Studmann. He would have been glad to get away. This well-built cow of a woman bored him to death.

"Only now and again," she admitted, "when I'm tired out. And that's no different from taking pyramidon, is it? You can ruin yourself with pyramidon, too. I once had a girl-friend who took twenty a day. And she—"

"Yes, yes, my dear!" said Pagel. "I'm not interested. Don't you want to go and play a bit?"

But she was not to be got rid of so easily. Nor was she in the least bit hurt; the only time she was offended was when no one intended it.

"You've already finished playing?" she asked.

"Yes. No more cash left. Absolutely broke."

"You little leg-puller!" she laughed foolishly.

He looked at her. She did not believe him. She had heard something about the contents of his pockets, otherwise she would never have wasted so much time and pleasantness on a shabby fellow in a soldier's tunic, since she deigned to consider only gentlemen in evening dress.

"Please do me a favor!" she cried suddenly. "Stake once for me!"

"What good will that be?" he asked crossly. This Studmann was taking an eternity, and he couldn't get rid of the woman. "I think you know the game well enough without me."

"You are bound to bring me luck."

"Possibly. But I'm not playing anymore."

"Oh, please—be nice to me for once!"

"You heard me. I'm not playing anymore."

"Really not?"

"No!"

She laughed.

"Why do you laugh so stupidly?" said Pagel crossly. "I'm not playing any more!"

"You—and not playing! I don't think!" She gave her voice a soft persuasive tone. "Come, darling, stake once for me; then I'll be very nice to you, too."

"Thanks very much for your favors," said Pagel gruffly. "God, can't I get rid of her at all? Go away, I tell you. I'm not playing any more, and as for you, I can't stand you at any price—you disgust me!" he cried.

She regarded him attentively. "You look attractive now, sonny. I never noticed before how handsome you really are. You always sat at the table like a fool." She tried to flatter him. "Come, darling, stake once for me! You'll bring me luck!"

Pagel threw his cigarette away and bent very close to her. "If you speak another word to me, you damned whore, I'll sock your teeth in!" His whole body trembled with senseless rage. Her eyes were right close to his. They were brown—suffused now with a yielding moistness.

"Hit me, then!" she whispered. "But stake for me once, darling."

He turned round with a jerk and went quickly to the table. Seizing von Studmann by the elbow and breathing rapidly, he asked: "Are we going or aren't we?"

"I can't get the Rittmeister away!" von Studmann whispered back as excitedly. "Just look at him!"

IX

It was with extreme reluctance that Rittmeister von Prackwitz had accompanied young Pagel on his mysterious journey through Berlin at night. Already in Lutter and Wegner's he had borne his company and provoking chatter only with great repugnance, hardly forgiving him the insult of the proffered money. His friend's interest in this completely dissipated fellow, whose ample funds seemed to be questionable at the very least, he found completely out of place. If to von Studmann the little incident of the retrieved shell splinter in the skirmish before Tetelmünde appeared a little ridiculous, yet also—and especially in the case of such a young fellow—rather heroic, to von Prackwitz the ridiculous outweighed all the heroic; moreover, a character which was capable of such extravagance could seem only suspicious to him.

The worthy Rittmeister Joachim von Prackwitz found only the extravagances of others suspicious; his own he regarded with perfect benevolence. From the moment he heard that the excursion had nothing to do with some filthy naked-woman business, his pet aversion—but it was merely a little game, or to put it better, a *jeu*—from that moment the two policemen with their hobnailed boots lost all their terror, the dark house acquired something inviting, the cheeky spotter became enveloped in humor, and Second Lieutenant Pagel changed from a tempter and doubtful character into a decent fellow and an experienced man of the world.

And when the Rittmeister had found himself standing in the little homely anteroom with its overcrowded clothes hooks, and the mustached man behind the small folding table had pleasantly asked: "Counters, gentlemen?" and the Rittmeister, after a scrutinizing glance, had said: "Seen service, eh? Where?" and the mustached fellow, clicking his heels together, had replied: "Nineteenth Saxon Transport Section—Leipzig," then the Rittmeister had felt himself in the best of moods and completely at home.

No thought of the prohibition of such games had disturbed this good mood. With excited interest he had asked to have explained to him the use and value of the unfamiliar counters—in his time one had played only with cash, or with visiting cards bearing a number scribbled on them. Had he thought of young Pagel at all, it would have been with extreme benevolence. But no thought of this young person crossed his mind. He found the game and the players much too interesting for that. With regret he had to admit that the people here were far from being as distinguished as those in the Officers' Casino in peace time. Here at the gaming table, for example, sat a fat red-faced man who kept on murmuring aloud to himself, and distributed his stakes with plump, jewel bedecked fingers. When he considered his bull neck with its many folds, there could be no doubt that this was a kind of brother or cousin of that cattle dealer from Frankfurt whom he never cared to admit into his house. What was more, the fellow had also swindled him a few times—the one in Frankfurt, of course. The Rittmeister stared at the fat man with hostility. So it was here that the profits unjustly squeezed from the landowners went—and the man couldn't even lose with decency! His fear of each loss was clearly noticeable, and yet he renewed it with every fresh stake.

The Rittmeister was also disturbed by the large number of women who thronged round the gaming table; women, in his opinion, had no business gambling, which was purely a man's affair. Only a man summoned up sufficient cold-bloodedness and intelligence to gamble with success. The women were, indeed, very elegant, but a little too extravagantly dressed, or rather undressed, for his taste. This mode of exhibiting a pair of young breasts in a gaping silk case, so to speak, for the inspection of every onlooker, made him think of the streetwalkers he hated so much. Such women certainly were not allowed admittance here, but even to be reminded of them was painful.

Yet there were also pleasant things to be seen; a fair-skinned old gentleman, for example, with a curiously sharp-pointed nose and monocle. Where this gentleman played, where this gentleman sat, where this gentleman was a guest, there a Rittmeister von Prackwitz could also be present. It was significant that Prackwitz completely failed to see young Pagel, who sat next to him; his eye, usually so sharp, noticed shabbily dressed people only with difficulty.

As far as the roulette was concerned—and the Rittmeister sat down with polite thanks on a chair that was apparently free, but was of course only vacated for him on a sign from the management—as far as the roulette was concerned, it appeared difficult to get used to. There were a surprising number of possibilities—and moreover it was played with such unseemly haste. He had hardly begun to perceive how the stakes were distributed when the wheel already hummed, the ball rolled, the croupier called, here came a rain of counters, there a drought broke out, the game finished, started again, people betting, disk turning, ball rolling, wheel humming, croupier calling—bewildering!

The Rittmeister's own experience of roulette lay far back in his lieutenant years. Even so, it had been little enough; the game hadn't been played more than three or four times. That was due to the fact that it had been very strictly forbidden, more strictly, indeed, than all other games of chance, being regarded as particularly dangerous. As a matter of fact the young officers had then known only one gambling game, called "God's Blessing on Cohen," which was considered as relatively harmless. All the same it had become so dangerous for the Rittmeister, then unmarried, that after one turbulent night he had had to travel at breakneck speed to his father, a most hot-tempered gentleman holding the rank of general. There, within the space of half an hour's fury, he was disinherited and cast off, though in the end both of them—after ample shedding of tears—had signed a whole pile of promissory notes with a swarthy gentleman, for which they received so much money that the gambling debt was eventually cleared. Since that time the Rittmeister had not gambled.

And so he now sat confused before the green cloth, looked at the numbers, gently rattled the counters in his pocket, and did not know how to begin, however much he wished to.

But when von Studmann asked: "Well, Prackwitz, do you really want to play?" he answered crossly: "Don't you? What have we bought counters for?" And he staked on red. Naturally red turned up. Before he had properly collected his thoughts a little heap of counters fell with a dry rattle on to his own. The unpleasant fellow who looked like a ruffled vulture called out something, and the wheel went spinning again. The Rittmeister was still undecided as to what he should stake on next when the ball settled it for him.

Red had turned up again. Now he possessed a whole mountain of counters.

He withdrew them and looked around like a man waking up. The best player at the gaming table was still the gentleman with the monocle. The Rittmeister looked at the long, thin fingers that were bent slightly upwards and which distributed little heaps of counters with incredible rapidity over the various numbers and on the intersections of their fields; and without overmuch reflection he imitated the gentleman. He also placed bets on numbers, on intersections of numbers, but in doing so he avoided out of a feeling of chivalry the areas occupied by the master (so as not to upset him).

Again the croupier called out something, again counters were added to those he had staked, while other little piles disappeared under the rake and fell with a gentle clatter into a bag at the end of the table.

From now on the Rittmeister was as if bewitched. The rolling of the ball, the croupier's voice, the green cloth with its numbers, inscriptions, squares and rectangles on which multicolored counters were continuously being rearranged—all this held him completely spellbound. He forgot himself, forgot the time and space in which he sat. He no longer thought of Studmann or the questionable Pagel. Neulohe no longer existed. He had to be nimble; the eye, quicker even than the hand, had to spy out free fields onto which counters could be thrown; winnings had to be hurriedly swept up, and as hurriedly he must decide what should be left in.

Once there came a disagreeable pause because the Rittmeister, to his surprise, found himself completely without counters. Crossly he fumbled around in his jacket pocket, irritated at having to miss a game. The fact that he had no more counters did not, however, arouse in him any thought of the loss he had suffered. It was the interruption which upset him. Luckily it turned out that he had been observed; one of the croupier's assistants was already holding some fresh counters ready for him. And with an absent-mindedness which shut out even the thought that he was now handing over money—indeed, almost all the money he had with him—he took the notes out of his pocket and exchanged them for bone counters.

Shortly after this undesirable interruption of the game, and just when the Rittmeister was beautifully absorbed in placing his stakes, up came von Studmann suddenly and whispered over the player's shoulder that Pagel, thank Heaven, had now had enough and was wanting to go. What in the world did he care about young Pagel? the Rittmeister asked very testily. He was having a good time here and hadn't the least intention of going home so soon.

Quite taken aback, von Studmann asked the Rittmeister whether he really wanted to play, then.

Von Prackwitz believed—was almost certain—that that little heap of counters on the intersection of numbers thirteen, fourteen, sixteen and seventeen, which had just won, had been staked by himself—a woman's hand ornamented with a pearl ring had reached out and taken the little pile away. He encountered the glance of the croupier, who was calmly observing him. Very crossly he requested von Studmann to go away and leave him in peace.

Studmann made no reply and the Rittmeister went on playing, but it was impossible to concentrate on the game now; he felt, without seeing it, that Studmann was standing behind him and was watching his bets. Turning round abruptly he said in a sharp voice: "Lieutenant Studmann, you're not my nurse!"

This remark, which brought up again an old wartime disparity of rank, was effective. Studmann gave a very slight apologetic bow and withdrew.

The Rittmeister, with a sigh of relief, looked back at the green cloth and saw that in the meantime the very last of his counters had vanished. Throwing an angry glance at the croupier, he thought he noticed a smile hidden somewhere in the bristly mustache. He opened the inner pocket of his wallet, which was secured by a double fastener, and took from it seventy dollars, all that was left to him of foreign currency. With tremendous rapidity the croupier's assistant heaped up piles and piles of counters in front of him. Hastily the Rittmeister swept them into his pocket without stopping to count them. For a moment, when he noticed that many faces were regarding him critically, he had the vague feeling of something wrong.

Such a lot of counters, however, gave him a feeling of security; pleasure filled him. That idiot of a Studmann, always worried! Almost he smiled as he settled down in his chair and began to stake again.

Yet this good mood did not continue long. With increasing irritation he saw stake after stake vanish under the croupier's rake; he no longer heard the dry rattle of winning counters on the numbers he had backed. With increasing frequency he had to delve into a pocket which was no longer so full. It was not as yet the thought of his losses which irritated him; it was the incomprehensibly rapid waning of the game. . . . Already he saw the moment approaching when he would have to stand up and surrender this pleasure which he had but scarcely tasted. The more stakes, the more his prospects of winning, he thought, and with increasing haste he distributed counters over the whole table.

"That's not the way to play!" said a disapproving voice near him.

"What?" burst forth the Rittmeister, and looked indignantly at young Pagel, who had returned to the neighboring chair. But here young Pagel was neither uncertain nor embarrassed. "No, that's not the way to play!" he said again. "You're playing against yourself."

"What am I doing?" asked the Rittmeister, trying to be angry and wanting to snub the fellow just as thoroughly as he had snubbed Studmann. But to his surprise his anger, which usually was ever ready, failed him and he was seized with embarrassment, as if he had been behaving like a foolish child.

"If you stake on red and black simultaneously then you can't win," said Pagel reprovingly. "Either red wins or black—never both!"

"Where have I . . . ?" the Rittmeister asked in confusion and looked at the table, just as the croupier's rake intervened and the counters rattled.

"Go on, take them," whispered Pagel sternly. "You've had luck. That over there is yours! And that! Madam, if you don't mind, that is our stake!"

A woman's voice said something very heatedly, but Pagel paid no attention. He continued giving orders, and the Rittmeister followed his instructions like a child.

"That's right. And this time we won't bet at all. We shall first see how the game runs. How many counters have you left? That won't be enough for a big coup. Wait, I'll buy some more."

"You wanted to go, Pagel!" Studmann's unbearable nursery-governess voice made itself heard.

"One moment, Herr von Studmann," said Pagel, smiling pleasantly. "I just want to show the Rittmeister quickly how to play in a correct way. Please, fifty counters of five hundred thousand and twenty of a million."

Studmann made a gesture of despair. . . .

"Only one moment, really," said Pagel. "You can take it from me the game doesn't amuse me at all. I'm no gambler. It's just for the Rittmeister's sake."

But von Studmann was listening no longer. He had turned round angrily and was gone.

"Just watch, Rittmeister," said Pagel. "Now red will turn up."

They waited anxiously.

There came—red.

"If we had only staked then!" mourned the Rittmeister.

"Just be patient!" said Pagel comfortingly. "First we must see how the land lies. One can't yet say anything definite—anyway, it's very probable that black will turn up."

But it was red.

"You see!" said Pagel triumphantly. "What a good thing we didn't. We'll soon start, though, and you'll see, in a quarter of an hour . . ."

The croupier smiled imperceptibly. In a corner von Studmann was cursing the moment that he had spoken to young Pagel in Lutter and Wegner's.

Chapter Eight

He Goes Astray in the Night

I

In the bushes in front of the staff-house Violet von Prackwitz stood on guard; inside the office another girl, Amanda Backs, came out of her hiding place. She did not understand by a long way everything that these two, the Lieutenant and Fräulein Violet, were doing together. But much could be guessed. She had already heard of the Lieutenant who traveled the countryside gathering the people for some revolt; and at that time there was a saying current throughout Germany, darkly threatening: "Traitors will be punished by the secret tribunal, the Vehme!"

It is not pleasant to have to think of one's lover as a traitor; and though Amanda Backs might be as sturdy a piece of vulgarity as one could imagine, she would never be a traitress. She loved and she hated without restraint, with all her powerful and unbreakable nature; but she could never betray. Therefore she continued to stand by her Hans, despite everything she knew about him. He too was just a man, and one cannot make much show, God knows, of any man—a girl has to take them just as they are.

She stole quickly into the room, knelt down by the bed and shook the sleeper vigorously. But he was not so easily to be shaken from his drunkenness. Amanda had to adopt strong measures, and when the wet face-cloth also failed to work she simply decided to tug at his hair with one hand while cautiously placing the other over his mouth so that he couldn't make a noise.

And this succeeded—the furious pain woke up little Meier, for she pulled and tugged his hair with all her by no means insignificant strength. Like all men, and especially like Black Meier, he instinctively defended himself, biting the hand over his mouth.

She suppressed a cry and whispered in his ear: "Wake up! Wake up, Hans. It's me—Amanda!"

"I can feel that," he grunted angrily. "If you only knew how fed up I am with you women! You can never leave a chap in peace." Feeling unwell, his head aching abominally, he would have continued his grumbling but she was afraid of the girl spying outside, and again laid her hand firmly over his mouth. Immediately he bit it again.

And now her patience was gone. She tore her hand away from his teeth and struck out blindly in the darkness, not caring where. Her senses, however, guided her well; she found her mark beautifully, thick and fast the blows fell on him, left, right—there, that must have been his nose! And now the mouth. . . .

And all the time she moaned softly, breathless, carried away by this hitting in the darkness at something which groaned. "Will you be sensible? Will you shut up? Otherwise they'll kill you!" (She herself was well on the way to achieving this.)

Breathless, almost completely sober, frightened, unable to defend himself, Meier now begged: "But, Mandy! My little Mandy! I'll do everything you want. But stop it now. Oh, be a bit careful. . . ."

Her breast heaving, she stopped. "Will you listen to me, you fathead?" she gasped with angry tenderness. "The Lieutenant was here!"

"Where—here?" he asked stupidly.

"Here in your room! He was looking for something—he took a letter out of your jacket."

"A letter?" He still didn't understand. But then his memory gradually if incompletely returned. "Oh, that!" he said scornfully. "He can keep that rubbish."

"But, Hans, do be sensible! Think!" she begged. "You must have been up to something—he was so mad with you! He's coming again. Tonight."

"Let him," he bragged, although an unpleasant feeling crept over him. "I've got the monkey where I want him, him and his fine Fräulein von Prackwitz."

"But, Hans, she was here as well. She looked for the letter with him."

"Who? Fräulein Vi—the boss's daughter? In my room? With me lying drunk and naked in bed? Oh, dear, oh, dear."

"Yes, and now she's keeping watch outside your window so that you shan't run away!"

"Me, run away!" he sneered boastfully. He involuntarily lowered his voice, however. "That's what they'd like, for me to run away. That would please them both! But no fear, I'm staying; I'm going to the Rittmeister tomorrow morning, and I'll show her up, with her fine Lieutenant."

"Hans, stop this nonsense! He's coming again, tonight. He won't let you go to the Rittmeister tomorrow morning."

"What can he do? He can't tie me up!"

"No, he can't tie you up. . . ."

"Supposing I tell the Rittmeister about the letter."

"Oh, shut up about the silly letter! You haven't got it anymore! He's got it!"

"But Kniebusch can prove—"

"Nonsense, Hans. All nonsense. What sort of proof will the forester be, if it comes to telling on Fräulein Violet?"

Little Meier was silent for a moment, really beginning to think things over. Rather dejectedly he said: "But he can't want to do anything to me. He's up to the neck in it himself!"

"But, Hans, that's just why! Because he's up to the neck in it, he wants to settle with you. He's afraid you'll talk."

"What should I talk about? I'll keep my mouth closed about the silly letter."

"But it isn't only the letter, Hans," she cried in desperation. "It's the other thing, the *Putsch!*"

"What *Putsch?*" he asked bankly.

"Oh, Hans, don't pretend! You needn't pretend to me. The *Putsch* that's planned—he's afraid you'll betray it!"

"But I don't know anything of his silly *Putsch*, Mandy. Word of honor! I haven't the faintest idea what the chaps are planning to do."

She reflected for a moment. Almost she believed him. But her feeling again told her that all he was saying didn't matter, that danger threatened him, and that therefore he must get away.

"Hans," she said very seriously, "it makes no difference whether you really know anything or not. He thinks you do, and that you want to betray him. And he's mad with you because of the letter. He wants to do something to you, I tell you!"

"What can he do to me?" he said feebly.

"Hans, don't pretend like that! You know all right. And it was recently in the papers, with a picture, too, showing them all wearing white hoods so they shouldn't be recognized, and holding a court. Under it was 'Secret Tribunal.' Traitors are punished by the Vehme, Hans, that's what they say!"

"But I'm not a traitor," he replied. Yet he said it only to say something, said it without any real conviction.

Nor did she accept it. "Hans," she begged, "why won't you go away? He's gone to the village now, to a meeting, and I'll get her away from the window. You can easily get away now—why won't you? It isn't that you think so much of me that you want to stay, seeing that today you were even playing around with Hartig." (She had not managed to keep completely quiet about it, but already she was sorry.) "And look, the Rittmeister's coming tomorrow, and you've only messed about while he was away, and you also got drunk in the pub during working hours—why don't you go away of your own accord, seeing that he'll throw you out, anyhow?"

"I haven't a penny," he said. "Where shall I go?"

"Well, I was thinking that you might go to one of the villages around here and put up at a little inn—perhaps in Grünow—there's a nice inn there, where I've danced. And on Sunday when I'm free I'll come over and see you. I've got a little money; I'll bring it along. And then you can gradually look for a new job; there are always some in the paper. But not too near to—"

"Sunday in Grünow! Nothing doing!" he grumbled. "And I could whistle for the money!"

"But, Hans, don't be so silly! I don't need to offer it to you if I'm not coming! Well, then, are you going?"

"You seem to be in a devil of a hurry to get rid of me all of a sudden. Who have you got your eyes on now?"

"You've got a lot of reason to pretend to be jealous! Yes, to pretend, for you're not in the least bit jealous!"

After a while he asked: "How much money have you got?"

"Oh, it can't be much, because of the inflation. But I can always give you some more. I shall now see to it that the mistress pays me in goods—in Birnbaum they're already supposed to be getting their wages in rye."

"You and wages in rye. . . . The old woman would never dream of it. You're always giving yourself nonsensical ideas." He laughed scornfully. It was very necessary for him to feel superior. "Do you know what, Mandy? Go straight away and fetch your money now. After all, I can't stay in the inn without money. And you can send Vi away at the same time. I've got to pack and I can't do it in the dark. Oh, God!" he groaned suddenly. "Fancy dragging two heavy suitcases as far as Grünow! Only you could think of such a ridiculous thing!"

"Hans," she comforted him, "it's not so bad, so long as you get away safely. Just keep thinking of that. And I'll carry them for a bit, there's no need for me to go to bed now. You've no idea how fresh I'll be if I wash myself from head to foot in cold water in the morning."

"Yes, yes," he said peevishly. "So long as you're fresh, that's the chief thing. Well, are you going or not?"

"Yes, of course, at once. But I may take a little time, I've got to get the girl away first. And you will hurry a little, won't you, Hans? I don't know when the Lieutenant's coming back."

"Oh, him!" said Black Meier contemptuously. "He shouldn't brag so much. How long do you think a meeting like that will last? At least two or three hours! Peasants don't let themselves be persuaded so quickly!"

"Well, hurry up, Hans," she warned him again. "I'll be back very quickly. A kiss, Hans."

"Run along," he said crossly. "All you think of is your cuddling and with me it's a matter of life and death! But that's just how you women are. Your heads always full of your so-called love. Not for me, thank you!"

"Oh, you blockhead," she said and pulled his hair, but this time tenderly. "I'm just glad that you are getting away from here. At last I'll be able to do some proper work again. It's mad, but if you've got love in your blood and have to keep on stopping and staring . . . After all, what are you? You're nothing—do you think I don't know? But even knowing it doesn't change things. Life's just a monkey show, and you are certainly the biggest monkey of them all."

And with that she planted a kiss on him, whether he liked it or not, and went out of the room, almost gay, almost contented.

II

Bailiff Meier didn't wait long to make sure whether Amanda had really got Fräulein Violet away from her post. He cast a fleeting glance out of the window and, seeing no one, switched the light on. Like all unimaginative persons, he could form no idea of the danger threatening him. Everything had hitherto turned out quite well for him; one could go a long way by being thick-skinned, and things would be all right now, too.

As a matter of fact the prospects were not at all bad: it would be nice to play the *rentier* for a while—and of a sudden he even had his plans for the future! The Lieutenant had put ideas into his head. He still had a few things to settle before he departed, but he really ought to make haste. That was not so easy, however. His head was still hazy, and he found that putting on his town clothes, with shirt, collar and tie, presented some difficulty. His hands were trembling. "Must be the ether," he decided. "I've never yet had it from drinking."

With a sigh he set about packing. What a job, finding his few odds and ends in an untidy room and squeezing them, dirty and creased as they were, into two suitcases! He had got them in once (he had bought nothing in Neulohe), so in they must go again. By dint of much struggling he managed it at last, locked the cases and fastened the straps—his next girl would have nothing to laugh about, washing and ironing his things!

How much money would Mandy bring him? Efficient girl, Mandy, talked a bit too big, but otherwise quite nice! Well, she wouldn't bring a lot of money; a lot of money would require a cart—but it would be useful as a supplement.

Cursing savagely he discovered that he was standing around in his socks—and his shoes were in the suitcase! Blast it. He was so used to putting on his high farm boots right at the end, that he hadn't thought of his shoes. Naturally with his town clothes he wore his pointed shoes, the brownish patent ones. But which suitcase were they in? His farm boots looked out at him from the first case he half opened; after all, the patent shoes were rather narrow. But the thought of the figure he would cut for the girls in Grünow, in town clothes and farm boots, decided him. It must be the shoes.

Naturally they were in the second case! He got them on with some difficulty. "They'll stretch in walking," he consoled himself.

Then he strode into the office. He sorted his papers out of drawers and portfolios; he stamped his unemployment insurance card for six months ahead. There were stamps enough in this pigsty, and if the things became worth nothing afterwards it didn't matter. And he carefully wrote himself a police notification to the effect that Herr Hans Meier was going on a journey. The stamp of the farm superintendent was pressed below it—there, that was all right.

Yet a moment's reflection convinced him of the truth of the sentiment that two is always better than one, and so he wrote out a second notification. In this Meier became Schmidt . . . von Schmidt, Hans von Schmidt, occupation—farm manager, likewise on a journey. "There, you dolts, now try and find me!"

He grinned. Satisfaction at his great cunning banished the throb and ache in his head—it is a wonderful thing to be smarter than others and do them down! And now he began to type a testimonial for himself on a sheet of official Neulohe paper. Naturally, he was the pearl of all employees, knew everything, could do everything, did everything—and, moreover, was honest, reliable and industrious. It was rapture to give oneself all these things in writing. From the lines of the testimonial arose a new Meier with a fine, promising future, one fitted for the post of farm manager, the Meier he would like to be—in short the Meier of all Meiers!

This testimony was actually too good—it was not really comprehensible why one should ever let such an employee go; one ought to keep him to the end of his life. But clever, witty Meier was also able to deal with this. Owing to sale of lease, he wrote down. You see, the new boss would then not be able to ask the old one for further references. He had given up his lease, did not know where he had moved to. Now the stamp of the farm administration—the signature: Joachim von Prackwitz, captain (ret.) and tenant farmer—again the superintendent's stamp—stamps are always good. The thing looked fine—the smartest fellow would be taken in by it.

Into his wallet with the papers. We'll also put the supply of postage stamps in, we can always use stamps—why let them lie around here? The safe doesn't hold overmuch, but it'll do for a while. And if Mandy turns up trumps, then I'll be able to live well for a few weeks. God, my breast pockets do bulge; papers on the right, cash on the left—a bosom, my child, a bosom is essential! A bosom is the latest fashion—no, as a matter of fact it isn't. But as far as I'm concerned, a bosom is always nice. Now we'll just close the safe, it'll look better in the morning. . . .

"Leave it open, my lad! Always leave it open, young man—it looks better. Then tomorrow morning the Rittmeister will guess things at once!" cried the Lieutenant from the door.

For a moment Meier's face was distorted. But only for a moment. "I'll do just what I like," he said pertly, and shut the safe. "Anyway, you've got no business to be here at night. . . . You've just pinched a letter of mine from my room."

"My lad," said the Lieutenant threateningly and came two paces nearer. But he was a little nonplussed by this incredible cheekiness. "My lad, do you see this?"

"Of course I can see the thing," declared Meier, and scarcely a tremor in his voice betrayed how unpleasant he found the sight of the pistol. "And I could have also got myself one of those cannons; there are enough of them lying in the drawer there. But I decided I could get on without it—I knew you were coming," he added somewhat boastfully.

"Oh, you knew, did you?" said the Lieutenant slowly, observing the ugly little fellow intently.

"So you're a conspirator! You want to plan a *Putsch*, eh?" said Meier mockingly, beginning to feel sure of himself. "And yet you didn't notice that there was a girl in the next room the whole time, here in the office. While you were in my room. And she heard everything that you and Vi said. There, that surprises you!" But the Lieutenant did not seem at all surprised.

"So there was a girl hidden here, was there?" he said calmly. "And where's the girl now? Still in the next room?"

"No," said Meier boldly. "Not this time. We're quite alone, so you needn't be alarmed. Your lady fair's taking a little walk with my lady fair. But you can naturally imagine," he added warningly, when he saw the Lieutenant make an involuntary movement, "what my girl will say tomorrow if anything happens to me. Or do you want to shoot us both?" he said, tickled by his own impudence, and laughing.

The Lieutenant threw himself into a chair, crossed his legs and thoughtfully lit a cigarette. "You're by no means stupid, my lad," he said. "The only question is whether you're not too clever. May I inquire what your plans are?"

"Indeed you may," said Meier readily. Now that he had convinced the Lieutenant that it was wiser not to do anything to him, his only desire was to come to an understanding with the man. "I'm clearing out of here!" he said. "I've already knocked off—well, you saw it just now at the safe." But the Lieutenant did not move an eye. "I'm well within my rights to take the money. My wages are owing to me. Besides, can you imagine what miserable wages they've been paying me here on account of the inflation? If I am taking a little, then it's not so much by a long chalk as what the Rittmeister's stolen from me."

He looked at the Lieutenant challengingly, as if expecting him to agree. But the latter merely said: "That doesn't interest me. Where are you intending to go?"

"A little further away," said Meier with a laugh. "I find that the country around here smells sour. I was thinking of Silesia or perhaps Mecklenburg."

"Fine, fine," said the Lieutenant. "Very sensible. Silesia's not bad. But where are you going *now*?"

"Now?"

"Yes, now." The Lieutenant spoke a little impatiently. "I can quite understand that you're not taking a train tomorrow morning from the local town, where everybody knows you."

"Now? Oh, just to a village nearby."

"I see, to a village? Which, may I ask?"

"What's that got to do with you?" This interrogation, behind which something was hidden, made Meier quite nervous.

"Oh, it has a little to do with me, my lad!" answered the Lieutenant coolly.

"What do you mean?"

"Well, I like to know, for example, the whereabouts of someone who is aware of my relations with Fräulein von Prackwitz. In Silesia not a soul would be interested; but here in the vicinity he might hit on the idea of making money out of his knowledge."

"I would never think of such a thing," said Meier indignantly. "I'm not such a scoundrel as that. You can rest assured, Lieutenant, I'll keep my mouth shut. In such matters I'm a gentleman!"

"Yes, I know," said the Lieutenant unmoved. "Well—what's the name of the village?"

"Grünow," said Meier hesitating, not really knowing why he shouldn't give the name, seeing that the Lieutenant already knew everything.

"Grünow. Why particularly Grünow? I suppose you mean Grünow near Ostade?"

"Yes, my girl suggested it to me. She wants to visit me there on Sundays, for the dances."

"You want to dance there as well? Then you're going to stay there some time?"

"Just a few days. On Monday I shall be clearing off, leaving from Ostade. You can rely on that, Lieutenant."

"Can I?" said the Lieutenant thoughtfully. He stood up and went to the drawer which Meier had previously pointed out to him. He pulled it open and regarded its contents. "Yes, you've got a couple of very nice blunderbusses there," he said patronizingly. "You know what, Herr Meier? I'd take one of those things along if I were you."

"What should I do with it? No, thanks!"

"You are going through the forest, and there are all sorts of rogues on the prowl now. I'd take the thing with you, Herr Meier; I myself never go about without firearms. Nothing like being prepared." The young Lieutenant had become almost loquacious, so worried was he about the life of his friend Meier.

But the latter persisted in his refusal. "No one's going to do anything to me," he said. "No one's done anything to me yet. That old thing just tears your pocket."

"All right. Do what you like!" the Lieutenant said in sudden irritation and laid the pistol on the safe. He nodded curtly to little Meier, said, "Good evening," and was already out of the office before the other could reply.

"Queer," said Meier, and stared at the door. "He was very queer at the end. But still," he went on to comfort himself, "all these chaps are like that. They first talk big and then there's nothing behind it."

He turned round and regarded the pistol. No. He'd have nothing to do with such a thing. It might even go off in his pocket. Where was Mandy? He'd have to have a look. She was well able to carry the suitcases for a bit. . . .

He went to the door. No, first he'd better put the pistol away again. It would look so silly there tomorrow morning.

He had the weapon in his hand, and again he hesitated.

As a matter of fact, he's quite right, was the thought that darted through his head, a weapon is always handy.

He went to the door, switched the light out, left the house. At every step he noticed the weight of the pistol in his hip pocket.

Queer—gives you a feeling of strength, a thing like that, he thought, not dissatisfied.

III

And Meier had only to go a few steps to see the two girls sitting on a bench. Next to them stood the Lieutenant, talking. At his approach the fellow looked up and said: "Here he comes." His proximity to the two girls, his whispering with them, this remark, all irritated little Meier. Advancing, he said crossly: "If I'm intruding I can go away again."

No one seemed to have heard him, no one answered.

"I suppose you three have some nice secret among yourselves," he said provokingly.

Again no answer. But now Violet stood up and, addressing the Lieutenant in a polite and formal tone, said: "Are you coming?"

"You needn't be stand-offish to him on my account," cried little Meier angrily. "We know what you've been up to!"

With astonishing calm the Lieutenant took the girl's arm and walked away with her into the park, saying not a word.

"Good night, sir, good night, madam. Pleasant dreams!" Meier called after them contemptuously.

The Lieutenant turned round and called out to Amanda:

"Just try and persuade him. Persuasion always helps."

Amanda nodded thoughtfully.

Angrily Meier let fly at her. "What do you mean by nodding to the fool? What do you mean speaking to the fellow at all?"

"You think that everyone's a fool, except yourself!" she replied calmly.

"Oh! So in your eyes I'm a fool!"

"I didn't say that!"

"Shut up! You said it just now!"

"I didn't!" And after long reflection: "Fräulein Violet is quite right."

"What is Vi right about? All she can do is talk nonsense. She's just like a seven-months-old babe."

"That it's better not to get mixed up with a man like you."

"So that's what she said?" Meier almost burst with fury and injured conceit. "And her fellow, the Lieutenant—is he anything better than me? What? You think he is? A swine like that! Comes into my office and brandishes a revolver in front of my nose. But I told him where he got off! Just let him come again, the silly idiot. I've got a revolver now. And I won't just threaten like that fool. I'll shoot." He wrenched the pistol from his pocket and waved it in the air.

"Have you gone mad?" Amanda screamed at him furiously. "Put that thing away at once. Waving a thing like that in my face! I am pleased! You seem to think it impresses me."

He was startled by her angry, contemptuous words. Somewhat crestfallen, though of course still defiant, he stood before her, in his hand the pistol with its muzzle lowered.

"You're going in again at once and put the money back in the safe!" she ordered. "Heavens, I can put up with a lot, and I'm not at all squeamish, but stealing money—no, thanks! Not me! And you're not going to, either."

Meier went red—she could not see it, of course.

"So that's what he's been blabbing to you, the fine chap!" he cried angrily. "I just want to tell you one thing: it's no bloody business of his or of yours! That's my own affair with the Rittmeister. If I take my wages, there's no need for you to put your nose in—understand?"

"Hans," she said more gently, "you must put the money back; otherwise it is finished between us. I can't stand for that sort of thing."

"I don't bloody well care whether it's finished between us or not. I'm glad it's finished. Who do you think you are? Do you think I bother about you? I slept with Hartig tonight; yes, Hartig, so there! And an old girl like that with eight children—I prefer her ten times to you. Oh, damn!"

It was a blow with all her strength and it landed right in the middle of his face. Meier staggered.

"You swine, you!" she said breathlessly. "You miserable wretch!"

"You struck me?" He was half out of his mind with pain. "You—you low-down chicken girl—strike me, the bailiff? Now you shall see. . . ."

He himself could see almost nothing, however. Everything reeled before his eyes, her figure melted away in the moonlight; then she was there again. . . . And now he saw her quite clearly. . . . She had struck him!

He quickly raised the pistol and pressed the trigger, with trembling finger. . . .

The shot cracked unbearably loud in his ear.

Amanda's face came close to him, getting bigger all the time, white and black in the moonlight. . . .

"You!" she whispered. "You, Hans, shoot at me!"

And there was complete silence between the two. Each heard only the jerky breathing of the other. They stood like that for a long time. . . .

The echoes of the shot had long died away, to be replaced by gentler noises. . . . They again heard the soft wind in the treetops. . . . Back in the stable a halter chain rattled slowly through its ring.

"Mandy," said Black Meier. "Mandy . . . I . . . ."

"Finished!" she said with a hard voice. "Quite finished!"

She looked at him once again.

"He fires at me—and then he says 'Mandy.'" It was as if this thought took her breath away. "What would he have said if he had hit me?"

And the serious danger in which she had stood, her incredible escape, overwhelmed her so suddenly that she broke into a soft weeping. And weeping thus she ran away from him, her shoulders hunched. Under the light hem of her skirt he saw her strong legs moving faster and faster as she sped away. . . . She turned into the path leading to the Manor; he no longer saw her, heard only her weeping, that suppressed pitiful, sobbing—and then that, too, was gone. . . .

Meier stood for a moment longer, staring after her. Then he lifted the pistol, heavy in his hand, and regarded it. He moved the safety catch into place—there, now it was safe, nothing more could happen with the thing. . . .

With a peevish shrug of his shoulders he pushed it into his trouser pocket and went hastily into the office to get his suitcases.

IV

The Lieutenant and Vi were sitting on a bench in the park. They were not sitting there like a pair of lovers: or perhaps indeed they were—like lovers who have quarreled. That is to say, they sat far apart, silent.

"Fancy letting that coward say a thing like that to you," she had said at the conclusion of their argument. "I don't understand you."

"Of course you don't understand me, my little lamb," he had answered very patronizingly. "That's all to the good. That means he won't understand me either."

"Running away from the fellow! What airs he will give himself now! And I just can't bear the smell of him."

"Don't go so near him," he had said in a bored way. "Then his smell won't upset you."

"Excuse me, Fritz, when have I gone too near him? That was mean of you, Fritz!"

But Fritz returned no answer, and so they had fallen into silence. . . .

The echo of the shot interrupted this quarrel. The Lieutenant started out of his thoughts. "He has fired a pistol!" he cried and began running.

"Who?" she asked, received no answer, and ran after him.

Their course took them over the moonlit park. Its long grass wetted her stockings; then through bushes, across paths, right through flower beds. Vi panted, wanted to call out and could not, since she had to keep on running.

Then the Lieutenant paused and signaled to her to be quiet. She peered over his shoulder through lilac and guelder-rose bushes and just caught sight of the weeping poultry maid disappearing in the direction of the Manor. Bailiff Meier was standing motionless outside the house.

"Hasn't hit her, thank God!" whispered the Lieutenant.

"Then what's she crying for?"

"Fright."

"The fellow must go to jail," exclaimed Vi.

"Don't be so silly, Vi. Then he'd let his tongue wag a bit, wouldn't he? I suppose you'd like that?"

"Well, and now?"

"Now we'll wait and see what he's going to do."

The little dark figure went quickly up to the staff-house; even in the bushes they could hear the noise of the vigorously slammed door. Bailiff Meier was gone.

"Now he's gone," said Fräulein von Prackwitz disconsolately. "And from now on I shall have to be particularly polite to him, so that he won't tell Papa."

"Just wait a bit," was all the Lieutenant said.

They did not have long to wait. Hardly three or four minutes. Then the door opened again and out stepped Meier, a suitcase in his right hand, a suitcase in his left hand. He did not even waste time in closing the door again, but strode on, a little hampered, it is true, yet at a steady pace—toward the farmyard, out into the world—away.

"He's clearing out," whispered the Lieutenant.

"Thank God!"

"You won't see him again," he muttered, and fell silent, as if he was annoyed at what he had said.

"Let's hope so."

"Violet!" he said after a while.

"Yes, Fritz?"

"Wait here a minute, will you? I just want to find out something in the office."

"What do you want to find out there?"

"Oh, nothing much. . . . Just to see what it looks like."

"What do you mean? It doesn't matter to us."

"Still, let me. Excuse me—now, you wait here!"

Hurriedly the Lieutenant went over to the staff-house. He felt his way through the dark passage, switched the light on in the office and went straight to the drawer containing the weapons. It was half open, but this was not sufficient for him. He pulled it right out and regarded its contents very attentively.

No, the nine-millimeter Mauser was not there. He closed the drawer again, switched off the light and went out.

"Well, what does it look like in there?" Violet asked a little maliciously. "I suppose he tidied it up quickly?"

"What should it look like? Oh—I see—yes, of course. Pigsty, that's what it looks like, my little lamb." The Lieutenant was strangely cheerful.

She took advantage of this at once. "I say, Fritz."

"Yes, Violet?"

"Do you still remember what you wanted today?"

"Well, what did I want? To give you a kiss? All right, come along then!"

He seized her by the head, and for a while she lay completely breathless in his arms.

"There!" he said. "And now I must dash off to Ostade."

"To Ostade? Oh, Fritz—you wanted to look round my room to see whether I kept a diary."

"But, my lamb, not today. I really must dash off. I've got to be at Ostade at six!"

"Fritz!"

"What?"

"Isn't it possible at all?"

"No—completely impossible today. But I shall come, quite definitely. The day after tomorrow; perhaps tomorrow even."

"Oh, you're always saying that. You didn't say anything this evening about having to go at once to Ostade!"

"I must, I really must. . . . Come, Violet, walk along with me as far as my bicycle. Now, please don't start making a fuss, my lamb."

"Oh, Fritz, you . . . the way you treat me . . ."

V

For a long time Petra had sat as if benumbed. Her sick enemy also lay still for a long time, exhausted. She had hurled all the abuse of which she was capable into Petra's face; spitting at her, she had reminded Petra in an ecstasy of malicious exultation of how she had once dragged her out of a taxi. "Away from that fine rich bloke. And your umbrella also went flying!"

Mechanically Petra had done what was to be done: had given her a little water, laid a compress on her forehead and a towel over her mouth, which she kept pushing away. However much the other abused and reviled her, jeered and tried to hurt her, it no longer affected Petra, just as the noises of the city, growing ever quieter after midnight, no longer affected her. The city outside, her enemy here inside—neither meant anything.

A feeling of extreme loneliness had numbed everything in her. In the end everyone was completely alone with himself. What others did, asked, performed, was nothing. With a single solitary person on it the earth whirled along its path through the infinities of time and space, always with one mere solitary person on it.

Thus Petra sat, thinking and dreaming—Petra Ledig, spinster. She tried to convince her heart that she would never see Wolf again, that things had to be this way, that this was precisely her fate, and that she must resign herself to it. In the days and weeks to come she was often to dream and try to convince herself. Even if love, filled with longing, would not let itself be convinced, there was yet something like consolation, like a faint memory of happiness, in the mere fact that she could thus sit and dream.

Therefore she was almost annoyed when a hand placed itself on her shoulder and a voice roused her from her brooding with the words: "I say, jail-birdie, talk to me. I can't sleep. My head aches. Your girl-friend pulled my hair so hard, and I can't help thinking of my business, too. What are you thinking about?" It was the fat elderly woman from the lower bed, whom the Hawk had previously attacked. She pushed a stool next to Petra, scrutinized her with dark mouse-like eyes and, tired of sitting alone and brooding, whispered, with a nod of her head toward the sick woman: "She can sting like a wasp! Is it true, what she said about you, jail-birdie?" Of a sudden Petra was glad that the other had spoken, that there was some diversion in the long night; she found the woman not too bad, if only because she looked without animosity at the girl who had caused her no little pain.

"Some things are true and some things are not true," she answered readily.

"But that you go on the streets—that's not true, is it?"

"A few times," began Petra hesitatingly.

But the old woman understood at once. "Yes, yes, I know, my pet!" she said kindly. "I've also grown up in Berlin. I live in Fruchtstrasse. I've also lived through these times—such times as we've never had before! I know the world, and I know Berlin, too. You smiled at someone when you were hungry, eh?"

Petra nodded.

"And that's what a cow like that calls going on the streets. And she squeals on you for a thing like that. She did squeal on you, didn't she?"

Petra nodded again.

"There—she's such a greedy, jealous cat—you can see it by her nose. People who have such thin noses are always sour and don't like seeing anybody else have anything. But you mustn't take it to heart. She can't help being crazy; she didn't choose her nose herself. And what do you do otherwise?"

"Sell shoes. . . ."

"There, I know all about that; that's also an aggravating business for young girls. There are nasty old men who, when they get the itch, run from one shoe shop to another just trying on shoes, and then push the young girls with their toes. Well, I suppose you know all about that, too."

"Yes, there are people like that," said Petra, "and we know them. And if we don't know them, then we can see it in their faces, and no one wants to serve them. And some are still worse. They don't only push, they talk as well, more vulgarly than any girl on the streets . . . And if you won't stand for it, they complain that the assistants give bad service, and they get a real kick when the manager tells you off. . . . There's no use defending yourself, they don't believe you when you say that a fine gentleman has used such vulgar words."

"I know, girlie," said the old woman soothingly, for the memory of some of the insults she had suffered had become so vivid to Petra that she had spoken almost heatedly. "We know all about that! Do you think it's different in Fruchtstrasse? Not a bit. If we haven't got shoe shops there, we've got sweet shops and ice-cream parlors—the under-dog always gets it in the neck. But there won't be any more shoes for you now that you're in prison. Or will they take you back when you come out?"

"I've had nothing to do with shoes for a long time," declared Petra. "Nearly a whole year. I've been living with a boy-friend, and it was today—no, yesterday midday—that we were to have been married."

"You don't say!" said the old woman with wonderment. "And just on a red-letter day like that the little poisonous toad has to go and queer everything by peaching on you? Now, tell me, girlie, what mischief have you really been getting up to, for them to shove you straight away into prison rig? They only do that with real jail-birds, because they think they might escape in ordinary clothes. But if you don't want to tell me, all right then. I don't like being taken in, anyway, and I can always see if you're not telling the truth."

And so it came about that Petra Ledig, between one and two in the morning, related to a completely unknown elderly woman the rather wretched story of the collapse of her hopes, and how she now stood once again alone in life, and really did not quite know the why or the wherefore.

The old woman listened to it all quite patiently, now nodding her head, now shaking it vigorously and saying: "Yes, I know," and "That does happen," or "We ought to tell that to God, but he's got a bit fed up with his job in the last five years and he's deaf in one ear." But when Petra had finished and looked silently at the sick woman below her, or maybe just stared in front of her at all the rubbish she really only became aware of while telling her own story—she no longer understood why, how, for whom and where it all began. The old woman gently laid her hand on her arm and said: "My child—so you are called Petra and he always said 'Peter' to you?"

"Yes," said Petra Ledig rather morosely.

"Then I shall also say 'Peter' to you. I'm Frau Krupass—Ma Krupass, they call me in Fruchtstrasse, and you must call me that, too."

"Yes," answered Petra.

"I believe what you have told me, and that's more than the chief of police himself can say. And if what you've told me is true—and it is true, I can see it in your face—then today or tomorrow you'll be out again. For what can they want from you? They can't want anything! You're healthy and you haven't been on the streets, and your name's displayed in the registry office, too—don't forget to tell them that; the registry office always works with them."

"Yes."

"Well then, today or tomorrow you'll be out and they'll also find some things for you to wear from the welfare office—so you'll be out—and what will you do then?"

Petra shrugged her shoulders uncertainly, but now she regarded the speaker with great attention.

"Yes, that's the question. Nothing else counts. Thinking and fretting and regretting—that's all bunk. What are you going to do when you get out—that's the question!"

"Of course," said Petra.

"From the looks of you, you ain't the sort to gas yourself or jump into the canal; and then you want to have your baby, don't you?"

"Yes, I do!" said Petra with determination.

"And what about the shoes?" inquired Ma Krupass. "Do you want to start that again?"

"I won't get a job again," said Petra. "I've got no references for the last year; I simply stopped going to my last job, without notice. All my papers are still there. I told you, it all happened so quickly with Wolf . . ."

"I know, I know," said Frau Krupass. "But still, you'll fetch your papers; papers are always handy. So there's nothing more doing with the shoes, and even if there was, you wouldn't be earning enough, and then the other business would just happen again, and you don't want that just now, do you?"

"No, no," said Petra quickly.

"No, of course not, I know. I was only just saying it. And now there's one more thing, girlie. Do you know what? I shall call you girlie, and not Peter—Peter doesn't seem to come easy to my tongue. Well now, there's your boy-friend—how do things stand with him, girlie?"

"He hasn't come for me."

"That's the sort he is; you are right there. And probably he never will. He'll think he'll get into trouble with his gambling if he makes too many inquiries for you with the police, and perhaps he also thinks that you've squealed on him."

"Wolf would never think that!"

"All right, then he doesn't think that. Very good," said Frau Krupass submissively. "He may be just as fine a gentleman as you say; I don't dispute it at all—and yet he doesn't come. Men are all the same. Do you want to go and look for him, then?"

"No," said Petra. "Not look for him . . ."

"And if he comes tomorrow to visit you?" The old woman shot a quick dark glance at the girl, who began to walk up and down, stopping sometimes as if she were listening for sounds in the prison; then she shook her head dejectedly and began walking up and down again. Stopping, she leaned her head against the wall and stood like that for a long time.

"This is how it is," Frau Kraupass at last said knowingly. "The warder will knock on the door and say: 'Ledig, come along—visitor!' And then you will follow him in your slippers, dressed as you are now in your blue prison smock. And then you will come into a room. In the middle there's a wooden barrier, and he'll be standing on one side, smartly togged up, and you on the other in your prison dress, and in the middle a warder will be sitting and watching you. And then you will talk to each other and when the warder says: 'Time's up,' he will go out again into the free air and you will go back again to your cell."

Petra was watching the old woman tensely, with pale face. She moved her lips as if she wanted to say something, ask something, but she said nothing, asked nothing.

"Yes, jail-birdie," Frau Krupass said suddenly, in a hard angry voice, "now just tell me what mischief have you been up to then, to bring you shuffling back to the cell? And what marvelous thing has he done, so that he can go out into the free air again?"

It was very quiet in the cell. At last Petra said painfully: "But it isn't his fault."

"I see," said the old woman sneeringly. "It wasn't his fault, I suppose, that you were always hungry and always had to wait up for him, and that he pawned your clothes, though if it hadn't been for that you wouldn't have come here at all. It wasn't his fault, no! He wore the skin off his paws shuffling cards, he was always working night shift!"

Petra wanted to say something.

"Be quiet!" cried the old woman. "Let me tell you something. You're crazy. He had a good time with you, and when he'd finished having a good time, he hopped it and thought: We'll look for someone else now, she can go and look after herself—I like that, I must say! I tell you, it makes my gall rise. Haven't you any self-respect left in your body, girl, to want to stand there in the visitors' room like a primrose pot with a pink serviette and beam at him—just because he really comes to visit you? Is that marriage, I ask you? Is it comradeship? Is it even friendship? It's pure wanting to sleep with him, I tell you. You ought to be ashamed, girl."

Petra's whole body trembled. She had never yet been so rudely awakened; she had never seen her relationship with Wolf in this light—all the veils which love had drawn over it torn away. She would have liked to cry, "Stop!"

"It may be," Frau Krupass continued more calmly, "that he's quite a good man, as you say. He does something for your education, you say. All right, let him, if it amuses him. It would have been better if he had done something for your heart and your stomach, but there of course he doesn't find himself so clever as he does with books. A good man, you say. But, child, he's not a man. He might become one some day, perhaps. But you take an old woman's word for it: what seems like a man in bed is a long way from being one. That's just a silly idea you young girls have. If you go on with him in the same way, spoiling him and always doing what he wants, and a mother in the background, too, with a nice fat money bag—then he'll never become a man, but you'll become a door-mat. God forgive me for saying so!" She breathed hard with exasperation.

Petra stood pale and quiet against her wall.

"I'm not asking you never to see him again. Just let him shift for himself for a while. You can wait a year, or as far as I'm concerned six months (I'm not so particular) and see what he does. See whether he goes on gambling or whether he goes back to his Ma or whether he gets another girl—in that case he never had any serious intentions about you. Or whether he starts doing some sensible work."

"But I must at least tell him what's happened to me, or write to him," pleaded Petra.

"What for? How will that help? After all, he's been seeing you every day for a year, and if he doesn't know you yet, then writing's of no use. And he can ask at the police station—they'll soon tell him you are here, they won't keep it a secret. And if he does come to visit you, then as far as I'm concerned you can go down and say to him: 'This is the way things are, old chap. I shall show what I'm made of, and you shall show me what you are made of.' And besides that: 'I'm going to have a baby,' you will say—not 'We are going to have a baby.' For you're having it and you must keep it, too, and you'll say: 'I want the child to have a real man as his father, someone who can earn a bit of grub, something to eat, something to fill our tummies, so that I won't go fainting in the street.'"

"Ma Krupass," pleaded Petra, for the old woman was again becoming angry.

"Yes, yes, girlie," she growled, "you can say that safely. It won't rub the gilt off him, a man's got to hear that sort of thing now and again, it does him good."

"Yes, and what am I to do during the six months?"

"Now, girlie"—Frau Krupass was pleased—"that's the first sensible word you've said this evening. Here, come and make yourself comfortable near me on the bed and let's have a proper talk. We won't talk any more about men anyway, a real woman shouldn't talk so much about them, it only gives them swelled heads and they ain't really so important. . . . What are you going to do during the year? I'll tell you. You shall represent me."

"Oh!" said Petra, a little disappointed.

VI

"Yes, you say, 'Oh,'" said old Frau Krupass quite pleasantly. With a groan she crossed her legs, an action which revealed that she wore not only a very old-fashioned many-pleated skirt (she even had a petticoat underneath it) but also impossibly thick home-knitted woolen stockings—in the middle of summer. "You say, 'Oh,' girlie, and you are right. For how is a pretty young thing like you to take the place of an old scarecrow like me? I look like a keeper of a brothel or a flop house, don't I?"

Petra shook her head with an embarrassed smile.

"But you're wrong, girlie. And why are you wrong? Because you've written out bills in the shoe shop and can add up, and you've got eyes in your head that see what they look at. That's what I told myself as soon as you came into the cell. 'Look,' I said, 'here's another one who's got observant eyes, not bleary eyes like the idiots of today who look everywhere and see nothing.'"

"Have I really got such eyes?" Petra asked curiously, because her mirror had never given her the impression that her eyes were different from other people's, and Wolfgang Pagel hadn't yet said they were, although he had certainly from time to time felt their effect.

"If I say so, then you have," declared Ma Krupass. "I've learned to know eyes in Fruchtstrasse where I've got fifty or sixty people running around; they all tell me lies with their mouths, but they can't lie with their eyes! Well, here am I sitting in this miserable bug-hutch, brooding and wondering how much I'll get this time; I'd like to think it'll be three months, but it'll probably be six.

Killich also says it'll be six, and Killich seldom makes a mistake; he must know, he's my lawyer."

Petra wanted to interpose a question, but the old woman nodded her head vigorously. "That's all still to come. You'll get to know everything at its proper time, girlie. And just as you said 'Oh!' before, so you can afterwards say 'No!'; it won't bother me. Except that you won't say it." She seemed so certain and so energetic, and at the same time so kind, that Petra lost all the doubts which such acquiescence in a prison sentence had aroused in her.

"And so here I sit and think," Frau Krupass continued. "Six months in jail are all very well, and after all I do need some rest—but what'll happen to the business, especially in times like these? Randolf can be trusted, but he's weak in arithmetic; and now, when everything runs in millions and him using only slate and chalk—that won't do, child, you can see that for yourself."

Petra did see it.

"Yes, so here I sit and worry my head about managers, which is a nice word, except that they all steal like hungry crows and don't think of the old woman in jail. But then you come in, child, and I look at you and your eyes and I see what goes on with that wench and I hear what she calls you—not to mention the attack on me and having my hair pulled out, and wrapping her in blankets—everything done nicely, without temper and yet not like the Salvation Army. . . ."

Petra sat quite still. But it does every person good to be rewarded with a little recognition, and it does especial good if that person has been ill-treated.

"Yes, and so I thought: She's all right, she's the sort of person you want. But then she's in jail rig-out, you can't get her. Just drop the idea, Ma Krupass. She'll be patching shirts a long time after you've got out again. And then I hear what you've told me, and I wonder if there isn't just the possibility that they may have sent the child straight from heaven to me in my loneliness."

"Ma Krupass!" said Petra for the second time.

"There, Ma Krupass, of course, what else could it be?" said the old woman very pleased, and slapping Petra on the knee. "I told you a lot of unpleasant things before, didn't I? Well, forget it, it won't hurt you. When I was young I also had unpleasant things handed out to me, and afterwards, too, without stint: the boys were killed in the war and my old man was so depressed he hanged himself. But not at my place in Fruchtstrasse. He was already in Dalldorf, which is now called Wittenau. But don't worry about it, is what I think—a little bitterness gingers you up." She leaned forward. "But I am not so very cheerful even now, girlie, you understand that? I just seem cheerful. On the whole, I think the business ain't worth the candle."

And Petra nodded her head in complete agreement, and understood clearly that the business did not mean the police station in Alexanderplatz. She understood Ma Krupass's outlook perfectly; one could find life rather depressing and yet not hang one's head. In fact she had rather a similar attitude, and when you discover such feelings, you are always pleased.

"Yes, yes—but just because of that I carry on with the business. It keeps me alive. And if one doesn't keep alive and do something, girlie, then it's useless; you just rot alive. And what you've been doing, always squatting in a furnished room and perhaps, at the most, doing a bit of washing-up for the landlady—that's no life, girl; it would make anyone crazy."

Again Petra nodded her head. It was quite impossible to return to the old life. But she would have liked to know what sort of work it was which kept Frau Krupass so fresh and vigorous, and she hoped with all her heart that it was something decent and responsible.

And then Frau Krupass herself said: "Now I want to tell you, girlie, what sort of business I've got. Even if people do turn up their noses at it and say that it stinks, it's still a good business. And it's got nothing to do with my being in jail, for it's a decent business—my being in jail is just the result of my own stupidity, because I was greedy for money. I can't help it. I've said to myself a hundred times: 'Don't do it, Auguste (my name happens to be Auguste, but I never use it), don't do it, you earn enough money as it is.' But I can't help it. And then I go and get caught—for the third time! And Killich says it'll cost me six months."

Greedy Frau Krupass! She looked very depressed, and Petra could see that her previous talk about six months' rest was pure bravado—the old woman was by no means hard-boiled. On the contrary, she had an unearthly fear of six months in jail. She would like to have said something comforting to the old woman, but still didn't exactly know what it was all about. She also hadn't the faintest idea what the flourishing but dubious, yet apparently decent, business was that Frau Krupass ran.

"Lordy, now I'm sitting here in the dumps," said Frau Krupass with an almost apologetic smile. "That always happens when you boast about being cheerful and all that. But now listen to me, girlie. Do you know what a rag-and-bone business is?"

Petra, with visions of a musty cellar, nodded slightly.

"Well, girlie, that's what I've got, and there's no need for you to turn your nose up, it's a good business and gets one a living and you don't have to stand for any nonsense from old lechers. Waste paper and old iron and bones and rags, and I've got skins too. . . . But I don't push a little barrow to the rubbish dumps, not me! I've got a big yard, with a truck, and six men working for me. And then there's Randolf; he's my supervisor—a bit slow, but trustworthy, as I've already told you. Fifty or sixty barrows come to me every day. I pay what's proper, and they know that Ma Krupass pays the proper prices. And it's growing from day to day, now that everyone goes round with a barrow because there's less and less work."

"But, Ma Krupass, I don't know a thing about it," said Petra timidly.

"You don't need to, my girl. Randolf knows everything, except that he can't reckon and is slow. You'll do the reckoning; you'll keep the books and pay out the money. I've got a lot of confidence in you, girlie, and it'll go all right. In the evenings you'll phone up the spinning mills and the factories, to ask them what they're all paying for the stuff that concerns them. I'll tell you the names and telephone numbers of the people, and you'll pay according to what they say. And then the truck will deliver at the factories, and you'll get the money. We send off the paper when we've got enough for a truckload. Randolf will tell you all that. That again brings in more money. It cheers you up, girlie, when you take in money; and today any child can do business, when the dollar's always rising."

Seeing the old woman's enthusiasm, Petra felt that the plan was not impossible. After all, it was work. Let's say it's a kind of future. Then she remembered that they were in prison, and that there must be some catch in the thing, and her joy left her.

But what the old woman now said restored her joy. "You needn't think that there's anything shady in my place. Everything's honest and open. Proper bookkeeping, and no more bother with the income-tax people than everyone has. And a little house in the yard, slap-up, spotless, with flowers and summerhouse, the proper thing. Downstairs lives Randolf, and I live upstairs, three rooms with bath and kitchen—classy. Randolf's wife cooks my meals, and she shall cook them for you, too. I like eating nice things. She doesn't cook bad! I was thinking you could live in my flat, and you can wash in the bathroom. . . . But you mustn't use the bath, for then the enamel will get spoiled. I'm the only one who knows how to manage it. You must give me your solemn oath that you won't touch the bath. Anyway, you won't get so dirty that you'll have to take a bath—Randolf and the men do the dirty work."

Petra nodded. But there was still one thing, the one point.

"And tomorrow morning Killich's coming here at visiting time; he's my lawyer, and he's a sly dog, girlie. I'll say to him: 'Killich, Herr Killich, Solicitor Killich—tomorrow or the day after tomorrow or even today someone will come to you in office hours. Petra Ledig's her name. She is my business representative. Don't look at what she's wearing—that's from the Welfare Office or Provident Society—look at her face. And if she does me down, Killich, then I won't believe another person in the world, not myself, and you least of all, Herr Killich.'"

"Ma Krupass!" Petra laid her hand on the old woman's, convinced that her crime could not really be so bad.

"Well, my girl, that's how it is. And then Killich will take you to Randolf and tell him that you are to be like me as regards money and giving orders and rooms and food, just like me, and whatever clothes, underwear and things you need, you'll buy yourself. And in the Municipal Bank, where I have my account, you'll sign just like me; Killich will arrange all that for you."

"But, Ma Krupass . . ."

"Well, what are you 'butting' about? You'll have good food, you'll have clothes, and you'll have lodgings; and you can also have your baby in my place, though I hope I'll be outside again by that time. There's only one thing you won't get: you won't get wages. And why not? Because you'll only give them to him. You're that soft, I know. I'm a woman myself. If he comes and looks at you with a faithful doggy look, then you'll give him what you've got. But what you haven't got—that's to say, my money—that you won't give him—I know you well enough for that. That's why you'll get no wages. Not because I'm stingy! And now tell me, child, do you agree or don't you?"

"Yes, Ma Krupass, of course I agree. But there's still one other thing—*the* thing."

"What thing? The fellow? We'll not speak about him anymore. First let him become a fellow!"

"No; your affair, Ma Krupass—*yours!*"

"What do you mean, my affair? I've told you everything, girlie, and if that isn't enough for you—"

"No, *your* affair—the business you're in prison for, the business you want to get six months for."

"*Want* to, girlie! You're a nice one. A funny idea you've got of what I want, I must say! Now, that's no concern of yours. You've got nothing to do with it, nor has the business; it's only my greediness is responsible. It's like this. When we sort rags I usually stand by, so that no cotton gets mixed up with linen rags, because linen is dear and cotton's cheap. I suppose you understand that?"

"Yes."

"That's good," said the old woman, pacified. "You've got brains, you have. Well, there I'm standing, with the rags flying through the air, and my greedy eyes see something sparkling. I edge up to it cautious=like and there I find a real dress shirt, and the idiot who chucked it away—though it was probably his servant, wanting to make a little money out of linen rags—a lot of people do that today because wages won't go far—he's left three diamond studs sticking in the front. I see at once they're not duds, but real diamonds, and not little ones either! Well, I pretend I see nothing and pull them out quietly. Pleased as punch when I've got them home. That's the way I am; if something hasn't cost me a cent I'm as happy as a child. I know I mustn't do it—I've been caught twice already—but I can't stop myself. I always think no one's seen me . . ."

The two looked at each other. Petra was very relieved, and Frau Krupass was very worried.

"And that's the nasty thing about me, child: I can't stop myself. It worries me to death because I can't overcome it. Killich also says to me: 'What's the point of it, Frau Krupass? You're a rich woman; you can buy yourself a whole bagful of diamond studs! Stop doing things like that.' And he's right, but I can't stop. Not however much I try. What would you do in a case like that, child?"

"I would give them up," said Petra.

"Give them up? Those beautiful studs? I'm not as silly as that." Frau Krupass managed to control herself. "Well, let's say no more about them. I'm angry enough without talking about it. What else is there for me to say? One of my men must have seen me, and before I can turn round there's the copper, and he's very polite. 'Well, Frau Krupass, what's all this again about stealing by finding?' he says and grins, too, the fool! 'Have you put it in the wardrobe again? Open it!' And fathead that I am, I really have put the studs there again, like last time—the man's right and no fool at all! It's only me who's always the fool. Well, the person who isn't born a thief will never become one as long as he lives."

Ma Krupass sat lost in thought. One could see that, despite her self-knowledge and her fear of imprisonment, even now she regretted the loss of the studs. Petra could almost have laughed at the foolish old woman. But then she thought of Wolfgang Pagel, and although at first she wanted to say: "But that's different from studs!"—she yet thought: Perhaps I'm only imagining that it's different. What Wolf is to me, the studs are to Ma Krupass.

And then she remembered again that it was now over with Wolf. She thought of the little house in the rag-and-bone yard; she could already visualize it (scarlet-runners on the summerhouse), and knew for certain now that there would be no more Madame Po and sweltering back room, no more screaming of tin being cut in the factory below, no more staying in bed through lack of clothes, no more cadging for a few rolls. No more passive waiting. Instead of that, cleanliness and order, a day regularly divided up by work, meals and rest . . . a prospect so overwhelming that she almost wept for happiness. She gulped and gulped again, but then pulled herself together. Going to the old woman, she took her hand and said: "Yes, I'll do it, Ma Krupass, and gladly. I'm very grateful to you."

VII

For a long time, for an immeasurably long time, almost an hour, the Rittmeister and young Pagel had played together. They had communicated with each other in whispers. Pagel had listened to the Rittmeister's suggestions and had followed them or not, according to how he judged the state of play. Young Pagel, cool and calculating in his gambling, had not been a bad teacher. Herr von Prackwitz realized, when Pagel discussed the chances in a whisper, how foolishly he had been playing before. Now he could see that the sharp=nosed gentleman with the monocle, even though he seemed self-controlled, played like a fool. The Rittmeister was now able to make more sensible suggestions which, though noted, were often not accepted by the ex-officer cadet. And at first a slightly irritated, and then later a really bitter, attitude gradually became stronger in the Rittmeister. Young Pagel, on the whole, despite a few triumphs, was on the down-grade, however. If he himself was not aware of it, the Rittmeister noticed how he continually had to delve into his pocket for fresh counters. The young fellow had every cause to follow the advice of one who was an older man and his former superior. Time and again it had been on the tip of the Rittmeister's tongue to say: "Do for once what I tell you! There, you've lost again!" And if he continued to swallow those words (though with great difficulty), it was not because young Pagel, after all, might play as he liked with his own money. There was no doubt about this: the Rittmeister himself was merely a tolerated spectator with three or four counters in his pocket and hardly any cash in reserve. So it was not this which kept him as the superior from calling the second lieutenant to order. It was rather the vague fear that Pagel might stop playing on the slightest excuse and want to go home. He trembled at the thought. It was the worst thing he could imagine—not to be able to go on sitting here, not to be able to continue watching the ball, not to hear the voice of the croupier which would at last, perhaps next time, announce the great coup. It was this fear alone, vague though it was, which restrained the explosive Rittmeister. Yet it was doubtful how long even this would be effective in view of his ever-increasing embitterment. A conflict between the two men was inevitable. And it came, of course, in a manner quite different from that expected.

The ball had been thrown and was rattling, the wheel was whirring round, the croupier had called. People hurried to withdraw their chips and replace them. Time passed quickly, accelerated, always busy. That moment when the ball seemed to balance on the edge of a number, undecided whether to fall into it or continue—that moment, when time seemed to be suspended with one's breath and heartbeat, that one moment always seemed to be over too quickly.

Some games demand the complete attention of their devotees. The eye that wanders, if only for a moment, has already lost control. The context is lost—why are a heap of chips here, and player's eyes glazed over there. The game is a merciless god. Only he who completely surrenders himself to the game is granted all the ecstasies of heaven, all the doubts of hell. The half-hearted, the lukewarm, are here—as everywhere—cast aside.

It was already difficult enough for Pagel to play calmly with the Rittmeister constantly chattering. But when, right in front of his eyes intent on the ball, there appeared a highly scented woman's hand with several glittering rings, a hand holding a few counters, while a voice pleaded coaxingly: "There, you see, darling, I told you so. Now bet for me, too, as you promised"—then young Pagel's patience gave way. Turning round savagely, he stared at the graciously smiling Valuta Vamp and snapped: "Go to the devil!" He was almost choking with rage.

The way the Rittmeister saw this incident was as follows: a young, very charming-looking lady had wanted to make her stake, perhaps somewhat awkwardly, over Pagel's shoulder, and Pagel had thereupon shouted at her in the most discourteous, most insulting manner. Discourtesy toward women was hateful to the Rittmeister. Tapping Pagel on the shoulder, he said very sharply: "Herr Pagel, you, an officer! Apologize to the lady at once."

The croupier regarded this encounter not without apprehension. He knew the lady very well and was unaware of anything ladylike about her; an illegal gambling club of this kind, however, could not possibly allow a noisy quarrel. There were the neighbors in those once very smart west-end apartment blocks. There were the owners of these properties tucked up in their matrimonial beds. Only the emergencies of the inflation had led them to hire out their respectable premises for such dubious purposes. The porter in the lodge below had been paid, but only just. A loud argument could make all of these people curious, suspicious and anxious. Therefore he threw a warning glance to his two assistants. And the assistants hurried to the battlefield. One whispered to the white-nosed Valuta Vamp: "Don't make us any trouble, Walli," while he said aloud: "Excuse me, madam, would you like a chair?" The other forced his way up to Pagel who, red with rage, had jumped to his feet; gently but firmly he removed the Rittmeister's hand from the young fellow's shoulder, for he knew that nothing makes an angry man more angry than to be gripped. At the same time he was considering, in case the young chap in the shabby tunic caused further trouble, whether a strong hook to the jaw would be out of place or not in this elegant assembly.

The croupier himself would have liked to act as mediator, but could not for the moment leave his place. In a low voice he requested the players to take back their stakes until the little difference of opinion between the gentlemen over there was settled. He was wondering which of the two disputants he would have to throw out. For one of them had to leave, that much was clear.

The table in front of him was now almost bare, and he was just getting ready to carry out his resolve, which was to request young Pagel to leave (quietly or by force, it didn't matter which), when the tense situation settled itself in a way which, unfortunately, did not fully correspond to the croupier's intentions.

The Valuta Vamp, or Walli rather, who within the last hour had been able to buy from a late-comer a few doses of snow which she had consumed at a mad speed, insisted, for no reason at all, in the incalculable way of all drug addicts, on regarding the angry Pagel this time as merely comic. Terribly comic, divinely comic, devastatingly comic! She felt like bursting with laughter at his expression, she invited the others to laugh with her, she pointed her finger at him. "He's such a sweet kid when he's angry. I must give you a kiss, darling." And her hilarity was only increased when Pagel, mad with rage, called her a bloody whore before the whole assembly. Almost sobbing with hysterical laughter, she cried: "Not for you, dearie, not for you. *You* don't need to pay me anything!"

"I told you that I'd hit you one on the jaw," shouted Pagel and hit out. She screamed.

The tone of their dialogue, the way they abused each other, had long convinced the croupier's assistant that a hook to the jaw would be just as much in place here as in his home district in Wedding. He too hit out—and unfortunately struck Walli as she was staggering backwards. The woman collapsed without another sound.

Both the croupier and von Studmann, who had been leaning against the wall, came too late. The Valuta Vamp lay on the floor unconscious. The assistant was trying to explain how it had all happened. Von Prackwitz stood there darkly, biting his lip with anger.

Rather dictatorially Studmann asked: "Well, are we going at last, now?"

Pagel, breathing quickly, was very white, and was obviously not listening to the Rittmeister, now making sharp comments on his ungentlemanly behavior.

The croupier saw the evening threatened. Many guests were preparing to go, and precisely the more distinguished ones, the guests of substance, those who held the opinion that one may overstep the bounds of the law, but only if all outward forms are preserved. In a few curt words he issued orders to his men: the unconscious girl was taken away into a dark adjoining room, the wheel again buzzed round, the ball rattled and jumped. In the lamplight the green cloth shone magical, soft, tempting. "There are still two stakes lying here on the table," the croupier called out. "Make your game. Two gentlemen have forgotten their stakes."

Many turned back.

"Well, let's go then," Studmann cried impatiently. "I really don't understand you . . ." The Rittmeister looked at him sharply and angrily, but he followed when Pagel went out of the door without a word.

In the passage sat the sorrowful sergeant major at his little table. Fumbling in his pocket the Rittmeister fished out the two or three counters he had left, threw them on to the table and called in a tone that was meant to sound carefree: "There! For you, comrade. It's all I possess."

The sorrowful sergeant major slowly raised his round eyes toward the Rittmeister, shook his head and laid down three notes for the three counters.

Herr von Studmann had opened the door leading to the dark staircase and was peering down. "You must wait a moment," said the sergeant major. "He'll make a light for you at once. He's just gone down with a couple of gentlemen."

Pagel stood pale and worn-out in front of the greenish wardrobe mirror. He could distinctly hear the croupier calling: "Seventeen—red—odd."

Of course. Red. His color! Soon he would be going down the stairs and into the country with the Rittmeister, while inside they were playing his color. And for him there would be no more playing.

The Rittmeister, in a tone intended to indicate that the past was forgiven and forgotten, but which still sounded very angry, said: "Pagel, you've also got some counters to change. It's a pity to throw them away."

Pagel dived into his pocket. Why doesn't the fellow come to let us out? he thought. Naturally they want us to go on playing. He was trying to count the chips in his pocket. If there were seven or thirteen he would play one last time. He hadn't played properly at all yet, today.

There must be more than thirteen, he couldn't make out the number. Taking them out of his pocket he encountered the Rittmeister's glance, which seemed to motion him toward the door.

There were neither seven nor thirteen. I must go home after all, he thought sadly. But he no longer had a home! The unsuspecting Studmann now stepped into the staircase to call the man with the light. Pagel looked at the counters in his hand. There were seventeen. *Seventeen! His number!* At that moment an indescribable feeling of happiness was his. The great chance had come!

He walked up to the Rittmeister and said in an undertone, with a glance through the open door at the stairs: "I'm not leaving yet. I'm going on playing."

The Rittmeister said nothing, but his eye flickered once—as if something had flown into it.

Wolfgang stepped up to the change-table, drew out a packet of bank notes, the second. "Chips for the lot!" While the man counted and recounted, he turned to the Rittmeister and cried, almost exultingly: "Tonight I shall win a fortune. I know it."

The Rittmeister moved his head slightly, as if he too knew it, as if it was indeed a natural thing.

"And you?" asked Pagel.

"I've no more money with me." It sounded strangely guilty, and while saying it the Rittmeister glanced almost with fear at the open door.

"I can lend you some. Play on your own account." Pagel held out a packet of money.

"No, no," said the Rittmeister. "It's too much. I don't want so much."

(Neither remembered at that moment the scene in Lutter and Wegner's, when young Pagel had first offered him money and had been rebuked with the most scornful indignation.)

"If you really want to win," explained Pagel, "you must have sufficient capital. I know!"

Again the Rittmeister nodded. Slowly he reached for the packet.

When von Studmann returned, the anteroom was empty. "Where are the gentlemen?"

The sergeant major made a movement with his head in the direction of the roulette room.

Von Studmann stamped his foot and went toward it. Then he turned back. I wouldn't dream of it, he thought angrily; I'm not his governess, however much he needs one.

A door opened. The girl with whom Pagel had had the quarrel stepped out.

"Can you take me downstairs?" she asked tonelessly, speaking as if she were not quite conscious. "I feel bad, I would like some fresh air."

Von Studmann, the eternal nursery governess, offered her his arm. "Certainly. I wanted to go anyway." The sergeant major took a silver-gray wrap from the wardrobe and draped it over the woman's naked shoulders.

The two descended the stairs without saying a word, the girl leaning heavily on Studmann's arm.

VIII

The spotter, the same one who had shown them up, had been standing down-stairs, taking good care not to hear the calls for him. Every player who wanted to go had to be given the opportunity of changing his mind. But when von Stud-mann appeared in the passage with the girl on his arm, he was fully capable of dealing with the situation. The Valuta Vamp, or Walli, he knew, and also that gold and love often play ring-around-the-rosy with each other.

"Taxi?" he asked. And before Studmann could reply, said: "Just wait here. I'll get one from Wittenbergplatz." With that he vanished. In the dark open passage of an unknown house, an unknown girl on his arm, von Studmann had time to reflect on his ambiguous situation. And upstairs was a gambling club. Now only the cops were missing.

It was all very awkward, and today had already fully covered von Stud-mann's requirements so far as awkward situations were concerned. In these times a man never knew what was going to happen in the next quarter of an hour, whether things were what they seemed. He had honestly been pleased to meet his old regimental comrade that morning. Prackwitz had behaved with extraordinary decency; without his intervention nothing would have reached Studmann's ear of a Dr. Schröck; he would have been kicked out more or less with ignominy. The prospect, too, of going with him out of this bottomless pit into the peaceful country had been very agreeable—and now the selfsame Prackwitz was sitting upstairs, throwing away his money in the silliest manner, and had already called him a "children's nurse."

He required no children's nurse, he had said. Yet he did and at once. When Studmann recalled young Pagel's absurd bundles of money, and the vulture-like nose and rapacious glance of the croupier, then he knew that—children's nurse or no children's nurse—he ought to go back at once and put an end to this suicidal gambling. But this unfortunate girl on his arm! She didn't seem quite herself—and no wonder, after that heavy blow. She was trembling, her teeth chattered, she kept whispering something about snow. About *snow*—in a foul, damp heat that was enough to kill you! It was clear that Studmann ought to go upstairs at once and get his friend away, but it was just as necessary first to take this girl safely somewhere—to relatives. He wanted to learn her address, but she wouldn't listen. Her sole response was brusque. Let him leave her in peace! Where she lived was no business of his!

A taxi stopped outside. Studmann was not certain whether it was the one meant for him—the spotter was nowhere to be seen, the girl whispered something about snow, von Studmann stood, hesitating. Finally, however, he slouched out of the doorway into the taxi. "Sorry to have kept you waiting. I felt as if there was a nasty niff in the air. You know—the cops' gambling squad! Those chaps can't sleep quiet for one night; on their rotten wage, hunger keeps them awake." He whistled the tune of—"And I sleep so bad and I dream so much." "Well, hurry up, Count, into the bone-shaker with you. Don't forget me! There, that's nice. Some more cash the old woman doesn't know about. Well, where to, Fräulein?"

He waited in vain. Von Studmann looked doubtfully at the girl reclining next to him in the taxi.

"Going home, Walli?" the spotter bellowed. "Where do you sleep now?"

She murmured something about being left in peace.

"All right, hop it, mate," said the spotter to the driver. "Down Kurfürstendamm. She'll soon wake up there."

The taxi started, and Studmann was annoyed with himself for not getting out.

Later, when he looked back on it, it seemed as if they must have driven for hours and hours. Up streets, down streets—dark streets, brightly lit streets, empty streets, streets full of people. From time to time the girl tapped on the window, got out, went into a café or spoke to a man on the pavement . . .

She returned slowly, said to the chauffeur: "Drive on!" And the taxi set off again. She sobbed, her teeth chattered more and more, she muttered incoherently to herself.

"I beg your pardon?" said von Studmann.

She did not reply. As far as she was concerned he wasn't there. He could have got out long ago and driven back to his friends. If he remained it was not because of her; he was not such an uncritical admirer of the feminine as Rittmeister von Prackwitz. And he knew now what he was sitting next to. He had guessed what the girl was hunting for. "Snow," he remembered, had also been a subject of discussion in his hotel. A lavatory attendant in the café there had been trafficking in it recently. Of course, he had been dismissed—even the most modern hotel didn't go quite so far toward meeting the wishes of its guests in crazy times.

No, if he still drove on with the girl, if he waited with increasing tension to see whether her inquiries met with success, it was because he was struggling with a decision. As soon as she was successful he would decide one way or the other.

The spotter's remark about the cops' gambling squad had given von Studmann the idea that the best thing would be for him to telephone the squad and have the club raided. What he had previously heard about these things, and the taxi driver confirmed it, was that the players had hardly anything to fear. Their names were taken, at the worst they were punished with a small fine, and that was all. The ones severely dealt with were the exploiters, the club organizers—which was only just.

Again and again Studmann said to himself that this was the best solution. What sense is there in my going up again? he kept thinking. I shall merely quarrel with Prackwitz, and he'll just go on playing. No, I'll ring up the police at the next café. I know that would be the most effective lesson for him; there's nothing he hates more than being conspicuous, and if his identity were established by the police, that would rid him of any further desire to gamble. He still thinks he's sitting in the casino—surrounded by beggars and swindlers. . . . It will do him good!

Yes, the organizers would be punished, but both the indiscreet Prackwitz and young Pagel, who seemed to have lost all his bearings, would be warned. Nevertheless, Studmann continued to fight for the strength to carry out his decision. Yet he felt reluctant to do the right thing, because one didn't bring a friend into contact with the police—not even if one's intention was for the best. First let him settle with the girl, then decide.

He waited for her expectantly, but again she said nothing, and whispered for a long time with the chauffeur.

"That's too far, Fräulein," he heard the driver say. "I'm going off duty soon."

At last he gave way. "But, Fräulein, if that's also no good . . ."

They drove on, endlessly. Deserted, almost black streets. Broken street lamps. For economy's sake only every sixth or eighth one was burning.

The girl was muttering automatically "Oh, God—Oh, God," and after each "Oh, God" she knocked her head against the back of the cab.

Von Studmann could see himself in the telephone booth of a café: "Please give me the police station, gambling squad . . ." But perhaps there wouldn't be a telephone booth, and he'd have to phone at the counter; then the people would think he was a fleeced gambler wanting to revenge himself . . . It looked very indecent, but it was decent. "It—is—decent!" Studmann said it to himself again and again. Formerly people had been luckier; then decent things had also looked decent. He was decent as well this afternoon. He could have knocked this wretched Baron down dead. And he paid for his decency by rolling drunk down the steps—what a life!

If only he'd been in the country with the rescued Prackwitz—in the peace and quiet, with long-lasting patience.

At last the taxi stopped. The girl got out and stumbled toward a house, cursing. In the uncertain light von Studmann saw only dark house-fronts. Not one café. Not a soul. Something like a shop, a chemist's apparently. The girl knocked at a ground-floor window next to the shop door, waited, knocked again.

"Where are we?" von Studmann asked the driver.

"Near Warschauer Brücke," said the man sullenly. "Are you paying for the taxi? It'll cost you a mint of money."

"Yes," said Studmann.

The window on the ground floor had opened; a large pale head above a white nightshirt appeared and seemed to be whispering maledictions. The girl pleaded and begged in a mournful whine.

"He's not dishing any up," said the driver. "What do you expect, being dragged out of his bed in the middle of the night like that? And he can go to jail for it. A skirt like that won't keep her mouth shut. Well, what did I tell you!"

The nightshirt had angrily shouted, "No! No!" and slammed the window. The girl could be heard weeping, inconsolable and at the same time angry. Von Studmann could already see her collapsing. He got out of the taxi to help her.

But she was on him with several very quick, short steps.

"What's the idea?" he cried.

She had wrenched the walking stick from his hand and ran, before he could get it away from her, back to the window—all without a word, sobbing. This sobbing was particularly horrible. And now she had shattered the windowpane with one blow. Loudly the glass rattled on to the pavement . . .

"Swindler! Fat pig!" screamed the girl. "Are you going to give me the snow?"

"Let's shove off," suggested the driver. "The cops must have heard that. Look, now the windows are being lit up."

And, indeed, here and there in the dark house-fronts appeared lights. A weak high voice shouted, "Quiet!"

But it was quiet now, for the two by the broken window were whispering to each other. The pale-faced man was no longer cursing, or only softly.

"There you are!" drawled the driver. "Them that starts with such people have got to do what they want. She doesn't care whether the cops come and shut up his shop so long as she gets her dope. Shall we drive on?"

But Studmann could not make up his mind to do this. Even if the girl had behaved irresponsibly and meanly, he couldn't drive off and leave her in the street, when the police might come strolling round the corner at any moment. And then there was that other business—that if she got her snow, then he would ring up the police. Once again he saw himself with the receiver in hand: "Gambling division of the criminal police, please." There was nothing else for it. Prackwitz must be saved. One had one's obligations.

The girl was back, and von Studmann had no need to ask whether her expedition was successful. The way she suddenly regarded him, the way she addressed him, the way he began to exist for her again, made it easy to guess that she had got her snow and had already sniffed it.

"Well?" she asked challengingly and held his stick out to him. "Who are you? Oh, yes, you're the pal of the young man who hit me. Nice friends you have, I must say, hitting a lady in the kisser!"

"You are wrong," said von Studmann politely. "It was not the young man— who, by the way, isn't my friend—who hit you like that. It was someone else, one of the two men who always stand next to the croupier."

"Do you mean Curly Willi? No, don't spring any yarns on me—I wasn't born yesterday. It was your pal, the one who brought you along. Well, I'll pay him out!"

"Shall we drive on?" suggested von Studmann. He felt dog-tired, tired of this woman and of her cheeky, quarrelsome tone, tired of this aimless wandering about in the gigantic city, tired of all the disorder, the filth, the wrangling.

"Of course we'll drive on!" she said at once. "Do you think I'm going to pad the hoof to the West End? Driver, Wittenbergplatz."

But now the driver rebelled, and since he didn't find it necessary to speak like a gentleman, and since the gent had declared himself ready to pay the fare, he didn't mince his words, but told her plainly what he thought of an old doper like her who broke windows. He announced that he wouldn't drive her a step farther, not to save his life! He declared he would have chucked her out long ago if the gent hadn't been there . . .

This abuse made little impression on the lady. She was used to it; in some ways quarreling was her natural element. It enlivened her, and the drug she had just taken lent wings to a fancy which proved vastly superior to that of the rather dense driver. She would report him to his employer. She had a friend— she had noted the number of his car. He needn't be surprised if he found his tires slit tomorrow morning!

A silly, endless altercation. The exhausted von Studmann wanted to put an end to it, but he lacked animation and was no match for them. When would it end? Windows were being lit up again, voices were again calling for quiet . . .

"But I say, please . . ." he protested feebly.

Suddenly the noise was over, the quarrel at an end. It had not even been pointless: the parties had come to a friendly understanding. True, they were not going to drive as far as Wittenbergplatz, but all the same they were going to drive "a step," namely as far as Alexanderplatz.

"My garage is close by there," explained the driver, and this explanation prevented von Studmann from reflecting any further on their objective, Alexanderplatz. For otherwise it would undoubtedly have occurred to him that in

Alexanderplatz stood the very Police Headquarters whose gambling squad he now had to phone up, seeing that the girl had obtained what she wanted. But he could think of nothing except of getting into the taxi again and being able to settle down comfortably. He was really very tired. It would be good if he could now have forty winks. Sleep is never so good as in a softly rattling car. But it wasn't worth sleeping between here and Alexanderplatz—it would make him feel even more tired. He lit a cigarette.

"You might offer a lady a cigarette!"

"Help yourself!" said von Studmann, and offered her his case.

"No thanks!" she said sharply. "Do you think I need your rotten cigarettes? I've got some myself. You should be polite to a lady."

She fetched a case out of her bag, brusquely demanded a light, and then said: "How do you think I'm going to pay your friend out?"

"He's not my friend," said von Studmann mechanically.

"I'll give him something to remember me by, that lad! Sauce the chap's got, hitting a lady. How does he come to have so much cash this evening? He usually hasn't got any, the little squirt!"

"I really don't know," said von Studmann wearily.

"All right! If he doesn't have his money taken off him in the club, I'll see that he gets rid of it. You can be sure of that. When I'm through with him he won't have a penny left."

"My dear Fräulein!" pleaded von Studmann. "Won't you let me smoke my cigarette in peace? I've already told you the gentleman is not my friend."

"Yes, you and your friends!" she said angrily. "Hitting a lady! But I'll peach on him—your friend!"

Von Studmann remained silent.

"Don't you hear? I'll peach on your friend!"

Silence.

Scornfully: "Don't you know what peaching means? I'm going to squeal on your friend."

Through the open glass partition came the driver's voice: "Hit her one on the jaw. Right on the jaw. That's what she deserves. Your friend was quite right; he's a right 'un, he knows what to do! Keep hitting it till she shuts up. Here are you running up all this expense with the taxi, and then she comes out with a lot of common talk about squealing!"

The quarrel between the two sprang into life once more. The glass partition was repeatedly wrenched open and again slammed shut, the taxi echoed with the screaming and shouting.

He ought to pay a little more attention to his steering, thought von Studmann. But what does it matter? If we hit something, at least this noise will stop.

However, they arrived safely at Alexanderplatz. Still cursing, the girl clambered out of the taxi, stumbling over von Studmann's legs. "And a man like that thinks he's a gentleman," she shouted back into the car, and dashed off across the square toward a large building where only a few windows were lit up.

"There she goes!" said the driver. "And she'll do a whole lot of talking if the cop lets her in; she's really going to do what she said. And she's done some pretty shady things herself. If they ask her whether she dopes she'll be in the soup at once. Perhaps they'll pinch her on the spot. Well, I shan't be sorry."

"What's that?" von Studmann asked pensively, looking at the large building under whose gateway the girl had just whispered.

"Well, I say!" The driver was very astonished. "You must be a stranger here. Why, that's Police Headquarters! Where she's going to squeal on your friend."

"What's she going to do?" Von Studmann suddenly woke up.

"Squeal on your friend!"

"Why?"

"I think you must have been asleep during the row. Because he socked her! Even I understood that much."

"No?" said Studmann very excited. "What for? One doesn't go running to Police Headquarters because of a box on the ears."

"How should I know? Do I know what your friend's been getting up to? Anyway, you've been asking some funny questions yourself about gambling clubs and such-like. I suppose she's going to blow the gaff to the cops!"

"Here!" Von Studmann jumped out of the taxi. Resolved as he had been a moment ago to denounce the gambling club, he was now equally convinced that this malicious girl's denunciation must be prevented.

"Here!" also shouted the taxi driver, seeing his fare money, and a lot of fare money indeed, running away. And there came for the impatient feverish Studmann an endless arguing, a reckoning-up that went on and on. "Taxi comes to so much." Reckoned out in pencil, and reckoned out in three different ways. "And then the extras . . ."

At last Studmann was able to run across the square, and then again he had to argue with the policeman on duty, who couldn't understand what he wanted; whether he was looking for a lady or the gambling squad, whether he wanted to lay information or prevent its being laid. . . .

Ah, the placid, the cool, the calm, the collected ex-lieutenant and ex-hotel manager von Studmann! He had completely lost his head at the thought that someone wanted to report his friend Prackwitz and young Pagel for illegal gambling. Yet he had had the same idea himself only half an hour ago.

In the end, however, he obtained permission to enter, and the policeman told him how to get to the Night Division, for that seemed to be his objective and not the gambling squad, as he had hitherto believed. Nevertheless, not having paid attention to these directions, he soon lost himself in the huge, badly lit building. Through passages and up stairs he trotted, the hollow echo of his footsteps with him. He knocked at doors from behind which no answer came, and at others from which he was gruffly or sleepily sent on. In his weariness it seemed to him as if he were in a dream that would never end. Until at last he stood outside the right door and heard the sharp voice of the girl inside.

And at the same moment it occurred to him how senseless was his errand, for he could say no word to refute the denunciation; no, he would even have to confirm it. For it *was* a gambling club, and it *was* illegal gambling. He ought rather to run off as fast as he could to the club, and get the two of them away before the police came.

He retraced his footsteps, slunk guiltily past the policeman on duty. He would have to hurry in order to get there before the police; happily he remembered that here he was right next to the subway, and that he could get to the West End more quickly that way than by taxi. He ran over to the station and wandered around among the closed booking offices until it dawned on him that there were no more trains at this time of night. He would have to take a taxi after all. And at last he found one, and sank down in its cushions with relief.

Immediately he sat up again. Hadn't he heard a police car just then?

Suddenly he became conscious of the stupidity of his actions the whole evening. Am I the same Studmann who never lost his head in battle? he thought with horror. And he felt as if he were no longer himself, but a hateful, fidgety, senseless person. "Cursed times!" he said, beating himself on the breast. "Damnable times, which steal people from themselves. But I shall get out of it all—I'm going to the country, and shall become myself again, as truly as I'm Studmann! But I must get there first—I can't let them be caught."

IX

Certain of victory, Wolfgang Pagel stepped into the gambling room with the Rittmeister beside him. In his closed hand he loosely held the seventeen counters from the first game, shaking them with a saucy gay, rattle. He knew that this time he was going to the game in a different spirit. Always before he had played wrongly, devised idiotic systems which were bound to fail. But now he must do it as he had today; wait for an inspiration and then stake. Then wait until another inspiration came—perhaps endless waiting. But he must have patience.

"Yes, very nice. Very," he said in smiling reply to the Rittmeister, who had asked something. Prackwitz looked at him in astonishment. Probably he had made some ridiculous reply, but it didn't matter, he was really near the gambling table now.

At this time the table was more densely besieged than ever. It was the last hour; at three, or half-past three at the latest, they closed down here. All the players who, exhausted, had stood against the wall and smoked, all who had sat undecided in armchairs and on settees—all now thronged round the table. Time was escaping, but once again offering the prospect of great winnings. Take your chance! When the city awakes in a few hours, you'll either be rich or poor. Wouldn't you prefer rich? The incident with Pagel had long been forgotten; no one took any notice of him. Seeing no possibility of getting close to the table, he went right round it and with his shoulder he forced himself between croupier and assistants. Curly Willi, the thick-set bruiser from Wedding, was on the point of making an angry protest against this irregularity when a quiet word from the croupier stopped him.

Wolfgang Pagel shook his seventeen counters lightly in his hand. He wanted to make a bet. With a mocking smile under his moustache, the croupier reminded the old gambler that he couldn't make a bet while the ball was rolling.

Wolfgang had to wait, and it was as if time stood still. Finally the ball came to a halt. A number was called out. The other players raked in their profits, ridiculous, paltry, insignificant profits.

Wolfgang's hand descended upon the green cloth!

Seventeen counters lay on the number seventeen.

The croupier gave him a swift side glance and smiled slightly. Calling to the players for the last time to make their stakes, he seized the knob, the wheel began to turn, the ball rolled. . . .

His game began—the game of Wolfgang Pagel, at the time without occupation, ex-lover of a girl named Petra Ledig—that game for which he had been waiting a year, no, a lifetime, for which he had, in fact, become what he had become; for whose sake he had quarreled with his mother; for whose sake he had taken to himself a girl who had shortened for him the period of waiting, and who had gone when the time was right. We have staked on seventeen, seventeen counters on number seventeen . . .

Attention, we are playing! Seventeen brings a win of thirty-six to one—the ball rolls ceaselessly, rattling, rattling. . . . We still have time to reckon out in millions and milliards what we shall win when seventeen turns up . . . If the ball were made of bone we could say that the bones of the dead in their crypts rattle like it. But we are alive, and playing.

"Seventeen!" called the croupier.

There, is he not calling it out? It is the hour of judgment. The black sheep will be shorn but the just—they shall be crowned! There is a rattling down of counters, a rain, a flood, a deluge. Into my pockets with them! Wait. I also want to stake. Isn't there a chair free for a player like me? What am I staking on? I must be calm, reflect . . . I shall stake on red. Red is correct, I once reckoned it out, a long, long time ago. Look, there's a chair!

"Here, my son, here are ten dollars, good American dollars. Do you remember how you wanted to hit me on the jaw before? Ha-ha-ha!"

I mustn't make so much noise? I disturb the others? The others can go to the devil! What do I care about the others with their measly stakes. They play to win, to hoard filthy paper money. I play for the sake of the game, for the sake of life . . . I am King!

Red!

He sat there and stared, suddenly morose, mistrustful. Were those enough counters? He piled them up before him in heaps of ten and, his hands trembling with excitement immediately, pushed them over again. They all wanted to cheat him here, rob him. After all, he was only the Pari Panther, a nobody in a shabby tunic. That dog, the croupier, had always treated him like a thief—he would pay him back for it!

And he staked again and won again, and Fortune returned to him. Blissful ecstasy never before experienced, like a cloud in the summer sky, and underneath the heavy dark earth with its vulgar people and their heavy distorted faces. Fly away, heavenly clouds and heavenly gods—O happiness!

What fell there? What's gushing? What's falling?

Like a brook the counters fell merrily splashing through his arms onto the floor, for he could no longer gather them together. Let them fall, Fortune is smiling on me! Let others bend down for them . . . We have enough, and we shall get still more!

How morose the croupier looks, how his beard bristles! Yes, we're going to fleece you today, my son. You shall slink back to your hole as bare as a rat— soon you'll have no counters left and you'll have to bring out your paper money; today we're taking everything!

What does the Rittmeister want? He has lost everything? Yes, you must know how to play. Do it like me, Rittmeister; after all, I've shown you how.

Here you have paper money, American dollars, 250 dollars. No, ten were given to Curly Willi—240 then! Yes, tomorrow morning we'll settle it up, but in half an hour this money too will come back to me by way of the croupier.

The game is turning? The ball no longer rolls as he wants it to?

Yes, it is a fact: one shouldn't give away money in the middle of a game; it brings bad luck.

He sat there gloomily, he tried the pari chances again, the three-to-one chances. He played cautiously, with calculation. But the counters between his arms dwindled, the ranks became thin. Again and again the army of the defeated rattled away beneath the croupier's rake. The croupier smiled again.

And the players no longer looked at Pagel; they took no more notice of him. They boldly went on placing their stakes over his shoulder again. He was no longer a favored player; he was a player like the rest. Luck smiled on him once, then forgot him again; he was the plaything of fortune, not its bed-fellow.

What had he been doing the whole time? How long had he been sitting here?

Already he was fishing in his pockets, the stream had dried up. Had he immediately forgotten the lesson Fate had taught him? He must back seventeen—seventeen counters on seventeen—that's what it was.

Seventeen!

And the rattle of the counters!

The ecstasy returned, remoteness from the world, and sun. He sat there, his head bent slightly forward, a lost smile on his lips. He could stake as he liked, the stream now gushed again. And then happened what he had been expecting: the counters gave out. Now notes were coming to him, more and more. They crackled, they looked up at him with dull colors—ridiculous paper marks, valuable pound notes, exquisite dollars, fat contented gulden, substantial Danish kronen—booty from the wallets of fifty or sixty visitors. It all streamed to him.

The croupier looked as gloomy as death, as if he had been seized by a sickness and was suffering intolerable pains. He could hardly control himself. Curly Willi had already run twice into the anteroom for fresh money, the day's takings had to be brought. Soon you'll have to use your wallet, croupier!

Croupier murmured something about closing down, but the players protested, threatened. . . . Hardly any of them were playing now; they were watching the duel between croupier and Pagel. They trembled for the young man. Would luck remain true to him? He was one of them, the born gambler; he was revenging all their losses on the wicked old vulture, the croupier. This young man didn't love money as did the croupier—he loved the game! He was no exploiter.

And young Pagel sat there, ever more smiling, ever more calm. With excitement the Rittmeister whispered at his shoulder. Pagel merely shook his head with a smile.

The Rittmeister shouted: "Pagel, man, stop now. You've got a fortune!"

No, the Rittmeister was no longer embarrassed to shout in this room, but Pagel smiled unheedingly. He was here and yet was far away. He wanted this to go on forever, endlessly through the eternities. That's what we live for! The wave of Fortune bears us on. Inexpressible feeling of joy in existence. This is how a tree must feel which, after days of tormented rising of its sap, unfolds all its blossoms in an hour. What is the croupier? What is money? What is the game itself? Roll on, little ball, roll. Did I ever think that the bones of the dead rattled like that?

Glory of heaven! Red? Of course red, and once more red. And red again. But now we'll take black—otherwise life has no savor. Without a slight mingling of black, life has no savor. Still more bank notes. Where shall I put them all? I should have brought a suitcase with me—but who could anticipate a thing like this?

What does Studmann want again? What's the shouting? Police? What does he mean by police—what does he want police for? Where are they all running to? Stop, let the ball finish rolling! I win once more, I win again, always again! I am the eternal winner . . .

Here are the police! Now all the players are standing as silent as their own ghosts. What does the funny man with the bowler hat want? He is saying something to me. All gambling money is confiscated. All money? But, of course, it's all gambling money—money for gambling—otherwise it would have no sense. What else is it for?

We are to get ready and come along? Of course we are coming along; if there's to be no more playing we might as well come. Why is the Rittmeister arguing with the man in blue? There's no sense in that. If we can't play, nothing matters!

"Come along, Herr Rittmeister, be calm. Look, Studmann is also going along, and he hasn't played once. So let's go."

How deathly pale the croupier looks! Yes, for him it is bad. He was losing—I, however, won as I've never won in my life! It was wonderful beyond words. Good night!

At last I can sleep peacefully, I have achieved what I longed for; as far as I'm concerned, I can sleep forever. Good night!

X

In a little courtroom in Police Headquarters at Alexanderplatz a wretched old incandescent lamp cast its reddish light on the faces of those arrested in the gambling club, some scowling, some silent and depressed, others sleepy or eagerly chatting. Only the croupier and his two assistants had been led off separately—all the rest had been driven into this room as they got out of the police wagon, and the doors had been locked on the outside in order to dispense with a guard. Now wait until your turn comes!

At long intervals the door to an adjoining room opened, a weary-looking, wrinkled clerk motioned to the man standing nearest him, and that man vanished and did not return. Then after an interminable period, the next was summoned.

Headquarters were extremely busy. The murder of Oberwachtmeister Leo Gubalke had led to a series of raids, and there was no lack of objectives for these raids, unfortunately. Gangs were rounded up, receivers' dens visited, night clubs inspected, naked-dancing resorts combed out, accommodation and assignation hotels were searched, station waiting rooms and down-and-out shelters scanned. . . .

Incessantly was heard from the square the exciting, nervous trilling of the patrol wagons setting out or returning with fresh hordes of arrested. Every room, every hall was packed full. Exhausted secretaries, clerks half asleep; gray-looking typists kept inserting fresh sheets of paper in their typewriters; in hoarse voices officials asked questions so quietly that they could hardly be understood.

Assault.

Immorality.

Unnatural vice.

Petty larceny.

Pocket-picking.

Housebreaking.

Robbing drunks.

Begging.

Street robbery.

Illegal possession of firearms.

Cheating.

Illegal gambling.

Receiving.

Passing of counterfeit money.

Drug-trafficking.

Procuring, trivial and serious cases of.

Blackmail.

Living on immoral earnings.

An endless list, the wearisome deathly menu of crimes, vices, misdemeanors, trespasses . . . Over their charge-sheets the officials almost nodded to sleep. . . . Then suddenly they started shouting, until their voices once more gave way. . . . An ever-rising flood of lies, evasions, distortions, denunciations. (And in the Government printing works, in a hundred auxiliary ones, they were preparing for the coming day its new abundance of money, poured out in overwhelming superfluity upon a starving, brutalized people who from day to day increasingly lost all feeling of self-respect and propriety.)

"It's enough to drive one mad," cried Rittmeister von Prackwitz, jumping up for the tenth time to pace the room. The fact that, in doing so, he had to avoid half a dozen men likewise engaged by no means improved his temper. Snorting, he stopped in front of his old comrade. "How much longer do you think we'll have to stay here? Until the gentlemen condescend, eh? It's monstrous, arresting me."

"Now, just keep calm," pleaded von Studmann. "Anyway, I don't believe we're arrested."

"Of course we're arrested," cried the Rittmeister still more angrily. "The windows are barred and the doors locked. Don't you call that arrested? Ridiculous. I'd just like to know what you think an arrest looks like, then."

"Be calm, Prackwitz. Getting excited won't do any good."

"Be calm, of course, be calm! It's all very well for you to talk—you haven't got a family, you haven't got a father-in-law. I'd just like to see how calm you would be if you had Geheimrat Horst-Heinz von Teschow as your father-in-law."

"He won't find out. I tell you, we only have to show our identification papers and then they'll let us go. Nothing will happen."

"Then why don't they let me go? Here are my papers—I have them in my hand. I must get away, my train's going, I have to take my harvesters to the country—I say, you—listen, Herr what's-your-name?" He rushed upon the clerk who had just appeared. "I demand to be released at once. First they take all my money from me—"

"Later, later," said the clerk indifferently. "First calm yourself a little. *You* are to come along now," and he motioned to a fat man.

"First calm myself!" said von Prackwitz to Studmann. "That's simply ridiculous. How can I calm myself when I'm treated in this way?"

"No, really, Prackwitz, pull yourself together. If you go on fuming like this, they'll keep us to the last. And then I ask one more thing of you: don't shout at the officials."

"Why shouldn't I shout at them? I'll blow them up properly. Keeping me here for hours!"

"For half an hour."

"Anyway, they're used to being shouted at. They're all old noncoms and sergeants—you can see it."

"But you're not here as their superior, Prackwitz. It's not their fault that you were caught gambling."

"No. But just look at young Pagel, the roué. Sits there as if the business didn't trouble him at all, smirking and grinning like some Buddha. What are you grinning like that for, Pagel?"

"I was just thinking," said Pagel, smiling, "how crazily everything happened today. Over a year I've been struggling for a little money and today I get it, piles and piles. Snap! It's confiscated."

"And that makes you laugh? Well, you've got a funny sense of humor."

"And then another thing," Pagel went on, unheeding. "This afternoon I wanted to get married . . ."

"You see, Pagel," said Rittmeister triumphantly, suddenly in a good temper. "I guessed at once in Lutter and Wegner's that you were worried about a woman."

"Yes. And this evening I heard that my dear intended had been arrested for something and taken to Police Headquarters. . . . And now I'm sitting here, too."

"Why was she arrested?" asked the Rittmeister curiously, for the consideration of events did not interest him so much as the events themselves.

Von Studmann shook his head, and Pagel remained silent.

The Rittmeister recollected himself. "I'm sorry, Pagel; of course, it's no concern of mine. But it beats me why you sit there pleased and grinning just because of that, I must say. After all, it's an extremely sad business."

"Yes," said Pagel. "It is. It's funny. Very funny. If I had won the money only twenty-four hours earlier, she wouldn't have been arrested and we would now have been married. Really very funny."

"I wouldn't think about it any more, Pagel," suggested von Studmann. "That's all finished and done with now, thank God. In a few hours we'll all be sitting together in the train."

There was a silence. Then Prackwitz cleared his throat. "Give me a cigarette, Pagel. No, you'd better not. I owe you so much already."

Pagel waved his hand. "That's all gone."

"But, man, don't talk such nonsense! You lent me money. Do you remember how much you gave me?"

"Doesn't matter," said Pagel. "I wasn't meant to have any of it; that's been proved."

"Gambling debts are debts of honor, Herr Pagel," declared the Rittmeister sternly. "You shall get your money back, you can depend on that. Of course, it won't be possible at once. First we must have the harvest in and begin thresh-ing. . . . Are you coming with me?"

"What, just in order to wait for the money?" said Pagel sullenly. "I'd like to start doing something worth while at last . . . if I only knew what. But if you have some proper work for me, Herr Rittmeister—"

"Of course I've got work for you, man," said the Rittmeister excitedly. "You've no idea how much I've been wanting a couple of reliable men. To give out fodder, pay wages, distribute allowances, make a tour of inspection through the fields every now and again at night—you can't imagine the things that are stolen from me."

"And forests and fields," added von Studmann. "Trees, animals—no brick houses with falling façades, no cocaine, no gambling clubs."

"No, of course not," said the Rittmeister eagerly. "You would have to promise me, Pagel, that you won't gamble as long as you're with me. That's quite out of the question." He turned red. "It doesn't really matter if you don't promise," he said a little blusteringly. "I can't really insist on that. Well, what do you say?"

"I'll come to the station tomorrow morning in any case and tell you then," said Pagel hesitatingly. "Eight o'clock at Schlesische Bahnhof—that was it, wasn't it?"

Prackwitz and Studmann looked at each other. The Rittmeister made an almost angry gesture. "Hasn't Fate answered your question yet?" said Stud-mann. Pagel kept silent. "For the game was your question, wasn't it, Pagel?"

"But I won," said Wolfgang obstinately.

"And sit here without anything!" laughed the Rittmeister scornfully. "Be a man, Pagel! I find your indecision horrible. Pull yourself together. Give up gambling."

"Are you worried about the girl?" asked Studmann.

"A little," admitted Pagel. "It's really so strange for me to be sitting here, too."

"Well, do what you must do," cried the Rittmeister angrily. "I'm not going to beg you to come to Neulohe."

"In any case, we shall be seeing each other at the station," added von Stud-mann hastily, for someone was calling out. From the adjoining room came a thick-set man who ran to doors and windows, inspected them, shook his head. "Thieves! What a nerve, robbing the police!" he shouted.

He hammered against the door. Officer, open up! Hey, Tiede, see that no one escapes—!

Confusion, yells, laughter.

Policemen entered. The fat Criminal Commissar stormed up and down. "Get into line, all of you. We're going to search you. Will you be quiet over there? Look under the tables and chairs as well."

It appeared that one or two of these arrested had not known how to employ the time more usefully than by screwing off the bronze door- and window-fittings. There were no more door-handles, no more window-handles, no more lock-fittings. Even the policemen laughed. The Commissar himself could not but smile.

"What a nerve! Have you ever heard of such a thing? Of course the fellow's already gone, or the fellows, for there must have been a few of them—one man couldn't have hidden it all. I questioned them and noticed nothing! Well, I shall have to look through the identity lists at once."

"A moment, Herr Commissar!" called Studmann.

"What do you want? You heard, didn't you? I haven't any time now. Oh, it's you, man. I'm very sorry, Oberleutnant von Studmann. The light's so bad. What are you doing in our shop, my old friend of the Baltic Corps? Well, come along, then; of course it's your turn next. Only a few formalities, but you'll get a fine. Still, you needn't turn gray because of that; the currency devaluation will settle that. Your friends? How do you do, Rittmeister? How do you do, Lieutenant? I'm Commissar Künnecke, formerly quartermaster-sergeant in the Rathenower Hussars. . . . Yes, this is how we meet again. Wretched times, aren't they? So you're the young man who made that enormous pile? Incredible. And just then the wicked police had to come in! Yes, the money has gone bye-bye; we don't give it back again. What we have we keep. Ha, ha! But you shouldn't let it worry you. Money of that sort never yet brought any luck—thank your Creator you are rid of it! The doorknobs? Our colleagues will enjoy pulling our legs tomorrow. I still can't help laughing. It was good bronze—they'll get a sack of money from the old-iron merchant. All right, and now the personal details. Herr von Studmann—occupation?"

"Reception manager."

"You? Lordy, lordy, lordy! What have we come down to? You—reception manager! Excuse me, Herr Oberleutnant . . ."

"Certainly, certainly—and at that I am an ex-reception manager, now agricultural apprentice."

"Agricultural apprentice? That's better. Even very good. Land is the only real thing today. When were you born?"

XI

Outside a door lined with sheet-metal stood a table, an ordinary deal table, on which lay a packet of sandwiches and a thermos flask. At the table sat an old man in police uniform, reading a newspaper by the very weak illumination of a fanlight. Hearing footsteps coming along the passage, he lowered the paper and glanced up over his pince-nez.

The young man came slowly nearer. At first it seemed as if he was about to walk past the table. "Excuse me," he said, "does this lead to the police prison?"

"It does," said the official, folding his paper carefully and laying it on the table. "But it is only a door for those on duty," he added.

The young man hesitated. "Well, what's on your mind? Do you want to give yourself up?" the old man asked.

"What do you mean—give myself up?" asked Pagel.

"Well," said the old man slowly, "it's getting on for four. Sometimes about this hour someone who is troubled because he's been up to something comes and gives himself up. But then you must go to the Night Division. I'm only on duty at the door."

"No," said Pagel, "I've not been up to anything." He fell silent. Then, seeing the old man's calm glance: "I only want to speak to my girl-friend. She's inside there." And he motioned with his head toward the door.

"Now?" The old man was almost indignant. "At night, between three and four?"

"Yes."

"Then you have really been getting up to something which won't let you rest?"

Pagel made no reply.

"There's nothing doing. Visits aren't allowed now. And anyway . . ."

"Isn't it possible at all?"

"Absolutely impossible!" The old man reflected. At last he said: "And you know it as well as I do. You're just standing here like this because it won't let you rest."

"I'm here in the police station quite by accident. I didn't come here on purpose."

"But you came to this door on purpose? It wasn't easy to find at night, eh?"

"No."

"There, you see," said the old man. "It's just the same with you as with those who come to give themselves up; they also say that they don't come because of a bad conscience. Bad conscience! There's no such thing anymore. Why do you come, then, at two or three in the night? That's a strange time. A man's alone with himself then; he suddenly gets very different thoughts from the daytime. And then he comes here."

"I don't know," said Pagel gloomily. And he really did not. He didn't want to leave Berlin without at least having asked her whether it was true. Sometimes he told himself that the official must have misinformed him—it was preposterous. He knew Petra! And then again he told himself that an official wouldn't tell him anything that was untrue; he had no interest in telling him a lie. Yes, the game was finished; victory had turned into defeat. How alone Peter now is. Peter—someone was once with him, something alive, that clung to him. Is everything now lost?

"I am going away early tomorrow morning," he pleaded. "Can't anything be done tonight? No one need notice anything."

"What are you thinking?" cried the old man. "There are night warders inside. No, it's absolutely impossible." He thought for a moment, looked at Pagel critically. "And anyway . . ."

"What do you mean—'and anyway'?" Pagel asked, somewhat angrily.

"And anyway, visitors are not usually permitted."

"And unusually?"

"Unusually neither."

"I see," said Pagel.

"This is a police prison here," said the old man, feeling there was some need to explain the situation. "In the remand prison the examining magistrate can give permission for visits, but here it's not allowed. Most of them only stay with us a few days."

"A few days? . . ."

"Yes. Perhaps you can inquire next week in Moabit Prison."

"Is it quite certain that I can't visit her tomorrow morning? No exceptions are made?"

"None at all. But naturally, if you know something to prove that your girl-friend is inside without cause, and tell it to the Commissar tomorrow, then she'll come out—that's plain."

Pagel reflected.

"But you don't look as if you had any information of that sort, do you? Otherwise you wouldn't come here to me at night. You just want to have an ordinary talk with your girl-friend, don't you—in private?"

"I wanted to ask her something," said Pagel.

"Well, write her a letter, then," said the old man kindly. "If there's nothing in it about the charge she's here for, then it'll be handed over to her, and she'll also be allowed to reply."

"But it's precisely about the charge that I want to ask her!"

"Well, young fellow, then you'll have to be patient. If you want to inquire about that, you can't do it in the remand prison, either. Until the charge has been tried, nobody is allowed to discuss the matter with her."

"How long will that take?" asked Pagel desperately.

"Well, that depends entirely on the charge. Has she confessed?"

"That's just it. She has confessed, but I don't believe her. She's confessed something she hasn't done."

The old man seized his newspaper very angrily. "Now run along to bed," he said. "If you want to persuade a self-confessed prisoner to withdraw her confession, then you can wait a long time for permission to visit her. And you won't be allowed to write to her, either, which is to say, she won't get your letter. You certainly have a nerve. You want me to help you to visit her secretly. No, you go home. I've had enough."

Pagel stood there, uncertain. "But it does happen sometimes that someone confesses to a thing he hasn't done. I've often read it."

"So you've read that, have you?" asked the old man almost venomously. "Then let me tell you, young fellow, anyone who makes a false confession has always been up to something worse. Yes, a man confesses to housebreaking because at the same hour he committed a murder. That's how it is. And if your girl-friend's confessed, then she'll very well know why. I wouldn't do any persuading if I was you. Otherwise she'll find herself in a worse mess." The old man squinted angrily at Pagel through his pince-nez.

Pagel, however, stood as if thunder-struck. New light had been thrown on Petra's confession. Yes, she had confessed to street-walking in order to escape something worse; she had confessed to street-walking in order to escape him. Prison was better than living with Wolfgang Pagel. Faith lost, confidence lost—gone from him, gone from the world, away from the intolerable to that which could be tolerated! A big win lost again—gone, vanished. . . .

"Thank you very much," he said very politely. "You have given me good advice." And he went slowly down the passage, followed by the old man's suspicious glance.

It was the right hour to fetch his things from Tannenstrasse. At this hour his mother would certainly not be expecting him; she would be sound asleep. In Alexanderplatz he would certainly find a taxi. Thank God that Studmann had lent him some money. Studmann, the non-gambler, the only capitalist; Studmann the helpful. He could almost think of Studmann and Neulohe with pleasure.

Chapter Nine

A New Start to a New Day

I

A girl and a man are lying on a bed in a hotel room. The man is against the wall in the narrow bed. A light whistling accompanies his breathing through his nose. The girl has just awoken, her chin resting on her folded arms, lying on her stomach, blinking at the night table which is already bright.

Sophie Kowalewski had been on a jaunt in the old city and had then landed up in an hotel on Weidendamm Bridge. Hence the hooting of the steamer. Steamers sail on the Spree—or wasn't this the Spree?

Quietly, so as not to wake the man, Sophie Kowalewski slipped out of bed, ran to the window, and raised a corner of the curtain. The sky stood a bright blue above the iron curves of the bridge.

I shall have wonderful weather in Neulohe, she thought. Marvelous thing, to lie under a tree at the edge of the wood and let yourself roast. No mistress. No bathing suit, thank you. And when there's the moon, to bathe quite naked in the cold grayish pond in the middle of the forest. . . .

She let the curtain fall and quickly began to dress. She gave herself a slight rinse and gargled hastily—she could do all that thoroughly in the hostel; she would still have time before the train went. A joyful excitement, something like the anticipation of approaching happiness, filled her. Neulohe . . . the lilac bush behind the fire station, where she had experienced her first kiss—Oh, God! In the hostel she would put on fresh underwear. The things she had on filled her with disgust.

She was ready. Bag in hand, she peered hesitantly toward the bed. She made two steps in its direction and murmured very cautiously: "Dearie."

No answer.

"I'm going now, darling. . . ."

No answer, only a light whistling through his nose.

It was not a sudden inspiration which made Sophie look at the sleeper's clothes, untidily thrown over a chair. Ever since she woke she had been thinking that this stupid night might at least produce the fare to Neulohe. She had to be a little careful with her money now there were no fresh supplies to be got at home. In a flash she was by the chair. She found the wallet at once (she had watched last night where he put it).

There was not much money in it—very little for a man who had spent several millions on champagne last night. For a moment she hesitated. With a woman's eye she saw that his clothes were carefully kept, but were not new; perhaps he had scraped all his money together for this one big bust. There were such men, she knew. They saved and saved and promised themselves the world from such an evening, a happiness such as they had never yet experienced. Then they awoke next morning, sober, desperate, penniless. . . .

Sophie stood there undecided. Her glance wandered from the few bank notes to the clothes, to the sleeper. . . . This little bit of money wouldn't be any use to her. And she was on the point of putting the notes back into the wallet.

But Hans would laugh at me, she thought suddenly. Hans isn't so silly. "You must take everything," he always says. "It's the honest people who are soft." No, it serves him right, he'll take more care next time. . . . But I ought to leave him at least his fare. It's certain he's got to go to his office. At least I ought to let him get to his office in time. Oh, what do I care whether he gets there in time? Who ever bothered to see how I got home? The toffs left me standing in the street, too lazy to open the door for me; shoved me out of the taxi when they'd had what they wanted. What's the idea, fare money?

She was proud of her decision as she stuffed the miserable money into her bag. "You're right!" Hans would say. And she was right too. Whoever didn't steal got robbed. Whoever didn't bite got bitten. Good morning!

And nimbly she ran down the stairs.

II

It was already light even in the forest. Ex-bailiff Meier plodded along angrily: the suitcases were too heavy, his shoes pinched, he hadn't enough money, the road was much too far to Grünow, he hadn't slept enough, his head ached like seven monkeys.

In his path, as if sprung from the earth, suddenly stood the Lieutenant.

He was friendly, however. "Morning, Meier," he said. "I just wanted to say good-by to you."

Meier stared at him suspiciously. "Well, good-by, Lieutenant!"

"You can walk on. Take your bags and go on; we've got to go the same way for a bit."

Meier remained where he was. "I like walking alone," he said.

"Now, now!" said the Lieutenant laughing. His laugh sounded false, thought Meier, and his voice uneasy. "Surely you're not afraid of me now, when you've got a pistol in your pocket."

"It's none of your bloody business what I'm carrying in my pocket!" cried Meier angrily. But his voice trembled.

"As a matter of fact that's true," admitted the Lieutenant. "But it's important for me because now I won't fall under suspicion."

"What do you mean, fall under suspicion?" stammered Meier.

"If you are lying dead somewhere here in the forest, Herr Meier," said the Lieutenant very politely, but bitterly in earnest.

"Me—dead—ridiculous," stammered little Meier, deathly white, peering at the other's face. "I haven't done anything to you, Herr Lieutenant!"

Begging, anxious, Meier stared into the Lieutenant's eyes, but there was nothing in them, only an ice-cold look.

"Your pistol and mine, you see, are the same caliber," explained the Lieutenant pitilessly. "You're a big fool, Meier, to have taken the pistol. . . . And then you've also recently fired it. . . . But I aim better than you, Herr Meier. And I am standing so nicely to the right of you. A close shot at six inches in the right temple—every gun expert would say suicide, my dear Herr Meier. And at home the plundered safe . . . the shot at the girl. No, no, Herr Meier, don't you worry, there's no doubt about it: everything points to suicide."

The Lieutenant talked and talked. But he was not so calm as he pretended. It is one thing to shoot someone in battle or in passion; it's quite another thing to slaughter in cold blood as a result of rational considerations. Once more he reminded himself that he was risking nothing, that he was not endangering the Cause, but saving it from a traitor. And yet all the time he was wishing—gun experts and risk notwithstanding—that Meier would reach for his pistol. The bullet with which the Lieutenant would anticipate him would be so much easier than the cold-blooded bullet into that gray face.

But Meier was not thinking of the pistol in his hip pocket. "Herr Lieutenant," he stammered, "I swear to you I'll never say a word about you and Fräulein Vi. . . . Nor about the *Putsch*. . . . I'll keep to it, Herr Lieutenant. I would always be afraid you'd get me, you or one of your men. I'm a coward. Please don't shoot! I swear to you by everything that's holy to me . . ." His voice failed him, he gulped and stared fearfully at the other.

"But there's nothing that's holy to you, Meier," said the Lieutenant. He still couldn't make up his mind. "You're a thorough swine, Meier."

Black Meier stared breathlessly at the lieutenant's lips and whispered quickly, "But I can still turn over a new leaf. Believe me, Herr Lieutenant, I can still become different, I'm still young. Please, please say yes! I'll turn back, I'll confess to the Rittmeister that I stole the money. If he sends me to prison I'll go willingly. I want to reform. Please, please, Herr Lieutenant."

The Lieutenant morosely shook his head. Why had he started talking to this fellow in the first place? He should have fired at once, without a word. But now it was getting more and more repellent. The Lieutenant was not completely depraved, nor did he deceive himself; he knew that he alone had got the fellow into this mess. Meier had to die because he, the Lieutenant, couldn't restrain himself from an affair with the little Prackwitz girl. But it couldn't be helped. Meier knew too much now, he was too dangerous, even more dangerous since he had seen the pistol aimed at him.

"Pick up your bags, Meier, we're going along for a bit!"

Without a trace of resistance Meier obediently picked up his bags and looked at the Lieutenant questioningly.

"Up there along the glade!" came the order.

Meier went in front, his shoulders hunched up, as if that could stop the dreaded shot from behind. The bags were no longer heavy, his shoes no longer pinched; he walked quickly as though he could run away from the death that followed him.

If only it were over, thought the Lieutenant, his eyes never leaving the man in front. But this glade is really much too frequented. Better if they don't find him for three or four days, when there's no trace of me left.

These thoughts disgusted him. They seemed so unreal, like something from a wild dream. But here was the man before him, a real, living man. So it isn't a dream. At any minute it can come true.

"Now to the left, up the footpath, Meier!"

Obedient as a lamb! Sickening! Yes, there at the top he would do it, he must do it. . . . A traitor is always a traitor; they never change, they don't reform. . . . What's the matter with Meier? What's he shouting? Has he gone mad? Now he was running, shouting louder and louder. He had thrown down the bags at the Lieutenant's feet.

The Lieutenant jerked his pistol up—too late; he must shoot at close quarters to make it seem like suicide.

"We're coming, Herr Kniebusch!" shouted Meier, running.

There stood the forester. Beside him lay a man in the bilberries and moss, bound hand and foot.

"Thank God you've come. I couldn't drag him any further, gentlemen. I've been dragging the fellow for hours."

Freed at last from being alone with the dangerous fellow, the forester was quite talkative.

"It's Bäumer of Altlohe—you know, Meier, the worst of the whole gang! I've made a very good catch, Herr Lieutenant. This man's a criminal."

The Lieutenant stood leaning against a tree, his face rather white. But he said calmly: "Yes, you've made a good catch, forester. But I?" Full of hatred, he stared at little Meier, who returned his glance defiantly, triumphantly. . . .

"Well, good morning and good luck to you," said the Lieutenant suddenly, turning round and marching down to the glade again. Coming to the two cases, he could not restrain himself longer: he trod heavily first on one, then on the other.

"I say!" said the forester in amazement. "What's wrong with him? Why's he so queer? Did he have any trouble with his meeting? I ordered everybody to come, as he told me. Do you understand it, Meier?"

"Oh, yes," said little Meier, "I understand it. He's in a fearful temper with you."

"With me? Whatever for?"

"Because you haven't shot the stag, you know; for the young Fräulein, you know. Well, come along, Kniebusch, now we'll go together to the farm; I'll harness the hunting cart, and we'll fetch this fellow and my bags."

"Your bags? Are they yours? Are you going away, then?"

"Lord, no. . . . They're the Lieutenant's bags. I'll tell you all about it. Come along now, it's better if we walk side by side; I can't tell it so well walking behind each other like this."

III

The taxi stopped in Tannenstrasse. Only with difficulty could the driver be persuaded to come up and help carry the things.

"Yes, you say there's no one about now, but the thieves here in Berlin are always about. Especially now. And who's going to buy me a new tire, which you can't even get now? You won't, for certain."

"Well, all right, seeing as you're going on to the station, for a mug of beer and a schnapps, as they say, although I'd much rather have a coffee. I'm to be quiet? I'm as quiet as a Government when it's going to pinch money! You don't hear them, but you lose your money all right, take it from me."

"Nice house—bit gloomy, though . . . I suppose there's no central heating? But gas, you've got gas, ain't you? 'Cause gas in the house saves briquettes, and saves you buying a rope to hang yourself with. . . . Yes, I'm being quiet; you ain't half as quiet as I am. Take that lock, for instance; I'd have handled it more gently. . . . Doing a bunk, I suppose—bit behind with the rent, eh?

"Now, don't be stuck up, I was in the war, too; if you bark at me, I'll scream so loud that the pictures'll slide off the wall. I say—so this is what you call your den, eh? Marvelous, with knobs on. I didn't have this at my mother's. And a wardrobe trunk as well—that'll mean two journeys.

"I say! Who's that lying on the sofa? Gave me a start! An old woman—and she's sleeping quite peaceful. Well, I won't make another sound now; we'll let her sleep. She's earned her sleep—she's been packing the whole night, the old woman! She's your mother, ain't she? Well, I guessed it straight off. But here, I'd say good-by and bon voyage to her, seeing she's been waiting the whole night for you. . . . Been kicking over the traces, eh? Well, youngsters ain't got no feelings, I was no different when I was your age. . . . Now I'm sorry for it sometimes, now she's dead and buried in St. Matthew's churchyard. . . . Well, everybody keeps doing the same silly things; there's always mugs about.

"Well, hurry up, mate, get this traveling wardrobe on me back. I'll manage it by meself; I'll be back in a jiffy. . . . No? You want to help me down with it? Well, all right; let everyone do what he likes—let everyone be as silly as he likes, say I."

"Well, at least that's something. Write the old woman a few lines; something nice, understand! Even if it's a fib. Mothers are always pleased, they know the kids are fibbing, but still they're pleased. 'He doesn't want to hurt me,' they think.

"Well now, let's hop it. . . . Gently, young fellow, careful with the door. . . . If we wake her up now, it'll be tough luck. . . . Getting nabbed when you're doing a bunk ain't nice. Look out, can't you! Careful, idiot! You'll wake her up! Thank God, we've managed it. . . . Quietly with the passage door. . . . Quietly, I said. Quietly doesn't mean kicking up a row! Lord, is your heart hammering like mine? I was afraid we'd wake the old woman; I'm queer that way. I could bust a man like you right on the jaw—I wouldn't think twice about it—but an old woman like that . . ."

IV

It stank—it stank suffocatingly in all the corridors and stairways, in all the dormitories, in every cell, workroom and workshop of Meienburg prison. Of lavatory buckets, disinfectants, old oakum, dried vegetables that had gone moldy, dried fish and old socks, cocoa fiber and polish. Yesterday's thunderstorm had also passed over Meienburg prison, but the cool rainy air had not been able to penetrate into the white structure of cement, steel and glass dominating the town.

"Hell! What a stink again!" said the warders on morning duty, who came at a quarter to six.

"Man, how it stinks in your cell!" The station warder woke his orderly, Hans Liebschner, with a vigorous poke in the ribs. "Get up, man; in ten minutes they'll be emptying their buckets. Oh, God! It stinks so much already that all my breakfast is coming up."

"I don't smell anything, chief warder," protested Liebschner as he slid into his trousers.

"I've told you ten times that I'm a principal warder, not chief warder," growled the old man. "You won't get favors from me by sucking up, Liebschner."

"Yet there was one favor I wanted so much from you, chief warder," Liebschner said flatteringly, with an exaggerated roll of his eyes.

"And what's that, my lad?" The warder leaned against the door, swinging the heavy steel plate backwards and forwards with his shoulders, and looking not unkindly at his orderly. "You are a real gallows-bird."

"I'd like to go on outside work, with the harvest crew," begged Liebschner. "Would you suggest me for it, chief warder?"

"But why? You've got nothing to grumble about here as orderly."

"I can't stand the air," complained the prisoner in a pitiful voice. "My head's queer; I can't eat anything, and I always feel so bad from the stink. . . ."

"And just before you couldn't smell anything! No, my lad, I'll tell you what's on your mind. You want to make a getaway—you'd like to go off on the spree—with the little girls, eh? Well, you won't. You're staying here! Besides, a convict isn't permitted to go on outside labor before he's served at least half his sentence."

The prisoner, his head lowered, tied his shoes. The warder went on swinging the steel door, at the same time observing the closely cropped skull.

"Principal warder!" said the prisoner Liebschner, looking up with determination.

"Well?"

"I don't like squealing on anyone, but if I have to, then I must. I can't stand it any longer in the cell; I'm going mad."

"You don't go mad so easily, my lad."

"But I know someone who's got a steel saw. Will you swear that I shall go on outside labor if I tell you his name?"

"No one's got a steel saw here!"

"Yes—on your landing, too!"

"Nonsense. Besides, I don't arrange who goes on the outside gangs; the work inspector does that."

"But if you put in a good word for me, I'll get out."

Long pause.

"Who's got the saw?"

"Do I get into the outside gang?"

"As far as I'm concerned. Who has the saw?"

"Quietly, principal warder, please, quietly! I'll whisper it in your ear. But don't give me away. They'd kill me when I go to the workroom."

Softly the prisoner whispered in the warder's ear. The latter nodded, asked something in a whisper, listened, nodded again. Below the bell began ringing; from landing to landing echoed the cry, "Buckets! Buckets!"

The warder straightened himself. "Very well, then, Liebschner, if it's true you'll go on the outside gang. What a low-down trick! I'd have been in a nice mess! Now hurry up, man, quick, empty your bucket. Make it snappy, so that we'll get the stink over quickly!"

V

In Meienburg prison the morning bell rang at six o'clock; in Alexanderplatz police prison in Berlin it was half-past six before the prisoner was allowed to get up, before he knew that the night was over and something new would happen— perhaps even to him.

Petra was awakened by the hurried clanging; for a moment she still had Wolf's image before her. It laughed—then many things went dark. An old woman (Wolfgang's mother?) said many bad things to her in a harsh tone. A tree appeared out of the dark, leafless, with skeletal, threatening branches. A line of poetry that Wolfgang often sang sounded in her ear, *He doesn't hang from a tree, from rope hangs he.* Then her eyes were wide open. The gypsies were chattering again in the corner, gesticulating, crouched upon their mattress; the tall girl was still lying in bed, her shoulders shaking—so she was crying again; the little fat woman was standing in front of the cell mirror, no bigger than a hand, wetting her finger in her mouth and then smoothing her eyebrows with it. And Frau Krupass sat up in her bed, braiding her miserable plaits. On the floor the Hawk, in her bundle, lay motionless.

Outside, divided by iron window bars, the sky was pale blue and softly touched by sun. A new day. Now for new work! How was one to wash? There was hardly any water left in the jug. "Listen, girlie, what we agreed on last night stands, eh? Or have you changed your mind?" said the old woman.

"No," said Petra.

"I've got a feeling that you'll be getting out today. If we don't see each other again, you're to go to Killich—Lawyer Killich, on Warschauer Brücke. Will you remember that?"

"Lawyer Killich, Warschauer Brücke," repeated Petra.

"Good. You are to go there right away. But what a sight you are! Still thinking of that fellow?"

"No."

"Now, now!"

"But I believe I dreamed about him."

"Well, you won't be able to do anything about that for the moment. That'll go away by itself in time, that dreaming. But don't eat roast potatoes in the evening; tell Randolf's wife she's always to give you cold meat. Roast potatoes in the evening, and especially with onions, always bring on dreams; you mustn't eat anything like that, girlie—understand!"

"Yes," said Petra. "But I am really not so sensitive."

"What do you want to get all upset about a fellow like that for? There are plenty of men, much too many—don't you bother with them. Always cold meat and a glass of beer, then you'll go to sleep easier. Well, you'll get over it. I'm not worried about it."

"I'm not, either."

"Well, go and look after your patient; I can see you're dying to. Once a fool, always a fool. You'll never learn. I say, girlie!"

"Yes?" Petra turned round.

"I think you won't stick it, you know. If he's standing on the other side of the street and whistles and beckons, then you'll run off, out of my nice flat and away from the good food and the bath and the bed—you'd run to him just as you are, wouldn't you?" There was suspicion in the old woman's eyes.

"But Ma Krupass," said Petra smiling, "he no longer comes first now. Now I think first of *it*."

Then she started to unroll her enemy, the Hawk.

Hubert Räder was already up and at work when Vi with highly flushed cheeks entered the Villa.

"Morning, Hubert!" she cried. "Good Lord, are you making everything so terribly tidy again? Mamma has so often forbidden you to do it."

"Women don't understand anything about it," declared Räder unmoved, and regarded his work with a stern but approving eye. Since the Rittmeister was returning today, his room had to be thoroughly cleaned out. The manservant's procedure in this was first to sweep, wipe, wax, polish and dust one side of the room before beginning on the other half, by which he reduced Frau von Prackwitz to complete despair. Time and again she had explained to him that the clean side always got covered with dust again while the other half was being cleaned . . .

"Yes, madam," Räder would say obediently, "but if I am called away to some other work, the Rittmeister will at least have one clean side on which he can live." And obstinate as a mule he would go on cleaning in his own way.

Now he said meaningly: "Madam has already sneezed twice, Fräulein!"

"Yes, yes, Hubert," said Vi. "That will be all right. I shall go straight up to my room, wash, change and disarrange the bed to show I've slept in it. Oh, no, I don't think I need do that after all. I shan't need to have been lying in bed if Mamma and Papa hear of all that happened last night!"

"You'd better hurry up," said Räder. "Madam always gets up immediately after she has sneezed."

"Oh, Hubert, don't be so silly!" cried Vi reproachfully. "You are bursting with curiosity. Just imagine, little Meier ran off with the cash. But he's back again now. And old Kniebusch has caught Bäumer, but he hasn't got him here yet; he's lying tied up in the forest, and Hartig and Kniebusch and Meier have gone to fetch him with the cart. He's unconscious. Don't stand there so stupidly. Put that polisher down. What do you think about it, Hubert?"

"You talk to me too familiarly, Fräulein," said Räder coldly. "The Rittmeister won't have it, neither do I think it quite right."

"Oh, you old fathead! I don't care how I talk to you. I won't be polite to an old haddock, either. Yes, that's what you are—you're an old haddock! You'd better pay attention to what I tell you—you were there, too. And don't go and make a hash of it all if Mamma asks you. . . ."

"Excuse me, Fräulein, I was not there. If anything as outrageous as that happens then I am not there. I have got to think of my reputation. I don't mix with safe-breakers and poachers. It's just the same as with uniforms—I don't mix with them."

"But Hubert, you know that Mamma said you were to go with me. You are not going to let us down."

"Very sorry, Fräulein, it can't be done. Would you mind stepping off the rug? I have to comb its fringes. Why do people make fringes like that on carpets anyway? They always look untidy and bedraggled. I suppose it's just to give us more work."

"Hubert!" said Vi very appealingly, and suddenly despondent. "You won't tell Mamma that you didn't go with me because of the things that happened, will you?"

"No, Fräulein," said Hubert. "My nose began to bleed in the farmyard, and I said I'd come on later and didn't find you because you'd taken the path by the coach-house and I went up the glade by the deer's feeding ground."

which everything depends to an empty-headed fool for twenty-four hours, spend a mint of money, gamble away still more, return with a pile of debts to you and young Pagel, and then bring no men but have to do what my neighbors advised me to four weeks ago; that is, take a prison gang." Von Prackwitz smiled and so did Studmann, but very cautiously. "All right, then, I've done it all wrong again. But what now? We all make mistakes, Studmann. My father-in-law, too. But the main thing is to realize our mistakes. I realize mine and I shall correct them. I'm going to carry on, Studmann, and you are going to help me."

"Of course! But isn't it time for our train? You've still got to talk to the agent, haven't you? And young Pagel isn't here yet, either!"

But von Prackwitz was not listening. Was his friend talking? Or was it the upsetting experience in the night? Prackwitz was talkative. Prackwitz wanted to unburden himself. Prackwitz wanted to confess.

"You've been working now for so long in a hotel, Studmann, you must certainly have learned something about bookkeeping and budgeting and handling men. I just yell at them. We've got to manage it. What? Manage so that I can keep the farm! I know my father-in-law would be only too glad to have it back. Excuse me for talking so much about him, but he's my pet aversion. I can't stand him and he can't stand me. The old man can't bear seeing me run the farm. And if I don't scrape the rent together by the first of October, I've got to get out—and what shall I do then?" He looked at Studmann angrily. "But it's standing out there, Studmann, and we'll get it in; and now that I've got you we'll make Neulohe into a model farm. Studmann, it was a lucky stroke meeting you. But I must confess to you that I really had a shock when I saw you there, bowing obsequiously in your black coat to every loudly dressed female. How you've come down in the world, Studmann! I thought."

"There comes Pagel!" cried Studmann, all hot and cold at these confessions of a man who was usually so reserved. For the good fellow would bitterly regret it one day. And then he would be annoyed with his friend for having spoken to him like that.

But von Prackwitz was as if intoxicated. It must be the air at the Schlesische Bahnhof.

"You've got enough baggage, Pagel," he said very benevolently. "I hope you'll be able to stand it long enough to wear everything you've got there. In the country we work, you know, we don't play! All right, all right, I didn't really mean it that way! Come to that, I've been playing about myself. And now be so good as to get three second-class tickets at the booking office, as far as Frankfurt. Then we'll dash through at the last minute."

"But don't you want to talk to the agent first? After all, the men have been told to come here."

"Well, you go and get the tickets and then come straight back here, Pagel. What do you want me to say to the man? He tried to do me down; now I am doing him down."

"But that sort of thing isn't done, Prackwitz. You don't have to be afraid of explaining things. You are fully within your rights to refuse to have the men— they aren't land workers. One doesn't go sneaking off—like a schoolboy."

"Studmann, I am not a schoolboy! I must ask you . . ."

"*Like* a schoolboy, I said, Prackwitz."

"All right, then, Studmann, I shall do as I think fit."

"But I thought, Prackwitz, you wanted to have my advice."

"Of course, Studmann, of course! Now don't pull faces. I'm always glad to hear your advice, only this time, you see . . . the truth is I told the agent that the men could look as they liked so long as they had hands to work with."

"I see!"

"But I didn't think he'd send a gang like that. I can't pay a couple of hundred gold marks commission for that. Now please, go on ahead with Pagel, I'll come after you. Let me do the thing this once, as I like."

"All right, Prackwitz," said von Studmann after brief reflection. "Just this once. It isn't really right nor is it a good beginning to our co-operation but . . ."

"Off with you!" cried the Rittmeister. "Second-class smoker! Another eight minutes and good-by Berlin—thank God!"

Ascending the stairs to the platform with young Pagel, von Studmann was very thoughtful. So don't let's consider it the beginning of our cooperation. But rather the end of Berlin. He was glad that he need not see how his old comrade, by a dash to the train, avoided paying an agent's commission. Once the sight of the Rittmeister at other storming parties had helped him. What cursed times these were that could so change a man!

"So you have decided to come after all," he said to young Pagel. "It's very nice of you."

VIII

Left alone, the Rittmeister gnawed his lip and looked at the ticket in his hand, undecided. The enthusiastic mood which had made all his confessions easy vanished with his two companions. Now he was overwhelmed by the situation, which was simply sickening. Angrily wrinkling his brow, he peered into the station hall. The men had become uneasy with the approach of the time due for

departure; those sitting on the steps had got up; groups formed and were carrying on excited discussions; on the landing stood the bony agent attempting
to reassure those crowding round him. His eyes searched the hall.

The Rittmeister retreated further behind his pillar. He saw no possibility of getting through this gang of hooligans unseen. Why hadn't the damned
platform more entrances?

I'm not going to take the men, I won't take them under any circumstances.
I'm not going to make myself the laughing-stock of the whole district. Farming in silk dresses and high-heeled shoes! Not a spare shirt, not a spare pair
of trousers. If the rascals should ever get wet they'd all sit stark naked on their
bunks till their things were dry again. What a fine state of affairs! No, the convicts for me.

The Rittmeister peered round the pillar, drew back quickly. The agent had
left his elevated point of vantage; with the girl in the shabby blouse on one side
of him, the old boy with the botanist-box and frock coat on the other, he was
struggling toward the platform entrance, talking excitedly. The Rittmeister
would have liked to creep into the pillar, turn to stone, dissolve—so terrified
was he of this trio.

And just at that moment, at that most critical of critical moments, a girl's
voice, somewhat harsh but by no means unpleasant, sounded in his ear. "Oh,
the Rittmeister!"

He swung round and stared.

Yes, it was true; before him stood, as if she had fallen from heaven, the
daughter of his overseer Kowalewski, a girl whom he had always liked to see on
account of her fresh appearance and dainty beauty, so different from the rest
of the silly, clumsy girls working on the farm. He had often favored her with a
fatherly word.

"Sophie!" he said. "What are you doing here, Sophie?"

"I'm going to spend a holiday with my parents," she laughed, looking at
him in quite a daughterly way.

"Ah, Sophie," he said eagerly. "You come as if you were really sent from
heaven. See that man on the other side of the pillar, with a bald head, yes,
the tall one—don't stare like that, Sophie!—he mustn't see me under any circumstances. I've got to get to the train and there's only three minutes more.
Can't you get him away somehow, just long enough for me to flit through the
entrance hall? I have my ticket. Thanks, thanks, Sophie, I'll explain it all in the
train. You're still the same splendid girl. Hurry!"

He heard her voice, loud, very quarrelsome. "I say, don't stand in the way!
I've got to get to my train. Here, you'd better take my bags."

Fine girl! But she'd changed a lot. A bit flashy . . .

He raced off as fast as he could, not at all like a Rittmeister, not at all like an employer. The barrier. There in front was the barrier.

But perhaps the fellow had platform tickets. Queer shadows under her eyes. And her face had got fat, all its fineness gone. Bloated, yes, as if from drink . . . "I know, thanks; yes, I know, the train on the left—not the first time I'm traveling here. Thanks!"

Thank God he'd made it! But he would only be safe when the train was moving. . . . Yes, he was afraid little Sophie had already in the past got a little mixed up with the young fellows in the village, so he had heard—and Berlin was a very slippery place. He knew that to his own cost. . . . Thank God, there was Pagel waving! "Well, gentlemen, I've made it. Please, Studmann, please, Pagel—stand at the window so that no one can look in; the fellow's quite capable of inspecting the carriages. I must first mop myself; I'm simply dripping. What a run, early in the morning."

"So you got through without being molested?" asked Studmann.

"It wasn't easy! And do you know who helped me? My overseer's daughter! She happened to turn up, traveling home on holiday; she's maid to some countess here in Berlin. . . . As a matter of fact, you might keep an eye open to see whether she still makes the train; it's due to start at any moment now. You might ask her to get in here. I should like to find out how she's getting on. A fine girl—she understood straight away, without a word!"

"Yes, but what does she look like? Old, young? Fat, thin? Fair, dark?"

"Ah, Berlin hasn't done her much good. No, you'd better leave it. There would only be talk afterwards, and it would be awkward in Neulohe when we meet again. After all, she's only the daughter of my overseer! Always keep to that rule, Pagel. Keep your distance from the men—no familiarity, no mixing with them. Understand?"

"Yes, Herr Rittmeister."

"Thank God, we're off. There, spread yourselves out comfortably. Let's have a smoke. It's fine, though, to travel out of this city into the summer, eh, Studmann? Eh, Pagel?"

"Marvelous!" said Studmann. "Something has just occurred to me, Prack-witz—doesn't the man know your name?"

"Which man?"

"Why, the agent!"

"Yes, of course—why?"

"Well then, he'll write to you and ask for compensation."

"Damn it! I didn't think of that. All that farce for nothing! But I won't accept the letter; I'll refuse to take it—no one can compel me to accept it." The Rittmeister ground his teeth with rage.

"I'm very sorry, Prackwitz, but that will scarcely help."

"Yes, you are sorry, Studmann. But you should either have told me that downstairs in the station or not at all. Now it's too late! My whole journey's spoiled! And it's such nice weather!"

The Rittmeister stared angrily out of the window at his nice weather. Before Studmann could make any reply, however (and it was doubtful whether he had any great desire to do so), the door to the corridor opened and, instead of the guard, there appeared a very smart young girl. Smilingly she raised her hand to her little hat. "Orders executed, Herr Rittmeister!"

The Rittmeister jumped up, beaming. "This is fine, Sophie; so you caught the train, after all! I was already beginning to reproach myself. Gentlemen, this is Sophie Kowalewski, I've already told you . . . Herr von Studmann, Herr Pagel. The gentlemen are—ahem!—my guests. Well, that's that. And now sit down here, Sophie, and tell me all the news. Cigarette? No, of course not. Very sensible. Young girls shouldn't smoke at all, I always say that to my daughter. Fräulein Kuckhoff is right: women womanly—men manly. And you think so too, eh, Sophie?"

"Of course, Herr Rittmeister. Smoking is so unhealthy as well." And with a glance at the two men listening: "Are the gentlemen coming only for the week-end or are they staying longer in Neulohe?"

Part Two

The Land Afire

Chapter Ten

The Peace of the Fields

I

It was no longer the same office. The bookshelves of ugly yellowish-gray pinewood, the desk with its green ink-stained felt, the over-large safe, were still there—but it was no longer the same office.

The windows sparkled; clean bright curtains had been put up; a dull gleam had been given to the furniture by an application of oil; the worn splintery floor had been planed smooth, waxed and polished; and the wheelwright had painted the safe a silver gray. No, it was no longer the same office.

Rittmeister von Prackwitz had at first worried about putting his friend into such a squalid office to scan wages lists and corn accounts. He need not have worried. Herr von Studmann was not the man to sit in squalor—he drove out slovenliness, gently but inexorably.

On one of those early days Studmann had had to fetch a key from the office—and Frau Hartig was standing on a window seat cleaning the windows. Studmann stopped and watched her. "Do you tidy up here?" he asked.

"I see to that all right!" Hartig said pugnaciously, for firstly she was deceived by this man's gentleness and secondly she was angry with him because little Meier had gone. Even if she had solemnly renounced all right to the former bailiff, she couldn't forgive the gentleman there—people said he was a detective—for the fact that Meier was gone.

The supposed detective did not reply, but for no earthly reason smelled the water with which she was cleaning the windows. Then he took the chamois in his hand, which was, of course, no chamois, but a mere rag, for Armgard at the Villa was not parting with good chamois for a bad office. Next he swung the cleaned window to and fro in the sunshine—Hartig's whole body trembled with fury at a spy who now even sniffed round her work! His inspection finished, he raised his glance to the woman, seeming not to see that she was angry. "Your name is?"

"I am the coachman's wife," cried Hartig angrily and polished her window noisily.

"I see, the coachman's wife," said Studmann calmly. "And what is the coachman's name?"

Then Hartig very excitedly and quickly said many things one after another; for example, that she understood her work, that it wasn't necessary for anyone to come from Berlin to "learn" her how to work, that she had worked for four years in the Manor for the old lady before marrying Hartig, and that the old lady had always been satisfied with her, though she was actually hard to please . . .

"So your name is Frau Hartig," said Herr von Studmann, patient because he had worked a long time in the hotel business. "Listen, Frau Hartig, this window cleaning is useless. One doesn't clean windows in the sunshine—look, they are quite streaky."

And he swung the window to and fro. But the annoyed Frau Hartig didn't look. She knew quite well that the windows were streaky, but hitherto her work had been good enough for everyone. She said so, too.

Studmann was unmoved. "And it's better to put a drop of spirit in the water; that makes the panes bright. But even then all your work will be in vain if you haven't got a proper chamois. Look, the cloth is fluffy. There's lots of fluff sticking to the windows!"

At first Frau Hartig was speechless with indignation. Then she asked Herr von Studmann very scornfully where was she to get spirit from, eh? She couldn't sweat any through her ribs, and Armgard wouldn't give her a chamois. . . .

"You shall get spirit and also a chamois," said Studmann. "And if you haven't got a chamois, you take an old newspaper—look, like this." He seized an old newspaper and polished away. "See, like that! Isn't it clean now?"

"That was the *District Gazette!*" exclaimed Frau Hartig contemptuously. "They're collected and bound! No number must be missing."

"Oh!" said Studmann, embarrassed—in the early days both he and Pagel frequently made such mistakes out of sheer ignorance. He unfolded the damp paper ball. "The date is still readable—I'll order another." He made a note of the date.

This little blunder, however, had exhausted his patience. He spoke more curtly. "And now go home. This half-cleaning is useless. Come this evening at six. Then I'll show you how I want the office and the room cleaned."

And he went off with his key in his hand. Frau Hartig, though, was quite undisturbed by the talk of this ass from Berlin who would be hopping it in the next few days, anyway. She went on cleaning in her own way, and did not dream of appearing at six, as ordered.

When, however, curiosity impelled her to go to the staff-house towards seven, she saw to her indignation that Black Minna, that sanctimonious bitch, was pottering around, and when she entered quietly, seizing a pail and flannel as if nothing had happened, the detective merely turned round and said in his beastly gentle way: "You are dismissed, Frau Hartig. You don't clean here anymore." And before she was able to make any reply, he turned away. The wheelwright and his boy set their planes going with a shrap! shrap! shrip! Frau Hartig had stood there like Hagar driven into the wilderness. Tears had had no effect on the old lady, nor sobs on Frau Eva, nor pleadings on the Rittmeister; all had suddenly become different, a new wind was blowing. . . . "Yes, if Herr von Studmann doesn't want to have you, then you can't have done your work properly, Frieda. So we can't say anything, and we can't help you." Not even the information about the spoiled newspaper, not even the news that Herr von Studmann had had Amanda for over an hour in the office after midnight—nothing which was usually listened to so willingly—had effect. "No, go home now, Frieda! You mustn't gossip like that—gossiping is a very ugly habit. You must get out of it, Frieda."

And so she had had to go, to a grumbling husband who was very displeased with her, and she hadn't even been right in her prophecy that on Saturday evening, after the paying of all the many employees, the office would again look like a pigsty. No, it still looked spotless, for that ass from Berlin had placed a table and two chairs on the grass outside the door, and had paid out the wages there. The men, who were always ready to be impressed by anything new, had thought it wonderful.

"But what will he do when it rains? And in the winter?" Frau Hartig had screamed.

"Be quiet, Frieda," said the men. "You're just jealous. He's ten times cleverer than you. He's already kicked out Black Meier, and if you scream too much he'll kick you out as well!"

"He ordered the poultry maid to come to him in the office at midnight!" she cried angrily.

"You'd like to cut her out again, as you did with little Meier, wouldn't you?" the men had laughed. "Ah, Hartig, you're silly. He's really a fine gentleman, like the Rittmeister, and he doesn't think of you or Amanda. Just be quiet!"

II

And now it was Sunday, a Sunday afternoon after a really busy week, and Herr von Studmann and Pagel were sitting in the spick-and-span office. Studmann was smoking a fine smooth Havana from the Rittmeister's special box, for they had both been invited "over there" to lunch; young Pagel was smoking one of his own cigarettes.

Yes, both men, to the great awe of the Neulohe employees, had been invited to lunch in the Villa, having already been there twice for supper. This had never yet happened with farm officials, and it added to the rumors about their unusual mission. The elder of the two gentlemen, the one with the some-what egg-shaped head and brown eyes, had even lived in the Villa until the nocturnal disappearance of little Meier. Then, of course, he had at once moved over to the staff-house—to be sure, against the Rittmeister's will, who had actually asked him, as was learned from Armgard the cook, to stay. But no, the gentleman had said: "I'm sorry, Prackwitz, but I want to live where my work is. You can see me as often as you like!" And now the younger gentleman, Herr Pagel, lived in the bailiff's room and the older in the gable room. What work they had in Neulohe would also be discovered in time—for they understood nothing about farming, that much was certain!

Von Studmann, then, was smoking at his desk, going through the lists of specifications. This he did but superficially, for in the first place it was warm, and then the lunch had been excellent. One ate much too much here now that one was so often in the fresh air. Violently Studmann shut his corn account and said to Pagel, who was sitting at the window, blinking with half-closed eyes at the Geheimrat's sunlit park: "Well, what shall we do? Shall we hit the hay for a bit? God, I'm tired!"

Pagel must have been just as tired, for he did not even open his mouth. But he pointed to the ceiling from which hung a fly-catcher with flies buzzing and humming around it. Studmann looked thoughtfully at the joyful summer dances of these tormenters and then said: "You are right, they wouldn't let us sleep for a moment. Well, what then?"

"I haven't seen the forest properly yet," said Pagel. "Shall we go along and look it over? They say there are ponds there, crayfish ponds, icy cold. We could take our bathing suits with us."

"Fine!" agreed Studmann, and five minutes later the two left the staff-house.

The first person they met was the old gentleman, Geheimrat Horst-Heinz von Teschow. The cunning old man was plodding along in his shaggy green suit, oak stick in hand; and when the two, who hardly knew him, were passing on with a short greeting, he called to them: "But this is fine, gentlemen, meet-ing you! I was wondering, thinking, brooding: Have the gentlemen already departed again? Have they had enough of the country and farming?—Why, I haven't seen you for days!"

As was proper the two smiled at this joke of the Geheimrat's, Herr von Studmann very coldly, but Pagel with honest pleasure.

"And now the gentlemen want to take a little Sunday afternoon stroll, for recreation, eh? The village beauties walk along over there, young man—I don't dare bring that to Herr von Tutmann's notice."

"Studmann," corrected the one-time first lieutenant.

"Yes, of course, please excuse me, of course, dear sir. Of course I know. It just slipped out, because people around here call you that. 'Tut Du Man,' one of the drivers said yesterday, someone you must have ticked off for his driving. Many around here call you that."

"Yesterday," said Studmann.

"Why say yesterday? Or wasn't it yesterday? Of course it was yesterday. My head's still screwed on, Herr von Studmann."

Pagel burst out laughing.

The old man was still for a moment, puzzled. Then he laughed, too. Still laughing, he gave Pagel a very hefty pat on the shoulder. Pagel was tempted to reciprocate, but he didn't know the jolly old fellow very well yet, so he let it go.

"Magnificent," cried the Geheimrat. "He got me there. Cunning fellow, Herr von Studmann. No slouch he!" And suddenly the Geheimrat was serious, which convinced Studmann that the whole thing was an act put on for Pagel and himself for some temporarily inexplicable reason. Ready for battle, Studmann thought, "I'll catch you again."

"Yes, of course, please excuse me, of course." Suddenly the old gentleman became serious. "Have you gentlemen a moment to spare?" he asked. "I've a letter here for my son-in-law, had it for days; haven't been able to send it over; had so much to do recently. . . . If you would deliver it at the Villa when you pass by?"

"I can . . ." began Pagel, whom Herr von Teschow had chiefly been looking at.

But Studmann interrupted him. "Certainly, Herr Geheimrat. We shall tell the servant at the Villa to fetch it."

"Excellent! Fine!" cried the master of Neulohe, but his tone was no longer good-natured. "Besides, it occurs to me that my old Elias can stretch his legs for once. I'll send him." He nodded to the two men and stamped on through the bushes toward the Manor.

"Lord, Studmann," said Pagel a little breathlessly, "you've got into his bad books, I must say! Why so crusty with the gay old boy?"

"I'll give you the lease contract to read sometime," said Studmann, passing his hand over his sweating forehead, "which this gay old boy made his son-in-law sign. Only a child as completely devoid of business instincts as the Rittmeister could have put his name to such a thing. It comes pretty close to the Treaty of Versailles. Bound hand and foot!"

"But the jolly old chap makes such an honest impression."

"Don't trust him. Never tell him anything. Don't do anything he tells you. We are employed by the Rittmeister—the old man has nothing to do with us."

"Ah, Studmann, you're a pessimist—I'm convinced that he is a jolly old fellow."

"And I'm convinced that even the letter he wanted us to deliver has its own peculiarities. Well, we shall see. Let's get on."

In the meantime the old gentleman was standing in his study. He was ringing up the forester. At last he heard the quaking voice.

"Are you sitting on your ears, Kniebusch? Is sleeping the only thing you can do? Well, just wait, I'll soon see that you have a rest—without any money from me! Can you still hear there, Kniebusch?"

"Yes, Herr Geheimrat!"

"Well, praise be to God you can still hear. Then listen to me now! I've just seen those two idlers from Berlin, whom my beloved son-in-law has freshly imported, lounging round the farm with bathing suits under their arms. They undoubtedly want to go bathing in our forest, in the crayfish ponds. Stalk them quietly, and when the gentlemen are in the water, but not before, give them to understand that they are my ponds, and that they've got no damn business to be bathing there. And you can confiscate their clothes, that'll raise a laugh. I'll be responsible, Kniebusch, I'll protect you."

"But, Herr Geheimrat, I can't. One of them is a first lieutenant and a close friend of the Rittmeister's."

"Well, what about it, Kniebusch, what about it? What's that got to do with his bathing in my pond? I tell you to do what I say, and on your own—don't dare to say I sent you! Otherwise you'll hear something—no, otherwise you won't hear anything again."

"Yes, Herr Geheimrat."

"And one thing more, Kniebusch. Hi, man, what are you in such a hurry for? When your boss is talking to you wait till you are dismissed. Or perhaps you're in a hurry for your dismissal? Do you hear what I say, Kniebusch?"

"Yes, Herr Geheimrat."

"Well, yesterday the examining magistrate phoned me from Frankfurt—Bäumer has a temperature of over 104° and is still unconscious, said to be the result of your rough treatment."

"But I couldn't, Herr Geheimrat . . ."

"Of course you could, man! You should have run, made a bandage, fetched a doctor, nurses, even the mid-wife Müller if you like—poor fellow, he's just a simple honest poacher! If he shoots at you it's only because you, wicked man, begrudge him a roast venison—isn't that so? An examining magistrate can't blame him for that, can he? He's only a poor fellow-being, eh?"

"But, Herr Geheimrat, what am I to do?"

"Don't do anything. I'm looking after you, Kniebusch, I've already told Comrade Magistrate what I think! Now go and get this thing done for me! Off with you, Kniebusch, bathing forbidden, distraint of clothes customary. . . ."

The Geheimrat hung up and grinned, got himself a cigar and poured himself out a brandy. After his day's work he sat down in an armchair for a snooze.

Why did magistrate Haase write so unfavorably about Kniebusch to the court? he wondered. I don't like that. I'll show him where he gets off. He's got to make reports as I like. But something's rotten there—and what it is I'll find out, even if it takes me a whole day!

III

"There they go," said the people in the village, watching the two "Berlin detectives." "What fools they must think us to believe they're farmers!—Did you see the hands of the young one, Dad? He's never handled a pitchfork in his life!—But yesterday he shoveled away with the rest!—Oh, that's just eyewash! They've already put little Meier away. They say he was taken straight to Meienburg!—Then why are they still here?—Don't you know who's the next one?—The next is the Rittmeister.—The Rittmeister! You're crazy! The next one is Forester Kniebusch.—No, it's the Rittmeister, I tell you—they're expecting another *Putsch* now, and if there are weapons buried anywhere then it's in our district.—But the man with the egg-shaped head is pals with the Rittmeister.—That's just their cunning, that's what the old Geheimrat has schemed out, to hoodwink him."

"There they go!" said Amanda Backs, and watched the two of them go. But they hadn't seen her. "What do you think of them, Minna?"

"That I can't say, Amanda," said Minna cautiously. "But the big fellow knows everything about tidying-up. When he makes a bed you feel like rolling into it straight away."

"And the young one?"

"Of course you only see the young one, Amanda," said Black Minna with a pious roll of her eyes. "Don't you think of your Meier anymore? After you stood up for him in the evening service, Amanda, and pointed to me with your finger. After all, the detective stole him from you."

"Yes, thank God he did!" But Amanda sounded very gloomy. "What are you doing this afternoon?"

Minna was suddenly vexed. "What should I be doing? I've got to go to my kids. They're certain to be up to some mischief now that I'm away half the day with the cleaning in the staff-house."

"You ought to be glad you've got your kids. Sometimes I think it would have been better for me if I'd had one from him."

Minna became indignant. "Lord, how can you say that, Amanda, you an unmarried girl! And you've already got your eye on another fellow, too. I can understand people sinning, but one's got to repent of sins, Amanda."

"Oh, stop your drivel," said Amanda, angrily going off to the forest, as Minna observed with profound satisfaction.

"There they go," said Jutta von Kuckhoff to her friend Belinde von Teschow. "Herr von Teschow speaks badly of them—but I do think the older one looks really distinguished. What sort of nobility are the Studmanns—old or new? Do you know, Belinde?"

Frau von Teschow peered eagerly out of the window after the disappearing figures. "They're carrying bundles under their arms—yes, bathing suits. They had no time for divine service this morning, but for bathing they have time. And you say he's distinguished, Jutta!"

"You are right, Belinde. It must be very new nobility; our ancestors certainly never bathed. I once saw an old wash-basin at the Quitzows' in Castle Friesack—the sort of thing you nowadays put in the cage for your canary."

"Horst-Heinz says he can revoke the lease at once; there isn't a single farmer on the farm now!"

"I suppose he wants to have little Meier back, does he? The rings round Amanda's eyes are getting darker and darker."

"There she goes—the same way!"

"Who?"

"Amanda! But if anything starts again now—efficient or not—she'll have to go."

"And what's this about Fräulein Kowalewski?" asked Fräulein von Kuckhoff dreamily. "Wherever there's a carcass, the flies gather!"

"They're said to have traveled in the same compartment," replied Frau Belinde eagerly. "And even if she did sit on the box with the coachman afterwards, they're said to have spoken to each other quite intimately. And, up until the day before, the Kowalewski parents didn't know of her visit. Suddenly a telegram arrived, and—Jutta—my son-in-law was already in town when it was sent off."

"They say she's dressed like a cocotte. Her brassière is all lace. . . ."

"Brassière! Please don't say that indecent word, Jutta. When I was young, girls like that wore drill corsets with alternate stays of whalebone and steel—that was like armor, Jutta. Armor is moral, but lace is immoral."

"There they go," said the Rittmeister, having coffee on the veranda with his wife and daughter. "They look good. Quite different from that monster Meier."

"They're going bathing," said Frau von Prackwitz.

"They'll be back in time for the foddering," said the Rittmeister. "Studmann is punctuality and reliability itself."

"Oh, Mamma!" cried Vi.

"Well," asked Frau von Prackwitz very coldly, "do you want anything, Violet?"

"I was just thinking. . . . I'd also have liked to go bathing."

"You know, Violet, I have forbidden you to go out until you tell Papa and myself who the strange man was with whom you crossed the yard at night."

"But, Mamma," cried Vi, almost weeping. "I've already told you a hundred times that it wasn't a strange man. It was Kniebusch! Räder also told you that!"

"You are lying, and Räder is lying, too. You are not going out of the house until you've told me the truth, and the good Hubert can expect sudden dismissal if he goes on telling lies. It's shameful of you both to lie to me in this way." Frau von Prackwitz looked very angry. Her ample bosom heaved hastily. Sharp, angry looks shot from her eyes.

"But if it really was the forester, Mamma—really and truly!—I can't lie to you that it was someone else. Who else could it have been?"

"This is impudence!" cried Frau von Prackwitz breathlessly, trembling with rage. She controlled herself, however. "You are to go up to your room, Violet, and write out yesterday's French lesson ten times, and without a mistake."

"Even if I write it out a hundred times, Mamma," said Vi, white with rage, "it *was* the forester!"

The door slammed: she was gone.

The Rittmeister had listened to this dispute in silence. Only by the twitching of his face had he indicated how painful it was to him. A quarrel between others he always found distressing. But he knew from experience that his wife, on the rare occasions when she was angry, had to be handled with extreme care. "Aren't you being a little hard on Vi?" he therefore asked cautiously. "It might really have been the forester. Hartig is just a gossip. . . ."

"It wasn't the forester. He says so now, but he can't tell me why they went into the staff-house instead of the forest."

"Hubert says they went to see whether there were any more cartridges for Vi."

"Nonsense! You must excuse me, Achim, but don't let those two make a fool of you. Räder knows as well as Vi that the cartridges are in your rifle cupboard."

"They say they didn't want to disturb you."

"Disturb me! My light was on till after twelve—and Vi's never yet been considerate. If she's got a pimple on her neck she wakes me up at two in the night to have it rubbed with ointment. . . . All stupid lies!"

"But really, Eva, who could it have been, then? A stranger whom Hartig doesn't know? And going with Vi at night to the staff-house?"

"That's the worst of it, Achim: that's why I can't sleep. If it had been some young fellow from the district, someone we know, a farmer's son or something like that—he would never be dangerous for her. A harmless flirtation which we could put an end to at once. . . . But it's a stranger, a man of whom we haven't the faintest inkling. She went with him to the staff-house; she was alone with him during the night. For Räder was in bed. That's not a lie. Armgard confirms it, and she'd never lie for Hubert."

"You really think, then, that something could have happened? I'd kill the fellow."

"Yes, but you don't know who it is. Who can it be, for all of them to be afraid to speak about him—to lie so desperately? The forester, Amanda Backs, Räder—and Vi! I can't imagine."

"But, Eva, I'm convinced you are worrying yourself like this for nothing. Vi's still a mere child."

"That's what I also thought, Achim—but my eyes have been opened. She's no longer a child, but she pretends to be one, very impudently, and a child who knows all about things."

"Eva, you are exaggerating."

"No, unfortunately not. She isn't as clever as all that; sometimes she gives herself away. It's sickening, Achim, to have to spy on one's own daughter. . . . But I'm horribly afraid something may have happened to her. I searched her room to see whether a letter was lying around somewhere, some note, a picture of him—Vi's so untidy, you know."

She broke off and looked in front of her with dry, burning eyes. The Ritt-meister stood at the window with his white hair and brown face. He did what all husbands do when embarrassed by their wives' emotional outbursts. He drummed with his fingers lightly against the window pane.

"I thought she hadn't noticed anything. I was ashamed and took care to leave everything lying as it was. . . . But yesterday she came into her room very quietly just when I had her album in my hand. I was very embarrassed."

"And?" The Rittmeister was now very intent.

"And she said to me maliciously: 'No, Mamma, I don't keep a diary, either.'"

"But I don't understand."

"Oh, Achim, that showed me she understood quite well what I was looking for, that she was making fun of me. She was really proud of her cunning! . . . And that's the same girl, Achim, who asked you only three weeks ago about the stork. You told me so yourself. Inexperienced? She's crafty. She's been corrupted by these cursed times!"

The Rittmeister now stood there in a different way, expectant. His brown face looked gray—all his blood flowed to his heart. He made an angry step toward the bell. "Räder shall come here," he murmured. "I'll break every bone in the fellow's body if he doesn't confess."

She stepped in his way. "Achim! You'll spoil everything by that. I'll find it out, you'll see! I tell you they are all mortally afraid of him; there's some secret. But I'll find it out and then you can take action."

She forced him against a chair and he sat down. "And I thought she was still a child!"

"It's all bound up with little Meier somehow," she said broodingly. "He must know something. It was certainly very clever of Herr Studmann to get rid of him so quietly, but it would be better now if we knew where he was. Don't you know what he had in mind?"

"No—he wanted to get away, he was suddenly afraid." The Rittmeister became animated. "But that's just what you were saying! Meier, too, was mortally afraid. . . . Sacked by Studmann? No! He didn't want to stay! He pleaded with Studmann to let him go, to give him a little money for his fare. Studmann gave it to him."

"But why was Meier afraid so suddenly? He went off in the middle of the night, didn't he?"

"With Amanda Backs. Amanda went with him to the station. The thing was like this—wait, Studmann told me about it—everything was so topsy-turvy in the first few days, I hardly paid any attention, and I must confess I was glad that Meier had gone; I never could stand him. . . ."

"In the night, you were saying," prompted Frau Eva.

"Yes. In the night Pagel and Studmann were still in the office, looking at the books—Studmann's thoroughness itself. Meier was sleeping in the next room. He'd handed over the money in the safe to me and Studmann in the evening, not a penny missing. . . . Suddenly they heard him scream, frightfully, in mortal fear; 'Help! help! He'll kill me! . . .' They jumped up, dashed into Meier's room—he was sitting up in bed, as white as a sheet, stammering: 'Please help me! He wants to shoot me again!' 'Who?' asked Studmann. . . . 'There, at the window—I distinctly heard him. He knocked. If I go, he'll shoot! . . .' Studmann opened the window, looked out—nothing. . . . But Meier insisted he was there, that he wanted to kill him."

"But who?" asked Frau von Prackwitz, very excited.

The Rittmeister rubbed his nose thoughtfully. "Who? . . . Well, listen. Meier insisted so firmly that someone had been at the window to shoot him that at last Studmann sent Pagel outside to have a look. In the meantime he calmed Meier down a bit. The chap began to dress himself, and Pagel came back with a girl he had found in the bushes—Amanda Backs."

"I see," said Frau von Prackwitz, disappointed.

"Amanda Backs admitted straight away that she had knocked at the window. She said she had to speak to her friend. When Studmann saw it was only a love affair he left the two alone and went back to the office, with Pagel."

"If he had questioned them properly, he might have found out everything."

"Perhaps. After a while Meier came to the office with Amanda and said he must go away, at once. Studmann didn't want to let him. Studmann is exactitude itself. He said it was impossible without notice; he must first ask me. Meier was very quiet and diffident, which is usually not like him; he said he had to go away now, but he would like to have the wages due to him, as fare money. . . . Finally Amanda Backs pleaded that Meier must get away, otherwise a calamity would happen. . . . And Studmann didn't like to ask any more questions. He thought it was a case of love and jealousy. In the end he agreed because he knew I'd be glad to get rid of Meier, and the two went off."

"Studmann didn't behave very shrewdly there. Jealousy that shoots through the window doesn't exist with us. And if I understood you rightly, Meier called out: 'He wants to shoot me again.'"

"Yes, that's what Studmann told me."

"'Shoot me again'—so the stranger had already tried it once. And this happened after the night on which Vi went into the staff-house with a strange man."

There was silence. Neither of the married couple dared say a word of what they feared. The Rittmeister raised his head slowly and looked into the tearful eyes of his wife. "We always have misfortune, Eva. Nothing turns out well for us."

"Don't lose courage, Achim. For the moment these are all mere apprehensions. Let me handle the matter. Don't worry about anything. I promise you I'll tell you everything, even if it's the worst. I shan't lie to you."

"Good," he said. "I can easily wait." And after short consideration, "Are you going to let Studmann into this? Studmann is discretion itself."

"Perhaps. I must see first. The fewer who know the better. But perhaps I shall need him.'"

"Ah, Eva," he said, much relieved (it already seemed to him as if he had merely been having a bad dream), "you don't know how happy I am to have a real friend here."

"I do, I do," she said earnestly. "I know. I also thought . . ." But she broke off. She had been about to say that she also had believed she had a friend in her daughter who was now lost to her. . . . But she didn't say it. Instead she said, "Excuse me a moment. I'll just go and see Violet."

"Don't be hard on her," he said. "The poor child's already quite pale."

IV

So there they went, the two of them, along the path to the forest. It was a real country path, which knew nothing of townsmen (and there is nothing townsmen like more than something which wants to know nothing of them). It led to the forest, and far inside the forest lay the crayfish ponds, deep, cool, clear—wonderful!

"Did you see the Rittmeister and family on the veranda just now?" asked Pagel. "What do you think of the young Fräulein?"

"And you?" countered Studmann, smiling.

"Very young," declared Pagel. "I don't know, Studmann, but I must have changed tremendously. Fräulein von Prackwitz here, and Sophie who traveled with us, and Amanda Backs—how they would have delighted me a year ago! I think I'm getting old."

"You've forgotten to mention Black Minna who cleans up the office," said Studmann gravely.

"No, seriously," replied Pagel half crossly, half laughing. "I've got a sort of yardstick in me, and when I apply it, all girls seem to me too young, too stupid, too common."

"Pagel!" Studmann raised his arm and extended it ceremoniously over the farms of Neulohe. "Pagel! Over there is the west. Berlin! And there it can stay. I declare to you solemnly, I don't want to see or hear anything of the place. I live in Neulohe! No Berlin memories, no stories of Berlin, nothing of the merits of Berlin girls!" More seriously: "Of course you have a yardstick, you should be glad you have, you even wanted to marry it; but don't think of it anymore now! Try to forget Berlin and everything in it. Enter into the spirit of Neulohe! Be a farmer only. When you've succeeded in that, and if your yardstick still means something, then we can talk about it. Till then it's only sentimental moonshine."

Pagel's face looked sullen and obstinate. He knew quite well what Studmann meant, yet he found it disagreeable. From his mother's protective care he had passed to that of his sweetheart; every trifling worry had been listened to with sympathy. Suddenly all this was to end.

"All right, Studmann," he said at last. "As you like."

"Excellent," said Studmann. He considered it advisable to discontinue the subject; he had read sufficient in the young man's face. Raising his voice, he said: "And now, my worthy fellow farmer, tell me what sort of grain this is!"

"That's rye," said Pagel, letting an ear glide expertly through his fingers. "I know that stuff. I helped pile it in stacks yesterday." And he cast a stealthy glance at his blistered hands.

"That's my opinion too," said Studmann. "But if it's rye, we have to ask ourselves, is it our rye, that is to say, does the rye belong to the estate?"

"According to the plan of the holdings, no peasant has a field out here," said Pagel hesitantly. "It should be ours."

"Again my opinion. But if it's ours, why hasn't it been reaped yet? Seeing that we are already reaping oats? Has it been forgotten, perhaps?"

"Impossible. So near to the farm! We pass here every day with the teams. In that case I should have heard at least something about it from the men."

"Don't tell me anything about the men. In the country they'll be no different from those in the hotel. They grin up their sleeves whenever the boss forgets anything. The experiences I had in the hotel!"

"Herr Studmann! Over there in the west, there lies Berlin—let it stay there, let's not bring it up! We're living in Neulohe—I don't want to hear any tales about Berlin!"

"Excellent. So you accept my suggestion? Agreed! No more about Berlin!" . . . And with new eagerness: "Perhaps it isn't ripe yet?"

"It is ripe," cried Pagel, proud of his newly acquired knowledge. "Look, the grain should break clean over the nail—and this is already dry and as hard as a bone."

"Queer. We must ask the Rittmeister—remind me. Just watch how I'll impress him this evening with our vigilance! He shall learn that he now has employees with eyes in their heads and brains in their skulls, the beau ideal of all employees, employees of the first class. He shall weep with joy over us."

"You're right off your rocker, Studmann," said Pagel. "I've never known you like this."

"Pagel, don't you know what it is? The peace of the fields, the breath of nature, grassy soil under one's feet—you don't know what it means, doing eighteen miles a day up and down the stupid corridors of a hotel, with the soles of your feet burning."

"Berlin! Wicked, forgotten Berlin!"

"I already have an idea that even this peace is a fraud. In the houses of that charming little village which crouches so picturesquely in the forest, scandal, jealousy, and tale-telling are just as much at home as in any city tenement. Instead of the clanging streetcars there's a pump handle eternally squeaking; instead of the scolding old woman on the floor above, here a farm dog howls day in and day out. The kite over there means the death of a mouse. But, Pagel, leave me my happiness, don't pluck the young blossom of my faith! The peace of the fields, the harmony of the cottages, the quiet of nature . . ."

"Come and bathe, Studmann, a bathe will cool you down—the crayfish ponds are said to be very cold."

"Yet, let's go and bathe," agreed Studmann enthusiastically. "Let's plunge this hot body into the cool waters—let us wash from our worried brow the corroding sweat of doubt—Pagel, I must confess to you, I feel marvelous!"

V

Geheimrat Horst-Heinz von Teschow had once presented his old servant Elias with a stick, a yellowish brown malacca cane with a cylindrical golden knob. As a rule the old gentleman was not the one for giving presents, a problem he generally settled by asking: "Who gives me anything?" Sometimes, however, he was quite the opposite and presented someone with something (and then reminded him of it for the rest of his life).

The malacca cane had passed into the possession of Elias only when the gray lead filling was beginning to show through the knob's glittering gold. This did not prevent the old gentleman from often reminding Elias of the "real gold stick." "Do you polish it properly, Elias? You must grease the cane every four weeks. It's an heirloom, a gold stick like that, you can bequeath it to your children. Of course you haven't any (at least as far as I know), but I'm convinced that even my granddaughter Violet would be delighted with it if you left it to her in your will."

What Elias thought of the gold content of the knob remained unknown; he was too dignified to speak of such things. But he made much of the cane, and always carried it on his Sunday walks. Thus he had it today also. Cane in one hand and panama hat in the other, he bore his large yellowish skull in the afternoon sun through Neulohe village, on his way to the Villa. In the breast pockets of his ceremonial brown frock coat he carried in the left the wallet with the 1,000-mark notes, and in the right the Geheimrat's letter to his son-in-law.

Whenever he saw a face old Elias stopped and addressed it. If it was a child he asked for the first or fifth commandment; if it was a woman he inquired about her gout or whether there was enough milk to feed the baby. With the men, he asked about the progress of the harvest, said "Ah" or "Oh!" or "You don't say!" and always broke off the conversation after three or four sentences, swung his panama gently, jabbed his stick against the ground and passed on. No ruling prince could have wandered among his subjects more affably or with more dignity than did old Elias among the villagers, who yet mattered nothing to him and to whom he mattered nothing. All, however, readily accepted him as he was; if ever a newcomer felt aggrieved after the first interview—what the devil did the old donkey want of him, what in all the world did he think he was?—at the second or third time, at the latest, he had succumbed to the spell of philosophic detachment and answered as readily as the old guard.

Although he was no younger than Forester Kniebusch, Elias was quite different; whereas the former was ever trying to take color from others, echoing their sentiments, always worrying about his old age and his livelihood, old Elias wandered about with unruffled serenity, the things of this world meaning nothing to him, and managing his crafty master just as naturally as a child does a doll. That's how things are arranged in this strange world. The cares that press on the hearts of some are not even felt by others.

Having arrived at the Villa, Elias did not take his letter up the front stairs to the brass bell—which on Saturday had been given its Sunday polish by Räder—but went round the Villa and down into the basement, where he knocked at the door, not too loudly and not too softly, just as was proper. No one called, "Come in!" so Elias opened the door and found himself in the kitchen, where a complete Sunday silence and cleanliness prevailed. Only the kettle hummed softly over the dying flames. There was no one in the kitchen. Old Elias emptied the kettle in the sink and put it aside; he knew that Frau Eva liked to have her tea brewed only from freshly boiled water.

Then he went through a door at the back of the kitchen into the dark passage dividing the basement into two parts. His stick was clearly to be heard; he coughed, he also knocked on the door. But perhaps all these announcements of his presence were unnecessary, for Räder was sitting quite still and rigid in his bare room, his hands in his lap, staring with fishy eyes at the door, as if he had been sitting like that for hours.

When the servant Elias entered, however, the servant Räder got up, not too slowly and not too quickly, just as was proper, and said: "Good day, Herr Elias. Will you please take a seat?"

"Good day, Herr Räder," answered old Elias. "But I shall be depriving you . . ."

"I like standing," declared Räder. "Old age must be respected." And he took the other's hat and stick. Then he placed himself with his back against the door, facing Elias, but separated from him by the whole length of the room.

The old man mopped his forehead and said pleasantly, "Yes, yes—it's hot today. Marvelous weather for the harvest."

"I know nothing about that," said Räder coldly. "I sit here in my cellar. I've nothing to do with the harvest."

Elias folded his handkerchief carefully, put it into his coat pocket and brought out the letter. "I have a letter here for the Rittmeister."

"From our father-in-law?" asked Räder. "The Rittmeister is upstairs. I'll announce you at once."

"Ah yes, ah yes!" sighed old Elias, looking at the letter as if he were reading the address. "Here are relatives writing letters to each other now. What one can't say face to face, Herr Räder, ought not to be written either." He looked at the address once again with disapproval and laid the letter absent-mindedly on Räder's bed.

"Herr Elias, please take the letter off my bed," said Räder sternly.

The old man picked it up with a sigh.

Räder spoke more calmly. "The letters from our father-in-law have never yet brought any good—you can deliver it yourself. I'll announce you, Herr Elias."

"Let an old man get his breath back, can't you?" complained the old man. "There can't be such a hurry about it, on Sunday afternoon."

"Of course, so that the Rittmeister goes for a walk in the meantime, and I get the full force of his anger!" grumbled Räder.

"We're worried over there about our grandchild," said old Elias. "We haven't seen Fräulein Violet in the Manor for five days."

"Manor! It's a mud hut, Herr Elias!"

"Is our little Vi ill?" asked the old man wheedlingly.

"We haven't had the doctor here," said Herr Räder.

"But what can she be doing? A young girl—and sitting in the house in such fine weather!"

"Your Manor is also a house—whether she sits there or here, it's all the same!"

"So she really doesn't go out at all—not even in the garden?" The old man got up.

"If you call this a garden, Herr Elias! . . . Does the letter concern the young Fräulein, then?"

"That I can't say—but it's possible."

"Give it to me, Herr Elias, I'll see to it."

"You will give it to the Rittmeister?"

"I'll see to it all right. . . . I'll go upstairs at once."

"I can tell the Geheimrat, then, that you have delivered it."

"Yes, Herr Elias."

Tap, tap, tap went the malacca cane, with old Elias, out into the sun; and tap, tap, tap went the servant Räder up to the first floor. But when he was about to knock at the door he heard steps and, looking up, saw the feet of Frau von Prackwitz coming down the stairs. So he held the letter somewhat behind him. "Madam!"

Frau von Prackwitz had two red patches under the eyes, as if she had just been crying. She spoke quite brightly, however. "Well, Hubert, what is it?"

"A letter has come from over there for the Rittmeister," replied Räder, showing a corner of the letter.

"Yes? Why don't you go in and deliver it, Hubert?"

"I'm just about to," whispered Räder. "I'm braver than Herr Elias, who didn't have the courage to deliver it. He even came into my room about it, a thing he's never done before."

Frau von Prackwitz became so thoughtful that a small wrinkle appeared between her eyebrows. Hubert showed nothing of the letter except a corner. From his room the Rittmeister burst forth. "What's all this damned whispering and rustling outside my door? You know I can't stand it! Oh, I'm sorry, Eva!"

"That's all right, Achim. I have to discuss something with Hubert."

The Rittmeister withdrew and his wife took Hubert over to one of the windows. "Well, give me the letter, Hubert," she said.

"They're very worried in the Manor about Fräulein Violet," said Hubert bumptiously. "Herr Elias was only too eager to find out why the young Fräulein hasn't been there for five days."

"And what did you say, Hubert?"

"I, madam? I didn't say anything!"

"Yes, you are good at that, Hubert," affirmed Frau von Prackwitz bitterly. "You see how worried and distracted I am because of Violet. Won't you really tell me who the unknown gentleman was, Hubert? I appeal to you!"

But one should not appeal to a blockhead for anything. "I don't know of any unknown gentleman, madam."

"No, of course not, because to *you* he is known! Oh, what a cunning fellow you are, Hubert!" Frau von Prackwitz was very angry. "But if you carry on like this, Hubert, with these mysterious doings and untruthfulness—then we're no longer friends."

"Ah, madam," said Hubert sullenly.

"What do you mean by 'Ah, madam'?"

"Excuse me, here is the letter."

"No, I want to know what you meant just now, Hubert!"

"It is just a manner of speaking, as it were. . . ."

"What is a manner of speaking? Hubert, I insist!"

"That we shall no longer be friends, madam," said Hubert very fishily. "I'm just the servant, and you, madam, are Frau von Prackwitz—so there can't be any talk of friendship."

Frau von Prackwitz went crimson at this impertinence. In her confusion she seized the letter which the servant still held out to her, tore it open and read it. In the middle of her reading, however, she raised her head and said sharply: "Herr Räder! Either you are too stupid or too clever for a servant's position—in either case I fear we shall soon separate."

"Madam," said Räder, also a little angry now, "in my references I am recommended by persons of very high rank. And at the training school I received the golden diploma."

"I know, Hubert, I know. You are a pearl!"

"And if the Rittmeister wants me to leave, then I ask that I be told in time, so that I can give notice. It is always an obstacle in my profession, if I've been given notice."

"All right," said Frau von Prackwitz, glancing quickly through the short letter and looking at the figures in it without understanding them. "It shall be as you wish, Hubert. This," she said in explanation, "is just an unimportant business letter, nothing about Fräulein Violet. Elias was probably a bit inquisitive on his own account."

Hubert saw, however, that Frau von Prackwitz folded the letter several times and pushed it into a little pocket in her dress.

"If you see Herr von Studmann, Hubert, tell him to call in about seven, no, let's say at a quarter to seven." And with that she nodded curtly and went into the Rittmeister's room.

Hubert remained in the passage for a moment longer, until he heard husband and wife talking. Then he crept up the stairs with extreme caution, so that no board should creak. He knocked softly on a door, once only, and entered quickly.

In the room Violet was sitting at a little table; a crumpled damp handkerchief and red patches on her face revealed that she, too, had been crying.

"Well?" she said, curious nevertheless. "Did Mamma put you through it as well, Hubert?"

"The young Fräulein shouldn't be so careless when she's eavesdropping," rebuked Hubert. "I saw your foot the whole time on the top stair. And madam could also have seen it."

"Ah, Hubert, poor Mamma! She's just been crying here. Sometimes I'm terribly sorry for her, and I feel that I ought to be ashamed. . . ."

"There's no use being ashamed, Fräulein," said Hubert severely. "Either you live as the old people want you to—then you won't need to be ashamed—or else you live as we young people think right, and then you really don't need to be."

Vi looked at him searchingly. "Sometimes I think, though, you're a very bad man, Hubert, and that you have very bad plans," she said, but rather cautiously, almost anxiously.

"What I am must be no concern of yours, Fräulein," he said at once, as if he had thought it all out long ago. "And my plans are mine, after all. What you want, that's your concern."

"And what did Mamma want?"

"Just the usual questions about the unknown man. Your grandparents are also worried about you, Fräulein."

"Oh, God, if they could only get me out of here! I can't stand it any longer indoors. I shall weep myself to death! Was there really nothing in the tree again, Hubert?"

"No letter, no note!"

"When did you look, Hubert?"

"Just before serving coffee."

"Take another look now, Hubert. Go there immediately and let me know at once."

"But it's useless, Fräulein. He doesn't come into the village in the daytime."

"Do you keep a good look-out at night, Hubert? It's impossible that he hasn't come at all! He gave me his solemn promise! He was going to be here on the second night, no, the next night."

"He has definitely not been here. I would have met him, and I would also have heard about it if he had been here."

"Hubert, I simply can't stand it any longer . . . I see him day and night, as if he were really here, but if I try to touch him, there's nothing, and I seem to fall down a hundred stairs. . . . I feel quite different, it's as if I've been poisoned,

I can't sleep any more. . . . And then I see his hands, Hubert. They hold you so tightly, they send a thrill through you. . . . Oh, what can be the matter with me?" She stared at servant Hubert Räder with wide-open eyes. But it was not certain that she saw him at all.

Räder stood by the door like a stick. His gray complexion took on no color, his eye remained gray and lusterless even though he did not turn his gaze away from the soft, confiding girl.

"You mustn't think anything about it," he said in his usual didactic tone. "It is so!"

Vi looked at her confidant, her only confidant, as if he were a prophet bringing salvation.

Räder nodded significantly. "Those are physical processes," he explained. "That is physical desire. I can give you a book about it, written by a doctor, a specialist. In it everything is exactly described, how it comes, and where its seat is, and how it is cured. It is called deficiency-phenomena or abstinence-phenomena."

"Is that really so, Hubert? Is that in the book? You must bring it me, Hubert."

"That is it. Nothing to do with—the man." Hubert narrowed his eyes and observed the effect of his words. "It is just the body—the body is hungry, Fräulein!"

Vi, although as foolish and pleasure-seeking as any girl in those days, still had her illusions about love, and not every pleasant fancy was swept away by the tearing of a single veil. Only gradually did she grasp the full significance of Hubert's revelations; she shrank as if from a sudden pain; she moaned.

But then she drew herself up. "How disgusting!" she cried. "You are a swine, Räder, you dirty everything. Go away—don't touch me! Out of my room, at once!"

"But please, Fräulein! Please calm yourself—madam's coming! Tell some lie; if the Rittmeister finds out, the Lieutenant is lost."

He glided out, vanishing into the adjoining bedroom of Frau von Prackwitz, and stood behind the door. He heard the hurried step; then the door of Violet's room was shut. He could hear the mother's voice, and Violet sobbing . . .

That's the cleverest thing she can do, he thought with satisfaction. Cry! I was probably a bit too soon and too strong. Well, when she's been a week without news of the Lieutenant . . .

He heard the Rittmeister's footstep on the stairs and cowered well back between Frau von Prackwitz's bathrobe and dressing gown. However contemptible the Rittmeister was in his stupidity and temper, he remained almost the only person of whom one had to be afraid. He was quite capable of throwing someone out of the window—through the glass.

"I tell you you're exaggerating," he heard the Rittmeister say angrily. "The child is simply nervous. She must get into the fresh air. Come, Vi, let's go for a little walk."

Räder nodded. He slipped through the bathroom and the Rittmeister's bedroom to the stairs, down which he vanished into his own bare room. He unlocked the cupboard. With a second key he opened a suitcase from which he took out a well-thumbed book—*What a Young Man Must Know Before and About Marriage*. This he wrapped in a piece of newspaper. One evening he would place it under Violet's pillow. Perhaps not today or tomorrow, but the day after. He was convinced Vi would read it, despite her outburst.

VI

Sophie Kowalewski, ex-maid to the Countess Mutzbauer, had said to her parents this Sunday morning: "I'm going over to Birnbaum to see Emmi. Don't keep dinner waiting for me; perhaps I won't be back until evening." Her kindhearted old father had nodded his head. "Ride along the main road, Sophie, not the forest path. There are such a lot of fellows knocking around the district now." And her tremendously fat mother, interested only in food and digestion, had said: "Emmi has made a wonderful match. They already have a cow and two goats. They kill three pigs for their own use. They don't have to go around with hungry bellies; there's always something to eat. They've also got chickens and geese. If you would only have such luck!"

Sophie did not stay to hear it all. She duly let her friend, who was lending her the bicycle, admire her blue costume, swung on to the saddle and pedaled slowly through the village with bell ringing, so that all should see her. She turned into the quiet mossy forest path along which the cycle ran as silently as on velvet, a firm and very narrow path, close to the rutted cart track. Heather and broom kept brushing the pedals, casting drops of morning dew on to the toes of her shoes. The beautiful pillars of old pine trees wandered past her, tinged reddish by the morning sun—and sometimes the path went so narrowly between two trunks that she had to grip the handle bars firmly in order not to knock against them. The bilberries were thick and their berries already turning blue. The forest grass was still green, and the junipers stood dark and silent in the bright undergrowth; there was an incessant fluttering and twittering of little forest birds.

Here Sophie had passed her childhood; every sound was familiar to her. As a child she had heard the distant vague soughing of the forest, which came close, but could never come closer. The sun shone on her hair as it had shone on the child's. As she glided by, there opened and closed almost immediately glades which seemed to lead into the heart of the forest.

No one is all bad, and Sophie isn't either. Sophie was filled with a gaiety which had nothing in common with the boisterous merriment of a night spent drinking in a bar. It was as if her body had received new blood; joyful, serene thoughts streamed through her with every fresh breath she took; instead of a dreary dance hit she hummed the song of "May has come." . . . The clouds— they wander—in the canopy of heaven. . . . Oh, wonderful!

Suddenly Sophie laughed. She remembered how her mother once took her to pick berries in the forest. At that time she was eight or nine years old. The laborious picking soon bored her. Playing, humming to herself, she wandered away from her busy mother; ten times she heard herself being called, without paying any heed; the eleventh call no longer reached her. Singing softly, laughing with happiness, she wandered deeper and deeper into the forest, aimlessly on and on, from the sheer joy of movement, into the little valleys where the trees descended from flat hills like silent pilgrims. For a long time she listened to the gurgling of a hurrying brook. For a still longer time she watched a butterfly which flew from blossom to blossom in the heat of a forest clearing—and was not tempted to try and catch it.

At last she reached a beech wood. The trees towered high and silver-gray. The green above was so bright. They stood far from each other; everywhere sunbeams penetrated into the golden warm shadows; her bare feet sank deep into the soft brownish-green moss. Singing softly, almost without knowing what she was doing, Sophie stripped off her clothes. There lay her little dress; over a tree stump the bright patch of her little knickers; now her chemise fell upon the moss—and gaily whooping, the child danced naked through sun and shade, laughing.

It was the joy of living on this earth, of wandering in the light—the joy of life! The little heart in the thin body throbbed. Dancing into ever new greenness, into ever different worlds, into ever deeper mystery. With sounds such as the birds sing, interrupted to watch a beetle lost in a wheel track . . . and begun again, all without thinking, like breathing. . . .

It was the joy of life, the happiness of being—that for which grown-up people eternally yearn, whether they know it or not. Happiness—for which they are always seeking, and which they will never find again. Joy which vanishes with childhood—only to be glimpsed afterwards in the weak reflection of a lover's embrace, in the joy over some work.

The bicycle sang softly along the path, the chain grated. Passing over a root, the rear mudguard clattered and the saddle springs sighed. Sophie, wishing to sing, could not succeed, and remembered only how to the child the sun had suddenly become cold, and the familiar forest strange. She had burst into tears—she was lost. Everything was hostile: prickly brambles, pointed stones on the path, a swarm of horseflies blowing over from a herd of cattle. At last a woodsman, old Hofert, had found her . . .

"Aren't you ashamed, Sophie, to run around naked like that?" he had scolded her. "You're a human being, you know, not a little pig." And he had taken her back to her mother. Oh, her mother's anger. The long search for her clothes, which could not be found, the scolding, the blows. The return to the village, with her mother's kerchief round her hips. The mocking of the other children, the wise observations of the old people: "Look out, Kowalewski. That girl will bring you trouble some day."

Sophie pedaled faster, ringing the bell loudly in the forest silence. She shook her head, although no swarm of horseflies now buzzed round her—she wanted to shake her thoughts away. No person can say how he has become what he is, but sometimes a piece of the way is revealed to us. Then we become angry with ourselves, find it disagreeable, shake the tormenting thoughts from our head. We're all right as we are; it's no fault of ours if we haven't turned out differently. We needn't think about that.

Faster and faster sped the bicycle; glade after glade, path after path, glided by. Sophie was not cycling to Birnbaum to see Emmi. She was cycling to the prison to visit Hans Liebschner, a lawfully condemned swindler with previous convictions. Life is no holiday; it's an extremely deceitful business, and whoever doesn't cheat others gets cheated himself. Sophie had no time to waste on dreams. She had to work out how she could get a visitor's permit as Hans's sister—without identification papers!

Her eyes had a dry, hard gleam. True, she had certified on a sheet of notepaper from the Christian Hostel that she was the cook, Sophie Liebschner, working there. But she was quite aware that this badly written and perhaps not even properly spelled document would be worthless to an official eye. From what her father had told her, Meier, the little bailiff who had run away, would have been just the right man to have given her some sort of certificate with the farm stamp on it. But there again she had been unlucky; she hadn't been able to get hold of the fellow. And the other two, who had traveled in the train with her, they wouldn't do a girl a favor like that, as you could see at a glance. They'd been much too polite, just like those gentlemen in a bar who are so politely cold merely to save themselves buying a lady a whisky!

Sophie's thoughts, however, did not make her despondent. Up till now she had always had luck, and she knew very well what effect a proper glance at the proper time could have. Pretty girls always had luck.

Sophie as well, therefore. It was grand visiting day at the prison; over a hundred relatives were standing outside its iron gate. Forcing herself among them, Sophie was let in with the great rush. Warders ran to and fro, papers were examined, questions asked, and gently, gently, step by step, Sophie edged herself from the group which had not been questioned into that which had.

Then she was in the visitors' room. On one side of the bars stood the relatives, on the other the prisoners. The talk and chatter were deafening! The two poor warders who had to supervise every word couldn't but fulfill their duties badly. How wonderfully might Sophie now have chatted with her Hans, have said everything that she had in her heart! But of course there was no Hans Liebschner in the visitors' room, nor could she insist on seeing him, for he was not in the list of prisoners due for visits, naturally!

But here again it proved to be good that Liebschner was a swindler—that is to say, not a violent or dogmatic person, but a cunning fox, versed in all the crafty arts—that is to say, a submissive, well-behaved prisoner, the pattern of obedience. Which was why he had become an orderly and, as orderly, had work to do in the corridors, and from the corridors could see the visitors coming. A raven's eye is sharp: Sophie was the same Sophie. Yes, supposing Hans had not been in favor with the warder of his landing? But the steel saw had actually been found, and three bars already sawn through! To discover a thing like that in time is a feather in the cap of any warder. And this one had been commended and was therefore well disposed to his orderly—all the more because he hadn't been able to fulfill his promise about the outside gang, since none had yet been sent out.

So Sophie was suddenly beckoned onwards by a bearded old warder. "Just come along here, Fräulein." She was pushed into a narrow cell crammed full of dirty cordage, even bolted in; and just as she was beginning to think all sorts of things, wondering if her unauthorized entry had been discovered and if this was her punishment, the bolt rattled again and in slouched her Hans in a disgusting get-up. There were shadows under his eyes, his nose was thin—but the same mischievous smile, the same old Hans!

The warder raised his finger threateningly. "Don't get up to any silly tricks now, children!" But he looked at Sophie with a benevolent smirk, as if he wouldn't mind getting up to silly tricks with her himself.

Then the bolt rattled again, and she was in Hans's arms. It was like a storm, a hurricane. She lost all sense of sight and sound. Oh, this dear good face, so close! The familiar smell! The taste of his lips! A sigh, a laugh which soon choked, a few words. "Oh, you! You! Oh, darling!" They scarcely found time to speak. "How I've been longing for you!"

"I'm coming out, with a harvest crew. Then I'll make a break for it!"

"Oh—if you would come to us!"

"Where?"

"To Neulohe! I'm with my parents. Father says we need a harvest crew."

"I'm certain to go with the next one. Can't you put a little pressure on your people?"

"Perhaps. I'll see. God, Hans . . ."

"That did me good! Six months . . ."

Happy and contented, Sophie walked along the rough pavements of the little town of Meienburg, having first left her cycle in a small pub. She entered the Prince of Prussia, the best hotel in the town, for lunch. There the wealthy farmers ate; as a child she had often stood before it, admiring the sign. Now she walked through the place and sat down on the terrace. The hotel was almost empty. On Sunday the farmers ate at home; there was no farmers' union, no cattle-dealing to be used as a pretext for escaping from their families.

Sophie ate with relish everything that was brought her, and drank half a bottle of Rhine wine with it. There was some point in feeding well now—perhaps Hans would be coming to Neulohe. He must succeed! With her coffee she ordered a large glass of cognac, and leisurely smoked cigarette after cigarette. From the stream, which flowed below the terrace, came the dry wooden sound of oars in their rowlocks. The rowers could not be seen, but in the midday heat their voices were heard distinctly. "Pull a little quicker, Erna! We want to have a bathe."

Suddenly Sophie realized that she also wanted to bathe, to bathe and lie in the sun, and roast herself. But not here! Here it was certain to be crowded with fellows. That wasn't bathing! The ass at the next table had been goggling at her for the last half hour: strange that some men can never understand that one hasn't been waiting precisely for them.

But she had no bathing suit with her—nor, for that matter, one at home—but a bathing suit was not a problem in Meienburg, even on Sunday. She paid, and as she went out accidentally knocked the goggling gentleman's straw hat off his head into the cheese dish. "Oh, I'm so sorry!" she said graciously to the blushing man and hurried out.

The little needlework shop, of course, was still where it had been five years ago, ten years ago, where it had probably been ever since Meienburg was built; there where the needlework shop of Fräulein Otti Kujahn would forever be—in little Bergstrasse, directly opposite the Konditorei Köller (the Lover's Nook). Sophie did not try the shop door. In things like that the little villages are punctilious; on a Sunday afternoon the shop door is locked. But if you go round the back there is not the slightest difficulty. Little humpy Fräulein Kujahn with the same gray hair, the same languishing pigeon-glance of ten years ago, was very pleased. She stocked bathing suits. She was also ready to sell them on a Sunday afternoon.

They were not modern—they were not those aquatic garments which reveal a different part of the anatomy at every movement and seem to consist only of open-work—as Sophie discovered with a certain regret. They were costumes which covered the body, which clothed and did not unclothe. But perhaps it was better so. Sophie had no intention of offering a spectacle to the adolescents of Neulohe. She knew the habit these young gentlemen had of spying on the bathing places on their free afternoons, in order to get a glimpse of the village girls. Sophie selected therefore a completely decent black costume with white embroidery and a minimum of open-work. She also bought a bathing cap.

The price which Otti Kujahn asked for these two things, after long hesitation ("Yes, what shall I take for them? They cost me under three marks"), corresponded perhaps to the postage of a local letter. Sophie was now of the opinion that the Kujahn needlework shop would not exist forever. At these prices Fräulein Kujahn could not survive the inflation, but would soon be sold out and starving.

The bicycle sang gently, the chain grated softly, in the afternoon silence the woods lay as if sleeping; the birds were quiet, the heather brushing the toes of her shoes swept off the dust. Something like happiness filled Sophie, a peacefulness she had not felt for a long time. The sun stood still, the day proceeded no further—her happiness remained.

Deep within the forest lay the crayfish ponds, a chain of little pools, reedy and muddy. Only in the large one was it possible to bathe. For a while Sophie lay in the sun. But she had to go into the water, feel its coolness, experience its freshness.

The fine sandy bottom sloped away gently; cool and fresh, cooler and fresher than anything on this earth, the water rose round her. Once she shivered, when the coolness reached her waist, but even this shiver was pleasant. And it was gone immediately. She went deeper. In a long swimming stroke she glided into the coolness, became one with it, as cool!

Now she strove to maintain her balance lying on her back, gently paddling with her hands. Lying in one element, part of it, her eyes closed, she felt the other element on her face, a heavenly greeting, fire. The warmth of the sun penetrated her, warmth that had nothing withering in it like the artificial flames of mankind. A puff of wind seemed to waft it away, but it was back again, penetrating, something nourishing, a divine nectar. Yes, this gentle warmth had something of life, of eternal life—it dispensed happiness.

But the happiness Sophie Kowalewski now felt had nothing in common with the childish joy remembered that morning. The child had danced through the woods, blissful, unselfconscious, laughing, singing. The rapture of existence had seized her, as it seizes a bird or a calf in the meadow. The happiness Sophie now felt was conditioned by many experiences. After months of tormented longing, her body was again for the first time in harmony with itself; she was no longer aware of it, it made no demands on her, no longer tormented her soul. Resting quietly on the surface of the water, it also rested quietly in the eternal ocean of desire, longing, craving.

The child's blissful unconscious happiness can never be attained again. The gate had closed, innocence had departed—but life has many possibilities of happiness! She had thought it was in the cell, with him, in his arms.

And now it was here in the water, wave upon wave of warmth, of happiness . . .

In a dream she came out of the water and lay down on the sand, propped on one arm, her chin in her hand. She looks closely at the confusion of grasses. They fold into each other, creating little hollows. But she sees nothing. Real happiness has no name, no word, no picture. It is a gentle hovering in some indeterminate place; not a tune for the song "I am here!"—but something like a gentle lament to the words "I am I." For we know that we must grow old and ugly, and have to die.

When she heard steps Sophie scarcely looked up. Lazily she pulled her costume over her naked breasts, murmuring, "Good afternoon." At another time she would have welcomed the accident which brought her together here with the two new gentlemen from the estate. But now they were of no moment to her. In a few syllables she answered their inquiries: yes, this was the only bathing place, everywhere else was reedy. No, the gentlemen were not disturbing her. No, the water was not dangerous, no water plants. . . . She relapsed into silence. She hardly knew that the two of them were there. She looked again at the grass hollows, which then immediately vanished as if by magic, so she couldn't see anything anymore. The sun was wonderfully warm. She pushed her costume down from her breast again, the voices of the two men came distantly from the water—oh, heavenly!

With all the cunning in the world Sophie Kowalewski could not have behaved more shrewdly than she did in ignoring, however thoughtlessly, the two gentlemen. It is undeniable that both Studmann and Pagel had not received a too favorable impression of her in the train, although the easily enthusiastic Rittmeister had praised this jewel of a girl to the skies. Both had recognized only too well that affected manner of speaking put on by little adventuresses wanting to play the great lady. They were both disgusted by her simultaneously dried out and puffy facial skin, which still smelled of powder. They were not leaving Berlin for the peace of the fields in order to burden themselves with such a companion. They had been very reserved. They thought a bit differently from the Rittmeister about the distance you should keep from your employees. When they saw Sophie, the thought didn't go through their heads: in the end she's only overseer's daughter. That's not how they wanted to see her. They had nothing against the girl, but they had strong objections to transplanting Berlin tart-shops to Neulohe.

When, therefore, Sophie did not exploit the present encounter, that yet offered so much incentive and possibility to an experienced girl; when she did not presume upon an acquaintanceship made in peculiar circumstances and did not seem minded to draw any inferences from it, Studmann said very cheerfully to Pagel as they went into the water: "As a matter of fact, the girl looks quite nice."

"Yes, queer. She seemed quite different to me last time."

"Did you see, Pagel?" Studmann asked after a while. "A perfectly decent bathing suit."

"Yes," agreed Pagel. "And no glad eye. I think I'll never understand women." With this light reference to the tragedy he had recently suffered, Pagel plunged into the water. Five or ten minutes, even a quarter of an hour, went by in swimming and diving and floating side by side and talking; minutes in which they both felt stronger, fresher, more conscious than for years. Until a noise from the bank caught their attention—a woman's shrill voice, a man's suppressed mumble.

"That's Sophie," said Studmann.

"Oh, forget her!" cried Pagel angrily. "It's so nice here in the water. Probably some quarrel with a country lover. Ain't love grand!"

"No, no!" said Studmann, the nursemaid who always had to intervene wherever anything threatened to go wrong. "She made a very nice impression on me just now." And he swam rapidly toward the bank, followed by the reluctant Pagel.

Yes, there was Sophie shouting. "I say, you two! Here—he wants to take away your clothes!"

"Be quiet, Sophie, can't you?" whispered the forester, trying to make off with his booty. "Nothing will happen to you. I only want the gentlemen's clothes."

"Herr von Studmann! Herr Pagel! Hurry up!" called Sophie all the more loudly.

"Now, what's going on here?" asked von Studmann with extreme astonishment. And Pagel too looked more puzzled than was becoming to an intelligent face.

In the meadow stood the forester, whom they knew slightly, a worthy old dodderer, his gun over his shoulder, and under his arm the two men's things in a bundle. Facing him Sophie Kowalewski, a charming sight in her rage, an Artemis. With one hand she held her bathing suit over her breast, with the other a trouser leg from the forester's bundle—and von Studmann recognized that it was his.

"What's this supposed to be?" he asked, still extremely astonished.

The forester was as red as a tomato, and became redder. Perhaps he wished to speak—all that was heard was a babbling in the depths of his beard. Yet he continued holding on to the clothes, and Sophie Kowalewski continued to tug at the trouser leg.

But *she* spoke, and what she said had certainly no ladylike affectation about it now.

"I'm lying here and thinking of nothing, and I hear something rustling and I think it's a hedgehog or a fox and take no notice, and then I look over there and I'm flabbergasted. There's Kniebusch creeping behind the reeds after the gentleman's clothes, and sticks them under his arm. So I get up and say: 'Kniebusch, what are you doing, those are the gentlemen's clothes!' But he says nothing, puts his finger on his lips and wants to slink away. So I make a grab and manage to get hold of the trousers. Will you let go of the trousers now! They're not your trousers!" she screamed angrily at the forester.

"You seem fated to be our rescuer, Fräulein Sophie," said Studmann, smiling. "Here you are again helping us out of an embarrassing situation. We are very grateful. But I think you can now let go of the trousers. Herr Kniebusch won't run off with them under our eyes." Sharply: "May I ask you, Herr Kniebusch, what is the meaning of this? In case you've forgotten, my name is Studmann, von Studmann, and this gentleman's name is Pagel—we are employed by Rittmeister von Prackwitz."

"That's got nothing to do with me," muttered Kniebusch, looking at the clothes which Pagel, without more ado, had pulled from under his arm. "Bathing is prohibited here, and if anyone bathes here his clothes are taken away!"

"Since when?" cried Sophie Kowalewski angrily. "That's a new one!"

"Shut up, Sophie!" said the forester rudely. "It's one of the Geheimrat's orders, it's been in force a long time."

"If you tell me to shut up, then I'll talk!" cried the warlike Sophie. "And anyway you're lying. You told me specially that nothing would happen to me, you only wanted the gentlemen's clothes!"

"That's not true!" contradicted the forester hastily. "I didn't mean it that way."

"You did mean it that way! I just want the clothes of the gentlemen, you said!"

"No!"

"Yes!"

"No!"

"Yes!"

"Let's sit down!" suggested von Studmann. "Yes, you too, please, Herr Kniebusch. Pagel, give me the cigarettes from my jacket. Sit down, Kniebusch! That's right. Cigarette, Fräulein Sophie? Yes, of course I know you smoke. We're not as strict as the Rittmeister was in the train; we're the younger generation. So you were specially ordered to confiscate our things, Herr Kniebusch?"

"I wasn't! I always confiscate the things of people bathing here!" said the forester obstinately.

"Not those of Fräulein Sophie, for instance. Well, let's drop that. How often have you confiscated clothes here, then, Forester Kniebusch?"

"I don't have to tell you that. I'm employed by the Geheimrat, not the Rittmeister," said the forester defiantly, squinting at the clothes, squinting at the forest, and feeling as if he were slowly roasting in hell—the heat from below supplied by Herr von Studmann, the heat above from the Geheimrat.

"I am only asking," said Herr von Studmann, "because you must have already had a lot of unpleasantness with this confiscation, haven't you?"

The forester maintained an obstinate silence.

"Or are you an auxiliary police official?"

Kniebusch remained silent.

"But perhaps you have been previously convicted. Then confiscating clothes without any legal right wouldn't matter to you so much."

Sophie burst out laughing, Pagel loudly cleared his throat, and the forester blushed to his eyes, which had become small and gloomy. He kept silent, however.

"You know us by name, you could have reported us for illegal bathing. If we had been convicted, we would, of course, have paid the fine. Why confiscation, then?"

The three of them looked at the forester fidgeting about, wanting to say something. Once more he looked at the forest close by. He half got up, but between him and the salvation of cover was young Pagel's leg. The forester sat down again.

"Forester Kniebusch," said Herr von Studmann, in the same pleasant, patient tone, as if he were explaining something to an obstinate child, "won't you speak openly to us? Look, if you don't tell us all about it, we shall go to Geheimrat von Teschow. I shall explain to him the situation in which we caught you here, and then we *shall* hear what this is all about."

The forester had lowered his head; his face could not be seen.

"But if you tell us the truth, I promise you on my word of honor that we shall keep it to ourselves. I think I can also answer for Fräulein Sophie's keeping quiet?" Sophie nodded. "Yes, we should like to help you to get out of this situation honorably."

The forester raised his head. He stood up. In his eyes were tears, and while he spoke these tears broke free and ran down into his beard. Others followed. Tears of old age, a graybeard's tears, flowing of themselves.

"Yes, gentlemen," said Forester Kniebusch, "but no one can help me. I understand that you are being very friendly to me, and I accept with gratitude your promise to say nothing. But I am a finished man. I'm too old—and when one is too old, nothing goes right for him any more. Everything that once pleased him is gone. . . . I recently caught the worst poacher, Bäumer, and I want to tell the truth now. I didn't do anything; he simply fell from his bicycle onto a stone and was knocked unconscious at once. Everything I said about a struggle was only to praise myself . . . I wanted to be clever, but an old man shouldn't try to be clever."

Sophie and Wolfgang stared in front of them. They were ashamed of the weeping old man who so shamelessly poured out his heart. Herr von Studmann, however, had directed his brown eyes attentively on him, and now and again he nodded.

"Yes, gentlemen," continued the forester, "and now in the courts they want to twist a rope out of it for me, because Bäumer has a high temperature. And the only one who can defend me is the Geheimrat, and if I don't do what he wants, he won't defend me, but will even take away my livelihood. And what will then become of me and my sick wife?"

The forester stood as if he had forgotten what he wished to say, but at Herr von Studmann's glance he pulled himself together. "Yes, and today after lunch he phoned me up and told me that the gentlemen had gone bathing and that I was to be certain to take their clothes away, otherwise he wouldn't help me. But Sophie was sitting there and it came to nothing. Why he is so angry with the gentlemen I don't know; he didn't say a word about that." Kniebusch stared disconsolately before him.

"Well, Herr Kniebusch, there are other ponds here, aren't there? We needn't have come here," said Studmann.

The forester reflected, a glimmer of hope in his eyes. "In this direction it's difficult," he said. "Here, apart from this, it's all forest and sand."

"Birnbaum," said Sophie.

"Yes, the gentlemen might have gone to the Birnbaum ponds. But then the gentlemen mustn't be home before seven, because it's so far. Would they like to sit in the forest as long as that?"

"Oh, of course we'll do that," said Studmann pleasantly. "The men can feed the cattle without us for once."

"Then I thank the gentlemen very much," said the forester, no longer tearful. "You are being very kind to an old man. But still, it won't help much. I ought sometime to bring a real success home, but that's asking too much of an old man. No young person knows what an old man feels like." He stood a moment longer in thought. "However, through the kindness of the gentlemen, it hasn't been a failure."

He raised his hat and went.

Studmann gazed after him. Then he called out: "Wait, Herr Kniebusch, I'll come along with you for a bit!" And he ran after him, barefooted, in bathing costume, without any regard for his rather tender feet. A true nursemaid, however, doesn't think of herself when she sees others who need comforting.

Sophie and young Pagel were alone, and very pleasantly they conversed, first about Forester Kniebusch and then about the harvest. And because that afternoon Sophie was rested and happy, it did not occur to her to impress young Pagel with feminine tricks or even to make eyes at him, so that Wolfgang was continually obliged to marvel how wrongly he had judged this nice, intelligent girl in the train. And he was now tempted to blame his Berlin eyes for this false judgment.

As to the harvest, however, her father had said that in Neulohe they were at least three weeks behind, and they would never do it unless a proper reinforcement of strong men came. And no one in the village understood why the Rittmeister did not order a gang from Meienburg. They were the most industrious and most submissive of men, as long as they were given enough to eat and smoke. But the Rittmeister had to remember that all the farms in the neighborhood already had their gangs, and the prison was half empty. That's what her father said, for of course she knew nothing about it, she had only just come to the district herself. But she was sorry about the harvest. . . .

Pagel thought this very intelligently spoken and thought it very good of the girl to worry about the Neulohe harvest, which after all did not matter a jot to a Berlin lady's maid. He resolved to discuss the matter with Studmann that evening. Since, however, Studmann had not yet returned, they decided to go into the water once more.

There he saw that Sophie swam excellently, and that it was an effort for him to keep up with her. But he was able to show her something new, a style of swimming which had just begun to spread in Berlin, and which was called the crawl. It always does a young man good when he can do something a little better than a young girl; and if he can teach this young girl something he finds her extremely likeable.

And Sophie also was very much pleased with her disinterested swimming instructor, whom otherwise she had found altogether ill-mannered; and so the two of them were the best of friends when finally a limping, thoughtful Studmann appeared out of the forest.

"Well," he said, sitting down on the grass and lighting himself a cigarette, "it's a strange world, Pagel. The earth sweats fear instead of corn, and its fear infects everything. A generation full of fear, Pagel. As I suspected this afternoon, the peace of the fields is an illusion, and someone is not hesitating to make us understand that as quickly as possible."

"That old geezer," said Sophie very contemptuously, "has been chattering and gossiping again, I suppose? Perhaps it still works on you—we no longer pay any attention to his claptrap."

"No, Fräulein Sophie," countered Studmann, "the old man didn't chatter, unfortunately. I wish he had been more talkative, for queer things seem to be happening here. Well, I think I'll get to know them in time. But, Pagel, I ask you one thing: when you see the old man, be a little friendly. And if you can help him in anything, then do so. After all, he's only an infirm old bundle of fears—Fräulein Sophie is right about that; but when a ship sends out an S O S, one helps it and doesn't spend too much time asking about its cargo."

"Good Lord!" mocked Sophie. "I would never have believed that Forester Kniebusch would ever have got two such helpers." For Pagel had nodded in complete agreement with Studmann. "He certainly hasn't deserved it, the sneak and tell-tale that he is."

"Is there anyone here who deserves anything?" said Studmann. "Certainly not me, and probably not Pagel; and you, Fräulein Sophie, decent and good-hearted girl though you are, no doubt you also have not deserved an extra-special reward."

Here Sophie turned red and felt that the line had a hook, although there was none.

"Well, let's drop it. I really wanted to ask you, Fräulein Sophie, whether you wouldn't like to tell us something about the wood thieves. You see, Kniebusch is so worried about them. He says they go about in gangs, and he as an individual is powerless against them."

"What have the wood thieves got to do with me?" cried Sophie indignantly. "I'm not a spy!"

"I thought, Fräulein Sophie," said Studmann, as if he had heard nothing, "that you in the village would notice when a gang like that sets out sooner than we who live on the farm."

"I am not a spy," Sophie again cried heatedly. "I don't go around spying on poor people."

"Wood-stealing is wood-stealing," persisted Studmann. "Spy sounds ugly, but whoever reports wood-stealing is no spy. I think," he continued persuasively, "you are interested in the farm and its welfare. Your father has a position like that among the men; he has to report sometimes who's been working badly, without being called a sneak for it. And then you sat very comfortably next to the Rittmeister in the train and are sitting quite pleasantly here with us—one must know, after all, to whom one belongs."

Sophie had propped her head on her hands. She looked thoughtfully, now at Herr von Studmann, now at Herr Pagel. But at the same time it wasn't certain whether she had listened to Studmann's cunning words; she seemed to be thinking about something. At last she spoke: "Very well, I'll see. But it isn't certain whether I'll really find out anything. The people don't count me one of them anymore."

"Fine!" said Studmann and got up. "If you only think of us, that's already something. The rest will arrange itself. And now if you've no objection, let's all three go into the water again. My feet are in a bit of a mess; I'd like to cool them a little before going home. Our time ought to be up then, and we can go back without fear of reproach. And you must tell us about the Birnbaum pond, Fräulein Sophie. I believe the old gentleman's capable of not believing the mere word of his forester, but will try and pump us a bit. If he doesn't turn up here himself!"

And Studmann cast a suspicious glance at the forest.

VII

Herr von Studmann had no ground for his fear that the old Geheimrat might turn up in person at the crayfish ponds. In fact, he judged Herr von Teschow wrongly. The latter did not mind prying around quietly, but he preferred to leave things to his men when it came to open rows. Ten horses could not have dragged him to the crayfish ponds where, on this afternoon, a row was to be expected. Instead he wandered, serene and affable, through the village of Neulohe, stopped whenever he met someone, exchanged a few words, and was indeed just like a prince mingling with his subjects. Old Elias hadn't done it better three hours previously.

And while the Geheimrat chattered his way through the village, he was continually thinking what sort of business he could pretend to have at Haase's, for he didn't like doing things awkwardly. He had to find out what the magistrate had against Kniebusch; why he had submitted such an unfavorable report on him. If one doesn't know everything one knows nothing, he had always said, and from Fräulein Kuckhoff he had often heard that no filth is so filthy as to prevent someone coming and growing the finest cucumbers on it.

But he couldn't think of the slightest excuse and was becoming quite discouraged when, just in front of the village square, where the road descended to the cemetery, he saw old Leege. Old Leege was a very ancient woman; formerly, when she was still able to work, she had been employed on the farm, while her husband, now dead for a long time, had earned his bread partly in the parish as a gravedigger, partly in the forest as a woodman. That was all a long time ago, however, and old Leege had been dwelling for some ten years now, ever since her last grandchild went to America, in an old cottage by the cemetery wall. She was a little odd, and feared by everyone, for she had the reputation of being able to put a spell on cattle. This much was certain—warts and erysipelas disappeared at her incantations.

The old Geheimrat was not very fond of old women, a hunters' superstition; and so he hurried on his way when he saw old Leege. But she had spied him with her sharp black eyes. She darted across the village square so as to block his path, and began, weeping huskily, to mumble something about her cottage roof, through which the whole of the last rain had come as through a sieve.

"That's no business of mine, Leege," the Geheimrat shouted into her deaf ears. "You must go to the magistrate about it. It's a parish matter, not a farm matter."

But old Leege would not be put off so easily, for she was firmly convinced that Herr von Teschow was her master and responsible for her welfare, just as he had been thirty or forty years ago—nor would she let herself be hustled out of the way. She filled the whole square with her husky, wailing cries in such a way that the Geheimrat began to feel truly sorry about the business. And since he reflected that a bad excuse is always better than none at all—and why shouldn't one, after all, talk to Haase about the leaky roof of a poor superannuated farm worker—he yielded and set off with her to Hangman's Pines, as Leege's dwelling place was called.

"Well, don't any of your grandchildren ever write to you?" he asked in order to escape from the roof topic, about which he already knew everything—front, back and gable. Old Leege moaned happily that her grandsons wrote from time to time and also sent her little pictures.

Well, what did they write, and how were things over there?

Yes, what they wrote she couldn't say exactly, for her old cat had broken her glasses over a year ago; but if the berry crop was good this year, she might perhaps be able to afford a new pair!

Then why didn't she get someone to read the letters to her?

No, she wouldn't do that, for if her grandsons should ever write that they weren't getting on well, it would immediately be spread through the whole village, and she didn't want people to talk about her grandsons. She would have plenty of time to read them when she had new glasses.

Did they ever send anything for their old grandmother, a little money or a little packet of something to eat?

Oh, yes, they sent her nice pretty little pictures; but as to food, they probably hadn't got so much in the Indian country!

In the meantime they had reached the old cottage, which really looked uncannily like a veritable witch's hovel out of a fairy tale, there among the Hangman's Pines. The Geheimrat took a look at the ancient mossy thatched roof, from the front, from the back and from the gable side, always accompanied by the wailing complaints of the old woman. He had suddenly become very thorough and was no longer in such a hurry to escape from her. For a true fox will smell out a goose in a cartload of straw. So he pushed open the door and entered the old hovel—he had smelled something. The inside of the house under the Hangman's Pines looked exactly as one would expect from the outside; that is to say, just as a pigsty ought not to look if the pigs are to thrive.

But neither dirt nor stench could upset the Geheimrat now, nor the rags and rubbish of extreme poverty. With his cunning old eyes he looked around, and there on the wall he spotted what he wanted, namely, an old photograph behind which something had been stuffed.

"Yes, that's Ernie," moaned the old woman. "He was the last to go out there, just at the beginning of 'thirteen, just before the Great War broke out."

"And that's one of the little pictures that Ernest sent you, Leege, eh? Have you got any more?"

Yes, she had some more, and there were some still in the letters, and she had also made a border of the little pictures in the kitchen cupboard.

"Listen, Leege," said the Geheimrat. "You'll get a new roof, I promise you. And if you want a goat you'll get one, too. And enough to eat as well. And a pair of glasses also. And firewood. . . ."

The old woman raised her hands toward him, as if she wanted to push the abundance of all these gifts away from her breast, and she began to praise her good old master.

But the Geheimrat was in a hurry. "You stay here, Leege, and in half an hour at the latest I'll be here with the magistrate; perhaps I'll bring the pastor, too. And you are not to go out, nor are you to give any of the little pictures away."

Old Leege promised this solemnly.

And everything took place in proper and orderly manner. With the Geheimrat came the pastor and the magistrate, and a search was made, and old Leege could not marvel enough at the three gentlemen who wouldn't stop turning over and shaking out her things. They even messed her pair of winter stockings about; the magistrate pulled the bed straw from its frame—all in the search for these bright-colored little pictures.

As for old Leege, she understood nothing of this business, and although they trumpeted ten times into her ear that this was "proper" money, gold money, foreign currency—while the other was rubbishy money, worthless money, muck—it still seemed to her as if these worthy three—Wealth, Priesthood and Authority—had turned into little children looking for Easter eggs in her cottage.

Geheimrat von Teschow, however, was once more in his element, and now and again he bubbled over, with a remark to the effect that of course an old man like himself had had to come first and look after his old employee, who, legally speaking, was no concern of his, while the magistrate, who ought to look after the local poor in respect of his office, and the pastor, who ought to look after his parishioners as a religious duty, once again didn't know a thing about anything, and would have let the old woman, with all her wealth, drown from rain and perish from hunger.

Both the magistrate and the parson made the best reply they could to these continual and pointed remarks—namely, none; and scarcely was the old woman's fortune ascertained to be two hundred and eighty-five dollars and legally recorded, than the parson hastily departed, for the matter was now in the best hands. The magistrate took charge of the bank notes and in return for the little pictures promised the old woman the thatcher for the next day. Also a basket of provisions. "Also a goat, of course, Leege. Also a new pair of glasses. Very good, Leege."

"What are you going to do with the money, Haase?" asked the Geheimrat, on the way back.

"Yes, Herr Geheimrat, that's a business," said the magistrate. "I shall have to think about it first."

"I believe I've read somewhere that foreign currency must be handed over. To the bank. But that need not be true."

"Yes, Herr Geheimrat, if I take it to the bank I'll get a worthless bundle of money for it, and if old Leege wants some coffee next week, I shall have to say to her: 'The money's all gone, Leege.'"

"That's no good to the old woman, Haase. But I suppose there's no help for it, if that's the regulation."

"Perhaps it isn't so—the Geheimrat might have read it wrongly."

"Yes, of course, I might have. There's so much in the newspapers."

"That's true—one gets dizzy merely looking at them."

The two walked along thoughtfully. The tall, lean Haase with his ravaged, multi-lined face, and the short, fat Geheimrat with his bright red face—which, however, also had its lines.

"The fact is," began Haase again, "we're all busy with the harvest; who's got time to go to the bank in Frankfurt to change the money? And I must give the thatcher something and pay for the straw and the goat—I can't do that with dollars. In the first place there'd be talk, and anyway I mustn't do it."

"Well, in that case someone else must change the money until there is time to hand it in," said the Geheimrat.

"Yes. That's what I've been thinking all the time. Only, who's got so much money on hand in harvest time?"

"I think I've still got something in my safe. I'll have a look. I'll let you know this evening."

"I've been doing my threshing yesterday," said Haase, "and I think I'll deliver tomorrow. I'm only doing it, Herr Geheimrat, because I have to pay your forester the day after tomorrow."

The Geheimrat said not a word.

"I wonder whether the forester would perhaps wait a few days."

"I don't understand this. Excuse me, Haase, I'm probably deaf in both ears. I suppose you're talking about Kniebusch's mortgage for ten thousand prewar marks?"

The magistrate bit his lip. "I don't understand it either, Herr Geheimrat," he said sulkily, "but your Kniebusch is an old hound. He's swindled me. I can't cancel the mortgage now, and I have to give him forty hundredweights of rye a year as interest, and that's why the rye's going away tomorrow."

"Well, well!" grinned the old gentleman, extremely pleased that someone had been caught out (for there was nothing in life he esteemed so highly as swindling a person properly). "You do get up to mischief! . . . Now I understand why the examining judge in Frankfurt speaks so badly about Kniebusch."

"I only wrote what was right," cried the magistrate hotly.

"Of course, Haase, what else?" said the old Geheimrat, delighted. "Always in accordance with justice and law and order! But we'll talk about that this evening. For I'll bring you the money so that you can change the dollars, since what you get for your rye won't cover everything. I'm glad to help you, Haase. And if I go to Frankfurt I'll hand in my dollars, and when you go there you'll hand in yours—the Government will certainly have learned how to wait. And Kniebusch also. I'll see to that, you can rely on me. He's a cunning dog, old Kniebusch; I'd never have thought him capable of taking in a farmer. Well, you'll tell me all about it this evening, Haase."

"The dollar is now one million one hundred thousand marks—that's what we'll exchange at, I suppose?" asked the magistrate thoughtfully.

"Why, of course," said the Geheimrat. "What else?"

"And supposing it rises tomorrow? Then I'll be landed with all those marks and won't be able to buy her anything."

"Oh, you'll be able to buy something for a little while, and lay in a few supplies, anyway. When it's gone, it's gone. If someone else had seen the little pictures she would have got nothing. And, anyway, in the letters it says that the grandson sends her ten dollars every month, with twenty dollars extra on her birthday and at Christmas, so there's always something coming in. Why, old Leege's got more now than she had in her whole life!"

"We ought to be certain, though, that no one will talk," said Haase. "Otherwise there'll be trouble."

"Who's to talk, Haase? Pastor Lehnich will keep his trap shut, having made a fool of himself. And we two won't talk. As for old Leege, she didn't get wise—she thinks it's a holiday in heaven. If she does talk no one will understand, and supposing someone does, just let him come and say that Geheimrat Horst-Heinz von Teschow is up to something shady. We'll hand the dollars in—that's agreed, eh, Haase?"

"As soon as I go to Frankfurt, without fail, Herr Geheimrat."

And so the two separated, Haase not quite content, for he would have preferred to manage the business himself; but he knew that the fattest pigs squeal the loudest for food. The Geheimrat, however, was perfectly content; he had not only learned what he wanted to know, he had also done a little business. However rich a man may be, he never feels he is rich enough. Forester Kniebusch, though, was very much astonished at the indifference with which his surly master heard about his unsuccessful search of the crayfish ponds. And still more astonished was he that Herr von Teschow knew all about the readjustment of the mortgage and was even interceding on Haase's behalf, asking for him to be allowed to pay two weeks later. To this Kniebusch willingly agreed; but all the more obstinate did he prove when the Geheimrat wanted to discover how Haase had been moved to such an unheard-of concession.

The forester swore by all that was holy, his pale blue eyes becoming even bluer and more honest, that Haase was a thoroughly decent man and had done what was right out of sheer decency. "And as a matter of fact it should have been sixty hundredweights of rye, Herr Geheimrat, but I'm not so particular, like Haase."

"Kniebusch!" cried the old gentleman in a rage, "you can't pull a hunchback through a lattice fence! Where money begins, decency stops—and now you two old rogues want . . ."

But no, the forester stuck to it! His forehead was dripping with sweat, and his tone became so sincere and ingenuous that it smelled of lies and deceit for ten miles against the wind. And it must be said that the Kniebusch who had always been subservient to his master had never so impressed Herr von Teschow as did the Kniebusch who was obviously telling him a pack of lies.

"Well, I never!" said the old gentleman when he was alone again. "My Kniebusch is getting on. But just wait! What one won't tell, the other will babble—and I'll eat my hat if I don't worm everything out of Haase this evening."

But in this he was mistaken: the magistrate kept as mum as the forester, to the old gentleman's surprise. For such a thing had never happened before.

To be sure, he did not yet eat his hat on that account. The Geheimrat was not one to give up hope so easily.

VIII

Studmann and Pagel had taken leave of their fair companion outside her home, and the villagers had seen with astonishment that these suspicious gentlemen from Berlin had not simply passed on with a nod, as was usually done with a farm girl, but had shaken her hand properly, as if she were a real lady. The older one, with the egg-shaped head, had raised his cap. The younger was not wearing one.

Admiration for Sophie, who seemed to the villagers like a butterfly which has emerged dazzling and gay from its dull chrysalis, had immeasurably risen. What her clothes had begun (and the journey with the Rittmeister) was completed by this formal leave-taking. Mothers no longer found it necessary to admonish their urchins to behave themselves with Sophie—"She's a real lady now!" Henceforth she was as safe from their mischievous tricks as, say, the young Fräulein in the Villa. None of them wanted to get into trouble with the gentlemen from Berlin, who might be detectives. And the gentlemen had gone on their way without any inkling that they had achieved the isolation in the village of a dangerous enemy.

Räder was waiting for them in the office. Madam would like to speak to Herr von Studmann at a quarter to seven.

Herr von Studmann, glancing at his watch, saw that it was a quarter past seven already. He looked at Räder inquiringly. But the servant did not move a muscle or utter a word.

"Well, I'll go right away, Pagel," said Studmann. "Don't hold up supper because of me; you'd better begin."

Wolfgang Pagel remained alone in the office. He did not begin his supper, however, but paced up and down, contentedly smoking his cigarette and glancing every now and again through the wide-open windows at the green park loud with the song of birds.

As is the way with all young men, he didn't think about his situation. He just went to and fro, smoking, moving between light and shadow. Nothing weighed on him, and he desired nothing. If he had thought about his situation and summed it up in the shortest way, he would have said he was—almost—happy.

On closer examination he would perhaps have discovered a slight feeling of emptiness, like the convalescent who has survived a life-threatening illness and hasn't yet been counted among the living. He'd survived serious danger, but still had no purpose in life; indeed he didn't fully belong to it. A secret power which wanted him healthy led his actions and, even more, his thoughts. Quite unlike Herr von Studmann, he was not interested in whatever lay behind things; he was only interested in the exterior. He instinctively defended himself against having to worry. He didn't look at rental contracts and made no painful calculations about rent levels. He considered old Herr von Teschow a good-natured, bushy-bearded old man and didn't want to know about his cunning and sinister intentions. He was fully satisfied by the simple, tangible life-tasks—going out into the field, the stoking up of the barley, and the deep, dreamless sleep that comes from extreme physical exhaustion. He was carefree like a convalescent, superficial like a convalescent, and still felt, without being clear about it, again like a convalescent, that frightening hint of what he had only barely escaped from.

Tomorrow they would begin gathering in the sheaves again—excellent! They could, of course, have gathered them in today, as all the farms in the neighborhood were doing; but the old lady in the Manor (he had not yet seen her) was supposed to be against working on Sunday. Good. Studmann had planned something for this evening; what it was he didn't know, but it was bound to be pleasant. Everything was pleasant here. He hoped Studmann would soon return. Wolfgang didn't like to be alone. He felt best in the midst of people.

Thoughtfully he came to a stop in front of the pinewood bookshelf, where the black annual volumes of laws and decrees stood in long rows. Row upon row, volume upon volume, year upon year they decreed, proclaimed, threatened, regulated and punished from the beginning of time to the end of the world, and yet every individual continually battered his skull against this world of law and order.

Pagel lifted down one of the oldest volumes. From the spotty brown paper a decree spoke to him, forbidding that a servant or inmate be given more than six score crayfish a week to eat. He laughed. Today bathers were chased from the ponds, thus protecting the crayfish from the people; in those days people were protected from the crayfish!

He put the volume back in its place, and just below his eye-level was the top edge of another row of volumes of the official *District Gazette*. Out of one of them peeped the corner of a sheet of paper. He seized it with two fingers and found he held a piece of typewriting paper only a quarter covered with typing. "Dearest! My dearest darling! My only one!"

He glanced at the volume from which he had taken it. It was the *Gazette* for the year 1900. Pagel felt reassured and read on with a smile, tasting something of the charm which clings to love letters of a century ago, the letters of lovers whose voices have died away, whose love is extinguished, who lie cold in their graves. He read down to the name "Violet."

That was no common name in Germany; until recently he had come across it only in books. But he had heard it frequently in the last few days, usually in the form "Vi." In some families, however, names are handed down. . . . He rubbed his finger cautiously over the typescript. It was fresh! The fingertip showed a faint smear.

Tearing the cover from the typewriter, he typed the words "Dearest! My dearest darling! My only one!"—with repugnance. He, too, had once heard those similar words and did not like being reminded of them. There was no doubt about it. The letter had been typed on this machine, and very recently: the capital E was defective. . . .

His first impulse was to destroy the letter; his next, to put it back in the *Gazette*. He didn't want to know anything of this affair.

But steady, old chap, steady! he thought. This Vi is very young—sixteen, perhaps only fifteen. She won't like her letters lying about in an office. I ought . . . Pagel put the letter in his inside pocket. That was no mistrust of Studmann, but Pagel was determined to read this letter only after he had considered everything in detail. Perhaps he wouldn't even mention it to him. In any case he must be clear about everything first. It was not pleasant; he would have liked to have continued walking up and down in his office without a thought in the world. But that's life. It doesn't ask if it suits us. We're already engaged in it.

So Pagel went thoughtfully up and down his office, smoking. (If only Studmann doesn't suddenly turn up!)

First question: Was the letter really a letter? No, it was the carbon copy of a letter. Second question: Would the sender have made a copy? Very improbable. Firstly, it wasn't the sort of letter which is easily written on a typewriter—a thing like that had to be written by hand if it wasn't to look utterly idiotic. Secondly, it was very improbable that Fräulein Violet would have chosen the office to write her love letters in. Thirdly, she would never keep the carbon copy there. And why make a copy at all? Conclusion: It was therefore, in all probability, the carbon copy of a copy of a letter of Fräulein Vi's. (One could leave till later the consideration: Where was the copy itself?)

Third question: Could the recipient have made a copy and carbon for himself? There seemed to be no point in *his* making a copy, though. Because the recipient would have the original! No, it was quite clear—an unauthorized person was responsible. And it ought not to be difficult to find out who. This third party must have had regular access to the office, otherwise he would not have been able to type or keep anything there. No, there could be no doubt about it. It could only have been that ugly little fellow called Black Meier.

And Wolfgang now recalled Meier's nocturnal departure, his waking up in a fright, his "He wants to shoot me." They had thought it was a question of jealousy involving that chubby-cheeked poultry maid, and the Rittmeister had accepted this explanation. So he, too, had no inkling of the real truth. Yes, there was something mysterious and dangerous about the whole affair—although Meier, of course, was a coward who had only imagined he was going to be shot. One didn't murder people so lightly because of an intercepted love letter.

And there still remained the question whether he ought to say nothing and replace this carbon copy—better still, destroy it; or whether he ought to speak about it—with Studmann, perhaps. Or with the passionate little Fräulein Vi. One must not forget, either, that the absconding Herr Meier was carrying another copy around with him. But what, after all, could such a copy prove? Anyone might make up a thing like that on the typewriter. It mentions no name that refers to anybody.

All the same, this business could upset an inexperienced young girl. But perhaps she already knew that this letter had been intercepted and copied. Its intended recipient must have known about it—how else would Meier have been so frightened that night by a rustling at the window? Yes, thought Pagel, if I only knew exactly what Meier cried out then. Was it "He wants to shoot me" or "He wants to shoot me again?" Shooting *again* would mean that Herr Meier had already attempted something like blackmail—one doesn't copy a letter of this sort for purely literary reasons—and that he had received a rather violent answer, perhaps with gun in hand. . . .

Pagel racked his brains, but he could not remember what Meier had actually called out.

Herr von Studmann entered, returning from his meeting with Frau von Prackwitz. Pagel glanced at Studmann's face. Even Herr von Studmann looked rather lost in thought. Now he could ask him what Meier had shouted back then, but he thought better of it. Such an inquiry would provoke counter-questions. Perhaps he would have to reveal the copy of this letter—and he didn't want to do that. Its recipient, whoever that might be, had been warned, and Fräulein Vi presumably too. So Pagel decided for the moment to say nothing at all. He had no wish to get into trouble by letting himself be sucked into love intrigues. Nothing would be missed if this letter stayed hidden for the moment, namely, in his pocket.

IX

Studmann was so lost in thought that he did not notice Pagel had not yet eaten, and when the young man poured himself out a cup of tea and took some bread, he looked up. "Eating a second supper, Pagel?"

"I've not eaten yet, old man."

"Oh, so I see. I'm sorry! I was just thinking about something." Studmann relapsed into thoughtfulness.

After a while Pagel asked cautiously: "What's on your mind?"

Studmann answered with surprising violence. "The peace of the fields is a bigger fraud than we supposed, Pagel. These people have their troubles. But I expect you'd rather I didn't bother you with them—" He broke off.

Herr von Studmann also had a letter in his pocket, a letter which Frau von Prackwitz regarded as a rather harmless business communication. To Herr von Studmann, however, it seemed crafty and underhanded—he would rather have been carrying a hand grenade in his pocket. But he was much more preoccupied with something else. Frau von Prackwitz was still a good-looking woman; she had very beautiful eyes, and there had been tears in those eyes, tears which had not made them any the less beautiful. A woman who must always control herself in the presence of a hot-headed husband and a wayward daughter, who must never let her household notice anything, must be able to let herself go before a chosen confidant. This absence of restraint had only made Frau Eva the more charming. A warm sweetness, a helplessness which was all the more seductive in so mature a woman, had captivated von Studmann.

I must help the poor creature! he thought. What does that kid think she's doing, carrying on in this way! Why, she can't be more than fifteen!

At this moment Pagel, likewise wrapped in thought, looked up from his cheese. "How old do you reckon Fräulein Violet is?"

"What?" cried Herr von Studmann, dropping his knife and fork with a loud clatter on his plate. "What makes you ask, Pagel? What's it got to do with you?"

"Good Lord!" said Pagel, taken aback. "I can ask, can't I? All right, then—not!"

"I was just thinking of something else," explained Studmann, a little embarrassed.

"It looked damn well as if you had just been thinking of her age, too!" grinned Pagel.

"Not a bit. Little girls like that don't mean a thing to me—I'm not twenty-two, like you, Pagel."

"Twenty-three."

"All right. Well, it's now just after eight. I think it'll be a good idea if we toddle along and indulge in a drink at one of the two local inns."

"Fine. And how old do you think Fräulein Violet is?"

"Sixteen. Seventeen."

"Much too high! She's got such soft curves, it's deceptive. Fifteen at the most."

"Anyway, keep your hands off her, Herr Pagel!" cried Studmann with a fierce glint in his eyes.

"Why, of course," said Pagel with astonishment. "Heavens, Studmann, you're getting like the sphinx itself. Well, about the inns?"

Somewhat more calmly Studmann outlined his plan of getting to know the innkeeper, of becoming regular patrons, and thus trying to discover as much as possible from the village gossip. "Neulohe is much too big. Even if we were to run round night after night looking for field thieves, we might still never find one. And our Rittmeister wants to see results. So a hint from the inn-keeper would be worth its weight in gold."

"True!" agreed Pagel. "Are we taking a gun with us?"

"No use doing that tonight; tonight we just want to get pally. But if you'd like to take one along! You still want to be in full war paint. I dragged one of those things around for over five years."

It was half-past eight when the two finally set off. The sun had gone down, but it was scarcely dusk even in the shade of the trees. The road to the village was full of people: children ran about, old people sat on little benches outside their doors, the younger folk hung about in groups, a girl dragged a restive goat into its shed. When the two men passed by, the people fell silent, the children stopped running about, everyone stared after them.

"Come along, Studmann," suggested Pagel, "let's go on the outside of the village. We'll find our way somehow. This being stared at gets me down. And anyway they don't all have to know that the farm officials are going boozing."

"Very well," said Studmann, and they turned into a narrow path between the windowless gable walls of two laborers' houses, and came to a ridge. To the left lay deserted orchards, to the right stretched a flourishing potato field. They came to a churned-up cart track; on the right it led straight into the fields, on the left it approached the last houses in the village. The air was turning gray, one could feel the darkness coming on, the birds had become silent. From the village echoed a laugh which died away.

As Pagel and Studmann strolled along, each in a rut of the track, they encountered a troop of people, some six or seven, men and women, who went by quietly in single file, baskets on their backs, along the grassy strip between the ruts.

"Good evening!" said Pagel loudly.

There was a muffled response, and the ghostly procession was gone.

The two went on a few steps, uncertain, then stopped as if by agreement. They turned round and gazed after the silent wanderers. Yes, it was true, they hadn't gone to the village, but had turned into the path between the fields.

"Well!" said Pagel.

"That was queer!" replied Studmann.

"Where are they going to at this hour?"

"With baskets?"

"To steal!"

"They might be going over there into the forest to gather wood."

"Gather wood—at night!"

"Well, let's give up our drink and errand, and follow them."

"Yes, but wait a moment. Let them get over the crest first."

"I didn't recognize any of them," said Pagel thoughtfully.

"It's getting dark; you could hardly distinguish their faces."

"It would be marvelous if we caught six first go."

"Seven," said Studmann. "Three men and four women. Well, let's go."

But after the first few steps Studmann stopped again. "We haven't thought this out, Pagel. Even if we catch the people we won't know them. How are we to find out their names? They can tell us what they like."

"While you're holding a general staff meeting here, Studmann, the people will slip through our fingers," urged Pagel impatiently.

"To be well informed is half the battle, Pagel."

"Well?"

"You go to the village and get some old inhabitant who knows everyone. . . ."

"Kowalewski? The overseer?"

"Yes, that's right. He's a bit slack; it'll be good for him to come more into conflict with his men; it'll make him sharper. They'll be in a rage with him if he has to name them."

But Pagel had long stopped listening to the opinions of a former reception manager of a city hotel in a period of inflation. He was already running at a steady trot toward the village. It did him good to run. It had been an eternity since he had done anything like this. Not since his time in the Baltic. Since then, he'd always moved as slowly as possible. It was a long day, waiting for play to begin. Now he was glad to see how efficiently his body worked. The mild, somewhat cool damp air filled his lungs, and he was glad that he had such a broad chest; despite his running he inhaled deeply and slowly and pleasurably. In Berlin he had sometimes had a stitch in lungs or heart, and as is the way with young people who have never really been ill, he had then imagined some serious malady. Well, thank God, it had been nothing. He ran like Nurmi. I'm in good condition, he thought cheerfully.

In the village he slowed down to a walk, so as not to arouse attention. Nevertheless, his disappearance into Kowalewski's house attracted a lot of notice. "See that!" they said. "An hour and a half ago he was saying bye-bye to Sophie, and now he's calling on her again. He's got rid of that old egg-face he had with him, of course. Well, what do you expect of a Berliner? And he's a strong fellow, too. Sophie's also become a bit of a townee—if you're used to cream, you want cream!"

Unfortunately the young man came out of Kowalewski's house, accompanied only by the old man, immediately. He probably hadn't seen Sophie, who went on singing upstairs. Hastily the two left the village, Kowalewski keeping to the young man's side, half a pace behind, like a well-trained dog. When Pagel had burst into his Sunday quiet, merely saying: "Come along with me, Kowalewski," the old overseer had followed without a question. A poor man has not to reason why.

Studmann was waiting where the path turned into the fields.

"Good evening, Kowalewski. Glad you've come. Has Pagel told you? No? Good. Where does this path lead to?"

"To our outfields, sir, and then into the Geheimrat's forest."

"Any peasants' fields there?"

"No, only our land. Lots five and seven. And on the other side lots four and six."

"Good. If you had met six or seven people here half an hour ago, silent, with baskets that looked empty on their backs—what would you have thought, Kowalewski?"

Kowalewski pointed. "Going over there?"

"Yes, over there, toward the outfields."

Kowalewski pointed. "Coming from over there?"

"Yes, Kowalewski, that's about where they'll have come from, not from the village."

"Then they were from Altlohe, sir."

"And what do Altlohe people want on our field? Now, at nighttime?"

"Well, sir, there's nothing on the potatoes yet. But there are the beetroots; perhaps they want to pick the leaves. And then further over is the wheat which we cut on Friday and Saturday—perhaps they want a few ears."

"Stealing, eh, Kowalewski?"

"They need the beetroot leaves for goats' fodder, nearly all of them have a goat. And if the wheat's nice and dry, you can grind it in a coffee grinder—they learned that in the war."

"Very good. Well, let's follow them. You come with us, Kowalewski. But I suppose you don't like to?"

"It's not for me to say, sir."

"You needn't have any more to do with it, Kowalewski, than just to give me a dig in the ribs if one of the people tells me a false name."

"Yes, sir."

"But I suppose they'll have it in for you, Kowalewski?"

"Even if they're Altlohe people, they know I have to do what I'm ordered. They understand that much."

"But you don't like admitting that they are stealing, Kowalewski, do you?"

"You see, sir, it's bad if you've got a goat and have no fodder for it. And it's still worse if you've got no flour for the children's soup."

"But Kowalewski!" Studmann stopped abruptly, then went on into the growing darkness. "How are you going to preserve order if people simply steal what they need? That would ruin the farm, wouldn't it?"

Kowalewski kept obstinately silent, but Studmann was unyielding. "Well, Kowalewski?"

"That's no sort of order, sir, if you'll excuse me, when people work and yet can't give their children anything to eat."

"Why don't they buy things? If they work, they must have money to spend."

"They've only got paper money, sir. Everybody sticks tight to his goods and won't take the paper."

"I see! But still you must agree, Kowalewski, that the farm can't carry on if everyone takes what he needs. You want your wages when they're due, but where are they to come from if there are no profits? Take it from me, the Ritt-meister doesn't find it too easy."

"The old Geheimrat always did well; he made a lot of money."

"But perhaps the Rittmeister has more difficulties—he has to pay the old man rent."

"The people from Altlohe don't take any notice of that."

"You mean they don't care?"

"No, they don't care."

"And do you think it right for them to steal, Kowalewski?"

"If a man has no fodder for his goat . . ." began the obstinate old man again.

"Rubbish! Do you think it right, Kowalewski?"

"I wouldn't do it, sir. But of course I get my corn from the farm and pota-toes and free pasture for a cow . . ."

"Do you think it right, Kowalewski?" Herr von Studmann almost screamed. Pagel began to laugh.

"What are you laughing at, Pagel? Don't be an idiot! Here's an old man, who himself has never stolen, advocating the right to steal from his own employer. Have you ever stolen yourself, Kowalewski?"

It was laughable. Herr von Studmann screamed at the old man almost as Bailiff Meier used to. But this did not intimidate Kowalewski.

"Do you mean what you call stealing, sir, or what we call stealing?"

"Is there any difference?" growled Studmann. But he knew there was.

Pagel intervened. "May I put a question, Herr von Studmann?"

"If you like. This warped morality seems to amuse you very much, Herr Pagel!"

"It's now very dark," said Pagel cheerfully, "and Herr Kowalewski knows that neither of us is familiar with the fields. Tell me, Kowalewski, where does our beetroot field lie?"

"About five minutes' walk ahead and then to the right over the rye stubble. You can see it in the starlight."

"And the wheat field?"

"About three or four minutes' walk along the path. Then we'll be right on it."

"Well, Kowalewski," said Pagel mischievously, "if you think that these people have a right to take their fodder, why don't you lead us a bit zigzag in the dark. You know we haven't the faintest notion where things are!"

"Pagel!" cried Studmann.

"I can't do that, sir. That wouldn't be right. If you tell me to do something, I can't lead you around by the nose."

"Well, then," said Pagel with satisfaction, "now we've got the thing clear. You believe in what's right, Kowalewski. And what Herr von Studmann does is right. But what the people from Altlohe do is not right. You understand what they're doing, but you don't find it right, you don't find it proper . . ."

"Well, sir, that may be. But when the goat hasn't any fodder?"

"Stop!" shrieked Studmann. "Your success didn't last long, Pagel!"

The stars glimmered in the almost black vault of heaven, and they saw round them nothing but gradations of black and gray. After a while, Pagel began to speak again. Something had occurred to him, and that something made sense. Because he sensed that the rather didactic and pedantic Studmann had developed an anger for the soft Kowalewski, who only thought and felt in a vague and confused way. Pagel felt the urge to try to reconcile Herr von Studmann with Sophie's father.

"You know," he said, "Herr Kowalewski is rather worried about our harvest, Studmann. He says we're three weeks behind."

"That's so!" said the overseer.

"Sounds bad," growled Studmann.

"We've got to have men as quickly as possible, Kowalewski thinks. And since the Rittmeister couldn't dig any up in Berlin, Kowalewski thinks we ought to have a prison gang."

"Me, sir?" asked the old man, still more astonished.

"Yes, your daughter told me today that you thought since the prison's half empty on account of the number of gangs they've already sent out, we'd better get a move on, otherwise we'll be left empty-handed."

"Me, sir?" asked the old man still more astonished.

"Well," said Herr von Studmann, "I've already spoken to the Rittmeister about it. But he thinks it involves a lot of expense, especially as the convicts know nothing of farming. So you're in favor of it, Kowalewski?"

"Me? No, sir. They're just a lot of criminals."

"Quite so. Men who have stolen. But Herr Pagel just said that you told him . . ."

"His daughter Sophie, Studmann."

"Your daughter, then. Your daughter probably got it from you."

"From me, sir?"

"Now don't start acting the fool again. All right, Kowalewski, I shan't bother you again." He stopped. "How much farther have we to go?" he asked very crossly.

"Here to the right, sir, is the rye stubble. If we cross that we'll come to the beetroot field."

"Do you think the people are really there?" Herr von Studmann suddenly felt qualms.

"Our beetroots aren't much this year; we transplanted them a bit too late. I think if there are any people they'll be on the wheat."

"And the wheat is straight ahead, isn't it?"

"Another three or four minutes."

"You know what, Pagel—why should we all three make the detour? You dash across the rye stubble, check up on the beetroots, and then come after us as quickly as you can."

"Right, Herr von Studmann."

"And since you probably won't meet anyone there, let me have the gun. Thanks. Well, good hunting, Pagel!"

"Same to you, Studmann."

With his hands in his pockets, Pagel sauntered cross the stubble, his glance fixed on the starry sky rather than on the ground. The footsteps of the others had already died away. Through his shoes he felt the cold dew brushed from the stubble. For the first time he was glad he did not have to be with Herr von Studmann. Schoolmaster, nursemaid! But he immediately regretted this thought. Studmann was really a decent fellow, and his pedantry was merely the shadow cast by a perfect reliability, a quality that had almost vanished today. It'll only make things difficult for him, he thought. Now I'm just the opposite, I'm too lax, I let things slide. This isn't a hotel business with highly experienced headwaiters and cunning elevator boys—good old Studmann will have to adapt himself. I, on the other hand—well, take this case . . .

He looked around. The field of rye stubble stretched, gray-white, in front of him. The ground beneath his feet seemed to sink a little. The dark starless patch which he saw over there against the sky was the beetroot field, perhaps.

Take this case, he thought. I ought to get to the bottom of it. Me, sir? No, Kowalewski wasn't being stupid. He really didn't know anything about it. But why should Sophie try to fool me? What interest's she got in a prison gang, to make her tell me that tale? Oh, what nonsense! There's probably some very simple explanation. I've enough with this silly love letter in my pocket. I don't want any more worries. I'll do my work and worry about nothing. The beetroots . . .

He stood still. Only another fifty or sixty paces separated him from the beetroot field, which rose like a hill against the starry sky. But dark though the field was, he could make out darker points moving on it. Sometimes a clear echo resounded when a knife struck a stone. Darker points! Pagel tried to count them. Six or seven? Sixteen? Twenty-six? It could have been over thirty! A swarm of locusts, a flying plague, attacking the fields at night . . .

"If the goat has no fodder . . ." But these weren't hungry goats. This was a robber gang—and must be caught!

Pagel's hand went to his hip pocket. Then he remembered that he had no weapon. Walking more and more slowly, he wondered if he ought to run back and call the others. But he, who had been able to recognize the thieves against the dark background, must long since have been noticed by them, standing out as he did against the lighter rye stubble. If he went for help, they would be gone! The fact that they so calmly saw him approach proved that they thought he was one of them. Or they thought there was no need to be afraid of one man. That way it's also probably going to go wrong. But in making all these rash decisions he didn't even hesitate once.

Step by step he advanced, perhaps a little slowly, but not through fear. Now he was quite close. His feet had left the crackling rye stubble; the beet-root leaves hung over his shoes like wet rags. Soon he would have to call out to them.

If I only catch a few, six or eight . . . he thought. And an idea came to him. Wrenching his jacket open, he snatched the silver cigarette case from his waistcoat pocket and raised it. "Hands up, or I'll shoot," he roared.

The case glittered in the starlight.

If only they see it! he thought. If they only see it straight away! It all depends on the first moment. If those near me put their hands up, the others will do the same.

"Hands up!" he shouted again, as loudly as he could. "I'll put a bullet into the man who doesn't put his hands up!"

A woman gave a little scream. A man's very deep voice said: "Here, what's all this!" But they raised their hands. Scattered over the dark field, the shadowy horde stood, their hands reaching to the starry sky.

I must shout as loud as possible, he thought with feverish excitement, so that they'll hear in the wheat field. If only they come quick enough!

And he roared at a non-existent man in the rear that, if he lowered his hands again, he'd have a bullet through him. He was gripping the cigarette case so tightly that its sharp edge cut painfully into his flesh. The people, so many around one man, stood like stiff dolls. This attitude did not necessarily mean surrender to fate. It might also have been a threat, and he was overwhelmed by the helplessness of his position: he was holding up thirty people with a ridiculous cigarette case. Only one of them needed to go for him, and they would all be on him. He was not afraid they would beat him to death—but he would be thrashed, the women would tear his hair out, he would become a figure of ridicule, unable to show himself in the village again . . .

How much time had passed? Do the seconds pass slowly? The minutes? How long had he been standing here, with pretended power among the powerless, who only need remember their strength to humble him? He didn't know. Time passed so slowly. He stopped shouting and listened. Weren't they coming yet?

Someone coughed, someone else moved. The man with the deep voice, quite close to Pagel, spoke: "How much longer are we to stand like this, sir? My arms are beginning to ache. What's going to happen?"

"Be quiet!" shouted Pagel. "You're all to be quiet, otherwise you'll get a bullet!" He had to keep saying that. Since he couldn't even fire a warning shot he must convince them by words of his dangerousness.

But now rescue came! Across the rye stubble Studmann came running, with Kowalewski following.

Breathless, as if it were he who had been running so quickly, Pagel yelled: "Shoot! For God's sake shoot, Studmann, shoot into the air and show them that we can! I've been standing here for ten minutes with my cigarette case in my hand."

"Good work, Pagel," said Studmann—and a shot, strangely small and dry under the expanse of heaven, cracked over the heads of the people.

A few laughed. The deep voice said: "Look out, they're throwing crackers about!" More laughed.

"Form up in twos!" called Studmann. "Get your baskets on your backs! We're going to the farm, where we shall take your names. Then everyone can go home. Pagel, you lead the way; I'll bring up the rear. We'd better leave old Kowalewski out of it; he can shuffle along behind. I hope they obey. We can't go shooting people on account of a few beetroot leaves."

"Why not?" asked Pagel.

The roles were changed. Pagel still trembled from the excitement; having felt himself threatened, he regarded his supposed threateners as bad lots, almost criminals. Every measure against them seemed justified to him. Studmann, who had seen how the thirty had let themselves be held up by a cigarette case, inferred therefrom the harmlessness of their activities. It was all a mere trifle.

Neither Studmann nor Pagel was right. The men from Altlohe were certainly no criminals. Yet they were just as certainly determined not to starve, but to get their food where they could find it, since they couldn't buy anything. They accepted a first surprisal almost good-humoredly. A second might make them vicious. They were hungry—and saw the huge farm where abundance grew. The smallest fraction of the harvest, a little corner of one field, could still their hunger, silence their ever-gnawing worry. The Rittmeister didn't know how much a goat gobbled up, they said. What difference did a sack of potatoes make to him? This spring he had sent a thousand hundredweights of frozen potatoes to the starch factory. Last year the rye had been so wet when they brought it in that they couldn't thresh it. It was all rotten—afterwards it had been thrown on the manure heap!

As long as they had been able to purchase their requirements with their wages, they had bought and not stolen. A few lazy rogues had always done a bit of stealing, but they were rogues and regarded as such. But now the people couldn't buy anything—and there had been the war with its thousands of regulations which no one could ever remember, and its ration cards which only enabled one to go hungry. Many of the men had been at the front, where it had not been a disgrace to "forage" what you needed. The moral standard had gradually grown laxer; it was no longer thought shameful to break the law, unless one were caught doing it. "Don't let yourself get caught!"—this increasingly popular saying was an indication of the decay in morals. Everything was topsy-turvy. It was still war. Despite the armistice, the Frenchman was still the enemy. Now he had marched into the Ruhr; horrible things were said to be taking place there.

How could these people think otherwise than they did—behave otherwise? When they passed by the Villa and heard the plates rattling they said: "He doesn't starve! Do we do less work? No, we work more! Then why should we starve and not him?" From this thought sprang hatred. If they had heard the plates rattling like that ten years ago they would have said: "He eats roast lamb, and our salt meat's like straw." That was envy. Envy is not a feeling that makes a man pugnacious—but strong haters become strong fighters!

This time they had been caught—caught for the first time; so they went along quietly. After five minutes they were chatting and laughing. It was just a night adventure. What could happen to them? A few beetroot leaves!

They spoke to Wolfgang. "What are you going to do now, sir? A few beetroot leaves! You write our names down and report us to the police for field stealing; that used to cost three marks—today it costs a few million. Well? By the time we pay our fine it'll be nothing, not a penny—we'll be able to pay it with the smallest bank note! Is that why you have to go popping off guns?"

"Quiet!" ordered Pagel angrily. "Next time we won't shoot into the air."

"You want to do a man in for the sake of a few beetroot leaves, do you? That's the sort you are! So long as we know! Other people can also shoot."

"Shut up!" called the others. "There's no need to say things like that."

"Quiet!" cried Pagel sharply. He thought he had seen figures on the path. Could it have been the Rittmeister with his wife? Impossible. He would have said something.

In passable order they approached the farm. Now curses were raised when the people had to empty their baskets. They had thought their fine would have enabled them to take the leaves home.

"What shall we give our goats?"

"An animal like that won't understand. He wants his fodder!"

"We'll have to go foraging again!"

"Be quiet!"

Their good humor was gone; they said their names crossly, aggressively, snappishly, defiantly. But they said them. Kowalewski had no need to do any rib-digging.

"You won't get me next time!" declared one.

"Write Georg Schwarz II, bailiff," said another. "Don't forget the II. I don't want my cousin to get mixed up with such a bloody business."

"Next," said Studmann. "Pagel, hurry them up a bit, will you? Next!" Till at last he could say: "Good night, Kowalewski. Oh, and thanks very much. I hope this won't cause you any unpleasantness."

"No—not *me*. Good night."

Studmann and Pagel were left alone. The desk was untidy with papers, the nicely waxed floor was dirty and covered with sand, which grated at every step.

Studmann got up from the desk, glanced curtly at Pagel. "Actually we set forth in good spirits at half-past eight, didn't we?"

"Yes, it was a nice walk, too, despite your quarrel with the overseer."

"Oh, you can't make him understand. Nor these others. It's just like the hotel in Berlin: they consider everything we do as low-down trickery."

"You mustn't ask too much of them, Studmann. After all, they can't help it."

"No, these can't, but . . ."

"But?"

Studmann did not answer. He was leaning out of the window. After a while, he turned back into the office. "No, he's not coming," he said quietly.

"Who's not coming? Are you waiting for someone?"

Studmann waved the question aside. Then he recollected himself. "You played the chief part in this success, Pagel. I thought the Rittmeister would come to thank us, or rather you."

"The Rittmeister?"

"Didn't you see him?"

"I thought . . . on the path . . . was it really him?"

"Yes, it was. He tried to avoid us. I spoke to him, but he obviously felt awkward. He didn't want the people to see him."

"Why not?" asked Pagel, astonished. "He wants us to put an end to this field stealing, doesn't he?"

"Of course! But *we* have to do it. We, Pagel! Not him; he doesn't want to have anything to do with it."

Pagel whistled thoughtfully through his teeth.

"I'm afraid Pagel, we've got a boss who wants strict officials so that he can appear all the milder. I'm afraid we won't get much support from Herr von Prackwitz." Studmann stared once more at the window. "I thought at least he'd come here. But if not, all right! If we have to depend on each other, we can still carry on, eh?"

"Splendidly."

"No getting annoyed with one another, always say what's on your mind! No secrets, always tell everything, every trifle. To some extent we're in a besieged fortress, and I'm afraid it will be difficult to hold Neulohe for the Rittmeister. Anything wrong, Pagel?"

Pagel withdrew his hand from his pocket. It's not my secret, he thought. I must speak to the young Fräulein first.

"No, nothing," he said.

Newspapers, newspapers . . .

People, be it in Neulohe or Altlohe, in Berlin or anywhere else in the country, bought newspapers. They read these newspapers. More people bought newspapers than at any previous time, to find out the dollar rate—as yet there was no broadcasting. And as they turned the pages in their search for these figures running into millions, the events of the day, whether they liked it or not, leaped up at them in huge headlines. Many did not want to read them. For seven years they had been fed with ever-larger headlines, they wanted to hear no more of the world. The world brought nothing good. They wanted as much as possible to live alone. Alone. But there was no help for it; they could not free themselves from their time.

Much happened in these hot harvest days. People read that Cuno's Government was tottering; it was said to have abetted usurers, to have been responsible for the food shortage. The French still occupied the Ruhr with their black troops, not a man was working there, not a single factory stack was smoking. This was called passive resistance, and people thought they could finance this by new taxes, new duties, to be paid by property through devaluation. In the period between July 26th and August 8th the dollar rose from 760,000 to 4,860,000 marks! The bank rate had been raised from eighteen to thirty per cent.

Despite resistance, however, despite the protests of England and Italy that French action was unjust, France continued its war in peace time. Difficulties must be created for Germany, it declared; otherwise she would not pay. Up to date these difficulties included: over a hundred killed, ten death sentences, half a dozen sentences of life imprisonment, the taking of hostages, bank robbery, the expulsion of 110,000 people from house and home. Germany might break down, but pay she must!

People read of these things in the papers. They did not see, but they felt them. These things entered into men, became part of them, affected their sleeping and waking, their dreaming and drinking, their eating and living.

A desperate people in a desperate position; every despairing individual behaving desperately. . . .

Confused, chaotic times.

Chapter Eleven

The Devil's Hussars Come

I

"It's an impertinence!"

"I knew you'd get excited," said Frau von Prackwitz gently.

"I won't have it!" cried the Rittmeister still more violently.

"It was just a precaution," said Frau von Prackwitz soothingly.

"Where's the letter? I want to have my letter! It's my letter!" he roared.

"The matter has surely been dealt with long ago," conjectured Frau von Prackwitz.

"A three-weeks-old letter addressed to me—and I don't see it! Who is the master here?" thundered the Rittmeister.

"You!" said his wife.

"Yes, and I'll show him I am," he shouted and ran to the door. "He's getting too big for his boots!"

"You're forgetting your letter," his wife reminded him.

"What letter?" The Rittmeister stopped, dumbfounded. Apart from this letter he could remember no other.

"The one over there—from Berlin."

"Oh, yes." He stuffed it into his pocket, giving his wife a dark threatening look. "You're not to telephone the fellow!"

"Of course not. Don't get so excited. The men will be coming at any moment."

"The men can . . ." As befitted a well-bred gentleman, the Rittmeister did not say what the men could do until he was outside his wife's room. She smiled. Immediately afterwards she saw her husband, bare-headed, storming along the road to the farm.

Frau von Prackwitz went to the telephone. "Is that you, Herr Pagel? Could you give me Herr von Studmann quickly? Thanks. Herr von Studmann? My husband's coming in a frightful rage because we kept the letter about the electric current from him. Don't worry if he blows off a little steam. He's already got rid of the worst of it on me. Yes, of course, thanks. Oh, no, I'm used to it. Well, thanks very much."

She hung the receiver up. "Do you want anything, Vi?"

"Can I go out for a walk for half an hour?"

Frau von Prackwitz looked at her watch. "In ten minutes' time you can go with me to the Manor. I want to see whether anything has been arranged about the cooking for the men."

"Oh, always there, Mamma! I would so like to go to the forest again. Can't I go to the forest? And swim? I haven't been swimming for four weeks."

"You know, Violet . . ." In her driest tone, against her own heart.

"Oh, you torment me so! You torment me, Mamma. I can't stand it any longer! You shouldn't have let me have so much freedom before if you now want to keep me on a chain like this! Like a prisoner. But I can't stand it any longer! I'm going mad in my room. Sometimes I dream that the walls are fall-ing in on me and then I see the curtain cord and wonder whether it will hold. I feel like jumping out of the window. I feel like smashing the glass so that I can see my blood flowing and feel that I'm still living. . . . I shall do something, I don't care what I do, I don't care."

"Vi, Vi!" said her mother. "If you would only tell us the truth! Do you think it's easy for us? But as long as you go on lying to us we can't do anything else."

"It's you! Only you! Papa said you're being unjust. And Papa also believes I told the truth—it wasn't a strange man, but Kniebusch. Everybody believes me, except you. You want to domineer over us, Papa says so, too."

"All right, get ready," said Frau von Prackwitz wearily. "I'll arrange it so that we can go for a walk in the forest afterwards."

"I don't want to go there with you. I don't need a keeper . . . I won't be imprisoned by you! I—I hate you! I don't want even to see you anymore; I won't, I won't!" Once again she broke into hysterics, which always ended in a loud sobbing that prostrated her, changing into a pitiable whimpering.

Frau von Prackwitz had a firm heart. She did not weep because others wept. Filled though she was with an infinite pity for her helpless child, she also thought: You are lying! If you weren't trying to hide a secret you wouldn't get so worked up.

She rang the bell.

"Don't come in, Hubert. Call Armgard and Lotte—Fräulein Violet is feeling bad. Yes, and then bring me the Hoffmann drops from the medicine chest."

Frau von Prackwitz, gently closing the door again, smiled sadly. The whimpering had noticeably lessened while she was giving the manservant her instructions; it had almost stopped when she ordered the hated Hoffmann drops.

You are feeling bad, my child, she thought, but you don't feel so bad as not to be interested in what's going to happen to you. There's no help for it, we must keep on until one of us gives way. I hope it is you!

II

The Rittmeister stormed into the office.

"Hello," said Studmann. "That's what I call quick! Are the men coming?"

"To hell with the men!" shouted the Rittmeister, whose anger had been given fresh vigor by his dash here. "Where's my letter? I want my letter!"

"You needn't shout like that," said Studmann coolly. "I can still hear perfectly. What letter?"

"This is a nice thing!" bellowed the Rittmeister. "People hide my letters from me, and I'm not even allowed to say what I think! I demand my letter!"

"Herr Pagel, do you mind closing the window? It isn't necessary for all Neulohe to hear what . . ."

"Pagel, leave the window open! You work for *me*, understand? I want to have my letter—it's three or four weeks old."

"Oh, you mean that letter, Prackwitz."

"Do you mean to say you're hiding other letters from me? You are carrying on secret intrigues with my wife, Studmann!"

At this the young and frivolous Pagel burst out laughing.

The Rittmeister stood transfixed. Young Pagel had laughed. One could have heard a pin drop in the office.

He took two long paces toward Pagel. "You laugh, Pagel? You laugh, Herr Pagel, when I'm angry?"

"I'm sorry, Herr Rittmeister. I wasn't laughing at you, sir. Only it sounded so funny. Herr Studmann carrying on secret intrigues with your wife."

"So—so!" An icy look, a scrutiny from head to foot. "You are dismissed, Herr Pagel. You can get Hartig to drive you to the station to catch the three o'clock train. No contradiction, please. Leave the office! I have business to attend to here."

Somewhat pale, yet with dignity, young Pagel left the office.

Herr von Studmann, angry, leaned against the safe. He looked out of the window, his forehead wrinkled. The Rittmeister regarded him sideways. "He's an impertinent rascal!" he growled tentatively, but Studmann did not move.

"Now please give me my letter."

"I have already given the letter back to Herr von Teschow," announced von Studmann coolly. "I was able to convince the Geheimrat that his demands were unjust. He asked for the letter to be returned, so that the whole matter could be regarded as never having been raised."

"I can believe it," the Rittmeister said with a bitter laugh. "You let the old fox cheat you! He made a fool of himself and you give him back the proof of his blunder. Fine!"

"Negotiating with Geheimrat von Teschow was not very easy. He could still base himself legally on the confounded lease. What finally decided him was the question of his reputation, of your position as relations—"

"Position as relations! I am convinced you let yourself be hoodwinked, Studmann."

"He seems to think a lot of his daughter and granddaughter. And how could I have been hoodwinked, since everything has been left as it was?"

"That doesn't matter," declared the Rittmeister obstinately. "I should have read the letter."

"I thought I had full power to deal with it. You expressly asked me to keep all unpleasant things away from you."

"When did I say that?"

"When we captured the field thieves."

"Studmann, if I don't want to be bothered by these petty thefts, it doesn't mean that you are to hide letters from me."

"Good. It won't happen again." Studmann leaned against the safe, a little reserved, but not impolite. "I have just examined the cooking arrangements in the washhouse. They seem to be all right. Amanda Backs is very efficient."

"We'll raise a fine stink with these convicts! I ought never to have agreed to it. But when you get everyone nagging you! I would ten times have preferred to take the Berlin people; then I wouldn't have been obliged to turn my harvesters' barracks into a jail. What it's all cost! And now this impertinence from that Berlin fellow. Here, read that!"

He handed the letter to Studmann, who read it without moving a muscle, returned it and said: "That sort of thing was to be expected."

"Was to be expected?" the Rittmeister almost screamed. "You think it's all right, do you? The fellow demands seven hundred gold marks for wretches whom I wouldn't touch with a barge pole! And you think it's all right! Look here, Studmann—"

"The items are all there: ten gold marks agent's fee per man makes six hundred marks, sixty hours of lost time at one mark, other expenses forty marks . . ."

"But you saw them, Studmann; they weren't laborers. Seven hundred gold marks for a botanist's tin and a babe in arms! No, you must write a strong letter to the fellow, Studmann!"

"Of course. What would you like me to write?"

"You know that best yourself."

"Shall I reject his demands?"

"Of course!"

"Completely?"

"Absolutely! I won't pay the fellow a penny!"

"Very good."

"You think that's right, don't you?" asked the Rittmeister suspiciously.

"Right? Not at all, Prackwitz. You are bound to lose the case."

"Lose the case . . . But, Studmann, they weren't men—agricultural laborers."

"One moment, Prackwitz . . ."

"No, listen, Studmann . . ."

"Well."

And Rittmeister von Prackwitz was very angry with his friend von Studmann when the latter finally convinced him that they must try and come to an agreement. "It'll cost money," he sighed.

"Unfortunately I shall have to ask you for some more money today." Studmann bent over an account book in which he hastily scribbled figures, endless figures with very many noughts.

"What do you mean—money? I haven't anything worth mentioning. The bills can wait."

"Since you've dismissed young Pagel," said Herr von Studmann, apparently very busy with his figures, "you'll have to pay your gambling debt. I have just reckoned it out. According to yesterday's dollar rate it will be ninety-seven milliards two hundred million marks. Roughly one hundred milliards."

"A hundred milliards!" exclaimed the Rittmeister breathlessly. "A hundred milliards! And you say off-handedly: 'Prackwitz, I shall have to ask you for some money' . . . Look here, Studmann, old man, I've got a feeling that you are angry with me somehow."

"Me angry with you? Just now it looked as if you were angry with me."

The Rittmeister paid no heed. "As if you were purposely creating difficulties for me!"

"Me—create difficulties for you?"

"But, Studmann, think! Where am I to get the money from? First there are these crazy expenses for the reconstruction of the harvesters' barracks, then this Berlin fellow with seven hundred gold marks whom you think I shall have to pay something, and now Pagel. . . . My dear Studmann, I'm not made of money! I haven't got a machine for printing bank notes, I haven't got a mint,

I can't sweat money out of my ribs—yet you come along with these exorbitant demands. I don't understand you."

"Prackwitz," said Studmann eagerly, "Prackwitz, sit down at once in this chair at the desk. There—comfortable? Good! Wait a moment. You'll soon see something. I must just take a look at Pagel's room."

"But what's the idea?" The Rittmeister was completely bewildered.

Studmann had disappeared into Pagel's room and could be heard rummaging around. What was wrong with him? A serious business talk, and he started this nonsense!

"No, sit where you are," cried Studmann, hurrying back. "Now you'll see something. . . . What's this?"

Somewhat foolishly the Rittmeister said: "A shaving mirror. Probably Pagel's. But what in Heaven's name—"

"Wait, Prackwitz! Whom do you see in the mirror?"

"Why, myself." Like all men, he stroked his chin and listened to the soft scraping of the stubble. Then he shifted his tie. "But . . ."

"Who is this 'me'? Who are you?"

"Now, look here, Studmann . . ."

"Since you don't seem to know, Prackwitz, I'll tell you. The man looking at you in the mirror is the most unbusinesslike, the most childlike, the most inexperienced man I have ever met in my life."

"I beg you!" said the Rittmeister with injured dignity. "I certainly don't want to underestimate your services, Studmann, but I managed Neulohe successfully even before you came here."

"Hark at him!" said Studmann energetically. "In order to avoid hurting your feelings—for if I wasn't your real friend, Prackwitz, I would pack up and go this very minute—let's call the gentleman in question Herr Mirror. Herr Mirror goes to Berlin to engage men. He finds his way to a gambling den. Against the advice of his friend, he gambles. When he has been cleaned out he borrows about two thousand gold marks from a young man and loses that, too. The young man becomes Herr Mirror's employee. He is very decent, he never says a word about the money, although he probably needs money very badly, for his cigarettes get worse every day, Prackwitz. Then Herr Mirror kicks the young man out and complains at having to pay him."

"But he laughed at me, Studmann! Take your damn mirror away."

"Herr Mirror," continued Studmann pitilessly, keeping the mirror in front of the Rittmeister's face despite his attempts to avoid it, "Herr Mirror engages men in Berlin. He expressly tells the agent: 'Doesn't matter what they look like, doesn't matter what they know'! But when Herr Mirror sees the men he gets a shock, and rightly. But instead of trying to come to some settlement with the agent, Herr Mirror avoids the dispute, flies from the enemy, afraid of an open combat—"

"Studmann!"

"And then blames the whole world, with the exception of himself, because he has to pay."

"I'm not blaming you, Studmann. I'm only asking you: Where am I to get the money from?"

"But these are trifles," said Studmann, laying down the mirror. "The important thing, the unpleasant thing, comes now."

"Good Lord, Studmann. No, not now, please. I've had enough irritation for one morning. Besides, the men will be here at any moment."

"The men can . . ." said Herr von Studmann violently. "You've got to listen now, Prackwitz. It's no use your trying to get out of it; you can't run around in the world like a blind chicken." He went to the window. "Oh, Frau von Prackwitz, could you come in for a moment?"

Frau von Prackwitz looked doubtfully at Vi, then at Studmann. "Is it so important?"

"My wife isn't needed here," protested the Rittmeister. "She doesn't understand a thing about business."

"She understands more than you," Studmann whispered back. "Pagel! Look after the young Fräulein for a bit. Fine. Come along, Frau von Prackwitz."

A little reluctantly, Frau von Prackwitz stepped toward the office. From the threshold she looked back at the two young people.

"Where would the young Fräulein like to go?" asked Pagel.

"Oh, just up and down in front of the windows."

Frau von Prackwitz entered the office.

III

"Would you perhaps like to see the huge cooking arrangements in the Manor?" asked Pagel. "There's terrific activity there now."

"I've got to go there with Mamma afterwards. Who is doing the cooking?"

"Fräulein Backs and Fräulein Kowalewski."

"I can understand Amanda doing it. But I should have thought Sophie considered herself a cut above cooking for convicts!"

"Everyone likes to earn a little money nowadays."

"You don't seem to, if you run around here smoking during working hours," snapped Violet.

"Does my cigarette disturb you?" asked Pagel, taking it out of his mouth.

"Not at all. I like smoking myself. When the people in the office have forgotten us, we can sneak away into the park for a bit. Then you can give me one."

"We can go straight away. Or do you think your mother considers me too dangerous to be allowed to walk in the park with you?"

"You dangerous!" Vi laughed. "No, but, you see, I'm supposed to be confined to my room."

"You are allowed to go only with your Mamma, then?"

"How clever you are!" she cried mockingly. "For three weeks the whole district has been talking about my being confined to my room, and now you've noticed it, too."

But her irritation made no impression on him. He smiled cheerfully. "May one inquire why you are confined to your room? Was it for something very bad?"

"Don't be indiscreet!" she said very pertly. "A gentleman is never indiscreet."

"I suppose I shall never be a gentleman, Fräulein," confessed Pagel sadly, feeling his breast pocket with a secret smile. "But if you think the people in the office are talking loud enough, we might steal into the park and smoke a cigarette."

"Wait." She listened. Studmann's voice could be heard, calm but very emphatic. Then the Rittmeister was plaintively protesting against something— and now Frau von Prackwitz was saying a great deal, very determined, very clear. "Mamma's off, let's go!"

They walked along the broad path between the lawns into the park.

"They can't see us now. Now you can give me a cigarette. . . . Heavens, this is a wonderful brand you smoke. How much do they cost?"

"Some millions, I can't remember; it changes every day. Anyway I get them from a friend, a certain Herr von Zecke who lives in Haidar-Pascha. Do you know where Haidar-Pascha is?"

"How should I know? I'm not training to be a teacher of kids!"

"No, of course not. I'm sorry. . . . Haidar-Pascha is on the Asiatic side of the Bosphorus."

"Heavens, Herr Pagel, stop talking such rubbish! Why do you keep grinning like that? Whenever I look at you, you're grinning."

"It's a war injury, Fräulein. Injury of the nervus sympathicus in its central canal. You know, just as shell-shock cases shake, so I grin."

"Are you trying to pull my leg?" she cried indignantly. "I won't have it."

"But, Fräulein, word of honor, it's a war injury. When I cry it looks as if I were laughing tears—it has got me into the most unpleasant situations."

"One doesn't know where one is with you," she declared, dissatisfied. "Men like you are simply horrible."

"That makes me harmless; that's an advantage, Fräulein."

"Yes, I don't doubt it!" she said scornfully. "I'd really like to know how you would go about it if . . ."

"Go about what? Go on, say it! Or are you afraid?"

"Afraid of you? Don't be ridiculous! I was wondering how you'd look if you wanted to give a girl a kiss."

"I'm afraid I don't know," confessed Pagel miserably. "To tell you the truth, Fräulein, I've thought about it thousands of times, but I'm so shy, and then . . ."

"What!" Vi gave him a superior look. "You've never yet given a girl a kiss?"

"I've intended to hundreds of times, Fräulein, word of honor! But at the decisive moment my courage . . ."

"How old are you?"

"Nearly twenty-four."

"And you've never yet kissed a girl?"

"I'm telling you, Fräulein, my shyness . . ."

"Coward!" she cried with the deepest contempt. And for a while they walked in silence down the avenue of tall lime trees which led to the pond.

"Fräulein, may I ask you something?"

Ungraciously: "Well, what is it?—hero!"

"But you mustn't be angry with me."

"What is the question?"

"Sure you won't?"

Very impatiently: "No! What's the question?"

"Well—how old are you, Fräulein?"

"You idiot! Sixteen."

"You see, you are angry—and I'm just beginning my questions."

Stamping her foot: "Well, get on with them—you weakling!"

"You're sure you won't be angry?"

"Ask your questions!"

"Fräulein—have you ever kissed a man?"

"I?" She pondered. "Of course. Hundreds of times."

"I don't believe it."

"Thousands of times!"

"You're joking!"

"It's true. My Papa!" And she burst into a peal of laughter.

"There you are!" said Pagel when she had finally quieted down. "You haven't the courage either."

Vi was indignant. "I haven't got the courage?"

"No, you're just as afraid as I am."

"Well, I have kissed a man. And not just Papa. A young man, a brave man"—her voice almost sang now—"not a weakling like you."

"I don't believe it."

"It's true, it's true. He's even got a mustache, a little fair one, it prickles. And you haven't got one!"

"I see," said Pagel, crestfallen. "And you're really only sixteen, Fräulein?"

"I'm only fifteen, even," she declared in triumph.

"I say, but you have got courage," he said admiringly. "I could never be as brave as that. But, of course, you have never *kissed* a man. You only let yourself *be* kissed. That is quite different. To get hold of a man's head and smother him with kisses—you couldn't do that."

"I couldn't do that?" she cried with blazing eyes. "What do you think of me, then?"

He lowered his glance before hers. "Please, Fräulein! I haven't said anything. Of course you could do it, I believe you. Please, don't . . ." But he pleaded in vain. Her flaming eyes, her half-opened mouth, came closer to him, although he tried to retreat. Her mouth laid itself on his. . . .

And she felt a change come over him, as if her lips had given strength to him. She felt herself crushed in his arms, his lips returned her kiss. . . . Now she wanted to draw away, now she was afraid. . . . But the kiss of those lips grew hotter and hotter; she wanted to resist, and she felt herself yielding. Her head, which had been proudly erect, gave way, nestled. . . . Her back became soft, she hung in his arms. . . . "Oh!" she sighed and sank into the ecstasy she had missed for so long. "Oh, you . . ."

But his arms ceased to hold her. His face was again far away; it looked serious, no longer wearing the smile.

"Well, Fräulein, that was that!" he said calmly. "Anyone as weak as you shouldn't play with men."

"You are mean!" she cried with flaming cheeks, partly from anger and partly from shame. "A gentleman wouldn't do a thing like that."

"It was mean," he admitted. "But there was something I had to know about you, and you would never have told me the truth. Now I know it." He thrust his hand into his pocket. "I found this letter, this copy of a letter, in the office hidden in a book. I suppose it was yours?"

"Oh, that silly old letter!" she cried scornfully. "That's why you're carrying on this performance. Meier must be crazy, making a copy of it. You should have torn the thing up, instead of deceiving me so horribly."

Pagel looked at her critically while he tore the letter into tiny pieces. "There," he said, putting the little heap into his pocket. "I shall burn it at once. But there is at least still *one* copy in existence, and if this Herr Meier sends it to your father, what then?"

"Anyone could type out a thing like that!"

"Quite so! But you are confined to your room—it seems therefore that there is already a suspicion. Without the suspicion the copy would carry little weight. But with it?"

"I've got the original back. If I admit nothing, nothing can be proved."

"But you might be outwitted."

"Not me."

"I outwitted you very quickly."

"They're not all as crafty as you."

"Little Fräulein," said Pagel with kindly admonition, "let's agree that from now on you'll be just as polite to me as I am to you. Let's forget the letter which I have torn up. What I did, doesn't seem very nice. But it was better, anyway, than if I'd gone to your mother and told tales. Perhaps I ought to have done so, but I didn't care for that."

"Don't be so solemn!" she mocked. "You've probably also written love letters and received them." But her mockery no longer had its old force.

"Very true," he said calmly, "but I've never been a scoundrel. I've never yet corrupted fifteen-year-old girls. Come along," he seized her arm, "let's go to your mother. She's sure to be getting worried."

"Herr Pagel," she said imploring, resisting. "He's not a scoundrel."

"Of course he is, and you know it quite well, too."

"No," she declared, struggling with her tears. "Why are you all so unkind to me now? Before it was different!"

"Who is unkind to you?"

"Mamma, who is eternally tormenting me, and Hubert."

"Who is Hubert? Is *Hubert* his name?"

"No. Our servant, Hubert Räder."

"Does he know?"

"Yes," she said weeping. "Please let go my arm, Herr Pagel, you are crushing it."

"Sorry. So the servant torments you, does he?"

"Yes. . . . He is so mean."

"And who else knows?"

"No one that knows anything definite."

"Not Bailiff Meier?"

"Oh, him! But he's gone away!"

"Then he knows too? Who else?"

"The forester—but he doesn't know anything definite."

"Who else?"

"No one—really, Herr Pagel! Don't look at me like that, I've told you every-thing. Really I have."

"And the servant torments you? How does he torment you?"

"He is mean—he says mean things, and he puts dirty books under my pillow."

"What sort of books?"

"I don't know—about marriage, with pictures."

"Come along," said Pagel again, seizing her arm. "Be brave. Now we shall go to your parents and tell them everything. You have fallen into the hands of scoundrels who torture you till you no longer know what to do. Your par-ents will understand. They are only angry with you because they feel you are lying. . . . Come along, Fräulein, be brave—I'm the coward of the two." And he smiled at her.

"Please, please, dear Herr Pagel, don't do that!" Her face was streaming with tears; she had seized his hands as if he were wanting to run away with the bad news, she caressed him . . . "If you tell my parents, I swear to you I'll jump into the water. Why do you want to tell them? It's all over, anyway."

"It's all over?"

"Yes, yes," she wept. "He hasn't come for three weeks."

He became thoughtful. Inevitably the vanished Petra stood before his eyes. When he had felt those lips under his own, felt that body soften as it surrendered itself to the seduction of pleasure, not to the ecstasy of love—her picture had arisen, distant but clear; a face sweet and composed, greeting him from the past. Reluctantly he found himself forced to make comparisons. What would Petra have done here? Would she have said that? She would never have behaved so. . . .

And the sweet face, seen a thousand times, the face of the girl who had for-saken him, whom he had forsaken, triumphed over this other schoolgirl face, and seemed to admonish him to kindness. She triumphed—and this triumph of the one who had abandoned him at least warned him to be good to this new one, and not to burden her with everything. If you've been too hard on me, he heard in his head, don't do the same thing again to this one.

He reflected and considered. She read his face.

"What is he?" he asked.

"A Lieutenant."

"In the Reichswehr?"

"Yes."

"Do your parents know him?"

"I don't think so. I don't know for certain."

Again he pondered. The fact that it was an officer, that is to say a man who, whatever he might be, was subject to a certain code of honor, was a little reassuring. If the young fellow had once forgotten himself and had withdrawn in fright, then to some extent it wasn't so bad; just a momentary lapse, perhaps when he was drunk—no repetition need be feared. But he ought to find out. Could one, however, ask such a young girl whether it had only happened once, whether there had been any sequel? If it had happened several times, it was scoundrelism. Then he would have to tell her parents.

No, he did not like asking. Perhaps he would have to reproach himself afterwards, but he could not.

"You are sure it is over?"

"Quite sure!"

"You swear to that?" he asked, although he knew how useless such oaths were.

"I swear it!"

He had an uncomfortable feeling. Something was wrong; she must have lied to him somewhere. "If I am to keep quiet, you must promise me one thing. But on your word of honor."

"Yes, of course."

"If this man—this Lieutenant—should again approach you, you must let me know at once. Will you promise me that? Give me your hand."

"On my word of honor!" she said, giving him her hand.

"All right, then. Let's go. Try and find some pretext for sending your manservant Räder over to me this evening, as late as possible."

"Fine!" she cried enthusiastically. "What will you do to him?"

"I'll make the young fellow yelp," he said grimly. "He won't torment you again."

"And if he runs to Papa?"

"We've got to risk that. But he won't. I'll put such fear into him he won't want to. Blackmailers are always cowards."

"Can you hear whether they are still talking in the office? Heavens, I must be looking awful. Please give me your handkerchief quickly; I must have lost mine—no, I didn't bring one with me. I'll never lie to you again, not even about little things. You are so nice, I'd never have thought it. If I wasn't in love already, I'd fall in love with you on the spot."

"That's over, Fräulein," said Pagel dryly. "Please don't forget it—you swore that."

"Why, of course."

"All right, now let's go and show ourselves under the window. The debate in there seems to be endless."

IV

"Dear Lady," Herr von Studmann had said, straightening Frau von Prackwitz's desk chair, which he gladly granted her, "apologies for calling you. But we're having a meeting here which you have to attend. We're talking about money...."

"Really?" said Frau Eva, examining herself in the shaving mirror. "Of course, that's quite a new topic for me! Achim discusses it at least every day."

"Eva, please!" cried the Rittmeister.

"And why does my friend Prackwitz speak of money every day? Because he hasn't any. Because the smallest bill upsets him. Because the rent due on the first of October weighs on him like a nightmare. Because he is always wondering if he will be able to pay it."

"Quite right, Studmann, I'm worried. I'm a prudent businessman."

"Let's examine your financial position. You have no capital; current expenses are paid from current income—that is to say, by sales of cattle, of early potatoes, the harvest.... You have no capital reserves...." Studmann rubbed his nose thoughtfully. Frau von Prackwitz gazed at herself in the mirror. The bored Rittmeister leaned against the stove, hoping that Studman (this eternal nursemaid) would at least have sufficient tact not to talk of his gambling debts.

"Then comes the first of October," went on Studmann. "On that date the annual rent has to be handed over in cash to Geheimrat von Teschow. This, as you ought to know, is equivalent to three thousand hundredweights of rye, and as far as I've been able to find out, the price is round about seven or eight gold marks a hundredweight, which would mean a sum of twenty-five thousand gold marks, not to be expressed in milliards—if only because we don't know what the price of rye will be in paper marks on the first of October." Von Studmann gazed at his victims, but they were not yet aware of the significance of his words.

"I'm very much obliged to you, Studmann, for bothering with all these things. But, if you'll pardon me, we know them. The rent is somewhat high, but I've got a very nice crop standing in the fields, and now that I'm getting reapers—"

"Excuse me, Prackwitz, you don't see the problem. On October the first you've got to give Herr von Teschow the value of three thousand hundred-weights of rye. Since the gold mark is a fictitious standard, the price of rye in paper marks—"

"I understand all that, my dear Studmann, I know that."

"But," continued the inexorable Studmann, "you can't deliver three thousand hundredweights of rye to the dealer in one day. Judging by your books, you require about fourteen days for that. Now suppose you deliver three hundredweights of rye on September the twentieth. The dealer, let us say, will give you three hundred milliards for it. You put the three hundred milliards in your safe ready for payment on October the first. In the period between September the twentieth and thirtieth the mark continues to fall. On September the thirtieth you'll get from the dealer, let us say, six hundred milliards for the three hundred hundredweights. Then the three hundred milliards in safe will only represent the value of one hundred and fifty hundredweights. You would have to deliver another one hundred and fifty hundredweights. . . . That's clear, isn't it?"

"Just a minute," said the Rittmeister, perplexed. "How was that? Three hundred hundredweights are suddenly only one hundred and fifty?"

"Herr von Studmann is quite right," asserted Frau von Prackwitz. "But it's terrible. No one can afford that."

"It's a fourteen-day race with inflation," said Studmann. "And it will exhaust us."

"But the inflation won't necessarily keep on like this!" exclaimed the Ritt-meister indignantly.

"No, of course not. But one can't tell. It depends on so much: on the French in the Ruhr, on the firmness of the present government, which wants to continue the Ruhr struggle at all costs and so needs more and more money, on the attitude of England and Italy, who still oppose France's action. That is to say, on thousands of things we can't influence—yet we have to pay on October the first whatever happens."

"Can we do it, Herr von Studmann?"

"We can, Frau von Prackwitz."

"There you are!" cried the Rittmeister, half laughing, half angry. "Just like Studmann! First he frightens us, then he has the solution to hand."

"There are people," said Studmann, unperturbed, "who believe in the perpetual depreciation of our currency, who speculate on a fall. They'd be prepared to buy your rye from you today, Prackwitz, payment to be made on October the first, delivery to be made October to November. . . . I have a few offers here."

"The fellows will make a mint of money out of it," said the Rittmeister bitterly.

"But you'll be able to pay Papa the rent punctually and without loss, Achim! That's what we have to consider."

"Give me the offers, Studmann," said Prackwitz sullenly. "I'll look them through. Anyway, I'm very grateful to you."

"The second question is," went on Studmann, "whether it is any use paying the rent at all." He said nothing and looked at them both. Fallen from heaven, he thought, like children.

"But why?" asked Frau von Prackwitz, puzzled. "Papa must have his money, mustn't he?"

"That's a crazy idea, Studmann," objected the Rittmeister very crossly. "As if there weren't enough difficulties without that!"

"The contract states," said Frau von Prackwitz, "that we would immediately lose the lease if punctual and full payment is not made!"

"I shall fulfill my obligations!" declared the Rittmeister.

"If you can!" said Studmann. "Listen, Prackwitz, now don't interrupt me. You listen, too—it will be a little painful, as I must speak of your father. . . . Well, let's speak of the lessor and lessee. For you are coming in for a few hard things, too, my dear Prackwitz, you, the lessee. The study of this lease is not uninteresting. If you examine it, you will be reminded of the Treaty of Versailles, over which stands the motto: 'To hell with the conquered'! Over your lease stand the words: 'Woe to the lessee!'"

"My father—"

"The lessor, Frau von Prackwitz, the lessor! I don't want to speak of all the mean, petty conditions which might lead to disaster. The electric light incident opened my eyes. My dear Prackwitz, if I hadn't been here you would have come to grief over that, as you were intended to. But the enemy retreated. He's waiting for you to fall over the rent payment, and you will fall over it."

"My father-in-law . . ."

"My father . . ."

"The lessor," said von Studmann firmly, "fixed the rent at one and a half hundredweights of rye per acre. Is that a reasonable rent?"

"It is perhaps a little high," began the Rittmeister.

"The State lands in the neighborhood pay sixty pounds of rye per acre; you pay more than twice that. And remember—the lessees of the State lands had to pay only an installment at the last quarter, and next quarter they'll probably pay nothing. That won't lose them their leasehold; but if you don't pay the full amount punctually, well . . ."

"My brother in Birnbaum . . ."

"Quite so, Frau von Prackwitz; your brother in Birnbaum, as he always moans to everyone, pays the lessor the same rent. But what's right for one child is too dear for the other. That's to say, one hears everywhere that your brother actually pays only ninety pounds but has had to promise his father to say it's one hundred and fifty."

"My dear Studmann, that would be equivalent to fraud. I must ask you . . ."

"If, then, one can call the rent a very high one, it may be that Neulohe is such an excellent property that even an unusually high rent is justified. I did not find this office"—Studmann let a disapproving glance sweep over it—"a striking model of order. No, excuse me, Prackwitz. But one thing was very striking: there wasn't a book to be found from the time of your predecessor, nothing which could afford information as to Neulohe's productivity in previous years. However, there were other ways. The overseer kept threshing lists, there were records at the Treasury office, the dealers kept entry-books. Well, after some trouble I finally came to the conclusion that even in previous years Neulohe produced only an average crop of five to six hundredweights of rye per acre."

"Much too low, Studmann!" cried the Rittmeister triumphantly. "You're no farmer . . ."

"I carried out a test on the—lessor. He didn't know why I was asking and wanted to try and fool me; like you he thought I was no farmer. But I'm a man who can calculate; it was Herr von Teschow who was fooled. The lessor admitted against his will that only an average crop of five to six hundredweights is to be expected, not more. 'There's a lot of sand in the outfields,' he said."

"But then I'm paying . . ." The Rittmeister paused in dismay.

"Yes," said Studmann inexorably, "you pay twenty-five to thirty per cent of your crop as rent. That can hardly be called reasonable. If you will remember, Frau von Prackwitz, the peasants in the Middle Ages paid a tithe to their manorial lords, that's to say, a tenth of their produce. It was not tolerable, and in the end they rose and killed their lords. Your husband doesn't pay a tenth, no, he pays a quarter—even so, I wouldn't advise killing." Herr von Studmann smiled. He was happy. The nursemaid could instruct, the teacher could teach—forgetting, meanwhile, the despair of his listeners. A child whose toy has been broken does not find much consolation in being told how this could have been avoided.

"But what are we to do?" said Frau von Prackwitz tonelessly. "What can we do?"

"My father-in-law has certainly no inkling of all this," said the Rittmeister. "One must tell him. You're so clever and calm with it, Studmann. . . ."

"What about asking his son in Birnbaum to keep quiet?"

The Rittmeister said nothing.

"So far, one might still think the lessor was just a man eager to get money. Too eager. Somewhat greedy, eh? But unfortunately it is much worse."

"If you please, Herr Studmann! We've had enough now."

"Yes, you really must stop."

"One must know everything, otherwise one will do the wrong thing. The rent amounts to three thousand hundredweights—one and a half hundred-weights per acre, which corresponds to a farm of two thousand acres. And that is the area as given in the lease."

"Is that also false?"

"I always heard, long before, that Neulohe had two thousand acres of land," said Frau von Prackwitz.

"That's quite true, Neulohe has two thousand," replied Studmann.

"Well, then!" The Rittmeister heaved a sigh of relief.

"Neulohe has two thousand acres, but how large is the area you cultivate, Prackwitz? From the two thousand acres you must take away paths, unfertile land, the field-balks, ditches, heaps of stones. You must exclude, too, a few bits of arable land which have been planted with firs—you can get yourself a Christmas tree without having to ask the owner of the forest, Prackwitz . . ."

"Yes, I know. Nothing much."

"You must exclude also the huge farmyard, the laborers' houses, this staff-house, your Villa with its garden, and you must exclude too the Manor and the park! Yes, my dear Prackwitz, you even pay rent to your father-in-law for the house in which he lives!"

"I'll be damned if I'll do that!" cried the Rittmeister.

"Steady, steady—you want to get out of all your difficulties, don't you? I have reckoned it out on the ground-plan; the area actually cultivated amounts to a trifle over fifteen hundred acres, so you are really paying two hundred-weights of rye."

"I'll contest the contract, I'll sue the fellow!" The Rittmeister looked as if he were about to dash immediately to the nearest law court.

"Oh, Achim!" wailed Frau von Prackwitz.

"Sit down!" shouted Studmann. "Now you know everything, and we can sit in judgment on the culprit—that's you, Prackwitz. Steady, now! How could you have signed this disgraceful contract? You signed it as well, madam. Well, go on, Prackwitz. You can talk now."

"How could a man imagine he was being tricked in such a low-down way—by relatives!" cried the Rittmeister angrily. "I knew my father-in-law was a skin-flint and after money like a cat after canaries. But I still can't believe, Studmann, that he would cut his own daughter's throat."

"Herr von Teschow is no fool," said Studmann. "When he drew up this lease he knew it could never be carried out. He must have had some motive. Have you anything to say about that, Prackwitz? I'd like to hear your views, too, madam."

"I don't know what my father was thinking." But Frau von Prackwitz turned red under Studmann's scrutiny.

"I'll chuck the damn thing in his face! I'm going to court!"

"According to clause seventeen any objection to a condition of the contract dissolves the lease. Once you have lodged your complaint you are no longer the lessee. How did the contract come to be made? It's new, and you've been farming here a long time."

"Oh, that's got nothing to do with the case. After the war we had nothing. I wasn't going to be paid my pension—was I not a traitor? So we landed up here as visitors. I ran around the fields with my father-in-law—slaving like the devil. I found it fun at the time. Then one day he said: 'I'm getting old, take the place as it stands. Eva will inherit all one day.' So I started managing it alone."

"Without any contract?"

"Without a contract."

"What rent did you pay?"

"Nothing was settled. When he needed money I gave it to him if I had any; otherwise he just waited."

"And then?"

"Then one day he said: 'Let's draw up a contract,' and so we made this disgraceful lease with which I'm landed."

"He just said 'Draw up a contract'? But something must have happened?"

"Nothing happened."

"Something's missing," persisted Studmann. "Well, Frau von Prackwitz?"

She had flushed. "Well, Achim," she said hesitantly, "oughtn't we to tell him? It's better. . . ."

"Oh, the old story!" growled the Rittmeister. "Studmann, you're a real nagger. What good will it do you to know—it won't alter the lease."

"Frau von Prackwitz," pleaded Studmann.

"A short while before the lease was made," she said quietly, "I had a quarrel with Achim. He thought it was time he started being jealous again—"

"Please, Eva, don't be ridiculous!"

"Yes, Achim, it's true. Well, you know him, and I do too. He immediately flew into a temper—you'd have thought the world was coming to an end.

Screamed about divorce, adultery—well, it wasn't nice to listen to. But I've been used to it for nearly twenty years and know that he really doesn't mean it."

"My dear Eva," said the Rittmeister stiffly, "if you go on talking about me in this way I shall leave the office. And anyway, I was quite right. That affair with Truchsess—"

"Was years ago," interrupted Studmann. "Please sit down again, Prackwitz. Don't forget, it's your money we are discussing."

"I don't want to hear any more of these stories!" cried the Rittmeister fiercely, sitting down, however.

"Go on, Frau von Prackwitz. So there was a little domestic quarrel?"

"Yes, and unfortunately my father heard of it without our knowing. From that time onwards he was convinced that Achim tormented and ill-treated me."

"Ridiculous! I'm the most peaceful, most placable man."

"For weeks he urged me to divorce Achim—"

"What!" The Rittmeister jumped up. "That's the latest! He wanted you to divorce me?"

"Sit down, Prackwitz," urged Studmann. "As you say, these are very old stories. Your wife is not divorced . . ."

"No, Papa saw that I didn't want to. He thinks more of me than you'd expect." She had flushed again. "And then there came this lease."

"Now I understand him," said Herr von Studmann, feeling extremely pleased. "And I hope you understand him, too, Prackwitz, and know what your attitude is to be. Your husband was intended to lose his nerve, become unbearable, be economically ruined; his incapability was to be proved, he was to pile up debt after debt . . ."

"And that man calls himself my father-in-law! It's true I could never stand him, but I thought, after all, he's quite a good fellow in his own way . . ."

"My dear Prackwitz," said Studmann somewhat pointedly, "some people regard others as being good only because it is to their interest to do so. But if you don't pull yourself together now, and if you let your father-in-law notice that you know anything, then you're done for!"

"That's impossible!" cried the Rittmeister. "I must be able to tell him my opinion. It makes my blood boil just to think of him!"

"Then you must simply turn aside if you see him in the distance. Prackwitz, for your wife's sake, pull yourself together. Promise us you won't talk or begin a quarrel or let yourself be provoked. Go away, say: 'Herr von Studmann is looking after that.' Finished! Your father-in-law would find that much more unpleasant! Leave all business matters to me. I'll find a way out. Why not begin by taking some gold, plenty of gold—the outcome of your work. We'll see later what we'll do in the winter."

"Herr von Studmann is right," said Frau von Prackwitz eagerly. "This would be the worst moment to give up the lease. Leave everything to him."

"Well, I suppose I'm just a fool," growled the Rittmeister. "There's a man for you, that Studmann! Understands in three weeks more than I do in three years. I—"

"The men are coming!" Vi exclaimed, bursting into the office with Pagel following slowly.

"There," said the Rittmeister, glad to escape from the hated office, "they're coming at last! I was beginning to think there would be difficulties there, too! My dear Pagel, will you see that the fellows get some grub right away, that implements are properly distributed, and all that?"

Pagel looked cheerfully at his employer. "Yes, Herr Rittmeister." He clicked his heels and went.

"What are you doing, Prackwitz?" asked Studmann. "You've given Pagel the sack! He's supposed to take the three o'clock train."

"I sack Pagel? Don't be silly, Studmann! You saw that the boy understood me perfectly. A good dressing-down when a young rip like that gets cheeky—and finish! I'm not the one to bear a grudge, you know."

"No, you aren't!" said Studmann. "Well, let's have a look at the men. I'm anxious to know what a gang of fifty convicts looks like."

V

Yes, there they came. They emerged just where the highway to Meienburg-Ostade turns into Neulohe, in fours, a warder at the side of every fourth row—and they sang loudly and with feeling the song about the nicest place I have on earth, my mother's grave.

"Lord, they're singing, too!" groaned Frau Belinde von Teschow to her friend Jutta at the Manor window. "It isn't enough that the food for these murderers is to be cooked in my respectable washhouse, I've got to listen to their bawling as well! Elias, tell the Geheimrat to come to me. Murderers singing—it's preposterous!"

"They're coming! They're coming!" cried the children in the village, and all who were not at work in the fields left standing everything that stood, let fall everything that would not stand, took up positions in the street, and stared—stared open-eyed and open-mouthed.

The prison authorities had spared no pains in doing the thing well. Despite the bad times, they had given the men fresh clothes. There were no worn-out uniforms made up of patches, no trousers reaching only halfway down the calves of the tall men, or jackets which drowned the short ones—their clothes fitted well, were spick and span, and proudly they sang their song: "We're bold and bad hussars!"

The people in the village street opened their mouths still wider. Where were the cropped heads they had always heard about? Where were the chains and handcuffs? Where was the sinister brooding silence? Where the angry glance suffused with red? No brand of Cain, no wild-beast look. "Say, ma, going to close your mouth again when you've had it open long enough?" one of them shouted, and they all laughed.

No. Neulohe had been expecting too much, at any rate expecting something quite different. Large and small, fat and thin; handsome men, indifferent men, ugly men—all were in high spirits. They had escaped from the dead constraint of iron and cement, were able to see the world again, not merely the little section from the cell window, which even so was forbidden them. The fresh air had enlivened them, the sun had warmed them; no more of gray monotony, but new work, different diet, tobacco, the sight of young girls already, of a woman hastily pulling down her sleeve over a bare arm which had been dipped into the flour tub.

They sang:
The Devil's Hussars are we,
No deed makes us afraid.
We've sinned right merrily,
And loved as well, pretty maid.

The warders were smiling too, glad to escape from their monotonous duty, the continual quarrels, objections, complaints, the unceasing worries about breaches of regulations, the outbreaks and revolts. The men would get enough to eat and smoke, they would be contented, there would be no rows—although one could never be quite certain about that. Almost with benevolence the warders regarded their lads—those to whom they devoted their whole life. After having passed through despair, hatred, indifference, they had almost come to love them. The prisoners looked so smart in their new things, they were so merry, they sang so cheerfully. "Warder, did you see the hare?" "Warder, this lunch time I'm going to have three helpings!" "Warder, what have we got for lunch—roast goose?"

They were like children. There were no murderers, no long-sentence men at all in the gang. Four years was already a lot; most were in for short stretches, and all, or nearly all, had served half their time. There were no desperate criminals among them, none of the big shots of the underworld—but in spite of that, in spite of their singing and gaiety, they were still convicts, that is to say, men whose freedom had been taken from them, a freedom which many of them would do everything, or almost everything, to regain. The officials could never forget that they might perhaps have to risk their own lives in keeping those prisoners from a desired freedom.

My darling said: I love you so,
You must not go from me.
No woman's arms will hold me, though.
The Devil's Hussars are we!

"They're coming! They're coming!" cried Amanda Backs in the Manor washhouse, and threw the ladle into the pea soup with a splash. "Come on, Sophie, let's have a look at them. We can see the harvesters' barracks from the coal cellar."

"I don't know why you're so excited," replied Sophie coolly. "Convicts— I wouldn't budge an inch for them. The fellows will give us enough to worry about when they come to get their food. They're all criminals."

But she followed Amanda nonetheless, and leaned with her against the dirty coal-cellar hatch. Breathing quickly she looked over, saw the procession and heard the song; but could not see him. Supposing he was not there? Supposing they hadn't sent him?

"What are you groaning like that for, Sophie?" asked Amanda in surprise.

"I? What do you mean, groaning? I'm not groaning! Why should I be groaning?"

"That's what I'm asking," said Amanda rather sharply. For the two were not yet friends, because up to now the question as to who was the cook and who the cook's help had not been settled.

Behind the convicts came two of the farm wagons, bringing the men's things; blankets, basins, knives and forks, medicine, water cans, buckets, spades, rakes. . . . Between the first wagon and the men marched Principal Warder Marofke, alone—a little man but a fine one, commander-in-chief of harvest crew five, Meienburg Prison, in Neulohe, the supreme master of fifty prisoners and four warders. He had very thin, short legs, clad in well-pressed gray trousers. His boots were the only ones which were almost shiny—a prisoner had had to "elbow-grease" them just before the entry into Neulohe. Marofke had a huge potbelly which quivered inside a blue tunic and was belted with a sword strap whereon a saber hung. As for his face, it was as tenderly colored as a young girl's, white and pink despite his fifty years. At the slightest excitement, however, it turned scarlet. His cat-like bristling mustache was reddish-yellow, his eyes pale blue, his voice screeching and curt. Yet for all his curtness and sharpness, the principal warder was good-nature itself—so long as his authority was not impugned. Should that happen, he at once became as malicious, as crafty, as vengeful as a panther.

"Company halt!" he screeched.

The convicts stopped.

"About turn!"

They did so, but in no very military way, for in 1923 most men hated anything military. They turned their backs on the harvesters' barracks and looked toward the staff-house and the farm.

Young Pagel stepped up to the little despot. "Principal Warder Marofke? Your governor has written to us. My name is Pagel, I'm a sort of—apprentice here. If I may present you to the boss, he is standing over there." Under the last trees of the park, next to the staff-house, stood the Rittmeister with his family and Herr von Studmann.

Bloated with pride, as if every step lifted him from the lowly earth, Principal Warder Marofke approached the Rittmeister. He clicked his heels together, raised his hand to his cap and announced: "Principal Warder Marofke, at your service, Herr Rittmeister; with two warders, two assistant warders and fifty convicts forming harvest crew number five!"

"Thank you, principal warder," said the Rittmeister graciously, looking at the little fellow with amusement. "Ex-soldier, eh?"

"Yes, Herr Rittmeister. Twenty-third Transport Section."

"Transport, eh? Of course. Obvious." A spark glimmered in the principal warder's eye. "At the front?"

"No, Herr Rittmeister. I had . . ."

"Whooping-cough? All right! Well, let the men go to their quarters, principal warder. Lunch is probably ready. You'll look after everything, Pagel, eh? And see that they do some solid work, principal warder, I don't want to have spent all this money for nothing. Thank you."

Flaming red, the other went back to his men.

Studmann and Frau von Prackwitz exchanged a glance. Frau von Prackwitz in despair shrugged her shoulders. Studmann whispered soothingly: "I'll set it right again."

"Even you can't set everything right." Frau von Prackwitz had tears in her eyes.

"What are you pulling faces for?" the Rittmeister asked, turning round. "Queer stick, that principal warder. Got a big idea of himself. A shirker, of course. Well, I'll put the fellow through it, I'll show him what service is. Come along, Eva, come along, Vi. Afternoon, Studmann. Must try to get something into my stomach, too—you've successfully taken away my appetite this morning. Well, good afternoon!"

VI

"Why does he call me 'principal warder'—can you tell me that?" the little principal warder asked Pagel heatedly. "We're not on a parade ground here, he's not my superior!"

They were sitting in Marofke's room. In the barracks the prisoners were making an uproar, laughing, swearing, singing, nailing up on the wall photographs of their sweethearts and smuggled pictures of film stars, whistling, putting up beds, already clattering with their tinny knives and forks.

"We want grub!" shouted a voice.

"Like a cigarette?" But Herr Marofke politely refused. "You ought to have a nice cover on your table," said Pagel, surveying the room. "A few other things, too, mirror, pictures, ash trays. You should shake the young girls up a bit—well, you'll get round them all right. I suppose you've had plenty of experience with young girls."

"If the governor says to me 'principal warder,' then it's all right. But _he_—he hasn't any right to. I could also say to him 'Rittmeister.' I'd like to see what sort of face he'd make then!"

"We want grub!" Spoons began to beat on cooking utensils.

"The boss is a queer chap," said Pagel. "An hour ago he kicked me out. It's true, Herr Marofke, sacked me on the spot for laughing while on duty. I'm not pulling your leg, word of honor! Well, I suppose he felt sorry for me, and keeps me on because I've nowhere else to go. But since he's still angry he calls me 'Herr.' When he's in a good mood he just says 'Pagel' or 'young rip.'"

Pagel sprawled comfortably over the table, blowing very artistic smoke rings and not looking at Herr Marofke at all. The officer scrutinized him suspiciously. "Why does he talk about whooping-cough to me? When I've got a double rupture in the groin! It isn't everyone can get a wound!"

"Poof!" said Pagel scornfully. "Wounds are nothing to the Rittmeister! He calls them whooping-cough, too. It's just his way of speaking. Forget it."

"We want grub!" The shouts outside were louder.

"What does mean anything to the Rittmeister, then?" asked the principal warder curiously. "I never heard that before, calling wounds whooping-cough. Supposing a man's leg has been amputated?"

"He calls it whooping-cough, too. Well, forget it. It's not worth worrying about. Herr Marofke, I want to ask you a great favor."

"Yes?"

"When you take your men to fetch their food you'll see two girls in the kitchen. I've got a crush on one of them, so be a sport and don't queer my pitch for me. The other one's also quite pretty."

"My boy, it's as you say. Don't be afraid!" Herr Marofke felt very flattered.

"That's decent of you," Pagel blurted out in confusion.

"Man, when I was your age! I don't know what's wrong with you young men today. At your age I wouldn't have gone begging to a fifty-year-old like myself. Still, consider it done. No need to be embarrassed. I'll also keep an eye on the warders—two of them are unmarried; you tip me off which girl is yours. I think I'll fetch the food myself."

"We want grub! We want grub!"

"Yes, it's time. Tell me quickly, what's wrong with your boss? You don't mind if we're pals, do you? Of course, when the others are around we'll have to be a bit stand-offish to each other."

"Pals we are, Herr Marofke! And the boss—but you must promise not to breathe a word on any account."

"Me? I don't talk. I'm an official—even the public prosecutor can't get a word out of me."

"Good. Entirely between ourselves, the boss was buried alive in the war. When they dragged him from the dugout they thought he was dead. Ever since then—"

"Yes, that's what he looks like—a warmed-up corpse!"

"Ever since then he's got 'buried alive' on the brain. Everything else he calls whooping-cough!"

"So your boss is loony! All right—don't be afraid, I won't give you away."

"Good morning, gentlemen," said Herr von Studmann. "Well, everything in order? Satisfied, officer? House solid enough? I don't think any of your fellows will get away from here. Excuse me, my name is von Studmann. I'm sort of business manager here. If you need anything, no matter what, if there's anything wrong with the food, you can always come to me—it's better not to bother the Rittmeister with such matters."

The principal warder gave young Pagel a glance full of understanding. "Yes, sir; I wonder if I could have a tablecloth and an ash tray?"

"You shall have everything you want," said Herr von Studmann pleasantly. "We'd like you to feel comfortable here. Pagel, go and get your lunch; it's already on the table. The officer and I will supervise the sharing out of the food."

Pagel gave the principal warder a glance of profound disappointment, but, at the other's amiable nod, he said: "Right, Herr von Studmann," and disappeared.

"Warder Siemens!" the principal warder screeched into the passage. "Have four men ready to get the food. Choose old men, married; there are pretty girls in the kitchen."

Laughter and cat-calls arose in the barracks.

"Who told you about the pretty girls?" asked von Studmann in surprise. "Was it young Pagel?"

"A prison official has to know everything," smirked the principal warder. "I have to be on the look-out with the boys—they get up to all sorts of tricks!"

"You haven't told me where you got your information from, officer," said von Studmann dryly. "It was Pagel, wasn't it?"

"Well," said the principal warder patronizingly, "I think the young fellow is in love. Between ourselves, in strictest confidence, he asked me to keep an eye on his girl."

"Really!" Studmann was very surprised. "Which of the two is it? Amanda or Sophie? Of course, it's Sophie, isn't it?"

"He hasn't told me yet. He was going to point her out when we went to fetch the food, but then you came along."

"I'm terribly sorry," laughed Studmann. "Well, he'll be able to do it some other time." Thoughtfully he followed the principal warder, and listened to a somewhat excited dispute as to why there were not four elderly married men detailed to fetch the food, but only three—the fourth man was young, with an unpleasantly smooth handsome face, shifty eyes and a too strong chin.

"I don't want Liebschner!" shouted Herr Marofke. "When I say elderly men it doesn't mean Liebschner. He's wormed his way in—you don't belong to my gang at all; you should be in your cell making mats! Brandt's got boils on his feet and can't get the food. I've got a boil too—in my stomach—but I can get it." Applause and roars of laughter. "If I catch you fetching food again, Liebschner, you'll march straight back to solitary! Understand? Hey, you there, Wendt, grab hold of the food-bin! March!"

Herr Studmann listened attentively. But he completely misheard it. It went in one ear and out the other. Studmann was thinking about Pagel. Young Pagel interested him. Studmann was one of those men who have to think and brood over something, but never over themselves. He did everything that had to be done, quite naturally, and was a completely uninteresting man. Pagel, however, was very interesting. Studmann had observed him carefully; the youngster did his work well, was always good-tempered, and adapted himself surprisingly to the unaccustomed farm life. Pulled his weight. He had been a gambler, but nothing indicated that he was longing to gamble again. He had no weakness for alcohol. He smoked too much, but that was a modern disease from which even Studmann was not free. Continually lighting up, puffing away. Yes, there was nothing wrong with young Pagel. He did his job!

And yet there was something wrong. There was no life in him; he was never enthusiastic, never angry. The fellow was twenty-three years old—he couldn't go on running around with that half-hidden smile forever, regarding himself and everything as unimportant, as if the whole world were a swindle and he the one who had discovered it! He was, when you came to think of it, like a man seen through a veil, hazy, vague—as if he were just vegetating, as if his emotions were paralyzed.

Herr von Studmann had at first thought that this lack of vivacity was a temporary phase. Pagel was a convalescent. He had had a love affair from which he still suffered. Perhaps it had been wrong to forbid any mention of it, but Studmann was of the opinion that wounds should be left to heal.

And now came this news that Pagel was in love again, that he spoke to others about it, that he thought of a girl with anxiety. In that case everything was quite different; in that case something was rotten in the State of Denmark; in that case he was no convalescent, but merely a lazy-bones, an indolent fellow who must be urged into activity. Studmann decided to observe Pagel much more closely and to handle him in a more comradely way. There was still an invisible wall between them. A twenty-three-year-old lad with no close contact to any other person in the world, and didn't even want any contact—that was nothing but weird. Twenty-three is surely no age to be a hermit! As far as Studmann knew, Pagel had not even written to his mother yet—that was not right; he would start on that first. All his nursemaid's instincts were suddenly awakened. Herr von Studmann felt he had a task, and he would ponder over it and perform it.

Had Studmann ever thought about himself, he would have realized that he was eagerly rushing into this new task because he had failed with the old. After the morning's discussion he had, without knowing it, given the Rittmeister up. The Rittmeister could not be saved, he was an incorrigible hothead—rescued from one rashness, he plunged into the next. He was a child that would never learn its lesson and the teacher was obliged to give up his job. When the lieutenant thinks about the Rittmeister, he no longer thinks, another step forward, but, now what's he going to get up to? He did not want to forsake the Rittmeister (there was a wife and a daughter, both desirable problems), but a riddle that one wanted to solve, and which turns out to be no riddle at all, but a mass of contradictions, has no more attraction.

Thoughtfully Herr von Studmann let a friendly glance rest alternately on Amanda Backs and Sophie Kowalewski. Amanda, sturdy as a strong-boned Belgian horse, seemed to him out of the question, although one could never judge another's tastes. Sophie, however, was quite pretty, though on closer inspection he found that her girlish features now and then acquired something sharp and evil, when her eyes became like pin-points, her voice almost hoarse. As when she now said to Principal Warder Marofke: "Is that supposed to mean we're not trusted?"

Herr Marofke might perhaps be a queer stick, one that might break easily, but he was also an experienced prison official. One could have fared worse. He had made the four food carriers and his colleague Siemens wait outside the washhouse; he had made the girls give him a spoonful to taste; he had even praised them. "This is good stuff! This'll please my lads." Then he had told them to withdraw to the cellar passage before the men came in. At which Fräulein Sophie had asked very angrily: "Is that supposed to mean we're not trusted?"

"Of course not," said little Marofke very pleasantly. "That applies to all women—not just such pretty little ones!"

Sophie Kowalewski threw her head back angrily. "We wouldn't get mixed up with convicts like that! You needn't think that about us!"

"But my boys would be very glad to get mixed up with you, Fräulein," explained the principal warder.

"Come on, Sophie!" urged Amanda. "I'm not so keen on seeing the fellows."

Sophie was strangely obstinate—she had lost her head. Merely in order to discover at once whether he had come, she risked everything. Why had she asked for the job in this ugly old kitchen, disfigured her well-kept hands with potato peeling and splashing in cold water, given up her leisure—if she wasn't to meet him here? She had come off worse than all the others now: if she had stood outside the harvesters' barracks or in the village street, then at least she would have seen him marching by!

She risked everything, she even rashly tried to take advantage of her good relations with Herr von Studmann. "The warder can't send me out of my own kitchen, can he, Herr von Studmann?"

Studmann could not find the key to this riddle! "Be sensible, Fräulein Sophie," he said pleasantly, "don't make the officer's duty more difficult than it is."

And he was surprised at the angry look Sophie gave the principal warder, a look full of hatred. Why in all the world should Sophie hate this little potbellied fellow? But now, since everything had been in vain, Sophie put as good a face on it as she could.

"Of course I don't mind leaving my kitchen if I'm told," she said, withdrawing. "Only Amanda and I can't be responsible for anything—madam has checked up everything with us, cloths and pots." With that the two girls were gone.

The principal warder called in his men, who carefully transferred into their bin the food that was laid out. "I thought at first the slim one was Herr Pagel's girl," Herr Marofke whispered. "But it must be the other. The pretty one's keen on my boys, keen as poison. I'll keep an eye on her, she wants to get off."

"No, no," protested Herr von Studmann, not quite convinced. "I know Fräulein Sophie, she's a very decent girl." But was that true? In the train she had made an extremely bad impression on him.

"You've no idea," said the principal warder as they walked back to the barracks behind the food carriers, "how queer women are. Some of them go crazy for our lads . . . just because they're convicts! Previously in winter we swept the snow from the streets in Meienburg. You can't imagine the tricks some women got up to then, so as to smuggle in letters. Take it from me, Herr von Studmann, women are a perfect puzzle, and the pretty slim one . . ."

"Quite so," said Herr von Studmann from time to time. He also found it puzzling. But he would soon find the solution. For a while he stood in the common-room to see how the men liked their food. Yes, they liked it. While they were gobbling up one helping they were squinting at the bin, wondering whether there was a second and possibly a third helping in it. The climax, the tit-bit, however, was the salt potatoes. Potatoes not boiled in the soup, where they only got hard, but boiled separately in a huge pot. The lads hadn't had that since they had been "inside." Some rolled the hot potatoes from one hand to another, and ate them like that, without soup, as soon as they had cooled a little.

"Fine, governor!" they called out to Studmann. "Couldn't you get them to make us potatoes in their jackets, and herring?"

"You shall have it," promised Studmann.

"I like my herrings with cream," one voice cried.

"All nice on ice, eh, governor?"

"I must have a woman with my potatoes," called a third, "to peel the skins. Could you do that, governor?"

A burst of laughter.

That was how they were, no worse and no better. Familiar and impudent, easily contented and greedy. They're very like children, thought Herr von Studmann, but without their innocence. Now they clamoured around him. Their hunger satisfied, they begged for tobacco. Tobacco, the best thing in the world so long as one is deprived of it; a matter of course when one has it. They knew they had no claim on Studmann until they had worked a week: each man was due to have two packets of tobacco next Sunday. But in that they were like children; a joy which will only come tomorrow, which will only come on Sunday, is no joy—they must have it at once!

And Studmann let himself be persuaded, he promised to send over young Pagel with fifty packets of tobacco, and went off to the staff-house. The prisoners thought him a fine fellow. "We'll milk him properly," they said. "He's the sort you've got to treat nice." They gabbled away, making a terrific din, till the warders interfered. Discipline mustn't be relaxed. "You're not here on holiday, you've got to work!"

When Herr von Studmann entered the office, he saw Herr von Teschow and young Pagel in close conversation. The two men, the oldest and youngest farmers in Neulohe, seemed to be getting on excellently: they both had very pleased faces.

"I was just telling your friend," boomed out Herr von Teschow, "what I used to get to eat when I was a young rip like him. Pork cutlets with spinach on a blasted week-day? Heavens, no! Warmed up dumplings three times a week! In the end we threw them at the ceiling where they stuck, they were that pasty. When I left the farm they were still sticking there."

"And what did you actually eat?" asked Studmann politely, all the more so since he was extremely angry. For every possible document relating to that morning's discussion with the Rittmeister lay open on the desk. There was nothing suspicious, but the old man was cunning; he could guess a whole plan of campaign from a hint.

"We stole like ravens!" said Herr von Teschow. "Larder, smoke house, apple bin—we had pass-keys to every nook and cranny!"

"So that in the end pork cutlets with spinach is still more economical for the employer," said Studmann dryly. "Pagel, would you mind taking fifty packets of tobacco to the barracks?"

"They're starting well!" boomed the Geheimrat. "Not a stroke of work yet, the rascals, and already fifty packets of tobacco! I'd also like to be one of your workers. Well, I won't say anything."

Pagel disappeared, waving his hand cheerfully to the Geheimrat. Studmann looked at Herr von Teschow challengingly, for the old man had sat himself in Studmann's chair at the desk, immediately in front of the scattered letters. But the owner of Neulohe did not budge. Studmann picked up the letters and began putting them away.

"The rubbish wouldn't have bothered me," said the old man patronizingly. "No letters bother me if I don't have to answer them. But I suppose you like writing letters, eh?"

Studmann murmured something. It might have been a reply, or it might not.

"I always say a farmer needn't know how to write at all. Read a little, perhaps, so that he can follow the prices of corn and livestock in the papers, but write! What for? So that they can sign bad bills of exchange, eh? All education is an invention of the Reds! Tell me, what good does it do a farm hand to be able to write? It makes him dissatisfied, that's all."

"Was everybody satisfied before?" asked Studmann. He was now leaning against the stove, smoking. He really ought to have been out on the farm, to see how things were going, but he would wait patiently to hear what the old man wanted. If he himself did not listen to it, the Rittmeister would have to, and then the business would be certain to go wrong.

"Of course not!" said the old man. "Of course they weren't satisfied before. Men are born to bleat, Herr Studmann! When a man's born he bleats away like a kid, and when he dies he rattles like an old goat. And in between he just goes on bleating. No, of course we weren't satisfied before. But there's a difference. Before, everyone merely wanted more than he had; today everyone wants what someone else has got!"

"There's some truth in that," assented Studmann and horridly wondered what he would like that others now had. He even thought of something.

"Of course there's some truth in it," said the old man triumphantly, now very pleased. Young Pagel had done him good, and Herr von Studmann also. They were both decent chaps—not like his son-in-law.

"Listen, Herr von Studmann," he said good-naturedly, "we're talking of bleating. Now take my old woman, she bleats too. That's why I'm sitting here."

Studmann looked at him inquiringly.

"Yes, Herr von Studmann, you're lucky, you're a bachelor. But I'm an old man. This time it's your Devil's hussars!"

"Who?"

"Those convicts. That's what they call themselves. Since they arrived she won't let me rest! 'Horst-Heinz, I won't tolerate it, convicts in our dear Neulohe! Whenever I look out of the window I see them; and they are all murderers and thieves, and now they're singing, too—murderers shouldn't be allowed to sing.'"

"So far as I've heard, the songs they sing are quite clean."

"That's what I told her, Herr von Studmann! My very words! They even sing 'Sitting at my parents' grave,' I told her. But no, she won't hear of murderers singing. Murderers must repent for the rest of their lives, she thinks."

"There aren't any murderers among them!" Studmann spoke with a trace of irritation, for he noticed that this chatter was intended to lead up to something more serious. "They are thieves and swindlers, all with relatively short sentences and good-conduct marks."

"My very words, Herr von Studmann, exactly what I told my wife. But you try telling a woman something when she's got something else in her head! 'Why are they in the penitentiary if they aren't murderers?' she says. 'There are ordinary prisons for thieves.' I can't explain the whole penal code to the woman!"

"So what's to be done?" asked Studmann. "What does Frau von Teschow want?"

"Then there's the matter of our washhouse," continued the Geheimrat. "Well, my wife placed it at your disposal for the cooking. But now she doesn't want to. You don't know how these things are, you bachelors. She's moaning about her beautiful copper in which our washing's usually boiled, not the food for your lot. I'm sorry, I didn't mean it that way, of course they are not *your* lot. And she thinks it is not right for Amanda to spend only half her time on the poultry. This morning there weren't so many eggs as yesterday."

"The chickens certainly didn't know this morning that the convicts were coming," said Studmann with a smile.

"You're right there! Ha-ha-ha!" The old man slapped his hand resoundingly on the desk. "I must tell that to my wife. That'll put her back up! Marvelous! The chickens didn't know! My wife has a weak spot for you, Herr von Studmann—well, this'll cure her. Really excellent!"

Studmann was extremely annoyed at his mistake. The old man, with all his parade of honesty, was such a big scoundrel, exploiting every slip ruthlessly—well, one simply had to be more careful than ever. And never lose patience, for that was all he desired. "We don't want our men to be a burden to your wife," he said politely. "We'll do what we can. We'll give up the washhouse. We can set up a kitchen somewhere else, in the fodder room or in the Villa—I'll see. Amanda shall be released. I'll take Frau Hartig to help Fräulein Kowalewski."

"Sophie?" cried the old man in astonishment. "Didn't you know? Well, you do know a lot about your own business! Sophie was standing in the cellar passage, sobbing out that your warder had insulted her, she wasn't going to work any more. Of course, I tried to calm her down, but you know what these girls are . . ."

"Thanks for trying to calm her down, Herr Geheimrat," said Studmann a little sharply. "I'll also find a substitute for Sophie. I shall forbid singing in the barracks. That would dispose of every objection, wouldn't it?"

"That's nice of you," cried the old man, beaming. "It's a pleasure to deal with you. If it had been my son-in-law, there would have been a fine row. But," the Geheimrat shook his head sadly, "unfortunately that isn't all, Herr von Studmann. When my wife sits at the window and sees these convicts' uniforms, it upsets her. She's an old woman; I must be considerate with her."

"Unfortunately I am not allowed to dress the men differently," said Studmann. "Otherwise I would have done that, too, you may be sure. But the Manor has four fronts—couldn't your wife choose a window somewhere else?"

"My dear Herr von Studmann," replied the Geheimrat, "my wife has sat at her window for, let's say, roughly fifty years. You really can't expect her to change in her old days just because you've imported convicts into Neulohe!"

"What do you want us to do?" asked Studmann.

"Why, Herr von Studmann," said the old Geheimrat, beaming, "send the men back to where they belong—to the prison! Today, if possible!"

"What about the harvest?" cried Studmann, horrified.

The Geheimrat smiled and shrugged his shoulders.

"You don't ask this seriously, do you?" inquired Studmann incredulously.

"My dear sir!" said the Geheimrat rudely, "you don't think I'd spend half an hour of my lunch time chatting with you for the fun of it, do you? The men are to leave Neulohe, and today!" He had risen from his chair and was regarding Studmann with an angry gleam. But, since a battle seemed imminent, the other was calm.

"Herr Geheimrat," he said, "your objections come too late. You knew two weeks ago of our intention to bring a prison gang here. You raised no protest. On the contrary, you placed your washhouse and your poultry maid at our disposal. By doing so you expressed your agreement."

"Look at him!" mocked the Geheimrat. "The little vest-pocket lawyer! But if you are clever, I can be clever, too. According to clause twenty-one of the contract of lease, the lessee has to remove at once any disturbance of the lessor's right of residence. Your criminals are a disturbance of the right of residence. Immediately this disturbance was apparent I asked for redress. Well, let's have your redress. Out with the men!"

"We refuse! We shall prove that a barracks occupied by Polish reapers with their wives and children is much more disturbing than convicts subject to strict discipline. We shall prove further—"

"In court, eh?" said the Geheimrat contemptuously. "Just go to court, my clever fellow! Any appeal to law dissolves the lease. Clause seventeen of the contract. Go on, appeal—I'll be glad to take over the harvest."

Studmann mopped his brow. Poor Prackwitz. If only he were here! But he'd no notion, and never would have. The old man wanted everything. He must have read the letters with the offers made by the corn dealers. Pagel was much too unobservant, too trusting. The old man was greedy—he not only wanted to clear out his son-in-law, he wanted the harvest as well. One must think of a way out.

"Well, Herr von Studmann?" said the old man with satisfaction. "Farming is different from the hotel business, eh? Why do you want to worry yourself here? My son-in-law certainly gives you no thanks for it. Send the men away and, if you're sensible, go away yourself. This place is a burst balloon; even you won't put any air into it."

Studmann stood at the office window. "A moment," he said, looking over at the barracks. Out of the door came Pagel; one, two, three convicts, then a warder. They went off, disappearing down the drive, probably to the toolshed. . . . All that could be seen from the Manor. There was no way out. Of course, he thought, it's me he really wants out of the way. He'd make easy work of Prackwitz. Prackwitz would just throw the whole thing up and give him the harvest. . . . No, no.

A thought came to him which he immediately rejected. He looked more sharply at the barracks. Its pointed red gable faced the staff-house and the Manor. In the gable was a door and a fanlight; the two long sides were hidden by lilac and guelder-rose bushes. No, the idea was not bad; it was *the* idea.

He turned round abruptly. "The lessor raises four objections," he said. "First, Amanda."

"Right," assented the Geheimrat, looking pleased.

"Amanda will be released. Suit you?"

"Right." The old man grinned.

"The use of the washhouse will be given up."

"Good!" laughed the old man.

"There'll be no more singing."

"Fine, fine. But with all your cunning you won't fill the fourth hollow tooth, Studmann, my lad."

"I am not a dentist. Fourth objection: The men can be seen from the Manor."

"Right," grinned Herr von Teschow.

"Nothing else?"

"Nothing else!" laughed the old man.

"It shall bother you no longer." Herr von Studmann was unable to prevent a note of triumph creeping into his voice.

"How do you mean?" The old man was taken aback. "Are you going to . . ."

"Going to what?"

The old man mused to himself. "Transfer the barracks? Can't be done. Quarter the men elsewhere? Can't be done, either, since their quarters must be secure. What else?"

"You will excuse me, Herr Geheimrat," said Studmann, with all that pleasant graciousness of which only a victor is capable. "I must at once give all the necessary instructions, so that the objection will be removed by evening at latest."

"But I should like to know . . ." said the old man, letting Studmann hustle him out of the office without a protest. "You'd better see that everything is arranged by the evening, though!" he cried, relapsing into his threatening mood of before.

"Everything will be arranged by evening," declared the cheerful Studmann, ostentatiously pocketing the office key instead of placing it as usual in the tin letter box. "Please give my kindest regards to Frau von Teschow." And he strode toward the farm like a conqueror, the Geheimrat gazing after him open-mouthed.

VII

While Herr von Studmann was negotiating, discussing, disputing with the Geheimrat; while he was dashing over to the farmyard and rounding up men to whom he gave instructions; while in the barracks he was informing young Pagel of the turn of events, not omitting to warn him against any more familiarity with jovial old gentlemen; while he spoke with the prison warders, entreating them not to feel offended—that is to say, during the whole afternoon in which he was talking, flattering, scolding, exhorting, sweating and smiling, in order to save his friend Prackwitz from his father-in-law's persecution—all that time Rittmeister Joachim von Prackwitz lay in a temper on his couch, sulking over his friend Studmann. He was furious with Studmann the guardian; cursed Studmann the nursery-governess; laughed contemptuously at Studmann the know-all; smiled scornfully at Studmann the prophet of evil!

As for old Geheimrat von Teschow, he merely cast one glance through the curtain at the beginnings of Studmann's labors, and immediately nodded his head. "The fellow's got brains all right," he said. "I should have had a man like that for my son-in-law, not a long-shanked blunderbuss."

The Rittmeister realized that he had been made to look completely ridiculous. Wife and friend had entered into a competition to see who could shame him the more. While his wife had ridiculed him before his friend by accusing him of exaggerating a little domestic intermezzo, in which, after all, he had been perfectly justified, his friend had represented him to his wife as an absolute nincompoop in business matters. He had cunningly deprived him of the whole management, and had even made him promise not to tell his father-in-law what he thought! This talk about the pitfalls in the lease was utter nonsense. By carefully avoiding details, the Rittmeister came to the conclusion that he had always done quite well in Neulohe, had always made a living—he hadn't brought conceited fellows from Berlin to prove to him that he wasn't.

He had wanted a friend, a companion to talk to, not a guardian. He wouldn't put up with it, he shouted in his head. The fact that it was inaudible made it no less intense. The worthy Studmann had been afraid that he would be in an ungovernable rage with his father-in-law. What his father-in-law did, that ridiculous old man of seventy in breeches, didn't mean a thing to him—he was furious with his friend, the friend who had mortally offended him.

In the harvesters' barracks everything appeared to be in order. Studmann ran sweating to the Manor washhouse. Three village women, who had been hastily rounded up, followed him with flying apron strings, clucking like hens, full of noisy expectation as to what could be happening again. Having arranged the transfer of the cooking utensils to the fodder-kitchen in the cattle-shed, having ordered an almost religious purification of the Teschow copper, desecrated by the convicts' food, Studmann ran at full speed to the village, to the house of Overseer Kowalewski, to discover from Sophie what had been the matter. He wanted to put things right with the girl, and perhaps at the same time find out what form the Geheimrat's kind exhortation had taken. But Sophie, he was told, had gone to a friend at the other end of the village. Herr von Studmann had sweated a lot already; a little more sweat would not matter. Herr von Studmann ran to the other end of the village.

From the park the old Geheimrat saw how he ran. "You can run!" he said cheerfully to himself. "But even if you took along all my Belinde's archangels and heavenly hosts, you wouldn't save my son-in-law!" Saying which, the Geheimrat went deeper into the park, to a spot he knew well. He who digs a ditch twice gets what he wants.

"Madam says, would you please come to coffee, sir."

"Thanks, Hubert. Ask her to leave me alone. Don't want any coffee, I'm ill."

"Are you ill, Achim?"

"Leave me alone!"

"Hubert says you are ill."

"I know what I said! I'm not ill! I don't want to be eternally treated like a child."

"I'm sorry, Achim—you are right, you are really ill!"

"Heavens, woman, leave me alone, can't you? I'm not ill! I just want to be left in peace."

He was left in peace. He heard his wife talking quietly to Vi in the next room, at coffee. They ought to talk loudly; otherwise he would only think they were talking about him. Of course they were talking about him! They ought not

to whisper like that! He was not *ill!* He had told her he wasn't, hadn't he? God
in heaven, they were forcing him, although he needed peace and quiet, to get
up and sit at the table—just to have their own way! Well, he wasn't going to. But
they shouldn't whisper like that, otherwise he would have to.

"Talk louder, can't you!" roared the Rittmeister furiously through the
closed door. "That whispering gets on my nerves! How can a man rest when all
that rustling's going on!"

"What are the men doing, I wonder?" said Frau von Teschow to Fräulein
von Kuckhoff. "I think they're building something."

The two women were sitting in their window seats, gazing at the most
interesting spot on Neulohe today, the harvesters' barracks. (They usually
slept at this time.)

"Everything comes to him who waits," replied Jutta von Kuckhoff. But
even she found waiting difficult. "You're right, Belinde, they look as if they're
building something."

"But what can they be building?" The old lady was excited. "The barracks
has been like that ever since Horst-Heinz built it in 'ninety-seven. I've got
used to it. And now suddenly alterations without any warning! Please, Jutta,
ring for Elias."

Jutta rang.

"That young man, that so-called Herr Pagel, is directing the gang. I never
trusted his face, Jutta. Why does he always run about in a field gray tunic, when
they say he's got two trunks full of suits? Elias, hasn't that young man got some
other suits?"

"Yes, madam, in a traveling wardrobe and in a large suitcase. Minna says
he also has silk shirts which button all the way down like the Rittmeister's.
Silk, not linen. But he doesn't wear them."

"Why doesn't he wear them?"

Elias shrugged his shoulders.

"Can you understand it, Jutta? A young man having silk shirts and not
wearing them?"

"Perhaps they don't belong to him, Belinde?"

"Oh, not if he has them in his trunk! There's something behind it—mark
my words, Jutta, remember what I said. We must be watchful. The first time he
puts on a silk shirt something will be happening. I'm sure of it!"

The three old people looked at each other with gleaming eyes, greedy and
curious; old ravens scenting the corpse while it was still alive. They understood
each other; even Elias had been their servant long enough to know how to join

in the hunt. "This morning the young man was in the park with the young Fräulein," he said.

"With my granddaughter, with Fräulein Violet? You must be mistaken, Elias. Violet is confined to her room, she isn't even allowed to come to us."

"I know, madam."

"And?"

"They were in the park for at least twenty-two minutes, at the back behind the trees, not in front on the lawn."

"Elias! My granddaughter . . ."

"They smoked, too. He gave her a light, not with a match but with his cigarette. I'm just saying what happened, madam. I saw it. Afterwards, I couldn't see, because the trees hid them. So I can't say what happened then."

The three fell silent. They looked at each other, then they looked away again as if they had caught one another doing something. At last Frau von Teschow piped: "Where was my daughter?"

"Frau von Prackwitz was in the office—with Herr von Studmann."

The two old women sat motionless, not looking at each other. Then, when Elias was certain that the hook held firmly he said: "The Rittmeister was also in the office."

The two friends stirred slowly, as if waking from a deep sleep. Fräulein von Kuckhoff cleared her throat loudly and gave Elias a doubting look. Frau von Teschow preferred to gaze out of the window.

"What are they doing over there, Elias?" she asked.

Elias had no need to look, he knew, and whatever he did not know he guessed. "They're bricking-up the door, because madam is upset by the sight of the criminals."

Frau von Teschow tried to make up her mind whether this was an insult or a kindly considerateness. The two could be so similar, it all depended how one took it. "How are the men to get out of the barracks?" she asked at last.

"They are making a door out of the second window in the large common-room," explained Elias. "Just behind the bushes, no, on the other side, facing the farm. . . . Madam will not be able to see them anymore."

"It's very inconsiderate of my son-in-law to brick-up my view," began Frau von Teschow bitterly.

"The Rittmeister knows nothing about it," Elias hastened to say. "He went straight home when the—er—men came. Herr von Studmann ordered it."

"How did Herr von Studmann manage to block up my old view of the barracks?" shouted Frau von Teschow heatedly.

"Herr von Studmann makes a very pleasant impression," said Fräulein von Kuckhoff warningly.

"The Geheimrat spent a long time talking with Herr von Studmann at midday," reported Elias. "The Geheimrat—er—shouted very loudly."

"It was very considerate of Horst-Heinz to think of it," said Frau von Teschow. "I knew nothing about it—he wanted it to be a surprise."

She gazed thoughtfully at the barracks. Two layers of bricks were already in place. The young man in field gray was talking eagerly to the farm masons; a warder stood by with an inquisitive face. Then all four burst out laughing. Laughing, they looked over at the Manor, at the windows. Frau von Teschow hastily moved her head out of the sun, although, half hidden behind the curtain, she could not be seen.

Still laughing, the two masons ran over to the farm. Young Pagel held out his cigarette case to the warder. They too were laughing.

Horst-Heinz shouldn't have done this! thought Frau von Teschow angrily. I can't stare at a bare wall the whole summer. I'm certain to hear stories of all these criminals, what they've done, why they're in prison—and I won't even know what they look like. She felt tempted to send over Elias to say that the alteration was not necessary, but did not dare. Her husband was good-natured only as long as no one interfered with his plans, which were usually secret. He could bellow in such a nerve-racking way! And he went purple in the face—Dr. Hotop was always saying that a stroke would be dangerous for him.

"Ask the Geheimrat to come to me, Elias," said Frau von Teschow gently.

"The Geheimrat has gone out. Shall I tell him when he comes back?"

"No, no, it should be now." A door can be bricked up so quickly. "But you might go over to my daughter and tell her I would like her to send Fräulein Violet for a little while." Elias nodded. "If my daughter should say anything about the child's being confined to the house, just hint, Elias—but carefully, quite unnoticeably—that Fräulein Violet went for a walk in the park today."

Elias bowed.

"You needn't mention anything about the young man to my daughter," said Frau von Teschow. "I'll talk to my granddaughter about it myself."

Elias's face showed that he had understood everything, that everything would be carried out perfectly. He asked whether there was anything else she wanted. But there was nothing. Elias went, dignified and calm, every inch the possessor of an enormous fortune.

"If Violet doesn't come today I'm going to the Villa!" added Frau von Teschow energetically. "Even if Horst-Heinz grumbles. I'm not going to have my granddaughter disgraced!"

"May I come with you, Belinde?" asked Fräulein von Kuckhoff excitedly.

"I'll see. Anyway, we must wait until my son-in-law leaves the house. And go at once and see if you can find Minna. Perhaps she knows something."

Young Pagel had had a brain wave. Fifty men in the harvesters' barracks laughed, five warders laughed, the masons laughed—soon the whole village would be laughing.

At first the atmosphere had been very unpleasant. This order to brick up the door, certainly a good solution on the part of Herr von Studmann, had not been a pleasant welcome to the convicts. "If they don't want to see us then they shouldn't bring us here to do their work," they growled. "If we're not too bad to dig up the potatoes they eat, then they shouldn't feel bad at seeing us. Who knows how he made his money? He didn't make his little pile by saying prayers!"

And the warders, too, had shaken their heads and pursed their lips. They considered they had—with two or three exceptions—a very orderly gang. The labor detachments from Meienburg were often far different. If the men behaved decently and worked well there was no need to keep on reminding them that they were convicts. It only made them restless and the warders' duty more difficult.

And then Pagel had had his brain wave. They had all laughed. They had all grinned. "That will remind them to pray for us every day," they said. "That's the way to treat them. Always pull the leg of a sod like that—it's the best way." For sheer pleasure they would have liked to burst into song again, thunder out "Arise! ye starvelings from your slumbers!" or some such thing to make the ears in the Manor tingle. But they did not want to cause the young man any trouble. With cheerful faces they sawed their planks, drove nails into the shelves for the utensils, packed and checked the washing. Today they were only to work half a day; today they first had to get everything in order, a thing the principal warder regarded as indispensable, everything in rank and file, everything shipshape and polished—just as in Meienburg prison. Numbers on every eating bowl and numbers on every wash-basin; numbers on the beds, numbers on the stools, every place at the dining table numbered. Important deliberations in a whisper among the warders; who ought to sit next to whom at the table? Which men could share a room? A faulty distribution, and the germ of an attempt to escape or a mutiny would be created.

And all the time one or other of them would slink up to the slowly diminishing doorway to have a look. And on his return the others would ask with a grin: "How far have they got? Can you recognize it yet?"

"They're just putting in the sixth layer. They'll only be able to recognize it properly when the crossbeam comes."

Von Studmann did not recognize it, either. He came from the village where he had at last found Sophie; and this time she hadn't been at all to his liking. Stubborn, close, untruthful. What could have entered into the girl? She was quite changed. Was the Geheimrat the cause? Yes, he must have stirred her up somehow. It was just like him. The whole day he had only been thinking how to make trouble. Oh, yes. The harvest. It is harvest time. Every little bit that is threshed and sold gives him pain. I must go immediately to Prackwitz and see that he doesn't again do anything stupid. Oh, yes, and I must ask Amanda what's behind what Kowalewski said. Today's one of those days when, once again, no sensible work will get done. You run about the whole time chasing your own tail. I would never have believed it, but it's almost worse than working in a hotel.

"What's the meaning of this, Pagel?" he said somewhat crossly. "There are plenty of red stones behind the cattle-shed: why mix in these ugly white cement ones?"

The two masons looked at each other and grinned. As is the way with such people, they pretended not to hear, but calmly went on with their work. An assistant warder, who poked his inquisitive head through the opening, drew it back hastily on seeing Herr von Studmann.

"Well?" asked Studmann very irritably.

Young Pagel gazed at his friend and superior with twinkling eyes. He threw his cigarette into the bushes and said with a sigh: "It's a cross, Herr von Studmann."

"What is a cross?" asked Studmann very testily, for he hated to have to grumble at or criticize a necessary labor.

"That!" Pagel pointed at the doorway. The two masons burst into laughter.

Studmann stared at the wall, at the doorway, at the stones white and red. . . . Suddenly it dawned upon him. "You mean that is going to be a cross, Pagel?"

"I thought it would look nicer," said Pagel, grinning. "A blank red wall would be very boring to look at, I thought. But with a cross—a cross somehow inspires contemplation."

The masons were working away with an almost counter-revolutionary zeal, wanting to protect the cross as far as possible from any prohibition. After a moment of reflection Studmann also laughed. "You're a cheeky scamp, Pagel," he said. "But still, if the effect is too bad we can always paint the white stones red. . . . See that you get it finished soon," he said to the masons. "Put some beef into it, understand? I suppose they can't yet see from the Manor what it's going to be?"

"Not yet," they replied. "When we get to the crossbeam, could the young gentleman go away for a bit? If they send over, we'll say we're only doing what we've been told."

"Yes, do that!" Studmann did not want any conspiracy with the men against the Manor. "Listen, Pagel," he said. "I'm going over to the Villa now, to tell Prackwitz about this." With a gesture embracing the Manor and the barracks: "In the meantime you will, in all circumstances, maintain the position."

"Position will be maintained, Herr Oberleutnant!" said Pagel, clicking his heels and saluting.

Studmann, however, did not go to the Villa, but to the staff-house, having remembered that he might meet the ladies. He couldn't possibly appear covered with perspiration; at least he ought to put on a fresh collar. And with a von Studmann it is only a step from a fresh collar to a fresh shirt. So the ex-lieutenant washed himself from head to foot in cold water—and in the meantime Fate took its course. While he was washing, disaster crossed the path to the Villa, with a beating of wings.

Old Elias had not been mistaken: his master had gone into the park. If nothing at all occurs to us any more, we still have whatever is left over from our original plans. Something like that had just occurred to Herr Geheimrat. Without hesitation, but looking around carefully out of his round, reddish, seal-like eyes, he had betaken himself to that spot in the fence where he had once stood at night. As before, he brought no tools with him but his hands. But memory is a wonderful thing; what we want to remember, we do remember. Despite the darkness of that night and the days that had since elapsed, the Geheimrat had not forgotten where the loose slat was. A pull, a little leverage, and he held it in his hand.

Puffing a little, he looked round. Again his memory worked excellently: he looked sharply at the bush in which he had once thought he saw Amanda Backs. Now, in the daylight, he recognized that it was a witch-wood bush—and no one was hiding in it. He went and thrust the slat into the middle of the bush and walked round it. The bush fulfilled all that was expected of it—the slat was invisible.

Nodding with satisfaction, the Geheimrat went in search of Attila. It was not his way to make a hole in a fence and then leave it to the geese to find, probably at the wrong time—this was the moment! The geese were, so to speak, the drop that was to fill the Rittmeister's cup of bitterness to overflowing. *Now* the Geheimrat went looking for Attila.

He found the geese—eighteen in all—on the meadow by the swans' pond, moodily cropping the park's sour grass. They greeted him with a disapproving and excited cackling. They stretched their necks, laid their heads on one side, squinted at him wickedly with their blue eyes, and hissed. But the Geheimrat knew his geese, even if they did not recognize him. These angrily hissing ladies were temporary phenomena; God's vice-regent here on earth, in this case Frau von Teschow, delivered them annually to the cook's knife, with the exception of three or four kept to breed. They were merely fleeting guests on the Geheimrat's meadow; hardly were they grown up when their flesh changed into smoked breasts and salted legs.

The only one who remained, surviving generation after generation, was Attila the breeding gander, a heavy bird weighing twenty-one pounds. Proud and superior, he regarded himself as the center of creation, bit the children, fluttered angrily at the postman's bicycle, making him fall, hated women's legs, which of late revealed more and more of themselves from under their skirts, and snapped at them till they bled. A stern despot in his harem, absolute monarch and autocrat, he tolerated no contradiction, was inaccessible to flattery, and had only one soft spot in his goosey heart—for Geheimrat Horst-Heinz von Teschow. Two kindred souls had recognized and fallen in love with each other.

Standing apart from his foolish womenfolk, probably immersed in the consideration of goosey problems, he had not noticed the arrival of his good friend. Then, his attention having been attracted, he gazed for a moment with his pale, forget-me-not blue eyes at the noisy flock, recognized the cause of the row, and with outspread wings fluttered cackling toward the Geheimrat.

"Attila!" the latter called. "Attila!"

The geese cackled excitedly; the gander advanced in a haste that brooked no obstacle. . . . Struck by the powerful blows of his wings, his wives staggered aside—and nestling against the Geheimrat's leg, neck lying on his stomach, head beating gently against his paunch, the gander softly and tenderly cackled a lot of things, announcing in every tone the unrestricted love of a friend for a friend.

With head bent, slowly coiling their necks in a wave-like movement, the flock of geese stood around.

"Attila!" said the Geheimrat, scratching the place geese cannot scratch, just above the beak which the gander, with a drowsy cackle, pressed gently against the softly heaving belly. And when the scratching finger grew sluggish, Attila pushed his head between shirt and waistcoat in a sudden adroit movement and remained thus, blissful, enjoying once again the greatest happiness on earth.

For a time the Geheimrat had to grant his furry friend such harmless pleasure. He stood in the meadow stippled with summer shade and summer sun, puffing his cigar slowly, a bearded, rosy-cheeked old man in rather sweaty clothes. A creature of this earth, he willingly granted his fellow creature the peace on his belly. "Attila!" he said soothingly from time to time. "Attila!"

And from under his waistcoat came a peaceful hissing in reply. To deceive the love of his gander would have seemed villainous to the Geheimrat; about his relatives he thought differently.

At last, however, he gently pushed his friend away. Once again he scratched the beak, then said invitingly, "Attila!" and walked off. The gander instantly followed, cackling softly and contentedly. And, as may be seen in children's books, all the geese followed in single file. First the old laying geese, then the grown-up goslings of the spring brood, with the wretched laggards in the rear.

Thus they wandered through the summery park. An ignorant onlooker would have found it a gay spectacle; an expert, of course, an Amanda Backs, would have shaken her head in suspicion. Unfortunately at this moment Amanda Backs was occupied in detaining with her protests Herr von Studmann, who was already late; she had not wanted to be freed from the kitchen, she could do the work in addition to looking after her poultry, and she would gladly have earned the money. She needed money. But the Geheimrat had said . . .

So Amanda saw nothing, and at this hour there was usually no one else in the park; in the country a park becomes frequented only after dusk. Thus the procession reached the hole in the fence unseen and unobserved. The Geheimrat stepped aside, and Attila stood before the hole. . . .

"Nice vetch, Attila, juicy vetch and anyway they cost me nothing," said the Geheimrat persuasively. Attila laid his head on one side and looked at his friend critically. He seemed to prefer near-by tenderness to distant and uncertain food. Quickly the Geheimrat bent down and thrust his hand through the hole, explaining: "Look, Attila, you can get through here!"

The gander approached and seized tenderly but firmly a tuft of the yellow-gray beard.

"Let go, Attila!" said the Geheimrat angrily, and tried to straighten himself. He couldn't. Attila held tight. A twenty-one-pound gander can hold very tightly. There the Geheimrat stood, crouched awkwardly; to put it exactly, his head was lower than the end of his back, which is a position even younger men do not find comfortable for long. It can be imagined what it was like for a somewhat too full-blooded old man with a tendency to apoplexy. Softly and tenderly the gander cackled, through his nose presumably, for he did not let the beard go.

"Attila!" implored the Geheimrat.

The female geese began to inspect his bent body and his hindquarters.

"This is intolerable!" groaned the Geheimrat, the world going black before his eyes. With a jerk he straightened himself. He stood, giddy, staggering. His cheek burned like fire. Attila cackled a gentle reproach, the tuft of hair still stuck to his beak.

"Blasted animal!" growled the Geheimrat, and pushed the gander violently through the hole in the fence. Attila cackled a loud protest, but already his wives were following him. What he, who saw only his friend, was prevented by his love from seeing, his wives noticed at once—the expanse of fields they had missed so long. They spread their wings. Cackling excitedly and ever louder, they fluttered—a noisy white cloud—toward the potato allotment stretching behind the laborers' houses.

Attila saw his wives far ahead. He knew there was food in the offing, and his friend was forgotten—how can a goose fly ahead of a gander? He spread his wings. Fluttering and cackling, he hurried after them and put himself at their head. Past the rear of the laborers' houses they hastened toward the fields, the broad fertile fields. Hastened. They knew they were doing what was forbidden; they knew that, once they were noticed, the hated people would come hurrying with sticks and whips to drive them back to the sour park grass. This did not make them any quieter, only quicker. . . .

For a moment the Geheimrat gazed after them. He rubbed his cheek and hoped his beard was worth it. But in any case it would be best if he was not on hand for the next few hours. Should anything happen to the geese, Belinde would be able to look after herself.

He hurried through the park on his way to the forest. The wind was against him. . . . Therefore he did not hear the shots. With a sigh of relief he disappeared into the shadow of the trees.

Young Pagel and his masons were at the crossbeam. Now, even at a distance, there was no mistaking what it was going to be. Therefore there was no more laughing, therefore there was no more huddling together of heads, therefore there was no more squinting over at the Manor windows.

"They're sitting up there and looking," said mason Tiede. "And if we peep at them the fat will be in the fire."

But the fat was in the fire anyhow. Frau von Teschow trembled with indignation at the insult offered her. Maids and cook were running round the Manor like chickens, looking in turn for Elias and the Geheimrat. . . .

"Just when you need a man he's certain never to be there," croaked Jutta von Kuckhoff.

"They're making fun of the holiest thing," groaned the old woman. "But you'll see, Jutta, that young man will also end up in prison."

"Whoever wants to be a hog's bristle is never a downy feather in his youth," asserted Fräulein von Kuckhoff, pouring out a glass of port wine for her friend.

Two gunshots cracked out in the distance. But in the general upset no one noticed them.

Studmann heard the shots nearer at hand, very near. He had finally freed himself from Amanda by promising to talk to the Geheimrat and was walking in the afternoon heat, slowly, so that he should not begin perspiring again, on his way to the Villa. He started at hearing shots crack out in his immediate vicinity. What idiot's shooting right near the houses? he thought with sudden anger.

At first he did not connect the cackling noisy geese with the shots. Then he saw a straggler, wailing sadly, with a hanging wing, probably broken. He saw three, four, five white spots on the green field. One of these was moving its feet and head convulsively. It became still.

But they are tame geese, not wild geese! thought Studmann, in astonishment, who was by no means familiar with all Neulohe's customs. Then he caught sight of the Rittmeister at a ground-floor window, gun in hand. His face was white as snow, his whole body trembled with rage, and he stared at his friend as if he did not recognize him. "Present my compliments to my father-in-law—tell him I'm giving him roast goose!" he shouted much too loudly. And before Studmann could answer, the Rittmeister slammed down the window.

"Disaster, misfortune, catastrophe!" Studmann felt, still not understanding what was going on.

Studmann dashed up the stairs to the entrance. The door was open. In the little hall stood Frau von Prackwitz, Violet von Prackwitz, the old servant Elias. . . .

When troubles come they come in floods; no nursemaid of a Studmann, no patient wife can ward them off. Had Frau von Prackwitz remained at the coffee table she would have heard through the open window the cackling approach of the feared and hated geese; she might have been able to prevent the unfortunate rash shots. . . . But Elias had brought the message asking that the young Fräulein be allowed to come over to the Manor—it was wiser not to annoy the Rittmeister and better to speak to Elias confidentially. They had gone out into the hall. Not two minutes had passed when the disastrous shots rang out.

In tears Frau von Prackwitz hurried toward Studmann. Her grief had broken down all barriers. Seizing his hands she said in despair: "Studmann, Studmann, now everything is finished—he's shot them."

Studmann looked at the disturbed faces around him.

"Mamma's breeding geese! Papa's favorite gander Attila! It has just died."

"But they're only geese! We can settle the matter . . . compensation."

"My parents will never forgive him." She wept. "And it was also contemptible of him! It wasn't the little bit of vetch! He wanted to hurt my parents."

Studmann looked around inquiringly, but the serious faces of the old servant and the young girl told him that more than geese had been shot.

Hubert Räder came quietly up from the basement, on rubber soles. He took up a respectful attitude near the stairs, his face indifferent, yet ready for orders. He glanced neither at the weeping woman nor out of the window at the victims. But he was there in case he should be needed; he was ready.

"What shall I do? Oh, what shall I do?" wept Frau von Prackwitz. "Whatever I do will annoy them, and will annoy him, too."

The Rittmeister emerged from his room like a jack-in-the-box. His face was no longer white but flecked with red, betokening the transition from wordless fury to abusive rage. "Don't take on like that!" he shouted at his wife. "Blubbering before all the servants on account of a few ridiculous geese."

"I must ask you," cried Studmann outraged, "not to shout at your wife like that!" In his teacher's way he added a precept. "Men shouldn't shout at their wives."

"This is fine!" said the furious Rittmeister, looking around in protest. "Haven't I pleaded, implored, demanded a hundred times: repair your fence, keep your geese under guard, don't let them get at my vetch? Haven't I warned them a hundred times: something will happen if I catch them at my vetch again? And now that something's happened, my wife weeps as if the world was coming to an end and my friend shouts at me! This is really too much!" He threw himself into a hall chair, making it creak; he jerked at the crease of his trousers with long, trembling fingers.

"Oh, Achim!" wailed his wife. "You have shot away the lease. Papa will never forgive you for this."

The Rittmeister jumped up from his chair at once. "You don't think that the geese got at the vetch by accident, do you, after all that's happened today? No, they were brought there. They wanted to annoy me, to provoke me. Good—I shot them!"

"But, Achim, you can't prove it."

"If I'm right I don't need to prove it."

"The weaker is always wrong . . ." began Studmann wisely.

"We'll see whether I'm the weaker!" cried the Rittmeister, enraged afresh by this wise dictum. "I'm not going to have them jeer at me. Elias, go at once to the vetch, pick up the dead geese, take them to my mother-in-law and tell her . . ."

"Herr Rittmeister," said the old servant, "I was sent here on an errand by my mistress. With all due respect, Herr Rittmeister, I am employed at the Manor."

"You will do what I say, Elias!" cried the Rittmeister in a louder voice. "You will take the dead geese and tell my mother-in-law . . ."

"I shall not do it, Herr Rittmeister. I couldn't, even if I wanted to. Five or six geese are too much for an old man. Attila alone weighs a quarter of a hundredweight."

"Hubert shall help you. Hubert, help him carry the dead geese."

"Good day, madam. Good day, Herr Rittmeister." Elias went.

"Fool!—Hubert, present my mother-in-law with my compliments; those who won't listen to reason will have their knuckles rapped."

"The Rittmeister's compliments, and those who won't listen to reason will have their knuckles rapped," repeated Räder, his fishy eyes resting on his master.

"That's right." The Rittmeister spoke more calmly. "You can take a barrow, get a man from the farm to help you. . . ."

"Very good, Herr Rittmeister." Hubert went to the door.

"Hubert!"

The servant stopped. He looked at his mistress. "Yes, madam?"

"You're not to go, Hubert. I shall go myself. Please come with me, Herr von Studmann. . . . There will be a terrible quarrel, but we'll save what we can."

"Of course, Frau von Prackwitz," said Studmann.

"What about me?" cried the Rittmeister. "What about me? I suppose I'm not needed any more? I'm completely superfluous, eh? Hubert, you are to go at once with the geese or you are dismissed."

"Very good, Herr Rittmeister," said Hubert obediently, but looking at his mistress.

"Go along now, Hubert, or I'll throw you out!" yelled the Rittmeister in a final explosion.

"Do as the Rittmeister says, Hubert. Come along, Herr von Studmann, we must try if possible to get to my parents before Elias." She dashed away. Studmann glanced back at the two figures in the hall, shrugged his shoulders helplessly and followed.

"Papa!" said Vi, who had been waiting anxiously for her mother to forget her for the first time in two weeks, "may I go out for a bit, and bathe?"

"Well, Vi, those two are kicking up a fuss, aren't they? Because of a few geese! I'll tell you what'll happen. They'll talk all day and night, and then everything will be left where it is."

"Yes, Papa. And may I go bathing?"

"You know you are confined to your room, Vi," explained the consistent father. "I can't allow you to do what your mother has forbidden. But if you like, come with me; I'm going to the forest for a little."

"Yes, Papa." His daughter felt annoyed beyond measure at having spoken. For her father would certainly also have forgotten her.

VIII

What made the tearful negotiations in the Manor so difficult was the slaughtered geese. Not the fact that they had been shot by martial law, as it were, for field stealing—this news had already been brought to Frau von Teschow by old Elias, with a haste that was quite unusual and undignified. No, it was the corpses of the victims themselves, their departed souls, which kept flitting through Frau von Teschow's room, shaded so pleasantly by the lime trees. The noise of the masons' hammers had died away; the door was bricked up; the cross had been painted over red on an order from Studmann, hastily whispered in passing by. The old Geheimrat was still wandering among his pines, knowing nothing, fortunately, so that there was still time to pacify his wife.

And Frau von Teschow was, in fact, sitting much more calmly in her large armchair, only infrequently dabbing a handkerchief to her old eyes that wept so easily. Fräulein von Kuckhoff uttered every now and again an apt or inapt proverb, usually apt. Herr von Studmann sat with a suitably courteous and somewhat troubled face, interjecting a shrewd word from time to time, as soothing as balm.

Frau Eva was huddled at her mother's feet on a kind of little bolster, thus wisely indicating by her choice of seat how completely subordinate she was to the old lady, and revealing that she knew the chief precept of the marriage catechism inside out—that it is usually the wives who have to suffer for the vices and stupidities of their husbands. Not for one moment did she forget what she had said to Herr von Studmann as she left the Villa—namely that she wanted to rescue what could be rescued. Without flinching she let Frau von Teschow not only say things which do not matter very much to a woman, remarks on goose-slaughter, the brick cross, the convicts or the Rittmeister, but also things which a woman will not tolerate even from her mother: remarks about her extravagance in silk underwear, her expensive taste for lobster ("But, Mamma, they're just Japanese crabs!"), her lipstick, her tendency to fatness, the low necks of her blouses, and Violet's upbringing.

"Yes, Mamma, I'll pay more attention to it. You are right," said Frau von Prackwitz obediently. She was a heroine—Studmann admitted it frankly. She neither flinched nor hesitated. She certainly did not find the victor's yoke light, yet she did not betray the fact. And for whom was she suffering these bitter humiliations? For a man who would never appreciate it, who, when everything had been happily straightened out, would triumphantly claim: "Well, didn't I tell you so? A lot of fuss about nothing! I knew it, but you always have to lose your head; you will never listen to me!"

It was dreadful how quickly a comradeship dating from before the war broke down in times like these, under such conditions. Herr von Prackwitz had certainly never been a brilliant or even very capable officer; but he had been a reliable comrade, a brave man and a pleasant companion. And what was left of it? He was not reliable—he sent his officials out against field thieves, and when the thieves were caught he went and hid behind a bush. He was no longer a comrade—he was only a superior, and an unjustly critical superior at that. He was no longer brave—he preferred to let his wife go alone to a distressing interview. He was no longer pleasant society—he spoke only of himself, of the insults he suffered, of the troubles he had, of the money he lacked. One had to admit, though, that these defects had always been present, and that it was the badness of the times which had made them blossom so luxuriantly.

But there sat the Rittmeister's wife, and whereas her husband was cowardly, she was brave. Whereas he only thought of himself, she remained a comrade. Above sat the old woman, a lean, dry little bird with a pointed beak, good for pecking, and below sat the beautiful woman. She looked radiant, the country did her good, she was mature as gold-tinted wheat, there was a charm about her. When the old woman had spoken of the low-necked blouses, Studmann had not been able to prevent himself from glancing at the gently heaving silken bosom, and had lowered his eyes like a schoolboy caught in mischief.

He saw only virtues in this woman. The more distorted, the more imperfect he found the Rittmeister's once friendly figure, all the more perfect did his wife appear to him. To be sure she was a woman, a human being, and therefore in theory imperfect—yes, she probably had her bad side. But he might have racked his brains to the utmost without finding a fault in her. She was perfect, a gift from heaven—but for whom? For a fool! For a scatter-brain!

The way she not only bore everything silently, but even smiled, trying to turn her mother's sermon into a dialogue which would cheer up that old heap of poison! She isn't doing it for her husband at all, suddenly thought Studmann. She is doing it for her child. She can only think as I do about him; she just saw in the hall what sort of a man he is. There's nothing to bind them together any longer. It's only her daughter, Violet. . . . And naturally she wants to keep the farm on which she has grown up. . . .

From condemnation to betrayal of his friend was only a step. But it must be said in Herr von Studmann's favor that he did not think clearly about these things. The teacher was frightened at the chasm in his own heart. Herr von Studmann didn't think. He just saw. He saw this handsome woman sitting a little lower than himself; he saw how her hair was rolled up on her neck, the beautiful white shoulders which disappeared beneath her blouse. She moved her foot, and the ankle covered by the silk stocking was beautiful. She raised her hand, her bracelets tinkled softly, and her arm was round and spotlessly white—it was Eve, the ancient, ever-young Eve.

She'd paralyzed his ability to think, to analyze, and to explain himself. Herr von Studmann was over thirty-five and hadn't believed that he would experience this any more, with such spontaneity, such power. In fact, he didn't really know he was experiencing it. He sat there innocently, his eyes betraying nothing. His words remained thoughtful and moderate. Yet it had happened!

If only the cursed geese had not been there! Again and again their ghosts drifted into a conversation, now gradually growing calmer, and made the old woman's tears flow afresh. Elias came knocking, then the maid, then Amanda Backs—to say that the servant from the Villa was there with the dead geese—what should they do with them? Again and again Hubert Räder stormed the Manor, to be turned away each time. The inscrutable intriguer from the servants' quarters was always making further attempts to hand over the corpses—thereby adding fuel to the fire.

An imploring glance from Frau Eva decided Studmann. Leaving the room out of her sight, he was again the cool businessman, familiar, as the result of years of hotel work, with every kind of servant's trick.

He found the basement of the Manor in a state of siege. After Räder had vainly attempted to hand over the geese to each of the employees there, he had apparently undertaken to get rid of them by stealth, laying them on window sills and outside cellar doors—attempts which were, however, frustrated by the general watchfulness. But, obstinate as a mule, Hubert Räder still circled the Manor, followed by a laborer pushing the barrow with the victims. Gray, fishy, cold, the servant peered at an open window, weighed the possibilities of the hen coop.

Studmann put an end to this disorder; he sent the Manor servants about their work and gave Räder a dressing-down. But Räder was strangely cool and refractory. He seemed not to regard Herr von Studmann as having authority. He had been strictly ordered by the Rittmeister to deliver the geese—on pain of losing his job. And madam also had assented to this order.

In vain did Studmann assure him that he had just come from madam with the order that he was to take the geese away at once. Räder showed no inclination to accept this as an annulment of the Rittmeister's command. Where was he to go with the geese, anyway? To the Villa? The Rittmeister would fire him on the spot.

Studmann should have seen in Räder a very faithful servant, but he merely found him sickeningly recalcitrant. He wanted to go back, to know what was being arranged in the large greenish-golden room—and he had been standing here for five minutes talking to this ass. At last he ordered them to follow him to the staff-house; the laborer obeyed with squeaking barrow while from the Manor basement every face stared after the procession. Räder followed, protesting—Studmann felt that he was a rather ridiculous figure.

In the office he seized the telephone. "I shall speak to the Rittmeister," he said more mildly. "You needn't be afraid about your job."

Räder stood there as cool as ever. There was no reply from the Villa, and Studmann could not help casting angry glances at the servant. But they were lost on him; Räder was watching the antics of the flies round the flycatcher. When finally someone did answer, it was the cook Armgard, who announced that the Rittmeister had gone out with the young Fräulein. Räder looked as if he had been expecting this.

"Then take the geese to the Villa, Herr Räder," said Studmann mildly. "You can put them somewhere in the cellar. I'll arrange the matter with the Rittmeister—you need not worry."

"I have to deliver the geese at the Manor, otherwise I'll be sacked," explained Hubert Räder inexorably.

"Then leave the geese here in the office, for all I care!" cried Studmann angrily. "The things have to be got out of the way, even if I have to do it myself!"

"I'm sorry," contradicted the servant politely, "but I have to deliver them at the Manor."

"I'll be damned!" shouted Studmann at this pig-headedness.

"I'll be damned!" bellowed from the doorway a stronger voice, more practised in swearing. "What are my geese doing here? What are my geese doing on this barrow? Who has killed my geese?"

Studmann left the servant standing where he was and dashed from the office. Outside stood old Geheimrat von Teschow, scarlet with rage. He roared like a wounded lion, brandishing his stick. He threatened the estate's builder Tiede, who dodged out of the way with almost silent curses.

"If you please, Herr Geheimrat," said Studmann with all that painfully acquired calmness which had never deserted him, even when faced with hysterical women in the hotel, not to speak of the man with the geese, "I shall—"

"Did you kill my geese? My Attila? I'll teach you, my lad! Clear out of my farm at once! Leave my stick alone!" The stick had been dangerously near Studmann's face. With a quick movement Studmann had hold of it.

"If you please, Herr Geheimrat," he requested, while the other, turning blue with rage, tugged at the stick, "not here before the men!"

"The men can go to blazes!" panted the old man. "Did you worry about the men when you shot my geese? But I'm telling you I won't tolerate you a moment longer on this farm! Comes from Berlin, thinks he's so clever, babbles like a shyster lawyer . . ." The Geheimrat was delighted to be able to retaliate on Studmann for the several set-backs he had suffered, to be able to curse him in the passion of a semi-simulated rage. He was too clever actually to believe that Studmann had killed his geese, but he wanted to have full freedom to curse.

Studmann, who did not know all the implications of the goose massacre, thought the old gentleman had some reason to be enraged, but felt at the same time that this fit of passion was not quite genuine. Suddenly he let go the stick and revealed what the old man would find out anyhow. "You're mistaken, Herr Geheimrat. Your son-in-law shot the geese. He intended only to frighten them, but unfortunately—"

"You're lying!" shouted the old man still more angrily. "You're lying in your throat!"

"'I assume, anyway, that he intended to frighten them," said Studmann, turning white.

"My son-in-law? You're lying! I've just spent half an hour with him in the forest, and he didn't mention a word to me about the geese! Are you suggesting that he's a liar—a coward? No, you are lying! You are a coward!"

Studmann, very pale, had an overpowering impulse to turn round on the spot, pack his bags and depart to more peaceful fields—perhaps to Berlin. Or to stamp so hard on the old man's toes that he would collapse at once. There stood Tiede, the estate builder, who, with open mouth and flared nostrils, was the personification of listening. Räder in the office was certainly listening to everything, and quite close, just behind the nearest bushes, was the Manor—also, without a doubt, well supplied with ears. The raging old man became ever more insulting. But Herr von Studmann had the unmistakeable feeling that this old man was only raging in order to insult him for knowing the truth.

Yes, Studmann had every inclination to turn his abilities to a more fruitful field—he had had a letter in his pocket for two days, offering him another post—and the news that the Rittmeister had not told his father-in-law of his heroic deed did nothing to diminish this inclination.

He did not doubt for a moment that the old man was speaking the truth on this point.

If, then, Studmann did not go up to his room to pack his bags—if, instead of that, he abruptly left the dead geese and the fuming old man and went toward the Manor—he was not moved to do so by the bonds of friendship nor by the memory of a beautiful helpless woman nor by a feeling of duty, but purely by the stubbornness innate in every true man. He felt that the old fellow wanted to frighten him away forever, and so he remained. He would go when it suited him and not the old man.

"Look here, sir!" shouted the Geheimrat. "What are you doing there? I forbid you to go into my park!"

Studmann went on without a word, putting Herr von Teschow at a disadvantage. If his expostulations were to reach the trespasser he had to hurry after him. A man who is normally short-winded cannot curse very well when he is running. Between jerky breaths the Geheimrat shouted: "I forbid you—to go—in my park—you are—not—to enter—my house! Elias, don't let him in. It's a breach of the peace. Don't let him up!"

The door of his wife's room slammed upstairs.

Beckoning to Elias, the old man whispered: "What does he want here?"

"Frau von Prackwitz is upstairs," Elias whispered back.

"Breach of the peace!" bellowed the Geheimrat again. It was the cannon-shot to cover his retreat. "Been here a long time?" he whispered.

"Over two hours."

"And Frau von Teschow?"

"Heavens, sir, both of them are crying."

"Damn it!" whispered the old man.

"Papa," came a gentle call from upstairs, "won't you come up?"

"No!" he shouted. "Got to bury my Attila! Goose murderers, damn them!"

She came tripping down the stairs as quickly as if she were still seventeen, as if she were still living in his house, in that distant happy time . . . "Papa!" she said, taking his arm. "I need your help."

"Don't help murderers!" The Geheimrat flared up. "The fellow must clear out of the house, I won't move an inch as long as he's upstairs!"

"Now, Papa, come along."

He had one foot on the stairs.

"You know quite well that Herr von Studmann is one of the most decent and helpful men there are. You needn't pretend to me." There was a strange sad note in these words.

"You shouldn't get old, Evie," said the old man. Angrily he called over his shoulder: "Elias! If Herr von Prackwitz, my so-called son-in-law, comes, tell him I'm not at home to him! Let him go and get another farm—today!" Quietly to his daughter: "Evie, you think you can do what you like with me. But only if my son-in-law clears out of Neulohe, understand?"

"We'll discuss everything calmly, Papa."

"Yes, you want to get round me, Evie," growled the old man and squeezed her arm.

IX

Geheimrat von Teschow had spoken the truth. He had met his son-in-law in the forest, and even if the two had not chatted long, they had said "Good day" quite pleasantly. Two-fifths of the conversation that followed was devoted to deer, and three-fifths to Violet, whom her grandfather had not seen for a good while. So no time was left to speak about the goose massacre. The Geheimrat had been right on this point, too.

If, however, Herr von Studmann entertained a still lower opinion of his former friend Prackwitz because of this silence, and even cursed him for a coward, then he was scarcely in the right. Prackwitz was no coward, but moody—as moody as a young girl shedding her childhood, as moody as a young woman expecting her first baby, as moody as a prima donna who has never had one and never will. That is to say, the Rittmeister was as moody as only a woman can be. But he was no coward. He would not have hesitated a moment to tell his father-in-law about the geese and engage him in the most violent quarrel regardless of consequences—if he had felt like it. But having humored his quarrelsomeness the whole morning and a good part of the afternoon, he was now in a peaceful mood. He had spent himself; his fit of anger had vanished with the two shots.

He looked at the sweaty old man, whose forehead was covered with perspiration. The news waiting for you will make you still hotter, he thought, politely promising to ask Eva whether Violet's detention might not be relaxed so far as to permit her to visit her grandparents.

"You're looking thin and pale, Vi," said her grandfather. "Well, come along, give your old granddad a kiss. Here, not so fast, must dry myself a bit first." And he drew out a huge handkerchief, gaily printed with the insignia of St. Hubert. The Rittmeister looked away indignantly. It was revolting that this gross old man with printed cotton handkerchiefs could kiss his granddaughter and yet tease and worry him with a wretched lease. He gazed into the pines, where birds fluttered now and again in the sunny cones, and after a while he said dryly:

"We must be getting along now."

"Of course you must," said the old man gaily. He was by no means unaware of his son-in-law's feelings, often deriving an unsullied pleasure from his "finicky fineness." "Well, one last big hug for your granddad, Vi!" And he cried out in the drunken tones of a Berlin sausage seller: "They're warm, and fat too. . . ."

"Now please, Vi!" ordered the Rittmeister sharply. One couldn't be with the old man for five minutes without getting cross with him!

"Run along, Vi. I'm not fine enough for your father. Queer though, my farm's fine enough for him!" And with this Parthian shot the old man plodded off, chuckling with pleasure.

For a while the Rittmeister walked along in silence—he was getting annoyed again and he didn't want that—he couldn't stand being annoyed. With an effort he banished all thought of his father-in-law and brooded about the Horch car which he was so anxious to have. He had wanted to buy it this autumn after the first threshing, but Studmann had, of course, destroyed this hope by his long-winded calculations. And why? Just because that old miser had swindled him with a fraudulent lease!

"Your grandfather always tries to annoy me, Violet!" he complained.

"Grandpa doesn't mean it that way, Papa," said Violet consolingly. "Papa, I wanted to ask you something . . ."

"Oh, doesn't he! He means even more than he says!" Irritably the Rittmeister slashed at the weeds bordering the path. "Yes, what did you want to ask?"

"Irma has written to me, Papa," Violet lied boldly. "Just think, Gustel Gallwitz wants to marry!"

"Really?" asked the Rittmeister without interest, for the Gallwitzes lived in Pomerania and were in no way related to the Prackwitzes. "Whom?"

"Oh, I don't know. Someone or other—you don't know him, a lieutenant. But what I wanted to ask, Papa . . ."

"In the Reichswehr?"

"I don't know. I think so. But, Papa . . ."

"Then he must have means. Or the Gallwitzes are giving her a dowry. . . . He certainly won't be able to live on the miserable pittance he draws as a lieutenant."

"But, Papa," cried Vi in despair, since she saw her father continually going off on the wrong track, "that's not what I mean. I want to ask something quite different. Gustel is no older than I am!"

"Well—what of it?" asked the Rittmeister, not understanding.

"But, Papa!" Vi knew very well that she would not have been allowed to carry on such a conversation with her mother, who would have smelled a rat at once. But Papa never noticed anything. "Gustel is only just fifteen! Is one allowed to marry at fifteen?"

"No!" declared the Rittmeister firmly. "Absolutely impossible! That's seduction of min—" He bit his lips. "No, it's not allowed. It even says so in the penal code."

"What's in the penal code, Papa?" cried Vi, startled.

"That little kids like you ought not to know about such things," concluded the Rittmeister with a somewhat false heartiness. It had occurred to him just in time that Frau Eva would have been very displeased at this conversation, suspecting as she did that Violet was no longer so innocent as her parents had believed. So he added darkly: "And fellows who meddle with fifteen-year-old girls are scoundrels and go to prison—that's in the penal code."

"But the man might not know she is only fifteen!" cried Violet excitedly.

The Rittmeister stopped and looked at his daughter. "Whoever meddles with a girl without even knowing how old she is, is already a scoundrel. One doesn't defend fellows like that, Violet. Now come along."

They went on. The Rittmeister was thinking again of his father-in-law and the Horch car—there must be some way of getting it. All his acquaintances had cars; only he . . .

"But, Papa," Violet began again cautiously, "he wants to marry Gustel! So the marriage must be possible, even if she is only fifteen."

"All right, if it's possible then it is possible—that's his worry!" said the Rittmeister crossly. "I think you have to apply to the Home Secretary or something. Anyway, I wouldn't let my daughter do it."

"I wouldn't want to, Papa," laughed Violet. "Do you think I would? Heavens, Papa, I'm so glad to be able to walk in the forest with you. I think all men are terrible except you!" She hung on his arm and nestled against him.

"There, Vi, I've told your mother ten times already that your mind isn't on men yet!" he said with pleasure, giving her arm a strong squeeze.

"Oh, Papa, you're hurting me! But, Papa, I'm awfully interested in this about Gustel. If Irma writes it, it must be true. Tell me all about it, Papa, all about the laws, and what they have to do."

"Now, what next, Vi! You women are all the same; when it's a question of marriage you become as inquisitive as monkeys."

"Monkeys, Papa! I'm not a monkey. But if the Home Secretary says yes, must the father also say yes?"

"What do you mean?" The Rittmeister was getting more and more fogged about the relevance of this cursed Pomeranian marriage. "It's the father who first has to ask the Home Secretary for permission to marry!"

"The father? Not Gustel?"

"But she's only fifteen, child; she's not yet of age."

"Supposing he makes an application to the Home Secretary—the lieutenant, I mean?"

"Gustel can never marry without the consent of old Gallwitz. I'm amazed that he gave it!"

"Never, Papa?"

"Well, at least not before her twenty-first birthday."

"Why not before? A lot of girls marry at seventeen or eighteen, Papa."

"Heavens, Vi, you're driving me crazy! Those girls have obtained their father's consent."

"And without it . . ."

"Without it," cried the Rittmeister, "no decent girl marries at all. Understand, Vi?"

"Why, of course, Papa," she said innocently. "I'm just asking you because you know everything and no one can explain things to me as well as you can. Not even Mamma."

"Really, Vi," said the Rittmeister, half placated, "you've been asking enough today to last a lifetime."

"Because I want to know everything about Gustel! You see, Irma writes that old Gallwitz isn't so pleased about it, but the lieutenant is so much in love, and Gustel too—and they want to marry whatever happens. So it has to be possible, Papa!"

"Yes, Vi," said her father. "If she's a bad and disobedient child, she'll run away with him and go to England. In England there's a blacksmith, and he can marry them. But it would be a scandalous marriage—the girl would never be able to return to her parents' house, and the lieutenant would have to take off his uniform and could never be an officer again."

"But would they be properly married, Papa?" asked Vi sweetly.

"Yes, properly married!" cried her father, red with rage. "But without their parents' blessing!" (The Rittmeister never went to church.) "The parents' blessing builds up a house for the children, but the father's curse tears it down, as it says somewhere in the Bible." (The Rittmeister had never looked at a Bible since he had been confirmed.) "And I forbid you, Vi, ever to write to these silly geese who put such stupid thoughts into your head! You shall give me the letter as soon as we get home."

"Yes, Papa," said Vi obediently. "But I've already torn it up."

"The cleverest thing you could have done!" growled her unsuspecting father.

The two went on in silence. The Rittmeister tried in vain to think about his Horch—disturbing thoughts kept intervening. Only when he turned his mind actively to the car's inner arrangements and encountered the serious questions—upholstery or leather? and what color?—only then did he succeed in becoming calm again and able to walk with contentment through the beautiful sun-swept forest, at the side of a daughter who, thank Heaven, no longer asked questions.

And Violet was just as content. She knew at last what she had long wanted to know: that there was a possibility of marrying her Lieutenant. What her father had added about the parents' curse and the taking off of the uniform did not affect this wonderful news in the least. She had always got round her father, and why not after marriage? And her Fritz was so clever; he could become anything and did not need to be a lieutenant. Since she would one day inherit, as the only child, everything here, he could just as well settle down in Neulohe and help Papa, instead of always riding round the country on a bicycle. She really didn't know which way to turn, but didn't notice. Her whole future seemed like a mirror garlanded with may-branches, a mirror in which she saw only her own happy face. Even if the word scoundrel had fallen on her ears for the second time today, that did not bother her. One could apply here a proverb from Jutta von Kuckhoff's collection and say that love makes even a broomstick green: since he had become a scoundrel through love of her, she forgave him his scoundrelism. Nay, she admired the hero who, for her sake, feared neither penal code nor prison.

But all this was only vague and without any fixed form. What she saw more clearly in her daydream was the flight over land and sea to the distant kingdom of England. Suddenly she was glad that she had continued to learn English with her mother, for now she would be able to converse with the people there. And she was glad there was no more war, for then she could not have got married to him in that country.

The marrying blacksmith! Strange that it should be a smith! And she saw his smithy just like the farm smithy in Neulohe. Under a small roof were tied the horses that were to be shod, and to the right of the door leaned the huge cartwheels on which tires were to be fixed, and through the door could be seen the open fire which glowed red under the squeaking bellows. And then the smith came out, tall and dark, with a leather apron, and over the anvil Violet von Prackwitz and Lieutenant Fritz were married.

Oh, this wretched smith of Gretna Green—that it had to be a smith! Had he been a chimney sweep or a tailor he would never have caused such mischief in the heads of two generations or been the last hope of all desperate young lovers. But a smith! In this bureaucratic world of documents he appeared, to all who could not obtain documents, like a warrior of old—iron and blood, flesh and anvil-song, who married according to divine law, not according to a documentary one. He had turned so many heads, this marriage maker who grew fat on fees—why shouldn't he also turn Vi's? She saw the smithy and she saw the smith. He could marry, and he married. There would be no more secrecy, no desperate waiting, no confinement to her room, no shameless servant Räder and no cheeky Herr Pagel—there would only be Fritz, morning, noon and evening, day as well as night, week-days as well as Sundays. . . .

These dreams were so beautiful, and they had trapped Vi so completely, as if in a warm protective net, so that she no longer thought about the path or her father, but walked along quite unselfconsciously, softly humming to herself. With the daughter it was the Lieutenant; with the father it was the Horch car. Both dreamed dreams according to their age.

And thus they both received the same shock when a man stepped out of a bush, a man in a rather shabby field-gray uniform, a steel helmet on his head, a gun under his arm, and on his belt not only a holster but also half a dozen hand grenades.

This man gave the peremptory order: "Stand still!"

The Rittmeister's desire for solitude had led him unawares deeper and deeper into the forest; father and daughter had long ago left the beaten track and were now on a kind of stalking path in an unfrequented part called the Black Dale. Here, on the extreme edge of the Teschow forest preserve, it looked gloomy and wild; only seldom did the woodsmen come to clear up and thin out the trees. The otherwise almost flat country was here all undulation, humps between which were dark little valleys where springs trickled just strongly enough to survive the summer and form a morass in which the wild boars had their almost inaccessible retreats. The firs and pines towered high, all around blackberry bushes formed impassable thickets—there was nothing here even for poachers.

In the midst of this deep solitude there now stood a heavily armed man who, quite without any legal grounds, said to the son-in-law of its owner: "Stand still!" And said it discourteously, too.

On first being startled, Violet von Prackwitz had uttered a little cry. But now she stood there calm, though breathing deeply—something said to her that this soldier was connected with her Lieutenant, whom perhaps she might even get to see again after such a long separation. . . .

The Rittmeister, however, who had merely said "Well!" was not so angry as one would have thought at this "Stand still!" in a place where he himself should have been the one to give the order. The man who had spoken wore a uniform, and the Rittmeister did not. And if he subscribed to any tenet, it was to the one that a uniformed man gives orders to a civilian, any civilian. This tenet he had imbibed with his mother's milk, his whole life as officer had proved its truth—and so he immediately halted, looked at the sentry and waited for what was to happen. (Silence was appropriate. Real civilians would naturally have asked questions; an old soldier kept his mouth shut and waited.)

He was right. When the man saw that the two showed no signs of resisting or escaping, he blew a little whistle—not too loudly, not too softly. Then he said quite pleasantly: "The Lieutenant will be here at once!"

If the Rittmeister hadn't been so absorbed in this military procedure, so long missed, he would undoubtedly have been somewhat perplexed at his daughter. She turned red, she turned white, she seized his arm, she let it go again, she gulped, she almost laughed. . . . But he noticed nothing of this. He was pleased, as only an ex-officer can be, that he had, after all his civilian troubles, encountered military maneuvers. He looked at the sentry benevolently, and the sentry looked benevolently at the blushing girl.

There came a rustling in the bushes, and out stepped the Lieutenant, thin, with sharp cold glance, and on his chin red stubble. Vi gazed at him with eyes that grew ever more radiant, for here at last was the Lieutenant—her Lieutenant.

But he did not look at her, nor at the Rittmeister; he stepped up to the sentry.

"Two civilians, Herr Lieutenant!" the man reported.

The Lieutenant nodded, and, as if only just noticing the pair now, he directed his sharp glance at them. What a pity Fritz wasn't wearing a steel helmet also! She would so much have liked to see him wearing one!

But the Lieutenant, gazing thoughtfully from under a forage cap, seemed not to know Violet. He seemed also to know nothing of the Rittmeister. "Who are you?" he asked coldly.

The Rittmeister sprang to life, introduced himself, announced with military brevity that he was the son-in-law of the owner taking a walk through this, his forest—in short, highly pleased, military maneuvers—undoubtedly Reichswehr. . . .

"Thanks," said the Lieutenant curtly. "Will you please go back the way you came without delay? And will you please preserve the strictest silence about this encounter? The State's interests demand it!" He looked at the Rittmeister. "I should be obliged if you would impress this on the young lady as well."

Vi gazed at her Fritz reproachfully, imploringly. How could she betray him, she who had successfully resisted all the blackmailing attempts of her mother! No, it was not nice of him. He was right to make no sign of recognition in front of her father, although even this pretense would not have been affected by a wink. But it was not nice of him to think that she might blab, she who was so faithful to him.

Even the Rittmeister was not pleasantly moved by so much positive strictness. This young snipe of a lieutenant was wrong to treat him as a complete civilian. He should have sensed the old officer, the comrade, even in mufti. Did the young puppy think he could throw sand in the eyes of an experienced officer? He spoke of the State's interests. The Rittmeister, however, recognized from the patched, utterly disreputable uniforms, from the lack of any insignia, that this was not the Reichswehr, but at most what was called the "Black Reichswehr"—which hardly represented the interests of the present Government, of the present State.

His irritation at being treated in such an off-hand way, at being thought so stupid, was, however, mingled with curiosity. He wanted to find out what was going on in the district behind his back. He had already spoken in Berlin to Studmann about this disagreeable uncertainty, this foreboding ignorance— here he was at the source, here he could at last find out what was afoot, and adapt his movements accordingly.

When, therefore, the Lieutenant with renewed sternness said: "If you don't mind!" significantly pointing to the forest path, the Rittmeister said quickly: "As I told you, I'm the owner of Neulohe—or rather the lessee. I have heard something—of certain preparations. I am—ahem!—not without influence. If I could have a short talk . . ."

"To what purpose?" the Lieutenant asked curtly.

"Well," answered the Rittmeister eagerly, "I would like to know how the land lies, get a clear view of things, understand? A man has to make up his own mind. . . . Anyway, there are fifty men working on my farm, mostly ex-soldiers. . . . If necessary I could give very valuable assistance."

"Thanks." The Lieutenant brutally cut his stammering short. "In any case one doesn't discuss these things before young ladies! Sentry, see that the lady and gentleman leave the place at once. Good day." With that he dived into the bushes. . . .

"Fritz!" Vi had almost called, wanting to throw herself on his breast. Oh, she understood his coldness. It was as she had already feared, when he no longer came and there was no news of him: he had not forgiven her the vexation caused by her foolish love letter, he feared she might imperil his cause. For him she was a stupid blabbing little girl; he had given her up! Perhaps his heart ached too, but he gave no sign of it; he was as hard as steel. She had always known he was a hero. But she would prove that she was worthy of him; never would a soul learn anything from her, and one day . . .

"If you don't mind!" ordered the sentry almost menacingly.

"Well, come along, Violet," urged the Rittmeister, starting from his stupe-faction and taking his daughter's arm. "Why, child, you're looking quite pale, and just before you were as red as fire. You must have had a terrible fright."

"He was a bit rude, wasn't he, Papa?"

"He's an officer on duty, Vi! How would they get on if they had to give infor-mation to everyone? I'm convinced he will report to his superiors. They will make inquiries about me, and one of the gentlemen will then pay me a visit. . . . That's how it is in the Army, everything has to go according to regulation."

"But he was really nasty to you!"

"Well, a young lieutenant! Probably gets a bit too big for his boots some-times. He's only rude because he still feels uncertain."

"Was he really a lieutenant? He looked—so shabby."

"The sentry addressed him as that. They're not regular troops."

"What did you think of him?"

"Yes, Vi, I can understand you, you're angry with him because he was a little rude, not courteous to a lady. But as a matter of fact, I thought he made quite a smart impression. Probably a capable young officer."

"Really, Papa? Did you also see what beautiful well-kept hands he had?"

"No, Vi, I really didn't notice them. But I wouldn't have let him run around so unshaven; as I said, they're not regular troops."

"But, Papa . . ." Vi would have liked to go on playing this tender game of hide-and-seek with her father, so soothing to her heavy heart. Forester Knie-busch intervened, however. He stepped out from between two junipers and greeted them.

"Kniebusch!" cried the Rittmeister. "What are you doing here? I thought you never came to this part of the forest."

"One has to look at every place sometimes, Herr Rittmeister," said the forester significantly. "One thinks nothing is happening, but something always is."

"Why, were you also back there?"

"In the Black Dale? Yes, Herr Rittmeister," announced the forester, who was burning to reveal what he knew.

"Oh," said the Rittmeister indifferently. "See anything special?"

"Yes." The forester knew that a piece of news imparted at once is worth nothing. "I saw you, sir, and your daughter."

"In the Black Dale?"

"You didn't get as far as that, sir."

"Oh," said Herr von Prackwitz, displeased that another should have witnessed that annoying scene, "I suppose you saw how we were stopped?"

"Yes, Herr Rittmeister, I did."

"Did you also hear what we said?"

"No, Herr Rittmeister, I was too far away." There was a short anxious pause. "I was between the sentry and the other men."

"So there were others there?" asked the Rittmeister with as much indifference as possible. "How many?"

"Thirty, Herr Rittmeister."

"Is that so? I thought there were more. Perhaps you didn't see them all."

"But I was there from the beginning; I heard the car. I have to know what is going on in my forest, Herr Rittmeister. I hid myself from the beginning. Thirty men, including Lieutenant Fritz."

"The lieutenant's name is Fritz?" cried the Rittmeister in surprise.

"Yes," said the forester, turning scarlet at the young Fräulein's glance. "At least, that's what the men call him," he stammered in confusion. "That's what I heard."

"His men called him Fritz, Kniebusch?" asked the Rittmeister incredulously.

"No, no," the forester hastened to say. "The men said Herr Lieutenant, but there was another one there—perhaps he was a lieutenant, too—who said Fritz."

"I see," said the Rittmeister, satisfied. "It would have been preposterous if the men had called their officer Fritz. That sort of thing doesn't exist even among irregular troops."

"No." The forester corrected himself. "It was probably the other lieutenant, a very fat man."

"They had a car, too?"

"Yes, Herr Rittmeister." The forester was glad to get away from the dangerous topic—even at the cost of his secret. "A truck, loaded right up."

"Did you see it? What was it carrying?"

The forester looked around; but when he saw only high and scattered trees, where no eavesdropper could be hiding, he said very quietly: "Weapons, Herr Rittmeister! Guns, ammunition boxes, hand grenades. Two light machine guns, three heavy ones. . . . They're burying it all."

The Rittmeister knew everything he wanted to know. He drew himself up more stiffly. "Listen, forester," he said solemnly. "I hope you are aware that it will cost you your life if you talk about what you know. It is to the interest of the State that complete silence should be preserved as to what is happening here.

If the Entente Commission hears of it, you will be better off if you have seen nothing! You are much too inquisitive, Kniebusch. As soon as you saw they were soldiers, you should have known the thing was in order—you shouldn't have hidden in the bushes. Understand?"

"Yes, Herr Rittmeister," said the forester plaintively.

"You had better forget everything, Kniebusch. If you ever think of it, you must say to yourself: 'It was just a dream—it's not true.' Understand?"

"Yes, Herr Rittmeister."

"And one more thing, Kniebusch. One doesn't discuss such affairs of State before women—even if it is your own daughter! Remember that in future!"

"Yes, Herr Rittmeister."

Herr von Prackwitz had avenged himself. In accordance with an old precept he had passed on the kick received, and could now walk on contentedly at his daughter's side.

"How is your prisoner Bäumer getting on?" he asked affably.

"Oh, Herr Rittmeister, the scoundrel!" A deep sigh rent the forester's breast. Apparently Bäumer had at last recovered consciousness, and they were treating him like a prince. They had taken him to the clinic in Frankfurt, and in a few days the forester was to confront him at his bedside. . . ." And I know what will happen then, Herr Rittmeister. I shan't be allowed to speak about all the crimes he's committed, but he'll lie that I half killed him, although I can point out the stone in the forest on which he fell. But they won't listen to me. The gendarme officer says they are getting out a summons against me for bodily assault or abuse of official powers. And in the end I'll go to prison, although I'm seventy, and the poacher Bäumer—"

"Yes, yes, Kniebusch," said the Rittmeister, very pleased that others also had their troubles, "that is just how the world is today, but you don't understand it. We were victorious throughout the whole war and now we are the defeated. And you have been honest your whole life and are now going to prison. It's all quite normal—take me, for instance. My father-in-law . . ." And for the remainder of the journey, the Rittmeister spoke consoling words to the old forester.

X

It was dark when Herr von Prackwitz arrived home with his daughter, but in spite of that his wife had not yet returned from the Manor. Vi went up to her room, while the Rittmeister paced angrily up and down. He had returned from the forest in the best of moods. He had caught a glimpse of secret military operations which pointed to the coming overthrow of the present hated Government, and even if he was going to exercise discretion in all circumstances, he could still give Eva an inkling of his new knowledge, by delicate hints.

But no Eva was there. Instead, the gun he had fired stood in his study by the window, reminding him of the silly, irritating incident. His wife had been in the Manor for five or six hours on account of an affair in which he had been clearly in the right, and his efficient friend Studmann was bound to be with her, too. It was ridiculous, it was childish, it was intolerable. The Rittmeister rang for his manservant and inquired whether his wife had left any instructions regarding supper. In a reproachful, annoyed tone he said he was hungry. Madam had left no instructions, reported Räder. Should he lay supper for the Rittmeister and the young Fräulein?

The Rittmeister decided to become a martyr and said no, he would wait. But, as the servant was going out of the door, he blurted out the question he had wanted to suppress—had the geese been delivered at the Manor?

"No, Herr Studmann would not allow me to." The servant went.

Herr von Prackwitz found his life gray. He had been in the forest, seen interesting things, become cheerful. But hardly had he returned home when a gray pall fell over everything again. There was no escape. It was like a powerful, merciless bog which sucked him down deeper every day. He rested his head in his hands. He longed for another world in which not everything, even wife and friend, made difficulties for him. He would gladly have left Neulohe. Like all weak people, he accused an imaginary Fate: Why must all this happen to me? I don't hurt anyone. I'm a little quick-tempered, but I don't mean it badly, I always recover at once. I don't make any really great demands of life; I am quite modest. Others have big cars, go to Berlin every week, have affairs with women! I live decently and am always in difficulties. . . .

He groaned. He was very sorry for himself. He was also very hungry. But no one bothered. No one cared what happened to him. He might be dying; no one would pay any attention, not even his wife. Supposing, in his utter desperation, he put a bullet through his head—a weaker man than he would be quite capable of doing so in this situation. Then she would come home and find him lying there. She would pull a pretty face; then, when it was too late, she would be sorry. She would realize too late what he meant to her.

The picture of his lonely death, the thought of his despairing widow, affected the Rittmeister so much that he got up, put on the light and poured himself out a vodka. Then he lit a cigarette and extinguished the light again. Huddled in a chair, his long legs stretched in front of him, he tried once again to imagine his death. But to his regret he had to admit that the picture did not have such a strong effect the second time.

Räder, this wily diplomat of the servants' quarters, whose conduct was guided by no understandable motive, yet who had a very definite object which he pursued by thousands of stratagems and artifices—this man ascended quietly to the young Fräulein's room, after firing the arrow designed for Herr von Studmann into the heart of his employer. She sat at the table, writing furiously.

"Well, what did Papa want?" she asked.

"The Rittmeister did not know what was happening about supper."

"And what is happening?"

"The Rittmeister will wait."

"If Mamma should still be at the Manor, I could take the letter myself," she said hesitatingly.

"As the young Fräulein wishes," said Räder coldly.

Vi folded the letter and surveyed him. That morning she had planned to hand him over to young Pagel for a good thrashing, but one couldn't free oneself so easily from a fellow conspirator and confidant—she kept finding that she needed him. She was convinced that the Lieutenant would come to the village this evening, after burying the weapons. He hadn't shown his face in the village for a fortnight. He'd never been away so long. Unlike the others, he hadn't been wearing a steel helmet. Proof that he still intended to go somewhere. He would look into the tree for her message, but it would be still safer to hand him the letter personally. But she could not get away, Räder was the best messenger . . . and at present he was not at all impudent. . . .

Poor little misguided Vi! She had forgotten she had sworn to her Fritz never again to write a letter. She had forgotten she had sworn to Pagel that this affair was over. She had forgotten she had sworn to herself never again to get mixed up with Räder, who was becoming more and more uncanny. She had forgotten that she would endanger her father and her Fritz if she mentioned the buried weapons in a letter of this sort. Her heart made her forget everything, her heart prevailed over her common sense and understanding. All she thought was that she loved him, that she must justify herself to him, that she wanted to see him again at all costs, that he ought not to put her aside so coldly, that she could not wait any longer, that she needed him.

She handed the letter to the servant. "See that he gets it safely, Hubert."

Räder's leaden eyelids, almost violet at the corners, were lowered as he observed the young girl. He took the letter. "'I can't promise that I will find the Lieutenant."

"Oh, you will find him, Hubert!"

"I can't run around the whole night, Fräulein. Perhaps he won't come. When shall I put it in the tree?"

"If you haven't found him by twelve or one o'clock."

"But I can't run around as long as that, Fräulein. I have to get some sleep. I shall put it in the tree at ten."

"No, Hubert, that's much too early. It's nine now already and we haven't yet had supper. You won't get out of the house before ten."

"The doctors say, Fräulein, that the sleep before midnight is the healthiest sleep."

"Hubert, don't be so silly. You just want to annoy me again."

"I don't want to annoy the young Fräulein. . . . It's true about the sleep. And I'd like to know, anyway, what I'm to get for this. If your parents find out I shall be dismissed, and then I won't get a testimonial or reference."

"How should they find out, Hubert? And what can I give you? I never get any money."

"It needn't be money, Fräulein."

Hubert spoke in a low voice, and involuntarily Violet did the same. Between each quiet sentence the summer evening could be heard gliding into night with a cry from the village, with the clattering of a pail, with the buzzing amorous dance of the midges over the garden bushes.

"What do you want, then, Hubert? I really don't know . . ." She avoided looking into his face. She glanced round the room as if looking for something that she could give him. . . . He, however, watched her more and more intently. His dead eyes came to life, a red spot appeared on his cheekbones. . . . "Since I am risking my reputation and my job for the young Fräulein, there's something I should like to ask of her."

She cast a swift glance at him and instantly looked away. Something of the fear of him she had once felt again arose in her. She strove against it, she tried to laugh, she said provokingly: "I suppose it isn't a kiss you want from me, Hubert?"

He looked at her unmoved. Her laugh had already died away, it sounded so ugly and false. I don't feel like laughing, she thought.

"No, not a kiss," he said almost contemptuously. "I don't believe in cuddling."

"What then, Hubert? Go on, tell me." She was burning with impatience. He had achieved what he wanted: she preferred the most fantastic request to this painful uncertainty.

"It is nothing unfitting that I ask of the young Fräulein," he said in his cold, didactic tone. "Nor is it anything indecent. . . . I should just like to be allowed to place my left hand for a while on the young Fräulein's heart."

She said nothing. She moved her lips, she wanted to say something.

He made no movement to approach closer. He stood at the door in an attitude appropriate to a servant; he was wearing a kind of livery-jacket with gray armorial buttons; on his glistening oily head every hair was in its proper place.

"Now I have told the young Fräulein," he said in his lifeless tone, "may I say that I intend nothing unchaste? It isn't that I want to touch her breast. . . ."

She was still struck dumb. They were separated almost by the width of the room.

Hubert Räder made something like a very slight bow. She hadn't moved and was quite still. He walked slowly across the room toward her; rigid, she saw him coming closer; no differently does the horrified victim await the murderer's death blow.

He placed the letter on the table, turned round and walked toward the door.

She waited, waited an eternity. He had already grasped the doorknob when she moved. She cleared her throat—and Hubert Räder looked round at her. . . . She wanted to say something, but a spell lay over her. With a vague, unsteady movement she pointed at the letter—no longer thinking at all of letter or recipient. . . .

The man raised his hand to the switch near the door, and the room was in darkness.

It was so dark she could have screamed. She stood behind the table, she saw nothing of him; only the two windows on the left stood out grayly. She heard nothing of him, he always walked so quietly. If only he would come!

Not a sound, not a breath.

If only she could scream, but she couldn't even breathe!

And then she felt his hand on her breast. No butterfly could have settled more gently on a blossom, yet with a shudder that passed through her whole body she shrank back. . . . The hand followed her shrinking body, laid itself in coolness over her breast. . . . She could shrink back no farther. . . . Coolness penetrated her thin summer dress, her skin, penetrated to her heart. . . .

Her fear was gone, she no longer felt the hand, only an ever more penetrating coolness. . . .

And the coolness was peace.

She wanted to think of something, she wanted to say to herself: It is only Hubert, a disgusting ridiculous fellow. . . . But nothing came of it. The pictures in the book on marriage drifted through her head; for a moment she saw its pages as if in bright lamplight.

Then she heard a melody from downstairs and knew it was her father. Bored with waiting, he had turned on the phonograph.

But the melody seemed to grow fainter and fainter, as if she were losing her strength in the ever-pervasive coolness. Her senses were becoming dulled, she only felt the hand . . . And now she felt the other . . . Its fingers fumbled lightly on her neck, they pushed her hair back.

Then the hand glided right round her throat; the thumb rested with a light pressure on her larynx, while the pressure on her heart increased . . .

She made a quick movement with her head, to free her neck from the hand—in vain, the thumb pressed on it more firmly . . .

But it was only the servant Hubert—he couldn't want to choke her . . . She breathed with difficulty. The blood buzzed in her ears. Her head grew dizzy . . .

"Hubert!" she wanted to scream.

Then she was free. Struggling for breath, she stared into the darkness, which became light. At the switch stood the servant Räder, irreproachable, not a hair on his head out of place.

Downstairs could be heard the phonograph.

"Thank you very much, Fräulein," said Räder, as unemotionally as if she had given him a tip. "The letter will be seen to." It was in his hand again; he must have taken it from the table in the dark.

In the drive outside sounded her mother's voice, then that of Herr von Studmann.

"Supper will be ready at once, Fräulein," said Räder, gliding out of the room.

She looked around. It's her room, unaltered. It was also the old, unchanged, funny servant, Räder—and she hadn't changed either. A little painfully, as if her limbs had not yet regained their full life, she went to the mirror and looked at her throat. But nothing could be seen of the fiery red marks she had imagined. Not even the slightest reddening of the skin. He had only gripped her very gently, if indeed he had gripped her at all. Perhaps she had only imagined most of it. He was merely a crazy, disgusting fellow; when a little time had passed, so that he wouldn't think it came from her, she must persuade Papa and Mamma to get another servant. . . .

Suddenly—she had already washed her face—a feeling of absolute despair came over her, as if everything were lost, as if she had gambled with her life and had lost it. . . . She saw her Lieutenant Fritz, first passionate and then quite cold, almost nasty to her. . . . She heard Armgard whispering to her mother that Hubert was a fiend, and the thought darted through her head that perhaps Hubert had also laid his hand on the fat cook's breast, had encircled her throat—and that that was why she hated him.

Violet regarded herself in the mirror with an almost indifferent curiosity. She looked at her white flesh, she pushed down the neck of her dress. She felt so degraded that she thought the flesh must look sullied. (The same hands that had touched Armgard!) But it was white and healthy. . . .

"Supper, Vi!" cried her mother from downstairs.

She shook off the tormenting thoughts as a dog shakes off water from its coat. Perhaps all men were like that. All a little disgusting. She just mustn't think of them.

She ran down the stairs, humming the tune she had heard on the phonograph. *Up you go, my girl, raise your leg high!*

XI

It turned out that Frau Eva and Herr von Studmann had already had supper with the old Teschows. Deeply hurt, the Rittmeister sat at table with his daughter, while the two for whom he had so heroically waited talked quietly in the adjoining room. The door stood open; the Rittmeister, muttering and growling, let slip disjointed sentences about punctuality and consideration for others, and from time to time barked at his daughter, who pleaded she had no appetite. Räder, a napkin under his arm, was the only one who had his approval. With unerring instinct he guessed which dish was wanted; he refilled the beer glass to the second.

"My dear Studmann," shouted the Rittmeister, having at last distinctly sniffed tobacco smoke, "do me just one favor and don't smoke, at least while I'm eating!"

"Sorry, Achim, I am smoking!" called his wife.

"So much the worse," growled the Rittmeister.

At last he jumped up and went in to the others.

"Enjoy your supper?" asked his wife.

"Nice question when I've been waiting two hours for you for nothing!" Full of irritation, he poured himself out another vodka. "Listen, Eva," he said aggressively, "Studmann has to get up at four in the morning. You should have let him go to bed rather than drag him over here. Or are you perhaps going to start on those ridiculous geese again?"

"Violet!" cried Frau Eva. "Come along now, say good night. You can go to bed, it is almost ten. Hubert, lock the doors, you are at liberty now."

The three were alone. "Quite so, now we'll start on the ridiculous geese again. You should at least thank your friend von Studmann; without him we shouldn't need to discuss it, but just pack our bags and go. If it were not for him, it would have been all over with Neulohe." Frau von Prackwitz spoke more sharply than she had ever yet done to her husband. Six hours of battle with a tearful mother and a crafty father had exhausted her patience.

"That's fine!" cried the Rittmeister. "I'm to be thankful for being able to stay in Neulohe! What do I care for the place? I'd find a job anywhere better than the one I've got here. You don't know what's going on in the world. The Army needs officers again!"

"Let us talk calmly," pleaded Studmann, anxiously observing the approaching storm. "You are probably right, Prackwitz; an officer's job would suit you best. But with an army only a hundred thousand strong—"

"Ah! you already seem to think you're a better farmer than I am, eh?"

"If," said Frau von Prackwitz heatedly, "you care so little about Neulohe, then perhaps you'll agree to our suggestion that you should go away for a few weeks."

"Please, Prackwitz. Please, Frau von Prackwitz."

"I go away!" shouted the Rittmeister. "Never! I'm staying." And he sat down in haste, as if the two might even dispute his right to a chair. He glowered at them.

"It is unfortunately a fact," said Studmann quietly, "that your parents-in-law are both at the moment filled with a strong prejudice against you. Your father-in-law has only one desire: to annul the lease."

"Then let him annul it, damn him! He'll never find another fool like me to give him three thousand hundredweights of rye as rent. Fool!"

"Since it's impossible to keep a family today on a captain's pension . . ."

"Why impossible? Thousands do it!"

". . . and since the farm offers a certain basis of livelihood . . ."

"You were saying just the opposite this morning!"

"If the lessor is well disposed," interjected Frau Eva.

"Which your father never was in his life, my dear."

". . . your wife agreed to manage the farm alone for the next few weeks while you travel for a bit. Until your parents-in-law have calmed down sufficiently to be approached again, that is."

"She agreed, did she?" mocked the Rittmeister bitterly. "Without asking me. Not necessary, I suppose. You just dispose of me as you like. Pretty. Very pretty. May I perhaps also be allowed to know where I am to travel?"

"I thought of . . ." began Studmann and felt in his pocket.

"No, don't, Herr von Studmann," said Frau Eva, stopping him. "Since he doesn't want to go away, it's no use making any suggestions. My dear Achim," she said energetically, "if you don't want to realize that Herr von Studmann and I talked for six hours with my parents solely on your account, then it's useless to say another word. Who is always in difficulties with Papa? Who fired at the geese? You! And, after all, it is your future that is at stake. Violet and I can always stay in Neulohe. We annoy no one; we have no difficulties with my parents."

"That's enough! If I'm in your way, I can leave at once. Where to, Studmann?" The Rittmeister was mortally hurt.

"We-ell . . ." Studmann rubbed his nose and regarded his peevish friend. "I more or less thought . . . It was my idea . . ."

The Rittmeister gave him a dark look, but said nothing.

Studmann felt in his pocket and brought out a letter. "There's this queer old chap, Dr. Schröck, who amused you so much, Prackwitz."

The Rittmeister did not look like one who was amused.

"He has written to me a few times, about damages from that Baron—you remember, Prackwitz."

The Rittmeister gave no sign of remembering.

"Well, of course, I refused everything. You know my view of the matter."

Whether the Rittmeister knew it or not, he remained dark and silent.

Studmann continued more cheerfully, waving his letter. "And now there is this last letter from Dr. Schröck, which came the day before yesterday. . . . he seems to be a queer sort of chap, with strangely sudden sympathies and dislikes. You told me yourself how much he seemed to hate his patient—Baron von Bergen. Well, he seems to have taken a liking to me, which is very funny when you come to think that he's never seen me, and that all he knows is that I fell down the hotel stairs—drunk. Well, in this letter he makes me a proposal, nothing to do with Baron von Bergen . . ."

Studmann became doubtful. He looked at the letter, then at his unusually silent friend, then at Frau Eva, who nodded to him encouragingly. It was actually hardly a nod, more a closing of her eyelids to mean yes. Studmann glanced again at his friend, to see whether he had noticed this signal. But Prackwitz stood silent at the window.

"Of course, it's only an idea of mine, a suggestion . . . Dr. Schröck was thinking of appointing a business manager for his sanatorium. It is a rather large place, over two hundred patients, about seventy employees, huge park, a little farming, too . . . So, you understand, Prackwitz, there are all sorts of things to do there . . . And, as I said, Dr. Schröck thought of me."

Studmann gave his friend a friendly look, but his friend didn't return it. Instead he helped himself to another vodka and drank it down. Then he poured himself another, which he didn't drink down. Frau Eva fidgeted in her chair and cleared her throat, but she said nothing, including nothing against the vodkas. "Naturally, Dr. Schröck doesn't want to engage me without seeing what I'm like; even his sympathies don't go as far as that," continued Studmann. "He invites me to go as his guest first for a few weeks, and so that I shouldn't feel superfluous during that time, he complains movingly about an almost Australian plague of rabbits which despoil his park and fields. He suggests I might, with the help of his ferret keeper, deal with them. He seems to be quite a practical type, the old fellow. . . ."

Herr von Studmann again gave his friend a friendly look. The Rittmeister looked darkly back; instead of answering, he emptied his second vodka and poured himself a third. Frau von Prackwitz drummed lightly on the arm of her chair. The burden of talking continued to rest on Studmann, and it was gradually becoming oppressive.

"Well, you're such an enthusiastic hunter and such a fine shot, Prackwitz! And we thought—I thought—a little relaxation would do you a lot of good. Just think, the peacefulness, the good food in a sanatorium like that. And then out of doors the whole day—he says there are thousands of rabbits there." Studmann waved the letter cheerfully. "And since I have found an occupation here, and am not very well able to get away, because of your father-in-law . . . You see, he wants something like a firm business-like hand . . . I thought if you went along in my place . . . As I said, the peacefulness, no irritation—and I'm convinced you would recommend me warmly for the manager's job." Studmann tried to laugh, but did not quite succeed.

"Well, say something, Prackwitz," he called out with a somewhat artificial cheeriness. "Don't stand there so gloomy and pale. Your father-in-law will calm down . . ."

"Very well thought out," said the Rittmeister darkly. "Very cleverly contrived."

"But, Prackwitz!" Studmann was taken aback. "What's the matter with you?"

"I felt it coming," murmured Frau Eva, leaning back and placing her hands over her ears.

And the Rittmeister did indeed burst out with double fury after his long silence. "But nothing will come of it!" he shouted, raising in menace a trembling finger. His face was deathly white. "You want to get me certified as insane! You want to lock me up in a lunatic asylum! Very cunning. Marvelous."

"Prackwitz! I implore you! How can you think such a thing? Here, read the letter from Dr. Schröck."

The Rittmeister pushed letter and friend aside. "Very well thought out. No, thank you! I can see through you. It's a put-up job, a conspiracy with my father-in-law. I'm to be got out of the way. I'm to be divorced! My substitute's on the spot, eh, Eva? But I understand everything now! The talk about the lease this morning—was it actually the real lease? Was that faked, too, like the letter, just to provoke me? And the geese!—probably lured here by you yourselves. The gun!—how did the gun come to be loaded? I put it away unloaded. Everything prepared, and then, when I fall into your trap, when I really do shoot, against my will—I swear it, against my will!—then I'm to be declared insane! Pushed off into a madhouse! Put under guard—in a padded cell . . ."

He seemed overcome by grief. Rage seized him anew, however. "But I refuse! I'll not budge an inch from Neulohe! I'll stay. You can do what you like! But perhaps you've already got the keepers there—the strait-jacket . . ." He tried to a recall a name. It came to him in a flash of inspiration. "Where is Herr Türke? Where is the attendant Türke?"

He rushed to the door. In front of him was the little hallway, quiet and still.

"They might be hiding," he murmured to himself. "Come out, Herr Türke," he shouted into the dark house. "Come out. You know very well I'm here."

"Enough of this!" cried Frau Eva angrily. "There's no need to let all the servants know you are drunk. You're just drunk! He can never stand alcohol when he's excited; he simply goes into a frenzy," she whispered to Studmann.

"Mad!" the Rittmeister wailed. He stood at the window, leaning his head against the glass. "Betrayed by my own wife and friend! Put under guard! Locked up!"

"You had better go now," she whispered to Studmann, who was possessed with the thought of urging his friend to be sensible, of explaining everything. "The only place for him now is bed. Tomorrow he'll be sorry. He was like this once before. You know, that business with Herr von Truchsess that made my father so angry."

"I'm not going!" shouted the Rittmeister in a new fit of rage, beating on the glass. It broke. "O-ow!" he cried, and held out his bleeding hand to his wife. "I've cut myself."

She could almost have laughed at the doleful change on his face. "Yes, come upstairs, Achim; I'll bandage it. You must go to bed instantly. You need some sleep."

"I'm bleeding," he muttered, miserably supporting himself on her arm. This man who had been thrice wounded in the war turned pale at a cut scarcely half an inch long.

At this spectacle Studmann considered it advisable to go. It was not the woman who was in need of protection. In a last access of unbending determination the Rittmeister bellowed after him: "I'll never go!"

It was not surprising, it was in fact quite natural, that Rittmeister von Prackwitz should go after all—at noon the next day, in very high spirits even, and of course to Dr. Schröck, with three gun-cases and on his right hand a strip of plaster. Almost with enthusiasm he had agreed to it next morning. He had no wish to see a friend before whom he had let himself go so abominably. And he was delighted at the prospect of a change, a journey, some shooting instead of money worries; while by no means least was the thought of the elegant sanatorium, the convalescent home of aristocracy—a Baron instead of his sweating father-in-law. . . .

"Just see that I'm regularly sent sufficient money," he said anxiously to his wife. "I don't want to look a fool." Frau Eva promised. "I think I'll look up my tailor in Berlin," he went on pensively. "I really haven't got a decent hunting suit. . . . You've no objection, have you, Eva?"

Frau Eva had no objection.

"You've got to manage for yourselves here now. I'm only going away at your wish, don't forget that. So no complaining if anything goes wrong. I don't care two hoots about going away. I can shoot bunny-rabbits here, too."

"Aren't you going to say good-by to von Studmann, Achim?"

"Yes, of course, if you think I ought to. But I'll pack first. And the guns have to be greased. Anyway, give him my best regards if I don't see him. He'll probably always be asking your father for advice now; he can't tell winter from summer barley! You'll get into a mess, you see!" The Rittmeister smiled cheerfully. "Still, if it gets too bad you can send for me. I'd come at once, of course. I'm not the one to bear a grudge."

XII

Listening at the door, Violet had only heard the beginning of the quarrel. Convinced that it would go on for some time and keep her mother busy, she slipped out of the house, at the back. For a moment she stood irresolute. Ought she really to chance it? If it was found out that she had left the house at night instead of going to bed, the stubbornest lying wouldn't save her from being packed off to a strict boarding school, as her mother had threatened. Besides, if Hubert Räder found the Lieutenant and gave him her letter, Fritz would be under her window this very night. And there was the trellis on the wall! If she went away, she might miss him. . . .

Everything spoke in favor of staying and waiting. But there was the warm starry August night! The air seemed like a living thing, enveloping her body. It was like a link to him, who was also outside on this soft night, perhaps quite near her. She felt her blood singing in her ears that sweet alluring song which the body voices when it is ready. Perhaps she ought to go after all. . . . And she felt downcast at the thought that she might wait the whole night for him in vain. . . .

A little patch of light in the house, almost on the ground, attracted her attention. Uncertain what it was, she approached it, glad of any diversion which put off her decision. She knelt down and peered. It was Räder's room in the basement, empty. He must have gone out to deliver her letter, then, and she could go up to her room with an easy mind: if the Lieutenant was in Neulohe tonight, he would come to her window. The otherwise orderly Räder had forgotten in his hurry to switch off the light.

Violet was just about to get up when the door opened. It was strange and a little uncanny: she, with the whole night around her, was looking unobserved at a little bright stage. Queer and at the same time a little uncanny was also the scene which now presented itself: the person closing the door was Hubert Räder, no longer the punctilious young man in gray livery, but a somewhat ridiculous thing in a disproportionately large nightshirt with gaily trimmed border. Above this angels' raiment, however, was the sallow fishy head with its expressionless eyes—and Violet was no longer able to think this head stupid and silly. Something like horror filled her. . . .

Räder went to a cupboard in the corner. In his hand he carried a glass containing a tooth-brush. He unlocked the cupboard and placed the glass inside it. . . . That is how men are! After experiencing that evening a sensation which was perhaps unusual, something that might perhaps be termed the rehearsal of a murder, Hubert Räder put on a nightshirt and brushed his teeth as he did every other evening. . . . He was not always a murderer; normally he was a very ordinary citizen; and it was this which made him so dangerous. One recognizes a tiger by its stripes, but a murderer brushes his teeth like everyone else; he is unrecognizable.

And now Violet was to see something stranger still. . . .

But at the moment she was not thinking of Räder. I listened at the door for five minutes at the most, she calculated. Then I came out and stood say, for three minutes, wondering whether to chance it. Hubert still had to clear the table—he did that while I was saying good night—then put away the plates and things. But he couldn't possibly have left the house! Undress, wash, brush his teeth! And my letter?

"My letter!" she wanted to scream out; she wanted to bang on the window and ask for it back. What restrained her was not the fear of arousing the house, nor the dislike of a silly dispute with the crazy lying fellow. Oh, hang the letter! she thought suddenly, very calm. I don't need it, I'll find Fritz without it. . . . He's probably kept it, not in order to take it to my parents, but to demand a reward again! And she felt his hand on her heart, his cold, inhuman hand. If I tell Fritz, he'll kill him; Fritz wanted to kill little Meier for much less. . . . But she felt that she would not tell Fritz. This must always be kept a secret from him, whatever happened. Actually she should be horrified at having a secret in common with Räder, but she was not. There was a dismal seduction about this evil servant's hand. She did not understand it, but she felt it. . . .

While all this was going through her head—and such thoughts and fears don't take a second—Hubert Räder had knelt down at the foot of his bed. There he crouched in his long nightshirt, with clasped hands, saying his prayers like a child. But there was nothing childish about that evil head. When she saw him, scarcely three yards away, kneel down on the little stage visible only to herself, and pray, he who just before had put his hand round her throat—when she reflected that perhaps he was thanking God for being allowed to do that to her—then Violet could contain herself no longer but jumped up and ran into the night, not giving a thought to the people who ought not to see her, nor to Fritz, whom she had to see. . . .

She ran through the garden, on and on, and up a grass ridge between the fields. Her breast heaved. She felt as if she must run away from it all, from herself and everybody, and she threw herself down and gazed at the sky, whose impalpably deep background made the stars twinkle all the more brightly. At last she dozed off. . . .

But she could only have slept a very short time, the stars hadn't shifted. It was as if she had dreamed of something very light and happy, but knew nothing more about it. A feeling of approaching danger had awakened her. Yet around her was nothing but silence and rural night. The village, too, had gone to bed, there was not a sound. . . .

"No, there is no danger," she said, calming her throbbing heart. But suddenly she realized that she was alone in the fields and too far away for a cry to awake anyone in the village. . . . And she, who had been out in the fields and forest hundreds of times at night without even a thought of fear, was seized with a cowardly trembling that he might come in his white shirt, along the ridge, and want to lay his hand on her heart again. I would not be able to resist, she thought.

And she started to run again. Away from the Villa, whence he might follow her, she ran toward the dark mass of trees in the park. She clambered over the fence, her dress tearing on a nail, and tumbled into the grass on the other side, but jumped to her feet immediately and ran towards the swans' pond, to the hollow tree. . . . She thrust her hand into the hollow, but there was no letter there; so he had already taken it and was on his way to her. . . .

Then she started running again, but already while she ran she realized that he'd never received the letter, that it was still with Räder, and she was gripped by a furious anger against that crook. . . . But the anger passed and, while she ran, she began to wonder why she was still running. There was surely no point anymore. Of course he's no longer in the village. After such a burying of weapons you're more likely to go home and report back than look for romantic adventures in the surrounding villages. However, although she knew she no longer needed to run, she continued to do so, as if something were chasing her, and she only stopped in her tracks when she saw a bright yellow rectangle shining through the trees. She changed her step to a cautious creeping and approached the lighted window as quietly as a cat. It stood wide open, but the curtains were drawn. She crossed the path, stepped onto the narrow grass border under the window and pushed the curtains apart. She'd been so confused that night that she didn't for a moment think she was doing anything improper, just unusual. After casting an initial look into the room, she pushed her whole head through the curtains, and remained looking, standing, her body outside in the night, but her head in the brightly lit room.

At the table sat young Wolfgang Pagel, writing a letter. It had been a rather sad and gloomy day for him—in the morning the row with the Rittmeister, who'd thrown him out. Then the chaos with the prisoners, and the bricked-up door with the white cross, which had to be painted over. Then there was the crazy farm servant Räder with his cartload of dead geese, and Studmann with his mysterious consultations in the manor—it was all frantic and confused, as little like rural life as could be. As he eventually, angrily, swallowed down his lonely evening meal— the servant Elias had replaced Studmann—he confronted the evening, unable to sleep, unwilling to do any further work. He had thought of going to the inn or of wandering into the village and keeping an eye open for Sophie Kowalewski. All things considered, she was quite a nice girl and probably, since she had experience of Berlin, without too many airs and graces. Violet von Prackwitz, with her morning kisses, would have been more dangerous. But then he remembered that he couldn't leave the house. He had accepted a commission, he was expecting a visitor whom he had to thrash: the stupid servant with the fishlike head, Hubert Räder. For some time, Wolfgang Pagel paced up and down his two rooms in the dusk—now in his office, now in his living room. And a bad mood certainly doesn't improve when one paces up and down for a quarter of an hour, thinking how one is to threaten, intimidate and thrash a scoundrel. That sort of thing is best done off-hand, without any undue deliberation.

It was rather strange: whenever he occupied himself with any girl, be her name Violet, Amanda or Sophie, his thoughts always drifted in the end to Peter. Well, Peter was finally gone and forgotten, peace on her ashes; a good, pleasant girl but, as already said, peace on her ashes! Well, he could at least write to his mother, tell her something of his new life and announce for her greater comfort the liquidation of the affair with Petra Ledig. That would be much better, anyway, than merely waiting idly for a wretched fellow. Now determined, Pagel switched on the light in his living room, drew the curtains, and took his writing things from his office. He only had to remove his jacket and he was sitting comfortably and airily in casual shirt and trousers, beginning to write.

He wrote of his life in Neulohe, a little insolently, a little coarsely, as one writes when one is twenty-three years old and will not admit that anything amuses him. In five sentences he drew a picture of his employer, then of the old father-in-law who oozed craft and cunning from every buttonhole. Of past things he wrote nothing. Nothing of the picture he had taken, nothing of the disappearance of a considerable sum of money, nothing of a marriage that had vanished into air. Neither shame nor reticence prevented him from writing of these unpleasant things. But, so long as a man is young, he still believes that the past is really past, is completely finished with. He believes he can begin a new life every day and assumes fellow human beings think the same, including his mother. He does not yet know of that chain which he drags behind him his whole life long; every day, every experience, adding its new link. He doesn't yet hear its clanking; he has not yet understood the hopeless significance of the precept: because you do this thing, you must be that.

No, at twenty-three years what is done is done, what is past is past—Wolfgang's pen flew over the paper. Now it was busy on a picture of Studmann, the nursemaid and mentor *par excellence*. His mood became stimulated, his father's spirit entered into him. He caricatured Studmann in the margin, he drew him as a rabbit gloomily sitting outside its burrow. The rabbit looked at the world wisely, and at the same time foolishly. But above all, gloomily.

Pagel, whistling with satisfaction, raised his glance and encountered the eye of young Violet von Prackwitz. "Hallo!" he said without any undue surprise. "Isn't young Räder coming?"

She shook her head. At the same time she slid a shoulder between the curtains, and her breast laid itself gently on the window sill. This attitude opened wide the neck of her dress and gave a glimpse of her tender skin, so seductively milk-white against her throat's dark brown.

"No," she said, after a moment of hesitation, as if speaking reluctantly or in her sleep. "Räder still has something to do for Papa. I couldn't send him."

"And you, my girl?" asked Pagel with forced easiness. "Still about at this hour? Not confined to your room anymore?"

Again she delayed her answer. "I was over at my grandparents'," she explained at last. "I wanted to let you know."

"Thanks!" said Pagel, a little too late.

It is so quiet, warm and quiet. Her breast on the windowsill. Her mouth breathing, breathing secrets, promising fulfillment. It's been so long. . . .

All is growing, ripening, thriving. . . . "Stay awhile—!"

"Yes. . . ." said Pagel, after a while, lost and dreaming.

Then all was quiet again—a quiet, still darkness. Complicit night.

"Come over here," she whispered suddenly.

Though she whispered so softly, he started, like one who receives a blow. "Yes?" he asked, already getting up from his chair.

"Please, yes," she whispered again, and he slowly approached. Without his knowing it, his face had taken on a bitterly determined expression, as if he tasted fruit which could not be sweet. Her face, however, bore the same expression as when she had watched the servant at his prayers; she seemed to feel horror and despair, pleasure and desire.

"Closer!" she whispered, when he stopped a pace or two in front of her. "Still closer!"

It was the seduction of the hour, and it was the seduction of hungry flesh, and it was also the seduction of her desire, which was like a net, imperceptibly closing in on him.

"Well?" he asked softly, and his face was right next to hers.

"Wouldn't you . . ." she said haltingly, "wouldn't you like to kiss me again?" And she raised her head; with a resolute and yet childish movement she offered him her lips. Suddenly tears stood in her eyes. . . . It was not only depravity which made her seek the pleasure of another's embrace—it was also the fear of him who had placed his hand on her heart, and taken possession of her. . . .

"There!" she said faintly, and their lips met. Thus they remained for an interminable time. Her breast lay on his hand, which rested on the window sill; through her dress he felt its heaviness and ripeness, more beautiful than any fruit. . . . Were they crickets, chirping outside in the park?—a thin sweet melody, it might be in his blood, ever continuing without pause, as if the earth herself sang, this kind fertile mother earth which loves lovers. . . . His mouth remained endlessly on her lips.

Then he felt her growing uneasy. She wanted to say something. But he did not want to free her lips, did not want to interrupt the spell. . . . With a nimble movement she slipped her left shoulder out of her dress and with her right hand—her left was round his neck—freed her breast.

"There!" she said plaintively. "Put your hand on it—it is so cold." And before he knew what he was doing, his hand had closed round her breast.

"Oh!" she sighed and pressed her lips more firmly against his.

What was he thinking? Was he thinking of anything at all? A flame of desire rose and rose. He thought he saw images, flying images, of a ghostly play about old times, in the theater of his imagination. The room with Madame Po, when he woke up and met Peter's eyes. . . . The flame of desire continued to rise. Can't I come with you?—That's what she asked, or something like it, and she did go with him. And when they introduced themselves to each other in the splendour of a Berlin marble stairwell: Petra Ledig—unforgettable moments.

The crickets were still chirping away. Crickets? Crickets did not live in a park, but in houses—they were grasshoppers, locusts, that were singing outside, green, rather grotesque-looking creatures. . . .

There is the breast in your hand; it is only the seduction of the flesh, not love. Carefully, gently; loosen your mouth, we must not frighten the little girl—she is just depraved. But she has obtained nothing in exchange for her depravity, not even knowledge. She knows nothing of herself. She is like a sleep-walker: one must not wake her suddenly. Peter was different—oh, Peter was quite different. She knew everything—but she was as innocent as a child. What they told me at the police station can't possibly be true. Peter was not depraved. She knew, but she was always innocent. . . .

"What's the matter with you?" asked Vi, puzzled. "What are you thinking of?"

"Oh—" he said absently. "I just remembered something."

"Remembered?"

"Yes. Remembered. I belong to another woman." He saw the change in her face, the shock. "Just as you belong to another man," he added hastily.

"Yes?" she asked submissively. She was so easy to guide—a young horse whose mouth was still tender, obeying every tug of the reins. "And the other woman—is that also over?"

"I thought so. But it occurred to me just now that perhaps it wasn't."

"Just now?"

She stood between the curtains, just as he had left her in the middle of the kiss, her hair disarranged, her breast still uncovered, her underlip trembling: the abode of pleasure, by pleasure forsaken. . . . She looked a pitiful figure.

"It isn't really all over with you," he comforted her. "You only need to wait a little, you know. It's to his credit to have kept away for so long."

"Do you think so?" she asked more brightly. "Do you think he'll come again? Is it only my silly fifteen years?"

"Of course. Wait—I'll quickly get ready. I'll see you home. We can talk about it as we go along." He went to the mirror and combed his hair. "Do you want a comb, too?" he called. "Here!"

He put his jacket on, washed his hands. "Let's go!" he said, swinging himself through the window. "We can leave the light burning. I'll be back soon."

The night was mild and quiet, a perfect night for walking, and after their hands had twice brushed against each other he took hold of hers, and thus they continued their way, hand in hand, like two good friends.

"You know what, Vi?" said Pagel. "I want to tell you what I have just discovered. . . . As a matter of fact, it isn't fitting to talk about such a thing to a young girl, but who else would tell you? Your parents certainly won't."

"Oh, them!" said Vi contemptuously. "They think I still believe in the stork!"

"There, you see! Absolute stick-in-the-muds. What can they be thinking of? A young girl can't help getting ideas into her head with the popular songs nowadays. Well, listen—but how am I to tell you, my child? Damn difficult to speak about such things; one gets embarrassed, and angry at being embarrassed. . . ."

"Your discovery!" she reminded him.

"Oh, yes. Well, I've already told you I belong to another woman, but I assure you that a minute ago I didn't know it."

"Well!" cried Vi, stopping. "That's a nice thing to say to me."

"Nonsense, Vi; there's no need to get annoyed. It's no insult to you. You are young and pretty—and so on. Well, it's like this: I didn't know I belonged to the other woman. In the past, before I knew her, I just flirted around, and I thought it was always that way and always would be: one had a row, and then got another girl. Finished with one, on with the next! Girls are no different either," he said a little shamefacedly, to excuse his crude male standpoint. "Just remember the song: 'If I see a new man at the next street corner.'"

"It's quite true; if it isn't the one, then it's the other!" agreed Violet.

"There, you see! That's precisely the catch. It isn't true. When I started with Peter—I always called my girl-friend Peter—as a matter of fact, her name was Petra. . . ."

"Queer name!" said Vi disapprovingly.

"Well, Violet isn't exactly so charming either," said Pagel crossly, but recovered himself at once. "However, that's a matter of taste. I like the name Peter immensely. Anyway, after I'd been living with her for a year—"

"Did you really *live* with her?"

"Of course! What else? No one finds anything strange in that today. Well, I thought it was the same as with the previous girls; this one was nicer and that was why it was lasting a little longer. And when it did come to an end, just before I came here, I thought: All right! No use crying over spilt milk; I'll soon get another. You know," said Pagel pensively, "when you really come to think of it, that's a low-down way of looking at things. . . . But what is one to do? Everyone talks like that, everyone acts like that, and so you think it is true."

"It *is* true!" declared Vi defiantly.

"Not at all. It's a lot of tommy-rot! That's my discovery! I've been running around here in Neulohe for weeks now, and so far I've found it quite pleasant, but I haven't had a real kick out of it. . . . In the past, I only had to wake up to be thankful merely that I was here, completely without any particular reason. Now I think, oh another bloody day. Oh well, on with you shirt—the sooner it's used up. . . ."

"Just how I feel," said Vi. "Everything bores me, too."

"The same disease, my lady!" cried Pagel. "I'll give you the symptoms exactly. No more enthusiasm, no more fun, and you don't feel so fit, either."

"I'll tell you something," said Violet importantly. "I read it. You've simply got abstinence-phenomena—especially after having lived with her."

"Well, I'm blessed!" cried Wolfgang Pagel. "That's pretty good for your age, Fräulein!" He began to feel misgivings. Was it right for him to tell such a young girl, precisely this young girl, of his discovery? But if she were really what her remark led him to believe, she would not have said it! Really depraved persons try to conceal their depravity. "No," he said. "There are enough girls in the village, but I have discovered that there is not another girl at every corner. Or rather, it is *another*. But one is always looking for the same one; only she can make you happy. And you, too, are looking for the same one."

She thought for a while. "I don't know. I don't understand it. I'm so restless, it keeps urging me on. And just now when I looked in at your window I felt as if it didn't matter who it was, anyone could give me peace."

"I," said Pagel, "I have only just managed to understand it. If I see a girl, no matter how much she appeals to me, I have to compare her at once with Peter, and then I know she means nothing."

"Do you understand it?" asked Vi, scarcely paying any attention to him. "I can't ask anybody about such a thing. Not my parents, no one. I think of it all day, and at night I dream about it. Sometimes I think it will drive me mad. When my parents are out I creep into Papa's room and look in the encyclopedia. From that, and from reading Räder's book, it sounds as if it were all only the body. And often I feel it must be right, and I become sad. And at other times I say to myself: It can't be true."

"Of course it isn't only the body. That's just a silly idea people have got into their heads. If it was only the body, then everyone would suit everybody else, and yet you've only to look at other people to know that it can't be so."

"You are right," she said. "But—perhaps several people suit several other people? Perhaps a lot? Just not all. Of course not all."

"I now think, only one! I'm frightfully glad I've discovered that."

"Herr Pagel," she said softly.

"Yes?"

"I would very much have liked—before—to have gone into your room."

He said nothing.

"I know it sounds horribly bad of me to say so, but it's true," she said defiantly. "I have to lie to everybody, even to Fritz, so to you I want to be able to tell the truth for once."

"You'd have probably had a terrible recovery," he said cautiously. "And me too."

"Tell me," she began again. "Before, at your window—were you like that because I was only fifteen, and because a man would be a scoundrel to meddle with me?"

"No!" he said astounded. "I didn't think of that at all."

"You see! Then my Lieutenant isn't necessarily a scoundrel either."

She had stopped. They often stopped on this path through the village. It was after eleven o'clock, and everyone was asleep at this hour during harvest time. She'd let go of his hand and he knew she wanted to say something.

"Well?" he asked.

"I would ever so much like to go back with you again," she said haltingly, and yet with a desperate, imploring obstinacy.

"No, no." His voice was quiet.

She threw her arms round his neck, she pressed him to her, she laughed and wept in one breath, she smothered him with her kisses, she wanted to seduce him . . . But everything went cold within him. He didn't push her away, but held her loosely in his arms so that she didn't fall over. He no longer forgot that she was still half a child. His mouth remained cold, and his blood, too. There was no flame anymore. But out of the darkness emerged the picture of the other girl, the unprotected one, no favored daughter, no heiress. Not at all! There's something else, he thought suddenly, shattered and more shattered, upset now and gripped, it's possible to have been through dirt and to have experienced bad things without becoming either dirty or bad. She . . . she had loved me, and was pure—but I didn't know it! And everything she'd told him about illness and being on the game seemed not to matter. It wasn't true! While all this was passing fleetingly through his head, her kisses and caresses pressed ever more upon him.

And Violet—I wish she'd leave off! he thought in disgust. But her own caresses seemed to make her more and more foolish, more and more mad.

She moaned softly, she seized his hand and pressed it to her breast again. . . . I hope I won't have to get rough with her, he thought.

Then steps sounded, very near. . . . At once she let go of him, and glided to the nearest fence, where she stopped with her face turned away from the village street. . . . Pagel, too, half turned away.

And Herr von Studmann, the eternal nursemaid—this time without knowing it—walked past. He seemed to peer at them through the darkness; yes, he even raised his hat. "Good evening!"

Pagel mumbled something, and from the fence came a sound. Was it laughing? Was it weeping? The steps died away.

"That was Herr von Studmann, Fräulein Violet."

"Yes, I must go home quickly, my parents will be going to bed now. God, if Mamma looks into my room!" She ran along by his side. "And all for nothing! Everything goes wrong!" she burst out angrily.

"Didn't you visit your grandparents?" asked Pagel teasingly.

"Oh rubbish!" she exclaimed angrily. "All the worse for you if you haven't yet understood what I was looking for!"

Pagel didn't answer, and she also remained silent.

They reached the Villa. "Thank heavens! They're still downstairs!" But as she spoke, the Rittmeister's light went out. The gay little windows of the staircase, ascending obliquely, lit up. "Quick, up the trellis! Perhaps I can still do it," she cried.

They ran round the house.

"Bend down, I'll climb on your back," she said with a laugh. "That's the only thing you're good for!"

"Always glad to be of service," declared Pagel politely. Now she was standing on him, fumbling for a hold in the lattice work. You're no feather, he thought, noticing how cheerfully she made him feel her full weight. Then she clambered higher. He stepped into a bush, the wisteria rustled, and the bright shadow disappeared into the dark room. Pagel saw four more windows light up, and heard the Rittmeister complaining, cursing and moaning through the open window.

"Sounds pretty drunk," he said to himself, surprised.

He started for home. "I've still got to write to Mama about Petra," he thought. "She needs to make inquiries about what's happened to her. And if I have no news in a week, I'll go to Berlin. I'll find her all right . . . Vi is difficult. . . . Let's leave it. . . ."

The summer slowly turned to autumn, the yellow cornfields became empty, the plow made the light stubble brown. The country people said: "Yes, we've done it again!" spat on their hands and turned to the aftermath. Some had already started with their potatoes.

Yes, something had been achieved. A certain amount of work had been done. But when they opened the newspapers—seldom on work nights, more likely on Sundays—they read that the Cuno Government had been overthrown. The Stresemann Government was said to be more kindly disposed to the French—but the French became no friendlier. They read that there was now a strike in the Government printing department. For a while there would be no money, not even trash. They read that a war was brewing, at first only a paper war, between the Defense Minister and the President of Saxony. And they read about a battle between the Bavarian government and the central government. They read that England had given up her resistance to the occupation of the Ruhr; they read of separatist demonstrations in Aachen, Cologne, Wiesbaden, Trier; they read that the Reich had expended 3,500 billion marks in one week in subsidies for the Rhine and the Ruhr. Then they read that passive resistance there, the struggle against the unjust French occupation, had been given up at last. They read that exports had ceased, that the German economic system was destroyed; they also read of fights between separatists and police—the police, however, were bundled into prisons by the French.

At this time, during these few weeks of the harvest, the dollar had risen from 4,000,000 to 160,000,000 marks!

"What are we working for?" the people asked. "What are we living for? The world is coming to an end, everything is falling to pieces. Let us be gay and forget our shame, before we depart this world."

Thus they thought, spoke, and behaved.

communicative, how many an excellent piece of advice, born of experience, sprang from his lips. True, he was still a little lax and easy-going with the men, but there again it was amazing to see how young Pagel, sweating and lively, came sprinting up on his bicycle, cracked the most indecent jokes with the silliest of the women, but said firmly: "You've got to get as far as here by noon—and as far as there by evening."

If they protested that it was impossible—the young gentleman ought to make it half that; they were just women and not a strong fellow like him—then he mocked them. They were always boasting they were a match for any man, he would say, and according to them the fellow wasn't born who could make them tired. Well, let them prove it.

Amid their roars of laughter the young gentleman drove off, but by evening they had reached the point indicated. Or perhaps even a little bit farther, in which case he never neglected to acknowledge this with a word of praise or, better still, a coarse joke. He pleased them all, especially as none had cause to be jealous of another on his account. "He's a smart young fellow," they said. "He'll marry a lady some day—not a scarecrow like you!"—"You've got nothing to write home about. I can always run rings round you!" And now that he came so often with Fräulein Violet, it seemed as if they were the owner's son and daughter, for the women soon sensed that they were not lovers.

Yes, in her loneliness Vi had become Wolfgang Pagel's constant companion. Her mother had little time for her; she also was out in the fields a lot. Frau Eva had spent all her youth in Neulohe; in the past she had often gone about the farm with her father, the Geheimrat, had heard what the old man mumbled to himself, had seen what he regarded as important. Now she was amazed how much of it had stuck. With her husband, whatever she saw she should not have seen. He had always said: "You understand nothing about it. Please don't interfere with the way I run things." And had immediately become annoyed.

Studmann never became annoyed. He listened attentively to what she had to say; he even encouraged her suggestions. And though he did not always do what she suggested, he would explain his contrary opinion so fully and so well that she was forced to agree—if sometimes with a little yawn. Studmann was certainly a very reliable and efficient man, but he was a little too pedantic. No one could imagine what he would look like should he one day declare his love for her, explaining it, setting forth the motives, analyzing it, discussing his attitude to his friend, stating his precise demands for the future. It was inconceivable! With all his efficiency Studmann was the most inefficient man in the world for love-making. Yet Frau Eva had to admit that his way of letting his glance rove absent-mindedly from her toes to her

Chapter Twelve

The Quest Fails

I

Whenever Frau Eva came to the office in these weeks to discuss farm affair[s] Studmann never forgot to ask: "And your husband? What does Prackwi[tz] write?" Usually Frau Eva merely shrugged her beautiful full shoulders which so it seemed to Studmann, concealed themselves in ever more charming, eve[r] flimsier blouses. Sometimes, however, she would say: "Just another post card He's getting on all right. He has now shot his five-hundredth rabbit."

"That's fine!" Studmann would answer, after which they said nothing mor[e] about the Rittmeister, but discussed the harvest and the work. They were both contented with their progress, and they were also contented with each other. Whatever measure they considered practical was decided upon without any long palaver, and also carried out. If it afterwards proved not to have been practical, they did not spend a long time regretting it but tried something else.

Naturally mistakes occurred, both large and small. It was not easy for Studmann to take over and manage such an entirely unfamiliar business at the busiest time. Often he had to make the most difficult decisions within the space of a minute. The bridge to outfield five had broken down, twenty teams of horses and eighty men stood idle. They stared at the cart sunk in the ditch and lolled in the shade, saying: "You can't do anything about it."

Studmann did do something about it. Within a minute men were racing to the farm; in five minutes rakes, spades and shovels were on the field; in fif-teen minutes a dyke had been laid across the ditch; in twenty minutes a wagon brought logs from the wood—not half an hour and carts were again rumbling from outfield five to the farm . . .

"Fine fellow, that!" said the men.

"I'd almost like to have a child by him," said Frau Hartig admiringly (although she now had to labor in the fields instead of the office).

"We've no doubt about that, Frieda!" laughed the others. "He's quite a change from your little Black Meier."

Yes, Herr von Studmann turned out well, but he also had good help. It was a miracle how the intimidated, humble overseer Kowalewski suddenly became mouth, in the midst of a sober calculation concerning the mixture of fodder for the cows, had its charm.

Slowly but surely, she thought. She was in no hurry; she had had enough of haste for the time being. Moreover she had probably no fixed plans or intentions; Studmann's respectful admiration, after the storm-tide of quarreling these last few years, did her good. After the cascade of trouble, disagreement, and hurry of recent years, she was happy to be rocked and cradled by the stream of dependency and order emanating from Studmann. But it must be realized that a mother who had so many things to do hadn't much time for her daughter. At first she had tried taking Violet with her round the farm and on her visits to the office. But this contact revealed that their relationship had suffered a serious blow. With sadness Frau Eva saw that Vi obstinately rejected everything coming from her. If she said the weather was fine, Violet found it oppressive; if she suggested that Violet ought to go bathing again, Violet found bathing a bore. There was nothing to be done; there was in this resistance something like serious hostility.

Perhaps I really have been unjust to her, the mother reflected. Perhaps it was nothing—some harmless little affair—we have certainly heard nothing more of any stranger. And now her girl's sense of honor is mortally offended. Well, it will be best for me not to force matters, but to give her time to get over it. One day she'll come back to me.

Vi therefore regained her freedom; there was no more talk of her being confined to her room. But what was she to do now? How empty this life had become! She couldn't go on waiting like this forever—and perhaps in vain. In that case . . . but she didn't know what to do in that case. If only something would happen! But nothing did, absolutely nothing.

In the first days of her new freedom she ran to all the places where she had been with Fritz. For hours on end she wandered up and down in the forest at the spot where they had met. She remembered every single one of the places where they had lain. . . . It was as if the grass had only just straightened itself, as if the mossy bank had only just become smooth again. But he did not return. Sometimes it seemed as if he had been nothing but a dream.

She went also to the Black Dale, and after long searching found the cleverly concealed spot where the weapons were buried. There she stayed a long time; he was bound to come sooner or later to see if the secret was still kept. But he did not come.

Sometimes she met old Forester Kniebusch on her wanderings, and he poured out his heart to her. He had been brought face to face with the poacher Bäumer, but that scoundrel must have got wind of the forester's boasts.

Although he had not been conscious a moment after his fall, he had had the impudence to assert that the forester had thrown him from his bicycle and battered his head several times against the stone, hoping to beat his brains out. They had spoken to the old man very roughly, telling him that only his age protected him from immediate arrest. This is no time to talk of wild deer. The attempt on Bäumer's life had to be settled first. And in the meantime the poacher was living in the hospital like a prince; he had excellent food, careful treatment, a private room—to be sure, with bars in the windows. Never in all his life had the scoundrel been so well off.

Violet was bored by these tales of woe. The forester ought to know what to expect from boasting about his heroic battle with the poacher. But when he announced that he had also met little Bailiff Meier in Frankfurt, she began to pay attention. Little Meier was a little man no longer; he seemed to have become a big man; he had money, a lot of money. In detail the forester described how Herr Meier was dressed, his elegance, the valuable rings on his fingers, his gold watch with a spring lid. But little Meier hadn't become arrogant or haughty; he had invited Kniebusch to supper at a fine restaurant. There had been Rhine wine and afterwards champagne, finally capped with a red Burgundy which little Meier had called "Turk's blood." The forester licked his lips at the memory of this carousal.

"Just another profiteer!" said Vi contemptuously. "Black Meier's cut out for that. And of course in return for the booze you told him everything that's happening in Neulohe, I suppose?"

The forester turned red and protested vigorously against this imputation. He hadn't even said that the Rittmeister was no longer there. And besides, they had talked about very different things. . . .

"What did you talk about?" asked Vi aggressively.

But the forester was not able to remember so exactly.

"You were drunk, Kniebusch," she affirmed. "You've completely forgotten what you talked about. Well, so long."

"Good day, Fräulein!" stammered the old man, and Violet continued her way alone.

The forester's wretched babble bored her, the wood bored her, her grandmother's pious phrases bored her. Her grandfather was always away on mysterious journeys or shut up with the magistrate Haase or silent and thoughtful. She kept out of Räder's way and hadn't even asked him what he had done with her letter. (But now she locked her door, both day and night, despite her mother's astonished protests.) Oh, everything bored her, got on her nerves. . . . She asked herself what she used to do the whole day before she knew Fritz. She could not remember. Everything seemed hollow and empty—boring.

The only thing left was Wolfgang Pagel, whom she ought really to hate more than her mother. But she was quite indifferent to what he thought about her, what he said to her, or his mocking. It was as if she had no sense of shame where he was concerned, as if he were a sort of brother. The two spoke to each other in an incredible tone. Her grandmother would have fainted on the spot had she heard her grandchild (for whom she purified the works of that voluptuary, Wolfgang von Goethe) talking to young Pagel.

"None of your tender caresses, Fräulein," Pagel might say. "I can see you've got another of your strange days today. Black rings round your eyes. But remember, I'm just a weak frail man."

Violet could not quite cope with this tone. She hung on his arm, squeezed it hard and said: "You're a fine one! You might be a bit nice to me for once; there isn't any need for you to always save up everything for your Petra."

"Always to save up," corrected Pagel with Studmann-like pedantry. "You might perhaps try learning a little grammar sometime."

Oh, he could irritate her into a fury. He kept at a distance; there was no more kissing—he saw to that. Sometimes she fled from him with flushed cheeks and tears of rage. She swore that he was a coward, a wretch, a weakling; that she would never speak a word to him again. . . .

Next morning she was standing outside the office door, waiting for him.

"Well, am I in your good graces again?" he grinned. "I swear to you, Violet, today I'm more of a coward, more of a wretch and more of a weakling than ever."

"When my Fritz comes back," she said, with flashing eyes, "I'll tell him how you've treated me. Then he'll challenge you and kill you. I shall be glad!"

Pagel merely laughed.

"Do you think I won't do it? I will do it! You see!" she cried, angry again.

"You are quite capable of it," he laughed. "I've known for a long time that you are really an absolutely cold-blooded creature, and that you wouldn't care if the whole world pegged out so long as you got what you wanted."

"I hope *you* peg out!"

"Yes, yes, but not now. Now I've got to go to the stable. Senta foaled last night. Coming along?"

And of course she went with him. Almost overwhelmed by tenderness, she stood before the little long-legged creature with its large head. "Isn't it sweet?" she whispered excitedly. "Isn't it a darling? Oh, it's heavenly!"

And Wolfgang looked at his Violet askance. Yet she would take the same pleasure in seeing me lie in the dust with a bullet through my heart. Or rather a bullet through my stomach, so that she could hear me moan with agony. No; give me my Peter a thousand times over. You're no good; all dolled up outside, but rotten inside.

But however calm and self-assured he usually felt in her presence, she could always enrage him with one thing—her casting away of all sense of physical shame before him. If she nestled close to him, exhibiting a half-ironical tenderness and passion, it was bearable, though not pleasant. (And to act Joseph to Potiphar's wife is always a little ridiculous.) She had been awoken once and for all, but she hadn't learned to pull herself together, to deny herself things. But when, in the middle of a walk through the fields, she said to him with studied carelessness: "Go on ahead, Pagel, I want to do a wee-wee," or when, bathing, she undressed herself before him with as little embarrassment as if he were her grandmother—then he was seized with a wild rage, and could have struck her. Trembling with anger, he would upbraid her roundly.

"Damn it all, you're not a whore!" he shouted.

"And supposing I were!" she said, looking at him mockingly, amused. "You couldn't make any use of me." Or else she would say, "Always boasting! Aren't you spoken for? Why get so angry about such things?"

"You're rotten and stinking, spoilt to the marrow! There's not a speck of your body that isn't dreck!"

"Specks are usually dreck," she said coolly.

It was perhaps not so much the insult to his manhood which aroused him, although such things must infuriate any man, especially one of twenty-three; it was perhaps rather a sudden panic. Did she already regard herself as completely lost? Did she intentionally want to go to the dogs? Has this fifteen-year-old really already had enough of life? Every decent person feels himself a little responsible for his fellow-beings: only the wicked let their brethren run into the swamp without warning. Pagel felt his responsibility. He would try to talk to her, to warn her. But she affected a complete lack of understanding; she sat within a barbed-wire entanglement of foolish remarks: "All men are like that—one must be low-down, otherwise one just gets treated badly." Or else: "Do you think it decent, the way Herr Studmann shows off to Mamma as soon as Papa goes away—and do you expect me to be more decent?" Or: "You don't tell me, either, all the things you did with your Fräulein Petra before you broke it off. I don't suppose you were very decent in that, anyway. So you needn't have started talking about decency to me—even if I am only a country girl." Oh, she could be as cunning as the devil. Darting off at a tangent, she would say: "Is it true that there are places in Berlin where girls dance all naked? And you've been there? Well, then! And you want to tell me that you faint when you sometimes see a little bit of me? You are ridiculous!"

There was nothing to be done, she would not be persuaded. Hundreds of times Pagel was on the point of talking to Studmann or Frau Eva about the girl. If he didn't, it was not because of any silly feeling of gentlemanly discretion. But what good could the old people do if she wouldn't listen to a young person like himself? Punishments and sermons will merely make it worse, he thought. Perhaps I shall have to speak about it if she ever wants to run away, but she certainly won't get mixed up with any of the fellows here—she feels herself too much of the heiress for that and won't want to tarnish her glory as future proprietress. If this scamp of a Lieutenant Fritz should turn up again, I shall hear of it instantly. Then I'll give the rascal a good hiding and write down for him, in no uncertain terms, that he can forget any idea of returning to these happy pastures.

Pagel stretched himself. He wasn't afraid to scrap with the toughest man in the village. Three months of country life had developed his muscles; he felt himself strong enough for any Lieutenant, any adventurer.

"Well, whom would you like to embrace now?" asked Vi ironically.

"Your Lieutenant Fritz!" was the surprising answer. He leaped on his bicycle. "Cheerio, Fräulein. Our walk is off for this morning, I must get on to my Hussars. But perhaps at one o'clock." He was gone.

"Come along here, Violet!" called Frau Eva, who had observed this leave-taking from the office window and was sorry at the disappointed look on her daughter's face. "I'm going to town in a quarter of an hour to fetch the wages. Come along with me—we'll have pastry and cream at Kipferling's."

"Oh!" said Vi, pouting. "I don't know, Mamma. No thanks, cream just makes you fat." And in order not to be called back again she went quickly into the park.

"Sometimes I get very worried," declared Frau von Prackwitz.

"Yes?" said Studmann politely, busy with his wage lists. Although he hadn't nearly given the numbers all the noughts that belonged to them, no single column could contain the riches.

"She is so undecided, so slack. There's no life in her."

"It's a rather critical age for young girls, though, isn't it?" suggested Studmann.

"Perhaps it's really that," agreed Frau Eva, adding cautiously: "As a matter of fact, she's always with young Pagel and the tone between them seems to me rather familiar. Do you think there is anything in that?"

"Anything in what?" Studmann looked up from his wage lists a little distract-edly. If he used the sick-benefit column for writing down the net wages then he would have to use the disability column for the health contributions. The disability column was too narrow for all this wealth of noughts; he would use the wage-tax column instead. And now it turned out that the wages book was much too narrow. You would have to have a kind of atlas-sized wage list, including all the world's lon-gitude lines. What a damn mess! And nothing balanced. The orderly Studmann looked at his disorderly wage list with a stern, discouraged face.

"Herr von Studmann!" cooed Frau von Prackwitz with a dove-like soft-ness that would have frightened any man, as if he received an electric shock, "I was just asking you whether you had any doubts about young Pagel."

Studmann looked startled, just as was proper.

"Oh, I beg your pardon, Frau von Prackwitz, I'm terribly sorry! I was so preoccupied with these wretched lists. They get worse and worse, I can't make them balance anymore. And I'm beginning to realize that it's useless tormenting myself with them. I suggest that we only pay round sums now; for instance, a mil-liard for every married man. It's true we would be paying a little over, but I can't see any other way of doing it." He looked at Frau Eva, thoughtful and worried.

"Agreed," she said tranquilly. "And now that the money questions are settled, do you mind paying some attention to my worries as a mother? To my doubts about young Pagel?"

Studmann turned very red. "Frau von Prackwitz, I am a silly ass in some ways. When I get involved in something you can't do anything with me. I'll explain it to you. . . ."

"No, please don't, my dear Studmann!" cried Frau Eva in despair. "I don't want explanations, but an answer! Sometimes," she said pensively, "you are astonishingly like Achim, although you are such contrasts. With him I get no answer because of his hastiness, from you I get none because of your thor-oughness. The result for me is the same: I still don't know whether I ought to be worried about Herr Pagel."

"Of course not," declared Studmann hurriedly and guiltily. "Quite apart from the fact that Pagel is a man of honor, he is also perfectly harmless."

"I don't know," said Frau Eva doubtfully. "He is very young. And he's more or less in thoroughly high spirits now, looking really happy the last few weeks. I've noticed it, and a young girl will notice it, too."

"That is so, isn't it?" said Studmann, looking pleased. "He has quite recov-ered. I'm proud of my success. When he came from Berlin he was a wreck, ill, dispirited, lazy—almost ruined. And now? Even the convicts look cheery when they catch sight of him."

"And my Violet, too!" said Frau Eva drily. "You are not exactly giving me a proof of the young man's harmlessness."

"But, Frau von Prackwitz!" cried Studmann in reproach. "He's in love. Only a man in love is so pleased, so gay, so contented with everything. Anyone can see that. Why, even I can see it, a dry man of figures like myself." He flushed slightly under her gently mocking glance. "When he came here he thought the affair was over. He was gloomy, without life. No, I didn't ask him anything, I didn't want to. I think that discussions about love are pernicious, because . . ."

Frau Eva coughed warningly.

"But the affair seems to have got straightened out again, he receives and writes letters, he is as merry as a bird, he works with a will—he would like to embrace the whole world."

"But not my Vi, if you please!" cried Frau Eva with determination.

II

Yes, Wolfgang Pagel was writing and receiving letters. And Studmann was right in saying that Wolfgang's new pleasure in life was bound up with these letters, although not a line had come from Petra or had been written to her. Despite everything, happy. Despite everything, ready for action. Despite everything, expansive and all-embracing. Despite everything, patient with the child Violet.

When old Minna had received the young master's first letter from the postman, and had recognized the handwriting, her limbs had trembled so much that she had to sit down. And then she became quite calm.

I mustn't frighten the old lady like this, she thought. She doesn't eat anymore, doesn't drink anymore, doesn't do anything; just sits there and thinks. And when she believes I'm not looking she takes out the note which he left when he fetched his things, and in which he said that he was now going to work properly and wouldn't write before he'd found his feet again. And now he's written.

She looked at the letter mistrustfully. But perhaps there were only silly things in it which would upset his mother. Minna became more and more doubtful. And perhaps he only wanted money again, because he was in a fix somewhere. She turned the letter round, but on the back were only stamps. . . . The writing was quite neat, Wolf used to write much worse. And it was in ink, not scribbled off in a hurry. Perhaps there was good news in it.

For a moment Minna thought of opening the letter secretly and, if it was too bad, of answering it herself. Wolfi was also her child in a way. But if it was good news, let his mother be the first to enjoy it. "Oh, it can't be anything bad!" And thereupon she stood up from her chair, calm, determination restored.

And she placed the letter under the newspaper so that nothing of it could be seen, and when Frau Pagel had sat down sadly at the breakfast table, she left her post at the door—against all habit—mumbled something about "market" and disappeared, deaf to the calls of her mistress. And she actually did dash to the market, where she purchased a trout for 900,000,000 marks. Her mistress would at last have an appetite again.

When she returned, Frau Pagel was already on the look-out for her, her eyes sparkling as they had not sparkled in the last eight weeks.

"Silly old goose!" she greeted her faithful servant. "Do you really have to run away, so that I haven't anyone to say a word to? Yes, the young master has written, he's in the country now, on a large farm, something like an apprentice. But he has rather a lot of responsibility, I don't understand anything about it—you must read it yourself, the letter's on the table. He's getting on well and he sends his regards to you and it's the first letter, since I don't know how long, in which he writes nothing about money. With the inflation I really couldn't blame him if he did; even if he still had the money from the picture it would be worth nothing now. He writes ever so cheerfully, he has never written so cheerfully before; there must be a lot of queer people there, but he seems to get on with everybody. Well, you'll read it yourself, Minna; why should I tell you all of it? But he doesn't want to stay on the farm even though he does like it; he writes that it is like a sort of sanatorium. I'm not to mind, and if he really has become a taxi driver, I'm not to try and change his mind. But I'm not going to answer him, I've not forgotten how you told me that I made everything too easy for him. Yet it was you who always gave him sweets whenever he howled, you old know-all! I think that you should reply first and then we can see whether he gets sulky and hurt again. In that case he won't be cured yet. And, Minna, he wants some information. I don't agree with it, no, I don't agree with it at all, but I shan't say anything again, so you can take this afternoon off and make inquiries. And this evening write to him at once; if we post the letter today he'll get it tomorrow. But perhaps it's a country post there, in which case he'll get it a day later. Besides, I might write a line, perhaps, after all. . . ."

"Madam," said Minna, "madam—if you don't sit down at once and eat your egg and at least two rolls I won't read the letter or reply this evening. . . . This is really absolute foolishness: first you don't eat because of sorrow and then you eat nothing because of joy. Yet you expect Wolfgang to be a calm and sensible person!"

"Stop it, Minna, you drive anyone crazy with all your talk!" said Frau Pagel. "Read the letter. I'm eating now."

However, although Frau Pagel ate a really good breakfast, and also did every justice at midday to the 900,000,000 mark trout, her reply to Wolfgang was not written that day. The information he requested was not so easy to obtain; the trail from Georgenkirchstrasse to Fruchtstrasse was not so easy to discover. Minna had to make many a journey to the registration offices, spend many an hour patiently waiting for information, questioning and being questioned, before she at last found herself in front of the large plank fence on which (alongside the usual scribblings of children—"Whoever reads this is daft") was painted in large white letters "Emil Krupass, widow: rags, bottles and bones."

"Here?" Minna asked herself doubtfully. "They've sent me to the wrong place again!"

She peered through the gateway into the large yard, which certainly did not look very inviting with its mountains of rusty old iron, its multitude of dirty bottles and its heap of burst mattresses. "Look out!" shouted a young scamp dashing into the yard with a dog-drawn barrow, missing her by a hair's-breadth.

Minna followed him hesitatingly. But on her asking at a shed for Fräulein Ledig she was answered readily: "She's by the rags. Over there at the back—the black hut!"

Poor thing! thought Minna. I suppose she must be finding it hard to scrape up a bit of a living. It was frightfully dirty in the old hut, and the stink was even more frightful. With a feeling of comfort she thought of her pretty clean kitchen. And if Petra was really stuck in here, she was three times as sorry for her. "Fräulein Ledig!" she shouted into the gloom where figures crouched and dust whirled, making her cough.

"Yes?"

She wore a bluish-green overall and looked queerly changed, but there was still the simple clear face.

"Lord, Petra, child, is it really you?" said Minna staring at her.

"Minna!" cried Petra in joyful surprise. "Have you really found me then?"

(And neither had an inkling that they were suddenly using the informal "du" with each other, which they'd never done before. But that's life: There are people who only notice how much they like each other when they meet again, after not having seen each other for a long time.)

"Petra!" And Minna, of course, at once blurted out: "Look at you! You aren't—?"

"Yes, I am," she smiled.

"When?"

"At the beginning of December, I think," replied Petra.

"I must write and tell Wolfi about it at once!"

"You are not to tell him about it in any circumstances!"

"Petra," said Minna imploringly, "you're not angry with him, are you?" Petra merely smiled. "You don't bear him a grudge, do you? I would never have thought it of you." They regarded each other silently for a while in the dusty rag hut, where women monotonously sorted the rags. They looked critically, as if they wanted to see how much the other had changed. "Come out of the bad air, Petra. We can't talk here."

"Is he outside?" Petra thought of what Ma Krupass had once said, that she would run to him if he were standing on the other side of the street. She did not want to. Minna looked at Petra guardedly. Suddenly she knew that it was of no little importance what sort of stepdaughter she would have been. Wolfgang's mother had already born enough sorrow.

"Do you want us to stand till we take root in this muck and filth?" cried Minna, stamping her foot. "If he *is* outside he won't bite you!"

Petra turned pale. But she said firmly: "If he's outside then I am not going out. I promised."

"You won't go out, eh? That's a nice thing. You won't go to the father of your child? Whom do you promise such things to?"

"Oh, do be quiet, Minna." This time it was Petra who stamped her foot. "Why is he sending you, then? I thought he would have become a bit different, but that's the way he always was. If he found anything unpleasant to do, he got others to do it."

"You mustn't excite yourself so, Petra. That can't be good for *it*."

"I'm not excited in the least!" said Petra, growing ever angrier. "But can you expect anyone not to be annoyed if he never learns anything and never changes? I suppose he's crept under his mother's skirts again. It's all just as Ma Krupass said it would be."

"Ma Krupass?" asked Minna jealously. "Is that the widow whose name is on the fence outside? Do you tell her all the doings of our Wolfi? I would never have thought it of you, Petra!"

"One must have someone to talk to," said Petra firmly. "I couldn't go on waiting for you. What's he doing now?" And she motioned with her head toward the street.

"So you are really afraid of him and don't want to see him?" said Minna, terribly angry. "After all, he is the father of your child!"

But suddenly it seemed as if some thought had wiped all doubt, all fear and worry from Petra's face. Its former clear character traits were apparent again; in times of greatest distress at Madam Po's Minna had never seen that face look either angry or tearful. And there was the old tone in her voice, the old ring. It was the ring of the old bell—trust, love, patience. Petra quietly took Minna's shaking hand between her own and said, "You know him, too, Minna, you saw him grow up, and you know that one can't be angry with him when he laughs and cracks his jokes with us poor women. . . . Your heart goes out to him straight away, you feel happy and think no more of anything he might have done to you . . ."

"Yes, God knows!"

"But, Minna, now he'll have to be a father and think of others. It mustn't just be that everyone should look happy when he is there; he must help in sharing troubles and work and also put up with an angry face sometimes, instead of running off at once for the day. And Ma Krupass is right, I've thought of it hundreds of times these past weeks: he must become a man before he can be a father. At present he's merely a child whom we've all spoiled."

"You are right, Petra, God knows."

"And if I stand here with you and go all hot and cold, it isn't because I'm angry or bear him a grudge or want to punish him! If he came in here, Minna, and gave me his hand and smiled at me in his old way, I know that the first thing I'd do would be to hug him, I'd be so happy. But, Minna, that must not be. I've realized that I mustn't make things so easy for him again. In the first hour it would be wonderful, but in the next I should be thinking: Is my child to have such a spoiled darling for its father, one for whom I have no proper respect? No, Minna, God forbid! Even if I have to run away from here, run away from him and from my own weakness! I promised Ma Krupass and myself: he must first be something. Even if it's only something quite small. And anyway I don't want to see him at all for six months." She paused for a moment. "But now he's again crept under the skirts of you old women!"

"But he hasn't, Petra!" cried old Minna joyfully. "What silly ideas you've got! He hasn't done that at all."

"Now you're lying, Minna. You just told me yourself."

"I said nothing of the sort! No, just come out with me now. I've had enough of your stink and dust."

"I'm not going out. I'm not going to him!"

"But he isn't outside! You're just imagining it."

"You said it yourself, Minna—please, let us stay here."

"I said I wanted to write to him that you are expecting a baby. How can I want to write to him if he's standing outside? You're just imagining it all, Petra, because you are afraid, afraid of your own heart and afraid for the child. And because you're afraid, everything's all right. And now just let anyone, madam or anyone else, say anything against you—I know different. I'm glad you've spoken this way. I know now what I have to write to him, not too much and not too little. Now ask for an hour off and come out, there must be something like a café in the neighborhood. I pinched his letter for you, and madam didn't say a word although she saw me. But you must give it back; you can copy it quickly if you like. Well, where shall we go? Can you get the time off?"

"Why shouldn't I get the time off?" said Petra with bravado. "I take time off when I like! Everything you see here," and she went with Minna to the hut door, "everything, the rags, the paper, the old iron and the bottles—it's all under my management, and the men working here too, of course. Herr Randolph," she said to an old man, "I'm going up to my room for a bit with my friend. If there's anything special you've only got to call me."

"What do you call special, Fräulein? Do you think they'll be bringing in Kaiser Bill's crown this afternoon? You go and have a lie down. If I was you I wouldn't stick all afternoon among the rags!"

"Very well, Herr Randolph," said Petra happily. "After all, it's the first time I'm having a visitor here."

And the two of them went up to Ma Krupass's little flat, sat down, talked, and talked more.

When the time came for Minna to go home to make supper for her mistress, she did what she had not done since time immemorial; she went to the telephone and announced that she was not coming, that the key of the larder was in the right drawer of the kitchen sideboard behind the spoons, and that the key to the right drawer was in the pocket of her blue apron hanging up with the tea towels. And before Frau Pagel had quite grasped these clear instructions, Minna had already hung up. "Otherwise she'd start pumping me on the telephone, and she can wait for once. Now go on telling me about your Ma Krupass—pinches cuff links and yet has a good heart. Such things are neither in prayer book or bible. How long has she got, did you say?"

"Four months—and that's just as if the court had known, for I'll be confined at the beginning of December and she'll be coming out at the end of November. She didn't appeal—her lawyer said she ought to be glad. But still, it's a pity when an old woman like that is up before the judge. I was there, and he told her off properly, and all the time she was crying like a child."

It was half-past ten before Minna came home. She saw the light in her mistress's room, but "You can wait!" she told herself, and crept quietly to her bed. But not quietly enough. For Frau Pagel called out: "Is that you, Minna? Well, thank God for that. I was beginning to think you were taking to night life in your old age."

"Seems like it, madam," said Minna staunchly. And then, with affected innocence: "Is there anything else madam would like?"

"Why, you deceitful cat!" cried Frau Pagel angrily. "Are you pretending you don't know what's itching me? What have you found out?"

"Oh, nothing special," said Minna off-hand. "Just that madam will soon be a grandmother." And with that she fled into her room with a speed that one would never have thought possible in such an old bag of bones, and slammed the door, as if to say: "Consulting hours are over for this evening."

"Well, I never!" said old Frau Pagel, vigorously rubbing her nose and looking dreamily at the spot on the carpet where her vixen of a servant had been standing. "That's a nice way to tell me! Grandmother! A moment ago a widow without any encumbrances, and now suddenly a grandmother. . . . Oh, no, we shan't swallow that medicine, even if you do give it to me so craftily, you spiteful old devil!"

With that Frau Pagel shook her fist at the empty passage and withdrew into her room. But she could not have thought the news too bad, for she fell asleep so soundly that she did not hear Minna creeping out of the house with a letter. And it was now past midnight!

This letter was the beginning of that correspondence which, even though it did not contain a line from Petra Ledig, turned Wolfgang Pagel into a young man who, in Herr Studmann's words, looked as if he wanted to embrace the world.

III

When Wolfgang Pagel bicycled to the prisoners on his own, and Violet von Prackwitz agreed to this without demur, although she would rather have spent the morning with the young man herself, it was because a higher will prevailed to which everyone had to agree: That of the Principal Warder Marofke. This ridiculous, conceited little man with a potbelly not only made the faces of his convicts sullen—whenever he entered the farm office with one of his never-ending requests, Frau von Prackwitz groaned: "Lord, here he is again!" and Studmann frowned. The workers, the chief guards and their assistants cursed the principle—but quietly. The girls in the kitchen cursed "the conceited clown"—only very loudly.

Marofke was always finding something wrong. First the mutton was too fat, then the pork was too scanty. There had been no peas for three weeks, but white cabbage had been cooked twice a week. The men didn't return punctually from work, and the meals were not punctual. That window had to be walled up, otherwise the prisoners could see into a room occupied by girls. It was not permissible for the lavatory next to the barracks to be used by villagers—women, for instance. It was likewise not permissible for women to let themselves be seen near the gang at work; it might excite the men.

There was no end to it. Yet this potbellied rascal made life damned easy for himself. He usually left the supervision of the gang to his subordinates, the four warders, and sat almost the whole day in his barracks, drawing up lists in a self-important manner, or writing reports to the prison administration, or striding restlessly through the rooms, pulling every bed to pieces, for inspection. A spoon handle from which a prisoner had made himself a pipe cleaner aroused him to intense thought. What could it signify? A pipe cleaner, of course; but whoever could make that could also make a skeleton key! And he inspected every lock, every iron bar, every socket. Then he strode to the closet, lifted up the lavatory seat, and looked down to see if there was only toilet paper or perhaps the torn bits of a letter there.

But most of the time he sat outside the barracks in the sun, twiddling his thumbs over his fat belly, eyes half-closed, thinking. The people who saw him sitting there so comfortable and sleepy laughed at him contemptuously. For in the country it is a shame for any healthy man to laze during the harvest. Everyone is needed; there are not enough hands.

But it must be admitted that the principal warder was not daydreaming in the sun; he actually was thinking. He thought uninterruptedly of his fifty prisoners. He recalled their sentences, their crimes, their ages, their relations with the world, how much time each had still to serve. He examined their characters man by man, he thought of incidents in the prison, trifling events which, however, vividly revealed what a man was capable of. When the men ate, rested, talked, slept, he observed them. He noticed who spoke to whom; he noticed friendships, hostilities. And as a result of his observations and reflections there was a continuous redistribution; enemies were placed together, friendships were torn asunder. Those who hated each other had to sleep in neighboring beds. Continually Marofke changed the order of sitting at table; he decided who should work by himself, whom the warders must always keep their eyes on.

And the prisoners hated their Marofke like the plague; the warders, to whom he gave endless trouble, cursed him behind his back. At the slightest contradiction he went scarlet, his fat belly shook, his hanging chops trembled. "I make you responsible for it, warder!" he shouted. "You have sworn an oath to do your duty!"

"These fault-finders always exist!" said Studmann with disgust. "It's best to let them alone. Even God wouldn't do anything right for them!"

"No!" said Pagel. "This time you are wrong. He is a really cunning fox. And efficient."

"Now I ask you, Pagel!" said the irritated Studmann. "Have you ever seen this man doing regular duty like his colleagues? Yes, sit in the sun and think out new complaints, that's all he can do. Unfortunately, I can't say anything to the fellow; he's subject only to the prison authorities. But you can be certain if I were his superior I'd give that fat fellow a bit of exercise!"

"Very efficient," Pagel had persisted. "And cunning. And diligent. Well, you'll see."

Yes, Pagel was the only one who believed in the merits of this unbearable buffoon, and it was probably because of this that the two got on well together.

That morning, before riding out to the field, Pagel had paid the principal warder a short visit. Herr Marofke was very susceptible to such courtesies. He was sitting at his table, his face red, staring at a letter which the postman had probably just brought him. Pagel could see that there was a storm in the offing. "Well, any news from the western front, chief?" he asked.

The little man jumped to his feet so suddenly that his chair fell over with a crash. Slapping the letter, he cried: "Yes, news, but not good news! Rejected—my petition to be relieved is rejected!"

"Did you want to leave us?" said Pagel, astonished. "I didn't know that."

"Me leave? Nonsense! I wouldn't let myself be relieved of such a difficult post. Me a shirker? No, never have been—people can say what they like about me. No." He was calmer. "I can tell you about it—you'll keep your mouth shut. I made a request that five men should be relieved because they no longer seem safe to me. And the pen-pushers in the office have rejected it—they say my request has no grounds! They have to have a murdered warder in their office before they have their grounds. Idiots!"

"But everything is quite peaceful," said Pagel soothingly. "I haven't noticed the slightest thing. Or did anything happen last night?"

"You also think that something must happen first," growled the principal warder sullenly. "If anything happens in a prison gang, young man, then it is already too late. But I don't blame you for that; you've no experience, and you know nothing about convicts. . . . Even my colleagues don't see anything—only this morning they said again that I had a bee in my bonnet—but better to have a bee in your bonnet than be a night owl that sees nothing by day."

"But what in heaven's name is wrong?" asked Pagel, surprised at so much sullen rage. "What have you found, officer?"

"Nothing!" said the principal warder dully. "No note, no skeleton key, no money, no weapon—nothing to indicate escape or revolt. But it stinks of it. I've been smelling it for days. I notice things like that. Something is going on."

"But why? What makes you think so?"

"I've been in prison over twenty-five years," confessed Herr Marofke, and saw nothing objectionable in saying so. On the contrary! "I know my men.

During the whole of my time of service three have escaped. For two of them I was not responsible, and as for the third, I had only been in service for six months—one doesn't know anything in that time. But today I do know something, and I swear to you—those five have got something on, and until I get them out of my gang, my gang won't be clean!"

"Which five?" Pagel had the impression that the principal warder was imagining things.

"I made a request for the following men to be relieved," said Marofke solemnly. "Liebschner, Kosegarten, Matzke, Wendt, Holdrian."

"But those are just our pleasantest, most intelligent and handiest men! Except for old Wendt—he's a bit daft."

"They've only got him in it as a safety valve. He's to be their scapegoat if there's any danger. Wendt is their forfeit, as it were, but the other four . . ." He sighed. "I've tried everything to separate them. I've redistributed them, none of them sleeps in the same room as the others, I don't let them sit together, I show favor to one and treat the others severely, which usually makes them angry—but no, hardly do I turn my back when they're together again, whispering."

"Perhaps they just like each other?" suggested Pagel. "Perhaps they're friends."

"There are no friendships in prison," declared the principal warder. "In prison everyone is always the other's enemy. Whenever two stick together they are conspirators—for a definite purpose. No, it stinks; if I tell you that—I, Principal Warder Marofke—then you can believe it!"

For a while they were silent. "I'm going out to the men now," Pagel said finally in order to get away. "I'll keep my eyes open in case I see anything."

"What do you think you'll see?" said the principal warder. "They are tough lads—they'd make an old detective inspector sweat. Before you'd see anything you'd be lying there with a hole in your skull. No, I've thought it over. Since they've rejected my request, I'm going all out. I shall cause a mutiny at lunch time; I'll shove salt in their food, literally; I'll put so much salt in their grub that they won't be able to swallow it. And then I shall force them to eat. I'll taunt them and threaten them until they mutiny. And then I shall have my grounds; then I shall grab my five and send them back as mutineers. That'll cost them another year or two in prison." He giggled in scorn.

"Well, I'm damned!" Pagel was horrified. "But it might go wrong. Five men against fifty in that narrow room!"

"Young man!" said the principal warder, and he no longer appeared ridiculous to Pagel. "If you know for certain that someone wants to attack you from the back, what do you do? You turn round and attack him. That's the way I am. I'd rather be killed from the front than from behind."

"I'll come over at lunch time with my gun," said Pagel eagerly.

"You'll do nothing of the kind," growled the principal warder. "I've no use for an inexperienced chap in a business like this. One minute, and the nearest crook will have your gun, and then it'll be Good-by, my Fatherland! Oh, dear no, you just run along now; I've got to work out my table order so that I have the loudest shouters sitting just under my truncheon."

IV

A man's settled conviction has something in it which can affect even his opponent. Broodingly Wolfgang Pagel rode along the old familiar way to the ninth outfield, where the potatoes were being gathered. Now and then he met a dray loaded with them and, getting off his bicycle, asked the driver what the crop was like. Then, before mounting again, he would casually add: "Everything all right out there?" A silly question. Obviously everything was all right, and the only reply one got from the driver was a vague mumble.

He rode on. It was no good letting oneself be influenced by those who saw ghosts everywhere.

It was a fine autumn day toward the end of September, and if the east wind was a little fresh, it was pleasantly warm in the sun and out of the wind; now that he was in the wood there was not even a breeze. Outfield nine, the remotest of all the areas of the estate, bordered on the long and the short side of the wood. Its other short side bordered on the Birnbaumer field. Almost soundless, except for the whirring chain, his bicycle sped over the forest paths. Of course everything would be in order there, but Pagel had to admit that the outfield, almost four miles from the farm, hidden in the woods and far from all inhabited places, offered the convicts a splendid opportunity.

Instinctively he trod harder on the pedals, then, smiling at himself, put on the brakes. He must not let himself get nervous. The convicts had been working there over a week, without anything happening. What was the good, then, of hurrying just in order to get out there five minutes sooner? If nothing had happened in six working days it was not likely to do so in those five minutes.

He tried to imagine how something could happen. The convicts worked in the open field in four gangs of twelve and thirteen men. Ten paces behind each group stood the warder with his loaded carbine in hand, and in front of him, continually under his eyes, were the men on their knees. A convict might not even stand up without permission. And before he could take three steps he would be shot down. They all knew they would be fired on without warning. In theory, of course, it was possible that two or three might sacrifice themselves to obtain freedom for the others, and that once the warder had emptied his magazine, and before he could draw his pistol, the rest would be off. Actually, however, convicts were not self-sacrificing; each, you might be sure, was quite prepared to sacrifice anyone but number one.

No, it was not out here that things would happen, but in the barracks. Marofke was playing a dangerous game at midday, and Pagel resolved that he would at least be outside with his gun. Perhaps Marofke was venturing on this game for nothing, for illusions, phantoms . . .

Pagel rode on slowly, pondering. It was this habit of thought which distinguished him from many young people and most old ones—an independent, persistent brooding, a desire to understand. Not for him the beaten track, but his own path. In Neulohe everyone considered the principal warder to be a lazy, conceited ass; but that had no influence on Wolfgang Pagel, who was of a very different mind. When Marofke asserted there was something going on among his prisoners, it was stupid, however weak might be the ground for his opinion, simply to reply: Nonsense!

In one thing the principal warder could not be wrong. He himself knew nothing about convicts, but Marofke knew a great deal. They were very pleasant to Pagel, making little jokes and frankly telling him of their troubles in "stir," and in the world outside. They made a harmless, if somewhat too friendly, impression. This impression, however, must be wrong. One realized that as soon as one thought about it. How could they be so inoffensive and friendly?

"Don't let them pull wool over your eyes, Pagel," Marofke had told him a dozen times. "Don't forget they are convicts because they have all done something criminal. Once a crook, always a crook. There may be many in prison who got there because of misfortune or jealousy—but whoever's in a penitentiary has always done something pretty low."

Yes, and they make themselves look harmless. He was right; one must not be taken in. That was where Marofke was different from the other officers; he was always suspicious, he was not to be caught napping. Never for a moment did he forget that fifty dangerous criminals lived in what was, after all, an insecure harvesters' barracks, and that if those fifty men ever escaped it would mean incalculable misfortune for their fellow men.

"But they will be out, anyway, in a month, in three months, in half a year," Pagel had objected.

"Certainly—but registered by the police, in their civilian duds, and with a little money to start off with. If they give us the slip here, however, their first crime must be in getting proper clothes—theft, burglary, assault. . . . Wherever they live they daren't register, but must hide among criminals or prostitutes who don't do a thing for nothing. And so they have to get money—theft, fraud, swindling, burglary, hold-ups.... Now do you understand what the difference is between release and escape?"

"Quite understand!" said Pagel.

Markofke was right and the others were wrong.

And the others were wrong also when they declared that, because he stayed behind, Marofke was shirking his duty. (The Rittmeister had said at once that he was a shirker.) But Pagel now understood what a numbing, indifferent occupation could be made of standing behind the gang of prisoners. Marofke was not stupid; he racked his brains; several times he had groaned: "If only I was back safe and sound with my fifty blackguards. At the beginning you're glad to be outside in the fresh air; but now I go on counting, another six weeks, another five weeks and six days, and so on and so on, and most likely we shan't get in your potatoes before the first of November anyway."

"And there are still the turnips," said Pagel spitefully.

One ought not to be spiteful to the man, however. He was no coward, as his plan for midday showed—a plan requiring a fair amount of resolution and courage. He might be a little unhinged, though; twenty-five years of prison service were enough to make any man queer. Not that one altogether believed this, however. The principal warder was a keen observer and a clear thinker, and Pagel decided to keep his eyes wide open today, and find out if what the other thought was correct or not.

And in five minutes events were to show him the value of his own powers of observation and the utility of an outsider among convicts.

He leaned his bicycle against a tree which, incidentally, was something the principal warder had severely forbidden (since a bicycle left unattended could assist a man's escape), but this time Pagel's carelessness had no further consequences. He crossed by the potato mounds toward the gang, which was working in a long column, the convicts sliding forward on their knees, digging up and collecting the potatoes. Four men, walking to and fro, emptied the full baskets into sacks, and returned them to the diggers. Behind the chain stood four officers in the listless manner of people who for ten hours a day fear something that never comes. Two had their carbines under their arms; two had them slung over their shoulders—Pagel noticed it because Marofke had forbidden this also. The convicts were just working down from the top of a small hill into a hollow bordered by older plantations of pine trees. This hollow was overgrown with weeds which, because of all the water collecting there, were still half green and made digging hard.

This the men shouted to Pagel at once. "It's all rotten here, bailiff! We can't get on at all. The potatoes are still quite green. Just to save tobacco!" As an incentive Pagel had arranged that a bonus in tobacco should be given for a fixed yield in hundredweights.

"We'll see what can be done," he shouted, going up to the nearest officer, whom he at once asked the question which was constantly on his tongue today: "Everything all right?"

"Of course," replied the bored young assistant warder. "Why shouldn't it be?"

"I was only asking. . . . Digging's bad here?"

"I see Marofke's been at you. He's cracked! Always bleating and nosing around! I tell you, this detachment couldn't be better off. And still he's not satisfied! That's overdoing it."

"How overdoing?"

"Warder!" interrupted a prisoner. "Can I fall out for a minute?"

The warder looked first at him, then at the others. "All right, Kosegarten."

The prisoner gave Pagel an amused, familiar look, stepped behind the row, and, grinning, unbuttoned his trousers. Squatting down he kept his eyes on Pagel, who half turned away so as not to have this spectacle before him.

"How overdoing?" replied the assistant warder. "Because Marofke wants to suck up to the director, that's why. He's sworn that he'll take back every man to Meienburg twenty-five pounds heavier. 'Even if we have to eat you out of house and home,' he said yesterday; 'I keep on grumbling about the food, they just can't cook too well for us!'"

There was no time to reply to this denunciation, for dismay suddenly changed the warder's face. "Halt!" he bawled, tearing the carbine from his shoulder . . .

Pagel swung round and saw the prisoner Kosegarten running off into the pine trees . . .

"Out of the way!" roared the warder, hitting Pagel heavily on the breast with the barrel of his carbine.

"Don't shoot, warder!" shouted voices. "We'll fetch him."

The man hesitated a moment, and two, three more figures disappeared among the pines.

"Halt!" he shouted and fired.

The report sounded feeble beside the uproar of the prisoners. There was shooting now at the top also. "Form fours!" roared voices.

Pagel, seeing a fifth man running to the pines, set after him.

"Stand still, fool! How can I shoot?" bellowed the officer.

Pagel hesitated, threw himself down, and the bullets whistled over him. They could be heard pattering on the trees. Five minutes later the men were drawn up ready to march off, numbered, and the names of the missing ascertained. Five men. Their names were: Liebschner, Kosegarten, Matzke, Wendt, Holdrian.

Shrewd Marofke, thought Pagel, ashamed of his own stupidity. How often had the warder told him not to enter into conversation with officers while on duty! How damned idiotic he had been to run after a fugitive when two men had just shown him that such pursuit excellently covered up a flight!

The prisoners were buzzing with excitement or they were very gloomy and silent; the warders agitated, morose and furious.

"You, Herr Pagel, go like hell and tell Marofke the whole stinking mess. My God, what a row he'll make, how he'll curse us! And he'll be right—compared with him we're idiots. Well, it's all over with the harvest gang. Back to Meienburg this afternoon! Tell Marofke it'll be a good two hours before we come along. We shall march round by the open fields; I won't risk taking the lads through the woods. Now off with you!"

Pagel jumped on his bicycle and sped through the woods.

V

For the next three or four hours, Neulohe was buzzing and humming like a beehive before the queen leaves. Only here the leaving had already taken place—and not by the queen!

"I thought so," was all that the principal warder said before flinging himself into the office to ring up the prison authorities, followed by a perspiring and breathless Pagel.

"You ought to have been a bit more careful with your people," said Studmann angrily.

Conceited little Marofke, however, spent no time in justifying or clearing himself. "We must get them today before they're out of the woods, or we'll never get them!" he told Pagel. He did not so much as attempt to say, "I told you so."

While the warder was telephoning, Pagel whispered to Studmann, astonished to find that what he himself had most at heart was to defend little Marofke. Little Marofke, however, thought quite otherwise. He had only two ideas: to lead the remainder of his party back to Meienburg without further loss, and to catch the fugitives as rapidly as possible. Clearly he was getting a frightful dressing down on the phone, but he did not wince, he made no reference to his rejected application. What alone interested him was what was going to happen now.

"There's a man for you!" said Pagel.

"If he's such a fine fellow, he shouldn't have let them get away first," Studmann muttered.

The principal warder hung up the receiver. "Herr von Studmann," he reported in a very frigid and military manner, "the harvest gang at Neulohe will be withdrawn today. Warders for the removal of the men are coming at once from Meienburg. I should like to have ready at, say, three o'clock, two teams for the conveyance of effects. I myself will go to meet the gang and bring it to the barracks."

"You yourself? Oh, really!" said Studmann bitterly. "And what about our potatoes?" He could foresee evil consequences.

Marofke ignored the thrust. "Will you, Herr von Studmann, get into touch with the forester, and perhaps the owner of the forest? In the next half-hour we must ascertain from the forest map where the fellows are likely to be. When exactly did they get away, Herr Pagel?"

"Round about half-past ten."

"Well, we know the place; a plan must be drawn up—thus, they may have got as far as this, or here they have perhaps hidden themselves. Gendarmes will come, fifty, a hundred, perhaps soldiers, too. By evening it'll be a real hunt."

"Charming!" said Studmann.

"I myself will be back as soon as possible. You, Pagel, go at once to the Manor and ring up police headquarters in Frankfurt. They will give you instructions. Afterwards you will have to ring up all gendarme stations in the neighborhood. . . . The Polish frontier has to be watched and the way to Berlin cut off. The phone here is to be only for incoming calls, no out-going calls here at all; inform the post office of that."

"My God!" cried Studmann, infected at last by the little man's energy. "Is it really so dangerous?"

"Four of the men are relatively not dangerous," said the principal warder. "*Souteneurs*, swindlers and cheats. But there's one, Matzke—he wouldn't worry about murder so long as he got clothes and money. Well, gentlemen, let's get started." And he shot out of the office like a rocket.

"Off, Pagel!" cried Studmann. "Send the old gentleman to me!"

Pagel ran through the park. Passing Fräulein Violet, who said something, he called out: "Convicts escaped!" and ran on. Pushing aside old Elias, who let him in, he ran to the phone in the hall. "Hello, hello. Exchange. Police headquarters in Frankfurt-on-the-Oder. Urgent. Urgent. No, at once. I'll hold on. . . . " In the doorways appeared frightened and astonished faces. Two housemaids looked at each other. What's the meaning of that queer look? he thought. Then Violet came into the hall. "What's up, Herr Pagel? The convicts?"

Noisily the door of the Geheimrat's room opened. "Who's bellowing in my house? In my house I do the bellowing!"

"Herr Geheimrat, please go to the office at once. Five convicts have made off."

Upstairs a servant girl laughed hysterically.

"And because of that you want me to go to your office?" the Geheimrat beamed. "Do you think they're going to come in order to look at me in your office? I told you at the time—get respectable people! Now I suppose every night I and my wife must look under the bed with a revolver as a torch."

"This is Neulohe Estate," said Pagel on the phone. "Neu-lo-he! On behalf of the administration of Meienburg Penitentiary I want to—"

"It's all right!" came an equable voice at the end of the wire. "We've already heard from Meienburg. Who's speaking? The bailiff? Well, you seem to be up to some fine larks. Couldn't you have kept your eyes peeled a bit more? Now listen. Ring off, and in the meantime I'll inform your exchange, and when it rings again it'll be the exchange giving you all gendarme stations in your district. All you need say to them is: 'Five convicts escaped; send every man to Neulohe—and jump to it.' Do this as quickly as you can, all our lines are engaged; the frontier's not thirteen miles off. . . ."

The Geheimrat had gone with his granddaughter to the office, nevertheless. Young Pagel went on telephoning; the servants were running about quite brainlessly. Sometimes one stood by him, panting, watching him and reading from his lips a message which was always the same. What crazy faces women can make when they're frightened, he thought, himself genuinely excited, too. A little upset and a little unhappy. Is the lady upstairs in tears? She must already be fearing for her bit of life. And while he went on repeating the same old warning, he was able to hear in what different ways people reacted to it:

"*Donnerwetter!*"

"You don't say so!"

"Just when I've got rheumatism in my leg!"

"But what are convicts doing in Neulohe?"

"Is there a reward offered?"

"Well, well! But there, today's Friday! It would happen when my wife's cooked a chicken!"

"Anyone can ring up and say he's speaking on behalf of police headquarters! Who are you, anyway?"

"What do you think, Inspector—boots? Or can I come in drill trousers?"

"Five's bad!"

And the appalling remark: "The one they may kill, perhaps in the next ten minutes, is alive and hasn't heard anything yet." Something rather gruesome arose from these words—guilt and complicity.

Pagel, telephoning, was considering in what way he had failed in this affair. Not in much, only in trifles. Where so many of the experienced had failed, no reasonable person could reproach him, the inexperienced. Wolfgang Pagel, however, who only a few months before had been so prepared to condone all his own transgressions—Wolfgang Pagel now thought otherwise. Or rather, he felt otherwise. Was it the work in the fields, or recent events, or was it the mention in Minna's letters of him becoming a man? What did it matter if others had trespassed more? He didn't want to have to reproach himself in any degree.

The gendarme stations were still on the line, the telephone rang constantly, there was the same message, the same cries of anger, of astonishment, of action. And all the time he could see the five men in convict garb, crouching like deer in some concealed corner of the woods, without money or weapons and of no great intelligence, but with one thing which did distinguish them from ordinary people: they had no inhibitions to stop them from doing what they wanted.

Wolfgang Pagel reflected that, not long ago, he had thought with pride, "I'm not tied to anything. I can do what I want. I'm free. . . ." Yes, Wolfgang Pagel—now you understand, you were free, unfettered like a wild animal. But humanity is not about doing what you want, but rather about doing what you must. And while he went on with his calls, thirty, fifty, seventy of them, he could see the healthy powers of life about to do battle with the sick; and suddenly the jokes about the Devil's Hussars appeared unsavory and the convicts' song impudent. Fifty, a hundred gendarmes were mounting their bicycles; making from all directions for one goal—Neulohe. He saw the officials in the police administration at Frankfurt. Telephones were ringing in dozens of police stations; there was the tap-tap-tap of Morse. In customs posts on the border, officials were putting on their caps, buckling up their belts with great care, examining their pistols—death was about!

Death! Five men capable of anything! And at a time when there seemed no unity anywhere, when everything was rotten and in collapse, at that moment life was at least united against one thing—death! Life was blocking all the highways; its eyes were everywhere. Police stood on the roads leading into the big towns, inspecting every passer-by—a scarf, a trouser leg might betray something. The slums, the dens where criminals hide, were being more closely watched than ever, and in the small towns the police were going into the alleys behind the houses, where they opened on to the gardens and yards.

Along the main roads they were warning pedestrians, drivers of carts, and truck drivers. A whole region between the Polish frontier and Berlin had come into movement. From the great presses in the printing works flowed police notices, proclamations and personal descriptions; these by this afternoon would be stuck on walls and billboards. Officials were examining the files of Liebschner, Kosegarten, Matzke, Wendt, Holdrian—from the report of former crimes hoping for hints of possible new ones, trying to divine fresh clues from the old. Where would this man try to go? Who were his friends? Who wrote to him while he was imprisoned?

Perhaps life no longer had its former strength and soundness; so much had been overthrown in recent years that life itself was sick. What it was now doing was possibly to a great extent only habit. The machine creaked and groaned—but it still revolved. It reached out once more—would it lay hold?

VI

How long had Wolfgang Pagel been at the telephone? An hour? Two hours? He didn't know. But when he left the Manor he saw the first results of his telephoning. Bicycle after bicycle stood against the office wall; gendarmes were in groups near the door and by the roadside, smoking, talking, some laughing. And more were coming, met with a "Hello" or expectant silence or a joke.

In the office they were graver. Maps were spread over the table; tensely Frau von Prackwitz, the old Geheimrat and Herr von Studmann examined them. A gendarme officer was pointing at something. At the window stood Marofke, pale and downcast. Obviously things had fared ill with him.

"The Polish frontier, Poland—quite out of the question," said the gendarme officer. "So far as we know, none of the five speak Polish; and Poland, anyway, is no field for criminals of their type. I'm convinced they mean to make their way as quickly as possible to Berlin. By night, of course, and on footpaths. All but one of them, pimps, swindlers, frauds. It's Berlin that attracts such fellows."

"But—" began Marofke.

"Don't interrupt, please," said the gendarme officer sharply. "Undoubtedly they will lie low in the woods till night. I'll try to catch them there with some of my men, although it's pretty hopeless—the woods are too large. Our chief job is to keep our eye on the smaller roads and the isolated villages at night. That's where they'll attempt to pass and get clothes and food. . . . We might possibly catch them tonight even; they'll still be in the district."

"Only don't tell my wife that, my dear sir," said the Geheimrat.

"If there's any place between here and Berlin which is absolutely safe from the scoundrels, it's Neulohe," said the gendarme officer, smiling. "That's

certain. We've got our headquarters here! No, it'll be bad for the isolated villages; we'll have to watch those. And solitary farms—but we'll warn them! And
even if we don't catch a glimpse of the five, we shall still know roughly where
they are. I imagine about thirty miles a night on the average—at first less, then
a bit more. If they have to stop much for food it will be less again. I assume the
first night they'll go north rather than west, so as to avoid this disturbed region.
Though, to be sure, Meienburg's that way." He turned to Marofke. "Has any of
them connections in Meienburg? Relatives—a girl—friends?"

"No."

"What do you mean, no?" asked the gendarme officer in sharp reproof.
"Don't you know, or haven't they any connections?"

"They haven't any," said the warder angrily.

"That is, as far as you know," sneered the gendarme officer. "But you don't
know very much, do you? Well, thank you. We shan't need you any longer, principal warder. Report to me before you leave with your detachment."

"Yes, sir!" The principal warder saluted and left the office. They watched
him go but no one said a word of farewell. Not even Studmann. The Geheimrat
started to hum "How swiftly, how swiftly, do beauty and greatness vanish!"

The gendarme officer smiled benevolently.

"He made a bad impression on me from the first," said Frau von Prackwitz.

"Herr Pagel thinks differently," observed Studmann.

"Excuse me a moment." Pagel dashed from the office.

Through the crowd of gendarmes Marofke, looking neither to the right
nor left, had passed with his ridiculous potbelly, his thin legs in irreproachably pressed trousers, his purple cheeks like the pouches of a hamster; he
walked with such energy that his cheeks trembled at every step. But, if he saw
nothing, he could not avoid hearing a gendarme ask in astonishment: "Who
the devil is that chap?"

"Good Lord, he's the one who let them escape."

"Oh, so it's because of him we've got to lie around in the woods at night!"

Without the slightest change of expression, Marofke passed on to the barracks, and sat down on the bench where, to the annoyance of the people of
Neulohe, he had so often sat.

The barracks resounded with the noise of packing and moving. In angry,
excited voices the warders were giving their orders; enraged, the prisoners
answered back. Marofke didn't get up. He knew there was nothing missing.
Not a blanket had been exchanged for tobacco, no sheet torn up for wicks, not
a spade forgotten in the fields; all in the best of order—except that five men
were missing. And even if they were caught today, which he did not believe,

that would not remove his disgrace. Five convicts had got away from him, and he was the cause of a detachment being withdrawn. That shame could never be removed. There was, of course, his report to the prison authorities. He had proved observant, had asked for the removal of those very five; even that, however, wouldn't clear him. The same pen-pushers who had rejected his application would do their utmost to minimize its importance—it was absolutely groundless, arrangements for removal could not be made as a result of such applications, the men would have had every right to complain. If Herr Marofke had really mistrusted them so very much, why had he let them out of sight for a moment? He ought to have been beside them night and day, instead of entrusting them to an inexperienced assistant warder. Yes, they would put all the blame on him, and in addition there would be the reports from the farm management and the gendarme officer!

Marofke had been long enough in the service to know that he could not be pensioned off because of this affair; but he wouldn't be promoted. And he had counted on that this coming autumn. Krebs, the head warder, was retiring at Michaelmas, and he had expected to get the post; he ought to. It was not vanity or ambition which made him wish for this advancement; it was something else. At home he had a daughter, a somewhat old-maidish creature of whom he was very fond; and she would have liked passionately to become a teacher. With the salary of head warder he might perhaps have been able to help her—now she would have to become a cook. Life was idiotic. Five men had run away because a young fellow chattered to a warder on duty, and therefore he wouldn't be able to gratify his daughter's dearest wish.

He looked up. Young Pagel had joined him on the bench; with a smile he was holding out his cigarette case and saying: "Idiots!"

Marofke would have liked to refuse. Yet he felt obliged to this young fellow for following him from the office, for letting everyone see him sitting beside a disgraced man. He means well, he thought, and took a cigarette. How could the other know what were the consequences of his foolishness? Everyone committed blunders.

"I'll take care, officer," said Pagel, "that it's I who make the report to your administration. And it shall be of a kind to please you."

"That's nice of you. But it's not worth while your spoiling your own position here, since it won't help me much. But pay attention to what I'm now going to tell you. I won't speak to anyone else; they wouldn't listen to me anyway. Did you understand what the gendarme officer was saying?"

"I was only in there a minute, but what he said seemed clear to me, officer."

"Good. Not for me, though. And why not? Because they're the sort of things a man thinks of when he doesn't know convicts. I'd be all right if Wendt and Holdrian only were at large. They're stupid enough to carry out half a dozen bad burglaries and perhaps hold-ups, just for a little food and clothes on the way. Even if they do reach Berlin they'll have let themselves in for six to eight years' penal servitude, only to get there. But they'll never do it. Every burglary will be a clue."

"What will they do, then?"

"Well, Matzke, Liebschner and Kosegarten are with them. Bright lads who think a bit more about what they do. Their idea is always: whatever we take's got to be worth it. They won't break into any farmhouse at the risk of a year in jug at least, just to find some plowboy's old corduroy jacket, which they wouldn't even dream of wearing."

"But they'll have to obtain clothes somewhere. They won't get far in prison dress."

"Of course," said Marofke, putting his finger to his nose with that old superiority which looked so conceited. "And since they're cunning and have thought of that, and because they're prudent and don't want to steal clothes, what follows?"

Pagel didn't know.

"Someone will get clothes for them," Marofke gently explained. "They have accomplices here in Neulohe, one or several. You can take it from me that hard-boiled lads like Kosegarten and Liebschner don't take a powder without any preparation. It's all been arranged, and because I didn't find out how they arranged it—for it was done here by notes or signs, they couldn't have done it in Meienburg!—because I've been stupid, it's really quite right in the end for everyone to blame me."

"But, officer, how could they, here under all our eyes? And who in Neulohe would have lent themselves to such a thing?"

The warder shrugged his shoulders. "If you only knew how cunning someone is who wants to regain his freedom! You yourself spend your time thinking of a hundred different things, but a prisoner is thinking all day and half the night about one thing only: how to get away. You talk about our eyes! We see nothing. When a convict goes out to work and starts to roll himself a cigarette and finds he has no tobacco and chucks the cigarette paper down in the mud, right in front of you, you march on with the gang. And three minutes later along comes another in the know and picks it up and reads what's scribbled on it. . . . Perhaps nothing—it's only folded in such and such a way, which means this and that."

"It seems a little improbable."

"Nothing's improbable with them," said Marofke, now in his element. "You just think of a prison, Pagel: iron and cement, locks and bolts, and chains too. And walls and doors and threefold supervision and guards outside and inside! Yet you can take my word for it, there isn't a prison in the whole world which is absolutely shut. On one side an enormous organization, and on the other an individual in the middle of iron and stone! Yet time and again we hear that a letter's gone out and no one saw it, that money or a steel file has come in, and no knows how. If that can be done in prison with all its organization, isn't it possible out here in our unguarded work gangs, under our very eyes?"

"It's always possible," said Pagel, "that they could manage to write a letter. But there must be someone here also who is in league with them, who wants to read it."

"And why shouldn't there be someone, Pagel? What do you know about it? What do I? It's only necessary for someone to be living here who was in the war with one of my lads. They've only to look at each other and the glance of my one says, 'Help, comrade!'—and the plot is on foot. Someone here may once have been on remand, and my chap was in the next cell on the same business; and every night through the cell window they told one another about their troubles—the damage is done! But it needn't be that. That would be an accident, and it doesn't need to be that. Women are not accidents; everywhere and always they come into it."

"What women?" asked Pagel.

"What women, Pagel? All women. That is, I obviously don't mean all of them, but there's a certain type everywhere which is as fond of such fellows as many people are of venison when it's really high. They think a convict who has had time to rest himself is better than an ordinary man, is more knowing, so to speak—you understand what I mean. Women like that would do anything to get one in their bed all to themselves. Harboring felons and so on, they don't consider that, they've never heard of it. . . ."

"There may be such women in Berlin, officer," objected Pagel, "but surely not in the country?"

"How do you know, young man, what things are like here, or the women either?" asked Marofke, immensely superior. "You're a nice chap, the only one who's been decent to me here, but you're a bit hazy. You always think things aren't so bad after all, and that what's eaten isn't as hot as what's cooked. Young fellow, you ought to have grasped early this morning that sometimes it can be even hotter."

Pagel looked uncomfortable, with an expression like a cat's in a thunderstorm. And it really was thundering, and uncomfortably so.

"I explained to you this morning all my ideas about it," said Marofke, sighing. "I didn't believe you could help me much, but I did think, The young man'll keep his eyes open. But that's not exactly what you've done, Lieutenant; you wouldn't have got the Iron Cross for that in wartime. But there, it's all right, I know what a young man's like. But please do this for me now—do keep your eyes open a little the next few days. I don't think all the gendarmes together, whatever they say, will catch my five chaps. You're here, though, and it would be very nice if you could write to the administration in a few days' time: We've got the five and Marofke told us how to catch them. . . . What do you think?"

"Gladly, officer," said Pagel obligingly. "And what is it you think I ought to do?"

"Man, have you got cotton wool in your ears?" Marofke jumped up. "Haven't you any brains? I can't tell you anything more. Keep your eyes open, that's all. I don't ask anything else. No need to play the detective or skulk in corners, nor even try to be cunning—only keep your eyes open!"

"All right, then," said Pagel, rising. "I'll see what I can do."

"You know what to do," replied Marofke hurriedly. "I'm convinced that they have accomplices in the village, one or more, probably girls, but not necessarily. And while the police are all over the place here, they'll keep under cover in the woods, in the village, who knows! It's you who must use your eyes. In three or four days' time, when it's a bit quieter, our old pals will set forth, properly, by train, and well dressed. . . ."

"I'll look out," promised Pagel.

"Do it, too," Marofke begged. "Looking out is harder than you think. And there's another thing you ought to know. What they have on their backs. . . ."

"Yes?"

"That's State property. And every prisoner knows that if he makes away with one piece of it he'll be wanted for larceny. A missing scarf may mean six months' penal servitude. So when really experienced lads bolt they take care that their things get sent as soon as possible to the prison. Usually by post—in which case I'll let you know. If so much as a single piece turns up here, then you must keep watch like a pointer. Don't think that it's something I've left behind, because I never forget a thing. If it's only a gray prison sock with a red rim, there's something wrong. Do you even know what our shirts look like? Or the mufflers? Come along—I'll show you."

The principal warder did not, however, get as far as initiating Pagel into these secrets. Down the village street came ten bicycles, bringing nine warders from the prison, all belted, with rubber truncheons swinging and their faces dripping with sweat. In front rode a fat flabby man in a thick crumpled black suit. His belly almost rested on the handle bars. When the principal warder saw this threatening colossus he stared, forgetting everything else, including young Pagel, and murmured in dismay: "The labor inspector himself!"

Pagel saw the fat man, breathing heavily, descend from his bicycle, which a zealous warder held while he wiped the sweat from his forehead. He did not look at Marofke.

"Inspector," said Marofke imploringly with his hand still at his cap badge. "Report Harvest Detachment Five Neulohe, a senior warder, four warders . . . forty-five men . . ."

"Where is the Manor office, young fellow?" demanded the colossus distantly. "Please show me the way. As for you, Marofke"—the inspector seemed to be interested in the gabled wall of the barracks, on which the stone cross stood out with its somewhat lighter red—"as for you, Marofke, you will soon find out that you're finished." He went on looking at the wall, considering. Then, in an indifferent tone: "You will immediately, Marofke, see if the footwear of the prisoners has been greased according to regulations and if laced up in conformity with orders. That is, bow knots and no others!"

One of the warders sniggered. Marofke, the little vain potbellied principal warder, replied, pale: "Yes, inspector," and disappeared round the corner of the barracks.

Pagel, leading the way to the office, thought bitterly about the little man who, although he had taken the greatest trouble and borne the heaviest anxieties, was snubbed by everybody. No one, however, had cast any reproach at himself . . . despite all the mistakes he had made. He resolved, if an opportunity offered, to rehabilitate Herr Marofke. He could understand how difficult it was for anyone who looked so absurd to obtain respect—however efficient he might be. Efficiency was not at all the chief thing; it was more important to look like it.

"So this is the office," said the inspector. "Thank you, young man. Who are you?"

"A friend of Herr Marofke's," answered Pagel rudely.

The fat man was not to be put out. "I was thinking of your occupation," he said, still friendly.

"Pupil," replied Pagel with fury.

"There you are!" beamed the fat man. "Then you are certainly suited to Marofke. Pupil! He, too, has a lot to learn." And, nodding, he opened the door.

Wolfgang Pagel had had another lesson, which was that one should not vent ill-humor on those whom it delights.

VII

Half an hour later Harvest Detachment Five moved off from Neulohe, and a quarter of an hour afterwards the gendarmes set out on their battue through the woods. From the office windows all four—the Geheimrat, the gendarme officer, young Pagel and Frau von Prackwitz—watched the convicts' departure. It was very different from their arrival. There was no singing, no one smiled; they went away with lowered heads, sullen faces, and their feet dragging in the dust. This dull shuffling along had in it something despairing, an evil rhythm, a "We are the enemies of this world"—that was what it sounded like to Wolfgang.

No doubt the prisoners had been thinking about their escaped fellow sufferers; burning envy had filled them when they considered the freedom of those five who now haunted the woods, while they were to return, under an escort of loaded carbines, to their solitary stone cells—punished because the others had escaped. From them had been taken the sight of distant fields, a laughing girlish face, a hare jumping along the potato furrows—all exchanged for the faded yellow dreariness of cell walls, because five others were scampering about in freedom.

In front of the column went the principal warder, Marofke. On the right he had to push a bicycle, on the left another; he wasn't even allowed to watch over his men now. And behind the column trod the inspector, with spiky eyebrows and elephant feet, alone. His fat, white face raised, expressionless. Strong white teeth flashed in his mouth. At the side of the road Vi had stood to take stock. Seeing her there, Pagel had been angry.

The Geheimrat spoke to his daughter. "I should advise you, incidentally, not to sleep in the Villa alone with your stupid Räder the next few nights. All respect to our clever gendarme officer—but safe is safe."

"Perhaps one of the gentlemen would . . . ?" began Frau von Prackwitz, looking from Pagel, who was staring out of the window, to Studmann.

Although Marofke had specifically warned against any playing at being detective, Pagel preferred being free in the nights that followed, to do a bit of looking and hearing around—to keep his eyes open, as he'd been told. So he looked at no one but out of the window—but the convicts had left at last, and the barracks looked like an empty red box.

"I shall be very pleased to sleep with you," said von Studmann—and flushed terribly.

The old Geheimrat bleated, and looked out of the window, too. Pagel shrugged his shoulders. The awkwardnesses of the adroit are always the worst.

When a completely conventional man like Studmann makes a slip, everyone turns red.

"That's settled, then. Thanks very much, Herr von Studmann," said Frau von Prackwitz in her deep, even voice.

"It will cost you a heap of money to restore the barracks to its old condition," declared the Geheimrat. "All this trellis-work and bolts must disappear as soon as possible, and the doorway be made free again."

"Perhaps we could leave the place as it is for the moment," suggested Studmann cautiously. "It would be a pity to tear everything out and have to put it back next year."

"Next year? No detachment's coming to Neulohe again!" announced the Geheimrat. "I have had about enough of your mother's nervousness, Eva. Well, I'll go up now and see how she is. All these green police coats will have cheered her up, of course! What an upset! And I keep asking myself what you're going to do about your potatoes." With this last thrust he left the office. The jealous father had taken a sufficient revenge for Studmann's flush, for his daughter's momentary embarrassment (perceived only by him), and for the accentuated indifference with which young Pagel was staring out of the window.

"Yes, what's going to happen to our potatoes?" asked Frau von Prackwitz, looking doubtfully at Studmann.

"I don't think that will offer any great difficulty," said Studmann hurriedly, glad to have found something to talk about. "Unemployment and hunger are on the increase, and if we let it be known in the local town that we are digging potatoes, not paying cash, but giving ten or fifteen pounds in kind per hundredweight, we'll get all the people we want. We shall have to send, two, three, perhaps four carts into town every morning to fetch the people and take them back at night, but we can manage that."

"A nuisance—and expensive," sighed Frau von Prackwitz. "Oh, if those convicts . . ."

"But far cheaper than if the potatoes are frozen. You, Pagel, won't be a landed gentleman any longer. You will have to be in the fields all day and distribute tokens, one for every hundredweight. . . ."

"Thank Heaven!" said Pagel submissively.

"I have to be away tomorrow," went on Studmann, "so I will also get a start on with this business—put an advertisement in the town paper, and settle things with the labor exchange."

"You're going away? Now, when the convicts . . . !" Frau von Prackwitz was very annoyed.

"Only a day in Frankfurt," said Studmann. "Today is the twenty-ninth, you know." Frau von Prackwitz didn't understand. "The rent is due the day after tomorrow," he added with emphasis. "I've already been in negotiation about it, but now it's high time to scrape together the money. The dollar is a hundred and sixty million marks, and we shall have to raise an enormous amount—at any rate, an enormous amount of paper."

"Rent! Rent! When convicts are loose in the district!" cried Frau Eva impatiently. "Did my father press for—?"

"Herr Geheimrat said nothing, but . . ."

"I am certain my father would not approve of your going off at this moment. In a way, you have taken over the job of protecting us." She smiled.

"I shall be back by evening. In my opinion, the rent ought to be paid exactly on the minute. That is a point of honor with me."

"Herr von Studmann! Papa loses nothing if he gets the rent a week later at the current dollar exchange. I will speak with him."

"I don't think the old gentleman will prove very amenable. You have just heard him demand that the harvesters' barracks be immediately put into its former condition."

"Anything might happen now, any minute!" pleaded Frau von Prackwitz. "Please, Herr von Studmann, don't leave me alone now . . . I have such a disagreeable feeling."

Herr von Studmann was embarrassed. For a moment he looked at Pagel, who was himself looking silently out of the window, but he immediately forgot about him again. "I would really like to say yes, but I'm sure you'll understand; I don't want to have to ask the Geheimrat for a postponement. It is really a point of honor. I took the management over from Prackwitz, and I am responsible to him. We are able to pay—I've gone into that thoroughly. I don't want to look ridiculous. In life we have to be exact, punctual. . . ."

"Ridiculous!" cried Frau von Prackwitz angrily. "I tell you it's the same to my father when we pay, since my husband's not here. He's only like that in order to annoy him. I tell you, when I think of the Villa, alone there with Vi and those stupid servants and the still more stupid Räder, and over five hundred yards to the nearest cottage. . . . Oh, it's not that!" she exclaimed, irritated and surprised at meeting another Studmann and learning something at last of the drawbacks of pedantry and trustworthiness. "I have a disagreeable feeling, and I don't want to be alone these next few days."

"But you have nothing to fear," declared Studmann, with that obstinate gentleness which can drive excited persons mad. "The gendarme officer is also of the opinion that the convicts have left the district. After all, an agreement is an agreement, especially among relatives. It must be carried out to the letter, and I am ultimately answerable for that. Prackwitz would rightly be able to reproach me—"

"The Rittmeister!" said Pagel in a low voice from the window. "He's driving up to the farm now."

"Who?" asked Studmann, dumbfounded.

"My husband? I thought he was shooting his five-hundredth rabbit!"

"Impossible!" said Studmann, yet in that moment he saw the Rittmeister getting out of a car.

"I had this uneasy feeling all day," declared Frau von Prackwitz.

"Just what I thought," said the Rittmeister entering, to shake hands, beaming, with the surprised trio. "A full council meeting once more to debate those quite insoluble problems my friend Studmann always solves in the end. Fine! Just as I thought; everything the same. Don't pull such a face, Studmann. Your still unknown friend Schröck asks, by the way, to let you know you are, now as formerly, the right man for him. I'm good only to shoot rabbits. But, tell me, my dears, what are all the green frogs doing in Neulohe? I saw a whole section marching away into the woods. Is my father-in-law thinking of catching his poachers? That reminds me, I met our old Kniebusch this morning in the station at Frankfurt, quite broken up; his case is on today, about Bäumer. . . . So none of you, including my respected father-in-law, has been fretting himself much about the old chap. He might really have been spared that! Well, I shall have to get down to work again. And the gendarmes? Convicts have bolted? The gang's withdrawn?" He laughed heartily, dropping into a chair. And the more he caught sight of the surprised, embarrassed faces, the more he laughed.

"But, my dears, you didn't need to get rid of me for that. I could have committed such stupidities by myself. Magnificent. I suppose mother-in-law is shivering with fright as usual? And the young gentleman here doesn't think of joining in the drive? Well, if I was your boss, Pagel, you'd have to go. It's a question of honor; there ought to be someone at least from the estate. Otherwise they'll think we're afraid. . . ."

"Very good, sir," said Pagel. "I'll go." And went.

"There!" beamed the Rittmeister. "Now he's out of the way. The youngster can't be always standing round here without lifting a hand; after all, he's supposed to be working here. Well, children, now tell me your worries. You can't imagine how fit and rested and restored I feel. Every day a pine-needle bath and ten hours' sleep—that does one good! Now then, Studmann, out with the worst. What about the rent?"

"I am fetching the money tomorrow from Frankfurt," replied Studmann without glancing at Frau von Prackwitz.

Strange. All of a sudden he no longer felt so pleased that he had had his way about that trip.

VIII

When toward evening the milk cart came back to the farm, and the milkman handed over the postbag, Studmann found in it a letter from Dr. Schröck which threw some light on Rittmeister Joachim von Prackwitz's sudden return.

Dear Herr von Studmann [read the letter from the gruff and rather truculent consultant for nervous and mental disorders] this will reach you at the same time as your friend Prackwitz, who did not become mine. A visit from him as a paying patient will always be a pleasure to me, but to avoid misunderstandings I should like to inform you now that psychopathic persons like Rittmeister von Prackwitz, unstable and inclined to moods of depression and excitement, with a considerable craving for self-assertion together with weak intellect, are not really curable—certainly not at his age. What is required in most cases of this sort is to encourage interest in some harmless occupation, such as stamp collecting, cultivating black roses, or finding out the German for foreign words; then they can't do any damage and may even become bearable.

I had got Herr von Prackwitz almost as far as five hundred rabbits and was making extremely broad hints about the record being a thousand when he—devil take him!—hit on the idea that he ought to cure my patients, since I couldn't. This he set about doing with all the enthusiasm of the ignoramus. There is a Russian princess who has been with me for over eight years, believing herself pregnant all the time and who has been going round a pond in my park these eight years, convinced that, if she circles this pond ten times a morning, she will be delivered. What he did was actually to drag this excellently paying and completely satisfied patient, weighing two and a half hundredweight, ten times round the pond; whereupon, if she did not give birth, nevertheless her heart and mental condition are in a state of collapse. He asked a beautiful schizophrenic for a lock of hair, the girl cropped herself bald—and the visit of her relatives is expected. With his fists he attempted to change the peculiar disposition of an unfortunately abnormal gentleman who had made certain proposals to him; and in his innocence he helped Reichsfreiherr Baron von Bergen, whom you have met, to escape again. In short, through Herr von Prackwitz I have lost patients to the value of about three thousand gold marks monthly. Therefore I say, thus far and no farther. I have made it clear to him that his presence in Neulohe on the first of October is absolutely essential—I am aware, of course, of all his troubles—and he is in agreement with this.

Should you, dear Herr Studmann, be inconvenienced by his return, this will make me very glad, because I take it that you will then come here all the sooner.

Yours, etc., etc.

"Well, well," sighed Herr von Studmann, striking a match and setting fire to the letter. "So he's back again to help us over October first. It ought to be all right; at least he doesn't seem so touchy now. If only he won't do anything too silly. Considerable craving for self-assertion together with weak intelligence! Nasty, but I'll manage somehow."

Studmann was to make a mistake. Herr von Prackwitz had, on the very day, several irreparable blunders behind him.

IX

As the Rittmeister earlier that morning had jumped at the very last moment into a compartment of the train from Berlin to Frankfurt-on-the-Oder, he had been greeted by a very surly voice. "Beg pardon, full up."

Although an obvious lie, because only two of the eight seats were occupied in a compartment already in motion, it was not this which had made the Rittmeister flush. He had recognized the face of the man who was so impolite. "Oh, no, my dear Lieutenant, I am not always turned away so easily as from my own wood," he said smilingly.

The Lieutenant too flushed deeply, and replied also with an allusion to that earlier event: "Out of your father-in-law's wood, I think, Rittmeister?"

They smiled at each other, both recalling the scene in the Black Dale, the sentry's whistle, the Lieutenant's abrupt order to retire. Both gentlemen were thinking themselves very intelligent and superior to the other; the Lieutenant because he had concealed from the father his connection with the daughter, and the Rittmeister because, in spite of the other's rudeness, he had found out about the buried weapons.

Their next remarks were worthy of notice. The Lieutenant said in a friendly, innocent way: "And how is your daughter?"

"Thank you, quite well," replied the Rittmeister. Good bait catches fine fish, he thought and went on: "Everything all right in the Black Dale?"

"Yes," said the Lieutenant coldly.

Conversation was over. Each of the intelligent pair believed he had found out what he wanted—the Lieutenant that the daughter had not prattled—the Rittmeister that the arms were still in the wood. Instinctively both looked across at the third man in the compartment. He, busy with a paper, sat silently in his corner, but now looked up, lowering his paper.

Although he, like the Lieutenant, was in mufti, his face and the way he held himself betrayed one whom the constant wearing of uniform had made stiff. In spite of his far too large lounge suit, the officer could be seen in him—it was not necessary to observe the monocle hanging from a wide black cord or the Hohenzollern order in his buttonhole. His glance, heavy and slow, had been made cautious by endless experience. The bloodless face, with its thin skin, looked as if it were supported on the bones without interposing flesh; the scanty pale-blond hair was carefully flattened down in long wisps, through which a parchment-like skin gleamed. The most noticeable thing about this barely disguised death's head was the mouth, a mouth without lips, a line sharp as the slit of an automatic machine, a mouth which appeared to have tasted every bitterness.

I must have seen him somewhere, thought the Rittmeister, quickly visualizing the picture pages of those journals seen in recent weeks.

With a slender-fingered, trembling child's hand, the disguised officer raised his monocle and the Rittmeister felt himself scrutinized. But just as he was about to introduce himself, the glance passed on to the young Lieutenant.

"Herr von Prackwitz, tenant of an estate at Neulohe, retired cavalry officer," said the Lieutenant hurriedly. One felt that the glance had given him a jerk.

"Delighted," said the other without, however, giving his own name, which did not at all disturb the Rittmeister, who knew that it was really his duty to have recognized a high officer. The monocle fell. "But sit down! Had a good harvest?"

Rittmeister and Lieutenant sat down. "Oh, the harvest's not altogether bad," replied the Rittmeister with the caution usual among farmers, to whom praise of a harvest seems like a challenge to heaven. "I was not in Neulohe these last weeks," he added.

"Herr von Prackwitz is the son-in-law of Herr von Teschow," explained the Lieutenant.

"Evidently," said the officer mysteriously. To what this "evidently" referred, whether to the absence from Neulohe or to the family relationship, was not evident. Or it might refer to the harvest.

The Lieutenant, whose name—as the Rittmeister now noticed—had also not been mentioned, assisted again: "Herr von Prackwitz is the tenant of his father-in-law."

"Clever man," said he with the monocle. "Visited me once or twice recently. You know that?"

The Rittmeister did not, and couldn't imagine what his rustic father-in-law might have to do with this parchment-like soldier. "No," he said, confused. "I've been away, as I mentioned."

"Clever," said the other gratingly. "The kind who always pay only when they have the goods in their hand. Family feelings hurt?"

"Oh, no!" protested the Rittmeister. "I, too, am always having difficulties with—"

"Who wants to join the trip must first take his ticket," proclaimed the officer with a bitterness which no word in the conversation made understandable. "Won't perhaps even know the definition. You understand?"

The Rittmeister did not, but he nodded profoundly.

"Suppose," went on the officer, "you have a car . . ."

"I haven't," explained the Rittmeister. "But I shall buy one."

"Today? Tomorrow?"

"Certainly in a few days."

"Either today or tomorrow, otherwise no use," said the officer, seizing hold of his paper again.

"I don't know." The Rittmeister hesitated. Was this man with the monocle a representative of a motor-car factory? "After all, it's a large sum of . . . I don't know if the money . . ."

"Money!" cried the other contemptuously, crumpling his paper fiercely. "Who pays cash for cars? Give a bill!" He vanished behind his newspaper.

This time the Lieutenant gave no help, but sat in his corner with such an expression of repudiation that the Rittmeister withdrew into his, and, remembering his own newspaper, also began to crumple it fiercely. But somehow he couldn't read. Continually his thoughts strayed to those mysterious words about a too-clever father-in-law, a ticket which must be paid for first, and a car which need not be paid for . . . In spite of many weeks in a peaceful sanatorium he was seized by a very impulsive anger, and when he thought of how the young man had treated him in the wood, he discovered that that matter hadn't yet been settled; while, if he took into account his treatment today at the hands of the parchment-like man, he felt even more that something ought to be done. . . .

The pair opposite had begun to whisper, which was unmannerly, the more so because they were obviously whispering about him. He was, after all, a reputable officer and a successful farmer. If you don't discuss such things in front of ladies, you certainly don't whisper them in front of elderly gentlemen. He had had a good deal to drink, and he now gave his paper a powerful blow—the row could begin. But the train was slowing down—they were already at Frankfurt; he would have to get out and change. His anger ought to have been quicker.

"You're getting out, Rittmeister?" asked the Lieutenant politely and groped for the other's suitcase.

"I'm changing! Don't trouble yourself, please," exclaimed the Rittmeister angrily. Despite which the Lieutenant lowered the case from the rack. "I have been asked to inform you," he said in a low voice without looking at the Rittmeister, "that we are having a sort of old comrades' reunion the day after tomorrow, October the first, in Ostade. At six in the morning, please. Uniform. Weapons, if any, to be brought." Then he looked at the Rittmeister, who was overwhelmed; so overwhelmed that he said: "At your service!"

"Porter!" shouted the Lieutenant from the window and busied himself with the Rittmeister's luggage.

Just as things had become interesting one must leave. The Rittmeister looked at the gentleman in the corner. He had stretched out his legs, his monocle dangled from its band; he seemed to be sleeping. Hesitant but respectful, the Rittmeister stepped across the somnolent legs, murmuring: "Good morning!"

"But with a car, you understand?" muttered the sleeper and dozed off again.

The Rittmeister stood on the platform in a daze. For the third time the porter asked where he was to carry the luggage. First the Rittmeister said to the Neulohe train, then he said Ostade.

"Oh, you want to go to Ostade. Then you're on the wrong line. You ought to have gone by Landberg," said the porter.

"No, no!" cried the Rittmeister, impatient. "I want a car. Can I buy a car here?"

"Here?" asked the porter, looking first at the passenger and then at the platform. "Here?"

"Yes, in Frankfurt."

"Of course you can buy cars here, sir," the porter reassured him. "Here you can get anything that way. That's what they all do. They come by train from Berlin and buy their cars in Frankfurt . . ."

The Rittmeister followed the man. Everything was clear now. He had seen the officer who had been described to him a hundred times, whose face he had never before glimpsed: Major Rückert, who was plotting the big *Putsch* against the Government. It was coming off early the day after tomorrow, at six, in Ostade, and the Rittmeister was to be present, with a car.

Father-in-law was too clever. He wanted to wait and see if the *Putsch* was successful before he bought his ticket. The Rittmeister, however, wasn't so clever about money. He would buy a car at once, on credit. That might not be businesslike, but it was the right thing.

Docilely he let himself be taken to the waiting room, where he sat down pensively, tipped the porter, and ordered a coffee. He was not thinking now about the *Putsch* with Major Rückert and the impolite Lieutenant. That affair had been settled: he would be in Ostade the day after tomorrow at six o'clock. There would be no hitch, and no need to be uneasy about it. He was not the over-prudent, crafty Geheimrat Horst-Heinz von Teschow: he was Rittmeister von Prackwitz, and when an old comrade said to him: "Join us!" he went along, without inquisitiveness. The little he had heard was enough for him. The Reichswehr and the Black Reichswehr were in it; that is, the old soldiers and the young ones, against a Government which printed worthless money, which had given up the Ruhr fight, and which wanted to "agree" with the French. One didn't need to reflect about such things—the *Putsch* was in order.

What did absorb him, while he stirred the coffee, was his car! It was of course already "his," although he didn't even know yet what it should look like. He had wanted one for a long time, only he had never had the money—and, as a matter of fact, there was none now. Indeed, he was traveling to Neulohe so as to be on the spot when the rent for the farm fell due on October the first; that is, the day after tomorrow—a difficult time. The Rittmeister was like a child. When a child has managed ten times not to take off shoes and stockings and splash in the water, it only requires the boy from next door to say the eleventh time: "Ah, it's so warm today!" In a minute the child, in spite of all commands, goes bare-legged and splashing. The Major had said that he ought to buy a car. Money was scarce, scarcer than ever, and the car would have to go on a dangerous adventure at once. But the Rittmeister didn't think a moment of that. He didn't even think of the *Putsch* and the Government to be overthrown; all he thought of was that he could at last buy a car. This *Putsch* was a splendid affair; it procured him a car.

The Rittmeister reviewed all the cars of his friends and acquaintances. He hesitated between a Mercedes and a Horch. Cheap ones were not considered. If one was to have a car, it couldn't look like a country doctor's—it had to look good; and since it was bought on credit, a bit more or less didn't matter. . . . No, the problem was not the car—it was where to get a chauffeur quickly, one who would look all right at the wheel; otherwise the pleasure of sitting behind him was halved. And the thing had to be done quickly, because the Rittmeister wanted, at the least in two or three hours, to be on the way to Neulohe in his own car. . . . And then there was the garage. Which would be the best place for a garage, close to the Villa?

The Rittmeister, wrapped up in his thoughts, resembled extraordinarily that retired officer who, a few months before, had sat at the gaming table, and who, out of sheer longing not to miss a single stake, couldn't wait to learn the rules of play. Once again he didn't know the game, and he was staking higher than he could afford. He might indeed buy some sort of corrugated-iron garage, but such things looked like nothing at all. . . .

"Herr Rittmeister," said for the third time a humble voice at the next table.

"Well, I never!" Starting out of his dreams and projects, he stared in surprise at the forester, who sat in his best clothes behind a glass of beer. "What are you doing in Frankfurt, Kniebusch?"

"The court case, Herr Rittmeister!" said the forester reproachfully. "My case about Bäumer."

"Well," nodded the Rittmeister, "I'm glad the rascal's to be sentenced at last. What do you think he'll get, then?"

"But, Herr Rittmeister," declared the forester solemnly, "it's me who's accused. It's me they want to sentence. I'm supposed to have done him grievous bodily harm!"

"Hasn't that dirty business been settled yet?" The Rittmeister was amazed. "Herr von Studmann wrote nothing about it. Come and sit at my table and tell me about the case. The cart seems to have lost its way badly, but perhaps I've come just at the right time to pull it out of the mess."

"Oh, thank you, thank you, Herr Rittmeister! I always told my wife: 'If only the Rittmeister was here, he'd soon get me out of it.'" And having not ineffectually appealed to old soldierly sentiments, the forester fetched the stale dregs of his beer and poured out his heart slowly and with many lamentations. The Rittmeister listened. Then, with the same *élan* which had been his about the car, he threw himself into legal affairs. Nor did he refrain from some bitter reflections on how everything was neglected even by the most reliable people when he wasn't there, and how he had to do everything himself. Pettifogging lawyers, poachers, the dollar and the Socialists were cursed, and he did not forget to make it clear to the forester that his employer was actually Geheimrat von Teschow, and that the business really had nothing whatever to do with him, von Prackwitz.

"Listen, Kniebusch," he said finally. "Your case comes on at half-past ten, eh? Actually I have a lot to do—I'm going to buy a car, you know, and shall have to engage a chauffeur, too . . ."

"A car! That will please Frau von Prackwitz."

The Rittmeister was not so sure; it was a point he preferred not to discuss. "I'll go with you to the court and give the gentlemen there a real piece of my mind. . . . You may rely on it that the whole thing will be settled in ten minutes, Kniebusch; one has only to put matters in a proper light, and it's high time that this persecution of landed property was stopped. Well, all that is going to be changed the day after tomorrow—you'll be surprised, Kniebusch."

The other pricked up his ears.

But the Rittmeister changed the subject. "And immediately afterwards I'll buy the car, get a chauffeur—a good chauffeur's a condition of purchase—and then I'll take you to Neulohe. You can save your fare, Kniebusch."

The forester's thanks knew no limit; this program delighted him, and wisely he suppressed the doubt which he perhaps still entertained that his case, in spite of the Rittmeister's intervention, might not pass off so smoothly. Herr von Prackwitz was now in a hurry. With his long legs he steered himself through the town of Frankfurt as though each step brought him nearer the car he yearned for; and a little behind trotted Kniebusch, puffing.

And thus they got to the court fifteen minutes too early. Nevertheless the Rittmeister pressed on to the courtroom indicated in the summons—where they knocked, listened, warily opened the door. The room was dirty, dreary and empty. Intercepting an usher, they showed him the summons. He looked from one to the other. . . .

"Is it you?" he asked the Rittmeister.

"Good heavens, no!" The Rittmeister did not at all like this, however readily he might be espousing the case.

"Oh, you then! Well, just wait a little! It'll take a little time yet. Your case will be called."

Sighing, the Rittmeister sat down with the forester on one of those benches where, perhaps because of their construction, perhaps because of the situation, no person can keep still. The corridor was dingy and deserted. People kept coming; their steps, however softly they trod, reverberated from stone walls and floor and ceiling. In the gray light they peered short-sightedly at the numbers on the doors, made up their minds to knock, and listened a long while before they entered.

Angrily the Rittmeister stared at a notice on the wall opposite, announcing "No Smoking. No Spitting." Underneath was a spittoon. He might now have been running around Frankfurt acquiring a magnificent car and going for a trial drive, instead of sitting in this dreary corridor out of pure good nature. The affair had really nothing to do with him at all.

"What a time it's taking!" he cried angrily, although it was no more than twenty-five minutes past ten.

The forester perceived the restlessness of a companion whom it was so very important to retain. Moreover he had been meditating on what the Ritt-meister had alluded to.

"The weapons are still in the Black Dale," he said discreetly.

"Shush . . ." went the Rittmeister, so loudly that some one at the far end of the corridor started, and turned inquiringly. Waiting till the man had dis-appeared into a room, he asked in a low voice: "How do you know about that, Kniebusch?"

"I had another look yesterday afternoon," whispered the ever-inquisi-tive forester. "One likes to know what is happening in one's own wood, Herr Rittmeister!"

"Oh," said the Rittmeister importantly. "And if they are still there today, tomorrow they won't be."

The forester pondered. The Rittmeister had used the word "tomorrow" twice already.

"Are you buying a car because of that, sir?" he asked cautiously.

The Rittmeister had traveled in an express train with an important man, the leader of a *Putsch*; he had brand-new information. It was very irritating, then, for the forester to presume to know as much as he himself did.

"But what do you know about this business, Herr Kniebusch?" he asked ill-humoredly.

"Oh, nothing at all, Herr Rittmeister," replied the forester apologetically, aware that he had blundered somehow, and not wishing to admit that he was fully in the secret until he knew which way the wind was blowing. People in the village talked such a lot, however. They had been saying a long time that something was going to happen soon, but no one knew anything about the day or hour. Only the Rittmeister knew that!

"I have said nothing," declared the Rittmeister, who nevertheless felt flattered. "How have the villagers got hold of such an idea?"

"Oh . . . I don't know whether I ought to talk about it."

"You can with me."

"Well, there's this Lieutenant. . . . You know him too, Herr Rittmeister, the one who was so rude to you. . . . He's been in the village a few times and spoken to the people."

"Oh!" The Rittmeister was annoyed that the Lieutenant had spoken with the villagers and no doubt also with the forester, but not with him. He did not want to show this, however. "Well, I don't mind telling you, Kniebusch, that I have just come from Berlin with this Lieutenant."

"From Berlin!"

"You're not very quick on the uptake, Kniebusch," said the Rittmeister condescendingly. "You didn't even see that this rudeness had been agreed upon because we weren't safe from eavesdroppers. . . ."

"No!" The forester was overwhelmed.

"Yes, my dear Kniebusch," declared the Rittmeister conclusively. "And since you'll hear about it tomorrow, I may as well reveal to you that the day after there's an old comrades' meeting at Ostade at six in the morning."

"That's what I always say," muttered the forester. "Our troubles will never come to an end."

"But you must give me your word of honor on the spot that you won't tell a soul."

"Of course, Herr Rittmeister, my word of honor. How could I?"

The pair shook hands. Already the Rittmeister felt uncomfortable that he should have talked so much, especially to Kniebusch. But, after all, he had told him nothing he didn't already know. Or not much more. Anyhow, the forester was in the plot.

Nevertheless an uncomfortable silence fell between them.

Very opportunely a young man came down the corridor, a real dandy, with a little cane and a peaked cap, the sort of fellow one immediately hoped would get three years' military service. Tapping his cane against the peak of his cap he said: "'Scuse me. Where does one leave the Church here?"

"What?" the Rittmeister almost shouted.

"Where do you leave the Church—it's here somewhere."

"Why do you want to leave it?" The Rittmeister was indignant at such an intention on the part of a mere whippersnapper. "And smoking, by the way, is forbidden here."

"You've been lucky then, chief!" said the young fellow, sauntering off down the corridor, cigarette in mouth, quite free and easy.

"Nothing but louts nowadays!" burst out the furious Rittmeister. "Leave the Church! Smoking! That's what they're like." Every moment he was growing more excited, throwing indignant glances at the notices on the walls. If they were only to threaten him and not such louts, they were good for nothing.

"I say, you!" he shouted to the usher who at that moment appeared again like a ghost in the corridor. "When are things going to start here?"

"I've already told you that you must wait a little," said the usher, offended.

"But it should have started at half-past ten and now it's just on eleven."

"I have told you that your case will be called."

"You can't expect people to sit here for hours," said the Rittmeister, more and more provoked. "My time is valuable."

"Yes, but . . . I know nothing about it," hesitated the usher, touching his cap. "They said nothing definite about it. Perhaps . . . Show me your summons."

"I haven't been summoned at all," shouted the insulted Rittmeister. "I've only come along with . . ."

"Have you?" In his turn the usher became angry. "You haven't been summoned but you can shout at me! Go home if you can't wait! Things are getting pretty fine nowadays." And, shaking his head, he shuffled down the corridor.

"I tell you what," said the Rittmeister, seizing the forester's arm affectionately. "As a matter of fact the man's quite right. What's the good of my sitting here and waiting any longer? He says himself it can be quite a good while yet."

"But Herr Rittmeister," implored the old man, "you won't leave me in the lurch now! I was ever so happy to have met you, and you were going to take up the cudgels for me. . . ."

"Of course I was, Kniebusch," said the Rittmeister with all the cordiality associated with a bad conscience. "It's not my fault. I came along with you at once, and gladly."

"Herr Rittmeister, wait a little. Perhaps it's nearly time, and it would be so excellent if . . ."

"But Kniebusch!" The Rittmeister was reproachful. "You understand the reason. I'm not here in Frankfurt just for my own pleasure. I have to get the car in plenty of time. You know that!"

"But Herr Rittmeister! . . ."

"No, you must pull yourself together, Kniebusch," declared the Rittmeister, releasing his arm from the forester's hand. "Man, an old experienced non-commissioned officer like you—and afraid of a few conceited lawyers! I tell you, Kniebusch, if the case was called this very moment, I'd still go. It's a good thing for you to face danger once more. You've become too soft, man." And with this Herr von Prackwitz nodded to the forester, curtly yet not without affection, walked down the corridor and disappeared.

Kniebusch, however, sank down on his condemned bench, hid his face in his hands and thought despairingly: They're all like that, these gentlemen. All promise and all humbug. I told him exactly what my position was, that perhaps I might even go to prison. . . . But no, he can't wait to find out; he wants to buy a car. Just as if he couldn't buy it this afternoon or tomorrow morning! For people like that you risk your good bones and a bullet. I'll not forget it, though.

"Well, has he gone, your old broomstick?" asked a bumptious voice.

Kniebusch looked up, stupefied. Before him stood a little fellow hideous to look at, with blubber lips and protruding eyeballs behind owl-like glasses, but grandly dressed in a short fur jacket and plus-fours, golf stockings and brogues. "What are you doing here in the court, Meier?" he asked, adding enviously as he eyed the former bailiff: "Lord, Meier, how do you do it? Every time I see you, you're looking better off, while our like hardly knows where to get the money to have his shoes soled."

"Sure," grinned Meier, "the old head!" And he hit his pear-shaped skull so hard with the palm of his hand that it resounded. "Money's lying nowadays on the pavement. Do you need some, Kniebusch? I can easily help you out with a few millions or milliards."

"Money!" groaned the forester. "It's help I need. My case is on today. I told you about it, the one with Bäumer."

"Yes, I know all about it, old fellow!" said little Black Meier, laying his hand, glittering with rings, on Kniebusch's shoulder. "That's why I'm here. I saw it posted up yesterday in the hall: Criminal case against Kniebusch, private forester from Neulohe, Room 18. . . . So I thought to myself, You've got nothing on, why not go and stand by your old comrade? . . . And I should have been able to testify what an excellent employee you are."

"You really are a decent chap, Meier," said the forester, touched. "I should never have thought you would come to the court for my sake."

"I don't mind at all, Kniebusch," said little Meier complacently. "But I'm not wanted now, of course, when you can drag along such important witnesses as Rittmeister von Prackwitz."

"But he's left me in the lurch, Meier," groaned the forester. "He hadn't got time to wait a moment, because my case didn't come up at once. He's made up his mind to buy a car this very hour."

"You see, money's lying on the pavement, Kniebusch." Little Meier screwed up his eyes. "Even the Rittmeister has money enough for a car."

"I don't know whether he's got money or not. I shouldn't think so," said the forester. "Or it's possible they gave him the money in Berlin."

"Berlin? Who?"

"Oh, those—you know—the Lieutenant—when you set fire to the pines."

"Oh, that business!" Meier grinned contemptuously. "That's all nonsense, Kniebusch. It's not worth a paper mark."

"Oh no, Meier. You'll see, in the next few days. I can't say anything, though. . . . I've given my word. . . . I'm not talking!"

"No need to, Kniebusch. Not a word. Though I don't think it's very decent of you when you know that I also am very nationalist and would prefer to march against the Reds today rather than tomorrow."

"I promised most faithfully," said the forester obstinately. "Don't be angry, Meier."

"Good Lord! Why should I be angry?" Meier laughed. "In fact I'm inviting you to lunch; you know, just as before. Rhine wine, champagne, Türkenblut. . . . Come along, old chap." And he put his arm through the forester's and was dragging him away.

"But, Meier!" cried the other in a panic, "I have my case—"

"Come along, come along," persisted Meier. "Your case? As for that, there's nothing to stop you having a drink; all the more because of your case." He looked at the forester triumphantly. "Yes, you old boozer, you! That's a surprise, eh? If I was as unfriendly as you are, I'd hold my tongue and think: Let him go on sitting there, the old crow—but I'm different. Come along, Kniebusch, and have one."

"But, Meier—"

"Your case has been dropped, Kniebusch. It's vanished. It's blown up, Kniebusch; your case has bolted!"

"Man! Meier!" The forester was almost sobbing.

"Bäumer escaped this morning at nine, Kniebusch!"

"Meier! Young Meier, you're the best fellow in the world, the only friend I have." Great tears were rolling down the forester's cheeks into his beard; he was sobbing so much that Meier clapped him hard on the back. "Is it really true, Meier?"

"I saw it with my own eyes, Kniebusch. He's a cunning hound, Bäumer, always pretending to be at death's door. They were going to bring him in an ambulance to the court, and as they came out of the hospital with the stretcher—they hadn't even strapped him up, the poor chap was so ill—he gave one jump and the attendants went down with the stretcher and he went into the hospital garden. Shouts, chasing. . . . And I joined in the chase as well, but not in the right direction because I thought: Better for my old friend Kniebusch if they don't get him. . . ."

"Meier!"

"Obviously it was a put-up job. You know Bäumer's had repeated visits in the hospital. There was a car waiting for him."

"Meier, I'll never forget what you've done, man. You can ask me anything you like."

"I don't want to. You don't have to tell me anything. Only have lunch with me."

"I'll tell you everything. The others leave me in the lurch; you're the only one to help me. What do you want to know, then?"

"I don't want to know anything—unless you wish to ask me for advice or if you're worried about the *Putsch*. I'm only too pleased to help. But otherwise—I don't mind."

He stopped short. With a superior air he addressed the usher. "Look here, what do you think you're up to? Letting the old gentleman wait here over an hour when you know very well the chief witness for the prosecution has hopped it."

"Yes, sir," said the usher, "but we don't do things in a hurry here. Officially the case comes on today; officially we don't know yet of the disappearance of this particular witness. . . ."

"But don't you know all this?"

"We've known about it for quite a while! The judges have disappeared once again as well."

"Well, listen now, my man," said Meier, and the forester was quite enchanted with the unceremonious way in which he treated the court official. "Then my friend can go and wet his whistle to celebrate. . . ."

"Far as we're concerned," said the usher. "If I wasn't on duty I'd come too."

"Well, you go along later." Meier spoke like a prince, bringing out of his fur jacket a ball of carelessly crumpled notes, one of which he withdrew and, pressing it into the usher's hand, said genteelly: "Good appetite! . . . Come along now, Kniebusch." And went off with him.

Enraptured, Kniebusch followed his friend, the only person in the world whom he could really trust.

X

"Aren't you sending the car back?" asked Frau Eva. It stood in the courtyard and the chauffeur was smoking beside it.

The Rittmeister hesitated a moment. Face to face with his wife, it was not easy to confess the purchase. There would be endless discussion.

"I'll keep it—just for a few days to begin with," he said, "The day after tomorrow all kinds of things will be decided, and that includes us." He addressed the chauffeur. "Finger! Drive to the Villa. I don't exactly know where we're going to keep the car the next few days, but we'll manage somehow. You'll stay with us at first; my man will show you."

"Very good, Herr Rittmeister," replied the chauffeur, opening the door.

Frau Eva eyed the brilliantly finished, softly upholstered monster with a mixture of reluctance, fear and anger. "I can't understand it," she murmured as she got in. And she did not sit back in a corner, but bolt upright, despite cushions which invited her to relax.

The car roared out and swung, gently as a cradle, between the cottages. Because of the convicts' escape and the marching away of the gendarmes, everyone was out and about, and thus saw the car, the smiling Rittmeister and his very erect wife. She felt that all the windows in the Manor, too, were occupied—it was insupportable. I ought never to have got in this devilish thing, she thought bitterly. Achim has made a fool of himself again, and my parents will think that I agreed to it.

The weeks of separation and the contact with Studmann had had their effect—Frau von Prackwitz had changed too. Before, whenever her husband acted rashly, she thought, "How can I hush this up?" Now she thought, "Nobody should think I'm in agreement."

"Do you like the car, Eva?"

"I should like you please to explain to me, Achim," she said hotly, "what all this means. Is this car . . . ?"

The Rittmeister tapped the chauffeur on the back. "Now straight ahead. Yes, the white house in front on the right. . . . It's a Horch. Do you notice how smooth she is? Does twenty-eight to the gallon, no, twenty-five. . . . I've forgotten exactly, but it's all the same."

With a hoot the car swept up to the Villa.

"There'll have to be a drive here," said the Rittmeister, lost in his thoughts.

"What!" Frau Eva started. "For a few days! I thought you had hired it only for a few days."

Violet came running from the house.

"Oh, Papa! Papa! You've come back?" She embraced her father; he couldn't get out of the car quickly enough. "Have you bought it? Oh, how smart! What make is it? How fast can it go? Have you also learned to drive? Let me just sit in it, Mamma."

"There!" said the Rittmeister reproachfully to his wife. "That's what I call pleasure. . . . Violet, be so good as to take Herr Finger to Hubert. He's to have the little spare room in the attic for the moment. The car can stay here for the time being. Eva, please."

"Now, Achim," said Frau Eva, really upset. "Please explain to me what all this means." She sat down.

The worse the Rittmeister's conscience, the more amiable his manner. He, who could not bear even a hasty word in his presence, was now all softness before his wife's bad temper. It was precisely this, however, which made things look dubious to her.

"What it means?" he asked, smiling. "Actually we haven't said good day properly to one another yet, Eva. In the office the schoolmaster was staring at you all the time."

"Herr von Studmann! Yes, he likes to look at me and he's never impolite. And he doesn't shout, either." Frau Eva's eyes flashed.

The Rittmeister thought it better not to insist for the moment on a tender welcome. "I myself don't shout nowadays," he said with a smile. "For weeks I haven't shouted. Altogether I have picked up marvelously."

"Why have you come so suddenly?"

"Well, you see, Eva, I didn't think I was going to inconvenience you here. It simply occurred to me that October the first is, after all, an important day, and I thought perhaps you would want me here." It sounded very amiable and modest, and for that reason it displeased her.

"No notification whatever," she said. "You seem to have remembered this October the first very suddenly."

"Oh, well," he replied a little irritably, "I've never been one for writing, and then there was a slight bother. . . . That Baron von Bergen—you remember, the one who took in Studmann—well, he humbugged me, too. Nothing much—a few marks. But he got out because of them and Dr. Schröck was unbelievably upset about it."

"And then you remembered October the first," said Frau von Prackwitz coldly. "I understand."

The Rittmeister made an angry gesture.

She jumped up, seized him by the lapels of his coat and shook him gently. "Oh, Achim, Achim," she cried sadly, "if only you would not always go on deceiving yourself. You've done this for so many years and I keep on thinking: Now he has had a lesson—now he will change. But always it is the same, always."

"How do I deceive myself?" He was vexed. "Please, Eva, let go of my coat. It has just been pressed."

"I'm sorry. . . . How do you deceive yourself? Well, the truth is, Achim, you were sent away from there because of some folly or indiscretion. And because it's painful for you to admit so, and it occurred to you in the train that the rent falls due on October the first—therefore you try to bamboozle yourself and me."

"If that's how you interpret it . . ." he said, offended. "Very well, then; I'm sent away and now I'm here. Or should I not be here?"

"But, Achim, if it's not like that, say something, then. What is the help you intend to give? Are you going to get hold of the money? Have you any plans? You know that Papa made it a condition you should stay away for a good time, and yet you come back without a word of notice. We haven't even been able to break it to my parents. . . ."

"I certainly didn't think about my father-in-law's feelings. All I thought was, you would be pleased. . . ."

"But, Achim!" she cried despairingly. "Don't be a child. What have I to be pleased about? We're no longer a newly married couple, for me to beam with pleasure as soon as I see you."

"No, you certainly don't do that."

"Here we are struggling for the lease! That is the only thing which ensures us a small income such as we are accustomed to. What are we going to do if we lose it? I've learned nothing and there's nothing I can do—and you—"

"I can do nothing either, of course," said the Rittmeister bitterly. "What's come over you, Eva? You are quite changed. Well, I may have come back a bit sooner than expected and perhaps it was a little thoughtless. But anyway, is that a reason to tell me I've learned nothing and can do nothing?"

"You are forgetting the car in front, Achim!" she cried. "You know we have no money at all, but there in front of the house is a brand-new car that certainly cost ten thousand gold marks!"

"Seventeen, Eva, seventeen."

"Very well. Seventeen. Things are so bad I can say it's all the same whether it cost ten thousand or seventeen thousand. We can't pay either sum. What is the position with the car, Achim?"

"Everything is all right with it, Eva." The proximity of extreme danger had restored his calm. He didn't want another scene; he wished to hear no more unpleasant things. He had the right, surely, to do what he wanted. A man whose wife has done everything he wishes for twenty years can never understand why she so suddenly changes. The woman who for twenty years has been silent, forgiving, smiling, patient, becomes in his eyes a rebel when in the twenty-first year she loses her patience and argues, accuses, demands explanations. Then she is a mutineer against whom every stratagem is permissible. Twenty years of patience have only given her the right to be patient also in the twenty-first.

It was so easy for the Rittmeister. His nimble mind, his boundless optimism, made him see everything in the rosiest light. To put his wife in the wrong there was no need at all for him to give a false account of this car purchase; he only needed to say how it *could* have come about. Women didn't understand. "All is in order, Eva. I'm not really supposed to speak about it, but I can say this. I bought the car more or less on higher instructions."

"On higher instructions? What do you mean by that?"

"Well, on behalf of someone else. In short, for the military authorities."

Frau von Prackwitz looked at her husband uneasily. That incorruptible weapon of womankind, her sense of reality, was not to be duped. Something was wrong.

"For the military authorities?" she asked thoughtfully. "Why don't they buy their cars themselves?"

"My dear girl," explained the Rittmeister, "the military today are restrained by a thousand considerations. By the talking shop in Berlin which won't vote them any supplies. By the Treaty of Versailles. By the Commission of Control. By hundreds of spies. As a consequence they must, unfortunately, be secret in what they regard as indispensable."

Frau von Prackwitz looked at her husband sharply. "So the car has been paid for by the military authorities?"

The Rittmeister would have liked to say yes, but he knew that a payment of 5,000 gold marks was due on October the second. Yet he ventured something. "Not quite that. But I shall get the money back."

"Will you? I suppose, since the military have to be secret, there is consequently no written agreement either?"

The worst thing about the Rittmeister was that he became so quickly tired of anything, even of his lies. It was all so boring. "I am under official orders," he said irritably. "And thank God I am still officer enough to carry out unhesitatingly whatever a superior officer commands."

"But you're not an officer, Achim! You're a civilian, and if you as a civilian buy a car, you are answerable for it with your entire fortune."

"Listen, Eva." The Rittmeister was determined to put an end to all this questioning. "I ought not to speak about it, but I'll tell you everything. On October the first, the day after tomorrow, the present Government is going to be overthrown—by the Reichswehr and other military associations. Everything is prepared. And I have received the official command to appear on October the first at six o'clock in Ostade—with a motor car. This motor car."

"A different Government," she said. "That wouldn't be so bad. Instead of this mire into which we sink deeper every day. That would be a good thing." She was silent for a moment. "But . . ."

"No, please, Eva," he said resolutely. "No 'buts.' You know what is at stake. The thing's settled."

"And Herr von Studmann?" she asked suddenly. "He is also an officer. Does he know anything about it?"

"I couldn't say." The Rittmeister spoke stiffly. "I don't know what are the principles according to which gentlemen are called upon."

"I'm sure he knows nothing about it. And Papa? One of the richest men in the district? Hasn't he been called upon also?"

"Some mention was made of your father," retorted the Rittmeister bitingly. "Unfortunately, rather to his disfavor. It seems he has been the soul of caution, wanting to see the outcome first, before he joins."

"Papa's careful," reflected Frau von Prackwitz. Then, suddenly seized by a thought: "And supposing the *Putsch* fails? What then? Who's going to pay for your car then?"

"It won't fail."

"But it can," she insisted. "The Kapp *Putsch* failed. Just think, seventeen thousand marks!"

"It won't fail, however."

"But it's possible. And we should be ruined."

"I'd return the car in that case."

"If it's confiscated? Or wrecked? Seventeen thousand marks!"

"I buy a car," said the affronted Rittmeister, "and you go on talking about seventeen thousand marks! But when your dear father demands immense sums from us, simply ruinous, then you say we have to pay them without fail."

"Achim, the rent must be paid. But we don't need a car."

"It's an official command." He was as obstinate as a mule.

"I don't understand it at all. You have only just come out of the sanatorium, where you thought of nothing but shooting rabbits. And now, suddenly, you talk about a *Putsch* and buying a motor car, all at once."

She looked at him thoughtfully. Her instinct kept on warning her that something was wrong.

He had colored under her glance; hastily he bent forward and took a cigarette from his case. Lighting it, he said: "You must excuse me, but you know nothing about it. This business was arranged a long time ago. I knew about it before I went away."

"Achim, why do you say that? You would certainly have told me about it in that case."

"I was sworn to silence."

"I don't believe it!" she cried. "This whole business happened suddenly. If you hadn't quarreled with Dr. Schröck you would still be there shooting your rabbits, and there would have been no talk about a *Putsch*, buying a car, and all that."

"I'd rather not hear again," said the Rittmeister menacingly, "that you don't believe something I say, that I'm a liar, that is. As far as that goes, I can prove what I said. Go and ask the forester if a whole lot of men in Neulohe are not waiting only for the signal to burst forth. Ask Violet if there isn't a very large arms dump hidden in your father's forest."

"Violet knows about it, too?" she cried, mortally offended. "And that's what you both call trust! That's supposed to be a family! Here I work myself to death, I humble myself to Papa, I calculate and worry, I put up with everything, I cover up your blunders—and you've got secrets from me! You conspire behind my back, get into debt, endanger everything, play fast and loose with our existence, and I'm to know nothing about it!"

"Eva, I beg you." He was frightened at the effect of his words, and put out his hand to her.

She looked at him with fury. "No, my friend," she cried angrily, "that was a bit too much. Kniebusch, a doddering old chatterbox, and Violet, a mere slip of a girl, plotting with you—but as for me, there you plead your duty to be silent. I'm not to know anything. I don't deserve the confidences you give the other two. . . ."

"I beg you, Eva! If you'll let me tell you . . ."

"No. Tell me nothing! I don't want your confessions afterwards. I've had enough of that all my married life. I'm so tired of it all. I'm sick to death of it! Understand," she cried, stamping on the ground, "I'm sick to death of it. I've heard it all hundreds of times before, the pleas for forgiveness, the promises to pull yourself together, pleasant words—no, thank you!" She turned toward the door.

"Eva," he said, following her, "I can't understand your agitation." He was fighting with himself. After a hard struggle: "All right then, I'll send the car back to Frankfurt this very minute."

"The car!" she said contemptuously. "What do I care about the car?"

"But you yourself have just said . . . Do be logical for once, Eva."

"You haven't even understood what we're talking about. We are not talking about cars, we're talking about trust. Trust! Something that you have demanded for twenty years as a matter of course, and which you have never shown me."

"Very well, Eva," he said bitterly, "say precisely what it is you really want. I've already told you that I'm willing to send the car back to Frankfurt at once, although actually official instructions. . . . I really shouldn't know how to justify it. . . ." He was getting muddled again.

Her eyes were cold. Suddenly she saw, as he really was, the man at whose side she had lived for almost a quarter of a century: a weakling, spineless, without self-control, at the mercy of every influence, a babbler. . . . He hadn't always been like that. No, he had been different, but the times had been different, too—luck had been his, life had smiled, there were no difficulties, it had been easy to show only his good side. Even in the war. Then there had been superiors to tell him what he had to do, and discipline. Uniform, and everything connected with it, had kept him upright. But once he had taken that off, he collapsed, and showed that there was nothing in him, nothing, no core, no faith, no ambition, not one thing to give him the power to resist. Without a guide he had wandered, lost, in a lost age. . . .

But while all this flashed through her mind, and she saw that familiar face into which she had looked more frequently than any other, a voice within her whispered accusingly: Your work! Your creation! Your guilt!

All women who sacrifice themselves completely to their men, relieving them of all burdens, forgiving everything, enduring everything—all live to see their work turn against them. The creature rounds on its creator; tender indulgence and kindness turn to guilt.

She heard him continuing to speak, but hardly listened to what he said. She saw his lips opening and closing, and she saw the lines and folds of his face moving. That face had once been smooth when she had first looked at it. Alongside her, with her, through her, it had now become the face that it was.

"You keep on talking about trust." He was reproachful. "Surely I have shown trust enough? I left you alone here for weeks, I put the whole property in your charge. After all, it's I who am the tenant."

She smiled. "Oh, yes, you are the tenant, Achim!" She spoke in ridicule. "You are the master, and you left your poor weak wife all to herself. . . . Don't let us talk about it anymore now. Nor do I mind if you keep the car. Everything must be considered. I should like to talk it over thoroughly with Herr von Studmann, and perhaps sound Papa a little. . . ."

Wrong again! Always doing things the wrong way! No sooner was she gentler than he became harsher. "On no account do I wish Studmann to be told," said he, beginning to be irritated. "If he hasn't been called upon, there will be a reason for it. And as for your father . . ."

"Very well, leave Papa. But Herr von Studmann must be informed. He's the only one who has a real notion of our finances and can say whether it is possible to buy the car after all."

"Don't you understand, Eva?" he cried angrily. "I reject Studmann as competent judge of my actions. He is not my nurse."

"It is necessary to ask him," she persisted. "If the *Putsch* fails . . ."

"Listen! I forbid you to speak a word to Studmann about the matter. I forbid it."

"What right have you to tell me what not to do? Why should I do what you think is correct, since everything you do, everything, is wrong? Certainly I shall talk to Herrr von Studmann."

"You're very obstinate about your friend," he said suspiciously.

"Isn't he your friend also?"

"He's a self-opinionated fool, a know-all! An everlasting nursemaid!" he burst out. "If you say a word to him about this matter, I'll throw him out on the spot. We'll see who is the master here!" he shouted, holding himself rigid.

With pale and unmoving face she looked at him a long, long time, and once again he grew uncertain under this gaze.

"Do be sensible, Eva," he pleaded. "Admit that I am right."

Suddenly she turned away. "Very well, my friend, I won't say anything to Studmann. In future I won't say anything whatever." And before he could reply he was alone.

He looked around discontentedly. The lengthy quarrel had left a feeling of emptiness, of something unsatisfied. He had had his way, and for once this did not please him. He wanted to forget the quarrel—it had been an endless torrent of words, long disputes about nothing—and why? Because he had bought a car! If he could pay over twenty thousand gold marks in rent he could afford a car. There were peasants who had them. There was a peasant in Birnbaum who had a car and a tractor plow, and another had twenty-five sewing machines in his barn, just to have something for his money. Goods!

It was not as if he had bought the car for his own pleasure. He would never have thought of it had not Major Rückert instructed him to get one. He had done it for the Cause; a thing she, however, couldn't understand. And didn't want to understand. In her dressing table there was a drawer at least a yard long and twenty inches deep, crammed with stockings. Yet she was constantly buying herself new ones. There always had to be money for that! He himself had hardly spent a penny for weeks, only the few cartridges which he needed for the rabbits, and the wine at meal times—but the very first thing he did buy, she made a row!

Soft and musical, the car hooted in front; his car, his brilliant Horch. Glad of this diversion, the Rittmeister put his head out of the window. Violet sat at the wheel, playing with the knob of the horn. "Stop that, Vi!" he shouted. "You'll frighten the horses."

"The car's so smart, Papa. You really are the nicest man. It must be the finest car in the whole district."

"It's also pretty dear," whispered the Rittmeister, twisting his head to look at the floor above.

Vi screwed up her eyes laughingly. "Don't worry, Papa. Mother's gone to the farm. In the office again, of course."

"In the office? Oh!" The Rittmeister was annoyed.

"How much, Papa?"

"Frightful. Seventeen."

"Seventeen hundred? That's not so much for a swell car."

"My dear Vi! Seventeen thousand!"

"At any rate, Papa, for that we have the finest car in the district."

"You think so? That's what I say. If you're going to buy something, it may as well be something decent."

"I suppose Mamma is not quite in agreement?"

"Not yet. But she'll change her mind, you see, when she's been out in it."

"Papa?"

"Yes . . . ? What?"

"When can I go in it? Today?"

"Oh!" Both children were equally delighted. The nursemaids were absent, in the office.

"I know, Papa! Suppose we go quickly through the forest? The gendarmes are searching there for the convicts. We might catch the fellows. Our car's so silent and fast! And then we could drop in at Birnbaum. Uncle Egon and the cousins will burst with envy."

"I don't know," said the Rittmeister doubtfully. "Perhaps Mamma would like to come."

"Mamma? She'd rather be in the office."

"Oh? What's the chauffeur doing now?"

"He's having something to eat in the kitchen. But he can't be long now. Shall I call him?"

"All right. By the way, Vi, guess whom I met in the train today."

"Who then? How can I tell, Papa? All the neighbors might have been there. Uncle Egon?"

"What are you talking about? I shouldn't have asked you to guess about him. No. Our Lieutenant!"

"Who?" Violet turned crimson and lowered her head. Confused, she pressed the knob of the horn and the car hooted loudly.

"Don't make that noise, Vi, please. You know, the Lieutenant who was so rude . . ." In a whisper: "The one with the weapons."

"Oh, him!" She still kept her head down, and played with the wheel. "I thought you meant someone we knew. . . ."

"No, that ruffian. . . . You remember? 'Such things are not discussed in the presence of young ladies.'" The Rittmeister laughed. "Well, to do him justice, Vi, he seems to be a big pot, however young he is. And damned clever."

"Yes, Papa?" she said very softly.

"As a matter of fact, he's responsible for my buying the car." Very low and mysteriously: "Violet, they've got a big thing on hand—and your Papa's in it." This was only the third time that Rittmeister von Prackwitz had let out his secret; and for that reason he was still enjoying himself.

"Against the Socialists, Papa?"

"The Government's to be overthrown, my child." (This very solemnly.) "So the day after tomorrow, on October the first, I am going with this car to Ostade."

"And the Lieutenant?"

"Which Lieutenant? Oh, the Lieutenant! Well, he'll be with us, naturally."

"Will there be fighting, Papa?"

"Very likely. Highly probable. But, Violet, you are not afraid, surely? An officer's daughter! I survived the World War; a few small street fights like that won't harm me."

"No, Papa."

"Well, then. Stiff upper lip, Violet. Nothing venture, nothing win. I think the chauffeur ought to have finished his meal by now. Call him. We want to get back before it's quite dark."

He watched his daughter get out of the car and go into the house, slowly, thoughtfully, her head down. She really loves me, he thought proudly; what a shock it was when she heard there would be fighting. But she pulled herself together marvelously. He thought thus, not out of joy in his daughter's love, but so that he could, mentally at least, upbraid a wife who had not thought for a moment of the dangers to which he was about to expose himself, but only of buying cars, financial difficulties, rent, and questions of trust. . . .

And while he, proud of a daughterly love which fully appreciated his worth, got ready for the drive, Vi stood as if paralyzed in the small hall, with only one thought in her heart. The day after tomorrow! We have not seen one another again, and he may be killed. The day after tomorrow!

XI

Immediately after the quarrel with her husband Frau von Prackwitz had gone up to her room. She felt she had to cry. In the mirror over the wash-basin she saw a woman no longer young but still quite good-looking, with slightly bulging eyes which now had rather a torpid look. It seemed as if all life had gone out of her; she felt icy cold, her heart was dead as a stone. . . .

Then she forgot she was standing in front of the mirror looking at herself. What is the good of it all? she asked herself once more. There must have been something which made me love him. What could I have seen? For so long!

An endless series of pictures swirled by her, memories of the past when they were first married. The young first lieutenant. A call from the garden. His charmingly foolish behavior at Violet's birth. The first intoxicating homecoming after the banquet. A garden party in the garrison town—they had endangered position and reputation when a sudden and overwhelming passion had united the married pair in a park crowded with visitors. The discovery of his first gray hair—already at thirty he had begun to turn gray—a secret she alone knew. His affair with that Armgard von Burkhard; how he had brought her a basket of delicatessen and she had suddenly known that what she had cried about so much was at last definitely over.

A thousand memories, speeding by, happy or sad, but all in a faded, calamitous light. When love goes and the eyes are suddenly opened, and the once-loved is seen as others see him—an average person without special merits—seen with the merciless eyes of a woman who has lived beside him for two decades, knowing beforehand every word he will say, to whom every pettiness and fault is familiar—then arise the perplexed questions: Why? What is the good? Why have I borne so much, retrieving, forgiving? What was in him to make me sacrifice myself so?

No answer. The form to which love alone gave breath has become lifeless without it, a scurrilous figure made up of buffooneries, whims and misbehavior, an insupportable marionette, all its strings known!

Frau Eva heard the sound of feet on the stairs, and came to herself with a start. Two men were talking. It would be Hubert coming down from the attic with the chauffeur. For a moment she was seized with the idea of being truly her father's daughter, cunning and subtle. . . .

Oh, let him go ahead and manage! He insists on being the master here, she thought. Let him see how far he can get without me and—Studmann. The money for the car, the rent. . . . I will tell Studmann not to go tomorrow, not to look for money, not to make any arrangements about hands for the potato harvest. He'll find out in a week how irretrievably he'll be stuck in the mud. I'm really tired of having to beg him for permission to do what is right. . . . This *Putsch* he's so full of now is nothing but an adventure. Papa's not in it, nor Studmann nor my brother. They've talked him round at the last moment. He will find . . .

She examined her face in the mirror. There was a trace of self-righteousness about the mouth which she didn't like. Her eyes were bright, but neither did she care for that. The fires of malice shine thus.

No, she told herself resolutely, not that way. I don't want that. If, as it now appears to me, everything is really finished, it will collapse without my assistance. I shall go on doing everything I can. That won't be much; there's no longer any enthusiasm, any love in it, only duty. But I have always been as honest as I could, and all these years I have nothing grave with which to reproach myself. . . .

Once again she examined the mirror. Her face had a strained expression; the skin round the eyes looked drawn, heavily wrinkled and dry. Promptly she took up her pot of cream and greased her face. Massaging the skin gently, she thought: I'm not finished yet; I'm in the prime of life. And if I'm more careful with myself and what I eat, I can easily lose fifteen or twenty pounds—then I shall have exactly the right figure. . . .

Five minutes later Frau von Prackwitz was sitting in the office with Herr Studmann. Studmann, of course, hadn't the slightest notion of how she was feeling. Frau Eva, who in a quarter of an hour had discovered that she no longer loved her husband, who had decided that she would remain honest in all circumstances, but who had nevertheless conceded herself a quite joyous and hopeful life—Frau Eva had to listen to an exhaustive lecture on how Herr von Studmann proposed to raise the money for the rent the day after tomorrow.

The old schoolmaster! she thought, but not without sympathy. She was no girl now; she knew men (for to know one man properly is to know all) and she was aware that they possessed a bewildering lack of intuition. Under their very eyes a woman might expire from her desire for tenderness while they were demonstrating at length and in detail that they needed a new suit, and why they needed a new suit, and what color the new suit had to be. . . . And suddenly, very surprised and a little hurt, they say: "Aren't you listening at all? What's the matter with you? Aren't you well? You're looking so strange!"

Frau Eva had crossed her legs, which, her skirt being fashionably short, gave her the opportunity of studying them during the lecture. They were, she thought, still very nice to look at, and if she reduced, it would be better to do so on the hips and behind. But of course, one always got slimmer just where it was not so desirable.

Both suddenly noticed that neither was speaking.

"What was that, Herr von Studmann?" she asked and laughed. "Excuse me, my thoughts were elsewhere." She drew back her legs as much as possible beneath the skirt.

Studmann was fully prepared to excuse her; his thoughts also had strayed. Hastily he took up his lecture again. It appeared that in the town of Frankfurt-on-the-Oder there lived a deranged person who was ready the following day to provide the full sum of rent in the finest of notes, if only the management of Neulohe Farm engaged to deliver him in December fifty tons of rye in exchange.

"The man's mad!" exclaimed Frau von Prackwitz, puzzled. "He could have one hundred and fifty tons for his money tomorrow."

That, admitted Studmann, had also been his opinion at first. But it was like this. The man—a rich fishmonger, by the way—would only have to change his tons of grain into paper money tomorrow or in a week. Everyone today, though, fled from paper money, tried to lay it out on some commodity of permanent value, and so this man had hit upon grain, no doubt.

"But how can he know that it will be different in December?"

"Obviously he can't know. He hopes so, believes so; he is speculating on it. A little while back there were negotiations in Berlin about issuing a new currency. After all, the mark can't go on falling forever. But they are at variance over money based on grain or on gold. No doubt the man thinks we shall have the new currency in December."

"Would that change things for us?"

"As far as I can foresee, no. We should always have to deliver fifty tons of rye only."

"Then let's do it. We shall certainly never be able to rid ourselves of this nightmare more favorably."

"Perhaps we ought to ask Prackwitz about it first," proposed Studmann.

"Willingly. If you think so. Only—why? You have full authority."

Women are the devil. At this moment there were certainly no legs in a conversation devoted to business, rent and currency. But when Frau Eva threw doubt on the necessity of consulting her husband, something dark and suppressed crept into the matter-of-fact discussion. It really sounded a little as if, to speak frankly, they were talking of a dying person.

"Yes," said Studmann softly, "to be sure. Only, you both undertake the obligation to deliver in—December."

"Yes. And—?" She did not comprehend.

"December! You will have, in all circumstances, to deliver in December. Fifty tons of grain. In all circumstances. A good two months yet."

Frau von Prackwitz tapped a cigarette on the lid of the box. There was a small furrow between her eyebrows. For greater comfort she crossed her legs, without, however, thinking about it. Nor did Studmann notice it this time.

"You understand, madam," he explained, "it would be a personal obligation of yours and your husband's, not of the farm. You would have to deliver the fifty tons if—well, wherever you were."

A long pause.

Frau von Prackwitz stirred. "Accept, Herr von Studmann," she said vivaciously. "Accept in spite of that danger." She shut her eyes; she was a beautiful, plump, fair woman, withdrawing into herself. She was like a cat, a cat who is happy, a cat on the hunt for mice. "If we lose the tenancy by December," she said smilingly, "my father won't leave *me* in the lurch. I should then take it over and deliver the fifty tons."

Studmann sat like a lump of wood. Amazing tidings had reached his ears. These women!

Frau von Prackwitz smiled. She was not smiling at Studmann, but at something imaginary between the stove and the law shelves. Putting her hand out to him, she said: "And may I rely also on you not to leave me in the lurch, Herr von Studmann?"

Disconcerted, Studmann gazed at the hand. It is a large but very white woman's hand with rather too many rings. He felt exactly as if he'd been hit on the head. What had she said? Impossible! She couldn't have meant it like that. He was a donkey. . . .

"Donkey!" said she in a deep warm voice, and for one moment the hand gently touched his lips. He felt its fresh softness, perceived its scent, and looked up, crimson. He would have to turn things over in his mind—the position was difficult. Prackwitz was his old friend, after all. He encountered her look, in which was a blend of mocking superiority and tenderness.

"Dearest madam . . ." said he, confused.

"Yes," she smiled. "What I have always wanted to ask you was—what actually is your Christian name?"

"My Christian name? Well, it's a bit awkward . . . actually I don't use it. I'm called Etzel; that is—"

"Etzel? Etzel? Wasn't that—?"

"Correct!" he explained hurriedly. "Attila or Etzel, a prince of the Huns, who swept into Europe with his Mongolian hordes, robbing and murdering. About 450 A.D. Battle on the Catalaunian Plain. 'Savagery was as innate in him as dignity and sobriety.' But, as I say, I make no use of it. It's a sort of family tradition."

"No, Etzel is quite impossible. Papa called his gander Attila. And what did your friends call you? Prackwitz always only says Studmann."

"Like all the others do," he sighed. "I'm not really suited to intimacies." He turned a little red. "Sometimes I was called the Nursemaid. And in the regiment they called me Mummy."

"Studmann, Nursemaid, Mummy. . . ." She shook her head with irritation, "Herr von Studmann, you really are impossible. No, I must find something else."

"Dearest madam!" cried Studmann, enraptured. "Do you really mean that? I'm such a boring fellow, a pedant, a fussy old woman. And you—"

"Quiet," she urged, shaking her head. "Wait. Don't forget, Herr von Studmann, for the moment I have only asked you about your Christian name . . . nothing else." She paused, supporting her head in her hands, armlets gently tinkling. She sighed, she made the most enchanting beginning to a yawn. She was altogether the cat which cleans itself, stretches, and does everything but look at the sparrow it is going to devour the next moment. "And then there is also the car."

"What car?" He was confused again. Her transitions today were much too sudden for any sober-thinking man.

She pointed out of the window, though there was no car outside. But he understood. "Oh, the car! What about it?"

"He's bought it," she said.

"Oh?" He was thoughtful. "How much?"

"Seventeen thousand."

Studmann made a gesture of despair. "Absolutely impossible!"

"And by installments?"

"Also."

"Listen, Herr von Studmann," she said with vigor, though a little sullenly. "In all circumstances you will go to Frankfurt tomorrow and obtain the money, but no more."

"Certainly."

"Whatever you may be told, you will go and fetch only that. Is it agreed?"

"Certainly."

"You will hand over the money for the settlement of the rent to Herr von Prackwitz tomorrow evening. Do you understand? Herr von Prackwitz is to give my father the money himself. You understand?"

"Yes, certainly."

"Wait. Prackwitz has planned a small journey for the day after tomorrow. Well, that's nothing to do with us. He can pay the money over tomorrow evening. You understand me?"

"Not quite, but—"

"All right. If you only keep to what I say. . . . Herr von Prackwitz is to receive the money for the rent punctually—that's enough. Perhaps you'll ask for a receipt?"

"If you wish." Studmann hesitated. "Prackwitz and I haven't usually—"

"Of course not. But now!" She spoke sharply, stood up and gave him her hand. Once again she was the mistress of Neulohe. "Then *au revoir*, Herr von Studmann. I suppose I shan't see you till after your trip to Frankfurt. Well, good business!"

"Thank you very much," said Studmann, looking at her a little unhappily. There ought to be frankness, something positive discussed; but no, nothing! Etzel, and a hand kiss! Such things ought not to be done that way.

Shaking his head, Studmann set about composing an advertisement: "Hands wanted for potato digging . . ."

Outside blows the September wind, beginning to tear off and carry away the sere leaves. Something in Eva told her it was autumn and winter was coming. Her bearing is all the more erect, however. The wind pressed her clothes against her body. She felt its cool freshness on her skin. No, it's not autumn for everybody, only for things ripe enough to die. She felt herself still young, and walked into the wind. She has made an experiment; she has encroached on Fate. Will Prackwitz pay the rent? Yes or no? Everything depends on that.

XII

Tranquil and in good spirits, Pagel made for the wood, after the gendarmes, on the hunt for convicts. No Rittmeister von Prackwitz could upset him now, by a long way. What a child the man was, a silly thoughtless child! Came back with a brand-new car and at once set about showing the young man he was master! But the young man didn't care—he was glad to be in the woods; he had no wish to remain in the office with such a paltry employer. A queer fish, the governor! Damned rude to someone who could raise his finger any moment, point at the car and say: "Well—and my two thousand gold marks?"

Not that he would exactly do that. Studmann would take care that he got the money some day, when it was needed. There had been a time when one had said to the Rittmeister: "Oh, forget about the trash. I don't want the money back at all." Then the Rittmeister had flushed and excitedly spoken about "debts of honor." Time had passed since then, however. One thought quite differently about money when stamps and boot repairs and cigarettes and laundry had to be paid for out of a small monthly sum, graciously conceded by the Rittmeister (although one really did nothing at all for it, of course!)—in other words, out of a miserable pocket money. In fact, a small installment of that debt would often come in very pat, these days. But, at the slightest hint of that kind now, the Rittmeister would flush again and cry out, offended: "But, Pagel, you know very well what my financial position is at present, man!"

Yet a brand-new car stood in front of his house. And one was ordered out like some mere lad. Undoubtedly a queer fish!

Thus preoccupied, Pagel strolled through the woods. He had no idea in what parts the gendarmes were beating; but so long as he steered for the potato field, he would find them.

For the moment he therefore continued and thought as he went. He was comfortable and content. It would be a great mistake to suppose he was angry with the Rittmeister. Not a bit! People could only be what they were. Idiots formed a splendid background for Petra. The more foolish others were, the clearer that girl stood out. And Wolfgang thought about her with deeply grateful tenderness, an emotion which grew constantly stronger; since he had heard from Minna that he was to be a father there was more joy than longing or desire in it. An odd feeling! It was a confounded long time, three months, ninety-four days exactly, before she would let him go to her. He thought about everything they had experienced together, how it had come about and what had happened next. It had been good! Strange. Living with Petra, he hadn't really thought much about her. Gambling had been the chief thing. Now that he lived in Neulohe, he actually mainly lived at Madam Po's. Strange! Did there ever really come a time in life when a man had the feeling that experience and awareness were one? When he felt: Now you are happy, in a manner you can never again experience in the whole of your life? In the very second of experience! Not like this, when it was only afterwards discovered: in those days I was happy! As happy as we always were—? No! It was strange and dangerous!

Pagel whistled thoughtfully. And considered whether the capture of convicts in a wood was aided by whistling, whether they would sneak off at the sound or make an attack upon him, to get his money, clothes and pistol. In a flash he saw Marofke's face with its trembling baggy cheeks. But let the fellows come! he thought defiantly. Whistling louder, he grasped the pistol butt in his trouser pocket.

Yes, indeed! It was strange and dangerous, always to think of your sweetheart and compare her to all the others, and only in her favour. Once again Pagel asked himself if the image he now had of Peter was still true. Was she really pure gold? That couldn't be true either. She must have faults, too, and if he looked for them, he easily found some. For instance, her tendency to silence if something didn't suit her—if something annoyed her. He would ask her what was wrong? Nothing was wrong. But he could see, something was. He'd done something wrong. No definitely nothing. You had to talk to her for a full quarter of an hour. She could make you furious. Almost drive you insane with her eternal no! It was clear as clear. Well, there was a fault all right. In any case, he'll help her break this habit. A girl like Peter shouldn't have any faults. As for himself, it was different. He had so many that it wasn't even worth beginning to improve.

Pagel, busy with his thoughts, had long passed beyond the potato field into ever stranger and more remote parts of the wood. He had seen nothing of the convicts and nothing of the gendarmes either. Well, he would take a pleasant walk instead of joining in an idiotic hunt; for idiotic it must be, he decided. Woods upon woods, up and down, hour after hour, overgrown thickets, plantations of thousands of small straggling pines, high as a man, half as high again, hundreds and hundreds of acres, glens of fir so gloomy that even on the brightest day one hardly saw a foot in front—and the police were hoping in this wilderness to find five shrewd and desperate men whose intelligence would be concentrated on not letting themselves be found. Absolute nonsense! In the woods one really perceived how impossible the task was. He would go on alone, comfortably, instead of crawling around with the others among thorns and junipers!

But, turning the next corner, he exclaimed "Ah-ha!" and was no longer alone. A little man in a fur jacket was walking toward him, that is, walking was not quite the right word; he had a kind of quavering in his progress, a staccato. He, so to speak, yodeled somewhat with his legs. "Damned roots!" he said far too loudly, though there were none in that spot. And a pace in front of Pagel he stopped with so sudden a start that he almost fell over.

Wolfgang seized him just in time. "Ah-ha! Herr Meier," he said smiling, "Germans don't say 'cognac,' they say 'brandy.'"

Meier's small, reddened eyes contemplated his successor on the farm. Suddenly a gleam of recognition shone in them and, with a broad impudent grin, he screeched: "Oh, it's you. I thought . . . Doesn't matter. I'm a bit boozed. Seen my car anywhere?"

"What!" Pagel became suspicious. "Have you got a car, too, Herr Meier? What are you doing in our forest today with a car?"

"So you too say our forest now," laughed Meier. "That seems to be the fashion here. The forester says my forest, the Rittmeister says my woods, his wife sometimes takes a little walk in her plantations, and the one it really belongs to, the old Geheimrat, he only talks about a few pine trees!"

Out of politeness Pagel laughed also. But the other's presence here, particularly today, still seemed suspicious. "Where did you leave your car, Herr Meier?" he asked.

"If only I knew, blockhead that I am!" said Meier, thumping himself on the head. "So it's not up that way, then?" Pagel shook his head. "Well, let's go up here." He seemed to take it for granted that Wolfgang would accompany him, and this somewhat removed the suspicion that he might be an associate of the escaped convicts. Cheerful and fairly erect, he sauntered along, apparently glad to have found a listener.

"As a matter of fact, I'm a bit boozed, you know. I've been celebrating with a friend. Actually he isn't a friend, but he thinks he is. Well, let the child have its pacifier. So I found myself here, I don't know what it's called, it was somewhere near. But I'll find it all right. I've a marvelous memory for places."

"Surely."

"Let's take this path on the left. I've forgotten your name for the moment, one gets acquainted with too many people in life, particularly the last few weeks; one's got to work his way in first. But my memory for names is good, the Colonel's always saying so."

"What colonel? You're not with the Army now, are you?" Pagel encountered a glance which was wary, suspicious, and not in the least drunken. He's not so tipsy as he seems, he thought. Take care!

But Meier was laughing again. "Well, are you with the Army because you say Rittmeister to your boss?" he asked adroitly. "He's bought himself a fine car, the old sod. Saw him today in Frankfurt scorching on a trial run—the world's got to collapse nobly. What's little Vi doing now?"

"Well, your car doesn't seem to be here either."

"Don't pull a face or I'll laugh. So I suppose you've been dropped, too? Is the Lieutenant still the only one? Lordie, what a girl! Love must be wonderful. Well"—in quite a different, a threatening, tone—"soon the Lieutenant will be dropped; he's going to feel sick soon. He'd better wash his chest, he'll be shot."

"Perhaps you are rather jealous, Herr Meier?" inquired Pagel amiably. "That time you screamed in the night—I suppose that was because of him? Incidentally, I found the copy you made of the letter, inside the *District Gazette*."

"Oh, that stupid thing! Far as I'm concerned, you can blow your nose on it. Haven't got any time nowadays for flea bites like that. We've got other things on tap. But there, a young chap from the country won't understand about that. You've no idea what I'm earning now."

"Oh, I can see it, Herr Meier."

"Isn't it so? Look at the rings, all real good stones. I have a pal who gets 'em for me at half price. And since I always pay only in foreign money . . ." Once again he stopped short, with the same intensely suspicious side-glance. But Pagel had not heard the treasonable word; he was following up another clue.

"Isn't that a little dangerous, Herr Meier? To go walking about here alone in the forest with so much jewelry and money? Something might easily happen to you."

"Don't you believe it!" laughed Meier contemptuously. "What could happen then? Nothing's ever happened to me before. You haven't the least idea, man, of all I've been through—and nothing's happened to me yet. Here," he said, stamping with his foot on the earth, "here in this wood someone once walked behind me, for a quarter of an hour, with his revolver all the time on my nut—and was going to shoot me dead. Well, did he shoot me?"

"Funny things happen to you," laughed Pagel, somewhat uncomfortably. "One would never have thought it. No doubt he was not really in earnest . . ."

"Him? He meant it all right. . . . The thing was loaded, and he only let me keep on walking because he wanted to get to a place a bit more secluded. So that they wouldn't find my body straight away, of course."

In these words there was something sinister and horrible. Pagel looked at the little man askance. What he said need not be true, but the fellow believed it was. . . . Threats were forming themselves on his lips.

"I'll get the swine, though. If I was frightened, he's going to be a hundred times as frightened. I escaped, but he won't. . . ."

"Well, Herr Meier," said Pagel coldly, "if the Lieutenant is ever found dead somewhere you can be quite certain the police will be told at once by me."

Meier turned with a vicious stare. Of a sudden, however, his expression changed, his heavy blubber lips curled, his owl-like eyes smiled scornfully. "You think I'm such a fool as to shoot at the fellow? Shoot off the mark, most likely, and be done to death by the swine? That'd be a fine revenge! No, man! Trust old Meier! He's got to be afraid, the swine. I'll hound him down, rob him of his honor, everyone shall spit at him—and then, when there's no way out for him anymore—then he can shoot himself, the swine! That and no other way!"

Triumphantly he stood before Pagel. There was no more intoxication to be seen, except that possibly the alcohol had inflamed his revengefulness and made him blab of things he otherwise carried locked within him. Pagel, watchful, was taking care not to let his disgust for the fellow become visible; he felt certain that behind all the threats much was hidden which it would be good to know. One must be clever and pump him, this Meier! But he could not hold back his youthfulness, the abhorrence of the young for whatever is sick, impure and criminal.

"You're a fine lump of turd!" he said contemptuously, and turned to go.

"And what about it?" challenged Meier. "What's that to do with you? Have I made myself? Have you made *yourself*? I should like to know what you'd look like if you'd always been treated as dirt, as I've been treated! You're a precious mother's pet, anyone can see that; a fine school and everything else that goes with it. . . ." He quieted down a little.

"You believe that a good education drives all the swinishness out of one?" asked Pagel. "Some people feel quite happy even in filth."

Meier looked evilly at him for a minute. Then he laughed. "Look here, why quarrel about that? I always think it's a short life and a long death, so let's see that we too have a decent time. And since money's necessary for that, and a poor devil will never get any by being honest . . ."

"You get it by being dishonest. Only I don't understand, Herr Meier, why you have it in for the Lieutenant so much. You won't get any money, will you, if he's done for?"

Now, however innocently Pagel had said this, immediately there was that same suspicious glance. But this time Meier didn't reply. Growling, he turned into a fresh path. "Damn and blast it, where the devil's the bloody car! I must be quite crazy. Aren't we going round and round in a circle really?" Again he looked viciously at Pagel and murmured: "You needn't worry about letting me go on by myself. You're not a help to me, anyway."

"I am afraid something might happen to you," said Pagel politely. "Your fine rings, all that money . . ."

"I've already told you, nothing can happen. Who's going to pinch rings in a forest?"

"Convicts," said Pagel calmly, with a sharp eye on his man.

Meier did not turn a hair. "Convicts? What convicts?"

"Ours, from the harvest crew," replied Pagel, convinced that his suspicion had been unjust. (But what was little Meier doing in the forest?) "In fact, five of them ran away this morning."

"Damn and blast!" shouted Meier, and his fright was genuine. "They're hiding here in the forest? You—you're trying to be funny. Why, you yourself are walking about just the same."

"Not at all!" said Pagel, half pulling the pistol from his trousers. "Besides that, I'm looking for the gendarmes. There are fifty of them, you know, ransacking the forest."

"That beats everything," said Meier, coming to a stop. "Five lags and fifty frogs—and me right in it with my bone-shaker! That can be painful. Lord, man, I must get my car right away. What was it called now? I've got it. The Black Dale! Do you know it?"

Pagel felt that the little man had known this name all along, had he wished to come out with it. Meier was looking at him suspiciously, too. Why? It was only a forest name, like any other. "I've never been there," he said. "But I've seen it on the map. It's very near Birnbaum and we're going the whole time toward Neulohe."

"Fool that I am." Meier hit himself on the head with his fist. "Onwards then, man—what do you call yourself?"

"Pagel."

"Keep your eyes open. In this sand even a worm could find a wheel mark. This way? Good. But is it the right way?"

"Oh, yes," said Pagel. "But why are you so enormously upset all of a sudden? I thought that nothing could happen to you?"

"Yes, I'd like to see you in my place. Suppose everything's messed up! Damnation! This is always my luck. That cursed drunk . . ."

"What'll be messed up?"

"What's that to do with you?"

"Well, I'd really like to know."

"Then write to Aunt Dolly in Advice to the Lovelorn."

"As a matter of fact, it's not yet been settled that we're really going to the Black Dale now."

Meier, coming to a stop, fixed young Pagel with a look of hatred. He would certainly very much have liked to do something to him, but he thought better of it, and snarled: "What do you want to know, then?"

"Why are you in a hurry so suddenly?"

Meier reflected. "I've business in Frankfurt," he said in a surly voice.

"So you had five minutes ago, and you weren't in any hurry then."

"Would you let a new car be pinched by convicts? Even if it's not a tiptop Horch like your Rittmeister's—only a baby Opel."

"You were frightened when I talked about the gendarmes."

"No."

"Yes."

"All right. I haven't got a driving license. And anyway, I like to steer clear of the police."

"Because of your business?"

"If you like. I don't mind—I do a bit of business on the sly."

Pagel scrutinized the ugly little fellow. It might be the truth, but it was much more likely that he was lying. "And what are you doing here today in our wood?"

Meier, however, was cunning. Cursing his drunken revengeful rigmarole about the Lieutenant, he had seen this question coming a long time. But once he had noticed that Pagel did not move a muscle at the words "Black Dale"— once he was sure he knew nothing—he felt certain of victory. "What am I doing here in your wood? Actually you ought not to know, but you'll keep your mouth shut. I've brought back your forester, your Kniebusch. He's fast asleep in my car, drunk as a fiddler."

"Wasn't the forester in Frankfurt for his case?"

"That's right. You've got it." Meier had quite recovered. "And now let's get on—the proper way to the Black Dale. The forester was there for his case about Bäumer, and your Rittmeister, who is a great man, was going to back him up, but cleared off, the great man, so as to buy a car. . . ."

"And the case?"

"Fallen through! In default of interest in it. Because Bäumer ran away this morning. Everyone seems to be running away today. Me, too. At once. Hurrah! Here's the tracks of the car. Didn't I say so? It's hardly a step now; so come along and take a peep at your Kniebusch, so that you'll know I'm not fooling you."

"But why did you motor over here into the wood if you wanted to take Kniebusch home? How did your car come to be lost?"

"You've got a funny idea of being drunk, man! I suppose you've never been boozed? Well, we couldn't drive into the village soaked—we weren't quite soaked enough for that. So we drove about a bit. Well, when we got here in the forest I felt a natural urge and had to get out. Kniebusch was fast asleep. I tumbled out of the car, into the ditch, behind a bush—and I must have dozed off. Well, when I woke up, I didn't at first know what was what. . . . I just went off looking aimlessly, and then I met you. Hello, here's my car!"

It was certainly not so magnificent as the Rittmeister's. It was a genuine baby Opel, a Tin Lizzie. . . . But that didn't interest Pagel much at the moment. It was a very small, low car, with not much space between the ground and its floor. All the same, it was a very uncomfortable position in which the forester was asleep, his head in the wood and his feet in the car.

Pagel actually ought to have put a few more suspicious questions to Herr Meier. But Meier would always have an answer to everything, either true or invented. The very man was a tangled web of truth and lies. What he had said would be approximately true, even if not completely, because the secretive lieutenant was totally missing in the story, and Pagel felt he definitely belonged there. To drag the truth out of that fellow would take too long. The first thing to be done now was to take the forester home and put him to bed. The whole situation could not be good for a nearly-seventy-year-old. His face was purple.

"In with him! In!" ordered Pagel, seeing that Meier wanted to drag the old man away from the car.

"What do you mean—in? I'm clearing! I'm in a hurry. Out with him!"

"In, I say! No doubt you made Kniebusch drunk, and you can drive him home as well."

"Not likely! I'm in a hurry. I don't want to be seen in Neulohe, either."

"No need to. You can drive up to the forester's house through the wood. No one will see you."

"And supposing I'm grabbed on the way? By the gendarmes or the convicts? Nix, I'm clearing off."

"Herr Meier!" warned Pagel. "Don't be silly. Rather than let you go off I'd shoot your tires to pieces."

Furiously Meier looked at the hand with the pistol.

"Well, get hold of him!" he said sullenly. "But put that thing away. Up with you, into the corner! Oh, it's all the same how he sits, he'll fall over again immediately. The main thing is to get the door shut. I don't know," he cursed again, "but Neulohe brings me only bad luck. Whatever I start here always turns to dirt. But I'll get my revenge sometime. I'll make you people sick about me yet!"

"Are already, Herr Meier! More than enough!" said Pagel, sitting beside him, and pleased at the little man's rage. "Though if I were you I'd use the horn less; it might in the end occur to our convicts that one can get to Berlin more comfortably in a car. There, keep a little to the left . . . *Donnerwetter!* what's this?"

A large blue and white car hooted itself round the corner just ahead.

"The Rittmeister's Horch!" whispered Meier and drove his small car close to the trees.

The great car howled once more, rushing past.

"The Rittmeister and our charming Vi," grinned little Meier. "Well, they didn't recognize us. I put my hand in front of my face at once. Trying it out, I suppose. Good luck to them! The splendor certainly won't be lasting much longer."

"In what way, Herr Meier?" asked Pagel sarcastically. "You believe the Rittmeister will go bankrupt because you're no longer working for him?"

Meier made no reply. He was not a very experienced driver, and the rough, sandy path through the forest required all his attention.

At last they came to the forester's house, unloaded him and laid him on a bed. From her armchair his wife reviled them for bringing her husband home drunk, for putting him on the wrong bed, for not undressing him . . .

"Well, that's that, Herr Meier!" said Pagel. Little Meier was back in the car. Pagel stretched out his hand. "Well, a good trip!"

Meier looked at Pagel and Pagel's hand. "You know, man—I can never remember your name—you know, I'll not shake hands, and it's better like that. You think I'm a big swine. . . . But I'm not such a big swine as to shake hands with you now. So there!" And he slammed the door on the astonished Pagel and nodded through the window. It seemed to be quite another face which was nodding: a sad, wretched one. Then the car started. Pagel looked after it a while. Poor devil, he thought. Poor devil. And he meant both the "poor" and the "devil."

Then he returned to the farm, utterly uncertain whether he should say anything or what he should say or to whom he should say it.

He would think about it—just a little too long.

Chapter Thirteen

Lost and Forsaken

I

Dawn on the thirtieth of September was overcast and sullen. The wind threw itself on Neulohe. Much would be swept away this day, love and hate, treachery, jealousy, selfishness; much blown away and the people scattered like leaves. And this although it was not yet October the first, the fateful day.

Herr von Studmann was the first to awake. It was still dark when the alarm clock went off; wind shook the house. Studmann was a man who did what he had in mind very matter-of-factly. He arose in the chilly gray morning without regret for his warm bed—today he had to find the rent and would do so, although he was fairly certain that it was to be used for quite other purposes.

He shaved himself carefully. When he went into town he always shaved twice. Now it occurred to him that he could shave himself twice for Neulohe, for Eva. . . . But he rejected this thought immediately. He was neither a youngster nor a Don Juan. He wasn't going to preen like a peacock.

A little later he was in the office. On the desk lay a note. "Please wake me before you go. I've something to tell you, Pagel."

Studmann shrugged his shoulders. Could it be anything important? Cautiously he opened Pagel's door—the lamplight, entering, showed him peacefully asleep on his side. Over his forehead a great lock of hair rested on the closed eyelid, every hair gleamed like the very thinnest of gold thread, and the face was serene. All of a sudden some words came into Studmann's mind, probably from his schooldays. "Favored by fortune, nothing done, dead like all."

The important communication, he decided, was not important. It was only four o'clock, and another hour and a half's sleep wouldn't do the young man any harm. Gently he shut the door. Besides, he mustn't miss the early train to Frankfurt, because that was what Eva wanted. Even the most important communication could not change that, but could only upset it.

Black Minna now appeared in the office, still half awake and more slovenly than ever. And the coffee she served looked just as slovenly. Studmann, who from his work in the hotel was very sensitive to cleanliness, had it in mind to speak harshly, but refrained. Knowing the situation as he did, he was aware that his reproof would promptly be made known in Frau Eva's kitchen, and thus reach her. He didn't want her to have any more trouble at present.

Carriage wheels crunched on the gravel outside; Hartig, the coachman, was there. Abandoning the coffee and stale bread, Studmann lit a cigar, put on his overcoat and left the house.

The coachman on his high seat was talking with the gendarme. Studmann said hello and asked after any news. There was no news. The gendarme's all-night vigil had been as fruitless as beating through the woods the previous afternoon. Not the slightest trace of the fellows! The whole thing was stupid. They should have gone about things in quite another way, of course; numb and exasperated, the gendarme explained his own plan . . .

"Excuse me, officer, I have to go to the station now," interposed Studmann. "But my coffee's still standing in the office. It's not much good but it's warm—if you'd care to drink it. . . . But don't make a noise, please; the young man's asleep in the next room."

The officer thanked him and went to the office. The carriage with the smoking Studmann and the silent, ever-grumpy Hartig, rolled toward the station. It was quarter past four.

It's only a quarter past four, thought Frau Eva, looking unbelievingly at the small alarm clock on her night table. Had someone called her? Vi? Achim? She had started up in bed and had automatically turned on the light. Now she sat erect among the pillows, listening. Outside there was nothing but the howling of the wind. Not a cry. All were asleep. Frau Eva had slept well, and felt incredibly fresh, full of a vague happiness. But what on earth was she going to do in the four hours until her morning coffee?

She looked at her room, surprised, almost a little disappointed, that it could offer her neither distraction nor diversion. For a moment she considered getting up to see if Vi, perhaps, had called out in her sleep. But it was so warm in bed and Vi, anyway, was a grownup girl now; the time had passed when her mother, as a matter of course, rose five or six times a night, to tiptoe to her little one. Happy vanished times, obvious duties gladly performed, simple cares which life, because it was life, brought along with it . . . and nothing of all this unnecessary artificial worry, the least essential thing in the world.

Suddenly her face became drawn and she remembered what had been forgotten—that she lay in a decaying house, a member of a family in dissolution. And that the very floor which held her bed was decaying. The door leading to her husband's bedroom was locked, had been locked after the angry scene yesterday evening. She frowned; her pretty plump shoulders drooped. She had suddenly become an old woman. How could I have lived with him year in, year out, and put up with all this? Impossible to live with him one week longer—and she had put up with it for twenty years! Inconceivable! She felt that she had completely lost the charity to be patient or forbearing or, in feminine cunning, achieve something with him. It seemed that with her love had vanished all capacity for this.

My God, he had come home many a time before this somewhat the worse for drink. But a wife learned to put up with that, although the mixture of bragging and sudden tenderness was always a little hard to support. But it was precisely yesterday afternoon he had picked on for this; he in his extreme folly could not wait to show off the car to—her brother! He had sneaked out. In an almost stupidly cunning way he had incited Violet against her and won her over to his side, a foolish child who was naturally enthusiastic about everything new, and especially something as new as a car. Finally, he had, to put the finish on everything, allowed this child of fifteen several liqueurs—he said one, she said two, but for certain there were four or five. No, all that was far more than even a woman married for many years could bear.

Supper had been laid, the servant waited, the maids in the kitchen waited. It grew late; too late. She had never thought that she would one day be sitting thus, angry and like a *petite bourgeoise*, waiting for her husband to come home. That had always appeared to her as the peak of the ridiculous and contemptible. The other must lead his own life; he was not kept on a chain!

And now she was sitting there like that, drawing up a list against him: This, that and the other thing. This done for him, that renounced for him, something else lost because of him. And yourself? This "yourself" grew and grew, until it became a monstrous cloud casting a shadow over her whole life, a threatening storm cloud, full of evil foreboding. And then the pair had come in, with the silly, unembarrassed jollity of the slightly tipsy.

"Oh, dear! . . . Oh, dear! Uncle Egon couldn't find the corkscrew and knocked the neck off the bottle. Oh dear, oh dear!" Growling thunder from afar—who were you once upon a time? A slender, swift creature, no great thinker, for sure, but a knight without fear or reproach. . . . "And we passed a baby Opel in the wood, Mamma, and our worthy young Herr Pagel was in it; I'll take my oath, with a young lady. She was holding her hand in front of her face, though!"

"Enough!" Yes, indeed enough, and more than enough. Words, quarreling, the young girl's tears, the father's amiable bad conscience changing into a raging one. . . .

"Only because you grudge me the car!" And Vi sobbing: "You don't want us to have any pleasures! We can't do anything. And now you want to tyrannize over Papa as well."

Father and daughter in alliance against the mother, and the servants listening behind the door—that was the result of the home you had made, Eva! You had sworn to marry the first man who really had some style—you hated your father's want of polish. Yes. Was everybody mad then? Was everybody diseased? Was this inflation some plague carried in the atmosphere, which everyone caught? Was this girl with blotched face, unrestrained gestures—now sobbing, now shouting her accusations—was that your daughter, your young and sheltered Violet? Was that your husband, the well-bred, upright man, so careful of his appearance, so fastidious and neat, now blustering and shouting and waving his hands about—"You won't get the better of me"?

Yes, and was that you yourself, angrily replying, scornfully rebuking, and all the while thinking of another man? You, who had already arranged a substitute before this one had gone?

Shame, shame on all of us! One and all! She had rushed upstairs—she couldn't get to her room quickly enough; she had wanted to be alone. The windows were open; it was pleasantly cool and fresh. She smelled a hint of central heating warmth in the air, and a hint of her soaps and perfumes as well. Just enough to remind her that she was at home now . . . Most of all she would have liked to have a bath, but she didn't like the idea of seeing her body at the moment. It had seen too much of life, experienced too much, enjoyed too much for her to enjoy seeing it this evening. She slipped out of her clothes and in the darkness found the veronal which the doctor had once given her when an abscess in a tooth had been maddening. . . . She took a tablet—the smallest amount had its effect on her—and lay back to sleep.

She had almost dropped off, had almost banished the scenes of that evening from her mind—the deafening squabble no longer resounded in her ears—when the door opened. He was there. In a low, uncertain voice he asked: "Are you asleep, Eva? I thought I would just come in."

This life can be one of constant disgust. She felt she would laugh, seeing him standing there. Although his hair was gray, he had learned nothing. Yes, he actually had on his best pajamas, had made himself smart for her, this eternal schoolboy, forever kept back in the class of those who would never understand anything.

"Eva! . . . Eva! . . . Eva! . . ." In every tone, considerate, pleading, and then slightly louder, so that she might wake up without his having exactly wakened her. She could see him quite well, outlined against the light, but he could not see her. Her face was in the shadow. And that was how things had been throughout a long marriage. What sort of a wife was it he imagined he had?

"Eva!"

Accusingly. Full of a melancholy reproach. See, he didn't really believe she was asleep. But he perceived that she was unwilling, and murmured something. Whenever he was embarrassed he always muttered to himself, believing he thereby covered up his embarrassment.

She heard his door shut.

With a jump she was out of bed, running barefooted to the door. Loudly and unblushingly she turned the key and stood there listening, panting, triumphant. "Have we been plain enough, sir? Have you understood at last that it's finished, forever?"

Not a sound. Not even one of his passionate exclamations. Only silence. Slowly she had returned to her bed, had fallen asleep at once. . . .

And now it was twenty-five past four. She had woken up so happy. It seemed as if someone had called her. She remembered; neither father nor daughter would do that. Why on earth was she so happy?

She sat, bent over, but her limbs were relaxed, loose.

She buried herself in the bed again as if she were coiling and cuddling round something living, that could protect her. She wanted to go on sleeping. It seemed inconceivable, how she would pass the four hours until breakfast, haunted by such ghosts dancing around her.

God, what sort of face should she bring to this breakfast? What should she say? What should she do? She could go to the office. But Herr von Studmann was away, and young Pagel was too young. . . . Oh, well. We'll see. In the end everyday passes somehow or another.

Goodnight.

II

After her too-early awakening Frau Eva slept so soundly that for the second time she looked at the alarm clock unbelievingly. Half-past nine. A soporific, according to an accepted saying, should be slept off. Well, she had slept twelve hours, which ought to be enough for one tablet of veronal. When she at last got up, however, and began to wash, her body was weary and her eyes felt as if they had just been weeping. Hastily and with increasing irritation she put on her clothes, scolding herself, resolving never again to take that "filthy veronal." And she reviled her husband, Vi, the maids, Hubert, for letting her sleep on like that. With it all she had a mortal sadness, an intuition that the day which, rainless, was wetly dripping from the trees, would bring no good to her or others. . . .

The breakfast table was laid only for one; neither Achim nor Violet was there. Twice she had to ring the bell before the coffee and eggs were brought, not by Hubert but by Armgard, smiling in a way Frau Eva did not like at all.

"Have the Rittmeister and Fräulein Violet had their breakfast?" she asked while the girl poured out the coffee somewhat too primly.

"At seven o'clock, madam," reported Armgard surprisingly promptly. "The Rittmeister and Fräulein Violet went out with the motor car before half-past seven." The manner in which she articulated the words motor car showed that the new acquisition had her full approval; the Horch had brought pride and sumptuousness into the kitchen also. Opinion there, no doubt, was that at last they had really "fine people" to work for.

"Why wasn't I called this morning?" asked Frau Eva rather sharply.

"The Rittmeister gave an emphatic order not to!" replied Armgard, a little offended. "Rittmeister and Fräulein Violet were very careful indeed not to disturb madam. They came down the stairs on tiptoe and only whispered during breakfast."

Frau von Prackwitz could see all too well that heroic pair who out of pure charity would not wake her up. Yes, she might have interfered with their trip; she might even have gone with them! The cowards!

"Then there was, to be sure, the big rumpus," said Armgard softly, with a very sanctimonious face.

Frau von Prackwitz chose to ignore this. Yesterday she had had all the noise she wanted; she had no desire to hear about any more.

"Did my husband say at all when he would be back?"

"The Rittmeister thought that he wouldn't be here for dinner," replied Armgard, looking at her expectantly. It was obvious that she knew about the quarrel with Achim; no doubt all the village, her own parents as well, knew about it by now. She would have to accustom herself soon to having everyone looking at her as if she were now half a widow, half a deserted wife. . . .

"Very well, Armgard," said Frau Eva, enlivened in spite of herself by all this tomfoolery. "Then you can slice up the cold fillet from Sunday, with runner beans. There will be enough for our small number." She counted on her fingers. "Myself, Lotte, you, that's three, Hubert four—there will be quite enough."

There was a pause, the maid silently regarding her mistress, a look which was really just a trifle disturbing. Frau von Prackwitz was on the point of smiling when she put her cup down. She would not be looked at like that by anyone. "Well? Why are you looking at me like that, Armgard?" she demanded.

"Oh, Lord, madam!" Armgard turned red. "Madam need not count Hubert in; the Rittmeister gave him notice this morning. That's the reason there was such a rumpus. We could hear it even in the kitchen. Not that we wanted to, but—"

"Where is Hubert?" Frau von Prackwitz stopped the flow of words with a gesture. "Has he gone?"

"Oh, no, madam. He's downstairs, packing his things."

"Send him here. Tell him I want to speak with him."

"Madam, Hubert threatened the Rittmeister that he—"

"Armgard! I don't want any tales from you. Call Hubert."

"Very good, madam!" Armgard, deeply offended, withdrew.

Frau Eva walked to and fro, waiting. Breakfast, of course, was now over. She'd known ever since she got up that today would be a loss. She walked to and fro feeling as she had done last night—everything was crumbling, disintegrating, while she stood impotently to one side and could do nothing. It was certainly not this ninny of a Hubert! She had never been his friend. A dozen times it would have given her the greatest pleasure to be rid of the freakish perverse fellow; moreover she had a physical repulsion to him. As a healthy woman she had always felt that things were not altogether right with that young man, quite apart from the maids' talk of his strangeness.

Well, he had been dismissed, probably because of some enormous crime such as an egg too hard or a teaspoon not picked up when dropped. In his present humor Achim would find cause for an outburst of fury in anything. But it all happened so quickly, without warning; nothing new came into her life, only the old went away, constantly went away. It was like sitting on an ice floe from which piece after piece splits off until there is nothing left. Once you had parents with whom you got on not well but bearably—and now no longer. You had a husband and a daughter—and now no longer. You had a business in the country—when were you last there? You had a comfortable home. And now, here you are sitting alone at the breakfast table, your servant dismissed, and the doors between the individual bedrooms carefully locked during the night.

A feeling of despair, an impotent grief, rose in her. Had there ever been a time when life was so little worth living? It made you itch to do something. Something just had to be done to get out of this morass. But somehow everything one did mysteriously only sucked you deeper in. Any action turned against itself.

Armgard stood in the door—half embarrassed, half defiant. "Hubert says he is no longer in service here. He says it's not necessary for him to come."

"We'll see about that!" cried Frau Eva passionately, reaching the hall in five steps.

"Madam! Please, madam!" implored the maid.

"What is it then?" she asked crossly. "No more tittle-tattle, Armgard!"

"But madam ought to know," said the girl coming close in order to speak softly. "Hubert did threaten the Rittmeister so! About an arms dump. Rittmeister was quite pale."

"And you saw that from the kitchen in the basement?" asked Frau Eva sarcastically.

"But the dining-room door was open, madam!" Armgard was deeply insulted. "I was just going up to fetch a collared ham and the door happened to be open. I'm not inquisitive, madam. I only wanted to help."

"All right, Armgard," said Frau Eva, about to go.

"But, madam, you don't know! Hubert was talking about a letter. A letter from the Fräulein. It was something to do with an arms dump."

"Rubbish," said Frau Eva unceremoniously, and went down into the basement. All rubbish and keyhole eavesdropping. Hubert had obviously listened behind the door yesterday, when she was talking with her husband about the car and the *Putsch*, and he now wanted to be revenged for his dismissal. She would soon put Hubert in his place. But to say that Vi of all people had been writing letters about an arms dump! That was the sort of absolute nonsense which might be expected from keyholes.

The dismissed servant was bending over a suitcase on his bed, packing with laborious exactness a pair of carefully folded trousers; he was allowing, so to speak, for every millimeter. The bed on which his suitcase lay had already been stripped. Folded in their creases the sheets hung over a chair; nevertheless a large piece of paper was spread out under his suitcase to protect the bed. Minute preciseness to the end—Hubert Räder all over!

At this sight, and still more at seeing his fishlike, impassive face, she lost all desire to attack him. "So you want to leave us, Master Hubert?" she said, with a touch of humor.

Hubert was holding up a waistcoat, examining it against the light, before proceeding to fold it, as was proper, with the lining outside. But he made no attempt to answer, which was not at all proper.

"Well, Hubert?" Frau Eva smiled. "No reply? Are you angry with me, too?"

Hubert laid the waistcoat in the case and took up the jacket. A jacket is a difficult thing to fold. He bent low over it and said nothing.

"Hubert!" She spoke sharply. "Don't be stupid. Even if you're angry with the Rittmeister, that's no reason why you should be rude to me."

"Madam," began Hubert solemnly, raising his dejected gray eyes, "the Rittmeister treated me like a slave. . . ."

"Well, I don't suppose you said very friendly things to him, either. I've been told that you even threatened him."

"Yes, madam. That is so. Armgard was listening—but it's true. I am sorry for it. Perhaps madam will be good enough, when the Rittmeister returns, to say that I regret it. I spoke in passion." He looked as passionate as a lump of wood.

"All right, Hubert. I'll do that. Now tell me what happened."

"And the Fräulein's letter will not be made use of," went on Hubert unswervingly. "That I promise. Although I shan't burn it. Not yet."

"Hubert! Be a good fellow and remember that I am not only an employer against whom you must naturally have some complaints, but also a mother who is often very worried. What is this letter of Violet's in your possession? Do tell me the truth about it. Stop playing the fool for once, Hubert."

"Excuse me, madam, I am not playing the fool," explained Hubert unmoved. "I am like that."

"All right, then. Tell me in your own way. I shall understand. Please tell me what you know, Hubert."

He looked at her with his cold dead eyes. Perhaps the grisly fellow was a little happy to have a woman pleading with him; it was not observable, however. After a long silent inspection he shook his head. "No." And returned to his jacket.

"Hubert, why not, then? You are leaving us, and it can't do you any harm to tell me now. It would be so helpful perhaps."

But Hubert Räder was busy with his jacket; he behaved as if he hadn't heard a thing. After a long pause, however, he said "No" again.

"But why not?" she whispered. "I don't understand you. What is the matter? Hubert, be amiable. I will give you a splendid recommendation, I'll ask my relatives about another place for you. . . ."

"I'm not going into service again," he explained.

"Well then, Hubert, you've said that you don't want to burn the letter yet; that is, you intend perhaps to use it, perhaps to get money for it. Vi, I suppose, has done something silly. All right, Hubert, I will buy the letter from you, I'll pay you what you wish . . . a hundred gold marks . . . five hundred . . . a thousand gold marks for a silly letter from a young girl!" Her speech and the suspense in which she watched him were feverish. She hardly thought about what she said. She couldn't make a judgment any longer about what sort of a letter it might actually be. A mysterious anxiety had seized her, alone with this horrible fellow. How had she been able to put up with him so long? Evil! Evil!

Hubert Räder uncovered his teeth in what no doubt was meant for a smile. At his threatening glance, and the triumph in it, her agitation turned to a dull despair. Slowly he shook his head and for the third time said "No." Then he looked at the jacket near him on the bed, as if he did not quite understand what it was doing there.

"All right, Hubert," she said in sudden anger, "the letter isn't yours. At the moment there are gendarmes here in Neulohe. I will send for one and have your things searched."

It was the same now as at the beginning, though; the fellow appeared not to hear anything and was occupied only with his packing. Pleas, threats, money—all had been in vain. What else was there? To flatter him, she thought; the fellow must be morbidly conceited. That went against the grain, however; the very thought of humbling herself before him was repulsive. . . . But she remembered her daughter, the mysterious letter, and that this man perhaps had her in his power. . . .

"You ought not to lower yourself to this sort of thing, Hubert," she ventured. (She had wanted to say "Herr Räder," but it would not come out.) "Someone like you who sets a proper value on himself. . . ." Hopefully she watched him. His glance turned from the jacket to her; once more there was that lifting of the lips. He had seen through her, and she felt humiliated.

"Excuse me, madam, I don't think I set much value on myself any longer, which is why I have no more use for money either." He was apparently satisfied with the effect of his incomprehensible words, for, after a moment's brooding, he said: "I will send madam the letter on October the second, by post. Madam doesn't need to pay for it."

"The day after tomorrow?" She knew that he had not promised her anything good. There was an obscure threat behind his words, something she could not ward off. But when she made to speak, there was a gesture from him, and she was silent at once, because he, the servant, wished it.

"Madam must not question me. I say only what I want to. The Fräulein treated me very badly. I never betrayed her, yet she incited her father to throw me out. . . . You said I shouldn't lower myself. I know you only said so to get me to say something. If Fräulein Violet is not out of your sight till early the day after tomorrow, then nothing will happen."

"She's gone out. . . ." she whispered.

After the daughter, the mother. Somehow both came under the man's spell. What was he? A stupid and a not exceedingly capable servant—the mother had hitherto supported him only with ridicule—but now she wasn't thinking of making fun of him, she took him only too seriously. Fads and whims? Stupidities? No. Danger, threat, and something somber that only he could know. . . .

"She's gone out," she had whispered.

He nodded, curt, self-assured. "She will be back tonight. Don't let her out of your sight then, madam, till early the day after tomorrow." He returned to his packing, and she understood that this was final.

"The best of luck, then, Hubert," she said. "You will fetch your papers and money from the office?"

He did not reply; he was preoccupied with scrupulously folding up his jacket. A gray and fishlike face, with no discoverable expression—that was the picture of him she was to take away, which she was to see many times in the future—her last glimpse of Hubert Räder.

She would never forget it. . . .

III

Leaving his room, she pushed open the door almost into Armgard's face. The maid screamed and sought to escape, but Frau Eva was extremely indignant. Holding the girl firmly by the arm she gave her notice, abruptly.

"Get your wages and papers from the office. Pack at once. You can go with the milk cart."

And with that she left her cook, paying no attention to her whining. The thought of having humiliated herself before Räder was bad enough; but to have had an audience, and such a one, was unbearable. Out of my sight! A fierce satisfaction filled her. He had thrown out the servant, and she the cook; everything was falling to pieces. What sort of a household would it seem in the next few days? What sort of meals would the seventeen-year-old Lotte rake together, with seven rooms to look after at the same time? Herr von Prackwitz would be astonished!

She went to the kitchen and disclosed the state of affairs to Lotte. Seven rooms, the cold fillet of beef, the beans, there was some sauce left, asparagus soup and—well, of all things, there stood the washing-up from last night! "My dear girl, don't you wash up every evening, as I told you to? Why not, then?"

Whereupon Lotte promptly broke into tears. Sobbing, she declared she knew nothing about asparagus soup, that she would never be able to do it, that she wouldn't let herself be shouted at, that she too would rather leave at once. . . .

Frau Eva wanted to think over what she had heard from Hubert Räder, what she should do with her daughter, and say to her husband. There were a thousand things to occupy and torment Frau Eva. But no, she must console Lotte and initiate her into the secret of how to make "real" asparagus soup from dried parings, with the aid of a small glass jar of asparagus tips. Finally she promised the disconsolate girl to ask her mother for a maid from the Manor as assistant. . . . And all the while she had the feeling that the disgusting Armgard was listening behind the kitchen door, delighted at her mistress's embarrassment. . . . Seven rooms to be done were in truth a nightmare.

Frau Eva walked to the office; she had to inform young Pagel of the dismissals. But the place was closed and the customary notice dangling on the door: "Urgent inquiries at the Villa. . . ." But in the Villa there was only the disconsolate Lotte, and when the dismissed servants came to get their papers from the office they would see the notice inviting them back to the Villa. Confusion would be complete!

She shrugged her shoulders—things were like that—and she went on to the Manor, telling herself that there at least everything would be the same as ever. But in front stood a cart on which trunks were being loaded, and at that moment up drove the ancient landau with her father's fat Hanover horses.

"What's taking place here, Elias?" she asked, astonished.

"Good morning, madam. The lady and gentleman are going on a journey," reported old Elias, taking off his little cap.

She ran into the house and up the stairs to her mother's room. In her armchair Frau von Teschow was sitting in coat and hat; behind her was old Kuckhoff with a bundle of sticks and umbrellas under her arm. Frau von Teschow was directing the maids, who were drawing linen dustsheets over the furniture.

"So there you are, child," said the old lady. "We shouldn't have gone away, of course, without coming over to look in on you again."

"But where are you going to so suddenly, Mamma? Papa never said a word about it yesterday."

"My dear child! Last night! It was unbearable." Holding her head, the old lady sighed dolefully. "Oh, why did your husband also have to bring these convicts to our dear Neulohe?"

"But they've gone away now, Mamma."

"Run away! I never slept a wink all night. I could hear people prowling around all the time. The stairs creaked, and once I heard giggling there . . . Yes, exactly as you are giggling now, you stupid goose, Marta!" said Frau von Teschow, angrily rebuking a maid who turned crimson.

"You imagined that, Mamma. It would be the gendarme on guard in the street. Their officer said . . ."

"My dear child, I believe only my ears! I'm going away. Your father for once is thoughtfulness itself. We shall go first of all to Berlin. Hotel Kaiserhof, Eva, if there should be anything. We're not going to be murdered in our beds! Oh, no!" And encumbered with her sticks and umbrellas, Aunt Jutta emphatically announced that she preferred the Kaiserhof to the churchyard.

Frau Eva saw it was useless to speak against the journey. The only puzzling thing was her father's prompt consent, for usually no complaints whatever from his wife would drive him away from his beloved Neulohe. But there was one good thing about it: she would be able to get a maid from her mother without difficulty.

Frau von Teschow shook her head. "You are always having trouble with your servants. That comes of spoiling them. And you don't send them to my evening prayers anymore!" In the end, however, after many a pointed remark, she declared herself willing that Marta should help. Marta, though, showed opposition. No, she wouldn't. She had been taken on for the Manor, not the Villa. Frau von Teschow tried to talk her round, Frau von Prackwitz promised her a reward, Fräulein von Kuckhoff admonished her, but Marta remained obstinate. She would not. Very well, then Trudchen! But neither would Trudchen. Trudchen in fact had an excuse: the Villa was too gloomy for her. Too far from the village; and now, when convicts were loose. . . .

"I really can't blame her, Eva," whispered Frau von Teschow. "I don't know how you look on your responsibility for Violet, but you should let her go with us to Berlin."

For a moment Frau von Prackwitz thought this a good idea. But: "Violet has gone out with her father."

"Of course. In that new car of yours. Horst-Heinz phoned to Berlin at once; a car like that costs easily twenty thousand marks. How can you afford it, when you are moaning about the rent?"

"Well, what about one of the maids, Mamma?"

"My dear child, you hear yourself. In these circumstances I really can't compel them. If something happened to them in the Villa I should have to reproach myself forever."

"Oh, you mustn't do that, of course, Mamma. I'll make shift with Minna or Hartig."

"I do wish I could have helped you, Evchen. But you really must stand more on your authority with the servants. I hear that you often don't go into the kitchen for a whole week!" Little pin-pricks, protestations, farewells . . .

When they went down to the carriage, Geheimrat von Teschow was standing in the hall in his best suit, which clothed the hairy East Prussian even more dreadfully than his customary worsted. "A minute, Eva. Yes, get in, Belinde. I want to say something to Eva." And taking her arm he led her a few paces away into the park. "There's one thing I especially want to tell you, Eva. I wouldn't do so to your husband. He listens to nothing. Perhaps this trip of ours surprises you. . . ."

"Mamma said it was because of the convicts' escape."

"Rubbish! Do you think I should go away because of a few brainless convicts? To a miserable town like Berlin? Ha, ha! That looks like Horst-Heinz von Teschow! No! But have you heard anything about a *Putsch*?" He looked closely at his daughter, who did not reply. "Good, you don't need to tell me. I can recite it off pat. My son-in-law's unexpected return, the new car. . . . So your husband's joined with them? I hope that he managed at least to get the money for the car beforehand. Still, he's not quite as stupid as all that, to get himself into debt for those gentlemen."

Frau Eva was silent.

"So he has!" crowed Herr von Teschow, delighted. "Well, well. Everyone's as stupid as he must be. It's all the same to me. Only I don't understand *you*. All right. Good. Let's drop it. Well, here's a word for you. This *Putsch* will end in smoke. The gentlemen can say what they like, the Reichswehr won't join in. I've been out and about the last few days all the time, keeping my ears open everywhere. A still-born child! There are twenty fools from the village in it, the magistrate Haase, that ninny, right in front. And so the other ninny's my son-in-law, then?"

"Papa, the people ought to be warned!"

"What's that? Believe an old man, my child—no one's pleased if you try to interfere with his stupidities. There may be a bit of fighting—all right! They just can't stop fighting; they don't see that Messieurs Clemenceau and Poincaré are laughing fit to split at us killing one another here. So, Evchen, you talk your husband round cunningly and go away, too! If you remain here you will have to take sides one way or the other and be dragged into the mess. Better go away."

"He wants to join in, though," she said softly.

"Have I got to tell you, girl, how to get round a man? Say that you have to go to Frankfurt this evening, appendicitis if you like. But go away!"

"Let him join in, Papa."

The old man looked up. "I'll be damned!" he cried astonished. "So it's like that, is it? Well, Evchen, you've taken a damned long time about it. I always thought I had a clever daughter. . . ."

"Oh, Papa."

"All right, then. Let him join in. For all I care, the car can be lost, too." He stopped, alarmed by his own generosity. "Well, that's not altogether necessary. You must try and arrange somehow, Evchen, that the car can't be taken out tomorrow. Speak to Herr von Studmann. He's pretty wide awake, certainly."

"Oh, and Papa! you're going away—to whom are we to pay the rent tomorrow?"

"Oh, the rent! Have you got it then? Well, leave it till I get back."

"No, Papa, that won't do. Herr von Studmann is bringing the money back this afternoon. We can't risk any devaluation."

"I'll be damned!" cried the old gentleman, looking at his daughter nonplussed. "I didn't think for a moment that you'd have the money by tomorrow. What am I to do now?"

"Tell me whom we shall pay it to, Papa. I shan't let the money wait beyond October the first."

"And tomorrow there's the *Putsch*. Tomorrow the mark may fall and fall. I tell you what, Evchen, pay for the car with the money."

"Will you take it instead of the rent, then, Papa? You would have to give me that in writing."

"Eh? What will the car look like tomorrow, perhaps? There's no family feeling in money matters. I tell you what, I'll go to some expense about it. Send your young man—Pagel, isn't it?—send him to me in the Kaiserhof. I'll pay the fare, third class, of course, and a little for expenses."

"That won't do either, Papa. For particular reasons I want Achim to give you the money himself."

"Damnation!" cried the old gentleman in a rage. "I wish I had gone away without talking to you. Then you could all of you see for yourselves how to get rid of your money. Achim will have to follow me, that's all."

"Achim won't do that, Papa. You know what he has on hand tomorrow."

"He will have to. Debts come first."

"That's what we think, too. But here!"

"Oh, so you'd like me to stay here? No, my child, your father is not such a fool. Elias, come here. Now, Elias, you'll get from my son-in-law either this evening or tomorrow morning a mass of paper, what they call money nowadays. Do you understand?"

"Yes, Herr Geheimrat."

"Put it in my old brown leather money bag, go at once to the station and take the next train to me in the Hotel Kaiserhof. Do you know it, Elias?"

"In the Wilhelmplatz, Herr Geheimrat."

"Correct, Elias. Don't say a word to anyone. Take a taxi at Friedrichstrasse Station. But don't let go of the bag for a moment."

"That I would never do, Herr Geheimrat."

"Elias, plenty can cut away the bag in a crowd and then you turn up at the Kaiserhof with the handle. . . ."

"I shall come with the bag."

"Well, all right, Elias. Listen, put a stone in at the bottom so you can tell by the weight. . . ."

"Certainly, Herr Geheimrat."

"Good. Everything in order now, Evchen?"

"Only the receipt for the rent, Papa."

"This is the limit. Here's a trusting daughter for you. I can't give the receipt till I've counted if the money is correct."

"And we can't give Elias the money without a receipt."

"You hear, Elias, she doesn't trust you. How often have you put a pacifier in her mouth, when she was crying in her pram—and now she doesn't trust you! Very well, Elias, I'll scribble a receipt for you now. And you must write in the exact sum you get, milliards and millions, exactly, Elias!"

"For certain, Herr Geheimrat."

"And then the time, to the minute. Notice, for example, if it's round about twelve, when the dollar changes. Wait a moment. Does your old watch go properly?"

With exactitude the watches were compared, and Elias was given the receipt. From the landau Frau von Teschow had been crying for the last five minutes: "We shan't get the train, Horst-Heinz! Eva, how can you delay your father like that?"

The Geheimrat shook his daughter's hand, hesitated a second, then kissed her on the cheek.

Frau von Prackwitz walked back to the farm, to the Villa. . . . Everyone was fleeing from Neulohe as though it were accursed.

IV

Rittmeister von Prackwitz had that sense of gain which suddenly emerges in those who know nothing of business. When his brother-in-law in Birnbaum admired greatly the Horch car, although thinking it very expensive, it had occurred to him that he might achieve in fact what he had falsely boasted of to his wife. That is, have the car paid for by the rebel gentlemen at Ostade. With a superior air he had assured his brother-in-law that, in the case of those who really knew their way about, cars didn't cost as much as was supposed. Indeed, almost nothing—in fact, absolutely nothing. And by hints, winks and confidential disclosures he ended by creating in his brother-in-law's mind a connection between the new car and the coming *Putsch*. Egon had naturally already heard of that. Everyone seemed to have known about it for a long time; the Rittmeister, if anything, last of all. Even though his brother-in-law did not appear to think the *Putsch* very hopeful, as a true son of his father young Teschow considered that no undertaking could be totally bad which had brought to light such a motor car.

Driving home in high spirits, with Vi no less cheerful beside him, the Rittmeister was already firmly convinced that the Reichswehr was under an obligation to pay for his car. What did that little Major mean by ordering him to appear with one? His life was at the service of his country day and night, but with his fortune he had to be more prudent. The croakings of disaster coming from Eva and his brother-in-law had not been altogether in vain; the Rittmeister resolved to drive to Ostade tomorrow, before the *Putsch*, and sound the comrades in the Reichswehr about squeezing a small installment out of them. Punctually on October the second the first payment for the car would be demanded, and he hadn't the slightest notion where he was to get the money. But it was superfluous to worry about that. He would see to it in Ostade tomorrow.

He turned and inquired of his daughter, humming happily to herself, what she thought of making a trip there. Violet, naturally, was enthusiastic, embracing and kissing him with such warmth that the Rittmeister almost became suspicious. But it was the alcohol, of course, the delightful drive and the long monotonous weeks, now at an end, when she had been confined to her room. Nevertheless he had, for one moment, got on to the right scent. It was not the father but the sweetheart who was kissed. What did she care for the car or the trip? Ostade meant the Lieutenant. It was impossible to motor to Ostade and not see him. But the thought of her mother gave her some anxiety and she asked cautiously: "And Mamma?"

Her father was suitably annoyed. "Military enterprises are not for your Mamma. It would be as well not to trouble her with them. The best thing would be to do our job properly and surprise her later with its success."

"But perhaps Mamma would like to go as well." Violet was very anxious. She certainly didn't want her mother present at her reunion with the Lieutenant. "Perhaps otherwise she won't allow me to go."

"If I allow you, yes, Violet!" It sounded very much the master of the house. In his heart, however, the Rittmeister was not quite so certain of his right to decide about his daughter. He didn't understand much about young girls; the way in which Violet had just kissed him was really alarming. But Eva, no doubt, understood little more. That confinement to her room about absolutely nothing at all had been a ridiculous blunder, though fortunately Violet did not bear grudges. All the same—to make amends—Eva might well have been a little nicer to her recently. Yes, Violet had honestly earned this excursion to Ostade.

"I will speak to your mother this evening. But, as I said, it is not possible to take her with us. Be downstairs on time. We'll have coffee at seven and be off by half-past. And don't make a noise on the stairs. You know your mother likes to have a good sleep." Again a gibe, even though it sounded solicitous. Actually, in undermining the mother in her daughter's eyes, the Rittmeister did not feel altogether comfortable. Unfortunately, Eva did not want it otherwise. If she could treat him like a fool, send him to a sanatorium, exclude him from the management of his estate, then he had the right to show his daughter what sort of a man he was, and that her mother also was not without her little weaknesses. He went about things with the utmost discretion, however!

And then that evening there had been the quarrel, and Frau Eva hadn't been invited to go with them, or even informed. That was forgotten. But the appointment between father and daughter, and not making a noise—that was remembered. Vi had been up first, and down the stairs like a cat, without a sound.

In the dining room the servant was laying the breakfast. What more natural than for her to call him to account at last? For a long time she had avoided him, he was too creepy; and she was glad when she did not have to speak to him. She never again forgot to lock the door to her room, night and day. Her love affair with the Lieutenant had become so hopeless—even she had to admit he had given up on her. Not because of her, but because the question of the letter that had come into the hands of the little Meier had so angered him. Everything was changed now, however. She was going with her father to Ostade; she would see her Fritz again this morning. He was face to face with great events and his cause would be victorious. Tomorrow he would no longer be a conspirator, having to conceal himself from the world; tomorrow he would be an important man, and her father said so, too. A hero who could openly acknowledge his love, and her. There must be then no more secrecy, nothing which she would have to hide from him; there must be no servant like Räder, knowing things about her.

She demanded her letter back.

He knew nothing about a letter.

Very agitated, she told him he should not be so low.

He replied that he was only a low servant and no fine Lieutenant.

She said she was going to Ostade now to meet him, and she would send him back. "You will see then!"

Räder looked at her with his melancholy dead eyes. Too late she realized that she had set about it wrongly. Too late she began to plead, to offer, to promise money; promised him indeed old Elias's situation at the Manor. She could obtain that for him through her grandparents!

He only smiled.

She considered a long time, very pale. She must have the letter back. She knew that her Fritz would not forgive such thoughtlessness a second time. Speaking in a low voice, flaggingly, she promised to allow once more . . . what he before . . . he knew . . . in her room. . . . She gave him her word of honor. But he must hand over the letter at once. . . .

She got further than had her mother; she could see him begin to waver, as the memory of that dark hour and the highest gratification of his life rose in his thin cheeks, leaving red circular patches there. He gulped. Then he changed

his mind. He had calculated for a long time, weeks and weeks. He had a definite plan in which this letter played a definite rôle. Violet was not enough. She
alone was nothing, only a female a little better-looking than Armgard. No, it
was the Lieutenant who was concerned. Anguish for the Lieutenant, her love
for the fellow, her disgust for him the servant—all that was concerned in it.

"Is the Fräulein motoring today to Ostade?" he asked.

She was sure now of her victory. "You know that, Hubert! At once. Fetch
the letter quickly—before Papa comes down."

"If the Fräulein doesn't go to Ostade today and this evening allows what
has been promised, I will give up the letter then."

She almost laughed in his face. Not to make the trip to Ostade, for his
sake! He was a fool. Anger overwhelmed her. "If you don't give me the letter at
once, I shall tell Papa everything, and then out you'll go and never get another
situation in your life!"

"As the Fräulein wishes," said he, quite unshaken.

And then the Rittmeister had entered. He would never have noticed anything about his servant, who was, as usual, like a block of wood. But Violet was
seething with rage. Within three minutes she boiled over. That, perhaps, was
what Räder wanted. Impassively he had passed her dripping when she asked
for butter; and sugar instead of salt. Bursting into tears, Violet shouted that
unless her father turned out that scoundrel on the spot she couldn't stand it
any longer. For weeks he had tormented and provoked her. He had stolen a
letter of hers. . . .

Immovable and fishlike, the servant offered her father the tray with the
fried eggs. The Rittmeister, who had had a very bad night, was at once exasperated. With his fork he gave the egg dish a good hit and, shouting at his daughter,
demanded to know what was this about a letter. What letters, in Heaven's
name, did she have to write, even to the good manservant? He turned round
and glared at Räder.

Violet's explanation was hurried and disconnected. She had believed that
the arms dump was endangered by the forester's babbling, and so thought to
send the Lieutenant a few warning lines through Räder. But the letter had been
purloined by the man and he refused to give it back.

The Rittmeister stood up in fury. "You have intercepted a military communication from my daughter!" he shouted. "The buried weapons are in your
power!"

Hubert set down the tray of fried eggs on the sideboard. Coldly he
looked at the Rittmeister; and nothing more provokes anger than another's
composure.

"Excuse me, Herr Rittmeister," he said, "but they are illegal arms. . . ."

The Rittmeister seized his servant by the lapels of his dark-gray jacket and shook him. Hubert offered no opposition. The Rittmeister shouted; Hubert kept silent. (Armgard's statement that the Rittmeister had been threatened by his servant was, therefore, a lie. But then, she had never been able to support Räder's arrogance.)

"Traitors against the wall!" cried the Rittmeister. Then a minute later: "If you hand over the letter now, it shall be forgiven and forgotten."

"Turn him out, Papa," said Violet.

The Rittmeister let go of his servant and spoke grimly. "Have you anything to say in your defense? Otherwise you are dismissed on the spot."

Violet trembled. She knew that Hubert had only to open his mouth, say a few words to her father, and she was lost. But she had taken the risk, since she felt that he wouldn't talk, that he had no interest at all in exposing her secrets to her father. And she was right. Hubert said only: "Then I am dismissed on the spot!"

He looked round the dining room once more and laid his napkin, which he had kept under his arm throughout the scene, on the sideboard. His eye lit on the fried eggs. "Shall I have them warmed up again?" he coolly asked.

There was no reply.

He went to the door, made a slight bow and said imperturbably: "A pleasant drive, Herr Rittmeister!" Then he was gone, without one glance at Violet.

Plunged in thought, the Rittmeister turned to his meal, for anger did not destroy his appetite. Then he had two cognacs and got into the car. All he said was: "To Ostade then, Finger."

Herr von Prackwitz was so constituted that after the interval of action came inevitably that of reflection concerning his action. He had got rid of his servant; now he began to consider why he had, in fact, done so. On this question it was not so easy to shed light. Much that had seemed lucid in his rage was now rather obscure. Had the fellow been merely impertinent? Of course he had; the Rittmeister remembered it distinctly. But in what way impertinent? What had he actually said?

Violet sat beside him, careful not to interrupt his reflections with one of those girlish nonsensicalities which, because they could always put him in the best of humor, she usually had ready. A child knows the faults of its parents better than the parents know the faults of their children. A child's observation is mercilessly sharp. Its first voyage of discovery to the new world is not encumbered by love or sympathy. She saw that her father was thinking about her; any word that sought to distract him would only make for suspicion. She had to wait till he began to speak, to question. He was one of those who pass without effort from this question to that and so lose sight of their original goal completely.

Moreover she had done something, the idea of which had come on seeing her father drink the two cognacs. The afternoon before, at her uncle's, she had had quite a lot of liqueurs; how many she didn't know and neither did her father. But the drink had done her good. It had given her courage to defy her mother, which she would never otherwise have dared; it had made her combative and cheerful. And when her father after breakfast went out to put on his coat, she had swiftly poured herself a cognac in his glass, while watching the door. She had filled it to the brim and emptied it at a gulp. Almost automatically she had, like her father, let a second drink follow the first.

And now she was curled up comfortably in the car, warmly covered, while the country glided slowly across the windows—an endless expanse of fields deserted except for a few plow teams in the distance or the long rows of potato diggers shifting forward on their knees, the three-pronged hoe in hand. A moment they raised their heads and looked after the car speeding by. Next the almost unending woodlands, where trees were often so close to the road that branches rustled across the windows, startling the motorists, who then laughed at their fright and saw that the glass was bedewed with drops of water from the branch.

The roads from Neulohe to Ostade were bad, softened by rain and cut up by the potato carts, so that the powerful car could not show its speed; at barely twenty miles an hour Finger drove her cautiously over the potholes and through the puddles. Despite this low speed, however, the deep note of the engine, the car's elastic springing, its effortless gliding, produced in Violet a feeling of peaceful strength. The engine seemed to transfer a portion of its unused forces to her, and this sensation was heightened by the alcohol circulating through her tranquil body. First a warmth, then in the form of many different images which faintly and fleetingly arose in her, but nevertheless left her with a feeling of something like happiness. Her young body had greedily drunk down the poison. Her tastebuds had risen up against the alcohol, and her body had shaken as she quickly drank it down. But the more her tongue rejected it, the more another instinct in her had welcomed it, whether it was her brain or an even more mysterious center of the body, which often contradicts our sense of what we should hate or what we should love. To drive like this was complete happiness, and peace.

But it had to come. In the moment when she was thinking most pleasantly of the reunion with her Lieutenant, the Rittmeister asked rather abruptly: "How did you come to know this Lieutenant?"

"But, Papa, everyone knows him!"

"Everyone? I don't know him!" contradicted the Rittmeister, annoyed.

"Papa, you were praising him to me only yesterday."

"Maybe." The Rittmeister was to some extent hit. "But I don't know him—what we mean by knowing. We haven't even been introduced. I don't know his name, either."

"Nor do I, Papa."

"What? Nonsense. Don't lie, Violet."

"But it's true, Papa. On my honor. The whole village calls him only Lieutenant Fritz, Papa. The forester told you that, too."

"You never told me. You don't trust me, Violet."

"Of course I do, Papa. I tell you everything."

"Not this about the *Putsch* and the Lieutenant."

"But you were away, Papa."

"Wasn't he here before that?"

"No, Papa. Only the last few weeks."

"Then he was not the same man who went with you and Hubert at night across the yard?"

"That was the forester Kniebusch, Papa! I've told you that a hundred times."

"So your mother acted wrongly?"

"Of course, Papa."

"I always told her so."

The Rittmeister fell silent again. But this silence was no longer as somber as before. He felt that he had cleared up the matter in a very satisfying way; and what particularly pleased him was that once again he had proved his wife in the wrong. Because he felt inferior to her, especially now, he repeatedly had to prove that he was her superior. The only thought disturbing to this satisfaction was that Violet had wanted, behind his back, to send the letter of warning to the Lieutenant. That showed she had either no trust in him or that she was indeed secretly associated with the man.

Suddenly he turned hot at the thought that she was in any case lying to him. When she had met the Lieutenant near the arms dump, both had pretended not to know each other. Yes, the Lieutenant had been openly rude to her. Yet even so Vi had written him a letter! They had wanted to deceive him, therefore. Or the pair had actually only become acquainted later. In that case, why had she not given her warning about the forester verbally?

It was an extremely difficult case, a maddening and complicated affair. He would have to consider very deeply and be very cunning to get at the truth.

"Vi?" he said, frowning.

"Yes, Papa?" She was readiness itself.

"When we met the Lieutenant in the wood, did you know him then?"

"Of course not, Papa; otherwise he wouldn't have been like that." Violet felt her danger. Not desiring her father to follow up that line of thought too far, she decided on a counter-attack. "Papa," she said energetically, "it seems to me you think with Mamma that I'm having affairs with men."

"Not at all!" replied the Rittmeister hastily. The magic words "like Mamma" had broken down his defense at once. But he reflected a while before asking suspiciously: "What do you know about affairs with men, Violet?"

"Well, cuddling and so on, Papa," said Violet with that girlish defiance which seemed to her suitable.

"Cuddling is a nasty word," said the indignant Rittmeister. "Where do you hear that sort of thing?"

"From the maids, Papa. They all say that."

"Our maids, too? Armgard? Lotte?"

"Of course, Papa. They all say that. But I can't swear that I exactly heard it from Armgard or Lotte."

"I'll throw them out," murmured the Rittmeister to himself. That was his particular way of annihilating the unpleasant things in life.

Violet had not heard him. She was very well satisfied with the path this examination was taking. She laughed. "A little while ago, Papa, I heard one of the girls in the village say to another: 'Have you come to the pub to dance or to cuddle?'—I had to laugh so, Papa!"

"There's nothing funny in that, Violet!" cried the Rittmeister indignantly. "That sort of thing is simply disgusting. I don't want to hear anything more like that, and neither do I wish you to listen to such things again. Cuddling is an absolutely low word."

"Isn't it the same then as kissing, Papa?" she asked very surprised.

"Violet!" almost roared the Rittmeister.

The angry cry must have reached the chauffeur through the glass, for he turned round with a questioning face. By furious gestures Herr von Prackwitz showed him that he was to drive on and that it was nothing to do with him. But the chauffeur did not understand, put on his brakes, stopped, opened the window and said: "Excuse me, I haven't quite understood, Herr Rittmeister."

"You're to drive on, man!" roared the Rittmeister. "Go on driving."

"Yes, Herr Rittmeister," replied the chauffeur politely. "We shall be in Ostade in twenty minutes."

"Then get on."

The window was closed and the car went on.

"Blockhead!" swore the Rittmeister at the window. Then to his daughter in a milder tone: "There is a respectable and a not-respectable term for many things. You don't say, 'What will you booze?' but 'What will you drink?' So for kissing; a respectable person doesn't use that other not-respectable word."

Violet considered a moment. Then she said, smiling brightly at her father: "I understand, Papa. It's like this. When you're in good humor you say make water, and when you're in a temper you say the other word which I mustn't ever use, isn't that it, Papa?"

The Rittmeister said nothing more all the way to Ostade. Violet, not honored with any further harangue, was very satisfied.

Now they were driving along the Oder. Somewhat revived, the Rittmeister instructed his chauffeur to stop in the Old Market at The Golden Hat, which the officers frequented to read the newspapers and drink sherry or port before lunch. The country gentlemen, of course, also frequented the inn.

The Rittmeister took care that his car was not driven into the yard but left in front. "We shall be going on immediately," he told his chauffeur. That was not at all his intention, however. He wanted the splendor of his new car to be noticed.

In the dining room there was no one, at least no one who counted for the Rittmeister. Only a few civilians. Among whom he, although not in uniform, did not include himself. It was a little after eleven; the officers usually came about this time or perhaps not till half-past.

The Rittmeister collected all the illustrated, all the humorous, periodicals. Conversation with his daughter was out of the question; she had offended him too much. Ordering a glass of port for himself and a beef tea for her, he gave himself up to his reading.

It was absolutely disgusting that this girl had again spoilt this day. It was simply impossible to enjoy life in Neulohe. For three minutes the Rittmeister seriously considered giving up Neulohe and rejoining the army. He need only wait for the *Putsch* and everything would be possible! Glad that he only had to make the decision the day after tomorrow, he sank deeper into reading about the latest attacks on the government in *Kladderadatsch*.

Violet sat so that she could see the market place; it appeared surprisingly peaceful for a town which had to expect on the morrow a big *Putsch* which would completely change the constitution and government of sixty million people. In a row stood farmers' carts with potatoes or cabbages; women went to and fro with their market bags—but there was nothing out of the way, nothing different, and above all no uniforms.

"Papa! I don't see any uniforms at all."

"They have something else to do today than stroll about," replied the Rittmeister sharply. "Anyway, I'm reading."

But a little later he lowered his newspaper and himself looked out of the window. Glancing at the clock, he called to the waiter: "Where are the officers?"

"They ought to be here by now," said the waiter, also regarding the clock.

Fully satisfied with this definite information, the Rittmeister ordered a second port. Violet asked for one too, but he frowned. "Keep to your beef tea," he said. With a slight smile the waiter moved away.

Violet felt deeply disgraced. Never again could she enter this inn. Papa had been absolutely beastly. Tears in her eyes, she stared at the market place and the chauffeur sitting in the car.

"Where are you thinking of driving to now, Papa?" she asked.

The Rittmeister started. "I? I'm not thinking of driving anywhere. Why?"

"You told the chauffeur we were going on immediately, Papa!"

"Mind your own business!" said he, nettled. "What's more, alcohol is not for young girls in the morning."

For a long time they stared at the market place. In the end there was nothing for the Rittmeister to do but order a third port. Irritably he asked the waiter where on earth the officers could be.

The man regretted very much, but he couldn't explain it himself.

Wretched and more and more out of humor, the two gazed from the window. The civilians had long ago recaptured the periodicals; only *Kladderadatsch* remained with the Rittmeister, and from time to time he glanced at it but found the jokes stupid. The situation was certainly not one for humor. What on earth was he to do all day in a boring town like Ostade, if the officers weren't going to appear? There wouldn't be any lunch at home now; besides, he had not the slightest wish to drive back yet—this evening would be soon enough to hear what his wife had to say about Hubert's dismissal. Most of all he would have liked to drive to one or two barracks, and make some inquiries. Unfortunately he had just told Violet that he had no intention of driving on anywhere.

Her movement made him attentive. Utterly absorbed, she was gazing at the door, and the Rittmeister, forgetting his good manners, turned on his chair and stared also.

In the doorway stood a young man in gray knickerbockers and a greenish-yellow trench coat. He was looking round the dining room, then over at the buffet and the waiter. In his incongruous get-up he appeared so different that it was some time before the Rittmeister recognized him. Then he sprang up, rushed

toward the young man and, in his delight at this distraction, greeted him enthusiastically. "Good morning, Lieutenant. You see, I'm already here today . . ."

"Twenty cigarettes, waiter," the young man called sharply. Having looked
coolly at the Rittmeister he decided to say "Good morning," very reserved.

"Surely you remember me!" cried the Rittmeister, astonished at this
reception. "Rittmeister von Prackwitz. We met yesterday in the train. Major,"
he whispered the name, "Rückert. You . . . I . . ." Louder: "I've already bought
the car, a fairly good one. A Horch. No doubt you saw it outside."

"Yes, yes," said the Lieutenant absent-mindedly. The waiter coming up,
he took his cigarettes, gave a note, acknowledged the change and asked: "The
gentlemen not here yet?"

The waiter brought out his two sentences: "They ought to have been here
long before this. I don't understand it either."

"Hmmm!" was all the Lieutenant said, but even the Rittmeister felt that
this had not been good news for the young man.

The waiter had left. The two men looked at each other in silence a
moment.

The Lieutenant made up his mind. "You must excuse me, I am very busy."
He spoke mechanically and did not move, but remained looking at the Rittmeister as if he expected something.

That his announcement about the purchase of a car had made so little
impression offended Herr von Prackwitz very much. Nevertheless he did not
want the Lieutenant to go. At the moment he was the only person with whom
he could talk or from whom he could find out anything. "Perhaps you would
join me at my table for a moment, Lieutenant?" he said. "I have something to
tell you."

The Lieutenant was obviously deep in thought. He waved his hand. "I am
really very busy," he said. But when the Rittmeister made a gesture of invitation he went with him. Violet had not taken her eyes away the whole time.

"You have met my daughter, Herr . . ." The Rittmeister's laugh was embarrassed. "There now, I've forgotten your name, Lieutenant!"

Under Violet's glance the Lieutenant had become more alert. She looked
so fervent and affectionate that a strong repulsion stirred in him at once. She
hasn't even understood yet that she's finished for me, he thought. You've got
to be rude first to her.

"Meier," he introduced himself. "Meier. Meier is a very useful, a very
agreeable name, don't you think?"

He was aware of her glance, plainly begging for pardon and mercy.

"No, I don't believe that I know the young lady," he said more harshly. "Or perhaps yes."

"Yes—in Neulohe . . ." whispered Violet, cowering under that ruthless glance and remark.

"In Neulohe? Oh? Have we seen one another there? You must pardon me, Fräulein, but I for my part don't remember it." Turning to the Rittmeister, transfixed at this incomprehensible scene—for he saw that his daughter was stricken to the heart—the Lieutenant added: "No, please order nothing for me. I must go at once. You had something to say to me, Rittmeister?"

"I don't know . . ." began the Rittmeister slowly.

Violet sat there with a pale and lifeless face.

The Lieutenant crossed his legs, basely making show of an expression of boredom, as of one who knew only too well what was coming. Lighting a cigarette he said superciliously: "If you don't know, Herr—Herr—my excuses, the name escapes me" (with a vindictive look at Violet), "but if you don't know, I should like to depart, if you don't mind. As I told you, I am very busy." And continued to sit there with a provocative air. A little more and it could have been said that he was openly yawning.

The Rittmeister restrained himself; outside his home he could do that. "The long and the short of it is, my daughter wrote you a letter." He hesitated. "About the matter you know of, and which has got into the wrong hands."

It was all as had been expected. The Lieutenant, conscious of the girl's imploring gaze, put out his cigarette in the ash tray. Then he looked up from his dead butt, ran his eyes over the Rittmeister and said: "I am at your disposal, naturally, Rittmeister. I dispute nothing. Only," he went on more quickly, "I should be grateful if you would wait till tomorrow's action is over. My friends will call on you immediately afterwards."

The Rittmeister was a very old man; hollow temples, white hair, a ravaged face. In almost an unintelligible voice he said: "Do-I-understand-you-aright?"

"Papa! Fritz!" cried Violet.

"You have completely understood," the Lieutenant informed him in his supercilious and insolent voice.

"Oh, Fritz, Fritz! Papa . . ." the girl murmured, her eyes full of tears.

The Rittmeister seemed paralyzed. Holding his wineglass by the stem he turned it round and round, as if examining the color of the port. On his tongue was no taste of wine; only of bitterness and ashes . . . the bitterness and ashes of a whole life.

"Oh, Fritz." It was Violet's tearful voice.

In a flash he had thrown the remainder of his port in the impudent, conceited face. With great pleasure Joachim von Prackwitz saw the young fellow turn pale and the firm chin tremble. . . . "Have I understood you properly now, Lieutenant?" he asked.

Violet had moaned. The Lieutenant, before wiping the wine from his face, was young enough to look anxiously round the room—the civilians were sitting behind their newspapers. But the waiter at the buffet had given a start and was now rubbing the zinc bar with embarrassed vigor.

"That was unnecessary," whispered the Lieutenant, full of hatred, standing up. "Anyway, I have always loathed your daughter."

The Rittmeister groaned. He attempted to rise and strike the brutal odious face, but his legs were trembling, the room turned round and round and he had to hold on to the table. In his ears the blood roared like breakers on the shore—his daughter spoke from far away. Has she no pride at all? he thought. How can she still talk to him?

"Oh, Fritz! why have you done this? Now everything is ruined. Papa knew nothing." He was looking at her with his clear malicious eyes, full of contempt and disgust.

She advanced round the table; it did not matter to her that she was in a public place. She seized his hand, she implored him: "Fritz, be kind. . . . Papa will do everything I want. I will talk him round. . . . I can't be without you. . . . Even if I see you only once a week, once a month, we could still be married."

He was attempting to withdraw his hand. . . .

Her eyes were large with anxiety and tears. She was trying to collect herself. With an attempt at a smile she said: "I will convince Papa that it's all a mistake. He didn't know about it at all! He must ask your pardon, Fritz, about the wine. . . . That was very horrible of him. I swear to you he will beg your pardon."

"How do you mean, your father didn't know?" he asked. "He was talking about the letter, wasn't he?"

Thus his first words to her were a cold suspicious question, the sole reply to her stammering appeal. . . .

But she was happy to have him speak to her again; she pressed his hand, that bony cruel hand, and spoke rapidly. "Papa was talking about a quite different letter! I wrote to you again, about the arms, because the forester had seen you burying them. And the letter was intercepted. Don't look so terrible, Fritz! Fritz! The arms are still there. . . . I haven't done anything wrong, Fritz. Please. . . ."

She had spoken louder and louder, and now he put his hand over her mouth. From behind their newspapers the civilians had emerged to observe the scene with embarrassment, indignation or amusement. At his table the Rittmeister moved as if in sleep. "Let my daughter alone," he murmured. And believed he had shouted this. The waiter had taken a step toward the couple and now stood unable to make up his mind whether to interfere or not. . . .

The Lieutenant, however, now understood everything: the absence of the officers this morning, the broken-off communications with the Reichswehr. . . . He perceived that the whole *Putsch*, this action which had been prepared for months, was endangered—and he was to blame! No, she was.

His hand still on her mouth, he whispered in her ear: his hatred for her submissive face flamed higher every moment. "You," he whispered, "you've brought me only misfortune. I loathe you. I wouldn't want you even if you were smothered in gold. You make me sick. I shudder when I think of your whining. I could tear myself to pieces when I think that I once touched you. Do you hear? Do you understand?" He spoke louder, for her eyes were closed and she hung as if lifeless from his arm. "You have ruined everything for me with your cursed filthy love. Listen, you!" He was shaking her. "Listen well. If the weapons are still there, then I'll take care to get killed tomorrow. But if they've been found, I'll shoot myself this afternoon—because of you, do you hear? Because of your magnificent love." Triumphantly, full of hatred, he watched her. For a moment he grew confused; she hung so lifeless on his arm. But he still had something else to say to her, even though the waiter was shaking him roughly by the shoulder. In her ear he whispered: "Visit me this evening, do you understand, darling? There! I'll look nice. All your life you shall think of me lying there—with a smashed skull!"

At her scream everyone started up, rushed forward.

The Lieutenant looked around, as if waking up. "There, take her! I don't need her anymore," he shouted to the waiter and released the girl so suddenly that she fell to the ground.

"Hey, pick her up at least, you!" yelled the waiter furiously. The Lieutenant, however, was already running from the inn.

V

The Lieutenant, he did not know how, had reached his small hotel; to stand in his room looking at the distempered walls and listening to the babble downstairs in the bar. "Be quiet!" he shouted with a face distorted by fury; but the bawling continued. For a while he listened, seeming to hear Violet's humble, imploring voice. The whimpering of a slave! Damnation! He pulled himself together, drank a glass of stale water, looked round and noticed the pieces of field-gray uniform hanging up. He could not make up his mind how he would go "there," whether in uniform or in mufti. For a long time he considered which would be more correct, but could not decide.

"Life's a curse," he said, sitting down. But now he could not keep his thoughts on the question of what to wear; it occurred to him that he had been ordered to go with his men at nine that evening to fetch the arms from the dump. There was no compulsion for him to have a look at the place beforehand. If the arms were gone, well, it was just as bad at nine in the evening as at midday—he need not have known about them. The Rittmeister and his daughter would keep their mouths shut, for dirty linen wasn't washed in public. Scornfully he grinned at the thought of how dirty for the daughter this linen was.

"What a swine I am! What a swine!" he groaned, though he did not really mean it. In the end he was no lower than life had wished him to be. There he sat, head in his hands, the Don Juan of villages, the mysterious Lieutenant Fritz, as swift to act as to love. Flesh and hair, the smell of powder and the hot taste of long kisses—that had been his life—the smooth, cool stock of a weapon in his hand, the smooth, cool limbs of girls under their clothes, the blaze in the sky from a village set on fire—but also the eternally consuming flames in his body. Cold-bloodedly he could set on fire the farm of a Haase, if it suited him, but he could also spring into a blazing stable to fetch out the horses. That was the man he was, and he could not be any other.

Because of that, he would not wait till evening to make certain of the arms dump. No, he would go at once, and if all was lost there, then he was lost too, exactly as he had told that damned girl. He knew well that to many he was a man of questionable honor, one used by the Major only because he was suited to certain missions; but he had his own sort of honor and did not choose to be dependent on the silence of a Fräulein von Prackwitz.

He jumped up, his irresolution gone. From the cupboard he took out a suitcase and burrowing beneath the dirty linen in it fetched out his pistol. The safety-catch was up, but it was loaded from that time before—he remembered very well—when he had driven that little stinking beast Meier in front of him. He threw his case down at his feet—he was indecisive, a coward!

No, he had had no luck with her; she was associated with nothing but tremulous figures. Cowardly Meier, Kniebusch the chatterbox, that scoundrel of a Räder, the idiotic father who thought it was the thing to throw wine in other people's faces and was then prostrated by his own heroic deed. And the most tremulous of all, the girl herself, with her romantic pretensions to love. "I can't live without you!"—when every man in Neulohe and in the world could have given her what he himself had!

There was a knock. Swiftly, before calling "Come in," the Lieutenant slipped the pistol into the roomy pocket of his knickerbockers. But it was only Friedrich, the boots, come to announce that Herr Richter had sent round to ask if Herr Fritz would drop in on him at once.

"Yes, yes, that'll be all right, Friedrich," said the Lieutenant with the greatest ease, although in his heart he cursed.

Very punctiliously and with a firm hand he parted his hair before the mirror, attentively observed by Friedrich who, of course, was also in the plot, though only as a minor hanger-on. In the mirror the Lieutenant was watching the face of his rear-rank man; it was as if kneaded out of clay, a coarse face, with a shapeless nose. Nevertheless its expression was unmistakably anxious. He made up his mind. "Well, Friedrich, where's it burning?" he asked with a smile.

Friedrich looked at the Lieutenant in the mirror and said hurriedly: "The town has been put out of bounds to the troops."

The Lieutenant gave a superior smile. "We know all about that. That's all right, Friedrich. Did you think they'd let the men into the town beforehand, so that they could get drunk?"

Friedrich nodded a slow agreement with his shapeless head. "I understand that. But Herr Lieutenant, they say—"

"Do you listen to what people say? Then you have to listen to a lot, Friedrich."

"But—"

"Oh, shut up! It's all rubbish. We people obey and do our job."

"But they say a car from the Commission of Control stopped in front of the artillery barracks, Herr Lieutenant."

The boots, this insignificant something, one of hundreds, did not remove his glance from a Lieutenant who must not lose his self-possession or show dismay. For a moment only did the young man close his eyes, no more than a blink; then he was again looking at himself and the other in the mirror. Thoughtfully he tapped his comb on the rim of the washbowl. "Well, and what else? Is it still there?" he asked.

"No, sir, it went away again."

"You see, Friedrich!" explained the Lieutenant, reassuring himself too. "You see! It stopped there and has gone away again, Friedrich. That's all. The swine have to stick their noses in everything. Obviously they've heard something or other. It's impossible, when thousands know about our affair, for there not to be a little gossip. They were trying to hear something, and they've had to go away again. Would they have left if they had really known anything?" He turned round, looking straight at his man. And whether it was the nearness of his glance or the effect of his words, he saw that he had convinced the boots.

"The Lieutenant is quite right. One oughtn't to listen to what people say. One must just obey," said the man.

The other secretly grinned. What a rotten business! See, here was one man persuaded out of about three thousand; and Heaven only knew what the others were being told in the meantime. For affairs like this one wanted a regiment of more or less deaf mutes.

"It's not that I'm afraid, Herr Lieutenant. Only I'm so glad to have a job again at last, and the boss told me he'd throw me out if I joined in the *Putsch*." The Lieutenant made a gesture. "But I shall join in, Herr Lieutenant," Friedrich said hastily. "I'll bring also the two sporting guns of the boss's, as commanded. If everything goes all right tomorrow, he can chuck me out. Only, Herr Lieutenant, you'll understand that if it had been absolutely hopeless . . . It's no joke to be out of work."

"No, no, Friedrich," laughed the Lieutenant, clapping the man on his shoulder. "It's O.K. That I guarantee—with my life." Well, he had said it, he wanted to have said it like that; it was all bloody well the same, especially now. Should he be sorry for this fool? All were trying to cover themselves, the cowards.

"Thank you very much, Herr Lieutenant," said Friedrich, beaming.

"So you see, comrade," laughed the Lieutenant graciously, "never say die! Just think how pleased your boss will be the day after tomorrow that you joined in for him." His tone changed. "Oh, and Friedrich, is my bike ready? I have to make another trip shortly."

"Yes, of course, Herr Lieutenant. But first you were going to Herr Richter. . . ."

"That's right," said the Lieutenant, and left the room.

He strolled along, smoking. In the lavatory he quickly pushed back the safety catch and saw that there was a cartridge in the barrel. Then, with the pistol ready and gripped inside his trouser pocket, he went to Herr Richter. It was a strange thing; since he had heard about the Entente Commission's car his mood was a hundred times happier. If all those condemned to death felt as cheerful as he did, then all the drivel about the death penalty was utter nonsense. It was possible that a few minutes at Herr Richter's and things would explode. He with them!

Everything was quite friendly there, however. A crowd of discharged officers sat around Richter, some in mufti, some in threadbare uniforms without distinguishing marks. The Lieutenant knew them all. With an abrupt greeting he went at once to Richter, who was whispering with the one stranger, a genuine civilian.

Richter himself really looked like a civilian. Tall, dark, the young colts called him "God's pencil" among themselves; he was always writing everything down—it was certain that the fellow had never smelled powder. The Lieutenant couldn't bear him; and probably he could just as little bear the Lieutenant. He now signed to him brusquely to wait at a distance and went on whispering with the fat civilian. The Lieutenant turned round and in a bored way contemplated the room.

It was the back room of a public-house, dreary and discolored; and something dreary and discolored also appeared in the men there. It was revolting that he too should have to stand and wait with them. He fingered the pistol in his pocket; Richter's first words would tell him whether those men knew something about him or not. Two or three words of the fat civilian's reached his ear. He could not exactly make them out, but one word might have been "Meier" and the other "spy." To be sure, there were many Meiers in the world, but the Lieutenant was convinced immediately that only one Meier could be intended. The swine had been born to make difficulties for him. Why hadn't he let him roast in that forest fire which he had started? This was the result of a man's good deeds! Actually it was stupid to wait any longer. Everything was plain and decided. Out and finish with it! Why let himself be insulted as well?

He considered where the lavatory might be in this place—but that would only make trouble for his comrades. He must go somewhere farther away, somewhere in the wood, in the undergrowth—no, the best place would be where he had promised her. She must not be let off that!

"Herr Lieutenant, please."

He breathed freely again. Perhaps only a respite, but yet a little time longer to draw breath, to be himself, to have a future. Attentively he listened to Herr Richter explaining that since early that morning every communication with the Reichswehr had been broken. No one could get into the barracks, no one came out; officers were not to be seen on the streets. Telephone calls brought only evasive chatter. . . .

Ah, it was clear now how uncertain is all preparation. They were a handful of people, the remnants of *Freicorps* that had long been officially dissolved, together with a *Landsturm* of a few thousand men—strong if the Reichswehr joined them and, if it opposed them, a ridiculous mob. One had firmly counted on the Reichswehr. Naturally there had been nothing official; one had had the fullest comprehension of the difficulties which the comrades faced. From the debris of the army, from the ruins of revolution, a new army had to be created under the suspicious eyes of late enemies who were still hostile. Those outside were more than willing to take all the risk. The discharged officer had spoken with the one in service; the first had talked, the other had listened. "Yes" had not been said, but neither had "No." But one had been given the feeling—if we only carry out our job, they will not be against it.

And then, out of the blue sky, a day before the event, this incomprehensible silence, utterly undeserved coldness, emphatic withdrawal, almost refusal. Herr Richter went on to represent urgently that this mystery must be cleared up at once and the shadow dissipated. One couldn't lead people against the Reichswehr if it was to be hostile. He spoke very forcibly. The Lieutenant would surely understand what was desired?

With grave and attentive face the Lieutenant stood there. In the right places he nodded and said yes, but actually he heard nothing. Savage hatred filled him. Could so great and important a business be endangered through a little love-sick creature? Was everything to be in vain which hundreds of men had prepared for months, for which they had risked honor, life and fortune—all because a bitch like that couldn't hold her tongue? Impossible! It couldn't be. Oh, he should have said quite different things to her. He should have taken her by the hair and hit her love-filled face.

(But neither the Lieutenant nor his superior, now talking of treachery, arrived at the thought that a thing must indeed be rotten to be overthrown by the chatter of a fifteen-year-old girl; that it could only be an adventure without any life-giving spark of an idea; that they themselves were all trapped by the glittering and corrupt enchantments of a wicked age, and were thinking of the moment instead of the eternity beyond—even as the bank-note machines in Berlin were working only for the day and the hour.)

Herr Richter was silent. His talk at an end, he was hoping that this shady Lieutenant had understood him. But he merely looked questioningly at God's Pencil, who therefore had to make up his mind to go further—a disgusting business for a decent person.

"I have heard," he whispered with a cautious look at the fat civilian who still stood nearby waiting for something, "I have heard that you have the possibility of finding out a few . . . hmm . . . secrets. You are supposed to have some sort of connection. . . ." The disgust in his voice was so obvious that a little crimson crept into the Lieutenant's cheeks. But he said nothing, only regarded his superior attentively. "Very well, then," said Herr Richter impatiently, himself flushing. "Why beat about the bush? I ask you in the interests of the cause to make use of your connections, so that we can know where we stand."

"Now?" The truth was that the Lieutenant wished to ride past the hotel, see if the lordly Horch car was still there, and then go at once to the dump. If it was as he now almost expected it to be, then back to her at once and before her eyes do what he had promised. No, he wouldn't touch her, but she should carry with her that picture—much worse than any other—throughout her whole life. She was so impressionable, she would never get over it; day after day with that picture, starting up at night from sleep—screaming—with that picture before her. Therefore the Lieutenant hesitated. "Now?" he asked.

The dark haggard man became almost angry. "When would it be, then? Do you think we have much more time to lose? We've got to know what's going to happen."

"I don't think," said the Lieutenant, retaliating for his blush, "that the young lady has time for me at the moment. She's only a housemaid and will have to clean up now. And the cook bears me a grudge." That's the stuff, he thought. If they need me, let them stop being so genteel, and eat my dirt.

Herr Richter, however, had become quite cold and polite. "I am convinced, Herr Lieutenant," he said, "that you can arrange the matter. I shall therefore expect your report here—inside an hour."

The Lieutenant bowed, and Herr Richter was on the point of dismissing him when he caught a gesture from the fat man. "Oh, yes—one or two more questions, Herr Lieutenant, in another connection, with which this gentleman is dealing."

The fat man advanced, with a curt greeting. He had been watching the Lieutenant during the entire discussion, but now he hardly looked at him. Without circumlocution, without a trace of politeness, he asked: "Neulohe is in your district?"

"Certainly, Herr . . . ?"

"The arms dump in the Black Dale also?"

The Lieutenant threw an irritated questioning glance at Herr Richter, who with an impatient sign ordered him to reply.

"Yes."

"When was the last time you inspected the dump?"

"Three days ago. Tuesday."

"Everything all right then?"

"Yes."

"Had you set up secret marks?"

"I could see by the state of the ground that it had not been dug up since."

"Are your people trustworthy?"

"Completely."

"Do you think that anyone could have watched you while the arms were being buried?"

"That—no. Otherwise I would have shifted the dump at once."

"Did anyone come in the neighborhood of the sentinels during the concealment?"

The Lieutenant was trying to consider what reply would be helpful to him. But the questions followed one another so rapidly, the observant eye was so cold, that he replied hastily, without reflection or weighing the consequences: "Yes."

"Who?"

"Herr von Prackwitz and his daughter."

"Did you know them?"

"Only by sight."

"What did you tell them?"

"I sent them on."

"Did both go forthwith?"

"Yes."

"They asked for no explanation of what was taking place on their land?"

"Herr von Prackwitz is a former officer."

"And his daughter?"

The Lieutenant was silent. This is like the police, he thought. Only criminals are questioned in this manner. Is there a spy in our section then? I heard something of that kind once. . . .

"And the daughter?" persisted the fat man.

"Said nothing."

"You weren't otherwise acquainted with her?"

"Only by sight."

That look, that damned penetrating look! If only he had an idea what the fellow really knew! But, like this, one was groping in the dark completely. A single reply might have exposed him as a liar. And then . . . And then? Nothing more!

"You are certain that neither of the pair spied on your dump later?"

"Absolutely certain."

"Why?"

"I should have seen by the ground."

For the first time Herr Richter joined in. "I think we can be certain of Rittmeister von Prackwitz and his daughter. As a matter of fact they are now in town. I saw them go into The Golden Hat."

"We could question them," said the fat man thoughtfully, not removing his ice-cold glance from the Lieutenant.

"Certainly, question them! I'll come with you at once. Come along, we'll go," almost shouted the Lieutenant. "What's up? Am I a traitor? Have I blabbed? Come with me, you, Herr Policeman! Yes, I've just come from The Golden Hat; I was sitting there at a table with the Rittmeister and his daughter; I have—" He broke off, looking at his tormentor with hatred.

"Yes, what have you?" asked the fat man, quite unmoved by this outburst.

"I beg you, gentlemen," cried God's Pencil imploringly. "Don't misunderstand the situation, Herr Lieutenant. There is no desire to offend you, but we have reason to believe that an arms dump has been betrayed. A car from the Entente Commission has been seen there. As yet we don't know which dump is in question; we are inquiring of all the gentlemen to whom one has been entrusted. There is always the possibility that this is the reason for the peculiar behavior of our comrades opposite."

The Lieutenant drew a deep breath. "Inquire, then," he said to the other; and yet he felt that even that breath had been seen.

"You were speaking of The Golden Hat," said the fat man impassively. "You said 'I have' and stopped."

"Is that really necessary?" exclaimed Herr Richter in despair.

"I had some port with the Rittmeister, perhaps I was going to say that. I don't remember now. Why don't we go there?" he cried again, this time not desperately but in defiance, carrying on that game with death which had already been decided, however, as he well knew. "I'll be pleased to go. It doesn't matter to me. You can question Herr von Prackwitz in my presence."

"And his daughter," said the fat man.

"And his daughter," repeated the Lieutenant, but in a low voice.

There was a silence, oppressive and lengthy.

What do they want, he thought in despair. Do they want to arrest me? They can't do that. I am not a traitor; I have not lost my honor yet.

The fat man, without any embarrassment, whispered in Herr Richter's ear, on whose face was seen once more, but intensified, an expression of disgust. He appeared to be in disagreement, to be rejecting something. Suddenly the Lieutenant remembered a former comrade from whom the colonel had torn the epaulettes in front of the regiment. But I don't wear epaulettes, he thought forlornly; he can't do that to me.

He looked across the room—it was ten paces to the door and no one stood in the way. Hesitatingly he took a step in that direction.

"A moment," commanded the fat man roughly. His ice-cold eye saw everything, even when it was turned away.

"I answer for the dump with my honor," cried the Lieutenant, beginning to tremble. The two men turned their faces to him. "And with my life," he added, not so firmly.

It seemed as if the fat man made a slight negative gesture with his head, but Herr Richter said briskly: "Good. Good. Nobody mistrusts you, Herr Lieutenant." The fat man was silent. No muscle of his face moved, but it nevertheless said: "I mistrust you." I don't want to be judged by you, thought the Lieutenant, not your way.

"May I go now?" asked the Lieutenant.

Herr Richter looked at the fat man, who said: "A couple of questions more, Herr Lieutenant."

Hasn't the fellow any shame? thought the young man in despair. I wish to God I was on the street. But he did not move and replied: "By all means"—as if it were of no consequence to him.

And it started again. "You know a farm bailiff, Meier from Neulohe?"

"Slightly. He was proposed. I turned him down."

"Why?"

"I didn't like him. I thought him unreliable."

"Why?"

"I can't remember. That was my impression. I think he had a lot of affairs with women."

"Oh, affairs with women . . . You thought he was unreliable because of affairs with women?" The unbending cold glance rested on the Lieutenant.

"Yes."

"Could this Meier have observed the concealment of the arms?"

"Absolutely impossible!" declared the Lieutenant quickly. "He had been gone from Neulohe a long time then."

"Oh! Gone away? Why had he gone?"

"I really don't know. One would have to ask Herr von Prackwitz."

"Do you think there is anyone in Neulohe who is still in touch with this Meier?"

"I have no idea at all. Perhaps one of his girls."

"You don't know them?"

"I beg you!" said the Lieutenant heavily.

"It might be possible, don't you think . . . that you know the name of one or another?"

"No."

"So you can form no conjecture how this Meier might have heard of the arms dump?"

"But he can't know anything about it!" shouted the Lieutenant, bewildered. "It's weeks since he left Neulohe."

"And who does know about it?"

Silence again. The Lieutenant shrugged his shoulders furiously.

"Well, it has been stated," said Herr Richter placatingly, "that this Meier was sitting in the car of the Control Commission this morning. But it's not certain that it was he."

For the first time the fat man betrayed annoyance, and glanced at the too-talkative God's Pencil with irritation. The other, however, made an end. "We'll let that be enough of questioning now. It doesn't seem to me that much has come out of it. You know your instructions, Lieutenant. I shall expect you back in a hour's time, then. Perhaps you can learn what we haven't found out here." He made a sign of dismissal; the Lieutenant gave a slight bow and went to the door.

I am going to the door, he thought, remarkably relieved. Yet he was trembling lest the fat man, that terrible person, should say a word and detain him again.

But no word was spoken behind him; the uncomfortable chilliness in his back vanished, as if distance weakened the icy power of that glance. He saluted his comrades right and left, and by a great effort of will stopped at the door to light a cigarette. Then he seized the handle, opened and closed the door, crossed the taproom—and at last stood outside on the open street.

He felt as if he had been restored to freedom after a long excruciating imprisonment.

VI

Standing there he knew that never again would he return to Herr Richter in that room, would never make the awaited report, nor say comrade to comrade again. Honor lost, all lost! Yes, honor, which belonged to him in common with the other officers, had been lost. He had lied like a coward to escape the judgment of his comrades. But not because he feared death—he had already awarded himself death—but because he wanted to die in his own manner, so that she shouldn't forget him.

Hands in his pockets, cigarette in mouth, he sauntered in the gently drizzling midday toward that outlying part of the town where were the officers' villas. When he considered the matter, it was utterly foolish to take on himself this further humiliation of finding out from the maid Frieda what her employers had been saying, since he would never convey to Herr Richter the results of his investigation. Let them see how they would manage their *Putsch* themselves; he was only going to bother about his own affairs now.

As, apparently carefree and unbound by time, the Lieutenant strolled through the streets in his shabby clothes, entering a shop once and buying fifty cigarettes of a very much better kind than usual, there was a deep crease between his eyebrows, just above the bridge of the nose—a crease of intense brooding. It was, for a young man who throughout his life had preferred action to reflection, not very easy to understand what was really the matter with him, what he wanted and what he did not want.

Very surprising indeed was the thought of how indifferent he had now become toward that *Putsch* for which he had worked so many months, almost without money, denying himself everything that young men otherwise desire. Equally surprising was it how indifferent he felt at leaving his comrades, to whom he no longer belonged, and whose society had always been more important for him than the love of any girl.

He had had to endure a lot that morning, things he would normally never have borne, things which would have rendered him frantic: the wine thrown at him by the Rittmeister, the apprehensive queries of the contemptible Friedrich, Herr Richter's hardly-concealed disgust, and, to cap all, the shameful examination by the fat detective. But all this too had lapsed from the mind of one who otherwise could not forget an injury for years, but who now had to coerce himself if he wished to remember anything at all of these recent happenings.

It is strange, he thought; I feel as if I am quite out of things already, as if I have really nothing more to do with this world, like a dying man when all fades round him. Yes, now I remember again. When people die, there hands begin to move restlessly about their bedclothes. Some say the dying try to dig their own graves; others that they are trying to find something to hold on to in this world. Is that what's happening to me? Is everything withdrawing from me, and can I find nothing more on earth to hold on to? But I am no dying man; I am not the least bit ill. Is it that the cells in my body already know they must perish? Can death not only be annihilation through illness, but also the destruction of the body through thought? In that case am I really a traitor?

He looked around as if waking from a bad dream. He was on a large dismal ground stamped hard by the boots of many hundreds of soldiers, a yellow expanse of cheerless clay where hardly a weed ventured to grow. At the far end were the crude yellow barracks, surrounded by a high yellow wall topped with broken glass. The great iron gate, painted a dull gray, was shut; the sentry in steel helmet and with slung carbine was marching up and down to warm himself a little.

The Lieutenant contemplated this picture. In him a sullen resolution was forming, something evil and very somber. He crossed the ground. Now I'll see about it, he thought.

He stood right in the sentry's way and looked at him challengingly. "Well, comrade?" he said. He knew the man and the man knew him; many times had the Lieutenant stood a round for him and his friends. Occasionally they had sat together, and once, when there had been a fight at a country dance, they had cleared the hall side by side. They were therefore very good acquaintances, but now the man was acting as if he did not know of any Lieutenant. In a low voice he said: "Be off with you."

The Lieutenant did not move. He had become more sullen and addressed the sentry again, sneeringly. "Well, comrade, have you become so important that you don't know me now?"

The man's face did not change; he appeared not to have heard and marched past in silence. But after six paces he had to turn again and march back. "Listen, man," said the Lieutenant this time, "I have nothing to smoke. Give me a cigarette and I'll go away at once."

The man gave a quick look to the left. The small door for pedestrians was open, showing part of a gravel path and the windows of the guardroom. Then he turned to the Lieutenant, whose face bore an expression of contempt, despair and anxiety hard to decipher. The sentry could make little of this face, but it held something threatening; otherwise he might possibly have dared to hand over a cigarette. As it was, he passed by without a word and about-turned at the sentry box. Some premonition led him to remove the carbine from his shoulder before approaching again.

The Lieutenant was possessed by a savage and reckless despair. It was now clear that the Reichswehr did not want to have anything more to do with them, that the sternest orders had been given not to associate with the outsiders. He was determined, however, that, whatever the circumstances, the man should enter into conversation. He wanted to quarrel with him and be taken into the barracks, if need be under arrest. Then he could ask the officer on guard what they had against them. And if he then heard something about an arms dump . . . Very well. All over. All—over!

It was a completely insane thought which was keeping him there in its power; as though the officer on guard would be inclined to give to an arrested person information which had been denied the comrades in liberty. But the Lieutenant was no longer rational. He had been quite right that his body's cells could be infected by thought. . . . This time he let the sentry pass him unchallenged, but while his back was turned he lit a cigarette. Puffing away, he watched the man returning and enjoyed the astonished and slightly foolish expression on his face when he saw one who had just asked for a cigarette now smoking. The Lieutenant held out a second cigarette and said: "Here, comrade, a cigarette for you because you didn't have one for me."

The man came to a halt and said firmly: "Go away or I'll call the guard."

"I'll go when you've taken it," declared the Lieutenant.

The man looked at him, made no attempt to take the cigarette, but raised his carbine a little. "Do be sensible. Go away," he said at last.

The Lieutenant also desired to win over the other. "Comrade," he said, "take the cigarette. Oblige me and take it. So that I know you are still my comrade. There!" He held it toward him. "If you don't take it, I'll have to give you a punch in the mug," he added threateningly.

The man scrutinized him, serious and watchful. He made no attempt to take the cigarette but waited to see what the other would do.

A sudden thought made the Lieutenant almost mad with rage. "Ah!" he shouted. "I can see you think I'm drunk. . . . I'll show you how drunk I am!"

He dropped his cigarette and at the same moment hit out at the soldier's face. But, Heaven only knew why, the Lieutenant, usually a very skillful boxer, had no luck today. With a dull sound his fist struck the wood of the carbine stock, and a burning pain shot through his hand and arm. Then the butt hit him on the chest with great force and he tumbled over backwards. He felt that he would never be able to breathe again.

And as he lay there, battling for breath, with the sentry's watchful eye on him as if he were a savage beast, and considered that he had not been arrested or taken into the barracks or fired upon, and remembered in the hundredth of a second that in his pocket there was a pistol with which he could pay back the shameful blow—then he was pierced by the thought that he had not only deceived his comrades about the betrayal of the dump and made fresh difficulties for them quite unnecessarily, but that he was also nothing but a coward. He was doing all this only to delay the journey to the Black Dale, to postpone the discovery of the truth, to steal a few more hours of life. His outer varnish disintegrated, colour seemed to peel off him; his whole existence seemed like the rotten carcass of an old wooden shipwreck. This is what you are! said the voice within him.

And while he lifted himself gropingly from the earth, while he walked on with aching limbs, taking no notice of the sentry, not even thinking of him—so completely had his new understanding extinguished all that had just happened—he could not help recalling again and again that summer morning in the wood when he had driven little Meier before him with a pistol. How he had despised the pitiful coward; what disgust had overwhelmed him at his entreaties! And now the anxiety was gnawing at himself: Shall I be as cowardly? Will I even have the courage to press the trigger? How will I die?

This thought grew ever stronger in him, and in a few minutes was completely dominant.

How will I die? Like a man or a coward? Will my hand tremble perhaps? Will I shoot myself blind, as little Rakow did? God, how he screamed!

He shuddered, gripping the smooth pistol stock in his pocket as if it could give him that self-confidence which had never failed him his whole life long and which now, when death was near, so completely deserted him. I must be quick, he thought desperately. I must go quickly to the Black Dale, so that I can make certain. How can I live when I don't even know if I am courageous enough to die?

And all the time, while every fiber in him seemed to be urging a decision, he was going painfully but persistently away from the Black Dale, from death, farther and farther away, toward the carrying out of a repugnant job of spying which was already of no purpose to him. But he was no longer aware of this. When he saw a small public-house which he had sometimes visited, it occurred to him that he could not possibly appear before the servant-girl Frieda in such soiled clothes, and he entered. Ordering a glass of beer from the landlord, he asked if he hadn't some jacket which he could put on in place of his dirty one.

The landlord looked at him for a moment; he knew more or less, of course, whom the Lieutenant represented. He disappeared, to come back with a brand-new trench jacket. "I think it will fit you," he said. "What's happened to yours then?"

"Fell down," muttered the Lieutenant. He had stripped off his own jacket and saw on the outside of the lower arm a large, highly-colored bruise. Without thinking he opened his shirt over the chest and found there the marks of the gun butt. Doing up the shirt again, he encountered the landlord's eye.

"It hasn't started already, has it?" whispered the man.

"No." The Lieutenant put on the trench jacket. "Might be made for me."

"Yes, I saw at once you're about the same size as my boy. I bought him the jacket for tomorrow. My boy's also going, Herr Lieutenant."

"Good," said the Lieutenant, taking a gulp of beer.

"You will see that I have the jacket back this evening, won't you, Herr Lieutenant?" begged the landlord. "He wants to look decent when he goes tomorrow—it's the first time he's been in anything like this."

"That's all right," was all the Lieutenant said. "What do I owe?"

"Oh, nothing," replied the landlord quickly. "I'd like to ask, if you won't think it—"

"Well?"

"Were you in the barracks?"

"No, I wasn't in the barracks."

"Oh! Then you won't know, either. They say there's something wrong there." He looked expectantly at the other. Perhaps he was thinking of the blue-black patches on the Lieutenant's body. "You don't think, sir," he went on earnestly, "that it's likely to be serious tomorrow?"

"Be serious? How?"

"Oh, I only mean—serious. Fighting, shooting and so on. In that case I shouldn't let my boy go."

"Rubbish." The Lieutenant laughed heartily. "What are you thinking of? Fighting, shooting! There's nothing like that now. A *Putsch* like this is a really happy affair. There's no heroic dying either, now. Heroic dying has been dismissed since 1918." He stopped suddenly, as if disgusted.

"I don't know if you are in earnest," explained the landlord, "but I ask completely in earnest, Herr Lieutenant. Because I have only the one boy, that's why! If something happened to him, who'd take over this house? One doesn't want to have worked all one's life for nothing. You ought to have seen the place when I bought it twenty years ago. A pigsty! But now! No, if I knew that it might be serious tomorrow—it would be too much of a pity about my boy. Otherwise he can gladly go—it's also good for business, because we have so many customers among the military."

The Lieutenant repeated his assurance that everything was all right and not at all dangerous, and once again he promised to send back the jacket in proper time that evening. Then he left. He had lied to the landlord, but what did that matter? A few lies more or less were not important now. Seen close at hand, it was enough to make one sick, the motives leading such people to join in. But perhaps his own motives seen close at hand were equally nauseating to Herr Richter. The weakening of his self-esteem had already made such progress that the Lieutenant could conceive this.

The short halt in the public-house, the two gulps of beer, had done him good. Now he stepped out and soon came to the little street of villas which was his goal. Pulling his cap down over his brows, the Lieutenant hurried on; he did not wish to be seen and recognized, here where so many of the officers lived.

A colonel of the Reichswehr inhabited the villa he was making for. Socially the Lieutenant had every right to press the button where the notice read: "Visitors only." However, he didn't ring here but went ten paces farther, to a small iron garden door with the notice: "Tradesmen." He walked along a flagged path—the visitors' entry was laid with black and white gravel—round the back of the villa to where a clothes pole and dustbins stood. He did not, like the visitors, climb five steps up to the first floor with its mirrors, but went down five steps to the basement with its gratings on his way to the kitchen. . . .

The Lieutenant had always believed that the end justified the means. He had not been ashamed to turn the formerly very respectable Frieda into a contemptible house spy, since by this he had often learned garrison secrets of considerable utility. If he was now making this visit with less pleasure than formerly, that was not only because his whole state of mind was far from cheerful, but also mainly because he had never before come this way in daylight. Our daylight deeds bear one aspect, our deeds at night another. The colonel on the first floor had two daughters, and the Lieutenant had even danced with them in the past; it would be embarrassing should they see him on a visit to the kitchen. He was not ashamed of his actions, but he was ashamed of being discovered at them.

He was fortunate—stepping into the corridor he met no one other than the maid Frieda. She was coming out of her room, carrying a duster and dustpan.

"G'day, Friedel!"

Friedel, about twenty, full-breasted, with that somewhat sturdy rustic beauty of which not a trace is left in the twenty-fifth year, was a little startled. "Is that you, Fritz?" she asked. "Are you coming in the day as well, now? I've no time for you, though." But she put down the duster and dustpan against the wall.

"Well, Friedel," said the Lieutenant awkwardly, "aren't you pleased to see me?"

She made no attempt to approach him, take him in her arms, kiss as usual. Generally she was radiant whenever she saw her Lieutenant. Who knew what the girl had been imagining to herself? Devoted infatuation, humble readiness. . . . And now?

She spoke very pertly. "I knew all morning that you would come today."

"Oh-ho?" The Lieutenant aped astonishment. "Have you presentiments nowadays? Were you dreaming about me, eh, Frieda? Well, I felt that . . . I thought, see what's happening to Friedel . . ." It was frightful, but he could not get into swing. He observed the girl, observed her with deliberation. Yes, a girl; she had a pleasant bosom, powerful hips, fine legs and ankles just a little too heavy . . . oh, it was no good, he couldn't get going. Just a female, quite unimportant—and Friedel was not so stupid that she couldn't notice that.

"Oh, so you felt like that, Fritz?" she said derisively. "But perhaps you've also heard what's being noised around, that you've all slipped up on your *Putsch*—and now you want to hear what your Friedel's got to say, eh?"

"Slipped up? How?" he asked, hoping she would start talking.

"Yes, pretend to be stupid!" she cried out furiously. "You know very well indeed. You're in a funk, that's why you've come. You're a rotter. When I heard what the colonel was saying to madam this morning I thought at once, well, we'll see now. If he comes today then it's not because of you, Friedel; it'll be to get you to talk, and you are only his spy. And you see, just a couple of hours, and here you are already. And you try to tell me you felt like that!" She snorted; her sturdy bosom moved vehemently. Seeing this the Lieutenant thought help-lessly: It's no good going on talking—I've got to find out what the colonel told his wife.

Suddenly without a word he passed by her and entered her bedroom. The bed was not yet made. There she had lain, there she had slept . . .

"Now I'll show you how I feel," he said, seizing the girl in his arms with-out worrying about her resistance; he never paid any attention to feminine opposition—that was only maidenly primness, affectation. With her fists she was pushing against his chest, against the painful chest, but he covered her face with his, mouth to mouth, hers closed firmly in denial. But he kissed and kissed her. . . . Now I am kissing her, he thought. Soon she will give way, her lips will open—and then I shall have to die. Because of my kisses she will blab, she will tell me everything. And then I shall have to go to the Black Dale and do what I told Violet—damned Violet!

Unaware the Lieutenant had spoken the hateful name aloud. He'd already forgotten he was kissing a girl. He only held her lightly in his arms.

He felt himself pushed back with savage energy. He crashed into the wardrobe.

"Get out," the girl panted. "You liar! So I'm to spy for you while you are thinking about others!"

He stood with a helpless, embarrassed smile near the wardrobe. He made no further attempt to explain or justify himself.

"Oh, well, Friedel," he said at last, with the same embarrassed expression, "it's a funny world. You are quite right. We already learned that at school: *nemo ante mortem beatus*, or something like that, I don't remember exactly. That means: No one is to be esteemed happy before his death, and no one knows before his death what he's really like. You are quite right. I'm a liar. Cheerio, Friedelchen, and no offense."

He held out his hand and she took it hesitatingly. Her anger had died down; his embarrassment infected her. "Oh, God, Fritz," she said, and did not at all know what she should reply to his unintelligible mottoes. "You are so queer. I was only angry because you don't think anything of me. . . ."

He made a gesture of denial.

"All right, I won't speak about that. But if you would like to know what the colonel said this morning . . ."

He dropped her hand. "No, Friedel, thanks. That's no longer necessary. It's all really damned funny," he reflected again. "It's nothing to do with me anymore now. Well, cheerio, Friedel. See that you get married soon; that would be best for you." And with that he went, even forgetting to look at her in farewell again. Frieda too had vanished for him, and he did not hear what she called out. Lost in thought, he went along the corridor, up the little staircase, and down the tiled path onto the street. His cap was in his hand, and he was completely indifferent to being seen and recognized. At the moment he was not conscious of the existence of others; he had enough to do with himself.

All the same, at the first corner he had once again to return from the quiet world of his thoughts back to this venturesome and dangerous planet, for a hand was laid on his shoulder and a voice said: "A moment please, Herr Lieutenant."

He looked up into the icy gaze of the fat detective.

VII

Had it not been for the waiter in The Golden Hat, Violet would have remained a long time where she had fallen in the coffee room. Rittmeister von Prackwitz was of no assistance. First he wanted to rush after the Lieutenant and shoot it out with him, then he called the guests to witness how shamefully the man had treated his daughter. . . . Kneeling beside Violet, he wiped her mouth with his handkerchief and wailed: "Violet, pull yourself together—you're an officer's daughter!"

Springing up he demanded port wine for himself. But not in that glass. That glass had been dirtied and must be smashed. He smashed it. "Where is my wife? My wife's never there when she's really needed. I call you to witness, gentlemen, that my wife is not here."

The waiter sent for the chauffeur. The three of them lifted Violet up, to carry her outside, put her in the car and let her go home. But as she was being lifted she began to moan loudly—moaned without a pause or a word, a confused plaint, like an animal. The men nearly let her fall. She was laid on one of those horrible waxed fabric sofas, with recessed buttons, from which everything slides off. There they and a guest attempted to pull her dress down over her knees. Her eyes were closed. She was no longer a young girl. She was nothing but a thing of flesh that moaned, moaned terribly. . . .

Incoherent, the Rittmeister sat at a table, his almost white head in his hands. He had stopped his ears. "Take her away," he murmured. "Stop her moaning. I can't bear it. Take her to a hospital. Send for my wife."

The last wish was the only realizable one. In the glittering Horch, the latest and already forgotten toy, Finger the chauffeur drove off to fetch the mother.

The proprietors of the hotel appeared. On the second floor a room was got ready, a doctor was telephoned for, and Violet was carried up, still moaning. The Rittmeister refused to accompany her. "I can't bear the moaning," he said. He had so managed it that there was now a whole bottle of port in front of him. He had found the salvation of those unfit for life. Alcohol, the escape from worries, that brings forgetfulness—and an awakening the next day which is a thousand times worse.

The landlady with the help of a chambermaid undressed Violet. She moaned. Nor did she stop moaning in bed.

"Dora," said the landlady, "I must get back to my dishes; the gentlemen will be coming for lunch soon. You stay here for the moment and call me when the doctor comes."

Down below, the gentlemen were in agreement that, although one would never have thought so to look at her, it was labor pains which caused the girl to moan so. Tomorrow all the district would know what was the matter with the daughter of Rittmeister von Prackwitz, the heiress. And what a cad of a fellow!

The Rittmeister was paying no attention to the chatter. He had something to drink, and he drank.

Upstairs Violet was moaning. Once or twice the chambermaid had said to her: "Fräulein, don't do that. No one is harming you. . . . Why do you moan like that? Are you in pain?" Without success. With a shrug of her shoulders: "All right then, don't." And feeling that ingratitude had rewarded her friendliness, the chambermaid sat down beside the bed, but not before she had fetched her knitting. As Dora sat, knitting her pullover, in the bar room beneath Herr von Prackwitz sat and drank. Violet, mortally wounded at heart, could only cry. No one is born immune to misery: Young and playful Violet, a girl, still half a child, was used up, without any idea of real life. And now she had looked into the abyss. Only twilight and darkness remained, and out of that darkness only the repeated cry: Help me, I'm desperate.

The doctor was a long time coming. In vain the waiter and the landlady had suggested that the Rittmeister, who was drinking too much, should eat something, if only a plate of soup. Herr von Prackwitz stood by his port. Only a faint memory of all that had happened to him that morning remained undisturbed by the fumes of alcohol; but this faint memory that calamity had befallen him was somehow associated with port, to which he therefore clung. Gradually, as the first bottle was followed by a second and the second by a third, his face began to glow. He held his head erect again, looking straight in front of him.

Sometimes he laughed aloud suddenly, or with nimble forefinger wrote many numbers on the tablecloth, apparently calculating.

The waiter kept a watchful eye on him. The Golden Hat was a very reputable house, and its reputation was not easily undermined. But it was enough, after all, for one guest to have collapsed on its premises; it would not do for the father to go the same way as his daughter. Frau Eva von Prackwitz, handing over all the vexation with the Entente Commission to young Pagel, the only representative left of the estate's ownership and officialdom, hurried into the motor car without suspecting that neither husband nor daughter was yearning to see her, or that no one but a head waiter wanted her to come so that there shouldn't be another scene. "Drive quickly," she said. "Certainly, madam—but the roads!" replied the chauffeur.

She leaned back in her corner and surrendered to her worries, thoughts and anxieties. Doom was visiting her house, everything was collapsing. She was tempted ten times to bang on the window again and question Finger once more. But she stayed in her corner. It would be useless. The fellow knew nothing. They'd first called him when Violet lay unconscious in the bar room. It was only when they had wanted to take her away in the car that she'd began to cry out.

"Do you think that she broke anything?" Eva asked.

"Broken anything? No," answered Finger.

"But why, then, had she cried out, Finger?" asked Eva.

But he knew no answer to that.

And not a word, not a message, from her husband! "Oh, Achim, Achim!" sighed Frau Eva, not knowing how much reason she indeed had to sigh over him. For in the dining room the Rittmeister was now becoming furious. Once or twice he had got up from his chair, holding tightly to the table and peering out at the market place. "What's the matter? Is something wrong?" the waiter had asked anxiously. "Shall I bring you something to eat? Roast chicken's very good today."

The Rittmeister glared at him, flushed and unsteady. He turned away without a word, sat down and swallowed another glass of port, murmuring angrily. A minute later he was looking out of the window again, gripped by the thought that he had left a car in front of the hotel. Where was it? It had been stolen!

He threw a wary glance around. There they were, sitting and eating; but they could not be trusted. He encountered many glances. Why were they all staring at him? Perhaps they knew he had been robbed and were only waiting for him to notice it, too.

His glance returned to his own table, where the bottle of port swayed gently like a reed in the wind. Away went the glass and then it was suddenly quite close and very large. The Rittmeister seized his opportunity. He inclined the neck of his bottle over the glass, but only a miserable residue trickled out.

His eye searched for the waiter, who had left the room for the moment. The Rittmeister took advantage of this to stand up; thoughtfully he stopped before the clothes stand on which caps and overcoats hung next to Violet's hat and jacket. What's happened to her? he wondered.

Then a new wave of drunkenness washed this thought away. He had already forgotten that he wanted to put on his overcoat; and he left the dining room. With circumspection he went down a few steps. A door—and Herr von Prackwitz was in the street.

It was drizzling. Bareheaded, he stood looking up and down the street. Where should he go? At the corner he thought he saw a policeman's shako glitter. Carefully, very erect, but with knees a little uncertain, he approached this policeman. At the corner, however, he saw that the glittering shako was a brass basin hanging outside a barber shop. Thoughtfully the Rittmeister stroked his chin, and the stubble rasped his fingers. He hadn't managed to get a shave that morning, so he now entered the shop.

It did not look quite what the Rittmeister had expected. There were a few tables and chairs, but no mirrors. However, he didn't mind that; he was glad to sit down a little, supporting his head in his hand and at once sinking into the troubled sea of drunkenness again.

After a while he noticed that someone had laid a hand on his shoulder. He raised his eyes and spoke with a thick tongue up into a sallow young face. "Shave, please!" There was a burst of laughter behind him.

The Rittmeister felt like becoming angry. Had someone possibly laughed at him? He'd turn round and see.

The young chap spoke in quite an affable manner. "Been having one or two, eh, Count? You want to be shaved? You can get that done afterwards, you know. This is only a pub."

"We'll shave you all right! Be only too glad to fleece you!" shouted a cheeky voice behind the Rittmeister.

"Shut up!" hissed sallow face. "Count, don't listen to him, he's boozed. Can I bring you somethin' to drink?"

"Port," murmured the Rittmeister.

"Oh, yes, of course! Port. Right-o! Only we haven't got any port here. But the schnapps is first class. Can I bring one for myself, too? And for my friend? Fine. Here we're so snug all on our own, so's no reason why we shouldn't sink one. Landlord! August! Three double schnapps and give us the bottle on the table. The gentleman's invited us. That's so, you have invited us, eh, Count?"

The Rittmeister sat half-asleep between the two. Frequently he started to his feet, as the call to action seized him. He must look for his car!

The others calmed him down. They would go and help him look in a moment; just let him have another one first. "The schnapps is bloody good, eh, Count?"

Rittmeister von Prackwitz was prostrate once more.

When the waiter in The Golden Hat noticed his guest's disappearance, he was not immediately perturbed. He's gone to the lavatory, he thought, and busied himself with his luncheon customers. He would have a look immediately afterwards; intoxicated persons often fell asleep there. Not a bad thing either. He would at least be in good keeping there.

The waiter put verve into his service. He bustled about, staggering up with trays, brought beer, made out bills—business, although the officers hadn't turned up today, was excellent. Already they had had over sixty guests at table, almost all country gentlemen on their own, who no doubt had come to see if they could find out what was really going to happen tomorrow. Perhaps one would quickly have to link oneself up somehow.

In the meantime the doctor came, and was shown up to the second floor. There he found a young girl in bed who, at short intervals, gave an animal-like cry of pain, rolling her head to and fro with closed eyes. The maid at the bedside could not give him any information. She didn't know who was the sick person or what was the matter—but she would call the landlady.

The doctor stood alone beside the bed. He waited a while but nothing happened; the sick girl went on moaning and no one came. To have something to do, he felt her pulse and spoke to her. Had she pain? What had happened? There was no reply. As an experiment he almost shouted at her to be quiet, but she did not react; she didn't hear him. He held her head firmly so that it could not be moved, but as soon as he let go, it started to toss about again and moan.

The doctor shrugged his shoulders and stood waiting at the window, observing the dismal weather. It was not a consoling prospect, nor were the girl's cries of pain consoling; besides, after a difficult morning, the doctor was hungry. It was time the landlady came.

And at last she did. It had been awkward for her to leave the kitchen, and she was very much in a hurry. "Thank God, doctor, that you're here at last. What is the matter with the girl?"

Which was exactly what the doctor would have liked to know.

"Yes, and now the father's disappeared. Rittmeister von Prackwitz, from Neulohe; you know, the son-in-law of that old skinflint, Teschow. He drank three bottles of port and has gone out in the rain without his hat or coat, quite tipsy. I've sent out to look for him. What a business! Some days everything happens at once. What do you think of doing about the lass? The mother's on her way by car; she can be here in one or two hours."

"What has happened to the little Fräulein?"

The landlady didn't exactly know, and the waiter was sent for. "My whole establishment is upside down; of course, it would happen today, when we have so many for lunch!"

But the waiter, too, had nothing more to report than that there had been some sort of argument with a young man.

"A love affair, then," said the doctor. "Probably a bad nervous shock. I'll give the girl something to make her sleep first—and then, when the mother's here, I'll call in again."

"Yes, do see that she sleeps, doctor. I really can't listen any longer to that moaning, and I can't have someone sitting up here with her all the time. We've got our work to do, too—we're not a hospital." It was the sort of thing the doctor had to listen to a hundred times a day. He had never ceased to wonder why people did not get tired of explaining that, at the particular moment, they hadn't the slightest time for illness; that illness was not a welcome guest. People, however, keep on telling their doctors such things.

He now drew up a mild narcotic into his syringe. The girl, when he stuck the needle into her forearm, twitched and for a moment stopped moaning.

The doctor looked thoughtful. He hadn't yet pressed down the piston in his syringe. That twitch, that interruption, didn't fit in with such a bad nervous shock; she oughtn't to have felt the prick at all—yet she had done so. Therefore she was conscious; she was only simulating unconsciousness.

It was not a young doctor who stood by the sick-bed of Violet von Prackwitz, but an elderly man who was no longer annoyed when his patients humbugged him. So many people had passed through his hands—oh, heaps of them, heaps! He no longer had any didactic, educational, or moral purposes. If this young girl, this child of good family, could moan like that, seeking refuge thus in illness and unconsciousness, then an overwhelming fear of something evil must possess her—perhaps only because of an argument, perhaps because of something worse. The doctor knew how greatly people in their fear of the dark powers of life seek nirvana, and he also knew that a dreamless, all-forgetting slumber can give the new strength to bear what has been unbearable.

Gently he removed the syringe from its needle. He had intended to give the child rest for two or three hours; but it would be better to let her have a long deep sleep, so that she might thoroughly repose and evade the evil hours.

He filled a larger syringe. Before all the injection had entered the arm, her moans stopped. Violet von Prackwitz's head fell to one side, she stretched herself, put one arm under her head and fell asleep.

It was a little after half-past twelve.

"There," said the doctor to the landlady, "now she will sleep soundly for ten or twelve hours. So when the mother comes give me a ring." He left.

One and a half hours later Herr Finger and Frau Eva arrived. The lunches were over, the landlady had time, the waiter, too, had a little time.

Many were the things Frau Eva was told—of an unknown young man, of a glass of port emptied in his face, of an argument. Her daughter had called out: "Fritz, oh, Fritz!" Her husband had drunk a little, on an empty stomach, gone out and not returned. No, he had not left word where he was going. The doctor considered it was a nervous shock. He would be rung up at once. . . . Yes, he had left his hat and overcoat behind; he had been away at least two hours now. Had he gone to a friend's, perhaps?

Frau von Prackwitz heard this, item by item, but she could not give it a proper meaning. She was an active person; her family was in distress, the husband wandering about tipsily in the rain, the daughter in some unknown danger, yet sound asleep. She wanted to be doing something, changing things, improving them. But she had to sit inactive by the bedside and wait for a doctor, who could, of course, tell her nothing.

She stood at the window and looked out at the sad, rainswept hotel yard, its flat shining bitumin roofs. The porter greased the wheels of his trolley. With infinite slowness and pauses between each movement, he took a wheel from the axle and leaned it against the wall. He fetched a copper box with grease, put it next to the axle, then looked at the axle. Then he fetched a flat wooden stick, took some grease out of the box, and looked at the grease on the stick.—And then he slowly began to grease the axle. . . . And that's how we fritter our life away, thought Eva bitterly. So it was a love affair! "Fritz! Oh Fritz!"—I was right. But what good does it do me to be right—and, above all, what good does it do her?

Eva turned round and looked at the sleeping girl. A frenzy of impatience seized her. She would have liked to grab her by the shoulders, shake her awake, question, advise, deliberate, do something. But by her pallid brows and her deep, somewhat noisy breathing she saw that shaking Violet would be in vain, that the girl was as much removed from her impatience and energy as that person who alone could still have given information—Achim.

Why isn't Studmann here? she thought angrily. What's the good of being reliable if he is never there when one really needs him? I can't run all over town looking for Achim, I can't peep into every public-house; I can't even ring up our friends. Perhaps he's not drunk at all and I should only shame him.

But at last she had an idea; she rushed downstairs and ordered the chauffeur to drive slowly through the streets and look out for the Rittmeister. Perhaps she was mistaken, but it seemed as if Herr Finger looked at her a little doubtfully. She was still not altogether sure whether Herr Finger was a proper chauffeur or more of an agent sent by the motor firm to keep an eye on their unpaid car, a man who would suddenly present a bill. In either case, the Rittmeister's home must appear out of the ordinary to him, and a little disturbed; a lot had certainly happened in the bare two days he had been with them.

Frau Eva remained in the rain on the hotel steps. Finger took his dignified place at the wheel. The car rumbled and slowly drove off. Eva went back into the hotel. She ran back upstairs feeling that something must have happened in the meantime. Her heart beat faster. Ah, if only something had happened, if only Violet had waked up, so that one might talk with her! She could talk with her now. . . .

But Violet was sleeping soundly.

The mother sat by the bed, looking at her child—she ought to be able to explain to her—she had suddenly understood in how much she had acted wrongly. She could not understand now how she had descended to such undignified prying, which more than anything had alienated her daughter. This mistake she would never make again. She had learned that her child had her own interests, entrance to which was forbidden the mother, because she was not only mother but also woman.

There was a knock at the door.

The doctor had come then. He was a gaunt, elderly man with remarkably pale eyes behind impossible nickel spectacles, and a very awkward manner, obviously a bachelor. She grew impatient as soon as she saw him so precisely feeling the pulse, with such contented nods, as if he were God, responsible for its powerful throbbing. Obviously he didn't know a thing. He was saying something about a shock, the necessity of sleeping a long time, of allowing the girl an interval, and not asking her any questions when she awoke, so as to spare her wounded feelings. What did this tiresome old fool know about her daughter's wounded feelings? He had only seen her in a swoon! As it turned out, he hadn't even spoken with Achim. About him, too, he had no information to give.

How long would Violet sleep? Till midnight, perhaps till tomorrow? Really, so that was all this booby had been able to do, to withdraw Vi from her mother in that very hour when she most needed her mother's love!

Could one at least take the girl home today, away from this horrible hotel room? When? Well, as soon as her husband was back. That would be all right?

She would not wake up in the car? "Very well. Then we will go as soon as Herr von Prackwitz is back. Thank you, doctor. Shall I pay your fee now, or will you send your account?"

"It all depends on the moment of awakening, madam," said the doctor, sitting down without being invited. Pleasantly and without flinching he looked at her.

Of course, Frau von Prackwitz understood that. It was why she wanted to take Violet from this depressing room back to more familiar and happy surroundings.

"It is just that which may be wrong," said the doctor. "Perhaps she ought not to see anything familiar when she wakes up, neither her own room nor someone she knows; perhaps not even you, madam."

"Why do you think that, doctor?" There was an angry note in her voice. "I know what has happened. Some trifling love affair or other which my daughter has taken tragically. I'm no Puritan; I shan't reproach her in the slightest. . . ."

"Exactly, exactly." The doctor smiled. "You speak of a trifling love affair, when the girl is almost out of her reason about it. Two worlds, madam, two quite different worlds, unable to comprehend each other."

"Violet will get over it," began Frau von Prackwitz.

The doctor interrupted rudely. "I have been thinking about it this afternoon, madam. Perhaps I made a mistake. I ought to have let the child talk before I gave her an injection. She was not unconscious, madam. No, not at all. She was simulating unconsciousness. . . . Something terrible has happened, but she is even more afraid of something terrible which is going to happen. Please allow me, madam. I may be wrong, naturally. I explain it to myself thus— it is possible, there are indications, that by pretending to be unconscious she thinks to escape what she fears. We don't know; perhaps this dreaded harm is not imminent."

"But what further harm can there be, then?" Frau von Prackwitz was really annoyed. "The fellow's thrown her over, and I've thought so a long time. By chance she met him here again, and he had a row with my husband. He must have behaved like a blackguard; otherwise my husband wouldn't have thrown wine in his face. All this would upset her terribly, and she had a nervous collapse. Fine. Or rather, far from fine. But what further harm can happen now?"

"That's just the thing, madam, we don't know, and perhaps are not intended to know. If the facts are as you suppose," and the doctor became persuasive, since Frau Eva remained totally unconvinced by his words, "then the girl ought to have been relieved after the scene. The fact that her father, and thus her parents, knew her secret at last ought rather to have relieved her, surely. How is it then that a young girl like her should dissemble thus? Why should she adopt a remedy so unusual?"

"But you are only supposing that Violet was dissembling, doctor. You didn't talk with her."

"No, unfortunately not. It's pure assumption; there you are right, madam."

"Very well; what would you advise?"

"Put your daughter in the hospital here. She would be well looked after and possibly she will feel safe there. And you can be with her in ten minutes if she wakes up and asks for you. Should she want to go home—that can be done at once."

Frau Eva looked thoughtfully at the doctor, but she was not thinking about his proposal, the man being far too silly for that. She knew her Violet. A few words and all would be well again between mother and daughter. Naturally she would respect Violet's secret, as one woman to another; this she had already firmly resolved on without all this talk of harm and greater harm. No, if Frau Eva was now thoughtful, it was because she was wondering why the doctor had made a proposal behind which there must be something else. "And you would attend Violet in the hospital here?" she asked glibly.

"If you wish, madam," replied the unsuspicious doctor. "I would naturally keep an eye on her."

The thing was clear. The little panel doctor had smelled money; his warnings against approaching harm were meant to justify a long and expensive treatment. Frau Eva stood up. "Thank you very much, doctor. I will talk it over with Herr von Prackwitz. Should we decide for it, I will let you know."

It was a very definite rebuff. One can only be oneself. She was otherwise a sensible, clear-sighted woman, but in this moment she was only the daughter of a rich man, mistrusting the motives of all who were compelled to do something for money in order to live. "He only wants to earn some money." That foolish attitude converted his shrewd, solicitous advice into a mean and selfish transaction.

And in the end the old man understood her. With a faint flush in his thin cheeks he bowed forlornly and approached the bed. There was nothing more he could do. He had been able to give the girl a little sleep, but he was not allowed to make easier for her what was coming after it. The world was like that. With bound hands the willing helper had to see the condemned, the unhappy, those in peril, go their way. He could merely warn. But his voice was drowned by laughter and death-cries, and was unnoticed as he stood by the roadside.

"Take great care when she wakes up," he said, and went.

Restlessly Frau von Prackwitz walked up and down. Where was Achim? And no word from the chauffeur! She had been nearly an hour in this wretched hotel. To have something to do, she now went downstairs to the telephone. Though it was not possible to speak as she wished, for the telephone was too public, it did her good to hear young Pagel's restful and somewhat leisurely voice.

Yes, so far everything was in order. The Commission of Control had gone off in their car a long time ago. Yes, rumors. He had refused to sign their record of the investigations, on the ground that he had no authority. They had gone away without. One other thing, which would amuse madam. Amanda Backs, you know, the poultry maid, had given little Meier a box on the ears several times, before all the visitors. With the shout of "Traitor!" No, nothing had happened. Not one of the gentlemen had moved a finger in Meier's aid. Oh, yes, splendid, really splendid. A capital person in her way, a real bit of the people, but magnificent. . . . And how was Fräulein Violet, by the way?

Not well? Oh! Certainly, he would do that, and see about the heating for the bath also, of course. He wouldn't forget. No, there would be no trouble about girls for once. The women had all come back soaked from the potato lifting; it was raining very heavily now. He would pick out three or four of the most suitable and see that the Villa was cleaned in person.

An excellent young fellow. Almost smiling, Frau von Prackwitz left the telephone. Before she went up, she ordered another coffee. Yes, please, in her room. And now back to it. But, just as last time, she was overcome with a feeling of anxiety on the stairs. Her heart beat faster. What had happened to Vi? She ran in such a way that she could feel her skirts on her knees.

But then back in her room, unchanged, Vi was in a deep sleep.

The anxiety declined and was replaced by dark desperation, and she thought suddenly: it's like coming back to a dead person. And again she began the agonized wait.

Eva didn't yet know how good it can be to come back to a dead person.

VIII

"What does this mean?" shouted the indignant Lieutenant. "You've been following me, I suppose? You want to arrest me?"

"Don't talk nonsense, man," said the other calmly. "How can I arrest you? We're illegal."

"Am I only a man now, not an officer anymore?" asked the Lieutenant sarcastically. "Well, what do you want with me?"

"Like to know, for example, how you have succeeded here."

"I shall report on that to Herr Richter. As ordered."

"I merely thought you might possibly forget it. That's why I came to meet you."

"Why should I forget? In my duty I have never forgotten anything."

"I merely thought so," said the fat man in apology, "because we have now been informed which arms dump has been discovered." He stood still—but only because the Lieutenant had come to a stop—and directed his cold ruthless glance at him, saying very softly: "Yes, you know about it, my friend. You knew about it in there with Herr Richter. It's yours."

"I didn't know." The Lieutenant nearly shouted.

"Quietly, quietly, my friend," said the fat man, laying his hand on the other's shoulder, in such a way that the Lieutenant noticed he was as strong as an ox. "The question now is whether you will tell me who's blabbed. Oh, don't pretend you don't know. Either you know him or you know her, and we'd very much like to know, too. For the future, you understand?"

"I know nothing about it," said the Lieutenant obstinately.

"Rubbish. The former bailiff, Meier from Neulohe, was sitting in the Entente Commission's car, and he showed them the dump—we know that now, too. Don't make so much fuss, man. You're not telling me for my own profit but for your former comrades, so that they shan't get caught out again."

The Lieutenant shivered to hear the other speaking of his "former comrades," but he took the bull by the horns and declared defiantly: "I have said that I am answerable for the dump with my life. If it's really done for, I shall do what I said."

"My dear chap," smiled the fat man, laying his hand once again on the shoulder—gently, yet the Lieutenant trembled—"my dear chap, don't flatter yourself. You are finished, one way or the other. You've made a mess of things, you've lied. No, my friend, you're done for." His frozen glance rested on the Lieutenant, from whose thin white lips no word came forth.

"No," went on the fat man, drawing away his hand. "It's not a question of you anymore; it's a question of the others. They're the ones we want to know about."

"You know already," said the Lieutenant heavily. "You say little Meier was in the car—then you know the traitor."

"We've got to find out who was the link between you and the traitor."

"I'm no traitor!" shouted the Lieutenant.

"Did I say so?" The fat man spoke imperturbably. "Do you think I should have let you leave Richter's room if you were a traitor? Do you think I'd be here with you now if you were a traitor? No, you're only a windbag, and some sort of honor's still in you. Although it must be a peculiar sort of honor. Because you swore on it that the dump was safe, and knew all the time it was found out."

"I didn't know," cried the Lieutenant in despair.

"You're cowardly and stupid; you shouldn't think so much about yourself, Herr. It's not at all important if you live. Now show some guts and tell me everything you know."

The Lieutenant appeared to reflect. All he said, however, was: "Wait a minute. I'll just go in here." And he entered the small public-house before which they happened to be standing. But the fat man did not wait behind; he followed, to listen. "Landlord," said the Lieutenant, "here is your trench jacket again. I shan't need it anymore. Give me back my rags."

"But there was no hurry, Herr Lieutenant. Herr Lieutenant can't wear the dirty jacket. Wait at least till my wife has brushed it a bit."

"Give me back the old rag," persisted the Lieutenant. And while he was changing, he whispered: "No, I wouldn't let my boy put it on tomorrow."

The landlord's eyes looked stupid in their astonishment.

"Good-by and thank you, landlord," said the Lieutenant, leaving the public-house.

"Acting as usual," criticized the fat man. "The jacket wouldn't have been so important, anyway. In your lifetime you'll have spoiled more than a jacket. But to be noble in his own eyes, yes, everyone likes that. I never met a murderer who said he had murdered for money. They all had some noble excuse. . . ."

"Listen, you!" shouted the Lieutenant. "If you're going to follow me, shut your jaw. Or—"

"Or what?" The other gripped the Lieutenant's arm. And the pressure, seeming to crush the muscles, increased till the veins were almost bursting, and the Lieutenant had to grind his teeth together so as not to scream. "I know you've got a pistol in your trouser pocket. Well, try and get it out, now."

No, the Lieutenant would not even try. That terrible grip crushed even the instinct of combat which had always been his.

The fat man released his arm. "Besides, I'm not following you, but taking you," he said imperturbably.

"And where are you taking me?"

"To The Golden Hat. I accept your proposal. We'll ask Herr von Prackwitz and his daughter about the dump. Especially his daughter."

"No." The Lieutenant stopped.

"Why not? You yourself proposed it, Lieutenant."

"I'm not going to stand like a prisoner—and before those people."

"Whom you know only by sight." The fat man laughed. "Are you excited, young man, at the prospect of going with me to Fräulein von Prackwitz?"

"Fräulein von Prackwitz can—" shouted the Lieutenant.

"Correct. Exactly what I thought, Lieutenant. You have a little private animosity toward the Fräulein. I wonder why?"

"The Fräulein means nothing to me."

"Why, even now when you are being careful you can't speak of her without your face twitching. Well, Lieutenant, what is it to be? Golden Hat or private confession?"

"Golden Hat," replied the Lieutenant firmly. The Prackwitzes must have been gone a long time by now; how could they still be sitting there, two or three hours after that scene! No, she would have fled; she had her reputation to consider. And even if they hadn't fled, he wouldn't let himself be conducted into their presence by this fat detective. He'd find some opportunity to escape, he'd not let himself be deprived of all that remained to him—his deliberate revenge on her. Execution should not be done on him, but by him on her.

Human beings, before they depart this earth, want to know that they have not been wiped from the great slate of life without leaving some trace. The Lieutenant had no children, he had nothing to bequeath, no farewell letter to write. He would be as extinguished as if he had never walked the earth. Honor and ambition, self-respect and manliness, had fallen away from him while still among the living. But . . . Oh, stay a while, you are so lovely! Still so lovely! There was that white suggestive face, which you were never able to love. Now you can hate it. Behind the forehead is a brain in which you will be registered for as long as it thinks. In that bosom beats a heart which will become fearful at the thought of you, thirty years from now, when nothing more remains of you on this planet. A small eternity for the dead man in one who still wanders in the light; traces of the past in the surviving.

The two of them walked silently side by side, the Lieutenant with his hands in his pockets, with an ugly smile on his face. The detective, lively, with the cold-blooded look of a dog picking up a scent.

For the first time, however, the fat man was unlucky. The waiter, throwing a suspicious glance at the Lieutenant, stated that Herr von Prackwitz had gone out and the young lady was ill. No, no—impossible to see her. The doctor was there, the young lady was unconscious. Without even asking the wishes of these guests he turned away. It was obvious that he laid no value on their presence; he went back to his work.

"And what now?" asked the Lieutenant derisively.

"You're a bit too sarcastic," said the other with a trace of irritation. "That betrays how pleased you are that nothing's come of this visit. Well, we'll just wait here for Herr von Prackwitz. Waiter, a bitter."

The Lieutenant had prepared his plan. "Listen," he said, "there's still a little money in my pocket, and I want to give it to a girl. Let's go there quickly. It won't take half an hour."

"The maid at the colonel's? You could have settled that a little while ago. What did she tell you, by the way? Waiter, a bitter!"

"Nothing," replied the Lieutenant promptly. "She was in a rage with me because I only went when I wished to hear something, she said. We were shits and our *Putsch* was also shit, or something like that. But I mean another girl now, in the New-town."

"Shits and shit. Well, that's something. She got that from someone else; that's why she was angry with you perhaps. Women like that always get mad with their fellow if some idiot speaks badly of him. . . . Isn't the waiter going to bring me any beer? Waiter, a bitter, please."

"Leave the beer," begged the Lieutenant. "Let me go to the girl now. It won't take half an hour—we can always meet Herr von Prackwitz afterwards."

The waiter set down the glass of beer. "Twenty million," he said rudely.

"Twenty million!" The fat man was indignant. "What sort of bitter is it here, then? Everywhere else it costs thirteen million."

"Since midday. The dollar's now two hundred and forty-two million."

"Oh," growled the fat man, and paid. "If I'd known that I wouldn't have had a beer. Two hundred and forty-two million! You see what good it'll do giving the girl money; it won't make her any the happier! It's all just acting."

"There are also letters for me there, which I'd like to fetch."

"Letters! What letters? You only want to get away."

"All right, we'll sit here. I'll have a bottle of wine for my money then. Waiter!"

"Stop," said the fat man. "Where is it?"

"What?"

"Where the girl lives."

"In the New-town, Festungs Promenade. Not twenty minutes away."

"You said before it wasn't half an hour there and back. What sort of letters are they? Love letters?"

"I'd keep my love letters at a girl's, eh?"

"Let's go then." The fat man finished his drink and stood up. "But I tell you now, if you're going to make trouble, as you did a little while ago at the barracks . . ."

"So you saw that as well?"

"I'll not only smash you in the chest—I'll go for the stomach so that you'll never walk straight again." Something flared in the ice-cold glance which threatened the Lieutenant. But this time it had no effect on him; he merely smiled. "I'm not making any trouble," he said. "Anyway, as far as I can see, I haven't got much more walking straight to do, eh? Threats haven't really much point with someone like me, don't you think?"

The fat man shrugged his shoulders. Through the rainy, deserted streets the two walked side by side.

The Lieutenant was trying to think how to get away from his tormentor; there were no letters and no girl in the New-town. But out there it ought to be easier to escape, to shake off this spy somehow, so as to do what had to be done without fresh humiliation or harassing surveillance. (Shall I really have courage enough— for that?) It was not going to be so easy to deceive this watchdog, however. Though the man shambled along beside him nonchalantly, the Lieutenant knew quite well what that hand always in his trouser pocket meant; he knew why the other kept so close to him that their shoulders touched at each step. Should he make the slightest unexpected movement the other's fist would seize him in its demoralizing grip. Or there would be a report, once, twice, right here in the street, and then there would be something in the papers again about a political murder.

Not that! Not that! The Lieutenant was feverishly trying to form an idea of the geography of all the public-houses on their way and the possibility of escaping across the yard from the lavatory. But he could not concentrate on his task; his brain, despite all compulsion, refused to help him. Always the image of Violet von Prackwitz kept on coming between. The waiter had said that she was lying unconscious, and a fierce delight possessed him. Already, at my mere threats, you are unconscious. But wait and see how you will relish life when I have carried out my threat. . . . But I must think about escaping from some pub. Now we shall soon be passing The Fire Ball. . . .

Ah, the Lieutenant was obsessed with the girl. Now, death approaching, the scatterbrain had found a significance in life; this man of a hundred love affairs, who had never loved, had discovered hatred—a feeling which was worth living for! He pictured what it would be like when she saw him; it seemed to him he could hear her screams. It had to come to that; he wished it so strongly it couldn't be otherwise. The wishes of the dying are fulfilled, he thought. And gave a start.

"What's the matter?" The fat man was sharply on guard.

The wishes of the dying are fulfilled, thought the Lieutenant again, immensely delighted. "There you are. Herr von Prackwitz!" he said. "You wanted to speak to him. Please do."

Their way to the New-town had brought them into the old long-demol-ished, long-outgrown fortifications, where the city fathers had made out of rampart and fosse a promenade for the citizens. And they were now walking in the fosse, with the ramparts rising steeply to the right and left, covered with trees and bushes. They had turned a corner and could see a strip of pathway, a lonely and remote spot.

To one side was a bench dripping with rain, and on this bench sat Ritt-meister von Prackwitz, huddled, but not awake. His head was hanging over his chest; his sleep was the insensible wheezy sleep of the utterly drunken. Now and then, when his breathing became too embarrassed, his head gave a jerk, raised itself almost vertical and slowly sank, bumping at first on his shoulder, then back again onto his chest.

It was a deplorable, a shameful sight, which Herr von Prackwitz presented. For a moment the two spectators stood silent. The Rittmeister, searching for his car, had not been dumped in this solitary corner of the grounds for noth-ing. He had been robbed.

"They are like carrion kites!" exclaimed the fat man furiously. "The ver-min smell their prey faster than we ever do." And he threw a suspicious look up at the ramparts. But no branch crackled among the bushes, no retreating foot sent a stone rolling down the slope. The kites had long flown with their spoils. Plundered, stripped to his underclothes, a ridiculous and lamentable figure, Rittmeister Joachim von Prackwitz-Neulohe slept off his intoxication in the drizzle. Too feeble to resist and fight like the strong, he had collapsed and resorted to the dirty Nirvana of alcohol—to awaken, how?

"I thought you wished to speak to the gentleman?" jeered the Lieuten-ant. The wishes of the dying were fulfilled. If already this could happen to the father, how would the daughter be dishonored?

"What bloody beastliness!" raged the fat man, not taking his eye off the Lieutenant. He is in exactly the same situation as the ferryman who has to ferry a wolf, a goat and a cabbage, and only has one place left in his little craft. He could keep a watch on him or he could help the Rittmeister—both together were hardly possible. "Leave Herr von Prackwitz there," advised the Lieutenant maliciously. "No one has seen us find him. And I—well, I've got to hold my tongue."

The fat man stood thoughtfully there. "Lieutenant," he said after a while, "dig yourself in the ribs. Tell me who blabbed about the dump, and I'll let you go."

"It's my business," said the Lieutenant slowly. "I don't want anyone else sticking their nose into it. But I give you my word of honor it was all only stupid woman's gossip and twaddle, not meant badly. . . ."

The fat man brooded. "I must know the name," he said at last. "It wasn't only Fräulein von Prackwitz—"

"It wasn't Fräulein von Prackwitz!" the Lieutenant cried.

With a terrible blow in the pit of the stomach, the fat man was on him like a sudden storm; he couldn't even begin to defend himself from the hail of blows. Before he knew where he was, he had been knocked down—the other groped in his pocket, drew out the pistol. "And the safety catch not up, you bloody coward!" he cursed. "Well, my lad, do what you needs must do, without a weapon. But I'll get you again before you know about it."

The Lieutenant, unable even to reply, lay on the ground. His whole body was in pain, but far worse was the fury of despair. This fat man, this pitiless brutal giant—he was at the bench, he already had the Rittmeister in his arms.

I must get up, I must go, thought the Lieutenant.

The fat man in passing gave him a frightful kick in the side, and it appeared as if he laughed or sniggered as he hurried away.

He wishes to damage me so that I don't make off, thought the Lieutenant—and was alone. He lay there waiting for the return of his strength, for a little breath, for the blessing of a decision. . . . It is my chance, he thought. I must go away, to the Black Dale—the Black Dale. But I've no weapon and none of the comrades would give me one. They all know. . . . Oh, I must leave here.

Swaying, he got up. It was the second time he had been knocked down today, and it was the worse of the two.

"I mustn't crawl like this; I must hurry, I must run," he whispered and stood still, holding on to a tree. His face felt as if it had been flayed. I can't go like this into the town. I must look a sight. He's knocked me about horribly, the brutal swine. That's what he wanted.

He was almost in tears with self-pity, almost in tears because it was so cowardly to sob. "Oh, my God," he groaned, "my God! I want to die. Why don't they let me die in peace? Will no one help me, my God?"

A little later he found himself walking. He had left the fortifications, he was in the town.

But I must go faster, he thought. He'll catch me for certain, at the latest in my hotel. Yes, stare, you fool. That's the way a man looks who's been trimmed by them. And in a loud challenging voice, quarrelsome as a drunken man's: "Stare, fool!"

"Good day, Herr Lieutenant," said a polite, a very polite voice. "Perhaps the Lieutenant doesn't remember me?"

Befogged by pain and numbness, the Lieutenant sought to recall the face. The polite, dispassionate voice soothed his shameful degradation. It seemed as though no one had spoken to him in that way for ages.

"Räder," the other assisted him. "My name is Hubert Räder. I was in service at Neulohe, not with the Geheimrat but the Rittmeister."

"Oh," cried the Lieutenant, almost delighted, "you're the one who wouldn't help me up the chestnut tree. Yes, I remember."

"But I should now be glad to be of assistance to the Lieutenant. As I said, I'm not in service there now. You look as if you require some assistance, sir."

"Yes. I fell down." He thought a moment. "I was set upon."

"If I could be of service to you, sir—"

"Clear off, man! Don't you bother me," suddenly screamed the Lieutenant. "I don't want to have anything to do with you people from Neulohe. You all bring me bad luck." And he tried to go more quickly in order to get away from the fellow.

"But, Herr Lieutenant," said the calm, unimpassioned voice at his side, "I don't come from Neulohe. And, as I said, I'm not employed there anymore. In short, I've been thrown out."

The Lieutenant stopped. "Who threw you out?"

"The Rittmeister, sir. The Rittmeister engaged me and the Rittmeister threw me out—no one else would have been legally entitled to do so, otherwise." The man spoke with a certain foolish satisfaction.

The Lieutenant remembered something. Violet had spoken about this servant—a conceited fool. "Why were you thrown out?" he asked.

"The young lady wished it," replied the servant curtly. "The young lady didn't like me from the beginning. Antipathies like that do occur. I have read about it in a book. Scientifically they are called idio-syn-cra-sies."

The wishes of the dying are fulfilled. The Lieutenant would have liked to take advantage of this very timely help, but some instinct or other warned him that it was a little too timely, and he became suspicious. "Listen," he said. "Go quickly to The Golden Hat. The Rittmeister has met with an accident. You will be received there like the Saviour himself, and get your job back and your wages doubled, man."

For the first time the gray, murky, fishlike eye met his.

"No." The servant shook his head. "You must excuse me, sir, but we learned at the training school that one must never return to a situation. Practice has proved that it is not expedient."

The Lieutenant was utterly exhausted. "Then clear off, fellow," he said wearily. "I have no use for a servant, I can't pay for a servant. So leave me in peace." He walked on. He had wasted so much time, and it was so far to his hotel.

"What do you still want?" he shouted angrily at his silent companion.

"I should like to be of assistance to the Lieutenant. Herr Lieutenant needs assistance."

"No!" yelled the Lieutenant.

"If you will permit me, sir," whispered the obstinate voice, "I have taken a small room here close by. You could wash yourself quite undisturbed, sir. In the meantime I will clean your clothes. . . ."

"Blast the clothes!"

"Yes, Herr Lieutenant. Perhaps you could do with a strong coffee, sir, and a double cognac. I can believe that you will need all your energies today, sir," he suggested a little confidentially.

"You, what can you believe, you donkey?" cried the furious Lieutenant. "What do you know about my energies?"

"Well, about the dump that was betrayed," explained the cold, obsequious voice. "I can imagine that you will not so easily put up with what the young lady has let you in for, sir."

The Lieutenant stood as if struck by lightning. His most secret thoughts in the possession of this intruder, this idiot! He could not understand it. "All right then, come along, show me your room," he said abruptly. "But if there's the slightest dirty trick . . ."

"I will explain, sir. It is all comprehensible forthwith. This way, please, Herr Lieutenant. If I may take your arm, sir, it would be quicker. . . ."

Half an hour later the Lieutenant, somewhat restored, was sitting in the corner of a deep sofa in Räder's furnished room. He had had a coffee with a good deal of cognac, and the servant at the moment was preparing him a second.

Thoughtfully he watched the strange fellow's unruffled activity. "Listen a moment, Herr Räder," he said finally.

"A moment please, Herr Lieutenant. You must pardon me, it takes time here. Everything is very primitive here." And he surveyed the room with a contemptuous glance.

"Why have you really come to Ostade? Surely not because you wanted to meet me?" And the Lieutenant laughed, so unlikely did this suspicion seem.

"Oh, yes, sir," the servant replied earnestly. "I hoped to find you. Ostade is not a big place." He set the coffee before the Lieutenant, without paying any attention to the effect of his words. Then he pushed forward the bottle of cognac so that it was near at hand. "I would advise a little less cognac now, sir. You are quite fresh again. And you doubtless desire to keep a clear head, sir, I think?"

Under that fishlike, expressionless eye the young man gave a slight shudder. If the fellow isn't a fool, he thought, then he's an abysmal scoundrel. "And why did you want to find me?" he asked. "Don't tell me again that it was to assist me, though."

"Because I thought it would interest the Lieutenant to know how the dump was betrayed."

"And how was it betrayed?"

"Because you stopped coming to the young lady, sir, and didn't take the letters out of the hollow tree, the young lady wrote to Herr Meier about the dump, because the young lady knew that Herr Meier had such a hatred for you, sir."

"That's a lie."

"If you think so, sir." The reply seemed unperturbed. "How much cognac do you wish, sir? The coffee is exactly hot enough."

"Pour out, then. You can fill the cup safely; that won't lay me out." The Lieutenant looked keenly into the somber gray face. "Even if it were true, the Fräulein wouldn't have told you."

"Not when I had to ascertain Herr Meier's address for the young lady?"

The Lieutenant took a slow gulp. Then he lit a cigarette. "And so you come here just to tell me that? What do you gain by it?"

The cold, lifeless eye again rested on him. "Because I am a revengeful person, Herr Lieutenant. It is all easily comprehensible, as I mentioned."

"Because she wanted the Rittmeister to turn you out?"

"As well. And also because of something else, because of matters to some extent delicate, sir."

"Listen, my friend," exploded the Lieutenant. "Don't play the gentleman with me. Cough up what you know, or else you'll see something! I've got the feeling that you're a very cunning dog." He was astonished to see the gray face redden a little. An unpleasantly simpering, flattered expression appeared there.

"I try to educate myself," said the man. "I read books. No, not novels; scientific works, often several hundred pages in length. . . ."

If the fellow's no idiot he's an abysmal scoundrel, thought the Lieutenant again. But of course he's an idiot. "Well, relate your delicate concealments. Don't be afraid, I shan't blush."

"It's because the young lady didn't treat me like a human being," said the servant, once more lifeless. "She would dress and undress in my presence as if I was a lump of wood. And when the master and mistress were away, the parents I mean, then the young lady always used to order me into the bathroom, to dry her."

"And you were naturally in love with her?"

"Yes, Herr Lieutenant. I am still in love with the young lady."

"And she knew that? Just wanted to torment you?"

"Yes, Herr Lieutenant. That was the intention."

The Lieutenant looked sideways at the servant. A thing like that, he thought, a fool and idiot, also has feelings. Suffers and is tormented just like a real human being . . . "Why don't you take vengeance yourself?"

"I am more or less of a peaceable temperament, Herr Lieutenant. Violence is not in my nature."

"So you are cowardly?"

"Yes, Herr Lieutenant. I am quiet-minded."

The Lieutenant considered. Then he spoke vigorously. "Listen, Herr Räder. Go to The Golden Hat. There you will see a fat gentleman—you'll recognize him—a detective in a bowler hat. If you tell him about Violet's letter to Meier, then the young lady won't enjoy many more happy hours in life."

"Excuse me, Herr Lieutenant. I'm not for the police. I'm for you, sir."

It was quiet in the room. Thoughtfully the Lieutenant stirred his cup while the servant stood in a watchful, yet indifferent, posture. The Lieutenant reached across to the bottle of cognac, filled the cup and took a gulp. Then he said softly: "I shall perhaps settle this business not quite as you think, Räder."

"That will be all right, Herr Lieutenant."

"If you think I am going to use violence on the girl . . ."

"The gentleman will have considered what is most efficacious."

"Most efficacious, yes . . ."

There was a long silence. The Lieutenant sipped his cognac, the servant stood in the doorway.

"Räder!"

"Yes, Herr Lieutenant."

"When does it become dark now?"

Räder went to the window and peered out into the gloomy evening drizzle. "With a cloudy sky like this—soon after six."

"Well, you must get me a taxi for a quarter-past six, here. I must be driven to the border of Neulohe Forest. Agree on the charge beforehand."

"Certainly, Herr Lieutenant."

"When you leave the house and also in the streets have a look if that fat detective is spying around anywhere, the one I told you about. A plump, beardless man, pale bloated face, a peculiar glance like ice. Black overcoat with velvet collar, bowler hat . . . You'll recognize him, man," he ended impatiently.

"Certainly, Herr Lieutenant; should I see him I shall recognize him. May I go now?"

"Yes," replied the Lieutenant, brooding. Then he spoke briskly, yet with embarrassment: "Listen, Räder, there is something else for you . . ."

"Yes, sir?"

"I require"—he hesitated—"I require a weapon. I have lost mine."

"Yes, sir."

"Can you manage that?"

"Certainly, Herr Lieutenant."

"But it won't be so easy to get hold of a pistol here today. And some ammunition, of course, Räder!"

"Of course, sir."

"You are sure?"

"Quite sure, sir."

"About the money . . ."

"I shall be glad to assist the Lieutenant."

"I have a little. But whether it will be enough for the taxi and the pistol . . ."

"I will settle that, sir—I'll be back in an hour's time then, sir." Hubert Räder had gone without a sound.

The Lieutenant was alone. On the wall a little Black Forest clock was ticking. In the kitchen the landlady from time to time clattered about. He lay on the sofa in his underwear; his clothes were still drying in front of the stove.

He looked at the table where the empty cup stood next to the cognac bottle, three-quarters full yet. Slowly his hand groped over the table, and was withdrawn. "Herr Lieutenant requires a clear head." He could hear Räder's insufferable voice, always somewhat didactic.

Why should I want a clear head for that? he thought. Tell me why, you fool!

All the same, he didn't pour himself out any more. Drunkenness was rising like a wave in him, to fall again and rise once more, higher. He looked at the clock. Twenty-five past five. He still had a good three-quarters of an hour alone to himself, continuing to live to some extent—then he would be hastening faster and faster to his end. He fixed his eyes on the minute hand. It moved infinitely slowly; no, it was not moving at all. The decrease in the little space between the minute and the hour hands was not perceptible. Yet all too suddenly it would be a quarter past six, and the last independent moments of his life would have expired. To rekindle his wrath he tried to think about Violet von Prackwitz, but Räder's fishlike leathery face and dead gray eyes swung upwards on a new wave of drunkenness. The fellow never opened his mouth in talking, he thought in sudden disgust; I have never even seen his teeth. It's certain he has nothing but rotten black stumps in his jaws. That's why he doesn't open his mouth to talk. It's all moldy and putrid.

The Lieutenant wanted to look at the time again but couldn't lift his head from the sofa.

He was asleep. He was sleeping away his last independent moments, sleeping, sleeping. . . .

The car drove through the night. In its white headlights the sodden trunks gleamed and were dark at once, vanished before the weary tormented eyes had really perceived them. In the corner sat the Lieutenant, half recumbent, almost asleep still. A piercing headache hindered him from thinking clearly. He could not make out if it was true that in front, next to the chauffeur, the servant Räder was sitting. It seemed to him that he had not wanted this disgusting fellow to come. Then, however, it occurred to him that the servant was paying for the car, though. Let him, therefore, drive his car as much as he wished; the chief thing was that he should go back immediately.

The lieutenant was almost happy that he'd found this solution, despite his headache. All was in order and good; the fat man, too, had not caught him. From now on everything would go of itself; he would be driven right up to the place—and then it was nothing but a little click. Only a click, that was all. The simplest thing in the world, about which there was no need to trouble oneself. He had seen it many a time. . . .

Anxiously he felt in his pockets and on the seat. Had the servant given him the pistol or not? He had been so drowsy on coming away, he could not remember; and he felt angry at finding nothing but the bottle of cognac beside him. Look at that! Sleepy as he was, he had not forgotten that. Wet my whistle with cognac, he thought, taking a good gulp from the bottle.

The alcohol washed away his drowsiness. Like a flame the thought rose in him: I am nothing but a coward.

The flame died down. "But you will do it," whispered intoxication. "The chief thing is that you should do it. No one will ever know that you were cowardly about it."

"Yes, the fat detective knows it!" said his understanding.

"Fat lot I care about him!" whispered intoxication.

"Both of you leave me in peace!" grumbled the Lieutenant.

It was now light in the car, a sort of twilight rapidly becoming brighter.

What's that now, he thought wearily. Am I not going to be left in peace at all?

But the brightness became stronger; the servant was turning round, half standing up. Was the car on fire? Räder said something to the chauffeur, a horn sounded, a horn replied. And a large car passed swiftly by. Gone! The Lieutenant was in darkness again.

Räder opened the panel in front. "That was the Rittmeister's car," he shouted, and there seemed to be triumph in his words.

"Good," answered the Lieutenant indistinctly. "Good. I always told you so, Räder. The wishes of the dying are fulfilled."

On the unrepaired country road the car was bumping terribly. "The young lady must have recovered, then," shouted the servant.

"Hold your jaw!" he yelled, and Räder closed the panel.

He must have fallen asleep again, waking up because the car had come to a stop. Laboriously he heaved himself up; he was half off the seat. Managing to get hold of the door handle he stumbled out.

They were right in the forest, in an inconceivable stillness. No breath of wind, no drop of rain. In front, ten or twelve paces from the car, stood two men, who seemed to be examining the ground.

"Hi! You! What are you doing there?" shouted the Lieutenant, lowering his voice even as he shouted.

The servant turned, walked slowly up to him and stood a couple of paces in front. "Yes, we're there," he said softly. "You only need to follow the car tracks, Herr Lieutenant."

"What car tracks?"

"Of the car, Herr Lieutenant! Of the Entente Commission's car."

"How can I do that in the dark?" asked the Lieutenant impatiently.

"Oh, I have a flashlight," replied the servant patiently. He waited a moment, but the Lieutenant said nothing. "Are you going now, sir?" he asked at last.

"Yes, now," said the Lieutenant mechanically. "Give me the thing."

"Here is the torch, Herr Lieutenant, and here—you must excuse me, sir, I could only get a revolver. But it's quite new."

"Hand it over. I shall manage with it." Without examination he pushed the revolver into a pocket. "Well, I'll go now."

"Yes, Herr Lieutenant."

But he did not go.

"Listen," he ordered, suddenly vehement. "You're to drive back on the spot. I don't want you here, you understand? You're a swine. What you've told me is nothing but lies. But—it's all the same to me. You think you're very clever, don't you? But that's all the same, too. Clever or stupid, swine or decent—we've all got to die."

"If I might make an observation, Herr Lieutenant . . ."

"What else? You go away."

"It is always possible that there's somebody there. It's not nine yet. And people are inquisitive. I should go as quietly as possibly, Herr Lieutenant."

"Yes, yes." The Lieutenant suddenly laughed. "I'll be delighted to go as quietly as you wish, my clever Herr Räder. But you will allow me a little noise, surely, just once, just for once, eh?" He stared at the other with hatred. "Clear off, you. I can't bear the sight of your mug any longer. If you don't, I swear to God I'll fire on you first."

But when the pair were in the car, he made a sign to wait. He had forgotten something, something enormously important, something without which a man could on no account die; and he looked for it in the car, on the back seat, under the rug that had slipped down. Then he slammed the door. "Off with you! To hell, for all I care."

The car moved away, the noise of its engine loud among the trees. In his damp and imperfectly cleaned trench jacket the Lieutenant stood at the roadside, the bottle of cognac in his hand. The last two people he would see in this life had gone. Very well, what of that? The cognac had remained with him—faithful unto death!

He listened intently. He was trying to persuade himself that the sounds he heard came from a motor car, and that he was not altogether alone. But it was so still, so still! And what he heard, that was his own heart beating in his breast—in fear! In cowardice!

He shrugged his shoulders; he was not responsible for his heartbeats. He pushed out his lips as if he were going to whistle, but there was no sound. They trembled. . . . My lips are trembling, my mouth is parched.

He looked up but could not see the sky. Dark, an uncomforting starless dark. There was indeed nothing more for him but to go down into the Black Dale. There was no discoverable pretext why he should postpone this any longer. . . .

In the beam of his torch the Lieutenant made out the car tracks. He followed them stealthily and slowly. They were not the tracks of one car only. No, two had been there. And after a little consideration he nodded his head, satisfied. It was all in order, exactly as it ought to be—the car of the Control Commission, and the lorry which had taken away the weapons. That is, it had not been a proper lorry, as one could see by the tire tracks. It was more a large delivery van. Again he nodded his head with satisfaction. Yes, his brain was working magnificently. He was not going into the grave as a withered gaffer, in the full vigor of his years—or whatever it said in the death notices. There would be no death notice for him, however.

Ah-ha! This was where the car had stopped, not being able to go any lower into the Dale. A pedestrian, though, didn't need to hesitate over that; the path for pedestrians was trodden out clearly enough. The Lieutenant went to and fro, examining everything with his torch. Yes, all in the best of order once more. The visitors, after they had stopped here, had driven on in the direction of Neulohe. All had been carried out according to orders, "comprehensibly," as that swine Räder would have said. Oh, that swine, that dog!—thank Heaven he had cleared off. In the woods there was not the slightest smell of women, and thus a man could settle his affairs with himself at last, alone. No need to pull a handsome mug, strike a fine pose. If you itched, you scratched yourself. If you wanted a nip from the bottle you took it, and afterwards belched.

Quite free and easy. Oh, yes. A baby, hardly entering on life, behaved itself somewhat shamefully; and it was the same before death. Coming out of nothingness, going into nothingness, one conducted oneself pretty coarsely. It was all comprehensible. Said the scoundrelly Räder.

A ghostly pleasure penetrated the Lieutenant. His last draught of cognac had been a powerful one, and he fell rather than walked down the little footpath. But at the bottom his cheerfulness vanished, and his spinning inebriation turned into a viscous mush. . . .

His face became grave. What a havoc the fellows had made here! They had certainly not put themselves out, those people. Great holes in the ground, mounds of earth, the lids of cases—why, here in the light of the torch lay a spade. I hid everything so neatly, he thought. And these swine have turned it all upside down. You couldn't notice a thing when I'd finished, and look at it now!

Very depressed he sat down on a mound of earth, dangling his legs in a pit. One about to die could not really sit in a more suitable fashion—but he was not thinking about that now. He put the bottle beside him in the soft earth, dived into his trouser pocket and brought out the revolver. With one hand he shone the torch on it, with the other held it in the light and fingered it. Yes, he had thought as much—a bit of rubbish, factory trash, mass production—a popgun, good to scare away dogs or for youngsters who had stolen the petty cash to commit suicide with—but not for him, a man who understood weapons. Oh, his fine accurately finished pistol, a thing as precise as an airplane engine! The detective had hit him in the belly and stolen the magnificent thing.

Wretchedly the Lieutenant stared in front—and then discovered that there were only the six cartridges in the drum—that villain Räder hadn't given him any ammunition, although he had specially requested some.

"But I have to try the revolver, it's quite new, it's never been shot yet," he whispered. "I wanted to try it out first; otherwise I won't know whether it shoots too high or too low."

A voice sought to persuade him that it was quite indifferent, with a revolver placed against the temple, whether it shot too high or no, but he would not give way. "I was looking forward to trying it. A man ought to be allowed a little pleasure."

Grief overwhelmed him; he could have wept. It is possible to miss six times, he thought; it has happened before now. And what would I do then?

He sat there pale, with hanging underlip, his eyes wandering all round him. His face was distorted, not so much from the blows as from an expression of desperate fear; he knew that he was acting, that he was only seeking to postpone the end. But he would not acknowledge it. He was not thinking any longer about this end: oh, no, there was still so much to prepare, to consider. He remembered that he had not thought about Violet for a long time. Hate and loathing for the girl had possessed him. He would like to experience those emotions once more.

But there seemed to be room in his breast only for this wretched uneasiness, this damnable flabby feeling, this weakness! I'm no abomination of a Black Meier. No, I swear it, I do not want to be better, I do not want to change myself. I was all right as I was, with teeth to bite, a wolf among wolves.

He took a long pull at his bottle. It gurgled as he drank, it gurgled as he put it down—but, curse it, that wasn't the only noise he had heard! Up he jumped, revolver in one hand, torch in the other. "Who is there?" he screamed wildly into the wood. "Stand, or I'll shoot."

He listened. Nothing! But someone was prowling about. Where? Over there? In the bushes? "Stand or I'll shoot." Oh, I heard it all right, the noise of the engine suddenly ceasing in the forest; that swine, that Räder, must have stopped. He's dodged after me, he wants to see if I shoot myself, get his money's worth. There! There! I heard something then. "Stand." Bang!

See, this little pistol doesn't shoot so badly. It pops. Are you afraid? Did it tickle you? Ah, you're running. Wait. I'll run after you. "Stop!" Bang, smash! What's that? Someone running behind. Is someone coming there? "Who are you then?" Doesn't show himself, he's a coward too. Bang! Bumm . . .

It's the fat man, of course. The worthy comrades want to know if I am executing their unspoken sentence. Here's good health; I'm executing a fat fellow first. Bang! That cracked too much, the bullet's flattened itself against a tree.

Gentlemen, here I stand, have a look. Is the lady Violet also there? Have a look, my girl. Here's a drink to a long life for you! May you remember me very often and very long.

Away with the bottle! Smash—and bust! Pity, it was a good cognac in it.

Ladies and gentlemen, I regretted that I only had six shots in the drum. See, I fire my fifth into the sky, a salvo for my lady, that her ears may tingle forever because of me. And the sixth shot—one's enough for me. Like this, above the nose . . . like this . . . Should she herself really visit me, I shall be a magnificent sight for her.

Oh, my God, my God, is no one coming? Is nothing to happen? They can't let me perish like this. Someone must come and say it was all a mistake. I'll count up to three now, and if nothing's happened by then, I'll fire. One. Two. Three! Nothing? Nothing at all? The whole muck is nothing, then! It was all muck, my life, and death is also muck, cowardly vile muck, and afterwards more muck, I know that by now. I was too frightened; it's not worth being frightened about this muck. I'm quite calm now. It would have been decent of the sentry this morning if he had fired on me. He would have really spared me something. But I can do that, too. Lived alone, died alone. *Fire*! And what now? Oh. . . .

Yes, and what now? Oh!

In the Black Dale, at the bottom of the wood, lay a torch on the ground. Its faint beam fell on a plant or two, a mossy stone, some earth. . . . It was quite still, quite still. . . . The solitary gleam in the silent night that had been so loud recently. . . .

And now there comes a sound out of the bushes, someone clears his throat, coughs . . .

Deep silence, a long silence . . .

Softly, cautiously, a step approaches, hesitates, stops. Another cough.

Deep silence, nothing but silence . . .

The step comes nearer, a foot, a foot in a black leather shoe appears in the white torchlight.

A moment later the torch is picked up. Its beam wanders, ceases. Hesitant, as if stuck to the ground, the step advances; the silent visitor looks down on that which is more silent, lying there.

No sound, no sound . . .

The man clears his throat. The torchlight searches once more, to the right, to the left.

Can he have fallen on it?

The revolver is found, however. He who finds it examines the drum, ejects the empty cartridge cases. The revolver is loaded afresh. Once again the light of the torch is thrown on the dead. Then it goes away quickly, up the slope, along the footpath, to Neulohe.

In the Black Dale it is utterly dark.

IX

No housewife, no help, could have got the Villa ready more painstakingly than had young Pagel. The rooms were clean and warm, the bath stove hot. In the kitchen there was supper waiting, and the young man had even managed to collect a few bunches of flowers from a garden parched by the summer heat and deluged by autumn rains. Gladioli, dahlias, asters . . .

Where Frau Eva had left behind a desolation stripped of all help, she found a home; and even the disconsolate Lotte, who had been firmly resolved to go away, too, was merry and carefree as never before. For young Pagel had turned the riot of scrubbing into a frolic. He had gone round with the women, taking the portable phonograph with him; and the way the beds could be made and the sweeping done when accompanied by tunes like "Darling, you're the pupil of my eye" or "We're boozing away our Oma's little cottage" was unbelievable. On this one evening there was more laughter in the Villa than there had been in six months.

But laughter gave way to tears, rain drove away sunshine, and—not everyday is Sunday. As the splendid car drove up, no one could perceive from it what cargo of misfortune it held. Before young Pagel could hurry to it, however, its door was opened by a very troubled Herr Finger, and when one looked inside . . .

To be sure, Fräulein Violet was still asleep, and though her rigid, pale slumber had something alarming about it, that alone would not have made faces so grave and disconcerted. No, it was the Rittmeister, the unfortunate Rittmeister von Prackwitz! During the drive home he had begun to be sick and now, almost naked, groaning and befouled, he was carried from the car.

His wife must have passed through terrible hours; she looked faded and old, her expression sad and bitter. "Yes," she said austerely, "I am bringing affliction into the house." She glanced at the faces round her, ghostly in the meager light of the front-door lamp. Young Pagel, the chauffeur Finger, and Lotte, frightened and anxious, a few village women. No, there was no concealment possible. Affliction had taken up its quarters in the house. Frau Eva could endure that, however. Endure? No, it strengthened her. In true affliction pretense disappears.

"Herr Finger, Herr Pagel, be so kind as to carry my husband upstairs. The best thing would be to put him on the couch in the bathroom, till the bath is ready. It is? Good. You girls help me with Fräulein Violet. Don't be afraid, Lotte; she's not dead, only in a stupor. The doctor gave her an injection. That's right—go on now."

Did the lamps suddenly darken in the house? Had there a while before been singing and laughter here? What were flowers doing in the vases? Affliction had arrived—all went on tiptoe, whispering. Hush! What was that? Nothing, only the Rittmeister groaning. Outside the headlights of the car shone uselessly into the night.

The two men, Pagel and Finger, had undressed the Rittmeister and laid him in the bath.

"No, I have no time for him. You see to it. Violet is more important." Was Frau Eva thinking of a certain warning? Was Violet still not safe, here in her home? Forest surrounded Neulohe; the world was distant—how could still greater evil arrive? Evil greater than a dishonored, bewildered daughter and a husband who had at last lost all foothold? A still greater evil?

"Lotte," she said, "go downstairs at once and lock all the doors in the basement and on the ground floor. Make sure that all the windows are really shut. Don't open the door to anyone without asking me first." Alarmed and confused, the girl went.

Frau Eva sat by the bed. Her daughter would wake up at half-past twelve or one. Everything depended on that moment, as the doctor had told her, and she would be prepared for it. Not a step out of the room. Violet's room. Where she had slept as child, as young girl. What she had been such a short time ago! That had to give her strength to outgrow what she had become.

Wordless, the two men were busy with the Rittmeister. Young Pagel washed him while the chauffeur held him, for the slack unconscious limbs kept on losing their support in the bath. Nevertheless, it seemed as though consciousness was returning. The eyelids trembled, the lips, too.

"Yes, Herr Rittmeister?"

"Something to drink . . ."

Yes, in the dazed brain was stirring the first reawakened foreboding of the evil which had befallen. And he who could not yet think was again demanding fresh insensibility, renewed flight . . .

Pagel looked at Herr Finger, who shook his head. "He's bringing up bile already; his stomach won't stand anything more."

It was not easy to lift the slippery body from the bath. The Rittmeister resisted, muttering angrily, "Port! Waiter, another bottle."

"What is it?" cried Frau Eva from Violet's door.

"We're putting the Rittmeister to bed now," said Pagel. "He wants something to drink, madam."

"He'll get nothing. Not a drop. Look in my night table, Herr Pagel; there ought to be some veronal there. Give him a tablet."

At last the Rittmeister was in bed, exhausted, in a restless half-sleep. He had been given some veronal, and had been sick at once.

"I ought to bring my car out of the rain," said Herr Finger hesitatingly. "It's a brand-new car and it's a shame."

"Your firm will get the money all right."

"But it's a downright shame about the car," replied the chauffeur angrily. "The mess it's in! And I haven't had anything proper to eat the whole day, out all the time in the rain and cold . . ."

"I'll speak to madam," said Pagel obligingly. "Please stay with the Rittmeister till I return." He spoke to Frau von Prackwitz, and then let the chauffeur, the women, and Lotte, too, out of the house. All were in a hurry to get away; misfortune had descended on the Villa.

Wolfgang Pagel himself returned to watch over the Rittmeister. It was obvious that the man was very ill; but far worse than the illness of his body, poisoned by alcohol, was the illness of his soul. The man's self-respect had been mortally wounded; he writhed under the gloomy thoughts haunting him. All his transgressions rushed into his mind, and he closed his eyes.

That did not help. He sat up in bed, staring at the young man in the arm-chair near by. He wanted to know if he knew, if others knew, how pitiable, how small, how empty he was, had been, would be. But everything confused him. There was a hunt . . . the lamps burnt so low. There were pictures, shadows of pictures. . . . Why was the night so still? Why did he suffer alone?

"Where is my wife? Where is Vi? Doesn't anyone bother about me? Have I got to die utterly deserted, by myself? Oh, God."

"It's late in the night, Herr Rittmeister. Your wife and your daughter are asleep. Try to get a little rest yourself."

The sick man lay back in bed. He appeared to be thinking, to be calmed by the information. Then he sat up again and asked with a sly tone in his voice: "You're young Pagel, aren't you?"

"Yes, Herr Rittmeister."

"And you're my employee?"

"Yes, Herr Rittmeister."

"And you must do what I order?"

"Yes, Herr Rittmeister."

"Then"—there was a pause, till he said all the more haughtily—"then bring me up a bottle of cognac at once."

Yes, Wolfgang Pagel, here no amiability can help, no compliance, no avoidance; the Rittmeister looks at you tensely, with hatred. He wants his cognac, and if you are not firm he will get it.

"You are ill, Herr Rittmeister. You must sleep first. You shall have some cognac tomorrow morning."

"I want it now. I order you!"

"It's not possible, Herr Rittmeister. Madam has forbidden it."

"My wife has not to forbid anything. Fetch the cognac or . . ."

The two gazed at each other.

Ah, how naked the world had become, how the gilt came off! Within the home, the make-up is wiped off and the hollow skull of egotism grins at you with its black eye-sockets. Pagel suddenly saw himself lying next to Peter in Madam Po's room, the dingy curtains hanging in the sultry air. It seemed like a symbol to him now. No! Like the prelude to a difficult test or examination. In those days he could have picked up his suitcase and slunk away like a coward;

that was impossible here. Gone were the blessed lies that had tasted so sweet, up and away had gone the tender image of love. Man against man, wolf against wolves, he must make his decision if he was to respect himself.

"No, Herr Rittmeister. I am sorry, but . . ."

"Then I'll get my cognac myself. You are dismissed." In one jump the Rittmeister was out of bed. Never would Wolfgang have thought that the sick man, whom the two of them had only just managed to lift from the bath, could develop such mobility.

"Herr Rittmeister!" he begged.

"You'll not dare to lay hands on your employer, what?" screamed the Rittmeister with distorted face, running in his pajamas to the door.

It was the decisive moment. "Yes," replied Pagel, seizing him.

"Leave me alone!" Rage, the unprecedented indignity, the lust for alcohol, gave the Rittmeister strength.

"Achim, Achim! What's all this?" The noise of the struggle had fetched in Frau von Prackwitz from that sickbed which she had not intended to leave, her daughter's.

"You! You!" shouted the Rittmeister, struggling all the more fiercely to tear himself from Pagel's arms. "You've set this young fool against me. What do you mean, I'm not to have any cognac? Am I the master here or you? I . . ." It seemed as though he intended to throw himself on his wife.

"Put him to bed, Herr Pagel!" angrily ordered Frau Eva. "Don't be over-nice; get hold of him properly. Achim! Achim! Violet's lying there ill, pull yourself together, be a man for once. She's so ill!"

"I'm going," said the Rittmeister, suddenly almost in tears. "When it's I who am ill you don't make any fuss about it. I only want a cognac, one small cognac."

"Give him another tablet. Give him two tablets, Herr Pagel, so that he'll keep quiet," cried Frau Eva in despair. "I must go back to Violet." And, driven by fear, she hurried away. And as she ran across the passage, her heart beat so wildly. What was she going to see next?

But nothing had changed. Her daughter was sleeping peacefully, very pale, her face a trifle swollen and as if brooding. She felt the pulse. It was beating slowly but powerfully. No reason for fear. Violet would wake up; one could talk with her or not, whichever was indicated; she would be restored to health, and they would leave Neulohe and live in some quiet corner. As for money, her father would listen to reason. No one needed to despair because of a defeat— not even Violet. In reality life, looked at properly, was nothing but defeats. Man, however, survived and enjoyed life—man, this most tenacious, most resistant of all creatures. . . .

It was five minutes past twelve. The decisive, the fateful, hour had begun. Although the room was oppressively hot she shivered.

She opened the window. There was a gentle wind in the dark night, gently the raindrops fell from the trees, and she could perceive only shadows within shadows. Was the danger which threatened her family to come from out of that shadow world?

She shivered again. What am I doing? she thought, alarmed. I'm cold and I open the window. I'm mad, too. It's all too much for one person.

Carefully she put up the hook between the casements, so that they would not bang in the wind.

At this moment the bell in the hall rang loudly.

X

Across the passage, each in the doorway of a sickroom, Frau Eva and Pagel looked at one another. The young man could not account for the fear on the woman's face. "That was a ring," she murmured.

"It will be the chauffeur," he reassured her. "He's had supper somewhere in the village and now . . ."

"No, no," she cried in distress.

The bell rang loudly again.

"Don't open, please, Herr Pagel. An evil will come."

"Or it's Lotte. Lotte also went. We can't shut the girl out. Herr Rittmeister is quiet now; let me quickly open the door."

"Please don't, Herr Pagel," she pleaded, as if one could keep out the misfortune invited by a wrongly conducted life. But he was already running downstairs, prepared for any danger. It was foolish, but something like pleasure was his; he was not useless, he had a task in the world, even if it was only the trifling one of demonstrating to the woman upstairs that she had no need to be frightened. For the first time he understood with heart and soul that life brought happiness only to him who fulfilled a task unswervingly, whether large or small. Satisfaction could come only from oneself.

The bell rang for the third time.

From upstairs Frau Eva shouted something incomprehensible.

As Pagel passed the hat stand in the hall he saw a stout oak stick which the Rittmeister used to take with him on his forest excursions. He seized it, swung it round—thereby endangering the hall lamp—and, holding it ready, opened the door just as the bell rang once more.

Outside stood Herr von Studmann with a flushed rather angry face, and an obviously heavy suitcase in his hand.

"You, Herr von Studmann?" cried Pagel disconcerted, lowering his ridiculous weapon.

"Yes, indeed," said Studmann, as angry as he possibly could be. "I really don't know what's the matter today in Neulohe. I thought I should be expected with impatience and eagerness, bringing as I do what is after all a not inconsiderable sum of money—yet there's no vehicle at the station, the office is shut and in darkness, the Manor also in darkness but full of uproar, just as if there was an immense party on, although no one came to the door. . . . And here I've got to stand ten minutes in a downpour, ringing!" His voice had become more and more reproachful as the inconveniences caused him by the unreliability of others grew clearer in their recitation.

"Listen, Herr von Studmann," whispered Pagel hurriedly, drawing the startled man into the hall and carefully locking the door behind him. "Here, or rather in Ostade, there appears to have been an accident. Fräulein Violet was brought back from Ostade very ill, and the Rittmeister—badly drunk. That's all I know. The worst is that his wife is terribly upset and seems to fear a greater calamity, though I don't know what. . . . And I'm quite alone with them. Oh, and the Commission of Control was also here and dug up an arms dump in the forest. Did you know about it?"

"I?" cried Studmann indignantly, putting down his suitcase. "I should . . ."

"Yes, madam," Pagel shouted upstairs. "It's quite all right. Herr von Studmann's here. Shall he come up?"

"Herr von Studmann! Yes. At once. Thank God, Herr von Studmann, you're back. I need assistance so much. . . . I can't come down."

Pagel returned to the Rittmeister's room. His employer seemed asleep; he had managed to keep down two tablets of veronal this time. But he couldn't be trusted. His eyes were shut, his breathing regular; but Pagel felt that there was something wrong. Something told him that in the meantime the Rittmeister had been out of bed. His face bore a sullen, malicious expression, and Pagel resolved to be on his guard. The prison officer, Marofke, had not given him a tip or two for nothing.

And all this while his ear was aware of the voices in Violet's room. Studmann's voice was unmistakably a trifle offended, which was not surprising. He had run around, he had negotiated, he had shown his efficiency and his success, he had brought back a heap of money, very necessary and very eagerly awaited—and there was no vehicle at the station, no one to receive him, the money was unimportant, his success was unimportant! For there has been illness in the meantime; people are occupied with other matters; accidents, for example—one that has happened and one that is to come—more important matters. . . . Poor Studmann. Pagel could so clearly see him standing in front of the gloomy office, carrying the heavy case which he would not set down for a moment. A good nursemaid, experiencing the eternal disappointment of all nursemaids. He had obtained the wished-for toy, but the child did not even look at it; something else had been found long ago.

In this quiet hour of the night, a bit sleepily because he'd been on his feet since half past four in the morning, young Pagel understood why Studmann, friendly, capable, and ready to help others, had remained an elderly solitary bachelor. People do not love their saviors. Once out of danger they resent that superiority.

The voices came and went in the next room. Pagel looked at his wrist-watch—nearly half-past twelve. I shouldn't mind going to bed at all, he thought drowsily. The Rittmeister hasn't stirred in the last fifteen minutes; he's off at last. But I can't leave the women there in the lurch, and Studmann won't be staying much longer; Frau Eva's voice sounds more and more irritated. . . . If only I could have a coffee at least, a good thick black coffee! And he saw himself go down to the kitchen in the house. . . . They've got an immersion heater there. He saw it that afternoon. It works fast. He would grind himself a good portion of coffee—a good few grams—put them staight in the cup, pour boiling water over the them, let it draw for three minutes, put a bit of cold in, and then drink the lot, boiling hot, coffee grounds and all. Oh! I'll be as fresh as a fish in water!

But he had to stay up with this idiot who was certainly not asleep. Why was he keeping his hands like that under the bedclothes? Pagel, worn out, even believed it possible that the Rittmeister had got out of bed to fetch a knife. But had he really got out of bed?

Wolfgang's sleepy mind stoutly refused to interest itself in this question; he could not withstand the vision of a coffee cup—there it was, as if real! It was steaming, the brownish silvery surface made by fine ground, strained coffee in boiling water. . . . How good a thing like that is against tiredness! With deep relief it occurred to him that he wouldn't need to go downstairs at all to make coffee—Lotte would be coming. She'd make him some. Where on earth was the girl? It was half-past twelve. Well, she'd have to make him some coffee all the same. . . .

Pagel started. Perhaps it was a rustle of the bedclothes. Had it not seemed as if a bare foot had been thrust out of bed? No, the Rittmeister lay quite still, and the voices opposite were also still. Oh, yes, what was it Studmann had said? The Manor in darkness but full of uproar and no one at the door. . . . He'd not thought of it at the time, but it had remained in his mind, like a hook, to pull him suddenly out of his drowsiness. Lotte not back yet, and the Manor in darkness but full of uproar . . .

There would be nothing wrong, though. Old Elias was trustworthy, and the mice play when the cat's away. All the same, he would have to jog Studmann about it; for he couldn't help feeling a little uneasy. His experience with the Oberwachtmeister Marofke had awoken Pagel a little. He no longer ambled about the landscape among its people. He felt responsible. But for what? Responsible for his actions! For himself! No, he wouldn't forget to jog von Studmann.

It was twenty to one when von Studmann entered the room and said somewhat abruptly: "Will you please let me out, Pagel? And give me the key to the office? You're staying here, I suppose?"

Pagel threw a glance at his patient. "Do you think that the Rittmeister is sleeping? Fast asleep?" he whispered.

Studmann gave the Rittmeister a fleeting and very unfriendly glance. "Of course he's asleep," he said crossly. "Why?"

"It seems to me he's only pretending," Pagel whispered.

Studmann looked at Pagel very suspiciously. "Pagel, have you some understanding with Frau von Prackwitz? I don't understand it."

"Understanding? How?"

"Because she asked me at least a dozen times if I thought Fräulein Violet was really asleep. She had the impression the girl had been awake a long time and was only pretending. . . . And you ask the same thing."

The two men looked hard at one another for a moment. Then Pagel laughed with all his youthful amiability. "Well, let's go down, Studmann," he said. "You are over-tired and I can imagine that you haven't been greatly thanked for all your pains." He put his arm through von Studmann's. "Come along, I'll let you out now. You really must go to bed."

Slowly they went downstairs.

"I assure you it's pure chance that Frau von Prackwitz and I asked you the same question. Word of honor, Studmann. . . . There's a peculiar atmosphere in the house now. The daughter's a little ill—well, daughters sometimes are ill. The father's had a drink too much. Well, fathers often do that, too. Nothing out of the way then; but there's an atmosphere here as if all the fates were attacking the house."

"And do you understand that, Pagel?" Studmann stood in the hall, no longer angry but distressed. "I am enthusiastically received, but nobody worries a bit about what I've accomplished, and it was really difficult. I ask what's the matter, I'm told the situation—which doesn't strike me as alarming—I say a few calming words and am coolly rebuffed. Because I'm without understanding! Do you understand it? Do you know anything?"

"I understand nothing and I know nothing," said Pagel, smiling. "Since it appears to reassure the lady, I am sitting up with the Rittmeister and trying not to fall asleep. That's all."

Studmann scrutinized him, but young Pagel's eye was without guile. "Well, good night then, Pagel. Perhaps it will be cleared up in the morning."

"Good night, Studmann," Pagel replied mechanically. There was something else he had wanted to say, and he looked after the other carrying his heavy suitcase into the darkness. Then he remembered. "Herr von Studmann, one moment please!"

"Yes?" Studmann turned round.

The two men approached each other and met about ten paces from the door. "What is it?" asked Studmann somewhat peevishly.

"Yes, it just occurred to me. . . . Tell me, Herr von Studmann, are you very tired? Must you go to bed at once?"

"If there is anything I can do," began Studmann, immediately ready to assist.

"I can't help thinking about what you told me when you arrived. You remember? The Manor in darkness but full of uproar. That was what you said, wasn't it?" Pagel paused, then added: "You know that the owners are traveling?"

"That's right," said the astonished Studmann. "I never thought about that."

"It won't be anything much," said Pagel reassuringly. "Some little celebration of the servants. Old Elias will see to it that things don't get too bad. . . . But I'd make certain, Studmann; that is, of course, if you're not too tired."

"Lord, not a bit," declared Studmann, pleased at the prospect of something to do. "I'll have to put the money in the safe first, naturally."

"I wouldn't ring. Or call out. I've thought it over, Studmann." And Pagel was astonished to find that he had done so without knowing it. "Outside your window there's the tarred roof, and from there you can get without difficulty onto the veranda of the Manor. That will take you practically round the house, on the first floor, and you can look in all the windows without being seen. . . . Yes, that's the way I'd do it," he concluded with a certain emphasis.

Studmann gazed at him. "For Heaven's sake, why? What's your idea there? What do you think I shall see?"

"Listen, Studmann." Pagel was suddenly very serious. "I can't tell you. I know nothing. But that's what I'd do."

"This sort of spying round at night . . ." protested Studmann.

"Do you remember that night we met at Lutter and Wegner's? Then also I had the feeling that it was a very special night, a night of destiny, if I may say so. Why shouldn't there be something like that, after all? A night during which everything is decided? Now I have this feeling again. A bad night, a wicked . . ." He peered into the darkness as though he could somehow discover its face, its evilly lurking face. But that, of course, was absurd. He perceived only a gently rustling, dripping darkness.

"Well then, Herr von Studmann," Pagel ended suddenly, "so long now. I must get back to my Rittmeister. Good night."

"Good night." Studmann stared after Pagel, for such mystical fits meant nothing to him. He could hear the door being shut and locked; then the outside light was turned off and he was in darkness. With a little sigh he picked up his heavy bag and set out for the office, determined to scout round the Manor first and keep both his ears open before taking Pagel's advice. Climbing by night over someone else's property struck him as more than questionable.

In the hall young Pagel was standing, listening to the quiet house. He couldn't shake off the strange mood which had been his since the doze by the sickbed. A glance at the clock showed that he had not been with Studmann more than five minutes. It was a quarter to one. Nothing could have happened; he had kept his eye on the front door all the time and stood quite near it. No one could have slipped in there. The house was quiet.

Yet he had the feeling that something had happened.

Slowly, soundlessly—as slowly and soundlessly as in a dream—he went up the stairs. At the door of Violet's room appeared Frau Eva's pale, worried face. He nodded to her and said softly: "Everything is all right."

He went into the Rittmeister's room.

His first glance showed him that the bed was empty. Empty!

He came to a stop, searching the room with his eyes. Nobody there, and the windows shut. What would Marofke do in such a case? The reply to this question was only negative, however. Marofke wouldn't do anything rash.

Catching sight of the bathroom door, he pushed it open and turned on the light; the bathroom, too, was empty. He went back into the passage.

Violet's door was wide open now, and Frau Eva walking to and fro restlessly. She saw him at once and came to him, possessed by feverish agitation. "What's the matter, Herr Pagel? Something's happened, I can see it."

"I'm going to make myself a coffee, madam," lied Pagel. "I'm tired out."

"And my husband?"

"Everything in order, madam."

"I'm so frightened," she said agitatedly. "Dear Herr Pagel, according to the doctor she ought to have waked up now; and she is awake, I feel it. But she doesn't stir, whatever I say to her. She's pretending to sleep. Oh, Herr Pagel, what shall I do? I'm so frightened. As never before." Her pale face twitched; she was gripping his hand without knowing it. "Have a look at Violet, Herr Pagel," she begged. "Just say a word to her. Perhaps she'll take notice of you."

Young Pagel was going hot and cold. He had to find the Rittmeister—Heaven knew what he would be up to in the meantime! But he let himself be taken to the bed. Doubtfully he looked down on the still face. "She seems to be sleeping," he said uncertainly.

"You are wrong. You are certainly wrong. Speak to her! Violet, our little Vi, here is Herr Pagel. He'd like to say good morning to you. . . . You see, her eyelid moved!"

Pagel almost thought so, too, and the idea occurred to him of shouting: "The Lieutenant's here!"—an idea immediately rejected. Did one do that sort of thing? And did one do it in front of the mother? After all, why shouldn't she be left in peace if that was what she wanted? And he had to look for the Rittmeister.

"No, she's certainly sleeping, madam," he said again. "And I should let her sleep. Now I'll make some coffee for us." He smiled encouragement at Frau Eva.

It was a somewhat unhappy role he played in returning under her eyes into the Rittmeister's empty bedroom, coming out again and nodding: "In order." Then he went downstairs—her gaze following him—to the ground floor. Instinct guided him correctly. There were six doors in the hall. Of these he chose the one into the study where, that evening in cleaning up, he had seen the two things which, in the Rittmeister's state, were likely to come into question—the rifle cupboard and the liquor cabinet.

At the sound of the opening door, the Rittmeister spun round with the air of a surprised thief. He leaned against the table, one hand holding on to the back of a large leather chair, the other gripping the bottle of brandy so greatly desired.

Pagel gently closed the door. Since it was the bottle and not the revolver, he thought himself able to be jocular. "Hello, Herr Rittmeister," he called out cheerfully. "Leave some for me. I'm done up and could do with a little stimulation myself."

But the cheerful tone was unsuccessful. The Rittmeister, like many drunken persons under no illusions about the shabbiness of their conduct, laid great value on his dignity. In the young man's tone he felt only an impudent familiarity. "What are you doing here?" he shouted angrily. "Why are you creeping after me? I won't put up with it. Get to hell out of this at once." His voice was very loud and very indistinct; his tongue, almost crippled by schnapps and veronal, refused to articulate the words evenly; his swollen voice spoke as if from behind a muffler. And all this only increased his rage. With bloodshot eyes and twitching face he looked viciously at his tormentor, the young fellow he had picked up out of the morass of the great city, and who now wanted to order him about.

Pagel did not recognize his peril or that he had to do with a man almost out of his mind and capable of anything. Unsuspecting, he went up to the Rittmeister and said in friendly persuasion: "Come along, Herr Rittmeister, you must go back to bed. You know that your wife doesn't want you to drink anything more. Be nice and give me the bottle."

All things which the Rittmeister did not wish to hear and which deeply insulted him. Hesitatingly he held the bottle out. But in the moment when Pagel was about to take it, the bottle was raised and fell upon his skull with a crash in which the whole world seemed to be shattered.

"There you are, my little fellow!" roared the Rittmeister triumphantly. "I'll teach you to obey."

Pagel, his hands raised to his head, had fallen back. In that second he understood, in spite of a numbness and pain which rendered him almost unconscious, the magnitude of the disaster that had befallen this house. He understood what the woman upstairs had already known for some hours—that they had to do not with a drunken, but with a mentally deranged man. As for the young girl . . .

"Bear yourself properly, second lieutenant!" ordered the Rittmeister in a scream. "Don't stand so slackly before your superior."

Despite the maddening pain, and although he could hardly lift his head, Pagel forced himself to adopt a stiff military bearing. The woman upstairs must not be disturbed for anything. It could only be a matter of a few minutes before the schnapps and the veronal would have done their work on his employer. He would quiet down; Pagel mustn't let it get to fighting. His limbs were trembling—and the noise . . .

"Attention!" screamed the Rittmeister. Once more he might command and be himself. In his mouth had been put the word of ruthless power, to be obeyed without the flicker of an eyelash. More deeply than alcohol, power intoxicated him a last time.

"Attention, Lieutenant Pagel! Two paces—forward! About—turn. Attention! Attention, I say! Why are you wobbling, man?"

"What's this?" said the woman's voice from the door. "Achim, won't you give us any peace? How you torment me!"

The Rittmeister turned in a flash. "I torment you?" he shouted. "You all torment me. Leave me alone, let me croak, let me soak. What am I good for?"

His voice became softer. "You may stand at ease, Lieutenant Pagel. I hope I didn't strike you too badly, it wasn't my intention."

And now he was muddled again. "I don't know why I should do something like that. It's in me, it's always been in me; I repressed it, but now it's got to come out. No one can restrain it; it must out. But when it gets something to drink, it quiets down, goes to sleep. . . ." He went on murmuring to himself. With his foot he knocked against the bottle on the floor, which had emptied itself. He shook his head and turned again to the liquor cabinet.

"Take hold of him, Herr Pagel," said Frau von Prackwitz in a faint voice. "Can you grasp him on one side so that we can get him up the stairs? I'll attend to your head immediately after. I must go back. Oh, let him! Let him take his schnapps with him. What does it matter now? It's all over. Oh, Pagel, if it wasn't for Violet, why should I go on living? I'd prefer to do as the pair of them do, go to bed and sleep and not care about anything more. Oh, Herr Pagel, tell me what's the purpose of it, to marry and be fond of a man and have a child, and then it's all dashed to pieces, dust to dust, man and child, dust to dust. Tell me, Herr Pagel."

But Pagel made no reply.

The pitiful little procession stumbled up the stairs. The Rittmeister was hardly conscious, but he did not lose hold of his bottle. His wife was in such agitation that she kept coming to a halt, forgetting their burden, talking at Pagel, demanding a reply. And Pagel, half stunned, heard this gabble; but he also heard something else, and in his tortured brain the thought slowly took shape, that he was hearing something horrible, appalling.

No, the house was no longer quiet. Between the woman's broken sentences he could hear from the first floor a noise which he had not yet heard that night, a dreadful noise, wooden, dry, lifeless.

Clap . . . clap.

And again—clap . . . clap . . . clap.

In the middle of Frau Eva's chatter Pagel raised his hand (leaving the Rittmeister to sink down on the landing), looked fixedly at her and whispered: "There!"

And Frau Eva was silent at once, raised her head and looked at Pagel, listening at the same time. It was quite still.

Clap . . . clap.

Her chin began to tremble, her pale face turned yellow as if laid waste by a sudden illness, her eyes filled with slow tears. And it came again—clap!

In that same moment the spell was broken and together they dashed up the stairs, along the short passage and into Violet's room. . . .

Peaceful in the light of the lamp on the ceiling, the bed gleamed whitely. But it was empty. The unfastened windows were clapping in the night wind, slowly, lifelessly, woodenly. Clap, clap. . . .

And now came what Pagel had feared the whole time, that before which he had quaked and yet had expected . . . the woman's scream, the terrible unending scream which broke into a hundred, a thousand little screams, like a diabolic laughter . . . the creature shattered by her agony.

Pagel laid Frau Eva on the sofa, patting her hands, reasoning with her so that her ear might perceive near by a friendly human voice. Again and again he told himself that this was no conscious cry, that the woman was almost over-powered by the extreme pain. . . . But then, once again, he felt that this one voice contained the cries of all mothers who would lose their children, sooner or later, *for we tarry here not*. He went to the window and closed it to make an end of that unbearable clapping, and as he did so gave a glance at the lattice along the wall and thought he saw a trampled vine—and shut the window. He knew enough. The syllogism: arms dump—Lieutenant—Violet, was so easy for him. Half an hour ago he had been tempted to call out to the girl shamming sleep: "The Lieutenant's coming!" He hadn't done so, and now the Lieutenant really had come, he believed. Pagel had no doubt that he understood every-thing. But what could he say about it to the distressed woman?

He comforted her, repeating over and over again that the girl in her fever had run into the woods and that Frau Eva should go with him just for a moment down to the telephone, so that he could inform Herr Studmann. Then they would look for and find the girl. . . . But no kindly word, no persuasion, reached Frau Eva. She lay there and groaned and wept. He was alone in the house—on the landing the Rittmeister slept away the loss of his daughter. He could not leave her.

Till the telephone below rang shrilly. What had not been possible to the human voice was possible to this ringing. Frau von Prackwitz started up and cried: "Run to the telephone. They have found my Vi."

She came too, standing behind him, holding the second receiver. They stood very close, with burning eyes, like ghosts . . . listening. But there came only the voice of Studmann, excitedly reporting that in the Manor the maids were hold-ing an orgy with the escaped convicts, all of them blind drunk and—"Pagel, it is a magnificent opportunity!" With a quick movement Frau von Prackwitz hung up her receiver, and Pagel saw her go upstairs slowly and as if unconscious. In a low voice he told Studmann that Fräulein Violet had disappeared from the house. Police on motorcycles, and a bloodhound, would be needed at once, and two or three reliable women for the Villa. . . . The door would be open.

He hung up, unlocked the door and left it wide open to this night of calamity; more could not befall the house. Then he hurried upstairs, stepping without ceremony over the sleeping Rittmeister, and found Frau von Prackwitz kneeling before the bed of her vanished daughter. She had thrust her hands beneath the cover, perhaps to perceive all that now remained to her of her child, the faint warmth retained by the bed.

Wofgang Pagel sat motionless next to the motionless woman, his head in his hands. Here, confronted by the greatest pain he'd ever seen, he fell to thinking about another woman, one far off, and much beloved. Perhaps he thought about what man can do to man, in love, in indifference, and in hatred. He hardly came to any decision; calculated decisions hadn't gotten him very far. But he let something grow within him which had quietly always been there. He gave it all the space he could. It was something very simple: To be as good and as decent as possible. *Because we are all of one flesh.*

Then he heard the voices and the footsteps of the people below. Now everything immediately became confused, as always when people are involved. He got up and had the Rittmeister brought to bed. He rang the doctor, and the lady would go to bed, too. He himself had plenty to do

But all that only confused the essential thing. To be as good and decent as possible. That was what was important. That's valid for a whole life.

XI

The wind had become stronger around the third hour of morning. It flung itself booming into the forest and brought the rotten and dead branches crashing to the ground. Autumn was going over into winter. From the swift clouds fled occasional brief showers, but the bloodhound did not lose the scent.

How many people were out! All Neulohe was on foot, no one asleep in the houses; lamps were burning everywhere. An amazing, a prodigious thing! The escaped convicts had hidden themselves in the Manor; they hadn't gone away at all. Snug in the maids' bedrooms they had enjoyed love and good food. Then, when the owners went on their travels, there had been a big party. The wild mirth had gone to their heads; in their frenzy they had even made the worthy old Elias, wrapped in a carpet, his mouth gagged, the spectator of their bacchanal. The maids had been utterly shameless in making friends with the convicts. Their rooms had overlooked the harvesters' barracks; signs had been exchanged, at first only in jest, but afterwards both parties had come to understand one another very well. Old Marofke had been on the right track.

Yes, there had been something rotten, in the Manor as in the Villa. There had been a lot of prayer there, but that alone was of little avail. How would the old lady take the bad news? Her home must appear to her as desecrated.

It had been easy work for the gendarmes; in fact no work at all, as with shouts of "Hands up!" they rushed with Herr von Studmann into the large dining room. The convicts, thinking it a very good joke, had laughed. They had had a delightful time; they had luscious things to relate; they would be the heroes of the prison. And what could actually happen to them? Upstairs in the maids' rooms their prison dress was neatly put away, not a piece missing; there could be no question of theft or housebreaking. Six months—three months—would square the matter for them. It had been worth that!

The girls, to be sure, sobbed. Oh, how the fat cook howled when the handcuffs were put on her lover, the convict Matzke! She pulled her apron over her head, howling beneath it like a puppy—she was so ashamed.

Pagel, looking in to hurry up the gendarmes, for Fräulein Violet seemed more important now than these convicts, saw Amanda Backs, that strapping buxom wench, standing at a window, her face curiously tense. She was watching with furious eyes the drunken, sobbing, cursing, hilarious uproar in the room—since there were not enough gendarmes to shut off the place, far too many of the merely curious had entered.

Pagel had a feeling of disappointment. Only yesterday he had thought her splendid when, in front of the Entente Commission, she boxed the ears of the traitorous Meier. "You too?" he said in a troubled voice.

Amanda Backs looked him full in the face. "Your brain soft?" she said contemptuously. "I've had enough of rotters. No, thanks, I'm cured of that. If there isn't a decent one, then I'd rather not." Pagel nodded. "I sleep downstairs because of the hens," she explained. "I've got to get up early and mustn't disturb madam. But *they* all sleep upstairs. I knew about it, of course—they're nothing but a lot of geese, and there's no geese without cackling." She looked at the turmoil. "I wonder if they've noticed yet?" she said thoughtfully. "I can't understand it. There should be five of them, and they've only got four. I don't know whether the fifth has escaped or was never here at all."

Pagel's eyes shone. "Liebschner, Kosegarten, Matzke, Wendt and Holdrian," he said immediately. "Who's missing, Amanda?"

"Liebschner. The one with the uneasy black eyes, a skulking fellow, you know, Herr Pagel!"

He nodded and went up to the gendarmes, to make inquiries. But they had already noticed that a man was missing. Even if they hadn't, Studmann's excellent memory spoke as correctly as Pagel's—Holdrian, Wendt, Matzke, Kosegarten, Liebschner.

Yes, for a time it looked as if the search for Fräulein Violet, in spite of all Pagel's entreaties, would be forgotten because of this missing fifth man. But toward three o'clock more gendarmes hurriedly arrived, and the curious were ejected. Interrogations began, greatly facilitated by the sudden appearance of a detective or former detective, whom the gendarmes seemed to know; a fat man, exceedingly dirty and wet through, with a strangely frozen look.

Two minutes, and it was clear that Liebschner had not been present at the orgy. Three more minutes, and it was shown that he had never been in the Manor. Ah, the fat sobbing cook, that weeping mountain of flesh! Now she indeed started out from under her apron. "Only four of us sleep upstairs," she shouted. "What should we do with five chaps? For shame! What do these men think we are!" And she disappeared blubbering under her apron again.

Another two minutes and they knew that Liebschner had been lost by the other four immediately after the escape, in the woods. . . .

"What is he? Swindler? Let's not delay here any longer," said the fat detective. "The lad's a long time ago in Berlin. Neulohe's no place for a gentleman like that. He knew what he wanted. Our colleagues at headquarters will be hearing about him. Pretty soon, I hope. Away with those chaps! You, Herr von Studmann, please go over to the Villa and tell the doctor to come as well. It would be better— the girl's in her nightdress or pajamas, same thing this weather."

"Frau von Prackwitz . . ." objected Studmann.

"The lady is asleep, had a small injection. The gentleman's asleep, had enough, too. The doctor's got time, I tell you. Wait! Bring some piece of the girl's clothing so that the hound won't lose the scent; anything which the girl had next to her skin. And another thing. There's said to be a forester here, an old ass, Kniebusch or something like that. Get him out of bed—the man will know his own wood."

"I will fetch the forester," said Pagel.

"Wait, young man. Herr Pagel, isn't it? I was wanting to speak to you."

The big hall had emptied itself. Only two or three of the bulbs set up for the orgy were still alight; the air was icy and seemed dirty. A half torn-down curtain hung from a window revealing a night blind.

The fat man took Pagel gently by the arm, obliging him to walk up and down. "It's damned cold. My very marrow's ice. How that young girl must be freezing! She's been practically two hours outside now. Well, tell me all you know about the young lady. You're in employment on the estate, and young men are interested in young women. So out with it." His icy gaze penetrated the young man.

But Pagel had seen and observed a good deal; he was no longer the unsuspecting young man who submitted to every pretension made with authority. He had heard a gendarme exclaim peevishly: "What's that lump of fat want with us again?" and had noticed how the fat man gave instructions to civilians but never to a gendarme, and how the gendarmes acted as though he were not there, never speaking to him.

"First I should like to know in the name of what authority you are here," he replied slowly.

"You want to see a badge?" cried the other. "I could show you one, only it's not valid now. I've been kicked out. In the newspapers they call it disciplinary punishment on account of nationalist convictions."

"You are the only man here," said Wolfgang more rapidly, "who kept urging the search for Fräulein von Prackwitz. What is your interest in her?"

"None," said the man icily. He bent closer to Pagel, seized his jacket and said: "You are lucky, young man. You have a pleasant face, not a bulldog's mug like mine. People will always have confidence in you—don't misuse it. Well, I trust you, too, and I'll disclose something. I have a great interest in whatever is connected with arms dumps that have been carted away."

Wolfgang stared in front of him. Then he looked up. "Violet von Prackwitz is fifteen years old. I don't think that she . . ."

"Herr Pagel," said the detective with a cold look, "in every case of treachery there is a woman behind it, either as instigator or tool. Often an unconscious tool. Always! Tell me what you know."

So Pagel told what he knew.

The fat man walked beside him, snorting, clearing his throat, looking contemptuously at the walls, tugging furiously at the cord of a curtain, spitting. "Idiocy. Miserable idiocy!" he cried. Then, somewhat calmer: "Thank you, Herr Pagel, things are a little clearer now."

"Shall we find the girl? The Lieutenant . . ."

"Blind!" said the fat man. "Born blind in a world of the blind! You're thinking of the Lieutenant—well, Herr Pagel," he whispered, "you will be able to say good morning to this Lieutenant in an hour's time, but I'm afraid you won't like it."

It was completely quiet in the hall. Only the lamps still glimmered. Pagel stared at the fat pallid face. As if through a veil it seemed to nod to him, that face acquainted with all the baseness, all the naked brutality, all the sins of the human heart, and which lived on, acquiescent. He looked into that face, and did so again. I was on *that* road, he said. Did he say it out loud? He heard the wind outside; a dog howled; another answered. The fat man took him by the shoulder. "Let's go, young man. We've no more time."

They went into the forest. . . .

The wind blew. It whistled in the invisible treetops, it screamed; branches fell with a crash, showers of rain became spray. Without a word the men advanced.

The hound was straining at his leash, followed by his master whispering encouragement and praise. Then came Pagel and the detective, then the doctor with Studmann, and the two gendarmes. . . . The forester was not there. He could not be found; he was said to be out somewhere. "But I'll get him!" the detective said in a tone Pagel did not like; and after that he walked silently beside the young man. Once he switched on his flashlight, stood still and said calmly: "Please don't tread here," and let the others go on. "Look." He pointed to something on the ground which Pagel could not distinguish. "He's thought of everything. She's wearing shoes now, and he'll also have brought a coat or something for her."

"Who's thought of everything?" asked Pagel, wearied. He was terribly tired and his head more painful than ever. He'd afterwards ask the doctor about it.

"Don't you know even yet? You told me yourself."

"If it's not the Lieutenant," said Pagel annoyed, "I really don't know who it is. And I shan't be able to find out tonight, either, unless you tell me."

"When the blood becomes too thin," exclaimed the fat man enigmatically, "then it loses its strength. The blood wants to go back to where it comes from. But we must hurry. My colleagues are far enough ahead to enjoy the honor of the discovery."

"Do you know, then, what we're going to find?" asked Pagel, with the same weary annoyance.

"Yes, I know what we shall find *now*. But what we shall find afterwards, no, I don't know that. I can't even guess."

They quickened their steps, but those in front seemed also to have gone faster, and they were a minute too late; the others were all round him.

There was a murmur, the wind passed overhead. But it was quiet in the Black Dale as the circle of men swayed here and there—the white beam of the doctor's torch lay intolerably brilliant on that which had once been a face.

"Dug his own grave, too! Quite off his head."

"But where's the girl?"

Murmuring. Silence.

Yes, there was no doubt about it, this was the Lieutenant of whom Pagel had so often heard and had once so wished to meet. There he lay, a very quiet, a very dubious figure—to be frank, a pretty bemired heap of rags. It was incomprehensible that this should ever have been the object of hate and love. With an inexplicable feeling of indifference, almost of repulsion, Pagel looked down at the thing. "Were you worth such great things?" he might have asked.

The doctor stood up. "Undoubtedly suicide," he declared.

"Does any one of the gentlemen from Neulohe know the man?" asked a gendarme.

Pagel and von Studmann looked at one another across the circle.

"Never seen him," replied Studmann.

"No," said Pagel, and looked round for the fat detective. But, as he had expected, he was nowhere to be seen.

"This is the place, isn't it, where . . . ?"

"Yes," said Pagel. "Yesterday afternoon I had to come here to make a statement. This is the place where the Entente Commission confiscated an arms dump."

"The dead man unknown, then," said a voice in the background, decisively.

"But unmistakably suicide," burst forth the doctor, as if putting something right.

There was a long silence. In the feeble torch light the faces were almost surly.

"Where's the weapon?" finally asked the man with the bloodhound.

There was a stir.

"No, it's not here. We scoured the place. It couldn't fall far away."

Again that long reluctant silence. It's like an assembly of ghosts, thought Pagel, extremely unhappy. And he tried to get nearer the dog, so that he could stroke its beautiful head. Had they all forgotten the girl?

But one of them now spoke. "And where is the girl?"

Silence again, but tenser.

"Perhaps—it's quite simple," said a gendarme. "He shot himself first, and she picked up the weapon to do the same. But she wasn't able to, and has taken it with her."

A thoughtful silence.

"Yes, that would be it. You are right," said another.

"So we had better quickly carry on the search at once."

"That can take all night! We're never lucky at Neulohe."

"Off! No dawdling now."

A hand from behind gripped Pagel's shoulder, a voice whispered in his ear. "Don't turn your head. I'm not here! Ask the doctor how long the man's been dead."

"A moment, please," called out Pagel. "Can you tell us, doctor, how long the man here has been dead?"

The country doctor, a thick-set man with a peculiarly sparse black beard, looked hesitatingly at the body, then at Wolfgang. His face cleared a little. "I have not the experience of my colleagues attached to the police. May I inquire why you ask?"

"Because I saw Fräulein von Prackwitz asleep in her bed at half-past twelve."

The doctor looked at his watch. "It's half-past three now," he said quickly. "At half-past twelve this man had been dead for hours."

"Then someone else must have brought Fräulein von Prackwitz here," concluded Pagel.

The hand, the heavy hand which all this time had rested like a load on his shoulder, was removed and a slight noise in the rear betrayed the fat man's departure.

"That knocks out your explanation, Albert!" said an irritated gendarme.

"How?" retorted the other. "She could have come here alone and found the dead man. She takes the revolver, goes on . . ."

"Rubbish!" said the man with the bloodhound. "Are you blind? There were two trails, a man's and a woman's, all the way. This is a bad business and it goes far beyond our ability. . . . We shall have to report a murder."

"This is suicide," contradicted the doctor.

"We have to look for the girl," Pagel reminded them. "Quickly."

"Young gentleman," said he with the bloodhound, "you know something or you have a suspicion; otherwise you wouldn't have asked that question of the doctor. Tell us what you have in mind. Don't leave us in darkness!"

Everyone looked at Pagel, who was thinking of that time when Violet had kissed him. He would gladly have felt now the firm hand on his shoulder, the voice in his ear. But when we have to make a decision, we're on our own, and we have to be. The words "I just don't know" rang desperately in his head. He listened to the words. Then he heard the rough voice again, that evil yet sad sound with which she had spoken: Blood will flow. . . . Blood will flow. Then he looked from the dead into the faces of the men. "The blood wants to go back to where it comes from."

"I know nothing," he said. "But perhaps I have guessed something. . . . This morning Rittmeister von Prackwitz dismissed his servant after a serious quarrel. The maid there told me this evening that it was about a letter which the Fräulein had written. . . . The Fräulein was very young and this servant was, according to what I know of him, a very evil person. I could imagine . . ." He looked questioningly at the men.

"Blackmail then! That sounds a bit different," cried a gendarme. "None of these damned affairs of traitors, arms dumps, secret tribunals!"

His colleague cleared his throat loudly, almost menacingly. "Let the hound smell the vest. Don't move, anyone! Take Minka in a circle round the hollow; everything's stamped down here."

Within five minutes the hound, tugging at the lead, shot up a little path. The men hurried after it, out of the hollow and up a glade, further and further from Neulohe.

Suddenly the detective was at Pagel's side again. "You did that very well," he said approvingly. "Have you guessed it at last, then?"

"Is it really true?" In his shock Pagel stopped. "It can't be."

"On, young man! We're in a hurry now, though I'm convinced we'll be too late. Of course it's true—who would it be else?"

"I don't believe it. That gray, fishlike brute!"

"I must have seen him on the streets of Ostade yesterday," said the fat detective, "I had a sort of inkling of his face. But one sees too many faces these days which look like the faces of past or future criminals. God help the chap if I find him!"

"If we can only find her."

"Stop. Perhaps your wish has just been fulfilled."

There was a delay. At right angles to the glade the bloodhound, tugging, went into a thickly wooded coppice of firs. Battling with the branches and aided by the torch, the men pushed on. No one spoke. It was so quiet that the animal's impatient panting sounded like the strokes of a steam engine.

"The scent's quite fresh," whispered the fat man to Pagel, and forced his way through the undergrowth.

But the little clearing they came to, hardly larger than a boxroom, was empty. The hound with a yelp sprang forward, and its master bent down. "A woman's shoe," he cried.

"And another," exclaimed the fat detective. "Here he . . . On, gentlemen! We're just behind him. He won't be able to go very fast with the girl in stockings. You can praise your dog, man. Onward!"

They ran.

This way and that went the wild chase, between firs and junipers, the hound yelping, the men knocking in the dark against tree trunks. "I can hear her!" "Be quiet!" "Wasn't that a woman screaming?"

The forest became more open, they advanced faster, and suddenly, fifty or sixty yards in front, there was a light between the branches, a beam white and brilliant . . .

"A car. He has a car!" cried someone. And they stormed forward. The engine started up, it roared, the glare flickered, became weaker. . . . And they were running in darkness.

They came to a halt. In the distance a light traveled away. A gendarme lowered his pistol—impossible to hit the tires.

They must hurry back to Neulohe! They must telephone; the fugitives could be followed in the Rittmeister's car. All set off.

"Pagel," called out Studmann impatiently, "aren't you coming?"

"In a moment."

The fat man held Pagel by the arm. "Listen, young man," he whispered. "I won't come with you, I'll go back to Ostade. Those chaps are full of optimism because they're on the track and it's nothing to do with a traitor. Chasing political murderers is something they don't like, although they have to. But you, young man, are the only sensible-looking one on the farm. Don't deceive yourself or the others, especially the mother. Break it to her slowly."

"What is it I'm to break to her?"

"When we were pushing through the thicket I too thought that he'd done it. But when we found the shoes . . ."

"We had disturbed him."

"Perhaps. But he had calculated it to the minute. Pagel, I tell you in your worst dreams you couldn't dream of a fellow like that. It's possible, of course, that he will still do it, but I don't think so. It's much worse. . . . There are people like that. Generally, in healthy times, the others don't let them advance. In a rotten diseased age they flourish like weeds. . . . You needn't think, Pagel, that this fellow's a human being. He's a monster, a wolf who kills for the sake of killing."

"But you say he won't do it?"

"Do you know what that means, to be sexually enslaved? Can you imagine it? Dependent on the breath and the glance of such a monster, able to do nothing without his permission and will? There's your little girl! And now he's got away he will do the worst he can; continually he will almost murder her and then let her live a little. What he calls living! Just enough for the spark of life to experience the fear of death!"

There was a gust of wind in the trees.

"Pagel," said the fat man suddenly, "I'm going now. We're hardly likely to meet again, but it has been, as they say, a pleasure."

"Pagel," he said once again urgently, "pray to God that this mother never finds her daughter—she'd no longer be a daughter."

He was gone without a sound, leaving Wolfgang Pagel alone in the dark and windy forest.

Chapter Fourteen

Life Goes On

I

It was October. Neulohe grew increasingly damper, windier, colder. And more and more difficult did Wolfgang Pagel find it to collect the necessary people for the potato digging. Where in September three wagons packed with laborers had rattled on to the fields from the local town, in October it had come to one, bearing a few sullen women wrapped up in sacks and woolen shawls.

Swearing and complaining, they toiled through the sodden growth over fields which seemed only to grow larger. Already Pagel had had to raise their wages twice, and had this not been in kind, had he not paid them with potatoes—that support of life which can replace even bread itself—none would have come. In those October days the dollar rose from 242,000,000 marks to 73,000,000,000. Hunger crept through the entire country, followed by influenza. Unprecedented despair seized the people; every pound of potatoes was a fence between them and death.

Wolfgang Pagel was now the overlord of Neulohe Manor, the farm and the forest. No time now to stand among the potatoes and give out tokens. Next year's rye had to be sown and the fields plowed. In the forest the cutting down of firewood had started, and unless one gingered up Kniebusch every day the forester would have taken to his bed and died.

Pagel would come on his bicycle to the potato field where old Kowalewski would meet him ever more and more hollow-eyed. "We can't do it, young sir," was his lament. "This way we shall be digging in January in snow and ice."

Wolfgang would laugh. "We'll do it, Kowalewski. Because we've got to. Because potatoes are bitterly needed in the town." And because the estate bitterly needs the money for them, he thought.

"But we ought to have more people," moaned Kowalewski.

"And where shall I get them?" Pagel was a little impatient. "Shall I have another prison gang sent?"

"Oh, Lord, no!" exclaimed old Kowalewski, horrified—much too horrified, thought Pagel, looking at the diggers. "They're only townsfolk, they've no business here," he said discontentedly. "The work's too unfamiliar for them. If only we could get the people from Altlohe as well."

"We'll never get them!" declared Kowalewski angrily. "They steal their potato supplies from our clamps at night."

"They certainly do that," sighed Pagel. "Every day I see the holes and have to have them filled up. I am always intending to go out at night and see if I can catch one, Kowalewski, but I always fall asleep over supper."

"It's too much, what the young gentleman has to do. All the estate and the whole forest and all the pen-pushing—no one's done all that. You need help."

"Oh, nobody knows what will happen here."

Both were silent a moment. "But those miserable potato thieves—that's a matter for the police," said Kowalewski. "The young gentleman ought to apply to them."

"The police! Oh, no. We're not in favor with them anymore, Kowalewski. We've made too much work for them in the last six months." Both were silent. Each new load of potatoes seemed to emerge like a yellowish brown blessing from the darkness into the dawn. Now Pagel could leave again, having established how far the work had proceeded. He had something else to say, and he was no longer too weak to say something which might be unpleasant. It had to be said, and he would say it. "By the way, I saw your Sophie this morning in the village. So she's still at home?"

The old man grew very embarrassed. "She has to look after her mother—my wife is ill," he stuttered.

"You told me last time she was taking up a situation on the first of October. Now you say she has to look after her mother. You're not telling me the truth, Kowalewski. That won't do. If you occupy one of our cottages, she's got to work."

Kowalewski looked very pale. "I have no authority over the lass, young gentleman," he said in excuse. "She takes no notice of what I say."

"Kowalewski, old fellow, don't be so flabby! You know yourself how much we need every hand, and you know too that if the overseer's daughter is lazy, then those of the laborers will certainly be."

"I'll tell her what you say, young gentleman," said Kowalewski, distressed.

"Yes, do, and tell her that otherwise I'll put another family into your house as well. Then you'll only have a parlor, bedroom and kitchen. Good day, Kowalewski, I'm damned hungry."

Young Pagel got on his bicycle. He was satisfied that he'd finally brought the business with Sophie in order—one way or another. He'd rather let her get away with things lately, he had had so much to do. But whenever he saw the girl in the village it had occurred to him that such an example of laziness was intolerable. It was difficult enough to retain one's workers at that time—they never considered they were paid enough. However, they didn't only get their wretched money, they got extras, too. Nobody in the village lived the life of the lilies in the field—the good Lord fed them! On the contrary, my good Sophie, on the contrary, these were not the times to rely on God in heaven. These were times to work yourself until you drop.

He could not deny that he was extremely angry with Sophie. He had liked her in the beginning. He dimly recalled a certain scene at the crab pool. She boldly defended the men's clothes against the war, like Kniebusch. But either he had been mistaken in his liking or the girl had changed. She had such a confounded slovenly way of lounging about the village. Yes, she had once had the cheek to call after him as he sped by on his bicycle: "Always busy, Herr Pagel?"

When a thing was overdone it was time to stop it. If she wasn't digging potatoes tomorrow, he would put Black Minna with all her screaming, quarrelsome retinue in Kowalewski's attic.

He came into the farmyard. In the sheds the head carter spoke to him. It was too wet, he declared, to drill rye—the drills would foul. For Pagel, who understood nothing of farming and stock-raising, and yet had to supervise and decide, this sort of thing was difficult. In general the older people gladly helped him; had he passed himself off as experienced, then they would have taken pleasure in playing him trick after trick. But because he never behaved as though he knew something when he did not, they were helpful. The experience and perceptions of these old people was hardly appreciated. But Pagel liked to listen to them—he always just fell asleep over his thick textbooks.

"What shall we do then?" he asked, and the man suggested that plowing was possible on the lighter outfields. "Good," said Pagel. "We'll plow then."

And went to his lunch.

Lunch he always took in the office, which was his living room, work room, smoke room and study. Although Studmann was no longer in Neulohe, his meals were not solitary. He had a companion, Amanda Backs. "Thank God," she said, "that you're punctual for once, Herr Pagel. Put on some dry clothes quickly. I'll bring in the food at once."

"Fine." He went into his bedroom.

It was very likely, indeed it was almost certain, that the village scandalmongers, bearing in mind what was known of the girl's earlier life, misrepresented this table fellowship of Pagel and Backs as a bed fellowship. Actually it had all come about quite naturally after the arrest of the convicts. The girls at the Manor had, without notice, wage or reference, fled in fear of prosecution for abetting escaped prisoners, not to mention the dreaded mockery of the villagers—leaving behind the single irreproachable—that Amanda Backs once publicly reproached at evening prayers. And old Elias also, of course. He, however, left next day to report no doubt to his employers, for he had no rent to take them. And did not return.

Pagel, those first days in October, had his mind too much occupied with a multitude of affairs to worry overmuch about the Manor. One day, however, he ran into Amanda Backs, and she inquired very forcibly what he was really thinking about, what did he imagine? Even if she didn't actually shudder at being the sole occupant of that enormous old dungeon, all the same it wasn't pleasant. And something would have to be done upstairs before the old people came back; the convicts' party had left everything in a terrible mess, and two windows had been broken in the drawing room. Now the rain came in, and there had been puddles on the floor for a week.

Pagel, tired out and a little disheartened, not having had ten hours' sleep in three days, looked at the rosy-cheeked Amanda, rubbed his exceedingly unshaven chin, and asked: "Yes, don't you want to clear out as well, Amanda?"

"And who'll look after my poultry?" she indignantly demanded. "Especially now, with winter coming, when the ducks and geese ought to be fattened and one can't feed them enough! I clear out! Not on your life."

"In the Villa they're wringing their hands for a sensible housemaid," he said. "You've no doubt heard that Lotte has also gone off. Wouldn't you like to go there?"

"No." Amanda Backs was clear on that point. "I'm used to the stupidity of my poultry, but I'll never get used to that of my fellow-beings. They always make me boil with rage and then I'm not fit for anything."

"All right," Pagel had said hurriedly. "I'll let you know this evening."

He had intended to discuss this matter with Frau von Prackwitz; but she was out again in the car, and it was uncertain when she would return. The Rittmeister was withdrawn from all inquiries; he lay in bed, watched over by an attendant. There was no one in all populous Neulohe whom he could ask for advice.

And so, after some reflection, he rang up the Hotel Kaiserhof and asked to speak with Geheimrat von Teschow-Neulohe.

"We are very sorry. They have left."

"Left?" It was something of a blow. "When, please?"

"On the third of October." Immediately after the arrival of old Elias, that is!

"Will you give me his address, please?"

"We are very sorry, we were strictly forbidden to do so."

"This is the Management of Neulohe Estate speaking—the Management of the Geheimrat himself," said Pagel with all his self-control. "His address is indispensable for a very important decision. I must make you responsible for all damages arising out of your refusal."

"A moment, please. I'll inquire. Please hold on."

And after some hesitation the clerk gave him the address. He was interested to know where these people had gone to, when their daughter was in despair and their grandchild lost. The address was Hotel Imperial, Côte d'Azure, Nice, France.

He sat quietly for a while, his face alert. His eyes saw nothing on the desk. But he saw something else. He saw the little dried-up woman with her sharp bird's face and swift eyes; she drove the servants from one task to another; she was empty but she could make up for this with the life of others, any life, it didn't matter which. She used her religion to worm herself into people. She was like a maggot, living on the decomposed offal of other existences.

He saw the fierce Geheimrat with his false heartiness, sweating enormously, dressed in worsted. And though he wouldn't be wearing worsted down there on the Côte d'Azure, nothing would be changed by that. He would still sit and calculate, drawing up crafty agreements and writing business letters with catches in them. Everything he looked at was transformed into profit. Certainly people said that he loved his woods, and he did—but in his own fashion. He loved with his sense of gain, he loved so-and-so many cubic feet of timber. A thicket of young pines was not a green and golden mystery, but meant that at the thinning out, so-and-so many bean poles could be cut.

But one would have thought that at least they loved their daughter, their grandchild. One now saw what this love was worth. Fearing to be dragged into a disgraceful business, they fled, offering no help, showing neither kindliness nor charity—fled into the other corner of Europe, into that France which, still occupying the Ruhr, continued to refuse negotiations with a German Government.

So that's what they were like, the old people, or as they say, the retired people. But the woman never found a home for her shallowness, or the man for his money, which he didn't know how to use. . . .

Young Pagel, after he had thought enough, while still sitting by the telephone, did something remarkable: He took a mark note out of his pocket, lit a match, and burned it. Such was the action of the young Pagel, the very young Pagel. It was symbolic, as if to say: Oh Lord, let me never be so in love with money that I can't part with it.

Besides, in doing this, he was depriving himself of something. It was Saturday evening. Paying the wages had completely emptied the estate coffers.

That had been his last note, with which he wanted to get some cigarettes. Now he couldn't smoke until Monday. Yes, despite all his recent experiences, he was still juvenile! But then again, didn't it show how strong he was, too! He just whistled nonchalantly when he considered that he only had three or four cigarettes left.

And still whistling, he drummed up a crowd of women and fetched the maintenance man.

That same evening he had what was essential done in the Manor, the broken panes replaced, the doors locked. "Now we've finished with the Teschows! And you, Amanda, move over with your things into Herr von Studmann's room. That is, if you've no misgivings."

"Because of gossip, Herr Pagel? A fat lot I care! Talk and let talk, I say."

"That's right. And if at the same time you'd take pity on my food and laundry! They've looked somewhat woeful of late."

"Black Minna . . ."

"Black Minna has to help in the kitchen at the Villa, besides which she's the only one of the women who's not afraid of the Rittmeister. The attendant has to take the air sometimes, and she takes his place."

"As it should be!" said Amanda, deeply satisfied. "That's what suits her. She afraid of men! She's never been afraid enough of men, and you can hear any day you pass the almshouse, Herr Pagel, the squealing that comes from too little fear."

"You've a scandalous gift of gab, Amanda," Pagel said, half laughing. "The dangerously ill Rittmeister and Black Minna! No, I really don't know if the two of us will get on well for long."

"I'll let you talk and you let me talk," Amanda had replied, very contented. "That's simple enough. Why shouldn't we get on well, Herr Pagel?"

II

The bloated woman, who had no other job in life but to eat, was ladling soup from a tureen when Kowalewski came home tired and wet through. He looked into the tureen, knitted his brows, but restrained himself. Spreading lard on a crust of bread, he began to eat.

The woman, chewing, gave him a malicious look from her small eyes. In her case it was gluttony which kept her from talking. So the two old people sat silent, both eating; he the bread, she the chicken soup.

Only when her hunger was stilled did she open her mouth. "A fine fool you are!" she scolded. "The good chicken soup! It won't make it any different you not touching a morsel." She dipped the ladle in the soup and found a leg, at which she almost forgot to be angry. "What a fat hen it was, this! Yes, the Haases feed them well. It weighed over five pounds; and the beautiful pure yellow fat, that makes a rich soup!" She smacked her lips.

"Is our Sophie upstairs?" asked the dejected old man.

"Where should she be? They're still sleeping." Satiated, she was already luxuriating in the prospect of further meals. "Tonight we're going to have a joint of venison. I'm fond of venison when it's well done. And he's also going to bring us a fat pig."

"I don't need a pig, I won't have it!" cried old Kowalewski in despair. "We've always been honest. But now! Thieves and associates of thieves! We can't look people in the face anymore."

"Don't excite yourself," said his wife indifferently. "You know that he won't put up with anything from you. Thieves! It's only theft if one's caught; he's too clever for that. He's ten times cleverer than you. A hundred times!"

"I don't want him here anymore," he mumbled.

"Yes, that's like you!" shouted the glutton. "Someone at last who provides for us—and you want him to leave! But I tell you, if you start a row with him, I—" She waved the ladle, not knowing with what she should threaten him, while her little eyes, drowned in fat, searched the room. "I'll eat up everything, and you can starve!" This was the worst threat she could contrive.

Her husband looked at her gloomily. Like mother, like daughter, he thought. Selfish and greedy. Greedy!

He turned across the room to the stairs.

"Don't you go up! Don't start a row!" she screamed after him.

Kowalewski was already climbing the stairs. For a moment he stood breathing quickly outside his daughter's room, and almost lost his courage. Then he knocked.

"Who's there?" asked Sophie's angry voice after a while.

"Me—father!" he murmured.

There was whispering inside; the door was unlocked. Sophie looked into her father's face. "What do you want?" she complained. "You know that Hans needs his sleep. First you make such a row downstairs that one can't get a wink of sleep, then you come up here. What's the matter?"

"Come in, father-in-law!" shouted a falsely cordial voice. "An enormous pleasure. Sophie, shut up! Company has come. Our respected father-in-law! Sit down, please, old gentleman. Give him a chair, Sophie, so he can sit down. Do excuse us, father-in-law, that we're still in bed. Had I guessed the honor to be done us, I would have put on my frock coat." The speaker grinned at the intimidated old man. "That's to say, looked at strictly, it's not mine. But it fits me perfectly, Herr Rittmeister's frock coat. Herr von Prackwitz was so kind as to come to my aid. My wardrobe was a little empty."

Kowalewski had been so often and so thoroughly mocked and scolded in his life that, although it perhaps never ceased to hurt him, he never let this appear. He stood behind the chair, not looking at the bed or Hans Liebschner. "You, Sophie," he said in low tones. "Well, what, father? Go on! More grumbling, I suppose, because something's disappeared! Is Haase making such a row about the few hens that you can't sleep? He can have something quite different happen!"

"Sophie, Herr Pagel again asked why you weren't working."

"Let him ask! Those who ask a lot, get a lot of answers. I'll answer him all right if he comes to me."

"But he says if you aren't digging potatoes tomorrow, he'll put Black Minna in the attic here."

"The fellow can—"

"Yes, Hans. Give him one in his cheeky mug so he won't be able to open his mouth for six weeks. What does the fool think he is?"

"Not for me, thank you, Sophie, that's not my sort of job. That's something for Bäumer. He'll finish the chap with pleasure, so that he won't even know he's dead."

"If anything happens to Herr Pagel, I'll denounce you," said the old man quietly.

"What does Pagel matter to you, father?" began Sophie. "You're mad."

"I've held my tongue because you're my only daughter and because you've kept on promising to go away soon. It's almost broken my heart, to see you here with such a—"

"Drivel on as much as you like, old gentleman!" cried the man in bed. "Don't put yourself out among relatives. Convict, eh?"

"Yes, convict!" repeated old Kowalewski defiantly. "But it doesn't mean I think all in prison are as low as you. And the stealing! Always stealing. . . . Does a man do that merely out of pleasure in doing mischief? You don't gain anything by it. The money you get in Frankfurt and Ostade for the stolen things is worth nothing."

"Be patient, old fellow. Times will change again. As soon as I've collected the fare and some working funds we'll dash off. D'you think I'm so fond of your cottage? Or that I can't bear to part from your whining face?"

"Yes," cried the old man eagerly. "Go off. Go to Berlin."

"Father-in-law, you've just told me that we've got no money. Or will you give me the dowry for your daughter in cash? What, my dear man, go to Berlin without money and be arrested at once! No, thanks. We've waited so long that a few days or weeks till we—"

"But what will happen if he really does put Minna in here?" said Sophie angrily. "You've let us in for this, father, so as to get rid of us!"

Herr Liebschner whistled and exchanged a glance with the girl, who fell silent.

Kowalewski had noticed this glance. "As true as I stand here, and hope that God will forgive me my weakness—if anything happens to Herr Pagel I'll bring the gendarmes here myself!" There was such energy in the old man's outburst that the other two were convinced he would do it.

"And you always pretend you are something like a father!" said the girl contemptuously.

"It's no good talking, Sophie," said Liebschner, resigned. "The old fellow's taken a passion for the lout. There are things like that. Listen, Sophie. You shove off to the young man at once. He'll be alone now, at midday. Be a little nice to him, Sophie; you know I'm not jealous. Then he'll give way. . . . You'll be able to manage that, eh, Sophie?"

"That lout! He'll go on his knees if I want it. But the Backs will be there. He's got her!"

"The fat one with the hens? If you can't cut out that gawk, you can lose your job with me, too, Sophie."

"Go away! Please. Better go away before everything is discovered," pleaded Kowalewski.

"Before you catch on to something, the pastor's got to preach three times on Sunday, I suppose, eh? Money, I say! You won't get rid of us sooner. So set your mind at rest, father-in-law; we'll wangle it. We shall keep on our lodgings; we still like them. And nothing will happen to your young chap—agreed?"

"You should go away," said the old man obstinately.

"Show him the door, Sophie. Let him go away first! If I wasn't too lazy, I'd show you how to travel down the stairs, father-in-law. Good morning, it's been a pleasure. Give my regards to your friend Herr Pagel."

The old man stood wretchedly on the stairs. "Oh, Sophie," he muttered, "you were such a good child."

III

Amanda had been right; things went well with the pair of them. No, more than that, things went excellently. To his astonishment Pagel discovered that this female who he thought would get on his nerves within a week, did, on the contrary, help him over many difficulties. That she was cleanly, industrious, quick and skillful he had more or less known. But this young thing with the tongue of an old fishwife knew very well when to be silent, and could tolerate other points of view. This illegitimate child, the sport of adversity, who had in one year received more hard words and blows than most people in an entire lifetime, and whose experience of people and of men in particular had filled her whole existence with a grinding pessimism, had a sensitiveness to every kind word, every slight hint, that never failed to move him.

"My God!" he exclaimed the third day on seeing the desk covered with a tablecloth and respectable china and cutlery which must have been fetched from the Manor—she had divined how much he detested the chipped earthenware and the stained knives and forks.

Yes, she said provocatively. So what's wrong now? To each his own! What I always say is that I couldn't give a damn about the packaging. It's what's inside that counts. But if you want to do it differently, help yourself!

The two young people lived as on an island, without any company or friends. They were completely dependent on one another. When Pagel, worn down by the rush and scramble of his work, wished for a little private life, he had to find it at "home," that is, in the office. And when Amanda wished to hear a kind, a personal word, it had to be from Pagel.

So each became the savior of the other. Without her Pagel might have deserted like a Geheimrat von Teschow, a Herr von Studmann, or even a Rittmeister. That he should keep his flag flying—therein had Amanda Backs no little merit.

And who knows if she herself would have got over her experience with Meier if she had not had Wolfgang Pagel constantly before her eyes? There were, then, other men, decent men, men who did not run after every skirt or goggle at every bosom! It was foolish to be at odds with all the world because Meier had been a rascal. She ought to be angry only with herself, for such a bad choice. In the beginning almost everyone had it a little in his power to choose whom he would love—later, to be sure, it was usually too late. She had adored her little Hans after a time.

And so, as each of these two received something good from the other, it stood to reason that they were also good to each other. When Wolfgang, washed and changed, re-entered the office, he saw that the food was ready but the soup not yet served. "Well?" he smiled. "Aren't we starting?"

"Post for you, too, Herr Pagel," she said, holding out two letters, and went into the bedroom to remove the wet clothes and tidy up.

That's what one could call being good to one another. Pagel didn't think of it again, but felt it was true. He leaned against the pleasantly warm stove, put Studmann's letter unread in his pocket, and tore open his mother's. But before he began to read, he lit another cigarette. He knew he would be able to read in peace and complete comfort—that no cry of "your soup's getting cold!" would disturb him.

Amanda always sorted out the post into little heaps: farm management, forest management, the occupants of the Villa, the land steward (also represented by Pagel), and finally, sometimes, a letter for Pagel himself. That letter, however, she did not place on the table, but kept secret somewhere, waiting till he had washed himself and felt a little fresher; then she said: "Post for you, too, Herr Pagel," and disappeared. However, it was by no means the case that this had been agreed between them. Amanda had thought it up all by herself. It was astonishing that so blunt a woman could be so sensitive. Pagel had never told her about his home or sweetheart, yet she had guessed how it was with him, without having the slightest fact to go on; there was no bulky correspondence with a lady—except with a Frau Pagel who, from the writing and the name, could only be his mother. Yet Amanda could have sworn any oath that Herr Pagel, in her words, was "in firm hands." And that, however firmly those hands held him, there was something in this affair not quite in order.

The girl cleared away the washstand and turned round again. Everything was in order. If he wanted to he could sleep here in the afternoon. Hopefully he would. He needed to. She listened out for the other room, but everything was quiet there. This quietness didn't entirely satisfy her. But it continued. . . .

Amanda sat down. She felt neither upset by, jealous of, nor in love with the young Pagel. On the contrary, what she saw and learnt about him only did her good. It confirmed what was strong in her—her will to live.

Look, she thought roughly, here's a clean and decent fellow, and for neither of us have things gone exactly smoothly. Why should I give up courage and despair when I clawed myself out of the dirt only two years ago? Thus ran Amanda's thoughts. But now they were interrupted, because in the office next door sounded a penetrating whistle—not the tuneful notes of a contented man but a wild warlike shrill, something which even Amanda's unsoldierly mind felt as a signal for attack. On the attack, quick march! Up and at the enemy! Then: Victory, fame, glory!

In the same moment, just when Amanda jumped up from her chair, the door was torn open. Pagel pushed his head into the bedroom and shouted: "Amanda, wench! Hunger! Grub! Soup! On, on!"

She, with all the indignation people from the folk have for every exaltation, scrutinized his flushed face. "You're going crazy," she said aloofly, and passed by.

"What are we having, Amanda?" Pagel asked. Yet obviously he was indifferent.

"Goose giblets with barley."

"Goose giblets again! And today! Today there ought . . . Oh, I certainly haven't the patience to nibble at goose wings."

"If you don't soon stop the village urchins from forever crippling my geese by throwing stones at them, you'll have to eat goose giblets every day, Herr Pagel," replied the Backs with dangerous calmness.

"Amanda, couldn't you give me a rest today from nagging? This is the first time for a long while that I've been more or less happy."

"If my geese are to go on having their bones broken because you're happy, Herr Pagel, then it would be better if you went around unhappy and did something for farming. Because that's what you're here for; not to be happy."

Pagel's amused gaze rested on her angry face. "Don't go on pretending. I can see that you're not in the least annoyed, because you've filled my plate with the stomach and heart. Which, as a matter of fact, I'm fondest of. As for the other thing, I ought to tell you that I've just had news I'm soon to be a father."

"Oh!" Her tone sounded in no way pacified. "I didn't know till now that Herr Pagel was married."

This female response so surprised young Pagel that he put his spoon demonstratively into his goose stew, pushed back his chair and stared at Amanda with big eyes. "Married—me married? How do you arrive at that idiotic idea, Amanda?"

"Because you are shortly becoming a father, Herr Pagel," she replied maliciously. "Fathers are usually married—or at least ought to be."

"You're a goose, Amanda," said Wolfgang amused, returning to his soup. "You only want to pump me."

For a while all was quiet.

Then Amanda said stubbornly, "I'm wondering if the young lady, when she noticed she was going to become a mother, whistled so tremendously and talked such rubbish to people."

"Your wonder is quite correct, Amanda. The young lady was certainly not so pleased at the time, although she was also perhaps just a wee little bit happy."

"Then," said Amanda decidedly, "I would leave at once and marry her."

"That's what I should like to do. Unfortunately she has absolutely forbidden me to show my face."

"She's forbidden! And expecting a child from you?"

"That's right," nodded Pagel gravely. "You have completely grasped what I wanted to say."

"Then . . ." She turned crimson.

"Then . . ." She did not dare say it.

"Then I should . . ." She became speechless.

"What would you do, please?" he asked very gravely.

She examined him with an ungracious eye, angry with herself for embarking on this inquisition which had discovered something she hadn't wished to know. And she was angry with him because he spoke about these matters in just the same flippant, stupid way as other men—and she had thought him very different! So she looked at him testingly and unsparingly.

But seeing his twinkling eyes, she understood that he was actually very happy, and was only making fun of her and her stupid curiosity. And that he was exactly as she had thought he was. And, as is always the case, the happiness of the one was communicated to the other. She gulped suddenly.

She spoke quite as Amanda Backs, however. "If you've rummaged about enough in the giblets, I should now lie down for half an hour. It's warm in there, and I've put a blanket for you on the sofa."

"Good. I'll do that for once," he said obediently. "But wake me in half an hour." And at the door he turned round. "I'm thinking of having it about Christmas, the marriage I mean. The son's arriving three weeks earlier."

And with that he shut the door as a sign that he no longer valued any answer, and that this subject was now absolutely closed. And as Amanda now knew everything she urgently needed to know, she also felt no need to talk anymore. She quietly cleared the table, took away the cutlery and sat down at the tiled stove, so that he could have real quiet for the remaining half-hour.

But of course, he wouldn't sleep but would read his letter again!

IV

Pagel really had wanted to reread his letter but hardly had he lay down but a tiredness overcame him like a large, benign, warm, dark wave. The sentence informing him that he would be a father at the beginning of December and that Peter would soon be writing to him herself, was part of his dream. It produced a happy feeling of lightness, and he went to sleep smiling.

However, his dream was about a child, and that child was himself. With some amazement he saw himself standing on a grassy lawn in a white sailor suit with a blue collar and a sewn-on anchor. Over him a plum tree spread its branches laden with small yellow plums.

He saw himself stretching up to the branches. He saw his bare knees between his long socks and his trousers. And that one of his knees had been cut, but was already scarred over. I must have already dreamt that as a child, he said to himself in the dream, and saw himself reaching for the branches as a child. He was on tiptoe and still couldn't reach them.

Then a voice called him, and of course it had to be Mama's voice from the veranda, but no, the voice came from the thick crown of the tree itself, and it was Peter's voice:

Little tree, shake and shake—Throw down your plums for my sake!

And the little plum tree shook all its plums over him like a golden shower of rain, and they fell, ever more, ever thicker, ever more golden. The green lawn was quite yellow with then. As if hundreds and thousands of buttercups were blossoming, and the child that he was bent over them, shouting with joy.

"No, I can't disturb him now," said Amanda. "You'll have to come back later." She gave Sophie Kowalewski a bellicose look.

But Sophie was not at all bellicose. "Perhaps I could wait here," she said politely.

"When he wakes up he must go to the fields at once; he'll have no time for you."

"But he asked me to come here through my father," explained Sophie, not quite in accordance with truth. "Herr Pagel, in fact, wants me to dig potatoes!" She laughed bitterly.

"Dig potatoes," repeated Amanda. The pair stood, one at the stove, the other at the window. "Herr Pagel's right. Digging potatoes is certainly better than—" She broke off with telling effect.

"Than what, Fräulein? Than propping up the stove in case it falls over? There you are certainly right."

"Many a person thinks that she alone is cunning," said the Backs disdainfully. "But as Fräulein von Kuckhoff always said, too much cunning turns stupid. And that's a fact."

"And are you also cunning or are you stupid?" asked Sophie sweetly, sitting down at the desk.

"That's no place for you, Fräulein!" said Amanda angrily, shaking the back of the chair. "There's a place for you somewhere else."

Sophie was aware what the other was driving at. But she wasn't easily stopped in anything; she would sit where she was. "If I'm to go, Herr Pagel will tell me," she said coolly. "All you do here are the beds, Fräulein."

"But I don't get in them, I don't!" shouted Amanda, pulling at the chair furiously.

"That won't be your fault, Fräulein. The gentleman perhaps has better taste than his predecessor."

"You say that to me, Fräulein?" Amanda stepped back very pale.

The combat was now at its climax; the arrows had been loosed and many had gone home. Now must come the hand-to-hand fighting—it was a wonder that young Pagel hadn't been waked up by the noise.

"Why shouldn't I say that to you?" asked Sophie defiantly but less assured, for the expression on her opponent's face made her uneasy. "You said so yourself before everyone during evening prayers."

"Fräulein," said Amanda threateningly, "if others can't count up to five, I can. And if the five don't come out right, then one can stand at night beneath a window and hear them talking."

Now it was Sophie who turned pale. Then she bethought herself. "If one is decent," she said in quite another tone, "one doesn't need to have heard everything one hears."

"And somebody like that talks about beds and better taste!" burst out Amanda angrily. "I ought to go and tell him on the spot." She reflected. "I think I really ought to." She looked doubtfully at Pagel's door.

"Why should he know that?" asked Sophie. "He loses nothing by it."

Amanda regarded her, undecided.

"You could have had a friend," whispered Sophie, "just the same as . . . I can understand it if one sticks to a friend."

"He's not my friend any longer," protested Amanda. "I don't associate with a traitor."

"Others can never know what someone is really like," declared Sophie. "They only look at the outside. Someone may have had bad luck in his life."

"I've heard that anyone from a penitentiary is always bad. Only the worst get sent there."

"He can wish to improve. And there are such things as wrong verdicts."

"Was he wrongly condemned then, Fräulein?"

Sophie considered. "No," she said reluctantly.

"It's good you said that. Or I should have thought you only wanted to wheedle me."

"The sentence was too severe. He's only heedless, not bad."

Amanda thought. She couldn't think as she wanted to; the image of Hänsecken prevented her. She'd remained true to him even when she knew that he was not only shallow but bad. But she eventually found what she wanted to ask. "Then why does he still hole up there?" asked Amanda. "If he really wants to change, he's got to work. Is he lazy?"

"Not at all," cried Sophie. "He holes up there . . ." She thought a bit. "We haven't got the fare yet, and then he received a bullet in the escape—"

"A bullet? But the warders didn't hit anyone!"

"That's what they think! But he was shot in the leg, here in the thigh. And he's been lying up there all these weeks without a doctor or proper attention. I've been nursing him. And now I'm to dig potatoes!"

Amanda looked doubtfully at the other's face. "There's so much stolen in the district at present," she said. "I thought that would be your one, Fräulein."

"With him always in bed, Fräulein Backs, and perhaps even lame the rest of his life? My father says it's Bäumer up to his tricks again."

"I thought that Bäumer was only a poacher."

"That's all you know! Bäumer will do anything. Now when they're looking for him, and his relatives in Altlohe won't have him with them, and he doesn't know where to stay, he'll do anything, he said."

"How do you come to know that, Fräulein?" asked Amanda softly. "You are very well informed about him. You've even spoken to the man."

"I . . ." stammered Sophie. But she recovered herself immediately. "Yes," she whispered excitedly, "I lied. He wasn't shot in the leg, and he goes out to provide for us, so that we can get the fare together. What can we do when they're after him? You stood up for yours at evening prayers without being ashamed. One must stick by one's fellow particularly when things are bad for him. And I'll never believe that you'll betray us—why, you smacked Meier's face because he was a traitor!"

"Yes, I smacked my fellow's face for that," said Amanda. "Your friend—"

"And you would be a traitor after that?" interrupted Sophie. The two girls looked at one another. "You ought to know," she whispered hurriedly, "what a girl feels like when she's fond of someone and how one doesn't give a damn if others say he's no good. To them he may be bad, perhaps, but to me he's good—and I of all people must leave him in the lurch? No, you don't want that, nor do you want to betray us."

Amanda Backs stood silent.

"I'll see that he doesn't touch anything more in Neulohe, and that we leave as soon as possible, as soon as we have a little money—but you won't betray us, eh, Fräulein?"

"What is it Amanda's not to betray?" Wolfgang Pagel stood between the two girls, a flushed, somewhat excited Amanda and a Sophie who had made herself very ladylike for this visit, so that not much excitement was to be noticed beneath her lipstick and powder.

Sophie did not reply. "I'll just quickly make your coffee, Herr Pagel," said Amanda. And she left the office.

"What's the matter with her?" asked Pagel. "Have you quarreled?"

"Not a bit," said Sophie quickly. "I was only asking her to put in a word for me with you, bailiff. But you were not to know what I'd asked her." She shrugged her shoulders. "My father says that you want me for the potato digging. But father must have misunderstood. Just look at my hands; one can't dig potatoes with hands like that." And she stretched out hers, wonderfully manicured, nails brilliantly polished. But neither manicure nor polish could hide the fact that they had once been very robust country-girl's hands.

Pagel gave them a benevolent pat and said: "Very nice! Well, Sophie, take a seat and we'll talk reasonably with one another."

She obediently sat down, but her manner betrayed that she was not inclined to enter into reasonable talk.

"Now look here, Sophie," said Pagel amiably. "When you left Neulohe a few years back, those pretty hands looked a little different, don't you agree? And yet they've become so pretty. Now, for a while again, they won't look quite so beautiful, but you'll be helping your father to earn a bit. What do you think? When you return to Berlin your hands will quickly enough become spotless and clean again."

Sophie drew them back as if the theme was, in her view, done with. Almost in a whine she said: "But, bailiff, I must look after my mother. She can't get up or walk any more, there's so much dropsy in her legs."

"Oh, if that is the case, Sophie," he replied distressed, "then I'll send the doctor to her tomorrow. He'll be able to say if your mother requires constant attendance." The pretty face was distorted by chagrin. "Sophie," he went on more vigorously, "why are you trying to take me in? First you say you can't work because of your hands, and then it's because of your sick mother, and recently your father told me you wanted to go into service again. It's all untrue. I'll say nothing about the contract, according to which unmarried grown-up children must work as well; but is it right for you to idle around if everyone else is working himself to death? Is it right for a healthy young girl to live at the expense of her old worn-out father?"

"I don't live at his expense!" she burst out. Rather more slowly: "I brought money with me from Berlin."

"Lies, Sophie. Cheating again. We both arrived in Neulohe on the same day, have you forgotten? The dollar was then so-and-so many thousand marks, and now it's so-and-so many milliards. What can be left of your money then?" She started to speak. "Yes, go on and tell me that you're selling your jewelry or that as lady help or whatever you were in Berlin you got paid in foreign currency! All lies. No, Sophie," he said firmly, "it's settled: either you come to work tomorrow or I'll put Black Minna with all her children in your father's house."

Her face changed, showing impatience, annoyance, then anger. There was something wrong in that pretty face, as if the beauty were only skin-deep and another face might at any moment be seen behind it, a face neither good nor beautiful. She restrained herself, however. She even smiled and she pleaded: "Oh, bailiff, let me off! What potatoes could I dig? Be so kind!" Pagel grew perplexed.

"How much you could do, Sophie, is another matter," he said woodenly, feeling like Herr von Studmann. "The chief thing is the example."

"But I'm not strong enough for such work," she complained. "That's why I left for the town, because I was too weak for farm work. You feel, Herr Pagel! I've no muscles, it's all so tender. . . ."

She had approached, brushing against him. She was smaller than he. A fragrance came from her; she moved her arm to show that no biceps stood up. And all the while she was looking into his eyes, meekly, roguishly, pleadingly.

"Those who have to carry the sacks must have the muscles," objected Pagel. "You only have to gather the potatoes, Sophie—even children can do that."

"And my knees!" she wailed. "The kneeling will wear them out the first day. See, bailiff, how soft they are." Her skirt was very short, but she lifted it higher. She patted her garter; he saw a gleam of white . . .

There went the door! "Put your skirt down!" he ordered sharply.

Yes, that other face now appeared from beneath the pretty one—a coarse face indeed. "Leave me alone! So that's what you want! No, no!" she shouted and was out of the door, passing Amanda Backs.

Impassively Amanda put down the coffee things on the table. "Your coffee, Herr Pagel."

"The damnable wench!" cried Pagel, breathing hard. "Amanda, I was to have been seduced here just now!" Amanda looked at him speechless. "Or," he continued thoughtfully, "it was to look to you as if I were the seducer—that was the idea." He gave an incredulous smile. "And all about a little potato digging! I don't understand it."

"I'd let her be, Herr Pagel," said Amanda shortly.

"Yes, yes, Amanda, I've heard that you wished to put in a good word for her. But why? Is she to get off with her laziness?"

"I'm not putting in a word for her, Herr Pagel. I don't worry myself about her, and the best thing would be for you not to worry about her either. Your coffee's getting cold," she said and left the office.

Pagel watched her go. Some things seemed questionable to him, but he actually had too much to do to try and answer such questions. He'd rather finish his coffee and finally read Herr von Studmann's letter.

V

A quarter of an hour later Wolfgang Pagel was cycling through the woods. He must hurry, for it was dark at five, and as soon as twilight came nothing would keep Forester Kniebusch in the forest. He gave no explanation. At the first sign of dusk he would leave his men abruptly and go home.

"He's getting a little cracked," said some.

"He's just scared stiff when the forest's dark," said others.

Kniebusch let them talk. He himself hardly said a word, no longer listening when something was being said. He didn't want to know anymore, and didn't say anything more himself. This change, so astonishing in such an old man, this forsaking of a weakness which he had not been able to overcome in a lifetime, dated from that first of October when he had marched on the fortress of Ostade with a troop of young peasants from Neulohe—to overthrow the Red Government in a big *Putsch*.

Pagel, noting the gossipy forester's transformation, had believed that it was due to mortification over the shameful failure of the *Putsch*. Kniebusch indeed said nothing about the undertaking, but that could only strengthen this interpretation. One had learned enough from the newspapers without wanting personal accounts.

A few sections of militarized associations which had not been disbanded, together with many armed country folk, had appeared in front of the barracks and had summoned the Reichswehr to join in the fight against the Government. The Reichswehr had coldly replied no. In all probability those in the *Putsch* had held this to be a sort of formality, to save face, and after a brief delay, but hesitatingly, they had proceeded to something like an attack—again in order to save face, apparently. There had been half a dozen or even a dozen shots; the mass of the rebels had ebbed away in disorder; and thus an undertaking to which many capable men had for months devoted all their strength, intellect, courage and self-sacrifice, ended in confusion, rout, a dozen arrests and, unfortunately, two or three killed as well. However, it was a sign of these times, when everything seemed to dissolve—to collapse even as it was being born. The strongest will remained powerless. The idea of self-sacrifice seemed ridiculous—everyone for himself, but all against one.

(That trench jacket which a lieutenant had borrowed from a publican and had almost immediately returned so that it might not be dirtied—that trench jacket was none the less dirtied with soil as with blood. . . . In vain had the father turned a small beer shop into a respectable tavern. If, however, the lieutenant had not returned the new jacket, would the landlord's son have stayed away then?)

In this way, or something like it, had the *Putsch* run its course. It had been a beautiful, splendid dream into which many had thrown their heart and soul—and then it was over, and one could well understand that a man could be bitter and silent about it. But as Pagel came more frequently in contact with the forester and observed, besides his taciturnity, that lifeless yet constantly frightened glance and the perpetually trembling hands—as he reflected rather more deeply on the *Putsch* and the man—then he said to himself: It is all wrong, it is something quite different. One could easily drive for half an hour through the forest and think of nothing but the forester Kniebusch. A certain slow tenacity in thought could at no time have been altogether denied young Pagel, and if the tempo of recent events had somewhat repressed this characteristic and demanded an almost unreflecting activity, the reaction was all the stronger now that he had to cover considerable distances alone between field and wood. He was not happy only to be active in the world; he wished also to understand it. He was not content to see that the forester was silent and afraid; he wanted to know why he had changed.

And when he came to rummage in his memories, it was not surprising that he recalled an autumn day when, along a forest path, a little drunken fellow had staggered toward him; and in the drunken fellow's car the considerably drunker Kniebusch lay. That this scoundrel of a Meier bore the chief guilt for the discovery of the arms dump and therefore for the Lieutenant's end, Pagel had always known since the slapping by Amanda Backs. Strange! At the time he hadn't thought of the forester. But now he understood, of course, that Kniebusch had been Meier's informer, intentionally or, what was more probable, unintentionally.

And something else occurred to him. He saw the room where the convicts' orgy had taken place; he saw the cook howling under her apron and the fat detective. The man had sent someone to fetch the forester, who, however, was not at home.

Yes, why should the detective send for Kniebusch when he already knew what there was in the forest, and where? Only because he wanted to see him! To examine him! Because he was suspicious of him! And why was the forester not at home in the middle of the night? Why did that peaceable, timid man join in the *Putsch*? Because his fear of the *Putsch* was less than his fear of inquiries about the arms dump. Because he wanted to be absent!

And Pagel saw himself standing in the wood. The fat detective had gone on, soaked and dog-tired, toward Ostade. Kniebusch would have met none other than the questioner he wished to avoid; and what a ruthless questioner he could be Wolfgang knew well. That would have been a bad hour for Kniebusch, sealing his lips at last. Perhaps he had only escaped by the skin of his teeth—but he had escaped! He had returned home. Of what was he still afraid, then? Why couldn't he remain in the wood at twilight?

Pagel advanced considerably further with his own reflections, but he was still not satisfied with their result. Something remained to be solved. Pagel himself, for a while, hadn't been able to remain in the darkening wood after that night. All his nerves had begun to tremble as soon as the first twilight fell, and he would mount his bicycle and ride, as fast as his legs allowed, out into the open. But he had resisted this feeling of panic; reason told him that it was the same forest as before the thirtieth of September, that the dead do not walk, that we have only the living to fear. And gradually his common sense had won.

Now it might very well be that the forester on that fatal evening—having heard that the dump was discovered—had been driven by conscience to steal into the Black Dale, and had then found the Lieutenant. That discovery would have sent him home terror-stricken. Yes, it might be that.

Nevertheless a voice told Pagel that it was not so—the forester was afraid of something much more tangible than a dead man, long since buried somewhere or other. No, it was not the dead Lieutenant, and it was not the detective—who was undoubtedly a man who would strike at once, without torturing a victim for weeks or months. Nor could it be little Meier. He would never dare confront the forester again. No matter how run down Kniebush had become, Little Meier would take steps to defend himself against a man who made his life such a misery.

Well, the mystery was for the moment unsolvable. But one ought to be particularly nice to the old man. No doubt he was far from being a model of virtue, but, in the little time before he descended into the grave, he ought not to have to torment himself beyond all measure. One might try sometime to find out what it was that frightened him, whether it was something tangible which he might be talked out of, or something in himself, something intangible.

Pagel had now reached the place where the forester and his two overseers were working. It was not yet time for felling, of course; the great old beech trees which stood there had as yet hardly lost their foliage, and there was still too much sap in them. But all day the forester was out with these two, who would later have charge of the woodmen. He indicated the tree to be felled; the overseer's ax flashed and a broad strip of silver-gray bark flew to the ground. Yellow, with rapidly reddening scars, the white tree shone in the wood. There, accommodate yourself to the winter; you will never know another spring. The woodmen will recognize you by your scar.

In reality it is a very epic calling which the old forester carries on there as deputy of the reaper who is called Death. And since death does not immediately overtake the one marked for it, since a certain respite has been granted to that which is ignorant of the sentence just passed—this makes his occupation almost a little unearthly. When, however, Pagel sees the forester walking among the trees, muttering or coughing hollowly, the shadow of a man withered by age, anxieties and a never-conquered fear of life—when he sees him point at a trunk with a bony forefinger already trembling—then the epic becomes grotesque. Then this reaper Death is himself visibly marked by death, carries out his regency only in an uncertain reprieve and perhaps even knows this. The overseers go from tree to tree, the trembling finger points, the ax rings clear and silvery, and they advance, slowly, leaving behind them the gleaming scars.

Pagel said a very polite good day to the forester, who, out of the corner of his prominent seal-like eyes, examined him, muttered something in reply, then went on, pointing. At his side strolled young Pagel, his hands in his pockets, smoking—he did not want the old man to have the feeling that he was being supervised—yet he could not help noticing how seldom the axes obtained something to do, how seldom the finger pointed, although it was nearly all timber fit for felling, indeed almost overseasoned. "You're marking extremely few today, Herr Kniebusch," he said after a while.

The forester turned his face away, muttering, but did not reply. He made a concession, however; he pointed at a tree—but, as the ax was lifted, he exclaimed: "No! Better not." Nevertheless the ax was not lowered; it struck and the trunk was branded.

"It's already getting hollow, forester," shouted the overseer.

Murmuring something like a curse, the forester looked angrily at Pagel. Then he walked on slowly, head lowered without bothering about the trees, as if he had quite forgotten his work.

"Your job's to do what the forester tells you," Pagel shouted.

"Herr Pagel," replied the man in a tone not at all disagreeable, "what we're doing today is really utter nonsense. The last few days, this morning even, he let us mark again and again; but since midday not a thing! We point out to him rotten and overseasoned timber, but he shakes his head and goes on. It's childish what he's doing now; that's not why we scour the woods and get sixty milliards of marks a day . . ."

"Oh, shut up, Karl!" said the other overseer. "Herr Pagel knows what's wrong with the old fellow, he doesn't cycle into the wood every day just for pleasure. The old un's getting crazy, and since midday he's quite mad."

"Hold your tongue, man!" shouted Pagel. The forester had been standing two paces away and must have heard everything. He kept his face lowered;

one couldn't tell if the brutal words had hurt him. As if made aware of their glances, he lifted his head, said: "Time to knock off," and walked quickly out of the trees into the glade, one hand holding his gun sling.

"It's not half-past three yet," said the more tactful overseer, reaching for his watch, "and it's daylight till a quarter to five. It's absurd, Herr Pagel, for him to send us home now."

"Oh, shut up, Karl," again said the other, who preferred to talk himself. "He knows why he's afraid of the wood in the dark. People say that the dead man in the Black Dale walks about; and the one he wants to find knows it too and takes care to get out of the wood before it gets dark."

Pagel mastered his anger. "Listen, my man," he said, "the forester is your superior and you'll do what he tells you, you understand?"

"If a man's mad I've no intention of doing what he tells me," said the fellow. "The forester's mad, and I'll tell him so till he clears out of the forest."

"Listen, you!" began Pagel passionately.

The overseer interrupted him. "One can see that he's got a bad conscience," he declared. "No one's found the dead man's revolver, and a good many say it was nothing less than a rifle shot."

"Oh!" shouted Pagel. "Oh! You old washerwoman!" Then his anger broke out. "God, man, aren't you ashamed to repeat such stupid rubbish? There you have a decent old man; don't make his life any harder than it is already."

"There you're right, Herr Pagel," said the other overseer. "I always say . . ."

"Shut up, Karl! We all know officials stand by one another. But when something's pretty wrong, I say so; and there's something wrong with the forester."

"You are dismissed," bellowed Pagel. "You are dismissed on the spot. I'll give you a week to get out of your cottage. Good evening."

He turned and walked to his cycle, not feeling at all happy. But what was one to do? The poor devil was not to blame for being boorish. But then neither was the forester for being worn-out and ill. The young overseer, now it was time for felling, could find work anywhere, the old forester hardly ever again . . .

He trod hard on the pedals and tried to think for a moment about his mother's letter. Barely two hours ago he had been almost happy! But however hard he tried, the letter remained very remote, like a faint light seen through trees at night—a light one never reaches because dark bushes and branches get in the way and extinguishes the little glowing spot.

Pagel had overtaken Kniebusch, who was dragging himself along with lowered head, exactly like a dog which has lost its master. And when the young man sprang from his bicycle he didn't raise his head but trudged onward as though alone.

For some time they walked together without a word. Then Pagel spoke. "I've just got rid of Schmidt, Herr Kniebusch. He won't be at work tomorrow."

The forester kept silent for a long time. Then he sighed. "That won't help anything, Herr Pagel."

"Why won't it? A mischief-maker the less is an anxiety the less, Herr Kniebusch."

"Oh, for every anxiety which disappears there come ten new ones."

"And what ones came today? Has it something to do with your not marking any more timber?" That, however, was too blunt a question for the man Kniebusch had become; he did not reply.

After a while Pagel tried again. "I was thinking, Herr Kniebusch, of ringing up the doctor this evening and having a talk with him. Then you can go to him tomorrow and he'll put you down as ill and you can take a complete rest. I'll answer for it. You know you're entitled to sick benefit for twenty-six weeks."

"Oh, who's going to live on sick benefit?" said the old man despondently, yet no longer in despair.

"You have your allowance, Kniebusch. We should go on giving you that. We shouldn't let you starve, you know."

"And who will do my work in the woods?"

"I can also not mark the timber, Herr Kniebusch," said Pagel amiably. "And I can make good use of your woodmen on the farm for a while."

"The Geheimrat will never agree to that in his life," cried the forester.

"Oh, the Geheimrat!" said Pagel disdainfully, to make the forester understand how little importance was to be attached to the old gentleman. "We've heard nothing from him for a month, and so he'll have to be content if we settle his affairs here in the manner we think right."

"But we have heard from him," contradicted the forester. "He wrote a letter to me."

"What! All of a sudden? And what does Herr Horst-Heinz von Teschow want? Can it be that he's coming back to help look for his granddaughter?"

The forester did not react to this mockery. Fräulein Violet too did not interest him any longer, however much value he had formerly attached to getting on good terms with her. He was now only interested in himself. After a long while he said broodingly: "Do you really believe that the doctor will put me down as ill?"

"Of course! You are ill, Kniebusch."

"And you will go on giving me an allowance in spite of the sick benefit? But that's forbidden, Herr Pagel!"

"While I'm here you will get your allowance, Kniebusch."

"Then I'll go to the doctor tomorrow and have myself put down as ill." The forester's voice had quite another ring. But nothing more came. He was probably lost in dreams of a life free from anxieties, annoyance and fear.

"Well, what did the Geheimrat write about?" asked Pagel finally.

The forester started out of his visions. "If I'm ill I shan't need to do what he wrote about," he said unhelpfully.

"Perhaps I could do what he wants done," proposed Pagel.

The forester looked at him bewildered; then a slight smile started to creep over his face. Yes, a smile. It was not a pretty sight, rather as if a dead man were smiling; nevertheless it was meant for a smile. "You would be in a position to," he said, still smiling.

"Position for what?"

The forester was once again surly. "Oh, you will only go and talk about it."

"I'll hold my tongue, you know that, Herr Kniebusch."

"But you will tell madam."

"The lady at the moment is not in the mood to hear anything. What's more, I promise not to tell her."

The forester thought for a time. "I'd rather not," he said. "The less one says the better. I've learned that at last."

"You learned that in Ostade from the fat detective, didn't you?" asked Pagel. And was immediately sorry he had said this. It was more brutal than the jeers of the boorish overseer. The old man turned deathly pale; he laid a shaking hand on Pagel's shoulder and brought his face close. "You know that?" he asked trembling. "How did you know? Did he tell you?"

Pagel let go of his cycle and put his arm firmly round the forester. "I ought not to have said that, Herr Kniebusch," he said, distressed. "You see, my tongue too runs away with me sometimes. No, you need have no fear. No one's told me anything. I just worked it out myself, because you were so changed after coming back from Ostade."

"Is that really true?" whispered the forester, still shaking violently. "He didn't tell you about it?"

"No, on my word of honor."

"But if you guessed about it so can someone else," cried Kniebusch despairingly. "Everyone will point me out as a traitor to his country, and say I sold myself to the French."

"And you haven't done that, Kniebusch?" asked Pagel gravely. "Little Meier—"

"Little Meier made me drunk and pumped me!" cried the other. "He knew I was as talkative as an old woman and he took advantage of it. You must believe me, Herr Pagel! The detective believed me in the end. 'Run home, you old fool,' he said. 'And don't open your mouth again in your life!'"

"He said that? Then you don't need to be afraid anymore, Kniebusch."

"Oh, he was terrible," gasped out the old man. To be able at last to relieve himself from the burden which was crushing him seemed almost intoxicating. "If he'd shot me down at once he would have been more merciful. 'The dust of the man your tongue killed must grate on your teeth whenever you move your jaws,' he said."

"Quiet! Quiet!" Pagel laid his hand gently over the other's mouth. "He's a pitiless man, and also an unjust one. Others have more guilt toward the dead than you. Come along, Kniebusch. I'll chuck down my bike here and fetch it tomorrow. I'll take you home to your bed, and then I'll ring up the doctor at once and he'll visit you this evening and you'll feel at peace."

The man leaned on him like one seriously ill. Now that he had found someone whom he could trust, all resistance left him. What had kept him on his feet had been his isolation. Now he let himself sink into illness and prostration, confident that one stronger than he would care for him. Without check he prattled confusedly of the fear that people might learn of his shame; of his fear of the escaped poacher Bäumer, whose tracks he thought he had come across in the forest; of his fear that everything might yet come out if Fräulein Violet or the servant Räder were found; of his fear whether Haase the magistrate would go on paying the rent now that the Lieutenant was dead; of his fear that little Meier would turn up again; of his fear of the Geheimrat who would turn him out of the ranger's house tomorrow, if he learned that his forester was not doing what he had written. . . .

Fear . . . The man's entire life had become fear. So much could a man torment himself, then, about a meager life which had known little pleasure. And now that it was in decline, and had become quite flat and unblessed, the fear grew worse. From every side it assailed him; it was not the will to existence which kept him among the living, no, it was the fear of existence. Wolfgang Pagel soon gave up speaking to the old man comfortingly and consolingly. He clearly didn't want consolation. He sat as if in the middle of his worries, which came at him like waves from all sides, lifting him up, ready to drown him! "Yes, Herr Pagel, I read every day in the newspapers about suicides, and that there are so many old people who do it, seventy and eighty years old. But I can't, I just can't do it; I have a sick wife and I keep on thinking: What would become of her if I went first? There's not a soul who worries about her; they'd simply let her die like an animal. That's why I'm so afraid."

"Oh, stop talking, Kniebusch," said Pagel, wearied. "Get into bed now and the doctor will come this evening; once you've had a sleep everything will look different. And while you're undressing give me the Geheimrat's letter to read."

Kniebusch, the old forester, a little bad-tempered and complaining, clumsily removed his clothing. Pagel stood under the lamp and looked over the letter the Geheimrat Horst-Heinz von Teschow had written to his forester. In a big chair at the window sat the forester's wife, whom the people in the village said grew stranger and stranger. She was staring into the night. On her knees was a book with a golden cross on the cover, no doubt a hymnal.

"Who puts your wife to bed?" asked Pagel, interrupting his reading.

"Oh, she won't be going to bed today," replied the forester. "She often sits like that all night and sings. But when she wants to go to bed she can manage quite well by herself." The young man threw a quick searching look at the forester's wife who continued to look out into the night while he read further. The forester crept into his nightshirt and then into his bed. On the pillow his face, tanned by sun and wind, and his yellow-white beard, seemed strangely colored.

Just as young Pagel had reached the part of the letter that the forester had just given him which once and for all banned everyone from access to the Geheimrat's woods, starting with all those from Neulohe, including his son-in-law's family, as well as all staff from the Neulohe estate, including the little upstart Pagel—just as Pagel had got this far in the incendiary, provocative and completely antagonistic letter, the old woman began to sing.

She'd stuck one finger into her songbook but didn't look down at it. She continued to look out into the night, and with a shrill, broken voice sang lightly to herself from an old hymn, "Commit yourself and your cares to our true saviour who guides heaven. Through sky and clouds and tempests, he will guide your footsteps."

Pagel looked towards the forester, but the old man didn't move. His head was motionless on the pillow. "I'm going now, Herr Kniebusch," said Pagel. "Here is the letter. Thanks very much and, as I said, I shall keep silent."

"Shut the door from outside," replied the old man. "The key's in the lock. I have another, if the doctor comes. I shall hear him coming, I shan't sleep."

"The singing disturbs you, I suppose?"

"The singing? What singing? Oh, my wife's? No, that doesn't disturb me, I don't even hear it. I'm thinking the whole time. . . . When you leave, please turn out the light; we don't need a light."

"What do you think about then, Herr Kniebusch?" asked Pagel looking down on the forester, lying with his eyes shut, motionless.

"Oh, I've been thinking it out like this. I think, Supposing I hadn't done such and such a thing in my life or hadn't met such and such a person—what would have happened then? But it's a difficult matter."

"Yes, it is certainly difficult."

"For example, I think, If that rascal Bäumer hadn't ridden me down, how would things have been then? It could so easily have been like that, eh, Herr Pagel? I need only have been going a little faster. If it hadn't been so dark in the ravine I should have been out of it already; he would have seen from a distance and avoided me."

"And how would things have been different then, Herr Kniebusch?"

"Everything! Every single thing! Because if Bäumer hadn't run over me then I shouldn't have had a court case about him in Frankfurt. And if I hadn't been in Frankfurt, then I shouldn't have met Meier again. And if I hadn't met Meier again, then he wouldn't have betrayed the arms dump."

Pagel grasped the forester's dry bony hands, speckled with age. "I should try to find something else to think about, Herr Kniebusch," he suggested. "Imagine what it will be like when you are pensioned. And you've got your pension from the employees' insurance office. Then perhaps things really will be different with money. The Geheimrat writes about that in his letter, too. You must have read it. . . . I should think about how I'd arrange my life; some hobby or other."

"Bees," said the forester in a low voice.

"There you are then. Bees are supposed to be wonderful things. Whole books are supposed to have been written about them. Supposing you have a shot at something like that?"

"Yes, I could." The forester opened his eyes wide for the first time. "But you still don't understand why I do the other, Herr Pagel. Because if it only happened through Bäumer running me over, and I can think of a hundred such things in my life, then I'm not to blame for the other, either. And I haven't got to suffer any remorse, isn't that so?"

Pagel looked thoughtfully at the old man, who was once again lying with his eyes closed. At the window, her face turned toward the night, the old woman went on singing psalm after psalm in her grating voice, as if she were alone.

"Well, get a bit of rest before the doctor comes," said Pagel suddenly. "I'll ring him up now."

"But why don't you answer me, Herr Pagel?" complained the old man, half sitting up in bed and staring at him. "Isn't it like I said, then? If Bäumer hadn't run me down, everything would have been different!"

"You suffer remorse and wish to acquit yourself, isn't that it, Herr Knie-busch? But acquittal is no good unless one feels innocent. I should prefer to have a go at the bees. Good night." And with that Pagel turned out the light, locked the front door, and stood outside. It was already dark, but perhaps he would still find the men at the potato clamps.

VI

The clamps were some five minutes' distance from the farmyard, at a place bordered on two sides by forest. The situation was convenient for carting, because three field paths met there, and the wood protected the clamps from the icy east and north winds; but its remoteness permitted thieves to approach it unseen, while the neighborhood of the forest made their flight an easy one.

Pagel had had constant trouble with these clamps. Every morning there was a hole dug here or there in the soil that covered the potatoes against the frost. Already over five hundred tons were stored here—the theft of four or five hundredweights was of little importance compared with the work required to fill the hole again, or with the danger a clamp ran of being frozen because of it. A hundred times had Pagel blamed himself for thoughtlessly agreeing to the suggestion that the clamps be laid down in this place. An experienced man would have foreseen all the difficulties which had arisen this year from the shortage of food. He was convinced that all Altlohe would have helped with the potato crop had the clamps been situated under constant supervision right by the farmyard. But as things were, it was much simpler to take at night, without risk, that which one otherwise could have won only through many days of hard and freezing labor. And the people could not even be blamed for it. They lacked the barest necessities, they suffered hunger. If they took a trifle of the abundance, whom could that harm?

In growing darkness Pagel roamed between the long, almost man-high mounds. The laborers had already gone, of course, and the thieves not yet come; once again he had made a fruitless journey.

But not quite fruitless: his foot knocked against a forgotten shovel, which would not be improved by being left out in the damp night. He picked it up, to take it along to the tool room. But a minute later he stumbled on two spades stuck in the ground. He took them along, too. Immediately he came across two pitchforks and more shovels—it was impossible, he couldn't lug them all to the farm alone.

Suddenly, quite discouraged, he sat down on a bale of straw. It is often the case that someone bravely endures a host of troubles for a long time, only to be cast down by a trifle. Pagel had with unchanged amiability borne greater troubles these last weeks, but the thought that he was running about from dawn to well into the night while slovenliness and indolence increased—the thought that fifteen shovels, spades and forks would become rusty that night—utterly disheartened him.

He sat, his head propped in his hands. Behind him the wood rustled, mysterious; the trees dripped unceasingly. He felt none too warm. Had he only been a little more cheerful, he would have gone to the farm, whistled together the guilty men and driven them off to the clamps to fetch their implements themselves. But today he hadn't the least energy to face their sullen and spiteful arguments.

He sat like that for a long time. Then thoughts began to creep back into his brain, but they were not good thoughts. They were worries. He thought of the Geheimrat's letter. That was the beginning of the end. No. It was the end, absolutely. The Geheimrat had remembered himself. Himself—that was his money, the unpaid rent. But because he was certain of not getting it, he wanted to get rid of the tenant. Not only did he forbid all to enter the forest who belonged to his son-in-law or worked for his daughter; not only did he forbid the farm carts to use the forest paths, which would necessitate their going hours out of their way if they went to the outlying fields—he also ordered the forester to keep a watchful eye on the sales made by the farm. Should grain or potatoes or livestock be delivered, the forester was to report immediately by telephone to the old gentleman's lawyer, who would at once attach the moneys coming in.

It was now evident that from the business point of view Studmann had been right when he had insisted that old Elias be sent with the rent to Berlin on the second of October—the old gentleman would then have had to keep quiet!

"Do you think my father would make difficulties for me in my present situation?" Frau Eva had protested. "No, Herr von Studmann. You're a very conscientious, very thorough businessman. The rent can wait, but I need a car at once, all the time. No, I will buy the car." Between the absent father and the chauffeur who had presented the bill for the car with the threat, in case it was not settled, to return to Frankfurt immediately, Frau Eva had decided for the chauffeur.

"Perhaps we could manage by hiring a car," Studmann had suggested.

"Which will never be available when I want it. No, Herr von Studmann; you are always forgetting that I have to find my daughter."

Studmann had turned pale, had bitten his lip. He also didn't say a word about what he thought about these reconnoiters through the countryside. He accommodated himself to them. "As you wish, madam. I'll discharge the installment agreed upon, therefore. The remainder of the money will easily amount to three-quarters of the rent. . . ."

"Don't talk to me anymore about the rent! I've told you that my father . . . in my present situation. Don't you understand then?" Frau von Prackwitz had almost shouted. Oh, she was uncontrollable these days, so exceedingly irritable. Pagel also had been shouted at once or twice because he hadn't, when she called him, immediately left everything as it stood. But she was not so unfriendly to him as to Studmann. It seemed inexplicable. Hadn't she once had almost a weakness for the other? But perhaps she became so unfriendly just because of that weakness? Now she was nothing but a mother; and a mother who neglects her daughter because of her own love affair is surely contemptible!

"I should like you to pay for the car at once, Herr von Studmann. I want to be able to dispose of it freely. Settle that with Herr Finger and his firm. And give him notice. I shan't need him as chauffeur; I know someone else more agreeable to my wishes."

Studmann had replied with a bow, extremely pale.

"Pardon me for being a little out of temper, Herr von Studmann." She held out her hand. "Things are not very well with me—but I hardly need to say this at all."

Studmann hadn't realized the effort this little concession cost her. "If I am to settle accounts with Herr Finger I must more or less know what was arranged with him."

"Settle the whole thing as you think right; I shan't bother you about it. . . . Oh, Herr von Studmann," she had cried, suddenly almost in tears, "must you torment me as well? Have you no feeling at all?" And she had fled from the office. Herr von Studmann gestured heavily towards young Pagel, but remained silent. For a few moments he walked up and down in his office, then he sat down at his desk, unfasted his watch from its chain, and laid it before him.

Pagel had started to type again. During this argument he couldn't have left the office. Frau von Prackwitz had stood by the door as if she wanted to leave as soon as possible.

Studmann had sat steadily regarding his watch. After a very short time—he must have worked it out—he took the receiver out of the cradle, turned the handle, and gestured energetically to Pagel. Pagel stopped typing. He looked alarmingly forlorn. Whoever had seen him sitting thus, receiver in hand, waiting, would not have said that this man was without feeling. Perhaps he was awkward and annoying; a womanless life had erected so many barriers in the path of his emotions that he could no longer free himself alone; but one saw how the man trembled, and could hardly speak for agitation, when he began to ask Frau Eva for an immediate and quite private interview. Pagel had jumped up and gone to his room. The unhappy Studmann! Now that the battle was almost lost, he knew what he ought to have done. Talk to her as a human being, not as a businessman.

And a minute or two afterwards Studmann had asked Pagel to go to the Villa at once and make up accounts with the chauffeur. "Frau von Prackwitz would like to leave at once. Probably you must go, too. To the firm in Frankfurt. No, Pagel, please, I don't want to go myself. . . . Frau von Prackwitz will see me at six o'clock."

And Pagel had had to go to Frankfurt in charge of the attaché case with the money, Finger the chauffeur not having been authorized to receive the full sum. In the back Frau von Prackwitz sat alone, erect on the edge of the seat, her white face pressed against the window. From time to time she called, "Stop!" Then she would get out and inspect the ground. "Go on slowly!"

She had seen a piece of paper in the ditch; she ran after it. That she hadn't really expected to find there a message from her daughter was to be seen in the unhopeful way in which she unfolded it. "Go on slowly!"

Again and again she cried out: "Slower! Slower! I want to be able to see each face." At a speed of fifteen miles an hour the powerful car crept along the roads.

"Slower!"

Ten miles an hour. . . .

"This is what she always does now," the chauffeur had whispered. "It doesn't matter to her where I drive, as long as she can get out and look around. As if the fellow would be still here in the neighborhood!"

She had gone into a road warden's house. "I'm only allowed to go fast through villages and towns," explained the chauffeur. "She thinks no doubt that the pair are utterly alone. Well, I'm glad I'm through with it today."

"Aren't you at all sorry for her?"

"Sorry? Of course I'm sorry for her. But after all I'm driving a sixty-horse-power Horch and not a pram. Do you think that's a pleasure for a chauffeur, to loiter about like this?"

Frau von Prackwitz came out of the warden's house. "Go on slowly!"

Pagel would have liked to hurry. They had to pay for the car before twelve o'clock. Studmann had strictly enjoined this; at twelve the new dollar rate would be announced. . . . But he said nothing.

It was three o'clock before they reached the town. The dollar was then 320 milliards as against 242 that morning—payment had taken all the rent. In fact there was even a small debt remaining. "Of no importance," said the gentleman politely. "You can settle that at your discretion."

Pagel knew that this would be very important to Herr von Studmann. He had hoped Pagel would still bring back a considerable amount as a loan. It would of course be even more important to Studmann that nothing had come of the meeting he had requested at six o'clock. Frau von Prackwitz had stood Pagel up in a local bar. She'd left to fetch the new chauffeur. Hours passed until she returned; the big new car stood driverless on the street. "This is Oskar," she said and sat down exhausted. "Oskar is the son of a housekeeper of Papa's. I remembered him. He's a motor engineer by trade."

"I have a driver's license, also," said Oskar. He was a young fellow about twenty with enormous hands and a face which looked as if roughly formed from a lump of dough; but he appeared good-natured, if a trifle simple.

Frau von Prackwitz swallowed one cup of coffee after the other, eating nothing. "Make a good meal, Oskar. We've a long way before us."

"You ought to eat something, too, madam."

"No, thank you, Herr Pagel. . . . Oskar knew Violet; he will help me to find her. How old was Violet, Oskar, when you left Neulohe to be apprenticed?"

"Eight."

"At least he will drive as I want, isn't that so, Oskar?"

"Of course, Frau von Prackwitz. Always very slowly and looking at everyone. I understand. I read about it in the papers."

Frau von Prackwitz shut her eyes for a moment. Then she said emphatically to Pagel, "I noticed quite clearly how unwillingly this man Finger drove as I wished him to. You all now do what I want unwillingly—you too, Herr Pagel!"

He moved away.

She said, "For goodness sake, let me do what I want. Isn't it me who's lost a daughter, after all? If only one of you had been clever enough before! But being clever now? What's the point of that?"

Pagel was silent.

When they had at last driven off it was after six and quite dark. Wolfgang hadn't been able to understand why they didn't go direct to Neulohe instead of by a long roundabout way; why, in spite of the darkness, they seldom drove faster than fifteen miles an hour; why they had to stop again and again while Frau Eva went a few paces into some unknown wood. Wolfgang understood nothing of all that.

Perhaps she just wanted to be alone. Perhaps she only stood there waiting in the dark night, till the engine noise in her body had died away, and the beating of her own heart was again palpable. Did she think that if she felt her own true self that she would feel her daughter, once a part of that self, as well?

Did she stand there awaiting some vision in which they would come through the wood—he and she, the lost ones? Did she see him in front, his bloodless face lowered, the thin-lipped mouth compressed—and her daughter half a pace behind with closed eyes, still in sleep, as the mother had last seen her? Did she see the two wandering homeless over a cold and alien earth, where no hospitable door opened to them, no friendly word ever reached them?

It had been only a little while ago that Pagel had informed her that everything was different from what she feared, that no furtive lover was to be sought for, that the enemy was the manservant. "But that is impossible! I'll never believe that," she had cried.

Then she had believed it. She saw the two of them—and it seemed to her that they must eternally be together without a word, each silently chained to the other by the same hellish torment. She saw the pair so plainly that she imagined the servant must be wearing gray gym shoes with grooved rubber soles and Violet a man's faded overcoat above a dress which did not fit properly because he had put it on while she slept.

Oh, those men, those police, those people from the Public Prosecutor, with their important airs, always ringing up, sending messages, wanting to know this, or measure some shoe! They would never find Violet, she was certain. She alone would meet the girl, some day or other. It didn't matter where she waited. It just had to be outside—sometime, when the right moment came, she would be on the right spot. Hadn't those people even wanted to carry out a kind of search of Violet's room, fingerprints on the windowsill, a hunt for letters? She hadn't allowed it, but simply locked the room. What was the good of such investigations now? Violet's room belonged to her mother; when she came home utterly exhausted from her excursions, too tired even to weep, she would, after quickly looking at Achim, unlock the door and sit down by the bed. First she threw an anxious look at the window. But this was locked fast. She hadn't been careless. Her daughter could sleep on undisturbed. She lay in her bed. Gradually the mother went to sleep too, in the wicker chair next to the empty bed—wishes became dreams! Eventually she slept soundly. Only the next day, when she awoke, did she change, wash herself, and prepare herself for the new day. These mornings, which filled her whole room with a wretched gray pallor, when the childish squabbling of the Rittmeister and his caregiver could be heard so embarrassingly clearly, and when, after the oblivion of sleep, the sense of her loss made itself felt like a consuming fire in her slowly awaking brain . . . But then there was the car, she would set out at once; she must hurry, the reunion with her daughter was perhaps close at hand. That foolish pedant of a Studmann had no idea what this car meant to her! It was the bridge into the future, her only hope. Yes, indeed. He had asked for a very urgent, hurried and private interview with her, but here she was standing in the wood and it was nine or ten o'clock. He didn't understand that you don't leave someone who's been struck down by misfortune—! Perhaps she was only standing there because he was waiting for her!

Eventually she got back into the car again, and told the driver to continue. Neulohe approached, and then it really was ten o'clock.

Passing through the little town of Meienburg, she had asked to stop again. She was dying of hunger! There was a good hotel here, The Prince of Prussia; she had often been there as a young girl, with her parents.

It was a long time before she could make up her mind what to order; nothing on the menu was exactly right. She ordered wine, all the time watching Pagel out of the corner of her eye. He had said that he wasn't hungry. He was almost surly—oh, how transparent people had become to her! She saw that he knew about the interview promised Herr von Studmann. Perhaps he knew a good deal more, of glances, certain words, of hopes. A woman can never have any idea how much men confess to one another; it is unimaginable. . . . Yes, young Pagel was dying of impatience on behalf of his friend; couldn't he think of her for once? That she perhaps had reasons for hesitating, for waiting? He just didn't think of her.

She drank a glass or two of wine and also ate a little. Then she got the waiter to unlock the veranda, unused in winter. She stood there a while—tables were piled on one another, the small garden could not be seen, nor the meadows and poplars on the bank of the little river.

At her side stood young Pagel. He didn't understand why she had had to come here. "I came with Achim on our first outing together, just after we were engaged," she said in a low voice, on going out. And she turned round to look again. The veranda showed no trace of the almost twenty years which lay between. A whole marriage had slipped by since then, a child had been born, more than a war had been lost. Vanished youth, forgotten laughter—gone forever!

Quieted, she had returned to her table; broodingly she turned the stem of the wineglass in her fingers. She could tell by young Pagel's manner that he was no longer impatient or sulky or urgent—he had understood.

It is simply not true that youth is intolerant—a genuine young person will immediately understand a genuine feeling.

It had been after midnight when they arrived in Neulohe. "Please tell your friend," she said, "that I will ring him up early tomorrow as soon as I can see him."

Studmann without a movement had listened to the message. "I always thought, Pagel, that reliability was a desirable quality in this world," said he, smiling a little miserably. "Be everything you like, however, but not reliable!" He looked old and tired. "I wrote to Frau von Prackwitz this evening. She will find the letter over there. Well, I'll wait till tomorrow."

Morning came. After breakfast Studmann had stayed in the office, not bothering about the farm. At first he tried to keep up the impression that he was working—then he gave that up altogether, a miserable person waiting for sentence. . . .

However, he didn't go up to his room. He stayed in his office and walked up and down. His eyes, which now and then involuntarily fell upon the telephone, betrayed what he was thinking. Perhaps she'll ring after all?

Pagel lay down to sleep, listening to the other man going up and down, up and down, while he himself went to sleep.

At half-past ten Pagel saw the great car drive through Neulohe. He hurried to the office. "Frau von Prackwitz wasn't here? Hasn't she rung up?"

"No. Why?"

"The car's just gone out."

Studmann seized the telephone. This time his hand did not tremble nor his voice falter. "Studmann here—may I speak to Frau von Prackwitz please? . . . She's just gone out? . . . Good. Did she leave a message? . . . Yes, inquire please. I'll hold on." He sat there, his head bowed. "Yes, here. . . . Only that she's not coming back today? Nothing else? . . . Thank you very much."

He put the receiver down and spoke to Pagel without looking at him. "What was it Frau von Prackwitz told you yesterday evening?" Studmann stretched himself, almost smiling. "I've fallen down the stairs again, my dear Pagel, only somewhat more painfully than in the hotel. . . . Nevertheless I'm firmly convinced that there's a spot somewhere in the world where absolute reliability is valued. I have decided to accept a situation open to me a long time. I will work in Dr. Schröck's sanatorium. I am sure that the patients there will know how to value thorough reliability, evenness of temperament and inexhaustible patience."

Pagel stared at a Studmann who now wished to be the nursemaid of neuropathics and hypochondriacs; was he speaking ironically? Oh, he was absolutely in earnest, never more so. He was not inclined to go along with the madness of this mad era, to be mad himself. Tirelessly, he continued without despairing. He'd certainly experienced a setback, a hope had escaped him, but he bore it. "I'm not a ladies' man," he went on. "I'm not fitted for their society. I'm too methodical, too correct—somehow I make them desperate. Once, a long while ago"—a vague gesture to indicate in what nebulous distance it lay—"I was engaged once. I was younger then, perhaps more flexible. Well, she broke off the engagement, all of a sudden. I was very much surprised—'It's just as if I'm going to marry an alarm clock,' she told me. 'You are absolutely reliable, you don't go fast or slow, you ring exactly at the right time—you're simply enough to drive one mad!'—Do you understand that, Pagel?"

Pagel had listened with a polite, interested expression, a trifle unsympathetic. This was the same Studmann who, when he himself was in trouble, had brusquely repelled every confidence.

The setback must have hit him hard. The solution probably came to him as a complete surprise this time, too.

"Well, Pagel," said the changed and chatty Studmann, "you're a different type of person. You don't really live in a straight line—more hither and thither, up and down. You like to take yourself by surprise. I . . . I hate surprises!" His voice became a little icy and contrary. Pagel thought Studmann considered surprises above all vulgar, and therefore found them despicable. However, even at this urgent moment, Herr von Studmann did not pursue his intimate revelations. He soon returned to play the caring friend.

"You will be alone here now, Pagel. But I'm afraid not for long. I am sure that Frau von Prackwitz is mistaken in her judgment of her father. The rent ought absolutely to have been paid, on legal and personal grounds. Well, you'll soon know all about that and will, I hope, inform me by letter. My interest remains the same. And should there come a change—over in the Villa—and I am really needed—well, you'll let me know, won't you?"

"Of course. But when are you going, then, Herr von Studmann? Surely not soon?"

"At once. That is, by the afternoon train, I think. I got in touch from Berlin with Herr Geheimrat Schröck."

"And you won't say good-by to Frau von Prackwitz?"

"I will leave a few lines behind for her. That reminds me, my dear Pagel; I will fix up your business at the same time."

"What business? There's nothing unsettled that I know of."

"Oh, it'll occur to you. And if not, I'm all for reliability in settlements, as I told you."

And so Studmann had departed, a man of merit, a reliable friend, but a little withered; an unlucky fellow who thought himself a cornerstone of the universe. And, of course, in that business which he had wanted to fix up for Pagel he made a rare mess of things.

"What's this I hear?" Frau Eva had asked next morning, highly indignant. "My husband has a debt of honor to you of two thousand marks in foreign money? What's the meaning of that?"

It had been really painful for young Pagel. Secretly he cursed a friend who had not been able to omit speaking of that matter in a farewell letter to the woman of his heart. In these difficult times! Flatly he had left Studmann in the lurch. The matter had long ago been settled between him and the Rittmeister.

Incidentally it had never been a question of two thousand marks. A very debatable matter—half a drinking debt, traveling expenses, he couldn't remember just what. But, as mentioned, settled long ago.

Frau von Prackwitz looked at him steadfastly. "Why are you lying to me?" she said. "Herr von Studmann, a great psychologist, at least in business matters, foresaw that you would feel embarrassed about this affair. It's a matter then of two thousand gold marks which you lent Herr von Prackwitz at roulette, isn't it?"

"The devil take Studmann! I settle my affairs myself. Moreover, the police confiscated all the stake-money without exception—it was all lost!"

"Why are you embarrassed about money? You mustn't be. Perhaps in this respect I have inherited my father's practical sense."

"I'm not here because of money," Pagel had said sullenly. "Although it really looks like it now."

"I'm pleased," she said quietly, "if Neulohe has at least done someone good."

"I can't give you the money now, as you know, but I won't forget it. Then Herr von Studmann wrote that there is also the question of your salary to be settled." Pagel raged inwardly. "Up to now you have received only a sort of pocket money. That, of course, is impossible. I have thought it over—my father's officials always had roughly ten hundredweights of rye in monthly wages. You will pay out to yourself from now on the value of two and a half hundredweights of rye weekly."

"I'm not a skilled agriculturalist. There ought to be a bailiff here."

"I don't want to see any new faces now. Don't you make things hard for me, too, Herr Pagel! You'll do what I told you, won't you?"

He took her hand.

"And please see to business matters for the moment exactly as you think, without asking me everything. Perhaps my husband will recover much quicker than we think."

"I'm afraid, though, it won't work. It's too much, and I've no experience whatever."

"Oh, yes, it will," she had nodded. "Once you are acquainted with the work, we shall hardly miss Herr von Studmann." Poor Studmann! This was his valediction from a woman whom he had reverenced and perhaps even loved. However, it can well be assumed that Studmann's farewell letter contained not only business matters, like issues of salary and gambling debts, but also the type of emotional language that seems to refer rather to men's wounded pride than to their unrequited love, which women always find so insulting and so ridiculous. But then, from her point of view, she might well say that she had been deserted in the hour of her greatest distress, because she had insisted that two payments should be made in a different order from that which he desired. She might also add that this friend had tactlessly wished to force on her a discussion of emotional matters at a time when her daughter was in peril and her husband dangerously ill.

No, if things were looked at from the woman's standpoint, any woman's, then Studmann was completely in the wrong. From a business point of view, however, he was now beginning to prove himself right.

"Well, my dear old friend," he wrote in that letter which Wolfgang had stuffed into his pocket before the scene with Sophie, "no, dear young friend would be more correct, I am getting on excellently with Dr. Schröck. A droll creature, the old boy! But an organization which runs like a clock. . . . You ought to see the diet kitchen here, my dear Pagel. The best-conducted Berlin hotel can't compare with such precision in weighing out, preparation, serving up. By the way, I have become a complete vegetarian; no more tobacco or alcohol. Somehow this seems to suit my whole constitution better, and I am astonished that I didn't think of it before. Just consider for yourself—tobacco came to us from South America, Central America—tropical lands. And alcohol—that is, wine—from Palestine, according to the Bible—and thus cannot be suited to our northern character. But in no sense do I want to convert you! All the same, I must say however . . ." And so on and so on for four pages, to the memorable postscript: "Has the Geheimrat still not stirred himself about his rent? I should be very surprised."

Pagel, constantly damper on his bale of straw, sighed. He lit a cigarette. Well, Studmann need not be surprised any longer; Studmann was right. The Geheimrat had stirred himself about his rent. He had, in fact, stirred himself most maliciously. And the first steps would be followed by others; the affair would come to a crisis. Get out! Your affectionate father!

It is in the nature of every man, especially of a young one, not to like working for something which is a failure. The deep discouragement which had seized hold of Pagel at the sight of a few rusting shovels undoubtedly came from this in the main. If the Geheimrat was going to write finish to the whole business in two or three weeks, all this rushing around wasn't any longer amusing. No, thank you! Pagel wouldn't stir a finger. Pagel wouldn't bother himself anymore. Especially not for this declining patch of the German Reich, consisting of so many regions and fifty-four different parties! Good night!

As a proprietor, as a lessor, one couldn't assert that the Geheimrat was in the wrong. It was a devilish thing that most people in most things were simultaneously in the right and in the wrong. The tenant undoubtedly had failed to meet his financial obligations, permitting himself expensive tastes that encumbered a property which he mismanaged with unskilled assistance; moreover he was no longer capable of business. Devil take it, what lessor wouldn't be scared to death at having such a tenant?

If, on the other hand, one considered that the old landlord was very rich, that the real tenant was his daughter, and that at the moment she was in a pretty bad way, then again the lessor was damnably in the wrong. But, thought Pagel, it's also not at all like the disagreeable old boy to start this business with the forester so utterly without reason. He himself knows that he is socially, as a gentleman, done for in the whole district if he now makes it impossible for his daughter to carry on the farm, and puts her, so to speak, out on the street. . . . No, this bolt couldn't have come from a clear sky. There must have been something else before. It was a damned nuisance, that one had promised the forester not to speak about the letter to Frau von Prackwitz.

Pagel got up from his bale of straw. He was an idiot; he ought to have looked through the private letters which Amanda took to the Villa. Perhaps there was a letter from the Geheimrat among them; almost certainly his daughter would neither have read nor replied to it. Nowadays she did little but drive through the world in a car. I certainly saw a pretty good bundle of letters lying unopened on her desk, he thought. I can tell if there's something from the old boy by the postmark, and the handwriting. Then I could somehow approach the business from that side.

He walked up and down. A spade, there to make his life burdensome, was roughly kicked aside.

Oh, my God, he thought, I don't want to have worked here, damn it all, for nothing. I don't want to have merely sat dawdling here till Peter called me back. I want to have done something, to have laid down some little stone or other which the old fellow won't overturn immediately. Another, a more pleasurable thought occurred to him. His cigarette flew in an arch over the next potato clamp and went out in the night. Away with sinful, tropical nicotine! I have, at least, done something that's not so bad; I've packed our secret overseer Kniebusch off to bed for the next twenty-six weeks. That's settled the veto on carts in the woods and the control of sales, my dear Geheimrat. You wanted to be so cunning. You began by taking away his work in the forest and his tree-cutting, with a secretive hint about imminent financial developments. But I've been even more cunning. I've taken everything from him: the forest as well as the spying.

The brief hour of discouragement had passed. No longer does he feel exhausted and flat. He's a young man whose work suits him and who wants to bring it to a good end! With rapid steps Pagel made for the farm.

VII

But he did not get to the office at once. On the swiftest paths something always intervenes. This time it was the local veterinary surgeon, Herr Hoffart, whom the stableman had called in during Pagel's absence; the Rittmeister's saddle horse, an English thoroughbred mare called Mabel, had been foaling since the morning. Her throes came again and again, but the birth was no nearer.

Everything appropriate had been done: her box had been curtained off, because horses in foal are shamefaced and cannot bear to be observed by a human being; a curious glance can delay birth for hours. But this seclusion was now over. When Pagel and the vet entered the box the mare threw them a bloodshot look which spoke of torture and pleaded for help. As with human beings, shame had disappeared when pain became unbearable.

"Half an hour ago I could still hear the foal's heartbeats. Now there's nothing, and I'm convinced it's dead. Very likely it has strangled itself in the navel string. I was called in too late, unfortunately." Hoffart had the resigned air of one who is accustomed to having to enter every death as a debit in his accounts.

"And what is to be done?" asked Pagel, more interested in the beast's misery than in a question of guilt.

"I have had a look," said the vet, relieved and eager. "Unfortunately the mare is very narrow. I shall have to cut up the foal inside and fetch it out piece-meal. That, at least, would save the mare."

"It's only a broken-down thoroughbred. The Rittmeister's said to have bought it from some racing stable or other for a couple of hundred marks. But he was very fond of her. I know what, Herr Hoffart," said Pagel briskly, "have patience for another quarter of an hour or twenty minutes, and I'll inform you then."

"The throes have almost stopped and the heart's very feeble. Is there someone here, at least, who can prepare a strong coffee for the horse? I'll also give her a camphor injection. . . . But it must be done quickly."

"It will be. I'll send the coffee over to you. How much? A wine bottle full? Good." Pagel ran across to the staff-house.

In the darkness somebody spoke to him, blocking his way. It was Black Minna, moaning something about madam, about Sophie. . . . He ran past her into the office. . . . Giving Amanda instructions about the coffee, he got through to the panel doctor. The doctor could not come. In the doorway appeared Black Minna and began again to blubber out something. . . . Furiously he waved her aside. But the doctor decided to come after all; he'd be at the office at nine or half-past and would like Pagel to show him the way to the forester's house. Pagel called to Amanda: "Well, you get the coffee quickly to the stables," and darted past the two women into the night. No doubt Minna really had some complaint, demand or warning, but he had no time to listen now. He had to go further. Behind his back, he couldn't help feeling that a fine spat was brewing between the women. He had told the vet a quarter of an hour, and five minutes of that were already gone.

The Rittmeister's attendant let him into the Villa, an elderly, somewhat fat man, with a few graying wisps of hair on his skull. He always wore, as if he were in an institution, a jacket with white and blue stripes, leather sandals, and baggy gray trousers which had obviously never been pressed since they were bought. Pagel liked the placid man. Schümann had related to him what he had told no one, not even the wife, not even the doctor. "I don't believe," he had whispered, "that the Rittmeister is so ill, mentally ill, as the doctor thinks. He has had a shock—but deranged? No! He can't speak, he smiles at everything one says to him—but he's only pretending! He doesn't want to speak, he doesn't want to see or hear anything more; he's had enough of the world, that's what it is! He can talk in his sleep . . ."

"But isn't that illness?" Pagel had asked.

"Perhaps; I don't know. Perhaps he's only cowardly and discouraged. At first he was quite able to quarrel with me when he wanted his alcohol. Later he would only speak to beg for sleeping draughts, and when we also made him do without those, then he said to himself: There's no point in talking, they won't give me anything, so I'll shut my mouth . . ."

"So, Herr Schümann, do you think he still wouldn't drink anything, if he wasn't being supervised?"

"That's always difficult, Herr Pagel. You never know with such people! If everything went smoothly, perhaps he'd get through without drinking. But if he heard something unpleasant—and he hears everything, he's so alert—then it's possible he'd cave in again. That's why I'm still here."

"Well, what's the Rittmeister doing?" asked Pagel now. "Is he in bed? Is he up? Is madam at home?"

"Madam's gone out. The Rittmeister is up; I put on his collar and tie, and now he's reading."

"Reading?" Pagel found it difficult to imagine Prackwitz reading, even in health, unless it was the newspaper.

Herr Schümann grinned slightly. "If you hadn't told me that he had passed a few weeks this summer as a shooting guest in a madhouse I should undoubtedly have been fooled." The attendant did not hide his smile now. "I sat him in his study, I thrust a copy of *Illustrated Sport* in his hand, I said to him: 'Herr Rittmeister, have a look at the pictures'—I was interested to see what he'd do. Naturally he immediately thinks of the lunatics he's met and he's not content till he has the magazine upside down. He kept on peeping at the same page, frowning, muttering—and only when I said—'Herr Rittmeister, the next page!'—did he turn over."

"But what's the point of all that?" asked Pagel somewhat indignant.

"He's pretending to be mad!" Herr Schümann giggled. "He's very delighted to think how well he does it. When he believes I'm not looking he gives a side glance to see if I'm taking notice of what he's doing."

"But we'd leave him alone, without these stupid tricks!" said Pagel angrily.

"You wouldn't! He's right there. Once you noticed he's in his senses you'd demand that he should think a bit about his affairs, bother about money; madam would expect him to grieve about his daughter, to assist. But that's just what he doesn't want. He's run dry, has nothing more to give."

"Then he is ill after all," cried Pagel. "Well, we shall see. Listen, Herr Schümann." And he expounded his plan.

"One can try," said the attendant thoughtfully. "Of course, if it turns out badly we'll both get it in the neck—from the doctor as well as madam. Well, come in, we'll soon see how he reacts."

It was a pitiable sight, and also a very shameful one—if the Rittmeister was not really so ill as he pretended. There he sat in one of his irreproachable English suits, his eyes dark as ever, but hair and eyebrows snow-white. His formerly brown face looked yellow. He had a newspaper in his hand and was chuckling with delight over it. The paper shook in his hand and his whole body shook with it.

"Herr Rittmeister!" said the attendant. "Please put down the paper. You must dress and go out a little."

For a moment it looked as if the white bushy eyebrows were drawn closer together—then a fresh chuckle seized the man and the newspaper rustled.

"Herr Rittmeister," said Pagel, "your mare, Mabel, is foaling. But it's not going well and the vet is there. He says the foal is dead and the mare will peg out, too. Won't you have a look?"

With wrinkled brows the Rittmeister stared at his paper; he had stopped chuckling and appeared to contemplate a picture.

"Come along, Herr Rittmeister," said the attendant at last, amiably. "Give me the newspaper."

The Rittmeister, of course, heard nothing, and so it was taken from his hands. He was led into the hall, an overcoat put on him, and a cap. Then they left the house.

"Please take my arm, Herr Rittmeister," said the attendant with mild, somewhat professional, affability. "Herr Pagel, will you also give Herr

Rittmeister your arm?—Walking must be very troublesome for you; you have been very ill, of course." Almost imperceptibly the emphasis was on "been."

Perhaps it was chance, perhaps the sick man had felt the emphasis, had considered it a challenge; he began to chuckle again. Then he walked on silently, swaying between the two men. They were close to the village when Pagel noticed that the Rittmeister's arm was trembling in his; the whole man shook. Something like fear in regard to his venture threatened the young man. "You are trembling a lot—are you cold, Herr Rittmeister?" he said at last.

The Rittmeister, of course, did not reply. But the attendant had well understood what was in Pagel's mind. "That won't help us now, Herr Pagel," he said. "We can't turn back now. We must go through with it."

They crossed the yard, they entered the stable. In the faces of those who stood there could be seen fright. The Rittmeister was, according to gossip, insane. And now the madman had come to them in the stable!

"Everybody outside!" Pagel ordered. "Only you, stableman, and, if you like, you, Amanda, can stay. Shut the stable door." Thank goodness the vet behaved very sensibly. "Good evening, Herr Rittmeister," he said calmly, and stepped a little to one side, leaving the entrance to the box free.

It seemed to Pagel as if he had felt a slight tug on his arm. Yes, the Rittmeister drew near the box, they need not hold him; he stood there by himself.

The horse lay on her side, legs stretched out. She turned her head with its sad, helpless eyes. She had recognized her master, and whinnied feebly as if expecting only from him the help which did not come.

"Since I gave the mare coffee and camphor," reported the vet, "the throes have become stronger, and the heart's quite good now. I almost thought I heard feeble heartbeats from the foal again, but I may be mistaken."

There was a general silence.

What was the Rittmeister doing? He had taken off his overcoat, he looked round. The stableman—all were quiet, very quiet—took the coat. Rittmeister von Prackwitz also removed his jacket; the stableman took it. He fumbled with his cuff link—Amanda was there and helped him to roll up his sleeve. Yes, that was the real obstetrician's hand, slender, with long dexterous fingers; a wrist thin as a child's, but of steel. A long slender arm, not flesh, but of sinew, bone, muscle.

They held their breath as he knelt down behind the horse. He hesitated now, looked round displeased. What was the matter? What was lacking? Why didn't he speak?

But the vet had understood him; he knelt down beside the Rittmeister and rubbed his arm with oil till it was smooth and supple. "A little carefully, Herr

Rittmeister!" he whispered. "When the throes come, the mare will kick out; they have forgotten to unshoe her."

The Rittmeister frowned and compressed his almost bloodless lips. Then he set about his work. His long arm disappeared to the shoulder in the mare's body; mysteriously could be read on his face the groping and searching of his hand. Now his eyes shone with their old ardent gleam; he had found what he sought for.

Yes, yes—this Rittmeister—like a coward he had slunk away from his daughter's shameful ruin. He had whined for alcohol and veronal. He pretended to be a lunatic. But because a horse was in distress he left his self-chosen isolation and returned to his fellow-beings; he had found something on earth which was still worth effort. Oh, my god! That's people for you. That's what they're like—no better. But also, no worse!

Once or twice he had to discontinue his work. The mare kicked out in agony, but he did not withdraw his arm; he ducked down, for the throes which endangered him were also of help in releasing the fruit from the mother. His face had turned crimson; with all his power he withstood the throes which were forcing his arm, too, with enormous strength out of the mare's body. Pagel got down on the straw beside him, supporting with his shoulder the shoulder of the Rittmeister—and was met by a glance which was certainly not that of an idiot, though perhaps of someone who had suffered unutterably. . . .

As the foal's hoofs appeared, a stir went round the bystanders. See! now came the delicate silky muzzle; the head, the shoulders, followed only slowly. Then, swiftly, came the very long body—and the foal lay as if lifeless on the ground. The vet, kneeling down, examined it. "Living," he said.

Up jumped the Rittmeister, swaying. "Just hold firmly to me, Herr Rittmeister," said the attendant. "That was rather a lot for the beginning." And the Rittmeister understood and held fast.

Amanda Backs advanced with a basin and warm water; she washed the Rittmeister's blood-stained arm as if that also was something newborn and easily damaged. Then Herr von Prackwitz walked from the stable, led by the two men, went without looking at a person, without a word, with dragging feet as though he were already asleep. Slowly they passed between the farm buildings. Then, as the October wind, blowing from the woods, sprang at them with all its freshness, the Rittmeister came to a stop. A spasm shook his body and Joachim von Prackwitz said the first word after a long silence. It was only an exclamation, a cry of lament, of despair, of recollection—who knows? "My God!" he cried.

And after a while they went on their way again, the sick man walking heavily between them. Pagel helped to bring him to his bedroom; then, when the attendant started to undress Prackwitz, he went downstairs.

In the hall he sat for a time inactive. He was exhausted, but he had done a thing right and good. He thought of something, however, and, after a knock or two, went into Frau Eva's room. As soon as he turned on the light he saw the piles of letters on the desk. He had a slight repugnance to overcome, but in life one couldn't do only the things which were agreeable. He looked for the foreign stamp and postmark, but he glanced through the first pile in vain; the second also. There was nothing, either, in the third. As he put down the fourth and last, with as little result, his eye fell on a note pad. Without wishing to read it, he had done so. "Write to father" was written there. He returned to the hall.

That note could mean anything; Frau Eva might have thought herself of writing to her father, but equally she might not want to forget to reply. He'd conducted this rather depressing little rummage in vain, and didn't know quite how to continue, but only knew that he must. . . .

A little later the attendant came down. "He went to sleep at once. It was really a bit too much for him. Well, we must wait and see. Will you tell madam?"

"Oh, yes. One of us must tell her. She ought not to hear about it from others."

Herr Schümann looked thoughtful. "I tell you what, Herr Pagel. It was your doing, of course; but I'll tell her and take the responsibility." And when Pagel made a gesture: "I've heard there's some gossip going round. Women are funny, you know; at least I'll take that off your shoulders." He smiled. "Of course, if it's gone all right with the Rittmeister I shall get the credit. . . ."

"I can guess what's up now," said Pagel annoyed. "Just let them come to me, that's all!"

"Don't worry yourself about it, Herr Pagel. Well, good night for the present."

"Good night." Pagel set out again for the staff-house. It was after eight. Amanda would already be waiting with her evening meal. He had endless business mail to deal with and he also wanted to write his mother. The doctor was coming, he had to go to the forester, and he had to see to the foals. But he'd rather go straight to bed—and there's chattering in the corridor! Give us peace, dear Lord, give us peace!

If only others were peaceful. . . .

VIII

It was now after ten. Pagel sat in front of his books; sick-fund contributions must be reckoned up, wage-tax stamps stuck on, and the cash book had to be somehow

brought into agreement with the cashbox. All these were almost insuperable difficulties for a tired man; and in addition it was getting more and more difficult
about the money. He would reckon out a laborer's wage exactly according to the
scale—so-and-so many millions and milliards. But he couldn't give him the
money; there weren't enough notes! He had to take some large denomination,
one of those rubbishy 100- or 200-milliard-mark notes, and call in four men.
"Here, each of you take a corner, it belongs to you in common. As a matter of fact
it's a bit too much, I don't know exactly, two or three milliards; but off with you
into the town! Make your purchases together; you'll have to come to an agreement somehow. Curse me if you like—I can't get any other money."

All right, they would go at last and find some tradesman who changed their
note for them. But where could Pagel find someone to help him out with his
own accounts? Oh, he was a great man, he had a weekly salary of two and a
half hundredweights of rye—but that amount was regularly missing from his
accounts. Often much more. Little Meier certainly never wrote so many incorrect figures in his cash book. If an accountant ever saw them—off to prison with
this embezzler!

He propped his head in his hands; the wilderness of figures was sickening; there was something unclean in this parade of ever more astronomical
numbers. Every small man a millionaire—but all we millionaires would yet
starve! What had the doctor said to the forester just now? "We shall soon be
having billion notes—a billion is a thousand milliards—it can't go any higher!
Then we shall get a stable currency, you'll be pensioned off—and till then you
can stay snugly in bed."

"Shall we really have decent money again?" the forester had asked anxiously. "Shall I live to see it? I would truly like to see the day, Herr Doctor,
when one can go into a shop again and the tradesman sells something without
looking at the money in a fury, as if one's a swindler."

"You will certainly live to see it, old fellow!" the doctor had reassured him,
tucking up the blankets under the forester's chin. But outside he had said to
Pagel: "See that the old man doesn't take to his bed altogether. Give him some
little job so that he can putter around. Utterly tired out and used up! How he
ever ran about the woods for ten hours every day beats me. Once he's properly
on his back he won't get up again, that's certain."

"So he won't live to see the end of this inflation? I know from school that
there are billiards and trillions and quadrillions and . . ."

"Come to a stop, man!" cried out the doctor, "or I'll strike you down
immediately with my reflex hammer! You want to go through all this misery?
Such an appetite for life, young man, could give one indigestion!"

"No," he whispered, "I have it from a man in the bank—the dollar will be stabilized at four hundred and twenty milliards."

"Oh, I've heard that sort of talk the last half-year. I don't believe a word of it."

"Young man," had declared the doctor solemnly, his eyes flashing behind his glasses, "let me tell you this. On the day when the dollar goes above four hundred and twenty milliards I'll put on a mask and chloroform myself out of this life. Because then I shall have had enough of it."

"So," said Pagel, "we'll speak together later."

"Not as you think," shouted the doctor angrily. "You modern youth are disgusting! Even hundred-year-old men weren't as cynical as that in my time!"

"So when exactly was your time, Herr Doctor?" asked Pagel, grinning. "Pretty much a long time ago, eh?"

"I mistrusted you from the very beginning," said the doctor sadly and climbed into his OpelLaubfrosch, "when you so shamefacedly asked me just how long the man could have been dead."

"Quiet please, Doctor!"

"All right, I agree. On this point I'm a cynic myself. It's the profession. Good night. And, as I said, if the dollar isn't stabilized at four hundred and twenty. . . ."

"Then we'll wait a little longer," Pagel shouted after the departing doctor.

It would have been good if there had been a coffee in the office, but there was naturally none at this time of night. Amanda Backs had long gone to bed. However, Pagel had once again underestimated Amanda: Coffees stood on the table. Unfortunately the coffee was no longer in a state to really cheer him up, or else Pagel was simply too tired. In any case, he sat, miserable, over his books. He got no further, wanted to go to bed, but wanted nevertheless to write to his mother, and tortured his conscience with the sentence: If I'm not too tired to write to Mama, I can't be too tired to finish the wage-books.

This strange sentence, lacking all logic, a distortion of an overtired mind, tortured the young Pagel so persistently that he was unable either to do his accounts or write, and couldn't sleep either. Eventually, he sank into a condition of semi-conscious misery and dazed numbness in which horrible thoughts crept into his mind. Doubts about life, doubts about himself, doubts about Petra.

"Damnation!" he cried and stood up. "I'd prefer to spring into the worthy Geheimrat's swannery and take the coldest bath of my life than sit around here gloomy and sleepy-headed."

And in this moment the telephone rang. A hurried feminine voice, familiar and yet strange, desired that Herr Pagel would come at once to the Villa; madam wished to speak to him.

"I'll come at once," he replied. Who was the woman who had spoken? Her voice had sounded disguised.

It was a quarter to eleven. Rather a little late, surely, for a man who got up at five, at half-past four, at four! Well, there was trouble again over there. The business with the Rittmeister had gone badly, or Frau Eva had at last learned something about Violet; or she only wanted to know how many potatoes had been dug up that day—she was often like that. At times she was her father's daughter, and then she thought she had to supervise her young employee. Whistling happily, Pagel wandered through the estate out to the Villa. Although he was supposed to go straight to Madam, he made a detour via the stables. The Ostler was startled—but everything was in perfect order. The stallion was back in his stall and turned round to look at Pagel with its lively eyes. The foal with the unbelievably long legs was asleep. And Pagel sent the Ostler off to bed too.

Frau Eva herself opened the door. She had changed greatly in the last weeks. Her daily trips with their harrowing senseless hopes, their apathetic returns, the agonizing uncertainty day in day out, to which the worst certainty would have been preferable—all this had laid its mark on her features. Her eye, formerly so amiable and feminine, had now a dry burning glance. But it was not only this. Now that she no longer took care of herself or ate regularly, her skin had become flabby. . . . Formerly she had been able to laugh pleasantly, a woman in harmony with herself and the world; her voice had sweetness and vibration. Now it sounded as if her throat were parched. Her angry eyes examined him. "I am very sorry, Herr Pagel, but I can't possibly put up with it. I have heard today that you are having affairs with women and taking advantage of your position to force girls . . ."

Oh, the poor transformed woman! "I'm very sorry." Oh, no. She was furious. This woman who only a few weeks ago had been ready to close a smiling eye to everything must now revenge her daughter on men. Everything was dirty wherever she looked; but she wouldn't put up with it in her neighborhood!

Pagel smiled; wrinkles appeared in the corners of his eyes. He couldn't understand how a woman prostrate with anxiety for her family could still lend an ear to gossip. . . . Smilingly he shook his head. "No, madam," he said, "I'm quite sure that I'm having no affairs with women."

"But I was told so!" she cried. "You have . . ."

"Why should we listen to lies?" he asked, still amiably. "Seeing that I have no affairs with women whatever? I'd really rather we didn't talk about such things, madam."

Frau Eva made an impatient gesture. Some hatred or fury was driving her to tell that young fellow to his face what she had heard about him. And she wished to hear explanations, excuses—most of all a confession.

Pagel, however, swung round; he had understood why this conversation was taking place in the hall. Yes, Sophie Kowalewski stood where the kitchen stairs went down into the basement. She made to hide herself, but it was too late. Doubtless it was she who had phoned. "Come out, Sophie," he called. "You're the only one from whom I'd like to hear the story. Please relate in front of madam what you did so that you wouldn't have to dig potatoes."

Frau Eva flushed and made a gesture to stop him. But Pagel had walked toward the girl, not at all fiercely, but pleasantly. "Now, Sophie," he said. "Come, my girl, talk, talk! Or better still, let madam see how you tried to show me your knees."

And then it was shown that Sophie Kowalewski was not complete, either in goodness or in evil. She had slipped up and fallen into bad ways—beautiful, wrong, but not even really that bad. She hadn't the courage even for her malice; she was cowardly. She screamed, ran down the kitchen stairs, and a door slammed.

Pagel turned back. He now showed nothing more of a bragging unconcern, but spoke in explanation, almost in excuse. "As a matter of fact, I had told her to appear early tomorrow for the potato harvest. Her laziness is a bad example to the village."

Frau von Prackwitz looked at him. The flush of anger and shame had left her face, but not completely. Something remained, a hint of a healthier color. No, life—despite everything—was not just old, ugly and stale, it could still also be young, fresh and clean. Almost apologetically she said: "I've taken on Sophie here in the house. She offered, and I was in such a quandary. But please do come in, Herr Pagel." She led the way, a little disconcerted. Shouldn't she be ashamed? Her lack of belief, her doubt—they were so ugly compared to his belief and rectitude. "I didn't know the circumstances," she explained.

"Sophie will certainly be better suited to housework than to potato digging. The main thing is that she shouldn't idle around any longer."

"But to make up for it I have dismissed Black Minna," reported Frau Eva guiltily. "The woman's so ghastly."

Pagel's mouth had shut tightly; the lazy one got the good situation and the diligent, who worked herself to death, had to return to the icy potatoes. But there was no sense in arguing about it with Frau Eva. The good-looking Sophie pleased her better. "I'll employ Minna, with your permission, in the Manor," he proposed. "It's very neglected, and some time or other the old people will be coming back."

"Yes, do that, Herr Pagel! I'm so grateful to you. That will certainly be the best solution." She looked at him almost guiltily. "You're not angry with me about just now?"

"No. No. But perhaps you will be, when I tell you that I was here in your room a few hours ago," he said a little embarrassed. "I was looking for a particular letter. I didn't want to read it or anything, I only wanted to see if it was there. Then by mistake I read the note "Write to Father" on your notepad. I felt a despicable spy; but I wasn't doing it for myself . . ."

"Why then? You only needed to ask me."

"It is," he said, annoyed and rubbing his nose, "a rather difficult case. I had intended to tell you that the forester had become bedridden and that we therefore had to write to the Geheimrat, which we will. However, it would be a fraud. The forester really is ill, but we needn't worry about the forest on that account."

"And what has actually happened?" she asked.

"Well, that's the point. I've given my word not to tell anybody, including yourself. I had to," he said more emphatically, "otherwise I would have learnt nothing."

"But what happened then?" she asked uneasily. Was she always to expect new worries? She got up and walked up and down. "Can't you tell me anything at all, Herr Pagel?"

"I should like to ask you something, madam. Has your father written to you since his departure?"

"Yes." So it's something to do with Father, she thought, but her tone was lighter. She didn't take it seriously.

"Have you replied?"

"No," she said curtly. He noticed that even the memory of the letter annoyed her. She looked at him expectantly, but he didn't ask anything else. He seemed to have said all that he wanted to say. Finally, she decided: "Herr Pagel, I will tell you. Papa demands that I divorce the Rittmeister. He has always wished it. But can I? Can I desert him like that? Does one desert a friend in distress? Had he been in health or if I was anyway sure that he could live without me, then yes. But like this—no! Now definitely not! For better, for worse, as they say in the English marriages. I'm like that. Especially for the worse, explicitly for the worse!" Her face twitched. "Oh, Herr Pagel, I know you tried this evening to bring him back to the world. Of course, you would do that. How can something like that occur to an attendant?! I was very angry at first; you must see yourself that the poor fellow's an invalid. Then I thought, Well, it was meant kindly. But all my father wants is for me to leave him, put him in some asylum, appoint a guardian. But we've lived together almost twenty years, Herr Pagel!"

"He said, 'Oh God!'"

"Yes, I heard him. It doesn't mean anything. He no longer knows what he's saying. But you're still young. You have hope. Oh, when I now drive round the country and see the people walking along the highroads in the frightful weather! There are so many of them, not only tramps. This terrible time makes everyone restless. This morning, there was such an icy rain, I saw two young people. The man was pushing a very old pram, and the woman was walking beside it talking to the child. I thought, My Violet is perhaps tramping round like that, but she has no child to whom she can speak, no one! Oh, Herr Pagel, what am I to do?"

"Hope," he said.

"Ought I to? Is it right, for her sake, even to still wish she is alive? Isn't it merely selfishness for me to hope she is still alive? Oh, I never cease to wish to find her, and at the same time I shudder from it. Herr Pagel, it's now over four weeks she's been away!"

"She has no will of her own," he said softly. "One day she will find it again, and then she'll come back."

"Isn't it so? You say that too? She's still asleep. She's still fast asleep! If you're asleep, fast asleep, you don't feel anything. Yes, she will come back unchanged. She will wake up in her room and believe that nothing has happened and that she went to sleep the evening before." Frau Eva was radiant and young again. Hope and her unquenchable will to life have awoken her. She's young again—life has abundant gifts ready for her. "I will tell you something else, Herr Pagel," she whispered, with a glance at the door. "I'm not searching for them alone; there's someone else, too. He stopped my car; a man with a bloated face, wearing a bowler hat—perhaps you know him?"

"Yes, I know him."

"Don't tell about him!" she exclaimed. "I don't want to know. He stops my car, asks no questions, gives no greetings, only says: 'Drive there, or there!' Then I see him again, on some road or other in some little town; he, too, is always on his way somewhere. He only shakes his head when I look at him and goes on . . . Herr Pagel, if I don't find her, he will! They talk so much about love, but hate is far stronger."

"Yes. That man hates evil. His hate urges him on without rest."

"It's over four weeks now that *he's* been with Violet; he must provide for her somehow or other." This mother abominated the wretch who had made her daughter miserable, but because he permitted the girl to live she did not like to think of his falling into the hands of that pitiless fat man.

Pagel stood up. "Madam, at least don't worry about the Geheimrat. For the moment nothing will happen. Something has intervened. Plans do exist. . . ."

"Yes, we're supposed to leave this place."

"But they can't be carried out for the moment. If anything happens, I'll let you know."

He looked at her thoughtfully for a moment. Then he added, "You needn't trouble your father with a letter either. As you can't do what he wants anyway, you could do just as well not to write him."

"Thank you, Herr Pagel. Thank you for everything." She gave him her hand, smiling at him. "It has done me good to talk to you."

And with that sudden, inexplicable woman's transition, she said, "And now, Herr Pagel, you must do me a favor too."

"Yes, please," he said, "gladly."

"Don't put up with this wretched woman Backs anymore! It's said you eat with her and that she's always sitting with you in the office. Oh, don't be angry with me, Herr Pagel!" she cried hastily. "I've absolutely no mistrust for you. You simply haven't noticed that the girl is in love with you. . . ."

"Amanda Backs is not in love with me, Madam," said Pagel. "I only do her good because she's been left on the shelf. What's more, she does me good. Life in Neulohe is sometimes a bit too much for a young man like me. I sometimes like to have someone around with whom I can exchange a word."

"Oh, God, Herr Pagel!" she cried, genuinely shocked. "I really didn't mean that. I only meant Backs, because she's with that Meier—and he really is horrible. . . ."

Pagel looked at her, but she didn't notice. She really noticed nothing; she saw absolutely no parallels.

In the hall outside the clock struck midnight.

"Well, Herr Pagel," she said earnestly, "see that you get to bed now. It's really too late for you. I can believe that the work here is often a bit too much for a single person. Have a thorough sleep for once. Let the laborers manage for a bit alone; I'm agreeable to anything. Good night, Herr Pagel, and my best thanks again."

"Good night, madam. I have to thank you."

"A thorough sleep, then, without fail!" she called out after him.

Pagel smiled to himself in the dark. He didn't hold it against her; in many respects this clever, alert woman was a child. By work, she always meant something like schoolwork. You can't do much about it, but a teacher can occasionally grant a whole day free and then the children are happy! She had not yet understood (and probably never would) that life, that every day, has its tasks which no one is spared.

In the office building above, a white shadow appeared in the window. The faithful concierge was checking up on him.

"Everything shipshape, Amanda," murmured Pagel in her direction. Sophie had put herself out in vain. "Go to sleep, get warm, and wake me tomorrow morning early at half past five—but with a coffee."

"Good night, Herr Pagel" was heard from above.

IX

The next morning this takes place in front of the Villa:

Frau Eva is already in the car, giving Oskar directions, when the front door opens and out steps the Rittmeister, followed by his attendant. He walks with a queerly stumbling gait to the car. The attendant remains standing at the top of the steps.

Like a guilty child the Rittmeister asks: "May I drive with you, Eva?"

Frau Eva throws an astonished glance at the attendant, who nods emphatically.

"But, Achim!" she cries, "won't it be too much for you?"

He shakes his head. His eyes are full of tears, his mouth trembles.

"Oh, Achim! Achim—I'm so happy indeed. All will be right again, you see. Sit down next to me. Herr Schümann, please help the Rittmeister into the car. Oskar, fetch another rug, the fur one. Herr Schümann, you must then go at once to Herr Pagel and tell him; he'll be so pleased."

The car starts. The Rittmeister makes an apologetic gesture. "Sorry, Eva," he says quietly. And again with much effort, "I can't speak properly yet. I don't quite understand, but. . . ."

"But what do you need to speak for, Achim?" she says, taking his hand. "Surely, as long as we are together, everything will be easier?"

He nods vigorously.

Chapter Fifteen

The Last Does Not Remain Alone

I

Soon it would be December. With storms of ice, snow and sleet the year was approaching its end. The last of the potato diggers had fled—a great blow—ten thousand hundredweight and more were still in the earth. Angry shame seized Pagel when he saw the leaves rotting in the fields and thought that, while people were dying of hunger in the towns, the potatoes themselves were rotting underground.

I have done a lot of things wrong, he thought. But how the devil could I have known better? Nobody told me, and I had so much to do I couldn't think a day ahead. I ought to have had the potatoes taken straight to the station; then we should now have the little bit of money which is always lacking. Stored in the clamps they are threatened by frost and thieves, and won't be saleable till spring. And who will have this place then?

The threshing machine hummed outside—but it was too loud, too noticeable. There was a man in Frankfurt who had once furnished a large sum of inflation money, and a car had been purchased with it; now the man wanted his goods. The times were beginning to change. In Berlin they had at last stopped the note presses, so people said, and the mark wouldn't be falling any lower: it had stopped falling when for one American dollar 4,200 milliard marks were given. And perhaps it would stay at that level.

The threshing machine hummed—sometimes it was busy with rye for the man in Frankfurt; sometimes he went away empty-handed because another had been quicker. Geheimrat von Teschow had left the beautiful region of Nice and now lived in the agreeable town of Dresden—to be more exact, at The White Hart, in Loschwitz. Perhaps he wanted to lose weight, or his gallstones gave him trouble if he thought of Neulohe. Or the old lady was having trouble with her nerves. Emissaries of his frequently visited Neulohe—they were bailiffs; and a certain attorney had become a familiar figure to Wolfgang, for the Geheimrat had a writ of execution—oh, everything was in the best of order. Once again he had snapped up three hundred hundredweights of rye which the man in Frankfurt should have had. . . .

Pagel sat at his typewriter; it was only half-past eight in the morning and the letter must go by the next post, without fail.

Dear Herr So-and-so, I regret to have to inform you that the wagonload of rye (Baden 326485, 15 tons), concerning which you had already been apprised, was seized at the goods station here by that other creditor of Herr von Prackwitz already known to you. I beg you to be patient a few days longer; as quickly as possible I will send you a delivery in replacement. In the meantime I would beg you to consider whether the grain assigned you could not be fetched direct from the threshing machine by truck. I have already verbally explained to you that there is no lack either of goodwill on our part or of the possibility . . .

But what did the two people in the Villa say to that? Nothing. The Rittmeister preferred to sit silently beside his wife. "Do just as you think best, Herr Pagel," she said. "You have the authorization."

"But your father . . ."

"Oh, father doesn't mean it so badly! You will see. When everything's in a complete muddle, he will come and put everything to rights—beaming because of the chance to be so clever. Isn't that so, Achim? Papa was always like that."

The Rittmeister nodded and smiled.

"But I have no money for wages!" cried Pagel despairingly.

"Sell something or other—sell cows, sell horses! What do we need with horses at the beginning of winter, when work's at an end? Don't you think so, Achim? In winter one doesn't need horses."

"No." He is of the same opinion; in winter one doesn't need horses.

"The lease prohibits the sale of livestock. Live and dead stock, madam, does not belong to you; it belongs to the Geheimrat."

"Have you become Herr von Studmann? Why, you're already talking of the lease! Dear Herr Pagel, don't make difficulties for us. You have full authority! It's only a question of a few days more. . . ." Pagel looked questioningly at Frau Eva. "Yes," she went on suddenly fervent, "I am convinced that our search will soon be successful. The fat man has turned up again in his bowler hat. . . . We hadn't seen him for a time, and we had almost given up hope. . . ."

Pagel went. Pagel raised money and paid the wages. Or Pagel could not raise money and he paid the people with grain and potatoes, a sucking pig, butter, a goose . . .

He sat at the typewriter: "We have still roughly four thousand hundred-weights of grain lying unthreshed. . . ." Is that true or is it a lie? he thought.

I don't know. I haven't kept the grain books for weeks; I'd never get them right now. Whoever takes over from me can only believe that I'm criminally thoughtless. Nothing balances. . . . If the Geheimrat gets to see it . . . He sighed. Oh, life's no fun, I don't enjoy it. Even when I think of Petra, I no longer enjoy it. If I ever really do reach her, I'm sure I'll cry and cry purely because of loss of nerve. But I can't run away now, though. I can't leave them in the lurch. They wouldn't even be able to borrow the petrol for their damned car!

"That's the third time you've sighed, Herr Pagel," said Amanda Backs from the window, "and it's only half-past eight in the morning. How are you going to get through the day?"

"That's what I often ask myself," replied Wolfgang, grateful for the distraction. "On the whole, however, the day itself sees to it that you get through it, and usually no day is as bad as I feared it would be in the morning, and none so good as I had hoped, either."

Amanda Backs looked impatiently out of the window; this sententiousness did not please her. Then she screamed, in horror. "Herr Pagel, look!"

Pagel sprang to the window . . .

He saw something coming across the Geheimrat's park, creeping on arms and legs.

For a moment he stood transfixed.

Then he shouted: "The forester! Now they've killed the forester, too!" and he ran from the room.

II

It had not been very hard for Pagel to get the old forester out of his sickbed again—not half so difficult as the doctor had thought. A man who had passed his whole life in the fresh air felt his head swim when he was always shut up in a stuffy room. "I'm afraid the walls will collapse on me," he complained to Pagel. "It's all so small—and she won't have a window open."

Perhaps it was not the confinement or the lack of air, or the bees who had to be prepared for the winter, or the hunting dog who wanted to be fed every day, that brought the forester so quickly out of his bed—perhaps it was "she," his wife, who more than anything sickened him of his room. They had spent a whole lifetime side by side—till they couldn't bear the sight of each other. Day after day they passed by one another without exchanging a word. He would go into the kitchen, make his coffee and butter his bread, and then, when he had left, she came and made her coffee and buttered her bread. They had long passed beyond disgust, hate and aversion; now they did not exist for one another at all. For a very long time. Before he opened his mouth she knew what he would say, and he knew everything about his wife; how peas agreed with her, and that when the wind was in the south she couldn't hear with the left ear, and that lampreys tasted much better with than without a bay leaf.

"Move into another room," proposed Pagel. "There are enough empty rooms in the house."

"But my bed has always stood in this room! I can't move it about at my time of life. I would never get to sleep."

"Then go for a little walk," replied Pagel. "Fresh air and a little exercise can only do you good, the doctor says."

"Yes? Does he really think so?" asked the forester anxiously. "Then I'll do it." He was very willing to do whatever was ordered by the doctor who had procured so many good things for him: rest from work, sick benefit, splendid medicine that brought a man tranquil sleep. And he had promised even better things: the end of inflation, a pension, a peaceful evening to his life. So the forester went for a walk. But that again was a difficult matter. At no price would he go into the forest, which came right up to his house. He had seen enough forest in his life, much too much. Actually he couldn't see the wood for the trees. He saw only so-and-so many cubic feet of timber, railway sleepers, wood for fellies, shafts for the wheelwright, stakes . . . And if he took a walk in the forest it would look, not as if he were ill, but as if he were on duty again. It would have been the same as for a sick clerk to go to his office for recreation.

In the other direction, however—toward the village—he also did not go. All his life the people had kept repeating that he was merely a lazybones who did nothing but walk about. He didn't intend now to go for real walks under their very eyes; that would look as if they had been right in the end.

There remained then only one way for him, that which led past the potato clamps fairly directly to Neulohe Farm and the staff-house. Kniebusch therefore went only this way, with great regularity, several times a day; and with the greatest regularity he arrived several times a day in the staff-house.

With the forester it had come to pass that he, a very old man, had at last found a real friend—and Pagel did not want to disappoint this simple faith. Yet he sighed whenever he saw the old man approaching, to sit down and not take his eyes off him for half an hour at a time. He did not exactly intrude; he never spoke if Pagel was busy—at the most he let himself be carried away into a rare exclamation of rapture when Pagel was typing, such as: "Oh, how fast he does that! Like machine-gun fire! Splendid!" No, he did not intrude, but it was a little disturbing to have those seal-like eyes fixed upon one in a glance of unbounded devotion, enthusiastic friendship. Perhaps it was disturbing precisely because Pagel did not in any way return this emotion. He had no particular love for the aged, timorous forester. And what had he done to earn such friendship, after all? Practically nothing: a talk on the telephone with the doctor, a little charity, two or three short sickbed visits. . . .

When things got too bad Pagel would interrupt his work. "Come along, Herr Kniebusch; I must see if there are any more mouse holes in my potato clamps; I'll accompany you the little distance."

The forester always got up at once and came away willingly. It never entered his head that his friend wanted to get rid of him. When this had happened three or four times, however, it occurred to the old man that at least he could take one job off this friend's hands, and now on his morning walk to the office he would go from one clamp to the other. "Stacks six, seven, eleven each have a hole," he would report. "At the north end, middle, south end." He was very exact.

"Yes, you sigh, Herr Pagel," said Amanda exasperated, "but you could easily tell him that the constant sitting around and staring is no good to you in the office. That Kniebusch is certainly no soft touch, and if he lays into someone, that someone definitely knows it. And if you don't like to tell him, then I will."

"You'll do nothing of the sort, Amanda." And Pagel spoke with such emphasis that Amanda did nothing of the sort.

When the forester had left his house that morning there was a very fine rain falling and no breath of wind. It was one of those mournful autumn days which lie on the hearts of young people like a nightmare, but the weather pleased the old forester, certain that his young friend could be found in the office, under shelter. Throwing a rain cape round his shoulders, he set forth.

Slowly and comfortably he shuffled toward the farm. His hands, clasped over his belly, were dry and warm under the cape. If he weighed up things closely, he had never been better off in his life, or felt better. He hadn't even to fear the Geheimrat's return. At Pagel's instigation the doctor had written to the old gentleman, who had sent an amiable note to Kniebusch—he should see if he couldn't get about a little again, so as to initiate his successor in the hiding places of the game, the ins and outs of the forest, and the artfulness of the population. But he shouldn't bother himself any more about his work.

A fat lot the old gentleman knew! The forester wasn't bothering himself or worrying a bit—least of all about the forest. But was he not perhaps a trifle sorry when he found holes in the potato clamps? That vexed and troubled his best and only friend, Pagel, as he knew; but it delighted him, because when there were holes he had something to report and was of use.

So he walked quite contentedly up one side of the clamps and down the other. Unfortunately, however, as he might almost have imagined, the people hadn't, in this beastly weather, the heart even to steal; clothing was so scarce that men didn't like to expose to rain the single gray uniform they had brought back with them from the war.

It looked then as if there would be nothing to report today, and that was annoying—till old Kniebusch came to the very last clamp, on the other side of which, next to the forest, he found the wished-for hole; and a splendid one, too. Six or eight hundredweights of potatoes had been taken out of it at least.

Satisfied, he might now have made his report. Instead, he looked thoughtfully at a small path trodden out from the hole into the pine plantation. The soft ground betrayed clearly that the potatoes had not been taken straight on a handcart to the road and thus to the village—the still quite fresh marks showed that they had been taken into the plantation and were probably still there.

The inquisitiveness of old men, as tormenting as an eczema, plagued him, and the hunter's instinct urged him on—one doesn't track game a whole lifetime to pass heedlessly over a trail in one's old age. The thought of being able to report something very special to his friend Pagel also encouraged him. Not for a moment did he think that this investigation could prove dangerous. Potato thieves were harmless people; their theft was merely of food and was punished with a paper fine, so that they had little to dread if caught. If anything caused the forester to hesitate, it was his firm decision not to bother about other things. However, he wanted to do Pagel a favor, so gently, on tiptoe, he took up the trail. Over the years people had provided themselves with so many poles and faggots from the plantation that the place had become thinned out, and the forester arrived very quickly at the spot where a small mound of potatoes lay. They were Red Professor Wohltmanns. Wanted, no doubt, to fatten his pigs with them!

Kniebusch, feeling that he was not alone, raised his eyes and saw a man squatting under the pines. His trousers were down and he looked calmly at the forester.

"Hi! What are you doing here?" shouted the surprised Kniebusch.

"I'm shitting," replied the man with a friendly grin.

"I can see that," said the forester, amused. Oh, what a lot he would have to tell Pagel! "Was it you who pinched the potatoes?"

"Of course," declared the man, taking his time.

"But who are you? I don't know you at all!" The forester thought he knew every soul for twenty kilometers round, but he had certainly never seen this man before.

"Take a good look at me," said the man, standing and pulling up his trousers. "You'll know me next time."

It was all so friendly and good-tempered—and potato theft was, after all, not really a capital crime—that the forester continued to stand with his hands clasped under the cape, and saw without misgiving the man saunter toward him. If there was no apprehension in his mind, there was certainly astonishment. He was familiar with that jacket and knickerbockers of gray-patterned cloth. "But you are wearing a suit of the Rittmeister's!" he exclaimed bewildered.

"You miss nothing, forester," said the man grinning. "It fits me, don't you think?" He was now standing right in front, laughing. But something in this laughter, in the tone of his words, in his nearness, displeased old Kniebusch. "Well, tell me your name," he ordered. "I certainly don't know you."

"Then you shall," cried the other. In a flash his expression changed into one of hate; in a flash he had his arms round the forester—who couldn't move under his cape.

"What's the meaning of this?" exclaimed the helpless Kniebusch, still not thinking it serious.

"Here's a greeting from your old friend Bäumer!" the man shouted right in his face. And in the same moment the forester heard a terrible crack, right in his skull, a blinding whiteness. . . . There must have been two of them, he thought. One has knocked me on the head from behind. . . .

All became red and then gradually black—he felt himself falling—he lost consciousness.

Slowly memory returned to his brain. It attached itself to what he had last thought. There were two of them, he told himself. One I don't know, but the other who hit me on the head from behind must have been Bäumer. . . . It's not so bad to be killed like this—all my life I've gone in fear of it, and now it's not so terrible at all. . . .

Not for a moment did he believe that he would escape with his life. That villain must have broken his skull. So the fellow had got him in the end! But it was not very painful. The warmth running over his skull was troublesome, though. That was the blood welling out. He was getting giddy from it. Had the fellows gone?

He listened, he heard nothing. No step, no rustling; not a twig snapped.

Painfully he moved his head to and fro; he could not move his eyes properly; he must move the whole head. He saw no one. Thought I was already done for; but it hasn't been as quick as all that.

In truth he was lying there comfortably, old Forester Kniebusch; he had lain worse than that in his life. His limbs were getting heavy, but his head and something in his breast were getting lighter and lighter. For a moment he considered whether he should do something, and what he should do. . . . But why do anything?

The cold was increasing, that icy cold which was creeping up from the extremities of his limbs, but one could endure that; sooner or later in the morning people would come to the clamps; he was close by, he had only to shout. Then they would find him, carry him home, put him to bed—he had always wished to die in his bed.

The old forester, whose vital strength was slowly trickling from the terrible skull wound, pushed an arm under his head. It isn't so bad at all, he thought again. If only one knew how little unpleasant even the most unpleasant thing is, one wouldn't need to have any fears in life.

He tried to reckon out when the laborers would be likely to come. Potatoes had to be fetched for the pigs. At the most it would be another two hours; he would remain alive as long as that, surely, so that he could die in his own bed. . . .

But Pagel! he thought suddenly. My friend Pagel will be waiting for me. Every morning I've been there early and informed him of the holes—and today I don't turn up! He'll miss me!

Kniebusch shut his eyes. It was pleasant to feel that someone would miss him. He could hear that youthful, invariably friendly voice asking the Backs: "Where's our old Kniebusch got to this morning? Why, he hasn't made his report yet, Amanda!"

He smiled.

But an agonized feeling began to stir in him; he hadn't yet made his report! Today he really had something to report, and today he failed to appear. They would soon find him, though. But this didn't comfort him. I'm getting weaker all the time, he thought. I'm getting colder and colder. Perhaps I won't be able to call out later on—they will find me too late.

He tried to move his head forward. He wanted to estimate, from the quantity of blood he had lost, the quantity of life which still remained to him; but he could not, it was too difficult.

A terrible struggle starts in him: the dying man wants only to lie quietly, to feel himself gently flowing away, to be at peace. . . . And something else tells him that he must get up and make his report. Bäumer is back again and someone else, a stranger—two dangerous people, two ravenous wolves.

I can't get there! he groaned. I can't walk even!

If you can't walk, you must crawl, spoke the pitiless voice.

I never had any peace in my life; let me at least die in peace.

You will have peace in the grave—now make your report! said the voice without pity.

And the worn-out old man, the coward, the babbler, rolled over on his belly and drew up his icy limbs. Will-power, the ruthless will-power of duty—it was this which had always strengthened him against his entire nature. Now once more it drove him to a last extreme effort; old Kniebusch crawled on all fours across the forest and, coming to a sack, he took hold of it and dragged it with him, in the obscure feeling that he had snatched up some evidence.

He crawled up to the potato clamps and hopefully raised his head. No one was to be seen. "Oh, my God, my God! Will no one help me?" he wailed.

But he crawled onward. He crawled down from the clamps onto the path, and when he was alongside the park he saw in the hedge a hole and squeezed through this, to shorten his journey. . . . He did everything correctly, exactly, as if his brain were still functioning. But his brain was only in its twilight. Everything his mind and body could give was made possible by the massive will that forced him constantly to crawl forward. He no longer thought of Pagel, of Bäumer, of icy coldness, of wounds. He had forgotten the sack which, in the midst of torments, he went on dragging with him—he thought of nothing but that he must crawl on. Crawl—till he collapsed.

And collapse he did, in that moment when Pagel shouted to him: "My God, Kniebusch, dear Kniebusch—what have they done to you?" At that moment, hearing that familiar voice, his will gave way, his body failed him, and he stopped crawling forward. Together Amanda and he dragged the old man indoors. But they couldn't get the sack out of his hand; it was as if his fingers had grown into the material.

III

It would certainly have been the bitterest irony in the world had Forester Kniebusch died in a strange bed without being able to make that report for which he had suffered so heroically. But Death was not so severe. Once again he was to open his eyes and see close above him his friend's pale face and hear his kind voice. "Old Kniebusch, what a fright you gave us! Just wait a bit, the doctor will be here in a moment. He'll patch you up again. Are you in bad pain?"

The forester moved his head angrily. Doctors and pain didn't concern him any longer. He had been plunged into the darkness and only returned from it because he had something to settle, his report. And in disjointed words he whispered into Pagel's ear, and Pagel nodded again and again and said: "Good, Kniebusch, good. Quietly—don't tax yourself, I can understand everything."

The forester went on whispering. Every word hurt him, but every word was necessary. When, however, he at last finished, he looked at Pagel with such imploring eyes that even the most callous would have understood the urgent question in that glance. And Pagel was by no means the most callous. "Good man," he said, and gently pressed the forester's hand. "Very good man." Like one set free, the old forester smiled as he perhaps had never smiled in his life before. And then he seemed to sleep.

Holding the limp hand Pagel reflected on what he had heard; it was little enough, for the forester hadn't seen one of the men, and the other he hadn't known.

Sitting there dolefully, however, Pagel's eye now alighted on the dirty old potato sack at his feet. For the dying man had let it fall as he groped for his friend's hand. With his foot Pagel pushed at the sack and turned it about, and it looked to him as if, under all the dirt, there were black characters forming a name. Of course forage sacks were marked with their owner's name.

He bent down and with his free hand laid the sack across his knee and wiped away the dirt—not letting go of the dying man's hand. Letter by letter the writing became legible—legible with difficulty, but legible: Kowalewski.

Pagel stared dejectedly at this name. What could the old and honest overseer have to do with potato thieves and murderers? Undoubtedly it was a stolen sack.

In this moment the office door opened, and Amanda Backs came in. She had been telephoning; the doctor would come in a quarter of an hour and the police perhaps in half an hour. . . .

In reply Pagel lifted the sack, showed her the name and said: "They all come too late. He didn't see his murderer and didn't recognize the one who held him. And the name on this sack doesn't help us further. . . ."

Amanda turned very pale, looked at him with large terrified eyes and began to tremble.

"What's the matter?" he asked. "Do you understand what the name Kowalewski is doing on the sack?"

Amanda had laid her hand on her breast and was looking from the dying man to the sack, and from the sack to Pagel.

"Speak, Amanda! What do you know about it?"

"I know," she whispered, "that the runaway convict is living in Sophie Kowalewski's room."

With a white face Pagel regarded the trembling girl.

"Yes, and I know that Liebschner has been out stealing, together with Bäumer, and so one of the pair held the forester fast, while the other hit—"

"Amanda!" he shouted.

"Yes, Amanda!" she repeated and burst into tears. "And now I've become an accomplice of murderers just when I thought I was quite out of the dirt."

He listened to her sobbing. "You ought certainly to have told me about that, Amanda."

"Yes," she cried in despair, "I know that now. But at the time she gave me so many good words. And I couldn't help thinking of my Hans, of Bailiff Meier, and what I should have felt like if someone had betrayed him to the police. I already helped him away from here as soon as he shot at me! You can't let down a friend. And she told me, Sophie told me, her Liebschner is good to her and they were going away at once as soon as the fare money had been saved, that means stolen. He's good to her! That's why it was; because she told me he was good to her, that's why I held my tongue."

"But you ought to have felt, Amanda," insisted Pagel, "that it was wrong to keep silent."

"Yes, you may say that now!" she cried wildly. "Sometimes it almost broke my heart, especially when Sophie acted so despicably against you. But how do I know what's right and not right in the world? You've always said: 'Amanda, that won't do!' and 'Amanda, please don't do that!' And when you turned up your nose without a word, that was even worse. And you've always done that whenever I start to talk about someone else. In the end I thought: Hold your tongue, he's the only person who is decent to you, and he'll think that treachery is treachery, and even a convict shouldn't be betrayed. I didn't know where I was any longer."

"I'm very sorry, Amanda. You are right, I ought to have talked with you differently. And before everything, I ought not to have stopped you from talking. I am certainly the more guilty. But I must go at once! Sit down and hold his hand. He won't notice the difference, and when he wakes up, tell him that I hadn't wanted to wait for the police. Perhaps I'll catch the fellows. . . ."

And Pagel ran out into the farmyard and drummed together a few sturdy fellows. Softly they entered the Kowalewski home and in the upper story they seized Bäumer and Liebschner, at that moment engaged in packing their things. They had believed there was no need to hurry, for they were certain they had killed the forester and that he would not be found so quickly. Thus they were caught, overcome, manacled and handed over to the police. And thus they were prosecuted and sentenced to life imprisonment, because they couldn't avoid the charge of murder.

Pagel, however, left to others the arrest of the still-unsuspecting Sophie and went back to the forester. But in his room there was only the doctor—the forester had already departed.

IV

It was not, however, on the evening of this day, it was not till the evening of the next, that Wolfgang learned beyond any doubt who the Prackwitzes were and who the Pagels, and what was actually the part he was playing on this estate and the value of all he had done there. Not only must mankind ponder its good deeds a while, before resolving for them; its basenesses great and small also require time. Frau Eva had required a good thirty-six hours.

When the large car stopped in front of the staff-house it was dark. But of course it was dark; mankind sins by night rather than by day, seeming to think that it need not be ashamed of an unseen iniquity. The car stopped—but neither Frau Eva nor the Rittmeister got out.

They waited.

"Sound your horn again, Oskar!" she cried, vexed. "He must have heard us stop. Why doesn't he come out?"

Pagel had heard the car stop; he had heard the horn, too. But he did not go out. He was depressed and angry. He had sacrificed his relaxed happiness. Life no longer tasted good to him. It was as if he were grinding dust and ashes between his teeth. Yesterday and today he had knocked ten times at the Villa, twenty times had asked for Frau Eva on the telephone; he wanted to know what was to be done about the forester's funeral, and what help given the destitute widow. But madam was not to be spoken with. Perhaps she resented his having taken away Sophie so inconsiderately, which meant that once again Black Minna was working in the Villa, that dirty wench with her heap of illegitimate brats.

Oh, let them all go to the devil. Probably Frau Eva was not so bad. Earlier he had found her really nice. Maternal, sensible, also friendly, and thoughtful towards others—as long as she was all right herself. But no doubt wealth had spoiled her; she had always had what she wanted, and now that things went badly for her she thought only of herself. She blamed the whole world, and let the world know it.

Let them hoot away, he wasn't going out. In reality she was excellently suited to the Rittmeister. Both were made of the same stuff. Before the war they were on top, they were of the nobility, they had money. Let the so-called people see for themselves how they got on! . . . Undoubtedly a damned similarity with her husband. Naturally she didn't behave so badly; she was a woman, after all, and could be amiable if she wanted something; feminine charm, a leg stretched out, a melodious voice—smiles. But in the end it came to the same thing. If she wanted a motor car she bought it, and the young bailiff, without money for wages, must do the best he could to get fifty families enough to eat.

"You will arrange that for me, won't you? I don't need to worry myself about it, then? You are so capable!" Yes, they wouldn't be able to arrange it themselves, didn't even want to—they had people to see to such things. Between Wolfgang Pagel and Black Minna there was (for madam) not such a great difference, by a long way, as between herself and him—the disparity was simply enormous!

I am unjust, he thought, and the car hooted again peremptorily. Unjust. She genuinely has a heavy affliction—and if wealth makes people selfish, if happiness makes them selfish, affliction does it so much the more. Ought I not to go out, after all?

It was no longer necessary to decide this. The chauffeur Oskar entered the office. "Herr Pagel, would you come outside to madam?"

Pagel stood up and looked thoughtfully at him. "All right."

Oskar, made by the grace of Frau von Prackwitz chauffeur to the gentility, whispered: "Be careful, Herr Pagel, she's going to slip off! But don't give me away." And went. Pagel smiled. There you were! Oskar, who only four weeks ago had beamed on Frau Eva as on a blessed angel, no longer appreciated the sweet cake of daily intercourse with gentlepeople. He felt that he was a hundred times closer to this almost unknown Herr Pagel than to the lady he saw daily.

"Good evening, madam," said Pagel. "I was wanting to speak to you."

"We've been hooting in front of your window for five minutes!" she cried, invisible in the dark car. "Were you sleeping? Do you go to sleep at eight in the evening?"

"Yesterday," replied Pagel unmoved, "I tried twenty times to get in touch with you, madam. Arrangements must be made about the forester. . . ."

"My husband is quite ill! Both of us are ill from all these terrible excitements. I must beg you not to speak to me about these things now." Her voice became gentler. "You have always been so considerate otherwise, Herr Pagel."

Unbribed, he said: "I should have been glad of fifteen minutes' talk, madam." He was looking at the back of the car, enormously swollen. Oskar had spoken the truth. That monstrous heap of trunks was clear evidence of flight.

"I haven't possibly got time this evening!"

"And when will you have time?" he inquired inexorably.

"I can't tell you any exact hour." The reply was evasive. "You know how irregularly I come and go. Oh, God, Herr Pagel, are you going to make difficulties for me, too? Do be independent. You have full authority!"

Of course he had full authority. He was authorized to settle everything independently (in the way madam wished) and to be landed because of it in a mess (in the way the Geheimrat wished). But he said nothing. One must not attribute too much baseness to a person. In the last resort she wouldn't leave him in the lurch. Or would she?

"Herr Pagel," said Frau von Prackwitz, "for a week you have given me no money. I need money."

"There's hardly anything in the cashbox," he replied, understanding now why the car had stopped at the staff-house.

"Then give me a check," she cried impatiently. "Oh, God, what a fuss! I must have money."

"Neither in the bank nor elsewhere have we a balance," he protested. "I'm sorry, I can't make out a check."

"But I must have money. You can't leave me without! I don't know how you can think so!"

"I'll see about selling something tomorrow. . . . Then I can give you some money, if it needn't be a lot, madam."

"But it must be a lot! And this evening!" she cried angrily.

Pagel was silent for a time. Then he asked casually: "Are you leaving?"

"No! Who told you such a thing? Are you having me spied on? I won't have that!"

"The trunks," explained Pagel, pointing to the rear of the car.

There was a long silence. Then Frau Eva spoke in a very different tone. "Dear Herr Pagel, how can you find me some money?"

"May I have a talk with you for ten minutes?"

"But there's nothing to talk about. We shall be back tomorrow, or the day after at the latest. I know, Herr Pagel, give me a postdated check. Start selling tomorrow and the day after, pay the money into the bank, and I won't present the check till the end of the week."

"Madam was going to be back at the latest the day after tomorrow. I am not an employee here; there was no agreement between me and the Rittmeister when I came—no period of notice. I therefore will also leave Neulohe tomorrow."

"Achim! Wait here. Oskar, turn out the headlights. Herr Pagel, help me out of the car." She led the way to the office. She looked magnificent in her rage. "So you want to desert, Herr Pagel, you want to leave me in the lurch—after all we've gone through together?"

"We haven't gone through anything together, madam," said Pagel somberly. "When you needed me you sent for me. And when you didn't need me you forgot me on the spot. You have never cared an atom whether I was sad or happy."

"I have been pleased about you so often, Herr Pagel. In all my worries and troubles I always thought: There's someone here on whom you can absolutely depend. Decent, honest . . ."

"Thank you, madam," he said with a slight bow. "But when a Sophie Kowalewski came and told you the decent, honest fellow was having affairs with women, then you immediately credited him with them."

"Why are you so nasty to me, Herr Pagel? What have I done? All right, I'm a woman and no doubt I'm like most women—I listen to gossip. But I also admit it when I'm wrong. Very well, then, I beg your pardon for that."

"I don't want you to beg my pardon, madam," he called out in despair. "Don't humiliate yourself so. I'm not asking to see you on your knees before me! It's not that at all. But now, for the first time since we know one another, you are thinking about me, about my feelings, and would like to see me in a good humor. . . . And why? Because you need me, because only I can find the money which you require for your flight from Neulohe."

"And don't you call that humiliation? You don't call that forcing someone on their knees? Yes, Herr Pagel, we are running away. . . . We hate Neulohe. Neulohe has brought us only bad luck. . . . And if I'm not to come to grief like my husband, I must go away this moment! Every second I tremble at the thought, What's coming next? If I hear someone shouting, my knees give way at once. What's the matter now? I think. . . . I must go away! And you must give me the money for that, Herr Pagel. You can't let me die here!"

"I must go, too," he said. "Life doesn't please me anymore. I'm at the end, too. Let me go tomorrow, madam. Why should I stay?"

She wasn't listening. Only one thought occupied her. "I must have money," she cried despairingly.

"There's none in the cashbox. And I won't make out any uncovered checks, it's too—dangerous. Madam, I can't get you the money for any lengthy stay at a distance from Neulohe, not in two days. Money has become scarce since the note presses stopped. Even if I stayed a few days more, however, I still couldn't satisfy your wishes."

"But I *must* have money," she repeated with unshakable obstinacy. "My God, money was always found when we really needed it! Think hard, Herr Pagel, you must manage it somehow. . . . I can't let myself be ruined just because a few marks aren't there!"

Many are ruined because a few marks are lacking, he thought. There was no point in saying such a thing, because it naturally didn't apply to her. "Madam, you have a rich brother in Birnbaum—he'll be sure to help you."

"I'm to ask my brother for money?" she cried angrily. "I'm to humiliate myself before my brother? Never!"

He took a quick, furious step forward. "But you can humiliate yourself before me, eh? A queen shows herself naked before the slaves, doesn't she? A slave is not human, what?"

She fell back before his indignation, deathly pale, trembling.

"There!" cried Pagel and pointed. "There in my bed in the next room the forester Kniebusch died yesterday morning, in your service, madam. You must have known him since your childhood; since you could speak the man ran about for you and your few marks, was frightened, worked himself to death—did you ever bother yourself at all about his sufferings, how he died, how he labored? Even by one word? Neulohe has become hell for you? Have you ever thought what sort of a hell it was for that old man? And he—he couldn't clear off—and neither did he! Almost crawling on his stomach, he did his duty right up to the last moment. . . ."

She stood against the wall, trembling.

"Desert? Be a coward?" His speech was more and more violent; he was increasingly aware that his nerves were giving way. Without wishing to, he yet had to speak, speak at last, once and for all. "What do you know of cowardice and courage? I also thought I knew something about it once. I used to think that courage meant standing up straight when a shell exploded and taking your share of the shrapnel. Now I know that's mere stupidity and bravado; Courage means keeping going when something becomes completely unbearable. Courage? That old coward who died in there had courage." He threw a sharp glance at her. "But it must be something which is worth it. There must be a flag there for which it is worth fighting. Where is your flag, madam? Why, you are the first to flee."

There was a long and gloomy silence. Then he walked slowly to his desk, sat down and propped his head in his hand. Everything which had accumulated these last weeks had been poured out—and what now?

Gently she laid her hand on his shoulder. "Herr Pagel," she said in a low voice, "Herr Pagel—what you said is certainly true. I'm selfish and cowardly and thoughtless. . . . I don't know if I have become so only recently, but you are right, I am like that. But you yourself are not. You are different, Herr Pagel, aren't you?"

She waited a long time, but he did not reply.

"Be once again what you were formerly; young, trusting, self-sacrificing. Not for me, Herr Pagel; I have indeed no flag for you, but I have the hope that you will remain here in Neulohe till my parents come back. I should like to ask you to move over into the Villa. Herr Pagel—I still have the hope that Violet will knock on the door there some day. . . . Don't you go away, too! Don't let the farm be utterly friendless if she comes. . . ."

Again a long silence, but of another sort—expectant. She took her hand from his shoulder and made a step to the door. He said nothing. She had her hand on the latch. . . . "When will your father come?" he asked.

"I have a letter to him in the car. I will post it today in Frankfurt. I take it my father will come immediately, once he learns that we've gone away. That's to say, in about three or four days."

"I will stay till then."

"Thank you. I knew you would." But she did not go; she waited.

He made it easy for her. He was tired of all beating about the bush. "And then there's the business of your money," he said abruptly. "I have about a hundred *Rentenmarks* in cash here, which I will give you. In the next few days I will sell everything which is saleable—do you know where you will be staying?"

"In Berlin."

"Where?"

"At first in a hotel."

"Studmann's hotel. Hotel Regina," he said. "I will telegraph you the money every day to the hotel. . . . What was the amount you had in mind?"

"Oh, a few thousand marks—just so that we can make a start."

He did not wince. "You know, of course, that I mustn't sell anything of the stock. That's forbidden. Since it's not your property I should render myself open to prosecution. You must now, madam, sign a declaration which will cover me as regards your father. You must testify that all illegal sales have arisen through your instigation. You must further testify that you know about the irregular, defective and also often incorrect way in which the books have been kept; in short, that all my proceedings have your full approval."

"You are very hard on me, Herr Pagel," she said. "Do you mistrust me so much?"

"It's possible that your father may say I've embezzled money, that I've engaged in underhand dealings. My God!" he said impatiently, "why a lot of talk? Yes, I mistrust you! I have lost all trust."

"Then write out the declaration," she said.

While he was typing she walked to and fro. Suddenly an idea struck her, she turned briskly to him, about to say something. . . . But when she saw his gloomy, unfriendly face she sat down at the desk and wrote, too. Her face was smiling. She had thought of something; she was no egoist, there he was wrong— she was thinking of him, doing him a kindness. . . .

That declaration which a moment ago she had found so shaming she now merely glanced through and carelessly signed. Then she took up her note. . . . "Here, Herr Pagel, I have something for you. See, I forget nothing. As soon as I can I'll settle it. Au revoir, Herr Pagel, and once again many thanks."

She went.

He stood in the middle of the office, staring at the scrawl in his hand. He felt that never in his life had he looked such an ass. He held an acknowledgment in which Frau Eva von Prackwitz, also in the name of her husband, testified to the receipt of a loan of 2,000 gold marks, in full letters, two thousand gold marks, from Wolfgang Pagel. Pagel appeared ludicrous to himself. He screwed up the note furiously. But then he thought again. He smoothed it out carefully and laid it together with the Declaration of Honor in his briefcase. Valuable travel momento! he grinned. Now he was almost pleased.

V

What friendship and respect young Pagel had gained in the four months of his Neulohe labors were utterly lost in the last four days. For a long time afterwards people told one another that little Black Meier had been bad enough, but such an unfeeling hypocrite as Pagel!—no, they certainly wouldn't see something like that again, for the lad was ashamed of nothing. He stole publicly—in broad daylight!

"I'm not going to lose my temper," he said to Amanda Backs the second evening, "but I'd like to explode sometimes. That old idiot Kowalewski actually has the cheek to say, when I'm selling the five hogs to the butcher: 'You oughtn't to be doing that, Herr Pagel. Supposing the police heard!' That's fine, from him!"

"Yes, lose your temper, lose your temper thoroughly," she said. "Why have you always been so nice and friendly to all of them? That's your thanks! They asked me in the village today what it's like sleeping in madam's bed, and if I won't soon be wearing her clothes, too."

"It's a trusting world!" he complained bitterly. "Everything bad is believed of one on the spot. They think I'm selling the livestock for my own account behind the owner's back, and that our moving over into the Villa is done on the quiet, an impudence. Doesn't it occur to any of the blackguards that I may by chance be acting on instructions? I can't stick my authorization under the nose of every washerwoman, surely?"

"They don't want to know anything different," said Amanda triumphantly. "If you're doing just what madam told you to, then that's merely a matter of course and boring. But if in broad daylight you're making away with half the estate, then that's something grand—something to talk about."

"Amanda!" said Pagel prophetically, "I've a damned rotten feeling. If the old Geheimrat comes and sees what I've been doing, and his wife hears what the women are saying, I don't know whether the scrawl in my pocket will be very effective. I'm afraid I shall leave Neulohe amid thunder and lightning."

"Just let things take their course, Herr Pagel. Up till now it's always been you who had the most trouble—and why should it be any different toward the end?"

"You're right. She rang up twice today from Berlin to ask where the money was—she says she needs a lot more. I think she wants to buy a business, although I find it hard to imagine the business in which Frau von Prackwitz stands behind the counter. I'm very much afraid I shall have to make up my mind to dispose of the threshing machine. And what the old gentleman will say then..."

But someone else said something first. Next day the local gendarme came stumbling into the threshing-machine negotiations. He was so awkwardly polite and so falsely amiable that it was not hard for Pagel to be aware that something was up. And when at last the gendarme came out with it, saying he would be glad to have the address of the owners, Pagel flatly refused it. "Herr and Frau von Prackwitz do not wish to be disturbed. I am their representative; anything you have to tell them you can please tell me."

Which was what the gendarme did not wish to do. Very annoyed, he retired, and Pagel went back to his negotiations. The dealer from the local town would not offer the tenth part of the threshing machine's real value, first because money was unbelievably scarce these days, and secondly because word was going round that a crazy rascal was selling Neulohe, lock, stock and barrel, for a song.

"A moment, you!" said a very indignant voice. "You want to sell the threshing mill?"

"Do you want to buy it?" Pagel looked with interest at the newcomer, a gentleman in reed linen and leggings. He could more or less guess who it was. In the distance stood a racing car which had once been much discussed.

"Allow me," cried the gentleman. "I am the son of Geheimrat von Teschow!"

"Then you must be the brother of Frau von Prackwitz." Pagel turned again to the dealer. "Well, say a reasonable word, Herr Bertram, or the mill stays here."

"Indeed it will stay here," cried the heir angrily.

"If you say a word, Herr Bertram, I'll never do any more business with you."

Intimidated, the dealer looked from one to the other. Pagel smiled. And so the confused Herr Bertram murmured the illuminating sentence: "Oh, if it's like that," and disappeared.

"Eight hundred *Rentenmarks* chucked away!" said Pagel regretfully. "I would have got him up to eight hundred. Your sister will regret that very much."

"Like hell she will!" shouted the other. "Eight hundred *Rentenmarks* for an almost new Schütte-Lanz, which, as it stands here, is worth its six thousand? Why, you're . . ."

"I hope it's not me you're shouting at, Herr von Teschow," said Pagel amiably. "Otherwise I shan't give you those explanations for which you have undoubtedly come, but will have to turn you off the farm."

"Turn me off my father's farm?" There was something in Pagel's eye which made the other lower his voice, however. "Well then, where can we speak about the mill? But I'm not to be made a fool of by words, Herr . . ."

Pagel led the way to the office.

"Well, if it's like that!" said young Herr von Teschow, and examined once more the two documents, authorization and declaration. "Then you are fully covered, and I beg your pardon. But my sister and my brother-in-law must be mad. My father will never forgive them the damage they have done here. Why does she need so much money? A few hundred marks would be enough for the first weeks, and by then she'll be reconciled to my father somehow or other. It's not as if he would leave her without a penny."

"If I understood your sister rightly on the telephone yesterday," said Pagel cautiously, "she seems to have the intention of purchasing a business."

"A business! Why, does Eva want to be a shopgirl?"

"I don't know. But at all events she seems to want to have a small capital to begin with. Of course, it's clear to me that what I am doing now for Frau von Prackwitz is legally not permissible, but it's her firm determination not to return to Neulohe. She's, so to speak, foregoing her share of the inheritance, and for that reason I thought one could answer for this irregularity."

"You mean," burst out the younger Herr von Teschow, "she will renounce Neulohe?"

"I think so. After her recent experiences . . ."

"I understand. Very sad indeed. Any news of my niece Violet?"

"No."

"Yes, yes," said the other lost in thought. "Yes, yes." He stood up. "Well, once again I beg your pardon. A false alarm—someone whispered something in my ear. Between us, I think as you do; see if you can't still squeeze out a tidy sum of money for my sister. It won't make any difference now; my father'll be in a rage in any case, whether the threshing machine's there or not. Eight hundred *Rentenmarks*. I could take it for that," he added thoughtfully. "But no, I can't, unfortunately. You'll understand, of course, Herr Pagel, that I can't take my sister's part in front of my father—her behavior is, in any case, incorrect."

With almost unconcealed disgust Pagel looked into the other's eyes. He thought he had never heard anything so hateful as the question: "Any news of my niece Violet?"—young Herr von Tesechow having understood how much there might be to inherit now. But this disgust was unnoticed. The younger von Teschow was much too busy to worry about Pagel. "So see then that you squeeze something more out," he said absently. "I think my father won't come for three or four days."

"Good."

"Well, I don't know whether it will be exactly good for you. But, anyway, you are covered against the worst. You don't know my father when he's really upset."

"Well, I shall get to know him then," said Pagel, smiling. "I will await him in calm."

But he was wrong there. He had already gone when the Geheimrat came.

"Hopped it, the cunning rogue!" laughed the people.

VI

It began with the telephone ringing in the office.

At that moment Wolfgang Pagel was filling out a telegraphic money order to Frau Eva, and upstairs Amanda Backs was wrapping herself up to cycle through winter winds and autumn rains to the local town. For the money order had to be given in at the post office there, and the pair knew no one else to whom they cared to entrust a good two thousand *Rentenmarks.* . . .

The telephone rings variously, sometimes loud, sometimes low, now indifferent, then peremptory. . . . And accordingly we have our presentiments what kind of conversation will follow.

That's something, thought Pagel, lifting the receiver.

A rather rough voice demanded to speak to Frau von Prackwitz.

"That is not possible. Frau von Prackwitz is away."

"Oh." The rough voice seemed somewhat disappointed. "She would be away now, of course! When is she coming back?"

"I couldn't say. Not this week. Can I deliver a message for her? This is the bailiff at Neulohe speaking."

"So you're still there?"

"I don't know what you want," cried Pagel a little annoyed. "Who are you?"

"Then stay on there!" said the rough voice.

"Wait!" yelled Pagel. "I want to know who you are."

But the other had rung off.

"Listen, Amanda." And Pagel related what had just happened.

"That's someone who may have wanted to play a joke on you."

"No, no," he said in an absent-minded way. "I think . . ."

"Well, what do you think?"

"I think it might be in connection with Fräulein Violet."

"But how? Why should anyone behave so stupidly on the telephone about her? Well, give me the two thousand marks; you've finished the money order, I suppose? I must be off. I don't want to have to pedal back in complete darkness in this weather."

"I'll be finished in a moment."

The telephone rang. It rang loud and long, monotonously.

"A dealer," said Pagel.

But it was from Berlin . . .

"Frau Eva," he whispered to Amanda.

It was a dealer, however, a great businessman. "Are you there, young man?" asked the familiar screech.

"Oh yes, Herr Geheimrat," said Pagel, grinning and throwing Amanda an amused glance. "My name's Pagel, by the way."

"Oh, that's all right then. . . . You see, I've quite forgotten it again. Impolite, but what can we do? Now give me your full attention, young man. . . ."

"Pagel's my name."

"Of course, I know that by now!" The Geheimrat was a little irritated. "There's no need for me to learn it by heart on the telephone! Don't forget that this talk's costing one mark twenty. And my money, unfortunately. So give me your full attention. . . ."

"I'm giving it, Herr Geheimrat."

"I shall come by the ten o'clock train this evening. Send Hartig to the station with the two old bays. . . ."

Pagel wanted to say: "But they're sold."

Better not; he would soon find that out for himself.

"And send covers along, horse-covers—so that they are properly covered at the station. Hartig's only a fool—he's doubtless divided up all his brains among the numerous children." Pagel burst into a laugh. "There, you see, now you're laughing," said the Geheimrat, pleased. "Let's hope you'll laugh tomorrow, too, when I'm there. I'm bringing an auditor along. It's not a vote of censure on you, but since my good son-in-law's cleared off on the quiet, we've got to make some kind of stock-taking and transfer of funds and books. You understand that, don't you, young man?"

"I understand completely, Herr Geheimrat. My name is Pagel."

"Is everything in order, man?" asked the Geheimrat, suddenly anxious.

"Everything in order," said Pagel, grinning. "You will see for yourself, Herr Geheimrat."

"There you are! Yes, miss, I've had good news, I'll go on another three minutes. Well, and now look sharp, young man. Have two rooms heated, my bedroom and the little guest room. My wife will be staying here for the moment. She wants to know first whether the coast is clear again with you people in Neu-lohe." His voice was anxious again: "There's nothing more happened to you?"

"Oh, yes, all sorts of things, Herr Geheimrat."

"Well, don't tell me about them on the telephone, man; I shall hear soon enough tomorrow. Amanda, the fat girl with the rosy cheeks, y'know. . . . She can turn into a general servant for once. Yes, and let her heat my study. But not the dining room. We've got to economize; there's less and less money. Tell me, Herr Pagel, have you a little money or so in the cashbox?"

"Very little, Herr Geheimrat. To speak more exactly—nothing!"

"But what are you all thinking of, then? I suppose you've raked together a little rent? You can't just simply . . . Oh, well, we'll talk that over seriously tomorrow. Hey, and something else, Herr Pagel! The forester, old Kniebusch, is he still shamming sick in bed?"

"No, Herr Geheimrat. I thought that your daughter had written to you about that. The forester is dead, the forester is—"

"Stop!" shouted the furious Geheimrat. "Stop! I wish I hadn't had the other three minutes now. Nothing but bad news . . . Well, then, at ten—ten o'clock at the station. Good-by."

"And not an inquiry after his granddaughter!" said Pagel, hanging up the receiver. "Like son, like father—both wretches."

"Ah, well," said Amanda, "what do you expect? All he thinks about is getting his farm back again. But how am I to go to the post office now and get the rooms ready in the Manor?"

"Give me back the money," said Pagel, putting it in his pocketbook. "I have a kind of feeling that I shall be turned out tomorrow, and in that case I can, after all, hand it over to madam personally. Let us save the postage."

"Good," said Amanda. "I will get hold of a few women in the village. There will have to be something to eat there as well."

"Go to it then! I'll sit down for a little while with my books; it won't help, of course, I'll never get them in order, but I can try anyway to arrive at something like a balance in hand." Pagel's good temper had evaporated. When he remembered how the old Geheimrat became red with fury and gave no quarter, and how he shouted down every contradiction, and how he spluttered in one's face when in a rage . . . Curse it all, tomorrow wasn't going to be much of a day, with himself as the scapegoat. What was worse, he wasn't altogether sure of his nerves any longer; and he hated to lose self-control.

But to back out because of that?

Never!

In the meantime the news that the old gentleman was coming back that evening spread through the village like wildfire. . . . And twenty villagers, male and female, pretended to have some business, and passed by the Manor, and when they saw the old gentleman's room lit up they nodded their heads in satisfaction, and looked forward very happily to what would take place the next morning. They had all forgotten how warmly they had once greeted the young Pagel, how much they had liked him and called him "Little Junker," and how happy they had been to have gotten decent Pagel instead of the indecent Black Meier. They strolled by the office window also, and attempted to peep in, and the most curious thought out a request; never before had Pagel been so often and so senselessly disturbed.

And when the spies came out again, the others would ask: "Is he still there?" And on the reply: "He's sitting and writing," then they shook their heads and said: "Why, he is utterly shameless! Isn't he packing at least?" "Why should he pack?" the spies in turn inquired. "You can be certain he's got his stuff in safety, going to town as often as he's done the last few days!"

And they could not agree on what they actually ought to wish for now, whether Pagel should remain and be sent to prison after a gigantic row, or whether he should run away and leave the old gentleman to burst with rage. Both were good!

"You watch, he won't be here in the morning!" said some.

"Rubbish," declared the others. "He's so cunning, even the old gentleman won't get the better of him. He's the smartest one we've ever had on the farm."

"Of course. And that's why he won't be here in the morning."

Neither was he.

VII

At seven o'clock that evening Pagel closed his books for the last time, sighing: "It's no good at all!" He cast a glance round the office, at the safe, the clumsy pigeonholes, the law volumes, the local newspaper files. The typewriter was covered over. He'd written many letters to his mother on it—for Petra. I'll be fired tomorrow, he thought, downcast. Not a glorious end, actually—on the whole I liked the work. It would have been nicer to have had someone standing here tomorrow and saying: "Thank you, Herr Pagel, you did your job well." Instead of that the Geheimrat will be screaming for the police and justice.

He turned the light out, locked up, put the key in his pocket and went through the pitch-dark night over to the Villa. It was influenza weather. The doctor had told him that people were dying like flies, young and old. Undernourished too long, first the war, then this inflation. . . . Poor devils. Will it really be any better with the new money?

In the Villa Amanda had food ready and a thousand bits of gossip passed on to her by the women. "Just think, Herr Pagel, what they've imagined now! They say you were hand in glove with Sophie—as for the forester dying in your room, you only did that so that he shouldn't talk."

"Amanda," said Pagel bored, "all that is so stupid and dirty. Can't you think of something nice to tell me, say, from your youth?"

"Something nice? From my youth?" The amazed Amanda was on the point of setting to with a will and telling him what sort of a childhood she had had . . .

Then the doorbell rang—and over their supper the pair looked at one another like detected criminals.

"That can't be the Geheimrat yet?" she whispered.

"Rot! It's not yet half-past seven—it'll be something in the stables. Open the door." However, growing impatient, he followed her, and arrived just as the violently protesting Amanda was pushed aside by a man, thick-set, with a bowler hat on a head like a bull's—his glance, icy and unforgettable, met young Pagel's. "I have a word to say to you," said the fat detective. "But send this girl away. Hold your tongue, you clacker!" And Amanda was silent at once.

"Wait in the hall, Amanda," begged Pagel. "Come along, please." And, with beating heart, he led the way into the dining room.

The man shot a glance at the table laid for two. "Is that your girl outside?" he asked.

"No. That was Bailiff Meier's girl. But she is a decent girl."

"Another swine I'd like to catch," said the fat man, sitting down at the table. "Don't waste any time laying a place for me; I'm hungry and have to go on immediately. Tell me what's up here, why Frau Eva is away, why you are staying in the Villa—all. Clear, brief, and to the point." He ate as was his nature—ruthlessly, greedily. And Pagel talked.

"So she let you down in the end, your employer; I might have known it. Give me a cigar now. Did you notice that it was me who rang you up this afternoon?"

"I thought so. And?"

"And you yourself are now in a tight place, eh? Show me the two statements Frau von Prackwitz scribbled for you."

Pagel did so.

The fat man read them. "In order," he said. "You've only forgotten to safeguard yourself about selling after her departure as well."

"Damnation!"

"Doesn't matter. You can get that later."

"But the Geheimrat will be here this evening."

"You won't see the Geheimrat any more. This evening you will go to Berlin and get Frau von Prackwitz to set down in writing that she's in agreement with recent sales. This very night. Promise me that! You are flippant about such things!"

"You have news of Fräulein Violet?" cried Pagel.

"Sitting in the taxi below," said the fat man.

"What!" Pagel jumped up, trembling. "And you let me sit here and her wait there?"

"Stop!" The fat man laid his hand, like a shackle not to be thrown off, on Pagel's shoulder. "Stop, young man!" Pagel tried to free himself, furious. "What I just told you is not quite correct. She who is sitting in the car is not the Fräulein Violet you remember. Don't forget that for two whole months she has been systematically terrified out of her mind. Out of her mind! You understand? I don't know," he said darkly, "if I'm doing her mother a service in bringing her back. But I haven't gone out of my way to seek her—don't you think that. If you travel round as much as I do, however, you hear a lot; old colleagues still count me in with them, even if the bigwigs have lopped me off. I just ran into her. What am I to do with the girl? As it is, I don't even know whether you can take her to the mother; you must decide that for yourself. Only she mustn't remain here with the old people. Get her away in a car within an hour. . . . Any place which is quiet and safe. Why let yourself be snapped at here by that old clodhopper? Get away!"

"Yes," said Pagel thoughtfully.

"Take that fat wench in the hall, if only to have a woman's help during the journey and not give people something else to say about you."

"Good."

"Don't speak kindly or strictly to the girl. Say only what is essential. 'Sit down. Eat. Go to sleep.' She does everything like a lamb. Not a trace of her own will. And don't call her Violet—otherwise she'll be frightened. He never called her anything but whore."

"And he?" asked Pagel in a low voice.

"He? Who? Who do you mean?" said the fat man and clapped Pagel on the shoulder so that he swayed. "That's all," said he more calmly. "Pack your things; you can go in the taxi outside. I will come as far as Frankfurt. And one other thing, young man; have you money?"

"Yes." It was some time since Pagel had admitted that willingly.

"My expenses have been eighty-two marks. Give me them back now. . . . Thanks. I won't give you a receipt; I haven't a name which I care to sign any longer. But if the mother asks, say I had to dress her out—she was pretty tattered—and then a little money for fares and traveling expenses. And now off with you! Hurry up that fat girl—in half an hour I shall stop with the taxi between here and the wood. We don't want people to notice."

"But can't I see Fräulein Violet now?"

"Young fellow, don't be in such a hurry. That won't be a very cheerful meeting. It'll come soon enough. March! I give you half an hour."

And he went.

VIII

Of the thirty minutes granted Pagel, eight were lost in letting Amanda Backs know what had happened and in convincing her that for Violet's sake she would have to abandon her poultry to a completely uncertain future. Going to the staff-house took another five minutes. And since the same time must be allowed to get to the car, only twelve minutes remained for the packing. Thus there could only be two suitcases, one for Amanda, one for himself. Wolfgang Pagel, who had arrived in Neulohe with a monster of a trunk, went away with almost nothing. Should he leave behind a few explanatory lines for the Geheimrat? He very much disliked to think that next morning he would be torn to pieces by every tongue as an unfaithful employee and miserable coward. He consulted Amanda.

"Write? Why do you want to write to him? He won't believe a word when he sees the mess here. No, you leave that to madam to settle later. . . . But, Herr Pagel," she said tearfully, "for you to ask me to leave my best things lying around, and then some wench like Black Minna comes and turns everything over and very likely puts my clean linen on her filthy body . . ."

"Oh, don't worry yourself about your things, Amanda," said Pagel abstractedly. "One can always buy some more."

"Oh!" Amanda was indignant. "Perhaps you can go on buying new clothes, but not me! And how pleased one is to have an extra pair of silk stockings in the cupboard for special occasions, you have absolutely no idea! And let me tell you that if the old grumbler doesn't pay to have my things sent on at once, then I shall come here myself and tell him off."

"Amanda, only three minutes more!"

"Oh, only three minutes more! And you tell me that so casually! What about my wages? Yes, Herr Pagel, you've thought of everyone, but these last months you've completely forgotten that I too would like to get something for my work. We don't suffer from the same disease, however, Herr Pagel. If you're silly in money matters there's no need for me to be, and I want my wages for the last three months, with a receipt, all done properly—and you enter it in your cash book too! I like everything done fairly."

"Oh, dear, Amanda," sighed Pagel. But he did what she wanted.

Then for the last time he locked his office door and threw the key into the small tin letter box. And now they hurried away, suitcases in their hands, through the pitch-dark night, though in the village there were lights in almost all the houses—it must be pretty close to nine o'clock now. Neulohe was tensely awaiting the Geheimrat's arrival.

"Careful!" said Pagel and pulled Amanda into a dark corner.

Someone came down Dorfstrasse and they stood anxiously in the dark like real criminals, and only walked on after hearing a front door close behind the nocturnal wanderer. Then they passed by the Villa—dark standing in the darkness.

The taxi was standing with dimmed lights by the forest. "Eight minutes late!" growled the fat man. "If I'd had any idea what to do with her I should have cleared off! . . . You, girl, sit beside her, and let me tell you you'll get something on the snout if you start jabbering."

With this he opened the door. The moment had come—and nothing happened. Something dark stirred in the corner, but the fat man merely said: "Don't move. Go on sleeping." And the darkness did not stir again. "Off!" he shouted to the driver. "As fast as you can to Frankfurt. If we're there by eleven the young man will give you a tip."

The car shot into the night. The Villa glided by again. Then came the lights of the apartment blocks. Pagel strained to make out the office building, but it wasn't recognizable in the dark. Now came the castle. . . .

"That's a light," cried Amanda, excited. "Black Minna is waiting for me. How she's going to set things right alone with the Geheimrat"—"Schnabel," said the fat man, but it didn't sound nasty.

"You may smoke without worry, young man. It won't disturb her. I'm going to smoke, too."

Not far from the local town they came very near to having an accident, almost running into a coach. That, however, was because the coachman Hartig had given the horses the rein while he kept his head turned round to his employer, telling him something of the lively events which had taken place at home.

"That was the Geheimrat," explained Pagel as the raging abuse of coachman and master died away behind them.

"Well, well," said the fat man, pondering, "I wouldn't like to be that man's bed tonight!"

After the Kreisstadt they entered Staatsstrasse. After the bumps and stops and starts of the minor roads, the car went easily and ever faster over the smooth metal road—farther and farther. Troubled, Pagel thought what an odd crew they were—each completely for himself. He was wondering what he was to do with the girl, that night. . . .

The fat man spoke. "You will hardly get to Berlin before two. Have you decided where you will take her? To the mother?"

The dark form in the corner did not stir.

"I don't know," Pagel whispered. "The mother's in a hotel. Ought I to go there in the middle of the night with a—an invalid? Or to my mother? It will be upsetting enough for her as it is, my blowing in without warning."

The fat man said nothing.

"I also thought of a sanatorium. I have an old acquaintance who is employed in one. But tonight I should never get so far."

"Sanatoriums cost a lot of money. And money's scarce with you people."

"Well, where shall I take her?"

"To madam," said Amanda. "To her mother."

"Yes," said the fat man. "What you said about hotels and midnight is complete nonsense. She's the mother after all. And even if she is clapped out and has acted like a slattern, she is a mother, and now she won't be a slattern."

"Good," said Pagel. But he began to think once more what answers he should give to all Frau von Prackwitz's questions, because he knew absolutely nothing, and the fat man would certainly not give him any more information.

The detective tapped on the glass in front, on which the street lamps of Frankfurt shone. "I'm getting out here," he said. "Listen, driver. The young man here will pay all the fare. You get eighty pfennigs a kilometer—a lot, young man, but that includes the return empty. When we started your meter was at 43,750. Make a note of that, lad."

"All correct," said the driver. "And you will have enough money, sir? It'll come to over three hundred marks."

"Got enough," said Pagel.

"Then it's all right," said the driver. "I was a bit leery, though."

"Get her a cup of coffee here in Frankfurt and something to eat, but not in an inn. Fetch it out to her in the car. Good night." And with this the fat man turned away. . . .

Strangely excited, Pagel shouted after him. The other made a sign with his hand, and turned a corner—never to be seen again.

"Driver," said Pagel, "once we're more or less through the town, stop at some little public-house. We want to eat something."

It was now lighter in the taxi but the dark figure, its face pressed in the cushions, did not stir.

"Fräulein—Fräulein Violet, would you like to eat something?" said Pagel, oppressed. He had forgotten about it—no, he hadn't forgotten about it, but he hadn't wanted to talk to her as one talks to a stupid child or a simple dog.

She trembled in her corner. Did she understand? Or did she not want to understand? Or could she not?

The trembling increased, a moan of grief was heard, nothing articulate— as a bird in the night sometimes laments alone.

Amanda made a movement. Warningly Pagel laid his hand on hers and endeavored to strike the fat man's cold passionless tones. "Keep quiet now. Sleep. . . ."

Later they stopped.

Amanda went inside and brought out what was necessary. "Eat—drink now," said Pagel.

The taxi drove on again. "Go to sleep now."

They drove a long way. It was dark and quiet. Was not Pagel also a son who had been lost and was now going home? She was also going home! Stranger— estranged, children don't know their parents anymore. Is that you? asks a mother. Oh, life, life! We can't hang on to it, whether we want to or not. We glide through it, we rush—restless, always changing. Of yesterday we ask, is that you? I no longer know you! Stop, oh, stop! Now, go on!

The car drives on. Sometimes the walls of the sleeping villages magnify the noise of the engine, which alternates with the purring quiet of the country roads.

Had Pagel believed that he would bring back a daughter to her mother, joyfully? He was merely tired and low-spirited, carrying on with Amanda a conversation drowsy and often a little irritable. What was she really going to do in Berlin if madam didn't want her assistance? "I don't know, Amanda. You are quite right; it was thoughtless."

Then even that conversation died away, as if there were nobody special in the taxi, no daughter who was restored to life, but rather some indifferent, almost troublesome, occupant. Nothing more. . . .

At last he stood in the hotel lobby. It was half-past two in the morning. Only with trouble had he got the night porter to connect him with Frau van Prackwitz's room.

"Yes, what is it then?" inquired the startled woman's voice.

"This is Pagel—I am below in the lobby—I am bringing Fräulein Violet." He broke off. He didn't know what else to say.

A long, long silence.

Then came a distant low voice. "I'm—coming."

And—only a few minutes could have passed—Frau Eva came down the stairs, those same red-carpeted stairs down which Herr von Studmann had once fallen. (But Pagel did not think of that now—although that fall, and a few other things, had taken him to Neulohe.)

She advanced, pale, very calm. She hardly looked at him. "Where?" was all she asked.

"In the taxi." He led the way. Oh, he would have had so much to say and he had believed she would have had so much to ask—but no, nothing. Only this single "Where?"

He opened the door.

The woman pushed him aside. "Come, Violet."

The figure stood up, came out of the taxi. For a moment Pagel saw the profile, the shut mouth, the lowered eyelids. . . .

"Come, child," said the woman and gave her her arm. They went into the hotel, went out of Pagel's life—he stood forgotten in the street.

"And where now, sir?" asked the driver.

"What?" said Pagel coming to himself. "Oh, yes. Some small hotel in the neighborhood. It doesn't matter."

And softly, taking Amanda's hand: "But don't cry, Amanda. Why are you crying?" And yet he too felt as though he must weep. And did not know why.

Chapter Sixteen

The Miracle of the Rentenmark

I

We have gone far, and have often had to stop on the way—now we're in a hurry. When we began it was summer; almost a year has passed since then. Once more it is green outside, it is flowering, a harvest is approaching, and inside the town, in Frau Thumann's room, the Pottmadam, the yellow-grey curtains once more hang motionless in the sticky heat. We don't know, but we assume. Outside and in—it's all the same. And everything is quite different. So little has happened: a man came and all was up with the senseless, the contemptible notes, the astronomical figures. To begin with, people looked at the new money in amazement. There was only a One on it or a Two or a Ten; if there were two noughts behind the number then it was a very large note indeed. How strange! When one had got used to counting in milliards and billions!

Coins came into circulation again, real money. One was to calculate not only in marks, but with groschen, no, with pfennigs also. There were men who, when they got their wages, built little towers with the money, playing with it. It seemed to them as though they had returned into childhood from a stormy, ruined age, from the terribly complicated into the simple.

And out of these low numbers, out of these coins and small notes, there came a magic. People began to calculate and suddenly they perceived—it tallies! I earn such and such a week, therefore I can spend so and so much—see, it tallies! For years people had been calculating—and it had never tallied. They had calculated themselves out of their minds; in the pockets of those who had starved to death had been found 1,000-mark notes; the poorest tramp on the highway had been a millionaire.

And now they all awoke from a confused torturing dream. They stood still and looked around. Yes, they could stand still and remember. Money would not run away from them now. Alarmed, they looked one another in the familiar, yet strange, faces. Was that you? they asked hesitatingly. Was that I? . . . Already those memories, still so near, were beginning to dissolve away like a fog. . . .

No, that wasn't I, they declared. And with new courage they set upon their work; once more there was a meaning in work and life.

Oh, everything has become very different!

II

A man leaves the University building, crosses the outer court, and steps into Unter den Linden.

The street is in full sunshine. He blinks a little in the light. Hesitantly he watches a bus, a bus which drives the students home to wives and children. He makes up his mind, shakes his briefcase a little, holding it by the handle, and with an easy yet swift step he goes along toward the Brandenburger Tor, toward the Tiergarten park. All his life he has been a city dweller. And for a short time has lived in the country. From that brief stay there has remained the need for peaceful, solitary paths, which recall the time when he rushed about the fields, supervising the farm laborers. Now he supervises his own thoughts, his own labors, his relations to the world around. He has a thoughtful, friendly face. He walks upright and quietly, but his eyes remain bright, shining. They are still quite young. In the bad days an antique business or dealing in pictures had seemed to him the highest that could be obtained. But on his return to Berlin he had said: "If you could do it, Mamma, I should like most to be a doctor. Psychiatrist. For mental diseases. Once I wanted to be an officer, and then it looked as though I would be nothing, a gambler, played out, hollow. Later agriculture gave me much satisfaction, but what I would like to be is: a real doctor."

"Oh, Wolfi, exactly the longest course!" She had been quite frightened.

"Yes, admittedly," he smiled. "When my son goes to school I shall still be learning. It's taking rather a time for his father to become something and earn money. But I've always liked to have to do with people. I've always liked to consider how matters are with them, and why they do this and that. I'm happy if I can help them. . . ." He looked in front of him.

"Stop, Wolfi!" said his mother. "Now you're thinking of Neulohe again."

"Why shouldn't I? Do you think it hurt me? I was much too young! To really help people, you must know a lot, have experienced a lot—and you mustn't be soft. I was much too soft!"

"They behaved shamefully toward you!"

"They behaved according to their natures, the shameful shamefully, the decent decently. . . . So, Mamma, it is not essential, but if you can and wish to . . ."

"Can and wish, Wolfi," she growled. "You're a donkey and will be one all your life. When you have a right to something then you are modest. And when you haven't, then you stick to it obstinately. I'm convinced that if you ought to ask your patient for fifty marks, you'll settle for five after long consideration."

"Peter is there now for the mathematics," he had cried. "I have had enough of reckoning up for a time."

"Oh, Peter!" growls the old lady. "She's a still greater donkey than you. She'll do whatever you want."

III

Frau Pagel has always disapproved of young Petra Ledig. Nor does she disapprove any the less, now she is called Frau Pagel the younger. She declared that the girl who transformed her own sinful past into a famous one, and who passively lets her mother-in-law slap her about, would herself cease clipping her husband round the ear. In the end it has got to the point where Frau Pagel senior visits the younger woman's household not more than week-days only. Sundays it isn't necessary; Sundays the young people take their meal with her.

She has a perfectly shameless manner of sitting stiff as a poker at the table, of drumming her fingers on it and of following every movement of Petra's with her glowing black eyes—all of which would throw any other young woman into a frenzy.

"I wouldn't put up with that from her," says the old servant Minna indignantly. "And I'm only the house-servant; you, however, the daughter-in-law."

"Nice weather today." That was the most conversation that the old woman would have with Wolfgang's wife. "There's fresh flounder in the market. Do you know what flounders are? You've got to cut their heads off. Yes, yes." And she'd rub her nose energetically with her finger.

She made Minna and Wolfgang completely crazy and desperate, but Petra just laughed.

"A very ordinary child," declares the mother-in-law whenever she sees the baby. "Nothing of the Pagels. Sold by the dozen."

Poor Petra—for Wolfgang is mostly in the University when his mother comes, and the old woman takes care that Minna should not often be present—Petra has to bear all this patiently. When she puts the child to her breast the old woman has a way of staring and of asking in the most impertinent tone in the world: "Well, Fräulein, is he getting on?"

The milk in any other woman would turn to bile. "Thanks, he is getting on, madam," smiles Petra.

"He has lost weight," declares the old lady, drumming on the table.

"Oh, no, he's put on ten ounces; the scale . . ."

"I don't go by baby scales, they're never right. I go by my own eyes. He has lost weight, Fräulein!"

"Yes, he has lost weight," replies Petra.

Frau Pagel the elder obstinately adheres to the viewpoint that Petra, in spite of the registry office, is a single girl.

"Yes, and didn't you already wait around a year ago, also to no effect. All just smoke and mirrors."

"But, mother, I really wish! . . ."

"Wishes are for Christmas, kid!"

"That you can all be so deceived," said Petra laughing. "Mother enjoys it most. Sometimes, when she thinks I don't see, she really shakes with laughter."

"Yes, she laughs at you because you let her get away with everything!" cried Minna shocked. "A sheep like you is just what she lacked for bullying!"

"Really, Petra," said Wolfgang, "you really shouldn't let Mama get away with it! She always takes more!"

"Oh, Wolfi!" said Petra amused. "Didn't I also let you get away with it, and snapped you up all the same?"

And when one considers that Frau Pagel senior lives in Tannenstrasse near Nollendorfplatz, and that the young people live right outside in Kreuznacherstrasse near Breitenbachplatz, one can only marvel at the perseverance with which the old lady daily makes the long journey to such an unpleasant young woman. The house is new, a product of the inflation, and already in decay.

"There, look," she says this morning. "I've hurt myself in your disgusting hole." And she shows Petra her hand, the palm of which is pierced by a large splinter. "The banisters! Respectable people don't live in such a hole. It's dangerous! Splinters can lead to blood poisoning."

"Wait, I'll get it out. I do that sort of thing very well."

"If you hurt me, though!" threatens the old lady, her grim eyes watching Petra fetch a needle and tweezers. Like many who endure great sorrows heroically, old Frau Pagel in respect of the little tribulations of life is squeamish, almost cowardly. . . . "I won't be ill-treated by you," she cries.

"If you will only keep your hand still, then it will hardly hurt."

"But it mustn't hurt at all! The beastly splinter is bad enough without your bungling!"

"You must hold the hand still! Better look away."

"I . . ." says Frau Pagel feebly and winces again. "I won't have it. . . . Leave the splinter in. . . . Perhaps it will come out alone." She tries to draw away her hand.

"Keep still!" Petra is vexed. "Behaving like this. Don't be so stupid."

"Petra!" says the old lady stiffly. "Petra! The idea!"

"There!" Petra triumphantly lifts the splinter in her tweezers. "You see how easy it is when you keep still."

"She says I'm not to act stupidly. Petra, aren't you afraid of me at all?"

"Not a bit," laughs Petra.

"Silly wench," says the old lady, irritated. "I won't have you laughing at me. You're to stop it. Petra, there'll be a box on the ears. Petra! Oh, how you treat an old woman like me! Is that right? Once they knelt down and implored the old mother's blessing—at least I've read such nonsense—and you laugh at me instead. Petra! Oh, you miserable siren, you! Have you got round me, too? Poor Wolfgang!"

IV

We've come a long way. We must go further. We're in a hurry! If one goes down Kurfürstendamm from the Gedächtniskirche toward Halensee, there is, on the left, a little street, Meinekestrasse—we must go down that; we shall meet acquaintances. Almost on the corner of Kurfürstendamm, only a house or two along Meinekestrasse, is a small shop whose sign bears the name: Eva von Prackwitz.

It is a little millinery business where a lady can buy a Viennese knitted dress or have a silk blouse made up; and for gentlemen there are wonderful gloves or a pair of elegant cuff links or a shirt of pure silk, made to measure, forty or fifty marks. Here no importance is attached to cheapness, and no one can count on getting any particular object: one can't go in and ask for collars, size forty; the young ladies with the nicely varnished nails would only make an amused face at such a customer. Here there are only knick-knacks to intrigue a mood, a sudden whim—a moment ago that lady hadn't known that she needed a woolen jumper—now she knows that the rest of her life will be empty and wearisome without it.

In this shop Frau von Prackwitz rules. Over the door is the name Prackwitz, but it would be more correct were it Teschow, for the one in power here is the authentic daughter of old Teschow. She keeps her amiability, her smiles, for the customers; her staff tremble before her. She has a cold, sharp tone, she is niggardly, she sweats overtime, she has an eye that sees all. And she has fallen out with her father—it has been agreed that she will not receive more than her strict inheritance—nevertheless she is a Teschow. She can be miserly when she has a purpose.

She has a purpose. She must earn money, a lot of money; she has to support two who are minors. Should she die there must be enough for them. She hates youth and health now; it makes her ill to see her young saleswomen exchange glances with gentlemen. She thinks only of husband and daughter now. All three of them have been betrayed by life, so she grudges others everything. All that remains is to snatch, and she snatches.

Frequently, in the evening, a slender, white-haired gentleman stands in the shop; he has dark eyes—he looks distinguished. He seldom says anything, but he has a gracious, somewhat shadowy smile—the customers like him very much. A gentleman of the old school—a *grand seigneur*—one sees what blue blood is.

The old gentleman chuckles. He accompanies a shopper almost to the door of the shop, and confirms that it is really warm out. Then he makes a little bow, watches the woman open the shop door, turns back in, and returns to his wife. His brain is asleep; an ice-age has set in. Once he was the Rittmeister and gentleman farmer, Joachim von Prackwitz—now he is only a very, very old man. He no longer marches, either on his own or in formation. He is declining. But some little remnant of former times remains—he does not open the shop door for ladies nor shut it behind them. If he were at home in his flat in Bleibtreustrasse, he would be helpful, be the host, the gentleman, the cavalier. But he is not and will not be a businessman "serving" customers. He won't have that. This little remnant of self-will has remained. It is not much, but it is something.

His daughter through weeks and months has grown accustomed to people again; now she can, without tears, listen to a kind word. She sits the whole day in the room behind the shop with the girls who carry out the hurried alterations. The machines hum, the girls whisper to one another, "Madam" is in the shop in front.

Violet von Prackwitz looks out of the window or at the flowers which stand before her in a little vase. She smiles, sometimes she cries a little, but she never speaks. A curse was laid upon her once; all her life she is to have a picture before her—she saw a dead man, and then came a period of which nothing is known.

Does she herself know anything about it? Does she remember anything about the man or his curse? The doctor says no; but why does she weep then? She weeps quietly, so that the girls at first often do not notice. But then one of them calls out: "Our Fräulein is crying." And all stop speaking and look. They have tried everything already. Given her flowers and chocolate, cracked jokes—one cackled like a hen, the other danced about her paper doll—but nothing worked.

Madam has been called; she has left her best customer in the shop. She takes her child in her arms and covers her eyes. "Don't cry, Violet. You must be merry." And gradually the sick girl is soothed; she smiles, she watches the girls again. Frau von Prackwitz returns to the shop. . . .

The girls in the cutting room in the front of the shop are Berliners. They have the gift of gab, and speak often and harshly about the harsh woman who tortures them. . . . But there is always one who says, "But, oh, God—what that woman has to put up with! That husband *and* the daughter. We would certainly be no different. . . ."

"No, we wouldn't be. Violet is now sixteen and has a long life before her. . . ."

"Yes," say the doctors, "who can tell? Wait and hope—it is not impossible, madam."

She waits and she hopes. She looks ahead, she economizes. All the gentleness and goodness she may have is devoted to the daughter. Her husband is barely noticed. Does she sometimes think of a certain Herr von Studmann? How far away—how foolish!

Sometimes she happens to meet a Herr Pagel in the street. She looks him coldly in the eye, she looks through him. She is sufficiently the daughter of her father to be able at last to see through that young fellow. He fraudulently obtained power of attorney from her, he misused this power; large sums of money found their way into his pockets. There are accounts made out by her father concerning the value of the things which that young man sold; there are statements of the amounts which he forwarded to her—enormous discrepancies! And these are charged to her inheritance! She also remembers that this Pagel has in his possession an IOU of hers for 2,000 marks. Let him keep it, she will never redeem it—a little punishment for all the mischief he has caused her.

He seemed so young, so amiable, so decent—one must beware of all youth, all amiability, all decency. This evening she must once more check the cash—Fräulein Degelow always wears new silk stockings now. She may have a friend, but she may also be delving into the till—be careful!

V

"Come in, young man. Step in the parlor. Of course she's there. Why shouldn't she be?" cries Frau Krupass in a loud, cheerful voice. But in a whisper: "Be a little nice to her today: she heard this morning that her old flame is dead."

"At last?" asks the young man joyfully. "Well, thank God."

"For heaven's sake, don't be so heartless, Herr Schulze! Even if he was a swine, she's upset just the same."

"Hello, Amanda," says Herr Schulze, truck driver at the paper factory, Korte & Körtig, into the kitchen where Amanda Backs is still washing up. "What have you been eating? Kippers? Shouldn't eat them in hot weather; fish always stinks at once."

"Eh, no! Not if it's smoked!" objects Krupass.

"Don't pretend, Schulzing, that you don't know. I heard her whispering secretly with you at the door. Yes, he's dead, my Hans—and if he was a rascal, all the same he loved me in his way just as I was, without anything."

"If you think, Amanda, it's because of that I . . ."

"Who says so? Who's talking of you then?" Amanda throws the dish cloth in the dish water, with a splash. "You men always think people are talking about you. No, I was speaking about my Meier and that I can't get over his dying a rascal. They killed him at Pirmasens; he was a Separatist—always with the French and against the Germans, just as in Neulohe, where I already gave him what-for for the same reason."

"At Pirmasens!" says Herr Schulze, embarrassed. "Just the same, it's a bloody while ago. . . ."

"The twelfth of February, a good four months back. But because he was only called Meier and they also had to find me, it took such a long time before they could inform me officially. And there it said in his pocketbook that I was his fiancée!" Amanda curls her lip in contempt. "What's more, I never was; I only slept with him."

There is a rather heavy silence, and the young man fidgets on his kitchen chair. At last Frau Krupass is heard.

"It's very nice, Amanda, that you're such a frank person, but too much of a thing is unhealthy. You're stepping quite needlessly on Herr Schulze's corns, when he's only trying to be fair to you."

"Now, say no more, Krupass, say no more!" says the driver. "I know Amanda; she doesn't mean that at all."

"What do I mean then?" cries Amanda with red cheeks. "That's exactly what I do mean, exactly as I said it. You needn't talk about Amanda and knowing her."

"All right. Then that's what you did mean. We won't quarrel about that."

"There you have it, Krupass! And he's supposed to be a man! No, Schulzing," she exclaims, genuinely grieved, "you're a good fellow, but you're too soft for me. I admit you're reliable and you save up and you don't drink, and as soon as possible you'll buy a truck and I could be the wife of a truck owner, as you told me. . . . But, Schulzing, the whole day I've been turning it over in my mind. We won't hit it off. To be caring is fine, but only to be caring, that's no good either. I'm only twenty-three, and I'm not in such a hurry. Perhaps someone else will come along who can make my heart throb a bit. You don't, Schulzing."

"Amanda, you only think that now because you got that letter. I know I'm a little slow; but in my business that's what's wanted. Smart driving, they can do all that; but drive carefully and turn with a truck and a trailer in a yard not much larger than your kitchen without a scratch, only I can do that."

"There you go speaking again about your stupid truck. Go and marry one."

"Certainly I'm speaking about my truck, but you must let me say what I have to, Amanda. I'm slow, as I said, but just as I succeed with my truck because I'm capable, so I'll succeed in marriage. Take it from me, Amanda, it's like this: they can all cut a great dash and drive up smartly, but you look at that sort of marriage months later! Driven into a smash-up. With me you'll keep safe; nothing'll happen to you with me—I'm as certain of that as of my driving license."

"Yes, you're a good fellow, Schulzing. But fire and water don't mix. You say nothing'll happen to me—good, but I don't know if that'll be all right for me. Too quiet is no good either."

"Oh, well." Young Schulze stands up. "I won't try to persuade you. What isn't, isn't. Oh, no, I don't take it bad of you, Amanda, not a bit. The bakers don't all bake the same bread. You can't help it, and I can't help it. Good evening, Frau Krupass. Thank you, too, for letting me sit here in the evening and for all the good food. . . ."

"Now he's talking of the food as well!"

"Why shouldn't I talk about it? One ought to return thanks for everything given us in life. I haven't been given such a lot for me to find thanks too much. Good night, Amanda, I wish you everything good also."

"Thank you, Schulzing. You too—and most of all a nice wife."

"Well, no doubt I shall find someone else. But I would have liked it the other way, Amanda. Good night."

Not till they hear him say good night to the foreman outside in the square does Frau Krupass say: "Was that right, Amanda? He's a very respectable young man, really." Amanda Backs says nothing. "Not that I'm complaining. It's all right as far as I'm concerned if you stay here another ten years in the yard with me. I like Petra very much, but I can't talk to her as I do to you. And you're better in the business." Ma Krupass stands up yawning. "Well, I'm going to hit the hay now. We've got the truckload of bottles tomorrow, and we must get up by five—aren't you going yet?"

"I'll sit here a little while and look out of the window. And I'm not angry with you. I know very well that I alone am guilty with him."

"Don't get in the dumps now. Think of Petra—she was properly in the dirt, worse than you; and what is she now? A real lady."

"Oh, lady!" says Amanda contemptuously. "I don't give a damn for that. But he loves her, that's it—and Schulze was thinking more of your depot here, and you saying you'd provide for me, than of love."

"Lawd, Amanda, love! Now don't start about love, too. Staring in the sky at evening and love as well! That's not healthy; all you'll get is a cold. A real good sleep's better than all your love. Love only makes people stupid."

"Good night, Ma Krupass. But I'd like to know what you'd have said if someone had told you that forty years ago."

"Ah, dear, why that's quite different. Forty years ago and love! They were other times then. But nowadays even love's good for nothing."

"Rubbish," says Amanda, pulling her chair up to the window.

VI

We must go on. We're in a hurry! Must we still go to Neulohe? Hello, hello! Careful! Get out of the way—here comes a cart heavily laden with sacks. They have no horses. All the horses are at work in the fields, not one can be spared— and so the people are pushing the fifty hundredweights over the bumpy yard toward the barn.

Who is coming across the yard? Who is shouting that it must go quicker? Old Geheimrat von Teschow. He has become his own bailiff, forester, clerk; now he becomes his own draught horse, too. He strains at the shaft. "Push, men. I'm seventy and you—you can't even do a few hundredweights? Weaklings!"

Hardly is the cart at rest than he must be off. Oh, he has so much to do, exhorting, supervising, calculating; from early morning onwards he is half dead from overwork. That delights him. He has two tasks. He must build up Neulohe again, despoiled by his son-in-law and his own daughter, in conjunction with a gang of thieves and criminals. And he must refill his money chests emptied by the Reds!

His activity is tireless; he is miserly, close-fisted. He robs his own wife of the eggs in the larder, to sell them; he is constantly inventing new ways of economizing. When the men complain: "Herr Geheimrat, you must let us live," he shouts: "Who lets me live, then? I have nothing more. I'm a poor man. I have debts—that's how much they robbed me!"

"But, Herr Geheimrat, you have the forest."

"The forest? A few pine trees! And what do you think the Treasury demands from me? Before the war I paid eighteen marks income tax a year. And now? The scoundrels want thousands! Well, they don't get them! No, you economize; I have to."

He is full of ideas. If in the mornings he has the bell to start work rung five minutes too early, he'll sweat five hours' unpaid overtime out of sixty people. He cheats them in the wages; if he diddles everyone once a week over no more than a pfennig, he'll have saved thirty marks in the year. He must hurry up; the shares which he purchased during the inflation are worth nothing.

"But a bit more, Elias, than you get for your thousand-mark notes."

"You wait, Herr Geheimrat, just you wait."

But he can't wait, the old Geheimrat. His property, in shares, in cash, has dwindled away. When he dies there must be at least as much as he received from his father. Why? For whom? The daughter is restricted to her inheritance, and from this are deducted all amounts already received. He has also fallen out with the son. For whom? He doesn't know. But he rushes around, he calculates—and apart from that he'll grow very old. He has no intention of departing these next twenty years; he'll see many a young man die yet.

Upstairs, at her window in the Manor, sits the old lady, his wife. But not as formerly is her friend Jutta von Kuckhoff at her side. Jutta has fallen into disfavor; Jutta has been sent away. Jutta must see how she gets on by herself in this world; she has set herself against her heavenly welfare, she has opposed Herr Herzschlüssel.

Herr Herzschlüssel is a bearded man in a black coat, the leader of a strict sect—consisting, probably, only of himself—devoted solely to repentance and contrition. He has freed Frau Belinde from the "petrified" Church; he has proved to her that he alone embodies the true gospel of Jesus. Now she may hold as many prayer meetings as she will; no longer need she fear pastor or superintendent.

But Jutta mutinied against Herr Herzschlüssel. She declared that he stole, drank, had affairs with women. Jutta, however, is merely a soured old spinster, and Herr Herzschlüssel has a beautifully tended beard, a gentle voice. When he carries Frau Belinde in his strong arms to the deck chair, she is as happy as this sinful flesh is allowed to be in this life.

In a last battle Jutta von Kuckhoff tried to push the Geheimrat towards Herr Herzschlüssel. But the Geheimrat merely laughed. "Herzschlüssel," he croaked, "ah, Jutta, he's a good man. He saved us a girl at least, and we're at last out of the church, and pay no more church taxes. Belinde's always in a good mood—and all for a bit of food. No Jutta, such a man should stay!" And thus the two old people have been provided with an occupation—they don't need to think about their children any longer.

VII

On his free days Herr von Studmann likes to take a walk to the graveyard of a neighboring village. There he sits on a bench before an ancient grave. This, when he first discovered it, was overgrown with ivy; he has had the stone cleared. On it can be read that Helene Siebenrot, sixteen years of age, was herself drowned in the rescue of a drowning child. "She was ignorant of swimming."

Herr von Studmann likes to sit here. It is quiet; in the summer no one has time to come to the churchyard, no one disturbs him. The birds sing. On the other side of the rubble wall, in the village street, the harvest wagons creak. He thinks about the young girl. Helene Siebenrot was her name—she was ignorant of swimming. She was ready to help, but she herself needed help. He, too, was ready to help, but he didn't know how to swim either.

Dr. Schröck is very satisfied with him, the patients like him, the staff have no complaints to make about him—Herr von Studmann can grow old in this sanatorium, he can die here. The thought has nothing terrifying for him. He has no wish to be outside again in the world of the healthy. He has discovered that he cannot accommodate himself to life. He had his standards, wished life to adapt itself to them. Life didn't do this, and Herr von Studmann foundered. In great and in little things. He could make no concessions. "Eh, what!" the old doctor says, "you're simply an old maid in trousers."

Herr von Studmann merely chuckled. He made no answer. He's reached the point when he didn't try to teach those who are unteachable.

He couldn't swim. That was it. For the rest Herr von Studmann will prove an excellent uncle for the Pagel children. He intends to spend his leave with them.

Only the thought of the woman still unknown to him disturbed him. Women are so . . . incomprehensible! No, there was nothing of women about him. The medical orderly had talked nonsense. Women, whether married or single, were completely alien to him. But that doesn't stop you being an uncle—without submitting to such difficult relationships. Perhaps he would be able to travel with the Pagels—without knowing how to swim!

VIII

A fresher wind stirs the white curtains. The woman has waked up, she has lit the small night lamp, she looks over to the other bed.

The man is asleep. He lies on his side, doubled up a little, his face peaceful. The somewhat curly blond hair gives him a boyish appearance; the lower lip is pushed out.

The woman examines this familiar face, but it is undisturbed by worry, and untroubled by cares. Sometimes in the night he starts to speak. He's frightened, he cries out. . . . then she wakes him and says only, "You're thinking about it again." There was a time when great burdens were loaded on him, but he endured. Endured only? No, he was made strong, he discovered something in himself which gave him a foothold, something indestructible—a will. Once he had been merely lovable—then he became worthy of love.

The young wife smiles—at life, at her husband, at happiness. . . . It is not a happiness dependent on external things; it rests in herself as the kernel in the nut. A woman who loves and knows herself to be loved feels the happiness which is always with her as a blessed whispering in her ear—drowning the noise of the day—the tranquil happiness which has nothing more to desire.

She hears the man's breathing; then, softer and faster, that of the child. Gently the white curtains stir.

Everything has quite changed.

She puts out the light.

Good, good night!

Afterword

Among German novelists of the first half of the twentieth century, Hans Fallada stands out as the chronicler of the proverbial little man and his fight for happiness and dignity in times of severe hardship. In *Wolf Among Wolves*, first published in 1937, Fallada presents us with an inspiring tale of perseverance in an era of political, social and economic upheaval. Set in 1923 amidst the rampant inflation that gripped Germany following World War I, *Wolf Among Wolves* has been referred to by literary critics as "a masterpiece of critical realism" and "one of the major novels published in fascist Germany." It is now regarded as the author's most ambitious literary achievement.

With *Wolf Among Wolves*, Fallada returned, after a foray into children's literature, to the gritty and ethically infused realism that had established him as one of the few bestselling German authors of the 1920s and 1930s. For all its unrestrained epic power, the novel is a compelling example of his concern with the intricacies of composition. What is striking from the beginning is the symphonic quality of the text. In Part One of the novel, covering only twenty-four hours, the omniscient narrator weaves a web of interrelated characters and stories. "A girl and a man were sleeping on a narrow iron bed. [. . .] The dollar stands for the moment at 414,000 marks." From the very first sentences, Fallada's epic throws the reader into the middle of things: a dingy Berlin boarding house, on a hot day in July 1923, at six o'clock in the morning. From here, the reader is taken on a journey to varied locales that are linked in one way or another to the story that is about to unfold: apartments and avenues, police stations and prison cells, roulette parlors and hotel cafés, and, eventually, the countryside. With its swift fluctuation between places and characters, the novel reads almost like a movie script. Throughout, *Wolf Among Wolves* is long on action, short on reflection, and one of Fallada's greatest strengths as a writer is his ability to gradually build up narrative tension. Providing the reader with glimpses into the lives of his main characters, he successfully appropriates the montage style that was highly popular in Weimar cinema.

The protagonist is Wolfgang Pagel, the man on the "narrow iron bed," a young former soldier who inhabits a corrupt world, in which the miseries of inflation have created an atmosphere of cynical self-advancement. Immature and selfish at the outset of the story, Pagel undergoes a fundamental transformation that allows him to embark upon the humanist mission of the novel, which is to find "something on earth which was still worth [the] effort." As one character says about the resilient Pagel: "You want to go through all this misery? Such an appetite for life, young man, could give one indigestion!" Pagel spends four months on the Neulohe estate east of the Elbe because, in the words of his pregnant girlfriend Petra Ledig, he "must become a man before he can be a father." Pagel meets this challenge, and by the end of the novel he is working toward a medical degree at Berlin's Humboldt University. His development from a drifting gambler, who sees in roulette "the prospect of something big," to a medical student eager to devote his life to helping others is unparalleled in Fallada's work. The narrator comments emphatically, "Once he had been merely lovable—then he became worthy of love."

As the action proceeds, the novel becomes more relentless in its depiction of people "who from day to day increasingly lost all feeling of self-respect and propriety." The loss of moral rectitude parallels currency devaluation, the dispiriting effect of which is evoked in an early passage:

> A feeling of impotent hatred overcame Rittmeister Joachim von Prackwitz. Somewhere in this town there was a machine—naturally a machine, for men would never submit to be prostituted for such a purpose—which vomited paper day and night over the city and the people. "Money" they called it; they printed figures on it, beautiful neat figures with many noughts, which became increasingly rounder. And when you had worked and sweated to put by a little for your old age, it all became worthless paper, paper muck.

The Berlin of the inflation years as depicted in *Wolf Among Wolves* is one of moral depravity—a place known for "heroin and cocaine, 'snow,' nude dances, French champagne and American cigarettes, influenza, hunger, despair, fornication and crime." In one of the most powerful passages in the novel, the narrator describes the city as a veritable "Oriental bazaar": "Dealers, beggars, strumpets: almost shoulder to shoulder they stood on both sides of the pavement." As Joachim von Prackwitz, the farmer from the Neulohe estate, promenades through Friedrichstraße, then and now one of Berlin's bustling avenues, he is appalled by "the misery, the indecency, the demoralization which manifest[s] itself in Berlin in broad daylight." Judging from their suggestive glances, even the young salesgirls are already trapped in this urban netherworld: "Why save oneself up for tomorrow? Who knows where the dollar will stand, who knows whether we shall be still alive tomorrow?" Forcing his way through the crowd, Prackwitz arrives at the arcade passing from Unter den Linden to Friedrichstraße and enters, sensing that "he might have come from purgatory into hell":

> The shops paraded huge pot-boiler pictures of naked women, repulsively naked, with revoltingly sweet pink breasts. Chains of indecent picture-postcards hung everywhere. [. . .] But the young boys were by far the worst of all. In their sailor suits, with smooth bare chests, cigarettes impudently sticking in their lips, they glided about everywhere; they did not speak, but they looked at you and touched you.

Overcome with "shuddering nausea," Prackwitz, who throughout the novel is characterized by his childlike naïveté, finally comes to think of Neulohe "as an untouched island of purity," a provincial refuge from Berlin, that "morass of infamy."

Fallada's Berlin is not the right place for Wolfgang Pagel to mature and develop into a responsible, compassionate man. It is in the country, at the estate in East Prussia, that Pagel learns the benefits of hard work. As the narrator puts it in one of the hundreds of passages that was left out in the 1938 translation: ". . . these were not the times to rely on God in Heaven. These were times to work yourself until you drop." By the end of the novel, Pagel, whom we first meet gambling in the Berlin night clubs, is in charge of the estate's accounts. He is the last man standing, desperately trying to manage a farm that has been ruined by the incompetence, indifference, and greed of almost everybody around him.

Reviewing *Wolf Among Wolves* in *The New Yorker* in 1938, Clifton Fadiman criticized the novel for its "somewhat unconvincing notion that the countryside possesses magical curative values for those rotted by the vices of the city." However, there is nothing in *Wolf Among Wolves* that indicates a simplistic economy of geographical disparities. In fact, Pagel is quick to realize that the country is no less corrupt than the city and that the idyllic vision of a "peace of the fields," which Studmann had conjured upon their arrival in Neulohe, is a mere delusion. Both metropolis and countryside are places of extreme disillusionment, of social, economic and political uncertainty. A few years prior to *Wolf Among Wolves*, Fallada had argued that the way of life of farmers had yet to be convincingly captured by German artists. Working on farms in northern and eastern Germany during the immediate postwar years, he witnessed both the plight of the laborers and the economic forces affecting farmers. *Wolf Among Wolves* illustrates that, as H.J. Schueler sums up in his seminal study on Fallada's fiction, "the times were just as terribly out of joint on the land as in the cities."

Fallada depicts a society in which each individual pursues his or her own self-interest—a pack of lone and hungry wolves, as the title suggests. As Schueler puts it, "The quest for survival proves to be the paramount concern of all the parties involved in the bitter battle of all against all." Wolfgang Pagel lives among these wolves, but he will not become one of them. Rising above the feverish roulette rooms, he overcomes the temptation to succumb to society's demoralizing influence. In spite of his surroundings, Pagel forges ahead, managing to find values worth holding onto, and proving that he is more than just a "leaf on life's stream." In Fallada's view, the individual is not determined by society, but rather has the chance to shape his own fate. It is up to him how he responds to social and moral ills. And yet, some are too weak to meet the challenges, as the example of the Rittmeister Joachim von Prackwitz, the Neulohe farmer, illustrates. Amidst the chaos of the inflation year, with the estate in desperate need of responsible management, his wife realizes how incompetent he is: "a weakling, spineless, without self-control, at the mercy of every influence, a babbler." The uniform and the firm world-view that came with it had provided him with security, but now it becomes clear that there is "nothing in him, nothing, no core, no faith, no ambition, not one thing to give him the power to resist." The Prackwitz family is at the center of the descent into moral turpitude, and the kidnapping of their daughter by one of their servants is the painful culmination of the family's disintegration.

While the Rittmeister is shattered by the challenges of the times, "lost, in a lost age," Wolfgang Pagel emerges morally invigorated from his stay in the country. Unlike Prackwitz, he will learn how to assume responsibility for his own actions. As the former soldier matures, he comes to rethink his definition of courage:

> I used to think that courage meant standing up straight when a shell exploded and taking your share of the shrapnel. Now I know that's mere stupidity and bravado; courage means keeping going when something becomes completely unbearable.

The end of the novel mirrors the beginning. One year has passed, it is once more summer in the city, and Wolfgang and Petra are lying in bed. And yet, the narrator informs us, "everything has become very different." Most importantly, they have both repudiated their previous behavior. Petra, the girl from the streets, has spent the intervening time working in a rag-and-bone business, determined not to see Wolfgang again until he grew up: "Is my child to have such a spoiled darling for its father," she had asked herself, "one for whom I have no proper respect?" Wolfgang has struggled to prove himself worthy of Petra's respect, realizing that assuming the role of husband and father requires him to accept responsibility for his own actions. Fallada was no doubt a "dedicated humanist," as Schueler writes, and it is through sincere commitment to others that Wolfgang can redeem himself. This central lesson is spelled out in a passage that was omitted in the 1938 translation:

> Wolfgang Pagel reflected that, not long ago, he had thought with pride: "I'm not tied to anything; I can do what I want; I'm free . . ." Yes, Wolfgang Pagel—now you understand: you were free, unfettered like a wild animal. But humanity is not about doing what you want, but rather about doing what you must.

* * *

Hans Fallada wrote *Wolf unter Wölfen* in a frenzy. Convinced that the book would end up "in the drawer" anyway, Fallada worked with unchecked ingenuity, temporarily relieved from the depressive illness that had already resulted in several stays in sanatoriums, an illness that can be detected in personal letters such as the one he wrote to fellow writer Hermann Broch: "I must write, narrate, tell stories, but basically it is a sad business; it won't make you happier, and it has no meaning." Fallada began *Wolf Among Wolves* on July 27, 1936, without having a clear idea of the scope of what he had undertaken. Since he was inventing the plot and characters as he moved along, the introduction—intended as the novel's rather brief opening chapter—eventually grew into the entire first book. Getting up at four o'clock in the morning, he managed, at the pinnacle of his creative powers, to produce 123 handwritten pages a week: a personal record, "which I do pride myself on," as he acknowledged in a letter to his publisher Ernst Rowohlt on May 9, 1937. Two days later, Fallada finished the manuscript, which by now comprised 1,400 pages. With the first print-run of 10,000 copies selling out by mid-November, *Wolf Among Wolves* proved an instant, if surprising, success for Rowohlt.

Wolf Among Wolves is a *Zeitroman*—a historical novel, providing an elaborate account of a particular moment in time and of how a diverse group of characters, taken from all walks of life, cope with that time. Unlike more theoretical writers, whose fiction is shaped by a coherent worldview, Fallada is not concerned with exploring the political and economic context of the inflation years. His focus is on action, and his love for storytelling is everywhere apparent in his work. *Wolf Among Wolves* occupies an exceptional position within Fallada's oeuvre, as the author successfully combines the two strands that run throughout his prose: reportage and narration. The objective and disaffected voice of the chronicler mixes with the emphatic and deeply involved voice of the storyteller. Stylistically, Fallada chose to throw all modernist pretenses overboard. His language is rooted in the everyday, and as with his other novels, the strength of *Wolf Among Wolves* lies in the close-up characterization. There is nothing artificial, nothing academic about his characters; they are presented "with such closeness to life," as Hermann Hesse once put it, that the reader cannot but feel invested in their fictional fate.

In *Wolf Among Wolves*, we witness the culmination of a theme that was at the heart of the two novels *Little Man, What Now?* and *The World Outside*. As the German weekly *Der Spiegel* put it in 1947, these works depicted "the individual's helpless entanglement in the prevailing circumstances of his times." It is his profound understanding of the varied problems that arise out of economic misery that accounts for Fallada's ongoing relevance up to the present day. He has been compared to predecessors such as Dickens, Flaubert and the German realist writers Wilhelm Raabe and Theodor Fontane—authors he read when he was still in his teenage years. But none of these writers, who are now credited with heralding the start of literary modernism, ever wrote fiction that could be called strictly realist in the sense of being a photographic, non-ambivalent representation of the world outside.

The same holds true of Hans Fallada. While Fallada's famed novels of the 1930s are often classified as prime examples of the Neue Sachlichkeit (New Objectivity), his work transcends straightforward realism limited to the depiction of real-life events in a real-life world. It is in brief hallucinatory statements and other deviations from our shared reality that the complex undercurrents of his fiction manifest themselves. The present edition is the first-ever unexpurgated English translation of *Wolf unter Wölfen*. Numerous passages that were omitted in the 1938 edition, published by Putnam's in London and New York, have been newly translated, and it is astonishing to observe how one's overall impression of the novel is altered once the "lost" passages are restored to the text.

What, then, are the politics of translation that account for the numerous cuts in the first English edition? The omitted passages share certain features. To begin with, the 1938 edition dispenses on several occasions with paragraphs that, while not advancing the plot, elaborate on the characters' feelings or behavior. Take this omitted passage, for example, in which the narrator provides us with an important comment on one of the main characters' attitude to Frau von Prackwitz:

> She'd paralyzed his ability to think, to analyse, and to explain himself. Herr von Studmann was over thirty-five and hadn't believed that he

would experience this any more, with such spontaneity, such power. In fact, he didn't really know he was experiencing it. He sat there innocently, his eyes betraying nothing. His words remained thoughtful and moderate. Yet it had happened!

Recently, critics have pointed out how fairy-tales and myths provide important subtexts for Fallada's fiction. It is often those passages that contradict the claim to naturalistic representation that were cut from the 1938 translation. Take for instance the following paragraph, which exhibits an almost surreal mode of perception:

> Occasionally, in the midst of some work or worry, she would glance from the narrow prison of herself at one such picture on the wall as if seeing it for the first time. Then something seemed to want to lightly touch her, as if something asleep were waking. . . . Stop! Oh, please stop! Everything was very bright. A tree, for instance, in the sun, in the air, against a clear summer sky. But the tree seemed to rise up, the wind to blow gently. The tree moved. Was it flying? Yes, the whole earth was flying, the sun, the play of light and air—everything was light, swift, soft. Oh, stop, you relentless, bright world!

In short, the fully reconstructed text, with its enhanced inconsistency, provides the reader with insight into a literary aesthetics that is unique among the novels of German modernism: Fallada combines realist prose and ethical concerns with a narrative technique that renders ambiguous what is supposedly a semi-documentary representation, shaped by his very own experiences in the country.

The last chapter of the novel is called "The Miracle of the Rentenmark," and while the title refers to the introduction of a stable currency and the return to rationality, it also refers to the miraculous outcome of a novel shaped by an atmosphere of impending doom. But the couple's "tranquil happiness" in the novel's final scene, embodied in the soft breathing of their child, is complicated by traumatic memory and its purchase on the present. Strikingly, the short passage that fleshes out this adverse undercurrent was omitted in the 1938 translation:

> The woman examines this familiar face, but it is undisturbed by worry, and untroubled by cares. Sometimes in the night he starts to speak. He's frightened, he cries out . . . Then she wakes him and says: 'You're thinking about it again.'

It is in this passage that the narrative comes full circle. While at the beginning of the novel Pagel had been tortured by nightmares about gambling, his sleep is now perturbed by the memory of Neulohe.

Reviewing the novel in 1938, some American critics complained about the sentimental, love-conquers-all ending. As the culmination of Pagel's personal development, reviewers found this outcome unconvincing. Interestingly enough, Fallada himself shared these concerns. In a letter to Hermann Broch, he conceded it might have been better to let his hero founder. This statement is complicated, however, by several other private comments that suggest Fallada's ambivalence about his work. Writing to his mother in May and August 1937, he repeatedly called *Wolf Among Wolves* "an absolutely positive" book, maintaining that "the brave manage to keep afloat, whereas the unfit fail." This contrasts with Fallada's remarks about the book being "very pessimistic" and full of "dark undertones." The German people, especially Wolfgang Pagel and Petra Ledig, may have awoken "from a confused torturing dream," as the narrator suggests in the last chapter, but this dream will continue to haunt them. On a larger historical scale, the fact that the stabilization of the economy was rather short-lived markedly undermines the narrator's firm declaration that "once more there was a meaning in work and life." But the "fresher wind," which stirs the curtains in the novel's final section and thus contrasts with the stifling heat and the "dull vapor" of the first chapter, was soon to be contaminated by the advance of Hitler and the NSDAP. The same reservations about the book's supposedly hopeful ending hold true with regard to its protagonist: Wolfgang Pagel's ethics of responsibility are called into question by his financial reliance on his mother. It is therefore important to note, as Geoff Wilkes reminds us, "how the novel's optimism about personal relationships and personal morality was undermined by the very existence of the oppressive Nazi regime."

Perhaps the finest aspect of *Wolf Among Wolves* is the character of Etzel von Studmann, and it is Fallada's portrayal of this "eternal nursemaid" that further corroborates *Der Spiegel*'s 1947 verdict that this book could, in fact, be seen as "hopelessly depressing." Though Studmann, who is "always ready to help," embodies the humanist core of the novel, he finally withdraws from society, taking up a position as resident administrator in a sanatorium where he might as well spend the rest of his life:

> The thought has nothing terrifying for him. He has no wish to be outside again in the world of the healthy. He has discovered that he cannot accommodate himself to life. He had his standards, wished

life to adapt itself to them. Life didn't do this, and Herr von Studmann foundered. In great and in little things.

By the time he started work on *Wolf Among Wolves*, Fallada had already experienced the full impact of Nazi cultural propaganda, having received several particularly vicious reviews from right wing critics for his previous book. This is the context of the peculiar "Word to the Reader" which precedes the novel. Fallada here justifies his decision to render the protagonist of that previous novel, *Once We Had a Child*, "such a brute." Eager to subvert similar complaints about his new book, Fallada warns his readers "that *Wolf Among Wolves* deals with sinful, weak, sensual, erring unstable men, the children of an age disjointed, mad and sick." A slap at Weimar, to placate the Nazis? The foreword was deleted from the novel after 1945. And yet, Fallada scholars such as Geoff Wilkes consider the preface to be ambiguous. As Wilkes has noted, "All this *could* be taken as referring to the economic and political turmoil of 1923 specifically, rather than to the Republic as such, and therefore not as placating the Nazis."

Ultimately, one must consider whether Fallada's note accurately reflects the attitude of the book, which it clearly does not. If anything, the note, as Wilkes suggests, is "an authentic expression of how Fallada had to walk a political tightrope in 1936–37." And while he was not like his character Studmann—who, as it says in the book, "could make no concessions"—Fallada did walk the line with bravery. The note's celebration of the rescue from the perils of inflation, a "both recent and yet entirely eclipsed" time, encapsulates his position in Nazi Germany rather succinctly: while at times writing warily with the official ideology in mind, he also asserted his own humane values. Utterly convinced that he had taken "a formidable risk," Fallada himself regarded the novel as the uncompromising product of his newly awakened will to write, "regardless of the consequences" his words might have: "I was once again gripped by the old familiar passion; I wrote without looking up, nor did I look round either— neither to the left, nor to the right."

THORSTEN CARSTENSEN,
New York University